Mon cher Paul,

J'ai pensé à toi en lisant

ce livre.

Le code des Samouraï Musashi

est le même que le tien.

Force, élégance, détermination.

Deux guerriers, deux époques.

Ton ami

Claude

3-11-01

MUSASHI

MUSASHI

By Eiji Yoshikawa

Translated from the Japanese by Charles S. Terry

Foreword by Edwin O. Reischauer

Kodansha International
Tokyo • New York • London

Poem on page 471, from *The Jade Mountain: A Chinese Anthology*, translated by
Witter Bynner from the texts of Kiang Kang-Hu, copyright 1929 and renewed by
Alfred A. Knopf, Inc. Reprinted by permission of the publisher.

Publication of this book was assisted by a grant from the Japan Foundation.

First published in the Japanese language, © Fumiko Yoshikawa 1971.

ISBN 4-7700-1813-4

Contents

Foreword
by Edwin O. Reischauer*

Musashi might well be called the *Gone with the Wind* of Japan. Written by Eiji Yoshikawa (1892–1962), one of Japan's most prolific and best-loved popular writers, it is a long historical novel, which first appeared in serialized form between 1935 and 1939 in the *Asahi Shimbun*, Japan's largest and most prestigious newspaper. It has been published in book form no less than fourteen times, most recently in four volumes of the 53-volume complete works of Yoshikawa issued by Kodansha. It has been produced as a film some seven times, has been repeatedly presented on the stage, and has often been made into television mini-series on at least three nationwide networks.

Miyamoto Musashi was an actual historical person, but through Yoshikawa's novel he and the other main characters of the book have become part of Japan's living folklore. They are so familiar to the public that people will frequently be compared to them as personalities everyone knows. This gives the novel an added interest to the foreign reader. It not only provides a romanticized slice of Japanese history, but gives a view of how the Japanese see their past and themselves. But basically the novel will be enjoyed as a dashing tale of swashbuckling adventure and a subdued story of love, Japanese style.

Comparisons with James Clavell's *Shōgun* seem inevitable, because for most Americans today *Shōgun*, as a book and a television mini-series, vies with samurai movies as their chief source of knowledge about Japan's past. The two novels concern the same period of history. *Shōgun*, which takes place in the year 1600, ends with Lord Toranaga, who is the historical Tokugawa Ieyasu, soon to be the Shōgun, or military dictator of Japan, setting off for the fateful battle of Sekigahara. Yoshikawa's story begins with the youthful Takezō, later to be renamed Miyamoto Musashi, lying wounded among the corpses of the defeated army on that battlefield.

With the exception of Blackthorne, the historical Will Adams, *Shōgun* deals largely with the great lords and ladies of Japan, who appear in thin disguise under names Clavell has devised for them. *Musashi*, while mentioning many great historical figures under their true names, tells about a broader range of Japanese and particularly about the rather extensive group who lived on the ill-defined borderline between the hereditary military aristocracy and the

*Edwin O. Reischauer was born in Japan in 1910. He was a professor at Harvard University and was Professor Emeritus until his death in 1990. He was the United States Ambassador to Japan from 1961 to 1966, and was one of the best-known authorities on the country. Among his numerous works are *Japan: The Story of a Nation* and *The Japanese*.

commoners—the peasants, tradesmen and artisans. Clavell freely distorts historical fact to fit his tale and inserts a Western-type love story that not only flagrantly flouts history but is quite unimaginable in the Japan of that time. Yoshikawa remains true to history or at least to historical tradition, and his love story, which runs as a background theme in minor scale throughout the book, is very authentically Japanese.

Yoshikawa, of course, has enriched his account with much imaginative detail. There are enough strange coincidences and deeds of derring-do to delight the heart of any lover of adventure stories. But he sticks faithfully to such facts of history as are known. Not only Musashi himself but many of the other people who figure prominently in the story are real historical individuals. For example, Takuan, who serves as a guiding light and mentor to the youthful Musashi, was a famous Zen monk, calligrapher, painter, poet and teamaster of the time, who became the youngest abbot of the Daitokuji in Kyoto in 1609 and later founded a major monastery in Edo, but is best remembered today for having left his name to a popular Japanese pickle.

The historical Miyamoto Musashi, who may have been born in 1584 and died in 1645, was like his father a master swordsman and became known for his use of two swords. He was an ardent cultivator of self-discipline as the key to martial skills and the author of a famous work on swordsmanship, the *Gorin no sho*. He probably took part as a youth in the battle of Sekigahara, and his clashes with the Yoshioka school of swordsmanship in Kyoto, the warrior monks of the Hōzōin in Nara and the famed swordsman Sasaki Kojirō, all of which figure prominently in this book, actually did take place. Yoshikawa's account of him ends in 1612, when he was still a young man of about 28, but subsequently he may have fought on the losing side at the siege of Osaka castle in 1614 and participated in 1637–38 in the annihilation of the Christian peasantry of Shimabara in the western island of Kyushu, an event which marked the extirpation of that religion from Japan for the next two centuries and helped seal Japan off from the rest of the world.

Ironically, Musashi in 1640 became a retainer of the Hosokawa lords of Kumamoto, who, when they had been the lords of Kumamoto, had been the patrons of his chief rival, Sasaki Kojirō. The Hosokawas bring us back to *Shōgun*, because it was the older Hosokawa, Tadaoki, who figures quite unjustifiably as one of the main villains of that novel, and it was Tadaoki's exemplary Christian wife, Gracia, who is pictured without a shred of plausibility as Blackthorne's great love, Mariko.

The time of Musashi's life was a period of great transition in Japan. After a century of incessant warfare among petty daimyō, or feudal lords, three successive leaders had finally reunified the country through conquest. Oda Nobunaga had started the process but, before completing it, had been killed by a treacherous vassal in 1582. His ablest general, Hideyoshi, risen from the rank of common foot soldier, completed the unification of the nation but died in 1598 before he could consolidate control in behalf of his infant heir. Hideyoshi's strongest vassal, Tokugawa Ieyasu, a great daimyō who ruled much of eastern Japan from his castle at Edo, the modern Tokyo, then won supremacy by defeating a coalition of western daimyō at Sekigahara in 1600. Three years later he took the traditional title of Shōgun, signifying his military dictatorship over the whole land, theoretically in behalf of the ancient but impotent imperial line in Kyoto. Ieyasu in 1605 transferred the position of Shōgun to his son, Hidetada, but remained in actual control himself until he had destroyed the supporters of Hideyoshi's heir in sieges of Osaka castle in 1614 and 1615.

The first three Tokugawa rulers established such firm control over Japan that their rule was to last more than two and a half centuries, until it finally collapsed in 1868 in the tumultuous aftermath of the reopening of Japan to contact with the West a decade and a half earlier. The Tokugawa ruled through semi-autonomous hereditary daimyō, who numbered around 265 at the end of the period, and the daimyō in turn controlled their fiefs through their hereditary samurai retainers. The transition from constant warfare to a closely regulated peace brought the drawing of sharp class lines between the samurai, who had the privilege of wearing two swords and bearing family names, and the commoners, who though including well-to-do merchants and land owners, were in theory denied all arms and the honor of using family names.

During the years of which Yoshikawa writes, however, these class divisions were not yet sharply defined. All localities had their residue of peasant fighting men, and the country was overrun by rōnin, or masterless samurai, who were largely the remnants of the armies of the daimyō who had lost their domains as the result of the battle of Sekigahara or in earlier wars. It took a generation or two before society was fully sorted out into the strict class divisions of the Tokugawa system, and in the meantime there was considerable social ferment and mobility.

Another great transition in early seventeenth century Japan was in the nature of leadership. With peace restored and major warfare at an end, the dominant warrior class found that military prowess was less essential to successful rule than administrative talents. The samurai class started a slow transformation from being warriors of the gun and sword to being bureaucrats of the writing brush and paper. Disciplined self-control and education in a society at peace was becoming more important than skill in warfare. The Western reader may be surprised to see how widespread literacy already was at the beginning of the seventeenth century and at the constant references the Japanese made to Chinese history and literature, much as Northern Europeans of the same time continually referred to the traditions of ancient Greece and Rome.

A third major transition in the Japan of Musashi's time was in weaponry. In the second half of the sixteenth century matchlock muskets, recently introduced by the Portuguese, had become the decisive weapons of the battlefield, but in a land at peace the samurai could turn their backs on distasteful firearms and resume their traditional love affair with the sword. Schools of swordsmanship flourished. However, as the chance to use swords in actual combat diminished, martial skills were gradually becoming martial arts, and these increasingly came to emphasize the importance of inner self-control and the character-building qualities of swordsmanship rather than its untested military efficacy. A whole mystique of the sword grew up, which was more akin to philosophy than to warfare.

Yoshikawa's account of Musashi's early life illustrates all these changes going on in Japan. He was himself a typical rōnin from a mountain village and became a settled samurai retainer only late in life. He was the founder of a school of swordsmanship. Most important, he gradually transformed himself from an instinctive fighter into a man who fanatically pursued the goals of Zen-like self-discipline, complete inner mastery over oneself, and a sense of oneness with surrounding nature. Although in his early years lethal contests, reminiscent of the tournaments of medieval Europe, were still possible, Yoshikawa portrays Musashi as consciously turning his martial skills from service in warfare to a means of character building for a time of peace. Martial skills, spiritual self-discipline and aesthetic sensitivity became merged into a single indistinguishable whole. This picture of Musashi may not be far from the historical truth. Musashi is known to have been a skilled painter and an accomplished sculptor as well as a swordsman.

The Japan of the early seventeenth century which Musashi typified has lived on strongly in the Japanese consciousness. The long and relatively static rule of the Tokugawa preserved much of its forms and spirit, though in somewhat ossified form, until the middle of the nineteenth century, not much more than a century ago. Yoshikawa himself was a son of a former samurai who failed like most members of his class to make a successful economic transition to the new age. Though the samurai themselves largely sank into obscurity in the new Japan, most of the new leaders were drawn from this feudal class, and its ethos was popularized through the new compulsory educational system to become the spiritual background and ethics of the whole Japanese nation. Novels like *Musashi* and the films and plays derived from them aided in the process.

The time of Musashi is as close and real to the modern Japanese as is the Civil War to Americans. Thus the comparison to *Gone with the Wind* is by no means far-fetched. The age of the samurai is still very much alive in Japanese minds. Contrary to the picture of the modern Japanese as merely group oriented "economic animals," many Japanese prefer to see themselves as fiercely individualistic, high-principled, self-disciplined and aesthetically sensitive modern-day Musashis. Both pictures have some validity, illustrating the complexity of the Japanese soul behind the seemingly bland and uniform exterior.

Musashi is very different from the highly psychological and often neurotic novels that have been the mainstay of translations of modern Japanese literature into English. But it is nevertheless fully in the mainstream of traditional Japanese fiction and popular Japanese thought. Its episodic presentation is not merely the result of its original appearance as a newspaper serial but is a favorite technique dating back to the beginnings of Japanese storytelling. Its romanticized view of the noble swordsman is a stereotype of the feudal past enshrined in hundreds of other stories and samurai movies. Its emphasis on the cultivation of self-control and inner personal strength through austere

Zen-like self-discipline is a major feature of Japanese personality today. So also is the pervading love of nature and sense of closeness to it. *Musashi* is not just a great adventure story. Beyond that, it gives both a glimpse into Japanese history and a view into the idealized self-image of the contemporary Japanese.

January 1981

Book I   EARTH

The Little Bell

Takezō lay among the corpses. There were thousands of them.

"The whole world's gone crazy," he thought dimly. "A man might as well be a dead leaf, floating in the autumn breeze."

He himself looked like one of the lifeless bodies surrounding him. He tried to raise his head, but could only lift it a few inches from the ground. He couldn't remember ever feeling so weak. "How long have I been here?" he wondered.

Flies came buzzing around his head. He wanted to brush them away, but couldn't even muster the energy to raise his arm. It was stiff, almost brittle, like the rest of his body. "I must've been out for quite a while," he thought, wiggling one finger at a time. Little did he know he was wounded, with two bullets lodged firmly in his thigh.

Low, dark clouds shifted ominously across the sky. The night before, sometime between midnight and dawn, a blinding rain had drenched the plain of Sekigahara. It was now past noon on the fifteenth of the ninth month of 1600. Though the typhoon had passed, now and then fresh torrents of rain would fall on the corpses and onto Takezō's upturned face. Each time it came, he'd open and close his mouth like a fish, trying to drink in the droplets. "It's like the water they wipe a dying man's lips with," he reflected, savoring each bit of moisture. His head was numb, his thoughts the fleeting shadows of delirium.

His side had lost. He knew that much. Kobayakawa Hideaki, supposedly an ally, had been secretly in league with the Eastern Army, and when he turned on Ishida Mitsunari's troops at twilight, the tide of battle turned too. He then attacked the armies of other commanders—Ukita, Shimazu and Konishi—and the collapse of the Western Army was complete. In only half a day's fighting, the question of who would henceforth rule the country was settled. It was Tokugawa Ieyasu, the powerful Edo daimyō.

Images of his sister and the old villagers floated before his eyes. "I'm dying," he thought without a tinge of sadness. "Is this what it's really like?" He felt drawn to the peace of death, like a child mesmerized by a flame.

Suddenly one of the nearby corpses raised its head. "Takezō."

The images of his mind ceased. As if awakened from the dead, he turned his head toward the sound. The voice, he was sure, was that of his best friend. With all his strength he raised himself slightly, squeezing out a whisper barely audible above the pelting rain. "Matahachi, is that you?" Then he collapsed, lay still and listened.

"Takezō! Are you really alive?"

"Yes, alive!" he shouted in a sudden outburst of bravado. "And you? You'd better not die either. Don't you dare!" His eyes were wide open now, and a smile played faintly about his lips.

"Not me! No, sir." Gasping for breath, crawling on his elbows and dragging his legs stiffly behind him, Matahachi inched his way toward his friend. He made a grab for Takezō's hand but only caught his small finger with his own. As childhood friends they'd often sealed promises with this gesture. He came closer and gripped the whole hand.

"I can't believe you're all right too! We must be the only survivors."

"Don't speak too soon. I haven't tried to get up yet."

"I'll help you. Let's get out of here!"

Suddenly Takezō pulled Matahachi to the ground and growled, "Play dead! More trouble coming!"

The ground began to rumble like a caldron. Peeking through their arms, they watched the approaching whirlwind close in on them. Then they were nearer, lines of jet-black horsemen hurtling directly toward them.

"The bastards! They're back!" exclaimed Matahachi, raising his knee as if preparing for a sprint. Takezō seized his ankle, nearly breaking it, and yanked him to the ground.

In a moment the horses were flying past them—hundreds of muddy lethal hooves galloping in formation, riding roughshod over the fallen samurai. Battle cries on their lips, their armor and weapons clinking and clanking, the riders came on and on.

Matahachi lay on his stomach, eyes closed, hoping against hope they would not be trampled, but Takezō stared unblinkingly upward. The horses passed so close they could smell their sweat. Then it was over.

Miraculously they were uninjured and undetected, and for several minutes both remained silent in disbelief.

"Saved again!" exclaimed Takezō, reaching his hand out to Matahachi. Still hugging the ground, Matahachi slowly turned his head to show a broad, slightly trembling grin. "Somebody's on our side, that's for sure," he said huskily.

The two friends helped each other, with great difficulty, to their feet. Slowly they made their way across the battlefield to the safety of the wooded hills, hobbling along with arms around each other's shoulders. There they collapsed but after a rest began foraging for food. For two days they subsisted on wild chestnuts and edible leaves in the sodden hollows of Mount Ibuki. This kept them from starving, but Takezō's stomach ached and Matahachi's bowels tormented him. No food could fill him, no drink quench his thirst, but even he felt his strength returning bit by bit.

The storm on the fifteenth marked the end of the fall typhoons. Now, only two nights later, a cold white moon glared grimly down from a cloudless sky.

They both knew how dangerous it was to be on the road in the glaring moonlight, their shadows looming like silhouette targets in clear view of any patrols searching for stragglers. The decision to risk it had been Takezō's. With Matahachi in such misery, saying he'd rather be captured than continue trying to walk, there really didn't seem to be much choice. They had to move on, but it was also clear that they had to find a place to lie low and rest. They made their way slowly in what they thought was the direction of the small town of Tarui.

"Can you make it?" Takezō asked repeatedly. He held his friend's arm around his own shoulder to help him along. "Are you all right?" It was the labored breathing that worried him. "You want to rest?"

"I'm all right." Matahachi tried to sound brave, but his face was paler than the moon above them. Even with his lance for a walking stick, he could barely put one foot in front of the other.

He'd been apologizing abjectly over and over. "I'm sorry, Takezō. I know it's me who's slowing us down. I'm really sorry."

The first few times Takezō had simply brushed this off with "Forget it." Eventually, when they stopped to rest, he turned to his friend and burst out, "Look, I'm the one who should be apologizing. I'm the one who got you into this in the first place, remember? Remember how I told you my plan, how I was finally going to do something that would really have impressed my father? I've never been able to stand the fact that to his dying day he was sure I'd never amount to anything. I was going to show him! Ha!"

Takezō's father, Munisai, had once served under Lord Shimmen of Iga. As soon as Takezō heard that Ishida Mitsunari was raising an army, he was convinced that the chance of a lifetime had finally arrived. His father had been a samurai. Wasn't it only natural that he would be made one too? He ached to enter the fray, to prove his mettle, to have word spread like wildfire through the village that he had decapitated an enemy general. He had wanted desperately to prove he was somebody to be reckoned with, to be respected—not just the village troublemaker.

Takezō reminded Matahachi of all this, and Matahachi nodded. "I know. I know. But I felt the same way. It wasn't just you."

Takezō went on: "I wanted you to come with me because we've always done everything together. But didn't your mother carry on something awful! Yelling and telling everybody I was crazy and no good! And your fiancée Otsū, and my sister and everybody else crying and saying village boys should stay in the village. Oh, maybe they had their reasons. We are both only sons, and if we get ourselves killed there's no one else to carry on the family names. But who cares? Is that any way to live?"

They had slipped out of the village unnoticed and were convinced that no 5 further barrier lay between themselves and the honors of battle. When they reached the Shimmen encampment, however, they came face to face with the realities of war. They were told straightaway they would not be made samurai, not overnight nor even in a few weeks, no matter who their fathers had been. To Ishida and the other generals, Takezō and Matahachi were a pair of country bumpkins, little more than children who happened to have got their hands on a couple of lances. The best they could wangle was to be allowed to stay on as common foot soldiers. Their responsibilities, if they could be called that, consisted of carrying weapons, rice kettles and other utensils, cutting grass, working on the road gangs and occasionally going out as scouts.

"Samurai, ha!" said Takezō. "What a joke. General's head! I didn't even get near an enemy samurai, let alone a general. Well, at least it's all over. Now what are we going to do? I can't leave you here all alone. If I did, I could never face your mother or Otsū again."

"Takezō, I don't blame you for the mess we're in. It wasn't your fault we lost. If anybody's to blame, it's that two-faced Kobayakawa. I'd really like to get my hands on him. I'd kill the son of a bitch!"

A couple of hours later they were standing on the edge of a small plain, gazing out over a sea of reedlike miscanthus, battered and broken by the storm. No houses. No lights.

There were lots of corpses here too, lying just as they had fallen. The head of one rested in some tall grass. Another was on its back in a small stream. Still another was entangled grotesquely with a dead horse. The rain had washed the blood away, and in the moonlight the dead flesh looked like fish scales. All around them was the lonely autumn litany of bellrings and crickets.

A stream of tears cleared a white path down Matahachi's grimy face. He heaved the sigh of a very sick man.

"Takezō, if I die, will you take care of Otsū?"

"What are you talking about?"

"I feel like I'm dying."

Takezō snapped, "Well, if that's the way you feel, you probably will." He was exasperated, wishing his friend were stronger, so he could lean on him once in a while, not physically, but for encouragement. "Come on, Matahachi! Don't be such a crybaby."

"My mother has people to look after her, but Otsū's all alone in the world. Always has been. I feel so sorry for her, Takezō. Promise you'll take care of her if I'm not around."

"Get hold of yourself! People don't die from diarrhea. Sooner or later we're going to find a house, and when we do I'll put you to bed and get some medicine for you. Now stop all this blubbering about dying!"

A little farther on, they came to a place where the piles of lifeless bodies made it look as if a whole division had been wiped out. By this time they were callous to the sight of gore. Their glazed eyes took in the scene with cold indifference and they stopped to rest again.

While they were catching their breath, they heard something move among the corpses. Both of them shrank back in fright, instinctively crouching down with their eyes peeled and senses alerted.

The figure made a quick darting movement, like that of a surprised rabbit. As their eyes focused, they saw that whoever it was was squatting close to the ground. Thinking at first it was a stray samurai, they braced themselves for a dangerous encounter, but to their amazement the fierce warrior turned out to be a young girl. She seemed to be about thirteen or fourteen and wore a kimono with rounded sleeves. The narrow obi around her waist, though patched in places, was of gold brocade; there among the corpses she presented a bizarre sight indeed. She looked over and stared at them suspiciously with shrewd catlike eyes.

Takezō and Matahachi were both wondering the same thing: what on earth could bring a young girl to a ghost-ridden, corpse-strewn field in the dead of night?

For a time they both simply stared back at her. Then Takezō said, "Who are you?"

She blinked a couple of times, got to her feet and sped away.

"Stop!" shouted Takezō. "I just want to ask you a question. Don't go!"

But gone she was, like a flash of lightning in the night. The sound of a small bell receded eerily into the darkness.

"Could it have been a ghost?" Takezō mused aloud as he stared vacantly into the thin mist.

Matahachi shivered and forced a laugh. "If there were any ghosts around here, I think they'd be those of soldiers, don't you?"

"I wish I hadn't scared her away," said Takezō. "There's got to be a village around here somewhere. She could've given us directions."

They went on and climbed the nearer of the two hills ahead of them. In the hollow on the other side was the marsh that stretched south from Mount Fuwa. And a light, only half a mile away.

When they approached the farmhouse, they got the impression that it wasn't of the run-of-the-mill variety. For one thing, it was surrounded by a thick dirt wall. For another, its gate verged on being grandiose. Or at least the remains of the gate, for it was old and badly in need of repair.

Takezō went up to the door and rapped lightly. "Is anybody home?"

Getting no answer, he tried again. "Sorry to bother you at this hour, but my friend here is sick. We don't want to cause any trouble—he just needs some rest."

They heard whispering inside and, presently, the sound of someone coming to the door.

"You're stragglers from Sekigahara, aren't you?" The voice belonged to a young girl.

"That's right," said Takezō. "We were under Lord Shimmen of Iga."

"Go away! If you're found around here, we'll be in trouble."

"Look, we've very sorry to bother you like this, but we've been walking a long time. My friend needs some rest, that's all, and—"

"Please go away!"

"All right, if you really want us to, but couldn't you give my friend some medicine? His stomach's in such bad shape it's hard for us to keep moving."

"Well, I don't know. . . ."

After a moment or two, they heard footsteps and a little tinkling sound receding into the house, growing fainter and fainter.

Just then they noticed the face. It was in a side window, a woman's face, and it had been watching them all along.

"Akemi," she called out, "let them in. They're foot soldiers. The Tokugawa patrols aren't going to be wasting time on them. They're nobodies."

Akemi opened the door, and the woman, who introduced herself as Okō, came and listened to Takezō's story.

It was agreed that they could have the woodshed to sleep in. To quiet his bowels, Matahachi was given magnolia charcoal powder and thin rice gruel with scallions in it. Over the next few days, he slept almost without interruption, while Takezō, sitting vigil by his side, used cheap spirits to treat the bullet wounds in his thigh.

One evening about a week later, Takezō and Matahachi sat chatting.

"They must have a trade of some kind," Takezō remarked.

"I couldn't care less what they do. I'm just glad they took us in."

But Takezō's curiosity was aroused. "The mother's not so old," he went on. "It's strange, the two of them living alone here in the mountains."

"Umm. Don't you think the girl looks a little like Otsū?"

"There is something about her that puts me in mind of Otsū, but I don't think they really look alike. They're both nice-looking, that's about it. What do you suppose she was doing the first time we saw her, creeping around all those corpses in the middle of the night? It didn't seem to bother her at all. Ha! I can still see it. Her face was as calm and serene as those dolls they make in Kyoto. What a picture!"

Matahachi motioned for him to be quiet.

"Shh! I hear her bell."

Akemi's light knock on the door sounded like the tapping of a woodpecker. "Matahachi, Takezō," she called softly.

"Yes?"

"It's me."

Takezō got up and undid the lock. She came in carrying a tray of medicine and food and asked them how they were.

"Much better, thanks to you and your mother."

"Mother said that even if you feel better, you shouldn't talk too loud or go outside."

Takezō spoke for the two of them. "We're really sorry to put you to so much trouble."

"Oh, that's okay, you just have to be careful. Ishida Mitsunari and some of the other generals haven't been caught yet. They're keeping a close watch on this area and the roads are crawling with Tokugawa troops."

"They are?"

"So even though you're only foot soldiers, Mother said that if we're caught hiding you, we'll be arrested."

"We won't make a sound," Takezō promised. "I'll even cover Matahachi's face with a rag if he snores too loudly."

Akemi smiled, turned to go and said, "Good night. I'll see you in the morning."

"Wait!" said Matahachi. "Why don't you hang around and talk awhile?"

"I can't."

"Why not?"

"Mother'd be angry."

"Why worry about her? How old are you?"

"Sixteen."

"Small for your age, aren't you?"

"Thanks for telling me."

"Where's your father?"

"I don't have one anymore."

"Sorry. Then how do you live?"

"We make moxa."

"That medicine you burn on your skin to get rid of pain?"

"Yes, the moxa from hereabouts is famous. In spring we cut mugwort on Mount Ibuki. In summer we dry it and in fall and winter make it into moxa. We sell it in Tarui. People come from all over just to buy it."

"I guess you don't need a man around to do that."

"Well, if that's all you wanted to know, I'd better be going."

"Hold on, just another second," said Takezō. "I have one more question."

"Well?"

"The other night, the night we came here, we saw a girl out on the battle-field and she looked just like you. That was you, wasn't it?"

Akemi turned quickly and opened the door.

"What were you doing out there?"

She slammed the door behind her, and as she ran to the house the little bell rang out in a strange, erratic rhythm.

The Comb

At five feet eight or nine, Takezō was tall for people of his time. His body was like a fine steed's: strong and supple, with long, sinewy limbs. His lips were full and crimson, and his thick black eyebrows fell short of being bushy by virtue of their fine shape. Extending well beyond the outer corners of his eyes, they served to accentuate his manliness. The villagers called him "the child of a fat year," an expression used only about children whose features were larger than average. Far from an insult, the nickname nonetheless set

9

him apart from the other youngsters, and for this reason caused him considerable embarrassment in his early years.

Although it was never used in reference to Matahachi, the same expression could have been applied to him as well. Somewhat shorter and stockier than Takezō, he was barrel-chested and round-faced, giving an impression of joviality if not downright buffoonery. His prominent, slightly protruding eyes were given to shifting when he talked, and most jokes made at his expense hinged on his resemblance to the frogs that croaked unceasingly through the summer nights.

Both youths were at the height of their growing years, and thus quick to recover from most ailments. By the time Takezō's wounds had completely healed, Matahachi could no longer stand his incarceration. He took to pacing the woodshed and complaining endlessly about being cooped up. More than once he made the mistake of saying he felt like a cricket in a damp, dark hole, leaving himself wide open to Takezō's retort that frogs and crickets are supposed to like such living arrangements. At some point, Matahachi must have begun peeping into the house, because one day he leaned over to his cellmate as if to impart some earth-shattering news. "Every evening," he whispered gravely, "the widow puts powder on her face and pretties herself up!" Takezō's face became that of a girl-hating twelve-year-old detecting defection, a budding interest in "them," in his closest friend. Matahachi had turned traitor, and the look was one of unmistakable disgust.

Matahachi began going to the house and sitting by the hearth with Akemi and her youthful mother. After three or four days of chatting and joking with them, the convivial guest became one of the family. He stopped going back to the woodshed even at night, and the rare times he did, he had sake on his breath and tried to entice Takezō into the house by singing the praises of the good life just a few feet away.

"You're crazy!" Takezō would reply in exasperation. "You're going to get us killed, or at least picked up. We lost, we're stragglers—can't you get that through your head? We have to be careful and lie low until things cool down."

He soon grew tired of trying to reason with his pleasure-loving friend, however, and started instead to cut him short with curt replies:

"I don't like sake," or sometimes: "I like it out here. It's cozy."

But Takezō was going stir-crazy too. He was bored beyond endurance, and eventually showed signs of weakening. "Is it really safe?" he'd ask. "This neighborhood, I mean? No sign of patrols? You're sure?"

After being entombed for twenty days in the woodshed, he finally emerged like a half-starved prisoner of war. His skin had the translucent, waxen look of death, all the more apparent as he stood beside his sun-and-sake-reddened friend. He squinted up at the clear blue sky, and stretching his arms broadly, yawned extravagantly. When his cavernous mouth finally came closed, one noticed that his brows had been knit all the while. His face wore a troubled air.

10

"Matahachi," he said seriously, "we're imposing on these people. They're taking a big risk having us around. I think we should start for home."

"I guess you're right," said Matahachi. "But they're not letting anyone through the barriers unchecked. The roads to Ise and Kyoto are both impossible, according to the widow. She says we should stay put until the snow comes. The girl says so too. She's convinced we should stay hidden, and you know she's out and about every day."

"You call sitting by the fire drinking being hidden?"

"Sure. You know what I did? The other day some of Tokugawa's men— they're still looking for General Ukita—came snooping around. I got rid of the bastards just by going out and greeting them." At this point, as Takezō's eyes widened in disbelief, Matahachi let out a rolling belly laugh. When it subsided, he went on. "You're safer out in the open than you are crouching in the woodshed listening for footsteps and going crazy. That's what I've been trying to tell you." Matahachi doubled up with laughter again, and Takezō shrugged.

"Maybe you're right. That could be the best way to handle things."

He still had his reservations, but after this conversation he moved into the house. Okō, who obviously liked having people, more specifically men, around, made them feel completely at home. Occasionally, however, she gave them a jolt by suggesting that one of them marry Akemi. This seemed to fluster Matahachi more than Takezō, who simply ignored the suggestion or countered it with a humorous remark.

It was the season for the succulent, fragrant *matsutake*, which grows at the bases of pine trees, and Takezō relaxed enough to go hunting the large mushrooms on the wooded mountain just behind the house. Akemi, basket in hand, would search from tree to tree. Each time she picked up their scent, her innocent voice reverberated through the woods.

"Takezō, over here! Lots of them!"

Hunting around nearby, he invariably replied, "There are plenty over here too."

Through the pine branches, the autumn sun filtered down on them in thin, slanting shafts. The carpet of pine needles in the cool shelter of the trees was a soft dusty rose. When they tired, Akemi would challenge him, giggling. "Let's see who has the most!"

"I do," he'd always reply smugly, at which point she'd begin inspecting his basket.

This day was no different from the others. "Ha, ha! I knew it!" she cried. Gleefully triumphant, the way only girls that young can be, with no hint of self-consciousness or affected modesty, she bent over his basket. "You've got a bunch of toadstools in your batch!" Then she discarded the poisonous fungi one by one, not actually counting out loud, but with movements so slow and deliberate Takezō could hardly ignore them, even with his eyes closed. She flung each one as far as she could. Her task completed, she looked up, her young face beaming with self-satisfaction.

"Now look how many more I have than you!"

"It's getting late," Takezō muttered. "Let's go home."

"You're cross because you lost, aren't you?"

She started racing down the mountainside like a pheasant, but suddenly stopped dead in her tracks, an expression of alarm clouding her face. Approaching diagonally across the grove, halfway down the slope, was a mountain of a man; his strides were long and languorous, and his glaring eyes were trained directly on the frail young girl before him. He looked frighteningly primitive. Everything about him smacked of the struggle to survive, and he had a distinct air of bellicosity: ferocious bushy eyebrows and a thick, curling upper lip; a heavy sword, a cloak of mail, and an animal skin wrapped around him.

"Akemi!" he roared, as he came closer to her. He grinned broadly, showing a row of yellow, decaying teeth, but Akemi's face continued to register nothing but horror.

"Is that wonderful mama of yours home?" he asked with labored sarcasm.

"Yes," came a peep of a reply.

"Well, when you go home, I want you to tell her something. Would you do that for me?" He spoke mock politely.

"Yes."

His tone became harsh. "You tell her she's not putting anything over on me, trying to make money behind my back. You tell her I'll be around soon for my cut. Have you got that?"

Akemi said nothing.

"She probably thinks I don't know about it, but the guy she sold the goods to came straight to me. I bet you were going to Sekigahara too, weren't you, little one?"

"No, of course not!" she protested weakly.

"Well, never mind. Just tell her what I said. If she pulls any more fast ones, I'll kick her out of the neighborhood." He glared at the girl for a moment, then lumbered off in the direction of the marsh.

Takezō turned his eyes from the departing stranger and looked at Akemi with concern. "Who on earth was that?"

Akemi, her lips still trembling, answered wearily, "His name is Tsujikaze. He comes from the village of Fuwa." Her voice was barely above a whisper.

"He's a freebooter, isn't he?"

"Yes."

"What's he so worked up about?"

She stood there without answering.

"I won't tell anybody," he assured her. "Can't you even tell me?"

Akemi, obviously miserable, seemed to be searching for words. Suddenly she leaned against Takezō's chest and pleaded, "Promise you won't tell anyone?"

"Who am I going to tell? The Tokugawa samurai?"

"Remember the night you first saw me? At Sekigahara?"

"Of course I remember."

"Well, haven't you figured out yet what I was doing?"

"No. I haven't thought about it," he said with a straight face.

12   "Well, I was stealing!" She looked at him closely, gauging his reaction.

"Stealing?"

"After a battle, I go to the battlefield and take things off the dead soldiers: swords, scabbard ornaments, incense bags—anything we can sell." She looked at him again for a sign of disapproval, but his face betrayed none. "It scares me," she sighed, then, turning pragmatic, "but we need the money for food and if I say I don't want to go, Mother gets furious."

The sun was still fairly high in the sky. At Akemi's suggestion, Takezō sat down on the grass. Through the pines, they could look down on the house in the marsh.

Takezō nodded to himself, as if figuring something out. A bit later he said, "Then that story about cutting mugwort in the mountains. Making it into moxa. That was all a lie?"

"Oh, no. We do that too! But Mother has such expensive tastes. We'd never be able to make a living on moxa. When my father was alive, we lived in the biggest house in the village—in all seven villages of Ibuki, as a matter of fact. We had lots of servants, and Mother always had beautiful things."

"Was your father a merchant?"

"Oh, no. He was the leader of the local freebooters." Akemi's eyes shone with pride. It was clear she no longer feared Takezō's reaction and was giving vent to her true feelings, her jaw set, her small hands tightening into fists as she spoke. "This Tsujikaze Temma—the man we just met—killed him. At least, everyone says he did."

"You mean your father was murdered?"

Nodding silently, she began in spite of herself to weep, and Takezō felt something deep inside himself start to thaw. He hadn't felt much sympathy for the girl at first. Though smaller than most other girls of sixteen, she talked like a grown woman much of the time, and every once in a while made a quick movement that put one on guard. But when the tears began to drop from her long eyelashes, he suddenly melted with pity. He wanted to hug her in his arms, to protect her.

All the same, she was not a girl who'd had anything resembling a proper upbringing. That there was no nobler calling than that of her father seemed to be something she never questioned. Her mother had persuaded her that it was quite all right to strip corpses, not in order to eat, but in order to live nicely. Many out-and-out thieves would have shrunk from the task.

During the long years of feudal strife, it had reached the point where all the shiftless good-for-nothings in the countryside drifted into making their living this way. People had more or less come to expect it of them. When war broke out, the local military rulers even made use of their services, rewarding them generously for setting fire to enemy supplies, spreading false rumors, stealing horses from enemy camps and the like. Most often their services were bought, but even when they were not, a war offered a host of opportunities; besides foraging among corpses for valuables, they could sometimes even wangle rewards for slaying samurai whose heads they'd merely stumbled upon and picked up. One large battle made it possible for these unscrupulous pilferers to live comfortably for six months or a year.

During the most turbulent times, even the ordinary farmer and woodcutter had learned to profit from human misery and bloodshed. The fighting on the outskirts of their village might keep these simple souls from working, but they had ingeniously adapted to the situation and discovered how to pick over the remains of human life like vultures. Partly because of these intrusions, the professional looters maintained strict surveillance over their respective territories. It was an ironclad rule that poachers—namely, brigands who trespassed on the more powerful brigands' turf—could not go unpunished. Those who dared infringe on the assumed rights of these thugs were liable to cruel retribution.

Akemi shivered and said, "What'll we do? Temma's henchmen are on their way here, I just know it."

"Don't worry," Takezō reassured her. "If they do show up, I'll greet them personally."

When they came down from the mountain, twilight had descended on the marsh, and all was still. A smoke trail from the bath fire at the house crept along the top of a row of tall rushes like an airborne undulating snake. Okō, having finished applying her nightly makeup, was standing idly at the back door. When she saw her daughter approaching side by side with Takezō, she shouted, "Akemi, what have you been doing out so late?"

There was sternness in her eye and voice. The girl, who had been walking along absentmindedly, was brought up short. She was more sensitive to her mother's moods than to anything else in the world. Her mother had both nurtured this sensitivity and learned to exploit it, to manipulate her daughter like a puppet with a mere look or gesture. Akemi quickly fled Takezō's side and, blushing noticeably, ran ahead and into the house.

The next day Akemi told her mother about Tsujikaze Temma. Okō flew into a rage.

"Why didn't you tell me immediately?" she screamed, rushing around like a madwoman, tearing at her hair, taking things out of drawers and closets and piling them all together in the middle of the room.

"Matahachi! Takezō! Give me a hand! We have to hide everything."

Matahachi shifted a board pointed to by Okō and hoisted himself up above the ceiling. There wasn't much space between the ceiling and the rafters. One could barely crawl about, but it served Okō's purpose, and most likely that of her departed husband. Takezō, standing on a stool between mother and daughter, began handing things up to Matahachi one by one. If Takezō hadn't heard Akemi's story the day before, he would've been amazed at the variety of articles he now saw.

Takezō knew the two of them had been at this for a long time, but even so, it was astonishing how much they had accumulated. There was a dagger, a spear tassel, a sleeve from a suit of armor, a helmet without a crown, a miniature, portable shrine, a Buddhist rosary, a banner staff. . . . There was even a lacquered saddle, beautifully carved and ornately decorated with gold, silver and mother-of-pearl inlay.

From the opening in the ceiling Matahachi peered out, a perplexed look on his face. "Is that everything?"

"No, there's one thing more," said Okō, rushing off. In a moment she was back, bearing a four-foot sword of black oak. Takezō started passing it up to Matahachi's outstretched arms, but the weight, the curve, the perfect balance of the weapon impressed him so deeply that he could not let it go.

He turned to Okō, a sheepish look on his face. "Do you think I could have this?" he asked, his eyes showing a new vulnerability. He glanced at his feet, as if to say he knew he'd done nothing to deserve the sword.

"Do you really want it?" she said softly, a motherly tone in her voice.

"Yes . . . Yes . . . I really do!"

Although she didn't actually say he could have it, she smiled, showing a dimple, and Takezō knew the sword was his. Matahachi jumped down from the ceiling, bursting with envy. He fingered the sword covetously, making Okō laugh.

"See how the little man pouts because he didn't get a present!" She tried to placate him by giving him a handsome leather purse beaded with agate. Matahachi didn't look very happy with it. His eyes kept shifting to the black-oak sword. His feelings were hurt and the purse did little to assuage his wounded pride.

When her husband was alive, Okō had apparently acquired the habit of taking a leisurely, steaming hot bath every evening, putting on her makeup, and then drinking a bit of sake. In short, she spent the same amount of time on her toilette as the highest-paid geisha. It was not the sort of luxury that ordinary people could afford, but she insisted on it and had even taught Akemi to follow the same routine, although the girl found it boring and the reasons for it unfathomable. Not only did Okō like to live well; she was determined to remain young forever.

That evening, as they sat around the recessed floor hearth, Okō poured Matahachi's sake and tried to persuade Takezō to have some as well. When he refused, she put the cup in his hand, seized him by the wrist and forced him to raise it to his lips.

"Men are supposed to be able to drink," she chided. "If you can't do it alone, I'll help."

From time to time, Matahachi stared uneasily at her. Okō, conscious of his gaze, became even more familiar with Takezō. Placing her hand playfully on his knee, she began humming a popular love song.

By this time, Matahachi had had enough. Suddenly turning to Takezō, he blurted out, "We ought to be moving on soon!"

This had the desired effect. "But . . . but . . . where would you go?" Okō stammered.

"Back to Miyamoto. My mother's there, and so is my fiancée."

Momentarily taken by surprise, Okō swiftly regained her composure. Her eyes narrowed to slits, her smile froze, her voice turned acid. "Well, please accept my apologies for delaying you, for taking you in and giving you a home. If there's a girl waiting for you, you'd better hurry on back. Far be it from me to keep you!"

After receiving the black-oak sword, Takezō was never without it. He derived an indescribable pleasure from simply holding it. Often he'd squeeze the handle tightly or run its blunt edge along his palm, just to feel the perfect proportion of the curve to the length. When he slept, he hugged it to his body. The cool touch of the wooden surface against his cheek reminded him of the floor of the dōjō where he'd practiced sword techniques in winter. This nearly perfect instrument of both art and death reawakened in him the fighting spirit he had inherited from his father.

Takezō had loved his mother, but she had left his father and moved away when he was still small, leaving him alone with Munisai, a martinet who wouldn't have known how to spoil a child in the unlikely event that he had wanted to. In his father's presence, the boy had always felt awkward and frightened, never really at ease. When he was nine years old, he'd so craved a kind word from his mother that he had run away from home and gone all the way to Harima Province, where she was living. Takezō never learned why his mother and father had separated, and at that age, an explanation might not have helped much. She had married another samurai, by whom she had one more child.

Once the little runaway had reached Harima, he wasted no time in locating his mother. On that occasion, she took him to a wooded area behind the local shrine, so they wouldn't be seen, and there, with tear-filled eyes, hugged him tightly and tried to explain why he had to go back to his father. Takezō never forgot the scene; every detail of it remained vividly in his mind as long as he lived.

Of course, Munisai, being the samurai he was, had sent people to retrieve his son the moment he learned of his disappearance. It was obvious where the child had gone. Takezō was returned to Miyamoto like a bundle of firewood, strapped on the back of an unsaddled horse. Munisai, by way of greeting, had called him an insolent brat, and in a state of rage verging on hysteria, caned him until he could cane no more. Takezō remembered more explicitly than anything else the venom with which his father had spat out his ultimatum: "If you go to your mother one more time, I'll disown you."

Not long after this incident, Takezō learned that his mother had fallen ill and died. Her death had the effect of transforming him from a quiet, gloomy child into the village bully. Even Munisai was intimidated eventually. When he took a truncheon to the boy, the latter countered with a wooden staff. The only one who ever stood up to him was Matahachi, also the son of a samurai; the other children all did Takezō's bidding. By the time he was twelve or thirteen, he was almost as tall as an adult.

One year, a wandering swordsman named Arima Kihei put up a gold-emblazoned banner and offered to take on challengers from the village. Takezō killed him effortlessly, eliciting praise for his valor from the villagers. Their
16 high opinion of him, however, was short-lived, since as he grew older, he

became increasingly unmanageable and brutal. Many thought him sadistic, and soon, whenever he appeared on the scene, people gave him a very wide berth. His attitude toward them grew to reflect their coldness.

When his father, as harsh and unrelenting as ever, finally died, the cruel streak in Takezō widened even more. If it had not been for his older sister, Ogin, Takezō would probably have gotten himself into something far over his head and been driven out of the village by an angry mob. Fortunately, he loved his sister and, powerless before her tears, usually did whatever she asked.

Going off to war with Matahachi was a turning point for Takezō. It indicated that somehow he wanted to take his place in society alongside other men. The defeat at Sekigahara had abruptly curtailed such hopes, and he found himself once again plunged into the dark reality from which he thought he had escaped. Still, he was a youth blessed with the sublime lightheartedness that flourishes only in an age of strife. When he slept, his face became as placid as an infant's, completely untroubled by thoughts of the morrow. He had his share of dreams, asleep or awake, but he suffered few real disappointments. Having so little to begin with, he had little to lose, and although he was in a sense uprooted, he was also unfettered by shackles.

Breathing deeply and steadily, holding on to his wooden sword tightly, Takezō at this moment may well have been dreaming, a faint smile on his lips as visions of his gentle sister and his peaceful hometown cascaded like a mountain waterfall before his closed, heavily lashed eyes. Okō, carrying a lamp, slipped into his room. "What a peaceful face," she marveled under her breath; she reached out and lightly touched his lips with her fingers.

Then she blew out the lamp and lay down beside him. Curling up catlike, she inched closer and closer to his body, her whitened face and colorful nightgown, really too youthful for her, hidden by the darkness. The only sound that could be heard was that of dewdrops dripping onto the windowsill.

"I wonder if he's still a virgin," she mused as she reached out to remove his wooden sword.

The instant she touched it, Takezō was on his feet and shouting, "Thief! Thief!"

Okō was thrown over onto the lamp, which cut into her shoulder and chest. Takezō was wrenching her arm without mercy. She screamed out in pain.

Astonished, he released her. "Oh, it's you. I thought it was a thief."

"Oooh," moaned Okō. "That hurt!"

"I'm sorry. I didn't know it was you."

"You don't know your own strength. You almost tore my arm off."

"I said I was sorry. What are you doing here, anyway?"

Ignoring his innocent query, she quickly recovered from her arm injury and tried to coil the same limb around his neck, cooing, "You don't have to apologize. Takezō . . ." She ran the back of her hand softly against his cheek.

"Hey! What are you doing? Are you crazy?" he shouted, shrinking away from her touch.

"Don't make so much noise, you idiot. You know how I feel about you." She *17*

The men barged rudely into the main part of the house. They didn't even stop to remove their sandals, a sure sign of habitual uncouthness. They began poking around everywhere—in the closets, in the drawers, under the thick straw tatami covering the floor. Temma seated himself royally by the hearth and watched as his henchmen systematically ransacked the rooms. He thoroughly enjoyed being in charge but soon seemed to tire of his own inactivity.

"This is taking too long," he growled, pounding his fist on the tatami. "You must have some of it here. Where is it?"

"I don't know what you're talking about," replied Okō, folding her hands over her stomach forbearingly.

"Don't give me that, woman!" he bellowed. "Where is it? I know it's here!"

"I don't have a thing!"

"Nothing?"

"Nothing."

"Well, then, maybe you don't. Maybe I have the wrong information. . . ." He eyed her warily, tugging and scratching at his beard. "That's enough, men!" he thundered.

Okō had meanwhile sat down in the next room, with the sliding door wide open. She had her back to him, but even so she looked defiant, as though telling him he could go ahead and search wherever he had a mind to.

"Okō," he called gruffly.

"What do you want?" came the icy reply.

"How about a little something to drink?"

"Would you like some water?"

"Don't push me . . ." he warned menacingly.

"The sake's in there. Drink it if you want to."

"Aw, Okō," he said, softening, almost admiring her for her coldhearted stubbornness. "Don't be that way. I haven't been to visit for a long time. Is this any way to treat an old friend?"

"Some visit!"

"Now, take it easy. You're partly to blame, you know. I've been hearing about what the 'moxa man's widow' has been up to from too many different people to think it's all lies. I hear you've been sending your lovely daughter out to rob corpses. Now, why would she be doing a thing like that?"

"Show me your proof!" she shrieked. "Where's the proof!"

"If I'd been planning to dig it out, I wouldn't have given Akemi advance warning. You know the rules of the game. It's my territory, and I've got to go through the motions of searching your house. Otherwise, everybody'd get the idea they could get away with the same thing. Then where'd I be? I've gotta protect myself, you know!"

She stared at him in steely silence, her head half turned toward him, chin and nose proudly raised.

"Well, I'm going to let you off this time. But just remember, I'm being especially nice to you."

"Nice to me? Who, you? That's a laugh!"

"Okō," he coaxed, "come here and pour me a drink."

19

When she showed no sign of moving, he exploded. "You crazy bitch! Can't you see that if you were nice to me, you wouldn't have to live like this?" He calmed down a bit, then advised her, "Think it over for a while."

"I'm overcome by your kindness, sir," came the venomous reply.

"You don't like me?"

"Just answer me this: Who killed my husband? I suppose you expect me to believe that you don't know?"

"If you want to take revenge on whoever it was, I'll be happy to help. Any way I can."

"Don't play dumb!"

"What do you mean by that?"

"You seem to hear so much from people. Haven't they told you that it was you yourself who killed him? Haven't you heard that Tsujikaze Temma was the murderer? Everyone else knows it. I may be the widow of a freebooter, but I haven't sunk so low that I'd play around with my husband's killer."

"You had to go and say it, didn't you—couldn't leave well enough alone, eh!" With a rueful laugh, he drained the sake cup in one gulp and poured another. "You know, you really shouldn't say things like that. It's not good for your health—or your pretty daughter's!"

"I'll bring Akemi up properly, and after she's married, I'll get back at you. Mark my word!"

Temma laughed until his shoulders, his whole body, shook like a cake of bean curd. After he'd downed all the sake he could find, he motioned to one of his men, who was positioned in a corner of the kitchen, his lance propped vertically against his shoulder. "You there," he boomed, "push aside some of the ceiling boards with the butt of your lance!"

The man did as he was told. As he went around the room, poking at the ceiling, Okō's treasure trove began falling to the floor like hailstones.

"Just as I suspected all along," said Temma, getting clumsily to his feet. "You see it, men. Evidence! She's broken the rules, no question about it. Take her outside and give her her punishment!"

The men converged on the hearth room, but abruptly came to a halt. Okō stood statuesquely in the doorway, as though daring them to lay a hand on her. Temma, who'd stepped down into the kitchen, called back impatiently, "What are you waiting for? Bring her out here!"

Nothing happened. Okō continued to stare the men down, and they remained as if paralyzed. Temma decided to take over. Clicking his tongue, he made for Okō, but he, too, stopped short in front of the doorway. Standing behind Okō, not visible from the kitchen, were two fierce-looking young men. Takezō was holding the wooden sword low, poised to fracture the shins of the first comer and anyone else stupid enough to follow. On the other side was Matahachi, holding a sword high in the air, ready to bring it down on the first neck that ventured through the doorway. Akemi was nowhere to be seen.

"So that's how it is," groaned Temma, suddenly remembering the scene on the mountainside. "I saw that one walking the other day with Akemi—the one with the stick. Who's the other one?"

Neither Matahachi nor Takezō said a word, making it clear that they intended to answer with their weapons. The tension mounted.

"There aren't supposed to be any men in this house," roared Temma. "You two . . . You must be from Sekigahara! You better watch your step—I'm warning you."

Neither of them moved a muscle.

"There isn't anybody in these parts who doesn't know the name of Tsujikaze Temma! I'll show you what we do to stragglers!"

Silence. Temma waved his men out of the way. One of them backed straight into the hearth, in the middle of the floor. He let out a yelp and fell in, sending a shower of sparks from the burning kindling up to the ceiling; in seconds, the room filled completely with smoke.

"Aarrgghh!"

As Temma lunged into the room, Matahachi brought down his sword with both hands, but the older man was too fast for him and the blow glanced off the tip of Temma's scabbard. Okō had taken refuge in the nearest corner while Takezō waited, his black-oak sword horizontally poised. He aimed at Temma's legs and swung with all his strength. The staff whizzed through the darkness, but there was no thud of impact. Somehow this bull of a man had jumped up just in time and on the way down threw himself at Takezō with the force of a boulder.

Takezō felt as though he were tangling with a bear. This was the strongest man he had ever fought. Temma grabbed him by the throat and landed two or three blows that made him think his skull would crack. Then Takezō got his second wind and sent Temma flying through the air. He landed against the wall, rocking the house and everything in it. As Takezō raised the wooden sword to come down on Temma's head, the freebooter rolled over, jumped to his feet, and fled, with Takezō close on his tail.

Takezō was determined to not let Temma escape. That would be dangerous. His mind was made up; when he caught him, he was not going to do a halfway job of killing him. He would make absolutely certain that not a breath of life was left.

That was Takezō's nature; he was a creature of extremes. Even when he was a small child, there had been something primitive in his blood, something harking back to the fierce warriors of ancient Japan, something as wild as it was pure. It knew neither the light of civilization nor the tempering of knowledge. Nor did it know moderation. It was a natural trait, and the one that had always prevented his father from liking the boy. Munisai had tried, in the fashion typical of the military class, to curb his son's ferocity by punishing him severely and often, but the effect of such discipline had been to make the boy wilder, like a wild boar whose true ferocity emerges when it is deprived of food. The more the villagers despised the young roughneck, the more he lorded it over them.

As the child of nature became a man, he grew bored with swaggering about the village as though he owned it. It was too easy to intimidate the timid villagers. He began to dream of bigger things. Sekigahara had given him his first lesson in what the world was really like. His youthful illusions were shattered—not that he'd really had many to begin with. It would never have occurred to him to brood over having failed in his first "real" venture, or to muse on the grimness of the future. He didn't yet know the meaning of self-discipline, and he'd taken the whole bloody catastrophe in stride.

And now, fortuitously, he'd stumbled onto a really big fish—Tsujikaze Temma, the leader of the freebooters! This was the kind of adversary he had longed to lock horns with at Sekigahara.

"Coward!" he yelled. "Stand and fight!"

Takezō was running like lightning through the pitch-black field, shouting taunts all the while. Ten paces ahead, Temma was fleeing as if on wings. Takezō's hair was literally on end, and the wind made a groaning noise as it swept past his ears. He was happy—happier than he'd ever been in his life. The more he ran, the closer he came to sheer animal ecstasy.

He leapt at Temma's back. Blood spurted out at the end of the wooden sword, and a bloodcurdling scream pierced the silent night. The freebooter's hulking frame fell to the ground with a leaden thud and rolled over. The skull was smashed to bits, the eyes popped out of their sockets. After two or three more heavy blows to the body, broken ribs protruded from the skin.

Takezō raised his arm, wiping rivers of sweat from his brow.

"Satisfied, Captain?" he asked triumphantly.

He started nonchalantly back toward the house. An observer new on the scene might have thought him out for an evening stroll, with not a care in the world. He felt free, no remorse, knowing that if the other man had won, he himself would be lying there, dead and alone.

Out of the darkness came Matahachi's voice. "Takezō, is that you?"

"Yeah," he replied dully. "What's up?"

Matahachi ran up to him and announced breathlessly, "I killed one! How about you?"

"I killed one too."

Matahachi held up his sword, soaked in blood right down to the braiding on the hilt. Squaring his shoulders with pride, he said, "The others ran away. These thieving bastards aren't much as fighters! No guts! Can only stand up to corpses, ha! Real even match, I'd say, ha, ha, ha."

Both of them were stained with gore and as contented as a pair of well-fed kittens. Chattering happily, they headed for the lamp visible in the distance, Takezō with his bloody stick, Matahachi with his bloody sword.

A stray horse stuck his head through the window and looked around the house. His snorting woke the two sleepers. Cursing the animal, Takezō gave him a smart slap on the nose. Matahachi stretched, yawned and remarked on how well he'd slept.

"The sun's pretty high already," said Takezō.

"You suppose it's afternoon?"

"Couldn't be!"

After a sound sleep, the events of the night before were all but forgotten. For these two, only today and tomorrow existed.

Takezō ran out behind the house and stripped to the waist. Crouching down beside the clean, cool mountain stream, he splashed water on his face, doused his hair and washed his chest and back. Looking up, he inhaled deeply several times, as though trying to drink in the sunlight and all the air in the sky. Matahachi went sleepily into the hearth room, where he bid a cheery good morning to Okō and Akemi.

"Why, what are you two charming ladies wearing sour pusses for?"

"Are we?"

"Yes, most definitely. You look like you're both in mourning. What's there to be gloomy about? We killed your husband's murderer and gave his henchmen a beating they won't soon forget."

Matahachi's dismay was not hard to fathom. He thought the widow and her daughter would be overjoyed at news of Temma's death. Indeed, the night before, Akemi had clapped her hands with glee when she first heard about it. But Okō had looked uneasy from the first, and today, slouching dejectedly by the fire, she looked even worse.

"What's the matter with you?" he asked, thinking she was the most difficult woman in the world to please. "What gratitude!" he said to himself, taking the bitter tea that Akemi had poured for him and squatting down on his haunches.

Okō smiled wanly, envying the young, who know not the ways of the world. "Matahachi," she said wearily, "you don't seem to understand. Temma had hundreds of followers."

"Of course he did. Crooks like him always do. We're not afraid of the kind of people who follow the likes of him. If we could kill him, why should we be afraid of his underlings? If they try to get at us, Takezō and I will just—"

"—will just do nothing!" interrupted Okō.

Matahachi pulled back his shoulders and said, "Who says so? Bring on as many of them as you like! They're nothing but a bunch of worms. Or do you think Takezō and I are cowards, that we're just going to slither away on our bellies in retreat? What do you take us for?"

"You're not cowards, but you are childish! Even to me. Temma has a younger brother named Tsujikaze Kōhei, and if *he* comes after you, the two of you rolled into one wouldn't have a chance!"

This was not the kind of talk Matahachi especially liked to hear, but as she went on, he started thinking that maybe she had a point. Tsujikaze Kōhei apparently had a large band of followers around Yasugawa in Kiso, and not only that: he was expert in the martial arts and unusually adept at catching people off their guard. So far, no one Kōhei had publicly announced he would kill had lived out his normal life. To Matahachi's way of thinking, it was one thing if a person attacked you in the open. It was quite another thing if he snuck up on you when you were fast asleep.

"That's a weak point with me," he admitted. "I sleep like a log."

23

As he sat holding his jaw and thinking, Okō came to the conclusion that there was nothing to do but abandon the house and their present way of life and go somewhere far away. She asked Matahachi what he and Takezō would do.

"I'll talk it over with him," replied Matahachi. "Wonder where he's gone off to?"

He walked outside and looked around, but Takezō was nowhere in sight. After a time he shaded his eyes, looked off into the distance and spotted Takezō riding around in the foothills, bareback on the stray horse that had woken them with his neighing.

"He doesn't have a care in the world," Matahachi said to himself, gruffly envious. Cupping his hands around his mouth, he shouted, "Hey, you! Come home! We've got to talk!"

A little while later they lay in the grass together, chewing on stalks of grass, discussing what they should do next.

Matahachi said, "Then you think we should head home?"

"Yes, I do. We can't stay with these two women forever."

"No, I guess not."

"I don't like women." Takezō was sure of that at least.

"All right. Let's go, then."

Matahachi rolled over and looked up at the sky. "Now that we've made up our minds, I want to get moving. I suddenly realized how much I miss Otsū, how much I want to see her. Look up there! There's a cloud that looks just like her profile. See! That part's just like her hair after she's washed it." Matahachi was kicking his heels into the ground and pointing to the sky.

Takezō's eyes followed the retreating form of the horse he had just set free. Like many of the vagabonds who live in the fields, stray horses seemed to him to be good-natured things. When you're through with them, they ask for nothing; they just go off quietly somewhere by themselves.

From the house Akemi summoned them to dinner. They stood up.

"Race you!" cried Takezō.

"You're on!" countered Matahachi.

Akemi clapped her hands with delight as the two of them sped neck and neck through the tall grass, leaving a thick trail of dust in their wake.

After dinner, Akemi grew pensive. She had just learned that the two men had decided to go back to their homes. It had been fun having them in the house, and she wanted it to go on forever.

"You silly thing!" chided her mother. "Why are you moping so?" Okō was applying her makeup, as meticulously as ever, and as she scolded the girl, she stared into her mirror at Takezō. He caught her gaze and suddenly recalled the pungent fragrance of her hair the night she invaded his room.

Matahachi, who had taken the big sake jar down from a shelf, plopped down next to Takezō and began filling a small warming bottle, just as though he were master of the house. Since this was to be their last night all together, they planned to drink their fill. Okō seemed to be taking special care with her face.

24

"Let's not leave a drop undrunk!" she said. "There's no point in leaving it here for the rats."

"Or the worms!" Matahachi chimed in.

They emptied three large jars in no time. Okō leaned against Matahachi and started fondling him in a way that made Takezō turn his head in embarrassment.

"I . . . I . . . can't walk," mumbled Okō drunkenly.

Matahachi escorted her to her pallet, her head leaning heavily on his shoulder. Once there, she turned to Takezō and said spitefully, "You, Takezō, you sleep over there, by yourself. You like sleeping by yourself. Isn't that right?"

Without a murmur, he lay down where he was. He was very drunk and it was very late.

By the time he woke up, it was broad daylight. The moment he opened his eyes, he sensed it. Something told him the house was empty. The things Okō and Akemi had piled together the day before for the trip were gone. There were no clothes, no sandals—and no Matahachi.

He called out, but there was no reply, nor did he expect one. A vacant house has an aura all its own. There was no one in the yard, no one behind the house, no one in the woodshed. The only trace of his companions was a bright red comb lying beside the open mouth of the water pipe.

"Matahachi's a pig!" he said to himself.

Sniffing the comb, he again recalled how Okō had tried to seduce him that evening not long ago. "This," he thought, "is what defeated Matahachi." The very idea made him boil with anger.

"Fool!" he cried out loud. "What about Otsū? What do you plan to do about her? Hasn't she been deserted too many times already, you pig?"

He stamped the cheap comb under his foot. He wanted to cry in rage, not for himself, but out of pity for Otsū, whom he could picture so clearly waiting back in the village.

As he sat disconsolately in the kitchen, the stray horse looked in the doorway impassively. Finding that Takezō would not pat his nose, he wandered over to the sink and began lazily to lick some grains of rice that had stuck there.

The Flower Festival

In the seventeenth century, the Mimasaka highroad was something of a major thoroughfare. It led up from Tatsuno in Harima Province, winding through a terrain proverbially described as "one mountain after another." Like the stakes marking the Mimasaka-Harima boundary, it followed a seemingly endless series of ridges. Travelers emerging from Nakayama Pass looked down into the valley of the Aida River, where, often to their surprise, they saw a sizable village.

Actually, Miyamoto was more a scattering of hamlets than a real village. One cluster of houses lay along the riverbanks, another huddled farther up in the hills, and a third sat amid level fields that were stony and hence hard to plow. All in all, the number of houses was substantial for a rural settlement of the time.

Until about a year before, Lord Shimmen of Iga had maintained a castle not a mile up the river—a small castle as castles go, but one that nonetheless attracted a steady stream of artisans and tradespeople. Farther to the north were the Shikozaka silver mines, which were now past their prime but had once lured miners from far and wide.

Travelers going from Tottori to Himeji, or from Tajima through the mountains to Bizen, naturally used the highroad. Just as naturally, they stopped over in Miyamoto. It had the exotic air of a village often visited by the natives of several provinces and boasted of not only an inn, but a clothing store as well. It also harbored a bevy of women of the night, who, throats powdered white as was the fashion, hovered before their business establishments like white bats under the eaves. This was the town Takezō and Matahachi had left to go to war.

Looking down on the rooftops of Miyamoto, Otsū sat and daydreamed. She was a wisp of a girl, with fair complexion and shining black hair. Fine of bone, fragile of limb, she had an ascetic, almost ethereal air. Unlike the robust and ruddy farm girls working in the rice paddies below, Otsū's movements were delicate. She walked gracefully, with her long neck stretched and head held high. Now, perched on the edge of Shippōji temple porch, she was as poised as a porcelain statuette.

A foundling raised in this mountain temple, she had acquired a lovely aloofness rarely found in a girl of sixteen. Her isolation from other girls her age and from the workaday world had given her eyes a contemplative, serious cast which tended to put off men used to frivolous females. Matahachi, her betrothed, was just a year older, and since he'd left Miyamoto with Takezō the previous summer, she'd heard nothing. Even into the first and second months of the new year, she'd yearned for word of him, but now the fourth month was at hand. She no longer dared hope.

Lazily her gaze drifted up to the clouds, and a thought slowly emerged. "Soon it will have been a whole year."

"Takezō's sister hasn't heard from him either. I'd be a fool to think either of them is still alive." Now and then she'd say this to someone, longing, almost pleading with her voice and eyes, for the other person to contradict her, to tell her not to give up. But no one heeded her sighs. To the down-to-earth villagers, who had already gotten used to the Tokugawa troops occupying the modest Shimmen castle, there was no reason in the world to assume they'd survived. Not a single member of Lord Shimmen's family had come back from Sekigahara, but that was only natural. They were samurai; they had lost. They wouldn't want to show their faces among people who knew them. But common foot soldiers? Wasn't it all right for them to come home? Wouldn't they have done so long ago if they had survived?

"Why," wondered Otsū, as she had wondered countless times before, "why do men run off to war?" She had come to enjoy in a melancholy way sitting alone on the temple porch and pondering this imponderable. Lost in wistful reverie, she could have lingered there for hours. Suddenly a male voice calling "Otsū!" invaded her island of peace.

Looking up, Otsū saw a youngish man coming toward her from the well. He was clad in only a loincloth, which barely served its purpose, and his weathered skin glowed like the dull gold of an old Buddhist statue. It was the Zen monk who, three or four years before, had wandered in from Tajima Province. He'd been staying at the temple ever since.

"At last it's spring," he was saying to himself with satisfaction. "Spring—a blessing, but a mixed one. As soon as it gets a little warm, those insidious lice overrun the country. They're trying to take it over, just like Fujiwara no Michinaga, that wily rascal of a regent." After a pause, he went on with his monologue.

"I've just washed my clothes, but where on earth am I going to dry this tattered old robe? I can't hang it on the plum tree. It'd be a sacrilege, an insult to nature to cover those flowers. Here I am, a man of taste, and I can't find a place to hang this robe! Otsū! Lend me a drying pole."

Blushing at the sight of the scantily clad monk, she cried, "Takuan! You can't just walk around half naked till your clothes dry!"

"Then I'll go to sleep. How's that?"

"Oh, you're impossible!"

Raising one arm skyward and pointing the other toward the ground, he assumed the pose of the tiny Buddha statues that worshipers anointed once a year with special tea.

"Actually, I should have just waited till tomorrow. Since it's the eighth, the Buddha's birthday, I could have just stood like this and let the people bow to me. When they ladled the sweet tea over me, I could've shocked everyone by licking my lips." Looking pious, he intoned the first words of the Buddha: "In heaven above and earth below, only I am holy."

Otsū burst out laughing at his irreverent display. "You do look just like him, you know!"

"Of course I do. I am the living incarnation of Prince Siddartha."

"Then stand perfectly still. Don't move! I'll go and get some tea to pour over you."

At this point, a bee began a full-scale assault on the monk's head and his reincarnation pose instantly gave way to a flailing of arms. The bee, noticing a gap in his loosely hung loincloth, darted in, and Otsū doubled up with laughter. Since the arrival of Takuan Sōhō, which was the name he was given on becoming a priest, even the reticent Otsū went few days without being amused by something he'd do or say.

Suddenly, however, she stopped laughing. "I can't waste any more time like this. I have important things to do!"

As she was slipping her small white feet into her sandals, the monk asked innocently, "What things?"

"What things? Have you forgotten too? Your little pantomime just reminded me. I'm supposed to get everything ready for tomorrow. The old priest asked me to pick flowers so we can decorate the flower temple. Then I have to set everything up for the anointing ceremony. And tonight I've got to make the sweet tea."

"Where are you going flower-picking?"

"Down by the river, in the lower part of the field."

"I'll come with you."

"Without any clothes on?"

"You'll never be able to cut enough flowers by yourself. You need help. Besides, man is born unclothed. Nakedness is his natural state."

"That may be, but I don't find it natural. Really, I'd rather go alone."

Hoping to elude him, Otsū hurried around to the rear of the temple. She strapped a basket on her back, picked up a sickle and slipped out the side gate, but only moments later turned to see him close behind her. Takuan was now swathed in a large wrapping cloth, the kind people used to carry their bedding.

"Is this more to your liking?" he called with a grin.

"Of course not. You look ridiculous. People will think you're crazy!"

"Why?"

"Never mind. Just don't walk next to me!"

"You never seemed to mind walking beside a man before."

"Takuan, you're perfectly horrible!" She ran off ahead, with him following in strides that would have befitted the Buddha descending from the Himalayas. His wrapping cloth flapped wildly in the breeze.

"Don't be angry, Otsū! You know I'm teasing. Besides, your boyfriends won't like you if you pout too much."

28 Eight or nine hundred yards down from the temple, spring flowers were

blooming profusely along both banks of the Aida River. Otsū put her basket down and, amid a sea of fluttering butterflies, began swinging her sickle in wide circles, cutting the flowers off near their roots.

After a while, Takuan grew reflective. "How peaceful it is here," he sighed, sounding both religious and childlike. "Why, when we could live out our lives in a flower-filled paradise, do we all prefer to weep, suffer and get lost in a maelstrom of passion and fury, torturing ourselves in the flames of hell? I hope that you, at least, won't have to go through all that."

Otsū, rhythmically filling her basket with yellow rape blossoms, spring chrysanthemums, daisies, poppies and violets, replied, "Takuan, instead of preaching a sermon, you'd better watch out for the bees."

He nodded his head, sighing in despair. "I'm not talking about bees, Otsū. I simply want to pass on to you the Buddha's teaching on the fate of women."

"This woman's fate is none of your business!"

"Oh, but you're wrong! It's my duty as a priest to pry into people's lives. I agree it's a meddlesome trade, but it's no more useless than the business of a merchant, clothier, carpenter or samurai. It exists because it is needed."

Otsū softened. "I suppose you're right."

"It does happen, of course, that the priesthood has been on bad terms with womankind for some three thousand years. You see, Buddhism teaches that women are evil. Fiends. Messengers of hell. I've spent years immersed in the scriptures, so it's no accident that you and I fight all the time."

"And why, according to your scriptures, are women evil?"

"Because they deceive men."

"Don't men deceive women too?"

"Yes, but . . . the Buddha himself was a man."

"Are you saying that if he'd been a woman, things would be the other way around?"

"Of course not! How could a demon ever become a Buddha!"

"Takuan, that doesn't make any sense."

"If religious teachings were just common sense, we wouldn't need prophets to pass them on to us."

"There you go again, twisting everything to your own advantage!"

"A typical female comment. Why attack me personally?"

She stopped swinging her sickle again, a world-weary look on her face.

"Takuan, let's stop it. I'm not in the mood for this today."

"Silence, woman!"

"You're the one who's been doing all the talking."

Takuan closed his eyes as if to summon patience. "Let me try to explain. When the Buddha was young, he sat under the bo tree, where she-demons tempted him night and day. Naturally, he didn't form a high opinion of women. But even so, being all-merciful, he took some female disciples in his old age."

"Because he'd grown wise or senile?"

"Don't be blasphemous!" he warned sharply. "And don't forget the Bodhisattva Nagarjuna, who hated—I mean feared—women as much as the Buddha   *29* did. Even he went so far as to praise four female types: obedient sisters, loving companions, good mothers and submissive maidservants. He extolled their virtues again and again, and advised men to take such women as wives."

"Obedient sisters, loving companions, good mothers and submissive maid-servants . . . I see you have it all worked out to men's advantage."

"Well, that's natural enough, isn't it? In ancient India, men were honored more and women less than in Japan. Anyway, I'd like you to hear the advice Nagarjuna gave women."

"What advice?"

"He said, 'Woman, marry thyself not to a man—'"

"That's ridiculous!"

"Let me finish. He said, 'Woman, marry thyself to the truth.'"

Otsū looked at him blankly.

"Don't you see?" he said, with a wave of his arm. "'Marry thyself to the truth' means that you shouldn't become infatuated with a mere mortal but should seek the eternal."

"But, Takuan," Otsū asked impatiently, "what is 'the truth'?"

Takuan let both arms fall to his sides and looked at the ground. "Come to think of it," he said thoughtfully, "I'm not really sure myself."

Otsū burst out laughing, but Takuan ignored her. "There is something I know for certain. Applied to your life, wedding honesty means that you shouldn't think of going off to the city and giving birth to weak, namby-pamby children. You should stay in the country, where you belong, and raise a fine, healthy brood instead."

Otsū raised her sickle impatiently. "Takuan," she snapped, exasperated, "did you come out here to help me pick flowers or not?"

"Of course I did. That's why I'm here."

"In that case, stop preaching and grab this sickle."

"All right; if you don't really want my spiritual guidance, I won't impose it on you," he said, pretending hurt.

"While you're busy at work, I'll run over to Ogin's house and see if she's finished the obi I'm supposed to wear tomorrow."

"Ogin? Takezō's sister? I've met her, haven't I? Didn't she come with you once to the temple?" He dropped the sickle. "I'll come with you."

"In that outfit?"

He pretended not to hear. "She'll probably offer us some tea. I'm dying of thirst."

Totally spent from arguing with the monk, Otsū gave a weak nod and to-gether they set out along the riverbank.

Ogin was a woman of twenty-five, no longer considered in the bloom of youth but by no means bad-looking. Although suitors tended to be put off by her brother's reputation, she suffered no lack of proposals. Her poise and good breeding were immediately evident to everyone. She'd turned down all offers thus far simply on the grounds that she wanted to look after her younger brother a bit longer.

The house she lived in had been built by their father, Munisai, when he was in charge of military training for the Shimmen clan. As a reward for his excellent service, he'd been honored with the privilege of taking the Shimmen name. Overlooking the river, the house was surrounded by a high dirt wall set on a stone foundation and was much too large for the needs of an ordinary country samurai. Although once imposing, it had become run down. Wild irises were sprouting from the roof, and the wall of the dōjō where Munisai once taught martial arts was completely plastered with white swallow droppings.

Munisai had fallen from favor, lost his status, and died a poor man, not an uncommon occurrence in an age of turmoil. Soon after his death, his servants had left, but since they were all natives of Miyamoto, many still dropped in. When they did, they would leave fresh vegetables, clean the unused rooms, fill the water jars, sweep the path, and in countless other ways help keep the old house going. They would also have a pleasant chat with Munisai's daughter.

When Ogin, who was sewing in an inner room, heard the back door open, she naturally assumed it was one of these former servants. Lost in her work, she gave a jump when Otsū greeted her.

"Oh," she said. "It's you. You gave me a fright. I'm just finishing your obi now. You need it for the ceremony tomorrow, don't you?"

"Yes, I do. Ogin, I want to thank you for going to so much trouble. I should have sewn it myself, but there was so much to do at the temple, I never would have had time."

"I'm glad to be of help. I have more time on my hands than is good for me. If I'm not busy, I start to brood."

Otsū, raising her head, caught sight of the household altar. On it, in a small dish, was a flickering candle. By its dim light, she saw two dark inscriptions, carefully brush-painted. They were pasted on boards, an offering of water and flowers before them:

The Departed Spirit of Shimmen Takezō, Aged 17.

The Departed Spirit of Hon'iden Matahachi, Same Age.

"Ogin," Otsū said with alarm. "Have you gotten word they were killed?"

"Well, no . . . But what else can we think? I've accepted it. I'm sure they met their deaths at Sekigahara."

Otsū shook her head violently. "Don't say that! It'll bring bad luck! They aren't dead, they aren't! I know they'll show up one of these days."

Ogin looked at her sewing. "Do you dream about Matahachi?" she asked softly.

"Yes, all the time. Why?"

"That proves he's dead. I dream of nothing but my brother."

"Ogin, don't say that!" Rushing over to the altar, Otsū tore the inscriptions from their boards. "I'm getting rid of these things. They'll just invite the worst."

Tears streamed down her face as she blew out the candle. Not satisfied with that, she seized the flowers and the water bowl and rushed through the next room to the veranda, where she flung the flowers as far as she could and poured the water out over the edge. It landed right on the head of Takuan, who was squatting on the ground below.

"Aaii! That's cold!" he yelped, jumping up, frantically trying to dry his head with an end of the wrapping cloth. "What're you doing? I came here for a cup of tea, not a bath!"

Otsū laughed until fresh tears, tears of mirth, came. "I'm sorry, Takuan. I really am. I didn't see you."

By way of apology, she brought him the tea he'd been waiting for. When she went back inside, Ogin, who was staring fixedly toward the veranda, asked, "Who is that?"

"The itinerant monk who's staying at the temple. You know, the dirty one. You met him one day, with me, remember? He was lying in the sun on his stomach with his head in his hands, staring at the ground. When we asked him what he was doing, he said his lice were having a wrestling match. He said he'd trained them to entertain him."

"Oh, him!"

"Yes, him. His name's Takuan Sōhō."

"Kind of strange."

"That's putting it mildly."

"What's that thing he's wearing? It doesn't look like a priest's robe."

"It isn't. It's a wrapping cloth."

"A wrapping cloth? He is eccentric. How old is he?"

"He says he's thirty-one, but sometimes I feel like his older sister, he's so silly. One of the priests told me that despite his appearance, he's an excellent monk."

"I suppose that's possible. You can't always judge people by their looks. Where's he from?"

"He was born in Tajima Province and started training for the priesthood when he was ten. Then he entered a temple of the Rinzai Zen sect about four years later. After he left, he became a follower of a scholar-priest from the Daitokuji and traveled with him to Kyoto and Nara. Later on he studied under Gudō of the Myōshinji, Ittō of Sennan and a whole string of other famous holy men. He's spent an awful lot of time studying!"

"Maybe that's why there's something different about him."

Otsū continued her story. "He was made a resident priest at the Nansōji and was appointed abbot of the Daitokuji by imperial edict. I've never learned why from anyone, and he never talks about his past, but for some reason he ran away after only three days."

Ogin shook her head.

Otsū went on. "They say famous generals like Hosokawa and noblemen like Karasumaru have tried again and again to persuade him to settle down. They even offered to build him a temple and donate money for its upkeep, but he's just not interested. He says he prefers to wander about the countryside like a beggar, with only his lice for friends. I think he's probably a little crazy."

"Maybe from his viewpoint we're the ones who are strange."

"That's exactly what he says!"

"How long will he stay here?"

"There's no way of knowing. He has a habit of showing up one day and disappearing the next."

Standing up near the veranda, Takuan called, "I can hear everything you're saying!"

"Well, it's not as though we're saying anything bad," Otsū replied cheerfully.

"I don't care if you do, if you find it amusing, but you could at least give me some sweet cakes to go with my tea."

"That's what I mean," said Otsū. "He's like this all the time."

"What do you mean, I'm 'like this'?" Takuan had a gleam in his eye. "What about you? You sit there looking as though you wouldn't hurt a fly, acting much more cruel and heartless than I ever would."

"Oh, really? And how am I being cruel and heartless?"

"By leaving me out here helpless, with nothing but tea, while you sit around moaning about your lost lover—that's how!"

The bells were ringing at the Daishōji and the Shippōji. They had started in a measured beat just after dawn and still rang forth now and then long past noon. In the morning a constant procession flowed to the temples: girls in red obis, wives of tradesmen wearing more subdued tones, and here and there an old woman in a dark kimono leading her grandchildren by the hand. At the Shippōji, the small main hall was crowded with worshipers, but the young men among them seemed more interested in stealing a glimpse of Otsū than in taking part in the religious ceremony.

"She's here, all right," whispered one.

"Prettier than ever," added another.

Inside the hall stood a miniature temple. Its roof was thatched with lime leaves and its columns were entwined with wild flowers. Inside this "flower temple," as it was called, stood a two-foot-high black statue of the Buddha, pointing one hand to heaven and the other to earth. The image was placed in a shallow clay basin, and the worshipers, as they passed, poured sweet tea over its head with a bamboo ladle. Takuan stood by with an extra supply of the holy balm, filling bamboo tubes for the worshipers to take home with them for good luck. As he poured, he solicited offerings.

"This temple is poor, so leave as much as you can. Especially you rich folks—I know who you are; you're wearing those fine silks and embroidered obis. You have a lot of money. You must have a lot of troubles too. If you leave a hundredweight of cash for your tea, your worries will be a hundredweight lighter."

On the other side of the flower temple, Otsū was seated at a black-lacquered table. Her face glowed light pink, like the flowers all around her. Wearing her new obi and writing charms on pieces of five-colored paper, she wielded her brush deftly, occasionally dipping it in a gold-lacquered ink box to her right. She wrote:

Swiftly and keenly,
On this best of days,
The eighth of the fourth month,
Bring judgment to bear on those
Insects that devour the crops.

From time immemorial it had been thought in these parts that hanging this practical-minded poem on the wall could protect one from not only bugs, but disease and ill fortune as well. Otsū wrote the same verse scores of times—so often, in fact, that her wrist started to throb and her calligraphy began to reflect her fatigue.

Stopping to rest for a moment, she called out to Takuan: "Stop trying to rob these people. You're taking too much."

"I'm talking to those who already have too much. It's become a burden. It's the essence of charity to relieve them of it," he replied.

"By that reasoning, common burglars are all holy men."

Takuan was too busy collecting offerings to reply. "Here, here," he said to the jostling crowd. "Don't push, take your time, just get in line. You'll have your chance to lighten your purses soon enough."

"Hey, priest!" said a young man who'd been admonished for elbowing in.

"You mean me?" Takuan said, pointing to his nose.

"Yeah. You keep telling us to wait our turn, but then you serve the women first."

"I like women as much as the next man."

"You must be one of those lecherous monks we're always hearing stories about."

"That's enough, you tadpole! Do you think I don't know why *you're* here! You didn't come to honor the Buddha, or to take home a charm. You came to get a good look at Otsū! Come on now, own up—isn't that so? You won't get anywhere with women, you know, if you act like a miser."

Otsū's face turned scarlet. "Takuan, stop it! Stop right now, or I'm really going to get mad!"

To rest her eyes, Otsū again looked up from her work and out over the crowd. Suddenly she caught a glimpse of a face and dropped her brush with a clatter. She jumped to her feet, almost toppling the table, but the face had already vanished, like a fish disappearing in the sea. Oblivious of all around her, she dashed to the temple porch, shouting, "Takezō! Takezō!"

34

The Dowager's Wrath

Matahachi's family, the Hon'iden, were the proud members of a group of rural gentry who belonged to the samurai class but who also worked the land. The real head of the family was his mother, an incorrigibly stubborn woman named Osugi. Though nearly sixty, she led her family and tenants out to the fields daily and worked as hard as any of them. At planting time she hoed the fields and after the harvest threshed the barley by trampling it. When dusk forced her to stop working, she always found something to sling on her bent back and haul back to the house. Often it was a load of mulberry leaves so big that her body, almost doubled over, was barely visible beneath it. In the evening, she could usually be found tending her silkworms.

On the afternoon of the flower festival, Osugi looked up from her work in the mulberry patch to see her runny-nosed grandson racing barefoot across the field.

"Where've you been, Heita?" she asked sharply. "At the temple?"

"Uh-huh."

"Was Otsū there?"

"Yes," he answered excitedly, still out of breath. "And she had on a very pretty obi. She was helping with the festival."

"Did you bring back some sweet tea and a spell to keep the bugs away?"

"Unh-unh."

The old woman's eyes, usually hidden amid folds and wrinkles, opened wide in irritation. "And why not?"

"Otsū told me not to worry about them. She said I should run right home and tell you."

"Tell me what?"

"Takezō, from across the river. She said she saw him. At the festival."

Osugi's voice dropped an octave. "Really? Did she really say that, Heita?"

"Yes, Granny."

Her strong body seemed to go limp all at once, and her eyes blurred with tears. Slowly she turned, as though expecting to see her son standing behind her.

Seeing no one, she spun back around. "Heita," she said abruptly, "you take over and pick these mulberry leaves."

"Where're you going?"

"Home. If Takezō's back, Matahachi must be too."

"I'll come too."

"No you won't. Don't be a nuisance, Heita."

The old woman stalked off, leaving the little boy as forlorn as an orphan. The farmhouse, surrounded by old, gnarled oaks, was a large one. Osugi ran past it, heading straight for the barn, where her daughter and some tenant farmers were working. While still a fair distance away, she began calling to them somewhat hysterically.

"Has Matahachi come home? Is he here yet?"

Startled, they stared at her as though she'd lost her wits. Finally one of the men said "no," but the old woman seemed not to hear. It was as though in her overwrought state she refused to take no for an answer. When they continued their noncommittal gaze, she began calling them all dunces and explaining what she'd heard from Heita, how if Takezō was back, then Matahachi must be too. Then, reassuming her role as commander in chief, she sent them off in all directions to find him. She herself stayed behind in the house, and every time she sensed someone approaching, ran out to ask if they had found her son yet.

At sunset, still undaunted, she placed a candle before the memorial tablets of her husband's ancestors. She sat down, seemingly lost in prayer, as immobile as a statue. Since everyone was still out searching, there was no evening meal at the house, and when night fell and there was still no news, Osugi finally moved. As if in a trance, she walked slowly out of the house to the front gate. There she stood and waited, hidden in the darkness. A watery moon shone through the oak tree branches, and the mountains looming before and behind the house were veiled in a white mist. The sweetish scent of pear blossoms floated in the air.

Time, too, floated by unnoticed. Then a figure could be discerned approaching, making its way along the outer edge of the pear orchard. Recognizing the silhouette as Otsū's, Osugi called out and the girl ran forward, her wet sandals clomping heavily on the earth.

"Otsū! They told me you saw Takezō. Is that true?"

"Yes, I'm sure it was him. I spotted him in the crowd outside the temple."

"You didn't see Matahachi?"

"No. I rushed out to ask Takezō about him, but when I called out, Takezō jumped like a scared rabbit. I caught his eye for a second and then he was gone. He's always been strange, but I can't imagine why he ran away like that."

"Ran away?" asked Osugi with a puzzled air. She began to muse, and the longer she did so, the more a terrible suspicion took shape in her mind. It was becoming clear to her that the Shimmen boy, that ruffian Takezō she so hated for luring her precious Matahachi off to war, was once more up to no good.

At length she said ominously, "That wretch! He's probably left poor Matahachi to die somewhere, then sneaked back home safe and sound. Coward, that's what he is!" Osugi began to shake in fury and her voice rose to a shriek. "He can't hide from me!"

36   Otsū remained composed. "Oh, I don't think he'd do anything like that.

Even if he did have to leave Matahachi behind, surely he'd bring us word or at least some keepsake from him." Otsū sounded shocked by the old woman's hasty accusation.

Osugi, however, was by now convinced of Takezō's perfidy. She shook her head decisively and went on. "Oh, no he wouldn't! Not that young demon! He hasn't got that much heart. Matahachi should never have taken up with him."

"Granny . . ." Otsū said soothingly.

"What?" snapped Osugi, not soothed in the least.

"I think that if we go over to Ogin's house, we just might find Takezō there."

The old woman relaxed a bit. "You might be right. She is his sister, and there really isn't anyone else in this village who'd take him in."

"Then let's go and see, just the two of us."

Osugi balked. "I don't see why I should do that. She knew her brother had dragged my son off to war, but she never once came to apologize or to pay her respects. And now that he's back, she hasn't even come to tell me. I don't see why I should go to her. It's demeaning. I'll wait here for her."

"But this isn't an ordinary situation," replied Otsū. "Besides, the main thing at this point is to see Takezō as soon as we can. We've got to find out what happened. Oh, please, Granny, come. You won't have to do anything. I'll take care of all the formalities if you like."

Grudgingly, Osugi allowed herself to be persuaded. She was, of course, as eager as Otsū to find out what was going on, but she'd die before begging for anything from a Shimmen.

The house was about a mile away. Like the Hon'iden family, the Shimmen were country gentry, and both houses were descended from the Akamatsu clan many generations back. Situated across the river from one another, they had always tacitly recognized each other's right to exist, but that was the extent of their intimacy.

When they arrived at the front gate, they found it shut, and the trees were so thick that no light could be seen from the house. Otsū started to walk around to the back entrance, but Osugi stopped mulishly in her tracks.

"I don't think it's right for the head of the Hon'iden family to enter the Shimmen residence by the back door. It's degrading."

Seeing she wasn't going to budge, Otsū proceeded to the rear entrance alone. Presently a light appeared just inside the gate. Ogin herself had come out to greet the older woman, who, suddenly transformed from a crone plowing the fields into a great lady, addressed her hostess in lofty tones.

"Forgive me for disturbing you at this late hour, but my business simply could not wait. How good of you to come and let me in!" Sweeping past Ogin and on into the house, she went immediately, as though she were an envoy from the gods, to the most honored spot in the room, in front of the alcove. Sitting proudly, her figure framed by both a hanging scroll and a flower arrangement, she deigned to accept Ogin's sincerest words of welcome.

The amenities concluded, Osugi went straight to the point. Her false smile disappeared as she glared at the young woman before her. "I have been told that young demon of this house has crawled back home. Please fetch him."

Although Osugi's tongue was notorious for its sharpness, this undisguised maliciousness came as something of a shock to the gentle Ogin.

"Whom do you mean by 'that young demon'?" asked Ogin, with palpable restraint.

Chameleon-like, Osugi changed her tactics. "A slip of the tongue, I assure you," she said with a laugh. "That's what the people in the village call him; I suppose I picked it up from them. The 'young demon' is Takezō. He is hiding here, isn't he?"

"Why, no," replied Ogin with genuine astonishment. Embarrassed to hear her brother referred to in this way, she bit her lip.

Otsū, taking pity on her, explained that she had spotted Takezō at the festival. Then, in an attempt to smooth over ruffled feelings, she added, "Strange, isn't it, that he didn't come straight here?"

"Well, he didn't," said Ogin. "This is the first I've heard anything about it. But if he is back, as you say, I'm sure he'll be knocking at the door any minute."

Osugi, sitting formally on the floor cushion, legs tucked neatly beneath her, folded her hands in her lap and with the expression of an outraged mother-in-law, launched into a tirade.

"What is all this? Do you expect me to believe you haven't heard from him yet? Don't you understand that I'm the mother whose son your young ne'er-do-well dragged off to war? Don't you know that Matahachi is the heir and the most important member of the Hon'iden family? It was your brother who talked my boy into going off to get himself killed. If my son is dead, it's your brother who killed him, and if he thinks he can just sneak back alone and get away with it . . ."

The old woman stopped just long enough to catch her breath, then her eyes glared in fury once more. "And what about you? Since he's obviously had the indecency to sneak back by himself, why haven't you, his older sister, sent him immediately to me? I'm disgusted with both of you, treating an old woman with such disrespect. Who do you think I am?"

Gulping down another breath, she ranted on. "If your Takezō is back, then bring my Matahachi back to me. If you can't do that, the least you can do is set that young demon down right here and make him explain to my satisfaction what happened to my precious boy and where he is—right now!"

"How can I do that? He isn't here."

"That's a black lie!" she shrieked. "You must know where he is!"

"But I tell you I don't!" Ogin protested. Her voice quivered and her eyes filled with tears. She bent over, wishing with all her might her father were still alive.

Suddenly, from the door opening onto the veranda, came a cracking noise, followed by the sound of running feet.

Osugi's eyes flashed, and Otsū started to stand up, but the next sound was a hair-raising scream—as close to an animal's howl as the human voice is capable of producing.

A man shouted, "Catch him!"

Then came the sound of more feet, several more, running around the house, accompanied by the snapping of twigs and the rustling of bamboo.

"It's Takezō!" cried Osugi. Jumping to her feet, she glared at the kneeling Ogin and spat out her words. "I knew he was here," she said ferociously. "It was as clear to me as the nose on your face. I don't know why you've tried to hide him from me, but bear in mind, I'll never forget this."

She rushed to the door and slid it open with a bang. What she saw outside turned her already pale face even whiter. A young man wearing shin plates was lying face up on the ground, obviously dead but with fresh blood still streaming from his eyes and nose. Judging from the appearance of his shattered skull, someone had killed him with a single blow of a wooden sword.

"There's . . . there's a dead . . . a dead man out there!" she stammered.

Otsū brought the light to the veranda and stood beside Osugi, who was staring terror-stricken at the corpse. It was neither Takezō's nor Matahachi's, but that of a samurai neither of them recognized.

Osugi murmured, "Who could've done this?" Turning swiftly to Otsū, she said, "Let's go home before we get mixed up in something."

Otsū couldn't bring herself to leave. The old woman had said a lot of vicious things. It would be unfair to Ogin to leave before putting salve on the wounds. If Ogin had been lying, Otsū felt she must doubtless have had good reason. Feeling she should stay behind to comfort Ogin, she told Osugi she would be along later.

"Do as you please," snapped Osugi, as she made her departure.

Ogin graciously offered her a lantern, but Osugi was proudly defiant in her refusal. "I'll have you know that the head of the Hon'iden family is not so senile that she needs a light to walk by." She tucked up her kimono hems, left the house and walked resolutely into the thickening mist.

Not far from the house, a man called her to a halt. He had his sword drawn, and his arms and legs were protected by armor. He was obviously a professional samurai of a type not ordinarily encountered in the village.

"Didn't you just come from the Shimmen house?" he asked.

"Yes, but—"

"Are you a member of the Shimmen household?"

"Certainly not!" Osugi snapped, waving her hand in protest. "I am the head of the samurai house across the river."

"Does that mean you are the mother of Hon'iden Matahachi, who went with Shimmen Takezō to the Battle of Sekigahara?"

"Well, yes, but my son didn't go because he wanted to. He was tricked into going by that young demon."

"Demon?"

"That . . . Takezō!"

"I gather this Takezō is not too well thought of in the village."

"Well thought of? That's a laugh. You never saw such a hoodlum! You can't imagine the trouble we've had at my house since my son took up with him."

"Your son seems to have died at Sekigahara. I'm—"

"Matahachi! Dead?"

"Well, actually, I'm not sure, but perhaps it'll be some comfort to you in your grief to know that I'll do everything possible to help you take revenge."

Osugi eyed him skeptically. "Just who are you?"

"I'm with the Tokugawa garrison. We came to Himeji Castle after the battle. On orders from my lord, I've set up a barrier on the Harima Province border to screen everyone who crosses.

"This Takezō, from that house back there," he continued, pointing, "broke through the barrier and fled toward Miyamoto. We chased him all the way here. He's a tough one, all right. We thought that after a few days of walking he'd collapse, but we still haven't caught up with him. He can't go on forever, though. We'll get him."

Nodding as she listened, Osugi realized now why Takezō hadn't appeared at the Shippōji, and more importantly, that he probably hadn't gone home, since that was the first place the soldiers would search. At the same time, since it seemed he was traveling alone, her fury wasn't diminished in the least. But as for Matahachi being dead, she couldn't believe that either.

"I know Takezō can be as strong and cunning as any wild beast, sir," she said coyly, "But I shouldn't think that samurai of your caliber would have any trouble capturing him."

"Well, frankly, that's what I thought at first. But there aren't many of us and he's just killed one of my men."

"Let an old woman give you a few words of advice." Leaning over, she whispered something in his ear. Her words seemed to please him immensely.

He nodded his approval and enthusiastically exclaimed, "Good idea! Splendid!"

"Be sure to do a thorough job of it," urged Osugi as she took her leave.

Not long afterward, the samurai regrouped his band of fourteen or fifteen men behind Ogin's house. After he briefed them, they piled over the wall, surrounding the house and blocking all exits. Several soldiers then stormed into the house, leaving a trail of mud, and crowded into the inner room where the two young women sat commiserating and dabbing at their tear-stained faces.

Confronted by the soldiers, Otsū gasped and turned white. Ogin, however, proud to be the daugher of Munisai, was unperturbed. With calm, steely eyes, she stared indignantly at the intruders.

"Which one of you is Takezō's sister?" asked one of them.

"I am," replied Ogin coldly, "and I demand to know why you've entered this house without permission. I will not stand for such brutish behavior in a house occupied only by women." She had turned to face them directly.

The man who had been chatting with Osugi a few minutes earlier pointed to Ogin. "Arrest her!" he ordered.

Barely were the words out of his mouth before violence erupted, the house began to shake and the lights went out. Uttering a cry of terror, Otsū stumbled out into the garden, while at least ten of the soldiers fell upon Ogin and began tying her up with a rope. Despite her heroic resistance, it was all over in a few seconds. They then pushed her down onto the floor and began kicking her as hard as they could.

Otsū couldn't recall afterward which way she had come, but somehow she managed to escape. Barely conscious, she ran barefoot toward the Shippōji in the misty moonlight, relying completely on instinct. She had grown up in peaceful surroundings and now felt as though the world were caving in.

When she reached the foot of the hill where the temple stood, someone called to her. She saw a shape sitting on a rock among the trees. It was Takuan.

"Thank heaven it's you," he said. "I was really starting to worry. You never stay out this late. When I realized the time, I came out looking for you." He looked down toward the ground and asked, "Why are you barefoot?"

He was still gazing at Otsū's bare white feet when she rushed headlong into his arms and began wailing.

"Oh, Takuan! It was awful! What can we do?"

In a calm voice, he tried to soothe her. "There, there. What was awful? There aren't many things in this world that are all that bad. Calm down and tell me what happened."

"They tied Ogin up and took her away! Matahachi didn't come back, and now poor Ogin, who's so sweet and gentle—they were all kicking her. Oh, Takuan, we've got to do something!"

Sobbing and trembling, she clung desperately to the young monk, her head resting on his chest.

It was noon on a still, humid spring day, and a faint mist rose from the young man's sweating face. Takezō was walking alone in the mountains, whither he knew not. He was tired almost beyond endurance, but even at the sound of a bird alighting, his eyes would dart around. Despite the ordeal he'd been through, his mud-spattered body came alive with pent-up violence and the sheer instinct to survive.

"Bastards! Beasts!" he growled. In the absence of the real target of his fury, he swung his black-oak sword screeching through the air, slicing a thick branch off a large tree. The white sap that poured from the wound reminded him of a nursing mother's milk. He stood and stared. With no mother to turn to, there was only loneliness. Instead of offering him comfort, even the running streams and rolling hills of his own home seemed to mock him.

"Why are all the villagers against me?" he wondered. "The minute they see me, they report me to the guards on the mountain. The way they run when they catch sight of me, you'd think I was a madman."

He'd been hiding in the Sanumo mountains for four days. Now, through the veil of the midday mist, he could make out the house of his father, the house where his sister lived alone. Nestled in the foothills just below him was the Shippōji, the temple's roof jutting out from the trees. He knew he could approach neither place. When he'd dared go near the temple on the Buddha's birthday, crowded though it was, he'd risked his life. When he heard his name called, he had no choice but to flee. Aside from wanting to save his own neck, he knew that being discovered there would mean trouble for Otsū.

41

That night, when he'd gone stealthily to his sister's house, Matahachi's mother—as luck would have it—had been there. For a while he'd just stood outside, trying to come up with an explanation of Matahachi's whereabouts, but as he was watching his sister through a crack in the door, the soldiers had spotted him. Again he had to flee without having the chance to speak to anyone. Since then, it appeared from his refuge in the mountains that the Tokugawa samurai were keeping a very sharp eye out for him. They patrolled every road he might take, while at the same time the villagers had banded together to form search parties and were scouring the mountains.

He wondered what Otsū must think of him and began to suspect that even she had turned against him. Since it appeared that everyone in his own village regarded him as an enemy, he was stymied.

He thought: "It'd be too hard to tell Otsū the real reason her fiancé didn't come back. Maybe I should tell the old woman instead. . . . That's it! If I explain everything to her, she can break it gently to Otsū. Then there won't be any reason for me to hang around here."

His mind made up, Takezō resumed walking, but he knew that it would not do to go near the village before dark. With a large rock he broke another into small pieces and hurled one of them at a bird in flight. After it fell to earth, he barely paused to pluck its feathers before sinking his half-starved teeth into the warm, raw flesh. As he was devouring the bird, he started walking again but suddenly heard a stifled cry. Whoever had caught sight of him was scrambling away frantically through the woods. Angered at the idea of being hated and feared—persecuted—for no reason, he shouted, "Wait!" and began running like a panther after the fleeing form.

The man was no match for Takezō and was easily overtaken. It turned out to be one of the villagers who came to the mountains to make charcoal, and Takezō knew him by sight. Grabbing his collar, he dragged him back to a small clearing.

"Why are you running away? Don't you know me? I'm one of you, Shimmen Takezō of Miyamoto. I'm not going to eat you alive. You know, it's very rude to run away from people without even saying hello!"

"Y-y-y-y-yes, sir!"

"Sit down!"

Takezō released his grip on the man's arm, but the pitiful creature started to flee, forcing Takezō to kick his behind and make as if to strike him with his wooden sword. The man cringed on the ground like a simpering dog, his hands over his head.

"Don't kill me!" he screamed pathetically.

"Just answer my questions, all right?"

"I'll tell you anything—just don't kill me! I have a wife and family."

"Nobody's going to kill you. I suppose the hills are crawling with soldiers, aren't they?"

"Yes."

"Are they keeping close watch on the Shippōji?"

"Yes."

"Are the men from the village hunting for me again today?"

Silence.

"Are you one of them?"

The man jumped to his feet, shaking his head like a deaf-mute.

"No, no, no!"

"That's enough," shouted Takezō. Taking a firm grip on the man's neck, he asked, "What about my sister?"

"What sister?"

"*My* sister, Ogin, of the House of Shimmen. Don't play dumb. You promised to answer my questions. I don't really blame the villagers for trying to capture me, because the samurai are forcing them to do it, but I'm sure they'd never do anything to hurt her. Or would they?"

The man replied, too innocently, "I don't know anything about that. Nothing at all."

Takezō swiftly raised his sword above his head in position to strike. "Watch it! That sounded very suspicious to me. Something has happened, hasn't it? Out with it, or I'll smash your skull!"

"Wait! Don't! I'll talk! I'll tell you everything!"

Hands folded in supplication, the trembling charcoal-maker told how Ogin had been taken away a prisoner, and how an order had been circulated in the village to the effect that anyone providing Takezō with food or shelter would automatically be regarded as an accomplice. Each day, he reported, the soldiers were leading villagers into the mountains, and each family was required to furnish one young man every other day for this purpose.

The information caused Takezō to break out in goose pimples. Not fear. Rage. To make sure he'd heard right, he asked, "What crime has my sister been charged with?" His eyes were glistening with moisture.

"None of us knows anything about it. We're afraid of the district lord. We're just doing what we're told, that's all."

"Where have they taken my sister?"

"Rumor has it that they've got her in Hinagura stockade, but I don't know if that's true."

"Hinagura . . ." repeated Takezō. His eyes turned toward the ridge that marked the provincial border. The backbone of the mountains was already spotted with the shadows of gray evening clouds.

Takezō let the man go. Watching him scramble away, grateful to have his meager life spared, made Takezō's stomach turn at the thought of the cowardice of humanity, the cowardice that forced samurai to pick on a poor helpless woman. He was glad to be alone again. He had to think.

He soon reached a decision. "I have to rescue Ogin, and that's that. My poor sister. I'll kill them all if they've harmed her." Having chosen his course of action, he marched down toward the village with long manly strides.

A couple of hours later, Takezō again furtively approached the Shippōji. The evening bell had just stopped tolling. It was already dark and lights could be seen coming from the temple itself, the kitchen and the priests' quarters, where people seemed to be moving about.

"If only Otsū would come out," he thought.

He crouched motionless under the raised passageway—it was of the sort that had a roof but no walls—which connected the priests' rooms with the main temple. The smell of food being cooked floated in the air, conjuring up visions of rice and steaming soup. For the past few days, Takezō had had nothing in his stomach but raw bird meat and grass shoots, and his stomach now rebelled. His throat burned as he vomited up bitter gastric juices, and in his misery he gasped loudly for breath.

"What was that?" said a voice.

"Probably just a cat," answered Otsū, who came out carrying a dinner tray and started crossing the passageway directly over Takezō's head. He tried to call to her, but was still too nauseated to make an intelligible sound.

This, as it happened, was a stroke of luck, because just then a male voice just behind Otsū inquired, "Which way is the bath?"

The man was wearing a kimono borrowed from the temple, tied with a narrow sash from which dangled a small washcloth. Takezō recognized him as one of the samurai from Himeji. Evidently he was of high rank, high enough to lodge at the temple and pass his evenings eating and drinking his fill while his subordinates and the villagers had to scour mountainsides day and night searching for the fugitive.

"The bath?" said Otsū. "Come, I'll show you."

She set her tray down and began leading him along the passageway. Suddenly the samurai rushed forward and hugged her from behind.

"How about joining me in the bath?" he suggested lecherously.

"Stop that! Let go of me!" cried Otsū, but the man, turning her around, held her face in both big hands and brushed his lips against her cheek.

"What's wrong!" he cajoled. "Don't you like men!"

"Stop it! You shouldn't do that!" protested the helpless Otsū. The soldier then clapped his hand over her mouth.

Takezō, oblivious of the danger, leapt up onto the passageway like a cat and thrust his fist at the man's head from behind. The blow was a hard one. Momentarily defenseless, the samurai fell backward, still clinging to Otsū. As she tried to break away from his hold, she let out a shrill scream. The fallen man began shouting, "It's him! It's Takezō! He's here! Come and take him!"

The rumble of feet and the roar of voices thundered from inside the temple. The temple bell began signaling the alarm that Takezō had been discovered, and from the woods throngs of men began converging on the temple grounds. But Takezō was already gone, and before long search parties were once again sent out to scour the hills of Sanumo. Takezō himself hardly knew how he'd slipped through the swiftly tightening net, but by the time the chase was in full swing he found himself standing far away, at the entrance to the large dirt-floored kitchen of the Hon'iden house.

Looking into the dimly lit interior, he called out, "Granny!"

"Who's there!" came the shrill reply. Osugi ambled out from a back room. Lit from below by the paper lantern in her hand, her gnarled face paled at the sight of her visitor.

44

"You!" she cried.

"I have something important to tell you," Takezō said hurriedly. "Matahachi isn't dead, he's still very much alive and healthy. He's staying with a woman. In another province. That's all I can tell you, because that's all I know. Will you please somehow break the news to Otsū for me? I couldn't do it myself."

Immensely relieved to have unburdened himself of the message, he started to leave, but the old woman called him back.

"Where do you plan to go from here?"

"I have to break into the stockade at Hinagura and rescue Ogin," he replied sadly. "After that, I'll go away somewhere. I just wanted to tell you and your family, as well as Otsū, that I didn't let Matahachi die. Other than that, I have no reason to be here."

"I see." Osugi shifted the lantern from one hand to the other, playing for time. Then she beckoned to him. "I'll bet you're hungry, aren't you?"

"I haven't had a decent meal for days."

"You poor boy! Wait! I'm in the midst of cooking right now, and I can give you a nice warm dinner in no time. As a going-away present. And wouldn't you like to take a bath while I'm getting it ready?"

Takezō was speechless.

"Don't look so shocked. Takezō, your family and ours have been together since the days of the Akamatsu clan. I don't think you should leave here at all, but I certainly won't let you go without giving you a good hearty meal!"

Again Takezō was unable to reply. He raised his arm and wiped his eyes. No one had been this kind to him for a long, long time. Having come to regard everybody with suspicion and distrust, he was suddenly remembering what it was like to be treated as a human being.

"Hurry on round to the bathhouse, now," urged Osugi in grandmotherly tones. "It's too dangerous to stand here—someone might see you. I'll bring you a washcloth, and while you're washing, I'll get out Matahachi's kimono and some underwear for you. Now take your time and have a good soak."

She handed him the lantern and disappeared into the back of the house. Almost immediately, her daughter-in-law left the house, ran through the garden and off into the night.

From the bathhouse, where the lantern swung back and forth, came the sound of splashing water.

"How is it?" Osugi called jovially. "Hot enough?"

"It's just right! I feel like a new man," Takezō called back.

"Take your time and get good and warm. The rice isn't ready yet."

"Thanks. If I'd known it'd be like this, I'd have come sooner. I was sure you'd have it in for me!" He spoke two or three more times, but his voice was drowned out by the sound of the water and Osugi didn't answer.

Before long, the daughter-in-law reappeared at the gate, all out of breath. She was followed by a band of samurai and vigilantes. Osugi came out of the house and addressed them in a whisper.

"Ah, you got him to take a bath. Very clever," said one of the men admiringly. "Yes, that's fine! We've got him for sure this time!"

Splitting into two groups, the men crouched and moved cautiously, like so many toads, toward the fire blazing brightly under the bath.

Something—something indefinable—pricked Takezō's instincts, and he peeped out through a crack in the door. His hair stood on end.

"I've been trapped!" he screamed.

He was stark naked, the bathhouse was tiny, and there was no time to think. Beyond the door he'd spotted what seemed like hordes of men armed with staffs, lances and truncheons.

Still, he wasn't really afraid. Any fear he might have had was blotted out by his anger toward Osugi.

"All right, you bastards, watch this," he growled.

He was well beyond caring how many of them there were. In this situation, as in others, the only thing he knew how to do was to attack rather than be attacked. As his would-be captors made way for each other outside, he abruptly kicked open the door and jumped out and into the air, bellowing a fearsome war whoop. Still naked, his wet hair flying in every direction, he seized and wrenched loose the shaft of the first lance thrust at him, sending its owner flying into the bushes. Taking a firm grip on the weapon, he thrashed about like a whirling dervish, swinging with complete abandon and hitting anyone who came near. He'd learned at Sekigahara that this method was startlingly effective when a man was outnumbered, and that the shaft of a lance could often be used more tellingly than the blade.

The attackers, realizing too late what a blunder they'd made by not sending three or four men charging into the bathhouse in the first place, shouted encouragement to one another. It was clear, however, they'd been out-maneuvered.

About the tenth time Takezō's weapon came in contact with the ground, it broke. He then seized a large rock and threw it at the men, who were already showing signs of backing down.

"Look, he's run inside the house!" shouted one of them, as simultaneously Osugi and her daughter-in-law scrambled out into the back garden.

Making a tremendous clatter as he stormed through the house, Takezō was yelling, "Where are my clothes? Give me back my clothes!"

There were work clothes lying about, not to speak of an elaborate kimono chest, but Takezō paid them no attention. He was straining his eyes in the dim light to find his own ragged garment. Finally spotting it in the corner of the kitchen, he seized it in one hand and finding a foothold atop a large earthenware oven, crawled out of a small high window. While he made his way onto the roof, his pursuers, now totally confused, cursed and made excuses to each other for their failure to ensnare him.

Standing in the middle of the roof, Takezō unhurriedly donned his kimono. With his teeth, he tore off a strip of cloth from his sash, and gathering his damp hair behind, tied it near the roots so tightly that his eyebrows and the corners of his eyes were stretched.

46   The spring sky was full of stars.

The Art of War

The daily search in the mountains continued, and farm work languished; the villagers could neither cultivate their fields nor tend to their silkworms. Large signs posted in front of the village headman's house and at every crossroads announced a substantial reward for anyone who captured or killed Takezō, as well as suitable recompense for any information leading to his arrest. The notices bore the authoritative signature of Ikeda Terumasa, lord of Himeji Castle.

At the Hon'iden residence, panic prevailed. Osugi and her family, trembling in mortal dread lest Takezō come to take his revenge, bolted the main gate and barricaded all entrances. The searchers, under the direction of troops from Himeji, laid fresh plans to trap the fugitive. Thus far all their efforts had proved fruitless.

"He's killed another one!" a villager shouted.

"Where? Who was it this time?"

"Some samurai. No one's identified him yet."

The corpse had been discovered near a path on the village outskirts, its head in a clump of tall weeds and its legs raised skyward in a bafflingly contorted position. Frightened but incurably nosy, villagers milled about, babbling among themselves. The skull had been smashed, evidently with one of the wooden reward signs, which now lay across the body soaked in blood. Those gawking at the spectacle could not avoid reading the list of promised rewards. Some laughed grimly at the blatant irony.

Otsū's face was drawn and pale as she emerged from the crowd. Wishing she hadn't looked, she hurried toward the temple, trying to somehow blot out the image of the dead man's face lingering before her eyes. At the foot of the hill, she ran into the captain who was lodging at the temple and five or six of his men. They had heard of the gruesome killing and were on their way to investigate. Upon seeing the girl, the captain grinned. "Where've you been, Otsū?" he said with ingratiating familiarity.

"Shopping," she replied curtly. Without bestowing so much as a glance upon him, she hurried up the temple's stone steps. She hadn't liked the man to begin with—he had a stringy mustache which she took particular exception to—but since the night he'd tried to force himself on her, the sight of him filled her with loathing.

Takuan was sitting in front of the main hall, playing with a stray dog. She 47 was hurrying by at some distance to avoid the mangy animal when the monk looked up and called, "Otsū, there's a letter for you."

"For me?" she asked incredulously.

"Yes, you were out when the runner came, so he left it with me." Taking the small scroll out of his kimono sleeve and handing it to her, he said, "You don't look too good. Is something wrong?"

"I feel sick. I saw a dead man lying in the grass. His eyes were still open, and there was blood—"

"You shouldn't look at things like that. But I guess the way things are now, you'd have to walk around with your eyes closed. I'm always tripping over corpses these days. Ha! And I'd heard this village was a little paradise!"

"But why is Takezō killing all these people?"

"To keep them from killing him, of course. They don't have any real reason to kill him, so why should he let them?"

"Takuan, I'm scared!" she said pleadingly. "What would we do if he came here?"

Dark cumulus clouds were drawing their cloak over the mountains. She took her mysterious letter and went to hide in the loom shed. On the loom was an unfinished strip of cloth for a man's kimono, part of the garment which, since the year before, she'd been spending every spare moment spinning silk yarn for. It was for Matahachi, and she was excited by the prospect of sewing all the pieces together into a full kimono. She had woven every strand meticulously, as if the weaving itself were drawing him closer to her. She wanted the garment to last forever.

Seating herself before the loom, she gazed intently at the letter. "Whoever could have sent it?" she whispered to herself, sure that the letter must have really been meant for someone else. She read the address over and over, searching for a flaw.

The letter had obviously made a long journey to reach her. The torn and crumpled wrapper was smudged all over with fingerprints and raindrops. She broke the seal, whereupon not one but two letters fell into her lap. The first was in an unfamiliar woman's hand, a somewhat older woman, she quickly guessed.

> I am writing merely to confirm what is written in the other letter, and will therefore not go into details.
> I am marrying Matahachi and adopting him into my family. However, he still seems concerned about you. I think it would be a mistake to let matters stand as they are. Matahachi is therefore sending you an explanation, the truth of which I hereby witness.
> Please forget Matahachi.
>
> Respectfully, Okō

The other letter was in Matahachi's scrawl and explained at tiresome length all the reasons why it was impossible for him to return home. The gist of it, of course, was that Otsū should forget about her betrothal to him and find an-

48

other husband. Matahachi added that since it was "difficult" for him to write directly to his mother of these matters, he would appreciate her help. If Otsū happened to see the old woman, she was to tell her Matahachi was alive and well and living in another province.

Otsū felt the marrow of her spine turn to ice. She sat stricken, too shocked to cry or even to blink. The nails of the fingers holding the letter turned the same color as the skin of the dead man she had seen less than an hour before.

The hours passed. Everyone in the kitchen began wondering where she'd gone. The captain in charge of the search was content to let his exhausted men sleep in the woods, but when he himself returned to the temple at dusk, he demanded comforts befitting his status. The bath had to be heated just so; fresh fish from the river had to be prepared to his specifications and someone had to fetch sake of the highest quality from one of the village homes. A great deal of work was entailed in keeping the man happy, and much of it naturally fell to Otsū. Since she was nowhere to be found, the captain's dinner was late.

Takuan went out to search for her. He had no concern whatsoever for the captain, but he was beginning to worry about Otsū herself. It just wasn't like her to go off without a word. Calling her name, the monk crossed the temple grounds, passing by the loom shed several times. Since the door was shut, he didn't bother to look inside.

Several times the temple priest stepped out onto the raised passageway and shouted to Takuan, "Have you found her yet? She's got to be around here somewhere." As time went on, he grew frantic, calling out, "Hurry up and find her! Our guest says he can't drink his sake without her here to pour it for him."

The temple's manservant was dispatched down the hill to search for her, lantern in hand. At almost the same moment he took off, Takuan finally opened the loom shed door.

What he saw inside gave him a start. Otsū was drooped over the loom in a state of obvious desolation. Not wanting to pry, he remained silent, staring at the two twisted and torn letters on the ground. They had been trampled on like a couple of straw effigies.

Takuan picked them up. "Aren't these what the runner brought today?" he asked gently. "Why don't you put them away somewhere?"

Otsū shook her head feebly.

"Everyone's half crazy with worry about you. I've been looking all over. Come, Otsū, let's go back. I know you don't want to, but you really do have work to do. You've got to serve the captain, for one thing. That old priest is nearly beside himself."

"My . . . my head hurts," she whispered. "Takuan, couldn't they let me off tonight—just this once?"

Takuan sighed. "Otsū, I personally think you shouldn't have to serve the captain's sake tonight or any night. The priest, however, is of a different mind. He is a man of this world. He's not the type who can gain the daimyō's respect or support for the temple through high-mindedness alone. He believes he has to wine and dine the captain—keep him happy every minute." He patted Otsū on the back. "And after all, he did take you in and raise you, so you do owe him something. You won't have to stay long."

She consented reluctantly. While Takuan was helping her up, she raised her tear-stained face to him and said, "I'll go, but only if you promise to stay with me."

"I have no objection to that, but old Scraggly Beard doesn't like me, and every time I see that silly mustache I have an irresistible urge to tell him how ridiculous it looks. It's childish, I know, but some people just affect me that way."

"But I don't want to go alone!"

"The priest is there, isn't he?"

"Yes, but he always leaves when I arrive."

"Hmm. That's not so good. All right, I'll go with you. Now stop thinking about it, and go wash your face."

When Otsū finally appeared at the priest's quarters, the captain, already slouching drunkenly, immediately perked up. Straightening his cap, which had been listing noticeably, he became quite jovial and called for refill after refill. Soon his face glowed scarlet and the corners of his bulging eyes began to sag.

He was not enjoying himself to the full, however, and the reason was a singularly unwanted presence in the room. On the other side of the lamp sat Takuan, bent over like a blind beggar, absorbed in reading the book open on his knees.

Mistaking the monk for an acolyte, the captain pointed at him, bellowing, "Hey, you there!"

Takuan continued reading until Otsū gave him a nudge. He raised his eyes absently, and looking all around, said, "You mean me?"

The captain spoke gruffly. "Yes, you! I have no business with you. Leave!"

"Oh, I don't mind staying," Takuan replied innocently.

"Oh, you don't, do you?"

"No, not at all," Takuan said, returning to his book.

"Well, I mind," the captain blustered. "It spoils the taste of good sake to have someone around reading."

"Oh, I'm sorry," responded Takuan with mock solicitude. "How rude of me. I'll just close the book."

"The very sight annoys me."

"All right, then. I'll have Otsū put it away."

"Not the book, you idiot! I'm talking about you! You spoil the setting."

Takuan's expression became grave. "Now, that is a problem, isn't it? It's not as though I were the sacred Wu-k'ung and could change myself into a puff of smoke, or become an insect and perch on your tray."

The captain's red neck swelled and his eyes bulged. He looked like a blow-fish. "Get out, you fool! Out of my sight!"

"Very well," said Takuan quietly, bowing. Taking Otsū's hand, he addressed her. "The guest says he prefers to be alone. To love solitude is the mark of the sage. We mustn't bother him further. Come."

"Why . . . why, you . . . you . . ."

"Is something wrong?"

"Who said anything about taking Otsū with you, you ugly moron!"

Takuan folded his arms. "I've observed over the years that not many priests or monks are particularly handsome. Not many samurai either, for that matter. Take you, for example."

The captain's eyes nearly leapt from their sockets. "What!"

"Have you considered your mustache? I mean, have you ever really taken the time to look at it, to evaluate it objectively?"

"You crazy bastard," shouted the captain as he reached for his sword, which was leaning against the wall. "Watch yourself!"

As he got to his feet, Takuan, keeping one eye on him, asked placidly, "Hmm. How do I go about watching myself?"

The captain, who was by now screaming, had his sheathed sword in hand. "I've taken all I can take. Now you're going to get what's coming to you!"

Takuan burst out laughing. "Does that mean you plan to cut off my head? If so, forget it. It would be a terrible bore."

"Huh?"

"A bore. I can't think of anything more boring than cutting off a monk's head. It would just fall to the floor and lie there laughing up at you. Not a very grand accomplishment, and what good could it possibly do you?"

"Well," growled the captain, "let's just say I'd have the satisfaction of shutting you up. It'd be pretty hard for you to keep up your insolent chatter!" Filled with the courage such people derive from having a weapon in hand, he laughed a mean belly laugh and moved forward threateningly.

"But, captain!"

Takuan's offhand manner had so enraged him that the hand in which he held his scabbard was shaking violently. Otsū slipped between the two men in an effort to protect Takuan.

"What are you saying, Takuan?" she said, hoping to lighten the mood and slow the action. "People don't talk like that to warriors. Now, just say you're sorry," she entreated. "Come on, apologize to the captain."

Takuan, however, was anything but finished.

"Get out of the way, Otsū. I'm all right. Do you really think I'd let myself be beheaded by a dolt like this, who though commanding scores of able, armed men has wasted twenty days trying to locate one exhausted, half-starved fugitive? If he hasn't enough sense to find Takezō, it would indeed be amazing if he could outwit me!"

"Don't move!" commanded the captain. His bloated face turned purple as he moved to draw his sword. "Stand aside, Otsū! I'm going to cut this big-mouthed acolyte in two!"

Otsū fell at the captain's feet and pleaded, "You have every reason to be angry, but please be patient. He's not quite right in the head. He talks to everybody this way. He doesn't mean anything by it, really!" Tears began gushing from her eyes.

"What are you saying, Otsū?" objected Takuan. "There's nothing wrong with my mind, and I'm not joking. I'm only telling the truth, which no one seems to like to hear. He's a dolt, so I called him a dolt. You want me to lie?"

"You'd better not say that again," thundered the samurai.

"I'll say it as often as I wish. By the way, I don't suppose it makes any difference to you soldiers how much time you squander looking for Takezō, but it's a terrible burden on the farmers. Do you realize what you're doing to them? They won't be able to eat soon if you keep this up. It probably hasn't even occurred to you that they have to neglect their field work completely to go out on your disorganized wild-goose chases. And with no wages, I might add. It's a disgrace!"

"Hold your tongue, traitor. That's outright slander against the Tokugawa government!"

"It isn't the Tokugawa government I'm criticizing; it's bureaucratic officials like you who stand between the daimyō and the common people, and who might as well be stealing their pay for all they do to earn it. For one thing, exactly why are you lounging around here tonight? What gives you the right to relax in your nice, comfortable kimono all snug and warm, take leisurely baths and have your bedtime sake poured for you by a pretty young girl? You call that serving your lord?"

The captain was speechless.

"Is it not the duty of a samurai to serve his lord faithfully and tirelessly? Isn't it your job to exercise benevolence toward the people who slave on the daimyō's behalf? Look at yourself! You just close your eyes to the fact that you're keeping the farmers from the work which gives them daily sustenance. You don't even have any consideration for your own men. You're supposed to be on an official mission, so what do you do? Every chance you get, you literally stuff yourself with other people's hard-earned food and drink and use your position to get the most comfortable quarters available. I should say you are a classic example of corruption, cloaking yourself with the authority of your superior to do nothing more than dissipate the energies of the common people for your own selfish ends."

The captain was by now too stunned to close his gaping mouth. Takuan pressed on.

"Now just try cutting off my head and sending it to Lord Ikeda Terumasa! That, I can tell you, would surprise him. He'd probably say, 'Why, Takuan! Has only your head come to visit me today? Where in the world is the rest of you?'

"No doubt you'd be interested to learn that Lord Terumasa and I used to partake of the tea ceremony together at the Myōshinji. We've also had several long and pleasant chats at the Daitokuji in Kyoto."

Scraggly Beard's virulence drained from him in an instant. His drunkenness had worn off a bit too, though he still appeared incapable of judging for himself whether Takuan was telling the truth or not. He seemed paralyzed, not knowing how to react.

"First, you'd better sit down," said the monk. "If you think I'm lying, I'll be happy to go with you to the castle and appear before the lord himself. As a gift, I could take him some of the delicious buckwheat flour they make here. He's particularly fond of it.

"However, there's nothing more tedious, nothing I like less, than calling on a daimyō. Moreover, if the subject of your activities in Miyamoto should happen to come up while we were chatting over tea, I couldn't very well lie. It would probably end up with your having to commit suicide for your incompetence. I told you from the beginning to stop threatening me, but you warriors are all the same. You never think about consequences. And that's your greatest failing.

"Now put your sword down and I'll tell you something else."

Deflated, the captain complied.

"Of course, you are familiar with General Sun-tzu's *Art of War*—you know, the classic Chinese work on military strategy? I assume any warrior in your position would be intimately acquainted with such an important book. Anyway, the reason I mention it is that I'd like to give you a lesson illustrating one of the book's main principles. I'd like to show you how to capture Takezō without losing any more of your own men or causing the villagers any more trouble than you have already. Now, this has to do with your official work, so you really should listen carefully." He turned to the girl. "Otsū, pour the captain another cup of sake, will you?"

The captain was a man in his forties, ten years or so older than Takuan, but it was clear from their faces at this moment that strength of character is not a matter of age. Takuan's tongue-lashing had humbled the older man and his bluster had evaporated.

Meekly he said, "No, I don't want any more sake. I hope you'll forgive me. I had no idea you were a friend of Lord Terumasa. I'm afraid I've been very rude." He was abject to the point of being comical, but Takuan refrained from rubbing it in.

"Let's just forget about that. What I want to discuss is how to capture Takezō. That is what you have to do to carry out your orders and maintain your honor as a samurai, isn't it?"

"Yes."

"Of course, I also know you don't care how long it takes to catch the man. After all, the longer it takes, the longer you can stay on at the temple, eating, drinking and ogling Otsū."

"Please, don't bring that up anymore. Particularly before his lordship." The soldier looked like a child ready to burst into tears.

"I'm prepared to consider the whole incident a secret. But if this running around in the mountains all day long keeps up, the farmers will be in serious trouble. Not only the farmers but all the rest of the people as well. Everyone in this village is too upset and frightened to settle down and get on with their normal work. Now, as I see it, your trouble is that you have not employed the proper strategy. Actually, I don't think you've employed any strategy at all. I take it that you do not know *The Art of War?*"

"I'm ashamed to admit it, but I don't."

"Well, you should be ashamed! And you shouldn't be surprised when I call you a dolt. You may be an official, but you are sadly uneducated and totally ineffectual. There's no use in my beating you over the head with the obvious, however. I'll simply make you a proposition. I personally offer to capture Takezō for you in three days."

"*You* capture him?"

"Do you think I'm joking?"

"No, but . . ."

"But what?"

"But counting the reinforcements from Himeji and all the farmers and foot soldiers, we've had more than two hundred men combing the mountains for nearly three weeks."

"I'm well aware of that fact."

"And since it's spring, Takezō has the advantage. There's plenty to eat up there this time of year."

"Are you planning on waiting till it snows, then? Another eight months or so?"

"No, uh, I don't think we can afford to do that."

"You certainly can't. That's precisely why I'm offering to catch him for you. I don't need any help; I can do it alone. On second thoughts, though, maybe I should take Otsū along with me. Yes, the two of us would be enough."

"You aren't serious, are you?"

"Would you please be quiet! Are you implying that Takuan Sōhō spends all his time making up jokes?"

"Sorry."

"As I said, you don't know *The Art of War*, and as I see it, that is the most important reason for your abominable failure. I, on the other hand, may be a simple priest, but I believe I understand Sun-tzu. There's only one stipulation, and if you won't agree to it, I'll just have to sit back and watch you bumble about until the snow falls, and maybe your head as well."

"What's the condition?" said the captain warily.

"If I bring back the fugitive, you'll let me decide his fate."

"What do you mean by that?" The captain pulled at his mustache, a string of thoughts racing through his mind. How could he be sure that this strange monk wasn't deceiving him completely? Although he spoke eloquently, it could be that he was completely insane. Could he be a friend of Takezō's, an accomplice? Might he know where the man was hiding? Even if he didn't, which was likely at this stage, there was no harm in leading him on, just to see whether he'd go through with this crazy scheme. He'd probably worm out of it at the last minute anyway. With this in mind, the captain nodded his assent. "All right, then. If you catch him, you can decide what to do with him. Now, what happens if you *don't* find him in three days?"

54

"I'll hang myself from the big cryptomeria tree in the garden."

Early the next day, the temple's manservant, looking extremely worried, came rushing into the kitchen, out of breath and half shouting: "Has Takuan lost his mind? I heard he promised to find Takezō himself!"

Eyes rounded.

"No!"

"Not really!"

"Just how does he plan to do it?"

Wisecracks and mocking laughter followed, but there was also an undercurrent of worried whispering.

When word reached the temple priest, he nodded sagely and remarked that the human mouth is the gateway to catastrophe.

But the person most genuinely disturbed was Otsū. Only the day before, the farewell note from Matahachi had hurt her more than news of his death could ever have. She had trusted her fiancé and had even been willing to suffer the formidable Osugi as a slave-driving mother-in-law for his sake. Who was there to turn to now?

For Otsū, plunged into darkness and despair, Takuan was life's one bright spot, her last ray of hope. The day before, weeping alone in the loom shed, she'd seized a sharp knife and cut to shreds the kimono cloth into which she'd literally woven her soul. She'd also considered plunging the fine blade into her own throat. Though she was sorely tempted to do so, Takuan's appearance had finally driven that thought from her mind. After soothing her and getting her to agree to pour the captain's sake, he'd patted her on the back. She could still feel the warmth of his strong hand as he led her out of the loom shed.

And now he'd made this insane agreement.

Otsū wasn't nearly as concerned over her own safety as she was over the possibility that her only friend in the world might be lost to her because of his silly proposal. She felt lost and utterly depressed. Her common sense alone told her it was ridiculous to think that she and Takuan could locate Takezō in so short a time.

Takuan even had the audacity to exchange vows with Scraggly Beard before the shrine of Hachiman, the god of war. After he returned, she took him severely to task for his rashness, but he insisted there was nothing to worry about. His intention, he said, was to relieve the village of its burden, to make travel on the highways safe once more and to prevent any further waste of human life. In view of the number of lives that could be saved by quickly apprehending Takezō, his own seemed unimportant, she must see that. He also told her to get as much rest as she could before the evening of the following day, when they would depart. She was to come along without complaint, trusting in his judgment completely. Otsū was too distraught to resist, and the alternative of staying behind and worrying was even worse than the thought of going.

Late the following afternoon, Takuan was still napping with the cat in the corner of the main temple building. Otsū's face was hollow. The priest, the manservant, the acolyte—everybody had tried to persuade her not to go. "Go and hide" was their practical advice, but Otsū, for reasons she herself could hardly fathom, didn't feel the least inclined to do so.

The sun was sinking fast, and the dense shadows of evening had begun to envelop the crevices in the mountain range that marked the course of the Aida River. The cat sprang down from the temple porch, and presently Takuan himself stepped onto the veranda. Like the cat before him, he stretched his limbs, with a great yawn.

"Otsū," he called, "we'd better get going."

"I've already packed everything—straw sandals, walking sticks, leggings, medicine, paulownia-oil paper."

"You forgot something."

"What? A weapon? Should we take a sword or a lance or something?"

"Certainly not! I want to take along a supply of food."

"Oh, you mean some box lunches?"

"No, good food. I want some rice, some salty bean paste and—oh, yes—a little sake. Anything tasty will do. I also need a pot. Go to the kitchen and make up a big bundle. And get a pole to carry it with."

The nearby mountains were now blacker than the best black lacquer, those in the distance paler than mica. It was late spring, and the breeze was perfumed and warm. Striped bamboo and wisteria vines entrapped the mist, and the farther Takuan and Otsū went from the village, the more the mountains, where every leaf shone faintly in the dim light, seemed to have been bathed by an evening shower. They walked through the darkness in single file, each shouldering an end of the bamboo pole from which swung their well-packed bundle.

"It's a nice evening for a walk, isn't it, Otsū?" Takuan said, glancing over his shoulder.

"I don't think it's so wonderful," she muttered. "Where are we going, anyway?"

"I'm not quite sure yet," he replied with a slightly pensive air, "but let's go on a bit farther."

"Well, I don't mind walking."

"Aren't you tired?"

"No," replied the girl, but the pole obviously hurt her, for every once in a while she shifted it from one shoulder to the other.

"Where is everyone? We haven't seen a soul."

"The captain didn't show his face at the temple all day today. I bet he called the searchers back to the village so we can have three days all to ourselves. Takuan, just how do you propose to catch Takezō?"

"Oh, don't worry. He'll turn up sooner or later."

"Well, he hasn't turned up for anyone else. But even if he does, what are we going to do? With all those men pursuing him for so long, he must be desperate by now. He'll be fighting for his life, and he's very strong to begin with. My legs start shaking just thinking about it."

"Careful! Watch your step!" Takuan shouted suddenly.

"Oh!" Otsū cried in terror, stopping dead in her tracks. "What's the matter? Why did you scare me like that?"

"Don't worry, it's not Takezō. I just want you to watch where you walk. There are wisteria-vine and bramble traps all along the side of the road here."

"The searchers set them there to catch Takezō?"

"Uh-huh. But if we're not careful, we'll fall into one ourselves."

"Takuan, if you keep saying things like that I'll be so nervous I won't be able to put one foot in front of the other!"

"What are you worried about? If we do walk into one, I'll fall in first. No need for you to follow me." He grinned back at her. "I must say, they went to an awful lot of trouble for nothing." After a moment's silence, he added, "Otsū, doesn't the ravine seem to be getting narrower?"

"I don't know, but we passed the back side of Sanumo some time ago. This should be Tsujinohara."

"If that's the case, we may have to walk all night."

"Well, I don't even know where we're going. Why talk to me about it?"

"Let's put this down for a minute." After they'd lowered the bundle to the ground, Takuan started toward a nearby cliff.

"Where are you going?"

"To relieve myself."

A hundred feet below him, the waters that joined to form the Aida River were crashing thunderously from boulder to boulder. The sound roared up to him, filling his ears and penetrating his whole being. As he urinated, he gazed at the sky as if counting the stars. "Oh, this feels good!" he exulted. "Am I one with the universe, or is the universe one with me?"

"Takuan," called Otsū, "aren't you finished yet? You certainly do take your time!"

Finally he reappeared and explained himself. "While I was about it, I consulted the Book of Changes, and now I know exactly what course of action we have to take. It's all clear to me now."

"*The Book of Changes?* You aren't carrying a book."

"Not the written one, silly, the one inside me. My very own original Book of Changes. It's in my heart or belly or somewhere. While I was standing there, I was considering the lay of the land, the look of the water and the condition of the sky. Then I shut my eyes, and when I opened them, something said, 'Go to that mountain over there.'" He pointed to a nearby peak.

"Are you talking about Takateru Mountain?"

"I have no idea what it's called. It's that one, with the level clearing about halfway up."

"People call that Itadori Pasture."

"Oh, it has a name, does it?"

When they reached it, the pasture proved to be a small plain, sloping to the southeast and affording a splendid view of the surroundings. Farmers usually turned horses and cows loose here to graze, but that night not an animal could be seen or heard. The stillness was broken only by the warm spring breeze caressing the grass.

"We'll camp here," announced Takuan. "The enemy, Takezō, will fall into my hands just as General Ts'ao Ts'ao of Wei fell into the hands of Ch'u-ko K'ung-ming."

As they laid down their load, Otsū inquired, "What are we going to do here?"

"We are going to sit," replied Takuan firmly.

"How can we catch Takezō by just sitting here?"

"If you set up nets, you can catch birds on the wing without having to fly around yourself."

"We haven't set up any nets. Are you sure you haven't become possessed by a fox or something?"

"Let's build a fire, then. Foxes are afraid of fire, so if I am I'll soon be exorcised."

They gathered some dry wood, and Takuan built a fire. It seemed to lift Otsū's spirits.

"A good fire cheers a person up, doesn't it?"

"It warms a person up, that's for sure. Anyway, were you unhappy?"

"Oh, Takuan, you can see the mood I've been in! And I don't think anyone really likes to spend a night in the mountains like this. What would we do if it rained right now?"

"On the way up I saw a cave near the road. We could take shelter there till it stopped."

"That's what Takezō probably does at night and in bad weather, don't you think? There must be places like that all over the mountain. That's probably where he hides most of the time, too."

"Probably. He doesn't really have much sense, but he must have enough to get in out of the rain."

She grew pensive. "Takuan, why do the people in the village hate him so much?"

"The authorities make them hate him. Otsū, these people are simple. They're afraid of the government, so afraid that if it so decrees, they'll drive away their fellow villagers, even their own kin."

"You mean they only worry about protecting their own skins."

"Well, it's not really their fault. They're completely powerless. You have to forgive them for putting their own interests first, since it's a case of self-defense. What they really want is just to be left alone."

"But what about the samurai? Why are they making such a fuss about an insignificant person like Takezō?"

"Because he's a symbol of chaos, an outlaw. They have to preserve the peace. After Sekigahara, Takezō was obsessed with the idea that the enemy was chasing him. He made his first big mistake by breaking through the barrier at the border. He should've used his wits somehow, snuck through at night or gone through in disguise. Anything. But not Takezō! He had to go and kill a guard and then kill other people later on. After that it just snowballed. He thinks he has to keep on killing to protect his own life. But he's the one who started it. The whole unfortunate situation was brought about by one thing: Takezō's complete lack of common sense."

"Do you hate him too?"

"I loathe him! I abhor his stupidity! If I were lord of the province, I'd have him suffer the worst punishment I could devise. In fact, as an object lesson to the people, I'd have him torn limb from limb. After all, he's no better than a wild beast, is he? A provincial lord cannot afford to be generous with the likes of Takezō, even if he does seem to some to be no more than a young ruffian. It would be detrimental to law and order, and that's not good, particularly in these unsettled times."

"I always thought you were kind, Takuan, but deep down you're quite hard, aren't you? I didn't think you cared about the daimyō's laws."

"Well, I do. I think that good should be rewarded and evil punished, and I came here with the authority to do just that."

"Oh, what was that?" cried Otsū, jumping up from her place by the fire. "Didn't you hear it? It was a rustling sound, like footsteps, in those trees over there!"

"Footsteps?" Takuan, too, became alert, but after listening closely for a few moments he burst into laughter. "Ha, ha. It's only some monkeys. Look!" They could see the silhouettes of a big monkey and a little one, swinging through the trees.

Otsū, visibly relieved, sat down again. "Whew, that scared me half to death!"

For the next couple of hours, the two sat silently, staring at the fire. Whenever it would dwindle, Takuan would break some dry branches and throw them on.

"Otsū, what are you thinking about?"

"Me?"

"Yes, you. Although I do it all the time, I really hate holding conversations with myself."

Otsū's eyes were puffy from the smoke. Looking up at the starry sky, she spoke softly. "I was thinking of how strange the world is. All those stars way up there in the empty blackness— No, I don't mean that.

"The night is full. It seems to embrace everything. If you stare at the stars a long time, you can see them moving. Slowly, slowly moving. I can't help thinking the whole world is moving. I feel it. And I'm just a little speck in it all—a speck controlled by some awesome power I can't even see. Even while I sit here thinking, my fate is changing bit by bit. My thoughts seem to go round and round in circles."

"You're not telling the truth!" said Takuan sternly. "Of course those ideas entered your head, but you really had something much more specific on your mind."

Otsū was silent.

"I apologize if I violated your privacy, Otsū, but I read those letters you received."

"You did? But the seal wasn't broken!"

"I read them after finding you in the loom shed. When you said you didn't want them, I stuck them in my sleeve. I guess it was wrong of me, but later, when I was in the privy, I took them out and read them just to pass the time."

"You're awful! How could you do such a thing! And just to pass the time!"

"Well, for whatever reason. Anyway, now I understand what started that flood of tears. Why you looked half dead when I found you. But listen, Otsū, I think you were lucky. In the long run, I think it's better that things turned out the way they did. You think I'm awful? Look at him!"

"What do you mean?"

"Matahachi was and still is irresponsible. If you married him, and then one day he surprised you with a letter like that, what would you do then? Don't tell me, I know you. You'd dive into the sea from a rocky cliff. I'm glad it's all over before it could come to that."

"Women don't think that way."

"Oh, really? How do they think?"

"I'm so angry I could scream!" She tugged angrily at the sleeve of her kimono with her teeth. "Someday I'll find him! I swear I will! I won't rest until I've told him, to his face, exactly what I think of him. And the same goes for that Okō woman."

She broke into tears of rage. As Takuan stared at her, he mumbled cryptically, "It's started, hasn't it?"

She looked at him dumbfounded. "What?"

He stared at the ground, seemingly composing his thoughts. Then he began. "Otsū, I'd really hoped that you, of all people, would be spared the evils and duplicities of this world. That your sweet, innocent self would go through all the stages of life unsullied and unharmed. But it looks like the rough winds of fate have begun to buffet you, as they buffet everyone else."

"Oh, Takuan! What should I do! I'm so . . . so . . . angry!" Her shoulders shook with her sobbing as she buried her face in her lap.

By dawn, she'd cried herself out, and the two of them hid in the cave to sleep. That night they kept watch by the fire and slept through the next day in the cave again. They had plenty of food, but Otsū was baffled. She kept saying she couldn't see how they'd ever capture Takezō at this rate. Takuan, on the other hand, remained sublimely unperturbed. Otsū hadn't a clue to what he was thinking. He made no move to search anywhere, nor was he the slightest bit disconcerted by Takezō's failure to appear.

On the evening of the third day, as on the previous nights, they kept vigil by the fireside.

"Takuan," Otsū finally blurted, "this is our last night, you know. Our time is up tomorrow."

"Hmm. That's true, isn't it?"

"Well, what do you plan to do?"

"Do about what?"

"Oh, don't be so difficult! You do remember, don't you, the promise you made to the captain?"

"Why, yes, of course!"

"Well, if we don't bring Takezō back—"

He interrupted her. "I know, I know. I'll have to hang myself from the old cryptomeria tree. But don't worry. I'm not ready to die just yet."

"Then why don't you go and look for him?"

"If I did, do you really think I'd find him? In these mountains?"

"Oh, I don't understand you at all! And yet somehow, just sitting here, I feel like I'm getting braver, mustering up the nerve to let things turn out whatever way they will." She laughed. "Or maybe I'm just going crazy, like you."

"I'm not crazy. I just have nerve. That's what it takes."

"Tell me, Takuan, was it nerve and nothing else that made you take this on?"

"Yes."

"Nothing but nerve! That's not very encouraging. I thought you must have some foolproof scheme up your sleeve."

Otsū had been on her way toward sharing her companion's confidence, but his disclosure that he was operating on sheer audacity sent her into a fit of despondency. Was he totally insane? Sometimes people who are not quite right in the mind are taken by others to be geniuses. Takuan might be one of those. Otsū was beginning to think this was a distinct possibility.

The monk, serene as ever, continued to gaze absently into the fire. Presently he mumbled, as though he'd just noticed, "It's very late, isn't it?"

"It certainly is! It'll be dawn soon, " snapped Otsū with deliberate tartness. Why had she trusted this suicidal lunatic?

Paying no attention to the sharpness of her response, he muttered, "Funny, isn't it?"

"What *are* you muttering about, Takuan?"

"It just occurred to me that Takezō has to show up pretty soon."

"Yes, but maybe he doesn't realize you two have an appointment." Looking at the monk's unsmiling face, she softened. "Do you really think he will?"

"Of course I do!"

"But why would he just walk right into a trap?"

"It's not exactly that. It has to do with human nature, that's all. People aren't strong at heart, they're weak. And solitude is not their natural state, particularly when it involves being surrounded by enemies and chased with swords. You may think it's natural, but I'd be very much surprised if Takezō manages to resist the temptation to pay us a call and warm himself by the fire."

"Isn't that just wishful thinking? He may be nowhere near here."

Takuan shook his head and said, "No, it is not just wishful thinking. It isn't even my own theory, it's that of a master of strategy." He spoke so confidently that Otsū found herself relieved that his disagreement was so definite.

"I suspect that Shimmen Takezō is somewhere very close by, but hasn't yet decided whether we're friends or enemies. He's probably plagued, poor boy, by a multitude of doubts, struggling with them, unable to advance or retreat. It'd be my guess he's hiding in the shadows right now, looking out at us furtively, wondering desperately what to do. Ah, I know. Let me have the flute you carry in your obi!"

"My bamboo flute?"

"Yes, let me play it for a while."

"No. Impossible. I never let anyone touch it."

"Why?" Takuan insisted.

"Never mind why!" she cried with a shake of her head.

"What harm would it do to let me use it? Flutes improve the more they're played. I won't hurt it."

"But . . ." Otsū clasped her right hand firmly on the flute in her obi.

She always carried it next to her body, and Takuan knew how much she treasured the instrument. He had never imagined, however, she would refuse to let him play it.

"I really won't break it, Otsū. I've handled dozens of flutes. Oh, come now, at least let me hold it."

"No."

"Whatever happens?"

"Whatever happens."

"You're stubborn!"

"Okay, I'm stubborn."

Takuan gave up. "Well, I'd just as soon listen to you play it. Will you play me just one little piece?"

"I don't want to do that either."

"Why not?"

"Because I'd start to cry, and I can't play the flute when I'm crying."

"Hmm," mused Takuan. While he felt pity for this obstinate tenacity, so characteristic of orphans, he was aware of a void deep within their stubborn hearts. They seemed to him doomed to yearn desperately for that which they could not have, for the parental love with which they were never blessed.

Otsū was constantly calling out to the parents she'd never known, and they to her, but she had no firsthand knowledge of parental love. The flute was the only thing her parents had left her, the only image of them she'd ever had. When, barely old enough to see the light of day, she'd been left like an abandoned kitten on the porch of the Shippōji, the flute had been tucked in her tiny obi. It was the one and only link that might in the future enable her to seek out people of her own blood. Not only was it the image, it was the voice of the mother and father she'd never seen.

"So she cries when she plays it!" thought Takuan. "No wonder she's so reluctant to let anyone handle it, or even to play it herself." He felt sorry for her.

On this third night, for the first time, a pearly moon shimmered in the sky, now and then dissolving behind misty clouds. The wild geese that always migrate to Japan in fall and go home in spring were apparently on their way back north; occasionally their quacking reached them from among the clouds.

Rousing himself from his reverie, Takuan said, "The fire's gone down, Otsū. Would you put some more wood on it? . . . Why, what's the matter? Is something wrong?"

Otsū didn't answer.

"Are you crying?"

Still she said nothing.

"I'm sorry I reminded you of the past. I didn't mean to upset you."

"It's nothing," she whispered. "I shouldn't have been so stubborn. Please take the flute and play it." She brought the instrument out from her obi and offered it to him across the fire. It was in a wrapper of old, faded brocade; the cloth was worn, the cords tattered, but there still remained a certain antique elegance.

"May I look at it?" asked Takuan.

"Yes, please do. It doesn't matter anymore."

"But why don't you play it instead of me? I think I really would rather listen. I'll just sit here like this." He turned sideways and clasped his arms around his knees.

"All right. I'm not very good," she said modestly, "but I'll try."

She knelt in formal fashion on the grass, straightened her kimono collar and bowed to the flute laying before her. Takuan said no more. He seemed no longer to even be there; there was only the great lonely universe enveloped in night. The monk's shadowy form might well have been a rock that had rolled down from the hillside and settled on the plain.

Otsū, her white face turned slightly to one side, put the cherished heirloom to her lips. As she wetted the mouthpiece and prepared herself inwardly to play, she seemed a different Otsū altogether, an Otsū embodying the strength and dignity of art. Turning to Takuan, she once again, in proper fashion, disavowed any claim to skill. He nodded perfunctorily.

The liquid sound of the flute began. As the girl's thin fingers moved over the seven holes of the instrument, her knuckles looked like tiny gnomes absorbed in a slow dance. It was a low sound, like the gurgling of a brook. Takuan felt that he himself had turned into flowing water, splashing through a ravine, playing in the shallows. When the high notes sounded, he felt his spirit wafted into the sky to gambol with the clouds. The sound of earth and the reverberations of heaven mingled and were transformed into the wistful sighs of the breeze blowing through the pines, lamenting the impermanence of this world.

As he listened raptly, his eyes closed, Takuan could not help but recall the legend of Prince Hiromasa, who, while strolling on a moonlit night at Suzaku Gate in Kyoto and playing his flute as he walked, heard another flute harmonizing with his. The prince searched out the player and found him in the upper story of the gate. Having exchanged flutes, the two played music together throughout the night. Only later did the prince discover that his companion had been a devil in human form.

"Even a devil," thought Takuan, "is moved by music. How much more deeply must a human being, subject to the five passions, be affected by the 63 sound of the flute in the hands of this beautiful girl!" He wanted to weep but shed no tears. His face sank deeper between his knees, which he unconsciously hugged more tightly.

As the light from the fire gradually faded, Otsū's cheeks turned a deeper red. She was so absorbed in her music that it was difficult to distinguish her from the instrument she was playing.

Was she calling to her mother and father? Were these sounds ascending into the sky really asking, "Where are you?" And was there not mingled with this plea the bitter resentment of a maiden who'd been deserted and betrayed by a faithless man?

She seemed intoxicated by the music, overwhelmed by her own emotions. Her breathing began to show signs of fatigue; tiny beads of sweat appeared around the edges of her hair. Tears flowed down her face. Though the melody was broken by stifled sobs, it seemed to go on and on forever.

And then suddenly there was a movement in the grass. It was no more than fifteen or twenty feet from the fire and sounded like a creeping animal. Takuan's head shot up. Looking straight at the black object, he quietly raised his hand and waved a greeting.

"You over there! It must be chilly in the dew. Come over here by the fire and warm yourself. Come and talk with us, please."

Startled, Otsū stopped playing and said, "Takuan, are you talking to yourself again?"

"Didn't you notice?" he asked, pointing. "Takezō has been over there for some time, listening to you play the flute."

She turned to look, and then, with a shriek, threw her flute at the black form. It was indeed Takezō. He jumped like a startled deer and started to flee.

Takuan, as astonished as Takezō by Otsū's scream, felt as though the net he was so carefully hauling in had broken and the fish escaped. Jumping to his feet, he called out at the top of his lungs, "Takezō! Stop!"

There was overpowering strength in his voice, a commanding force that could not easily be ignored. The fugitive stopped as though nailed to the ground and looked back, a little stupefied. He stared at Takuan with suspicious eyes.

The monk said no more. Slowly crossing his arms on his chest, he stared back at Takezō as steadily as Takezō was staring at him. The two seemed even to be breathing in unison.

Gradually there appeared at the corners of Takuan's eyes the wrinkles that mark the beginning of a friendly smile. Unfolding his arms, he beckoned to Takezō and said, "Now, come here."

At the sound of the words, Takezō blinked; a strange expression came over his dark face.

"Come on over here," Takuan urged, "and we can all talk to each other."

There followed a puzzled silence.

"There's lots to eat and we even have some sake. We're not your enemies, you know. Come over by the fire. Let's talk."

More silence.

64 "Takezō, aren't you making a big mistake? There's a world outside where

there are fires and food and drink and even human sympathy. You persist in driving yourself about in your own private hell. You're taking a pretty warped view of the world, you know.

"But I'll stop trying to argue with you. In your condition, you could hardly have much of an ear for reason. Just come over here by the fire. Otsū, warm up the potato stew you made a while ago. I'm hungry too."

Otsū put the pot on the fire, and Takuan placed a jar of sake near the flames to heat it. This peaceful scene allayed Takezō's fears, and he inched nearer. When he was almost on top of them, he stopped and stood still, apparently held back by some inner embarrassment.

Takuan rolled a rock up near the fire and patted Takezō on the back. "You sit here," he said.

Abruptly, Takezō sat down. Otsū, for her part, couldn't even look her ex-fiance's friend in the face. She felt as though she were in the presence of an unchained beast.

Takuan, lifting the lid of the pot, said, "It seems to be ready." He stuck the tips of his chopsticks into a potato, drew it out, and popped it into his mouth. Chewing heartily, he proclaimed, "Very nice and tender. Won't you have some, Takezō?"

Takezō nodded and for the first time grinned, showing a set of perfect white teeth. Otsū filled a bowl and gave it to him, whereupon he began alternately to blow on the hot stew and slurp it up in big mouthfuls. His hands trembled and his teeth clattered against the edge of the bowl. Pitifully hungry as he was, the trembling was uncontrollable. Frighteningly so.

"Good, isn't it?" asked the monk, putting down his chopsticks. "How about some sake?"

"I don't want any sake."

"Don't you like it?"

"I don't want any now." After all that time in the mountains, he was afraid it might make him sick.

Presently he said, politely enough, "Thank you for the food. I'm warmed up now."

"Have you had enough?"

"Plenty, thank you." As he handed his bowl back to Otsū, he asked, "Why did you come up here? I saw your fire last night too."

The question startled Otsū and she had no answer ready, but Takuan came to the rescue by saying forthrightly, "To tell the truth, we came here to capture you."

Takezō showed no particular surprise, though he seemed hesitant to take what Takuan had said at face value. He hung his head in silence, then looked from one to the other of them.

Takuan saw that the time had come to act. Turning to face Takezō directly, he said, "How about it? If you're going to be captured anyway, wouldn't it be better to be tied up with the bonds of the Buddha's Law? The daimyō's regulations are law, and the Buddha's Law is law, but of the two, the bonds of the Buddha are the more gentle and humane."

"No, no!" said Takezō, shaking his head angrily.

Takuan continued mildly. "Just listen for a minute. I understand that you are determined to hold out to the death, but in the long run, can you really win?"

"What do you mean, can I win?"

"I mean, can you successfully hold out against the people who hate you, against the laws of the province and against your own worst enemy, yourself?"

"Oh, I know I've already lost," groaned Takezō. His face was sadly contorted and his eyes brimmed with tears. "I'll be cut down in the end, but before I am I'll kill the old Hon'iden woman and the soldiers from Himeji and all the other people I hate! I'll kill as many as I can!"

"What will you do about your sister?"

"Huh?"

"Ogin. What are you going to do about her? She's locked up in the stockade at Hinagura, you know!"

Despite his earlier resolve to rescue her, Takezō could not answer.

"Don't you think you should start considering the well-being of that good woman? She's done so much for you. And what about your duty to carry on the name of your father, Shimmen Munisai? Have you forgotten that it goes back through the Hirata family to the famous Akamatsu clan of Harima?"

Takezō covered his face with his blackened, now nearly clawed hands, his sharp shoulders piercing upward as they shook in his haggard, trembling body. He broke into bitter sobs. "I . . . I . . . don't know. What . . . what difference does it make now?"

At that, Takuan suddenly clenched his fist and let go with a solid punch to Takezō's jaw.

"Fool!" the monk's voice thundered.

Taken by surprise, Takezō reeled from the blow and before he could recover took another punch on the other side.

"You irresponsible oaf! You stupid ingrate! Since your father and mother and ancestors are not here to punish you, I'll do it for them. Take that!" The monk struck him again, this time knocking him all the way to the ground. "Does it hurt yet?" he asked belligerently.

"Yes, it hurts," the fugitive whined.

"Good. If it hurts, you may still have a little human blood coursing through your veins. Otsū, hand me that rope, please. . . . Well, what are you waiting for? Bring me the rope! Takezō already knows I'm going to tie him up. He's prepared for it. It's not the rope of authority, it's the rope of compassion. There's no reason for you to either fear or pity him. Quick, girl, the rope!"

Takezō lay still on his stomach, making no effort to move. Takuan easily straddled his back. If Takezō had wanted to resist, he could have kicked Takuan in the air like a little paper ball. They both knew that. Yet he lay passively, arms and legs outstretched, as though he'd finally surrendered to some invisible law of nature.

The Old Cryptomeria Tree

Although it was not the time of the morning when the temple bell was usually rung, its heavy, regular gonging resounded through the village and echoed far into the mountains. This was the day of reckoning, when Takuan's time limit was up, and the villagers raced up the hill to find out whether he'd done the impossible. The news that he had spread like wildfire.

"Takezō's been captured!"

"Really! Who got him?"

"Takuan!"

"I can't believe it! Without a weapon?"

"It can't be true!"

The crowd surged up to the Shippōji to gawk at the collared outlaw, who was tied like an animal to the stair railing in front of the main sanctuary. Some gulped and gasped at the sight, as though they were beholding the countenance of the dreaded demon of Mount Ōe. As if to deflate their exaggerated reaction, Takuan sat a bit farther up the stairs, leaning back on his elbows and grinning amiably.

"People of Miyamoto," he shouted, "now you can go back to your fields in peace. The soldiers will be gone soon!"

To the intimidated villagers, Takuan had become a hero overnight, their savior and protector from evil. Some bowed deeply to him, their heads nearly touching the ground of the temple courtyard; others pushed their way forward to touch his hand or robe. Others knelt at his feet. Takuan, appalled at this display of idolatry, pulled away from the mob and held up his hand for silence.

"Listen, men and women of Miyamoto. I have something to say, something important." The hue and cry died down. "It is not I who deserve the credit for capturing Takezō. It was not I who accomplished it, but the law of nature. Those who break it always lose in the end. It is the law that you should respect."

"Don't be ridiculous! You caught him, not nature!"

"Don't be so modest, monk!"

"We give credit where it's due!"

"Forget the law. We have you to thank!"

"Well, then thank me," continued Takuan. "I don't mind that. But you should pay homage to the law. Anyway, what's done is done, and right now   67 there's something very important I'd like to ask you about. I need your help."

"What is it?" came the question from the curious crowd.

"Just this: what shall we do with Takezō now that we've got him? My agreement with the House of Ikeda's representative, who I'm sure you all know by sight, was that if I didn't bring the fugitive back in three days' time, I'd hang myself from that big cryptomeria. If I did succeed, I was promised, I could decide his fate."

People started to murmur.

"We heard about that!"

He assumed a judicial pose. "Well, then, what shall we do with him? As you see, the dreaded monster is here in the flesh. Not very fearsome, really, is he? In fact, he came along without a fight, the weakling. Shall we kill him, or let him go?"

There was a rumble of objections at the idea of setting Takezō free. One man shouted, "We've got to kill him! He's no good, he's a criminal! If we let him live, he'll be the curse of the village."

While Takuan paused, seeming to consider the possibilities, angry, impatient voices from the rear shouted, "Kill him! Kill him!"

At that point, an old woman pushed her way to the front, shoving aside men twice her size with sharp jabs of her elbows. It was, of course, the irate Osugi. When she reached the steps, she glared at Takezō for a moment, then turned and faced the villagers. Waving a mulberry branch in the air, she cried, "I won't be satisfied with just killing him! Make him suffer first! Just look at that hideous face!" Turning back to the prisoner, she raised her switch, screaming, "You degenerate, loathsome creature!" and brought it down on him several times, until she ran out of breath and her arm dropped to her side. Takezō cringed in pain as Osugi turned to Takuan with a menacing look.

"What do you want from me?" the monk asked.

"It was because of this murderer that my son's life has been ruined." Shaking violently, she screeched, "And without Matahachi there is no one to carry on our family name."

"Well," countered Takuan, "Matahachi, if you don't mind my saying so, never amounted to much anyway. Won't you be better off in the long run taking your son-in-law as heir? Giving him the honored Hon'iden name?"

"How dare you say such a thing!" Suddenly the proud dowager burst into sobs. "I don't care about what you think. Nobody understood him. He wasn't really bad; he was my baby." Her fury rose again and she pointed at Takezō. "He led him astray, he made him a good-for-nothing like himself. I have the right to take my revenge." Addressing the crowd, she beseeched them, "Let me decide. Leave it to me. I know what to do with him!"

Just then a loud and angry shout from the back cut the old woman off. The crowd parted like rent cloth, and the latecomer marched quickly to the front. It was Scraggly Beard himself, in a towering rage.

"What's going on here? This isn't a sideshow! All of you, get out of here. Go back to work. Go home. Immediately!" There was shuffling, but no one turned to go. "You heard what I said! Get a move on! What are you waiting for?" He stepped threateningly toward them, his hand poised above his sword. Those in the front shrank back wide-eyed.

"No!" interrupted Takuan. "There's no reason for these good people to go. I called them here for the express purpose of discussing what's to be done with Takezō."

"You be quiet!" commanded the captain. "You have nothing to say in this matter." Drawing himself up and glaring first at Takuan, then at Osugi, and finally at the crowd, he boomed, "This Shimmen Takezō has not only committed grave and serious crimes against the laws of this province; he is also a fugitive from Sekigahara. His punishment cannot be decided by the people. He must be turned over to the government!"

Takuan shook his head. "Nonsense!" Seeing that Scraggly Beard was ready to respond, he raised a silencing finger. "That's not what you agreed to!"

The captain, his dignity seriously threatened, started to argue. "Takuan, you will no doubt receive the money the government has offered as a reward. But as an official representative of Lord Terumasa, it is my duty to take charge of the prisoner at this point. His fate need no longer be of any concern to you. Don't trouble yourself even thinking about it."

Takuan, making no effort to answer, broke into peals of laughter. Every time it seemed to subside, it would come rolling up again.

"Watch your manners, monk!" warned the captain. He started to spit and sputter. "What's so funny? Huh? You think this is all a joke?"

"My manners?" repeated Takuan, cracking up in laughter again. "My manners? Look, Scraggly Beard, are you thinking of breaking our agreement, going back on your sacred word? If you are, I warn you, I'll turn Takezō loose here and now!"

With a unanimous gasp, the villagers began edging away.

"Ready?" asked Takuan, reaching toward the rope that bound Takezō.

The captain was speechless.

"And when I unleash him, I'm going to sic him on you first. You can fight it out between yourselves. Then arrest him, if you can!"

"Now hold on—just a minute!"

"I kept my part of the bargain." Takuan continued to make as if he were about to remove the prisoner's fetters.

"Stop, I say." The samurai's forehead beaded with sweat.

"Why?"

"Well, because—because—" He was almost stuttering. "Now that he's tied up, there's no point in letting him go, just to cause more trouble—now, is there? I'll tell you what! You can kill Takezō yourself. Here—here's my sword. Just let me have his head to take back with me. That's fair, isn't it?"

"Give you his head! Not on your life! It's the business of the clergy to conduct funerals, but giving away the corpses, or parts of them . . . Well, that'd give us priests a bad name, wouldn't it? No one would trust us with their dead, and anyway, if we started to just give them away, the temples would go broke in no time." Even with the samurai's hand resting on his sword handle, Takuan couldn't resist baiting him.

Turning to the mob, the monk became serious again. "I ask you to talk it over among yourselves and give me an answer. What shall we do? The old woman says it's not enough to kill him outright, we should torture him first. What do you think of lashing him to a branch of the cryptomeria tree for a few days? We could bind him hand and foot, and he would be exposed to the elements day and night. The crows will probably gouge out his eyeballs. How does that sound?"

His proposal struck his listeners as so inhumanly cruel that at first no one could answer.

Except Osugi, who said, "Takuan, this idea of yours shows what a wise man you really are, but I think we should string him up for a week—no, more! Let him hang there ten or twenty days. Then I myself will come and strike the fatal blow."

Without further ado, Takuan nodded. "All right. So be it!"

He took hold of the rope after freeing it from the railing and dragged Takezō, like a dog on a leash, to the tree. The prisoner went meekly, head bowed, uttering not a sound. He seemed so repentant that some of the softer-hearted members of the crowd felt a bit sorry for him. The excitement of capturing the "wild beast" had hardly worn off, however, and with great gusto everyone joined in the fun. Having tied several lengths of rope together, they hoisted him up to a branch about thirty feet from the ground and lashed him tightly. So bound, he looked less like a living man than a big straw doll.

After Otsū came back to the temple from the mountains, she began feeling a strange and intense melancholy whenever she was alone in her room. She wondered why, since being alone was nothing new to her. And there were always some people around the temple. She had all the comforts of home, yet felt lonelier now than she had at any time during those three long days on the desolate hillside with only Takuan as a companion. Sitting at the low table by her window, her chin resting on her palms, she reflected on her feelings for half a day before coming to a conclusion.

She felt that this experience had given her an insight into her own heart. Loneliness, she mused, is like hunger; it isn't outside but inside oneself. To be lonely, she thought, is to sense that one lacks something, something vitally necessary, but what she knew not.

Neither the people around her nor the amenities of life at the temple could assuage the feeling of isolation she now felt. In the mountains there had only been the silence, the trees and the mist, but there had also been Takuan. It came to her like a revelation that he was not entirely outside herself. His words had gone straight to her heart, had warmed and lighted it as no fire or lamp could. She then came to the innocent realization that she was lonely because Takuan was not around.

Having made this discovery, she stood up, but her mind still grappled with the problem at hand. After deciding Takezō's punishment, Takuan had been closeted in the guest room with the samurai from Himeji a good deal of the time. What with having to go back and forth to the village on this errand and that, he'd had no time to sit down and talk with her as he had in the mountains. Otsū sat down again.

If only she had a friend! She didn't need many; just one who knew her well, someone she could lean on, someone strong and completely trustworthy. That was what she longed for, craved so badly that she was nearly at her wit's end.

There was always, of course, her flute, but by the time a girl is sixteen, there are questions and uncertainties inside her that can't be answered by a piece of bamboo. She needed intimacy and a sense of partaking in, not just observing, real life.

"It's all so disgusting!" she said out loud, but voicing her feeling in no way mitigated her hatred for Matahachi. Tears spilled onto the little lacquered table; the angry blood coursing through her veins turned her temples blue. Her head throbbed.

Silently the door behind her slid open. In the temple kitchen, the fire for the evening meal burned brightly.

"Ah ha! So this is where you've been hiding! Sitting here letting the whole day slip through your fingers!"

The figure of Osugi appeared at the door. Startled out of her abstraction, Otsū hesitated a moment before welcoming the old woman and putting a cushion down for her to sit on. Without so much as a by-your-leave, Osugi seated herself.

"My good daughter-in-law . . ." she began in grandiose tones.

"Yes, ma'am," answered Otsū, cowed into bowing deeply before the old harridan.

"Now that you have acknowledged the relationship, there's a little something I want to talk to you about. But first bring me some tea. I've been talking till now with Takuan and the samurai from Himeji, and the acolyte here didn't even serve us refreshments. I'm parched!"

Otsū obeyed and brought her some tea.

"I want to talk about Matahachi," the old woman said without prelude. "Of course, I'd be a fool to believe anything that lying Takezō says, but it seems Matahachi is alive and staying in a different province."

"Is that so?" said Otsū coldly.

"I can't be sure, but the fact remains that the priest here, acting as your guardian, agreed to your marriage to my son, and the Hon'iden family has already accepted you as his bride. Whatever happens in the future, I trust you don't have any ideas about going back on your word."

"Well . . ."

"You'd never do such a thing, would you?"

Otsū let out a soft sigh.

"All right then, I'm glad of that!" She spoke as though adjourning a meeting. "You know how people talk, and there's no telling when Matahachi will be back, so I want you to leave this temple and come live with me. I've more work than I can handle, and since my daughter-in-law's got so much on her hands with her own family, I can't drive her too hard. So I need your help."

"But I—"

"Who else but Matahachi's bride could come into the Hon'iden house?"

"I don't know, but—"

"Are you trying to say you don't want to come? Don't you like the idea of living under my roof? Most girls would jump at the chance!"

"No, it's not that. It's—"

"Well, then, stop dawdling! Get your things together!"

"Right now? Wouldn't it be better to wait?"

"Wait for what?"

"Until . . . until Matahachi comes back."

"Absolutely not!" Her tone was final. "You just might start getting ideas in your head about other men before that. It's my duty to see that you don't misbehave. In the meantime, I'll also see that you learn how to do field work, care for the silkworms, sew a straight seam and act like a lady."

"Oh. I . . . see." Otsū had no strength to protest. Her head still pounded and with all this talk of Matahachi, her chest tightened. She feared saying another word lest she release a torrent of tears.

"And there's one other thing," said Osugi. Heedless of the girl's distress, she raised her head imperiously. "I'm still not quite sure what that unpredictable monk plans to do with Takezō. It worries me. I want you to keep a sharp eye on the two of them until we're sure Takezō is dead. At night as well as in the daytime. If you don't take special care at night, there's no telling what Takuan might do. They may be in cahoots!"

"So you don't mind if I stay here?"

"For the time being, no, since you can't be in two places at once, can you? You will come with your belongings to the Hon'iden house the day that Takezō's head is separated from his body. Understand?"

"Yes, I understand."

"Make sure you don't forget!" Osugi barked as she whooshed out of the room.

Thereupon, as though waiting for the chance, a shadow appeared on the paper-covered window and a male voice called softly, "Otsū! Otsū!"

Hoping it was Takuan, she hardly looked at the shape of the shadow before rushing to open the window. When she did, she jerked back in surprise, for the eyes meeting hers were the captain's. He reached through, grabbing her hand and squeezing it hard.

"You've been kind to me," he said, "but I've just received orders from Himeji to go back."

"Why, that's too bad." She tried to pull her hand from his, but the grip was too firm.

"They seem to be conducting an investigation into the incident here," he explained. "If only I had Takezō's head, I could say I had discharged my duty with honor. I'd be vindicated. That crazy, stubborn Takuan won't let me take it. He won't listen to anything I say. But I think you're on my side; that's why I've come here. Take this letter, will you, and read it later, somewhere where no one will see you?"

72

He pressed the letter into her hand and was off in a shot. She could hear him hurriedly walking down the steps to the road.

It was more than a letter, for a large gold piece was enclosed. But the message itself was straightforward enough: it asked Otsū to cut off Takezō's head within the next few days and bring it to Himeji, where the writer would make her his wife, and she would live amid wealth and glory for the rest of her days. The missive was signed "Aoki Tanzaemon," a name that, according to the writer's own testimony, belonged to one of the most celebrated warriors of the region. She wanted to burst out laughing, but was too indignant.

As she finished reading, Takuan called, "Otsū, have you eaten yet?"

Slipping her feet into her sandals, she went out to talk with him.

"I don't feel like eating. I have a headache."

"What's that in your hand?"

"A letter."

"Another one?"

"Yes."

"From whom?"

"Takuan, you're so nosy!"

"Curious, my girl, inquisitive. Not nosy!"

"Would you like to have a look at it?"

"If you don't mind."

"Just to pass the time?"

"That's as good a reason as any."

"Here. I don't mind at all."

Otsū handed him the letter, and after reading it, Takuan laughed heartily. She couldn't help but let the corners of her mouth turn up too.

"That poor man! He's so desperate he's trying to bribe you with both love and money. This letter is hilarious! I must say, our world is fortunate indeed to be blessed with such outstanding, upright samurai! He's so brave he asks a mere girl to do his beheading for him. And so stupid as to put it in writing."

"The letter doesn't bother me," said Otsū, "but what am I going to do with the money?" She handed Takuan the gold piece.

"This is worth quite a lot," he said, weighing it in his hand.

"That's what bothers me."

"Don't worry. I never have any trouble disposing of money."

Takuan walked around to the front of the temple, where there was an alms box. Preparing to toss the coin in, he touched it to his forehead in deference to the Buddha. Then he changed his mind. "On second thought, you keep it. I daresay it won't be in the way."

"I don't want it. It'll just cause trouble. I might be questioned about it later. I'd rather just pretend I never saw it."

"This gold, Otsū, no longer belongs to Aoki Tanzaemon. It has become an offering to the Buddha, and the Buddha has bestowed it on you. Keep it for good luck."

Without further protest, Otsū tucked the coin into her obi; then, looking up at the sky, she remarked, "Windy, isn't it? I wonder if it'll rain tonight. It hasn't rained for ages."

"Spring's almost over, so we're due for a good downpour. We need it to wash away all the dead flowers, not to mention relieving the people's boredom."

"But if it's a heavy rain, what'll happen to Takezō?"

"Hmm. Takezō . . ." the monk mused.

Just as the two of them turned toward the cryptomeria, a call came from its upper branches.

"Takuan! Takuan!"

"What? Is that you, Takezō?"

As Takuan squinted to look up into the tree, Takezō hurled down a stream of imprecations. "You swine of a monk! You filthy impostor! Come and stand under here! I have something to say to you!"

The wind was beating at the tree's branches violently, and the voice came through broken and disjointed. Leaves swirled around the tree and onto Takuan's upturned face.

The monk laughed. "I see you're still full of life. That's okay; that suits me fine. I hope it's not just the false vitality that comes from the knowledge that you're soon going to die."

"Shut up!" cried Takezō, who was not so much full of life as full of anger. "If I were afraid to die, why would I have just kept still while you tied me up?"

"You did that because I am strong and you are weak!"

"That's a lie, and you know it!"

"Then I'll put it another way. I'm clever, and you are unspeakably stupid!"

"You might be right. It was certainly stupid of me to let you catch me."

"Don't squirm so much, monkey in the tree! It won't do you any good, it'll make you bleed if you've any blood left, and frankly, it's quite unbecoming."

"Listen, Takuan!"

"I'm listening."

"If I had wanted to fight you on the mountain, I could've easily squashed you under one foot like a cucumber."

"That's not a very flattering analogy. In any case you didn't, so you'd be better off leaving that line of thought. Forget about what happened. It's too late for regrets."

"You tricked me with your high-sounding priest talk. That was pretty mean, you bastard. You got me to trust you and you betrayed me. I let you capture me, yes, but only because I thought you were different from the others. I never thought I'd be humiliated like this."

"Get to the point, Takezō," Takuan said impatiently.

"Why are you doing this to me?" the straw bundle shrieked. "Why don't you just cut off my head and get it over with! I thought that if I had to die, it'd be better to let you choose how to execute me than let that bloodthirsty mob do it. Although you are a monk, you also claim to understand the Way of the Samurai."

74

"Oh, I do, you poor misguided boy. Much better than you!"

"I would've been better off letting the villagers catch up with me. At least they're human."

"Was that your only mistake, Takezō? Hasn't just about everything you've ever done been some kind of mistake? While you're resting up there, why don't you try thinking about the past a little."

"Oh, shut up, you hypocrite! I'm not ashamed! Matahachi's mother can call me anything she wants, but he is my friend, my best friend. I considered it my responsibility to come and tell the old hag what happened to him and what does she do? She tries to incite that mob to torture me! Bringing her news of her precious son was the only reason I broke through the barrier and came here. Is that a violation of the warrior's code?"

"That's not the point, you imbecile! The trouble with you is that you don't even know how to think. You seem to be under the misconception that if you perform one brave deed, that alone makes you a samurai. Well, it doesn't! You let that one act of loyalty convince you of your righteousness. The more convinced you became, the more harm you caused yourself and everyone else. And now where are you? Caught in a trap you set for yourself, that's where!" He paused. "By the way, how's the view from up there, Takezō?"

"You pig! I won't forget this!"

"You'll forget everything soon. Before you turn into dried meat, Takezō, take a good look at the wide world around you. Gaze out onto the world of human beings, and change your selfish way of thinking. And then, when you arrive in that other world beyond and are reunited with your ancestors, tell them that just before you died a man named Takuan Sōhō told you this. They'll be overjoyed to learn you had such excellent guidance, even if you did learn what life was all about too late to bring anything but shame to your family name."

Otsū, who had been standing transfixed some distance away, came running forward and attacked Takuan in shrill tones.

"You're carrying this too far, Takuan! I've been listening. I heard everything. How can you be so cruel to someone who can't even defend himself? You're a religious man, or you're supposed to be! Takezō's telling the truth when he says he trusted you and let you take him without a struggle."

"Now what's all this? Is my comrade in arms turning against me?"

"Have a heart, Takuan! When I hear you talk like that, I hate you, I really do. If you intend to kill him, then kill him and be done with it! Takezō is resigned to dying. Let him die in peace!" She was so outraged she grabbed frantically at Takuan's chest.

"Be quiet!" he said with uncharacteristic brutality. "Women know nothing of these matters. Hold your tongue, or I'll hang you up there with him."

"No, I won't, I won't!" she screamed. "I should have a chance to speak too. Didn't I go to the mountains with you and stay there three days and three nights?"

"That has nothing to do with it. Takuan Sōhō will punish Takezō as he sees fit."

75

"So punish him! Kill him! Now. It's not right for you to ridicule his misery while he's lying up there half dead."

"That happens to be my only weakness, ridiculing fools like him."

"It's inhuman!"

"Get out of here, now! Go away, Otsū; leave me alone."

"I will not!"

"Stop being so stubborn," Takuan shouted, giving Otsū a hard shove with his elbow.

When she recovered, she was slumped against the tree. She pressed her face and chest to its trunk and began wailing. She had never dreamed Takuan could be so cruel. The people in the village believed that even if the monk had Takezō tied up for a while, eventually he'd soften and lighten the punishment. Now Takuan had admitted that it was his "weakness" to enjoy seeing Takezō suffer! Otsū shuddered at the savagery of men.

If even Takuan, whom she'd trusted so deeply, could become heartless, then the whole world must indeed be evil beyond comprehension. And if there was no one at all whom she could trust . . .

She felt a curious warmth in this tree, felt somehow that through its great, ancient trunk, so thick that ten men with arms outstretched could not encompass it, there coursed the blood of Takezō, flowing down into it from his precarious prison in the upper branches.

How like a samurai's son he was! How courageous! When Takuan had first tied him up, and again just now, she had seen Takezō's weaker side. He, too, was able to weep. Until now, she'd gone along with the opinion of the crowd, been swayed by it, without having any real idea of the man himself. What was there about him that made people hate him like a demon and hunt him down like a beast?

Her back and shoulders heaved with her sobs. Clinging tightly to the tree trunk, she rubbed her tear-stained cheeks against the bark. The wind whistled loudly through the upper branches, which were waving broadly to and fro. Large raindrops fell on her kimono neck and flowed down her back, chilling her spine.

"Come on, Otsū," Takuan shouted, covering his head with his hands. "We'll get soaked."

She didn't even answer.

"It's all your fault, Otsū! You're a crybaby! You start weeping, the heavens weep too." Then, the teasing tone gone from his voice: "The wind's getting stronger, and it looks like we're in for a big storm, so let's get inside. Don't waste your tears on a man who's going to die anyway! Come on!" Takuan, sweeping the skirt of his kimono up over his head, ran toward the shelter of the temple.

Within seconds it was pouring, the raindrops making little white spots as they pummeled the ground. Though the water was streaming down her back, Otsū didn't budge. She couldn't tear herself away, even after her drenched kimono was clinging to her skin and she was chilled to the marrow. When her thoughts turned to Takezō, the rain ceased to matter. It didn't occur to her to wonder why she should suffer simply because he was suffering; her mind was consumed by a newly formed image of what a man should be. She silently prayed his life would be spared.

She wandered in circles round the foot of the tree, looking up to Takezō often, but unable to see him because of the storm. Without thinking, she called his name, but there was no answer. A suspicion arose in her mind that he might regard her as a member of the Hon'iden family, or as just another hostile villager.

"If he stays out in this rain," she thought in despair, "he's sure to die before morning. Oh, isn't there anyone in the world who can save him?"

She started running at full speed, partially propelled by the raging wind. Behind the main temple, the kitchen building and the priests' quarters were tightly shuttered. Water overflowing from the roof gutters slashed deep gullies in the ground as it rushed downhill.

"Takuan!" she screamed. She'd reached the door of his room, and began banging on it with all her strength.

"Who is it?" came his voice from within.

"It's me—Otsū!"

"What are you doing still out there?" He quickly opened the door and looked at her in astonishment. Despite the building's long eaves, rain showered in on him. "Come inside quick!" he exclaimed, making a grab for her arm, but she pulled back.

"No. I came to ask a favor, not to dry off. I beg you, Takuan, take him down from that tree!"

"What? I'll do no such thing!" he said adamantly.

"Oh, please, Takuan, you must. I'd be grateful to you forever." She fell on her knees in the mud and lifted her hands in supplication. "It doesn't matter about me, but you must help him! Please! You can't just let him die—you can't!"

The sound of the torrent nearly blotted out her tearful voice. With her hands still raised before her, she looked like a Buddhist practicing austerities by standing under a freezing waterfall.

"I bow before you, Takuan. I beg you. I'll do anything you ask, but please save him!"

Takuan was silent. His eyes were tightly closed, like the doors to the shrine where a secret Buddha is kept. Heaving a deep sigh, he opened them and breathed fire.

"Go to bed! This minute! You're weak to begin with, and being out in this weather is suicidal."

"Oh, please, please," she pleaded, reaching for the door.

"I'm going to bed. I advise you to do the same." His voice was like ice. The door slammed shut.

Still, she would not give up. She crawled under the house till she reached the spot she guessed was beneath where he slept. She called up to him:

"Please! Takuan, it's the most important thing in the world to me! Takuan, can you hear me? Answer me, please! You're a monster! A heartless, cold-blooded fiend!"

For a while, the monk listened patiently without replying, but she was making it impossible for him to sleep. Finally, in a fit of temper, he jumped out of bed, shouting, "Help! Thief! There's a thief under my floor. Catch him!"

Otsū scrambled out into the storm again and retired in defeat. But she was not finished yet.

The Rock and the Tree

By early morning, wind and rain had washed spring away without a trace. A throbbing sun beat down furiously and few villagers walked around without a wide-brimmed hat for protection.

Osugi made her way uphill to the temple, arriving at Takuan's door thirsty and breathless. Beads of sweat emerged from her hairline, converged in rivulets and coursed straight down her righteous nose. She took no notice of this, for she was brimming over with curiosity about her victim's fate.

"Takuan," she called, "did Takezō survive the storm?"

The monk appeared on his veranda. "Oh, it's you. Terrific downpour, wasn't it?"

"Yes." She smiled crookedly. "It was murderous."

"I'm sure you know, however, that it isn't very difficult to live through a night or two of even the heaviest rain. The human body can take a lot of buffeting. It's the sun that's really deadly."

"You don't mean he's still alive?" said Osugi in disbelief, at once turning her wrinkled face toward the old cryptomeria. Her needlelike eyes squinted in the glare. She raised a hand to shield them and in a moment relaxed a bit. "He's just drooping up there like a wet rag," she said with renewed hope. "He can't have any life left in him, he can't."

"I don't see any crows picking at his face yet." Takuan smiled. "I think that means he's still breathing."

"Thank you for telling me. A man of learning like you must surely know more than I do about such matters." She craned her neck and peered around him into the building. "I don't see my daughter-in-law anywhere. Would you please call her for me?"

"Your daughter-in-law? I don't believe I've ever met her. In any case, I don't know her name. How can I call her?"

"Call her, I say!" Osugi repeated impatiently.

"Who on earth are you talking about?"

"Why, Otsū, of course!"

"Otsū! Why do you call her your daughter-in-law? She hasn't entered the Hon'iden family, has she?"

"No, not yet, but I plan to take her in very soon as Matahachi's bride."

"That's hard to imagine. How can she marry someone when he's not around?"

Osugi became more indignant. "Look, you vagabond! This has nothing to do with you! Just tell me where Otsū is!"

"I imagine she's still in bed."

"Oh, yes, I should've thought of that," the old woman muttered, half to herself. "I did tell her to watch Takezō nights, so she must become pretty tired by daybreak. Incidentally," she said accusingly, "aren't you supposed to be watching him during the day?"

Without waiting for an answer, she did an about-face and marched under the tree. There she stared upward for a long time, as if in a trance. When it finally broke, she plodded off toward the village, mulberry stick in hand.

Takuan returned to his room, where he stayed until evening.

Otsū's room was not far from his, in the same building. Her door was also closed all day except when opened by the acolyte, who several times brought her medicine or an earthenware pot full of thick rice gruel. When they had found her half dead in the rain the night before, they'd had to drag her in kicking and screaming and force her to swallow some tea. The priest had then given her a severe scolding while she sat mutely propped against a wall. By morning she had a high fever and was hardly able to lift her head to drink the gruel.

Night fell, and in sharp contrast to the previous evening, a bright moon shone like a clearly cut hole in the sky. When everyone else was sound asleep, Takuan put down the book he was reading, slipped into his wooden clogs and went out into the yard.

"Takezō!" he called.

High above him a branch shook and glistening dewdrops fell.

"Poor boy, I guess he doesn't have the strength to reply," Takuan said to himself. "Takezō! Takezō!"

"What do you want, you bastard of a monk?" came the ferocious response.

Takuan was seldom taken off guard, but he could not conceal his surprise. "You certainly howl loudly for a man at death's door. Sure you're not really a fish or some kind of sea monster? At this rate you ought to last another five or six days. By the way, how's your stomach? Empty enough for you?"

"Forget the small talk, Takuan. Just cut my head off and get it over with."

"Oh, no! Not so fast! One has to be careful about things like that. If I cut your head off right now, it'd probably fly down and try to bite me." Takuan's voice trailed off and he stared at the sky. "What a beautiful moon! You're lucky to be able to view it from such an excellent vantage point."

"Okay, just watch me, you filthy mongrel of a monk! I'll show you what I can do if I put my mind to it!" With every ounce of strength in him, Takezō then began to shake himself violently, flinging his weight up and down and nearly breaking off the branch he was bound to. Bark and leaves rained down on the man below, who remained unruffled but perhaps a bit affectedly nonchalant.

The monk calmly brushed his shoulders clean, and when he was finished he looked up again. "That's the spirit, Takezō! It's good to get as angry as you are now. Go ahead! Feel your strength to the fullest, show you're a real man, show us what you're made of! People these days think it's a sign of wisdom and character to be able to control their anger, but I say they're foolish. I hate seeing the young being so restrained, so proper. They have more spirit than their elders and they should show it. Don't hold back, Takezō! The madder you get, the better!"

"Just wait, Takuan, just wait! If I have to chew through this rope with my bare teeth, I will, just to get my hands on you and tear you limb from limb!"

"Is that a promise or a threat? If you really think you can do it, I'll stay down here and wait. Are you sure you can keep it up without killing yourself before the rope breaks?"

"Shut up!" Takezō screamed hoarsely.

"Say, Takezō, you really are strong! The whole tree is swaying. But I don't notice the earth shaking, sorry to say. You know, the trouble with you is that, in reality, you're weak. Your kind of anger is nothing more than personal malice. A real man's anger is an expression of moral indignation. Anger over petty emotional trifles is for women, not men."

"It won't be long now," he threatened. "I'll go straight for the neck!"

Takezō struggled on, but the thick rope showed no sign of weakening. Takuan looked on for a time, then offered some friendly advice. "Why don't you cut that out, Takezō—you're getting nowhere. You'll just wear yourself out, and what good is that going to do you? Squirm and wriggle all you like, you couldn't break a single branch of this tree, much less make a dent in the universe."

Takezō gave out a mighty groan. His tantrum was over. He realized the monk was right.

"I daresay all that strength would be put to better use working for the good of the country. You really should try doing something for others, Takezō, although it is a little late to start now. If you'd just tried, you'd have had a chance at moving the gods or even the universe, not to mention plain, everyday people." Takuan's voice took on a slightly pontifical tone. "It's a pity, a great pity! Though you were born human, you're more like an animal, no better than a boar or wolf. How sad it is that a handsome young man like you has to meet his end here, without ever having become truly human! What a waste!"

"You call yourself human?" Takezō spat.

"Listen, you barbarian! All along you've had too much confidence in your own brute strength, thinking you didn't have a match in the world. But look where you are now!"

"I've got nothing to be ashamed of. It wasn't a fair fight."

"In the long run, Takezō, it doesn't make any difference. You were outwitted and outtalked instead of being outpummeled. When you've lost, you've lost. And whether you like it or not, I'm sitting on this rock and you're lying up there helpless. Can't you see the difference between you and me!"

"Yeah. You fight dirty. You're a liar and a coward!"

"It would have been crazy of me to try to take you by force. You're too strong physically. A human being doesn't have much chance wrestling a tiger. Luckily, he rarely has to, being the more intelligent of the two. Not many people would argue with the fact that tigers are inferior to humans."

Takezō gave no indication that he was still listening.

"It's the same with your so-called courage. Your conduct up till now gives no evidence that it's anything more than animal courage, the kind that has no respect for human values and life. That's not the kind of courage that makes a samurai. True courage knows fear. It knows how to fear that which should be feared. Honest people value life passionately, they hang on to it like a precious jewel. And they pick the right time and place to surrender it, to die with dignity."

Still no answer.

"That's what I meant when I said it's a pity about you. You were born with physical strength and fortitude, but you lack both knowledge and wisdom. While you managed to master a few of the more unfortunate features of the Way of the Samurai, you made no effort to acquire learning or virtue. People talk about combining the Way of Learning with the Way of the Samurai, but when properly combined, they aren't two—they're one. Only one Way, Takezō."

The tree was as silent as the rock on which Takuan sat. The darkness, too, was still. After several moments, Takuan rose slowly and deliberately. "Think about it one more night, Takezō. After you do, I'll cut off your head for you." He started walking away, taking long, thoughtful strides, his head bowed. He hadn't gone more than twenty paces when Takezō's voice rang out urgently.

"Wait!"

Takuan turned and called back, "What do you want now?"

"Come back."

"Mm. Don't tell me you want to hear more? Could it be that at last you're beginning to think?"

"Takuan! Save me!" Takezō's cry for help was loud and plaintive. The branch began to tremble, as though it, as though the whole tree, were weeping.

"I want to be a better man. I realize now how important it is, what a privilege it is to be born human. I'm almost dead, but I understand what it means to be alive. And now that I know, my whole life will consist of being tied to this tree! I can't undo what I've done."

"You're finally coming to your senses. For the first time in your life, you're talking like a human being."

"I don't want to die," Takezō cried. "I want to live. I want to go out, try again, do everything right this time." His body convulsed with his sobbing. "Takuan . . . please! Help me . . . help me!"

The monk shook his head. "Sorry, Takezō. It's out of my hands. It's the law of nature. You can't do things over again. That's life. Everything in it is for keeps. Everything! You can't put your head back on after the enemy's cut it off. That's the way it is. Of course, I feel sorry for you, but I can't undo that rope, because it wasn't me who tied it. It was you. All I can do is give you some advice. Face death bravely and quietly. Say a prayer and hope someone bothers to listen. And for the sake of your ancestors, Takezō, have the decency to die with a peaceful look on your face!"

The clatter of Takuan's sandals faded into the distance. He was gone, and Takezō cried out no more. Following the spirit of the monk's advice, he shut the eyes that had just experienced a great awakening and forgot everything. He forgot about living and about dying, and under the myriad tiny stars lay perfectly still as the night breeze sighed through the tree. He was cold, very cold.

After a while, he sensed that someone was at the base of the tree. Whoever it was was clutching the broad trunk and trying frantically but not very adroitly to climb up to the lowest branch. Takezō could hear the climber slipping downward after almost every upward advance. He could also hear chips of bark falling to the ground and was sure that the hands were being skinned much worse than the tree was. But the climber kept at it doggedly, digging into the tree again and again until finally the first branch was within reach. Then the form rose with relative ease to where Takezō, barely distinguishable from the branch he was stretched on, lay depleted of every ounce of strength. A panting voice whispered his name.

With great difficulty he opened his eyes and found himself face to face with a veritable skeleton; only the eyes were alive and vibrant. The face spoke. "It's me!" it said with childlike simplicity.

"Otsū?"

"Yes, me. Oh, Takezō, let's run away! I heard you scream out that you wanted with all your heart to live."

"Run away? You'll untie me, set me free?"

"Yes. I can't stand this village anymore either. If I stay here—oh, I don't even want to think about it. I have my reasons. I just want to get out of this stupid, cruel place. I'll help you, Takezō! We can help each other." Otsū was already wearing traveling clothes, and all her worldly possessions hung from her shoulder in a small fabric bag.

"Quick, cut the rope! What are you waiting for? Cut it!"

"It won't take a minute."

She unsheathed a small dagger and in no time severed the captive's bonds. Several minutes passed before the tingling in his limbs eased and he could flex his muscles. She tried to support his entire weight, with the result that when he slipped, she went down with him. The two bodies clung to each other, bounced off a limb, twisted in the air and crashed to the ground.

82

Takezō stood up. Dazed from the thirty-foot fall and numbingly weak, he nevertheless planted his feet firmly on the earth. Otsū writhed in pain on her hands and knees.

"O-o-h-h," she moaned.

Putting his arms around her, he helped her up.

"Do you think you broke something?"

"I have no idea, but I think I can walk."

"We had all those branches to break the fall, so you're probably not too badly hurt."

"What about you? You okay?"

"Yes . . . I'm . . . I'm okay. I'm . . . " He paused a second or two, then blurted out, "I'm alive! I'm really alive!"

"Of course you are!"

"It's not 'of course.'"

"Let's get out of here fast. If anybody finds us here, we'll be in real trouble."

Otsū started limping away and Takezō followed . . . slowly, silently, like two frail wounded insects walking on the autumn frost.

They proceeded as best they could, hobbling along in silence, a silence broken only much later, when Otsū cried, "Look! It's getting light over toward Harima."

"Where are we?"

"At the top of Nakayama Pass."

"Have we really come that far?"

"Yes." Otsū smiled weakly. "Surprising what you can do when you're determined. But, Takezō . . . " Otsū looked alarmed. "You must be famished. You haven't eaten anything for days."

At the mention of food, Takezō suddenly realized his shrunken stomach was cramped with pain. Now that he was aware of it, it was excruciating, and it seemed like hours before Otsū managed to undo her bag and take out the food. Her gift of life took the form of rice cakes, stuffed generously with sweet bean paste. As their sweetness slid smoothly down his throat, Takezō grew giddy. The fingers holding the cake shook. "I'm alive," he thought over and over, vowing that from that moment on he'd live a very different sort of life.

The reddish clouds of morning turned their cheeks rosy. As he began to see Otsū's face more clearly and hunger gave way to a sated calm, it seemed like a dream that he was sitting here safe and sound with her.

"When it gets light, we'll have to be very careful. We're almost at the provincial border," said Otsū.

Takezō's eyes widened. "The border! That's right, I forgot. I have to go to Hinagura."

"Hinagura? Why?"

"That's where they've got my sister locked up. I have to get her out of there. Guess I'll have to say good-bye."

Otsū peered into his face in stunned silence. "If that's the way you feel about it, go! But if I'd thought you were going to desert me, I wouldn't have left Miyamoto."

"What else can I do? Just leave her there in the stockade?"

With a look that pressed in on him, she took his hand in hers. Her face, her whole body, was aflame with passion. "Takezō," she pleaded, "I'll tell you how I feel about this later, when there's time, but please, don't leave me alone here! Take me with you, wherever you go!"

"But I can't!"

"Remember"—she gripped his hand tight—"whether you like it or not, I'm staying with you. If you think I'll be in the way when you're trying to rescue Ogin, then I'll go to Himeji and wait."

"All right, do that," he agreed instantly.

"You'll definitely come, won't you?"

"Of course."

"I'll be waiting at Hanada Bridge, just outside Himeji. I'll wait for you there, whether it takes a hundred days or a thousand."

Answering with a slight nod, Takezō was off without further ado, racing along the ridge leading from the pass into the far-distant mountains. Otsū raised her head to watch him till his body melted into the scenery.

Back in the village, Osugi's grandson came charging up to the Hon'iden manor house, shouting, "Grandma! Grandma!"

Wiping his nose with the back of his hand, he peered into the kitchen and said excitedly, "Grandma, have you heard? Something awful's happened!"

Osugi, who was standing before the stove, coaxing a fire with a bamboo fan, barely looked his way. "What's all the fuss about?"

"Grandma, don't you know? Takezō's escaped!"

"Escaped!" She dropped the fan in the flames. "What are you talking about?"

"This morning he wasn't in the tree. The rope was cut."

"Heita, you know what I said about telling tales!"

"It's the truth, Grandma, honest. Everybody's talking about it."

"Are you absolutely sure?"

"Yes, ma'am. And up at the temple, they're searching for Otsū. She's gone too. Everybody's running around shouting."

The visible effect of the news was colorful. Osugi's face whitened shade by shade as the flames of her burning fan turned from red to blue to violet. Her face soon seemed drained of all blood, so much so that Heita shrank in fear.

"Heita!"

"Yes?"

"Run as fast as your legs can carry you. Fetch your daddy right away. Then go down to the riverbank and get Uncle Gon! And hurry!" Osugi's voice quivered.

Before Heita even reached the gate, a crowd of muttering villagers had arrived. Among them were Osugi's son-in-law, Uncle Gon, other relatives and a number of tenants.

"That girl Otsū's run away too, hasn't she?"

84 "And Takuan's not around either!"

"Looks pretty funny if you ask me!"

"They were in it together, that's for sure."

"Wonder what the old woman'll do? Her family honor's at stake!"

The son-in-law and Uncle Gon, carrying lances passed down to them from their ancestors, stared blankly toward the house. Before they could do anything, they needed guidance, so they stood there restlessly waiting for Osugi to appear and issue orders.

"Granny," someone finally shouted, "haven't you heard the news?"

"I'll be there in a minute," came the reply. "All of you, just be quiet and wait."

Osugi quickly rose to the occasion. When she'd realized the awful news had to be true, her blood boiled, but she managed to control herself enough to kneel before the family altar. After silently saying a prayer of supplication, she raised her head, opened her eyes and turned around. Calmly she opened the doors of the sword chest, pulled out a drawer and withdrew a treasured weapon. Having already donned attire suitable for a manhunt, she slipped the short sword in her obi and went to the entranceway, where she tied her sandal thongs securely round her ankles.

The awed hush that greeted her as she approached the gate made clear they knew what she was dressed for. The stubborn old woman meant business and was more than ready to avenge the insult to her house.

"Everything's going to be all right," she announced in clipped tones. "I'm going to chase down that shameless hussy myself and see to it she receives her proper punishment." Her jaw clamped shut.

She was already walking briskly down the road before someone in the crowd spoke up. "If the old woman is going, we should go too." All the relatives and tenants stood up, and fell in behind their doughty matriarch. Arming themselves as they went with sticks, fashioning bamboo lances hastily as they walked, they marched directly to Nakayama Pass, not even pausing to rest on the way. They reached it just before noon, only to find that they were too late.

"We've let them get away!" one man shouted. The crowd seethed with anger. To add to their frustration, a border official approached to inform them such a large group could not pass through.

Uncle Gon came forward and pleaded earnestly with the official, describing Takezō as a "criminal," Otsū as "evil" and Takuan as "crazy." "If we drop this matter now," he explained, "it will sully the name of our ancestors. We'll never be able to hold up our heads. We'll be the laughingstock of the village. The Hon'iden family might even have to abandon its land."

The official said he understood their predicament but could do nothing to help. The law's the law. He could perhaps send an inquiry on to Himeji and get them special permission to cross the border, but that would take time.

Osugi, after conferring with her relatives and tenants, stepped in front of the official and asked, "In that case, is there any reason why two of us, myself and Uncle Gon, can't go through?"

"Up to five people are permitted."

Osugi nodded her acquiescence. Then, although it looked as if she was about to deliver a moving farewell, she instead called her followers together in a very matter-of-fact way. They lined up before her, staring attentively at her thin-lipped mouth and large protruding teeth.

When they were all quiet, she said, "There's no reason for you to be upset. I anticipated something like this happening before we even set out. When I put on this short sword, one of the most prized Hon'iden heirlooms, I knelt before our ancestors' memorial tablets and bade them a formal farewell. I also made two vows.

"One was that I would overtake and punish the brazen female who has smeared our name with mud. The other was that I'd find out for sure, even if I died trying, whether my son Matahachi is alive. And if he is, I'll bring him home to carry on the family name. I swore to do this, and I will do it, even if it means tying a rope around his neck and dragging him all the way back. He has an obligation not only to me and to those departed, but to you as well. He will then find a wife a hundred times better than Otsū and blot out this disgrace for all time, so that the villagers will once again recognize our house as a noble and honorable one."

As they were applauding and cheering, one man uttered something sounding like a groan. Osugi stared fixedly at her son-in-law.

"Now Uncle Gon and I," she went on, "are both old enough to retire. We are both in agreement on everything I've vowed to do, and he, too, is resolved to accomplish them, even if it means spending two or three years doing nothing else, even if it means walking the length and breadth of the country. While I'm gone, my son-in-law will take my place as head of the house. During that time, you must promise to work as hard as ever. I don't want to hear of any of you neglecting the silkworms or letting weeds grow wild in the fields. Do you understand?"

Uncle Gon was nearly fifty, Osugi ten years older. The crowd seemed hesitant to let them go it alone, since they were obviously no match for Takezō in the event that they should ever find him. They all imagined him to be a madman who would attack and kill for the smell of blood alone.

"Wouldn't it be better," someone suggested, "if you took three young men along with you? The man said that five can pass through."

The old woman shook her head with vehemence. "I don't need any help. I never have, and never will. Ha! Everyone thinks Takezō is so strong, but he doesn't scare me! He's only a brat, with not much more hair on him than when I knew him as a baby. I'm not his equal in physical strength, of course, but I haven't lost my wits. I can still outsmart an enemy or two. Uncle Gon's not senile yet either.

"Now I've told you what I'm going to do," she said, pointing her index finger at her nose. "And I'm going to do it. There's nothing left for you to do but go home, so go and take care of everything till we return."

She shooed them away and walked up to the barrier. No one tried to stop her again. They called their good-byes and watched as the old couple started their journey eastward down the mountainside.

"The old lady really has guts, doesn't she?" someone remarked.

Another man cupped his hands and shouted, "If you get sick, send a messenger back to the village."

A third called solicitously, "Take care of yourselves!"

When she could no longer hear their voices, Osugi turned to Uncle Gon. "We don't have a thing to worry about," she assured him. "We're going to die before those young people anyway."

"You're absolutely right," he replied with conviction. Uncle Gon made his living hunting, but in his younger days he had been a samurai involved, to hear him tell it, in many a gory battle. Even now his skin was healthily ruddy and his hair as black as ever. His surname was Fuchikawa; Gon stood for Gonroku, his given name. As Matahachi's uncle, he was naturally quite concerned and upset about the recent goings-on.

"Granny," he said.

"What?"

"You had the foresight to dress for the road, but I'm just wearing my everyday clothes. I'll have to stop somewhere for sandals and a hat."

"There's a teahouse about halfway down this hill."

"So there is! Yes, I remember. It's called the Mikazuki Teahouse, isn't it? I'm sure they'll have what I need."

By the time they reached the teahouse they were surprised to see that the sun was beginning to set. They had thought they had more daylight hours ahead of them, since the days were growing longer with the approach of summer—more time to search on this, their first day in pursuit of their lost family honor.

They had some tea and rested for a while. Then, as Osugi laid down the money for the bill, she said, "Takano's too far to reach by nightfall. We'll have to make do with sleeping on those smelly mats at the packhorse driver's inn in Shingū, although not sleeping at all might be better than that."

"We need our sleep now more than ever. Let's get going," said Gonroku, rising to his feet and clutching the new straw hat he had just bought. "But wait just a minute."

"Why?"

"I want to fill this bamboo tube with drinking water."

Going around behind the building, he submerged his tube in a clear running brook till the bubbles stopped rising to the surface. Walking back toward the road in front, he glanced through a side window into the dim interior of the teahouse. Suddenly he came to a halt, surprised to see a figure lying on the floor, covered with straw matting. The smell of medicine permeated the air. Gonroku couldn't see the face, but he could discern long black hair strewn every which way on the pillow.

"Uncle Gon, hurry up!" Osugi cried impatiently.

"Coming."

"What kept you?"

"There seems to be a sick person inside," he said, walking behind her like a chastened dog.

"What's so unusual about that? You're as easy to distract as a child."

"Sorry, sorry," he apologized hastily. He was as intimidated by Osugi as anyone else but knew better than most how to manage her.

They set off down the fairly steep hill leading to the Harima road. The road, used daily by packhorses from the silver mines, was pitted with potholes.

"Don't fall down, Granny," Gon advised.

"How dare you patronize me! I can walk on this road with my eyes closed. Be careful yourself, you old fool."

Just then a voice greeted them from behind. "You two are pretty spry, aren't you?"

They turned to see the owner of the teahouse on horseback.

"Oh, yes; we just had a rest at your place, thank you. And where are you off to?"

"Tatsuno."

"At this hour?"

"There's no doctor between here and there. Even on horseback, it'll take me at least till midnight."

"Is it your wife who's sick?"

"Oh, no." His brows knitted. "If it were my wife, or one of the children, I wouldn't mind. But it's a lot of trouble to go to for a stranger, someone who just stopped in to take a rest."

"Oh," said Uncle Gon, "is it the girl in your back room? I happened to glance in and see her."

Osugi's brows now knitted as well.

"Yes," the shopkeeper said. "While she was resting, she started shivering, so I offered her the back room to lie down in. I felt I had to do something. Well, she didn't get any better. In fact, she seems much worse. She's burning up with fever. Looks pretty bad."

Osugi stopped in her tracks. "Is the girl about sixteen and very slender?"

"Yes, about sixteen, I'd say. Says she comes from Miyamoto."

Osugi, winking at Gonroku, began poking around in her obi. A look of distress came over her face as she exclaimed, "Oh, I've left them back at the teahouse!"

"Left what?"

"My prayer beads. I remember now—I put them down on a stool."

"Oh, that's too bad," said the shopkeeper, turning his horse around. "I'll go back for them."

"Oh, no! You've got to fetch the doctor. That sick girl's more important than my beads. We'll just go back and pick them up ourselves."

Uncle Gon was already on his way, striding rapidly back up the hill. As soon as Osugi disposed of the solicitous teahouse owner, she hurried to catch up. Before long they were both puffing and panting. Neither spoke.

It had to be Otsū!

Otsū had never really shaken off the fever she caught the night they dragged her in out of the storm. Somehow she forgot about feeling sick during the few hours she was with Takezō, but after he left her she'd walked only a short way before beginning to give in to pain and fatigue. By the time she got to the teahouse, she felt miserable.

She did not know how long she had been lying in the back room, deliriously begging for water time and time again. Before leaving, the shopkeeper had looked in on her and urged her to try to stick it out. Moments later she had forgotten he'd ever spoken to her.

Her mouth was parched. She felt as if she had a mouthful of thorns. "Master, water, please," she called out feebly. Hearing no reply, she raised herself on her elbows and craned her neck toward the water basin just outside the door. Slowly she managed to crawl to it, but as she put her hand on the bamboo dipper at the side, she heard a rain shutter fall to the ground somewhere behind her. The teahouse was little more than a mountain hut to begin with, and there was nothing to prevent anyone from simply lifting out any or all of the loosely fitted shutters.

Osugi and Uncle Gon stumbled in through the opening.

"I can't see a thing," complained the old woman in what she thought was a whisper.

"Wait a minute," Gon replied, heading toward the hearth room, where he stirred up the embers and threw on some wood to get a bit of light.

"She's not in here, Granny!"

"She must be! She can't have gotten away!" Almost immediately, Osugi noticed that the door in the back room was ajar.

"Look, out there!" she shouted.

Otsū, who was standing just outside, threw the dipperful of water through the narrow opening into the old woman's face and sped downhill like a bird in the wind, sleeves and skirt trailing behind her.

Osugi ran outside and spat out an imprecation.

"Gon, Gon. Do something, do something!"

"Did she get away?"

"Of course she did! We certainly gave her enough warning, making all that noise. You would have to drop the shutter!" The old woman's face contorted with rage. "Can't you do something?"

Uncle Gon directed his attention to the deerlike form flying in the distance. He raised his arm and pointed. "That's her, right? Don't worry, she doesn't have much of a head start. She's sick and anyway she only has the legs of a girl. I'll catch up with her in no time." He tucked his chin in and broke into a run. Osugi followed close behind.

"Uncle Gon," she cried, "you can use your sword on her, but don't cut off her head until after I've had a chance to give her a piece of my mind."

Uncle Gon suddenly let out a scream of dismay and fell to his hands and knees.

"What's the matter?" cried Osugi, coming up behind him.

"Look down." Osugi did. Directly in front of them was a steep drop into a bamboo-covered ravine.

"She dived into that?"

"Yes. I don't think it's very deep, but it's too dark to tell. I'll have to go back to the teahouse and get a torch."

As he knelt staring into the ravine, Osugi cried, "What are you waiting for, you dolt?" and gave him a violent shove. There was the sound of feet trying to gain a footing, scrambling desperately before coming to a stop at the bottom of the ravine.

"You old witch!" shouted Uncle Gon angrily. "Now just get on down here yourself! See how you like it!"

Takezō, arms folded, sat atop a large boulder and stared across the valley at the Hinagura stockade. Under one of those roofs, he reflected, his sister was imprisoned. But he'd sat there from dawn to dusk the previous day and all day today, unable to devise a plan to get her out. He intended to sit until he did.

His thinking had progressed to the point where he was confident he could outmaneuver the fifty or a hundred soldiers guarding the stockade, but he continued to ponder the lay of the land. He had to get not only in but out. It was not encouraging: behind the stockade was a deep gorge, and at the front the road into the stockade was well protected by a double gate. To make matters worse, the two of them would be forced to flee across a flat plateau, which offered not a single tree to hide behind; on a cloudless day such as this, a better target would be hard to find.

The situation thus called for a night assault, but he'd observed that the gates were closed and locked before sunset. Any attempt to jimmy them open would doubtless set off a cacophonous alarm of wooden clappers. There seemed no foolproof way to approach the fortress.

"There's no way," Takezō thought sadly. "Even if I just took a long shot, risked my life and hers, it wouldn't work." He felt humiliated and helpless. "How," he asked himself, "did I get to be such a coward? A week ago I wouldn't have even thought about the chances of getting out alive."

For another half day his arms remained folded over his breast as if locked. He feared something he couldn't define and hesitated getting any closer to the stockade. Time and time again he upbraided himself. "I've lost my nerve. I never used to be this way. Maybe staring death in the face makes cowards out of everyone."

He shook his head. No, it wasn't that, not cowardice.

He had simply learned his lesson, the one Takuan had taken so much trouble to teach, and could now see things more clearly. He felt a new calm, a sense of peace. It seemed to flow in his breast like a gentle river. Being brave was very different from being ferocious; he saw that now. He didn't feel like an animal, he felt like a man, a courageous man who's outgrown his adolescent recklessness. The life that had been given to him was something to be treasured and cherished, polished and perfected.

He stared at the lovely clear sky, whose color alone seemed a miracle. Still, he could not leave his sister stranded, even if it meant violating, one last time, the precious self-knowledge he'd so recently and painfully acquired.

A plan began to take shape. "After nightfall, I'll cross the valley and climb the cliff on the other side. The natural barrier may be a blessing in disguise; there's no gate at the back, and it doesn't seem heavily guarded."

He had hardly arrived at this decision when an arrow whizzed toward him and thudded into the ground inches from his toes. Across the valley, he saw a crowd of people milling about just inside the stockade. Obviously they'd spotted him. Almost immediately they dispersed. He surmised it had been a test shot, to see how he'd react, and deliberately remained motionless upon his perch.

Before long, the light of the evening sun began to fade behind the peaks of the western mountains. Just before darkness dropped, he arose and picked up a rock. He had spotted his dinner flying in the air over his head. He downed the bird on the first try, tore it apart and sank his teeth into the warm flesh.

While he ate, twenty-odd soldiers moved noisily into position and surrounded him. Once in place, they let out a battle cry, one man shouting, "It's Takezō! Takezō from Miyamoto!"

"He's dangerous! Don't underestimate him!" someone else warned.

Looking up from his feast of raw fowl, Takezō trained a murderous eye on his would-be captors. It was the same look animals flash when disturbed in the midst of a meal.

"Y-a-a-h-h!" he yelled, seizing a huge rock and hurling it at the perimeter of this human wall. The rock turned red with blood, and in no time he was over it and away, running straight toward the stockade gate.

The men were agape.

"What's he doing?"

"Where's the fool going?"

"He's out of his mind!"

He flew like a crazed dragonfly, with the war-whooping soldiers in full chase. By the time they reached the outer gate, however, he'd already leapt over it. But now he was between the gates, in what was in fact a cage. Takezō's eyes took in none of this. He could see neither the pursuing soldiers nor the fence, nor the guards inside the second gate. He wasn't even conscious of knocking out, with a single blow, the sentinel who tried to jump him. With almost superhuman strength, he wrenched at a post of the inner gate, shaking it furiously till he was able to pull it out of the ground. Then he turned on his pursuers. He didn't know their number; all he knew was that something big and black was attacking him. Taking aim as best he could, he struck at the amorphous mass with the gatepost. A good number of lances and swords broke, flew into the air and fell useless to the ground.

"Ogin!" cried Takezō, running toward the rear of the stockade. "Ogin, it's me—Takezō!"

He glared at the buildings with fiery eyes, calling out repeatedly to his sister. "Has it all been a trick?" he wondered in panic. One by one he began battering down doors with the gatepost. The guards' chickens, squawking for dear life, flew in every direction.

"Ogin!"

When he failed to locate her, his hoarse cries became nearly unintelligible.

In the shadows of one of the small, dirty cells he saw a man trying to sneak away.

"Halt!" he shouted, throwing the bloodstained gatepost at the weasel-like creature's feet. When Takezō leaped at him, he began to cry shamelessly. Takezō slapped him sharply on the cheek. "Where's my sister?" he roared. "What have they done to her? Tell me where she is or I'll beat you to death!"

"She . . . she's not here. Day before yesterday they took her away. Orders from the castle."

"Where, you stupid bastard, where?"

"Himeji."

"Himeji?"

"Y-y-yes."

"If you're lying, I'll . . ." Takezō grabbed the sniveling mass by its hair.

"It's true—true. I swear!"

"It better be, or I'll come back just for you!"

The soldiers were closing in again, and Takezō lifted the man and hurled him at them. Then he disappeared into the shadows of the dingy cells. Half a dozen arrows flew by him, one sticking like a giant sewing needle in the skirt of his kimono. Takezō bit his thumbnail and watched the arrows speed by, then suddenly dashed for the fence and was over it in a flash.

Behind him there was a loud explosion. The echo of the gunshot roared across the valley.

Takezō sped down the gorge, and as he ran, fragments of Takuan's teachings were racing through his head: "Learn to fear that which is fearsome. . . . Brute strength is child's play, the mindless strength of beasts. . . . Have the strength of the true warrior . . . real courage. . . . Life is precious."

The Birth of Musashi

Takezō waited on the outskirts of the castle town of Himeji, sometimes keeping out of sight under Hanada Bridge but more often standing on the bridge unobtrusively surveying the passersby. When not in the immediate vicinity of the bridge, he would make short excursions around town, careful to keep his hat low and his face concealed, like a beggar's, behind a piece of straw matting.

It baffled him that Otsū had not yet appeared; only a week had gone by since she swore to wait there—not a hundred but a thousand days. Once Takezō had made a promise, he was loath to break it. But with every passing moment he grew more and more tempted to be on the move, though his promise to Otsū was not the only reason he made his way to Himeji. He also had to find out where they were keeping Ogin.

He was near the center of town one day when he heard a voice shouting his name. Footsteps came running after him. He looked up sharply, to see Takuan approaching, calling, "Takezō! Wait!"

Takezō was startled, and as usual in the presence of this monk, felt slightly humiliated. He had thought his disguise was foolproof and had been sure that no one, not even Takuan, would recognize him.

The monk grabbed him by the wrist. "Come with me," he commanded. The urgency in his voice was impossible to ignore. "And don't make any trouble. I've spent a lot of time looking for you."

Takezō followed meekly. He had no idea where they were going, but he once again found himself powerless to resist this particular man. He wondered why. He was free now, and for all he knew they were headed straight back to the dreaded tree in Miyamoto. Or perhaps into a castle dungeon. He had suspected they had his sister locked up somewhere in the castle's confines, but he hadn't a shred of evidence to back this up. He hoped he was right: if he, too, was taken there, at least they could die together. If they had to die, he could think of no one else he loved enough to share the final moments of precious life with.

Himeji Castle loomed before his eyes. He could see now why it was called the "White Crane Castle": the stately edifice stood upon huge stone ramparts, like a great and proud bird descended from the heavens. Takuan preceded him across the wide arcing bridge spanning the outer moat. A row of guards stood at attention before the riveted iron gate. The sunlight glancing off their drawn lances made Takezō, for a split second, hesitant to pass. Takuan, without even turning, sensed this and with a slightly impatient gesture urged him to keep moving. Passing under the gate turret, they approached the second gate, where the soldiers looked even more tense and alert, ready to fight at a moment's notice. This was the castle of a daimyō. It would take its inhabitants a while to relax and accept the fact that the country was successfully unified. Like many other castles of the time, it was far from accustomed to the luxury of peace.

Takuan summoned the captain of the guard. "I've brought him," he announced. Handing Takezō over, the monk advised the man to take good care of him as previously instructed, but added, "Be careful. He's a lion cub with fangs. He's far from tamed. If you tease him, he bites."

Takuan went through the second gate to the central compound, where the daimyō's mansion was located. Apparently he knew the way well; he needed neither a guide nor directions. He barely raised his head as he walked and not a soul interrupted his progress.

Heeding Takuan's instructions, the captain didn't lay a finger on his charge. He simply asked Takezō to follow him. Takezō silently obeyed. They soon arrived at a bathhouse, and the captain instructed him to go in and get cleaned up. At this point Takezō's spine stiffened, for he remembered all too well his last bath, at Osugi's house, and the trap from which he had narrowly escaped. *93*

He folded his arms and tried to think, stalling for time and inspecting the surroundings. It was all so peaceful—an island of tranquillity where a daimyō could, when not plotting strategies, enjoy the luxuries of life. Soon a servant bearing a black cotton kimono and *hakama* arrived, bowing and saying politely, "I'll lay these here. You can put them on when you come out."

Takezō nearly wept. The outfit included not only a folding fan and some tissue paper, but a pair of long and short samurai swords. Everything was simple and inexpensive, but nothing was lacking. He was being treated like a human being again and wanted to lift the clean cotton to his face, rub it to his cheek and inhale its freshness. He turned and entered the bathhouse.

Ikeda Terumasa, lord of the castle, leaned on an armrest and gazed out into the garden. He was a short man, with a cleanly shaven head and dark pockmarks lining his face. Although not dressed in formal attire, his countenance was stern and dignified.

"Is that him?" he asked Takuan, pointing his folding fan.

"Yes, that's him," answered the monk with a deferential bow.

"He has a good face. You did well to save him."

"He owes his life to you, your lordship. Not me."

"That's not so, Takuan, and you know it. If I just had a handful of men like you under my command, no doubt a lot of useful people would be saved, and the world would be the better for it." The daimyō sighed. "My trouble is that all my men think their sole duty is to tie people up or behead them."

An hour later, Takezō was seated in the garden beyond the veranda, his head bowed and his hands resting flat on his knees in an attitude of respectful attentiveness.

"Your name is Shimmen Takezō, isn't it?" Lord Ikeda asked.

Takezō glanced up quickly to see the face of the famous man, then respectfully cast his eyes downward again.

"Yes, sir," he answered clearly.

"The House of Shimmen is a branch of the Akamatsu family, and Akamatsu Masanori, as you well know, was once lord of this castle."

Takezō's throat went dry. He was, for once, at a loss for words. Having always thought of himself as the black sheep of the Shimmen family, with no particular feelings of respect or awe for the daimyō, he was nonetheless filled with shame at having brought such complete dishonor on his ancestors and his family name. His face burned.

"What you have done is inexcusable," continued Terumasa in a sterner tone.

"Yes, sir."

"And I am going to have to punish you for it." Turning to Takuan, he asked, "Is it true that my retainer, Aoki Tanzaemon, without my leave, promised you that if you captured this man, you could decide and mete out his punishment?"

"I think you can best find that out by asking Tanzaemon directly."

"I've already questioned him."

"Then did you think I would lie to you?"

94

"Of course not. Tanzaemon has confessed, but I wanted your confirmation. Since he is my direct vassal, his oath to you constitutes one from me. Therefore, even though I am lord of this fief, I have lost my right to penalize Takezō as I see fit. Of course, I will not permit him to go unpunished, but it is up to you what form the punishment is to take."

"Good. That is exactly what I had in mind."

"Then I assume you have given it some thought. Well, what shall we do with him?"

"I think it would be best to place the prisoner in—what shall we say?—'straitened circumstances' for a while."

"And how do you propose to do that?"

"I believe you have somewhere in this castle a closed room, one long rumored to be haunted?"

"Yes, I do. The servants refused to enter it, and my retainers avoided it consistently, so it went unused. I now leave it as it is, since there is no reason to open it again."

"But don't you think it's beneath the dignity of one of the strongest warriors in the Tokugawa realm, you, Ikeda Terumasa, to have a room in your castle where a light never shines?"

"I never thought of it that way."

"Well, people think of things like that. It's a reflection on your authority and prestige. I say we should put a light there."

"Hmm."

"If you'll let me make use of that chamber, I'll keep Takezō there until I'm ready to pardon him. He's had enough of living in total darkness. You hear that, don't you, Takezō?"

There was not a peep from Takezō, but Terumasa began laughing and said, "Fine!"

It was obvious from their excellent rapport that Takuan had been telling Aoki Tanzaemon the truth that night at the temple. He and Terumasa, both followers of Zen, seemed to be on friendly, almost brotherly, terms.

"After you've taken him to his new quarters, why don't you join me in the teahouse?" Terumasa asked the monk as he rose to leave.

"Oh, are you planning to demonstrate once again how inept you are at the tea ceremony?"

"That's not even fair, Takuan. These days I've really started to get the knack of it. Come along later and I'll prove to you I'm no longer simply an uncouth soldier. I'll be waiting." With that, Terumasa retired to the inner part of the mansion. Despite his short stature—he was barely five feet tall—his presence seemed to fill the many-storied castle.

It was always pitch dark high in the donjon, where the haunted room was located. There was no calendar here: no spring, no fall, no sounds of everyday life. There was only one small lamp, lighting a pale and sallow-cheeked Takezō.

The topography section of Sun-tzu's *Art of War* lay open on the low table before him.

> Sun-tzu said: "Among topographical features,
>> There are those that are passable.
>> There are those that suspend.
>> There are those that confine.
>> There are those that are steep.
>> There are those that are distant."

Whenever he came to a passage that particularly appealed to him, like this one, he would read it aloud over and over, like a chant.

> He who knows the art of the warrior is not confused in his movements. He acts and is not confined.
> Therefore Sun-tzu said, "He who knows himself and knows his enemy wins without danger. He who knows the heavens and the earth wins out over all."

When his eyes blurred from fatigue, he rinsed them with cool water from a small bowl he kept beside him. If the oil ran low and the lamp wick sputtered, he simply put it out. Around the table was a mountain of books, some in Japanese, some in Chinese. Books on Zen, volumes on the history of Japan. Takezō was virtually buried in these scholarly tomes. They had all been borrowed from Lord Ikeda's collection.

When Takuan had sentenced him to confinement, he had said, "You may read as much as you want. A famous priest of ancient times once said, 'I become immersed in the sacred scriptures and read thousands of volumes. When I come away, I find that my heart sees more than before.'

"Think of this room as your mother's womb and prepare to be born anew. If you look at it only with your eyes, you will see nothing more than an unlit, closed cell. But look again, more closely. Look with your mind and think. This room can be the wellspring of enlightenment, the same fountain of knowledge found and enriched by sages in the past. It is up to you to decide whether this is to be a chamber of darkness or one of light."

Takezō had long since stopped counting the days. When it was cold, it was winter; when hot, summer. He knew little more than that. The air remained the same, dank and musty, and the seasons had no bearing on his life. He was almost positive, however, that the next time the swallows came to nest in the donjon's boarded-over gun slots, it would be the spring of his third year in the womb.

"I'll be twenty-one years old," he said to himself. Seized by remorse, he groaned as if in mourning. "And what have I done in those twenty-one years?" Sometimes the memory of his early years pressed in on him unrelentingly, engulfing him in grief. He would wail and moan, flail and kick, and sometimes sob like a baby. Whole days were swallowed up in agony, which, once it subsided, left him spent and lifeless, hair disheveled and heart torn apart.

Finally, one day, he heard the swallows returning to the donjon eaves. Once again, spring had flown from across the seas.

Not long after its arrival, a voice, now sounding strange, almost painful to the ears, inquired, "Takezō, are you well?"

The familiar head of Takuan appeared at the top of the stairs. Startled and much too deeply moved to utter a sound, Takezō grabbed hold of the monk's kimono sleeve and pulled him into the room. The servants who brought his food had never once spoken a word. He was overjoyed to hear another human voice, especially this one.

"I've just returned from a journey," said Takuan. "You're in your third year here now, and I've decided that after gestating this long, you must be pretty well formed."

"I am grateful for your goodness, Takuan. I understand now what you've done. How can I ever thank you?"

"Thank me?" Takuan said incredulously. Then he laughed. "Even though you've had no one to converse with but yourself, you've actually learned to speak like a human being! Good! Today you will leave this place. And as you do so, hug your hard-earned enlightenment to your bosom. You're going to need it when you go forth into the world to join your fellow men."

Takuan took Takezō just as he was to see Lord Ikeda. Although he had been relegated to the garden in the previous audience, a place was now made for him on the veranda. After the salutations and some perfunctory small talk, Terumasa lost no time in asking Takezō to serve as his vassal.

Takezō declined. He was greatly honored, he explained, but he did not feel the time was yet right to go into a daimyō's service. "And if I did so in this castle," he said, "ghosts would probably start appearing in the closed room every night, just as everyone says they do."

"Why do you say that? Did they come to keep you company?"

"If you take a lamp and inspect the room closely, you'll see black spots spattering the doors and beams. It looks like lacquer, but it's not. It's human blood, most likely blood spilled by the Akamatsu, my forebears, when they went down to defeat in this castle."

"Hmm. You may very well be right."

"Seeing those stains infuriated me. My blood boiled to think that my ancestors, who once ruled over this whole region, ended up being annihilated, their souls just blown about in the autumn winds. They died violently, but it was a powerful clan and they can be roused.

"That same blood flows in my veins," he went on, an intense look in his eyes. "Unworthy though I am, I am a member of the same clan, and if I stay in this castle, the ghosts may rouse themselves and try to reach me. In a sense, they already have, by making it clear to me in that room just who I am. But they could cause chaos, perhaps rebel and even set off another bloodbath. We are not in an era of peace. I owe it to the people of this whole region not to tempt the vengeance of my ancestors."

Terumasa nodded. "I see what you mean. It's better if you leave this castle, but where will you go? Do you plan to return to Miyamoto? Live out your life there?"

Takezō smiled silently. "I want to wander about on my own for a while."

"I see," the lord replied, turning to Takuan. "See that he receives money and suitable clothing," he commanded.

Takuan bowed. "Let me thank you for your kindness to the boy."

"Takuan!" Ikeda laughed. "This is the first time you've ever thanked me twice for anything!"

"I suppose that's true." Takuan grinned. "It won't happen again."

"It's all right for him to roam about while he's still young," said Terumasa. "But now that he's going out on his own—reborn, as you put it—he should have a new name. Let it be Miyamoto, so that he never forgets his birthplace. From now on, Takezō, call yourself Miyamoto."

Takezō's hands went automatically to the floor. Palms down, he bowed deep and long. "Yes, sir, I will do that."

"You should change your first name too," Takuan interjected. "Why not read the Chinese characters of your name as 'Musashi' instead of 'Takezō'? You can keep writing your name the same as before. It's only fitting that everything should begin anew on this day of your rebirth."

Terumasa, who was by this time in a very good mood, nodded his approval enthusiastically. "Miyamoto Musashi! It's a good name, a very good name. We should drink to it."

They moved into another room, sake was served, and Takezō and Takuan kept his lordship company far into the night. They were joined by several of Terumasa's retainers, and eventually Takuan got to his feet and performed an ancient dance. He was expert, his vivid movements creating an imaginary world of delight. Takezō, now Musashi, watched with admiration, respect and enjoyment as the drinking went on and on.

The following day they both left the castle. Musashi was taking his first steps into a new life, a life of discipline and training in the martial arts. During his three-year incarceration, he had resolved to master the Art of War.

Takuan had his own plans. He had decided to travel about the countryside, and the time had come, he said, to part again.

When they reached the town outside the castle walls, Musashi made as if to take his leave, but the monk grabbed his sleeve and said, "Isn't there someone you'd like to see?"

"Who?"

"Ogin?"

"Is she still alive?" he asked in bewilderment. Even in his sleep, he'd never forgotten the gentle sister who'd been a mother to him so long.

Takuan told him that when he'd attacked the stockade at Hinagura three years earlier, Ogin had indeed already been taken away. Although no charges were pressed against her, she had been reluctant to return home and so went instead to stay with a relative in a village in the Sayo district. She was now living comfortably there.

98   "Wouldn't you like to see her?" asked Takuan. "She's very eager to see you.

I told her three years ago that she should consider you dead, since in one sense, you were. I also told her, however, that after three years I'd bring her a new brother, different from the old Takezō."

Musashi pressed his palms together and raised them in front of his head, as he would have done in prayer before a statue of the Buddha. "Not only have you taken care of me," he said with deep emotion, "but you've seen to Ogin's well-being too. Takuan, you are truly a compassionate man. I don't think I'll ever be able to thank you for what you've done."

"One way to thank me would be to let me take you to your sister."

"No . . . No, I don't think I should go. Hearing about her from you has been as good as meeting her."

"Surely you want to see her yourself, if only for a few minutes."

"No, I don't think so. I did die, Takuan, and I do feel reborn. I don't think that now is the time to return to the past. What I have to do is take a resolute step forward, into the future. I've barely found the way along which I'll have to travel. When I've made some progress toward the knowledge and self-perfection I'm seeking, perhaps I'll take the time to relax and look back. Not now."

"I see."

"I find it hard to put into words, but I hope you'll understand anyway."

"I do. I'm glad to see you're as serious about your goal as you are. Keep following your own judgment."

"I'll say good-bye now, but someday, if I don't get myself killed along the way, we'll meet again."

"Yes, yes. If we have a chance to meet, let's by all means do so." Takuan turned, took a step, and then halted. "Oh, yes. I suppose I should warn you that Osugi and Uncle Gon left Miyamoto in search of you and Otsū three years ago. They resolved never to return until they've taken their revenge, and old as they are, they're still trying to track you down. They may cause you some inconvenience, but I don't think they can make any real trouble. Don't take them too seriously.

"Oh, yes, and then there's Aoki Tanzaemon. I don't suppose you ever knew his name, but he was in charge of the search for you. Perhaps it had nothing to do with anything you or I said or did, but that splendid samurai managed to disgrace himself, with the result that he's been dismissed permanently from Lord Ikeda's service. He's no doubt wandering about too." Takuan grew grave. "Musashi, your path won't be an easy one. Be careful as you make your way along it."

"I'll do my best." Musashi smiled.

"Well, I guess that's everything. I'll be on my way." Takuan turned and walked westward. He didn't look back.

"Keep well," Musashi called after him. He stood at the crossroads watching the monk's form recede until it was out of sight. Then, once again alone, he started to walk toward the east.

"Now there's only this sword," he thought. "The only thing in the world I have to rely on." He rested his hand on the weapon's handle and vowed to 99 himself, "I will live by its rule. I will regard it as my soul, and by learning to master it, strive to improve myself, to become a better and wiser human being. Takuan follows the Way of Zen, I will follow the Way of the Sword. I must make of myself an even better man than he is."

After all, he reflected, he was still young. It was not too late.

His footsteps were steady and strong, his eyes full of youth and hope. From time to time he raised the brim of his basket hat, and stared down the long road into the future, the unknown path all humans must tread.

He hadn't gone far—in fact, he was just on the outskirts of Himeji—when a woman came running toward him from the other side of Hanada Bridge. He squinted into the sunlight.

"It's you!" Otsū cried, clutching his sleeve.

Musashi gasped in surprise.

Otsū's tone was reproachful. "Takezō, surely you haven't forgotten? Don't you remember the name of this bridge? Did it slip your mind that I promised to wait here for you, no matter how long it took?"

"You've been waiting here for the last three years?" He was astounded.

"Yes. Osugi and Uncle Gon caught up with me right after I left you. I was sick and had to take a rest. And I almost got myself killed. But I got away. I've been waiting here since about twenty days after we said good-bye at Nakayama Pass."

Pointing to a basket-weaving shop at the end of the bridge, a typical little highroad stall selling souvenirs to travelers, she continued: "I told the people there my story, and they were kind enough to take me on as a sort of helper. So I could stay and wait for you. Today is the nine hundred and seventieth day, and I've kept my promise faithfully." She peered into his face, trying to fathom his thoughts. "You will take me with you, won't you?"

The truth, of course, was that Musashi had no intention of taking her or anyone else with him. At this very moment, he was hurrying away to avoid thinking about his sister, whom he wanted to see so badly and felt so strongly drawn toward.

The questions raced through his agitated mind: "What can I do? How can I embark on my quest for truth and knowledge with a woman, with anyone, interfering all the time? And this particular girl is, after all, still betrothed to Matahachi." Musashi couldn't keep his thoughts from showing on his face.

"Take you with me? Take you where?" he demanded bluntly.

"Wherever you go."

"I'm setting out on a long, hard journey, not a sightseeing trip!"

"I won't get in your way. And I'm prepared to endure some hardships."

"Some? Only some?"

"As many as I have to."

"That's not the point. Otsū, how can a man master the Way of the Samurai with a woman tagging along? Wouldn't that be funny. People'd say, 'Look at Musashi, he needs a wet nurse to take care of him.'" She pulled harder at his kimono, clinging like a child. "Let go of my sleeve," he ordered.

"No, I won't! You lied to me, didn't you?"

"When did I lie to you?"

"At the pass. You promised to take me with you."

"That was ages ago. I wasn't really thinking then either, and I didn't have time to explain. What's more, it wasn't my idea, it was yours. I was in a hurry to get moving, and you wouldn't let me go until I promised. I went along with what you said because I had no choice."

"No, no, no! You can't mean what you're saying, you can't," she cried, pinning him against the bridge railing.

"Let go of me! People are watching."

"Let them! When you were tied up in the tree, I asked you if you wanted my help. You were so happy you told me twice to cut the rope. You don't deny that, do you?"

She was trying to be logical in her argument, but her tears betrayed her. First abandoned as an infant, then jilted by her betrothed and now this. Musashi, knowing how alone she was in the world and caring for her deeply, was tongue-tied, though outwardly more composed.

"Let go!" he said with finality. "It's broad daylight and people are staring at us. Do you want us to be a sideshow for these busybodies?"

She released his sleeve and fell sobbing against the railing, her shiny hair falling over her face.

"I'm sorry," she mumbled. "I shouldn't have said all that. Please forget it. You don't owe me anything."

Leaning over and pushing her hair from her face with both hands, he looked into her eyes. "Otsū," he said tenderly. "During all that time you were waiting, until this very day, I've been shut up in the castle donjon. For three years I haven't even seen the sun."

"Yes, I heard."

"You knew?"

"Takuan told me."

"Takuan? He told you everything?"

"I guess so. I fainted at the bottom of a ravine near the Mikazuki Teahouse. I was running away from Osugi and Uncle Gon. Takuan rescued me. He also helped me make arrangements to work here, at the souvenir shop. That was three years ago. And he's stopped in several times. Only yesterday, he came and had some tea. I wasn't sure what he meant, but he said, 'It's got to do with a man and a woman, so who can say how it'll turn out?'"

Musashi dropped his hands and looked down the road leading west. He wondered if he'd ever again meet the man who'd saved his life. And again he was struck by Takuan's concern for his fellow man, which seemed all-encompassing and completely devoid of selfishness. Musashi realized how narrow-minded he himself had been, how petty, to suppose that the monk felt a special compassion for him alone; his generosity encompassed Ogin, Otsū, anyone in need whom he thought he could help.

"It has to do with a man and a woman. . . ." Takuan's words to Otsū sat heavily on Musashi's mind. It was a burden for which he was ill prepared, since in all the mountains of books he'd pored over those three years, there wasn't one word about the situation he was in now. Even Takuan had shrunk from becoming involved in this matter between him and Otsū. Had Takuan meant that relationships between men and women had to be worked out alone by the people involved? Did he mean that no rules applied, as they did in the Art of War? That there was no foolproof strategy, no way to win? Or was this meant as a test for Musashi, a problem only Musashi would be able to solve for himself?

Lost in thought, he stared down at the water flowing under the bridge.

Otsū gazed up into his face, now distant and calm. "I can come, can't I?" she pleaded. "The shopkeeper's promised to let me quit whenever I wish. I'll just go and explain everything and then pack my things. I'll be back in a minute."

Musashi covered her small white hand, which was resting on the railing, with his own. "Listen," he said plaintively. "I beg of you, just stop and think."

"What's there to think about?"

"I told you. I've just become a new man. I stayed in that musty hole for three years. I read books. I thought. I screamed and cried. Then suddenly the light dawned. I understood what it means to be human. I have a new name, Miyamoto Musashi. I want to dedicate myself to training and discipline. I want to spend every moment of every day working to improve myself. I know now how far I have to go. If you chose to bind your life to mine, you'd never be happy. There will be nothing but hardship, and it won't get easier as it goes along. It'll get more and more difficult."

"When you talk like that, I feel closer to you than ever. Now I'm convinced I was right. I've found the best man I could ever find, even if I searched for the rest of my life."

He saw he was just making things worse. "I'm sorry, I can't take you with me."

"Well, then, I'll just follow along. As long as I don't interfere with your training, what harm would it do? You won't even know I'm around."

Musashi could find no answer.

"I won't bother you. I promise."

He remained silent.

"It's all right then, isn't it? Just wait here; I'll be back in a second. And I'll be furious if you try to sneak away." Otsū ran off toward the basket-weaving shop.

Musashi thought of ignoring everything and running too, in the opposite direction. Though the will was there, his feet wouldn't move.

Otsū looked back and called, "Remember, don't try to sneak off!" She smiled, showing her dimples, and Musashi inadvertently nodded. Satisfied by this gesture, she disappeared into the shop.

If he was going to escape, this was the time. His heart told him so, but his body was still shackled by Otsū's pretty dimples and pleading eyes. How sweet she was! It was certain no one in the world save his sister loved him so much. And it wasn't as though he disliked her.

He looked at the sky, he looked into the water, desperately gripped the railing, troubled and confused. Soon tiny bits of wood began floating from the bridge into the flowing stream.

Otsū reappeared on the bridge in new straw sandals, light yellow leggings and a large traveling hat tied under the chin with a crimson ribbon. She'd never looked more beautiful.

But Musashi was nowhere to be seen.

With a cry of shock, she burst into tears. Then her eyes fell upon the spot on the railing from which the chips of wood had fallen. There, carved with the point of a dagger, was the clearly inscribed message. "Forgive me. Forgive me."

Book II WATER

The Yoshioka School

The life of today, which cannot know the morrow . . .

In the Japan of the early seventeenth century, an awareness of the fleeting nature of life was as common among the masses as it was among the elite. The famous general Oda Nobunaga, who laid the foundations for Toyotomi Hideyoshi's unification of Japan, summed up this view in a short poem:

> Man's fifty years
> Are but a phantom dream
> In his journey through
> The eternal transmigrations.

Defeated in a skirmish with one of his own generals, who attacked him in a sudden fit of revenge, Nobunaga committed suicide in Kyoto at the age of forty-eight.

By 1605, some two decades later, the incessant warring among the daimyō was essentially over, and Tokugawa Ieyasu had ruled as shōgun for two years. The lanterns on the streets of Kyoto and Osaka glowed brightly, as they had in the best days of the Ashikaga shogunate, and the prevailing mood was lighthearted and festive.

But few were certain the peace would last. More than a hundred years of civil strife had so colored people's view of life that they could only regard the present tranquillity as fragile and ephemeral. The capital was thriving, but the tension of not knowing how long this would last whetted the people's appetite for merrymaking.

Though still in control, Ieyasu had officially retired from the position of shōgun. While still strong enough to control the other daimyō and defend the family's claim to power, he had passed on his title to his third son, Hidetada. It was rumored that the new shōgun would visit Kyoto soon to pay his respects to the emperor, but it was common knowledge that his trip west meant more than a courtesy call. His greatest potential rival, Toyotomi Hideyori, was the son of Hideyoshi, Nobunaga's able successor. Hideyoshi had done his best to ensure that power remain with the Toyotomis until Hideyori was old enough to exercise it, but the victor at Sekigahara was Ieyasu.

Hideyori still resided at Osaka Castle, and although Ieyasu, rather than have him done away with, permitted him to enjoy a substantial annual income, he was aware that Osaka was a major threat as a possible rallying point of resistance. Many feudal lords knew this too, and hedging their bets, paid equal court to both Hideyori and the shōgun. It was often remarked that the former had enough castles and gold to hire every masterless samurai, or rōnin, in the country, if he wanted to.

Idle speculation on the country's political future formed the bulk of gossip in the Kyoto air.

"War's bound to break out sooner or later."

"It's just a matter of time."

"These street lanterns could be snuffed out tomorrow."

"Why worry about it? What happens happens."

"Let's enjoy ourselves while we can!"

The bustling nightlife and booming pleasure quarters were tangible evidence that much of the populace were doing just that.

Among those so inclined was a group of samurai now turning a corner into Shijō Avenue. Beside them ran a long wall of white plaster, leading to an impressive gate with an imposing roof. A wooden plaque, blackened with age, announced in barely legible writing: "Yoshioka Kempō of Kyoto. Military Instructor to the Ashikaga Shōguns."

The eight young samurai gave the impression of having practiced sword fighting all day without respite. Some bore wooden swords in addition to the two customary steel ones, and others were carrying lances. They looked tough, the kind of men who'd be the first to see bloodshed the moment a clash of arms erupted. Their faces were as hard as stone and their eyes threatening, as if always on the brink of exploding in a rage.

"Young Master, where are we headed tonight?" they clamored, surrounding their teacher.

"Anywhere but where we were last night," he replied gravely.

"Why? Those women were falling all over you! They barely looked at the rest of us."

"Maybe he's right," another man put in. "Why don't we try someplace new, where no one knows the Young Master or any of the rest of us." Shouting and carrying on among themselves, they seemed totally consumed by the question of where to go drinking and whoring.

They moved on to a well-lit area along the banks of the Kamo River. For years the land had been vacant and weed-filled, a veritable symbol of wartime desolation, but with the coming of peace, its value had shot up. Scattered here and there were flimsy houses, red and pale yellow curtains hanging crookedly in their doorways, where prostitutes plied their trade. Girls from Tamba Province, white powder smeared carelessly on their faces, whistled to prospective customers; unfortunate women who had been purchased in droves plunked on their shamisens, a newly popular instrument, as they sang bawdy songs and laughed among themselves.

The Young Master's name was Yoshioka Seijūrō, and a tasteful dark brown kimono draped his tall frame. Not long after they'd entered the brothel district, he looked back and said to one of his group, "Tōji, buy me a basket hat."

"The kind that hides your face, I suppose?"

"Yes."

"You don't need one here, do you?" Gion Tōji replied.

"I wouldn't have asked for one if I didn't!" Seijūrō snapped impatiently. "I don't care to have people see the son of Yoshioka Kempō walking about in a place like this."

Tōji laughed. "But it just attracts attention. All the women around here know that if you hide your face under a hat, you must be from a good family and probably a rich one. Of course, there are other reasons why they won't leave you alone, but that's one of them."

Tōji was, as usual, both teasing and flattering his master. He turned and ordered one of the men to get the hat and stood waiting for him to thread his way through the lanterns and merrymakers. The errand accomplished, Seijūrō donned the hat and began to feel more relaxed.

"In that hat," commented Tōji, "you look more than ever like the fashionable man about town." Turning to the others, he continued his flattery indirectly. "See, the women are all leaning out their doors to get a good look at him."

Tōji's sycophancy aside, Seijūrō did cut a fine figure. With two highly polished scabbards hanging from his side, he exuded the dignity and class one would expect from the son of a well-to-do family. No straw hat could stop the women from calling out to him as he walked.

"Hey there, handsome! Why hide your face under that silly hat?"

"Come on, over here! I want to see what's under there."

"Come on, don't be shy. Give us a peek."

Seijūrō reacted to these teasing come-ons by trying to look even taller and more dignified. It had only been a short time since Tōji had first persuaded him to set foot in the district, and it still embarrassed him to be seen there. Born the eldest son of the famous swordsman Yoshioka Kempō, he had never lacked money, but he had remained until recently unacquainted with the seamier side of life. The attention he was getting made his pulse race. He still felt enough shame to hide, though as a rich man's spoiled son he'd always been something of a show-off. The flattery of his entourage, no less than the flirting of the women, bolstered his ego like sweet poison.

"Why, it's the master from Shijō Avenue!" one of the women exclaimed. "Why are you hiding your face? You're not fooling anybody."

"How does that woman know who I am?" Seijūrō growled at Tōji, pretending to be offended.

"That's easy," the woman said before Tōji could open his mouth. "Everybody knows that the people at the Yoshioka School like to wear that dark brown color. It is called 'Yoshioka dye,' you know, and it's very popular around here."

"That's true, but as you say, a lot of people wear it."

"Yes, but they don't have the three-circle crest on their kimonos."

Seijūrō looked down at his sleeve. "I must be more careful," he said as a hand from behind the lattice reached out and latched onto the garment.

"My, my," said Tōji. "He hid his face but not his crest. He must have wanted to be recognized. I don't think we can really avoid going in here now."

"Do whatever you want," said Seijūrō, looking uncomfortable, "but make her let go of my sleeve."

"Let go, woman," Tōji roared. "He says we're coming in!"

The students crowded in under the shop curtain. The room they entered was so tastelessly decorated with vulgar pictures and messily arranged flowers that it was difficult for Seijūrō to feel at ease. The others, however, took no notice of the shabbiness of their surroundings.

"Bring on the sake!" Tōji demanded, also ordering assorted tidbits.

After the food arrived, Ueda Ryōhei, who was Tōji's match with a sword, cried, "Bring on the women!" The order was given in exactly the same surly tone Tōji had used to order their food and drink.

"Hey, old Ueda says bring the women!" the others chorused, mimicking Ryōhei's voice.

"I don't like being called old," Ryōhei said, scowling. "It's true I've been at the school longer than any of you, but you won't find a gray hair on my head."

"You probably dye it."

"Whoever said that come forward and drink a cup as punishment!"

"Too much trouble. Throw it here!"

The sake cup sailed through the air.

"Here's the repayment!" And another cup flew through the air.

"Hey, somebody dance!"

Seijūrō called out, "You dance, Ryōhei! Dance, and show us how young you are!"

"I am prepared, sir. Watch!" Going to the corner of the veranda, he tied a maid's red apron around the back of his head, stuck a plum blossom in the knot and seized a broom.

"Why, look! He's going to do the Dance of the Hida Maiden! Let's hear the song too, Tōji!"

He invited them all to join in, and they began rapping rhythmically on the dishes with their chopsticks, while one man clanged the fire tongs against the edge of the brazier.

> Across the bamboo fence, the bamboo fence, the bamboo fence,
> I caught sight of a long-sleeved kimono,
> A long-sleeved kimono in the snow....

Drowned in applause after the first verse, Tōji bowed out, and the women took up where he had left off, accompanying themselves on shamisen.

> The girl I saw yesterday
> Is not here today.
> The girl I see today,
> She'll not be here tomorrow.
> I know not what the morrow will bring,
> I want to love her today.

In one corner, a student held up a huge bowl of sake to a comrade and said, "Say, why don't you down this in one gulp?"

"No, thanks."

"No, thanks? You call yourself a samurai, and you can't even put this away?"

"Sure I can. But if I do, you have to too!"

"Fair enough!"

The contest began, with them gulping like horses at the trough and dribbling sake out of the corners of their mouths. An hour or so later a couple of them started vomiting, while others were reduced to immobility and blankly staring bloodshot eyes.

One, whose customary bluster became more strident the more he drank, declaimed, "Does anyone in this country besides the Young Master truly understand the techniques of the Kyōhachi Style? If there is—*hic*—I want to meet him. . . . Oops!"

Another stalwart, seated near Seijūrō, laughed and stammered through his hiccups. "He's piling on the flattery because the Young Master's here. There are other schools of martial arts besides the ones here in Kyoto, and the Yoshioka School's not necessarily the greatest anymore. In Kyoto alone, there's the school of Toda Seigen in Kurotani, and there's Ogasawara Genshinsai in Kitano. And let's not forget Itō Ittōsai in Shirakawa, even though he doesn't take students."

"And what's so wonderful about them?"

"I mean, we shouldn't get the idea we're the only swordsmen in the world."

"You simple-minded bastard!" shouted a man whose pride had been offended. "Come forward!"

"Like this?" retorted the critic, standing up.

"You're a member of this school, and you're belittling Yoshioka Kempō's style?"

"I'm not belittling it! It's just that things aren't what they used to be in the old days when the master taught the shōguns and was considered the greatest of swordsmen. There are far more people practicing the Way of the Sword these days, not only in Kyoto but in Edo, Hitachi, Echizen, the home provinces, the western provinces, Kyushu—all over the country. Just because Yoshioka Kempō was famous doesn't mean the Young Master and all of us are the greatest swordsmen alive. It's just not true, so why kid ourselves?"

"Coward! You pretend to be a samurai, but you're afraid of other schools!"

"Who's afraid of them? I just think we should guard ourselves against becoming complacent."

"And who are you to be giving warnings?" With this the offended student punched the other in the chest, knocking him down.

"You want to fight?" growled the fallen man.

"Yeah, I'm ready."

The seniors, Gion Tōji and Ueda Ryōhei, intervened. "Stop it, you two!" Jumping to their feet, they pulled the two men apart and tried to smooth their ruffled feathers.

"Quiet down now!"

"We all understand how you feel."

111

A few more cups of sake were poured into the combatants, and presently things were back to normal. The firebrand was once again eulogizing himself and the others, while the critic, his arm draped around Ryōhei, pleaded his case tearfully. "I only spoke up for the sake of the school," he sobbed. "If people keep spouting flattery, Yoshioka Kempō's reputation will eventually be ruined. Ruined, I tell you!"

Seijūrō alone remained relatively sober. Noticing this, Tōji said, "You're not enjoying the party, are you?"

"Unh. Do you think they really enjoy it? I wonder."

"Sure; this is their idea of a good time."

"I don't see how, when they carry on like that."

"Look, why don't we go someplace quieter? I've had enough of this too."

Seijūrō, looking much relieved, quickly assented. "I'd like to go to the place we were at last night."

"You mean the Yomogi?"

"Yes."

"That's much nicer. I thought all along you wanted to go there, but it would've been a waste of money to take along this bunch of oafs. That's why I steered them here—it's cheap."

"Let's sneak out, then. Ryōhei can take care of the rest."

"Just pretend you're going to the toilet. I'll come along in a few minutes."

Seijūrō skillfully disappeared. No one noticed.

Outside a house not far away, a woman stood on tiptoe, trying to hang a lantern back on its nail. The wind had blown out the candle, and she had taken it down to relight it. Her back was stretched out under the eaves, and her recently washed hair fell loosely around her face. Strands of hair and the shadows from the lantern made lightly shifting patterns on her outstretched arms. A hint of plum blossoms floated on the evening breeze.

"Okō! Shall I hang it for you?"

"Oh, it's the Young Master," she said with surprise.

"Wait a minute." When the man came forward, she saw that it was not Seijūrō but Tōji.

"Will that do?" he asked.

"Yes, that's fine. Thank you."

But Tōji squinted at the lantern, decided it was crooked, and rehung it. It was amazing to Okō how some men, who would flatly refuse to lend a hand in their own homes, could be so helpful and considerate when visiting a place like hers. Often they would open or close the windows for themselves, get out their own cushions, and do a dozen other little chores they'd never dream of doing under their own roofs.

Tōji, pretending not to have heard, showed his master indoors.

Seijūrō, as soon as he was seated, said, "It's awfully quiet."

"I'll open the door to the veranda," said Tōji.

Below the narrow veranda rippled the waters of the Takase River. To the south, beyond the small bridge at Sanjō Avenue, lay the broad compound of the Zuisenin, the dark expanse of Teramachi—the "Town of Temples"—and a field of miscanthus. This was near Kayahara, where Toyotomi Hideyoshi's troops had slain the wife, concubines and children of his nephew, the murderous regent Hidetsugu, an event still fresh in many people's memory.

Tōji was getting nervous. "It's still too quiet. Where are the women hiding? They don't seem to have any other customers tonight." He fidgeted a bit. "I wonder what's taking Okō so long. She hasn't even brought us our tea." When his impatience made him so jumpy he could no longer sit still, he got up to go see why the tea hadn't been served.

As he stepped out onto the veranda, he nearly collided with Akemi, who was carrying a gold-lacquered tray. The little bell in her obi tinkled as she exclaimed, "Be careful! You'll make me spill the tea!"

"Why are you so late with it? The Young Master's here; I thought you liked him."

"See, I've spilled some. It's your fault. Go fetch me a rag."

"Ha! Pretty sassy, aren't you? Where's Okō?"

"Putting on her makeup, of course."

"You mean she's not finished yet?"

"Well, we were busy during the daytime."

"Daytime? Who came during the daytime?"

"That's none of your business. Please let me by."

He stepped aside and Akemi entered the room and greeted the guest. "Good evening. It was good of you to come."

Seijūrō, feigning nonchalance, looked aside and said, "Oh, it's you, Akemi. Thanks for last night." He was embarrassed.

From the tray she took a jar that looked like an incense burner and placed on it a pipe with a ceramic mouthpiece and bowl.

"Would you like a smoke?" she asked politely.

"I thought tobacco was recently banned."

"It was, but everybody still smokes anyway."

"All right, I'll have some."

"I'll light it for you."

She took a pinch of tobacco from a pretty little mother-of-pearl box and stuffed it into the tiny bowl with her dainty fingers. Then she put the pipe to his mouth. Seijūrō, not being in the habit of smoking, handled it rather awkwardly.

"Hmm, bitter, isn't it?" he said. Akemi giggled. "Where did Tōji go?"

"He's probably in Mother's room."

"He seems fond of Okō. At least, it looks that way to me. I suspect he comes here without me sometimes. Does he?" Akemi laughed but did not answer. "What's funny about that? I think your mother rather likes him too."

"I really wouldn't know!"

"Oh, I'm sure of it! Absolutely sure! It's a cozy arrangement, isn't it? Two happy couples—your mother and Tōji, you and me."

Looking as innocent as he could, he put his hand on top of Akemi's, which was resting on her knee. Primly, she brushed it away, but this only made Seijūrō bolder. As she started to rise, he put his arm around her thin waist and drew her to him.

"You don't have to run away," he said. "I'm not going to hurt you."

113

"Let go of me!" she protested.

"All right, but only if you sit down again."

"The sake . . . I'll just go and get some."

"I don't want any."

"But if I don't bring it, Mother'll get angry."

"Your mother's in the other room, having a nice chat with Tōji."

He tried to rub his cheek against her lowered face, but she turned her head away and called frantically for help. "Mother! *Mother!*" He released her and she flew toward the back of the house.

Seijūrō was becoming frustrated. He was lonely but didn't really want to force himself on the girl. Not knowing what to do with himself, he grunted out loud, "I'm going home," and started tramping down the outer corridor, his face growing more crimson with each step.

"Young Master, where are you going? You're not leaving, are you?" Seemingly from out of nowhere, Okō appeared behind him and rushed down the hall. As she put her arm about him, he noticed that her hair was in place and her makeup was in order. She summoned Tōji to the rescue, and together they persuaded Seijūrō to go back and sit down. Okō brought sake and tried to cheer him up, then Tōji led Akemi back into the room. When the girl saw how crestfallen Seijūrō was, she flashed a smile at him.

"Akemi, pour the Young Master some sake."

"Yes, Mother," she said obediently.

"You see how she is, don't you?" said Okō. "Why does she always want to act like a child?"

"That's her charm—she's young," said Tōji, sliding his cushion up closer to the table.

"But she's already twenty-one."

"Twenty-one? I didn't think she was that old. She's so small she looks about sixteen or seventeen!"

Akemi, suddenly as full of life as a minnow, said, "Really? That makes me happy, because I'd like to be sixteen all my life. Something wonderful happened to me when I was sixteen."

"What?"

"Oh," she said, clasping her hands to her breast. "I can't tell anybody about it, but it happened. When I was sixteen. Do you know what province I was in then? That was the year of the Battle of Sekigahara."

With a menacing look, Okō said, "Chatterbox! Stop boring us with your talk. Go and get your shamisen."

Pouting slightly, Akemi stood up and went for her instrument. When she returned, she started playing and singing a song, more intent, it seemed, upon amusing herself than upon pleasing the guests.

> Tonight then,
> If it's to be cloudy,
> Let it be cloudy,
> Hiding the moon
> I can see only through my tears.

114

Breaking off, she said, "Do you understand, Tōji?"
"I'm not sure. Sing some more."

> Even in the darkest night
> I do not lose my way.
> But oh! How you fascinate me!

"She is twenty-one, after all," said Tōji.

Seijūrō, who had been sitting silently with his forehead resting on his hand, came to life and said, "Akemi, let's have a cup of sake together."

He handed her the cup and filled it from the sake warmer. She drank it down without flinching and briskly handed him back the cup to drink from.

Somewhat surprised, Seijūrō said, "You know how to drink, don't you."

Finishing off his draft, he offered her another, which she accepted and downed with alacrity. Apparently dissatisfied with the cup's size, she took out a larger one and for the next half hour matched him drink for drink.

Seijūrō marveled. There she was, looking like a sixteen-year-old girl, with lips that had never been kissed and an eye that shrank with shyness, and yet she was putting away her sake like a man. In that tiny body, where did it all go?

"You may as well give up now," Okō said to Seijūrō. "For some reason the child can drink all night without getting drunk. The best thing to do is to let her play the shamisen."

"But this is fun!" said Seijūrō, now thoroughly enjoying himself.

Sensing something strange in his voice, Tōji asked, "Are you all right? Sure you haven't had too much?"

"It doesn't matter. Say, Tōji, I may not go home tonight!"

"That's all right too," replied Tōji. "You can stay as many nights as you wish—can't he, Akemi?"

Tōji winked at Okō, then led her off to another room, where he began whispering rapidly. He told Okō that with the Young Master in such high spirits, he would certainly want to sleep with Akemi, and that there would be trouble if Akemi refused; but that, of course, a mother's feelings were the most important thing of all in cases like this—or in other words, how much?

"Well?" Tōji demanded abruptly.

Okō put her finger to her thickly powdered cheek and thought.

"Make up your mind!" urged Tōji. Drawing closer to her, he said, "It's not a bad match, you know. He's a famous teacher of the martial arts, and his family has lots of money. His father had more disciples than anybody else in the country. What's more, he's not married yet. Any way you look at it, it's an attractive offer."

"Well, I think so too, but—"

"But nothing. It's settled! We'll both spend the night."

There was no light in the room, and Tōji casually rested his hand on Okō's shoulder. At just that moment, there was a loud noise in the next room back.

"What was that?" asked Tōji. "Do you have other customers?"

Okō nodded silently, then put her moist lips to his ear and whispered, *115*

"Later." Trying to appear casual, the two went back to Seijūrō's room, only to find him alone and sound asleep.

Tōji, taking the adjacent room, stretched out on the pallet. He lay there, drumming his fingers on the tatami, waiting for Okō. She failed to appear. Eventually his eyelids grew heavy and he drifted off to sleep. He woke up quite late the next morning with a resentful look on his face.

Seijūrō had already arisen and was again drinking in the room overlooking the river. Both Okō and Akemi looked bright and cheerful, as though they'd forgotten about the night before. They were coaxing Seijūrō into some sort of promise.

"Then you'll take us?"

"All right, we'll go. Put together some box lunches and bring some sake."

They were talking about the Okuni Kabuki, which was being performed on the riverbank at Shijō Avenue. This was a new kind of dance with words and music, the current rage in the capital. It had been invented by a shrine maiden named Okuni at the Izumo Shrine, and its popularity had already inspired many imitations. In the busy area along the river, there were rows of stages where troupes of women performers competed to attract audiences, each trying to achieve a degree of individuality by adding special provincial dances and songs to their repertoire. The actresses, for the most part, had started out as women of the night; now that they had taken to the stage, however, they were summoned to perform in some of the greatest mansions in the capital. Many of them took masculine names, dressed in men's clothing, and put on stirring performances as valiant warriors.

Seijūrō sat staring out the door. Beneath the small bridge at Sanjō Avenue, women were bleaching cloth in the river; men on horseback were passing back and forth over the bridge.

"Aren't those two ready yet?" he asked irritably. It was already past noon. Sluggish from drink and tired of waiting, he was no longer in the mood for Kabuki.

Tōji, still smarting from the night before, was not his usual ebullient self. "It's fun to take women out," he grumbled, "but why is it that just when you're ready to leave, they suddenly start worrying about whether their hair is just right or their obi straight? What a nuisance!"

Seijūrō's thoughts turned to his school. He seemed to hear the sound of wooden swords and the clack of lance handles. What were his students saying about his absence? No doubt his younger brother, Denshichirō, was clicking his tongue in disapproval.

"Tōji," he said, "I don't really want to take them to see Kabuki. Let's go home."

"After you've already promised?"

"Well . . ."

"They were so thrilled! They'll be furious if we back out. I'll go and hurry them up."

On his way down the hallway, Tōji glanced into a room where the women's clothes were strewn about. He was surprised to see neither of them. "Where can they have got to?" he wondered aloud.

They weren't in the adjoining room either. Beyond that was another gloomy little room, sunless and musty with the odor of bedclothes. Tōji opened the door and was greeted with an angry roar: "Who's there?"

Jumping back a step, Tōji peered into the dark cubbyhole; it was floored with old tattered mats and was as different from the pleasant front rooms as night is from day. Sprawled on the floor, a sword handle lying carelessly across his belly, was an unkempt samurai whose clothing and general appearance left no doubt that he was one of the rōnin often seen roaming the streets and byways with nothing to do. The soles of his dirty feet stared Tōji in the face. Making no effort to get up, he lay there in a stupor.

Tōji said, "Oh, I'm sorry. I didn't know there was a guest in here."

"I'm not a guest!" the man shouted toward the ceiling. He reeked of sake, and though Tōji had no idea who he was, he was sure he wanted nothing more to do with him.

"Sorry to bother you," he said quickly, and turned to leave.

"Hold on there!" the man said roughly, raising himself up slightly. "Close the door behind you!"

Startled by his rudeness, Tōji did as he was told and left.

Almost immediately Tōji was replaced by Okō. Dressed to kill, she was obviously trying to look the great lady. As though tut-tutting a child, she said to Matahachi, "Now what are you so angry about?"

Akemi, who was just behind her mother, asked, "Why don't you come with us?"

"Where?"

"To see the Okuni Kabuki."

Matahachi's mouth twisted with repugnance. "What husband would be seen in the company of a man who's chasing after his wife?" he asked bitterly.

Okō had the feeling that cold water had been thrown in her face. Her eyes lighting up with anger, she said, "What are you talking about? Are you implying that there's something going on between Tōji and me?"

"Who said anything was going on?"

"You just said as much."

Matahachi made no reply.

"And you're supposed to be a man!" Though she hurled the words at him contemptuously, Matahachi maintained his sullen silence. "You make me sick!" she snapped. "You're always getting jealous over nothing! Come, Akemi. Let's not waste our time on this madman."

Matahachi reached out and caught her skirt. "Who're you calling a madman? What do you mean, talking to your husband that way?"

Okō pulled free of him. "And why not?" she said viciously. "If you're a husband, why don't you act like one? Who do you think's keeping you in food, you worthless layabout!"

"Heh!"

"You've hardly earned anything since we left Ōmi Province. You've just been living off me, drinking your sake and loafing. What've you got to complain about?"

"I told you I'd go out and work! I told you I'd even haul stones for the castle wall. But that wasn't good enough for you. You say you can't eat this, you can't wear that, you can't live in a dirty little house—there's no end to what you can't put up with. So instead of letting me do honest labor, you start this rotten teahouse. Well, stop it, I tell you, stop it!" he shouted. He began to shake.

"Stop what?"

"Stop running this place."

"And if I did, what would we eat tomorrow?"

"I can make enough for us to live on, even hauling rocks. I could manage for the three of us."

"If you're so eager to carry rocks or saw wood, why don't you just go away? Go on, be a laborer, anything, but if you do, you can live by yourself! The trouble with you is that you were born a clod, and you'll always be a clod. You should have stayed in Mimasaka! Believe me, I'm not begging you to stay. Feel free to leave anytime you want!"

While Matahachi made an effort to hold back his angry tears, Okō and Akemi turned their backs on him. But even after they were out of sight, he stood staring at the doorway. When Okō had hidden him at her house near Mount Ibuki, he'd thought he was lucky to have found someone who would love and take care of him. Now, however, he felt that he might as well have been captured by the enemy. Which was better, after all? To be a prisoner, or to become the pet of a fickle widow and cease to be a real man? Was it worse to languish in prison than to suffer here in the dark, a constant object of a shrew's scorn? He had had great hopes for the future, and he had let this slut, with her powdered face and her lascivious sex, pull him down to her level.

"The bitch!" Matahachi trembled with anger. "The rotten bitch!"

Tears welled up from the bottom of his heart. Why, oh, why, hadn't he returned to Miyamoto? Why hadn't he gone back to Otsū? His mother was in Miyamoto. His sister too, and his sister's husband, and Uncle Gon. They'd all been so good to him.

The bell at the Shippōji would be ringing today, wouldn't it? Just as it rang every day. And the Aida River would be flowing along its course as usual, flowers would be blooming on the riverbank, and the birds would be heralding the arrival of spring.

"What a fool I am! What a crazy, stupid fool!" Matahachi pounded his head with his fists.

Outside, mother, daughter and the two overnight guests strolled along the street, chatting merrily.

"It's just like spring."

"It ought to be. It's almost the third month."

"They say the shōgun will come to the capital soon. If he does, you two ladies should take in a lot of money, eh?"

"Oh, no, I'm sure we won't."

"Why? Don't the samurai from Edo like to play?"

"They're much too uncouth—"

118   "Mother, isn't that the music for the Kabuki? I hear bells. And a flute too."

"Listen to the child! She's always like this. She thinks she's already at the theater!"

"But, Mother, I can hear it."

"Never mind that. Carry the Young Master's hat for him."

The footsteps and voices drifted into the Yomogi. Matahachi, with eyes still red with fury, stole a look out the window at the happy foursome. He found the sight so humiliating he once again plopped down on the tatami in the dark room, cursing himself.

"What are you doing here? Have you no pride left? How can you let things go on this way? Idiot! *Do* something!" The speech was addressed to himself, his anger at Okō eclipsed by his indignation at his own craven weakness.

"She said get out. Well, get out!" he argued. "There's no reason to sit here gnashing your teeth. You're only twenty-two. You're still young. Get out and do something on your own."

He felt he couldn't abide staying in the empty, silent house another minute, yet for some reason, he couldn't leave. His head ached with confusion. He realized that living the way he had been for the past few years, he had lost the ability to think clearly. How had he stood it? His woman was spending her evenings entertaining other men, selling them the charms she had once lavished on him. He couldn't sleep nights, and in the daytime he was too dispirited to go out. Brooding here in this dark room, there was nothing to do but drink.

And all, he thought, for that aging whore!

He was disgusted with himself. He knew that the only way out of his agony was to kick the whole ugly business sky high and return to the aspirations of his younger days. He must find the way he had lost.

And yet . . . and yet . . .

Some mysterious attraction bound him. What sort of evil spell was it that held him here? Was the woman a demon in disguise? She would curse him, tell him to go away, swear he was nothing but trouble to her, and then in the middle of the night she would melt like honey and say it had all been a joke, she really hadn't meant any of it. And even if she was nearly forty, there were those lips—those bright red lips that were as appealing as her daughter's.

This, however, was not the whole story. In the final analysis, Matahachi did not have the courage to let Okō and Akemi see him working as a day laborer. He had grown lazy and soft; the young man who dressed in silk and could distinguish Nada sake from the local brew by its taste was a far cry from the simple, rugged Matahachi who had been at Sekigahara. The worst aspect was that living this strange life with an older woman had robbed him of his youthfulness. In years he was still young, but in spirit he was dissolute and spiteful, lazy and resentful.

"But I'll do it!" he vowed. "I'll get out now!" Giving himself a final angry blow on the head, he jumped to his feet, shouting, "I'll get out of here this very day!"

As he listened to his own voice, it suddenly sank in that there was no one around to hold him back, nothing that actually bound him to this house. The only thing he really owned and could not leave behind was his sword, and this he quickly slipped into his obi. Biting his lips, he said determinedly, "After all, I am a man."

He could have marched out the front door waving his sword like a victorious general, but by force of habit he jumped into his dirty sandals and left by the kitchen door.

So far, so good. He was out of doors! But now what? His feet came to a halt. He stood motionless in the refreshing breeze of early spring. It was not the light dazzling his eyes that kept him from moving. The question was, where was he headed?

At that moment it seemed to Matahachi that the world was a vast, turbulent sea on which there was nothing to cling to. Aside from Kyoto, his experience encompassed only his village life and one battle. As he puzzled over his situation, a sudden thought sent him scurrying like a puppy back through the kitchen door.

"I need money," he said to himself. "I'll certainly have to have some money."

Going straight to Okō's room, he rummaged through her toilet boxes, her mirror stand, her chest of drawers, and everywhere else he could think of. He ransacked the place but found no money at all. Of course, he should have realized Okō wasn't the type of woman who would fail to take precautions against something like this.

Frustrated, Matahachi flopped down on the clothes that still lay on the floor. The scent of Okō lingered like a thick mist about her red silk underrobe, her Nishijin obi and her Momoyama-dyed kimono. By now, he reflected, she would be at the open-air theater by the river, watching the Kabuki dances with Tōji at her side. He formed an image of her white skin and that provoking, coquettish face.

"The evil slut!" he cried. Bitter and murderous thoughts arose from his very bowels.

Then, unexpectedly, he had a painful recollection of Otsū. As the days and months of their separation added up, he had grown at last to understand the purity and devotion of this girl who had promised to wait for him. He would gladly have bowed down and lifted his hands in supplication to her, if he'd thought she would ever forgive him. But he had broken with Otsū, abandoned her in such a way that it would be impossible to face her again.

"All for the sake of that woman," he thought ruefully. Now that it was too late, everything was clear to him; he should never have let Okō know that Otsū existed. When Okō had first heard of the girl, she had smiled a little smile and pretended not to mind in the slightest, but in fact, she was consumed with jealousy. Afterward, whenever they quarreled, she would raise the subject and insist that he write a letter breaking his engagement. And when he finally gave in and did so, she had brazenly enclosed a note in her own obviously feminine hand, and callously had the missive delivered by an impersonal runner.

120   "What must Otsū think of me?" groaned Matahachi sorrowfully. The image

of her innocent girlish face came to his mind—a face full of reproach. Once again he saw the mountains and the river in Mimasaka. He wanted to call out to his mother, to his relatives. They had been so good. Even the soil now seemed to have been warm and comforting.

"I can never go home again!" he thought. "I threw all of it away for . . . for . . ." Enraged afresh, he dumped Okō's clothes out of the clothes chests and ripped them apart, strewing strips and pieces all over the house.

Slowly he became aware of someone calling from the front door.

"Pardon me," said the voice. "I'm from the Yoshioka School. Are the Young Master and Tōji here?"

"How should I know?" replied Matahachi gruffly.

"They must be here! I know it's rude to disturb them when they've gone off to have some fun, but something terribly important has happened. It involves the good name of the Yoshioka family."

"Go away! Don't bother me!"

"Please, can't you at least give them a message? Tell them that a swordsman named Miyamoto Musashi has appeared at the school, and that, well, none of our people can get the better of him. He's waiting for the Young Master to return—refuses to budge until he's had a chance to face him. Please tell them to hurry home!"

"Miyamoto? Miyamoto?"

The Wheel of Fortune

It was a day of unforgettable shame for the Yoshioka School. Never before had this prestigious center of the martial arts suffered such total humiliation.

Ardent disciples sat around in abject despair, long faces and whitened knuckles mirroring their distress and frustration. One large group was in the wood-floored anteroom, smaller groups in the side rooms. It was already twilight, when ordinarily they would have been heading home, or out to drink. No one made a move to leave. The funereal silence was broken only by the occasional clatter of the front gate.

"Is that him?"

"Is the Young Master back?"

"No, not yet." This from a man who had spent half the afternoon leaning disconsolately against a column at the entranceway.

Each time this happened, the men sank deeper into their morass of gloom. Tongues clicked in dismay and eyes shone with pathetic tears.

The doctor, coming out of a back room, said to the man at the entranceway, "I understand Seijūrō isn't here. Don't you know where he is?"

"No. Men are out looking for him. He'll probably be back soon."

The doctor harrumphed and departed.

In front of the school, the candle on the altar of the Hachiman Shrine was surrounded by a sinister corona.

No one would have denied that the founder and first master, Yoshioka Kempō, was a far greater man than Seijūrō or his younger brother. Kempō had started life as a mere tradesman, a dyer of cloth, but in the course of endlessly repeating the rhythms and movements of paste-resist dyeing, he had conceived of a new way of handling the short sword. After learning the use of the halberd from one of the most skillful of the warrior-priests at Kurama and then studying the Kyōhachi style of swordsmanship, he had then created a style completely his own. His short-sword technique had subsequently been adopted by the Ashikaga shōguns, who summoned him to be an official tutor. Kempō had been a great master, a man whose wisdom was equal to his skill.

Although his sons, Seijūrō and Denshichirō, had received training as rigorous as their father's, they had fallen heir to his considerable wealth and fame, and that, in the opinion of some, was the cause of their weakness. Seijūrō was customarily addressed as "Young Master," but he had not really attained the level of skill that would attract a large following. Students came to the school because under Kempō the Yoshioka style of fighting had become so famous that just gaining entrance meant being recognized by society as a skilled warrior.

After the fall of the Ashikaga shogunate three decades earlier, the House of Yoshioka had ceased to receive an official allowance, but during the lifetime of the frugal Kempō, it had gradually accumulated a great deal of wealth. In addition, it had this large establishment on Shijō Avenue, with more students than any other school in Kyoto, which was by far the largest city in the country. But in truth, the school's position at the top level in the world of swordsmanship was a matter of appearances only.

The world outside these great white walls had changed more than most of the people inside realized. For years they had boasted, loafed, and played around, and time had, as it will, passed them by. Today their eyes had been opened by their disgraceful loss to an unknown country swordsman.

A little before noon, one of the servants came to the dōjō and reported that a man who called himself Musashi was at the door, requesting admittance. Asked what sort of a fellow he was, the servant replied that he was a rōnin, that he hailed from Miyamoto in Mimasaka, was twenty-one or twenty-two years old, about six feet tall, and seemed rather dull. His hair, uncombed for at least a year, was carelessly tied up behind in a reddish mop, and his clothing was too filthy to tell whether it was black or brown, plain or figured. The servant, while admitting that he might be mistaken, thought he detected an odor about the man. He did have on his back one of the webbed leather sacks people called warriors' study bags, and this did probably mean he was a *shu-gyōsha*, one of those samurai, so numerous these days, who wandered about devoting their every waking hour to the study of swordsmanship. Nevertheless, the servant's overall impression was that this Musashi was distinctly out of place at the Yoshioka School.

If the man had simply been asking for a meal, there would have been no problem. But when the group heard that the rustic intruder had come to the great gate to challenge the famous Yoshioka Seijūrō to a bout, they burst into uproarious laughter. Some argued for turning him away without further ado, while others said they should first find out what style he employed and the name of his teacher.

The servant, as amused as anyone else, left and came back to report that the visitor had, as a boy, learned the use of the truncheon from his father and had later on picked up what he could from warriors passing through the village. He left home when he was seventeen and "for reasons of his own" spent his eighteenth, nineteenth and twentieth years immersed in scholarly studies. All the previous year he had been alone in the mountains, with the trees and the mountain spirits as his only teachers. Consequently, he couldn't lay claim to any particular style or teacher. But in the future he hoped to learn the teachings of Kiichi Hōgen, master the essence of the Kyōhachi Style, and emulate the great Yoshioka Kempō by creating a style of his own, which he had already decided to call the Miyamoto Style. Despite his many flaws, this was the goal toward which he proposed to work with all his heart and soul.

It was an honest and unaffected answer, the servant conceded, but the man had a country accent and stammered at almost every word. The servant obligingly provided his listeners with an imitation, again throwing them into gales of laughter.

The man must be out of his senses. To proclaim that his goal was to create a style of his own was sheer madness. By way of enlightening the lout, the students sent the servant out again, this time to ask whether the visitor had appointed anyone to take his corpse away after the bout.

To this Musashi replied, "If by any chance I should be killed, it makes no difference whether you discard my body on Toribe Mountain or throw it into the Kamo River with the garbage. Either way, I promise not to hold it against you."

His way of answering this time, said the servant, was very clear, with nothing of the clumsiness of his earlier replies.

After a moment's hesitation, someone said, "Let him in!"

That was how it started, with the disciples thinking they would cut the newcomer up a bit, then throw him out. In the very first bout, however, it was the school's champion who came away the loser. His arm was broken clean through. Only a bit of skin kept his wrist attached to his forearm.

One by one others accepted the stranger's challenge, and one by one they went down in ignominious defeat. Several were wounded seriously, and Musashi's wooden sword dripped with blood. After about the third loss, the disciples' mood turned murderous; if it took every last one of them, they would not let this barbaric madman get away alive, taking the honor of the Yoshioka School with him.

Musashi himself ended the bloodshed. Since his challenge had been accepted, he had no qualms about the casualties, but he announced, "There's no point in continuing until Seijūrō returns," and refused to fight anymore. There being no alternative, he was shown, at his own request, to a room where he could wait. Only then did one man come to his senses and call for the doctor.

It was soon after the doctor left that voices screaming out the names of two of the wounded brought a dozen men to the back room. They clustered around the two samurai in stunned disbelief, their faces ashen and their breathing uneven. Both were dead.

Footsteps hurried through the dōjō and into the death room. The students made way for Seijūrō and Tōji. Both were as pale as though they'd just emerged from an icy waterfall.

"What's going on here?" demanded Tōji. "What's the meaning of all this?" His tone was surly, as usual.

A samurai kneeling grim-faced by the pillow of one of his dead companions fixed accusing eyes on Tōji and said, "You should explain what's going on. You're the one who takes the Young Master out carousing. Well, this time you've gone too far!"

"Watch your tongue, or I'll cut it out!"

"When Master Kempō was alive, a day never passed when he wasn't in the dōjō!"

"What of it? The Young Master wanted a little cheering up, so we went to the Kabuki. What do you mean, talking that way in front of him? Just who do you think you are?"

"Does he have to stay out all night to see the Kabuki? Master Kempō must be turning in his grave."

"That's enough!" cried Tōji, lunging toward the man.

As others moved in and tried to separate and calm down the two, a voice heavy with pain rose slightly above the sound of the scuffle. "If the Young Master's back, it's time to stop squabbling. It's up to him to retrieve the honor of the school. That rōnin can't leave here alive."

Several of the wounded screamed and pounded on the floor. Their agitation was an eloquent rebuke to those who had not faced Musashi's sword.

To the samurai of this age, the most important thing in the world was honor. As a class, they virtually competed with each other to see who would be the first to die for it. The government had until recently been too busy with its wars to work out an adequate administrative system for a country at peace, and even Kyoto was governed only by a set of loose, makeshift regulations. Still, the emphasis of the warrior class on personal honor was respected by farmers and townsmen alike, and it played a role in preserving peace. A general consensus regarding what constituted honorable behavior, and what did not, made it possible for the people to govern themselves even with inadequate laws.

The men of the Yoshioka School, though uncultured, were by no means shameless degenerates. When after the initial shock of defeat they returned to their normal selves, the first thing they thought of was honor. The honor of their school, the honor of the master, their own personal honor.

Putting aside individual animosities, a large group gathered around Seijūrō to discuss what was to be done. Unfortunately, on this of all days, Seijūrō felt bereft of fighting spirit. At the moment when he should have been at his best, he was hung over, weak and exhausted.

"Where is the man?" he asked, as he hitched up his kimono sleeves with a leather thong.

"He's in the small room next to the reception room," said one student, pointing across the garden.

"Call him!" Seijūrō commanded. His mouth was dry from tension. He sat down in the master's place, a small raised platform, and prepared himself to receive Musashi's greeting. Choosing one of the wooden swords proffered by his disciples, he held it upright beside him.

Three or four men acknowledged the command and started to leave, but Tōji and Ryōhei told them to wait.

There ensued a good deal of whispering, just out of Seijūrō's earshot. The muted consultations centered around Tōji and other of the school's senior disciples. Before long family members and a few retainers joined in, and there were so many heads present that the gathering split into groups. Though heated, the controversy was settled in a relatively short time.

The majority, not only concerned about the school's fate but uncomfortably aware of Seijūrō's shortcomings as a fighter, concluded that it would be unwise to let him face Musashi man to man, then and there. With two dead and several wounded, if Seijūrō were to lose, the crisis facing the school would become extraordinarily grave. It was too great a risk to take.

The unspoken opinion of most of the men was that if Denshichirō were present, there would be little cause for alarm. In general, it was thought that he would have been better suited than Seijūrō to carry on his father's work, but being the second son and having no serious responsibilities, he was an exceedingly easygoing type. That morning he had left the house with friends to go to Ise and hadn't even bothered to say when he'd return.

Tōji approached Seijūrō and said, "We've reached a conclusion."

As Seijūrō listened to the whispered report, his face grew more and more indignant, until finally he gasped with barely controlled fury, "Trick him?"

Tōji tried to silence him with his eyes, but Seijūrō was not to be silenced. "I can't agree to anything like that! It's cowardly. What if word got out that the Yoshioka School was so afraid of an unknown warrior that it hid and ambushed him?"

"Calm down," Tōji pleaded, but Seijūrō continued to protest. Drowning him out, Tōji said loudly, "Leave it to us. We'll take care of it."

But Seijūrō would have none of it. "Do you think that I, Yoshioka Seijūrō, would lose to this Musashi, or whatever his name is?"

"Oh, no, it's not that at all," lied Tōji. "It's just that we don't see how you would gain any honor by defeating him. You're of much too high a status to take on a brazen vagabond like that. Anyway, there's no reason why anybody   *125* outside this house should know anything about it, is there? Only one thing is important—not to let him get away alive."

Even while they argued, the number of men in the hall shrank by more than half. As quietly as cats, they were disappearing into the garden, toward the back door and into the inner rooms, fading almost imperceptibly into the darkness.

"Young Master, we can't put it off any longer," Tōji said firmly, and blew out the lamp. He loosened his sword in its scabbard and raised his kimono sleeves.

Seijūrō remained seated. Though to some extent relieved at not having to fight the stranger, he was by no means happy. The implication, as he saw it, was that his disciples had a low opinion of his ability. He thought back on how he had neglected practice since his father's death, and the thought made him despondent.

The house grew as cold and quiet as the bottom of a well. Unable to sit still, Seijūrō got up and stood by the window. Through the paper-covered doors of the room given Musashi, he could see the softly flickering light of the lamp. That was the only light anywhere.

Quite a number of other eyes were peering in the same direction. The attackers, their swords on the ground in front of them, held their breath and listened intently for any sound that might tell them what Musashi was up to.

Tōji, whatever his shortcomings, had experienced the training of a samurai. He was trying desperately to figure out what Musashi might do. "He's completely unknown in the capital, but he's a great fighter. Could he just be sitting silently in that room? Our approach has been quiet enough, but with this many people pressing in on him, he must have noticed. Anyone trying to make it through life as a warrior would notice; otherwise he'd be dead by now.

"Mm, maybe he's dozed off. It rather looks that way. After all, he's been waiting a long time.

"On the other hand, he's already proved he's clever. He's probably standing there fully prepared for battle, leaving the lamp lit to put us off guard, just waiting for the first man to attack.

"That must be it. That *is* it!"

The men were edgily cautious, for the target of their murderous intent would be just as eager to slay them. They exchanged glances, silently asking who would be the first to run forward and risk his life.

Finally the wily Tōji, who was just outside Musashi's room, called out, "Musashi! Sorry to have kept you waiting! Could I see you for a moment?"

There being no answer, Tōji concluded that Musashi was indeed ready and waiting for the attack. Vowing not to let him escape, Tōji signaled to right and left, then aimed a kick at the shoji. Dislodged from its groove by the blow, the bottom of the door slid about two feet into the room. At the sound, the men who were supposed to storm into the room unintentionally fell back a pace. But in a matter of seconds, someone shouted for the attack, and all the other doors of the room clattered open.

126

"He's not here!"

"The room's empty!"

Voices full of restored courage muttered disbelievingly. Musashi had been sitting there just a short while ago, when someone had brought him the lamp. The lamp still burned, the cushion he had been sitting on·was still there, the brazier still had a good fire in it, and there was a cup of untouched tea. But no Musashi!

One man ran out on the veranda and let the others know that he had gotten away. From under the veranda and from dark spots in the garden, students and retainers assembled, stamping the ground angrily and cursing the men who had been standing guard on the small room. The guards, however, insisted that Musashi could not have gotten away. He had walked down to the toilet less than an hour earlier but had returned to the room immediately. There was no way he could have gotten out without being seen.

"Are you saying he's invisible, like the wind?" one man asked scornfully.

Just then a man who had been poking around in a closet shouted, "Here's how he got away! See, these floorboards have been ripped up."

"It hasn't been very long since the lamp was trimmed. He can't have gone far!"

"After him!'

If Musashi had indeed fled, he must at heart be a coward! The thought fired his pursuers with the fighting spirit that had been so notably lacking a bit earlier. They were streaming out the front, back and side gates when someone yelled, "There he is!"

Near the back gate, a figure shot out of the shadows, crossed the street and entered a dark alley on the other side. Running like a hare, it swerved off to one side when it reached the wall at the end of the alley. Two or three of the students caught up with the man on the road between the Kūyadō and the burned ruins of the Honnōji.

"Coward!"

"Run away, will you?"

"After what you did today?"

There was the sound of heavy scuffling and kicking, and a defiant howl. The captured man had regained his strength and was turning on his captors. In an instant, the three men who had been dragging him by the back of his neck plummeted to the ground. The man's sword was about to descend on them when a fourth man ran up and shouted, "Wait! It's a mistake! He's not the one we're after."

Matahachi lowered his sword and the men got to their feet.

"Hey, you're right! That's not Musashi."

As they were standing there looking perplexed, Tōji arrived on the scene. "Did you catch him?" he asked.

"Uh, wrong man—not the one who caused all the trouble."

Tōji took a closer look at the captive and said with astonishment, "Is that the man you were chasing?"

"Yes. You know him?'

127

"I saw him just today at the Yomogi Teahouse."

While they eyed Matahachi silently and suspiciously, he calmly straightened his tousled hair and brushed off his kimono.

"Is he the master of the Yomogi?"

"No, the mistress of the place told me he wasn't. He seems to be just a hanger-on of some sort."

"He looks shady, all right. What was he doing around the gate? Spying?"

But Tōji had already started to move on. "If we waste time with him, we'll lose Musashi. Split up and get moving. If nothing else, we can at least find out where he's staying."

There was a murmur of assent and they were off.

Matahachi, facing the moat of the Honnōji, stood silently with his head bowed while the men ran by. As the last one passed, he called out to him.

The man stopped. "What do you want?" he asked.

Going toward him, Matahachi asked, "How old was this man called Musashi?"

"How would I know?"

"Would you say he was about my age?"

"I guess that's about right. Yes."

"Is he from the village of Miyamoto in Mimasaka Province?"

"Yes."

"I guess 'Musashi' is another way of reading the two characters used to write 'Takezō,' isn't it?"

"Why are you asking all these questions? Is he a friend of yours?"

"Oh, no. I was just wondering."

"Well, in the future, why don't you just stay away from places where you don't belong? Otherwise you might find yourself in some real trouble one of these days." With that warning, the man ran off.

Matahachi started walking slowly beside the dark moat, stopping occasionally to look up at the stars. He didn't seem to have any particular destination.

"It is him after all!" he decided. "He must have changed his name to Musashi and become a swordsman. I guess he must be pretty different from the way he used to be." He slid his hands into his obi and began kicking a stone along with the toe of his sandal. Every time he kicked, he seemed to see Takezō's face before him.

"It's not the right time," he mumbled. "I'd be ashamed for him to see me the way I am now. I've got enough pride not to want him to look down on me. . . . If that Yoshioka bunch catches up with him, though, they're likely to kill him. Wonder where he is. I'd like to at least warn him."

Encounter and Retreat

Along the stony path leading up to the Kiyomizudera Temple stood a row of shabby houses, their planked roofs lined up like rotten teeth and so old that moss covered their eaves. Under the hot noonday sun, the street reeked of salted fish broiling over charcoal.

A dish flew through the door of one of the ramshackle hovels and broke into smithereens on the street. A man of about fifty, apparently an artisan of sorts, came tumbling out after it. Close on his heels was his barefooted wife, her hair a tangled mess and her tits hanging down like a cow's.

"What're you saying, you lout?" she screamed shrilly. "You go off, leave your wife and children to starve, then come crawling back like a worm!"

From inside the house came the sound of children crying and nearby a dog howled. She caught up with the man, seized him by his topknot and began beating him.

"Now where do you think you're going, you old fool?"

Neighbors rushed up, trying to restore order.

Musashi smiled ironically and turned back toward the ceramics shop. For some time before the domestic battle erupted, he had been standing just outside it, watching the potters with childlike fascination. The two men inside were unaware of his presence. Eyes riveted on their work, they seemed to have entered into the clay, become a part of it. Their concentration was complete.

Musashi would have liked to have a try at working with the clay. Since boyhood he had enjoyed doing things with his hands, and he thought he might at least be able to make a simple tea bowl. Just then, however, one of the potters, an old man of nearly sixty, started fashioning a tea bowl. Musashi, observing how deftly he moved his fingers and handled his spatula, realized he'd overestimated his own abilities. "It takes so much technique just to make a simple piece like that," he marveled.

These days he often felt deep admiration for other people's work. He found he respected technique, art, even the ability to do a simple task well, particularly if it was a skill he himself had not mastered.

In one corner of the shop, on a makeshift counter made of an old door panel, stood rows of plates, jars, sake cups, and pitchers. They were sold as souvenirs, for the paltry sum of twenty or thirty pieces of cash, to people on their way to and from the temple. In stark contrast to the earnestness the potters devoted to their work was the humbleness of their boarded shack. Musashi wondered whether they always had enough to eat. Life, it appeared, wasn't as easy as it sometimes seemed.

Contemplating the skill, concentration and devotion put into making wares, even as cheap as these, made Musashi feel he still had a long way to go if he was ever to reach the level of perfection in swordsmanship that he aspired to. The thought was a sobering one, for in the past three weeks he'd visited other well-known training centers in Kyoto besides the Yoshioka School and had begun to wonder whether he had not been too critical of himself since his confinement at Himeji. His expectation had been to find Kyoto full of men who had mastered the martial arts. It was, after all, the imperial capital, as well as the former seat of the Ashikaga shogunate, and it had long been a gathering place for famous generals and legendary warriors. During his stay, however, he had not found a single training center that had taught him anything to be genuinely grateful for. Instead, at each school he had experienced disappointment. Though he always won his bouts, he was unable to decide whether this was because he was good or his opponents were bad. In either case, if the samurai he had met were typical, the country was in sorry shape.

Encouraged by his success, he had reached the point of taking a certain pride in his expertise. But now, reminded of the danger of vanity, he felt chastened. He mentally bowed in deep respect to the clay-smudged old men at the wheel and started up the steep slope to Kiyomizudera.

He had not gone far when a voice called to him from below. "You there, sir. The rōnin!"

"Do you mean me?" asked Musashi, turning around.

Judging from the man's padded cotton garment, his bare legs, and the pole he carried, he was a palanquin bearer by trade. From behind his beard, he said, politely enough for one of his lowly status, "Sir, is your name Miyamoto?"

"Yes."

"Thank you." The man turned and went down toward Chawan Hill.

Musashi watched him enter what appeared to be a teahouse. Passing through the area a while earlier, he had noticed a large crowd of porters and palanquin bearers standing about in a sunny spot. He couldn't imagine who had sent one of them to ask his name but supposed that whoever it was would soon come to meet him. He stood there awhile, but when no one appeared, resumed his climb.

He stopped along the way to look at several well-known temples, and at each of them he bowed and said two prayers. One was: "Please protect my sister from harm." The other was: "Please test the lowly Musashi with hardship. Let him become the greatest swordsman in the land, or let him die."

Arriving at the edge of a cliff, he dropped his basket hat on the ground and sat down. From there he could look out over the whole city of Kyoto. As he sat clasping his knees, a simple, but powerful, ambition welled up in his young breast.

"I want to lead an important life. I want to do it because I was born a human being."

He had once read that in the tenth century two rebels named Taira no Masa-kado and Fujiwara no Sumitomo, both wildly ambitious, had gotten together and decided that if they emerged from the wars victorious, they would divide Japan up between them. The story was probably apocryphal to begin with, but Musashi remembered thinking at the time how stupid and unrealistic it would have been for them to believe they could carry out so grandiose a scheme. Now, however, he no longer felt it laughable. While his own dream was of a different sort, there were certain similarities. If the young cannot harbor great dreams in their souls, who can? At the moment Musashi was imagining how he could create a place of his own in the world.

He thought of Oda Nobunaga and Toyotomi Hideyoshi, of their visions of unifying Japan and of the many battles they had fought to that end. But it was clear that the path to greatness no longer lay in winning battles. Today the people wanted only the peace for which they'd thirsted so long. And as Musa-shi considered the long, long struggle Tokugawa Ieyasu had had to endure to make this desire a reality, he realized once again how hard it was to hold fast to one's ideal.

"This is a new age," he thought. "I have the rest of my life before me. I came along too late to follow in the footsteps of Nobunaga or Hideyoshi, but I can still dream of my own world to conquer. No one can stop me from doing that. Even that palanquin bearer must have a dream of some sort."

For a moment he put these ideas out of his mind and tried to view his situation objectively. He had his sword, and the Way of the Sword was the way he had chosen. It might be fine to be a Hideyoshi or an Ieyasu, but the times no longer had use for people of their particular talents. Ieyasu had ev-erything neatly tied up; there was no more need for bloody wars. In Kyoto, stretched out below him, life was no longer a touch-and-go affair.

For Musashi, the important thing from now on would be his sword and the society around him, his swordsmanship as it related to existing as a human being. In a moment of insight, he was satisfied that he had found the link between the martial arts and his own visions of greatness.

As he sat lost in thought, the palanquin bearer's face came into view be-neath the cliff. He pointed his bamboo pole at Musashi and shouted, "There he is, up there!"

Musashi looked down to where the porters were milling about and shout-ing. They began climbing the hill toward him. He got to his feet and, trying to ignore them, walked farther up the hill, but soon discovered that his path was blocked. Locking arms and thrusting out their poles, a sizable group of men had encircled him at a distance. Looking over his shoulder, he saw that the men behind him had come to a halt. One of them grinned, showing his teeth, and informed the others that Musashi seemed to be "staring at a plaque or something."

Musashi, now before the steps of the Hongandō, was indeed gazing up at a weatherbeaten plaque hanging from the crossbeam of the temple entrance. He felt ill at ease and wondered if he should try frightening them away with a battle cry. Even though he knew he could make quick work of them, there was no point in brawling with a bunch of lowly laborers. It was probably all a mistake anyway. If so, they would disperse sooner or later. He stood there patiently, reading and rereading the words on the plaque: "Original Vow."

"Here she comes!" one of the porters cried.

They began talking among themselves in hushed tones. Musashi's impression was that they were working themselves into a frenzy. The compound within the western gate of the temple had quickly filled with people, and now priests, pilgrims and vendors were straining their eyes to see what was going on. Their faces brimming with curiosity, they formed circles outside the ring of porters surrounding Musashi.

From the direction of Sannen Hill came the rhythmical, pace-setting chants of men carrying a load. The voices came closer and closer until two men entered the temple grounds bearing on their backs an old woman and a rather tired-looking country samurai.

From her porter's back, Osugi waved her hand briskly and said, "This will do." The bearer bent his legs, and as she jumped spryly to the ground, she thanked him. Turning to Uncle Gon, she said, "We won't let him get away this time, will we?" The two were clothed and shod as though they expected to spend the rest of their lives traveling.

"Where is he?" called Osugi.

One of the bearers said, "Over there," and pointed proudly toward the temple.

Uncle Gon moistened the handle of his sword with spittle, and the two pushed through the circle of people.

"Take your time," cautioned one of the porters.

"He looks pretty tough," said another.

"Just make sure you're well prepared," advised still another.

While the laborers offered words of encouragement and support to Osugi, the spectators looked on in dismay.

"Is the old woman actually planning to challenge that rōnin to a duel?"

"Looks that way."

"But she's so old! Even her second is shaky on his legs! They must have good reason to try taking on a man so much younger."

"Must be a family feud of some kind!"

"Look at that now, will you! She's lighting into the old man. Some of these old grannies really have guts, don't they!"

A porter ran up with a dipper of water for Osugi. After drinking a mouthful she handed it to Uncle Gon and addressed him sternly. "Now see that you don't get flustered, because there's nothing to be flustered about. Takezō's a man of straw. Oh, he may have learned a little about using a sword, but he couldn't have learned all that much. Just stay calm!"

Taking the lead, she went straight to the front staircase of the Hongandō and sat down on the steps, not ten paces from Musashi. Paying no attention whatever either to him or to the crowd watching her, she took out her prayer beads, and closing her eyes, began moving her lips. Inspired by her religious fervor, Uncle Gon put his hands together and did likewise.

The sight proved to be a little too melodramatic, and one of the spectators started snickering. Immediately, one of the porters spun around and said challengingly, "Who thinks this is funny? This is no laughing matter, you imbecile! The old woman's come all the way from Mimasaka to find the good-for-nothing who ran off with her son's bride. She's been praying at the temple here every day for almost two months and today he finally showed up."

"These samurai are different from the rest of us," was the opinion of another porter. "At that age, the old woman could be living comfortably at home, playing with her grandchildren, but no, here she is, in place of her son, seeking to avenge an insult to her family. If nothing else, she deserves our respect."

A third one said, "We're not supporting her just because she's been giving us tips. She's got spirit, she has! Old as she is, she's not afraid to fight. I say we should give her all the help we can. It's only right to help the underdog! If she should lose, let's take care of the rōnin ourselves."

"You're right! But let's do it now! We can't stand here and let her get herself killed."

As the crowd learned of the reasons for Osugi's being there, the excitement mounted. Some of the spectators began goading the porters on.

Osugi put her prayer beads back into her kimono, and a hush fell over the temple grounds. "Takezō!" she called loudly, putting her left hand on the short sword at her waist.

Musashi had all the while been standing by in silence. Even when Osugi called out his name, he acted as if he hadn't heard. Unnerved by this, Uncle Gon, at Osugi's side, chose this moment to assume an attacking stance, and thrusting his head forward, uttered a cry of challenge.

Musashi again failed to respond. He couldn't. He simply did not know how to. He recalled Takuan's having warned him in Himeji that he might run into Osugi. He was prepared to ignore her completely, but he was very upset by the talk the porters had been spreading among the mob. Furthermore, it was difficult for him to restrain his resentment at the hatred the Hon'idens had harbored against him all this time. The whole affair amounted to nothing more than a petty matter of face and feelings in the little village of Miyamoto, a misunderstanding that could be easily cleared up if only Matahachi were present.

Nevertheless, he was at a loss as to what to do here and now. How was one to respond to a challenge from a doddering old woman and a shrunken-faced samurai? Musashi stared on in silence, his mind in a quandary.

"Look at the bastard! He's afraid!" a porter shouted.

"Be a man! Let the old woman kill you!" taunted another.

There was not a soul who was not on Osugi's side.

The old woman blinked her eyes and shook her head. Then she looked at the bearers and snapped angrily, "Shut up! I just want you as witnesses. If the two of us should happen to be killed, I want you to send our bodies back to Miyamoto. Otherwise I don't need your talk, and I don't want your help!" Pulling her short sword partway out of its scabbard, she took a couple of steps in Musashi's direction.

"Takezō!" she said again. "Takezō was always your name in the village, so why don't you answer to it? I've heard you've taken a fine new name—Miyamoto Musashi, is it?—but you'll always be Takezō to me! Ha, ha, ha!" Her wrinkled neck quivered as she laughed. Evidently she hoped to kill Musashi with words before swords were drawn.

"Did you think you could keep me from tracking you down just by changing your name? How stupid! The gods in heaven have guided me to you, as I knew they would. Now fight! We'll see whether I take your head home with me, or you manage somehow to stay alive!"

Uncle Gon, in his withered voice, issued his own challenge. "It's been four long years since you gave us the slip, and we've been searching for you all this time. Now our prayers here at the Kiyomizudera have brought you into our grasp. Old I may be, but I'm not going to lose to the likes of you! Prepare to die!" Whipping out his sword, he cried to Osugi, "Get out of the way!"

She turned on him furiously. "What do you mean, you old fool? You're the one who's shaking."

"Never mind! The bodhisattvas of this temple will protect us!"

"You're right, Uncle Gon. And the ancestors of the Hon'idens are with us too! There's nothing to fear."

"Takezō! Come forward and fight!"

"What are you waiting for?"

Musashi did not move. He stood there like a deaf-mute, staring at the two old people and their drawn swords.

Osugi cried, "What's the matter, Takezō! Are you scared?"

She edged sideways, preparing to attack, but suddenly tripped on a rock and pitched forward, landing on her hands and knees almost at Musashi's feet.

The crowd gasped, and someone screamed, "She'll be killed!"

"Quick, save her!"

But Uncle Gon only stared at Musashi's face, too stunned to move.

The old woman then startled one and all by snatching up her sword and walking back to Uncle Gon's side, where she again took a challenging stance. "What's wrong, you lout?" Osugi cried. "Is that sword in your hand just an ornament? Don't you know how to use it?"

Musashi's face was like a mask, but he spoke at last, in a thunderous voice. "I can't do it!"

He started walking toward them, and Uncle Gon and Osugi instantly fell back to either side.

"Wh-where are you going, Takezō?"

"I can't use my sword!"

"Stop! Why don't you stop and fight?"

"I told you! I can't use it!"

He walked straight ahead, looking neither right nor left. He marched directly through the crowd, without once swerving.

Recovering her senses, Osugi cried, "He's running away! Don't let him escape!"

134   The crowd now moved in on Musashi, but when they thought they had him

hemmed in, they discovered he was no longer there. Their bewilderment was acute. Eyes flared in surprise, then became dull patches in blank faces.

Breaking up into smaller groups, they continued until sunset to run about, searching frantically under the floors of the temple buildings and in the woods for their vanished prey.

Still later, as people were going back down the darkened slopes of Sannen and Chawan hills, one man swore that he had seen Musashi jump with the effortlessness of a cat to the top of the six-foot wall by the western gate and disappear.

Nobody believed this, least of all Osugi and Uncle Gon.

The Water Sprite

In a hamlet northwest of Kyoto, the heavy thuds of a mallet pounding rice straw shook the ground. Unseasonal torrents of rain soaked into the brooding thatched roofs. This was a sort of no-man's-land, between the city and the farming district, and the poverty was so extreme that at twilight the smoke of kitchen fires billowed from only a handful of houses.

A basket hat suspended under the eaves of one small house proclaimed in bold, rough characters that this was an inn, albeit one of the cheapest variety. The travelers who stopped here were impecunious and rented only floor space. For pallets they paid extra, but few could afford such luxury.

In the dirt-floored kitchen beside the entranceway, a boy leaned with his hands on the raised tatami of the adjoining room, in the center of which was a sunken hearth.

"Hello! . . . Good evening! . . . Anybody here?" It was the errand boy from the drinking shop, another shabby affair just down the road.

The boy's voice was too loud for his size. He could not have been more than ten or eleven years old, and with his hair wet from the rain and hanging down over his ears, he looked no more substantial than a water sprite in a whimsical painting. He was dressed for the part too: thigh-length kimono with tubular sleeves, a thick cord for an obi, and mud splattered clear up his back from running in his wooden clogs.

"That you, Jō?" called the old innkeeper from a back room.

"Yes. Would you like me to bring you some sake?"

"No, not today. The lodger isn't back yet. I don't need any."

"Well, he'll want some when he does come back, won't he? I'll bring the usual amount."

"If he does, I'll come get it myself."

Reluctant to leave without an order, the boy asked, "What are you doing in there?"

"I'm writing a letter, going to send it by the packhorse up to Kurama tomorrow. But it's a bit difficult. And my back's getting sore. Be quiet, don't bother me."

"That's pretty funny, isn't it? You're so old you're beginning to stoop, and you still don't know how to write properly!"

"That's enough out of you. If I hear any more sass, I'll take a stick of firewood to you."

"Want me to write it for you?"

"Ha, as if you could."

"Oh, I can," the boy asserted as he came into the room. He looked over the old man's shoulder at the letter and burst into laughter. "Are you trying to write 'potatoes'? The character you've written means 'pole.'"

"Quiet!"

"I won't say a word, if you insist. But your writing's terrible. Are you planning to send your friends some potatoes, or some poles?"

"Potatoes."

The boy read a moment longer, then announced, "It's no good. Nobody but you could guess what this letter's supposed to mean!"

"Well, if you're so smart, see what you can do with it, then."

"All right. Just tell me what you want to say." Jōtarō sat down and took up the brush.

"You clumsy ass!" the old man exclaimed.

"Why call me clumsy? You're the one who can't write!"

"Your nose is dripping on the paper."

"Oh, sorry. You can give me this piece for my pay." He proceeded to blow his nose on the soiled sheet. "Now, what is it you want to say?" Holding the brush firmly, he wrote with ease as the old man dictated.

Just as the letter was finished, the lodger returned, casually throwing aside a charcoal sack he had picked up somewhere to put over his head.

Musashi, stopping by the door, wrung the water out of his sleeves and grumbled, "I guess this'll be the end of the plum blossoms." In the twenty-odd days Musashi had been there, the inn had come to seem like home. He was gazing out at the tree by the front gate, where pink blossoms had greeted his eye every morning since his arrival. The fallen petals lay scattered about in the mud.

Entering the kitchen, he was surprised to catch a glimpse of the boy from the sake shop, head to head with the innkeeper. Curious as to what they were doing, he stole up behind the old man and peered over his shoulder.

Jōtarō looked up into Musashi's face, then hastily hid the brush and paper behind him. "You shouldn't sneak up on people like that," he complained.

"Let me see," said Musashi teasingly.

"No," said Jōtarō with a defiant shake of his head.

"Come on, show me," said Musashi.

"Only if you buy some sake."

"Oh, so that's your game, is it? All right, I'll buy some."

"Five gills?"

"I don't need that much."

"Three gills?"

"Still too much."

"Well, how much? Don't be such a tightwad!"

"Tightwad? Now, you know I'm only a poor swordsman. Do you think I have money to throw away?

"All right. I'll measure it out myself, give you your money's worth. But if I do, you have to promise to tell me some stories."

The bargaining concluded, Jōtarō splashed cheerfully off into the rain.

Musashi picked up the letter and read it. After a moment or two, he turned to the innkeeper and asked, "Did he really write this?"

"Yes. Amazing, isn't it? He seems very bright."

While Musashi went to the well, poured some cold water over himself and put on dry clothes, the old man hung a pot over the fire and set out some pickled vegetables and a rice bowl. Musashi came back and sat down by the hearth.

"What's that rascal up to?" muttered the innkeeper. "He's taking a long time with the sake."

"How old is he?"

"Eleven, I think he said."

"Mature for his age, don't you think?"

"Mm. I suppose it's because he's been working at the sake shop since he was seven. He runs up against all kinds there—wagon drivers, the paper-maker down the way, travelers, and what have you."

"I wonder how he learned to write so well."

"Is he really that good?"

"Well, his writing has a certain childish quality, but there's an appealing—what can I say?—directness about it. If I had a swordsman in mind, I would say it shows spiritual breadth. The boy may eventually be somebody."

"What do you mean?"

"I mean become a real human being."

"Oh?" The old man frowned, took the lid off the pot and resumed his grumbling. "Still not back. I'll bet he's dawdling somewhere."

He was about to put on his sandals and go for the sake himself when Jōtarō returned. "What have you been up to?" he asked the boy. "You've been keeping my guest waiting."

"I couldn't help it. There was a customer in the shop, very drunk, and he grabbed hold of me and started asking a lot of questions."

"What kind of questions?"

"He was asking about Miyamoto Musashi."

"And I suppose you did a lot of blabbering."

"It wouldn't matter if I did. Everybody around here knows what happened at Kiyomizudera the other day. The woman next door, the daughter of the lacquer man—both of them were at the temple that day. They saw what happened."

"Stop talking about that, won't you?" Musashi said, almost in a pleading tone.

The sharp-eyed boy sized up Musashi's mood and asked, "Can I stay here for a while and talk with you?" He started washing off his feet, preparing to come into the hearth room.

"It's all right with me, if your master won't mind."

"Oh, he doesn't need me right now."

"All right."

"I'll warm up your sake for you. I'm good at that." He settled a sake jar into the warm ashes around the fire and soon announced it was ready.

"Fast, aren't you?" said Musashi appreciatively.

"Do you like sake?"

"Yes."

"But being so poor, I guess you don't drink very much, do you?"

"That's right."

"I thought men who were good at the martial arts served under great lords and got big allowances. A customer at the shop told me once that Tsukahara Bokuden always used to go around with seventy or eighty retainers, a change of horses and a falcon."

"That's true."

"And I heard that a famous warrior named Yagyū, who serves the House of Tokugawa, has an income of fifty thousand bushels of rice."

"That's true too."

"Then why are you so poor?"

"I'm still studying."

"How old will you have to be before you have lots of followers?"

"I don't know if I ever will."

"What's the matter? Aren't you any good?"

"You heard what the people who saw me at the temple said. Any way you look at it, I ran away."

"That's what everybody's saying: that *shugyōsha* at the inn—that's you—is a weakling. But it makes me mad to listen to them." Jōtarō's lips tightened in a straight line.

"Ha, ha! Why should you mind? They're not talking about you."

"Well, I feel sorry for you. Look, the paper-maker's son and the cooper's son and some of the rest of the young men all get together sometimes behind the lacquer shop for sword practice. Why don't you fight one of them and beat him?"

"All right. If that's what you want, I will."

Musashi was finding it difficult to refuse anything the boy asked, partly because he himself was in many ways still a boy at heart and was able to sympathize with Jōtarō. He was always looking, mostly unconsciously, for

138

something to take the place of the family affection lacking from his own boyhood.

"Let's talk about something else," he said. "I'll ask you a question for a change. Where were you born?"

"In Himeji."

"Oh, so you're from Harima."

"Yes, and you're from Mimasaka, aren't you? Somebody said you were."

"That's right. What does your father do?"

"He used to be a samurai. A real honest-to-goodness samurai!"

At first Musashi looked astonished, but actually the answer explained several things, not the least of which was how the boy had learned to write so well. He asked the father's name.

"His name is Aoki Tanzaemon. He used to have an allowance of twenty-five hundred bushels of rice, but when I was seven he left his lord's service and came to Kyoto as a rōnin. After all his money was gone, he left me at the sake shop and went to a temple to become a monk. But I don't want to stay at the shop. I want to become a samurai like my father was, and I want to learn swordsmanship like you. Isn't that the best way to become a samurai?"

The boy paused, then continued earnestly: "I want to become your follower—go around the country studying with you. Won't you take me on as your pupil?"

Having blurted out his purpose, Jōtarō put on a stubborn face reflecting clearly his determination not to take no for an answer. He could not know, of course, that he was pleading with a man who had caused his father no end of trouble. Musashi, for his part, could not bring himself to refuse out of hand. Yet what he was really thinking of was not whether to say yes or no but of Aoki Tanzaemon and his unfortunate fate. He could not help sympathizing with the man. The Way of the Samurai was a constant gamble, and a samurai had to be ready at all times to kill or be killed. Mulling over this example of life's vicissitudes, Musashi was saddened, and the effect of the sake wore off quite suddenly. He felt lonely.

Jōtarō was insistent. When the innkeeper tried to get him to leave Musashi alone, he replied insolently and redoubled his efforts. He caught hold of Musashi's wrist, then hugged his arm, finally broke into tears.

Musashi, seeing no way out, said, "All right, all right, that's enough. You can be my follower, but only after you go and talk it over with your master."

Jōtarō, satisfied at last, trotted off to the sake shop.

The next morning, Musashi rose early, dressed, and called to the innkeeper, "Would you please fix me a lunch box? It's been nice staying here these few weeks, but I think I'll go on to Nara now."

"Leaving so soon?" asked the innkeeper, not expecting the sudden departure. "It's because that boy was pestering you, isn't it?"

"Oh, no, it's not his fault. I've been thinking about going to Nara for some time—to see the famous lance fighters at the Hōzōin. I hope he doesn't give you too much trouble when he finds out I'm gone."

"Don't worry about it. He's only a child. He'll scream and yell for a while, then forget all about it."

"I can't imagine that the sake man would let him leave anyway," said Musashi as he stepped out onto the road.

The storm had passed, as if wiped away, and the breeze brushed gently against Musashi's skin, quite unlike the fierce wind of the day before.

The Kamo River was up, the water muddy. At one end of the wooden bridge at Sanjō Avenue, samurai were examining all the people who came and went. Asking the reason for the inspection, Musashi was told it was because of the new shōgun's impending visit. A vanguard of influential and minor feudal lords had already arrived, and steps were being taken to keep dangerous unattached samurai out of the city. Musashi, himself a rōnin, gave ready answers to the questions asked and was allowed to pass.

The experience set him to thinking about his own status as a wandering masterless warrior pledged neither to the Tokugawas nor to their rivals in Osaka. Running off to Sekigahara and taking sides with the Osaka forces against the Tokugawas was a matter of inheritance. That had been his father's allegiance, unchanged from the days when he served under Lord Shimmen of Iga. Toyotomi Hideyoshi had died two years before the battle; his supporters, loyal to his son, made up the Osaka faction. In Miyamoto, Hideyoshi was considered the greatest of heroes, and Musashi remembered how as a child he had sat at the hearth and listened to tales of the great warrior's prowess. These ideas formed in his youth lingered with him, and even now, if pressed to say which side he favored, he'd probably have said Osaka.

Musashi had since learned a few things and now recognized that his actions at the age of seventeen had been both mindless and devoid of accomplishment. For a man to serve his lord faithfully, it was not enough to jump blindly into the fray and brandish a lance. He must go all the way, to the brink of death.

"If a samurai dies with a prayer for his lord's victory on his lips, he has done something fine and meaningful," was the way Musashi would have put it now. But at the time neither he nor Matahachi had had any sense of loyalty. What they had been thirsting for was fame and glory, and more to the point, a means of gaining a livelihood without giving up anything of their own.

It was odd that they should have thought of it that way. Having since learned from Takuan that life is a jewel to be treasured, Musashi knew that far from giving up nothing, he and Matahachi had unwittingly been offering their most precious possession. Each had literally wagered everything he had on the hope of receiving a paltry stipend as a samurai. In retrospect, he wondered how they could have been so foolish.

He noticed that he was approaching Daigo, south of the city, and since he'd worked up quite a sweat, decided to stop for a rest.

From a distance, he heard a voice shouting, "Wait! Wait!" Gazing far down
the steep mountain road, he made out the form of the little water sprite Jōtarō,

running for all he was worth. Presently the boy's angry eyes were glaring into his.

"You lied to me!" Jōtarō shouted. "Why did you do that!" Breathless from running, face flushed, he spoke with belligerence, though it was clear he was on the verge of tears.

Musashi had to laugh at his getup. He had discarded the work clothes of the day before in favor of an ordinary kimono, but it was only half big enough for him, the skirt barely reaching his knees and the arms stopping at the elbows. At his side hung a wooden sword that was longer than the boy was tall, on his back a basket hat that looked as big as an umbrella.

Even as he shouted at Musashi for having left him behind, he burst into tears. Musashi hugged and tried to comfort him, but the boy wailed on, apparently feeling that in the mountains, with no one around, he could let himself go.

Finally Musashi said, "Does it make you feel good, acting like a crybaby?"

"I don't care!" Jōtarō sobbed. "You're a grownup, and yet you lied to me. You said you'd let me be your follower—then went off and left me. Are grownups supposed to act like that?"

"I'm sorry," said Musashi.

This simple apology turned the boy's crying into a pleading whine.

"Stop it now," said Musashi. "I didn't mean to lie to you, but you have a father and you have a master. I couldn't bring you with me unless your master consented. I told you to go and talk with him, didn't I? It didn't seem likely to me that he'd agree."

"Why didn't you at least wait until you heard the answer?"

"That's why I'm apologizing to you now. Did you really discuss this with him?"

"Yes." He got his sniffling under control and pulled two leaves from a tree, on which he blew his nose.

"And what did he say?"

"He told me to go ahead."

"Did he now?"

"He said no self-respecting warrior or training school would take on a boy like me, but since the samurai at the inn was a weakling, he ought to be just the right person. He said maybe you could use me to carry your luggage, and he gave me this wooden sword as a going-away present."

Musashi smiled at the man's line of reasoning.

"After that," continued the boy, "I went to the inn. The old man wasn't there, so I just borrowed this hat from off the hook under the eaves."

"But that's the inn's signboard; it has 'Lodgings' written on it."

"Oh, I don't mind. I need a hat in case it rains."

It was clear from Jōtarō's attitude that as far as he was concerned, all necessary promises and vows had been exchanged, and he was now Musashi's disciple. Sensing this, Musashi resigned himself to being more or less stuck with the child, but it also occurred to him that maybe it was all for the best. Indeed, when he considered his own part in Tanzaemon's loss of status, he concluded that perhaps he should be grateful for the opportunity to see to the boy's future. It seemed the right thing to do.

Jōtarō, now calm and reassured, suddenly remembered something and reached inside his kimono. "I almost forgot. I have something for you. Here it is." He pulled out a letter.

Eyeing it curiously, Musashi asked, "Where did you get that?"

"Remember last night I said there was a rōnin drinking at the shop, asking a lot of questions?"

"Yes."

"Well, when I went home, he was still there. He kept on asking about you. He's some drinker, too—drank a whole bottle of sake by himself! Then he wrote this letter and asked me to give it to you."

Musashi cocked his head to one side in puzzlement and broke the seal. Looking first at the bottom, he saw it was from Matahachi, who must have been drunk indeed. Even the characters looked tipsy. As Musashi read the scroll, he was seized with mixed feelings of nostalgia and sadness. Not only was the writing chaotic; the message itself was rambling and imprecise.

> Since I left you at Mount Ibuki, I haven't forgotten the village. And I haven't forgotten my old friend. By accident I heard your name at the Yoshioka School. At the time, I got confused and couldn't decide whether to try to see you. Now I'm in a sake shop. I've had a lot to drink.

Thus far the meaning was clear enough, but from this point on the letter was difficult to follow.

> Ever since I parted from you, I've been kept in a cage of lust, and idleness has eaten into my bones. For five years I've spent my days in a stupor, doing nothing. In the capital, you are now famous as a swordsman. I drink to you! Some people say Musashi is a coward, good only at running away. Some say you're an incomparable swordsman. I don't care which is true, I'm just happy that your sword has the people in the capital talking.
>
> You're smart. You should be able to make your way with the sword. But as I look back, I wonder about me, the way I am now. I'm a fool! How can a stupid wretch like me face a wise friend like you without dying of shame?
>
> But wait! Life is long, and it's too early to say what the future will bring. I don't want to see you now, but there will come a day when I will.
>
> I pray for your health.

Then came a rapidly scrawled postscript informing him, at some length, that the Yoshioka School took a serious view of the recent incident, that they were looking everywhere for him, and that he should be careful about his movements. It ended: "You mustn't die now that you're just beginning to make a name for yourself. When I, too, have made something of myself, I want to see you and talk over old times. Take care of yourself, stay alive, so you can be an inspiration to me."

Matahachi had no doubt meant well, but there was something twisted about his attitude. Why must he praise Musashi so and in the next breath carry on so about his own failings? "Why," wondered Musashi, "couldn't he just write and say that it's been a long time, and why don't we get together and have a long talk?"

"Jō, did you ask this man for his address?"

"No."

"Did the people at the shop know him?"

"I don't think so."

"Did he come there often?"

"No, this was the first time."

Musashi was thinking that if he knew where Matahachi lived, he would go back to Kyoto right now to see him. He wanted to talk to his childhood comrade, try to bring him to his senses, reawaken in him the spirit he had once had. Since he still considered Matahachi to be his friend, he would have liked to pull him out of his present mood, with its apparently self-destructive tendencies. And of course, he would also have liked to have Matahachi explain to his mother what a mistake she was making.

The two walked on silently. They were on their way down the mountain at Daigo, and the Rokujizō crossing was visible below them.

Abruptly Musashi turned to the boy and said, "Jō, there's something I want you to do for me."

"What is it?"

"I want you to go on an errand."

"Where to?"

"Kyoto."

"That means turning around and going back where I just came from."

"That's right. I want you to take a letter from me to the Yoshioka School on Shijō Avenue."

Jōtarō, crestfallen, kicked a rock with his toe.

"Don't you want to go?" asked Musashi, looking him in the face.

Jōtarō shook his head uncertainly. "I don't mind going, but aren't you just doing this to get rid of me?"

His suspicion made Musashi feel guilty, for wasn't he the one who had broken the child's faith in adults?

"No!" he said vigorously. "A samurai does not lie. Forgive me for what happened this morning. It was just a mistake."

"All right, I'll go."

Entering a teahouse at the crossroads known as Rokuamida, they ordered tea and ate lunch.

Musashi then wrote a letter, which he addressed to Yoshioka Seijūrō:

> I am told that you and your disciples are searching for me. As it happens, I am now on the Yamato highroad, my intention being to travel around in the general area of Iga and Ise for about a year to continue my study of swordsmanship. I do not wish to change my plans at this time, but since I regret as much as you do that I was unable to meet you during my previous visit to your school, I should like to inform you that I shall certainly be back in the capital by the first or the second month of next year. Between now and then, I expect to improve my technique considerably. I trust that you yourself will not neglect your practice. It

143

would be a great shame if Yoshioka Kempō's flourishing school were to suffer a second defeat like the one it sustained the last time I was there. In closing, I send my respectful wishes for your continued good health.

Shimmen Miyamoto Musashi Masana

Though the letter was polite, it left little doubt as to Musashi's confidence in himself. Having amended the address to include not only Seijūrō but all the disciples in the school, he laid down his brush and gave the letter to Jōtarō.

"Can I just throw it in at the school and come back?" the boy asked.

"No. You must call at the front entrance and hand it personally to the servant there."

"I understand."

"There's something else I want you to do, but it may be a little difficult."

"What is it?"

"I want you to see if you can find the man who gave you the letter. His name is Hon'iden Matahachi. He's an old friend of mine."

"That should be no trouble at all."

"You think not? Just how do you propose to do it?"

"Oh, I'll ask around at all the drinking shops."

Musashi laughed. "That's not a bad idea. I gather from Matahachi's letter, however, that he knows somebody at the Yoshioka School. I think it would be quicker to ask about him there."

"What do I do when I find him?"

"I want you to deliver a message. Tell him that from the first to the seventh day of the new year, I'll go every morning to the great bridge at Gojō Avenue and wait for him. Ask him to come on one of those days to meet me."

"Is that all?"

"Yes, but also tell him that I want very badly to see him."

"All right, I think I have it. Where will you be when I come back?"

"I'll tell you what. When I get to Nara, I'll arrange it so that you can find out where I am by asking at the Hōzōin. That's the temple that's famous for its lance technique."

"You'll really do that?"

"Ha, ha! You're still suspicious, aren't you? Don't worry. If I don't keep my promise this time, you can cut off my head."

Musashi was still laughing as he left the teahouse. Outside, he turned toward Nara, and Jōtarō set off in the opposite direction, toward Kyoto.

The crossroads was a jumble of people under basket hats, of swallows and of neighing horses. As the boy made his way through the throng, he looked back and saw Musashi standing where he had been, watching him. They smiled a distant farewell, and each went on his way.

144

A Spring Breeze

On the bank of the Takase River, Akemi was rinsing a strip of cloth and singing a song she had learned at the Okuni Kabuki. Each time she pulled at the flower-patterned cloth, it created an illusion of swirling cherry blossoms.

> The breeze of love
> Tugs at the sleeve of my kimono.
> Oh, the sleeve weighs heavy!
> Is the breeze of love heavy?

Jōtarō stood on top of the dike. His lively eyes surveyed the scene and he smiled amicably. "You sing well, Auntie," he called out.

"What's that?" asked Akemi. She looked up at the gnomelike child with his long wooden sword and his enormous basket hat. "Who are you?" she asked. "And what do you mean, calling me Auntie? I'm still young!"

"Okay—Sweet Young Girl. How's that?"

"Stop it," she said with a laugh. "You're much too little to be flirting. Why don't you blow your nose instead?"

"I only wanted to ask a question."

"Oh, my!" she cried in consternation. "There goes my cloth!"

"I'll get it for you."

Jōtarō chased down the riverbank after the cloth, then fished it out of the water with his sword. At least, he reflected, it comes in handy in a situation like this one. Akemi thanked him and asked what he wanted to know.

"Is there a teahouse around here called the Yomogi?"

"Why, yes, it's my house, right over there."

"Am I glad to hear that! I've spent a long time looking for it."

"Why? Where do you come from?"

"Over that way," he replied, pointing vaguely.

"And just where might that be?"

He hesitated. "I'm not really sure."

Akemi giggled. "Never mind. But why are you interested in our teahouse?"

"I'm looking for a man named Hon'iden Matahachi. They told me at the Yoshioka School that if I went to the Yomogi, I'd find him."

"He's not there."

"You're lying!"

"Oh, no; it's true. He used to stay with us, but he went off some time ago."

"Where to?"

145

"I don't know."

"But someone at your house must know!"

"No. My mother doesn't know either. He just ran away."

"Oh, no." The boy crouched down and stared worriedly into the river. "Now what am I supposed to do?" he sighed.

"Who sent you here?"

"My teacher."

"Who's your teacher?"

"His name is Miyamoto Musashi."

"Did you bring a letter?"

"No," said Jōtarō, shaking his head.

"A fine messenger you are! You don't know where you came from, and you don't have a letter with you."

"I have a message to deliver."

"What is it? He may never come back, but if he does, I'll tell him for you."

"I don't think I should do that, do you?"

"Don't ask me. Make up your own mind."

"Maybe I should, then. He said he wanted to see Matahachi very much. He said to tell Matahachi that he'd wait on the great bridge at Gojō Avenue every morning from the first day to the seventh day of the new year. Matahachi should meet him there on one of those days."

Akemi broke into uncontrollable laughter. "I never heard of such a thing! You mean he's sending a message *now* telling Matahachi to meet him next year? Your teacher must be as strange as you are! Ha, ha!"

A scowl came over Jōtarō's face, and his shoulders tensed with anger. "What's so funny?"

Akemi finally managed to stop laughing. "Now you're angry, aren't you?"

"Of course I am. I just asked you politely to do me a favor, and you start laughing like a lunatic."

"I'm sorry, I really am. I won't laugh anymore. And if Matahachi comes back, I'll give him your message."

"Is that a promise?"

"Yes, I swear." Biting her lips to avoid smiling, Akemi asked, "What was his name again? The man who sent you with the message."

"Your memory's not too good, is it? His name is Miyamoto Musashi."

"How do you write Musashi?"

Picking up a bamboo stick, Jōtarō scratched the two characters in the sand.

"Why, those are the characters for Takezō!" exclaimed Akemi.

"His name isn't Takezō. It's Musashi."

"Yes, but they can also be read Takezō."

"Stubborn, aren't you?" snapped Jōtarō, tossing the bamboo stick into the river.

Akemi stared fixedly at the characters in the sand, lost in thought. Finally she lifted her gaze from the ground to Jōtarō, reexamined him from head to toe, and in a soft voice asked, "I wonder if Musashi is from the Yoshino area in Mimasaka."

146

"Yes. I'm from Harima; he's from the village of Miyamoto in the neighboring province of Mimasaka."

"Is he tall and manly? And does he leave the top of his head unshaved?"

"Yes. How did you know?"

"I remember him telling me once that when he was a child he had a carbuncle on the top of his head. If he shaved it the way samurai usually do, you would see an ugly scar."

"Told you? When?"

"Oh, it's been five years now."

"Have you known my teacher that long?"

Akemi did not answer. The memory of those days evoked stirrings in her heart that made even speaking difficult. Convinced from the little the boy had said that Musashi was Takezō, she was gripped by a yearning to see him again. She had seen her mother's way of doing things, and she had watched Matahachi go from bad to worse. From the first, she had preferred Takezō and had since grown more and more confident in the rightness of his choice. She was glad to be still single. Takezō—he was so different from Matahachi.

Many were the times she had resolved to never let herself wind up with the likes of the men who always drank at the teahouse. She scorned them, holding on firmly to the image of Takezō. Deep within her heart, she nourished the dream of finding him again; he, only he, was the lover in her mind when she sang love songs to herself.

His mission fulfilled, Jōtarō said, "Well, I'd better be going now. If you find Matahachi, be sure to tell him what I told you." He hurried off, trotting along the narrow top of the dike.

The oxcart was loaded with a mountain of sacks, containing rice perhaps, or lentil beans, or some other local product. On top of the pile, a plaque proclaimed that this was a contribution being sent by faithful Buddhists to the great Kōfukuji in Nara. Even Jōtarō knew of this temple, for its name was virtually synonymous with Nara.

Jōtarō's face lit up with childish joy. Chasing after the vehicle, he climbed up on back. If he faced backward, there was just enough room to sit down. As an added luxury, he had the sacks to lean against.

On either side of the road, the rolling hills were covered with neat rows of tea bushes. The cherry trees had begun to bloom, and farmers were plowing their barley—praying, no doubt, that this year it would once again be safe from the trampling feet of soldiers and horses. Women knelt by the streams washing their vegetables. The Yamato highroad was at peace.

"What luck!" thought Jōtarō, as he settled back and relaxed. Comfortable on his perch, he was tempted to go to sleep but thought better of it. Fearing they might reach Nara before he awoke, he was thankful every time the wheels struck a rock and the wagon shook, since it helped him keep his eyes open. Nothing could have given him more pleasure than to be not only moving along like this but actually heading toward his destination.

Outside one village, Jōtarō lazily reached out and plucked a leaf from a camellia tree. Putting it to his tongue, he began to whistle a tune.

The wagon driver looked back, but could see nothing. Since the whistling went on and on, he looked over his left shoulder, then his right shoulder, several more times. Finally he stopped the wagon and walked around to the back. The sight of Jōtarō threw him into a rage, and the blow from his fist was so sharp the boy cried out in pain.

"What're you doing up there?" he snarled.

"It's all right, isn't it?"

"It is not all right!"

"Why not? You're not pulling it yourself!"

"You impudent little bastard!" shouted the driver, tossing Jōtarō onto the ground like a ball. He bounced and rolled against the foot of a tree. Starting off with a rumble, the wheels of the wagon seemed to be laughing at him.

Jōtarō picked himself up and began to search carefully around on the ground. He'd just noticed he no longer had the bamboo tube containing the reply from the Yoshioka School to Musashi. He had hung it from his neck with a cord, but now it was gone.

As the totally distraught boy gradually widened the area of his search, a young woman in traveling clothes, who had stopped to watch him, asked, "Did you lose something?"

He glanced at her face, which was partially hidden by a broad-brimmed hat, nodded and resumed his search.

"Was it money?"

Jōtarō, thoroughly absorbed, paid little attention to the question, but managed a negative grunt.

"Well, was it a bamboo tube about a foot long with a cord attached?"

Jōtarō jumped up. "Yes! How did you know?"

"So it was you the drivers near the Mampukuji were yelling at for teasing their horse!"

"Ah-h-h . . . well . . . "

"When you got scared and ran, the cord must've broken. The tube fell on the road, and the samurai who'd been talking to the drivers picked it up. Why don't you go back and ask him about it?"

"Are you sure?"

"Yes, of course."

"Thanks."

Just as he started to run off, the young woman called after him. "Wait! There's no need to go back. I can see the samurai coming this way. The one in the field *hakama*." She pointed toward the man.

Jōtarō stopped and waited, eyes wide.

The samurai was an impressive man of about forty. Everything about him was a little bigger than life—his height, his jet-black beard, his broad shoulders, his massive chest. He wore leather socks and straw sandals, and when he walked, his firm footsteps seemed to compact the earth. Jōtarō, certain at a glance that this was a great warrior in the service of one of the more prominent daimyō, felt too frightened to address him.

Fortunately, the samurai spoke first, summoning the boy. "Weren't you the imp who dropped this bamboo tube in front of the Mampukuji?" he asked.

"Oh, that's it! You found it!"

"Don't you know how to say thank you?"

"I'm sorry. Thank you, sir."

"I daresay there's an important letter inside. When your master sends you on a mission, you shouldn't be stopping along the way to tease horses, hitching rides on wagons, or loafing by the wayside."

"Yes, sir. Did you look inside, sir?"

"It's only natural when you've found something to examine it and return it to its owner, but I did not break the seal on the letter. Now that you have it back, you should check and see that it's in good order."

Jōtarō took the cap from the tube and peered inside. Satisfied that the letter was still there, he hung the tube from his neck and swore not to lose it a second time.

The young woman looked as pleased as Jōtarō. "It was very kind of you, sir," she said to the samurai, in an attempt to make up for Jōtarō's inability to express himself properly.

The bearded samurai started walking along with the two of them. "Is the boy with you?" he asked her.

"Oh, no. I've never seen him before."

The samurai laughed. "I thought you made a rather strange pair. He's a funny-looking little devil, isn't he—'Lodgings' written on his hat and all?"

"Perhaps it's his youthful innocence that's so appealing. I like him too." Turning to Jōtarō, she asked, "Where are you going?"

Walking along between them, Jōtarō was once again in high spirits. "Me? I'm going to Nara, to the Hōzōin." A long, narrow object wrapped in gold brocade and nestled in the girl's obi caught his eye. Staring at it, he said, "I see you have a letter tube too. Be careful you don't lose it."

"Letter tube? What do you mean?"

"There, in your obi."

She laughed. "This isn't a letter tube, silly! It's a flute."

"A flute?" Eyes burning with curiosity, Jōtarō unabashedly moved his head close to her waist to inspect the object. Suddenly, a strange feeling came over him. He pulled back and seemed to be examining the girl.

Even children have a sense of feminine beauty, or at least they understand instinctively whether a woman is pure or not. Jōtarō was impressed with the girl's loveliness and respected it. It seemed to him an unimaginable stroke of good luck that he should be walking along with one so pretty. His heart throbbed and he felt giddy.

"I see. A flute . . . Do you play the flute, Auntie?" he asked. Then, obviously remembering Akemi's reaction to the word, he abruptly changed his question. "What's your name?"

The girl laughed and cast an amused glance over the boy's head at the samurai. The bearlike warrior joined in the laughter, displaying a row of strong white teeth behind his beard.

"You're a fine one, you are! When you ask someone's name, it's only good manners to state your own first."

"My name's Jōtarō."

This brought forth more laughter.

"That's not fair!" cried Jōtarō. "You made me tell my name, but I still don't know yours. What's your name, sir?"

"My name's Shōda," said the samurai.

"That must be your family name. What's your other name?"

"I'll have to ask you to let me off on that one."

Undaunted, Jōtarō turned to the girl and said, "Now it's your turn. We told you our names. It wouldn't be polite for you not to tell us yours."

"Mine is Otsū."

"Otsū?" Jōtarō repeated. He seemed satisfied for a moment, but then chattered on. "Why do you go around with a flute in your obi?"

"Oh, I need this to make my living."

"Are you a flute player by profession?"

"Well, I'm not sure there's any such thing as a professional flute player, but the money I get for playing makes it possible for me to take long trips like this one. I suppose you could call it my profession."

"Is the music you play like the music I've heard at Gion and the Kamo Shrine? The music for the sacred dances?"

"No."

"Is it like the music for other kinds of dancing—Kabuki maybe?"

"No."

"Then what kind do you play?"

"Oh, just ordinary melodies."

The samurai had meanwhile been wondering about Jōtarō's long wooden sword. "What's that you've got stuck in your waist?" he asked.

"Don't you know a wooden sword when you see one? I thought you were a samurai."

"Yes, I am. I'm just surprised to see one on you. Why are you carrying it?"

"I'm going to study swordsmanship."

"Oh, are you now? Do you have a teacher yet?"

"I do."

"And is he the person to whom the letter is addressed?"

"Yes."

"If he's your teacher, he must be a *real* expert."

"He's not all that good."

"What do you mean?"

"Everybody says he's weak."

"Doesn't it bother you to have a weak man for a teacher?"

"No. I'm no good with the sword either, so it doesn't make any difference."

The samurai could hardly contain his amusement. His mouth quivered as if to break into a smile, but his eyes remained grave. "Have you learned any techniques?"

"Well, not exactly. I haven't learned anything at all yet."

The samurai's laughter finally burst forth. "Walking with you makes the road seem shorter! . . . And you, young lady, where are you going?"

"Nara, but exactly where in Nara I don't know. There's a rōnin I've been trying to locate for a year or so, and since I've heard that a lot of them have gathered in Nara recently, I'm planning to go there, though I admit the rumor's not much to go on."

The bridge at Uji came into view. Under the eaves of a teahouse, a very proper old man with a large teakettle was purveying his stock-in-trade to his customers, who were seated around him on stools. Catching sight of Shōda, he greeted him warmly. "How nice to see someone from the House of Yagyū!" he called. "Come in, come in!"

"We'd just like to take a short rest. Could you bring the boy here some sweet cakes?"

Jōtarō remained on his feet while his companions sat. To him, the idea of sitting down and resting was a bore; once the cakes arrived, he grabbed them and ran up the low hill behind the teahouse.

Otsū, sipping her tea, inquired of the old man, "Is it still a long way to Nara?"

"Yes. Even a fast walker'd probably get no farther than Kizu before sunset. A girl like you should plan to spend the night at Taga or Ide."

Shōda spoke up immediately. "This young lady has been searching for someone for months. But I wonder, do you think it's safe these days for a young woman to travel to Nara alone, with no place to stay in mind?"

The old man grew wide-eyed at the question. "She shouldn't even consider it!" he said decisively. Turning to Otsū, he waved his hand back and forth before his face and said, "Give the idea up entirely. If you were sure you had someone to stay with, it'd be a different matter. If you don't, Nara can be a very dangerous place."

The proprietor poured a cup of tea for himself and told them what he knew of the situation in Nara. Most people, it seemed, had the impression that the old capital was a quiet, peaceful place where there were lots of colorful temples and tame deer—a place undisturbed by war or famine—but in fact the town was no longer like that at all. After the Battle of Sekigahara, nobody knew how many rōnin from the losing side had come to hide there. Most of them were Osaka partisans from the Western Army, samurai who now had no income and little hope of finding another profession. With the Tokugawa shogunate growing in power year by year, it was doubtful whether these fugitives would ever again be able to make a living out in the open with their swords.

According to most estimates, 120,000 to 130,000 samurai had lost their positions. Being the victors, the Tokugawas had confiscated estates representing an annual income of 33 million bushels of rice. Even if the feudal lords who had since been allowed to reestablish themselves on a more modest scale were taken into consideration, at least eighty daimyō, with incomes thought to total 20 million bushels, had been dispossessed. On the basis that for every 500 bushels, three samurai had been cut loose from their moorings and forced into hiding in various provinces—and including their families and retainers—the total number could not be less than 100,000.

The area around Nara and Mount Kōya was full of temples and therefore difficult for the Tokugawa forces to patrol. By the same token, it was an ideal hiding place, and the fugitives moved there in droves.

"Why," said the old man, "the famous Sanada Yukimura is in hiding at Mount Kudo, and Sengoku Sōya is said to be in the vicinity of the Hōryūji, and Ban Dan'emon at the Kōfukuji. I could name many more." All these were marked men, who would be killed instantly if they showed themselves; their one hope for the future was for war to break out again.

The old man's opinion was that it wouldn't be so bad if it were only these famous rōnin hiding out, since they all had a degree of prestige and could make a living for themselves and their families. Complicating the picture, however, were the indigent samurai who prowled the city's back streets in such straits that they'd sell their swords if they could. Half of them had taken to picking fights, gambling and otherwise disturbing the peace, in the hope that the havoc they caused would make the Osaka forces rise up and take arms. The once tranquil city of Nara had turned into a nest of desperadoes. For a nice girl like Otsū to go there would be tantamount to her pouring oil on her kimono and jumping into a fire. The teahouse proprietor, stirred by his own recitation, concluded by strongly begging Otsū to change her mind.

Now doubtful, Otsū sat silently for a while. If she had had the slightest indication that Musashi might be in Nara, she would not have given danger a second thought. But she really had nothing to go on. She had merely wandered toward Nara—just as she had wandered around to various other places in the year since Musashi had left her stranded at the bridge in Himeji.

Shōda, seeing the perplexity on her face, said, "You said your name is Otsū, didn't you?"

"Yes."

"Well, Otsū, I hesitate to say this, but why don't you give up the idea of going to Nara and come with me to the Koyagyū fief instead?" Feeling obliged to tell her more about himself and assure her that his intentions were honorable, he continued, "My full name is Shōda Kizaemon, and I'm in the service of the Yagyū family. It happens that my lord, who's now eighty, is no longer active. He suffers terribly from boredom. When you said you make your living by playing the flute, it occurred to me that it might be a great comfort to him if you were around to play for him from time to time. Do you think you'd like that?"

The old man immediately chimed in with enthusiastic approval. "You should definitely go with him," he urged. "As you probably know, the old lord of Koyagyū is the great Yagyū Muneyoshi. Now that he's retired, he's taken the name Sekishūsai. As soon as his heir, Munenori, lord of Tajima, returned from Sekigahara, he was summoned to Edo and appointed an instructor in the shōgun's household. Why, there's no greater family in Japan than the Yagyūs. To be invited to Koyagyū is an honor in itself. Please, by all means, accept!"

On hearing that Kizaemon was an official in the famous House of Yagyū, Otsū congratulated herself for having guessed that he was no ordinary samurai. Still, she found it difficult to reply to his proposal.

Faced with her silence, Kizaemon asked, "Don't you want to come?"

"It's not that. I couldn't wish for a better offer. I'm simply afraid my playing isn't good enough for a great man like Yagyū Muneyoshi."

"Oh, don't give it a second thought. The Yagyūs are very different from the other daimyō. Sekishūsai in particular has the simple, quiet tastes of a tea-master. He would be more upset, I think, by your diffidence than by what you fancy to be your lack of skill."

Otsū realized that going to Koyagyū, rather than wandering aimlessly to Nara, offered some hope, however slight. Since the death of Yoshioka Kempō, the Yagyūs had been considered by many to be the greatest exponents of the martial arts in the country. It was only to be expected that swordsmen from all over the country would call at their gate, and there might even be a registry of visitors. How happy she would be if on that list she found the name of Miya-moto Musashi!

With that possibility foremost in mind, she said brightly, "If you really think it's all right, I'll go."

"You will? Wonderful! I'm very grateful. . . . Hmm, I doubt that a woman could walk all the way there before nightfall. Can you ride a horse?"

"Yes."

Kizaemon ducked under the eaves of the shop and raised his hand toward the bridge. The groom waiting there came running forward with a horse, which Kizaemon let Otsū ride, while he himself walked along beside her.

Jōtarō spotted them from the hill behind the teahouse and called, "Are you leaving already?"

"Yes, we're off."

"Wait for me!"

They were halfway across Uji Bridge when Jōtarō caught up with them. Kizaemon asked him what he had been up to, and he answered that a lot of men in a grove on the hill were playing some kind of game. He didn't know what game it was, but it looked interesting.

The groom laughed. "That would be the rōnin riffraff having a gambling session. They don't have enough money to eat, so they lure travelers into their games and take them for everything they're worth. It's disgraceful!"

"Oh, so they gamble for a living?" asked Kizaemon.

"The gamblers are among the better ones," replied the groom. "Many others have become kidnappers and blackmailers. They're such a rough lot nobody can do anything to stop them."

"Why doesn't the lord of the district arrest them or drive them away?"

"There are too many of them—far more than he can cope with. If all the rōnin from Kawachi, Yamato and Kii joined together, they'd be stronger than his own troops."

"I hear Kōga's swarming with them too."

"Yes. The ones from Tsutsui fled there. They're determined to hang on until the next war."

"You keep talking that way about the rōnin," Jōtarō broke in, "but some of them must be good men."

"That's true," agreed Kizaemon.

153

"My teacher's a rōnin!"

Kizaemon laughed and said, "So that's why you spoke up in their defense. You're loyal enough. . . . You did say you were on your way to the Hōzōin, didn't you? Is that where your teacher is?"

"I don't know for sure, but he said if I went there, they'd tell me where he is."

"What style does he use?"

"I don't know."

"You're his disciple, and you don't know his style?"

"Sir," the groom put in, "swordsmanship is a fad these days; everybody and his brother's going around studying it. You can meet five or ten wandering on this road alone any day of the week. It's all because there are so many more rōnin around to give lessons than there used to be."

"I suppose that's part of it."

"They're attracted to it because they hear somewhere that if a fellow's good with a sword, the daimyō will fall all over each other trying to hire him for four or five thousand bushels a year."

"A quick way to get rich, uh?"

"Exactly. When you think about it, it's frightening. Why, even this boy here has a wooden sword. He probably thinks he just has to learn how to hit people with it to become a real man. We get a lot like that, and the sad part is, in the end, most of them will go hungry."

Jōtarō's anger rose in a flash. "What's that? I dare you to say that again!"

"Listen to him! He looks like a flea carrying a toothpick, but he already fancies himself a great warrior."

Kizaemon laughed. "Now, Jōtarō, don't get mad, or you'll lose your bamboo tube again."

"No I won't! Don't worry about me!"

They walked on, Jōtarō sulking silently, the others looking at the sun as it slowly set. Presently they arrived at the Kizu River ferry landing.

"This is where we leave you, my boy. It'll be dark soon, so you'd better hurry. And don't waste time along the way."

"Otsū?" said Jōtarō, thinking she would come with him.

"Oh, I forgot to tell you," she said. "I've decided to go along with this gentleman to the castle at Koyagyū." Jōtarō looked crushed. "Take good care of yourself," Otsū said, smiling.

"I should've known I'd wind up alone again." He picked up a stone and sent it skimming across the water.

"Oh, we'll see each other again one of these days. Your home seems to be the road, and I do a bit of traveling myself."

Jōtarō didn't seem to want to move. "Just who are you looking for?" he asked. "What sort of person?"

Without answering, Otsū waved farewell.

Jōtarō ran along the bank and jumped into the very middle of the small ferryboat. When the boat, red in the evening sun, was halfway across the river, he looked back. He could just make out Otsū's horse and Kizaemon on the

Kasagi Temple road. They were in the valley, beyond the point where the river suddenly grows narrower, slowly being swallowed up by the early shadows of the mountain.

The Hōzōin

Students of the martial arts invariably knew of the Hōzōin. For a man who claimed to be a serious student to refer to it as just another temple was sufficient reason for him to be regarded as an impostor. It was well known among the local populace too, though, oddly enough, few were familiar with the much more important Shōsōin Repository and its priceless collection of ancient art objects.

The temple was located on Abura Hill in a large, dense forest of cryptomeria trees. It was just the kind of place goblins might inhabit. Here, too, were reminders of the glories of the Nara period—the ruins of a temple, the Ganrin'in, and of the huge public bathhouse built by the Empress Kōmyō for the poor—but today all that was left was a scattering of foundation stones peeking out through the moss and weeds.

Musashi had no difficulty getting directions to Abura Hill, but once there he stood looking all around in bewilderment, for there were quite a few other temples nestled in the forest. The cryptomerias had weathered the winter and been bathed in the early spring rains, and their leaves were now at their darkest. Above them one could make out in the approaching twilight the soft feminine curves of Mount Kasuga. The distant mountains still lay in bright sunlight.

Although none of the temples looked like the right one, Musashi went from gate to gate inspecting the plaques on which their names were inscribed. His mind was so preoccupied with the Hōzōin that when he saw the plaque of the Ōzōin, he at first misread it, since only the first character, that for Ō, was different. Although he immediately realized his mistake, he took a look inside anyway. The Ōzōin appeared to belong to the Nichiren sect; as far as he knew, the Hōzōin was a Zen temple having no connection with Nichiren.

As he stood there, a young monk returning to the Ōzōin passed by him, staring suspiciously.

Musashi removed his hat and said, "Could I trouble you for some information?"

"What would you like to know?"

"This temple is called the Ōzōin?"

"Yes. That's what it says on the plaque."

"I was told that the Hōzōin is on Abura Hill. Isn't it?"

"It's just in back of this temple. Are you going there for a fencing bout?"

"Yes."

"Then let me give you some advice. Forget it."

"Why?"

"It's dangerous. I can understand someone born crippled going there to get his legs straightened out, but I see no reason why anyone with good straight limbs should go there and be maimed."

The monk was well built and somehow different from the ordinary Nichiren monk. According to him, the number of would-be warriors had reached the point where even the Hōzōin had come to regard them as a nuisance. The temple was, after all, a holy sanctuary for the light of the Buddha's Law, as its name indicated. Its real concern was religion. The martial arts were only a sideline, so to speak.

Kakuzenbō In'ei, the former abbot, had often called on Yagyū Muneyoshi. Through his association with Muneyoshi and with Lord Kōizumi of Ise, Muneyoshi's friend, he had developed an interest in the martial arts and eventually taken up swordsmanship as a pastime. From that he had gone on to devise new ways of using the lance, and this, as Musashi already knew, was the origin of the highly regarded Hōzōin Style.

In'ei was now eighty-four years old and completely senile. He saw almost no one. Even when he did receive a caller, he was unable to carry on a conversation; he could only sit and make unintelligible movements with his toothless mouth. He didn't seem to comprehend anything said to him. As for the lance, he had forgotten about it completely.

"And so you see," concluded the monk after explaining all this, "it wouldn't do you much good to go there. You probably couldn't meet the master, and even if you did, you wouldn't learn anything." His brusque manner made it clear that he was eager to be rid of Musashi.

Though aware he was being made light of, Musashi persisted. "I've heard about In'ei, and I know what you've said about him is true. But I've also heard that a priest named Inshun has taken over as his successor. They say he's still studying but already knows all the secrets of the Hōzōin Style. According to what I've heard, although he already has many students, he never refuses to give guidance to anyone who calls on him."

"Oh, Inshun," said the monk disdainfully. "There's nothing in those rumors. Inshun is actually a student of the abbot of the Ōzōin. After In'ei began to show his age, our abbot felt it would be a shame for the reputation of the Hōzōin to go to waste, so he taught Inshun the secrets of lance fighting—what he himself had learned from In'ei—and then saw to it that Inshun became abbot."

"I see," said Musashi.

"But you still want to go over there?"

"Well, I've come all this distance. . . ."

"Yes, of course."

"You said it's behind here. Is it better to go around to the left or to the right?"

"You don't have to go around. It's much quicker just to walk straight through our temple. You can't miss it."

Thanking him, Musashi walked past the temple kitchen to the back of the compound, which with its woodshed, a storehouse for bean paste and a vegetable garden of an acre or so, very much resembled the area around the house of a well-to-do farmer. Beyond the garden he saw the Hōzōin.

Walking on the soft ground between rows of rape, radishes and scallions, he noticed, off to one side, an old man hoeing vegetables. Hunched over his hoe, he was looking intently at the blade. All Musashi could see of his face was a pair of snow-white eyebrows, and save for the clank of the hoe against the rocks, it was perfectly quiet.

Musashi assumed that the old man must be a monk from the Ōzōin. He started to speak, but the man was so absorbed in his work that it seemed rude to disturb him.

As he walked silently by, however, he suddenly became aware that the old man was staring out of the corner of his eye at Musashi's feet. Although the other man neither moved nor spoke, Musashi felt a terrifying force attack him—a force like lightning splitting the clouds. This was no daydream. He actually felt the mysterious power pierce his body and, terrified, he leaped into the air. He felt hot all over, as if he'd just narrowly avoided a death blow from a sword or lance.

Looking over his shoulder, he saw that the hunched back was still turned toward him, the hoe continuing its unbroken rhythm. "What on earth was that all about?" he wondered, dumbfounded by the power he'd been hit with.

He found himself in front of the Hōzōin, his curiosity unabated. While waiting for a servant to appear, he thought: "Inshun should still be a young man. The young monk said In'ei was senile and had forgotten all about the lance, but I wonder. . . ." The incident in the garden lingered in the back of his mind.

He called out loudly two more times, but the only reply was an echo from the surrounding trees. Noticing a large gong beside the entrance, he struck it. Almost immediately an answering call came from deep inside the temple.

A priest came to the door. He was big and brawny; had he been one of the warrior-priests of Mount Hiei, he might well have been the commander of a battalion. Accustomed as he was to receiving visits from people like Musashi day in and day out, he gave him a brief glance and said, "You're a *shugyōsha?*"

"Yes."

"What are you here for?"

"I'd like to meet the master."

The priest said, "Come in," and gestured to the right of the entrance, suggesting obliquely that Musashi should wash his feet first. There was a barrel overflowing with water supplied by a bamboo pipe and, pointing this way and that, about ten pairs of worn and dirty sandals.

Musashi followed the priest down a wide dark corridor and was shown into an anteroom. There he was told to wait. The smell of incense was in the air, and through the window he could see the broad leaves of a plantain tree. Aside from the offhand manner of the giant who'd let him in, nothing he saw indicated there was anything unusual about this particular temple.

When he reappeared, the priest handed him a registry and ink box, saying, "Write down your name, where you studied, and what style you use." He spoke as though instructing a child.

The title on the registry was: "List of Persons Visiting This Temple to Study. Steward of the Hōzōin." Musashi opened the book and glanced over the names, each listed under the date on which the samurai or student had called. Following the style of the last entry, he wrote down the required information, omitting the name of his teacher.

The priest, of course, was especially interested in that.

Musashi's answer was essentially the one he'd given at the Yoshioka School. He had practiced the use of the truncheon under his father, "without working very hard at it." Since making up his mind to study in earnest, he had taken as his teacher everything in the universe, as well as the examples set by his predecessors throughout the country. He ended up by saying, "I'm still in the process of learning."

"Mm. You probably know this already, but since the time of our first master, the Hōzōin has been celebrated everywhere for its lance techniques. The fighting that goes on here is rough, and there are no exceptions. Before you go on, perhaps you'd better read what's written at the beginning of the registry."

Musashi picked up the book, opened it and read the stipulation, which he had skipped over before. It said: "Having come here for the purpose of study, I absolve the temple of all responsibility in the event that I suffer bodily injury or am killed."

"I agree to that," said Musashi with a slight grin—it amounted to no more than common sense for anyone committed to becoming a warrior.

"All right. This way."

The dōjō was immense. The monks must have sacrificed a lecture hall or some other large temple building in favor of having it. Musashi had never before seen a hall with columns of such girth, and he also observed traces of paint, gold foil and Chinese-white primer on the frame of the transom—things not to be found in ordinary practice halls.

He was by no means the only visitor. More than ten student-warriors were seated in the waiting area, with a similar number of student-priests. In addition, there were quite a few samurai who seemed to be merely observers. All were tensely watching two lancers fighting a practice bout. No one even glanced Musashi's way as he sat down in a corner.

According to a sign on the wall, if anyone wanted to fight with real lances, the challenge would be accepted, but the combatants now on the floor were using long oak practice poles. A strike could, nevertheless, be extremely painful, even fatal.

158   One of the fighters was eventually thrown in the air, and as he limped back

to his seat in defeat, Musashi could see that his thigh had already swollen to the size of a tree trunk. Unable to sit down, he dropped awkwardly to one knee and extended the wounded leg out before him.

"Next!" came the summons from the man on the floor, a priest of singularly arrogant manner. The sleeves of his robe were tied up behind him, and his whole body—legs, arms, shoulders, even his forehead—seemed to consist of bulging muscles. The oak pole he held vertically was at least ten feet in length.

A man who seemed to be one of those who'd arrived that day spoke up. He fastened up his sleeves with a leather thong and strode into the practice area. The priest stood motionless as the challenger went to the wall, chose a halberd, and came to face him. They bowed, as was customary, but no sooner had they done this than the priest let out a howl like that of a wild hound, simultaneously bringing his pole down forcefully on the challenger's skull.

"Next," he called, reverting to his original position.

That was all: the challenger was finished. While he did not appear to be dead yet, the simple act of lifting his head from the floor was more than he could manage. A couple of the student-priests went out and dragged him back by the sleeves and waist of his kimono. On the floor behind him stretched a thread of saliva mixed with blood.

"Next!" shouted the priest again, as surly as ever.

At first Musashi thought he was the second-generation master Inshun, but the men sitting around him said no, he was Agon, one of the senior disciples who were known as the "Seven Pillars of the Hōzōin." Inshun himself, they said, never had to engage in a bout, because challengers were always put down by one of these.

"Is there no one else?" bellowed Agon, now holding his practice lance horizontally.

The brawny steward was comparing his registry with the faces of the waiting men. He pointed at one.

"No, not today. . . . I'll come again some other time."

"How about you?"

"No. I don't feel quite up to it today."

One by one they backed out, until Musashi saw the finger pointing at him.

"How about you?"

"If you please."

" 'If you please'? What's that supposed to mean?"

"It means I'd like to fight."

All eyes focused on Musashi as he rose. The haughty Agon had retired from the floor and was talking and laughing animatedly with a group of priests, but when it appeared that another challenger had been found, a bored look came over his face, and he said lazily, "Somebody take over for me."

"Go ahead," they urged. "There's only one more."

Giving in, Agon walked nonchalantly back to the center of the floor. He took a fresh grip on the shiny black wooden pole, with which he seemed totally familiar. In quick order, he assumed an attacking stance, turned his back on Musashi, and charged off in the other direction.

"Yah-h-h-h!" Screaming like an enraged roc, he hurtled toward the back wall and thrust his lance viciously into a section used for practice purposes. The boards had been recently replaced, but despite the resilience of the new wood, Agon's bladeless lance plowed straight through.

"Yow-w-w!" His grotesque scream of triumph reverberated through the hall as he disengaged the lance and started to dance, rather than walk, back toward Musashi, steam rising from his muscle-bound body. Taking a stance some distance away, he glared at his latest challenger ferociously. Musashi had come forward with only his wooden sword and now stood quite still, looking a little surprised.

"Ready!" cried Agon.

A dry laugh was heard outside the window, and a voice said, "Agon, don't be a fool! Look, you stupid oaf, look! That's not a board you're about to take on."

Without relaxing his stance, Agon looked toward the window. "Who's there?" he bellowed.

The laughter continued, and then there came into view above the window-sill, as though it had been hung there by an antique dealer, a shiny pate and a pair of snow-white eyebrows.

"It won't do you any good, Agon. Not this time. Let the man wait until the day after tomorrow, when Inshun returns."

Musashi, who had also turned his head toward the window, saw that the face belonged to the old man he had seen on his way to the Hōzōin, but no sooner had he realized this than the head disappeared.

Agon heeded the old man's warning to the extent of relaxing his hold on his weapon, but the minute his eyes met Musashi's again, he swore in the direction of the now empty window—and ignored the advice he had received.

As Agon tightened his grip on his lance, Musashi asked, for the sake of form, "Are you ready now?"

This solicitude drove Agon wild. His muscles were like steel, and when he jumped, he did so with awesome lightness. His feet seemed to be on the floor and in the air at the same time, quivering like moonlight on ocean waves.

Musashi stood perfectly still, or so it seemed. There was nothing unusual about his stance; he held his sword straight out with both hands, but being slightly smaller than his opponent and not so conspicuously muscular, he looked almost casual. The greatest difference was in the eyes. Musashi's were as sharp as a bird's, their pupils a clear coral tinted with blood.

Agon shook his head, perhaps to shake off the streams of sweat pouring down from his forehead, perhaps to shake off the old man's warning words. Had they lingered on? Was he attempting to cast them out of his mind? Whatever the reason, he was extremely agitated. He repeatedly shifted his position, trying to draw out Musashi, but Musashi remained motionless.

Agon's lunge was accompanied by a piercing scream. In the split second that decided the encounter, Musashi parried and counterattacked.

160   "What happened?"

Agon's fellow priests hastily ran forward and crowded around him in a black circle. In the general confusion, some tripped over his practice lance and went sprawling.

A priest stood up, his hands and chest smeared with blood, shouting, "Medicine! Bring the medicine. Quick!"

"You won't need any medicine." It was the old man, who had come in the front entrance and quickly assessed the situation. His face turned sour. "If I'd thought medicine would save him, I wouldn't have tried to stop him in the first place. The idiot!"

No one paid any attention to Musashi. For lack of anything better to do, he walked to the front door and began putting his sandals on.

The old man followed him. "You!" he said.

Over his shoulder, Musashi replied, "Yes?"

"I'd like to have a few words with you. Come back inside."

He led Musashi to a room behind the practice hall—a simple, square cell, the only opening in the four walls being the door.

After they were seated, the old man said, "It would be more proper for the abbot to come and greet you, but he's on a trip and won't be back for two or three days. So I'll act on his behalf."

"This is very kind of you," said Musashi, bowing his head. "I'm grateful for the good training I received today, but I feel I should apologize for the unfortunate way it turned out—"

"Why? Things like that happen. You have to be ready to accept it before you start fighting. Don't let it worry you."

"How are Agon's injuries?"

"He was killed instantly," said the old man. The breath with which he spoke felt like a cold wind on Musashi's face.

"He's dead?" To himself, he said: "So, it's happened again." Another life cut short by his wooden sword. He closed his eyes and in his heart called on the name of the Buddha, as he had on similar occasions in the past.

"Young man!"

"Yes, sir."

"Is your name Miyamoto Musashi?"

"That's correct."

"Under whom did you study the martial arts?"

"I've had no teacher in the ordinary sense. My father taught me how to use the truncheon when I was young. Since then, I've picked up a number of points from older samurai in various provinces. I've also spent some time traveling about the countryside, learning from the mountains and the rivers. I regard them, too, as teachers."

"You seem to have the right attitude. But you're so strong! Much too strong!"

Believing he was being praised, Musashi blushed and said, "Oh, no! I'm still immature. I'm always making blunders."

"That's not what I mean. Your strength is your problem. You must learn to control it, become weaker."

161

"What?" Musashi asked perplexedly.

"You will recall that a short while ago you passed through the vegetable garden where I was at work."

"Yes."

"When you saw me, you jumped away, didn't you?"

"Yes."

"Why did you do that?"

"Well, somehow I imagined that you might use your hoe as a weapon and strike my legs with it. Then, too, though your attention seemed to be focused on the ground, my whole body felt transfixed by your eyes. I felt something murderous in that look, as though you were searching for my weak spot—so as to attack it."

The old man laughed. "It was the other way around. When you were still fifty feet from me, I perceived what you call 'something murderous' in the air. I sensed it in the tip of my hoe—that's how strongly your fighting spirit and ambition manifest themselves in every step you take. I knew I had to be prepared to defend myself.

"If it had been one of the local farmers passing by, I myself would have been no more than an old man tending vegetables. True, you sensed belligerence in me, but it was only a reflection of your own."

So Musashi had been right in thinking, even before they first exchanged words, that here was no ordinary man. Now he keenly felt that the priest was the master, and he the pupil. His attitude toward the old man with the bent back became appropriately deferential.

"I thank you for the lesson you have given me. May I ask your name and your position in this temple?"

"Oh, I don't belong to the Hōzōin. I'm the abbot of the Ōzōin. My name is Nikkan."

"I see."

"I'm an old friend of In'ei, and since he was studying the use of the lance, I decided to study along with him. Later, I had an afterthought or two. Now I never touch the weapon."

"I guess that means that Inshun, the present abbot here, is your disciple."

"Yes, it could be put that way. But priests shouldn't have any use for weapons, and I consider it unfortunate that the Hōzōin has become famous for a martial art, rather than for its religious fervor. Still, there were people who felt that it would be a pity to let the Hōzōin Style die out, so I taught it to Inshun. And to no one else."

"I wonder if you'd let me stay in your temple until Inshun returns."

"Do you propose to challenge him?"

"Well, as long as I'm here, I'd like to see how the foremost master uses his lance."

Nikkan shook his head reproachfully. "It's a waste of time. There's nothing to be learned here."

"Is that so?"

162   "You've already seen the Hōzōin lancemanship, just now, when you fought

Agon. What more do you need to see? If you want to learn more, watch me. Look into my eyes."

Nikkan drew up his shoulders, put his head slightly forward, and stared at Musashi. His eyes seemed about to jump from their sockets. As Musashi stared back, Nikkan's pupils shone first with a coral flame, then gradually took on an azure profundity. The glow burned and numbed Musashi's mind. He looked away. Nikkan's crackling laugh was like the clatter of bone-dry boards.

He relaxed his stare only when a younger priest came in and whispered to him. "Bring it in," he commanded.

Presently the young priest returned with a tray and a round wooden rice container, from which Nikkan scooped rice into a bowl. He gave it to Musashi. "I recommend the tea gruel and pickles. It's the practice of the Hōzōin to serve them to all those who come here to study, so don't feel they're going to any special trouble for you. They make their own pickles—called Hōzōin pickles, in fact—cucumbers stuffed with basil and red pepper. I think you'll find they taste rather good."

As Musashi picked up his chopsticks, he felt Nikkan's keen eyes on him again. He could not tell at this point whether their piercing quality originated within the priest or was a response to something he himself emitted. As he bit into a pickle, the feeling swept over him that Takuan's fist was about to smite him again, or perhaps the lance near the threshold was about to fly at him.

After he had finished a bowl of rice mixed with tea and two pickles, Nikkan asked, "Would you care for another helping?"

"No, thank you. I've had plenty."

"What do you think of the pickles?"

"Very good, thank you."

Even after he'd left, the sting of the red pepper on Musashi's tongue was all he could recall of the pickles' flavor. Nor was that the only sting he felt, for he came away convinced that somehow he'd suffered a defeat. "I lost," he grumbled to himself, walking slowly through a grove of cryptomerias. "I've been outclassed!" In the dim light, fleeting shadows ran across his path, a small herd of deer, frightened by his footsteps.

"When it was only a matter of physical strength, I won, but I left there feeling defeated. Why? Did I win outwardly only to lose inwardly?"

Suddenly remembering Jōtarō, he retraced his steps to the Hōzōin, where the lights were still burning. When he announced himself, the priest standing watch at the door poked his head out and said casually, "What is it? Did you forget something?"

"Yes. Tomorrow, or the next day, I expect someone to come here looking for me. When he does, will you tell him I'll be staying in the neighborhood of Sarusawa Pond? He should ask for me at the inns there."

"All right."

Since the reply was so casual, Musashi felt constrained to add, "It'll be a boy. His name is Jōtarō. He's very young, so please be sure you make the message clear to him."

163

Once again striding down the path he had taken earlier, Musashi muttered to himself, "That proves I lost. I even forgot to leave a message for Jōtarō. I was beaten by the old abbot!" Musashi's dejection persisted. Although he had won against Agon, the only thing that stuck in his mind was the immaturity he had felt in Nikkan's presence. How could he ever become a great swordsman, the greatest of them all? This was the question that obsessed him night and day, and today's encounter had left him utterly depressed.

During the past twenty years or so, the area between Sarusawa Pond and the lower reaches of the Sai River had been built up steadily, and there was a jumble of new houses, inns and shops. Only recently, Ōkubo Nagayasu had come to govern the city for the Tokugawas and had set up his administrative offices nearby. In the middle of the town was the establishment of a Chinese who was said to be a descendant of Lin Ho-ching; he had done so well with his stuffed dumplings that an expansion of his shop in the direction of the pond was under way.

Musashi stopped amid the lights of the busiest district and wondered where he should stay. There were plenty of inns, but he had to be careful about his expenses; at the same time, he wanted to choose a place not too far off the beaten track, so Jōtarō could find him easily.

He had just eaten at the temple, but when he caught a whiff of the stuffed dumplings, he felt hungry again. Entering the shop, he sat down and ordered a whole plateful. When they arrived, Musashi noted that the name Lin was burned into the bottom of the dumplings. Unlike the hot pickles at the Hōzōin, the dumplings had a flavor he could savor with pleasure.

The young girl who poured his tea asked politely, "Where are you planning to stay tonight?"

Musashi, unfamiliar with the district, welcomed the opportunity to explain his situation and ask her advice. She told him one of the proprietor's relatives had a private boardinghouse where he would be welcome, and without waiting for his answer, trotted off. She returned with a youngish woman, whose shaved eyebrows indicated she was married—presumably the proprietor's wife.

The boardinghouse was on a quiet alley not far from the restaurant, apparently an ordinary residence that sometimes took in guests. The eyebrowless mistress of the shop, who had shown him the way, tapped lightly on the door, then turned to Musashi and said quietly, "It's my elder sister's house, so don't worry about tipping or anything."

The maid came out of the house and the two of them exchanged whispers for a moment or two. Apparently satisfied, she led Musashi to the second floor.

The room and its furnishings were too good for an ordinary inn, making Musashi feel a bit ill at ease. He wondered why a house as well-off as this one would take in boarders and asked the maid about it, but she just smiled and said nothing. Having already eaten, he had his bath and went to bed, but the question was still on his mind when he went off to sleep.

Next morning, he said to the maid, "Someone is supposed to come looking for me. Will it be all right if I stay over for a day or two until he arrives?"

"By all means," she replied, without even asking the lady of the house, who soon came herself to pay her respects.

She was a good-looking woman of about thirty, with fine smooth skin. When Musashi tried to satisfy his curiosity about why she was accepting roomers, she laughingly replied, "To tell the truth, I'm a widow—my husband was a Nō actor by the name of Kanze—and I'm afraid to be without a man in the house, what with all these ill-bred rōnin in the vicinity." She went on to explain that while the streets were full of drinking shops and prostitutes, many of the indigent samurai were not satisfied with these diversions. They would pump information from the local youths and attack houses where there were no men about. They spoke of this as "calling on the widows."

"In other words," said Musashi, "you take in people like me to act as your bodyguard, right?"

"Well," she said, smiling, "as I said, there are no men in the household. Please feel free to stay as long as you like."

"I understand perfectly. I hope you'll feel safe as long as I'm here. There's only one request I'd like to make. I'm expecting a visitor, so I wonder if you'd mind putting a marker with my name on it outside the gate."

The widow, not at all unhappy to let it be known that she had a man in the house, obligingly wrote "Miyamoto Musashi" on a strip of paper and pasted it on the gatepost.

Jōtarō did not show up that day, but on the next, Musashi received a visit from a group of three samurai. Pushing their way past the protesting maid, they came straight upstairs to his room. Musashi saw immediately that they were among those who had been present at the Hōzōin when he had killed Agon. Sitting down around him as though they'd known him all their lives, they started pouring on the flattery.

"I never saw anything like it in my life," said one. "I'm sure nothing of the kind ever happened at the Hōzōin before. Just think! An unknown visitor arrives and, just like that, downs one of the Seven Pillars. And not just any-one—the terrifying Agon himself. One grunt and he was spitting blood. You don't often see sights like that!"

Another went on in the same vein. "Everyone we know is talking about it. All the rōnin are asking each other just who this Miyamoto Musashi is. That was a bad day for the Hōzōin's reputation."

"Why, you must be the greatest swordsman in the country!"

"And so young, too!"

"No doubt about it. And you'll get even better with time."

"If you don't mind my asking, how does it happen that with your ability you're only a rōnin? It's a waste of your talents not to be in the service of a daimyō!"

They paused only long enough to slurp some tea and devour the tea cakes with gusto, spilling crumbs all over their laps and on the floor.

Musashi, embarrassed by the extravagance of their praise, shifted his eyes from right to left and back again. For a time, he listened with an impassive

165

face, thinking that sooner or later their momentum would run down. When they showed no signs of changing the subject, he took the initiative by asking their names.

"Oh, I'm sorry. I'm Yamazoe Dampachi. I used to be in the service of Lord Gamō," said the first.

The man next to him said, "I'm Ōtomo Banryū. I've mastered the Bokuden Style, and I have a lot of plans for the future."

"I'm Yasukawa Yasubei," said the third with a chuckle, "and I've never been anything but a rōnin, like my father before me."

Musashi wondered why they were taking up their time and his with their small talk. It became apparent that he would not find out unless he asked, so the next time there was a break in the conversation, he said, "Presumably you came because you had some business with me."

They feigned surprise at the very idea but soon admitted they had come on what they regarded as a very important mission. Moving quickly forward, Yasubei said, "As a matter of fact, we do have some business with you. You see, we're planning to put on a public 'entertainment' at the foot of Mount Kasuga, and we wanted to talk to you about it. Not a play or anything like that. What we have in mind is a series of matches that would teach the people about the martial arts, and at the same time give them something to lay bets on."

He went on to say that the stands were already being put up, and that the prospects looked excellent. They felt, however, that they needed another man, because with just the three of them, some really strong samurai might show up and beat them all, which would mean that their hard-earned money would go down the drain. They had decided that Musashi was just the right person for them. If he would join in with them, they would not only split the profits but pay for his food and lodging while the matches were in progress. That way he could easily earn some fast money for his future travels.

Musashi listened with some amusement to their blandishments, but by and by he grew tired and broke in. "If that's all you want, there's no point in discussing it. I'm not interested."

"But why?" asked Dampachi. "Why aren't you interested?"

Musashi's youthful temper erupted. "I'm not a gambler!" he stated indignantly. "And I eat with chopsticks, not with my sword!"

"What's that?" protested the three, insulted by his implication. "What do you mean by that?"

"Don't you understand, you fools? I am a samurai, and I intend to remain a samurai. Even if I starve in the process. Now clear out of here!"

One man's mouth twisted into a nasty snarl, and another, red with anger, shouted, "You'll regret this!"

They well knew that the three of them together were no match for Musashi, but to save face, they stamped out noisily, scowling and doing their best to give the impression they weren't through with him yet.

That night, as on other recent nights, there was a milky, slightly overcast moon. The young mistress of the house, free from worry as long as Musashi

166

was in residence, was careful to provide him with delicious food and sake of good quality. He ate downstairs with the family and in the process drank himself into a mellow mood.

Returning to his room, he sprawled on the floor. His thoughts soon came to rest on Nikkan.

"It's humiliating," he said to himself.

The adversaries he had defeated, even the ones he had killed or half killed, always disappeared from his mind like so much froth, but he couldn't forget anyone who got the better of him in any way or, for that matter, anyone in whom he sensed an overpowering presence. Men like that dwelt in his mind like living spirits, and he thought constantly of how one day he might be able to overshadow them.

"Humiliating!" he repeated.

He clutched at his hair and pondered how he could get the better of Nikkan, how he could face that unearthly stare without flinching. For two days this question had gnawed at him. It wasn't that he wished Nikkan any harm, but he was sorely disappointed with himself.

"Is it that I'm no good?" he asked himself ruefully. Having learned swordsmanship on his own, and thus lacking an objective appraisal of his own strength, he couldn't help but doubt his own ability to ever achieve power such as the old priest exuded.

Nikkan had told him he was too strong, that he had to learn to become weaker. This was the point that sent his mind off on tangent after tangent, for he couldn't fathom the meaning. Wasn't strength a warrior's most important quality? Was that not what made one warrior superior to others? How could Nikkan speak of it as a flaw?

"Maybe," thought Musashi, "the old rascal was toying with me. Maybe he considered my youth and decided to talk in riddles just to confuse me and amuse himself. Then after I left, he had a good laugh. It's possible."

At times like this, Musashi wondered whether it had been wise to read all those books at Himeji Castle. Until then, he had never bothered much about figuring things out, but now, whenever something happened, he couldn't rest until he'd found an explanation satisfying to his intellect. Previously he'd acted on instinct; now he had to understand each small thing before he could accept it. And this applied not only to swordsmanship but to the way he viewed humanity and society.

It was true that the daredevil in him had been tamed. Yet Nikkan said he was "too strong." Musashi assumed that Nikkan was referring not to physical strength but to the savage fighting spirit with which he had been born. Could the priest really have perceived it, or was he guessing?

"The knowledge that comes from books is of no use to the warrior," he reassured himself. "If a man worries too much about what others think or do, he's apt to be slow to act. Why, if Nikkan himself closed his eyes for a moment and made one misstep, he'd crumble and fall to pieces!"

The sound of footsteps on the stairs intruded upon his musings. The maid appeared, and after her Jōtarō, his dark skin further blackened by the grime

167

acquired on his journey, but his spritelike hair white with dust. Musashi, truly happy to have the diversion of his little friend, welcomed him with open arms.

The boy plopped down on the floor and stretched his dirty legs out straight. "Am I tired!" he sighed.

"Did you have trouble finding me?"

"Trouble! I almost gave up. I've been searching all over!"

"Didn't you ask at the Hōzōin?"

"Yes, but they said they didn't know anything about you."

"Oh, they did, did they?" Musashi's eyes narrowed. "And after I said specifically that you'd find me near Sarusawa Pond. Oh, well, I'm glad you made it."

"Here's the answer from the Yoshioka School." He handed Musashi the bamboo tube. "I couldn't find Hon'iden Matahachi, so I asked the people at his house to give him the message."

"Fine. Now run along and have a bath. They'll give you some dinner downstairs."

Musashi took the letter from its container and read it. It said that Seijūrō looked forward to a "second bout"; if Musashi didn't show up as promised the following year, it would be assumed that he'd lost his nerve. Should that happen, Seijūrō would make sure that Musashi became the laughingstock of Kyoto. This braggadocio was set down in clumsy handwriting, presumably by someone other than Seijūrō.

As Musashi tore the letter to bits and burned it, the charred pieces fluttered up into the air like so many black butterflies.

Seijūrō had spoken of a "bout," but it was clear that it was going to be more than that. It would be a battle to the death. Next year, as a result of this insulting note, which one of the combatants would end up in ashes?

Musashi took it for granted that a warrior must be content to live from day to day, never knowing each morning if he'd live to see nightfall. Nevertheless, the thought that he might really die in the coming year worried him somewhat. There were so many things he still wanted to do. For one thing, there was his burning desire to become a great swordsman. But that wasn't all. So far, he reflected, he hadn't done any of the things people ordinarily do in the course of a lifetime.

At this stage of his life, he was still vain enough to think he'd like to have retainers—a lot of them—leading his horses and carrying his falcons, just like Bokuden and Lord Kōizumi of Ise. He would like, too, to have a proper house, with a good wife and loyal servants. He wanted to be a good master and to enjoy the warmth and comfort of home life. And of course, before he settled down, he had a secret longing to have a passionate love affair. During all these years of thinking solely about the Way of the Samurai he had, not unnaturally, remained chaste. Still, he was struck by some of the women he saw on the streets of Kyoto and Nara, and it was not their aesthetic qualities alone that pleased him; they aroused him physically.

His thoughts turned to Otsū. Though she was now a creature of the distant past, he felt closely bound to her. How many times, when he was lonely or melancholy, had the vague recollection of her alone cheered him up.

Presently he came out of his reverie. Jōtarō had rejoined him, bathed, satiated and proud to have carried out his mission successfully. Sitting with his short legs crossed and his hands between his knees, he didn't take long to succumb to fatigue. He was soon snoozing blissfully, his mouth open. Musashi put him to bed.

When morning came, the boy was up with the sparrows. Musashi also arose early, since he intended to resume his travels.

As he was dressing, the widow appeared and said in a regretful tone, "You seem in a hurry to leave." In her arms she was carrying some clothing, which she offered him. "I've sewn these things together for you as a parting gift—a kimono with a short cloak. I'm not sure you'll like them, but I hope you'll wear them."

Musashi looked at her in astonishment. The garments were much too expensive for him to accept after having stayed there only two days. He tried to refuse, but the widow insisted. "No, you must take them. They aren't anything very special anyway. I have a lot of old kimono and Nō costumes left by my husband. I have no use for them. I thought it would be nice for you to have some. I do hope you won't refuse. Now that I've altered them to fit you, if you don't take them, they'll just go to waste."

She went behind Musashi and held up the kimono for him to slip his arms into. As he put it on, he realized that the silk was of very good quality and felt more embarrassed than ever. The sleeveless cloak was particularly fine; it must have been imported from China. The hem was gold brocade, the lining silk crepe, and the leather fastening straps had been dyed purple.

"It looks perfect on you!" exclaimed the widow.

Jōtarō, looking on enviously, suddenly said to her, "What're you going to give me?"

The widow laughed. "You should be happy for the chance to accompany your fine master."

"Aw," grumbled Jōtarō, "who wants an old kimono anyway?"

"Is there anything you do want?"

Running to the wall in the anteroom and taking a Nō mask down from its hook, the boy said, "Yes, this!" He'd coveted it since first spying it the night before, and now he rubbed it tenderly against his cheek.

Musashi was surprised at the boy's good taste. He himself had found it admirably executed. There was no way of knowing who had made it, but it was certainly two or three centuries old and had evidently been used in actual Nō performances. The face, carved with exquisite care, was that of a female demon, but whereas the usual mask of this type was grotesquely painted with blue spots, this was the face of a beautiful and elegant young girl. It was peculiar only in that one side of her mouth curved sharply upward in the eeriest fashion imaginable. Obviously not a fictitious face conjured up by the artist, it was the portrait of a real, living madwoman, beautiful yet bewitched.

"That you cannot have," said the widow firmly, trying to take the mask away from the boy.

Evading her reach, Jōtarō put the mask on the top of his head and danced about the room, shouting defiantly, "What do you need it for? It's mine now; I'm going to keep it!"

Musashi, surprised and embarrassed by his ward's conduct, made an attempt to catch him, but Jōtarō stuffed the mask into his kimono and fled down the stairs, the widow giving chase. Although she was laughing, not angry at all, she clearly didn't intend to part with the mask.

Presently Jōtarō climbed slowly back up the stairs. Musashi, ready to scold him severely, was seated with his face toward the door. But as the boy entered, he cried, "Boo!" and held the mask out before him. Musashi was startled; his muscles tensed and his knees shifted inadvertently.

He wondered why Jōtarō's prank had such an effect on him, but as he stared at the mask in the dim light, he began to understand. The carver had put something diabolical into his creation. That crescent smile, curving up on the left side of the white face, was haunted, possessed of a devil.

"If we're going, let's go," said Jōtarō.

Musashi, without rising, said, "Why haven't you given the mask back yet? What do you want with a thing like that?"

"But she said I could keep it! She gave it to me."

"She did not! Go downstairs and give it back to her."

"But she gave it to me! When I offered to return it, she said that if I wanted it so badly, I could keep it. She just wanted to make sure I'd take good care of it, so I promised her I would."

"What am I going to do with you!" Musashi felt ashamed about accepting, first, the beautiful kimono and then this mask that the widow seemed to treasure. He would have liked to do something in return, but she was obviously not in need of money—certainly not the small amount he could have spared—and none of his meager possessions would make a suitable gift. He descended the stairs, apologizing for Jōtarō's rudeness and attempting to return the mask.

The widow, however, said, "No, the more I think of it, the more I think I'd be happier without it. And he does want it so badly. . . . Don't be too hard on him."

Suspecting the mask had some special significance for her, Musashi tried once more to return it, but by this time Jōtarō had his straw sandals on and was outside waiting by the gate, a smug look on his face. Musashi, eager to be off, gave in to her kindness and accepted the gift. The young widow said she was sorrier to see Musashi go than she was to lose the mask, and begged him several times to come back and stay there whenever he was in Nara.

Musashi was tying the thongs of his sandals when the dumpling-maker's wife came running up. "Oh," she said breathlessly, "I'm so glad you haven't left yet. You can't go now! Please, go back upstairs. Something terrible is going on!" The woman's voice trembled as though she thought some fearful ogre was about to attack her.

170

Musashi finished tying his sandals and calmly raised his head. "What is it? What's so terrible?"

"The priests at the Hōzōin have heard you're leaving today, and more than ten of them have taken their lances and are lying in wait for you in Hannya Plain."

"Oh?"

"Yes, and the abbot, Inshun, is with them. My husband knows one of the priests, and he asked him what was going on. The priest said the man who's been staying here for the last couple of days, the man named Miyamoto, was leaving Nara today, and the priests were going to waylay him on the road."

Her face twitching with fright, she assured Musashi that it would be suicide to leave Nara this morning and fervently urged him to lie low for another night. It would be safer, in her opinion, to try and sneak away the next day.

"I see," said Musashi without emotion. "You say they plan to meet me on Hannya Plain?"

"I'm not sure exactly where, but they went off in that direction. Some of the townspeople told me it wasn't only the priests. They said a whole lot of the rōnin, too, had got together, saying they'd catch you and turn you over to the Hōzōin. Did you say something bad about the temple, or insult them in some way?"

"No."

"Well, they say the priests are furious because you hired somebody to put up posters with verses on them making fun of the Hōzōin. They took this to mean you were gloating over having killed one of their men."

"I didn't do anything of the sort. There's been a mistake."

"Well, if it's a mistake, you shouldn't go out and get yourself killed over it!"

His brow beaded with sweat, Musashi looked thoughtfully up at the sky, recalling how angry the three rōnin had been when he turned down their business deal. Maybe he was indebted to them for all this. It would be just like them to put up offensive posters and then spread the word that he'd done it.

Abruptly he stood up. "I'm leaving," he said.

He strapped his traveling bag to his back, took his basket hat in hand, and turning to the two women, thanked them for their kindness. As he started toward the gate, the widow, now in tears, followed along, begging him not to go.

"If I stay over another night," he pointed out, "there's bound to be trouble at your house. I certainly wouldn't want that to happen, after you've been so good to us."

"I don't care," she insisted. "You'd be safer here."

"No, I'll go now. Jō! Say thank you to the lady."

Dutifully, the boy bowed and did as he was told. He, too, appeared to be in low spirits, but not because he was sorry to leave. When it came right down to it, Jōtarō did not really know Musashi. In Kyoto, he had heard that his master was a weakling and a coward, and the thought that the notorious lancers of the Hōzōin were set to attack him was very depressing. His youthful heart was filled with gloom and foreboding.

171

Hannya Plain

Jōtarō trudged along sadly behind his master, fearing each step was taking them closer to certain death. A little earlier, on the damp, shady road near the Tōdaiji, a dewdrop falling on his collar had almost made him cry out. The black crows he saw along the way gave him an eerie feeling.

Nara was far behind them. Through the rows of cryptomeria trees along the road, they could make out the gently sloping plain leading up to Hannya Hill; to their right were the rolling peaks of Mount Mikasa, above them the peaceful sky.

That he and Musashi were heading straight for the place where the Hōzōin lancers were waiting in ambush made absolutely no sense to him. There were plenty of places to hide, if one put one's mind to it. Why couldn't they go into one of the many temples along the way and bide their time? That would surely be more sensible.

He wondered if perhaps Musashi meant to apologize to the priests, even though he hadn't wronged them in any way. Jōtarō resolved that if Musashi begged their forgiveness, he would too. This was no time to be arguing about the right and wrong of things.

"Jōtarō!"

The boy started at the sound of his name being called. His eyebrows shot up and his body became tense. Realizing his face was probably pale from fright and not wanting to appear childish, he turned his eyes bravely toward the sky. Musashi looked up at the sky too, and the boy felt more dispirited than ever.

When Musashi continued, it was in his usual cheerful tone. "Feels good, doesn't it, Jō? It's as though we were walking along on the songs of the nightingales."

"What?" asked the boy, astonished.

"Nightingales, I said."

"Oh, yeah, nightingales. There are some around here, aren't there?"

Musashi could see from the paleness of the boy's lips that he was dejected. He felt sorry for him. After all, in a matter of minutes he might be suddenly alone in a strange place.

"We're getting near Hannya Hill, aren't we?" said Musashi.

"That's right."

"Well, now what?"

Jōtarō didn't reply. The singing of the nightingales fell coldly on his ears. He couldn't shake off the foreboding that they might soon be parted forever. The eyes that had bristled with mirth when surprising Musashi with the mask were now worried and mournful.

"I think I'd better leave you here," said Musashi. "If you come along, you may get hurt accidentally. There's no reason to put yourself in harm's way."

Jōtarō broke down, tears streaming down his cheeks as if a dam had broken. The backs of his hands went up to his eyes and his shoulders quivered. His crying was punctuated by tiny spasms, as if he had the hiccups.

"What's this? Aren't you supposed to be learning the Way of the Samurai? If I break and run, you run in the same direction. If I get killed, go back to the sake shop in Kyoto. But for now, go to that little hill and watch from there. You'll be able to keep an eye on everything that happens."

Having wiped his tears away, Jōtarō grabbed Musashi's sleeves and blurted out, "Let's run away!"

"That's no way for a samurai to talk! That's what you want to be, isn't it?"

"I'm afraid! I don't want to die!" With trembling hands, he kept trying to pull Musashi back by the sleeve. "Think about me," he pleaded. "Please, let's get away while we can!"

"When you talk like that, you make me want to run too. You've got no parents who'll look after you, just like me when I was your age. But—"

"Then come on. What are we waiting for?"

"No!" Musashi turned, and planting his feet wide apart, faced the child squarely. "I'm a samurai. You're a samurai's son. We're not going to run away."

Hearing the finality in Musashi's tone, Jōtarō gave up and sat down, dirty tears rolling off his face as he rubbed his red and swollen eyes with his hands.

"Don't worry!" said Musashi. "I have no intention of losing. I'm going to win! Everything will be all right then, don't you think?"

Jōtarō took little comfort from this speech. He couldn't believe a word of it. Knowing that the Hōzōin lancers numbered more than ten, he doubted whether Musashi, considering his reputation for weakness, could beat them one at a time, let alone all together.

Musashi, for his part, was beginning to lose patience. He liked Jōtarō, felt sorry for him, but this was no time to be thinking about children. The lancers were there for one purpose: to kill him. He had to be prepared to face them. Jōtarō was becoming a nuisance.

His voice took on a sharp edge. "Stop your blubbering! You'll never be a samurai, carrying on this way. Why don't you just go on back to the sake shop?" Firmly and not too gently, he pushed the boy from him.

Jōtarō, stung to the core, suddenly stopped crying and stood straight, a surprised look on his face. He watched his master stride off toward Hannya Hill. He wanted to call out after him, but resisted the urge. Instead he forced himself to remain silent for several minutes. Then he squatted under a nearby tree, buried his face in his hands, and gritted his teeth.

Musashi did not look back, but Jōtarō's sobs echoed in his ears. He felt he

173

could see the hapless, frightened little boy through the back of his head and regretted having brought him along. It was more than enough just to take care of himself; still immature, with only his sword to rely on and no idea of what the morrow might bring—what need had he of a companion?

The trees thinned out. He found himself on an open plain, actually the slightly rising skirt of the mountains in the distance. On the road branching off toward Mount Mikasa, a man raised his hand in greeting.

"Hey, Musashi! Where are you going?"

Musashi recognized the man coming toward him; it was Yamazoe Dampachi. Though Musashi sensed immediately that Dampachi's objective was to lead him into a trap, he nevertheless greeted him heartily.

Dampachi said, "Glad I ran into you. I want you to know how sorry I am about that business the other day." His tone was too polite, and as he spoke, he was obviously examining Musashi's face with great care. "I hope you'll forget about it. It was all a mistake."

Dampachi himself was none too sure what to make of Musashi. He had been very impressed by what he had seen at the Hōzōin. Indeed, just thinking about it sent chills up his spine. Be that as it may, Musashi was still only a provincial rōnin, who couldn't be more than twenty-one or twenty-two years old, and Dampachi was far from ready to admit to himself that anyone of that age and status could be his better.

"Where are you going?" he asked again.

"I'm planning to go through Iga over to the Ise highroad. And you?"

"Oh, I have some things to do in Tsukigase."

"That's not far from Yagyū Valley, is it?"

"No, not far."

"That's where Lord Yagyū's castle is, isn't it?"

"Yes, it's near the temple called Kasagidera. You must go there sometime. The old lord, Muneyoshi, lives in retirement, like a tea master, and his son, Munenori, is in Edo, but you should still stop in and see what it's like."

"I don't really think Lord Yagyū would give a lesson to a wanderer like me."

"He might. Of course, it'd help if you had an introduction. As it happens, I know an armorer in Tsukigase who does work for the Yagyūs. If you'd like, I could ask if he'd be willing to introduce you."

The plain stretched out broadly for several miles, the skyline broken occasionally by a lone cryptomeria or Chinese black pine. There were gentle rises here and there, however, and the road rose and fell too. Near the bottom of Hannya Hill, Musashi spotted the brown smoke of a fire rising beyond a low hillock.

"What's that?" he asked.

"What's what?"

"That smoke over there."

"What's so strange about smoke?" Dampachi had been sticking close to Musashi's left side, and as he stared into the latter's face, his own hardened perceptibly.

Musashi pointed. "That smoke over there: there's something suspicious about it," he said. "Doesn't it look that way to you?"

"Suspicious? In what way?"

"Suspicious—you know, like the look on your face right now," Musashi said sharply, abruptly sweeping his finger toward Dampachi.

A sharp whistling sound broke the stillness on the plain. Dampachi gasped as Musashi struck. His attention diverted by Musashi's finger, Dampachi never realized that Musashi had drawn his sword. His body rose, flew forward, and landed face down. Dampachi would not rise again.

From the distance there was a cry of alarm, and two men appeared at the top of the hillock. One of the men screamed, and both spun round and took to their heels, their arms flailing the air wildly.

The sword that Musashi was pointing toward the earth glittered in the sunlight; fresh blood dripped from its tip. He marched directly on toward the hillock, and although the spring breeze blew softly against his skin, Musashi felt his muscles tauten as he ascended. From the top, he looked down at the fire burning below.

"He's come!" shouted one of the men who had fled to join the others. There were about thirty men. Musashi picked out Dampachi's cohorts, Yasukawa Yasubei and Ōtomo Banryū.

"He's come!" parroted another.

They'd been lolling in the sun. Now they all jumped to their feet. Half were priests, the other half nondescript rōnin. When Musashi came into view, a wordless but nonetheless savage stir went through the group. They saw the bloodstained sword and suddenly realized that the battle had already begun. Instead of challenging Musashi, they had been sitting around the fire and had let him challenge them!

Yasukawa and Ōtomo were talking as fast as they could, explaining with broad rapid gestures how Yamazoe had been cut down. The rōnin scowled with fury, the Hōzōin priests eyed Musashi menacingly while grouping themselves for battle.

All of the priests carried lances. Black sleeves tucked up, they were ready for action, apparently set upon avenging the death of Agon and restoring the temple's honor. They looked grotesque, like so many demons from hell.

The rōnin formed a semicircle, so they could watch the show and at the same time keep Musashi from escaping.

This precaution, however, proved unnecessary, for Musashi showed no sign of either running or backing down. In fact, he was walking steadily and directly toward them. Slowly, pace by pace, he advanced, looking as if he might pounce at any moment.

For a moment, there was an ominous silence, as both sides contemplated approaching death. Musashi's face went deadly white and through his eyes stared the eyes of the god of vengeance, glittering with venom. He was selecting his prey.

Neither the rōnin nor the priests were as tense as Musashi. Their numbers gave them confidence, and their optimism was unshakable. Still, no one wanted to be the first attacked.

A priest at the end of the column of lancers gave a signal, and without breaking formation, they rushed around to Musashi's right.

"Musashi! I am Inshun," shouted the same priest. "I'm told that you came while I was away and killed Agon. That you later publicly insulted the honor of the Hōzōin. That you mocked us by having posters put up all over town. Is this true?"

"No!" shouted Musashi. "If you're a priest, you should know better than to trust only what you see and hear. You should consider things with your mind and spirit."

It was like pouring oil on the flames. Ignoring their leader, the priests began to shout, saying talk was cheap, it was time to fight.

They were enthusiastically seconded by the rōnin, who had grouped themselves in close formation at Musashi's left. Screaming, cursing and waving their swords in the air, they egged the priests on to action.

Musashi, convinced that the rōnin were all mouth and no fight, suddenly turned to them and shouted, "All right! Which one of you wants to come forward?"

All but two or three fell back a pace, each sure that Musashi's evil eye was upon him. The two or three brave ones stood ready, swords outstretched, issuing a challenge.

In the wink of an eye, Musashi was on one of them like a fighting cock. There was a sound like the popping of a cork, and the ground turned red. Then came a chilling noise—not a battle cry, not a curse, but a truly blood-curdling howl.

Musashi's sword screeched back and forth through the air, a reverberation in his own body telling him when he connected with human bone. Blood and brains spattered from his blade; fingers and arms flew through the air.

The rōnin had come to watch the carnage, not to participate in it, but their weakness had led Musashi to attack them first. At the very beginning, they held together fairly well, because they thought the priests would soon come to their rescue. But the priests stood silent and motionless as Musashi quickly slaughtered five or six rōnin, throwing the others into confusion. Before long they were slashing wildly in all directions, as often as not injuring one other.

For most of the time, Musashi wasn't really conscious of what he was doing. He was in a sort of trance, a murderous dream in which body and soul were concentrated in his three-foot sword. Unconsciously, his whole life experience—the knowledge his father had beaten into him, what he had learned at Sekigahara, the theories he had heard at the various schools of swordsmanship, the lessons taught him by the mountains and the trees—everything came into play in the rapid movements of his body. He became a disembodied whirlwind mowing down the herd of rōnin, who by their stunned bewilderment left themselves wide open to his sword.

For the short duration of the battle, one of the priests counted the number of times he inhaled and exhaled. It was all over before he had taken his twentieth breath.

Musashi was drenched with the blood of his victims. The few remaining rōnin were also covered with gore. The earth, the grass, even the air was bloody. One of their number let out a scream, and the surviving rōnin scattered in all directions.

While all this was going on, Jōtarō was absorbed in prayer. His hands folded before him and his eyes lifted skyward, he implored, "Oh, God in heaven, come to his aid! My master, down there on the plain, is hopelessly outnumbered. He's weak, but he isn't a bad man. Please help him!"

Despite Musashi's instructions to go away, he couldn't leave. The place where he had finally chosen to sit, his hat and his mask beside him, was a knoll from which he could see the scene around the bonfire in the distance.

"Hachiman! Kompira! God of Kasuga Shrine! Look! My master is walking directly into the enemy. Oh, gods of heaven, protect him. He isn't himself. He's usually mild and gentle, but he's been a little bit strange ever since this morning. He must be crazy, or else he wouldn't take on that many at once! Oh, please, please, help him!"

After calling on the deities a hundred times or more, he noticed no visible results of his efforts and started getting angry. Finally, he was shouting: "Aren't there any gods in this land? Are you going to let the wicked people win, and the good man be killed? If you do that, then everything they've always told me about right and wrong is a lie! You can't let him be killed! If you do, I'll spit on you!"

When he saw that Musashi was surrounded, his invocations turned to curses, directed not only at the enemy but at the gods themselves. Then, realizing that the blood being spilled on the plain was not his teacher's, he abruptly changed his tune. "Look! My master's not a weakling after all! He's beating them!"

This was the first time Jōtarō had ever witnessed men fighting like beasts to the death, the first time he had ever seen so much blood. He began to feel that he was down there in the middle of it, himself smeared with gore. His heart turned somersaults, he felt giddy and light-headed.

"Look at him! I told you he could do it! What an attack! And look at those silly priests, lined up like a bunch of cawing crows, afraid to take a step!"

But this last was premature, for as he spoke the priests of the Hōzōin began moving in on Musashi.

"Oh, oh! This looks bad. They're all attacking him at once. Musashi's in trouble!" Forgetting everything, out of his senses with anxiety, Jōtarō darted like a fireball toward the scene of impending disaster.

Abbot Inshun gave the command to charge, and in an instant, with a tremendous roar of voices, the lancers flew into action. Their glittering weapons whistled in the air as the priests scattered like bees sprung from a hive, shaved heads making them appear all the more barbaric.

The lances they carried were all different, with a wide variety of blades—the usual pointed, cone-shaped ones, others flat, cross-shaped or hooked—each priest using the type he favored most. Today they had a chance to see how the techniques they honed in practice worked in real battle.

As they fanned out, Musashi, expecting a trick attack, jumped back and stood on guard. Weary and a little dazed from the earlier bout, he gripped his sword handle tightly. It was sticky with gore, and a mixture of blood and sweat clouded his vision, but he was determined to die magnificently, if die he must.

To his amazement, the attack never came. Instead of making the anticipated lunges in his direction, the priests fell like mad dogs on their erstwhile allies, chasing down the rōnin who had fled and slashing at them mercilessly as they screamed in protest. The unsuspecting rōnin, futilely trying to direct the lancers toward Musashi, were slit, skewered, stabbed in the mouth, sliced in two, and otherwise slaughtered until not one of them was left alive. The massacre was as thorough as it was bloodthirsty.

Musashi could not believe his eyes. Why had the priests attacked their supporters? And why so viciously? He himself had only moments earlier been fighting like a wild animal; now he could hardly bear to watch the ferocity with which these men of the cloth slew the rōnin. Having been transformed for a time into a mindless beast, he was now restored to his normal state by the sight of others similarly transformed. The experience was sobering.

Then he became aware of a tugging at his arms and legs. Looking down, he found Jōtarō weeping tears of relief. For the first time, he relaxed.

As the battle ended, the abbot approached him, and in a polite, dignified manner, said, "You are Miyamoto, I assume. It is an honor to meet you." He was tall and of light complexion. Musashi was somewhat overcome by his appearance, as well as by his poise. With a certain amount of confusion, he wiped his sword clean and sheathed it, but for the moment words failed him.

"Let me introduce myself," continued the priest. "I am Inshun, abbot of the Hōzōin."

"So you are the master of the lance," said Musashi.

"I'm sorry I was away when you visited us recently. I'm also embarrassed that my disciple Agon put up such a poor fight."

Sorry about Agon's performance? Musashi felt that perhaps his ears needed cleaning. He remained silent for a moment, for before he could decide on a suitable way to respond to Inshun's courteous tone, he had to straighten out the confusion in his mind. He still couldn't figure out why the priests had turned on the rōnin—could imagine no possible explanation. He was even somewhat puzzled to find himself still alive.

"Come," said the abbot, "and wash off some of that blood. You need a rest." Inshun led him toward the fire, Jōtarō tagging along close behind.

The priests had torn a large cotton cloth into strips and were wiping their lances. Gradually they gathered by the fire, sitting down with Inshun and Musashi as though nothing unusual had occurred. They began chatting among themselves.

"Look, up there," said one, pointing upward.

"Ah, the crows have caught the whiff of blood. Cawing over the dead bodies, they are."

"Why don't they dig in?"

"They will, as soon as we leave. They'll be scrambling to get at the feast."

The grisly banter went on in this leisurely vein. Musashi got the impression that he wasn't going to find out anything unless he asked. He looked at Inshun and said, "You know, I thought you and your men had come here to attack me, and I'd made up my mind to take along as many of you as I could to the land of the dead. I can't understand why you're treating me this way."

Inshun laughed. "Well, we don't necessarily regard you as an ally, but our real purpose today was to do a little housecleaning."

"You call what's been going on housecleaning?"

"That's right," said Inshun, pointing toward the horizon. "But I think we might as well wait and let Nikkan explain it to you. I'm sure that speck on the edge of the plain is he."

At the same moment, on the other side of the plain, a horseman was saying to Nikkan, "You walk fast for your age, don't you?"

"I'm not fast. You're slow."

"You're nimbler than the horses."

"Why shouldn't I be? I'm a man."

The old priest, who alone was on foot, was pacing the horsemen as they advanced toward the smoke of the fire. The five riders with him were officials.

As the party approached, the priests whispered among themselves, "It's the Old Master." Having confirmed this, they fell back a good distance and lined themselves up ceremoniously, as for a sacred rite, to greet Nikkan and his entourage.

The first thing Nikkan said was, "Did you take care of everything?"

Inshun bowed and replied, "Just as you commanded." Then, turning to the officials, "Thank you for coming."

As the samurai jumped one by one off their horses, their leader replied, "It's no trouble. Thank *you* for doing the real work! . . . Let's get on with it, men."

The officials went about inspecting the corpses and making a few notes; then their leader returned to where Inshun was standing. "We'll send people from the town to clean up the mess. Please feel free to leave everything as it is." With that, the five of them remounted their horses and rode off.

Nikkan let the priests know that they were no longer needed. Having bowed to him, they started walking away silently. Inshun, too, said good-bye to Nikkan and Musashi and took his leave.

As soon as the men were gone, there was a great cacophony. The crows descended, flapping their wings joyfully.

Grumbling over the noise, Nikkan walked over to Musashi's side and said casually, "Forgive me if I offended you the other day."

"Not at all. You were very kind. It is I who should thank you." Musashi knelt and bowed deeply before the old priest.

"Get off the ground," commanded Nikkan. "This field is no place for bowing."

Musashi got to his feet.

"Has the experience here taught you anything?" the priest asked.

"I'm not even sure what happened. Can you tell me?"

"By all means," replied Nikkan. "Those officials who just left work under Ōkubo Nagayasu, who was recently sent to administer Nara. They're new to the district, and the rōnin have been taking advantage of their unfamiliarity with the place—waylaying innocent passersby, blackmailing, gambling, making off with the women, breaking into widows' houses—causing all sorts of trouble. The administrator's office couldn't bring them under control, but they did know that there were about fifteen ringleaders, including Dampachi and Yasukawa.

"This Dampachi and his cohorts took a disliking to you, as you know. Since they were afraid to attack you themselves, they concocted what they thought was a clever plan, whereby the priests of the Hōzōin would do it for them. The slanderous statements about the temple, attributed to you, were their work; so were the posters. They made sure everything was reported to me, presumably on the theory that I'm stupid."

Musashi's eyes laughed as he listened.

"I thought about it for a while," said the abbot, "and it occurred to me that this was an ideal opportunity to have a housecleaning in Nara. I spoke to Inshun about my plan, he agreed to undertake it, and now everybody's happy—the priests, the administrators; also the crows. Ha, ha!"

There was one other person who was supremely happy. Nikkan's story had wiped away all of Jōtarō's doubts and fears, and the boy was ecstatic. He began singing an improvised ditty while dancing about like a bird flapping its wings:

> A housecleaning, oh,
> A housecleaning!

At the sound of his unaffected voice, Musashi and Nikkan turned to watch him. He was wearing his mask with the curious smile and pointing his wooden sword at the scattered bodies. Taking an occasional swipe at the birds, he continued:

> Yes, you crows,
> Once in a while
> There's a need for housecleaning,
> But not only in Nara.
> It's nature's way
> To make everything new again.
> So spring can rise from the ground,
> We burn leaves,
> We burn fields.
> Sometimes we want snow to fall,
> Sometimes we want a housecleaning.
> Oh, you crows!
> Feast away! What a spread!
> Soup straight from the eye sockets,
> And thick red sake.
> But don't have too much
> Or you'll surely get drunk.

"Come here, boy!" shouted Nikkan sharply.

"Yes, sir." Jōtarō stood still and turned to face the abbot.

"Stop acting the fool. Fetch me some rocks."

"This kind?" asked Jōtarō, snatching a stone that lay near his feet and holding it up.

"Yes, like that. Bring lots of them!"

"Yes, sir!"

As the boy gathered the stones, Nikkan sat down and wrote on each one "Namu Myōhō Renge-kyō," the sacred invocation of the Nichiren sect. Then he gave them back to the boy and ordered him to scatter them among the dead. While Jōtarō did this, Nikkan put his palms together and chanted a section of the Lotus Sutra.

When he had finished, he announced, "That should take care of them. Now you two can be on your way. I shall return to Nara." As abruptly as he had come, he departed, walking at his customary breakneck speed, before Musashi had a chance to thank him or make arrangements to see him again.

For a moment, Musashi just stared at the retreating figure, then suddenly he darted off to catch up with it. "Reverend priest!" he called. "Haven't you forgotten something?" He patted his sword as he said this.

"What?" asked Nikkan.

"You have given me no word of guidance, and since there is no way of knowing when we'll meet again, I'd appreciate some small bit of advice."

The abbot's toothless mouth let out its familiar crackling laugh. "Don't you understand *yet?*" he asked. "That you're too strong is the only thing I have to teach you. If you continue to pride yourself on your strength, you won't live to see thirty. Why, you might easily have been killed today. Think about that, and decide how to conduct yourself in the future."

Musashi was silent.

"You accomplished something today, but it was not well done, not by a long shot. Since you're still young, I can't really blame you, but it's a grave error to think the Way of the Samurai consists of nothing but a show of strength.

"But then, I tend to have the same fault, so I'm not really qualified to speak to you on the subject. You should study the way that Yagyū Sekishūsai and Lord Kōizumi of Ise have lived. Sekishūsai was my teacher, Lord Kōizumi was his. If you take them as your models and try to follow the path they have followed, you may come to know the truth."

When Nikkan's voice ceased, Musashi, who had been staring at the ground, deep in thought, looked up. The old priest had already vanished.

The Koyagyū Fief

Yagyū Valley lies at the foot of Mount Kasagi, northeast of Nara. In the early seventeenth century, it was the site of a prosperous little community, too large to be described as a mere village, yet not populous or bustling enough to be called a town. It might naturally have been called Kasagi Village, but instead its inhabitants referred to their home as the Kambe Demesne, a name inherited from the bygone age of the great privately owned manorial estates.

In the middle of the community stood the Main House, a castle that served as both a symbol of governmental stability and the cultural center of the region. Stone ramparts, reminiscent of ancient fortresses, surrounded the Main House. The people of the area, as well as their lord's ancestors, had been comfortably settled there since the tenth century, and the present ruler was a country squire in the best tradition, who spread culture among his subjects and was at all times prepared to protect his territory with his life. At the same time, however, he carefully avoided any serious involvement in the wars and feuds of his fellow lords in other districts. In short, it was a peaceful fief, governed in an enlightened manner.

Here one saw no traces of the depravity or degeneracy associated with foot-loose samurai; it was quite unlike Nara, where ancient temples celebrated in history and folklore were being left to go to seed. Disruptive elements simply were not permitted to enter into the life of this community.

The setting itself militated against ugliness. The mountains in the Kasagi Range were no less strikingly beautiful at eventide than at sunrise, and the water was pure and clean—ideal water, it was said, for making tea. The plum blossoms of Tsukigase were nearby, and nightingales sang from the season of the melting snow to that of the thunderstorms, their tones as crystal clear as the waters of the mountain streams.

A poet once wrote that "in the place where a hero is born, the mountains and rivers are fresh and clear." If no hero had been born in Yagyū Valley, the poet's words would have been empty; but this was indeed a birthplace of heroes. No better proof could be offered than the lords of Yagyū themselves. In this great house even the retainers were men of nobility. Many had come from the rice fields, distinguished themselves in battle, and gone on to become loyal and competent aides.

Yagyū Muneyoshi Sekishūsai, now that he'd retired, had taken up residence in a small mountain house some distance behind the Main House. He no longer showed any interest in local government, and had no idea who was in direct control at the moment. He had a number of capable sons and grandsons, as well as trustworthy retainers to assist and guide them, and he was safe in assuming that the people were being as well governed as they had been when he was in charge.

When Musashi arrived in this district, about ten days had passed since the battle on Hannya Plain. On the way he had visited some temples, Kasagidera and Jōruriji, where he'd seen relics of the Kemmu era. He put up at the local inn with the intention of relaxing for a time, physically and spiritually.

Dressed informally, he went out one day for a walk with Jōtarō. "It's amazing," said Musashi, his eyes roving over the crops in the fields and the farmers going about their work. "Amazing," he repeated several times.

Finally Jōtarō asked, "What's amazing?" For him, the most amazing thing was the way Musashi was talking to himself.

"Since leaving Mimasaka, I've been in Settsu, Kawachi and Izumi provinces, Kyoto and Nara, and I've never seen a place like this."

"Well, so what? What's so different about it?"

"For one thing, there are lots of trees in the mountains here."

Jōtarō laughed. "Trees? There are trees everywhere. Well, aren't there?"

"Yes, but here it's different. All the trees in Yagyū are old. That means there haven't been any wars here, no enemy troops burning or cutting down the forests. It also means there haven't been any famines, at least for a long, long time."

"That's all?"

"No. The fields are green too, and the new barley has been well trampled to strengthen the roots and make it grow well. Listen! Can't you hear the sound of spinning wheels? It seems to be coming from every house. And haven't you noticed that when travelers in fine clothing pass by, the farmers don't look at them enviously?"

"Anything else?"

"As you can see, there are many young girls working the fields. This means that the district is well off, that life is normal here. The children are growing up healthy, the old people are treated with due respect, and the young men and women aren't running off to live uncertain lives in other places. It's a safe bet that the lord of the district is wealthy, and that the swords and guns in his armory are kept polished and in the best condition."

"I don't see anything so interesting in all that," complained Jōtarō.

"Hmm, I don't imagine you would."

"Anyway, you didn't come here to admire the scenery. Aren't you going to fight the samurai in the House of Yagyū?"

"Fighting isn't all there is to the Art of War. The men who think that way, and are satisfied to have food to eat and a place to sleep, are mere vagabonds. A serious student is much more concerned with training his mind and disciplining his spirit than with developing martial skills. He has to learn about all sorts of things—geography, irrigation, the people's feelings, their manners and customs, their relationship with the lord of their territory. He *183* wants to know what goes on inside the castle, not just what goes on outside it. He wants, essentially, to go everywhere he can and learn everything he can."

Musashi realized this lecture probably meant little to Jōtarō, but he felt it necessary to be honest with the child and not give him halfway answers. He showed no impatience at the boy's many questions, and as they walked along, he continued to give thoughtful and serious replies.

After they had seen what there was to see of the exterior of Koyagyū Castle, as the Main House was properly known, and taken a good look all around the valley, they started back to the inn.

There was only one inn, but it was a large one. The road was a section of the Iga highroad, and many people making pilgrimages to the Jōruriji or Kasagi-dera stayed the night here. In the evening, ten or twelve packhorses were always to be found tied to the trees near the entrance or under the front eaves.

The maid who followed them to their room asked, "Have you been out for a walk?" In her mountain-climbing trousers, she might have been mistaken for a boy, were it not for her girl's red obi. Without waiting for an answer, she said, "You can take your bath now, if you like."

Musashi started for the bathroom, while Jōtarō, sensing that here was a new friend of his own age, asked, "What's your name?"

"I don't know," answered the girl.

"You must be crazy if you don't know your own name."

"It's Kocha."

"That's a funny name." Jōtarō laughed.

"What's funny about it?" demanded Kocha, striking him with her fist.

"She hit me!" yelled Jōtarō.

From the folded clothing on the floor of the anteroom, Musashi knew there were other people in the bath. He took off his own clothes and opened the door into the steamy bathroom. There were three men, talking jovially, but catching sight of his brawny body, they stopped as though a foreign element had been introduced into their midst.

Musashi slipped into the communal bath with a contented sigh, his six-foot frame causing the hot water to overflow. For some reason, this startled the three men, and one of them looked straight at Musashi, who had leaned his head against the edge of the pool and closed his eyes.

Gradually they took up their conversation where they had left off. They were washing themselves outside the pool; the skin on their backs was white and their muscles pliant. They were apparently city people, for their manner of speech was polished and urbane.

"What was his name—the samurai from the House of Yagyū?"

"I think he said it was Shōda Kizaemon."

"If Lord Yagyū sends a retainer to convey a refusal to a match, he can't be as good as he's said to be."

"According to Shōda, Sekishūsai's retired and never fights anyone anymore. Do you suppose that's the truth, or was he just making it up?"

"Oh, I don't think it's true. It's much more likely that when he heard the second son of the House of Yoshioka was challenging him, he decided to play it safe."

"Well, he was tactful at least, sending fruit and saying he hoped we'd enjoy our stopover."

Yoshioka? Musashi lifted his head and opened his eyes. Having overheard someone mention Denshichirō's trip to Ise while he was at the Yoshioka School, Musashi assumed that the three men were on their way back to Kyoto. One of them must be Denshichirō. Which one?

"I don't have much luck with baths," thought Musashi ruefully. "First Osugi tricked me into taking a bath, and now, again with no clothes on, I run into one of the Yoshiokas. He's bound to have heard of what happened at the school. If he knew my name was Miyamoto, he'd be out that door and back with his sword in no time."

But the three paid him no attention. To judge from their talk, as soon as they had arrived they had sent a letter to the House of Yagyū. Apparently Sekishūsai had had some connection with Yoshioka Kempō back in the days when Kempō was tutor to the shōguns. No doubt because of this, Sekishūsai could not let Kempō's son go away without acknowledging his letter and had therefore sent Shōda to pay a courtesy call at the inn.

In response to this, the best these city youths could say was that Sekishūsai was "tactful," that he had decided to "play it safe," and that he couldn't be "as good as he's said to be." They seemed exceedingly satisfied with themselves, but Musashi thought them ridiculous. In contrast to what he had seen of Koyagyū Castle and the enviable state of the area's inhabitants, they appeared to have nothing better to offer than clever conversation.

It reminded him of a saying about the frog at the bottom of a well, unable to see what was going on in the outside world. Sometimes, he was thinking, it works the other way around. These pampered young sons of Kyoto were in a position to see what was happening at the center of things and to know what was going on everywhere, but it would not have occurred to them that while they were watching the great open sea, somewhere else, at the bottom of a deep well, a frog was steadily growing larger and stronger. Here in Koyagyū, well away from the country's political and economic center, sturdy samurai had for decades been leading a healthy rural life, preserving the ancient virtues, correcting their weak points and growing in stature.

With the passage of time, Koyagyū had produced Yagyū Muneyoshi, a great master of the martial arts, and his son Lord Munenori of Tajima, whose prowess had been recognized by Ieyasu himself. And there were also Muneyoshi's older sons, Gorōzaemon and Toshikatsu, famous throughout the land for their bravery, and his grandson Hyōgo Toshitoshi, whose prodigious feats had earned him a highly paid position under the renowned general Katō Kiyomasa of Higo. In fame and prestige, the House of Yagyū did not rank with the House of Yoshioka, but in terms of ability, the difference was a thing of the past. Denshichirō and his companions were blind to their own arrogance. Musashi, nevertheless, felt a little sorry for them.

185

He went over to a corner where water was piped into the room. Undoing his headband, he seized a handful of clay and began scrubbing his scalp. For the first time in many weeks, he treated himself to the luxury of a good shampoo.

In the meantime, the men from Kyoto were finishing their bath.

"Ah, that felt good."

"Indeed it did. Now why don't we have some girls in to pour our sake for us?"

"Splendid idea! Splendid!"

The three finished drying themselves and left. After a thorough wash and another soak in the hot water, Musashi too dried off, tied up his hair, and went back to his room. There he found the boyish-looking Kocha in tears.

"What happened to you?"

"It's that boy of yours, sir. Look where he hit me!"

"That's a lie!" Jōtarō cried angrily from the opposite corner.

Musashi was about to scold him, but Jōtarō protested, "The dope said you were weak!"

"That's not true. I didn't."

"You did too!"

"Sir, I didn't say you or anybody else was weak. This brat started bragging about how you were the greatest swordsman in the country, because you'd killed dozens of rōnin at Hannya Plain, and I said there wasn't anybody in Japan better with the sword than the lord of this district, and then he started slapping me on the cheeks."

Musashi laughed. "I see. He shouldn't have done that, and I'll give him a good scolding. I hope you'll forgive us. Jō!" he said sternly.

"Yes, sir," said the boy, still sulking.

"Go take a bath!"

"I don't like to take baths."

"Neither do I," Musashi lied. "But you, you're so sweaty you stink."

"I'll go swimming in the river tomorrow morning."

The boy was becoming more and more stubborn as he grew more accustomed to Musashi, but Musashi did not really mind. In fact, he rather liked this side of Jōtarō. In the end, the boy did not go to the bath.

Before long Kocha brought the dinner trays. They ate in silence, Jōtarō and the maid glaring at each other, while she served the meal.

Musashi was preoccupied with his private objective of meeting Sekishūsai. Considering his own lowly status, perhaps this was asking too much, but maybe, just maybe, it was possible.

"If I'm going to match arms with anybody," thought Musashi, "it should be with somebody strong. It's worth risking my life to see whether I can overcome the great Yagyū name. There's no use in following the Way of the Sword if I haven't the courage to try."

Musashi was aware that most people would laugh outright at him for entertaining the idea. Yagyū, though not one of the more prominent daimyō, was the master of a castle, his son was at the shōgun's court, and the whole family was steeped in the traditions of the warrior class. In the new age now dawning, they were riding the crest of the times.

"This will be the true test," thought Musashi, who, even as he ate his rice, was preparing himself for the encounter.

The Peony

The old man's dignity had grown with the years, until now he resembled nothing so much as a majestic crane, while at the same time retaining the appearance and manner of the well-bred samurai. His teeth were sound, his eyes wonderfully sharp. "I'll live to be a hundred," he frequently assured everyone.

Sekishūsai firmly believed this himself. "The House of Yagyū has always been long-lived," he liked to point out. "The ones who died in their twenties and thirties were killed in battle; all the others lived well beyond sixty." Among the countless wars he himself had taken part in were several major ones, including the revolt of the Miyoshi and the battles marking the rise and fall of the Matsunaga and Oda families.

Even if Sekishūsai had not been born in such a family, his way of life, and especially his attitude after he reached old age, gave reason to believe he would live to reach a hundred. At the age of forty-seven, he had decided for personal reasons to give up warfare. Nothing since had altered this resolution. He had turned a deaf ear to the entreaties of the shōgun Ashikaga Yoshiaki, as well as to repeated requests from Nobunaga and Hideyoshi to join forces with them. Though he lived almost in the shadow of Kyoto and Osaka, he refused to become embroiled in the frequent battles of those centers of power and intrigue. He preferred to remain in Yagyū, like a bear in a cave, and tend his fifteen-thousand-bushel estate in such a way that it could be handed on to his descendants in good condition. Sekishūsai once remarked, "I've done well to hold on to this estate. In this uncertain age, when leaders rise today and fall tomorrow, it's almost incredible that this one small castle has managed to survive intact."

This was no exaggeration. If he had supported Yoshiaki, he would have fallen victim to Nobunaga, and if he had supported Nobunaga, he might well have run afoul of Hideyoshi. Had he accepted Hideyoshi's patronage, he would have been dispossessed by Ieyasu after the Battle of Sekigahara.

His perspicacity, which people admired, was one factor, but to survive in such turbulent times, Sekishūsai had to have an inner fortitude lacking in the ordinary samurai of his time; they were all too apt to side with a man one day and shamelessly desert him the next, to look after their own interests—with no thought to propriety or integrity—or even to slaughter their own kinsmen should they interfere with personal ambitions.

"I am unable to do things like that," Sekishūsai said simply. And he was telling the truth. However, he had not renounced the Art of War itself. In the alcove of his living room hung a poem he had written himself. It said:

> I have no clever method
> For doing well in life.
> I rely only
> On the Art of War.
> It is my final refuge.

When he was invited by Ieyasu to visit Kyoto, Sekishūsai found it impossible not to accept and emerged from decades of serene seclusion to make his first visit to the shōgun's court. With him he took his fifth son, Munenori, who was twenty-four, and his grandson Hyōgo, then only sixteen. Ieyasu not only confirmed the venerable old warrior in his landholdings but asked him to become tutor in the martial arts to the House of Tokugawa. Sekishūsai, declining the honor on grounds of age, requested that Munenori be appointed in his stead, and this met with Ieyasu's approval.

The legacy Munenori carried with him to Edo encompassed more than a superb ability in martial arts, for his father had also passed on to him a knowledge of the higher plane of the Art of War that enables a leader to govern wisely.

In Sekishūsai's view, the Art of War was certainly a means of governing the people, but it was also a means of controlling the self. This he had learned from Lord Kōizumi, who, he was fond of saying, was the protective deity of the Yagyū household. The certificate Lord Kōizumi had given him to attest to his mastery of the Shinkage Style of swordsmanship was always kept on a shelf in Sekishūsai's room, along with a four-volume manual of military techniques presented him by his lordship. On anniversaries of Lord Kōizumi's death, Sekishūsai never neglected to place an offering of food before these treasured possessions.

In addition to descriptions of the hidden-sword techniques of the Shinkage Style, the manual contained illustrative pictures, all by the hand of Lord Kōizumi himself. Even in his retirement, Sekishūsai took pleasure in rolling the scrolls out and looking through them. He was constantly surprised to rediscover how skillfully his teacher had wielded the brush. The pictures showed people fighting and fencing in every conceivable position and stance. When Sekishūsai looked at them, he felt that the swordsmen were about to descend from heaven to join him in his little mountain house.

Lord Kōizumi had first come to Koyagyū Castle when Sekishūsai was thirty-seven or thirty-eight and still brimming with military ambition. His lordship, together with two nephews, Hikida Bungorō and Suzuki Ihaku, was going around the country seeking experts in the martial arts, and one day he arrived at the Hōzōin. This was in the days when In'ei often called at Koyagyū Castle, and In'ei told Sekishūsai about the visitor. That was the beginning of their relationship.

Sekishūsai and Kōizumi held matches for three days in a row. In the first bout, Kōizumi announced where he would attack, then proceeded to take the match doing exactly as he had said.

The same thing happened the second day, and Sekishūsai, his pride injured, concentrated on figuring out a new approach for the third day.

Upon seeing his new stance, Kōizumi merely said, "That won't do. If you are going to do that, I will do this." Without further ado, he attacked and defeated Sekishūsai for the third time. From that day on, Sekishūsai gave up the egotistic approach to swordsmanship; as he later recalled, it was on that occasion that he first had a glimpse of the true Art of War.

At Sekishūsai's strong urging, Lord Kōizumi remained at Koyagyū for six months, during which time Sekishūsai studied with the single-minded devotion of a neophyte. When they finally parted, Lord Kōizumi said, "My way of swordsmanship is still imperfect. You are young, and you should try to carry it to perfection." He then gave Sekishūsai a Zen riddle: "What is sword fighting without a sword?"

For a number of years, Sekishūsai pondered this, considering it from every angle and finally arriving at an answer that satisfied him. When Lord Kōizumi came to visit again, Sekishūsai greeted him with clear, untroubled eyes and suggested that they have a match. His lordship scrutinized him for a moment, then said, "No, it would be useless. You have discovered the truth!"

He then presented Sekishūsai with the certificate and the four-volume manual, and in this fashion the Yagyū Style was born. This in turn gave birth to Sekishūsai's peaceful way of life in his old age.

That Sekishūsai lived in a mountain house was due to his no longer liking the imposing castle with all its elaborate trappings. Despite his almost Taoist love of seclusion, he was happy to have the company of the girl Shōda Kizaemon had brought to play the flute for him, for she was thoughtful, polite and never a nuisance. Not only did her playing please him immensely, but she added a welcome touch of youth and femininity to the household. Occasionally she would talk of leaving, but he would always tell her to stay a little longer.

Putting the finishing touches on the single peony he was arranging in an Iga vase, Sekishūsai asked Otsū, "What do you think? Is my flower arrangement alive?"

Standing just behind him, she said, "You must have studied flower arranging very hard."

"Not at all. I'm not a Kyoto nobleman, and I've never studied either flower arranging or the tea ceremony under a teacher."

"Well, it looks as though you had."

"I use the same method with flowers that I use with the sword."

Otsū looked surprised. "Can you really arrange flowers the way you use the sword?"

189

"Yes. You see, it's all a matter of spirit. I have no use for rules—twisting the flowers with your fingertips or choking them at the neck. The point is to have the proper spirit—to be able to make them seem alive, just as they were when they were picked. Look at that! My flower isn't dead."

Otsū felt that this austere old man had taught her many things she needed to know, and since it had all begun with a chance meeting on the highroad, she felt she had been very lucky. "I'll teach you the tea ceremony," he would say. Or: "Do you compose Japanese poems? If you do, teach me something about the courtly style. The Man'yōshū is all well and good, but living here in this secluded place, I'd rather hear simple poems about nature."

In return, she did little things for him that no one else thought of. He was delighted, for example, when she made him a little cloth cap like the tea masters wore. He kept it on his head much of the time now, treasuring it as though there were nothing finer anywhere. Her flute playing, too, pleased him immensely, and on moonlit nights, the hauntingly beautiful sound of her flute often reached as far as the castle itself.

While Sekishūsai and Otsū were discussing the flower arrangement, Kizaemon came quietly to the entrance of the mountain house and called to Otsū. She came out and invited him in, but he hesitated.

"Would you let his lordship know I've just come back from my errand?" he asked.

Otsū laughed. "That's backwards, isn't it?"

"Why?"

"You're the chief retainer here. I'm only an outsider, called in to play the flute. You're much closer to him than I. Shouldn't you go to him directly, rather than through me?"

"I suppose you're right, but here in his lordship's little house, you're special. Anyway, please give him the message." Kizaemon, too, was pleased by the way things had turned out. He had found in Otsū a person whom his master liked very much.

Otsū returned almost immediately to say that Sekishūsai wanted Kizaemon to come in. Kizaemon found the old man in the tea room, wearing the cloth cap Otsū had made.

"Are you back already?" asked Sekishūsai.

"Yes. I called on them and gave them the letter and the fruit, just as you instructed."

"Have they gone?"

"No. No sooner had I arrived back here than a messenger came from the inn with a letter. It said that since they'd come to Yagyū, they didn't want to leave without seeing the dōjō. If possible, they'd like to come tomorrow. They also said they'd like to meet you and pay their respects."

"Impudent boors! Why must they be such a nuisance?" Sekishūsai looked extremely annoyed. "Did you explain that Munenori is in Edo, Hyōgo in Kumamoto, and that there's no one else around?"

"I did."

"I despise people like that. Even after I send a messenger to tell them I can't see them, they try to push their way in."

"I don't know what—"

"It would appear that Yoshioka's sons are as shiftless as they're said to be."

"The one at the Wataya is Denshichirō. He didn't impress me."

"I'd be surprised if he did. His father was a man of considerable character. When I went to Kyoto with Lord Kōizumi, we saw him two or three times and drank some sake together. It appears that the house has gone downhill since then. The young man seems to think that being Kempō's son gives him the right not to be refused entry here, and so he's pressing his challenge. But from our viewpoint, it makes no sense to accept the challenge and then send him away beaten."

"This Denshichirō seems to have a good deal of self-confidence. If he wants so badly to come, perhaps I myself should take him on."

"No, don't even consider it. These sons of famous people usually have a high opinion of themselves; moreover, they're prone to try and twist things to their own advantage. If you were to beat him, you can depend on it that he'd try to destroy our reputation in Kyoto. As far as I'm concerned, it makes no difference, but I don't want to burden Munenori or Hyōgo with something like that."

"What shall we do, then?"

"The best thing would be to appease him in some way, make him feel he's being treated the way a son from a great house should be treated. Maybe it was a mistake to send a man to see him." Shifting his gaze to Otsū, he continued: "I think a woman would be better. Otsū is probably just the right person."

"All right," she said. "Do you want me to go now?"

"No, there's no hurry. Tomorrow morning will do."

Sekishūsai quickly wrote a simple letter, of the sort a tea master might compose, and handed it to Otsū, with a peony like the one he had put in the vase. "Give these to him, and tell him that you've come in my stead because I have a cold. Let's see what his answer is."

The next morning, Otsū draped a long veil over her head. Although veils were already out of style in Kyoto, even among the higher classes, the upper- and middle-class women in the provinces still prized them.

At the stable, which was in the outer grounds of the castle, she asked to borrow a horse.

The keeper of the stables, who was busy cleaning up, asked, "Oh, are you going somewhere?"

"Yes, I have to go to the Wataya on an errand for his lordship."

"Shall I go with you?"

"There's no need for that."

"Will you be all right?"

"Of course. I like horses. The ones I used to ride in Mimasaka were wild, or nearly so."

As she rode off, the reddish-brown veil floated in the wind behind her. She rode well, holding the letter and the slightly weary peony in one hand and deftly handling the horse with the other. Farmers and workers in the field waved to her, for in the short time she had been here, she had already become fairly well known among the local people, whose relations with Sekishūsai were much friendlier than were usual between lord and peasants. The farmers here all knew that a beautiful young woman had come to play the flute for their lord, and their admiration and respect for him were extended to Otsū.

Arriving at the Wataya, she dismounted and tied her horse to a tree in the garden.

"Welcome!" called Kocha, coming out to greet her. "Are you staying for the night?"

"No, I've just come from Koyagyū Castle with a message for Yoshioka Denshichirō. He's still here, isn't he?"

"Would you wait a moment, please?"

In the brief time Kocha was gone, Otsū created a mild stir among the travelers who were noisily putting on their leggings and sandals and strapping their luggage to their backs.

"Who's that?" asked one.

"Who do you suppose she's come to see?"

Otsū's beauty, a graceful elegance seldom encountered in the country, kept the departing guests whispering and ogling until she followed Kocha out of sight.

Denshichirō and his companions, having drunk until late the night before, had only just arisen. When told that a messenger had come from the castle, they assumed it would be the man who had come the day before. The sight of Otsū with her white peony came as a distinct surprise.

"Oh, please forgive the room! It's a mess."

With abjectly apologetic faces, they straightened their kimonos and sat properly and a little stiffly on their knees.

"Please, come in, come in."

"I've been sent by the lord of Koyagyū Castle," Otsū said simply, placing the letter and the peony before Denshichirō. "Would you be so kind as to read the letter now?"

"Ah, yes . . . this is the letter? Yes, I'll read it."

He opened the scroll, which was no more than a foot long. Written in thin ink, suggestive of the light flavor of tea, it said: "Forgive me for sending my greetings in a letter, rather than meeting you in person, but unfortunately I have a slight cold. I think a pure white peony will give you more pleasure than the runny nose of an old man. I send the flower by the hand of a flower, with the hope that you will accept my apology. My ancient body rests outside the everyday world. I hesitate to show my face. Please smile with pity on an old man."

Denshichirō sniffed with contempt and rolled up the letter. "Is that all?" he asked.

"No, he also said that although he'd like to have a cup of tea with you, he hesitates to invite you to his house, because there is no one there but warriors ignorant of the niceties of tea. Since Munenori is away in Edo, he feels that the serving of the tea would be so crude as to bring laughter to the lips of

192

people from the imperial capital. He asked me to beg your pardon, and tell you that he hopes to see you on some future occasion."

"Ha, ha!" exclaimed Denshichirō, putting on a suspicious face. "If I understand you correctly, Sekishūsai is under the impression we were looking forward to observing the niceties of the tea ceremony. To tell the truth, being from samurai families, we don't know anything about tea. Our intention was to inquire personally after Sekishūsai's health and persuade him to give us a lesson in swordsmanship."

"He understands that perfectly, of course. But he's spending his old age in retirement and has acquired the habit of expressing many of his thoughts in terms of tea."

In obvious disgust, Denshichirō replied, "Well, he hasn't left us any choice but to give up. Please tell him that if we come again, we'd like to see him." He handed the peony back to Otsū.

"Don't you like it? He thought it might cheer you up on the road. He said you might hang it in the corner of your palanquin, or if you're on horseback, attach it to your saddle."

"He meant it to be a souvenir?" Denshichirō lowered his eyes as though insulted, then with a sour face said, "This is ridiculous! You can tell him we have peonies of our own in Kyoto!"

If that was the way he felt, Otsū decided, there was no point in pressing the gift on him. Promising to deliver his message, she took her leave as delicately as she would have removed the bandage from an open sore. In ill temper, her hosts barely acknowledged her departure.

Once in the hallway, Otsū laughed softly to herself, glanced at the shiny black floor leading to the room where Musashi was staying, and turned in the other direction.

Kocha came out of Musashi's room and ran to catch up with her.

"Are you leaving already?" she asked.

"Yes, I've finished what I came to do."

"My, that was fast, wasn't it?" Looking down at Otsū's hand, she asked, "Is that a peony? I didn't know they bloomed white."

"Yes. It's from the castle garden. You can have it, if you like."

"Oh, please," said Kocha, stretching out her hands.

After bidding Otsū good-bye, Kocha went to the servants' quarters and showed everyone the flower. Since no one was inclined to admire it, she went disappointedly back to Musashi's room.

Musashi, sitting by the window with his chin in his hands, was gazing in the direction of the castle and thinking hard about his objective: how could he manage, first, to meet Sekishūsai and, second, to overcome him with his sword?

"Do you like flowers?" Kocha asked as she entered.

"Flowers?"

She showed him the peony.

"Hmm. It's nice."

"Do you like it?"

"Yes."

"It's supposed to be a peony, a white peony."

"Is it? Why don't you put it in that vase over there."

"I don't know how to arrange flowers. You do it."

"No, you do it. It's better to do it without thinking how it's going to look."

"Well, I'll go and get some water," she said, taking the vase out with her.

Musashi's eye happened to light on the cut end of the peony stem. His head tilted in surprise, though he couldn't pinpoint what it was that attracted his attention.

Casual interest had become intent scrutiny by the time Kocha came back. She put the vase in the alcove and tried sticking the peony in it, but with poor results.

"The stem's too long," said Musashi. "Bring it here; I'll cut it. Then when you stand it up, it'll look natural."

Kocha brought the flower over and held it up to him. Before she knew what had happened, she had dropped the flower and burst into tears. Small wonder, for in that split second Musashi had whipped out his short sword, uttered a vigorous cry, slashed through the stem between her hands, and resheathed his sword. To Kocha, the glint of steel and the sound of the sword snapping back into its scabbard seemed simultaneous.

Making no attempt to comfort the terrified girl, Musashi picked up the piece of stem he had cut off and began comparing one end of it with the other. He seemed completely absorbed. Finally, taking notice of her distraught state, he apologized and patted her on the head.

Once he had coaxed her out of her tears, he asked, "Do you know who cut this flower?"

"No. It was given to me."

"By whom?"

"A person from the castle."

"One of the samurai?"

"No, it was a young woman."

"Mm. Then you think the flower came from the castle?"

"Yes, she said it did."

"I'm sorry I scared you. If I buy you some cakes later, will you forgive me? In any case, the flower should be just right now. Try putting it in the vase."

"Will this do?"

"Yes, that's fine."

Kocha had taken an instant liking to Musashi, but the flash of his sword had chilled her to the marrow. She left the room, unwilling to return until her duties made it absolutely unavoidable.

Musashi was far more fascinated by the eight-inch piece of stem than by the flower in the alcove. He was sure the first cut had not been made with either scissors or a knife. Since peony stems are lithe and supple, the cut could only have been made with a sword, and only a very determined stroke would have made so clean a slice. Whoever had done it was no ordinary person. Although he himself had just tried to duplicate the cut with his own sword, upon com-

194

paring both ends he was immediately aware that his own cut was by far the inferior one. It was like the difference between a Buddhist statue carved by an expert and one made by a craftsman of average skill.

He asked himself what it could mean. "If a samurai working the castle garden can make a cut like this, then the standards of the House of Yagyū must be even higher than I thought."

His confidence suddenly deserted him. "I'm nowhere near ready yet."

Gradually, however, he recovered from this feeling. "In any event, the Yagyū people are worthy opponents. If I should lose, I can fall at their feet and accept defeat with good grace. I've already decided I'm willing to face anything, even death." Sitting and mustering up his courage, he felt himself grow warmer.

But how was he to go about it? Even if a student arrived at his doorstep with a proper introduction, it seemed unlikely Sekishūsai would agree to a match. The innkeeper had said as much. And with Munenori and Hyōgo both away, there was no one to challenge but Sekishūsai himself.

He again tried to devise a way of gaining admittance to the castle. His eyes returned to the flower in the alcove, and the image of someone the flower unconsciously reminded him of began to take form. Seeing Otsū's face in his mind's eye quieted his spirit and soothed his nerves.

Otsū herself was well on her way back to Koyagyū Castle when suddenly she heard a raucous shout behind her. She turned to see a child emerging from a clump of trees at the base of a cliff. He was clearly coming after her, and since children of the area were much too timid to accost a young woman such as herself, she brought her horse to a halt out of sheer curiosity.

Jōtarō was stark naked. His hair was wet, and his clothes were rolled up in a ball under his arm. Unabashed by his nudity, he said, "You're the lady with the flute. Are you still staying here?" Having eyed the horse with distaste, he looked directly at Otsū.

"It's you!" she exclaimed, before averting her eyes in embarrassment. "The little boy who was crying on the Yamato highroad."

"Crying? I wasn't crying!"

"Never mind. How long have you been here?"

"Just came the other day."

"By yourself?"

"No; with my teacher."

"Oh, that's right. You did say you were studying swordsmanship, didn't you? What are you doing with your clothes off?"

"You don't think I'd jump in the river with my clothes on, do you?"

"River? But the water must be freezing. People around here would laugh at the idea of going swimming this time of year."

"I wasn't swimming; I was taking a bath. My teacher said I smelled sweaty, so I went to the river."

Otsū chuckled. "Where are you staying?"

"At the Wataya."

"Why, I've just come from there."

"Too bad you didn't come to see us. How about coming back with me now?"

"I can't now. I have an errand to do."

"Well, bye!" he said, turning to go.

"Jōtarō, come see me at the castle sometime."

"Could I really?"

The words were barely out before Otsū began to regret them, but she said, "Yes, but make sure you don't come dressed the way you are now."

"If that's the way you feel about it, I don't want to go. I don't like places where they make a fuss about things."

Otsū felt relieved and still had a smile on her face when she rode back through the castle gate. After returning her horse to the stable, she went to report to Sekishūsai.

He laughed and said, "So they were angry! Fine! Let them be angry. There's nothing they can do about it." After a moment, he seemed to remember something else. "Did you throw the peony away?" he asked.

She explained that she had given it to the maid at the inn, and he nodded his approval. "Did the Yoshioka boy take the peony in his hand and look at it?" he asked.

"Yes. When he read the letter."

"And?"

"He just handed it back to me."

"He didn't look at the stem?"

"Not that I noticed."

"He didn't examine it, or say anything about it?"

"No."

"It's just as well that I refused to meet him. He's not worth meeting. The House of Yoshioka might just as well have ended with Kempō.

The Yagyū dōjō could quite appropriately be described as grand. Situated in the outer grounds of the castle, it had been rebuilt around the time when Sekishūsai was forty, and the sturdy timber used in its construction gave it an air of indestructibility. The gloss of the wood, acquired over the years, seemed to echo the rigors of the men who had undergone training here, and the building was ample enough to have served as samurai barracks during times of war.

"Lightly! Not with your sword point! With your gut, your gut!" Shōda Kizaemon, seated on a slightly elevated platform and clad in underrobe and *hakama*, was roaring angry instructions at two aspiring swordsmen. "Do it again! You don't have it right at all!"

The target of Kizaemon's scolding was a pair of Yagyū samurai, who though dazed and bathed in sweat fought doggedly on. Stances were taken, weapons readied, and the two came together again like fire against fire.

"A-o-o-oh!"

"Y-a-a-ah!"

At Yagyū, beginners were not allowed to use wooden swords. Instead they used a staff devised specifically for the Shinkage Style. A long, thin leather

196

bag filled with strips of bamboo, it was, in effect, a leather stick, with no handle or sword guard. Though less dangerous than a wooden sword, it could still remove an ear or turn a nose into a pomegranate. There were no restrictions regarding what part of the body a combatant could attack. Knocking down an opponent by striking him horizontally in the legs was permitted, and there was no rule against hitting a man once he was down.

"Keep it up! Keep at it! Same as last time!" Kizaemon drove the students on.

The custom here was not to let a man quit until he was ready to drop. Beginners were driven especially hard, never praised and treated to no small amount of verbal abuse. Because of this, the average samurai knew that entering into the service of the House of Yagyū was not something to be taken lightly. Newcomers rarely lasted long, and the men now serving under Yagyū were the result of very careful sifting. Even the common foot soldiers and stablemen had made some progress in the study of swordsmanship.

Shōda Kizaemon was, needless to say, an accomplished swordsman, having mastered the Shinkage Style at an early age and, under the tutelage of Sekishūsai himself, gone on to learn the secrets of the Yagyū Style. To this he had added some personal techniques of his own, and he spoke proudly now of the "True Shōda Style."

The Yagyū horse trainer, Kimura Sukekurō, was also an adept, as was Murata Yozō, who, though employed as keeper of the storehouse, was said to have been a good match for Hyōgo. Debuchi Magobei, another relatively minor official, had studied swordsmanship from childhood and wielded a powerful weapon indeed. The Lord of Echizen had tried to persuade Debuchi to come into his service, and the Tokugawas of Kii had tried to lure Murata away, but both of them had chosen to stay in Yagyū, though the material benefits were fewer.

The House of Yagyū, now enjoying a peak in its fortunes, was turning out a seemingly unending stream of great swordsmen. By the same token, the Yagyū samurai were not recognized as swordsmen until they had proved their ability by surviving the merciless regimen.

"You there!" called Kizaemon to a guard passing by outside. He had been surprised by the sight of Jōtarō following along after the soldier.

"Hello!" shouted Jōtarō in his friendliest manner.

"What are you doing inside the castle?" asked Kizaemon sternly.

"The man at the gate brought me in," answered Jōtarō, truthfully enough.

"He did, did he?" To the guard, he said, "Why did you bring this boy here?"

"He said he wanted to see you."

"Do you mean to say you brought this child here on his word alone? . . . Boy!"

"Yes, sir."

"This is no playground. Get along with you."

"But I didn't come to play. I brought a letter from my teacher."

"From your teacher? Didn't you say he was one of those wandering students?"

"Look at the letter, please."

"I don't need to."

"What's the matter? Can't you read?"

Kizaemon snorted.

"Well, if you can read, read it."

"You're a tricky brat. The reason I said I don't need to read it is that I already know what it says."

"Even so, wouldn't it be more polite to read it?"

"Student warriors swarm here like mosquitoes and maggots. If I took time to be polite to all of them, I wouldn't be able to do anything else. I feel sorry for you, however, so I'll tell you what the letter says. All right?

"It says that the writer would like to be allowed to see our magnificent dōjō, that he would like to bask, even for a minute, in the shadow of the greatest master in the land, and that for the sake of all those successors who will follow the Way of the Sword, he would be grateful to have a lesson bestowed upon him. I imagine that's about the long and short of it."

Jōtarō's eyes rounded. "Is that what the letter says?"

"Yes, so I don't need to read it, do I? Let it not be said, however, that the House of Yagyū coldheartedly turns away those who call upon it." He paused and continued, as though having rehearsed the speech: "Ask the guard there to explain everything to you. When student warriors come to this house, they enter through the main gate and proceed to the middle gate, to the right of which is a building called the Shin'indō. It is identified by a hanging wooden plaque. If they apply to the caretaker there, they are free to rest for a time, and there are facilities for them to stop over for a night or two. When they leave, they are given a small amount of money to help them along the way. Now, the thing for you to do is to take this letter to the caretaker at the Shin'indō—understand?"

"No!" said Jōtarō. He shook his head and raised his right shoulder slightly. "Listen, sir!"

"Well?"

"You shouldn't judge people by their appearance. I'm not the son of a beggar!"

"I do have to admit you have a certain knack with words."

"Why don't you just take a look at the letter? It may say something completely different from what you think. What would you do then? Would you let me cut off your head?"

"Hold on a minute!" Kizaemon laughed, and his face, with its red mouth behind his spiky beard, looked like the inside of a broken chestnut burr. "No, you can't cut my head off."

"Well, then, look at the letter."

"Come in here."

"Why?" Jōtarō had a sinking feeling he'd gone too far.

"I admire your determination not to let your master's message go undelivered. I'll read it."

"And why shouldn't you? You're the highest-ranking official in the House of Yagyū, aren't you?"

"You wield your tongue superbly. Let's hope you can do the same with your sword when you grow up." He broke the seal of the letter and silently read Musashi's message. As he read, his face became serious. When he was finished, he asked, "Did you bring anything along with this letter?"

"Oh, I forgot! I was to give you this too." Jōtarō quickly pulled the peony stem from his kimono.

Silently, Kizaemon examined both ends of the stem, looking somewhat puzzled. He could not completely understand the meaning of Musashi's letter.

It explained how the inn's maid had brought him a flower, which she said had come from the castle, and that upon examining the stem, he had discovered that the cut had been made by "no ordinary person." The message continued: "After putting the flower in a vase, I sensed some special spirit about it, and I feel that I simply have to find out who made that cut. The question may seem trivial, but if you would not mind telling me which member of your household did it, I would appreciate your sending a reply by the boy who delivers my letter."

That was all—no mention of the writer's being a student, no request for a bout.

"What an odd thing to write," thought Kizaemon. He looked at the peony stem again, again examining both ends closely, but without being able to discern whether one end differed from the other.

"Murata!" he called. "Come look at this. Can you see any difference between the cuts at the ends of this stem? Does one cut, perhaps, seem to be keener?"

Murata Yozō looked at the stem this way and that, but had to confess that he saw no difference between the two cuts.

"Let's show it to Kimura."

They went to the office at the back of the building and put the problem to their colleague, who was as mystified as they were. Debuchi, who happened to be in the office at the time, said, "This is one of the flowers the old lord himself cut the day before yesterday. Shōda, weren't you with him at the time?"

"No, I saw him arranging a flower, but I didn't see him cut it."

"Well, this is one of the two he cut. He put one in the vase in his room and had Otsū take the other one to Yoshioka Denshichirō with a letter."

"Yes, I remember that," said Kizaemon, as he started to read Musashi's letter again. Suddenly, he looked up with startled eyes. "This is signed 'Shimmen Musashi,'" he said. "Do you suppose this Musashi is the Miyamoto Musashi who helped the Hōzōin priests kill all that riffraff at Hannya Plain? It must be!"

Debuchi and Murata passed the letter back and forth, rereading it. "The handwriting has character," said Debuchi.

"Yes," mumbled Murata. "He seems to be an unusual person."

"If what the letter says is true," Kizaemon said, "and he really could tell that this stem had been cut by an expert, then he must know something we don't. The old master cut it himself, and apparently that's plain to someone whose eyes really see."

Debuchi said, "Mm. I'd like to meet him. . . . We could check on this and also get him to tell us what happened at Hannya Plain." But rather than commit himself on his own, he asked Kimura's opinion. Kimura pointed out that since they weren't receiving any *shugyōsha*, they couldn't have him as a guest at the practice hall, but there was no reason why they couldn't invite him for a meal and some sake at the Shin'indō. The irises were already in bloom there, he noted, and the wild azaleas were about to blossom. They could have a little party and talk about swordsmanship and things like that. Musashi would in all likelihood be glad to come, and the old lord certainly wouldn't object if he heard about it.

Kizaemon slapped his knee and said, "That's a splendid suggestion."

"It'll be a party for us too," Murata added. "Let's send him an answer right away."

As he sat down to write the reply, Kizaemon said, "The boy's outside. Have him come in."

A few minutes earlier, Jōtarō had been yawning and grumbling, "How can they be so slow," when a big black dog caught his scent and came over to sniff at him. Thinking he had found a new friend, Jōtarō spoke to the dog and pulled him forward by the ears.

"Let's wrestle," he suggested, then hugged the dog and threw him over. The dog went along with this, so Jōtarō caught him in his hands and threw him two or three more times.

Then, holding the dog's jaws together, he said, "Now, bark!"

This made the dog angry. Breaking away, he caught the skirt of Jōtarō's kimono with his teeth and tugged tenaciously.

Now it was Jōtarō's turn to get mad. "Who do you think I am? You can't do that!" he shouted.

He drew his wooden sword and held it menacingly over his head. The dog, taking him seriously, started barking loudly to attract the attention of the guards. With a curse, Jōtarō brought his sword down on the dog's head. It sounded as though he had hit a rock. The dog hurled himself against the boy's back, and catching hold of his obi, brought him to the ground. Before he could get to his feet, the dog was at him again, while Jōtarō frantically tried to protect his face with his hands.

He tried to escape, but the dog was right on his heels, the echoes of his barking reverberating through the mountains. Blood began to ooze between the fingers covering his face, and soon his own anguished howls drowned out those of the dog.

200

Jōtarō's Revenge

On his return to the inn, Jōtarō sat down before Musashi and with a smug look reported that he had carried out his mission. Several scratches criss-crossed the boy's face, and his nose looked like a ripe strawberry. No doubt he was in some pain, but since he offered no explanation, Musashi asked no questions.

"Here's their reply," said Jōtarō, handing Musashi the letter from Shōda Kizaemon and adding a few words about his meeting with the samurai, but saying nothing about the dog. As he spoke, his wounds started to bleed again.

"Will that be all?" he asked.

"Yes, that's all. Thanks."

As Musashi opened Kizaemon's letter, Jōtarō put his hands to his face and hurriedly left the room. Kocha caught up with him and examined his scratches with worried eyes.

"How did that happen?" she asked.

"A dog jumped on me."

"Whose dog was it?"

"One of the dogs at the castle."

"Oh, was it that big black Kishū hound? He's vicious. I'm sure, strong as you are, you wouldn't be able to handle him. Why, he's bitten prowlers to death!"

Although they were not on the best of terms, Kocha led him to the stream out back and made him wash his face. Then she went and fetched some oint-ment, which she applied to his face. For once, Jōtarō behaved like a gentle-man. When she had finished her ministrations, he bowed and thanked her over and over again.

"Stop bobbing your head up and down. You're a man, after all, and it looks ridiculous."

"But I appreciate what you've done."

"Even if we do fight a lot, I still like you," she confessed.

"I like you too."

"Really?"

The parts of Jōtarō's face that showed between the patches of ointment turned crimson, and Kocha's cheeks burst into subdued flame. There was no one around. The sun shone through the pink peach blossoms.

"Your master will probably be going away soon, won't he?" she asked with a trace of disappointment.

"We'll be here for a while yet," he replied reassuringly.

"I wish you could stay for a year or two."

The two went into the shed where the fodder for the horses was kept and lay down on their backs in the hay. Their hands touched, sending a warm tingle through Jōtarō. Quite without warning, he pulled Kocha's hand toward him and bit her finger.

"Ouch!"

"Did that hurt? I'm sorry."

"It's all right. Do it again."

"You don't mind?"

"No, no, go on and bite! Bite harder!"

He did just that, tugging at her fingers like a puppy. Hay was falling over their heads, and soon they were hugging each other, just for the sake of hugging, when Kocha's father came looking for her. Appalled at what he saw, his face took on the stern expression of a Confucian sage.

"You idiots, what are you up to? Both of you, still only children!" He dragged them out by the scruff of the neck and gave Kocha a couple of smart whacks on the behind.

The rest of that day, Musashi said very little to anyone. He sat with his arms folded and thought.

Once, in the middle of the night, Jōtarō woke up and, raising his head a little, stole a look at his master. Musashi was lying in bed with his eyes wide open, staring at the ceiling with intense concentration.

The next day, too, Musashi kept to himself. Jōtarō was frightened; his master might have heard about his playing with Kocha in the shed. Nothing was said, however. Late in the afternoon, Musashi sent the boy to ask for their bill and was making preparations to depart when the clerk brought it. Asked if he would need dinner, he said no.

Kocha, standing idly in a corner, asked, "Won't you be coming back to sleep here tonight?"

"No. Thank you, Kocha, for taking such good care of us. I'm sure we've been a lot of trouble for you. Good-bye."

"Take good care of yourself," said Kocha. She was holding her hands over her face, hiding her tears.

At the gate, the manager of the inn and the other maids lined up to see them off. Their setting off just before sunset seemed very odd.

After walking a bit, Musashi looked around for Jōtarō. Not seeing him, he turned back toward the inn, where the boy was under the storehouse, saying farewell to Kocha. When they saw Musashi approaching, they drew hastily away from each other.

"Good-bye," said Kocha.

"Bye," called Jōtarō, as he ran to Musashi's side. Though fearful of Musashi's eyes, the boy could not resist stealing backward glances until the inn was out of sight.

Lights began to appear in the valley. Musashi, saying nothing and not once looking back, strode on ahead. Jōtarō followed along glumly.

After a time, Musashi asked, "Aren't we there yet?"

"Where?"

"At the main gate of Koyagyū Castle."

"Are we going to the castle?"

"Yes."

"Will we stay there tonight?"

"I have no idea. That depends on how things turn out."

"There it is. That's the gate."

Musashi stopped and stood before the gate, feet together. Above the moss-grown ramparts, the huge trees made a soughing sound. A single light streamed from a square window.

Musashi called out, and a guard appeared. Giving him the letter from Shōda Kizaemon, he said, "My name is Musashi, and I've come on Shōda's invitation. Would you please tell him that I'm here?"

The guard had been expecting him. "They're waiting for you," he said, motioning for Musashi to follow him.

In addition to its other functions, the Shin'indō was the place where the young people in the castle studied Confucianism. It also served as the fief's library. The rooms along the passageway to the rear of the building were all lined with bookshelves, and though the fame of the House of Yagyū stemmed from its military prowess, Musashi could see it also placed great emphasis on scholarship. Everything about the castle seemed to be steeped in history.

And everything seemed to be well run, to judge from the neatness of the road from the gate to the Shin'indō, the courteous demeanor of the guard, and the austere, peaceful lighting visible in the vicinity of the keep.

Sometimes, upon entering a house for the first time, a visitor has the feeling he's already familiar with the place and its inhabitants. Musashi had that impression now, as he sat down on the wooden floor of the large room to which the guard brought him. After offering him a hard round cushion of woven straw, which he accepted with thanks, the guard left him alone. On the way, Jōtarō had been dropped off at the attendants' waiting room.

The guard returned a few minutes later and told Musashi that his host would arrive soon.

Musashi slid the round cushion over to a corner and leaned back against a post. From the light of the low lamp shining into the garden, he saw trellises of blossoming wisteria vines, both white and lavender. The sweetish scent of wisteria was in the air. He was startled by the croak of a frog, the first he had heard that year.

Water gurgled somewhere in the garden; the stream apparently ran under the building, for after he was settled, he noticed the sound of flowing water beneath him. Indeed, before long it seemed to him that the sound of water was coming from the walls, the ceiling, even the lamp. He felt cool and relaxed. Yet simmering deep inside him there was an unsuppressible sense of disquiet. It was his insatiable fighting spirit, coursing through his veins even in this quiet atmosphere. From his cushion by the post, he looked questioningly at his surroundings.

203

"Who is Yagyū?" he thought defiantly. "He's a swordsman, and I'm a swordsman. In this respect we are equal. But tonight I will advance a step farther and put Yagyū behind me."

"Sorry to have kept you waiting."

Shōda Kizaemon entered the room with Kimura, Debuchi and Murata.

"Welcome to Koyagyū," Kizaemon said warmly.

After the other three men had introduced themselves, servants brought in trays of sake and snacks. The sake was a thick, rather syrupy, local brew, served in large old-style sake bowls with high stems.

"Here in the country," said Kizaemon, "we aren't able to offer you much, but please feel at home."

The others too, with great cordiality, invited him to make himself comfortable, not to stand on ceremony.

With a little urging, Musashi accepted some sake, though he was not particularly fond of it. It was not so much that he disliked it as that he was still too young to appreciate its subtlety. The sake this evening was palatable enough but had little immediate effect on him.

"Looks as though you know how to drink," said Kimura Sukekurō, offering to refill his cup. "By the way, I hear the peony you asked about the other day was cut by the lord of this castle himself."

Musashi slapped his knee. "I thought so!" he exclaimed. "It was splendid!"

Kimura moved closer. "What I'd like to know is just how you could tell that the cut in that soft, thin stem had been made by a master swordsman. We, all of us, were deeply impressed by your ability to discern that."

Uncertain as to where the conversation was leading, Musashi said, to gain time, "You were? Really?"

"Yes, no mistake about it!" said Kizaemon, Debuchi and Murata almost simultaneously.

"We ourselves couldn't see anything special about it," said Kizaemon. "We arrived at the conclusion that it must take a genius to recognize another genius. We think it would be of great help in our future studies if you'd explain it to us."

Musashi, taking another sip of sake, said, "Oh, it wasn't anything in particular—just a lucky guess."

"Come now, don't be modest."

"I'm not being modest. It was a feeling I got—from the look of the cut."

"Just what sort of feeling was it?"

As they would with any stranger, these four senior disciples of the House of Yagyū were trying to analyze Musashi as a human being and at the same time test him. They had already taken note of his physique, admiring his carriage and the expression in his eyes. But the way he held his sake cup and his chopsticks betrayed his country upbringing and made them inclined to be patronizing. After only three or four cups of sake, Musashi's face turned copper red. Embarrassed, he touched his hand to his forehead and cheeks two or three times. The boyishness of the gesture made them laugh.

204

"This feeling of yours," repeated Kizaemon. "Can't you tell us more about it? You know, this building, the Shin'indō, was built expressly for Lord Kōizumi of Ise to stay in during his visits. It's an important building in the history of swordsmanship. It's a fitting place for us to hear a lecture from you tonight."

Realizing that protesting their flattery was not going to get him off the hook, Musashi decided to take the plunge.

"When you sense something you sense it," he said. "There's really no way to explain it. If you want me to demonstrate what I mean, you'll have to unsheath your sword and face me in a match. There's no other way."

The smoke from the lamp rose as black as squid ink in the still night air. The croaking frog was heard again.

Kizaemon and Debuchi, the two eldest, looked at each other and laughed. Though he had spoken quietly, the statement about testing him had undeniably been a challenge, and they recognized it as such.

Letting it pass without comment, they talked about swords, then about Zen, events in other provinces, the Battle of Sekigahara. Kizaemon, Debuchi and Kimura had all taken part in the bloody conflict, and to Musashi, who had been on the opposing side, their stories had the ring of bitter truth. The hosts appeared to be enjoying the conversation immensely, and Musashi found it fascinating just to listen.

He was nonetheless conscious of the swift passage of time, knowing in his heart that if he did not meet Sekishūsai tonight, he would never meet him.

Kizaemon announced it was time for the barley mixed with rice, the customary last course, to be served, and the sake was removed.

"How can I see him?" thought Musashi. It became increasingly clear that he might be forced to employ some underhanded scheme. Should he goad one of his hosts into losing his temper? Difficult, when he was not angry himself, so he purposefully disagreed several times with what was being said and spoke in a rude and brash manner. Shōda and Debuchi chose to laugh at this. None of these four was about to be provoked into doing anything rash.

Desperation set in. Musashi could not bear the idea of leaving without accomplishing his objective. For his crown, he wanted a brilliant star of victory, and for the record, he wanted it known that Musashi had been here, had gone, had left his mark on the House of Yagyū. With his own sword, he wanted to bring Sekishūsai, this great patriarch of the martial arts, this "ancient dragon" as he was called, to his knees.

Had they seen through him completely? He was considering this possibility when matters took an unexpected turn.

"Did you hear that?" asked Kimura.

Murata went out on the veranda, then, reentering the room, said, "Tarō's barking—not his usual bark, though. I think something must be wrong."

Tarō was the dog Jōtarō had had a run-in with. There was no denying that the barking, which seemed to come from the second encirclement of the castle, was frightening. It sounded too loud and terrible to be coming from a single dog.

Debuchi said, "I think I'd better have a look. Forgive me, Musashi, for spoiling the party, but it may be important. Please go on without me."

Shortly after he left, Murata and Kimura excused themselves, politely begging Musashi's forgiveness.

The barking grew more urgent; the dog was apparently trying to give warning of some danger. When one of the castle's dogs acted this way, it was almost a sure sign something untoward was going on. The peace the country was enjoying was not so secure that a daimyō could afford to relax his vigilance against neighboring fiefs. There were still unscrupulous warriors who might stoop to anything to satisfy their own ambition, and spies roamed the land searching out complacent and vulnerable targets.

Kizaemon seemed extremely upset. He kept staring at the ominous light of the little lamp, as if counting the echoes of the unearthly noise.

Eventually there was one long, mournful wail. Kizaemon grunted and looked at Musashi.

"He's dead," said Musashi.

"Yes, he's been killed." No longer able to contain himself, Kizaemon stood up. "I can't understand it."

He started to leave, but Musashi stopped him, saying, "Wait. Is Jōtarō, the boy who came with me, still in the waiting room?"

They directed their inquiry to a young samurai in front of the Shin'indō, who after searching reported the boy was nowhere to be found.

A look of concern came over Musashi's face. Turning to Kizaemon, he said, "I think I know what happened. Would you mind my going with you?"

"Not at all."

About three hundred yards from the dōjō, a crowd had gathered, and several torches had been lit. Besides Murata, Debuchi and Kimura, there were a number of foot soldiers and guards, forming a black circle, all talking and shouting at once.

From the outer rim of the circle, Musashi peered into the open space in the middle. His heart sank. There, just as he had feared, was Jōtarō, covered with blood and looking like the devil's own child—wooden sword in hand, his teeth tightly clenched, his shoulders rising and falling with his heavy breathing.

By his side lay Tarō, teeth bared, legs outstretched. The dog's sightless eyes reflected the light of the torches; blood trickled from his mouth.

"It's his lordship's dog," someone said mournfully.

A samurai went toward Jōtarō and shouted, "You little bastard! What have you done? Are you the one who killed this dog?" The man brought his hand down in a furious slap, which Jōtarō just managed to dodge.

Squaring his shoulders, he shouted defiantly, "Yes, I did it!"

"You admit it?"

"I had a reason!"

"Ha!"

"I was taking revenge."

"What?" There was general astonishment at Jōtarō's answer; the whole crowd was angry. Tarō was the favorite pet of Lord Munenori of Tajima. Not only that; he was the pedigreed offspring of Raiko, a bitch belonging to and much loved by Lord Yorinori of Kishū. Lord Yorinori had personally given the pup to Munenori, who had himself reared it. The slaying of the animal would consequently be investigated thoroughly, and the fate of the two samurai who had been paid to take good care of the dog was now in jeopardy.

The man now facing Jōtarō was one of these two.

"Shut up!" he shouted, aiming his fist at Jōtarō's head. This time Jōtarō did not duck in time. The blow landed in the vicinity of his ear.

Jōtarō raised his hand to feel his wound. "What are you doing?" he screamed.

"You killed the master's dog. You don't mind if I beat you to death the same way, do you? Because that's exactly what I'm going to do."

"All I did was get even with him. Why punish me for that? A grown man should know that's not right!"

In Jōtarō's view, he had only protected his honor, and risked his life in doing so, for a visible wound was a great disgrace to a samurai. To defend his pride, there was no alternative to killing the dog: indeed, in all likelihood he had expected to be praised for his valiant conduct. He stood his ground, determined not to flinch.

"Shut your impudent mouth!" screamed the keeper. "I don't care if you are only a child. You're old enough to know the difference between a dog and a human being. The very idea—taking revenge on a dumb animal!"

He grabbed Jōtarō's collar, looked to the crowd for approval, and declared it his duty to punish the dog's murderer. The crowd silently nodded in agreement. The four men who had so recently been entertaining Musashi looked distressed but said nothing.

"Bark, boy! Bark like a dog!" the keeper shouted. He swung Jōtarō around and around by his collar and with a black look in his eye threw him to the ground. Seizing an oak staff, he raised it above his head ready to strike.

"You killed the dog, you little hoodlum. Now it's your turn! Stand up so I can kill you! Bark! Bite me!"

Teeth tightly clenched, Jōtarō propped himself up on one arm and struggled to his feet, wooden sword in hand. His features had not lost their spritelike quality, but the expression on his face was anything but childlike, and the howl that issued from his throat was eerily savage.

When an adult gets angry, he often regrets it later, but when a child's wrath is aroused, not even the mother who brought him into the world can placate him.

"Kill me!" he screamed. "Go on, kill me!"

"Die, then!" raged the keeper. He struck.

The blow would have killed the boy if it had connected, but it didn't. A sharp crack reverberated in the ears of the bystanders, and Jōtarō's wooden sword went flying through the air. Without thinking about it, he had parried the keeper's blow.

Weaponless, he closed his eyes and charged blindly at the enemy's midriff, latching on to the man's obi with his teeth. Holding on for dear life, he tore with his nails at the keeper's groin, while the keeper made futile swings with his staff.

Musashi had remained silent, arms folded and face expressionless, but then another oak staff appeared. A second man had dashed into the ring and was on the verge of attacking Jōtarō from behind. Musashi moved into action. His arms came down and in no time he forced his way through the solid wall of men into the arena.

"Coward!" he shouted at the second man.

An oak stick and two legs described an arc in the air, coming to rest in a clump about four yards away.

Musashi shouted, "And now for you, you little devil!" Gripping Jōtarō's obi with both hands, he lifted the boy above his head and held him there. Turning to the keeper, who was taking a fresh grip on his staff, he said, "I've been watching this from the start, and I think you're going about it the wrong way. This boy is my servant, and if you're going to question him, you ought to question me too."

In fiery tones, the keeper answered, "All right, we'll do that. We'll question the two of you!"

"Good! We'll take you on together. Now, here's the boy!"

He threw Jōtarō straight at the man. The crowd let out an appalled gasp and fell back. Was the man mad? Who ever heard of using one human being as a weapon against another human?

The keeper stared in disbelief as Jōtarō sailed through the air and rammed into his chest. The man fell straight back, as though a prop holding him up had suddenly been removed. It was difficult to tell whether he had struck his head against a rock, or whether his ribs had been broken. Hitting the ground with a howl, he began vomiting blood. Jōtarō bounced off the man's chest, did a somersault in the air, and rolled like a ball to a point twenty or thirty feet away.

"Did you see that?" a man shouted.

"Who is this crazy rōnin?"

The fracas no longer involved only the dog's keeper; the other samurai began abusing Musashi. Most of them were unaware that Musashi was an invited guest, and several suggested killing him then and there.

"Now," said Musashi, "everybody listen!"

They watched him closely as he took Jōtarō's wooden sword in his hand and faced them, a terrifying scowl on his face.

"The child's crime is his master's crime. We are both prepared to pay for it. But first let me tell you this: we have no intention of letting ourselves be killed like dogs. We are prepared to take you on."

Instead of acknowledging the crime and taking his punishment, he was challenging them! If at this point Musashi had apologized for Jōtarō and spoken in his defense, if he had made even the slightest effort to soothe the ruffled feelings of the Yagyū samurai, the whole incident might have passed by quietly. But Musashi's attitude precluded this. He seemed set on creating a still greater disturbance.

Shōda, Kimura, Debuchi and Murata all frowned, wondering anew what sort of freak they had invited to the castle. Deploring his lack of sense, they gradually edged around the crowd while keeping a watchful eye on him.

The crowd had been seething to begin with, and Musashi's challenge exacerbated their anger.

"Listen to him! He's an outlaw!"

"He's a spy! Tie him up!"

"No, cut him up!"

"Don't let him get away!"

For a moment it looked as though Musashi and Jōtarō, who was again by his side, would be swallowed up by a sea of swords, but then an authoritative voice cried, "Wait!"

It was Kizaemon, who together with Debuchi and Murata was trying to hold the crowd in check.

"This man seems to have planned all this," said Kizaemon. "If you let him entice you and you're wounded or killed, we shall have to answer to his lordship for it. The dog was important, but not as important as a human life. The four of us will assume all responsibility. Rest assured no harm will befall you because of anything we do. Now calm down and go home."

With some reluctance, the others dispersed, leaving the four men who had entertained Musashi in the Shin'indō. It was no longer a case of guest and hosts, but one of an outlaw facing his judges.

"Musashi," said Kizaemon, "I'm sorry to tell you your plot has failed. I suppose someone put you up to spying on Koyagyū Castle or just stirring up trouble, but I'm afraid it didn't work."

As they pressed in on Musashi, he was keenly aware that there was not one among them who was not an expert with the sword. He stood quite still, his hand on Jōtarō's shoulder. Surrounded, he couldn't have escaped even if he'd had wings.

"Musashi!" called Debuchi, working his sword a little way out of its scabbard. "You've failed. The proper thing for you to do is commit suicide. You may be a scoundrel, but you showed a great deal of bravery coming into this castle with only that child at your side. We had a friendly evening together; now we'll wait while you prepare yourself for harakiri. When you're ready, you can prove that you're a real samurai!"

That would have been the ideal solution; they had not consulted with Sekishūsai, and if Musashi died now, the whole affair could be buried along with his body.

Musashi had other ideas. "You think I should kill myself? That's absurd! I have no intention of dying, not for a long time." His shoulders shook with laughter.

"All right," said Debuchi. The tone was quiet, but the meaning was crystal clear. "We've tried to treat you decently, but you've done nothing but take advantage of us—"

Kimura broke in, saying, "There's no need for further talk!"

He went behind Musashi and pushed him. "Walk!" he commanded.

209

"Walk where?"

"To the cells."

Musashi nodded and started walking, but in the direction of his own choice, straight toward the castle keep.

"Where do you think you're going?" cried Kimura, jumping in front of Musashi and stretching his arms out to block him. "This isn't the way to the cells. They're in back of you. Turn around and get going!"

"No!" cried Musashi. He looked down at Jōtarō, who was still clinging to his side, and told him to go sit under a pine tree in the garden in front of the keep. The ground around the pine trees was covered with carefully raked white sand.

Jōtarō darted from under Musashi's sleeve and hid behind the tree, wondering all the while what Musashi intended to do next. The memory of his teacher's bravery at Hannya Plain came back to him, and his body swelled with excitement.

Kizaemon and Debuchi took positions on either side of Musashi and tried to pull him back by the arms. Musashi didn't budge.

"Let's go!"

"I'm not going."

"You intend to resist?"

"I do!"

Kimura lost patience and started to draw his sword, but his seniors, Kizaemon and Debuchi, ordered him to hold off.

"What's the matter with you? Where do you think you're going?"

"I intend to see Yagyū Sekishūsai."

"You *what?*"

Never had it crossed their minds that this insane youth could have even thought of anything so preposterous.

"And what would you do if you met him?" asked Kizaemon.

"I'm a young man, I'm studying the martial arts, and it is one of my goals in life to receive a lesson from the master of the Yagyū Style."

"If that's what you wanted, why didn't you just ask?"

"Isn't it true that Sekishūsai never sees anyone and never gives lessons to student warriors?"

"Yes."

"Then what else can I do but challenge him? I realize, of course, that even if I do, he'll probably refuse to come out of retirement, so I'm challenging this whole castle to a battle instead."

"A battle?" chorused the four.

His arms still held by Kizaemon and Debuchi, Musashi looked up at the sky. There was a flapping sound, as an eagle flew toward them from the blackness enveloping Mount Kasagi. Like a giant shroud, its silhouette hid the stars from view before it glided noisily down to the roof of the rice storehouse.

To the four retainers, the word "battle" sounded so melodramatic as to be laughable, but to Musashi it barely sufficed to express his concept of what was to come. He was not talking about a fencing match to be decided by technical skill only. He meant total war, where the combatants concentrate every ounce of their spirit and ability—and their fates are decided. A battle between two armies might be different in form, but in essence it was the same. It was simple: a battle between one man and one castle. His willpower was manifest in the firmness with which his heels were now implanted in the ground. It was this iron determination that made the word "battle" come naturally to his lips.

The four men scrutinized his face, wondering again if he had an iota of sanity left.

Kimura took up the challenge. Kicking his straw sandals into the air and tucking up his *hakama,* he said, "Fine! Nothing I like better than a battle! I can't offer you rolling drums or clanging gongs, but I can offer you a fight. Shōda, Debuchi, push him over here." Kimura had been the first to suggest that they should punish Musashi, but he had held himself back, trying to be patient. Now he had had his fill.

"Go ahead!" he urged. "Leave him to me!"

At exactly the same time, Kizaemon and Debuchi shoved Musashi forward. He stumbled four or five paces toward Kimura. Kimura stepped back a pace, lifted his elbow above his face, and sucking in his breath, swiftly brought his sword down toward Musashi's stumbling form. There was a curious gritty sound as the sword flashed through the air.

At the same time a shout was heard—not from Musashi but from Jōtarō, who had jumped out from his position behind the pine tree. The handful of sand he had thrown was the source of the strange noise.

Realizing that Kimura would be gauging the distance so as to strike effectively, Musashi had deliberately added speed to his stumbling steps and at the time of the strike was much closer to Kimura than the latter had anticipated. His sword touched nothing but air, and sand.

Both men quickly jumped back, separating themselves by three or four paces. There they stood, staring menacingly at one another in the tension-filled stillness.

"This is going to be something to watch," said Kizaemon softly.

Debuchi and Murata, though not within the sphere of battle, both took up new positions and assumed defensive stances. From what they had seen so far, they had no illusions about Musashi's competence as a fighter. His evasion and recovery had already convinced them he was a match for Kimura.

Kimura's sword was positioned slightly lower than his chest. He stood motionless. Musashi, equally still, had his hand on the hilt of his sword, right shoulder forward and elbow high. His eyes were two white, polished stones in his shadowy face.

For a time, it was a battle of nerves, but before either man moved, the darkness around Kimura seemed to waver, to change indefinably. Soon it was obvious that he was breathing faster and with greater agitation than Musashi.

A low grunt, barely audible, issued from Debuchi. He knew now that what had started as a comparatively trivial matter was about to turn into a catastrophe. Kizaemon and Murata, he felt sure, understood this as well as he. It was not going to be easy to put an end to this.

The outcome of the fight between Musashi and Kimura was as good as decided, unless extraordinary steps were taken. Reluctant as the three other men were to do anything that suggested cowardice, they found themselves forced to act to prevent disaster. The best solution would be to rid themselves of this strange, unbalanced intruder as expeditiously as possible, without themselves suffering needless wounds. No exchange of words was needed. They communicated perfectly with their eyes.

Acting in unison, the three moved in on Musashi. At the same instant, Musashi's sword, with the twang of a bowstring, pierced the air, and a thunderous shout filled the empty space. The battle cry came not from his mouth alone but from his whole body, the sudden peal of a temple bell resounding in all directions. From his opponents, arrayed to both sides of him, to front and back, came a hissing gurgle.

Musashi felt vibrantly alive. His blood seemed about to burst from every pore. But his head was as cool as ice. Was this the flaming lotus of which the Buddhists spoke? The ultimate heat made one with the ultimate cold, the synthesis of flame and water?

No more sand sailed through the air. Jōtarō had disappeared. Gusts of wind whistled down from the peak of Mount Kasagi; tightly held swords glinted luminescently.

One against four, yet Musashi felt himself at no great disadvantage. He was conscious of a swelling in his veins. At times like this, the idea of dying is said to assert itself in the mind, but Musashi had no thought of death. At the same time, he felt no certainty of his ability to win.

The wind seemed to blow through his head, cooling his brain, clearing his vision, though his body was growing sticky, and beads of oily sweat glistened on his forehead.

There was a faint rustle. Like a beetle's antennae, Musashi's sword told him that the man on his left had moved his foot an inch or two. He made the necessary adjustment in the position of his weapon, and the enemy, also perceptive, made no further move to attack. The five formed a seemingly static tableau.

Musashi was aware that the longer this continued, the less advantageous it was for him. He would have liked somehow to have his opponents not around him but stretched out in a straight line—to take them on one by one—but he was not dealing with amateurs. The fact was that until one of them shifted of his own accord, Musashi could make no move. All he could do was wait and hope that eventually one would make a momentary misstep and give him an opening.

His adversaries took little comfort from their superiority in numbers. They knew that at the slightest sign of a relaxed attitude on the part of any one of them, Musashi would strike. Here, they understood, was the type of man that one did not ordinarily encounter in this world.

Even Kizaemon could make no move. "What a strange man!" he thought to himself.

212   Swords, men, earth, sky—everything seemed to have frozen solid. But then

into this stillness came a totally unexpected sound, the sound of a flute, wafted by the wind.

As the melody stole into Musashi's ears, he forgot himself, forgot the enemy, forgot about life and death. Deep in the recesses of his mind, he knew this sound, for it was the one that had enticed him out of hiding on Mount Takateru—the sound that had delivered him into the hands of Takuan. It was Otsū's flute, and it was Otsū playing it.

He went limp inside. Externally, the change was barely perceptible, but that was enough. With a battle cry rising from his loins, Kimura lunged forward, his sword arm seeming to stretch out six or seven feet.

Musashi's muscles tensed, and the blood seemed to rush through him toward a state of hemorrhage. He was sure he had been cut. His left sleeve was rent from shoulder to wrist, and the sudden exposure of his arm made him think the flesh had been cut open.

For once, his self-possession left him and he screamed out the name of the god of war. He leaped, turned suddenly, and saw Kimura stumble toward the place where he himself had been standing.

"Musashi!" shouted Debuchi Magobei.

"You talk better than you fight!" taunted Murata, as he and Kizaemon scrambled to head Musashi off.

But Musashi gave the earth a powerful kick and sprang high enough to brush against the lower branches of the pine trees. Then he leaped again and again, and off he flew into the darkness, never looking back.

"Coward!"

"Musashi!"

"Fight like a man!"

When Musashi reached the edge of the moat around the inner castle, there was a cracking of twigs, and then silence. The only sound was the sweet melody of the flute in the distance.

The Nightingales

There was no way of knowing how much stagnant rainwater might be at the bottom of the thirty-foot moat. After diving into the hedge near the top and rapidly sliding halfway down, Musashi stopped and threw a rock. Hearing no splash, he leapt to the bottom, where he lay down on his back in the grass, not making a sound.

After a time his ribs stopped heaving and his pulse returned to normal. As the sweat cooled, he began to breathe regularly again.

"Otsū couldn't be here at Koyagyū!" he told himself. "My ears must be playing tricks on me. . . . Still, it's not impossible. It could have been her."

As he debated with himself, he envisioned Otsū's eyes among the stars above him, and soon he was carried away by memories: Otsū at the pass on the Mimasaka-Harima border, where she had said she could not live without him, there was no other man in the world for her. Then at Hanada Bridge in Himeji, when she had told him how she had waited for him for nearly a thousand days and would have waited ten years, or twenty—until she was old and gray. Her begging him to take her with him, her assertion that she could bear any hardship.

His headlong flight at Himeji had been a betrayal. How she must have hated him after that! How she must have bit her lips and cursed the unpredictability of men.

"Forgive me!" The words he had carved on the railing of the bridge slipped from his lips. Tears seeped from the corners of his eyes.

He was startled by a cry from the top of the moat. It sounded like, "He's not here." Three or four pine torches flickered among the trees, then disappeared. They hadn't spotted him.

He was annoyed to find himself weeping. "What do I need with a woman?" he said scornfully, wiping his eyes with his hands. He jumped to his feet and looked up at the black outline of Koyagyū Castle.

"They called me a coward, said I couldn't fight like a man! Well, I haven't surrendered yet, not by a long shot. I didn't run away. I just made a tactical retreat."

Almost an hour had passed. He began walking slowly along the bottom of the moat. "No point in fighting those four anyway. That wasn't my aim to begin with. When I find Sekishūsai himself, then the real battle will start."

He stopped and began gathering fallen branches, which he broke into short sticks over his knee. Shoving them one by one into cracks in the stone wall, he used them for footholds and climbed out of the moat.

He could no longer hear the flute. For a second he had the vague feeling Jōtarō was calling, but when he stopped and listened closely, he could hear nothing. He wasn't really worried about the boy. He could take care of himself; he was probably miles away by now. The absence of torches indicated the search had been called off, at least for the night.

The thought of finding and defeating Sekishūsai was once again his controlling passion, the immediate shape taken by his overpowering desire for recognition and honor.

He had heard from the innkeeper that Sekishūsai's retreat was in neither of the castle encirclements but in a secluded spot in the outer grounds. He walked through the woods and valleys, at times suspecting he had strayed outside the castle grounds. Then a bit of moat, a stone wall or a rice granary would reassure him he was still inside.

All night he searched, compelled by a diabolic urge. He intended, once he had found the mountain house, to burst in with his challenge on his lips. But as the hours wore on, he would have welcomed the sight of even a ghost appearing in Sekishūsai's form.

It was getting on toward daybreak when he found himself at the back gate of the castle. Beyond it rose a precipice and above that Mount Kasagi. On the verge of screaming with frustration, he retraced his steps southward. Finally, at the bottom of a slope inclined toward the southeast quarter of the castle, well-shaped trees and well-trimmed grass told him he'd found the hideaway. His conjecture was soon confirmed by a gate, with a thatched roof, in the style favored by the great tea master Sen no Rikyū. Inside he could make out a bamboo grove shrouded in morning mist.

Peeking through a crack in the gate, he saw that the path meandered through the grove and up the hill, as in Zen Buddhist mountain retreats. For a moment he was tempted to leap over the fence, but he checked himself; something about the surroundings held him back. Was it the loving care that had been lavished on the area, or the sight of white petals on the ground? Whatever it was, the sensitivity of the occupant came through, and Musashi's agitation subsided. He suddenly thought of his appearance. He must look like a tramp, with his disheveled hair and his kimono in disarray.

"No need to rush," he said to himself, conscious now of his exhaustion. He had to pull himself together before presenting himself to the master inside.

"Sooner or later," he thought, "someone's bound to come to the gate. That'll be time enough. If he still refuses to see me as a wandering student, then I'll use a different approach." He sat down under the eaves of the gate, leaned his back against the post and dropped off to sleep.

The stars were fading and white daisies swaying in the breeze when a large drop of dew fell coldly on his neck and woke him up. Daylight had come, and as he stirred from his nap, his head was cleansed by the morning breeze and the singing of the nightingales. No vestige of weariness remained: he felt reborn.

Rubbing his eyes and looking up, he saw the bright red sun climbing over the mountains. He jumped up. The sun's heat had already rekindled his ardor, and the strength stored up in his limbs demanded action. Stretching, he said softly, "Today's the day."

He was hungry, and for some reason this made him think about Jōtarō. Perhaps he had treated the boy too roughly the night before, but it had been a calculated move, a part of the lad's training. Musashi again assured himself that Jōtarō, wherever he was, wasn't in any real danger.

He listened to the sound of the brook, which ran down the mountainside, detoured inside the fence, circled the bamboo grove and then emerged from under the fence on its journey toward the lower castle grounds. Musashi washed his face and drank his fill, in lieu of breakfast. The water was good, so good that Musashi imagined it might well be the main reason Sekishūsai had chosen this location for his retirement from the world. Still, knowing nothing of the art of the tea ceremony, he had no inkling that water of such purity was in fact the answer to a tea master's prayer.

He rinsed his hand towel in the stream, and having wiped the back of his neck thoroughly, cleaned the grime from his nails. He then tidied his hair with the stiletto attached to his sword. Since Sekishūsai was not only the master of the Yagyū Style but one of the greatest men in the land, Musashi intended to look his best; he himself was nothing but a nameless warrior, as different from Sekishūsai as the tiniest star is from the moon.

Patting his hair and straightening his collar, he felt inwardly composed. His mind was clear; he was resolved to knock at the gate like any legitimate caller.

The house was quite a way up the hill, and it wasn't likely an ordinary knock would be heard. Looking around for a clapper of some kind, he saw a pair of plaques, one on either side of the gate. They were beautifully inscribed, and the carved writing had been filled in with a bluish clay which gave off a bronzelike patina. On the right were the words:

> Be not suspicious, ye scribes,
> Of one who likes his castle closed.

And on the left:

> No swordsman will you find here,
> Only the young nightingales in the fields.

The poem was addressed to the "scribes," referring to the officials of the castle, but its meaning was deeper. The old man had not shut his gate merely to wandering students but to all the affairs of this world, to its honors as well as its tribulations. He had put behind him worldly desire, both his own and that of others.

"I'm still young," thought Musashi. "Too young! This man is completely beyond my reach."

The desire to knock on the gate evaporated. Indeed, the idea of barging in on the ancient recluse now seemed barbarian, and he felt totally ashamed of himself.

Only flowers and birds, the wind and the moon, should enter this gate. Sekishūsai was no longer the greatest swordsman in the land, no longer the lord of a fief, but a man who had returned to nature, renouncing the vanity of human life. To upset his household would be a sacrilege. And what honor, what distinction, could possibly be derived from defeating a man to whom honor and distinction had become meaningless?

"It's a good thing I read this," Musashi said to himself. "If I hadn't, I'd have made a perfect fool of myself!"

With the sun now fairly high in the sky, the nightingales' singing had subsided. From a distance up the hill came the sound of rapid footsteps. Apparently frightened by the clatter, a flock of little birds arced up into the sky. Musashi peeped through the gate to see who was coming.

It was Otsū.

So it had been her flute he had heard! Should he wait and meet her? Go away? "I want to talk with her," he thought. "I must!"

Indecision seized him. His heart palpitated and his self-confidence fled.

Otsū ran down the path to a point a few feet from where he stood. Then she stopped and turned back, uttering a little cry of surprise.

"I thought he was right behind me," she murmured, looking all around. Then she ran back up the hill, calling, "Jōtarō! Where are you?"

Hearing her voice, Musashi flushed with embarrassment and began to sweat. His lack of confidence disgusted him. He couldn't move from his hiding place in the shadow of the trees.

After a short interval, Otsū called again, and this time there was an answer. "I'm here. Where are you?" shouted Jōtarō from the upper part of the grove.

"Over here!" she replied. "I told you not to wander off like that."

Jōtarō came running toward her. "Oh, is this where you are?" he exclaimed.

"Didn't I tell you to follow me?"

"Well, I did, but then I saw a pheasant, so I chased it."

"Of all things, chasing after a pheasant! Did you forget you have to go look for somebody important this morning?"

"Oh, I'm not worried about him. He's not the kind to get hurt."

"Well, that's not the way it was last night when you came running to my room. You were ready to burst into tears."

"I was not! It just happened so fast, I didn't know what to do."

"I didn't either, especially after you told me your teacher's name."

"But how do you know Musashi?"

"We come from the same village."

"Is that all?"

"Of course that's all."

"That's funny. I don't see why you should start crying just because somebody from the same village turned up here."

"Was I crying that much?"

"How can you remember everything I did, when you can't remember what you did yourself? Anyway, I guess I was pretty scared. If it'd just been a matter of four ordinary men against my teacher, I wouldn't have worried, but they say all of them are experts. When I heard the flute I remembered you were here in the castle, so I thought maybe if I could apologize to his lordship—"

"If you heard me playing, Musashi must have heard it too. He may even have known it was me." Her voice softened. "I was thinking of him as I played."

"I don't see what difference that makes. Anyway, I could tell from the sound of the flute where you were."

"And that was quite a performance—storming into the house and screaming about a 'battle' going on somewhere. His lordship was pretty shocked."

"But he's a nice man. When I told him I'd killed Tarō, he didn't get mad like all the others."

Suddenly realizing she was wasting time, Otsū hurried toward the gate. "We can talk later," she said. "Right now there are more important things to do. We've got to find Musashi. Sekishūsai even broke his own rule by saying he'd like to meet the man who'd done what you said."

Otsū looked as cheerful as a flower. In the bright sun of early summer, her cheeks shone like ripening fruit. She sniffed at the young leaves and felt their freshness fill her lungs.

Musashi, hidden in the trees, watched her intently, marveling at how   217 healthy she looked. The Otsū he saw now was very different from the girl who had sat dejectedly on the porch of the Shippōji, looking out at the world with vacant eyes. The difference was that then Otsū had had no one to love. Or at least, such love as she had felt had been vague and difficult to pin down. She had been a sentimental child, self-conscious about being an orphan, and somewhat resentful of the fact.

Coming to know Musashi, having him to look up to, had given birth to the love that now dwelt inside her and gave meaning to her life. During the long year she'd spent wandering around in search of him, body and mind had developed the courage to face anything fate might fling at her.

Quickly perceiving her new vitality and how beautiful it made her, Musashi yearned to take her somewhere where they could be alone and tell her everything—how he longed for her, how he needed her physically. He wanted to reveal that hidden in his heart of steel was a weakness; he wanted to retract the words he had carved on Hanada Bridge. If no one were to know, he could show her how tender he could be. He would tell her he felt the same love for her that she felt for him. He could hug her, rub his cheek against hers, cry the tears he wanted to cry. He was strong enough now to admit to himself that these feelings were real.

Things Otsū had said to him in the past came back to him and he saw how cruel and ugly it was for him to reject the simple, straightforward love she had offered.

He was miserable, yet there was something in him that couldn't surrender to these feelings, something that told him it was wrong. He was two different men, one longing to call out to Otsū, the other telling him he was a fool. He couldn't be sure which was his real self. Staring from behind the tree, lost in indecision, he seemed to see two paths ahead, one of light and another of darkness.

Otsū, unaware of his presence, walked a few paces out from the gate. Looking back, she saw Jōtarō stooping to pick something up.

"Jōtarō, what on earth are you doing? Hurry up!"

"Wait!" he cried excitedly. "Look at this!"

"It's nothing but a dirty old rag! What do you want that for?"

"It belongs to Musashi."

"To Musashi?" she exclaimed, running back to him.

"Yes, it's his," replied Jōtaro as he held the hand towel up by the corners for her to see. "I remember it. It came from the widow's house where we stayed in Nara. See, here: there's a maple leaf design dyed on it and a character reading 'Lin.' That's the name of the owner of the dumpling restaurant there."

"Do you think Musashi was right here?" Otsū cried, looking frantically around.

Jōtarō drew himself up almost to the girl's height and at the top of his voice yelled, "*Sensei!*"

In the grove there was a rustling sound. With a gasp, Otsū spun around and darted toward the trees, the boy chasing after her.

"Where are you going?" he called.

"Musashi just ran away!"

"Which way?"

"That way."

"I don't see him."

"Over there in the trees!"

She had caught a glimpse of Musashi's figure, but the momentary joy she experienced was immediately replaced by apprehension, for he was rapidly increasing the distance between them. She ran after him with all the strength her legs possessed. Jōtarō ran along with her, not really believing she'd seen Musashi.

"You're wrong!" he shouted. "It must be somebody else. Why would Musashi run away?"

"Just look!"

"Where?"

"There!" She took a deep breath, and straining her voice to the utmost, screamed, "Mu—sa—shi!" But no more had the frantic cry come from her lips than she stumbled and fell. As Jōtarō helped her up, she cried, "Why don't you call him too? Call him! Call him!"

Instead of doing as she said, he froze in shock and stared at her face. He had seen that face before, with its bloodshot eyes, its needlelike eyebrows, its waxen nose and jaw. It was the face of the mask! The madwoman's mask the widow in Nara had given him. Otsū's face lacked the curiously curved mouth, but otherwise the likeness was the same. He quickly withdrew his hands and recoiled in fright.

Otsū continued her scolding. "We can't give up! He'll never come back if we let him get away now! Call him! Get him to come back!"

Something inside Jōtarō resisted, but the look on Otsū's face told him it was useless to try to reason with her. They started running again, and he, too, began to shout for all he was worth.

Beyond the woods was a low hill, along the bottom of which ran the back road from Tsukigase to Iga. "It is Musashi!" cried Jōtarō. Having reached the road, the boy could see his master clearly, but Musashi was too far ahead of them to hear their shouts.

Otsū and Jōtarō ran as far as their legs would carry them, shouting themselves hoarse. Their screams echoed through the fields. At the edge of the valley they lost sight of Musashi, who ran straight into the heavily wooded foothills.

They stopped and stood there, forlorn as deserted children. White clouds stretched out emptily above them, while the murmuring of a stream accented their loneliness.

"He's crazy! He's out of his mind! How could he leave me like this?" Jōtarō cried, stamping the ground.

Otsū leaned against a large chestnut tree and let the tears gush forth. Even her great love for Musashi—a love for which she would have sacrificed anything—was incapable of holding him. She was puzzled, bereft and angry. She knew what his purpose in life was, and why he was avoiding her. She had known since that day at Hanada Bridge. Still, she could not comprehend why he considered her a barrier between him and his goal. Why should his determination be weakened by her presence?

Or was that just an excuse? Was the real reason that he didn't like her enough? It would make more sense perhaps. And yet ... and yet ... Otsū had come to understand Musashi when she had seen him tied up in the tree at the Shippōji. She could not believe him to be the sort who would lie to a woman. If he didn't care about her, he would say so, but in fact he had told her at Hanada Bridge that he did like her very much. She recalled his words with sadness.

Being an orphan, she was prevented by a certain coldness from trusting many people, but once she trusted someone, she trusted him completely. At this moment, she felt there was no one but Musashi worth living for or relying on. Matahachi's betrayal had taught her, the hard way, how careful a girl must be in judging men. But Musashi was not Matahachi. She had not only decided that she would live for him, whatever happened, but had already made up her mind never to regret doing so.

But why couldn't he have said just one word? It was more than she could bear. The leaves of the chestnut tree were shaking, as though the tree itself understood and sympathized.

The angrier she became, the more she was possessed by her love for him. Whether it was fate or not, she couldn't say, but her grief-torn spirit told her there was no real life for her apart from Musashi.

Jōtarō glanced down the road and muttered, "Here comes a priest." Otsū paid no attention to him.

With the approach of noon, the sky above had turned a deep, transparent blue. The monk descending the slope in the distance had the look of having stepped down from the clouds, of having no connection whatever with this earth. As he neared the chestnut tree, he looked toward it and saw Otsū.

"What's all this?" he exclaimed, and at the sound of his voice, Otsū looked up.

Her swollen eyes wide with astonishment, she cried, "Takuan!" In her present condition, she saw Takuan Sōhō as a savior. She wondered if she was dreaming.

Although the sight of Takuan was a shock to Otsū, the discovery of Otsū was for Takuan no more than confirmation of something he had suspected. As it happened, his arrival was neither accident nor miracle.

Takuan had been on friendly terms with the Yagyū family for a long time, his acquaintance with them going back to the days when, as a young monk at the Sangen'in in the Daitokuji, his duties had included cleaning the kitchen and making bean paste.

In those days, the Sangen'in, then known as the "North Sector" of the Daitokuji, had been famous as a gathering place for "unusual" samurai, which is to say, samurai who were given to thinking philosophically about the meaning of life and death; men who felt the need to study affairs of the spirit, as well as the technical skills of the martial arts. Samurai flocked there in greater numbers than did Zen monks, and one result of this was that the temple became known as a breeding ground for revolt.

Among the samurai who came frequently were Suzuki Ihaku, the brother of Lord Kōizumi of Ise; Yagyū Gorōzaemon, the heir of the House of Yagyū; and Gorōzaemon's brother Munenori. Munenori had quickly taken a liking to Takuan, and the two had remained friends ever since. In the course of a number of visits to Koyagyū Castle, Takuan had met Sekishūsai and had acquired great respect for the older man. Sekishūsai had also taken a liking to the young monk, who struck him as having a great deal of promise.

Recently Takuan had stopped for a time at the Nansōji in Izumi Province and from there had sent a letter to inquire after the health of Sekishūsai and Munenori. He had received a long reply from Sekishūsai, saying in part:

> I have been very fortunate lately. Munenori has taken a post with the To-
> kugawas, in Edo, and my grandson, who left the service of Lord Katō of Higo and
> went out to study on his own, is making progress. I myself have in my service a
> beautiful young girl who not only plays the flute well but talks with me, and
> together we have tea, arrange flowers and compose poems. She is the delight of
> my old age, a flower blooming in what might otherwise be a cold, withered old
> hut. Since she says that she comes from Mimasaka, which is near your birthplace,
> and was brought up in a temple called the Shippōji, I imagine that you and she
> have much in common. It is unusually pleasant to drink one's evening sake to
> the accompaniment of a flute well played, and since you are so close to here, I
> hope you will come and enjoy this treat with me.

It would have been difficult for Takuan to refuse the invitation under any circumstances, but the certainty that the girl described in the letter was Otsū made him all the more eager to accept.

As the three of them walked toward Sekishūsai's house, Takuan asked Otsū many questions, which she answered without reservation. She told him what she'd been doing since last seeing him in Himeji, what had happened that morning, and how she felt about Musashi.

Nodding patiently, he heard out her tearful story. When she was finished, he said, "I guess women are able to choose ways of life that would not be possible for men. You want me, I take it, to advise you on the path that you should follow in the future."

"Oh, no."

"Well . . ."

"I've already decided what I'm going to do."

Takuan scrutinized her closely. She had stopped walking and was looking at the ground. She seemed to be in the depths of despair, yet there was a certain strength in the tone of her voice that forced Takuan to a reappraisal.

"If I'd had any doubts, if I'd thought I'd give up," she said, "I'd never have left the Shippōji. I'm still determined to meet Musashi. The only question in my mind is whether this will cause him trouble, whether my continuing to live will bring him unhappiness. If it does, I'll have to do something about it!"

"Just what does that mean?"

"I can't tell you."

"Be careful, Otsū!"

"Of what?"

"Under this bright, cheerful sun, the god of death is tugging at you."

"I . . . I don't know what you mean."

"I don't suppose you would, but that's because the god of death is lending you strength. You'd be a fool to die, Otsū, particularly over nothing more than a one-sided love affair." Takuan laughed.

Otsū was getting angry again. She might as well have been talking to thin air, she thought, for Takuan had never been in love. It was impossible for anyone who'd never been in love to understand how she felt. For her to try to explain her feelings to him was like him trying to explain Zen Buddhism to an imbecile. But just as there was truth in Zen, whether an imbecile could understand it or not, there were people who would die for love, whether Takuan could understand it or not. To a woman at least, love was a far more serious matter than the troublesome riddles of a Zen priest. When one was swayed by a love that meant life or death, what difference did it make what the clapping of one hand sounded like? Biting her lips, Otsū vowed to say no more.

Takuan became serious. "You should have been born a man, Otsū. A man with the kind of willpower you have would certainly accomplish something for the good of the country."

"Does that mean it's wrong for a woman like me to exist? Because it might bring harm to Musashi?"

"Don't twist what I said. I wasn't talking about that. But no matter how much you love Musashi, he still runs away, doesn't he? And I daresay you never will catch him!"

"I'm not doing this because I enjoy it. I can't help it. I love him!"

"I don't see you for a while, and the next thing I know, you're carrying on like all the other women!"

"But can't you see? Oh, never mind, let's not talk about it anymore. A brilliant priest like you would never understand a woman's feelings!"

"I don't know how to answer that. It's true, though; women do puzzle me."

Otsū turned away from him and said, "Let's go, Jōtarō!"

As Takuan stood watching, the two of them started down a side road. With a sad flicker of his eyebrows, the monk came to the conclusion that there was nothing more for him to do. He called after her, "Aren't you going to say good-bye to Sekishūsai before setting out on your own?"

"I'll say good-bye to him in my heart. He knows I never meant to stay at his house this long anyway."

"Won't you reconsider?"

"Reconsider what?"

"Well, it was nice living in the mountains of Mimasaka, but it's nice here too. It's peaceful and quiet, and life is simple. Instead of seeing you go out in the ordinary world, with all its misery and hardships, I'd like to see you live your life out in peace, among these mountains and streams, like those nightingales we hear singing."

222 "Ha, ha! Thanks so much, Takuan!"

Takuan sighed, realizing he was helpless before this strong-willed young woman, so determined to go blindly on her chosen way. "You may laugh, Otsū, but the path you are embarking on is one of darkness."

"Darkness?"

"You were brought up in a temple. You should know that the path of darkness and desire leads only to frustration and misery—frustration and misery beyond salvation."

"There's never been a path of light for me, not since I was born."

"But there is, there is!" Putting his last drop of energy into this plea, Takuan came up to the girl and took her hand. He wanted desperately for her to trust him.

"I'll talk to Sekishūsai about it," he offered. "About how you can live and be happy. You can find yourself a good husband here in Koyagyū, have children, and do the things that women do. You'd make this a better village. That would make you happier too."

"I understand you're trying to be helpful, but—"

"Do it! I beg you!"

Pulling her by the hand, he looked at Jōtarō and said, "You come too, boy!"

Jōtarō shook his head decisively. "Not me. I'm going to follow my master."

"Well, do as you like, but at least go back to the castle and say good-bye to Sekishūsai."

"Oh, I forgot!" gasped Jōtarō. "I left my mask there. I'll go get it." He streaked off, untroubled by paths of darkness and paths of light.

Otsū, however, stood still at the crossroads. Takuan relaxed, becoming again the old friend she had known before. He warned her of the dangers lurking in the life she was trying to lead and tried to convince her there were other ways to find happiness. Otsū remained unmoved.

Presently Jōtarō came running back with the mask over his face. Takuan froze when he saw it, instinctively feeling that this was the future face of Otsū, the one he would see after she had suffered on her long journey along the path of darkness.

"I'll go now," said Otsū, stepping away from him.

Jōtarō, clinging to her sleeve, said, "Yes, let's go! Now!"

Takuan lifted his eyes to the white clouds, lamenting his failure. "There's nothing more I can do," he said. "The Buddha himself despaired of saving women."

"Good-bye, Takuan," said Otsū. "I'm bowing here to Sekishūsai, but would you also tell him thank you and good-bye for me?"

"Ah, even I'm beginning to think priests are crazy. Everywhere they go, they meet no one but people rushing toward hell." Takuan raised his hands, let them drop and said very solemnly, "Otsū, if you begin to drown in the Six Evil Ways or the Three Crossings, call out my name. Think of me, and call my name! Until then, all I can say is, travel on as far as you can and try to be careful!"

Book III   FIRE

Sasaki Kojirō

Just south of Kyoto, the Yodo River wound around a hill called Momoyama (the site of Fushimi Castle), then flowed on through the Yamashiro Plain toward the ramparts of Osaka Castle, some twenty miles farther to the southwest. Partly owing to this direct water link, each political ripple in the Kyoto area produced immediate repercussions in Osaka, while in Fushimi it seemed that every word spoken by an Osaka samurai, let alone an Osaka general, was reported as a portent of the future.

Around Momoyama, a great upheaval was in progress, for Tokugawa Ieyasu had decided to transform the way of life that had flourished under Hideyoshi. Osaka Castle, occupied by Hideyori and his mother, Yodogimi, still clung desperately to the vestiges of its faded authority, as the setting sun holds fast to its vanishing beauty, but real power resided at Fushimi, where Ieyasu had chosen to live during his extended trips to the Kansai region. The clash between old and new was visible everywhere. It could be discerned in the boats plying the river, in the deportment of the people on the highways, in popular songs, and in the faces of the displaced samurai searching for work.

The castle at Fushimi was under repair, and the rocks disgorged from the boats onto the riverbank formed a virtual mountain. Most of them were huge boulders, at least six feet square and three or four feet high. They fairly sizzled under a boiling sun. Though it was autumn by the calendar, the sweltering heat was reminiscent of the dog days immediately following the early summer rainy season.

Willow trees near the bridge shimmered with a whitish glint, and a large cicada zigzagged crazily from the river into a small house near the bank. The roofs of the village, deprived of the gentle colors their lanterns swathed them in at twilight, were a dry, dusty gray. In the heat of high noon, two laborers, mercifully freed for half an hour from their backbreaking work, lay sprawled on the broad surface of a boulder, chatting about what was on everybody's lips.

227

"You think there'll be another war?"

"I don't see why not. There doesn't seem to be anybody strong enough to keep things under control."

"I guess you're right. The Osaka generals seem to be signing up all the rōnin they can find."

"They would, I suppose. Maybe I shouldn't say this too loud, but I heard the Tokugawas are buying guns and ammunition from foreign ships."

"If they are, why is Ieyasu letting his granddaughter Senhime marry Hideyori?"

"How should I know? Whatever he's doing, you can bet he has his reasons. Ordinary people like us can't be expected to know what Ieyasu has in mind."

Flies buzzed about the two. A swarm covered two nearby oxen. Still hitched to empty timber carts, the beasts lazed in the sun, stolid, impassive and drooling at the mouth.

The real reason the castle was undergoing repairs was not known to the lowly laborer, who assumed that Ieyasu was to stay there. Actually, it was one phase of a huge building program, an important part of the Tokugawa scheme of government. Construction work on a large scale was also being carried out in Edo, Nagoya, Suruga, Hikone, Ōtsu and a dozen other castle towns. The purpose was to a large extent political, for one of Ieyasu's methods of maintaining control over the daimyō was to order them to undertake various engineering projects. Since none was powerful enough to refuse, this kept the friendly lords too busy to grow soft, while simultaneously forcing the daimyō who'd opposed Ieyasu at Sekigahara to part with large portions of their incomes. Still another aim of the government was to win the support of the common people, who profited both directly and indirectly from extensive public works.

At Fushimi alone, nearly a thousand laborers were engaged in extending the stone battlements, with the incidental result that the town around the castle experienced a sudden influx of peddlers, prostitutes and horseflies—all symbols of prosperity. The masses were delighted with the good times Ieyasu had brought, and merchants relished the thought that on top of all this there was a good chance of war—bringing even greater profits. Goods were moving briskly, and even now the bulk of them were military supplies. After fingering their collective abacus, the larger entrepreneurs had concluded that this was where the big money was.

City folk were fast forgetting the balmy days of Hideyoshi's regime and instead speculating on what might be gained in the days ahead. It made little difference to them who was in power; so long as they could satisfy their own petty wants, they saw no reason to complain. Nor did Ieyasu disappoint them in this respect, for he contrived to scatter money as he might pass out candy to children. Not his own money, to be sure, but that of his potential enemies.

In agriculture, too, he was instituting a new system of control. No longer were local magnates allowed to govern as they pleased or to conscript farmers at will for outside labor. From now on, the peasants were to be permitted to farm their lands—but to do very little else. They were to be kept ignorant of politics and taught to rely on the powers that be.

228

The virtuous ruler, to Ieyasu's way of thinking, was one who did not let the tillers of the soil starve but at the same time ensured that they did not rise above their station; this was the policy by which he intended to perpetuate Tokugawa rule. Neither the townspeople nor the farmers nor the daimyō realized that they were being carefully fitted into a feudal system that would eventually bind them hand and foot. No one was thinking of what things might be like in another hundred years. No one, that is, except Ieyasu.

Nor were the laborers at Fushimi Castle thinking of tomorrow. They had modest hopes of getting through the day, the quicker the better. Though they talked of war and when it might break out, grand plans to maintain peace and increase prosperity had nothing to do with them. Whatever happened, they could not be much worse off than they were.

"Watermelon! Anybody want a watermelon?" called a farmer's daughter, who came around at this time every day. Almost as soon as she appeared, she managed to make a sale to some men matching coins in the shadow of a large rock. Jauntily, she went on from group to group, calling, "Won't you buy my melons?"

"You crazy? You think we've got money for watermelons?"

"Over here! I'll be glad to eat one—if it's free."

Disappointed because her initial luck had been deceptive, the girl approached a young worker sitting between two boulders, his back propped against one, his feet against the other, and his arms around his knees. "Watermelon?" she asked, not very hopefully.

He was thin, his eyes sunken, and his skin ruddily sunburned. A shroud of fatigue dimmed his obvious youth; still, his closer friends would have recognized him as Hon'iden Matahachi. Wearily he counted some grimy coins into the palm of his hand and gave them to the girl.

When he leaned back against the rock again, his head drooped morosely. The slight effort had exhausted him. Gagging, he leaned to one side and began to spit up on the grass. He lacked the little strength it would have taken to retrieve the watermelon, which had tumbled from his knees. He stared dully at it, his black eyes revealing no trace of strength or hope.

"The swine," he mumbled weakly. He meant the people he would like to strike back at: Okō, with her whitened face; Takezō, with his wooden sword. His first mistake had been to go to Sekigahara; his second to succumb to the lascivious widow. He had come to believe that but for these two events, he would be at home in Miyamoto now, the head of the Hon'iden family, a husband with a beautiful wife, and the envy of the village.

"I suppose Otsū must hate me now . . . though I wonder what she's doing." In his present circumstances, thinking occasionally of his former fiancée was his only comfort. When Okō's true nature had finally sunk in, he had begun to long for Otsū again. He had thought of her more and more since the day he'd had the good sense to break loose from the Yomogi Teahouse.

On the night of his departure, he had discovered that the Miyamoto Musashi who was acquiring a reputation as a swordsman in the capital was his old friend Takezō. This severe shock was followed almost immediately by strong waves of jealousy.

229

With Otsū in mind, he had stopped drinking and attempted to slough off his laziness and his bad habits. But at first he was unable to find any suitable work. He cursed himself for having been out of the swim of things for five years, while an older woman supported him. For a time it appeared as though it was too late to change.

"*Not* too late," he'd assured himself. "I'm only twenty-two. I can do whatever I want, if I try!" While anyone might experience this sentiment, in Matahachi's case it meant shutting his eyes, leaping over an abyss of five years, and hiring himself out as a day laborer at Fushimi.

Here he had worked hard, slaving steadily day after day while the sun beat down on him from summer into fall. He was rather proud of himself for sticking to it.

"I'll show them all!" he was thinking now, despite his queasiness. "No reason I can't make a name for myself. I can do anything Takezō can do! I can do even more, and I will. Then I'll have my revenge, despite Okō. Ten years is all I need."

Ten years? He stopped to calculate how old Otsū would be by then. Thirty-one! Would she stay single, wait for him all that time? Not likely. Matahachi had no inkling of recent developments in Mimasaka, no way of knowing that his was but a pipe dream, but ten years—never! It would have to be no more than five or six. Within that time he would have to make a success of himself; that was all there was to it. Then he could go back to the village, apologize to Otsū and persuade her to marry him. "That's the only way!" he exclaimed. "Five years, six at most." He stared at the watermelon and a glimmer of light returned to his eyes.

Just then one of his fellow workers rose up beyond the rock in front of him, and resting his elbows on the boulder's broad top, called, "Hey, Matahachi. What're you mumbling to yourself about? Say, your face is green. Watermelon rotten?"

Matahachi, though he forced a wan smile, was seized by another wave of dizziness. Saliva streamed from his mouth as he shook his head. "It's nothing, nothing at all," he managed to gasp. "Guess I got a little too much sun. Let me take it easy here for an hour or so."

The burly stone haulers gibed at his lack of strength, albeit good-naturedly. One of them asked, "Why'd you buy a watermelon when you can't eat it?"

"I bought it for you fellows," answered Matahachi. "I thought it'd make up for not being able to do my share of the work."

"Now, that was smart. Hey, men! Watermelon! Have some, on Matahachi."

Splitting the melon on the corner of a rock, they fell to it like ants, snatching greedily at the sweet, dripping hunks of red pulp. It was all gone when moments later a man jumped up on a rock and yelled, "Back to work, all of you!"

The samurai in charge emerged from a hut, whip in hand, and the stench of sweat spread over the earth. Presently the melody of a rock haulers' chantey rose from the site, as a gigantic boulder was shifted with large levers onto rollers and dragged along with ropes as thick as a man's arm. It advanced ponderously, like a moving mountain.

With the boom in castle construction, these rhythmical songs proliferated. Though the words were rarely written down, no less a personage than Lord Hachisuka of Awa, who was in charge of building Nagoya Castle, quoted several verses in a letter. His lordship, who would hardly have had occasion to so much as touch construction materials, had apparently learned them at a party. Simple compositions, like the following, they'd become something of a fad in society as well as among work crews.

> From Awataguchi we've pulled them—
> Dragged rock after rock after rock.
> For our noble Lord Tōgorō.
> Ei, sa, ei, sa . . .
> Pull—ho! Drag—ho! Pull—ho! Drag—ho!
> His lordship speaks,
> Our arms and legs tremble.
> We're loyal to him—to the death.

The letter writer commented, "Everybody, young and old alike, sings this, for it is part of the floating world we live in."

While the laborers at Fushimi were not aware of these social reverberations, their songs did reflect the spirit of the times. The tunes popular when the Ashikaga shogunate was in decline had been on the whole decadent and had been sung mostly in private, but during the prosperous years of Hideyoshi's regime, happy, cheerful songs were often heard in public. Later, with the stern hand of Ieyasu making itself felt, the melodies lost some of their rollicking spirit. As Tokugawa rule became stronger, spontaneous singing tended to give way to music composed by musicians in the shōgun's employ.

Matahachi rested his head on his hands. It burned with fever, and the heave-ho singing buzzed indistinctly in his ears, like a swarm of bees. All alone now, he lapsed into depression.

"What's the use," he groaned. "Five years. Suppose I do work hard—what'll it get me? For a whole day's work, I make only enough to eat that day. If I take a day off, I don't eat."

Sensing someone standing near him, he looked up and saw a tall young man. His head was covered with a deep, coarsely woven basket hat, and at his side hung a bundle of the sort carried by *shugyōsha*. An emblem in the form of a half-open steel-ribbed fan adorned the front of his hat. He was gazing thoughtfully at the construction work and sizing up the terrain.

After a time he seated himself next to a flat, broad rock, which was just the right height to serve as a writing table. He blew away the sand on top, along with a line of ants marching across it, then with his elbows propped on the rock and his head on his hands, resumed his intense survey of the surroundings. Though the sun's glare hit him full in the face, he remained motionless, seemingly impervious to the discomforting heat. He did not notice Matahachi, who was still too miserable to care whether anyone was around or not. The other man meant nothing to him. He sat with his back to the newcomer and spasmodically retched.

By and by the samurai became aware of his gagging. "You there," he said. "What's the matter?"

"It's the heat," answered Matahachi.

"You're in pretty bad shape, aren't you?"

"I'm a little better than I was, but I still feel dizzy."

"I'll give you some medicine," said the samurai, opening his black-lacquered pillbox and shaking some black pills into the palm of his hand. He walked over and put the medicine in Matahachi's mouth.

"You'll be all right in no time," he said.

"Thanks."

"Do you plan to rest here for a while longer?"

"Yes."

"Then do me a favor. Let me know if anybody comes—throw a pebble or something."

He went back to his own rock, sat down, and took a brush from his writing kit and a notebook from his kimono. He opened the pad on the rock and began to draw. Under the brim of his hat, his eyes moved back and forth from the castle to its immediate surroundings, taking in the main tower, the fortifications, the mountains in the background, the river and the smaller streams.

Just before the Battle of Sekigahara, this castle had been attacked by units of the Western Army, and two compounds, as well as part of the moat, had suffered considerable damage. Now the bastion was not only being restored but also being strengthened, so that it would outclass Hideyori's stronghold at Osaka.

Quickly but in great detail, the student warrior sketched a bird's-eye view of the entire castle and on a second page began making a diagram of the approaches from the rear.

"Uh-oh!" exclaimed Matahachi softly. From out of nowhere the inspector of works appeared and was standing behind the sketcher. Clad in half-armor, with straw sandals on his feet, he stood there silently, as if waiting to be noticed. Matahachi felt a pang of guilt for not having seen him in time to give warning. It was too late now.

Presently the student warrior lifted his hand to brush a fly off his sweaty collar and in doing so caught sight of the intruder. As he looked up with startled eyes, the inspector stared back angrily for a moment before stretching out a hand toward the drawing. The student warrior grabbed his wrist and jumped up.

"What do you think you're doing?" he shouted.

The inspector seized the notebook and held it high in the air. "I'd like to have a look at this," he barked.

"You have no right."

"Just doing my job!"

"Butting into other people's business—is that your job?"

"Why? Shouldn't I look at it?"

"An oaf like you wouldn't understand it."

"I think I'd better keep it."

"Oh, no you don't!" cried the student warrior, making a grab for the notebook. Both pulled at it, ripping it in half.

"Watch yourself!" shouted the inspector. "You'd better have a good explanation, or I'll turn you in."

"On whose authority? You an officer?"

"That's right."

"What's your group? Who's your commander?"

"None of your business. But you might as well know that I'm under orders to investigate anyone around here who looks suspicious. Who gave you permission to make sketches?"

"I'm making a study of castles and geographic features for future reference. What's wrong with that?"

"The place is swarming with enemy spies. They all have excuses like that. It doesn't matter who you are. You'll have to answer some questions. Come with me!"

"Are you accusing me of being a criminal?"

"Just hold your tongue and come along."

"Rotten officials! Too used to making people cringe every time you open your big mouths!"

"Shut up—let's go!"

"Try and make me!" The student warrior was adamant.

Angry veins popping up in his forehead, the inspector dropped his half of the notebook, ground it under foot, and pulled out his truncheon. The student warrior jumped back a pace to improve his position.

"If you're not going to come along willingly, I'll have to tie you up and drag you," said the inspector.

Before the words were out, his adversary went into action. Uttering a great howl, he seized the inspector by the neck with one hand, grabbed the lower edge of his armor with the other, then hurled him at a large rock.

"Worthless lout!" he screamed, but not in time to be heard by the inspector, whose head split open on the rock like a watermelon. With a cry of horror, Matahachi covered his face with his hands to protect it from the globs of red pasty matter flying his way, while the student warrior quickly reverted to an attitude of complete calm.

Matahachi was appalled. Could the man be accustomed to murdering in this brutal fashion? Or was his sangfroid merely the letdown that follows an explosion of rage? Matahachi, shocked to the core, began to sweat profusely. From all he could tell, the other man could hardly have reached the age of thirty. His bony, sunburned face was blemished by pockmarks, and he appeared to have no chin, though this may have been due to a curiously shrunken scar from a deep sword wound.

The student warrior was in no hurry to flee. He gathered up the torn fragments of his notebook. Then he began looking quietly about for his hat, which had flown off when he made his mighty throw. After finding it, he placed it with care upon his head, once again concealing his eerie face from view. At a brisk pace he took his leave, gathering speed until he seemed to be flying on the wind.

The whole incident had happened so fast that neither the hundreds of laborers in the vicinity nor their overseers had noticed it. The workmen continued to toil like drones, as the supervisors, armed with whips and truncheons, bellowed orders at their sweating backs.

But one particular pair of eyes had seen it all. Standing atop a high scaffold commanding a view of the whole area was the general overseer of carpenters and log cutters. Seeing that the student warrior was escaping, he roared out a command, setting into motion a group of foot soldiers who had been drinking tea below the scaffold.

"What happened?"

"Another fight?"

Others heard the call to arms and soon stirred up a cloud of yellow dust near the wooden gate of the stockade, which divided the construction site from the village. Angry shouts rose from the gathering swarm of people.

"It's a spy! A spy from Osaka!"

"They'll never learn."

"Kill him! Kill him!"

Rock haulers, earth carriers and others, screaming as though the "spy" were their personal enemy, bore down on the chinless samurai. He darted behind an oxcart shambling through the gate and tried to slip out, but a sentinel caught sight of him and tripped him with a nail-studded staff.

From the overseer's scaffold came the cry: "Don't let him escape!"

With no hesitation, the crowd fell upon the miscreant, who counterattacked like a trapped beast. Wresting the staff from the sentinel, he turned on him and with the point of the weapon knocked him down headfirst. After downing four or five more men in similar fashion, he drew his huge sword and took an offensive stance. His captors fell back in terror, but as he prepared to cut his way out of the circle, a barrage of stones descended on him from all directions.

The mob vented its wrath in earnest, its mood all the more murderous because of a deep-seated distaste for all *shugyōsha*. Like most commoners, these laborers considered the wandering samurai useless, nonproductive and arrogant.

"Stop acting like stupid churls!" cried the beleaguered samurai, appealing for reason and restraint. Though he fought back, he seemed more concerned with chiding his attackers than with avoiding the rocks they hurled. More than a few innocent bystanders were injured in the melee.

Then, in a trice, it was all over. The shouting ceased, and the laborers began moving back to their work stations. In five minutes, the great construction site was exactly as it had been before, as though nothing had happened. The sparks flying from the various cutting instruments, the whinnying of horses half addled by the sun, the mind-numbing heat—all returned to normal.

Two guards stood over the collapsed form, which had been trussed up with a thick hemp rope. "He's ninety percent dead," said one, "so we may as well leave him here till the magistrate comes." He looked around and spotted Matahachi. "Hey, you there! Stand watch over this man. If he dies, it doesn't make any difference."

234   Matahachi heard the words, but his head could not quite take in either their

import or the meaning of the event he had just witnessed. It all seemed like a nightmare, visible to his eyes, audible to his ears, but not comprehensible to his brain.

"Life's so flimsy," he thought. "A few minutes ago he was absorbed in his sketching. Now he's dying. He wasn't very old."

He felt sorry for the chinless samurai, whose head, lying sideways on the ground, was black with dirt and gore, his face still contorted with anger. The rope anchored him to a large rock. Matahachi wondered idly why the officials had taken such precautions when the man was too near death to make a sound. Or maybe already dead. One of his legs lay grotesquely exposed through a long rip in his *hakama*, the white shinbone protruding from the crimson flesh. Blood was sprouting from his scalp, and wasps had begun to hover around his matted hair. Ants nearly covered his hands and feet.

"Poor wretch," thought Matahachi. "If he was studying seriously, he must have had some great ambition in life. Wonder where he's from . . . if his parents are still alive." Matahachi was seized by a peculiar doubt: was he really bemoaning the man's fate, or was he bothered by the vagueness of his own future? "For a man with ambition," he reflected, "there ought to be a cleverer way to get ahead."

This was an age that fanned the hopes of the young, urged them to cherish a dream, prodded them to improve their status in life. An age, indeed, in which even someone like Matahachi might have visions of rising from nothing to become the master of a castle. A modestly talented warrior could get by simply by traveling from temple to temple and living on the charity of the priests. If he was lucky, he might be taken in by one of the provincial gentry, and if he was still more fortunate, might receive a stipend from a daimyō.

Still, of all the young men who set out with high hopes, only one in a thousand actually ended up finding a position with an acceptable income. The rest had to be content with what satisfaction they could derive from the knowledge that theirs was a difficult and dangerous calling.

As Matahachi contemplated the samurai lying before him, the whole idea began to seem utterly stupid. Where could the path Musashi was following possibly lead? Matahachi's desire to equal or surpass his boyhood friend hadn't abated, but the sight of the bloodied warrior made the Way of the Sword seem vain and foolish.

Horror-stricken, he realized that the warrior was moving, and his train of thought stopped short. The man's hand reached out like a turtle's flipper and clawed at the ground. Feebly he lifted his torso, raised his head and pulled the rope taut.

Matahachi could hardly believe his eyes. As the man inched along the ground, he dragged behind him the four-hundred-pound rock securing his rope. One foot, two feet—it was a display of superhuman strength. No muscle man on any rock-hauling crew could have done it, though many boasted of the strength of ten or twenty men. The samurai lying on the threshold of death was possessed by some demonic force, which enabled him to far surpass the power of an ordinary mortal.

A gurgle came from the dying man's throat. He was trying desperately to speak, but his tongue had turned black and dry, making it impossible for him to form the words. Breath came in cracked, hollow hisses; eyes popping from their sockets stared imploringly at Matahachi.

"Pl—lul—poo—loo—ees . . ."

Matahachi gradually understood he was saying "please." Then a different sound, all but inarticulate, Matahachi made out to be "beg you." But it was the man's eyes that really spoke. Therein were the last of his tears and the certainty of death. His head fell back; his breathing ceased. As more ants started coming out of the grass to explore the dust-whitened hair, a few even entering a blood-caked nostril, Matahachi could see the skin under his kimono collar take on a blackish-blue cast.

What had the man wanted him to do? Matahachi felt haunted by the thought that he had incurred an obligation. The samurai had come upon him when he was sick and had had the kindness to give him medicine. Why had fate blinded Matahachi when he should have been warning the man of the inspector's approach? Was this destined to have occurred?

Matahachi tentatively touched the cloth-wrapped bundle on the dead man's obi. The contents would surely reveal who the man was and where he was from. Matahachi suspected that his dying wish had been to have some memento delivered to his family. He detached the bundle, as well as the pillbox, and stuffed them quickly inside his own kimono.

He debated whether to cut off a lock of hair for the man's mother, but while staring into the fearsome face, he heard footsteps approaching. Peeking from behind a rock, he saw samurai coming for the corpse. If he were caught with the dead man's possessions, he'd be in serious trouble. He crouched down low and made his way from shadow to shadow behind the rocks, sneaking away like a field rat.

Two hours later he arrived at the sweetshop where he was staying. The shopkeeper's wife was by the side of the house, rinsing herself off from a washbasin. Hearing him moving about inside, she showed a portion of her white flesh from behind the side door and called, "Is that you, Matahachi?"

Answering with a loud grunt, he dashed into his own room and grabbed a kimono and his sword from a cabinet; he then knotted a rolled towel around his head and prepared to slip into his sandals again.

"Isn't it dark in there?" called the woman.

"No, I can see well enough."

"I'll bring you a lamp."

"No need to. I'm going out."

"Aren't you going to wash?"

"No. Later."

He rushed out into the field and swiftly moved away from the shabby house. A few minutes later he looked back to see a group of samurai, no doubt from the castle, come from beyond the miscanthus in the field. They entered the sweetshop from both front and rear.

"That was a close call," he thought. "Of course, I didn't really steal anything. I just took it in custody. I had to. He begged me to."

236

To his way of thinking, as long as he admitted that the articles were not his, he had committed no crime. At the same time, he realized he could never again show his face at the construction site.

The miscanthus came up to his shoulders, and a veil of evening mist floated above it. No one could see him from a distance; it would be easy to get away. But which way to go was a difficult choice, all the more so since he strongly felt that good luck lay in one direction and bad luck in another.

Osaka? Kyoto? Nagoya? Edo? He had no friends in any of those places; he might as well roll dice to decide where to go. With dice, as with Matahachi, all was chance. When the wind blew, it would waft him along with it.

It seemed to him that the farther he walked, the deeper he went into the miscanthus. Insects buzzed about him, and the descending mist dampened his clothes. The soaked hems curled around his legs. Seeds caught at his sleeves. His shins itched. The memory of his noonday nausea was gone now and he was painfully hungry. Once he felt himself out of the reach of his pursuers, it became agony to walk.

An overwhelming urge to find a place to lie down and rest carried him the length of the field, beyond which he spotted the roof of a house. Drawing nearer, he saw that the fence and gate were both askew, apparently damaged by a recent storm. The roof needed fixing too. Yet at one time the house must have belonged to a wealthy family, for there was a certain faded elegance about it. He imagined a beautiful court lady seated in a richly curtained carriage approaching the house at a stately pace.

Going through the forlorn-looking gate, he found that both the main house and a smaller detached house were nearly buried in weeds. The scene reminded him of a passage by the poet Saigyō that he had been made to learn as a child:

> I heard that a person I knew lived in Fushimi and went to pay him a call, but the garden was so overgrown! I couldn't even see the path. As the insects sang, I composed this poem:

> Pressing through the weeds,
> I hide my tearful feelings
> In the folds of my sleeve.
> In the dew-laden garden
> Even lowly insects weep.

Matahachi's heart was chilled as he crouched near the house, whispering the words so long forgotten.

Just as he was about to conclude the house was empty, a red light appeared from deep inside. Presently he heard the pining strains of a *shakuhachi*, the bamboo flute mendicant priests played when begging on the streets. Looking inside, he discovered the player was indeed a member of that class. He was seated beside the hearth. The fire he had just lit grew brighter, and his shadow loomed larger on the wall. He was playing a mournful tune, a solitary lament on the loneliness and melancholy of autumn, intended for no ears but his own. The man played simply, without flourish, giving

Matahachi the impression he took little pride in his playing.

When the melody came to an end, the priest sighed deeply and launched into a lament.

"They say when a man is forty, he is free from delusion. But look at me! Forty-seven when I destroyed my family's good name. Forty-seven! And still I was deluded; contrived to lose everything—income, position, reputation. Not only that; I left my only son to fend for himself in this wretched world. . . . For what? An infatuation?

"It's mortifying—never again could I face my dead wife, nor the boy, wherever he is. Ha! When they say you're wise after forty, they must be talking about great men, not dolts like me. Instead of thinking myself wise because of my years, I should have been more careful than ever. It's madness not to, where women are concerned."

Standing his *shakuhachi* on end in front of him and propping both hands on the mouthpiece, he went on. "When that business with Otsū came up, nobody would forgive me any longer. It's too late, too late."

Matahachi had crept into the next room. He listened but was repelled by what he saw. The priest's cheeks were sunken, his shoulders had a pointed, stray-dog air, and his hair was sheenless. Matahachi crouched in silence; in the flickering firelight the man's form summoned up visions of demons of the night.

"Oh, what am I to do?" moaned the priest, lifting his sunken eyes to the ceiling. His kimono was plain and dingy, but he also wore a black cassock, indicating he was a follower of the Chinese Zen master P'u-hua. The reed matting on which he sat, and which he rolled up and carried with him wherever he went, was probably his only household possession—his bed, his curtain, and in bad weather, his roof.

"Talking won't bring back what I've lost," he said, "Why wasn't I more careful! I thought I understood life. I understood nothing, let my status go to my head! I behaved shamelessly toward a woman. No wonder the gods deserted me. What could be more humiliating?"

The priest lowered his head as though apologizing to someone, then lowered it still farther. "I don't care about myself. The life I have now is good enough for me. It's only right I should do penance and have to survive without outside help.

"But what have I done to Jōtarō? He'll suffer more for my misconduct than I. If I were still in Lord Ikeda's service, he'd now be the only son of a samurai with an income of five thousand bushels, but because of my stupidity, he's nothing. What's worse, one day, when he's grown, he'll learn the truth."

For a time he sat with his hands covering his face, then suddenly stood up. "I must stop this—feeling sorry for myself again. The moon's out; I'll go walk in the field—rid myself of these old grievances and ghosts."

The priest picked up his *shakuhachi* and shuffled listlessly out of the house. Matahachi thought he saw a hint of a stringy mustache under the emaciated nose. "What a strange person!" he thought. "He's not really old, but he's so unsteady on his feet." Suspecting the man might be a little insane, he felt a tinge of pity for him.

Fanned by the evening breeze, the flames from the broken kindling were beginning to scorch the floor. Entering the empty room, Matahachi found a pitcher of water and poured some on the fire, reflecting as he did so on the priest's carelessness.

It wouldn't matter much if this old deserted house burned to the ground, but what if instead it were an ancient temple of the Asuka or Kamakura period? Matahachi felt a rare spasm of indignation. "It's because of people like him that the ancient temples in Nara and on Mount Kōya are destroyed so often," he thought. "These crazy vagabond priests have no property, no family of their own. They don't give a thought to how dangerous fire is. They'll light one in the main hall of an old monastery, right next to the murals, just to warm their own carcasses, which are of no use to anyone.

"Now, there's something interesting," he mumbled, turning his eyes toward the alcove. It wasn't the graceful design of the room nor the remains of a valuable vase that had attracted his attention, but a blackened metal pot, beside which stood a sake jar with a chipped mouth. In the pot was some rice gruel, and when he shook the jar, it made a cheerful gurgling sound. He smiled broadly, grateful for his good fortune and oblivious, as any hungry man might be, to the property rights of others.

He promptly drained off the sake in a couple of long swallows, emptied the rice pot and congratulated himself on the fullness of his belly.

Nodding sleepily beside the hearth, he became conscious of the rainlike buzz of insects coming from the dark field outside—not only from the field but from the walls, the ceiling and the rotting tatami mats.

Just before drifting off to sleep, he remembered the bundle he had taken from the dying warrior. He roused himself and untied it. The cloth was a soiled piece of crepe dyed with a dark red sappanwood dye. It contained a washed and bleached undergarment, together with the usual articles travelers carry. Unfolding the garment, he found an object the size and shape of a letter scroll, wrapped with great care in oil paper. There was also a purse, which fell with a loud clink from a fold in the fabric. Made of purple-dyed leather, it contained enough gold and silver to make Matahachi's hand shake with fear. "This is someone else's money, not mine," he reminded himself.

Undoing the oil paper around the longer object revealed a scroll, wound on a Chinese-quince roller, with a gold brocade end cloth. He immediately sensed that it contained some important secret and with great curiosity put the scroll down in front of him and slowly unrolled it. It said:

CERTIFICATE

On sacred oath I swear that I have transmitted to Sasaki Kojirō the following seven secret methods of the Chūjō Style of swordsmanship:

Overt—Lightning style, wheel style, rounded style, floating-boat style
Secret—The Diamond, The Edification, The Infinite

Issued in the village of Jōkyōji in the Usaka Demesne of Echizen Province on the —— day of the —— month.

Kanemaki Jisai, Disciple of Toda Seigen   239

On a piece of paper that seemed to have been attached later, there followed a poem:

> The moon shining on
> The waters not present
> In an undug well
> Yields forth a man
> With neither shadow nor form.

Matahachi realized he was holding a diploma given to a disciple who had learned all his master had to teach, but the name Kanemaki Jisai meant nothing to him. He would have recognized the name of Itō Yagorō, who under the name Ittōsai had created a famous and highly admired style of swordsmanship. He did not know that Jisai was Itō's teacher. Nor did he know that Jisai was a samurai of splendid character, who had mastered the true style of Toda Seigen and had retired to a remote village to pass his old age in obscurity, thereafter transmitting Seigen's method to only a few select students.

Matahachi's eyes went back to the first name. "This Sasaki Kojirō must have been the samurai who was killed at Fushimi today," he thought. "He must have been quite a swordsman to be awarded a certificate in the Chūjō Style, whatever that is. Shame he had to die! But now I'm sure of it. It's just as I suspected. He must've wanted me to deliver this to somebody, probably someone in his birthplace."

Matahachi said a short prayer to the Buddha for Sasaki Kojirō, then vowed to himself that somehow he would carry out his new mission.

To ward off the chill, he rebuilt the fire, then lay down by the hearth and presently fell asleep.

From somewhere in the distance came the sound of the old priest's *shakuhachi*. The mournful tune, seemingly searching for something, calling out to someone, went on and on, a poignant wave hovering over the rushes of the field.

Reunion in Osaka

The field lay under a gray mist, and the chill in the early morning air hinted that autumn was beginning in earnest. Squirrels were up and about, and in the doorless kitchen of the deserted house, fresh fox tracks crossed the earthen floor.

The beggar priest, having stumbled back before sunrise, had succumbed to fatigue on the pantry floor, still clutching his *shakuhachi*. His dirty kimono and cassock were wet with dew and spotty with grass stains picked up while he wandered like a lost soul through the night. As he opened his eyes and sat up, his nose crinkled, his nostrils and eyes opened wide, and he shook with a mighty sneeze. He made no effort to wipe off the snot trickling from his nose into his wispy mustache.

He sat there for a few minutes before recalling that he still had some sake left from the night before. Grumbling to himself, he made his way down a long hallway to the hearth room at the back of the house. By daylight, there were more rooms than there had seemed to be at night, but he found his way without difficulty. To his astonishment, the sake jar was not where he had left it.

Instead there was a stranger by the hearth, with his head on his arm and saliva seeping from his mouth, sound asleep. The whereabouts of the sake was all too clear.

The sake, of course, was not all that was missing. A quick check revealed that not a drop of the rice gruel intended for breakfast remained. The priest turned scarlet with rage; he could get by without the sake, but rice was a matter of life and death. With a fierce yelp, he kicked the sleeper with all his might, but Matahachi grunted sleepily, took his arm from underneath him, and lazily raised his head.

"You . . . you . . . !" sputtered the priest, giving him another kick.

"What are you doing?" cried Matahachi. The veins popped out on his sleepy face as he jumped to his feet. "You can't kick me like that!"

"Kicking's not good enough for you! Who told you you could come in here and steal my rice and sake?"

"Oh, were they yours?"

"Of course they were!"

"Sorry."

"You're sorry? What good does that do me?"

"I apologize."

"You'll have to do more than that!"

"What do you expect me to do?"

"Give them back!"

"Heh! They're already inside me; they kept me alive for a night. Can't get them back now!"

"I have to live too, don't I? The most I ever get for going around and playing music at people's gates is a few grains of rice or a couple of drops of sake. You imbecile! Do you expect me to stand silently by and let you steal my food? I want it back—give it back!" His tone as he made his irrational demand was imperious, and his voice sounded to Matahachi like that of a hungry devil straight from hell.

"Don't be so stingy," said Matahachi disparagingly. "What's there to get so upset about—a little rice and less than half a jar of third-rate sake."

"You ass, maybe you turn your nose up at leftover rice, but for me it's a day's food—a day's life!" The priest grunted and grabbed Matahachi's wrist. "I won't let you get away with this!"

241

"Don't be a fool!" countered Matahachi. Wresting his arm free and seizing the old man by his thin hair, he tried to throw him down with a quick yank. To his surprise, the starved-cat body didn't budge. The priest got a firm grip on Matahachi's neck and clung to it.

"You bastard!" barked Matahachi, reassessing his opponent's fighting power.

He was too late. The priest, planting his feet solidly on the floor, sent Matahachi stumbling backward with a single push. It was a skillful move, utilizing Matahachi's own strength, and Matahachi did not stop until he banged against the plastered wall on the far side of the adjacent room. The posts and lathing being rotten, a good part of the wall collapsed, showering him with dirt. Spitting out a mouthful, he jumped up, drew his sword and lunged at the old man.

The latter prepared to parry the attack with his *shakuhachi*, but he was already gasping for air.

"Now see what you've got yourself into!" yelled Matahachi as he swung. He missed but went on swinging relentlessly, giving the priest no chance to catch his breath. The old man's face took on a ghostly look. He jumped back time and again, but there was no spring in his step; he appeared to be on the verge of collapse. Each time he dodged, he let out a plaintive cry, like the whimper of a dying man. Still, his constant shifting made it impossible for Matahachi to connect with his sword.

Eventually Matahachi was undone by his own carelessness. When the priest jumped into the garden, Matahachi followed blindly, but the moment his foot hit the rotted floor of the veranda, the boards cracked and gave way. He landed on his backside, one leg dangling through a hole.

The priest leaped to the attack. Grabbing the front of Matahachi's kimono, he started beating him on the head, the temples, the body—anywhere his *shakuhachi* happened to fall—grunting loudly with each whack. With his leg caught, Matahachi was helpless. His head seemed ready to swell to the size of a barrel, but luck was with him, for at this point pieces of gold and silver began dropping from his kimono. Each new blow was followed by the happy tinkling of coins falling on the floor.

"What's this?" gasped the priest, letting go of his victim. Matahachi hastily freed his leg and jumped clear, but the old man had already vented his anger. His aching fist and labored breathing didn't stop him from staring in wonder at the money.

Matahachi, hands on his throbbing head, shouted, "See, you old fool? There was no reason to get excited over a little bit of rice and sake. I've got money to throw away! Take it if you want it! But in return you're going to get back the beating you gave me. Stick out your silly head, and I'll pay you with interest for your rice and booze!"

Instead of responding to this abuse, the priest put his face to the floor and began weeping. Matahachi's wrath abated somewhat, but he said venomously, "Look at you! The minute you see money, you fall apart."

242   "How shameful of me!" wailed the priest. "Why am I such a fool?" Like the

strength with which he had so lately fought, his self-reproach was more violent than that of an ordinary man. "What an ass I am!" he continued. "Haven't I come to my senses yet? Not even at my age? Not even after being cast out of society and sinking as low as a man can sink?"

He turned toward the black column beside him and started beating his head against it, all the time moaning to himself. "Why do I play this *shakuhachi*? Isn't it to expel through its five openings my delusions, my stupidity, my lust, my selfishness, my evil passions? How could I possibly have allowed myself to get into a life-and-death struggle over a bit of food and drink? And with a man young enough to be my son?"

Matahachi had never seen anyone like this. The old man would weep for a moment, then ram his head against the column again. He seemed intent on beating his forehead until it split in two. More numerous by far were his inflictions on himself than the blows he had dealt Matahachi. Presently, blood began to flow from his brow.

Matahachi felt obliged to prevent him from torturing himself further. "Look now," he said. "Stop that. You don't know what you're doing!"

"Leave me alone," pleaded the priest.

"But what's wrong with you?"

"Nothing's wrong."

"There must be something. Are you sick?"

"No."

"Then what is it?"

"I'm disgusted with myself. I'd like to beat this evil body of mine to death and feed it to the crows, but I don't want to die a stupid fool. I'd like to be as strong and upright as the next person before I discard this flesh. Losing my self-control makes me furious. I guess you could call it sickness after all."

Feeling sorry for him, Matahachi picked up the fallen money and tried to press some of it into his hand. "It was partly my fault," he said apologetically. "I'll give you this, and then maybe you'll forgive me."

"I don't want it!" cried the priest, quickly withdrawing his hand. "I don't need money. I tell you, I don't need it!" Though he had previously exploded in anger over a bit of rice gruel, he now looked at the money with loathing. Shaking his head vigorously, he backed away, still on his knees.

"You're an odd one," said Matahachi.

"Not really."

"Well, you certainly act strange."

"Don't let it worry you."

"You sound like you come from the western provinces. Your accent, I mean."

"I guess I would. I was born in Himeji."

"Is that so? I'm from that area too—Mimasaka."

"Mimasaka?" repeated the priest, fixing his eye on Matahachi. "Just where in Mimasaka?"

"The village of Yoshino. Miyamoto, to be exact."

The old man seemed to relax. Sitting down on the porch, he spoke quietly.

"Miyamoto? That's a name that brings back memories. I was once on guard duty at the stockade in Hinagura. I know that area fairly well."

"Does that mean you used to be a samurai in the Himeji fief?"

"Yes. I suppose I don't look it now, but I used to be something of a warrior. My name is Aoki Tan—"

He broke off, then just as abruptly went on: "That's not true. I just made it up. Forget I said anything at all." He stood up, saying, "I'm going into town, play my *shakuhachi* and get some rice." With that, he turned and walked rapidly toward the field of miscanthus.

After he was gone, Matahachi started wondering whether it had been right of him to offer the old priest money from the dead samurai's pouch. Soon he'd solved his dilemma by telling himself there couldn't be any harm in just borrowing some, provided it wasn't a lot. "If I deliver these things to the dead man's home, the way he wanted me to," he thought, "I'll have to have money for expenses, and what choice do I have but to take it out of the cash I have here?" This easy rationalization was so comforting that from that day on he began using the money little by little.

There remained the question of the certificate made out to Sasaki Kojirō. The man appeared to have been a rōnin, but mightn't he instead have been in the service of some daimyō? Matahachi had found no clue to where the man was from, hence had no idea where to take the certificate. His only hope, he decided, would be to locate the master swordsman Kanemaki Jisai, who no doubt knew all there was to know about Sasaki.

As Matahachi made his way from Fushimi toward Osaka, he asked at every teahouse, eating house and inn whether anyone knew of Jisai. All the replies were negative; even the added information that Jisai was an accredited disciple of Toda Seigen elicited no response.

Finally, a samurai with whom Matahachi struck up an acquaintance on the road displayed a glimmer of recognition. "I've heard of Jisai, but if he's still alive, he must be very old. Somebody said he went east and became a recluse in a village in Kōzuke, or somewhere. If you want to find out more about him, you should go to Osaka Castle and talk to a man named Tomita Mondonoshō." Mondonoshō, it seemed, was one of Hideyori's teachers in the martial arts, and Matahachi's informant was fairly sure he belonged to the same family as Seigen.

Though disappointed at the vagueness of his first real lead, Matahachi resolved to follow it up. Upon his arrival in Osaka, he took a room at a cheap inn on one of the busier streets and as soon as he was settled in asked the innkeeper whether he knew of a man named Tomita Mondonoshō at Osaka Castle.

"Yes, I've heard the name," replied the innkeeper. "I believe he's the grandson of Toda Seigen. He's not Lord Hideyori's personal instructor, but he does teach swordsmanship to some of the samurai in the castle. Or at least he used to. I think he might have gone back to Echizen some years ago. Yes, that's what he did.

"You could go to Echizen and look for him, but there's no guarantee he's still there. Instead of taking such a long trip on a hunch, wouldn't it be easier to look up Itō Ittōsai? I'm pretty sure he studied the Chūjō Style under Jisai before developing his own style."

The innkeeper's suggestion seemed sensible, but when Matahachi began looking for Ittōsai, he found himself in another blind alley. As far as he could learn, the man had until recently been living in a small hut in Shirakawa, just east of Kyoto, but he was no longer there and hadn't been seen in Kyoto or Osaka for some time.

Before long, Matahachi's resolution flagged and he was ready to drop the whole business. The bustle and excitement of the city rekindled his ambition and stirred his youthful soul. In a wide-open town like this, why should he spend his time looking for a dead man's family? There were plenty of things to do here; people were looking for young men like him. At Fushimi Castle, the authorities had been single-mindedly implementing the policies of the Tokugawa government. Here, however, the generals running Osaka Castle were searching out rōnin to build up an army. Not publicly, of course, but openly enough so that it was common knowledge. It was a fact that rōnin were more welcome and could live better here than in any other castle town in the country.

Heady rumors circulated among the townspeople. It was said, for instance, that Hideyori was quietly providing funds for such fugitive daimyō as Gotō Matabei, Sanada Yukimura, Akashi Kamon and even the dangerous Chōsokabe Morichika, who now lived in a rented house in a narrow street on the outskirts of town.

Chōsokabe had, despite his youth, shaved his head like a Buddhist priest and changed his name to Ichimusai—"The Man of a Single Dream." It was a declaration that the affairs of this floating world no longer concerned him, and ostensibly he passed his time in elegant frivolities. It was widely known, however, that he had in his service seven or eight hundred rōnin, all of them firm in their confidence that when the proper time came, he would rise up and vindicate his late benefactor Hideyoshi. It was rumored that his living expenses, including the pay for his rōnin, all came from Hideyori's private purse.

For two months Matahachi wandered about Osaka, increasingly confident that this was the place for him. Here was where he would catch the straw that would lead to success. For the first time in years he felt as brave and dauntless as when he'd gone off to war. He was healthy and alive again, unperturbed by the gradual depletion of the dead samurai's money, for he believed luck was finally turning his way. Every day was a joy, a delight. He was sure he was about to stumble over a rock and come up covered with money. Good fortune was on the verge of finding him.

New clothes! That was what he needed. And so he bought himself a complete new outfit, carefully choosing material that would be suitable in the cold of approaching winter. Then, having decided living in an inn was too expensive, he rented a small room belonging to a saddle-maker in the vicinity of the 245

Junkei Moat and began taking his meals out. He went to see what he wanted to see, came home when he felt like it, and stayed out all night from time to time, as the spirit moved him. While basking in this happy-go-lucky existence, he remained on the lookout for a friend, a connection who would lead him to a good paying position in the service of a great daimyō.

It required a certain amount of self-restraint for Matahachi to live within his means, but he felt he was behaving himself better than ever before. He was repeatedly buoyed up by stories of how this or that samurai had not long ago been hauling dirt away from a construction site but was now to be seen riding pompously through town with twenty retainers and a spare horse.

At other times he felt a trace of dejection. "The world's a stone wall," he would think. "And they've put the rocks so close together there's not a chink where anybody can get in." But his frustration always eddied away. "What am I talking about? It just looks that way when you still haven't seen your chance. It's always difficult to break in, but once I find an opening . . ."

When he asked the saddle-maker whether he knew of a position, the latter replied optimistically, "You're young and strong. If you apply at the castle, they're sure to find a place for you."

But finding the right work was not as easy as that. The last month of the year found Matahachi still unemployed, his money diminished by half.

Under the wintry sun of the busiest month of the year, the hordes of people milling about the streets looked surprisingly unrushed. In the center of town there were empty lots, where in early morning the grass was white with frost. As the day progressed, the streets became muddy, and the feeling of winter was driven away by the sound of merchants hawking their goods with clanging gongs and booming drums. Seven or eight stalls, surrounded by shabby straw matting to keep outsiders from looking in, beckoned with paper flags and lances decorated with feathers to advertise shows being presented inside. Barkers competed stridently to lure idle passersby into their flimsy theaters.

The smell of cheap soy sauce permeated the air. In the shops, hairy-legged men, skewers of food stuffed in their mouths, whinnied like horses, and at twilight long-sleeved women with whitened faces simpered like ewes, walking together in flocks and munching on parched-bean tidbits.

One evening a fight broke out among the customers of a man who had set up a sake shop by placing some stools on the side of the street. Before anyone could tell who had won, the combatants turned tail and ran off down the street, leaving a trail of dripping blood behind them.

"Thank you, sir," said the sake vendor to Matahachi, whose glaring presence had caused the fighting townsmen to flee. "If you hadn't been here, they would have broken all my dishes." The man bowed several times, then served Matahachi another jar of sake, which he said he trusted was warmed to just the right temperature. He also presented some snacks as a token of his appreciation.

Matahachi was pleased with himself. The brawl had erupted between two

246

workmen, and when he had scowled at them, threatening to kill them both if they did any damage to the stall, they had fled.

"Lots of people around, aren't there?" he remarked amiably.

"It's the end of the year. They stay awhile and move on, but others keep coming."

"Nice that the weather's holding up."

Matahachi's face was red from drink. As he lifted his cup, he remembered having sworn off before he went to work at Fushimi, and vaguely wondered how he had started again. "Well, what of it?" he thought. "If a man can't have a drink now and then . . ."

"Bring me another, old boy," he said aloud.

The man sitting quietly on the stool next to Matahachi's was also a rōnin. His long and short swords were impressive; townsmen would be inclined to steer clear of him, even though he wore no cloak over his kimono, which was quite dirty around the neck.

"Hey, bring me another one too, and make it quick!" he shouted. Propping his right leg on his left knee, he scrutinized Matahachi from the feet up. When his eyes came to the face, he smiled and said, "Hello."

"Hello," said Matahachi. "Have a sip of mine while yours is being heated."

"Thanks," said the man, holding out his cup. "It's humiliating to be a drinker, isn't it? I saw you sitting here with your sake, and then this nice aroma floated through the air and pulled me over here—by the sleeve, sort of." He drained his cup in one gulp.

Matahachi liked his style. He seemed friendly, and there was something dashing about him. He could drink too; he put down five jars in the next few minutes, while Matahachi was taking his time over one. Yet he was still sober.

"How much do you usually drink?" asked Matahachi.

"Oh, I don't know," replied the man offhandedly. "Ten or twelve jars, when I feel like it."

They fell to talking about the political situation, and after a time the rōnin straightened up his shoulders and said, "Who's Ieyasu anyway? What kind of nonsense is it for him to ignore Hideyori's claims and go around calling himself the 'Great Overlord'? Without Honda Masazumi and some of his other old supporters, what have you got? Cold-bloodedness, foxiness and a little political ability—I mean, all he has is a certain flair for politics that you usually don't find in military men.

"Personally, I wish Ishida Mitsunari had won at Sekigahara, but he was too high-minded to organize the daimyō. And his status wasn't high enough." Having delivered himself of this appraisal, he suddenly asked, "If Osaka were to clash with Edo again, which side would you be on?"

Not without hesitation, Matahachi replied, "Osaka."

"Good!" The man stood up with his sake jar in his hand. "You're one of us. Let's drink to that! What fief do you— Oh, I guess I shouldn't ask that until I tell you who I am. My name is Akakabe Yasoma. I'm from Gamō. Perhaps you've heard of Ban Dan'emon? I'm a good friend of his. We'll be together again one of these days. I'm also a friend of Susukida Hayato Kanesuke, the distinguished general at Osaka Castle. We traveled together when he was still a rōnin. I've also met Ōno Shurinosuke three or four times, but he's too gloomy for me, even if he does have more political influence than Kanesuke."

He stepped back, paused for a moment, seemingly having second thoughts about talking too much, then asked, "Who are you?"

Matahachi, though he did not believe everything the man had said, felt somehow that he had been put temporarily in the shade.

"Do you know of Toda Seigen?" he asked. "The man who originated the Tomita Style."

"I've heard the name."

"Well, my teacher was the great and selfless hermit Kanemaki Jisai, who received the true Tomita Style from Seigen and then developed the Chūjō Style."

"Then you must be a real swordsman."

"That's right," replied Matahachi. He was beginning to enjoy the game.

"You know," said Yasoma, "I've been thinking that's what you must be. Your body looks disciplined, and there's an air of capability about you. What were you called when you were training under Jisai? I mean, if I'm not being too bold in asking."

"My name is Sasaki Kojirō," said Matahachi with a straight face. "Itō Yagorō, the creator of the Ittō Style, is a senior disciple from the same school."

"Is that a fact?" said Yasoma with astonishment.

For a jittery moment, Matahachi thought of retracting everything, but it was too late. Yasoma had already knelt on the ground and was making a deep bow. There was no turning back.

"Forgive me," he said several times. "I've often heard Sasaki Kojirō was a splendid swordsman, and I must apologize for not having spoken more politely. I had no way of knowing who you were."

Matahachi was vastly relieved. If Yasoma had happened to be a friend or acquaintance of Kojirō, he would have had to fight for his life.

"You needn't bow like that," said Matahachi magnanimously. "If you insist on standing on formalities, we won't be able to talk as friends."

"But you must have been annoyed by my spouting off so."

"Why? I have no particular status or position. I'm only a young man who doesn't know much about the ways of the world."

"Yes, but you're a great swordsman. I've heard your name many times. Now that I think about it, I can see you must be Sasaki Kojirō." He stared intently at Matahachi. "What's more, I don't think it's right that you should have no official position."

Matahachi replied innocently, "Well, I've devoted myself so single-mindedly to my sword that I haven't had time to make many friends."

"I see. Does that mean you aren't interested in finding a good position?"

"No; I've always thought that one day I'd have to find a lord to serve. I just haven't reached that point yet."

"Well, it should be simple enough. You have your reputation with the sword to back you up, and that makes all the difference in the world. Of course, if you remain silent, then no matter how much talent you have, nobody's likely to search you out. Look at me. I didn't even know who you were until you told me. I was completely taken by surprise."

Yasoma paused, then said, "If you'd like me to help you, I'd be glad to. To tell the truth, I've asked my friend Susukida Kanesuke to see whether he can find a position for me too. I'd like to be taken on at Osaka Castle, even though there might not be much pay in it. I'm sure Kanesuke would be happy to recommend a person like you to the powers that be. If you'd like, I'll be glad to speak to him."

As Yasoma waxed enthusiastic about the prospects, Matahachi could not avoid the feeling that he had stumbled straight into something it wouldn't be easy to get out of. Eager as he was to find work, he feared he'd made a mistake passing himself off as Sasaki Kojirō. On the other hand, if he had said he was Hon'iden Matahachi, a country samurai from Mimasaka, Yasoma would never have offered his help. Indeed, he probably would have looked down his nose at him. There was no getting around it: the name Sasaki Kojirō had certainly made a strong impression.

But then—was there actually anything to worry about? The real Kojirō was dead, and Matahachi was the only person who knew that, for he had the certificate, the dead man's only identification. Without it, there was no way for the authorities to know who the rōnin was; it was extremely unlikely they would have gone to the trouble of conducting an investigation. After all, who was the man but a "spy" who had been stoned to death. Gradually, as Matahachi convinced himself that his secret would never be discovered, a bold scheme took definite shape in his mind: he would become Sasaki Kojirō. As of this moment.

"Bring the bill," he called, taking some coins from his money pouch.

As Matahachi rose to leave, Yasoma, thrown into confusion, blurted, "What about my proposal?"

"Oh," replied Matahachi, "I'd be very grateful if you'd speak to your friend on my behalf, but we can't discuss this sort of thing here. Let's go somewhere quiet where we can have some privacy."

"Why, of course," said Yasoma, obviously relieved. He appeared to think it only natural that Matahachi paid his bill too.

Soon they were in a district some distance from the main streets. Matahachi had intended to take his newfound friend to an elegant drinking establishment, but Yasoma pointed out that going to such a place would be a waste of money. He suggested someplace cheaper and more interesting, and while singing the praises of the red-light district, led Matahachi to what was euphemistically called the Town of Priestesses. Here, it was said, with only slight exaggeration, there were a thousand houses of pleasure, and a trade so thriving that a hundred barrels of lamp oil were consumed in a single night. Matahachi was a little reluctant at first but soon found himself attracted by the gaiety of the atmosphere.

Nearby was an offshoot of the castle moat, into which tidewater flowed   *249* from the bay. If one looked very closely, one could discern fish lice and river crabs crawling about under the projecting windows and red lanterns. Matahachi did look closely and ended up slightly unsettled, for they reminded him of deadly scorpions.

The district was peopled to a large extent by women with thickly powdered faces. Among them a pretty face was to be seen now and then, but there were many others who seemed to be more than forty, women stalking the streets with sad eyes, heads wrapped in cloth to fend off the cold, teeth blackened, but trying wanly to stir the hearts of the men who gathered here.

"There sure are lots of them," said Matahachi with a sigh.

"I told you so," replied Yasoma, who was at pains to make excuses for the women. "And they're better than the next teahouse waitress or singing girl you might take up with. People tend to be put off by the idea of selling sex, but if you spend a winter's night with one of them and talk with her about her family and so on, you're likely to find she's just like any other woman. And not really to blame for having become a whore."

"Some were once concubines of the shōgun, and there are lots whose fathers were once retainers of some daimyō who have since lost power. It was the same centuries ago when the Taira fell to the Minamoto. You'll find, my friend, that in the gutters of this floating world, much of the trash consists of fallen flowers."

They went into a house, and Matahachi left everything to Yasoma, who seemed to be quite experienced. He knew how to order the sake, how to deal with the girls; he was flawless. Matahachi found the experience quite entertaining.

They spent the night, and even at noon on the next day, Yasoma showed no sign of tiring. Matahachi felt recompensed to some extent for all those times he had been pushed off into a back room at the Yomogi, but he was beginning to run down.

Finally, admitting he'd had enough, he said, "I don't want any more to drink. Let's go."

Yasoma did not budge. "Stay with me until evening," he said.

"What happens then?"

"I have an appointment to see Susukida Kanesuke. It's too early to go to his house now, and anyway I won't be able to discuss your situation until I have a better idea of what you want."

"I guess I shouldn't ask for too large an allowance at first."

"There's no point in selling yourself cheap. A samurai of your caliber should be able to command any figure he names. If you say you'll settle for any old position, you'll be demeaning yourself. Why don't I tell him you want an allowance of twenty-five hundred bushels? A samurai with self-confidence is always better paid and treated. You shouldn't give the impression you'd be satisfied with just anything."

As evening approached, the streets in this area, lying as they did in the immense shadow of Osaka Castle, darkened early. Having left the brothel, Matahachi and Yasoma made their way through the town to one of the more exclusive samurai residential areas. They stood with their backs to the moat, the cold wind driving away the effects of the sake they'd been pouring into themselves all day.

"That's Susukida's house there," said Yasoma.

"The one with the bracketed roof over the gate?"

"No, the corner house next to it."

"Hmm. Big, isn't it?"

"Kanesuke's made a name for himself. Until he was thirty or so, nobody had ever heard of him, but now . . ."

Matahachi pretended to pay no attention to what Yasoma was saying. Not that he did not believe it; on the contrary, he had come to trust Yasoma so thoroughly that he no longer questioned what the man said. He felt, however, that he should remain nonchalant. As he gazed at the mansions of the daimyō, which ringed the great castle, his still youthful ambition told him, "I'll live in a place like that too—one of these days."

"Now," said Yasoma, "I'll see Kanesuke and talk him into hiring you. But before that, what about the money?"

"Oh, sure," said Matahachi, aware that a bribe was in order. Taking the money pouch from his breast, he realized that it had shrunk to about a third of its original bulk. Pouring it all out in his hand, he said, "This is all I have. Is it enough?"

"Oh, sure, quite enough."

"You'll want to wrap it up in something, won't you?"

"No, no. Kanesuke's not the only man around here who takes a fee for finding somebody a position. They all do it, and very openly. There's nothing to be embarrassed about."

Matahachi kept back a little of the cash, but after handing over the rest began to feel uneasy. When Yasoma walked away, he followed for a few steps. "Do the best you can," he implored.

"Don't worry. If it looks as though he's going to be difficult, all I have to do is keep the money and return it to you. He's not the only influential man in Osaka. I could just as easily ask help from Ōno or Gotō. I've got lots of contacts."

"When will I get an answer?"

"Let's see. You could wait for me, but you wouldn't want to stand here in this wind, would you? Anyway, people might suspect you were up to no good. Let's meet again tomorrow."

"Where?"

"Come to that vacant lot where they're holding sideshows."

"All right."

"The surest way would be for you to wait at that sake vendor's where we first met."

After they settled on the time, Yasoma waved his hand and walked grandly through the gate to the mansion, swinging his shoulders and showing not the slightest hesitation. Matahachi, duly impressed, felt Yasoma must indeed have known Kanesuke since his less prosperous days. Confidence swept over him, and that night he dreamed pleasant dreams of his future.

At the appointed time, Matahachi was walking through the melting frost on the open lot. As on the previous day, the wind was cold, and there were a lot of people about. He waited until sundown but saw no sign of Akakabe Yasoma.

The day after that, Matahachi went again. "Something must have detained him," he thought charitably, as he sat staring at the faces of the passing crowd. "He'll show up today." But again the sun set without Yasoma's appearing.

On the third day, Matahachi said to the sake vendor, somewhat timidly, "I'm here again."

"Are you waiting for someone?"

"Yes, I'm supposed to meet a man named Akakabe Yasoma. I met him here the other day." Matahachi went on to explain the situation in detail.

"That scoundrel?" gasped the sake vendor. "Do you mean he told you he'd find you a good position and then stole your money?"

"He didn't steal it. I gave him some money to give to a man named Susukida Kanesuke. I'm waiting here to find out what happened."

"You poor man! You can wait a hundred years, but I daresay you won't see him again."

"Wh-what? Why do you say that?"

"Why, he's a notorious crook! This area's full of parasites like him. If they see anybody who looks a little innocent, they pounce on him. I thought of warning you, but I didn't want to interfere. I thought you'd know from the way he looked and acted what sort of character he was. Now you've gone and lost your money. Too bad!"

The man was all sympathy. He tried to assure Matahachi that it was no disgrace to be taken in by the thieves operating here. But it wasn't embarrassment that troubled Matahachi; it was finding his money gone, and with it his high hopes, that made his blood boil. He stared helplessly at the crowd moving about them.

"I doubt it'll do any good," said the sake vendor, "but you might try asking over there at the magician's stall. The local vermin often gather behind there to gamble. If Yasoma came by some money, he may be trying to build it into something bigger."

"Thanks," said Matahachi, jumping up excitedly. "Which is the magician's stall?"

The enclosure to which the man pointed was surrounded by a fence of pointed bamboo stakes. Out in front, barkers were drumming up trade, and flags suspended near the wooden gate announced the names of several famous sleight-of-hand artists. From within the curtains and strips of straw matting lining the fence came the sound of strange music, mingled with the loud, rapid patter of the performers and the applause of the audience.

Going around to the rear, Matahachi found another gate. When he glanced in, a lookout asked, "You here to gamble?"

He nodded and the man let him in. He found himself in a space surrounded

252

by tenting but open to the sky. About twenty men, all unsavory types, sat in a circle playing a game. All eyes turned toward Matahachi and one man silently made room for him to sit down.

"Is Akakabe Yasoma here?" Matahachi asked.

"Yasoma?" repeated one gambler in a puzzled tone. "Come to think of it, he hasn't been around lately. Why?"

"Do you think he'll come later?"

"How should I know? Sit down and play."

"I didn't come to play."

"What're you doing here if you don't want to play?"

"I'm looking for Yasoma. Sorry to bother you."

"Well, why don't you go look somewhere else!"

"I said I'm sorry," said Matahachi, exiting hastily.

"Hold on there!" commanded one of the gamblers, getting up and following him. "You can't get away with just saying you're sorry. Even if you don't play, you'll pay for your seat!"

"I don't have any money."

"No money! I see. Just waiting for a chance to swipe some cash, huh? Damned thief, that's what you are."

"I'm no thief! You can't call me that!" Matahachi pushed the hilt of his sword forward, but this merely amused the gambler.

"Idiot!" he barked. "If threats from the likes of you scared me, I wouldn't be able to stay alive in Osaka for one day. Use your sword, if you dare!"

"I warn you, I mean it!"

"Oh, you do, do you?"

"Do you know who I am?"

"Why should I?"

"I'm Sasaki Kojirō, successor of Toda Seigen of Jōkyōji Village in Echizen. He created the Tomita Style," Matahachi declared proudly, thinking this pronouncement alone would put the man to flight. It didn't. The gambler spat and turned back into the enclosure.

"Hey, come on, all of you! This guy's just called himself some fancy name; seems to want to pull his sword on us. Let's have a look at his swordsmanship. It ought to be fun."

Matahachi, seeing that the man was off guard, suddenly drew his sword and sliced across his backside.

The man jumped straight up in the air. "You son of a bitch!" he screamed.

Matahachi dived into the crowd. By sneaking from one cluster of people to the next, he managed to stay hidden, but every face he saw looked like one of the gamblers. Deciding he couldn't hide that way forever, he looked around for more substantial shelter.

Directly in front of him, draped on a bamboo fence, was a curtain with a large tiger painted on it. There was also a banner on the gate bearing a design of a forked spear and a snake-eye crest, and a barker standing on an empty box, shouting hoarsely, "See the tiger! Come in and see the tiger! Take a trip of a thousand miles! This enormous tiger, my friends, was captured personally by the great general Katō Kiyomasa in Korea. Don't miss the tiger!" His spiel was frenetic and rhythmical.

Matahachi threw down a coin and darted through the entrance. Feeling relatively safe, he looked around for the beast. At the far end of the tent a large tiger skin lay stretched out like laundry drying on a wooden panel. The spectators were staring at it with great curiosity, seemingly unperturbed by the fact that the creature was neither whole nor alive.

"So that's what a tiger looks like," said one man.

"Big, isn't it?" marveled another.

Matahachi stood a little to one side of the tiger skin, until suddenly he spotted an old man and woman, and his ears perked up in disbelief as he listened to their voices.

"Uncle Gon," said the woman, "that tiger there is dead, isn't it?"

The old samurai, stretching his hand over the bamboo railing and feeling the skin, replied gravely, "Of course it's dead. This is only the hide."

"But that man outside was talking as though it was alive."

"Well, maybe that's what they mean by a fast talker," he said with a little laugh.

Osugi didn't take it so lightly. Pursing her lips, she protested, "Don't be silly! If it's not real, the sign outside should say so. If all I was going to see was a tiger's skin, I'd just as soon see a picture. Let's go and get our money back."

"Don't make a fuss, Granny. People will laugh at you."

"That's all right. I'm not too proud. If you don't want to go, I'll go myself." As she started pushing her way back through the spectators, Matahachi ducked, but too late. Uncle Gon had already seen him.

"Hey, there, Matahachi! Is that you?" he shouted.

Osugi, whose eyes were none too good, stammered, "Wh-what's that you said, Uncle Gon?"

"Didn't you see? Matahachi was standing there, just behind you."

"Impossible!"

"He was there, but he ran away."

"Where? Which way?"

The two scampered out the wooden gate into the crowd, already veiled in the hues of evening. Matahachi kept bumping into people but disentangled himself and ran on.

"Wait, son, wait!" cried Osugi.

Matahachi glanced behind him and saw his mother chasing him like a madwoman. Uncle Gon, too, was waving his hands frantically.

"Matahachi!" he cried. "Why are you running away? What's wrong with you? Matahachi! Matahachi!"

Seeing she was not going to be able to catch him, Osugi stuck her wrinkled neck forward and, at the top of her lungs, screamed, "Stop, thief! Robber! Catch him!"

Immediately a throng of bystanders took up the chase, and those in the forefront soon fell upon Matahachi with bamboo poles.

"Keep him there!"

"The scoundrel!"

"Give him a good beating!"

The mob had Matahachi cornered, and some even spat on him. Arriving with Uncle Gon, Osugi quickly took in the scene and turned furiously on Matahachi's attackers. Pushing them away, she seized the hilt of her short sword and bared her teeth.

"What are you doing?" she cried. "Why are you attacking this man?"

"He's a thief!"

"He is not! He's my son."

"Your son?"

"Yes, he's my son, the son of a samurai, and you have no business beating him. You're nothing but common townspeople. If you touch him again I'll . . . I'll take you all on!"

"Are you joking? Who shouted 'thief' a minute ago?"

"That was me, all right, I don't deny it. I'm a devoted mother, and I thought if I cried 'thief,' my son would stop running. But who asked you stupid oafs to hit him? It's outrageous!"

Startled by her volte-face, yet admiring her mettle, the crowd slowly dispersed. Osugi seized her wayward son by the collar and dragged him to the grounds of a nearby shrine.

After standing and looking on from the shrine gate for a few minutes, Uncle Gon came forward and said, "Granny, you don't have to treat Matahachi like that. He's not a child." He tried to pull her hand away from Matahachi's collar, but the old woman elbowed him roughly out of the way.

"You stay out of this! He's my son, and I'll punish him as I see fit, with no help from you. Just keep quiet and mind your own business! . . . Matahachi, you ungrateful . . . I'll show you!"

It is said that the older people grow, the simpler and more direct they become, and watching Osugi, one could not help but agree. At a time when other mothers might have been weeping for joy, Osugi was seething with rage.

She forced Matahachi to the ground and beat his head against it.

"The very idea! Running away from your own mother! You weren't born from the fork of a tree, you lout—you're my son!" She began spanking him as though he were still a child. "I didn't think you could possibly be alive, and here you are loafing around Osaka! It's shameful! You brazen, good-for-nothing . . . Why didn't you come home and pay the proper respects to your ancestors? Why didn't you so much as show your face just once to your old mother? Didn't you know all your relatives were worried sick about you?"

"Please, Mama," begged Matahachi, crying like a baby. "Forgive me. Please forgive me! I'm sorry. I know what I did was wrong. It was because I knew I'd failed you that I couldn't go home. I didn't really mean to run away from you. I was so surprised to see you, I started running without thinking. I was so ashamed of the way I'd been living, I couldn't face you and Uncle Gon." He covered his face with his hands.

255

Osugi's nose crinkled, and she, too, started to bawl, but almost immediately she stopped herself. Too proud to show weakness, she renewed her attack, saying sarcastically, "If you're so ashamed of yourself and feel you've disgraced your ancestors, then you really must have been up to no good all this time."

Uncle Gon, unable to restrain himself, pleaded, "That's enough. If you keep on like that, it'll surely twist his nature."

"I told you to keep your advice to yourself. You're a man; you shouldn't be so soft. As his mother, I have to be just as stern as his father would be if he were still alive. I'll do the punishing, and I'm not finished yet! . . . Matahachi! Sit up straight! Look me in the face."

She sat down formally on the ground and pointed to the place where he was to sit.

"Yes, Mama," he said obediently, lifting his dirt-stained shoulders and getting into a kneeling position. He was afraid of his mother. She could on occasion be an indulgent parent, but her readiness to raise the subject of his duty to his ancestors made him uncomfortable.

"I absolutely forbid you to hide anything from me," said Osugi. "Now, what exactly have you been doing since you ran off to Sekigahara? Start explaining, and don't stop till I've heard all I want to hear."

"Don't worry, I won't hold anything back," he began, having lost the desire to fight. True to his word, he blurted out the whole story in detail: about escaping from Sekigahara, hiding at Ibuki, becoming involved with Okō, living off her—though hating it—for several years. And how he now sincerely regretted what he'd done. It was a relief, like throwing up bile from his stomach, and he felt much better after he'd confessed.

"Hmm . . ." mumbled Uncle Gon from time to time.

Osugi clicked her tongue, saying, "I'm shocked at your conduct. And what are you doing now? You seem to be able to dress well. Have you found a position that pays adequately?"

"Yes," said Matahachi. The answer slipped out without forethought, and he hastened to correct himself. "I mean, no, I don't have a position."

"Then where do you get money to live on?"

"My sword—I teach swordsmanship." There was the ring of truth in the way he said this, and it had the desired effect.

"Is that so?" said Osugi with obvious interest. For the first time, a glimmer of good humor appeared in her face. "Swordsmanship, is it? Well, it doesn't really surprise me that a son of mine would find time to polish his swordsmanship—even leading the kind of life you were. Hear that, Uncle Gon? He is my son, after all."

Uncle Gon nodded enthusiastically, grateful to see the old woman's spirits rise. "We might have known," he said. "That shows he does have the blood of his Hon'iden ancestors in his veins. So what if he went astray for a time? It's clear he's got the right spirit!"

"Matahachi," said Osugi.

"Yes, Mama."

"Here in this area, who did you study swordsmanship under?"

"Kanemaki Jisai."

"Oh? Why, he's famous." Osugi had a happy expression on her face. Matahachi, eager to please her even more, brought out the certificate and unrolled it, taking care to cover Sasaki's name with his thumb.

"Look at this," he said.

"Let me see," said Osugi. She reached for the scroll, but Matahachi kept a firm grip on it.

"See, Mama, you don't have to worry about me."

She nodded. "Yes, indeed, this is fine. Uncle Gon, look at this. Isn't it splendid? I always thought, even when Matahachi was a baby, that he was smarter and more capable than Takezō and the other boys." She was so overjoyed she began spitting as she spoke.

At just this moment, Matahachi's hand slipped, and the name on the scroll became visible.

"Wait a minute," said Osugi. "Why does it say 'Sasaki Kojirō'?"

"Oh, that? Why, uh, that's my nom de guerre."

"Nom de guerre? Why do you need that? Isn't Hon'iden Matahachi good enough for you?"

"Yes, fine!" replied Matahachi, thinking fast. "But when I thought it over, I decided not to use my own name. With my shameful past, I was afraid of disgracing our ancestors."

"I see. That was good thinking, I suppose. Well, I don't imagine you know anything about what's gone on in the village, so I'll tell you. Now pay attention; it's important."

Osugi launched into a spirited account of the incident that had occurred in Miyamoto, choosing her words in a way calculated to spur Matahachi to action. She explained how the Hon'iden family had been insulted, how she and Uncle Gon had been searching for years for Otsū and Takezō. Although she tried not to get emotional, she did get carried away with her story; her eyes moistened and her voice thickened.

Matahachi, listening with bowed head, was struck by the vividness of her narrative. At times like this, he found it easy to be a good and obedient son, but whereas his mother's main concern was family honor and the samurai spirit, he was most deeply moved by something else: if what she was saying was true, Otsū didn't love him anymore. This was the first time he had actually heard this. "Is that really true?" he asked.

Osugi, seeing his face change color, drew the mistaken conclusion that her lecture on honor and spirit was taking effect. "If you think I'm lying," she said, "ask Uncle Gon. That trollop abandoned you and ran off with Takezō. To put it another way, you could say Takezō, knowing you wouldn't be back for some time, lured Otsū into going away with him. Isn't that right, Uncle Gon?"

"Yes. When Takezō was tied up in the tree, he got Otsū to help him escape, and the two made off together. Everybody said there must have been something going on between them."

This brought out the worst in Matahachi and inspired a new revulsion against his boyhood friend.

Sensing this, his mother fanned the spark. "Do you see now, Matahachi! Do you understand why Uncle Gon and I left the village? We're going to have our revenge on those two. Unless I kill them, I can't ever show my face in the village again or stand before the memorial tablets of our ancestors."

"I understand."

"And do you see that unless we avenge ourselves, you can't return to Miyamoto either?"

"I won't go back. I'll never go back."

"That's not the point. You've got to kill those two. They're our mortal enemies."

"Yeah, I guess so."

"You don't sound very enthusiastic. What's the matter? Don't you think you're strong enough to kill Takezō?"

"Of course I am," he protested.

Uncle Gon spoke up. "Don't worry, Matahachi. I'll stick by you."

"And your old mother will too," added Osugi. "Let's take their heads back to the village as souvenirs for the people. Isn't that a good idea, son? If we do, then you can go ahead and find yourself a wife and settle down. You'll vindicate yourself as a samurai and earn a fine reputation as well. There's no better name in the whole Yoshino area than Hon'iden, and you will have proved that to everyone beyond a doubt. Can you do it, Matahachi? Will you do it?"

"Yes, Mama."

"That's a good son. Uncle Gon, don't just stand there, congratulate the boy. He's sworn to take revenge on Takezō and Otsū." Seemingly satisfied at last, she started to rise from the ground with visible difficulty. "Oh, that hurts!" she cried.

"What's the matter?" asked Uncle Gon.

"The ground is freezing. My stomach and hips ache."

"That's not so good. Are you coming down with piles again?"

Matahachi, in a show of filial devotion, said, "Climb on my back, Mama."

"Oh, you want to carry me? Isn't that nice!" Grasping his shoulders, she shed tears of joy. "How many years has it been? Look, Uncle Gon, Matahachi's going to carry me on his back."

As her tears fell on his neck, Matahachi himself felt strangely pleased. "Uncle Gon, where are you staying?" he asked.

"We still have to find an inn, but any will do. Let's go look for one."

"All right." Matahachi bounced his mother lightly on his back as he walked. "Say, Mama, you're light! Very light! Much lighter than a rock!"

The Handsome Young Man

Gradually obscured by the wintry noonday mist, the sunlit island of Awaji faded into the distance. The flapping of the great sail in the wind drowned out the sound of the waves. The boat, which plied several times each month between Osaka and Awa Province in Shikoku, was crossing the Inland Sea on its way to Osaka. Although its cargo consisted mostly of paper and indigo dye, a distinctive odor betrayed it was carrying contraband, in the form of tobacco, which the Tokugawa government had forbidden the people to smoke, sniff or chew. There were also passengers on board, mostly merchants, either returning to the city or visiting it for the year-end trading.

"How's it going? Making lots of money, I bet."

"Not at all! Everybody says things are booming in Sakai, but you couldn't prove it by me."

"I hear there's a shortage of workmen there. Heard they need gunsmiths."

Conversation in another group went along similar lines.

"I supply battle equipment myself—flagstaffs, armor, that sort of thing. I'm certainly not making as much as I used to, though."

"Is that so?"

"Yes, I guess the samurai are learning how to add."

"Ha, ha!"

"It used to be that when the freebooters brought in their loot, you could redye or repaint things and sell them right back to the armies. Then after the next battle, the stuff would come back and you could fix it up and sell it again."

One man was gazing out over the ocean and extolling the riches of the countries beyond it. "You can't make money at home anymore. If you want real profits, you have to do what Naya 'Luzon' Sukezaemon or Chaya Sukejirō did. Go into foreign trade. It's risky, but if you're lucky, it can really pay off."

"Well," said another man, "even if things aren't so good for us these days, from the samurai's viewpoint we're doing very well. Most of them don't even know what good food tastes like. We talk about the luxuries the daimyō enjoy, but sooner or later they have to put on their leather and steel and go out and get killed. I feel sorry for them; they're so busy thinking about their honor and the warrior's code they can't ever sit back and enjoy life."

"Isn't that the truth? We complain about bad times and all, but the only thing to be today is a merchant."

259

"You're right. At least we can do what we want."

"All we really have to do is make a show of bowing down before the samurai, and a little money makes up for a lot of that."

"If you're going to live in this world, might as well have a good time."

"That's the way I see it. Sometimes I feel like asking the samurai what they're getting out of life."

The woolen carpet this group had spread for themselves to sit on was imported—evidence that they were better off than other elements of the population. After Hideyoshi's death, the luxuries of the Momoyama period had passed largely into the hands of merchants, rather than samurai, and these days the richer townspeople were the ones with elegant sake-serving sets and beautiful, expensive travel equipment. Even a small businessman was normally better off than a samurai with an allowance of five thousand bushels of rice per year, which was considered a princely income by most samurai.

"Never much to do on these trips, is there?"

"No. Why don't we have a little card game to pass the time."

"Why not?"

A curtain was hung, mistresses and underlings brought sake, and the men began playing *umsummo*, a game recently introduced by Portuguese traders, for unbelievable stakes. The gold on the table could have saved whole villages from famine, but the players tossed it about like gravel.

Among the passengers were several people the rich merchants might well have questioned as to what they were getting out of life—a wandering priest, some rōnin, a Confucian scholar, a few professional warriors. Most of them, after witnessing the beginning of the ostentatious card game, sat down beside their baggage and stared disapprovingly at the sea.

One young man was holding something round and furry in his lap, telling it from time to time to "Sit still!"

"What a nice little monkey you have. Is it trained?" asked another passenger.

"Yes."

"You've had him for some time, then?"

"No, I found him not long ago in the mountains between Tosa and Awa."

"Oh, you caught him yourself?"

"Yes, but the older monkeys almost scratched me to pieces before I got away."

As he talked, the young man concentrated intently on picking fleas off the animal. Even without the monkey, he would have attracted attention, for both his kimono and the short red cloak he wore over it were decidedly fancy. His front hair wasn't shaved, and his topknot was tied with an unusual purple band. His clothing suggested he was still a boy, but these days it wasn't as easy as it used to be to tell a person's age from his apparel. With the rise of Hideyoshi, clothing in general had become more colorful. It was not unknown for men of twenty-five or so to continue to dress like boys of fifteen or sixteen and leave their forelocks uncut.

260 His skin glowed with youth, his lips were a healthy red, and his eyes were

bright. On the other hand, he was solidly built, and there was a certain adult severity about his thick eyebrows and the upward curve at the corners of his eyes.

"Why do you keep squirming?" he said impatiently, rapping the monkey sharply on the head. The innocence with which he was picking off the fleas added to the impression of youthfulness.

His social status was also difficult to ascertain. Since he was traveling, he wore the same straw sandals and leather socks everyone else wore. So there was no clue there, and he seemed perfectly at home among the wandering priest, the puppeteer, the ragged samurai and the unwashed peasants on board. He could easily be taken for a rōnin, yet there was something that hinted at a higher status, namely the weapon slung slantwise across his back on a leather strap. It was a long, straight battle sword, large and splendidly made. Nearly everyone who spoke to the youth remarked on its fineness.

Gion Tōji, standing some distance away, was impressed by the weapon. Yawning and thinking that not even in Kyoto were swords of such high quality often seen, he grew curious as to its owner's background.

Tōji was bored. His trip, which had lasted fourteen days, had been vexing, tiring and fruitless, and he longed to be once again among people he knew. "I wonder if the runner arrived in time," he mused. "If he did, she'll certainly be at the dock in Osaka to meet me." He tried, by conjuring up Okō's face, to alleviate his boredom.

The reason behind his trip was the shaky financial condition of the House of Yoshioka, brought on by Seijūrō's having lived beyond his means. The family was no longer wealthy. The house on Shijō Avenue was mortgaged and in danger of being seized by merchant creditors. Aggravating the situation were countless other year-end obligations; selling every single family possession would not produce enough funds to meet the bills that had already piled up. Faced with this, Seijūrō's only comment had been, "How did this happen?"

Tōji, feeling responsible for having encouraged the Young Master's extravagance, had said that the matter should be left up to him. He promised that he would settle things somehow.

After racking his brains, he'd come up with the idea of building a new and bigger school on the vacant lot next to the Nishinotōin, where a much larger number of students could be accommodated. According to his reasoning, this was no time to be exclusive. With all sorts of people around wanting to learn the martial arts and the daimyō crying for trained warriors, it would be in the interests of everyone to have a bigger school and turn out a great number of trained swordsmen. The more he thought about it, the more he deluded himself into thinking it was the school's sacred duty to teach Kempō's style to as many men as possible.

Seijūrō wrote a circular to that effect, and thus armed, Tōji set out to solicit contributions from former students in western Honshu, Kyushu and Shikoku. There were many men in various feudal domains who had studied under Kempō, and most of those still alive were now samurai of enviable status. As it turned out, however, for all the earnestness of Tōji's pleas, not many were   *261* ready to make substantial donations or subscribe on such short notice. With discouraging frequency, the answer had been, "I'll write you about it later," "We'll see about it the next time I'm in Kyoto," or something equally evasive. The contributions Tōji was returning with amounted to but a fraction of what he'd anticipated.

The endangered household was not, strictly speaking, Tōji's own, and the face that came to mind now was not Seijūrō's but Okō's. But even hers could divert him only superficially, and soon he became fidgety again. He envied the young man picking the fleas off his monkey. He had something to do to kill time. Tōji walked over and tried to strike up a conversation.

"Hello, there, young fellow. Going to Osaka?"

Without actually raising his head, the young man lifted his eyes a bit and said, "Yes."

"Does your family live there?"

"No."

"Then you must be from Awa."

"No, not there either." This was said with a certain finality.

Tōji lapsed into silence for a time before he made another try. "That's quite a sword you have there," he said.

Seemingly happy to have the weapon praised, the young man rearranged himself to face Tōji and replied genially, "Yes, it's been in my family a long time. It's a battle sword, but I plan to get a good swordsmith in Osaka to remount it, so I can draw it from my side."

"It's too long for that, isn't it?"

"Oh, I don't know. It's only three feet."

"That's pretty long."

Smiling, the youth replied confidently, "Anybody should be able to handle a sword that long."

"Oh, it could be used if it was three feet long, or even four feet," said Tōji reproachfully. "But only an expert could handle it with ease. I see a lot of fellows swaggering around with huge swords these days. They look impressive, but when the going gets rough, they turn and run. What style did you study?" In matters pertaining to swordsmanship, Tōji could not conceal a feeling of superiority over this mere boy.

The young man flashed a questioning look at Tōji's smug face and replied, "The Tomita Style."

"The Tomita Style is for use with a shorter sword than that," said Tōji authoritatively.

"The fact that I learned the Tomita Style doesn't mean I have to use a shorter sword. I don't like to be imitative. My teacher used a shorter sword, so I decided to use a long one. That got me thrown out of the school."

"You young people do seem to take pride in being rebellious. What happened then?"

"I left Jōkyōji Village in Echizen and went to Kanemaki Jisai. He'd also discarded the Tomita Style, then developed the Chūjō Style. He sympathized with me, took me in as a disciple, and after I'd studied under him four years, he said I was ready to go out on my own."

262

"These country teachers are all quick to pass out certificates."

"Oh, not Jisai. He wasn't like that. In fact, the only other person he had ever given his certificate to was Itō Yagorō Ittōsai. After I made up my mind to be the second man to get formally certified, I worked at it very hard. Before I was through, though, I was suddenly called home because my mother was dying."

"Where's your home?"

"Iwakuni in Suō Province. After I went home, I practiced every day in the neighborhood of Kintai Bridge, cutting down swallows on the wing and slicing willow branches. That way I developed some techniques of my own. Before my mother died, she gave me this sword and told me to take good care of it, because it was made by Nagamitsu."

"Nagamitsu? You don't say!"

"It doesn't bear his signature on the tang, but it's always been thought to be his work. Where I come from, it's a well-known sword; people call it the Drying Pole." Though reticent earlier, on subjects he liked he would talk at great length, even volunteer information. Once started, he rattled on, paying little attention to his listener's reaction. From this, as well as from his account of his earlier experiences, it appeared that he was of stronger character than might have been inferred from his taste in clothes.

At one point, the youth stopped talking for a moment. His eyes grew cloudy and pensive. "While I was in Suō," he murmured, "Jisai took sick. When I heard about it from Kusanagi Tenki, I actually broke down and cried. Tenki was at the school long before I was and was still there when the master was on his sickbed. Tenki was his nephew, but Jisai didn't even consider giving him a certificate. Instead he told him he'd like to give me a certificate, along with his book of secret methods. He not only wanted me to have them but had hoped to see me and give them to me personally." The young man's eyes moistened with the recollection.

Tōji had not the slightest whit of empathy with this handsome, emotional youth, but talking to him was better than being alone and bored. "I see," he said, feigning great interest. "And he died while you were away?"

"I wish I could have gone to him as soon as I heard of his illness, but he was in Kōzuke, hundreds of miles from Suō. And then my mother finally died about the same time, so it was impossible for me to be with him at the end."

Clouds hid the sun, giving the whole sky a grayish cast. The ship began to roll, and foam blew in over the gunwales.

The young man continued his sentimental tale, the gist of which was that he had closed up the family residence in Suō and, in an exchange of letters, had arranged to meet his friend Tenki on the spring equinox. It was unlikely that Jisai, who had no close kin, had left much property, but he had entrusted Tenki with some money for the young man, along with the certificate and the book of secrets. Until they met on the appointed day at Mount Hōraiji in Mikawa Province, halfway between Kōzuke and Awa, Tenki was supposedly traveling around studying. The young man himself planned to spend the time in Kyoto, studying and doing some sightseeing.

Having finished his story, he turned to Tōji and asked, "Are you from Osaka?"

263

"No, I'm from Kyoto."

For a while, they were both silent, distracted by the noise of the waves and the sail.

"Then you plan to try to make your way in the world through the martial arts?" said Tōji. While the remark was innocent enough in itself, the look on Tōji's face revealed condescension bordering on contempt. He had long since had his fill of conceited young swordsmen who went around bragging about their certificates and their books of secrets. It was his considered opinion that there could not possibly be all that many expert swordsmen just wandering around. Had not he himself been in the Yoshioka School for nearly twenty years, and was he not still only a disciple, although a highly privileged one?

The young man shifted his position and looked intently at the gray water. "Kyoto?" he muttered, then turned again to Tōji and said, "I'm told there's a man there named Yoshioka Seijūrō, the eldest son of Yoshioka Kempō. Is he still active?"

Tōji was in the mood to do some teasing.

"Yes," he replied simply. "The Yoshioka School seems to be flourishing. Have you visited the place?"

"No, but when I get to Kyoto, I'd like to have a match with this Seijūrō and see how good he is."

Tōji coughed to suppress a laugh. He was fast growing to detest the young man's brash self-confidence. Of course, he had no way of knowing Tōji's position in the school, but if he were to find out, he would no doubt regret what he had just said. With a twisted face and a contemptuous tone, Tōji asked, "And I suppose you think you'd come away unscathed?"

"Why not?" the youth snapped back. Now he was the one who wanted to laugh, and laugh he did. "Yoshioka has a big house and a lot of prestige, so I imagine Kempō must have been a great swordsman. But they say neither of his sons amounts to much."

"How can you be so sure before you've actually met them?"

"Well, that's what the samurai in the other provinces say. I don't believe everything I hear, but almost everybody seems to think the House of Yoshioka will come to an end with Seijūrō and Denshichirō."

Tōji longed to tell the youth to hold his tongue. He even thought for a moment of making his identity known, but to bring the matter to a head at this point would make him appear the loser. With as much restraint as he could manage, he replied, "The provinces seem to be full of know-it-alls these days, so I wouldn't be surprised if the House of Yoshioka is being underrated. But tell me more about yourself. Didn't you say a while ago you'd figured out a way to kill swallows on the wing?"

"Yes, I said that."

"And you did it with that great long sword?"

"That's right."

"Well, if you can do that, it should be easy for you to cut down one of the sea gulls swooping down over the ship."

The youth did not answer immediately. It had suddenly dawned on him that Tōji was up to no good. Staring at Tōji's grim lips, he said, "I could do it, but I think it would be silly."

"Well," said Tōji magniloquently, "if you're so good that you can disparage the House of Yoshioka without having been there . . ."

"Oh, have I annoyed you?"

"No; not at all," said Tōji. "But no one from Kyoto likes to hear the Yoshioka School talked down."

"Ha! I wasn't telling you what I thought; I was repeating what I'd heard."

"Young man!" said Tōji sternly.

"What?"

"Do you know what is meant by 'half-baked samurai'? For the sake of your future, I warn you! You'll never get anywhere underestimating other people. You brag about cutting down swallows and talk about your certificate in the Chūjō Style, but you'd better remember that not everybody is stupid. And you'd better start taking a good look at whoever you're talking to before you start boasting."

"You think it's only bragging?"

"Yes, I do." Thrusting out his chest, Tōji came closer. "Nobody really minds listening to a young man boast of his accomplishments, but you shouldn't carry it too far."

When the young man said nothing, Tōji continued. "From the beginning I've been listening to you carry on about yourself, and I haven't complained. But the fact of the matter is that I am Gion Tōji, the chief disciple of Yoshioka Seijūrō, and if you make one more disparaging remark about the House of Yoshioka, I'll have it out of your hide!"

By this time they had attracted the attention of the other passengers. Tōji, having revealed his name and exalted status, swaggered off toward the stern of the ship, growling ominously about the insolence of young people these days. The youth followed him in silence, while the passengers gaped from a safe distance.

Tōji was not at all happy about the situation. Okō would be waiting for him when the ship docked, and if he got into a fight now, there was bound to be trouble with the officials later. Looking as unconcerned as possible, he propped his elbows on the rail and gazed intently at the blue-black eddies forming under the rudder.

The youth tapped him on the back lightly. "Sir," he said, in a quiet voice that showed neither anger nor resentment.

Tōji did not answer.

"Sir," the young man repeated.

Unable to keep up his show of nonchalance, Tōji asked, "What do you want?"

"You called me a braggart in front of a lot of strangers, and I have my honor to uphold. I feel constrained to do what you challenged me to do a few minutes ago. I want you to be a witness."

"What did I challenge you to do?"

"You can't have forgotten already. You laughed when I told you I'd cut down swallows on the wing and dared me to try cutting down a sea gull."

"Hmm, I did suggest that, didn't I?"

"If I cut one down, will it convince you I'm not just talking?"

"Well . . . yes, it will."

"All right, I'll do it."

"Fine, splendid!" Tōji laughed sarcastically. "But don't forget, if you undertake this just for pride's sake and fail, you'll *really* be laughed at."

"I'll take that chance."

"I've no intention of stopping you."

"And you will stand by as a witness?"

"Why, I'd be only too glad to!"

The young man took a position on a lead plate in the center of the afterdeck and moved his hand toward his sword. As he did so, he called out Tōji's name. Tōji, staring curiously, asked what he wanted, and the youth, speaking with great seriousness, said, "Please have some sea gulls fly down in front of me. I'm ready to cut down any number of them."

Tōji suddenly recognized the similarity between what was going on and the plot of a certain humorous tale attributed to the priest Ikkyū; the young man had succeeded in making an ass of him. Angrily he shouted, "What sort of nonsense is this? Anyone who could make sea gulls fly in front of him would be able to cut them down."

"The sea stretches out for thousands of miles, and my sword is only three feet long. If the birds won't come near, I can't cut them down."

Advancing a couple of paces, Tōji gloated, "You're just trying to work yourself out of a bad spot. If you can't kill a sea gull on the wing, say you can't, and apologize."

"If I intended to do that, I wouldn't be standing here waiting. If the birds won't come near, then I'll cut something else for you."

"Such as . . . ?"

"Just come another five steps closer. I'll show you."

Tōji came nearer, growling, "What are you up to now?"

"I just want you to let me make use of your head—the head with which you dared me to prove I wasn't just boasting. When you consider the matter, it would be more logical to cut that off than to kill innocent sea gulls."

"Have you lost your mind?" shouted Tōji. His head ducked reflexively, for just at that instant, the young man whipped his sword from its scabbard and used it. The action was so fast that the three-foot sword seemed no larger than a needle.

"Wh-wh-what?" cried Tōji, as he staggered backward and put his hands to his collar. His head was still there, fortunately, and as far as he could tell, he was unharmed.

"Do you understand now?" asked the youth, turning his back and walking off between the piles of baggage.

Tōji was already crimson with embarrassment, when looking down at a sunlit patch of the deck, he saw a peculiar-looking object, something like a little brush. A horrible thought came into his mind, and he put his hand to the top of his head. His topknot was gone! His precious topknot—the pride and joy of any samurai! Horror on his face, he rubbed the top of his head and found that the band tying his hair at the back was undone. The locks it had held together had fanned out over his scalp.

"That bastard!" Unmitigated rage swept through his heart. He knew now, only too well, that the youth had been neither lying nor voicing an empty boast. Young he was, but he was a spectacular swordsman. Tōji was amazed that anyone so young could be so good, but the respect he felt in his mind was one thing, and the choler in his heart something else again.

When he raised his head and looked toward the bow, he saw that the youth had returned to his previous seat and was searching around on the deck for something. He was obviously off guard, and Tōji sensed that the opportunity for revenge had presented itself. Spitting on the hilt of his sword, he grasped it tightly and sneaked up behind his tormenter. He was not sure his aim was good enough to take off the man's topknot without taking off his head too, but he did not care. Body swollen and red, breathing heavily, he steeled himself to strike.

Just then, a commotion arose among the card-playing merchants.

"What's going on here? There aren't enough cards!"

"Where'd they go?"

"Look over there!"

"I've already looked."

As they were shouting and shaking out their carpet, one of them happened to glance skyward.

"Up there! That monkey has them!"

The other passengers, welcoming still another diversion, all looked up at the simian in question, which was perched at the very top of the thirty-foot mast.

"Ha, ha!" laughed one. "Quite a monkey—stole the cards, he did."

"He's chewing them up."

"No, he's making like he's dealing them."

A single card came floating down. One of the merchants swept it up and said, "He must still have three or four more."

"Somebody get up there and get the cards! We can't play without them."

"Nobody's going to climb up there."

"Why not the captain?"

"I guess he could if he wanted to."

"Let's offer him a little money. Then he'll do it."

The captain heard the proposal, agreed, and took the money, but apparently felt that as the master of the ship, he must first fix responsibility for the incident. Standing on a pile of cargo, he addressed the passengers. "Just who does that monkey belong to? Will the owner please come forward?"

Not a soul answered, but a number of people who knew the monkey belonged to the handsome young man eyed him expectantly. The captain also knew, and his anger rose when the youth did not reply. Raising his voice still higher, he said, "Isn't the owner here? . . . If nobody owns the monkey, I'll

267

take care of him, but I don't want any complaints afterward."

The monkey's owner was leaning against some luggage, apparently deep in thought. A few passengers began to whisper disapprovingly; the captain looked daggers at the youth. The cardplayers grumbled malevolently, and others began to ask whether the young man was deaf and dumb or just insolent. The youth, however, merely shifted his position a little to the side and acted as though nothing had happened.

The captain spoke again. "It appears that monkeys thrive on sea as well as on land. As you can see, one has wandered in on us. Since it is ownerless, I suppose we can do whatever we wish with it. Passengers, be my witness! As captain, I have appealed to the owner to make himself known, but he hasn't done so. If he later complains that he could not hear me, I ask you to stand by me!"

"We're your witnesses!" cried the merchants, who by this time were verging on apoplexy.

The captain disappeared down the ladder into the hold. When he reemerged, he was holding a musket with the slow-burning fuse already lit. There was no question in anybody's mind but that he was ready to use it. Faces turned from the captain to the monkey's owner.

The monkey was enjoying himself immensely. High in the air, he was playing with the cards and doing everything he could to annoy the people on deck. Suddenly he bared his teeth, chattered, and ran to the yardarm, but once there he did not seem to know what to do.

The captain raised the musket and took aim. But as one of the merchants pulled at his sleeve and urged him to fire, the owner called out, "Stop, Captain!"

It was now the captain's turn to pretend not to hear. He squeezed the trigger, the passengers bent down with their hands over their ears, and the musket fired with a huge bang. But the shot went high and wide. At the last instant, the young man had pushed the barrel of the gun out of line.

Screaming with rage, the captain caught hold of the young man's chest. He seemed for a time almost to be suspended there, for though he was strongly built, he was short by the side of the handsome youth.

"What's the matter with you?" shouted the young man. "You were about to shoot down an innocent monkey with that toy of yours, weren't you?"

"I was."

"That's not a very nice thing to do, is it?"

"I gave fair warning!"

"And just how did you do that?"

"Don't you have eyes and ears?"

"Shut up! I'm a passenger on this ship. What's more, I'm a samurai. Do you expect me to answer when a mere ship's captain stands up before his customers and bellows as though he were their lord and master?"

"Don't be impertinent! I repeated my warning three times. You must have heard me. Even if you didn't like the way I said it, you could have shown some consideration for the people who were inconvenienced by your monkey."

"What people? Oh, you mean that bunch of tradesmen who've been gambling behind their curtain?"

"Don't talk so big! They paid three times as much fare as the others."

"That doesn't make them anything but what they are—low-class, irresponsible merchants, throwing around their gold where everybody can see it, drinking their sake, and acting as though they owned the ship. I've been watching them, and I don't like them at all. What if the monkey did run away with their cards? I didn't tell him to. He was just imitating what they themselves were doing. I see no need for me to apologize!"

The young man looked fixedly at the rich merchants and directed a loud, sardonic laugh their way.

The Seashell of Forgetfulness

It was evening when the ship entered the harbor at Kizugawa, where it was met by the all-pervading odor of fish. Reddish lights twinkled onshore, and the waves hummed steadily in the background. Little by little, the distance between the raised voices coming from the ship and those issuing from the shore closed up. With a white splash, the anchor was dropped; ropes were cast and the gangplank was moved into place.

A flurry of excited cries filled the air.

"Is the son of the priest at the Sumiyoshi Shrine aboard?"

"Is there a runner around?"

"Master! Here we are, over here!"

Like a wave, paper lanterns bearing the names of various inns rolled across the dock toward the ship, as the touts vied with each other for business.

"Anyone for the Kashiwaya Inn?"

The young man with the monkey on his shoulder pushed his way through the crowd.

"Come to our place, sir—no charge for the monkey."

"We're right in front of Sumiyoshi Shrine. It's a great place for pilgrims. You can have a beautiful room with a beautiful view!"

No one had come to meet the youth. He walked straight away from the dock, paying no attention to the touts or anyone else.

"Who does he think he is?" growled one passenger. "Just because he knows a little swordsmanship!"

"If I weren't just a townsman, he wouldn't have gotten away without a fight."

"Oh, calm down! Let the warriors think they're better than anybody else. As long as they're strutting around like kings, they're happy. The thing for us townsmen to do is to let them have the flowers while we take the fruit. Why get excited over today's little incident?"

While talking on in this fashion, the merchants saw to it that their mountains of baggage were properly gathered together, then disembarked, to be met by swarms of people and lanterns and vehicles. There was not one among them who was not immediately surrounded by several solicitous women.

The last person off the ship was Gion Tōji, on whose face there was an expression of extreme discomfort. Never in all his life had he spent a more unpleasant day. His head was decently covered with a kerchief to conceal the mortifying loss of his topknot, but the cloth did nothing to hide his downcast eyebrows and sullen lips.

"Tōji! Here I am!" called Okō. Though her head was also covered with a kerchief, her face had been exposed to the cold wind while she was waiting, and her wrinkles showed through the white powder that was meant to hide them.

"Okō! So you came after all."

"Isn't that what you expected? You sent me a letter telling me to meet you here, didn't you?"

"Yes, but I thought it might not have reached you in time."

"Is something the matter? You look upset."

"Oh, it's nothing. Just a little seasick. Come on, let's go to Sumiyoshi and find a nice inn."

"Come this way. I have a palanquin waiting."

"Thanks. Did you reserve a room for us?"

"Yes. Everybody's waiting at the inn."

A look of consternation crossed Tōji's face. "*Everybody*? What are you talking about? I thought just the two of us were going to spend a couple of pleasant days here at some quiet place. If there are a lot of people around, I'm not going."

Refusing the palanquin, he strode angrily on ahead. When Okō tried to explain, he cut her off and called her an idiot. All the rage that had built up inside him on the ship exploded.

"I'll stay somewhere by myself!" he bellowed. "Send the palanquin away! How could you be such a fool? You don't understand me at all." He snatched his sleeve away from her and hurried on.

They were in the fish market by the waterfront; all the shops were closed, and the scales strewn about the street glittered like tiny silver seashells. Since there was virtually no one around to see them, Okō hugged Tōji and attempted to soothe him.

"Let go of me!" he shouted.

"If you go off by yourself, the others will think something's wrong."

"Let them think what they want!"

"Oh, don't talk like that!" she pleaded. Her cool cheek pressed against his. The sweetish odor of her powder and her hair penetrated his being, and gradually his anger and frustration ebbed.

270   "Please," begged Okō.

"It's just that I'm so disappointed," he said.

"I know, but we'll have other chances to be together."

"But these two or three days with you—I was really looking forward to them."

"I understand that."

"If you understood, why did you drag a lot of other people along? It's because you don't feel about me the way I feel about you!"

"Now you're starting on that again," said Okō reproachfully, staring ahead and looking as if the tears were about to flow. But instead of weeping, she made another attempt to get him to listen to her explanation. When the runner had arrived with Tōji's letter, she had, of course, made plans to come to Osaka alone, but as luck would have it, that very night Seijūrō had come to the Yomogi with six or seven of his students, and Akemi had let it slip out that Tōji was arriving. In no time at all, the men had decided that they should all accompany Okō to Osaka and that Akemi should come along with them. In the end, the party that checked into the inn in Sumiyoshi numbered ten.

While Tōji had to admit that under the circumstances there was not much Okō could have done, his gloomy mood did not improve. This had clearly not been his day, and he was sure there was worse to come. For one thing, the first question he expected to hear would concern how he had made out on his canvassing campaign, and he hated to have to give them the bad news. What he dreaded far more was the prospect of having to take the kerchief off his head. How could he ever explain the missing topknot? Ultimately he realized there was no way out and resigned himself to his fate.

"Oh, all right," he said, "I'll go with you. Have the palanquin brought here."

"Oh, I'm so happy!" cooed Okō, as she turned back toward the dock.

At the inn, Seijūrō and the others had taken a bath, wrapped themselves up snugly in the cotton-padded kimonos provided by the inn, and settled down to wait for Tōji and Okō's return. When, after a time, they failed to reappear, someone said, "Those two will be here sooner or later. There's no reason to sit here doing nothing."

The natural consequence of this statement was the ordering of sake. At first they drank merely to pass the time, but soon legs began to stretch out comfortably, and the sake cups to pass back and forth more rapidly. It was not long before everybody had more or less forgotten about Tōji and Okō.

"Don't they have any singing girls in Sumiyoshi?"

"Say, that's a good idea! Why don't we call in three or four nice girls?"

Seijūrō looked hesitant until someone suggested that he and Akemi retire to another room, where it would be quieter. The none-too-subtle move to get rid of him brought a wistful smile to his face, but he was nevertheless happy to leave. It would be far more pleasant to be alone with Akemi in a room with a warm *kotatsu* than to be drinking with this crew of ruffians.

As soon as he was out of the room, the party began in earnest, and before long several singing girls of the class known locally as the "pride of Tosamagawa" appeared in the garden outside the room. Their flutes and shamisen were old, of poor quality and battered from use.

"Why are you making so much noise?" one of the women asked saucily. "Did you come here to drink or to have a brawl?"

The man who had appointed himself ringleader called back, "Don't ask foolish questions. Nobody pays money to fight! We called you in so we could drink and have some fun."

"Well," said the girl tactfully, "I'm glad to hear that, but I do wish you'd be a little quieter."

"If that's the way you want it, fine! Let's sing some songs."

In deference to the feminine presence, several hairy shins were retracted under kimono skirts, and a few horizontal bodies became vertical. The music started, spirits rose, and the party gained momentum. It was in full swing when a young maid came in and announced that the man who had come in on the ship from Shikoku had arrived with his companion.

"What'd she say? Somebody coming?"

"Yeah, she said somebody named Tōji's coming."

"Great! Wonderful! Good old Tōji's coming. . . . Who's Tōji?"

Tōji's entrance with Okō did not interrupt the proceedings in the least; in fact, they were ignored. Having been led to believe the gathering was all for his sake, Tōji was disgusted.

He called back the maid who had shown them in and asked to be taken to Seijūrō's room. But as they went into the hall, the ringleader, reeking of sake, staggered over and threw his arms around Tōji's neck.

"Hey, Tōji!" he slurred. "Just get back? You must have been having a good time with Okō somewhere while we sat here waiting. Now, that's not the thing to do!"

Tōji tried unsuccessfully to shake him off. The man dragged him struggling into the room. In the process, he stepped on a tray or two, kicked over several sake jars, then fell to the floor, bringing Tōji down with him.

"My kerchief!" gasped Tōji. His hand sped to his head, too late. On his way down, the ringleader had snatched at the kerchief and now had it in his hand. With a collective gasp, all eyes looked straight at the spot where Tōji's topknot should have been.

"What happened to your head?"

"Ha, ha, ha! That's some hairdo!"

"Where did you get it?"

Tōji's face flushed blood red. Grabbing the kerchief and replacing it, he sputtered, "Oh, it's nothing. I had a boil."

To a man, they doubled up with laughter.

"He brought a boil back with him as a souvenir!"

"Cover the vile spot!"

"Don't talk about it. Show us!"

It was obvious from the feeble jokes that nobody believed Tōji, but the party went on, and no one had much to say about the topknot.

272 The next morning it was a different matter altogether. Ten o'clock found the

same group assembled on the beach behind the inn, sober now and engaged in a very serious conference. They sat in a circle, some with shoulders squared, some with arms crossed, but all looking grim.

"Any way you look at it, it's bad."

"The question is, is it true?"

"I heard it with my own ears. Are you calling me a liar?"

"We can't let it pass without doing anything. The honor of the Yoshioka School is at stake. We have to act!"

"Of course, but what do we do?"

"Well, it's still not too late. We'll find the man with the monkey and cut off *his* topknot. We'll show him that it's not just Gion Tōji's pride that's involved. It's a matter that concerns the dignity of the whole Yoshioka School! Any objections?" The drunken ringleader of the night before was now a gallant lieutenant, spurring his men on to battle.

Upon awakening, the men had ordered the bath heated, so as to wash away their hangovers, and while they were in the bath, a merchant had come in. Not knowing who they were, he told them about what had happened on the ship the day before. He furnished them with a humorous account of the cutting off of the topknot and concluded his tale by saying that "the samurai who had lost his hair claimed to be a leading disciple of the House of Yoshioka in Kyoto. All I can say is that if he really is, the House of Yoshioka must be in worse shape than anyone imagines."

Sobering up fast, the Yoshioka disciples had gone looking for their wayward senior to question him about the incident. They soon discovered he had risen early, spoken a few words with Seijūrō, and departed with Okō for Kyoto right after breakfast. This confirmed the essential accuracy of the story, but rather than pursue the cowardly Tōji, they decided it would make better sense to find the unknown youth with the monkey and vindicate the Yoshioka name.

Having agreed upon a plan at their seaside council of war, they now stood up, brushed the sand off their kimonos and moved into action.

A short distance away, Akemi, bare-legged, had been playing at the edge of the water, picking up seashells one by one, then discarding them almost immediately. Even though it was winter, the sun was shining warmly, and the smell of the sea rose from the froth of the breakers, which stretched out like chains of white roses as far as the eye could see.

Akemi, wide-eyed with curiosity, watched the Yoshioka men as they all ran off in different directions, the tips of their scabbards in the air. When the last of them passed her, she called out to him, "Where are you all going?"

"Oh, it's you!" he said. "Why don't you come search with me? Everybody's been assigned a territory to cover."

"What are you looking for?"

"A young samurai with a long forelock. He's carrying a monkey."

"What did he do?"

"Something that will disgrace the Young Master's name unless we act fast." He told her what had happened, but failed to raise even a spark of interest.   273

"You people are always looking for a fight!" she said disapprovingly.

"It's not that we like to fight, but if we let him get away with this, it'll bring shame on the school, the greatest center of the martial arts in the country."

"Oh, what if it does?"

"Are you crazy?"

"You men spend all your time running after the silliest things."

"Huh?" He squinted at her suspiciously. "And what have you been doing out here all this time?"

"Me?" She dropped her eyes to the beautiful sand around her feet and said, "I'm looking for seashells."

"Why look for them? There are millions of them all over the place. It just goes to show you—women waste their time in crazier ways than men."

"I'm looking for a very particular type of shell. It's called the seashell of forgetfulness."

"Oh? And is there really such a shell?"

"Yes, but they say you can only find it here on the shore at Sumiyoshi."

"Well, I'll bet there's no such thing!"

"There is too! If you don't believe it, come with me. I'll show you."

She pulled the reluctant youth over to a row of pine trees and pointed to a stone on which an ancient poem was carved.

> Had I but the time
> I'd find it on the Sumiyoshi shore.
> They say it comes there—
> The shell that brings
> Oblivion to love.

Proudly, Akemi said, "See? What more proof do you need?"

"Aw, that's only a myth, one of those useless lies they tell in poetry."

"But in Sumiyoshi they also have flowers that make you forget, and water too."

"Well, suppose it does exist. What magic will it work for you?"

"It's simple. If you put one in your obi or sleeve, you can forget everything."

The samurai laughed. "You mean you want to be more absentminded than you already are?"

"Yes. I'd like to forget everything. Some things I can't forget, so I'm unhappy in the daytime and lie awake nights. That's why I'm looking for it. Why don't you stay and help me look?"

"This is no time for child's play!" the samurai said scornfully, then suddenly remembering his duty, flew off at full speed.

When she was sad, Akemi often thought her problems would be solved if she could only forget the past and enjoy the present. Right now she was hugging herself and wavering between holding on to the few memories she cherished and wanting to cast them out to sea. If there really were such a thing as a seashell of forgetfulness, she decided, she wouldn't carry it herself, but instead sneak it into Seijūrō's sleeve. She sighed, imagining how lovely life would be if he would just forget all about her.

The very thought of him turned her heart cold. She was tempted to believe he existed for the sole purpose of ruining her youth. When he importuned her with his wheedling protestations of love, she comforted herself by thinking of Musashi. But if Musashi's presence in her heart was at times her salvation, it was also a frequent source of misery, for it made her want to run away to escape into a world of dreams. Yet she hesitated to give herself up entirely to fantasy, knowing it was likely that Musashi had forgotten her completely.

"Oh, if there was some way I could erase his face from my mind!" she thought.

The blue water of the Inland Sea looked suddenly tempting. Staring at it, she grew frightened. How easy it would be to run straight in and disappear.

Her mother had no idea Akemi entertained such desperate thoughts, let alone Seijūrō. All the people around her considered her a very happy creature, a little flippant perhaps, but nonetheless a bud still so far from blossoming that she couldn't possibly accept the love of a man.

To Akemi, her mother and the men who came to the teahouse were something outside her own self. In their presence, she laughed and joked, tinkled her bell and pouted as the occasion seemed to demand, but when she was alone, her sighs were care-filled and sullen.

Her thoughts were interrupted by a servant from the inn. Spotting her by the stone inscription, he ran up and said, "Young lady, where've you been? The Young Master's been calling for you, and he's getting very worried."

Back at the inn, Akemi found Seijūrō all alone, warming his hands under the red quilt covering the *kotatsu*. The room was silent. In the garden a breeze rustled through the withered pines.

"Have you been out in this cold?" he asked.

"What do you mean? I don't think it's cold. It's very sunny on the beach."

"What have you been doing?"

"Looking for seashells."

"You act like a child."

"I *am* a child."

"How old do you think you'll be on your next birthday?"

"It doesn't make any difference. I'm still a child. What's wrong with that?"

"There's a great deal wrong with it. You ought to think about your mother's plans for you."

"My mother? She's not thinking about me. She's convinced she's still young herself."

"Sit down here."

"I don't want to. I'd get too hot. I'm still young, remember?"

"Akemi!" He seized her wrist and pulled her toward him. "There's no one else here today. Your mother had the delicacy to return to Kyoto."

Akemi looked at Seijūrō's burning eyes; her body stiffened. She tried unconsciously to back away, but he held her wrist tightly.

"Why are you trying to run away?" he asked accusingly.

"I'm not trying to run away."

"There's no one here now. It's a perfect opportunity, isn't it, Akemi?"

"For what?"

"Don't be so obstinate! We've been seeing each other for nearly a year. You know how I feel about you. Okō gave her permission long ago. She says you won't give in to me because I don't go about it the right way. So today, let's—"

"Stop! Let go of my arm! Let go, I tell you!" Akemi suddenly bent over and lowered her head in embarrassment.

"You won't have me, whatever happens?"

"Stop! Let go!"

Though her arm had turned red under his grasp, he still refused to release her, and the girl was hardly strong enough to resist the military techniques of the Kyōhachi Style.

Seijūrō was different today from his usual self. He often sought comfort and consolation in sake, but today he had drunk nothing. "Why do you treat me this way, Akemi? Are you trying to humiliate me?"

"I don't want to talk about it! If you don't let me go, I'll scream!"

"Scream away! Nobody'll hear you. The main house is too far away, and anyway, I told them we were not to be disturbed."

"I want to leave."

"I won't let you."

"My body doesn't belong to you!"

"Is that the way you feel? You'd better ask your mother about that! I've certainly paid her enough for it."

"Well, my mother may have sold me, but I haven't sold myself! Certainly not to a man I despise more than death itself!"

"What's that?" shouted Seijūrō, throwing the red quilt over her head.

Akemi screamed for all she was worth.

"Scream, you bitch! Scream all you want! Nobody's coming."

On the shoji the pale sunlight mingled with the restless shadow of the pines as though nothing had happened. Outside, all was quiet, save for the distant lapping of the waves and the chatter of the birds.

Deep silence followed Akemi's muffled wails. After a time, Seijūrō, his face deathly pale, appeared in the outer corridor, holding his right hand over his scratched and bleeding left hand.

Shortly afterward, the door opened again with a bang, and Akemi emerged. With a cry of surprise, Seijūrō, his hand now wrapped in a towel, moved as though to stop her, but not in time. The half-crazed girl fled with lightning speed.

Seijūrō's face creased worriedly, but he did not pursue her as she crossed the garden and went into another part of the inn. After a moment, a thin, crooked smile appeared on his lips. It was a smile of deep satisfaction.

A Hero's Passing

"Uncle Gon!"

"What?"

"Are you tired?"

"Yes, a little."

"I thought so. I'm about walked out myself. But this shrine has splendid buildings, doesn't it? Say, isn't that the orange tree they call the secret tree of Wakamiya Hachiman?"

"Seems to be."

"It's supposed to be the first item in the eighty shiploads of tribute presented by the King of Silla to Empress Jingū when she conquered Korea."

"Look over there in the Stable of the Sacred Horses! Isn't that a fine animal? It'd certainly come in first at the annual horse race in Kamo."

"You mean the white one?"

"Yes. Hmm, what does that signboard say?"

"It says if you boil the beans used in the horse fodder and drink the juice, it'll keep you from crying or gritting your teeth at night. Do you want some?"

Uncle Gon laughed. "Don't be silly!" Turning around, he asked, "What happened to Matahachi?"

"He seems to have wandered off."

"Oh, there he is, resting by the stage for the sacred dances."

The old lady lifted her hand and called to her son. "If we go over that way, we can see the original Great Torii, but let's go to the High Lantern first."

Matahachi followed along lazily. Ever since his mother had collared him in Osaka, he'd been with them—walking, walking, walking. His patience was beginning to wear thin. Five or ten days of sightseeing might be all well and good, but he dreaded the thought of accompanying them to take their revenge. He had tried to persuade them that traveling together was a poor way to go about it, that it would be better for him to go and look for Musashi on his own. His mother wouldn't hear of it.

"It'll be New Year's soon," she pointed out. "And I want you to spend it with me. We haven't been together to celebrate the New Year holiday for a long time, and this may be our last chance."

Though Matahachi knew he couldn't refuse her, he had made up his mind to leave them a couple of days after the first of the year. Osugi and Uncle Gon, possibly fearing they hadn't long to live, had become so wrapped up in religion they stopped at every shrine or temple possible, leaving offerings and making long supplications to the gods and Buddhas. They had spent nearly all of the present day at Sumiyoshi Shrine.

Matahachi, bored stiff, was dragging his feet and pouting.

"Can't you walk faster?" Osugi asked in a testy voice.

Matahachi's pace did not change. Fully as annoyed with his mother as she was with him, he grumbled, "You hurry me along and make me wait! Hurry and wait, hurry and wait!"

"What am I to do with a son like you? When people come to a sacred place, it's only proper to stop and pray to the gods. I've never seen you bow before either a god or a Buddha, and mark my words, you'll live to regret it. Besides, if you prayed with us, you wouldn't have to wait so long."

"What a nuisance!" growled Matahachi.

"Who's a nuisance?" cried Osugi indignantly.

For the first two or three days everything had been as sweet as honey between them, but once Matahachi had got used to his mother again, he began to take exception to everything she did and said and to make fun of her every chance he got. When night came and they returned to the inn, she would make him sit down in front of her and give him a sermon, which served to put him in worse humor than before.

"What a pair!" Uncle Gon lamented to himself, trying to figure out a way to soothe the old woman's pique and restore a measure of calmness to his nephew's scowling face. Sensing yet another sermon in the making, he moved to head it off. "Oh," he called cheerily. "I thought I smelled something good! They're selling broiled clams at that teahouse over by the beach. Let's stop in and have some."

Neither mother nor son displayed much enthusiasm, but Uncle Gon managed to steer them to the seaside shop, which was sheltered with thin reed blinds. While the other two got comfortable on a bench outside, he went in and came back with some sake.

Offering a cup to Osugi, he said amiably, "This will cheer Matahachi up a little. Maybe you're being a little hard on him."

Osugi looked away and snapped, "I don't want anything to drink."

Uncle Gon, caught in his own web, offered the cup to Matahachi, who, though still grumpy, proceeded to empty three jars as fast as he could, knowing full well this would make his mother livid. When he asked Uncle Gon for a fourth, Osugi had had all she could take.

"You've had enough!" she scolded. "This isn't a picnic, and we didn't come here to get drunk! And you watch yourself too, Uncle Gon! You're older than Matahachi, and should know better."

Uncle Gon, as mortified as if only he had been drinking, tried to hide his face by rubbing his hands over it. "Yes, you're quite right," he said meekly. He got up and ambled off a few paces.

Then it began in earnest, for Matahachi had struck at the roots of Osugi's violent though brittle sense of maternal love and anxiety, and it was out of the question for her to wait until they returned to the inn. She lashed out furious-ly at him, not caring whether other people were listening. Matahachi stared at her with a look of sullen disobedience until she finished.

"All right," he said. "I take it you've made up your mind that I'm an un-grateful lout with no self-respect. Right?"

"Yes! What have you done up till now that shows any pride or self-respect?"

"Well, I'm not as worthless as you seem to think, but then you wouldn't have any way of knowing that."

"Oh, I wouldn't, would I? Well, nobody knows a child better than his par-ents, and I think the day you were born was a bad day for the House of Hon'iden!"

"You just wait and see! I'm still young. One day when you're dead and buried, you'll be sorry you said that."

"Ha! I wish that were so, but I doubt that would happen in a hundred years. It's so sad, when you think of it."

"Well, if it makes you so terribly sad to have a son like me, there's not much use in my hanging around any longer. I'm leaving!" Steaming with rage, he stood up and walked away in long, determined strides.

Taken by surprise, the old woman tried in a pitifully trembling voice to call him back. Matahachi paid no heed. Uncle Gon, who could have run and tried to stop him, stood looking intently toward the sea, his mind apparently occu-pied with other thoughts.

Osugi got up, then sat back down again. "Don't try to stop him," she said needlessly to Uncle Gon. "It's no use."

Uncle Gon turned toward her, but instead of answering, said, "That girl out there is acting very funny. Wait here a minute!" Almost before the words were out, he had chucked his hat under the eaves of the shop and headed like an arrow toward the water.

"Idiot!" cried Osugi. "Where are you going? Matahachi's—"

She chased after him, but about twenty yards from the shop, snagged her foot in a clump of seaweed and fell flat on her face. Mumbling angrily, she picked herself up, her face and shoulders covered with sand. When she caught sight of Uncle Gon again, her eyes opened like mirrors.

"You old fool! Where are you going? Have you lost your mind?" she screamed.

So excited that she looked as if she might be mad herself, she ran as fast as she could, following Uncle Gon's footsteps. But she was too late. Uncle Gon was already in up to his knees and pushing out farther.

Enveloped in the white spray, he seemed almost in a trance. Still farther out was a young girl, feverishly making her way toward deep water. When he had first spotted her, she had been standing in the shadow of the pines, looking blankly at the sea; then suddenly she sped across the sand and into the water, her black hair streaming out behind her. The water was now halfway up to her waist, and she was rapidly approaching the point where the bottom fell off sharply.

As he neared her, Uncle Gon called out frantically, but she pressed on. Suddenly, with an odd sound, her body disappeared, leaving a swirl on the surface.

"Crazy child!" cried Uncle Gon. "Are you determined to kill yourself?" Then he himself sank below the surface with a glug.

Osugi was running back and forth along the edge of the water. When she saw the two go down, her screaming turned to strident calls for help.

Waving her hands, running, stumbling, she ordered the people on the beach to the rescue as though they were the cause of the accident. "Save them, you idiots! Hurry, or they'll drown."

Minutes later, some fishermen brought the bodies in and laid them on the sand.

"A love suicide?" asked one.

"Are you joking?" said another, laughing.

Uncle Gon had caught hold of the girl's obi and was still holding it, but neither he nor she was breathing. The girl presented a strange appearance, for though her hair was matted and messy, her powder and lipstick had not washed away, and she looked as if she were alive. Even with her teeth still biting her lower lip, her purple mouth bore the suggestion of a laugh.

"I've seen her before somewhere," somebody said.

"Isn't she the girl who was looking for shells on the beach a while ago?"

"Yes, that's right! She was staying at the inn over there."

From the direction of the inn, four or five men were already approaching, among them Seijūrō, who breathlessly pushed his way through the crowd.

"Akemi!" he cried. His face went pale, but he stood perfectly still.

"Is she a friend of yours?" asked one of the fishermen.

"Y-y-yes."

"You'd better try and get the water out of her fast!"

"Can we save her?"

"Not if you just stand there gaping!"

The fishermen loosened Uncle Gon's grip, laid the bodies side by side, and began slapping them on the back and pressing them in the abdomen. Akemi regained her breathing fairly rapidly, and Seijūrō, eager to escape the stares of the bystanders, had the men from the inn carry her back.

"Uncle Gon! Uncle Gon!" Osugi had her mouth to the old man's ear and was calling to him through her tears. Akemi had come back to life because she was young, but Uncle Gon . . . Not only was he old, but he had had a fair amount of sake in him when he went to the rescue. His breath was stilled forever; no amount of urging on Osugi's part would open his eyes again.

The fishermen, giving up, said, "The old man's gone."

Osugi stopped crying long enough to turn on them as though they were enemies rather than people trying to help. "What do you mean? Why should he die when that young girl was saved?" Her attitude suggested she was ready to attack them physically. She pushed the men aside and said firmly, "I'll bring him back to life myself! I'll show you."

She set to work on Uncle Gon, putting to use every method she could think of. Her determination brought tears to the eyes of the onlookers, a few of whom stayed to help her. Far from being appreciative, however, she ordered them around like hired help—complained that they were not pressing the right way, told them that what they were doing would not work, ordered them to build a fire, sent them off for medicine. Everything she did, she did in the surliest fashion imaginable.

To the men on the shore, she was neither a relative nor a friend but just a stranger, and eventually even the most sympathetic became angry.

"Who is this old hag anyway?" growled one.

"Humph! Can't tell the difference between somebody who's unconscious and somebody who's dead. If she can bring him back, let her do it."

Before long, Osugi found herself alone with the body. In the gathering darkness, mist rose from the sea, and all that remained of the day was a strip of orange clouds near the horizon. Building a fire and sitting down beside it, she held Uncle Gon's body close to her.

"Uncle Gon. Oh, Uncle Gon!" she wailed.

The waves darkened. She tried and tried to bring warmth back to his body. The look on her face said that she expected him at any minute to open his mouth and speak to her. She chewed up pills from the medicine box in his obi and transferred them to his mouth. She held him close and rocked him.

"Open your eyes, Uncle Gon!" she pleaded. "Say something! You can't go away and leave me alone. We still haven't killed Musashi or punished that hussy Otsū."

Inside the inn, Akemi lay in a fretful sleep. When Seijūrō attempted to adjust her feverish head on the pillow, she mumbled deliriously. For a time, he sat by her side in utter stillness, his face paler than hers. As he observed the agony he himself had heaped on her, he suffered too.

It was he himself who by animal force had preyed on her and satisfied his own lust. Now he sat gravely and stiffly beside her, worrying about her pulse and her breathing, praying that the life that had for a time left her would be safely restored. In one short day, he had been both a beast and a man of compassion. But to Seijūrō, given as he was to extremes, his conduct didn't seem inconsistent.

His eyes were sad, the set of his mouth humble. He stared at her and murmured, "Try to be calm, Akemi. It's not just me; most other men are the same way. . . . You'll soon come to understand, though you must have been shocked by the violence of my love." Whether this speech was actually directed toward the girl or was intended to quiet his own spirit would have been difficult to judge, but he kept voicing the same sentiment over and over.

The gloom in the room was like ink. The paper-covered shoji muffled the sound of the wind and waves.

Akemi stirred and her white arms slipped out from under the covers. When Seijūrō tried to replace the quilt, she mumbled, "Wh-what's the date?"

"What?"

"How . . . how many days . . . till New Year's?"

"It's only seven days now. You'll be well by then, and we'll be back in Kyoto." He lowered his face toward hers, but she pushed it away with the palm of her hand.

"Stop! Go away! I don't like you."

He drew back, but the half-crazed words poured from her lips.

"Fool! Beast!"

Seijūrō remained silent.

"You're a beast. I don't . . . I don't want to look at you."

"Forgive me, Akemi, please!"

"Go away! Don't talk to me." Her hand waved nervously in the dark. Seijūrō swallowed sadly but continued to stare at her.

"What . . . what's the date?"

This time he did not answer.

"Isn't it New Year's yet? . . . Between New Year's and the seventh . . . Every day . . . He said he'd be on the bridge. . . . The message from Musashi . . . every day . . . Gojō Avenue bridge . . . It's so long till New Year's. . . . I must go back to Kyoto. . . . If I go to the bridge, he'll be there."

"Musashi?" said Seijūrō in wonderment.

The delirious girl was silent.

"This Musashi . . . Miyamoto Musashi?"

Seijūrō peered into her face, but Akemi said no more. Her blue eyelids were closed; she was fast asleep.

Dried pine needles tapped against the shoji. A horse whinnied. A light appeared beyond the partition, and a maid's voice said, "The Young Master is in here."

Seijūrō hastily went into the adjoining room, carefully shutting the door behind him. "Who is it?" he asked. "I'm in here."

"Ueda Ryōhei," came the answer. Clad in full travel garb and covered with dust, Ryōhei came in and sat down.

While they exchanged greetings, Seijūrō wondered what could have brought him here. Since Ryōhei, like Tōji, was one of the senior students and was needed at home, Seijūrō would never have brought him on a spur-of-the-moment excursion.

"Why have you come? Has something happened in my absence?" asked Seijūrō.

"Yes, and I must ask you to return immediately."

"What is it?"

As Ryōhei put both hands into his kimono and felt around, Akemi's voice came from the next room. "I don't like you! . . . Beast! . . . Go away!" The clearly spoken words were filled with fear; anyone would have thought she was awake and in real danger.

Startled, Ryōhei asked, "Who's that?"

"Oh, that? Akemi took sick after she got here. She's feverish. Every once in a while she gets a little delirious."

"That's Akemi?"

"Yes, but never mind. I want to hear why you came."

From the stomach wrapper under his kimono, Ryōhei finally extracted a letter and presented it to Seijūrō. "It's this," he said without further explanation, then moved the lamp the maid had left over to Seijūrō's side.

"Hmm. It's from Miyamoto Musashi."

"Yes!" said Ryōhei with force.

"Have you opened it?"

"Yes. I talked it over with the others, and we decided it might be important, so we opened and read it."

Instead of seeing for himself what was in the letter, Seijūrō asked, somewhat hesitantly, "What does it say?" Though nobody had dared mention the subject to him, Musashi had remained in the back of Seijūrō's mind. Even so, he had nearly convinced himself he'd never run into the man again. The sudden arrival of the letter right after Akemi had spoken Musashi's name sent chills up and down his spine.

Ryōhei bit his lip angrily. "It's finally come. When he went away talking so big last spring, I was sure he'd never set foot in Kyoto again, but—can you imagine the conceit? Go on, look at it! It's a challenge, and he has the gall to address it to the entire House of Yoshioka, signing it with only his own name. He thinks he can take us all on himself!"

Musashi hadn't written any return address, nor was there any clue to his whereabouts in the letter. But he had not forgotten the promise he had written to Seijūrō and his disciples, and with this second letter the die was cast. He was declaring war on the House of Yoshioka; the battle would have to be fought, and it would be a fight to the finish—one in which samurai struggle to the death to preserve their honor and vindicate their skill with the sword. Musashi was laying his life on the line and challenging the Yoshioka School to do the same. When the time came, words and clever technical ploys would count for little.

That Seijūrō still did not grasp this fact was the greatest source of danger to him. He did not see that the day of reckoning was at hand, that this was no time to be idling away his days on empty pleasures.

When the letter had arrived in Kyoto, some of the stauncher disciples, disgusted with the Young Master's undisciplined way of life, had grumbled angrily over his absence at so crucial a moment. Riled by the insult from this lone rōnin, they lamented that Kempō was no longer alive. After much discussion, they had agreed to inform Seijūrō of the situation and make sure he returned to Kyoto immediately. Yet now that the letter had been delivered, Seijūrō merely put it on his knees and made no move to open it.

With obvious irritation, Ryōhei asked, "Don't you think you ought to read it?"

"What? Oh, this?" said Seijūrō vacantly. He unrolled the letter and read it. His fingers began to tremble beyond his control, an unsteadiness caused not by the strong language and tone of Musashi's challenge but by his own feeling of weakness and vulnerability. Akemi's harsh words of rejection had already destroyed his composure and upset his pride as a samurai. He had never before felt so powerless.

283

Musashi's message was simple and straightforward:

> Have you been in good health since I last wrote? In accordance with my previous promise, I am writing to ask where, on what day and at what hour we will meet. I have no particular preference and am willing to hold our promised match at the time and place designated by you. I request that you post a sign by the bridge at Gojō Avenue giving me your reply sometime before the seventh day of the New Year.
>
> I trust that you have been polishing your swordsmanship as usual. I myself feel that I have improved to a certain small extent. Shimmen Miyamoto Musashi.

Seijūrō stuffed the letter into his kimono and stood up. "I'll return to Kyoto now," he said.

This was said less out of resolution than because his emotions were so tangled he couldn't bear to remain where he was a moment longer. He had to get away and put the whole dreadful day behind him as soon as possible.

With much commotion, the innkeeper was called and requested to take care of Akemi, a task he accepted only with reluctance, despite the money Seijūrō pressed on him.

"I'll use your horse," he said summarily to Ryōhei. Like a fleeing bandit, he jumped into the saddle and rode rapidly away through the dark rows of trees, leaving Ryōhei to follow along at a dead run.

The Drying Pole

"A guy with a monkey? Yes, he came by a while ago."

"Did you notice which way he went?"

"That way, toward Nōjin Bridge. Didn't cross it, though—looked like he went into the swordsmith's shop down there."

After conferring briefly, the Yoshioka students stormed off, leaving their informant gaping in wonder at what the fuss was all about.

Although it was just past closing time for the shops along the East Moat, the sword shop was still open. One of the men went in, consulted with the apprentice and emerged shouting, "Temma! He's headed toward Temma!" And away they raced.

The apprentice had said that just as he was about to hang the shutters for the night, a samurai with a long forelock had thrown a monkey down near the front door, seated himself on a stool and asked to see the master. Told he was out, the samurai had said that he wanted to have his sword sharpened, but that it was much too valuable to entrust to anyone but the master himself. He had also insisted on seeing samples of the swordsmith's work.

The apprentice had politely shown him some blades, but the samurai, after looking them over, showed nothing but disgust. "It seems all you handle here are ordinary weapons," he said dryly. "I don't think I'd better give you mine. It's much too good, the work of a Bizen master. It's called the Drying Pole. See? It's perfect." He had then held it up with obvious pride.

The apprentice, amused by the young man's boasting, mumbled that the only remarkable features of the sword seemed to be its length and its straightness. The samurai, apparently offended, abruptly stood up and asked directions to the Temma-Kyoto ferry landing.

"I'll have my sword taken care of in Kyoto," he snapped. "All the Osaka swordsmiths I've visited seem to deal only in junk for ordinary foot soldiers. Sorry to have bothered you." With a cold look in his eye, he had departed.

The apprentice's story infuriated them all the more, as fresh evidence of what they already considered to be the young man's excessive conceit. It was clear to them that cutting off Gion Tōji's topknot had made the braggart cockier than ever.

"That's our man for sure!"

"We've got him now. He's as good as caught."

The men continued their pursuit, not once stopping to rest, even when the sun began to set. Nearing the dock at Temma, someone exclaimed, "We've missed it," referring to the last boat of the day.

"That's impossible."

"What makes you think we've missed it?" another asked.

"Can't you see? Down there," said the first man, pointing to the wharf. "The teashops are piling up their stools. The boat must've already pulled out."

For a moment they all stood stock-still, the wind gone from their sails. Then, on making inquiries, they found that the samurai had indeed boarded the last boat. They also learned it had just left and wouldn't be docking at the next stop, Toyosaki, for some time. The boats going upstream toward Kyoto were slow; they would have plenty of time to catch it at Toyosaki without even hurrying.

Knowing this, they took their time over tea, rice cakes and some cheap sweets before setting off at a brisk pace up the road along the riverbank. Ahead the river looked like a silver snake winding away into the distance. The Nakatsu and Temma rivers joined to form the Yodo, and near this fork a light flickered midstream.

"It's the ship!" one man shouted.

The seven became animated and soon forgot the piercing cold. In the bare fields by the road, dry rushes covered with frost glittered like slender steel swords. The wind seemed laden with ice.

As the distance between themselves and the floating light narrowed, they were able to see the boat quite clearly. Soon one of the men, without thinking, shouted, "Hey, there. Slow down!"

"Why?" came a response from on board.

Annoyed at having attention drawn to themselves, his companions chided the loudmouth. The boat was stopping at the next landing anyway; it was sheer stupidity to give advance warning. Now that they had, however, everyone agreed that the best thing to do would be to make their demand for the passenger then and there.

"There's only one of him, and if we don't challenge him outright, he may get suspicious, jump overboard and escape."

Keeping pace with the boat, they again called out to those on board. An authoritative voice, undoubtedly the captain's, demanded to know what they wanted.

"Bring the boat to the bank!"

"What! Are you crazy?" came the reply, accompanied by raucous laughter.

"Land here!"

"Not on your life."

"Then we'll be waiting for you at the next landing. We have some business with a young man you've got on board. Wears a forelock and has a monkey. Tell him if he has any sense of honor, he'll show himself. And if you let him get away, we'll drag every one of you ashore."

"Captain, don't answer them!" pleaded a passenger.

"Whatever they say, just ignore it," counseled another. "Let's go on to Moriguchi. There are guards there."

Most of the passengers were huddled in fear and talking in subdued tones. The one who had spoken so jauntily to the samurai on shore a few minutes earlier now stood mute. For him as well as the others, safety lay in keeping some distance between the boat and the riverbank.

The seven men, sleeves hitched up and hands on their swords, stayed with the boat. Once they stopped and listened, apparently expecting an answer to their challenge, but heard none.

"Are you deaf?" one of them shouted. "We told you to tell that young braggart to come to the rail!"

"Do you mean me?" bellowed a voice from the boat.

"He's there, all right, and brazen as ever!"

While the men pointed their fingers and squinted toward the boat, the murmuring of the passengers grew frenzied. To them it looked as though the men on the shore might at any moment leap onto the deck.

The young man with the long sword stood firmly poised on the gunwale, his teeth shining like white pearls in the reflected moonlight. "There's no one else on board with a monkey, so I suppose it's me you're looking for. Who are you, freebooters down on your luck? A troupe of hungry actors?"

"You still don't know who you're talking to, do you, Monkey Man? Watch your tongue when you address men from the House of Yoshioka!"

As the shouting match intensified, the boat neared the dike at Kema, which had both mooring posts and a shed. The seven ran forward to seal off the landing, but no sooner reached it than the boat stopped midriver and began turning around in circles.

The Yoshioka men grew livid.

"What do you think you're doing?'"

"You can't stay out there forever!"

"Come in or we'll come out after you."

The threats continued unabated till the prow of the boat began to move toward the bank. A voice roared through the cold air: "Shut up, you fools! We're coming in! Better get ready to defend yourselves."

Despite the other passengers' pleas, the young man had seized the boatman's pole and was bringing the ferry in. The seven samurai immediately assembled around where the prow would touch shore and watched the figure poling the boat grow larger as he neared them. But then suddenly the boat's speed picked up, and he was upon them before they knew it. As the hull scraped bottom, they fell back, and a dark, round object came sailing across the reeds and locked itself around one man's neck. Before realizing it was only the monkey, they had all instinctively drawn their swords and sliced through the empty air around them. To disguise their embarrassment, they shouted impatient orders at one another.

Hoping to stay out of the fray, the passengers huddled in a corner of the boat. The mayhem among the seven on the bank was encouraging, if somewhat puzzling, but no one yet dared to speak. Then, in an instant, all heads turned with a gasp as the boat's self-appointed pilot rammed his pole into the riverbed and vaulted, more lightly than the monkey, over the rushes to shore.

This caused even greater confusion, and without pausing to regroup, the Yoshioka men scampered toward their enemy in single file. This couldn't have put him in a better position to defend himself.

The first man had already advanced too far to turn back when he realized the stupidity of his move. At that moment every martial skill he'd ever learned deserted him. It was all he could do to bare his teeth and wave his sword erratically in front of him.

The handsome young man, aware of his psychological advantage, seemed to grow in stature. His right hand was behind him, on his sword hilt, and his elbow protruded above his shoulder.

"So you're from the Yoshioka School, are you? That's good. I feel as if I know you already. One of your men was kind enough to allow me to remove his topknot. Apparently that wasn't enough for you. Have you all come for a haircut? If you have, I'm sure I can oblige you. I'm having this blade sharpened soon anyway, so I don't mind putting it to good use."

As the declaration ended, the Drying Pole split first the air and then the cringing body of the nearest swordsman.

Seeing their comrade slain so easily paralyzed their brains; one by one they backed into one another in retreat, like so many colliding balls. Taking advantage of their obvious disorganization, the attacker swung his sword sideways at the next man, delivering a blow so solid it sent him tumbling with a shriek into the rushes.

The young man glared at the remaining five, who had in the meantime arranged themselves around him like flower petals. Reassuring each other that their present tactic was foolproof, they regained their confidence to the point of taunting the young man again. But this time their words had a tremulous, hollow ring.

Finally, with a loud battle cry, one of the men sprang forward and swung. He was sure he had made a cut. In fact, his sword point fell short of its target by two full feet and finished its arc by clanging loudly against a rock. The man fell forward, leaving himself wide open.

Rather than slay such easy prey, the young man leaped sideways and swung at the next man over. While the death scream still rang through the air, the other three took to their heels.

The young man, looking murderous, stood holding his sword with both hands. "Cowards!" he shouted. "Come back and fight! Is this the Yoshioka Style you boast of? To challenge a person and then run away? No wonder the House of Yoshioka's become a laughingstock."

To any self-respecting samurai, such insults were worse than being spat on, but the young man's former pursuers were too busy running to care.

Just then, from the vicinity of the dike, the sound of a horse's bells rang out. The river and the frost in the fields reflected enough light for the young man to make out a form on horseback and another running along behind. Though frosty breath steamed from their nostrils, they seemed oblivious of the cold as they sped along. The three fleeing samurai nearly collided with the horse as his rider brutally reined him up short.

Recognizing the three, Seijūrō scowled furiously. "What are you doing here?" he barked. "Where are you running to?"

"It's . . . it's the Young Master!" one of them stammered.

Ueda Ryōhei, appearing from behind the horse, lit into them. "What's the meaning of this? You're supposed to be escorting the Young Master, you pack of fools! I suppose you were too busy getting yourselves into another drunken brawl."

The three, rattled but righteously indignant, spilled out the story of how, far from being in a drunken fight, they had been defending the honor of the Yoshioka School and its master and how they had come to grief at the hands of a young but demonic samurai.

"Look!" cried one of them. "He's coming this way."

Terrified eyes watched the approaching enemy.

"Quiet down!" Ryōhei ordered in a disgusted voice. "You talk too much. Fine ones you are to protect the honor of the school. We'll never be able to live down that performance. Stand aside! I'll take care of him myself." He took a challenging stance and waited.

The young man rushed toward them. "Stand and fight!" he was shouting. "Is running away the Yoshioka version of the Art of War? I personally don't want to kill you, but my Drying Pole's still thirsty. The least you can do, cowards that you are, is leave your heads behind." He was running along the dike with enormous, confident strides and seemed likely to leap right over the head of Ryōhei, who spat on his hands and regripped his sword with resolution.

288   At the moment the young man flew by, Ryōhei uttered a piercing cry, raised

his sword over the young man's gold-colored coat, brought it down fiercely, and missed.

Halting instantly, the young man turned around, crying, "What's this? A new one?"

As Ryōhei stumbled forward with the momentum of his swing, the young man swiped viciously at him. In all his life, Ryōhei had never seen such a powerful stroke, and although he managed to dodge it just in time, he plunged headfirst into the paddy field below. Luckily for him, the dike was fairly low and the field frozen over, but he lost his weapon as well as his confidence when he fell.

When he clambered back up, the young man was moving with the strength and speed of an enraged tiger, scattering the three disciples with a flash of his sword and making for Seijūrō.

Seijūrō hadn't yet felt any fear. He had thought it would be all over before he himself became involved. But now danger was rushing directly at him, in the form of a rapacious sword.

Moved by a sudden inspiration, Seijūrō cried, "Ganryū! Wait!" He disengaged one foot from its stirrup, put it on the saddle, and stood straight up. As the horse sprang forward over the young man's head, Seijūrō flew backward through the air and landed on his feet about three paces away.

"What a feat!" cried the young man in genuine admiration as he moved in on Seijūrō. "Even if you are my enemy, that was really magnificent! You must be Seijūrō himself. On guard!"

The blade of the long sword became the embodiment of the young man's fighting spirit. It loomed ever closer to Seijūrō, but Seijūrō, for all his failings, was Kempō's son, and he was able to face the danger calmly.

Addressing the young man confidently, he said, "You're Sasaki Kojirō from Iwakuni. I can tell. It is true, as you surmise, that I am Yoshioka Seijūrō. However, I have no desire to fight you. If it's really necessary, we can have it out some other time. Right now I'd just like to find out how all this came about. Put your sword away."

When Seijūrō had called him Ganryū, the young man had apparently not heard; now, being addressed as Sasaki Kojirō startled him. "How did you know who I am?" he asked.

Seijūrō slapped his thigh. "I knew it! I was only guessing, but I was right!" Then he came forward and said, "It's a pleasure to meet you. I've heard a good deal about you."

"Who from?" asked Kojirō.

"From your senior, Itō Yagorō."

"Oh, are you a friend of his?"

"Yes. Until last fall, he had a hermitage on Kagura Hill in Shirakawa, and I often visited him there. He came to my house a number of times too."

Kojirō smiled. "Well, then, this is not exactly like meeting for the first time, is it?"

"No. Ittōsai mentioned you rather often. He said there was a man from Iwakuni named Sasaki who had learned the style of Toda Seigen and then studied under Kanemaki Jisai. He told me this Sasaki was the youngest man in Jisai's school but would one day be the only swordsman who could challenge Ittōsai."

"I still don't see how you knew so quickly."

"Well, you're young and you fit the description. Seeing you wield that long sword reminded me that you're also called Ganryū—'The Willow on the Riverbank.' I had a feeling it must be you, and I was right."

"That's amazing. It really is."

As Kojirō chuckled with delight, his eyes dropped to his bloody sword, which reminded him that there had been a fight and made him wonder how they would straighten everything out. As it happened, however, he and Seijūrō hit it off so well that an understanding was soon reached, and after a few minutes they were walking along the dike shoulder to shoulder, like old friends. Behind them were Ryōhei and the three dejected disciples. The little group headed toward Kyoto.

Kojirō was saying, "From the beginning, I couldn't see what the fight was all about. I had nothing against them."

Seijūrō's thoughts were on Gion Tōji's recent conduct. "I'm disgusted with Tōji," he said. "When I get back, I'll call him to account. Please don't think I have any grudge against you. I'm simply mortified to find that the men in my school aren't better disciplined."

"Well, you can see what sort of man I am," Kojirō replied. "I talk too big and I'm always ready to fight anybody. Your disciples weren't the only ones to blame. In fact, I think you should give them some credit for trying to defend your school's good name. It's unfortunate they're not much as fighters, but at least they tried. I feel a little sorry for them."

"I'm the one to blame," Seijūrō said simply. The expression on his face was one of genuine pain.

"Let's just forget the whole thing."

"Nothing would please me more."

The sight of the two making up came as a relief to the others. Who would have thought this handsome, overgrown boy was the great Sasaki Kojirō, whose praises Ittōsai had sung? ("The prodigy of Iwakuni" were his actual words.) No wonder Tōji, in his ignorance, had been tempted to do some teasing. And no wonder he had ended up looking ridiculous.

It made Ryōhei and the other three shiver to think how close they had come to being mowed down by the Drying Pole. Now that their eyes had been opened, the sight of Kojirō's broad shoulders and sturdy back made them wonder how they could have been so stupid as to underestimate him in the first place.

After a time, they came again to the landing. The corpses were already frozen, and the three were assigned to bury them, while Ryōhei went to find the horse. Kojirō went about whistling for his monkey, which suddenly appeared out of nowhere and jumped on his master's shoulder.

Seijūrō not only urged Kojirō to come along to the school on Shijō Avenue and stay awhile but even proffered his horse. Kojirō refused.

"That wouldn't be right," he said, with unaccustomed deference. "I'm just a young rōnin, and you're the master of a great school, the son of a distinguished man, the leader of hundreds of followers." Taking hold of the bridle, he continued, "Please, you ride. I'll just hold on to this. It's easier to walk that way. If it's really all right for me to go with you, I'd like to accept your offer and stay with you in Kyoto for a time."

Seijūrō, with equal cordiality, said, "Well, then, I'll ride for now, and when your feet get tired, we can change places."

Seijūrō, faced with the certain prospect of having to fight Miyamoto Musashi at the beginning of the New Year, was reflecting that it was not a bad idea to have a swordsman like Sasaki Kojirō around.

Eagle Mountain

In the 1550s and 1560s, the most famous master swordsmen in eastern Japan were Tsukahara Bokuden and Lord Kōizumi of Ise, whose rivals in central Honshu were Yoshioka Kempō of Kyoto and Yagyū Muneyoshi of Yamato. In addition there was Lord Kitabatake Tomonori of Kuwana, a master of the martial arts and an outstanding governor. Long after his death, the people of Kuwana spoke of him with affection, since to them he symbolized the essence of good government and prosperity.

When Kitabatake studied under Bokuden, the latter passed on to him his Supreme Swordsmanship: his most secret of secret methods. Bokuden's son, Tsukahara Hikoshirō, inherited his father's name and estate but had not been bequeathed his secret treasure. It was for this reason that Bokuden's style spread not in the east, where Hikoshirō was active, but in the Kuwana region, where Kitabatake ruled.

Legend has it that after Bokuden's death, Hikoshirō came to Kuwana and tried to trick Kitabatake into revealing the secret method to him. "My father," he allegedly claimed, "long ago taught it to me, and I'm told he did the same with you. But lately I've been wondering whether what we were taught was, in fact, the same thing. Since the ultimate secrets of the Way are our mutual concern, I think we should compare what we've learned, don't you?"

Though Kitabatake immediately realized Bokuden's heir was up to no good, he quickly agreed to a demonstration, but what Hikoshirō then became privy to was only the outward form of the Supreme Swordsmanship, not its innermost secret. As a result, Kitabatake remained the sole master of the true Bokuden Style and to learn it students had to go to Kuwana. In the east, Hikoshirō passed on as genuine the spurious hollow shell of his father's skill: its form without its heart.

Or such, in any case, was the story told to any traveler who happened to set foot in the Kuwana region. It was not a bad story, as such stories go, and being based on fact, it was both more plausible and less inconsequential than most of the myriad local folk tales people told to reaffirm the uniqueness of their beloved towns and provinces.

Musashi, descending Tarusaka Mountain on his way from the castle town of Kuwana, heard it from his groom. He nodded and said politely, "Really? How interesting." It was the middle of the last month of the year, and though the Ise climate is relatively warm, the wind blowing up into the pass from Nako inlet was cold and biting.

He wore only a thin kimono, a cotton undergarment and a sleeveless cloak, clothing too light by any standard, and distinctly dirty as well. His face was not so much bronzed as blackened from exposure to the sun. Atop his weather-beaten head, his worn and frayed basket hat looked absurdly superfluous. Had he discarded it along the road, no one would have bothered to pick it up. His hair, which could not have been washed for many days, was tied in back, but still managed to resemble a bird's nest. And whatever he had been doing for the past six months had left his skin looking like well-tanned leather. His eyes shone pearly white in their coal-dark setting.

The groom had been worrying ever since he took on this unkempt rider. He doubted he would ever receive his pay and was certain he would see no return fare from their destination deep in the mountains.

"Sir," he said, somewhat timidly.

"Mm?"

"We'll reach Yokkaichi a little before noon and Kameyama by evening, but it'll be the middle of the night before we get to the village of Ujii."

"Mm."

"Is that all right?"

"Mm." Musashi was more interested in the view of the inlet than in talking, and the groom, try though he did, could elicit no more response than a nod and a noncommittal "Mm."

He tried again. "Ujii's nothing but a little hamlet about eight miles into the mountains from the ridge of Mount Suzuka. How do you happen to be going to a place like that?"

"I'm going to see someone."

"There's nobody there but a few farmers and woodcutters."

"In Kuwana I heard there's a man there who's very good with the chain-ball-sickle."

"I guess that would be Shishido."

"That's the man. His name is Shishido something or other."

"Shishido Baiken."

"Yes."

"He's a blacksmith, makes scythes. I remember hearing how good he is with that weapon. Are you studying the martial arts?"

"Mm."

"Well, in that case, instead of going to see Baiken, I'd suggest you go to Matsuzaka. Some of the best swordsmen in Ise Province are there."

"Who, for instance?"

"Well, there's Mikogami Tenzen, for one."

Musashi nodded. "Yes, I've heard of him." He said no more, leaving the impression that he was quite familiar with Mikogami's exploits.

When they reached the little town of Yokkaichi, he limped painfully to a stall, ordered a box lunch and sat down to eat. One of his feet was bandaged around the instep, because of a festering wound on the sole, which explained why he had chosen to rent a horse rather than walk. Despite his usual habit of taking good care of his body, a few days earlier in the crowded port town of Narumi, he had stepped on a board with a nail in it. His red and swollen foot looked like a pickled persimmon, and since the day before, he had had a fever.

To his way of thinking, he had had a battle with a nail, and the nail had won. As a student of the martial arts, he was humiliated at having let himself be taken unawares. "Is there no way to resist an enemy of this sort?" he asked himself several times. "The nail was pointed upward and plainly visible. I stepped on it because I was half asleep—no, blind, because my spirit is not yet active throughout my whole body. What's more, I let the nail penetrate deep, proof my reflexes are slow. If I'd been in perfect control, I would have noticed the nail as soon as the bottom of my sandal touched it."

His trouble, he concluded, was immaturity. His body and his sword were still not one; though his arms grew stronger every day, his spirit and the rest of his body were not in tune. It felt to him, in his self-critical frame of mind, like a crippling deformity.

Still, he did not feel he'd entirely wasted the past six months. After fleeing from Yagyū, he had gone first to Iga, then up the Ōmi highroad, then through the provinces of Mino and Owari. At every town, in every mountain ravine, he had sought to master the true Way of the Sword. At times he felt he had brushed up against it, but its secret remained elusive, something not to be found lurking in either town or ravine.

He couldn't remember how many warriors he had clashed with; there had been dozens of them, all well-trained, superior swordsmen. It was not hard to find able swordsmen. What was hard to find was a real man. While the world was full of people, all too full, finding a genuine human being was not easy. In his travels, Musashi had come to believe this very deeply, to the point of pain, and it discouraged him. But then his mind always turned to Takuan, for there, without doubt, was an authentic, unique individual.

"I guess I'm lucky," thought Musashi. "At least I've had the good fortune to know one genuine man. I must make sure the experience of having known him bears fruit."

Whenever Musashi thought of Takuan, a certain physical pain spread from his wrists throughout his body. It was a strange feeling, a physiological memory of the time when he had been bound fast to the cryptomeria branch. "Just wait!" vowed Musashi. "One of these days, I'll tie Takuan up in that tree, and

293

I'll sit on the ground and preach the true way of life to him!" It was not that he resented Takuan or had any desire for revenge. He simply wanted to show that the state of being one could attain through the Way of the Sword was higher than any one could reach by practicing Zen. It made Musashi smile to think he might someday turn the tables on the eccentric monk.

It could happen, of course, that things would not go exactly as planned, but supposing he did make great progress, and supposing he was eventually in a position to tie Takuan up in the tree and lecture him; what would Takuan be able to say then? Surely he would cry out for joy and proclaim, "It's magnificent! I'm happy now."

But no, Takuan would never be that direct. Being Takuan, he would laugh and say, "Stupid! You're improving, but you're still stupid!"

The actual words wouldn't really matter. The point was that Musashi felt, in a curious way, that hitting Takuan over the head with his personal superiority was something he owed to the monk, a kind of debt. The fantasy was innocent enough; Musashi had set out upon a Way of his own and was discovering day by day how infinitely long and difficult the path to true humanity is. When the practical side of his nature reminded him of how much farther along that path Takuan was than he, the fantasy vanished.

It unsettled him even more to consider how immature and inept he was compared to Sekishūsai. Thinking of the old Yagyū master both maddened and saddened him, making him keenly aware of his own incompetence to speak of the Way, the Art of War or anything else with any confidence.

At times like this, the world, which he had once thought so full of stupid people, seemed frighteningly large. But then life, Musashi would tell himself, is not a matter of logic. The sword is not logic. What was important was not talk or speculation but action. There may be other people much greater than he right now, but he, too, could be great!

When self-doubt threatened to overwhelm him, it was Musashi's habit to make straight for the mountains, in whose seclusion he could live to himself. His style of life there was evident from his appearance on returning to civilization—his cheeks hollow as a deer's, his body covered with scratches and bruises, his hair dry and stiff from long hours under a cold waterfall. He would be so dirty from sleeping on the ground that the whiteness of his teeth seemed unearthly, but these were mere superficialities. Inside he would be burning with a confidence verging on arrogance and bursting with eagerness to take on a worthy adversary. And it was this search for a test of mettle that always brought him down from the mountains.

He was on the road now because he wondered whether the chain-ball-sickle expert of Kuwana might do. In the ten days left before his appointment in Kyoto, he had time to go and find out whether Shishido Baiken was that rare entity a real man, or just another of the multitude of rice-eating worms who inhabit the earth.

It was late at night before he reached his destination deep in the mountains. After thanking the groom, he told him he was free to leave, but the groom said that since it was so late he would prefer to accompany Musashi to the house he was looking for and spend the night under the eaves. The next morning he could go down from Suzuka Pass and, if he was lucky, pick up a return fare on the way. Anyhow, it was too cold and dark to try making his way back before sunup.

Musashi sympathized with him. They were in a valley enclosed on three sides, and any way the groom went, he'd have to climb the mountains knee-deep in snow. "In that case," said Musashi, "come with me."

"To Shishido Baiken's house?"

"Yes."

"Thank you, sir. Let's see if we can find it."

Since Baiken ran a smithy, any of the local farmers would have been able to direct them to his place, but at this hour of the night, the whole village was in bed. The only sign of life was the steady thud of a mallet beating on a fulling block. Walking through the frigid air toward the sound, they eventually spied a light.

It turned out to be the blacksmith's house. In front was a pile of old metal and the underside of the eaves was smoke-stained. At Musashi's command, the groom pushed open the door and went in. There was a fire in the forge, and a woman with her back to the flames was pounding cloth.

"Good evening, ma'am! Oh! You've got a fire. That's wonderful!" The groom made straight for the forge.

The woman jumped at the sudden intrusion and dropped her work. "Who in the world are you?" she asked.

"Just a moment, I'll explain," he said, warming his hands. "I've brought a man from a long way off who wants to meet your husband. We just got here. I'm a groom from Kuwana."

"Well, of all . . ." The woman looked sourly in Musashi's direction. The frown on her face made it evident that she had seen more than enough *shugyōsha* and had learned how to handle them. With a touch of arrogance, she said to him, as though to a child, "Shut the door! The baby will catch cold with all that freezing air blowing in."

Musashi bowed and complied. Then, taking a seat on a tree stump beside the forge, he surveyed his surroundings, from the blackened foundry area to the three-room living space. On a board nailed to one section of the wall hung about ten chain-ball-sickle weapons. He assumed that was what they were, since if the truth be told, he'd never laid eyes on the device. As a matter of fact, another reason for his having made the journey here was that he thought a student like himself should become acquainted with every type of weapon. His eyes sparkled with curiosity.

The woman, who was about thirty and rather pretty, put down her mallet and went back into the living area. Musashi thought perhaps she would bring some tea, but instead she went to a mat where a small child was sleeping, picked him up and began to suckle him.

To Musashi she said, "I suppose you're another one of those young samurai who come here to get bloodied up by my husband. If you are, you're in luck. He's off on a trip, so you don't have to worry about getting killed." She laughed merrily.

Musashi did not laugh with her; he was thoroughly annoyed. He had not come to this out-of-the-way village to be made fun of by a woman, all of whom, he mused, tended to overestimate their husbands' status absurdly. This wife was worse than most; she seemed to think her spouse the greatest man on earth.

Not wanting to give offense, Musashi said, "I'm disappointed to learn that your husband's away. Where did he go?"

"To the Arakida house."

"Where's that?"

"Ha, ha! You've come to Ise, and you don't even know the Arakida family?" The baby at her breast began to fret, and the woman, forgetting about her guests, started to sing a lullaby in the local dialect.

> Go to sleep, go to sleep.
> Sleeping babies are sweet.
> Babies who wake and cry are naughty,
> And they make their mothers cry too.

Thinking he might at least learn something by taking a look at the black-smith's weapons, Musashi asked, "Are those the weapons your husband wields so well?"

The woman grunted, and when he asked to examine them, she nodded and grunted again.

He took one down from its hook. "So this is what they're like," he said, half to himself. "I've heard people are using them a good deal these days." The weapon in his hand consisted of a metal bar about a foot and a half long (easily carried in one's obi), with a ring at one end to which a long chain was attached. At the other end of the chain was a heavy metal ball, quite substantial enough to crack a person's skull. In a deep groove on one side of the bar, Musashi could see the back of a blade. As he pulled at it with his fingernails, it snapped out sideways, like the blade of a sickle. With this, it would be a simple matter to cut off an opponent's head.

"I suppose you hold it like this," said Musashi, taking the sickle in his left hand and the chain in his right. Imagining an enemy in front of him, he assumed a stance and considered what movements would be necessary.

The woman, who had turned her eyes from the baby's bed to watch, chided him. "Not that way! That's terrible!" Stuffing her breast back in her kimono, she came over to where he was standing. "If you do that, anyone with a sword can cut you down with no trouble at all. Hold it this way."

She snatched the weapon from his hands and showed him how to stand. It made him queasy to see a woman take a battle stance with such a brutal-looking weapon. He stared with open mouth. While nursing the baby, she had appeared distinctly bovine, but now, ready for combat, she looked handsome, dignified and, yes, beautiful. As Musashi watched, he saw that on the blade,

296

which was blackish blue like the back of a mackerel, there was an inscription reading "Style of Shishido Yaegaki."

She kept the stance only momentarily. "Well, anyway, it's something like that," she said, folding the blade back into the handle and hanging the weapon on its hook.

Musashi would have liked to see her handle the device again, but she obviously had no intention of doing so. After clearing up the fulling block, she clattered about near the sink, evidently washing pots or preparing to cook something.

"If this woman can take a stance as imposing as that," thought Musashi, "her husband must really be something to see." By this time he was nearly sick with the desire to meet Baiken and quietly asked the groom about the Arakidas. The groom, leaning against the wall and baking in the warmth of the fire, mumbled that they were the family charged with guarding Ise Shrine.

If this was true, Musashi thought, they would not be difficult to locate. He resolved to do just that, then curled up on a mat by the fire and went to sleep.

In the early morning, the blacksmith's apprentice got up and opened the outside door to the smithy. Musashi got up too and asked the groom to take him to Yamada, the town nearest Ise Shrine. The groom, satisfied because he'd been paid the day before, agreed at once.

By evening they had reached the long, tree-lined road that led to the shrine. The teashops looked particularly desolate, even for winter. There were few travelers, and the road itself was in poor condition. A number of trees blown down by autumn storms were still lying where they had fallen.

From the inn in Yamada, Musashi sent a servant to inquire at the Arakida house whether Shishido Baiken was staying there. A reply came saying that there must be some mistake; no one of that name was there. In his disappointment, Musashi turned his attention to his injured foot, which had swollen up considerably overnight.

He was exasperated, for only a few days remained before he was due in Kyoto. In the letter of challenge he had sent to the Yoshioka School from Nagoya, he had given them the choice of any day during the first week of the New Year. He couldn't very well beg off now because of a sore foot. And besides, he had promised to meet Matahachi at the Gojō Avenue bridge.

He spent the whole of the next day applying a remedy he had once heard about. Taking the dregs left after making bean curd, he put them in a cloth sack, squeezed the warm water out, and soaked his foot in it. Nothing happened, and to make matters worse, the smell of the bean curd was nauseating. As he fretted over his foot, he bemoaned his stupidity in making this detour to Ise. He should have gone to Kyoto straight away.

That night, with his foot wrapped up under the quilt, his fever shot higher and the pain became unendurable. The next morning, he desperately tried more prescriptions, including smearing on some oily medicine given him by the innkeeper, who swore his family had used it for generations. Still the swelling did not go down. The foot began to look to Musashi like a large, bloated wad of bean curd and felt as heavy as a block of wood.

The experience set him to thinking. He had never in his life been bedridden for three days. Aside from having a carbuncle on his head as a child, he couldn't remember ever having been ill.

"Sickness is the worst kind of enemy," he reflected. "Yet I'm powerless in its grip." Until now he had assumed his adversaries would be coming at him from without, and the fact of being immobilized by a foe within was both novel and thought-provoking.

"How many more days are there in the year?" he wondered. "I can't just stay here doing nothing!" As he lay there chafing, his ribs seemed to press in on his heart, and his chest felt constricted. He kicked the quilt off his swollen foot. "If I can't even beat this, how can I hope to overcome the whole House of Yoshioka?"

Thinking he would pin down and stifle the demon inside him, he forced himself to sit on his haunches in formal style. It was painful, excruciatingly so. He nearly fainted. He faced the window but closed his eyes, and quite some time passed before the violent redness in his face began to subside and his head to cool a bit. He wondered if the demon was yielding to his unflinching tenacity.

Opening his eyes, he saw before him the forest around Ise Shrine. Beyond the trees he could see Mount Mae, and a little to the east Mount Asama. Rising above the mountains between these two was a soaring peak that looked down its nose at its neighbors and stared insolently at Musashi.

"It's an eagle," he thought, not knowing its name actually was Eagle Mountain. The peak's arrogant appearance offended him; its haughty pose taunted him until his fighting spirit was once again stirred. He could not help thinking of Yagyū Sekishūsai, the old swordsman who resembled this proud peak, and as time passed, it began to seem the peak *was* Sekishūsai, looking down at him from above the clouds and laughing at his weakness and insignificance.

Staring at the mountain, he became for a time oblivious of his foot, but presently the pain reasserted its claim on his consciousness. Had he rammed his leg into the fire of the blacksmith's forge, it couldn't have hurt any more, he thought bitterly. Involuntarily he drew the big round thing out from under him and glared at it, unable to accept the fact that it was really a part of him.

In a loud voice he summoned the maid. When she did not appear promptly, he beat on the tatami with his fist. "Where is everybody?" he shouted. "I'm leaving! Bring the bill! Fix me some food—some fried rice—and get me three pairs of heavy straw sandals!"

Soon he was out on the street, limping through the old marketplace where the famous warrior Taira no Tadakiyo, the hero of the "Story of the Hōgen War," was supposed to have been born. But now little about it suggested a birthplace of heroes; it was more like an open-air brothel, lined with tea stalls and teeming with women. More temptresses than trees stood along the lane, calling out to travelers and latching on to the sleeves of passing prospects, as they flirted, coaxed and teased. To get to the shrine, Musashi had to literally

298

push his way through them, scowling and avoiding their impertinent stares.

"What happened to your foot?"

"Shall I make it feel better?"

"Here, let me rub it for you!"

They pulled at his clothing, grabbed at his hands, grasped his wrists.

"A good-looking man won't get anywhere frowning like that!"

Musashi reddened and stumbled along blindly. Utterly without defense against this kind of attack, he apologized to some and made polite excuses to others, which only made the women titter. When one of them said he was as "cute as a baby panther," the assault of the whitened hands intensified. Finally, he gave up all pretense of dignity and ran, not even stopping to retrieve his hat when it flew off. The giggling voices followed him through the trees outside the town.

It was impossible for Musashi to ignore women, and the frenzy their pawing hands aroused in him took long to subside. The mere memory of the scent of pungent white powder would set his pulse racing, and no amount of mental effort could calm it. It was a greater threat than an enemy standing with sword drawn before him; he simply did not know how to cope with it. Later, his body burning with sexual fire, he would toss and turn all night. Even innocent Otsū sometimes became the object of his lustful fantasies.

Today he had his foot to take his mind off the women, but running from them when he was barely able to walk, he might as well have been crossing a bed of molten metal. At every other step, a stab of anguish shot to his head from the sole of his foot. His lips reddened, his hands grew as sticky as honey, and his hair smelled acrid from sweat. Just lifting the injured foot took all the strength he could muster; at times he felt as if his body would suddenly fall apart. Not that he had any illusions. He knew when he left the inn that this would be torture and he intended to survive it. Somehow he managed to stay in control, cursing under his breath each time he dragged the wretched foot forward.

Crossing the Isuzu River and entering the precincts of the Inner Shrine brought a welcome change of atmosphere. He sensed a sacred presence, sensed it in the plants, in the trees, even in the voices of the birds. What it was, he could not say, but it was there.

He groaned and collapsed on the roots of a great cryptomeria, whimpering softly with pain and holding his foot in both hands. For a long time he sat there, motionless as a rock, his body aflame with fever even as his skin was bitten by the cold wind.

Why had he suddenly risen from his bed and fled the inn? Any normal person would have stayed there quietly until the foot healed. Was it not childish, even imbecilic, for an adult to allow impatience to overcome him?

But it was not impatience only that had moved him. It was a spiritual need, and a very deep one. For all the pain, all the physical torment, his spirit was tense and throbbing with vitality. He lifted his head and with keen eyes regarded the nothingness around him.

Through the bleak, ceaseless moaning of the great trees in the sacred forest, *299*

Musashi's ear caught another sound. Somewhere, not far away, flutes and reeds were giving voice to the strains of ancient music, music dedicated to the gods, while ethereal children's voices sang a holy invocation. Drawn by this peaceful sound, Musashi tried to stand. Biting his lips, he forced himself up, his unwilling body resisting every move. Reaching the dirt wall of a shrine building, he grasped it with both hands and worked his way along with an awkward crablike movement.

The heavenly music was coming from a building a little farther on, where a light shone through a latticed window. This, the House of Virgins, was occupied by young girls in the service of the deity. Here they practiced playing ancient musical instruments and learned to perform sacred dances devised centuries earlier.

Musashi made his way to the rear entrance of the building. He paused and looked in, but saw no one. Relieved at not having to explain himself, he removed his swords and the pack on his back, tied them together, and hung them on a peg on the inside wall. Thus unencumbered, he put his hands on his hips and began hobbling back toward the Isuzu River.

An hour or so later, completely naked, he broke the ice on the surface and plunged into the frigid waters. And there he stayed, splashing and bathing, dunking his head, purifying himself. Fortunately, no one was about; any passing priest would have thought him insane and driven him away.

According to Ise legend, an archer named Nikki Yoshinaga had, long ago, attacked and occupied a part of the Ise Shrine territory. Once ensconced, he fished in the sacred Isuzu River and used falcons to catch small birds in the sacred forest. In the course of these sacrilegious plunderings, the legend said, he went totally insane, and Musashi, acting as he was, could easily have been taken for the madman's ghost.

When finally he leaped onto a boulder, it was with the lightness of a small bird. While he was drying himself and putting on his clothes, the strands of hair along his forehead stiffened into slivers of ice.

To Musashi, the icy plunge into the sacred stream was necessary. If his body could not withstand the cold, how could it survive in the face of life's more threatening obstacles? And at this moment, it was not a matter of some abstract future contingency, but one of taking on the very real Yoshioka Seijūrō and his entire school. They would hurl every bit of strength they had at him. They had to, to save face. They knew they had no alternative but to kill him, and Musashi knew just saving his skin was going to be tricky.

Faced with this prospect, the typical samurai would invariably talk about "fighting with all his might" or "being prepared to face death," but to Musashi's way of thinking, this was a lot of nonsense. To fight a life-or-death struggle with all one's might was no more than animal instinct. Moreover, while not being thrown off balance by the prospect of death was a mental state of a higher order, it was not really so difficult to face death if one knew that one had to die.

Musashi was not afraid to die, but his objective was to win definitively, not just survive, and he was trying to build up the confidence to do so. Let others die heroic deaths, if that suited them. Musashi could settle for nothing less than a heroic victory.

Kyoto was not far away, no more than seventy or eighty miles. If he could keep up a good pace, he could get there in three days. But the time needed to prepare himself spiritually was beyond measuring. Was he inwardly ready? Were his mind and spirit truly one?

Musashi wasn't yet able to reply to these questions in the affirmative. He felt that somewhere deep inside himself there was a weakness, the knowledge of his immaturity. He was painfully aware that he had not attained the state of mind of the true master, that he was still far short of being a complete and perfect human. When he compared himself with Nikkan, or Sekishūsai, or Takuan, he could not avoid the simple truth: he was still green. His own analysis of his abilities and traits unveiled not only weaknesses in some areas but virtual blind spots in others.

But unless he could triumph throughout this life and leave an indelible mark on the world around him, he could not regard himself as a master of the Art of War.

His body shook as he shouted, "I will win, I will!" Limping on toward the upper reaches of the Isuzu, he cried out again for all the trees in the sacred forest to hear: "I will win!" He passed a silent, frozen waterfall and, like a primitive man, crawled over the boulders and pushed his way through thick groves in deep ravines, where few had ever gone before.

His face was as red as a demon's. Clinging to rocks and vines, he could with the utmost effort advance only one step at a time.

Beyond a point called Ichinose there was a gorge five or six hundred yards long, so full of crags and rapids that even the trout could not make their way through it. At the farther end rose an almost sheer precipice. It was said that only monkeys and goblins could climb it. Musashi merely looked at the cliff and said matter-of-factly, "This is it. This is the way to Eagle Mountain."

Elated, he saw no impassable barrier here. Seizing hold of strong vines, he started up the rock face, half climbing, half swinging, seemingly lifted by some upside-down gravity.

Having reached the cliff top, he exploded with a cry of triumph. From here he could make out the white flow of the river and the silver strand along the shore of Futamigaura. Ahead of him, through a sparse grove veiled in nocturnal mist, he saw before his eyes the foot of Eagle Mountain.

The mountain was Sekishūsai. As it had laughed while he'd lain in bed, the peak continued to mock him now. His unyielding spirit felt literally assaulted by Sekishūsai's superiority. It was oppressing him, holding him back.

Gradually his objective took form: to climb to the top and unleash his rancor, to trample roughshod on the head of Sekishūsai, to show him Musashi could and would win.

He advanced against the opposition of weeds, trees, ice—all enemies trying desperately to keep him back. Every step, every breath, was a challenge. His recently chilled blood boiled, and his body steamed as the sweat from his pores met the frosty air. Musashi hugged the red surface of the peak, groping for footholds. Each time he felt for a footing he had to struggle, and small rocks would go crashing down to the grove below. One hundred feet, two hundred, three hundred—he was in the clouds. When they parted, he appeared from below to be hanging weightless in the sky. The mountain peak stared coldly down at him.

Now, nearing the top, he hung on for dear life. One false move and he would come flying down in a cascade of rocks and boulders. He puffed and grunted, gasping for air with his very pores. So intense was the strain, his heart seemed about to rise up and explode from his mouth. He could climb but a few feet, then rest, climb a few feet more, then rest again.

The whole world lay beneath him: the great forest enclosing the shrine, the white strip that must be the river, Mount Asama, Mount Mae, the fishing village at Toba, the great open sea. "Almost there," he thought. "Just a little more!"

"Just a little more." How easy to say, but how difficult to achieve! For "just a little more" is what distinguishes the victorious sword from the vanquished.

The odor of sweat in his nostrils, he felt giddily that he was nestled in his mother's breast. The rough surface of the mountain began to feel like her skin, and he experienced an urge to go to sleep. But just then a piece of rock under his big toe broke off and brought him to his senses. He groped for another foothold.

"This is it! I'm almost there!" Hands and feet knotted with pain, he clawed again at the mountain. If his body or willpower weakened, he told himself, then as a swordsman he would surely one day be done in. This was where the match would be decided, and Musashi knew it.

"This is for you, Sekishūsai! You bastard!" With every pull and tug, he execrated the giants he respected, those supermen who had brought him here and whom he must and would conquer. "One for you, Nikkan! and you, Takuan!"

He was climbing over the heads of his idols, trampling over them, showing them who was best. He and the mountain were now one, but the mountain, as if astonished to have this creature clawing into it, snarled and spit out regular avalanches of gravel and sand. Musashi's breath stopped as though someone had clapped his hands over his face. As he clung to the rock, the wind gusted, threatening to blow him away, rock and all.

Then suddenly he was lying on his stomach, his eyes closed, not daring to move. But in his heart he sang a song of exultation. At the moment when he had flattened out, he had seen the sky in all directions, and the light of dawn was suddenly visible in the white sea of clouds below.

"I've done it! I've won!"

The instant he realized he had reached the top, his strained willpower snapped like a bowstring. The wind at the summit showered his back with sand and stones. Here at the border of heaven and earth, Musashi felt an indescribable joy swelling out to fill his whole being. His sweat-drenched body united with the surface of the mountain; the spirit of man and the spirit of the mountain were performing the great work of procreation in the vast expanse of nature at dawn. Wrapped in an unearthly ecstasy, he slept the sleep of peace.

When he finally lifted his head, his mind was as pure and clear as crystal. He had the impulse to jump and dart about like a minnow in a stream.

"There's nothing above me!" he cried. "I'm standing on top of the eagle's head!"

The pristine morning sun cast its reddish light on him and on the mountain as he stretched his brawny, savage arms toward the sky. He looked down at his two feet planted firmly on the summit, and as he looked, he saw what seemed like a bucketful of yellowish pus stream from his injured foot. Amid the celestial purity surrounding him, there arose the strange odor of humanity—the sweet smell of gloom dispelled.

The Mayfly in Winter

Every morning after finishing their shrine duties, the maidens living in the House of Virgins went, books in hand, to the schoolroom at the Arakida house, where they studied grammar and practiced writing poems. For their performances of religious dances, they dressed in white silk kimono with crimson widely flared trousers, called *hakama*, but now they had on the short-sleeved kimono and white cotton *hakama* they wore while studying or doing household chores.

A group of them was streaming out the back door when one exclaimed, "What's that?" She was pointing to the pack with the swords tied to it, hung up there by Musashi the night before.

"Whose do you think it is?"

"It must be a samurai's."

"Isn't that obvious?"

"No, it could have been left here by a thief."

They looked wide-eyed at each other and gulped, as though they had come across the robber himself—leather bandannaed and taking his noonday nap.

"Perhaps we should tell Otsū about it," one of them suggested, and by common consent they all ran back to the dormitory and called up from beneath the railing outside Otsū's room.

"*Sensei! Sensei!* There's something strange down here. Come and look!"

Otsū put her writing brush down on her desk and stuck her head out the window. "What is it?" she asked.

"A thief left his swords and a bundle behind. They're over there, hanging on the back wall."

"Really? You'd better take them over to the Arakida house."

"Oh, we can't! We're afraid to touch them."

"Aren't you making a big fuss over nothing? Run along to your lessons now, and don't waste any more time."

By the time Otsū came down from her room, the girls had gone. The only people in the dormitory were the old woman who did the cooking and one of the maidens who had taken ill. "Whose things are those hanging up here?" Otsū asked the cook.

The woman did not know, of course.

"I'll take them over to the Arakida house," Otsū said. When she took the pack and swords down, she nearly dropped them, they were so heavy. Lugging them with both hands, she wondered how men could walk about carrying so much weight.

Otsū and Jōtarō had come here two months earlier, after traveling up and down the Iga, Ōmi and Mino highroads in search of Musashi. Upon their arrival in Ise, they had decided to settle down for the winter, since it would be difficult to make their way through the mountains in the snow. At first Otsū had given flute lessons in the Toba district, but then she had come to the attention of the head of the Arakida family, who, being the official ritualist, ranked second only to the chief priest.

When Arakida asked Otsū to come to the shrine to teach the maidens, she had consented, not so much out of a desire to teach as out of her interest in learning the ancient, sacred music. Then, too, the peacefulness of the shrine's forest had appealed to her, as had the idea of living for a while with the shrine maidens, the youngest of whom was thirteen or fourteen, and the oldest around twenty.

Jōtarō had stood in the way of her taking the position, for it was forbidden to have a male, even of his age, living in the same dormitory as the maidens. The arrangement they arrived at was that Jōtarō could sweep the sacred gardens in the daytime and spend his nights in the Arakidas' woodshed.

As Otsū passed through the shrine gardens, a forbidding unearthly breeze whistled through the leafless trees. One thin column of smoke rose from a distant grove, and Otsū thought of Jōtarō, who was probably there cleaning the grounds with his bamboo broom. She stopped and smiled, pleased that Jōtarō, the incorrigible, was minding very well these days, applying himself dutifully to his chores at just the age when young boys think of nothing but playing and amusing themselves.

The loud cracking noise she heard sounded like a branch breaking off a tree. It came a second time, and clutching her load, she ran down the path through the grove, calling, "Jōtarō! J-ō-ō-t-a-r-ō-ō-ō!"

"Y-e-e-s?" came the lusty reply. In no time she heard his running footsteps. But when he drew up before her, he said merely, "Oh, it's you."

"I thought you were supposed to be working," said Otsū sternly. "What are you doing with that wooden sword? And dressed in your white work clothes too."

"I was practicing. Practicing on the trees."

"Nobody objects to your practicing, but not here, Jōtarō. Have you forgotten where you are? This garden symbolizes peace and purity. It's a holy area, sacred to the goddess who is the ancestress of us all. Look over there. Don't you see the sign saying it's forbidden to damage the trees or hurt or kill the animals? It's a disgrace for a person who works here to be breaking off branches with a wooden sword."

"Aw, I know all that," he grumbled, a look of resentment on his face.

"If you know it, why do you do it? If Master Arakida caught you at it, you'd really be in trouble!"

"I don't see anything wrong with breaking off dead limbs. It's all right if they're dead, isn't it?"

"No, it is not! Not here."

"That's how much you know! Just let me ask you a question."

"What might that be?"

"If this garden is so important, why don't people take better care of it?"

"It's a shame they don't. To let it run down this way is like letting weeds grow in one's soul."

"It wouldn't be so bad if it were only weeds, but look at the trees. The ones split by lightning have been allowed to die, and the ones blown over by the typhoons are lying right where they fell. They're all over the place. And the birds have pecked at the roofs of the buildings until they leak. And nobody ever fixes any of the stone lanterns when they get knocked out of shape.

"How can you think this place is important? Listen, Otsū, isn't the castle at Osaka white and dazzling when you see it from the ocean at Settsu? Isn't Tokugawa Ieyasu building more magnificent castles at Fushimi and a dozen other places? Aren't the new houses of the daimyō and the rich merchants in Kyoto and Osaka glittering with gold ornaments? Don't the tea masters Rikyū and Kobori Enshū say that even a speck of dirt out of place in the teahouse garden spoils the flavor of the tea?

"But this garden's going to ruin. Why, the only people working in it are me and three or four old men! And look how big it is!"

"Jōtarō!" said Otsū, putting her hand under his chin and lifting his face. "You're doing nothing but repeating word for word what Master Arakida said in a lecture."

"Oh, did you hear it too?"

"Indeed I did," she said reproachfully.

"Uh, well, can't win all the time."

"Parroting what Master Arakida says will carry no weight with me. I don't approve of it, even when what he says is right."

"He is right, you know. When I hear him talk, I wonder whether Nobunaga and Hideyoshi and Ieyasu are really such great men. I know they're supposed to be important, but is it really so wonderful to take control of the country if you get the idea that you're the only person in it who counts?"

"Well, Nobunaga and Hideyoshi weren't as bad as some of the others. At least they repaired the imperial palace in Kyoto and tried to make the people happy. Even if they did these things only to justify their conduct to themselves and others, they still deserve a lot of credit. The Ashikaga shōguns were much worse."

305

"How?"

"You've heard about the Ōnin War, haven't you?"

"Um."

"The Ashikaga shogunate was so incompetent, there was constant civil war—warriors fighting other warriors all the time to gain more territory for themselves. The ordinary people didn't get a moment's peace, and nobody had any real concern for the country as a whole."

"You mean those famous battles between the Yamanas and the Hosokawas?"

"Yes. . . . It was during those days, over a hundred years ago, that Arakida Ujitsune became the chief priest of the Ise Shrine, and there wasn't even enough money to continue the ancient ceremonies and sacred rites. Ujitsune petitioned the government twenty-seven times for help to repair the shrine buildings, but the imperial court was too poor, the shogunate was too weak, and the warriors so busy with their bloodbaths they didn't care what happened. In spite of all this, Ujitsune went around pleading his case till he finally succeeded in setting up a new shrine.

"It's a sad story, isn't it? But when you think about it, people when they grow up forget they owe their lifeblood to their ancestors, just as we all owe our lives to the goddess at Ise."

Pleased with himself for having elicited this long, passionate speech from Otsū, Jōtarō jumped in the air, laughing and clapping his hands. "Now who's parroting Master Arakida? You thought I hadn't heard that before, didn't you?"

"Oh, you're impossible!" exclaimed Otsū, laughing herself. She would have cuffed him one, but her bundle was in the way. Still smiling, she glared at the boy, who finally took notice of her unusual parcel.

"Whose are those?" he asked, stretching out his hand.

"Don't touch them! We don't know whose they are."

"Oh, I'm not going to break anything. I just want to look. I bet they're heavy. That long sword's really big, isn't it?" Jōtarō's mouth was watering.

"Sensei!" With a patter of straw sandals, one of the shrine maidens ran up. "Master Arakida is calling for you. I think there's something he wants you to do." Scarcely pausing, she turned and ran back.

Jōtarō looked around in all four directions, a startled expression on his face. The wintry sun was shining through the trees, and the twigs swayed like wavelets. His eyes looked as though they had spotted a phantom among the patches of sunlight.

"What's the matter?" asked Otsū. "What are you looking at?"

"Oh, nothing," replied the boy dejectedly, biting his forefinger. "When that girl called 'teacher,' I thought for a second she meant my teacher."

Otsū, too, suddenly felt sad and a little annoyed. Though Jōtarō's remark had been made in all innocence, why did he have to mention Musashi?

Despite Takuan's advice, she could not conceive of trying to expel from her heart the longing she cherished for Musashi. Takuan was so unfeeling; in a way she pitied him and his apparent ignorance of the meaning of love.

306 Love was like a toothache. When Otsū was busy, it did not bother her, but

when the remembrance struck her, she was seized by the urge to go out on the highways again, to search for him, to find him, to place her head on his chest and shed tears of happiness.

Silently, she started walking. Where was he? Of all the sorrows that beset living beings, surely the most gnawing, the most wretched, the most agonizing, was not to be able to lay eyes on the person one pined for. Tears streaming down her cheeks, she walked on.

The heavy swords with their worn fittings meant nothing to her. How could she have dreamed she was carrying Musashi's own belongings?

Jōtarō, sensing he had done something wrong, followed sadly a short distance behind. Then, as Otsū turned into the gate at the Arakida house, he ran up to her and asked, "Are you angry? About what I said?"

"Oh, no, it's nothing."

"I'm sorry, Otsū. I really am."

"It's not your fault. I just feel kind of sad. But don't worry about it. I'm going to find out what Master Arakida wants. You go back to your work."

Arakida Ujitomi called his home the House of Study. He had converted part of it into a school, attended not only by the shrine maidens but also by forty or fifty other children from the three counties belonging to Ise Shrine. He was trying to impart to the young a type of learning not currently very popular: the study of ancient Japanese history, which in the more sophisticated towns and cities was considered irrelevant. The early history of the country was intimately connected with Ise Shrine and its lands, but this was an age when people tended to confuse the fate of the nation with that of the warrior class, and what had happened in the distant past counted for little. Ujitomi was fighting a lonely battle to plant the seeds of an earlier, more traditional culture among the young people from the shrine area. While others might claim provincial regions had nothing to do with the national destiny, Ujitomi took a different view. If he could teach the local children about the past, perhaps, he thought, its spirit would one day thrive like a great tree in the sacred forest.

With perseverance and devotion, he talked to the children each day about the Chinese classics and the *Record of Ancient Matters*, the earliest history of Japan, hoping that his charges would eventually come to value these books. He had been doing this for more than ten years. To his way of thinking, Hideyoshi might seize control of the country and proclaim himself regent, Tokugawa Ieyasu might become the omnipotent "barbarian-subduing" shōgun, but young children should not, like their elders, mistake the lucky star of some military hero for the beautiful sun. If he labored patiently, the young would come to understand that it was the great Sun Goddess, not an uncouth warrior-dictator, who symbolized the nation's aspirations.

Arakida emerged from his spacious classroom, his face a little sweaty. As the children flew out like a swarm of bees and darted quickly off to their homes, a shrine maiden told him Otsū was waiting. Somewhat flustered, he said, "That's right. I sent for her, didn't I? I completely forgot. Where is she?"

Otsū was just outside the house, where she had been standing for some time listening to Arakida's lecture. "Here I am," she called. "Did you want me?"

307

"I'm sorry to have kept you waiting. Come inside."

He led her to his private study, but before sitting down, pointed to the objects she was carrying and asked what they were. She explained how she came to have them; he squinted and stared suspiciously at the swords. "Ordinary worshipers wouldn't come here with things like that," he said. "And they weren't there last evening. Somebody must have come inside the walls in the middle of the night."

Then, with a distasteful expression on his face, he grumbled, "This may be some samurai's idea of a joke, but I don't like it."

"Oh? Can you think of anyone who would want to suggest that a man had been in the House of Virgins?"

"Yes, I can. As a matter of fact, that's what I wanted to talk to you about."

"Does it concern me in some way?"

"Well, I don't want you to feel bad about it, but it's like this. There's a samurai who has taken me to task for putting you in the same dormitory with the shrine maidens. He says he's warning me for my own sake."

"Have I done something that reflects on you?"

"There's no reason to be upset. It's just that—well, you know how people talk. Now don't be angry, but after all, you're not exactly a maiden. You've been around men, and people say it tarnishes the shrine to have a woman who's not a virgin living together with the girls in the House of Virgins."

Although Arakida's tone was casual, angry tears flooded Otsū's eyes. It was true that she had traveled around a lot, that she was used to meeting people, that she had wandered through life with this old love clinging to her heart; maybe it was only natural for people to take her for a woman of the world. It was, nevertheless, a shattering experience to be accused of not being chaste, when in fact she was.

Arakida did not seem to attach much importance to the matter. It simply disturbed him that people were saying things, and since it was the end of the year "and all that," as he put it, he wondered if she would be so good as to discontinue the flute lessons and move out of the House of Virgins.

Otsū consented quickly, not as an admission of guilt, but because she had not planned to stay on and did not want to cause trouble, especially to Master Arakida. Notwithstanding her resentment at the falseness of the gossip, she promptly thanked him for his kindnesses during her stay and said that she would leave within the day.

"Oh, it's not all that urgent," he assured her, reaching out to his small bookcase and taking out some money, which he wrapped in paper.

Jōtarō, who had followed Otsū, chose this moment to put his head in from the veranda and whisper, "If you're going to leave, I'll go with you. I'm tired of sweeping their old garden anyway."

"Here's a little gift," said Arakida. "It's not much, but take it and use it for travel money." He held out the packet containing a few gold coins.

Otsū refused to touch it. With a shocked look on her face, she told him she deserved no pay for merely giving flute lessons to the girls; rather it was she who should be paying for her food and lodging.

"No," he replied. "I couldn't possibly take money from you, but there is something I'd like you to do for me in case you happen to be going to Kyoto. You can think of this money as payment for a favor."

"I'll be glad to do anything you ask, but your kindness is payment enough."

Arakida turned to Jōtarō and said, "Why don't I give him the money? He can buy things for you along the way."

"Thank you," said Jōtarō, promptly extending his hand and accepting the packet. As an afterthought, he looked at Otsū and said, "It's all right, isn't it?"

Confronted with a fait accompli, she gave in and thanked Arakida.

"The favor I want to ask," he said, "is that you deliver a package from me to Lord Karasumaru Mitsuhiro, who lives at Horikawa in Kyoto." While speaking, he took two scrolls down from the set of staggered shelves on the wall. "Lord Karasumaru asked me two years ago to paint these. They're finally done. He plans to write in the commentary to go with the pictures and present the scrolls to the Emperor. That's why I don't want to entrust them to an ordinary messenger or courier. Will you take them to him and make sure they don't get wet or soiled on the way?"

This was a commission of unexpected importance, and Otsū hesitated at first. But it would hardly do to refuse and after a moment she agreed. Arakida then took out a box and some oiled paper, but before wrapping and sealing the scrolls, said, "Perhaps I should show them to you first." He sat down and began unrolling the paintings on the floor before them. He was obviously proud of his work and wanted to take a last look himself before parting with it.

Otsū gasped at the beauty of the scrolls, and Jōtarō's eyes widened as he bent over to examine them more closely. Since the commentary had not yet been written in, neither of them knew what story was depicted, but as Arakida unrolled scene after scene, they saw before them a picture of life at the ancient imperial court, fastidiously executed in magnificent colors with touches of powdered gold. The paintings were in the Tosa style, which was derived from classic Japanese art.

Though Jōtarō had never been taught anything about art, he was dazzled by what he saw. "Look at the fire there," he exclaimed. "It looks like it's really burning, doesn't it?"

"Don't touch the painting," admonished Otsū. "Just look."

While they gazed in admiration, a servant entered and said something in a very low voice to Arakida, who nodded and replied, "I see. I suppose it's all right. Just in case, though, you'd better have the man make out a receipt." With that, he gave the servant the pack and the two swords Otsū had brought to him.

Upon learning that their flute teacher was leaving, the girls in the House of Virgins were disconsolate. In the two months she had been with them, they had come to regard her as an elder sister, and their faces as they gathered about her were full of gloom.

"Is it true?"

"Are you really going away?"

"Won't you ever come back?"

From beyond the dormitory, Jōtarō shouted, "I'm ready. What's taking you so long?" He had doffed his white robe and was once again dressed in his usual short kimono, his wooden sword at his side. The cloth-wrapped box containing the scrolls was suspended diagonally across his back.

From the window, Otsū called back, "My, that was fast!"

"I'm always fast!" retorted Jōtarō. "Aren't you ready yet? Why does it take women so long to dress and pack?" He was sunning himself in the yard, yawning lazily. But being impatient by nature, he quickly grew bored. "Aren't you finished yet?" he called again.

"I'll be there in a minute," Otsū replied. She'd already finished packing, but the girls wouldn't let her go. Attempting to break away, Otsū said soothingly, "Don't be sad. I'll come to visit one of these days. Till then, take good care of yourselves." She had the uncomfortable feeling that this was not true, for in view of what had happened, it seemed unlikely that she would ever return.

Perhaps the girls suspected this; several were crying. Finally, someone suggested that they all see Otsū as far as the holy bridge across the Isuzu River. They thereupon crowded around her and escorted her out of the house. They didn't see Jōtarō immediately, so they cupped their hands around their mouths and called his name, but got no reply. Otsū, too used to his ways to be disturbed, said, "He probably got tired of waiting and went on ahead."

"What a disagreeable little boy!" exclaimed one of the girls.

Another suddenly looked up at Otsū and asked, "Is he your son?"

"My son? How on earth could you think that? I won't even be twenty-one till next year. Do I look old enough to have a child that big?"

"No, but somebody said he was yours."

Recalling her conversation with Arakida, Otsū blushed, then comforted herself with the thought that it made no real difference what people said, so long as Musashi had faith in her.

Just then, Jōtarō came running up to them. "Hey, what's going on?" he said with a pout. "First you keep me waiting for ages, now you start off without me!"

"But you weren't where you were supposed to be," Otsū pointed out.

"You could have looked for me, couldn't you? I saw a man over there on the Toba highroad who looked a little like my teacher. I ran over to see whether it was really him."

"Someone who looked like Musashi?"

"Yes, but it wasn't him. I went as far as that row of trees and got a good look at the man from behind, but it couldn't have been Musashi. Whoever it was had a limp."

It was always like this when Otsū and Jōtarō were traveling. Not a day passed without their experiencing a glimmer of hope, followed by disappointment. Everywhere they went, they saw someone who reminded them of Musashi—the man passing by the window, the samurai in the boat that had just left, the rōnin on horseback, the dimly seen passenger in a palanquin. Hopes

soaring, they would rush to make sure, only to find themselves looking dejectedly at each other. It had happened dozens of times.

For this reason, Otsū was not as upset now as she might have been, though
Jōtarō was crestfallen. Laughing the incident off, she said, "Too bad you were
wrong, but don't get mad at me for going on ahead. I thought I'd find you at
the bridge. You know, everybody says that if you start out on a journey in a
bad mood, you'll stay angry all the way. Come now, let's make up."

Though seemingly satisfied, Jōtarō turned and cast a rude look at the girls
trailing along behind. "What are they all doing here? Are they coming with
us?"

"Of course not. They're just sorry to see me leave, so they're sweet enough
to escort us to the bridge."

"Why, that's so very kind of them," said Jōtarō, mimicking Otsū's speech
and throwing everyone into fits of laughter. Now that he had joined the
group, the anguish of parting subsided, and the girls recovered their good
spirits.

"Otsū," called one of them, "you're turning the wrong way; that's not the
path to the bridge."

"I know," said Otsū quietly. She had turned toward the Tamagushi Gate to
pay her respects to the inner shrine. Clapping her hands together once, she
bowed her head toward the sanctum and remained in an attitude of silent
prayer for a few moments.

"Oh, I see," murmured Jōtarō. "She doesn't think she should leave without
saying good-bye to the goddess." He was content to watch from a distance, but
the girls started poking him in the back and asking him why he did not follow Otsū's example. "Me?" asked the boy incredulously. "I don't want to bow
before any old shrine."

"You shouldn't say that. You'll be punished for that someday."

"I'd feel silly bowing like that."

"What's silly about showing your respect to the Sun Goddess? She's not like
one of those minor deities they worship in the cities."

"I know that."

"Well, then, why don't you pay your respects?"

"Because I don't want to!"

"Contrary, aren't you!"

"Shut up, you crazy females! All of you!"

"Oh, my!" chorused the girls, dismayed at his rudeness.

"What a monster!" exclaimed one.

By this time Otsū had finished her obeisance and was coming back toward
them. "What happened?" she asked. "You look upset."

One of the girls blurted, "He called us crazy females, just because we tried
to get him to bow before the goddess."

"Now, Jōtarō, you know that's not nice," Otsū admonished. "You really
ought to say a prayer."

"What for?"

"Didn't you say yourself that when you thought Musashi was about to be   *311* killed by the priests from the Hōzōin, you raised your hands and prayed as loudly as you could? Why can't you pray here too?"

"But . . . well, they're all looking."

"All right, we'll turn around so we can't see you."

They all turned their backs to the boy, but Otsū stole a look behind her. He was running dutifully toward the Tamagushi Gate. When he reached it, he faced the shrine and, in very boyish fashion, made a deep, lightning-quick bow.

The Pinwheel

Musashi sat on the narrow veranda of a little seafood shop facing the sea. The shop's specialty was sea snails, served boiling in their shells. Two women divers, baskets of freshly caught turban shells on their arms, and a boatman stood near the veranda. While the boatman urged him to take a ride around the offshore islands, the two women were trying to convince him he needed some sea snails to take with him, wherever he was headed.

Musashi was busily engaged in removing the pus-soiled bandage from his foot. Having suffered intensely from his injury, he could hardly believe that both the fever and the swelling were finally gone. The foot was again normal size, and though the skin was white and shriveled, it was only slightly painful.

Waving the boatman and divers away, he lowered his tender foot onto the sand and walked to the shore to wash it. Returning to the veranda, he waited for the shopgirl he'd sent to buy new leather socks and sandals. When she came back, he put them on and took a few cautious steps. He still had a slight limp, but nothing like before.

The old man cooking snails looked up. "The ferryman's calling you. Weren't you planning to cross over to Ōminato?"

"Yes. I think there's a regular boat from there to Tsu."

"There is, and there are also boats for Yokkaichi and Kuwana."

"How many days to the end of the year?"

The old man laughed. "I envy you," he said. "It's plain you don't have any year-end debts to pay. Today's the twenty-fourth."

"Is that all? I thought it was later."

"How nice to be young!"

As he trotted to the ferry landing, Musashi felt an urge to keep running, farther and farther, faster and faster. The change from invalid to healthy man had lifted his spirits, but what made him far happier was the spiritual experience he'd had that morning.

The ferry was already full, but he managed to make room for himself. Directly across the bay, at Ōminato, he changed to a bigger boat, bound for Owari. The sails filled and the boat glided over the glasslike surface of the Bay of Ise. Musashi stood huddled with the other passengers and gazed quietly across the water to his left—at the old market, Yamada and the Matsuzaka highroad. If he went to Matsuzaka, he might have a chance to meet the prodigious swordsman Mikogami Tenzen, but no, it was too soon for that. He disembarked at Tsu as planned.

No sooner was he off the boat than he noticed a man walking ahead of him with a short bar at his waist. Wrapped around the bar was a chain, and at the end of the chain was a ball. The man also wore a short field sword in a leather sheath. He looked to be forty-two or forty-three; his face, as dark as Musashi's, was pockmarked, and his reddish hair was pulled back in a knot.

He might have been taken for a freebooter were it not for the young boy following him. Soot blackened both cheeks, and he carried a sledgehammer; he was obviously a blacksmith's apprentice.

"Wait for me, master!"

"Get a move on!"

"I left the hammer on the boat."

"Leaving behind the tools you make your living with, huh?"

"I went back and got it."

"And I suppose that makes you proud of yourself. The next time you forget anything, I'll crack your skull open for you!"

"Master . . ." the boy pleaded.

"Quiet!"

"Can't we spend the night at Tsu?"

"There's still plenty of daylight. We can make it home by nightfall."

"I'd like to stop somewhere anyway. As long as we're on a trip, we might as well enjoy it."

"Don't talk nonsense!"

The street into the town was lined with souvenir shops and infested with inn touts, just as in other port towns. The apprentice again lost sight of his master and searched the crowd worriedly until the man emerged from a toy shop with a small, colorful pinwheel.

"Iwa!" he called to the boy.

"Yes, sir."

"Carry this. And be careful it doesn't get broken! Stick it in your collar."

"Souvenir for the baby?"

"Mm," grunted the man. After being away on a job for a few days, he was looking forward to seeing the child's grin of delight when he handed it over.

It almost seemed that the pair were leading Musashi. Every time he planned to turn, they turned ahead of him. It occurred to Musashi that this blacksmith was probably Shishido Baiken, but he could not be sure, so he improvised a simple strategy to make certain. Feigning not to notice them, he went ahead for a time, then dropped back again, eavesdropping all the while. They went through the castle town and then toward the mountain road to Suzuka, presumably the route Baiken would take to his house. Putting this together with snatches of overheard conversation, Musashi concluded that this was indeed Baiken.

He had intended to go straight to Kyoto, but this chance meeting proved too tempting. He approached and said in a friendly manner, "Going back to Umehata?"

The man's reply was curt. "Yes, I'm going to Umehata. Why?"

"I was wondering if you might be Shishido Baiken."

"I am. And who are you?"

"My name is Miyamoto Musashi. I'm a student warrior. Not long ago I went to your house in Ujii and met your wife. It looks to me as though fate brought us together here."

"Is that so?" Baiken said. With a look of sudden comprehension on his face, he asked, "Are you the man who was staying at the inn in Yamada, the one who wanted to have a bout with me?"

"How did you hear about that?"

"You sent someone to the Arakida house to find me, didn't you?"

"Yes."

"I was doing some work for Arakida, but I didn't stay at the house. I borrowed a work place in the village. It was a job nobody could do but me."

"I see. I hear you're an expert with the chain-ball-sickle."

"Ha, ha! But you said you met my wife?"

"Yes. She demonstrated one of the Yaegaki stances for me."

"Well, that should be enough for you. There's no reason to be following along after me. Oh, of course I could show you a great deal more than she did, but the minute you saw it, you'd be on your way to a different world."

Musashi's impression of the wife had been that she was pretty overbearing, but here was real arrogance. He was fairly sure from what he had seen already that he could take the measure of this man, but he cautioned himself not to be hasty. Takuan had taught him life's first lesson, namely that there are a lot of people in the world who may very well be one's betters. The lesson had been reinforced by his experiences at the Hōzōin and at Koyagyū Castle. Before letting his pride and confidence betray him into underestimating an adversary, he wanted to size him up from every possible angle. While laying his groundwork, he would remain sociable, even if at times this might strike his opponent as being cowardly or subservient.

In reply to Baiken's contemptuous remark, he said, with an air of respect befitting his youth, "I see. I did indeed learn a good deal from your wife, but since I've had the good fortune to meet you, I'd be grateful if you'd tell me more about the weapon you use."

"If all you want to do is talk, fine. Are you planning to stay overnight at the inn by the barrier?"

"That's what I had in mind, unless you'd be kind enough to put me up for another night."

"You're welcome to stay, if you're willing to sleep in the smithy with Iwa. But I don't run an inn and we don't have extra bedding."

At sunset they reached the foot of Mount Suzuka; the little village, under red clouds, looked as placid as a lake. Iwa ran on ahead to announce their arrival, and when they got to the house, Baiken's wife was waiting under the eaves, holding the baby and the pinwheel.

"Look, look, look!" she cooed. "Daddy's been away, Daddy's come back. See, there he is."

In a twinkling, Daddy ceased to be the epitome of arrogance and broke into a fatherly smile. "Here, boy, here's Daddy," he babbled, holding up his hand and making his fingers dance.

Husband and wife disappeared inside and sat down, talking only about the baby and household matters, paying no attention to Musashi.

Finally, when dinner was ready, Baiken remembered his guest. "Oh, yes, give that fellow something to eat," he told his wife.

Musashi was sitting in the dirt-floored smithy, warming himself by the forge. He hadn't even removed his sandals.

"He was just here the other day. He spent the night," the woman replied sullenly. She put some sake to warm in the hearth in front of her husband.

"Young man," Baiken called. "Do you drink sake?"

"I don't dislike it."

"Have a cup."

"Thanks." Moving to the threshold of the hearth room, Musashi accepted a cup of the local brew and put it to his lips. It tasted sour. After downing it, he offered the cup to Baiken, saying, "Let me pour you a cup."

"Never mind, I have one." He looked at Musashi for an instant, then asked, "How old are you?"

"Twenty-two."

"Where do you come from?"

"Mimasaka."

Baiken's eyes, which had wandered off in another direction, swung back to Musashi, reexamining him from head to toe.

"Let's see, you mentioned it a while ago. Your name—what's your name?"

"Miyamoto Musashi."

"How do you write Musashi?"

"It's written the same way as Takezō."

The wife came in and put soup, pickles, chopsticks and a bowl of rice on the straw mat before Musashi. "Eat!" she said unceremoniously.

"Thanks," replied Musashi.

Baiken waited a couple of breaths, then said, as though to himself, "It's hot now—the sake." Pouring Musashi another cup, he asked in an offhand manner, "Does that mean you were called Takezō when you were younger?"

"Yes."

"Were you still called that when you were seventeen or so?"

"Yes."

"When you were about that age, you weren't by any chance at the Battle of Sekigahara with another boy about your age, were you?"

It was Musashi's turn to be surprised. "How did you know?" he said slowly.

"Oh, I know a lot of things. I was at Sekigahara too."

Hearing this, Musashi felt better disposed toward the man; Baiken, too, seemed suddenly more friendly.

"I thought I'd seen you somewhere," said the blacksmith. "I guess we must have met on the battlefield."

"Were you in the Ukita camp too?"

"I was living in Yasugawa then, and I went to the war with a group of samurai from there. We were in the front lines, we were."

"Is that so? I guess we probably saw each other then."

"Whatever happened to your friend?"

"I haven't seen him since."

"Since the battle?"

"Not exactly. We stayed for a time at a house in Ibuki, waiting for my wounds to heal. We, uh, parted there. That was the last I saw of him."

Baiken let his wife know they were out of sake. She was already in bed with the baby. "There isn't any more," she answered.

"I want some more. Now!"

"Why do you have to drink so much tonight, of all nights?"

"We're having an interesting little talk here. Need some more sake."

"But there isn't any."

"Iwa!" he called through the flimsy board wall in a corner of the smithy.

"What is it, sir?" said the boy. He pushed open the door and showed his face, stooping because the lintel was so low.

"Go over to Onosaku's house and borrow a bottle of sake."

Musashi had had enough to drink. "If you don't mind, I'll go ahead and eat," he said, picking up his chopsticks.

"No, no, wait," said Baiken, quickly grabbing Musashi's wrist. "It's not time to eat. Now that I've sent for some sake, have a little more."

"If you were getting it for me, you shouldn't have. I don't think I can drink another drop."

"Aw, come now," Baiken insisted. "You said you wanted to hear more about the chain-ball-sickle. I'll tell you everything I know, but let's have a few drinks while we're talking."

When Iwa returned with the sake, Baiken poured some into a heating jar, put it on the fire, and talked at great length about the chain-ball-sickle and ways to use it to advantage in actual combat. The best thing about it, he told Musashi, was that, unlike a sword, it gave the enemy no time to defend himself. Also, before attacking the enemy directly, it was possible to snatch his weapon away from him with the chain. A skillful throw of the chain, a sharp yank, and the enemy had no more sword.

Still seated, Baiken demonstrated a stance. "You see, you hold the sickle in your left hand and the ball in your right. If the enemy comes at you, you take him on with the blade, then hurl the ball at his face. That's one way."

Changing positions, he went on, "Now, in this case, when there's some space between you and the enemy, you take his weapon away with the chain. It doesn't make any difference what kind of weapon it is—sword, lance, wooden staff, or whatever."

Baiken went on and on, telling Musashi about ways of throwing the ball, about the ten or more oral traditions concerning the weapon, about how the chain was like a snake, about how it was possible by cleverly alternating the movements of the chain and the sickle to create optical illusions and cause the enemy's defense to work to his own detriment, about all the secret ways of using the weapon.

Musashi was fascinated. When he heard talk like this, he listened with his whole body, eager to absorb every detail.

The chain. The sickle. Two hands . . .

As he listened, the seeds of other thoughts formed in his mind. "The sword can be used with one hand, but a man has two hands. . . ."

The second bottle of sake was empty. While Baiken had drunk a good deal, he pressed even more on Musashi, who had far surpassed his limit and was drunker than he ever had been before.

"Wake up!" Baiken called to his wife. "Let our guest sleep there. You and I can sleep in the back room. Go spread some bedding."

The woman did not budge.

"Get up!" Baiken said more loudly. "Our guest is tired. Let him go to bed now."

His wife's feet were nice and warm now; getting up would be uncomfortable. "You said he could sleep in the smithy with Iwa," she mumbled.

"Enough of your back talk. Do as I say!"

She got up in a huff and stalked off to the back room. Baiken took the sleeping baby in his arms and said, "The quilts are old, but the fire's right here beside you. If you get thirsty, there's hot water on it for tea. Go to bed. Make yourself comfortable." He, too, went into the back room.

When the woman came back to exchange pillows, the sullenness was gone from her face. "My husband's very drunk too," she said, "and he's probably tired from his trip. He says he plans to sleep late, so make yourself comfortable and sleep as long as you want. Tomorrow I'll give you a nice hot breakfast."

"Thanks." Musashi could think of nothing more to say. He could hardly wait to get out of his leather socks and cloak. "Thanks a lot."

He dived into the still warm quilts, but his own body was even hotter from drink.

The wife stood in the doorway watching him, then quietly blew out the candle and said, "Good night."

Musashi's head felt as if it had a tight steel band around it; his temples throbbed painfully. He wondered why he had drunk so much more than usual. He felt awful, but couldn't help thinking about Baiken. Why had the blacksmith, who had seemed hardly civil at first, suddenly grown friendly and sent out for more sake? Why had his disagreeable wife become sweet and solicitous all of a sudden? Why had they given him this warm bed?

It all seemed inexplicable, but before Musashi had solved the mystery, drowsiness overcame him. He closed his eyes, took a few deep breaths, and pulled the covers up. Only his forehead remained exposed, lit up by occasional sparks from the hearth. By and by, there was the sound of deep, steady breathing.

Baiken's wife retreated stealthily into the back room, the pit-a-pat of her feet moving stickily across the tatami.

Musashi had a dream, or rather the fragment of one, which kept repeating itself. A childhood memory flitted about his sleeping brain like an insect, trying, it seemed, to write something in luminescent letters. He heard the words of a lullaby.

> Go to sleep, go to sleep.
> Sleeping babies are sweet. . . .

He was back home in Mimasaka, hearing the lullaby the blacksmith's wife had sung in the Ise dialect. He was a baby in the arms of a light-skinned woman of about thirty . . . his mother. . . . This woman must be his mother. At his mother's breast, he looked up at her white face.

". . . naughty, and they make their mothers cry too. . . ." Cradling him in her arms, his mother sang softly. Her thin, well-bred face looked faintly bluish, like a pear blossom. There was a wall, a long stone wall, on which there was liverwort. And a dirt wall, above which branches darkened in the approaching night. Light from a lamp streamed from the house. Tears glistened on his mother's cheeks. The baby looked in wonder at the tears.

"Go away! Go back to your home!"

It was the forbidding voice of Munisai, coming from inside the house. And it was a command. Musashi's mother arose slowly. She ran along a long stone embankment. Weeping, she ran into the river and waded toward the center.

Unable to talk, the baby squirmed in his mother's arms, tried to tell her there was danger ahead. The more he fretted, the more tightly she held him. Her moistened cheek rubbed against his. "Takezō," she said, "are you your father's child, or your mother's?"

Munisai shouted from the bank. His mother sank beneath the water. The baby was cast up on the pebbly bank, where he lay wailing at the top of his lungs amid blooming primroses.

Musashi opened his eyes. When he started to doze off again, a woman—his mother? someone else?—intruded into his dream and woke him again. Musashi could not remember his mother's appearance. He thought of her often, but he couldn't have drawn her face. Whenever he saw another mother, he thought perhaps his own mother had looked the same.

"Why tonight?" he thought.

The sake had worn off. He opened his eyes and gazed at the ceiling. Amid the blackness of the soot was a reddish light, the reflection from the embers in the hearth. His gaze came to rest on the pinwheel suspended from the ceiling above him. He noticed, too, that the smell of mother and child still clung to the bedcovers. With a vague feeling of nostalgia, he lay half asleep, staring at the pinwheel.

The pinwheel started slowly to revolve. There was nothing strange about this; it was made to turn. But . . . but not unless there was a breeze! Musashi started to get up, then stopped and listened closely. There was the sound of a door being slid quietly shut. The pinwheel stopped turning.

Musashi quietly put his head back on the pillow and tried to fathom what was going on in the house. He was like an insect under a leaf, attempting to divine the weather above. His whole body was attuned to the slightest change in his surroundings, his sensitive nerves absolutely taut. Musashi knew that his life was in danger, but why?

"Is it a den of robbers?" he asked himself at first, but no. If they were professional thieves, they'd know he had nothing worth stealing.

"Has he got a grudge against me?" That did not seem to work either. Musashi was quite sure he had never even seen Baiken before.

Without being able to figure out a motive, he could feel in his skin and bones that someone or something was threatening his very life. He also knew that whatever it was was very near; he had to decide quickly whether to lie and wait for it to come, or get out of the way ahead of time.

Slipping his hand over the threshold into the smithy, he groped for his sandals. He slipped first one, then the other, under the cover and down to the foot of the bedding.

The pinwheel started to whirl again. In the light of the fire, it turned like a bewitched flower. Footsteps were faintly audible both inside and outside the house, as Musashi quietly wadded the bedding together into the rough shape of a human body.

Under the short curtain hanging in the doorway appeared two eyes, belonging to a man crawling in with his sword unsheathed. Another, carrying a lance and clinging closely to the wall, crept around to the foot of the bed. The two stared at the bedclothes, listening for the sleeper's breathing. Then, like a cloud of smoke, a third man jumped forward. It was Baiken, holding the sickle in his left hand and the ball in his right.

The men's eyes met and they synchronized their breathing. The man at the head of the bed kicked the pillow into the air, and the man at the foot, jumping down into the smithy, aimed his lance at the reclining form.

Keeping the sickle behind him, Baiken shouted, "Up, Musashi!"

Neither answer nor movement came from the bedding.

The man with the lance threw back the covers. "He's not here!" he shouted.

Baiken, casting a confused look around the room, caught sight of the rapidly whirling pinwheel. "There's a door open somewhere!" he shouted.

Soon another man cried out angrily. The door from the smithy onto a path that went around to the back of the house was open about three feet, and a biting wind was blowing in.

"He got out through here!"

"What are those fools doing?" Baiken screamed, running outside. From under the eaves and out of the shadows, black forms came forward.

"Master! Did it go all right?" asked a low voice excitedly.

Baiken glowered with rage. "What do you mean, you idiot? Why do you think I put you out here to keep watch? He's gone! He must have come this way."

"Gone? How could he get out?"

"You're asking me? You thick-headed ass!" Baiken went back inside and stamped around nervously. "There are only two ways he could have gone: he either went up to Suzuka ford or back to the Tsu highway. Whichever it was, he couldn't have gone far. Go get him!"

"Which way do you think he went?"

"Ugh! I'll go toward Suzuka. You cover the lower road!"

The men inside joined forces with the men outside, making a motley group of about ten, all armed. One of them, carrying a musket, looked like a hunter; another, with a short field sword, was probably a woodcutter.

As they parted, Baiken shouted, "If you find him, fire the gun, then everybody come together."

They set off at great speed, but after about an hour came straggling back, looking hangdog and talking dejectedly among themselves. They expected a tongue-lashing from their leader, but when they reached the house, they found Baiken sitting on the ground in the smithy, eyes downcast and expressionless.

When they tried to cheer him up, he said, "No use crying about it now." Searching about for a way to vent his wrath, he seized a piece of charred wood and broke it sharply over his knee.

"Bring some sake! I want a drink." He stirred up the fire again and threw on more kindling.

Baiken's wife, trying to quiet the baby, reminded him there was no more sake. One of the men volunteered to bring some from his house, which he did with dispatch. Soon the brew was warm, and the cups were being passed around.

The conversation was sporadic and gloomy.

"It makes me mad."

"The rotten little bastard!"

"He leads a charmed life. I'll say that for him."

"Don't worry about it, master. You did everything you could. The men outside fell down on their job."

Those referred to apologized shamefacedly.

They tried to get Baiken drunk, so he would go to sleep, but he just sat there, frowning at the bitterness of the sake, but taking no one to task for the failure.

Finally, he said, "I shouldn't have made such a big thing out of it, getting so many of you to help. I could have handled him all by myself, but I thought I'd better be careful. After all, he did kill my brother, and Tsujikaze Temma was no mean fighter."

"Could that rōnin really be the boy who was hiding in Okō's house four years ago?"

"He must be. My dead brother's spirit brought him here, I'm sure. At first the thought never crossed my mind, but then he told me he'd been at Sekigahara, and his name used to be Takezō. He's the right age and the right type of person to have killed my brother. I know it was him."

320

"Come on, master, don't think about it anymore tonight. Lie down. Get some sleep."

They all helped him to bed; someone picked up the pillow that had been kicked aside and put it under his head. The instant Baiken's eyes were closed, the anger that had filled him was replaced by loud snoring.

The men nodded to each other and drifted off, dispersing into the mist of early morning. They were all riffraff—underlings of freebooters like Tsujikaze Temma of Ibuki and Tsujikaze Kōhei of Yasugawa, who now called himself Shishido Baiken. Or else they were hangers-on at the bottom of the ladder in open society. Driven by the changing times, they had become farmers or artisans or hunters, but they still had teeth, which were only too ready to bite honest people when the opportunity arose.

The only sounds in the house were those made by the sleeping inhabitants and the gnawing of a field rat.

In the corner of the passageway connecting the workroom and kitchen, next to a large earthen oven, stood a stack of firewood. Above this hung an umbrella and heavy straw rain capes. In the shadows between the oven and the wall, one of the rain capes moved, slowly and quietly inching up the wall until it hung on a nail.

The smoky figure of a man suddenly seemed to come out of the wall itself. Musashi had never gone a step away from the house. After slipping out from under the covers, he had opened the outer door and then merged with the firewood, drawing the rain cape down over him.

He walked silently across the smithy and looked at Baiken. Adenoids, thought Musashi, for the snoring was thunderous. The situation struck him as humorous, and his face twisted into a grin.

He stood there for a moment, thinking. To all intents and purposes, he had won his bout with Baiken. It had been a clear-cut victory. Still, this man lying here was the brother of Tsujikaze Temma and had tried to murder him to comfort the spirit of his dead brother—an admirable sentiment for a mere freebooter.

Should Musashi kill him? If he left him alive, he would go on looking for an opportunity to take his revenge, and the safe course was doubtless to do away with him here and now. But there remained the question of whether he was worth killing.

Musashi pondered for a time, before hitting on what seemed exactly the right solution. Going to the wall by Baiken's feet, he took down one of the blacksmith's own weapons. While he eased the blade from its groove, he examined the sleeping face. Then, wrapping a piece of damp paper around the blade, he carefully laid it across Baiken's neck; he stepped back and admired his handiwork.

The pinwheel was sleeping too. If it were not for the paper wrapping, thought Musashi, the wheel might wake in the morning and turn wildly at the sight of its master's head fallen from the pillow.

When Musashi had killed Tsujikaze Temma, he had had a reason, and anyway, he had still been burning with the fever of battle. But he had nothing to

321

gain from taking the blacksmith's life. And who could tell? If he did kill him, the infant owner of the pinwheel might spend his life seeking to avenge his father's murder.

It was a night on which Musashi had thought time and again of his own father and mother. He felt a little envious as he stood here by this sleeping family, sensing the faint sweet scent of mother's milk about him. He even felt a little reluctant to take his leave.

In his heart, he spoke to them: "I'm sorry to have troubled you. Sleep well." He quietly opened the outer door and went out.

The Flying Horse

Otsū and Jōtarō arrived at the barrier late at night, stopped over at an inn and resumed their journey before the morning mist cleared. From Mount Fudesute, they walked to Yonkenjaya, where they first felt the warmth of the rising sun on their backs.

"How beautiful!" exclaimed Otsū, pausing to look at the great golden orb. She seemed full of hope and cheer. It was one of those wonderful moments when all living things, even plants and animals, must feel satisfaction and pride in their existence here on earth.

Jōtarō said with obvious pleasure, "We're the very first people on the road. Not a soul ahead of us."

"You sound boastful. What difference does it make?"

"It makes a lot of difference to me."

"Do you think it'll make the road shorter?"

"Oh, it's not that. It's just feels good to be first, even on the road. You have to admit it's better than following along behind palanquins or horses."

"That's true."

"When no one else is on the road I'm on, I have the feeling it belongs to me."

"In that case, why don't you pretend you're a great samurai on horseback, surveying your vast estates. I'll be your attendant." She picked up a bamboo stick, and waving it ceremoniously, called out in singsong fashion, "Bow down, all! Bow down for his lordship!"

A man looked out inquiringly from under the eaves of a teahouse. Caught playing like a child, she blushed and walked rapidly on.

"You can't do that," Jōtarō protested. "You mustn't run away from your master. If you do, I'll have to put you to death!"

"I don't want to play anymore."

"You're the one who was playing, not me."

"Yes, but you started it. Oh, my! The man at the teahouse is still staring at us. He must think we're silly."

"Let's go back there."

"What for?"

"I'm hungry."

"Already?"

"Couldn't we eat half of the rice balls we brought for lunch now?"

"Be patient. We haven't covered two miles yet. If I let you, you'd eat five meals a day."

"Maybe. But you don't see me riding in palanquins or hiring horses, the way you do."

"That was only last night, and then only because it was getting dark and we had to hurry. If you feel that way about it, I'll walk the whole way today."

"It should be my turn to ride today."

"Children don't need to ride."

"But I want to try riding a horse. Can't I? Please."

"Well, maybe, but only for today."

"I saw a horse tied up at the teahouse. We could hire it."

"No, it's still too early in the day."

"Then you didn't mean it when you said I could ride!"

"I did, but you're not even tired yet. It'd be a waste of money to rent a horse."

"You know perfectly well I never get tired. I wouldn't get tired if we walked a hundred days and a thousand miles. If I have to wait till I'm worn out, I'll never get to ride a horse. Come on, Otsū, let's rent the horse now, while there aren't any people ahead of us. It'd be a lot safer than when the road is crowded. Please!"

Seeing that if they kept this up, they would lose the time they had gained by making an early start, Otsū gave in, and Jōtarō, sensing rather than waiting for her nod of approval, raced back to the teahouse.

Although there actually were four teahouses in the vicinity, as the name Yonkenjaya indicated, they were located at various places on the slopes of mounts Fudesute and Kutsukake. The one they had passed was the only one in sight.

Running up to the proprietor and stopping suddenly, Jōtarō shouted, "Hey, there, I want a horse! Get one out for me."

The old man was taking down the shutters, and the boy's lusty cry jarred him into wakefulness. With a sour expression, he grumbled, "What's all this! Do you have to yell so loud?"

"I need a horse. Please get one ready right away. How much is it to Minakuchi? If it's not too much, I may even take it all the way to Kusatsu."

"Whose little boy are you anyway?"

"I'm the son of my mother and my father," replied Jōtarō impudently.

"I thought you might be the unruly offspring of the storm god."

"You're the storm god, aren't you? You look mad as a thunderbolt."

"Brat!"

"Just bring me the horse."

"I daresay you think that horse is for hire. Well, it isn't. So I fear I shall not have the honor of lending it to your lordship."

Matching the man's tone of voice, Jōtarō said, "Then, sir, shall I not have the pleasure of renting it?"

"Sassy, aren't you?" cried the man, taking a piece of lighted kindling from the fire under his oven and throwing it at the boy. The flaming stick missed Jōtarō, but struck the ancient horse tied under the eaves. With an air-splitting whinny, she reared, striking her back against a beam.

"You bastard!" screamed the proprietor. He leapt out of the shop sputtering curses and ran up to the animal.

As he untied the rope and led the horse around to the side yard, Jōtarō started in again. "Please lend her to me."

"I can't."

"Why not?"

"I don't have a groom to send with her."

Now at Jōtarō's side, Otsū suggested that if there was no groom, she could pay the fee in advance and send the horse back from Minakuchi with a traveler coming this way. Her appealing manner softened the old man, and he decided he could trust her. Handing her the rope, he said, "In that case, you can take her to Minakuchi, or even to Kusatsu if you want. All I ask is that you send her back."

As they started away, Jōtarō, in high dudgeon, exclaimed, "How do you like that! He treated me like an ass, and then as soon as he saw a pretty face . . . "

"You'd better be careful what you say about the old man. His horse is listening. She may get angry and throw you."

"Do you think this feeble-jointed old nag can get the best of me?"

"You don't know how to ride, do you?"

"Of course I know how to ride."

"What are you doing, then, trying to climb up from behind?"

"Well, help me up!"

"You're a nuisance!" She put her hands under his armpits and lifted him onto the animal.

Jōtarō looked majestically around at the world beneath him. "Please walk ahead, Otsū," he said.

"You're not sitting right."

"Don't worry. I'm fine."

"All right, but you're going to be sorry." Taking the rope in one hand, Otsū waved good-bye to the proprietor with the other, and the two started off.

Before they had gone a hundred paces, they heard a loud shout coming out of the mist behind them, accompanied by the sound of running footsteps.

"Who could that be?" asked Jōtarō.

"Is he calling us?" wondered Otsū.

They stopped the horse and looked around. The shadow of a man began to take form in the white, smoky mist. At first they could make out only contours, then colors, but the man was soon close enough for them to discern his general appearance and approximate age. A diabolic aura surrounded his body, as though he were accompanied by a raging whirlwind. He came rapidly to Otsū's side, halted and with one swift motion snatched the rope from her hand.

"Get off!" he commanded, glaring up at Jōtarō.

The horse skittered backward. Clutching her mane, Jōtarō shouted, "You can't do this! I rented this horse, not you!"

The man snorted, turned to Otsū and said, "You, woman!"

"Yes?" Otsū said in a low voice.

"My name's Shishido Baiken. I live in Ujii Village up in the mountains beyond the barrier. For reasons I won't go into, I'm after a man named Miyamoto Musashi. He came along this road sometime before daybreak this morning. Probably passed here hours ago, so I've got to move fast if I'm going to catch him in Yasugawa, on the Ōmi border. Let me have your horse." He talked very rapidly, his ribs heaving in and out. In the cold air, the mist was condensing into icy flowers on branches and twigs, but his neck glistened like a snakeskin with sweat.

Otsū stood very still, her face deathly white, as though the earth beneath her had drained all the blood from her body. Her lips quivering, she wanted desperately to ask and make sure that she had heard correctly. She couldn't utter a word.

"You said Musashi?" Jōtarō blurted out. He was still clutching the horse's mane, but his arms and legs were trembling.

Baiken was in too much of a hurry to notice their shocked reaction.

"Come on, now," he ordered. "Off the horse, and be quick about it, or I'll give you a thrashing." He brandished the end of the rope like a whip.

Jōtarō shook his head adamantly. "I won't."

"What do you mean, you won't?"

"It's my horse. You can't have it. I don't care how much of a hurry you're in."

"Watch it! I've been very nice and explained everything, because you're only a woman and a child traveling alone, but—"

"Isn't that right, Otsū?" Jōtarō interrupted. "We don't have to let him have the horse, do we?"

Otsū could have hugged the boy. As far as she was concerned, it was not so much a question of the horse as it was of preventing this monster from progressing any faster. "That's true," she said. "I'm sure you're in a hurry, sir, but so are we. You can hire one of the horses that travel up and down the mountain regularly. Just as the boy says, it's unfair to try to take our horse away from us."

"I won't get off," Jōtarō repeated. "I'll die before I do!"

"You've set your mind on not letting me have the horse?" Baiken asked gruffly.

"You should have known we wouldn't to begin with," replied Jōtarō gravely.

"Son of a bitch!" shouted Baiken, infuriated by the boy's tone.

325

Jōtarō, tightening his grip on the horse's mane, looked little bigger than a flea. Baiken reached up, took hold of his leg and started to pull him off. Now, of all times, was the moment for Jōtarō to put his wooden sword to use, but in his confusion he forgot all about the weapon. Faced with an enemy so much stronger than himself, the only defense that came to mind was to spit in Baiken's face, which he did, again and again.

Otsū was filled with grim terror. The fear of being injured, or killed, by this man brought an acid, dry taste to her mouth. But there was no question of giving in and letting him have the horse. Musashi was being pursued; the longer she could delay this fiend, the more time Musashi would have to flee. It didn't matter to her that the distance between him and herself would also be increased—just at a time when she knew at least that they were on the same road. Biting her lip, then screaming, "You can't do this!" she struck Baiken in the chest with a force that not even she realized she possessed.

Baiken, still wiping the spit off his face, was thrown off balance, and in that instant, Otsū's hand caught the hilt of his sword.

"Bitch!" he barked, grabbing for her wrist. Then he howled with pain, for the sword was already partly out of its scabbard, and instead of Otsū's arm, he'd squeezed his hand around the blade. The tips of two fingers on his right hand dropped to the ground. Holding his bleeding hand, he sprang back, unintentionally pulling the sword from its scabbard. The brilliant glitter of steel extending from Otsū's hand scratched across the ground, coming to rest behind her.

Baiken had blundered even worse than the night before. Cursing himself for his lack of caution, he struggled to regain his footing. Otsū, now afraid of nothing, swung the blade sidewise at him. But it was a great wide-bladed weapon, nearly three feet long, which not every man would have been able to handle easily. When Baiken dodged, her hands wobbled, and she staggered forward. She felt a quick wrenching of her wrists, and reddish-black blood spurted into her face. After a moment of dizziness, she realized the sword had cut into the rump of the horse.

The wound was not deep, but the horse let out a fearsome noise, rearing and kicking wildly. Baiken, yelling unintelligibly, got hold of Otsū's wrist and tried to recover his sword, but at that moment the horse kicked them both into the air. Then, rising on her hind legs, she whinnied loudly and shot off down the road like an arrow from a bow, Jōtarō clinging grimly to her back and blood spewing out behind.

Baiken stumbled around in the dust-laden air. He knew he couldn't catch the crazed beast, so his enraged eyes turned toward the place where Otsū had been. She wasn't there.

After a moment, he spotted his sword at the foot of a larch tree and with a lunge retrieved it. As he straightened up, something clicked in his mind: there must be some connection between this woman and Musashi! And if she was Musashi's friend, she would make excellent bait; at the very least she would know where he was going.

Half running, half sliding down the embankment next to the road, he strode around a thatched farmhouse, peering under the floor and into the storehouse, while an old woman stooped like a hunchback behind a spinning wheel inside the house looked on in terror.

Then he caught sight of Otsū racing through a thick grove of cryptomeria trees toward the valley beyond, where there were patches of late snow.

Thundering down the hill with the force of a landslide, he soon closed the distance between them.

"Bitch!" he cried, stretching out his left hand and touching her hair.

Otsū dropped to the ground and caught hold of the roots of a tree, but her foot slipped and her body fell over the edge of the cliff, where it swayed like a pendulum. Dirt and pebbles fell into her face as she looked up at Baiken's large eyes and his gleaming sword.

"Fool!" he said contemptuously. "Do you think you can get away now?"

Otsū glanced downward; fifty or sixty feet below, a stream cut through the floor of the valley. Curiously, she was not afraid, for she saw the valley as her salvation. At any moment she chose, she could escape simply by letting go of the tree and throwing herself on the mercy of the open space below. She felt death was near, but rather than dwell on that, her mind focused on a single image: Musashi. She seemed to see him now, his face like a full moon in a stormy sky.

Baiken quickly seized her wrists, and hoisting her up, dragged her well clear of the edge.

Just then, one of his henchmen called to him from the road. "What are you doing down there? We'd better move fast. The old man at the teahouse back there said a samurai woke him up before dawn this morning, ordered a box lunch, then ran off toward Kaga Valley."

"Kaga Valley?"

"That's what he said. But whether he goes that way or crosses Mount Tsuchi to Minakuchi doesn't matter. The roads come together at Ishibe. If we make good time to Yasugawa, we should be able to catch him there."

Baiken's back was turned to the man, his eyes fastened on Otsū, who crouched before him, seemingly trapped by his fierce glare. "Ho!" he roared. "All three of you come down here."

"Why?"

"Get down here, fast!"

"If we waste time, Musashi'll beat us to Yasugawa."

"Never mind that!"

The three men were among those who had been engaged in the fruitless search the night before. Used to making their way through the mountains, they stormed down the incline with the speed of so many boars. As they reached the ledge where Baiken was standing, they caught sight of Otsū. Their leader rapidly explained the situation to them.

"All right now, tie her up and bring her along," said Baiken, before darting off through the woods.

They tied her up, but they couldn't help feeling sorry for her. She lay helpless on the ground, face turned to the side; they stole embarrassed looks at her pale profile.

Baiken was already in Kaga Valley. He stopped, looked back at the cliff and 327 shouted, "We'll meet in Yasugawa. I'll take a shortcut, but you stay on the highway. And keep your eyes peeled."

"Yes, sir!" they chorused back.

Baiken, running between the rocks like a mountain goat, was soon out of sight.

Jōtarō was hurtling down the highroad. Despite her age, the horse was so maddened there was no stopping her with a mere rope, even if Jōtarō had known how to go about it. The raw wound burning like a torch, she sped blindly ahead, up hill, down dale, through villages.

It was only through sheer luck that Jōtarō avoided being thrown off. "Watch out! Watch out! *Watch out!*" he screamed repeatedly. The words had become a litany.

No longer able to stay on by clinging to the mane, he had his arms locked tightly around the horse's neck. His eyes were closed.

When the beast's rump rose in the air, so did Jōtarō's. As it became increasingly apparent that his shouts were not working, his pleas gradually gave way to a distressed wail. When he had begged Otsū to let him ride a horse just once, he had been thinking how grand it would be to go galloping about at will on a splendid steed, but after a few minutes of this hair-raising ride, he had had his fill.

Jōtarō hoped that someone—anyone—would bravely volunteer to seize the flying rope and bring the horse to a halt. In this he was overoptimistic, for neither travelers nor villagers wanted to risk being hurt in an affair that was no concern of theirs. Far from helping, everyone made for the safety of the roadside and shouted abuse at what appeared to them to be an irresponsible horseman.

In no time he'd passed the village of Mikumo and reached the inn town of Natsumi. If he had been an expert rider in perfect control of his mount, he could have shaded his eyes and calmly looked out over the beautiful mountains and valleys of Iga—the peaks of Nunobiki, the Yokota River and, in the distance, the mirrorlike waters of Lake Biwa.

"Stop! Stop! Stop!" The words of his litany had changed; his tone was more distraught. As they started down Kōji Hill, his cry abruptly changed again. "Help!" he screamed.

The horse charged on down the precipitous incline, Jōtarō bouncing like a ball on her back.

About a third of the way down, a large oak projected from a cliff on the left, one of its smaller branches extending across the road. When Jōtarō felt the leaves against his face, he grabbed with both hands, believing the gods had heard his prayer and caused the limb to stretch out before him. Perhaps he was right; he jumped like a frog, and the next instant he was hanging in the air, his hands firmly wrapped around the branch above his head. The horse went out from under him, moving a little faster now that she was riderless.

It was no more than a ten-foot drop to the ground, but Jōtarō could not bring himself to release his grip. In his badly shaken condition, he saw the

328

short distance to the ground as a yawning abyss and hung onto the branch for dear life, crossing his legs over it, readjusting his aching hands, and wondering feverishly what to do. The problem was solved for him when with a loud crack the branch broke off. For an awful instant, Jōtarō thought he was done for; a second later he was sitting on the ground unharmed.

"Whew!" was all he could say.

For a few minutes he sat inertly, his spirit dampened, if not broken, but then he remembered why he was there and jumped up.

Heedless of the ground he had covered, he shouted, "Otsū!"

He ran back up the slope, one hand firmly around his wooden sword.

"What could have happened to her? . . . Otsū! O-tsū-ū-ū!"

Presently he met a man in a grayish-red kimono coming down the hill. The stranger wore a leather *hakama* and carried two swords, but had on no cloak. After passing Jōtarō, he looked over his shoulder and said, "Hello, there!" Jōtarō turned, and the man asked, "Is something wrong?"

"You came from over the hill, didn't you?" Jōtarō asked.

"Yes."

"Did you see a pretty woman about twenty years old?"

"I did, as a matter of fact."

"Where?"

"In Natsumi I saw some freebooters walking along with a girl. Her arms were tied behind her, which naturally struck me as strange, but I had no reason to interfere. I daresay the men were from Tsujikaze Kōhei's gang. He moved a whole villageful of hoodlums from Yasugawa to Suzuka Valley some years ago."

"That was her, I'm sure." Jōtarō started to walk on, but the man stopped him.

"Were you traveling together?" he asked.

"Yes. Her name's Otsū."

"If you take foolish risks you'll get yourself killed before you can help anybody. Why don't you wait here? They'll come this way sooner or later. For now, tell me what this is all about. I may be able to give you some advice."

The boy immediately placed his trust in the man and told him everything that had happened since morning. From time to time, the man nodded under his basket hat. When the story ended, he said, "I understand your predicament, but even with your courage, a woman and a boy are no match for Kōhei's men. I think I'd better rescue Otsū—is that her name?—for you."

"Would they hand her over to you?"

"Maybe not for the mere asking, but I'll think about that when the time comes. Meanwhile, you hide in a thicket and stay quiet."

While Jōtarō selected a clump of bushes and hid behind it, the man continued briskly on down the hill. For a moment, Jōtarō wondered if he had been deceived. Had the rōnin just said a few words to cheer him up, then moved on to save his own neck? Seized by anxiety, he lifted his head above the shrubs, but hearing voices, ducked down again.

A minute or two later Otsū came into view, surrounded by the three men, her hands tied firmly behind her. Blood was encrusted on a cut on her white foot.

One of the ruffians, shoving Otsū forward by the shoulder, growled, "What are you looking around for? Walk faster!"

"That's right, walk!"

"I'm looking for my traveling companion. What could have happened to him? . . . Jōtarō!"

"Quiet!"

Jōtarō was all set to yell and jump out of his hiding place when the rōnin came back, this time without his basket hat. He was twenty-six or -seven and of a darkish complexion. In his eyes was a purposeful look that strayed neither right nor left. As he trotted up the incline, he was saying, as if to himself, "It's terrifying, really terrifying!"

When he passed Otsū and her captors, he mumbled a greeting and hastened on, but the men stopped. "Hey," one of them called. "Aren't you Watanabe's nephew? What's so terrifying?"

Watanabe was the name of an old family in the district, the present head of which was Watanabe Hanzō, a highly respected practitioner of the occult martial tactics known collectively as *ninjutsu*.

"Haven't you heard?"

"Heard what?"

"Down at the bottom of this hill there's a samurai named Miyamoto Musashi, all ready for a big fight. He's standing in the middle of the road with his sword unsheathed, questioning everybody who passes by. He has the fiercest eyes I ever saw."

"Musashi's doing that?"

"That's right. He came straight up to me and asked my name, so I told him that I was Tsuge Sannojō, the nephew of Watanabe Hanzō, and that I came from Iga. He apologized and let me by. He was very polite, in fact, said as long as I wasn't connected with Tsujikaze Kōhei, it was all right."

"Oh?"

"I asked him what had happened. He said Kōhei was on the road with his henchmen, out to catch him and kill him. He decided to entrench himself where he was and meet the attack there. He seemed prepared to fight to the finish."

"Are you telling the truth, Sannojō?"

"Of course I am. Why would I lie to you?"

The faces of the three grew pale. They looked at each other nervously, uncertain as to their next move.

"You'd better be careful," said Sannojō, ostensibly resuming his trip up the hill.

"Sannojō!"

"What?"

"I don't know what we should do. Even our boss said this Musashi is unusually strong."

"Well, he does seem to have a lot of confidence in himself. When he came up to me with that sword, I certainly didn't feel like taking him on."

"What do you think we should do? We're taking this woman to Yasugawa on the boss's orders."

"I don't see that that has anything to do with me."

"Don't be like that. Lend us a hand."

"Not on your life! If I helped you and my uncle found out about it, he'd disown me. I could, of course, give you a bit of advice."

"Well, speak up! What do you think we should do?"

"Um . . . For one thing, you could tie that woman up to a tree and leave her. That way, you could move faster."

"Anything else?"

"You shouldn't take this road. It's a little farther, but you could go up the valley road to Yasugawa and let people there know about all this. Then you could surround Musashi and gradually hem him in."

"That's not a bad idea."

"But be very, very careful. Musashi will be fighting for his life, and he'll take quite a few souls with him when he goes. You'd rather avoid that, wouldn't you?"

Quickly agreeing with Sannojō's suggestion, they dragged Otsū to a grove and tied her rope to a tree. Then they left but after a few minutes returned to tie a gag in her mouth.

"That should do it," said one.

"Let's get going."

They dived into the woods. Jōtarō, squatting behind his leafy screen, waited judiciously before raising his head for a look around. He saw no one—no travelers, no freebooters, no Sannojō.

"Otsū!" he called, prancing out of the thicket. Quickly finding her, he undid her bonds and took her hand. They ran to the road. "Let's get away from here!" he urged.

"What were you doing hiding in the bushes?"

"Never mind! Let's go!"

"Just a minute," said Otsū, stopping to pat her hair, straighten her collar and rearrange her obi.

Jōtarō clicked his tongue. "This is no time for primping," he wailed. "Can't you fix your hair later?"

"But that rōnin said Musashi was at the bottom of the hill."

"Is that why you have to stop and make yourself pretty?"

"No, of course not," said Otsū, defending herself with almost comic seriousness. "But if Musashi is so near, we don't have anything to worry about. And since our troubles are as good as over, I feel calm and safe enough to think of my appearance."

"Do you believe that rōnin really saw Musashi?"

"Of course. By the way, where is he?"

"He just disappeared. He's sort of strange, isn't he?"

"Shall we go now?" said Otsū.

"Sure you're pretty enough?"

"Jōtarō!"

"Just teasing. You look so happy."

"You look happy too."

"I am, and I don't try to hide it the way you do. I'll shout it so everybody can hear: *I'm happy!*" He did a little dance, waving his arms and kicking his legs, then said, "It'll be very disappointing if Musashi isn't there, won't it? I think I'll run on ahead and see."

Otsū took her time. Her heart had already flown to the bottom of the slope faster than Jōtarō could ever have run.

"I look frightful," she thought as she surveyed her injured foot and the dirt and leaves stuck to her sleeves.

"Come on!" called Jōtarō. "Why are you poking along?" From the lilt in his voice, Otsū felt certain that he had spotted Musashi.

"At last," she thought. Until now she'd had to seek comfort within herself, and she was tired of it. She felt a measure of pride, both in herself and toward the gods, for having remained true to her purpose. Now that she was about to see Musashi again, her spirit was dancing with joy. This elation, she knew, was that of anticipation; she could not predict whether Musashi would accept her devotion. Her joy at the prospect of meeting him was only slightly tarnished by a gnawing premonition that the encounter might bring sadness.

On the shady slope of Kōji Hill, the ground was frozen, but at the tea shop near the bottom, it was so warm flies were flying around. This was an inn town, so of course the shop sold tea to travelers; it also carried a line of miscellaneous goods required by the farmers of the district, from cheap sweets to straw boots for oxen. Jōtarō stood in front of the shop, a small boy in a large and noisy crowd.

"Where's Musashi?" She looked around searchingly.

"He's not here," replied Jōtarō dispiritedly.

"Not here? He must be!"

"Well, I can't find him anywhere, and the shopkeeper said he hasn't seen a samurai like that around. There must have been some mistake." Jōtarō, though disappointed, was not despondent.

Otsū would have readily admitted that she had had no reason on earth to expect as much as she had, but the nonchalance of Jōtarō's reply annoyed her. Shocked and a little angry at his lack of concern, she said, "Did you look for him over there?"

"Yes."

"How about behind the Kōshin milepost?"

"I looked. He's not there."

"Behind the tea shop?"

"I told you, he isn't here!" Otsū turned her face away from him. "Are you crying?" he asked.

"It's none of your business," she said sharply.

"I don't understand you. You seem to be sensible most of the time, but sometimes you act like a baby. How could we know if Sannojō's story was true or not? You decided all by yourself that it was, and now that you find it wasn't, you burst into tears. Women are crazy," Jōtarō exclaimed, bursting into laughter.

Otsū felt like sitting down right there and giving up. In an instant, the light had gone out of her life; she felt as bereft of hope as before—no, more so. The decaying milk teeth in Jōtarō's laughing mouth disgusted her. Angrily she asked herself why she had to drag a child like this around with her anyway. The urge swept over her to abandon him right there.

True, he was also searching for Musashi, but he loved him only as a teacher. To her, Musashi was life itself. Jōtarō could laugh everything off and return to his normal cheerful self in no time, but Otsū would for days be deprived of the energy to go on. Somewhere in Jōtarō's youthful mind, there was the blithe certainty that one day, sooner or later, he'd find Musashi again. Otsū had no such belief in a happy ending. Having been too optimistic about seeing Musashi today, she was now swinging toward the opposite extreme, asking herself if life would go on like this forever, without her ever again seeing or talking to the man she loved.

Those who love seek a philosophy and, because of this, are fond of solitude. In Otsū's case, orphan that she was, there was also the keen sense of isolation from others. In response to Jōtarō's indifference, she frowned and marched silently away from the tea shop.

"Otsū!" The voice was Sannojō's. He emerged from behind the Kōshin milepost and came toward her through the withered underbrush. His scabbards were damp.

"You weren't telling the truth," Jōtarō said accusingly.

"What do you mean?"

"You said Musashi was waiting at the bottom of the hill. You lied!"

"Don't be stupid!" said Sannojō reproachfully. "It was because of that lie that Otsū was able to escape, wasn't it? What are you complaining about? Shouldn't you be thanking me?"

"You just made up that story to fool those men?"

"Of course."

Turning triumphantly to Otsū, Jōtarō said, "See? Didn't I tell you?"

Otsū felt she had a perfect right to be angry with Jōtarō, but there was no reason to nurse a grudge against Sannojō. She bowed to him several times and thanked him profusely for having saved her.

"Those hoodlums from Suzuka are a lot tamer than they used to be," said Sannojō, "but if they're out to waylay somebody, he's not likely to get over this road safely. Still, from what I hear about this Musashi you're so worried about, it sounds to me like he's too smart to stumble into one of their traps."

"Are there other roads besides this one to Ōmi?" asked Otsū.

"There are," replied Sannojō, raising his eyes toward the mountain peaks sparkling dazzlingly in the midday sun. "If you go to Iga Valley, there's a road to Ueno, and from Ano Valley there's one that goes to Yokkaichi and Kuwana. There must be three or four other mountain paths and shortcuts. My guess is, Musashi left the highroad early on."

"Then you think he's still safe?"

333

"Most likely. At least, safer than the two of you. You've been rescued once today, but if you stay on this highway, Tsujikaze's men will catch you again at Yasugawa. If you can stand a rather steep climb, come with me, and I'll show you a path practically nobody knows."

They quickly assented. Sannojō guided them up above Kaga Village to Makado Pass, from which a path led down to Seto in Ōtsu.

After explaining in detail how to proceed, he said, "You're out of harm's way now. Just keep your eyes and ears open, and be sure to find a safe place to stay before dark."

Otsū thanked him for all he had done and started to leave, but Sannojō stared at her and said, "We're parting now, you know." The words seemed fraught with meaning, and there was a rather hurt look in his eyes. "All along," he continued, "I've been thinking, 'Is she going to ask now?' but you never did ask."

"Ask what?"

"My name."

"But I heard your name when we were on Kōji Hill."

"Do you remember it?"

"Of course. You're Tsuge Sannojō, and you're the nephew of Watanabe Hanzō."

"Thank you. I don't ask you to be eternally grateful to me or anything like that, but I do hope you'll always remember me."

"Why, I'm deeply indebted to you."

"That's not what I mean. What I want to say is, well, I'm still not married. If my uncle weren't so strict, I'd like to take you to my home right now.... But I can see you're in a hurry. Anyway, you'll find a small inn a few miles ahead where you can stay overnight. I know the innkeeper very well, so mention my name to him. Farewell!"

After he was gone, a strange feeling came over Otsū. From the outset, she had not been able to figure out what sort of person Sannojō was, and when they had parted, she felt as though she had escaped from the clutches of a dangerous animal. She had gone through the motions of thanking him; she did not really feel grateful in her heart.

Jōtarō, in spite of his tendency to take to strangers, reacted in much the same way. As they started down from the pass, he said, "I don't like that man."

Otsū did not want to speak badly of Sannojō behind his back, but she admitted she did not like him either, adding, "What do you suppose he meant by telling me that he was still single."

"Oh, he's hinting that one day he's going to ask you to marry him."

"Why, that's absurd!"

The two made their way to Kyoto without incident, albeit disappointed at not finding Musashi at any of the places where they had hoped to—neither on the lakeside in Ōmi nor at the Kara Bridge in Seta nor at the barrier in Osaka.

From Keage, they plunged into the year-end crowds near the Sanjō Avenue entrance to the city. In the capital, the housefronts were adorned with the pine-branch decorations traditional during the New Year's season. The sight of the decorations cheered Otsū, who, instead of lamenting the lost chances of the past, resolved to look forward to the future and the opportunities it held for finding Musashi. The Great Bridge at Gojō Avenue. The first day of the New Year. If he did not show up that morning, then the second, or the third ... He had said he would certainly be there, as she had learned from Jōtarō. Even though he wasn't coming to meet her, just to be able to see him and talk to him again would be enough.

The possibility that she might run into Matahachi was the darkest cloud shadowing her dream. According to Jōtarō, Musashi's message had been delivered only to Akemi; Matahachi might never have received it. Otsū prayed that he hadn't, that Musashi would come, but not Matahachi.

Otsū slowed her steps, thinking Musashi might be in the very crowd they were in. Then a chill ran up her spine and she started walking faster. Matahachi's dreadful mother might also materialize at any moment.

Jōtarō hadn't a care in the world. The colors and noises of the city, seen and heard after a long absence, exhilarated him no end. "Are we going straight to an inn?" he asked apprehensively.

"No, not yet."

"Good! It'd be dull being indoors while it's still light out. Let's walk around some more. It looks like there's a market over there."

"We haven't time to go to the market. We have important business to take care of."

"Business? We do?"

"Have you forgotten the box you're carrying on your back?"

"Oh, that."

"Yes, that. I won't be able to relax until we've found Lord Karasumaru Mitsuhiro's mansion and delivered the scrolls to him."

"Are we going to stay at his house tonight?"

"Of course not." Otsū laughed, glancing toward the Kamo River. "Do you think a great nobleman like that would let a dirty little boy like you sleep under his roof, lice and all?"

The Butterfly in Winter

Akemi slipped out of the inn at Sumiyoshi without telling anybody. She felt like a bird freed from its cage but was still not sufficiently recovered from her brush with death to fly too high. The scars left by Seijūrō's violence would not heal quickly; he had shattered her cherished dream of giving herself unblemished to the man she really loved.

On the boat up the Yodo to Kyoto, she felt that all the waters of the river would not equal the tears she wanted to shed. As other boats, loaded with ornaments and supplies for the New Year celebration, rowed busily past, she stared at them and thought: "Now, even if I do find Musashi . . ." Her troubled eyes filled and overflowed. No one could ever know how eagerly she had anticipated the New Year's morning when she would find him on the Great Bridge at Gojō Avenue.

Her longing for Musashi had grown deeper and stronger. The thread of love had lengthened, and she had wound it up into a ball inside her breast. Through all the years, she had gone on spinning the thread from distant memories and bits of hearsay and winding it around the ball to make it larger and larger. Until only a few days earlier, she had treasured her girlish sentiments and carried them with her like a fresh wild flower from the slopes of Mount Ibuki; now the blossom inside her was crushed. Though it was unlikely anyone was aware of what had occurred, she imagined everybody was looking at her with knowing eyes.

In Kyoto, in the fading light of evening, Akemi walked among the leafless willows and miniature pagodas in Teramachi, near Gojō Avenue, looking as cold and forlorn as a butterfly in winter.

"Hey, beautiful!" said a man. "Your obi cord is loose. Don't you want me to tie it for you?" He was thin, shabbily clothed and uncouth of speech, but he wore the two swords of a samurai.

Akemi had never seen him before, but habitués of the drinking places nearby could have told her that his name was Akakabe Yasoma, and that he hung around the back streets on winter nights doing nothing. His worn straw sandals flapped as he ran up behind Akemi and picked up the loose end of obi cord.

"What are you doing all by yourself in this deserted place? I don't suppose you're one of those madwomen who appear in the *kyōgen* plays, are you? You've got a pretty face. Why don't you fix your hair up a little and stroll about like the other girls?" Akemi walked on, pretending to have no ears, but Yasoma mistook this for shyness. "You look like a city girl. What did you do? Run away from home? Or do you have a husband you're trying to escape from?"

Akemi made no reply.

"You should be careful, a pretty girl like you, wandering around in a daze, looking as though you're in trouble or something. You can't tell what might happen. We don't have the kind of thieves and ruffians who used to hang out around Rashōmon, but there are plenty of freebooters, and their mouths water at the sight of a woman. And vagrants too, and people who buy and sell women."

Although Akemi said not a word, Yasoma persisted, answering his own questions when necessary.

"It's really quite dangerous. They say women from Kyoto are being sold for very high prices in Edo now. A long time ago, they used to take women from here up to Hiraizumi in the northeast, but now it's Edo. That's because the second shōgun, Hidetada, is building up the city as fast as he can. The brothels in Kyoto are all opening up branches there now."

Akemi said nothing.

"You'd stand out anywhere, so you should be careful. If you don't watch out, you might get involved with some scoundrel. It's terribly dangerous!"

Akemi had had enough. Throwing her sleeves up on her shoulders in anger, she turned and hissed loudly at him.

Yasoma just laughed. "You know," he said, "I think you really are crazy."

"Shut up and go away!"

"Well, aren't you?"

"You're the crazy one!"

"Ha, ha, ha! That as much as proves it. You're crazy. I feel sorry for you."

"If you don't get out of here, I'll throw a rock at you!"

"Aw, you don't want to do that, do you?"

"Go away, you beast!" The proud front she was putting up masked the terror she actually felt. She screamed at Yasoma and ran into a field of miscanthus, where once had stood Lord Komatsu's mansion and its garden filled with stone lanterns. She seemed to swim through the swaying plants.

"Wait!" cried Yasoma, going after her like a hunting dog.

Above Toribe Hill rose the evening moon, looking like the wild grin of a she-demon.

There was no one in the immediate vicinity. The nearest people were about three hundred yards away, in a group slowly descending a hill, but they wouldn't have come to her rescue even if they had heard her shouts, for they were returning from a funeral. Clad in formal white clothing and hats tied with white ribbons, they carried their prayer beads in their hands; a few of them were still weeping.

Suddenly Akemi, pushed sharply from behind, stumbled and fell.

"Oh, I'm sorry," said Yasoma. He fell on top of her, apologizing all the while. "Did it hurt?" he asked solicitously, hugging her to him.

337

Seething with anger, Akemi slapped his bearded face, but this did not faze him. Indeed, he seemed to like it. He merely squinted and grinned as she struck. Then he hugged her more closely and rubbed his cheek against hers. His beard felt like a thousand needles sticking into her skin. She could barely breathe. As she scratched desperately at him, one of her fingernails clawed the inside of his nose, bringing forth a stream of blood. Still, Yasoma did not relax the tight hold he had on her.

The bell at the Amida Hall on Toribe Hill was tolling a dirge, a lamentation on the impermanence of all things and the vanity of life. But it made no impression on the two struggling mortals. The withered miscanthus waved violently with their movements.

"Calm down, stop fighting," he pleaded. "There's nothing to be afraid of. I'll make you my bride. You'd like that, wouldn't you?"

Akemi screamed, "I just want to die!" The misery in her voice startled Yasoma.

"Why? Wh-what's the matter?" he stammered.

Akemi's crouching position, with her hands, knees and chest drawn tightly together, resembled the bud of a sasanqua flower. Yasoma began to comfort and cajole, hoping to soothe her into surrender. This did not seem to be the first time he had encountered a situation of this sort. On the contrary, it would appear that this was something he liked, for his face shone with pleasure, without losing its menacing quality. He was in no hurry; like a cat, he enjoyed playing with his victim.

"Don't cry," he said. "There's nothing to cry about, is there?" Giving her a kiss on the ear, he went on, "You must have been with a man before. At your age, you couldn't be innocent."

Seijūrō! Akemi recalled how stifled and miserable she had been before, how the framework of the shoji had blurred before her eyes.

"Wait!" she said.

"Wait? All right, I'll wait," he said, mistaking the warmth of her feverish body for passion. "But don't try to run away, or I'll really get rough."

With a sharp grunt, she twisted her shoulders and shook his hand off her. Glaring into his face, she slowly rose. "What are you trying to do to me?"

"You know what I want!"

"You think you can treat women like fools, don't you? All you men do! Well, I may be a woman, but I've got spirit." Blood seeped from her lip where she had cut it on a miscanthus leaf. Biting the lip, she burst into fresh tears.

"You say the strangest things," he said. "What else can you be but crazy?"

"I'll say whatever I please!" she screamed. Pushing his chest away from her with all her might, she scrambled away through the miscanthus, which stretched as far as she could see in the moonlight.

"Murder! Help! Murder!"

Yasoma lunged after her. Before she had gone ten steps, he caught her and threw her down again. Her white legs visible beneath her kimono, her hair falling around her face, she lay with her cheek pressed against the ground. Her kimono was half open, and her white breasts felt the cold wind.

Just as Yasoma was about to leap on her, something very hard landed in the vicinity of his ear. Blood rushed to his head, and he screamed out in pain. As he turned to look, the hard object came crashing down on the crown of his head. This time there could hardly have been any pain, for he immediately fell over unconscious, his head shaking emptily like a paper tiger's. As he lay there with his mouth slack, his assailant, a mendicant priest, stood over him, holding the *shakuhachi* with which he had dealt the blows.

"The evil brute!" he said. "But he went down easier than I expected." The priest looked at Yasoma for a time, debating whether it would be kinder to kill him outright. The chances were that even if he recovered consciousness, he would never be sane again.

Akemi stared blankly at her rescuer. Apart from the *shakuhachi*, there was nothing to identify him as a priest; to judge from his dirty clothes and the sword hanging at his side, he might have been a poverty-stricken samurai or even a beggar.

"It's all right now," he said. "You don't have to worry anymore."

Recovering from her daze, Akemi thanked him and began straightening her hair and her kimono. But she peered into the darkness around her with eyes still full of fright.

"Where do you live?" asked the priest.

"Eh? Live . . . do you mean where's my house?" she said, covering her face with her hands. Through her sobs, she tried to answer his questions, but she found herself unable to be honest with him. Part of what she told him was true—her mother was different from her, her mother was trying to exchange her body for money, she had fled here from Sumiyoshi—but the rest was made up on the spur of the moment.

"I'd rather die than go back home," she wailed. "I've had to put up with so much from my mother! I've been shamed in so many ways! Why, even when I was a little girl, I had to go out on the battlefield and steal things from the bodies of dead soldiers."

Her loathing for her mother made her bones tremble.

Aoki Tanzaemon helped her along to a little hollow, where it was quiet and the wind less chilly. Coming to a small dilapidated temple, he flashed a toothy grin and said, "This is where I live. It's not much, but I like it."

Though aware that it was a little rude, Akemi could not help saying, "Do you really live here?"

Tanzaemon pushed open a grille door and motioned for her to enter. Akemi hesitated.

"It's warmer inside than you'd think," he said. "All I have to cover the floor with is thin straw matting. Still, that's better than nothing. Are you afraid I might be like that brute back there?"

Silently Akemi shook her head. Tanzaemon did not frighten her. She felt sure he was a good man, and anyway he was getting on—over fifty, she thought. What held her back was the filthiness of the little temple and the smell of Tanzaemon's body and clothing. But there was nowhere else to go, no telling what might happen if Yasoma or someone like him were to find her. And her forehead was burning with fever.

"I won't be a bother to you?" she asked as she went up the steps.

"Not at all. No one will mind if you stay here for months."

The building was pitch black, the kind of atmosphere favored by bats.

"Wait just a minute," said Tanzaemon.

She heard the scratching of metal against flint, and then a small lamp, which he must have scavenged somewhere, cast a feeble light. She looked about and saw that this strange man had somehow accumulated the basic necessities for housekeeping—a pot or two, some dishes, a wooden pillow, some straw matting. Saying he would make a little buckwheat gruel for her, he began puttering around with a broken earthenware brazier, first putting in a little charcoal, then some sticks, and after raising a few sparks, blowing them into a flame.

"He's a nice old man," thought Akemi. As she began to feel calmer, the place no longer seemed so filthy.

"There now," he said. "You look feverish, and you said you were tired. You've probably caught a cold. Why don't you just lie down over there until the food is ready?" He pointed to a makeshift pallet of straw matting and rice sacks.

Akemi spread some paper she had with her on the wooden pillow and with murmured apologies for resting while he worked, lay down. For cover, there were the tattered remains of a mosquito net. She started to pull this over her, but as she did so, an animal with glittering eyes jumped out from under it and bounded over her head. Akemi screamed and buried her face in the pallet.

Tanzaemon was more astonished than Akemi. He dropped the sack from which he was pouring flour into the water, spilling half of it on his knees. "What was that?" he cried.

Akemi, still hiding her face, said, "I don't know. It seemed bigger than a rat."

"Probably a squirrel. They sometimes come when they smell food. But I don't see it anywhere."

Lifting her head slightly, Akemi said, "There it is!"

"Where?"

Tanzaemon straightened up and turned around. Perched on the railing of the inner sanctum, from which the image of the Buddha was long gone, was a small monkey, shrinking with fright under Tanzaemon's hard stare.

Tanzaemon looked puzzled, but the monkey apparently decided there was nothing to fear. After a few trips up and down the faded vermilion railing, he sat down again, and turning up a face like a peach with long hair, began blinking his eyes.

"Where do you suppose he came from? . . . Ah ha! I see now. I thought a good deal of rice had been scattered around." He moved toward the monkey, but the latter, anticipating his approach, bounded behind the sanctum and hid.

"He's a cute little devil," said Tanzaemon. "If we give him something to eat, he probably won't do any mischief. Let's let him be." Brushing the flour off his knees, he sat down before the brazier again. "There's nothing to be afraid of, Akemi. Get some rest."

"Do you think he'll behave himself?"

"Yes. He's not wild. He must be somebody's pet. There's nothing to worry about. Are you warm enough?"

"Yes."

"Then get some sleep. That's the best cure for a cold."

He put more flour in the water and stirred the gruel with chopsticks. The fire was burning briskly now, and while the mixture was heating up, he began chopping some scallions. His chopping board was the top of an old table, his knife a small rusted dagger. With unwashed hands, he scooped the scallions into a wooden bowl and then wiped off the chopping block, converting it into a tray.

The bubbling of the boiling pot gradually warmed the room. Seated with his arms around his spindly knees, the former samurai gazed at the broth with hungry eyes. He looked happy and eager, as though the pot before him contained the ultimate pleasure of mankind.

The bell of Kiyomizudera pealed as it did every night. The winter austerities, which lasted thirty days, had ended, and the New Year was at hand, but as always as the year drew to a close, the burden on people's souls seemed to grow heavier. Far into the night supplicants were sounding the tinny gong above the temple entrance as they bowed to pray, and wailing chants invoking the Buddha's aid droned on monotonously.

While Tanzaemon slowly stirred the gruel to keep it from scorching, he turned reflective. "I myself am receiving my punishment and atoning for my sins, but what has happened to Jōtarō? . . . The child did nothing blameworthy. Oh, Blessed Kannon, I beg you to punish the parent for his sins, but cast the eye of generous compassion on the son—"

A scream suddenly punctuated his prayer. "You beast!" Her eyes still closed in sleep, her face pressed hard against the wooden pillow, Akemi was weeping bitterly. She ranted on until the sound of her own voice woke her.

"Was I talking in my sleep?" she asked.

"Yes; you startled me," said Tanzaemon, coming to her bedside and wiping her forehead with a cool rag. "You're sweating terribly. Must be the fever."

"What . . . what did I say?"

"Oh, a lot of things."

"What sort of things?" Akemi's feverish face grew redder from embarrassment. She pulled the cover up over it.

Without answering directly, Tanzaemon said, "Akemi, there's a man you'd like to put a curse on, isn't there?"

"Did I say that?"

"Mm. What happened? Did he desert you?"

"No."

"I see," he said, jumping to his own conclusion.

Akemi, pushing herself up into a half-sitting position, said, "Oh, what should I do now? Tell me, what?" She had vowed she would reveal her secret shame to no one, but the anger and sadness, the sense of loss pent up inside her, were too much to bear alone. She sprawled on Tanzaemon's knee and blurted out the whole story, sobbing and moaning throughout.

"Oh," she wailed finally, "I want to die, die! Let me die!"

Tanzaemon's breath grew hot. It had been a long time since he had been this close to a woman; her odor burned his nostrils, his eyes. Desires of the flesh, which he thought he had overcome, began to swell as from an influx of warm blood, and his body, until now no more vibrant than a barren withered tree, took on new life. He was reminded, for a change, that there were lungs and a heart underneath his ribs.

"Mm," he muttered, "so that's the kind of man Yoshioka Seijūrō is." Bitter hatred for Seijūrō welled up in him. Nor was it only indignation; a kind of jealousy moved him to tighten his shoulders, as though it were a daughter of his own who had been violated. As Akemi writhed in tears on his knee, he experienced a feeling of intimacy, and a look of perplexity crept into his face.

"Now there, don't cry. Your heart is still chaste. It's not as if you'd permitted this man to make love to you, nor did you return his love. What's important to a woman is not her body but her heart, and chastity itself is a matter of the inner being. Even when a woman doesn't give herself to a man, if she regards him with lust, she becomes, at least as long as the feeling lasts, unchaste and unclean."

Akemi was not comforted by these abstract words. Hot tears seeped through the priest's kimono, and she went on repeating that she wanted to die.

"Now, now, stop crying," said Tanzaemon again, patting her on the back. But the trembling of her white neck did not move him to genuine sympathy. This soft skin, so sweet to the smell, had already been stolen from him by another man.

Noticing that the monkey had sneaked up to the pot and was eating something, he unceremoniously removed Akemi's head from his knee, shook his fist and cursed the animal roundly. Beyond the shadow of a doubt, food was more important than a woman's suffering.

The next morning Tanzaemon announced he was going to town with his beggar's bowl. "You stay here while I'm gone," he said. "I have to get some money to buy you medicine, and then we need some rice and oil so we can have something hot to eat."

His hat was not a deep one woven of reeds, like those of most itinerant priests, but an ordinary bamboo affair, and his straw sandals, worn and split at the heels, scraped against the ground as he shuffled along. Everything about him, not just his mustache, had an air of scruffiness. Yet, walking scarecrow that he was, it was his habit to go out every day, unless it rained.

Not having slept well, he was particularly bleary-eyed this morning. Akemi, after crying and carrying on so in the evening, had later sipped her gruel, broken into a heavy sweat and slept soundly through the rest of the night. He had hardly closed his eyes until dawn. Even walking under the bright morning sun, the cause of his sleeplessness remained with him. He could not get it out of his mind.

342   "She's about the same age as Otsū," he thought. "But they're completely

different in temperament. Otsū has grace and refinement, but there's something chilly about her. Akemi's appealing whether she's laughing, crying or pouting."

The youthful feelings aroused in Tanzaemon's desiccated cells by the strong rays of Akemi's charm had made him all too conscious of his advancing years. And during the night, as he had looked solicitously at her each time she stirred in her sleep, a different warning had sounded in his heart. "What a wretched fool I am! Haven't I learned yet? Though I wear the surplice of the priest and play the *shakuhachi* of the mendicant, I'm still a long way from achieving the clear and perfect enlightenment of P'u-hua. Will I never find the wisdom that will release me from this body?"

After castigating himself at length, he had forced his sad eyes shut and tried to sleep, but to no avail.

As dawn broke, he had again resolved, "I will—I must—put evil thoughts behind me!" But Akemi was a charming girl. She had suffered so. He must try to comfort her. He had to show her that not all the men in the world were demons of lust.

Besides the medicine, he was wondering what sort of present he could bring her when he came back in the evening. Throughout the day's alms-seeking, his spirit would be bolstered by this desire to do something to make Akemi a little happier. That would suffice; he cherished no greater desire.

At about the time he recovered his composure and the color returned to his face, he heard the flapping of wings above the cliff beside him. The shadow of a large falcon skimmed past, and Tanzaemon watched a gray feather from a small bird flutter down from an oak branch in the leafless grove above him. Holding the bird in its claws, the falcon rose straight up, exposing the undersides of its wings.

Nearby a man's voice said, "Success!" and the falconer whistled to his bird.

Seconds later, Tanzaemon saw two men in hunting outfits coming down the hill behind the Ennenji. The falcon was perched on the left fist of one of them, who carried a net bag for the catch on the side opposite his two swords. An intelligent-looking brown hunting dog trotted along behind.

Kojirō stopped and took in the surroundings. "It happened somewhere along here yesterday evening," he was saying. "My monkey was scrapping with the dog, and the dog bit his tail. He hid somewhere and never came out. I wonder if he's up in one of those trees."

Seijūrō, looking rather disgruntled, sat down on a rock. "Why would he still be here? He's got legs too. Anyway, I can't see why you bring a monkey along when you go hunting with falcons."

Kojirō made himself comfortable on the root of a tree. "I didn't bring him, but I can't keep him from tagging along. And I'm so used to him, I miss him when he's not around."

"I thought only women and people of leisure liked to have monkeys and lapdogs for pets, but I guess I was wrong. It's hard to imagine a student warrior like you being so attached to a monkey." Having seen Kojirō in action on the dike at Kema, Seijūrō had a healthy respect for his swordsmanship, but his tastes and his general way of life seemed all too boyish. Just living in the same house with him these past few days had convinced Seijūrō that maturity came only with age. While he found it difficult to respect Kojirō as a person, this, in a way, made it easier to associate with him.

Kojirō replied laughingly, "It's because I'm so young. One of these days, I'll learn to like women, and then I'll probably forget all about the monkey."

Kojirō chatted idly in a light vein, but Seijūrō's face seemed increasingly preoccupied. There was a nervous look in his eyes not unlike that of the falcon perched on his hand. All at once he said irritably, "What's that beggar priest over there doing? He's been standing there staring at us ever since we got here." Seijūrō glared suspiciously at Tanzaemon, and Kojirō turned around to have a look.

Tanzaemon turned his back and trudged off.

Seijūrō stood up abruptly. "Kojirō," he said, "I want to go home. Any way you look at it, this is no time to be out hunting. It's already the twenty-ninth of the month."

Laughing, with a touch of scorn, Kojirō said, "We came out to hunt, didn't we? We've only got one turtledove and a couple of thrushes to show for it. We should try farther up the hill."

"No; let's call it a day. I don't feel like hunting, and when I don't feel like it, the falcon doesn't fly right. Let's go back to the house and practice." He added, as though talking to himself, "That's what I need to do, practice."

"Well, if you must go back, I'll go with you." He walked along beside Seijūrō but did not seem very happy about it. "I guess I was wrong to suggest it."

"Suggest what?"

"Going hunting yesterday and today."

"Don't worry about it. I know you meant well. It's just that it's the end of the year, and the showdown with Musashi is creeping up on us fast."

"That's why I thought it'd be good for you to do some hunting. You could relax, get yourself into the proper spirit. I guess you're not the type who can do that."

"Umm. The more I hear about Musashi, the more I think it's just as well not to underrate him."

"Isn't that all the more reason to avoid getting excited or panicky? You should discipline your spirit."

"I'm not panicky. The first lesson in the Art of War is not to make light of your enemy, and I think it's only common sense to try to get in plenty of practice before the fight. If I should lose, then at least I'd know I'd done my best. If the man's better than I am, well . . . "

Though he appreciated Seijūrō's honesty, Kojirō sensed in him a smallness of spirit that would make it very difficult for Seijūrō to uphold the reputation of the Yoshioka School. Because Seijūrō lacked the personal vision needed to follow in his father's footsteps and run the huge school properly, Kojirō felt sorry for him. In his opinion, the younger brother, Denshichirō, had more strength of character, but Denshichirō was also an incorrigible playboy. And

344

though he was a more capable swordsman than Seijūrō, he had no stake in the Yoshioka name.

Kojirō wanted Seijūrō to forget about the impending bout with Musashi, for this, he believed, would be the best possible preparation for him. The question he wanted to ask, but didn't, was what could he hope to learn between now and the time for the match? "Well," he thought with resignation, "that's the way he is, so I suppose I can't be of much help to him."

The dog had run off and was barking ferociously in the distance.

"That means he's found some game!" said Kojirō, his eyes brightening.

"Let him go. He'll catch up with us later."

"I'll go have a look. You wait here."

Kojirō sprinted off in the direction of the barking and after a minute or two spotted the dog on the veranda of an ancient ramshackle temple. The animal leaped against the dilapidated grille door and fell back. After a few trials, he began scratching at the worn red-lacquered posts and walls of the building.

Wondering what he could possibly be so excited about, Kojirō went to another door. Peering through the grille was like looking into a black lacquer vase.

The rattle of the door as he pulled it open brought the dog running to his heels, wagging his tail. Kojirō kicked the dog away, but to little effect. As he entered the building, the dog streaked in past him.

The woman's screams were ear-splitting, the kind of screams that shatter glass. Then the dog started howling, and there was a battle of lung power between him and the shrieking woman. Kojirō wondered if the beams would split. Running forward, he discovered Akemi lying under the mosquito net and the monkey, which had jumped in the window to escape the dog, hiding behind her.

Akemi was between the dog and the monkey, blocking the dog's way, so he attacked her. As she rolled to one side, the howl of the dog reached a crescendo.

Akemi was now screaming from pain rather than fright. The dog had set his teeth around her forearm. Kojirō, with an oath, kicked him violently again in the ribs. The dog was already dead from the first kick, but even after the second, his teeth were solidly clamped on Akemi's arm.

"Let go! Let go!" she screamed, writhing on the floor.

Kojirō knelt beside her and pulled the dog's jaws open. The sound was like that of pieces of glued wood being wrenched apart. The mouth came open, all right; a little more force on Kojirō's part, and the dog's head would have split in two. He threw the corpse out the door and came back to Akemi's side.

"It's all right now," he said soothingly, but Akemi's forearm said otherwise. The blood flowing over the white skin gave the bite the appearance of a large crimson peony.

Kojirō shivered at the sight. "Isn't there any sake? I should wash it with sake. . . . No, I guess there wouldn't be any in a place like this." Warm blood flowed down the forearm to the wrist. "I have to do something," he said, "or poison from the dog's teeth might cause you to go mad. He has been acting peculiarly these past few days."

While Kojirō tried to decide what could be done in a hurry, Akemi screwed her eyebrows together, bent her lovely white neck backward and cried, "Mad? Oh, how wonderful! That's what I want to be—mad! Completely stark, raving mad!"

"Wh-wh-what's this?" stammered Kojirō. Without further ado, he bent over her forearm and sucked blood from the wound. When his mouth was full, he spat it out, put his mouth back to the white skin, and sucked until his cheeks bulged.

In the evening Tanzaemon returned from his daily round. "I'm back, Akemi," he announced as he entered the temple. "Were you lonesome while I was gone?"

He deposited her medicine in a corner, along with the food and the jar of oil he had bought, and said, "Wait a moment; I'll make some light."

When the candle was lit, he saw that she was not in the room. "Akemi!" he called. "Where could she have gone?"

His one-sided love turned suddenly to anger, which was quickly replaced by loneliness. Tanzaemon was reminded, as he had been before, that he would never be young again—that there was no more honor, no more hope. He thought of his aging body and winced.

"I rescued her and took care of her," he grumbled, "and now she's gone off without a word. Is that the way the world is always going to be? Is that the way she is? Or was she still suspicious of my intentions?"

On the bed he discovered a scrap of cloth, apparently torn from the end of her obi. The spot of blood on it rekindled his animal instincts. He kicked the straw matting into the air and threw the medicine out the window.

Hungry, but lacking the will to prepare a meal, he took up his *shakuhachi* and, with a sigh, went out onto the veranda. For an hour or more, he played without stopping, attempting to expel his desires and delusions. Yet it was evident to him that his passions remained with him and would remain with him until he died. "She'd already been taken by another man," he mused. "Why did I have to be so moral and upright? There was no need for me to lie there alone, pining all night."

Half of him regretted not having acted; the other half condemned his lecherous yearning. It was precisely this conflict of emotions, swirling incessantly in his veins, that constituted what the Buddha called delusion. He was trying now to cleanse his impure nature, but the more he strived, the muddier the tone of his *shakuhachi* became.

The beggar who slept beneath the temple poked his head from under the veranda. "Why are you sitting there playing your recorder?" he asked. "Did something good happen? If you made lots of money and bought some sake, how about giving me a drink?" He was a cripple, and from his lowly viewpoint, Tanzaemon lived like a king.

"Do you know what happened to the girl I brought home last night?"

"She was a nice-looking wench, wasn't she? If I'd been able, I wouldn't have let her get away. Not long after you left this morning, a young samurai with a long forelock and a huge sword on his back came and took her away. The monkey too. He had one of them on one shoulder, one on the other."

"Samurai . . . forelock?"

"Uh. And what a handsome fellow he was—handsomer by far than you and me!"

The humor of this sent the beggar into a paroxysm of laughter.

The Announcement

Seijūrō arrived back at the school in a foul mood. He thrust the falcon into a disciple's hands, curtly ordering him to put the bird back in its cage.

"Isn't Kojirō with you?" asked the disciple.

"No, but I'm sure he'll be along presently."

After changing his clothes, Seijūrō went and sat down in the room where guests were received. Across the court was the great dōjō, closed since the final practice on the twenty-fifth. Throughout the year, there was the coming and going of a thousand or so students; now the dōjō would not be open again until the first training session of the New Year. With the wooden swords silent, the house seemed coldly desolate.

Desperate to have Kojirō as a sparring partner, Seijūrō inquired of the disciple repeatedly whether he had returned. But Kojirō did not come back, neither that evening nor the following day.

Other callers came in force, however, it being the last day of the year, the day to settle up all accounts. For those in business, it was a question of collecting now or waiting until the *Bon* festival of the following summer, and by noon the front room was full of bill collectors. Normally these men wore an air of complete subservience in the presence of samurai, but now, their patience exhausted, they were making their feelings known in no uncertain terms.

"Can't you pay at least part of what you owe?"

"You've been saying the man in charge is out, or the master is away, for months now. Do you think you can keep putting us off forever?"

"How many times do we have to come here?"

"The old master was a good customer. I wouldn't say a word if it were only the last half year, but you didn't pay at midyear either. Why, I've even got unpaid bills from last year!"

347

A couple of them impatiently tapped on their account books and stuck them under the nose of the disciple. There were carpenters, plasterers, the rice man, the sake dealer, clothiers and sundry suppliers of everyday goods. Swelling their ranks were the proprietors of various teahouses where Seijūrō ate and drank on credit. And these were the small fry, whose bills could hardly be compared to those of the usurers from whom Denshichirō, unknown to his brother, had borrowed cash.

Half a dozen of these men sat down and refused to budge.

"We want to talk with Master Seijūrō himself. It's a waste of time to talk to disciples."

Seijūrō kept to himself in the back of the house, his only words being: "Tell them I'm out." And Denshichirō, of course, would not have come near the house on a day like this. The face most conspicuously absent was that of the man in charge of the school's books and the household accounts: Gion Tōji. Several days earlier, he had decamped with Okō and all the money he'd collected on his trip west.

Presently six or seven men swaggered in, led by Ueda Ryōhei, who even in such humiliating circumstances was swollen with pride at being one of the Ten Swordsmen of the House of Yoshioka. With a menacing look, he asked, "What's going on here?"

The disciple, while contriving to make it plain that he considered no explanation necessary, gave a brief rundown of the situation.

"Is that all?" Ryōhei said scornfully. "Just a bunch of moneygrubbers? What difference does it make as long as the bills are eventually paid? Tell the ones who don't want to wait for payment to step into the practice hall; I'll discuss it with them in my own language."

In the face of this threat, the bill collectors grew sulky. Owing to Yoshioka Kempō's uprightness in money matters, not to mention his position as a military instructor to the Ashikaga shōguns, they had bowed before the Yoshioka household, groveled, lent them goods, lent them anything, come whenever summoned, left when they were told, and said yes to anything and everything. But there was a limit to how long they could kowtow to these vain warriors. The day they allowed themselves to be intimidated by threats like Ryōhei's was the day the merchant class would go out of business. And without them, what would the samurai do? Did they imagine for a moment they could run things by themselves?

As they stood around grumbling, Ryōhei made it perfectly clear that he regarded them as so much dirt. "All right now, go on home! Hanging around here won't do you any good."

The merchants grew silent but made no move to leave.

"Throw them out!" cried Ryōhei.

"Sir, this is an outrage!"

"What's outrageous about it?" asked Ryōhei.

"It's completely irresponsible!"

"Who says it's irresponsible?"

"But it *is* irresponsible to throw us out!"

"Then why don't you leave quietly? We're busy."

"If it wasn't the last day of the year, we wouldn't be here begging. We need the money you owe to settle our own debts before the day is out."

"That's too bad. Too bad. Now go!"

"This is no way to treat us!"

"I think I've heard enough of your complaints!" Ryōhei's voice grew angry again.

"No one would complain—if you'd just pay up!"

"Come here!" commanded Ryōhei.

"Wh-who?"

"Anyone who's dissatisfied."

"This is crazy!"

"Who said that?"

"I wasn't referring to you, sir. I was talking about this . . . this situation."

"Shut up!" Ryōhei seized the man by his hair and threw him out the side door.

"Anybody else with complaints?" growled Ryōhei. "We're not going to have you riffraff inside the house claiming paltry sums of money. I won't permit it! Even if the Young Master wants to pay you, I won't let him do it."

At the sight of Ryōhei's fist, the bill collectors stumbled all over each other in their rush to get out of the gate. But once outside, their vilification of the House of Yoshioka intensified.

"Will I ever laugh and clap my hands when I see the 'For Sale' sign posted on this place! It shouldn't be long now."

"They say it won't be."

"How could it be?"

Ryōhei, vastly amused, held his stomach with laughter as he went to the back of the house. The other disciples went with him to the room where Seijūrō was bent, alone and silent, over the brazier.

"Young Master," said Ryōhei, "you're so quiet. Is something wrong?"

"Oh, no," replied Seijūrō, somewhat cheered by the sight of his most trusted followers. "The day's not far off now, is it?" he said.

"No," agreed Ryōhei. "That's what we came to see you about. Shouldn't we decide on the time and place and let Musashi know?"

"Why, yes, I suppose so," said Seijūrō pensively. "The place . . . Where would be a good place? How about the field at the Rendaiji, north of the city?"

"That sounds all right. What about the time?"

"Should it be before the New Year's decorations are taken down, or after?"

"The sooner the better. We don't want to give that coward time to worm his way out."

"How about the eighth?"

"Isn't the eighth the anniversary of Master Kempō's death?"

"Ah, so it is. In that case, how about the ninth? At seven o'clock in the morning? That'll do, won't it?"

"All right. We'll post a sign on the bridge this evening."

"Fine."

"Are you ready?" asked Ryōhei.

"I've been ready all along," replied Seijūrō, who was in no position to answer otherwise. He had not really considered the possibility of losing to Musashi. Having studied under his father's tutelage since childhood, and having never lost a match to anyone in the school, not even to the oldest and best-trained disciples, he couldn't imagine being beaten by this young, inexperienced country bumpkin.

His confidence, nonetheless, was not absolute. He felt a tinge of uncertainty, and characteristically, instead of attributing this to his failure to put into practice the Way of the Samurai, wrote it off as being due to recent personal difficulties. One of these, perhaps the greatest, was Akemi. He'd been ill at ease ever since the incident at Sumiyoshi, and when Gion Tōji had absconded, he had learned that the financial cancer in the Yoshioka household had already reached a critical stage.

Ryōhei and the others came back with the message to Musashi written on a freshly cut board.

"Is this what you had in mind?" asked Ryōhei.

The characters, still glistening wet, said:

> Answer—In response to your request for a bout, I name the following time and place. Place: Field of the Rendaiji. Time: Seven o'clock in the morning, ninth day of the first month. I swear on my sacred oath to be present.
>
> If, by some chance, you do not fulfill your promise, I shall consider it my right to ridicule you in public.
>
> If I break this agreement, may the punishment of the gods be visited upon me!
> Seijūrō, Yoshioka Kempō II, of Kyoto. Done on the last day of [1605].
> To the Rōnin of Mimasaka, Miyamoto Musashi.

After reading it, Seijūrō said, "It's all right." The announcement made him feel more relaxed, perhaps because for the first time it came home to him that the die was cast.

At sunset, Ryōhei put the sign under his arm and strode proudly along the street with a couple of other men to post it on the Great Bridge at Gojō Avenue.

At the foot of Yoshida Hill, the man to whom the announcement was addressed was walking through a neighborhood of samurai of noble lineage and small means. Conservatively inclined, they led ordinary lives and were unlikely to be found doing anything that would excite comment.

Musashi was going from gate to gate examining the nameplates. Eventually he came to a stop in the middle of the street, seemingly unwilling or unable to look further. He was searching for his aunt, his mother's sister and his only living relative besides Ogin.

His aunt's husband was a samurai serving, for a small stipend, the House of Konoe. Musashi thought it would be easy to find the house near Yoshida Hill but soon discovered there was very little to distinguish one house from another. Most were small, surrounded by trees, and their gates were shut tight as clams. Quite a few of the gates had no nameplates.

His uncertainty about the place he was seeking made him reluctant to ask directions. "They must have moved," he thought. "I may as well stop looking."

He turned back toward the center of town, which lay under a mist reflecting the lights of the year-end marketplace. Although it was New Year's Eve, the streets in the downtown area still hummed with activity.

Musashi turned to look at a woman who had just passed going the other way. He hadn't seen his aunt for at least seven or eight years, but he was sure this was she, for the woman resembled the image he had formed of his mother. He followed her a short distance, then called out to her.

She stared at him suspiciously for a moment or two, intense surprise reflected in eyes wrinkled by years of humdrum living on a tiny budget. "You're Musashi, Munisai's son, aren't you?" she finally asked.

He wondered why she called him Musashi rather than Takezō, but what actually disturbed him was the impression that he was not welcome. "Yes," he replied, "I'm Takezō from the House of Shimmen."

She looked him over thoroughly, without the customary "oh"s and "ah"s as to how large he had grown or how different he looked from before. "Why have you come here?" she asked coolly in a rather censorious tone.

"I had no special purpose in coming. I just happened to be in Kyoto. I thought it would be nice to see you." Looking at the eyes and hairline of his aunt, he thought of his mother. If she were still alive, surely she would be about as tall as this woman and speak with the same sort of voice.

"You came to see me?" she asked incredulously.

"Yes. I'm sorry it's so sudden."

His aunt waved her hand before her face in a gesture of dismissal. "Well, you've seen me, so there's no reason to go any farther. Please leave!"

Abashed at this chilly reception, he blurted out, "Why do you say that as soon as you see me? If you want me to leave, I'll go, but I can't see why. Have I done something you disapprove of? If so, at least tell me what it is."

His aunt seemed unwilling to be pinned down. "Oh, as long as you're here, why don't you come to our house and say hello to your uncle? But you know what kind of person he is, so don't be disappointed at anything he might say. I'm your aunt, and since you've come to see us, I don't want you to go away with hard feelings."

Taking what little comfort he could from this, Musashi walked with her to her house and waited in the front room while she broke the news to her husband. Through the shoji he could hear the asthmatic, grumbling voice of his uncle, whose name was Matsuo Kaname.

"What?" asked Kaname testily. "Munisai's son here? ... I was afraid he'd show up sooner or later. You mean he's *here*, in this house? You let him in without asking me?"

Enough was enough, but when Musashi called to his aunt to say good-bye, Kaname said, "You're in there, are you?" and slid the door open. His face wore not a frown but an expression of utter contempt—the look city people reserve for their unwashed country relatives. It was as though a cow had lumbered in and planted its hooves on the tatami.

"Why did you come here?" asked Kaname.

"I happened to be in town. I thought I'd just ask after your health."

"That's not true!"

"Sir?"

"You can lie all you want, but I know what you've done. You caused a lot of trouble in Mimasaka, made a lot of people hate you, disgraced your family's name and then ran away. Isn't that the truth?"

Musashi was nonplussed.

"How can you be so shameless as to come to call on relatives?"

"I'm sorry for what I did," said Musashi. "But I fully intend to make the proper amends to my ancestors and to the village."

"I suppose you can't go back home, of course. Well, we reap what we sow. Munisai must be weeping in his grave!"

"I've stayed too long," said Musashi. "I must be going now."

"Oh, no you don't!" said Kaname angrily. "You stay right here! If you go wandering around this neighborhood, you'll get yourself in trouble in no time. That cantankerous old woman from the Hon'iden family showed up here about a half year ago. Recently she's been around several times. She keeps asking us whether you've been here and trying to find out from us where you are. She's after you, all right—with a terrible vengeance."

"Oh, Osugi. Has she been here?"

"Indeed she has. I heard all about you from her. If you weren't a relative of mine, I'd tie you up and hand you over to her, but under the circumstances . . . Anyway, you stay here for now. It'll be best to leave in the middle of the night, so there won't be any trouble for your aunt and me."

That his aunt and uncle had swallowed every word of Osugi's slander was mortifying. Feeling terribly alone, Musashi sat in silence, staring at the floor. Eventually his aunt took pity on him and told him to go to another room and get some sleep.

Musashi flopped down on the floor and loosened his scabbards. Once again came the feeling that he had no one in the world to depend on but himself.

He reflected that perhaps his uncle and aunt were dealing with him frankly and sternly precisely because of the blood relationship. While he had been angry enough earlier to want to spit on the doorway and leave, he now took a more charitable view, reminding himself that it was important to give them the benefit of every doubt.

He was too naive to accurately judge the people around him. If he had already become rich and famous, his sentiments about relatives would have been appropriate, but here he was barging in out of the cold in a dirty rag of a kimono on New Year's Eve, of all times. Under the circumstances, his aunt and uncle's lack of familial affection was not surprising.

This was soon brought forcefully home to Musashi. He had lain down hungry on the guileless assumption that he would be offered something to eat. Though he smelled food cooking and heard the rattle of pots and pans in the kitchen, no one came near his room, where the flicker of the fire in the brazier was no larger than that of a firefly. He presently concluded that hunger and cold were secondary; what was most important now was to get some sleep, which he proceeded to do.

352

He awoke about four hours later to the sound of temple bells ringing out the old year. The sleep had done him good. Jumping to his feet, he felt that his fatigue had been washed away. His mind was fresh and clear.

In and around the city, huge bells bonged in slow and stately rhythm, marking the end of darkness and the beginning of light. One hundred and eight peals for the one hundred and eight illusions of life—each ring a call to men and women to reflect on the vanity of their ways.

Musashi wondered how many people there were who on this night could say: "I was right. I did what I should have done. I have no regrets." For him, each resounding knell evoked a tremor of remorse. He could conjure up nothing but the things he had done wrong during the last year. Nor was it only the last year—the year before, and the year before that, all the years that had gone by had brought regrets. There had not been a single year devoid of them. Indeed, there had hardly been one day.

From his limited perspective of the world, it seemed that whatever people did they soon came to regret. Men, for example, took wives with the intention of living out their lives with them but often changed their minds later. One could readily forgive women for their afterthoughts, but then women rarely voiced their complaints, whereas men frequently did so. How many times had he heard men disparage their wives as if they were old discarded sandals?

Musashi had no marital problems, to be sure, but he had been the victim of delusion, and remorse was not a feeling alien to him. At this very moment, he was very sorry he had come to his aunt's house. "Even now," he lamented, "I'm not free of my sense of dependence. I keep telling myself I must stand on my own two feet and fend for myself. Then I suddenly fall back on someone else. It's shallow! It's stupid!

"I know what I should do!" he thought. "I should make a resolution and write it down."

He undid his *shugyōsha*'s pack and took out a notebook made of pieces of paper folded in quarters and tied together with coiled paper strips. He used this to jot down thoughts that occurred to him during his wanderings, along with Zen expressions, notes on geography, admonitions to himself and, occasionally, crude sketches of interesting things he saw. Opening the notebook in front of him, he took up his brush and stared at the white sheet of paper.

Musashi wrote: "I will have no regrets about anything."

While he often wrote down resolutions, he found that merely writing them did little good. He had to repeat them to himself every morning and every evening, as one would sacred scripture. Consequently, he always tried to choose words that were easy to remember and recite, like poems.

He looked for a time at what he had written, then changed it to read: "I will have no regrets about my actions."

He mumbled the words to himself but still found them unsatisfactory. He changed them again: "I will do nothing that I will regret."

Satisfied with this third effort, he put his brush down. Although the three sentences had been written with the same intent, the first two could conceivably mean he would have no regrets whether he acted rightly or wrongly, whereas the third emphasized his determination to act in such a way as to make self-reproach unnecessary.

Musashi repeated the resolution to himself, realizing it was an ideal he could not achieve unless he disciplined his heart and his mind to the utmost of his ability. Nevertheless, to strive for a state in which nothing he did would cause regrets was the path he must pursue. "Someday I will reach that state!" he vowed, driving the oath like a stake deep into his own heart.

The shoji behind him slid open, and his aunt looked in. With a voice shivering around the roots of her teeth, she said, "I knew it! Something told me I shouldn't let you stay here, and now what I was afraid would happen is happening. Osugi came knocking at the door, and saw your sandals in the entrance hall. She's convinced you're here and insists we bring you to her! Listen! You can hear her from here. Oh, Musashi, do something!"

"Osugi? Here?" said Musashi, reluctant to believe his ears. But there was no mistake. He could hear her hoarse voice seeping through the cracks like an icy wind, addressing Kaname in her stiffest, haughtiest manner.

Osugi had arrived just as the pealing of the midnight bells had ended and Musashi's aunt was on the point of going to draw fresh water for the New Year. Troubled by the thought of her New Year being ruined by the unclean sight of blood, she made no attempt to hide her annoyance.

"Run away as fast as you can," she implored. "Your uncle's holding her off by insisting you haven't been here. Slip out now while there's still time." She picked up his hat and pack and led him to the back door, where she had placed a pair of her husband's leather socks, along with some straw sandals.

While tying the sandals, Musashi said sheepishly, "I hate to be a nuisance, but won't you give me a bowl of gruel? I haven't had a thing to eat this evening."

"This is no time for eating! But here, take these. And be off with you!" She held out five rice cakes on a piece of white paper.

Eagerly accepting them, Musashi held them up to his forehead in a gesture of thanks. "Good-bye," he said.

On his way down the icy lane, on the first day of the joyous New Year, Musashi walked sadly—a winter bird with feathers molted, flying off into a black sky. His hair and fingernails felt frozen. All he could see was his own white breath, quickly turning to frost on the fine hairs around his mouth. "It's cold!" he said out loud. Surely the Eight Freezing Hells could not be this numbing! Why, when he normally shrugged off the cold, did he feel it so bitterly this morning?

He answered his own question. "It's not just my body. I'm cold inside. Not disciplined properly. That's what it is. I still long to cling to warm flesh, like a baby, and I give in too quickly to sentimentality. Because I'm alone, I feel sorry for myself and envy people who have nice warm houses. At heart, I'm base and mean! Why can't I be thankful for independence and freedom to go where I choose? Why can't I hold on to my ideals and my pride?"

As he savored the advantages of freedom, his aching feet grew warm, down to the tips of his toes, and his breath turned to steam. "A wanderer with no ideal, no sense of gratitude for his independence, is no more than a beggar! The difference between a beggar and the great wandering priest Saigyō lies inside the heart!"

He suddenly became aware of a white sparkle under his feet. He was treading on brittle ice. Without noticing, he had walked all the way to the frozen edge of the Kamo River. Both it and the sky were still black, and there was as yet no hint of dawn in the east. His feet stopped. Somehow they had carried him without mishap through the darkness from Yoshida Hill, but now they were reluctant to go on.

In the shadow of the dike, he gathered together twigs, chips of wood and anything else that would burn, then began scratching at his flint. The raising of the first tiny flame required work and patience, but eventually some dry leaves caught. With the care of a woodworker, he began piling on sticks and small branches. After a certain point, the fire rapidly took on life, and as it drew the wind, it fanned out toward its maker, ready to scorch his face.

Musashi took the rice cakes his aunt had given him and toasted them one by one in the flames. They turned brown and swelled up like bubbles, reminding him of the New Year's celebrations of his childhood. The rice cakes had no flavor but their own; they were neither salted nor sweetened. Chewing them, he thought of the taste of the plain rice as the taste of the real world about him. "I'm having my own New Year's celebration," he thought happily. As he warmed his face by the flames and stuffed his mouth, the whole thing began to seem rather amusing. "It's a good New Year's celebration! If even a wanderer like me has five good rice cakes, then it must be that heaven allows everybody to celebrate the New Year one way or another. I have the Kamo River to toast the New Year with, and the thirty-six peaks of Higashiyama are my pine tree decorations! I must cleanse my body and wait for the first sunrise."

At the edge of the icy river, he untied his obi and removed his kimono and underwear; then he plunged in and, splashing about like a water bird, washed himself thoroughly.

He was standing on the bank wiping his skin vigorously when the first rays of dawn broke through a cloud and fell warmly on his back. He looked toward the fire and saw someone standing on the dike above it, another traveler, different in age and appearance, brought here by fate. Osugi.

The old woman had seen him, too, and cried out in her heart, "He's here! The troublemaker is here!" Overcome by joy and fear, she nearly fell down in a swoon. She wanted to call to him, but her voice choked; her trembling body would not do as it was told. Abruptly, she sat down in the shadow of a small pine.

"At last!" she rejoiced. "I've finally found him! Uncle Gon's spirit has led me to him." In the bag hanging from her waist she was carrying a fragment of Uncle Gon's bones and a lock of his hair.

Each day since his death she'd talked to the dead man. "Uncle Gon," she'd say, "even though you're gone, I don't feel alone. You stayed with me when I vowed not to go back to the village without punishing Musashi and Otsū. You're with me still. You may be dead, but your spirit is always beside me.

We're together forever. Look up through the grass at me and watch! I'll never let Musashi go unpunished!"

To be sure, Uncle Gon had been dead only a week, but Osugi was resolved to keep faith with him until she, too, was reduced to ashes. In the past few days, she had pressed her search with the furor of the terrible Kishimojin, who, before her conversion by the Buddha, had killed other children to feed to her own—said to have numbered five hundred, or one thousand, or ten thousand.

Osugi's first real clue had been a rumor she'd heard in the street that there was soon to be a bout between Musashi and Yoshioka Seijūrō. Then early the previous evening, she had been among the onlookers who watched the sign being posted on the Great Bridge at Gojō Avenue. How that had excited her! She had read it through time and time again, thinking: "So Musashi's ambition has finally got the better of him! They'll make a clown of him. Yoshioka will kill him. Oh! If that happens, how will I be able to face the people at home? I swore I myself would kill him. I must get to him before Yoshioka does. And take that sniveling face back and hold it up by the hair for the villagers to see!" Then she had prayed to the gods, to the bodhisattvas and to her ancestors for help.

For all her fury and all her venom, she had come away from the Matsuo house disappointed. Returning along the Kamo River, she had first taken the firelight to be a beggar's bonfire. For no particular reason, she had stopped on the dike and waited. When she caught sight of the muscular naked man emerging from the river, oblivious of the cold, she knew it was Musashi.

Since he had no clothes on, it would be a perfect time to catch him by surprise and cut him down, but even her old dried-up heart would not let her do that.

She put her palms together and offered a prayer of thanks, just as she would if she had already taken Musashi's head. "How happy I am! Thanks to the favor of the gods and bodhisattvas, I have Musashi before my eyes. It couldn't be mere chance! My constant faith has been rewarded; my enemy has been delivered into my hands!" She bowed before heaven, firm in her belief that she now had all the time in the world to complete her mission.

The rocks along the water's edge seemed to float above the ground one by one as the light struck them. Musashi put on his kimono, tied his obi tightly and girded on his two swords. He knelt on hands and knees and bowed silently to the gods of heaven and earth.

Osugi's heart leaped as she whispered, "Now!"

At that precise moment, Musashi sprang to his feet. Jumping nimbly over a pool of water, he started walking briskly along the river's edge. Osugi, taking care not to alert him to her presence, hurried along the dike.

The roofs and bridges of the city began to form gentle white outlines in the morning mist, but above, stars still hovered in the sky and the area along the foot of Higashiyama was as black as ink. When Musashi reached the wooden bridge at Sanjō Avenue, he went under it and reappeared at the top of the dike beyond, taking long, manly strides. Several times Osugi came close to calling him but checked herself.

Musashi knew she was behind him. But he also knew that if he turned around, she would come storming at him, and he'd be forced to reward her effort with some show of defense, while at the same time not hurting her. "A frightening opponent!" he thought. If he were still Takezō, back in the village, he would have thought nothing of knocking her down and beating her until she spat blood, but of course he could no longer do that.

In reality he had more right to hate her than she him, but he wanted to make her see that her feeling toward him was based on a horrible misunderstanding. He was sure that if he could just explain things to her she would cease regarding him as her eternal enemy. But since she'd carried her festering grudge for so many years, there was no likelihood that he himself could convince her now, not if he explained a thousand times. There was only one possibility; stubborn though she was, she would certainly believe Matahachi. If her own son told her exactly what had happened before and after Sekigahara, she could no longer consider Musashi an enemy of the Hon'iden family, let alone the abductor of her son's bride.

He was drawing near the bridge, which was in an area that had flourished in the late twelfth century, when the Taira family was at the peak of its fortunes. Even after the wars of the fifteenth century, it had remained one of the most populous sections of Kyoto. The sun was just beginning to reach the housefronts and gardens, where broom marks from the previous night's thorough sweeping were still visible, but at this early hour not a door was open.

Osugi could make out his footprints in the dirt. Even these she despised.

Another hundred yards, then fifty.

"Musashi!" screamed the old woman. Balling her hands into fists, she thrust her head forward and ran toward him. "You evil devil!" she shouted. "Don't you have ears?"

Musashi did not look back.

Osugi ran on. Old as she was, her death-defying determination lent her footsteps a brave and masculine cadence. Musashi kept his back to her, casting about feverishly in his mind for a plan of action.

All at once she sprang in front of him, screaming, "Stop!" Her pointed shoulders and thin, emaciated ribs trembled. She stood there a moment, catching her breath and gathering spit in her mouth.

Not concealing a look of resignation, Musashi said as nonchalantly as he could, "Well, if it isn't the Hon'iden dowager! What are you doing here?"

"You insolent dog! Why shouldn't I be here? I'm the one who should ask you that. I let you get away from me on Sannen Hill, but today I'll have that head of yours!" Her scrawny neck suggested a game rooster, and her shrill voice, which seemed set to whisk her protruding teeth out of her mouth, was more frightening to him than a battle cry.

Musashi's dread of the old woman had its roots in reminiscences from his childhood days, the times when Osugi had caught him and Matahachi engaged in some mischief in the mulberry patch or the Hon'iden kitchen. He had been eight or nine—just the age when the two of them were always up to something—and he still remembered clearly how Osugi had shouted at them. He had fled in terror, his stomach turning somersaults, and those memories made him shiver. He had regarded her then as a hateful, ill-tempered old witch, and even now he resented her betrayal of him when he returned to the village after Sekigahara. Curiously, he had also grown accustomed to thinking of her as one person he could never get the best of. Still, with the passage of time, his feelings toward her had mellowed.

With Osugi, it was quite the opposite. She could not rid herself of the image of Takezō, the obnoxious and unruly little brat she had known since he was a baby, the boy with the runny nose and sores on his head, his arms and legs so long that he looked deformed. Not that she was unconscious of the passage of time. She was old now; she knew that. And Musashi was grown. But she could not overcome the urge to treat him as a vicious urchin. When she thought of how this little boy had shamed her—revenge! It was not only a matter of vindicating herself before the village. She had to see Musashi in his grave before she ended up in her own.

"There's no need for talk!" she screeched. "Either give me your head, or prepare to feel my blade! Get ready, Musashi!" She wiped her lips with her fingers, spat on her left hand and grabbed her scabbard.

There was a proverb about a praying mantis attacking the imperial carriage. Surely it must have been invented to describe the cadaverous Osugi with her spindly legs attacking Musashi. She looked exactly like a mantis; her eyes, her skin, her absurd stance, were all the same. And as Musashi stood on guard, watching her approach as he might a child at play, his shoulders and chest gave him the invincibility of a sturdy iron carriage.

In spite of the incongruity of the situation, he was unable to laugh, for he was suddenly filled with pity. "Come now, Granny, wait!" he begged, grabbing her elbow lightly but firmly.

"Wh-what are you doing?" she cried. Both her powerless arm and her teeth shook with surprise. "C-c-coward!" she stammered. "You think you can talk me out of this? Well, I've seen forty more New Years than you, and you can't trick me. Take your punishment!" Osugi's skin was the color of red clay, her voice filled with desperation.

Musashi, nodding vigorously, said, "I understand; I know how you feel. You've got the fighting spirit of the Hon'iden family in you, all right. I can see you have the same blood as the first of the Hon'idens, the one who served so bravely under Shimmen Munetsura."

"Let go of me, you—! I'm not going to listen to flattery from somebody young enough to be my grandchild."

"Calm down. It doesn't become an old person like you to be rash. I have something to say to you."

"Your last statement before you meet your death?"

"No; I want to explain."

"I don't want any explanations from you!" The old woman drew herself up to her full height.

"Well, then, I'll just have to take that sword away from you. Then when Matahachi shows up, he can explain everything to you."

"Matahachi?"

"Yes. I sent him a message last spring."

"Oh, you did, did you?"

"I told him to meet me here on New Year's morning."

"That's a lie!" shrieked Osugi, vigorously shaking her head. "You should be ashamed, Musashi! Aren't you Munisai's son? Didn't he teach you that when the time comes to die, you should die like a man? This is no time for playing around with words. My whole life is behind this sword, and I have the support of the gods and bodhisattvas. If you dare face it, face it!" She wrested her arm away from him and cried, "Hail to the Buddha!" Unsheathing her sword and grasping it with both hands, she lunged at his chest.

He dodged. "Calm down, Granny, please!"

When he tapped her lightly on the back, she screamed and whirled around to face him. As she prepared to charge, she invoked the name of Kannon. "Praise to Kannon Bosatsu! Praise to Kannon Bosatsu!" She attacked again.

As she passed him, Musashi seized her wrist. "You'll just wear yourself out, carrying on like that. Look, the bridge is just over there. Come with me that far."

Turning her head back over her shoulder, Osugi bared her teeth and pursed her lips. "Phooey!" She spat with all the breath she had left.

Musashi let go of her and moved aside, rubbing his left eye with his hand. The eye burned as if a spark had struck it. He looked at the hand he had put to his eye. There was no blood on it, but he couldn't open the eye. Osugi, seeing he was off guard, charged with renewed strength, calling again on the name of Kannon. Twice, three times she swung at him.

On the third swing, preoccupied with his eye, he merely bent his body slightly from the waist. The sword cut through his sleeve and scratched his forearm.

A piece of his sleeve fell off, giving Osugi the chance to see blood on the white lining. "I've wounded him!" she screamed in ecstasy, waving her sword wildly. She was as proud as if she had felled a great tree in one stroke, and the fact that Musashi wasn't fighting back in no way dimmed her elation. She went on shouting the name of the Kannon of Kiyomizudera, calling the deity down to earth.

In a noisy frenzy, she ran around him, attacking him from front and back. Musashi did no more than shift his body to avoid the blows.

His eye bothered him, and there was the scratch on his forearm. Although he had seen the blow coming, he had not moved quickly enough to avoid it. Never before had anyone gotten the jump on him or wounded him even slightly, and since he had not taken Osugi's attack seriously, the question of who would win, who lose, had never crossed his mind.

But was it not true that by not taking her seriously, he had let himself be wounded? According to *The Art of War*, no matter how slight the wound, he had quite clearly been beaten. The old woman's faith and the point of her sword had exposed for all to see his lack of maturity.

"I was wrong," he thought. Seeing the folly of inaction, he jumped away from the attacking sword and slapped Osugi heavily on the back, sending her sprawling and her sword flying out of her hand.

With his left hand Musashi picked up the sword, and with his right, lifted Osugi into the crook of his arm.

"Let me down!" she screamed, beating the air with her hands. "Are there no gods? No bodhisattvas? I've already wounded him once! What am I going to do? Musashi! Don't shame me like this! Cut off my head! Kill me now!"

While Musashi, tight-lipped, strode along the path with the struggling woman under his arm, she continued her hoarse protest. "It's the fortunes of war! It's destiny! If this is the will of the gods, I'll not be a coward! ... When Matahachi hears Uncle Gon died and I was killed trying to take revenge, he'll rise up in anger and avenge us both; it'll be good medicine for him. Musashi, kill me! Kill me now! ... Where are you going? Are you trying to add disgrace to my death? Stop! Cut off my head now!"

Musashi paid no attention, but when he arrived at the bridge, he began to wonder what he was going to do with her.

An inspiration came. Going down to the river, he found a boat tied to one of the bridge piers. Gently, he lowered her into it. "Now, you just be patient and stay here for a while. Matahachi will be here soon."

"What are you doing?" she cried, trying to push aside his hands and the reed mats in the bottom of the boat at the same time. "Why should Matahachi's coming here make any difference? What makes you think he's coming? I know what you're up to. You're not satisfied with just killing me; you want to humiliate me too!"

"Think what you like. It won't be long before you learn the truth."

"Kill me!"

"Ha, ha, ha!"

"What's so funny? You should have no trouble cutting through this old neck with one swift stroke!"

For lack of a better way of keeping her put, he tied her to the raised keel of the boat. He then slid her sword back into its scabbard and laid it down neatly by her side.

As he started to leave, she taunted him, saying, "Musashi! I don't think you understand the Way of the Samurai! Come back here, and I'll teach you."

"Later."

He started up the dike, but she was making such a racket, he had to go back and pile several reed mats over her.

A huge red sun sprang up in flames above Higashiyama. Musashi watched fascinated as it climbed, feeling its rays pierce the inner depths of his being. He grew reflective, thinking that only once a year, when this new sun rose, did the little worm of ego that binds man to his tiny thoughts have the chance to melt and vanish under its magnificent light. Musashi was filled with the joy of being alive.

Exultant, he shouted in the radiant dawn, "I'm still young!"

The Great Bridge at Gojō Avenue

"Field of the Rendaiji . . . ninth day of the first month . . ."

Reading the words made Musashi's blood surge.

His attention was distracted, however, by a sharp, stabbing pain in his left eye. Lifting his hand to his eyelid, he noticed a small needle stuck into his kimono sleeve, and a closer look revealed four or five more embedded in his clothing, shining like slivers of ice in the morning light.

"So that's it!" he exclaimed, pulling one out and examining it. It was about the size of a small sewing needle but had no threading eye and was triangular instead of round. "Why, the old bitch!" he said with a shudder, glancing down toward the boat. "I've heard about blow needles, but whoever would have thought the old hag could shoot them? That was a pretty close call."

With his usual curiosity, he gathered the needles one by one, then pinned them securely into his collar with the intention of studying them later on. He'd heard that among warriors there were two opposing schools of thought regarding these small weapons. One held that they could be effectively employed as a deterrent by blowing them into an enemy's face, while the other maintained that this was nonsense.

The proponents held that a very old technique for the needles' employment had been developed from a game played by seamstresses and weavers who migrated from China to Japan in the sixth or seventh century. Although it was not considered a method of attack per se, they explained, it was practiced, up until the time of the Ashikaga shogunate, as a preliminary means of fending off an adversary.

Those on the other side of the fence went so far as to claim that no ancient technique ever existed, although they did admit that needle-blowing had been practiced as a game at one time. While conceding that women may have amused themselves in this fashion, they adamantly denied that needle-blowing could be refined to the degree necessary to inflict injury. They also pointed out that saliva could absorb a certain amount of heat, cold or acidity, but it could do little to absorb the pain caused by needles puncturing the inside of a person's mouth. The reply to this, of course, was that with enough practice, a person could learn to hold the needles in the mouth painlessly and to manipulate them with the tongue with a great deal of precision and force. Enough to blind a man.

The nonbelievers then countered that even if the needles could be blown hard and fast, the chances of hurting anyone were minimal. After all, they said, the only parts of the face vulnerable to such attack were the eyes, and the chances of hitting them weren't very good, even under the best conditions. And unless the needle penetrated the pupil, the damage would be insignificant.

After hearing most of these arguments at one time or another, Musashi had been inclined to side with the doubters. After this experience, he realized how premature his judgment had been and how important and useful randomly acquired bits of knowledge could subsequently prove to be.

The needles had missed his pupil, but his eye was watering. As he felt around his clothing for something to dry it with, he heard the sound of cloth being torn. Turning, he saw a girl ripping a foot or so of red fabric from the sleeve of her undergarment.

Akemi came running toward him. Her hair was not done up for the New Year's celebration, and her kimono was bedraggled. She wore sandals, but no socks. Musashi squinted at her and muttered; though she looked familiar, he couldn't place the face.

"It's me, Takezō . . . I mean Musashi," she said hesitantly, offering him the red cloth. "Did you get something in your eye? You shouldn't rub it. That'll only make it worse. Here, use this."

Musashi silently accepted her kindness and covered his eye with the cloth. Then he stared at her face intently.

"Don't you remember me?" she said incredulously. "But you must!"

Musashi's face was a perfect blank.

"You must!"

His silence broke the dam holding back her long-pent-up emotions. Her spirit, so accustomed to unhappiness and cruelty, had clung to this one last hope, and now the light was dawning that it was nothing more than a fantasy of her own making. A hard lump formed in her breast, and she made a choking sound. Though she covered her mouth and nose to suppress the sobs, her shoulders quivered uncontrollably.

Something about the way she looked when crying recalled the innocent girlishness of the days in Ibuki, when she'd carried the tinkling bell in her obi. Musashi put his arms around her thin, weak shoulders.

"You're Akemi, of course. I remember. How do you happen to be here? It's such a surprise to see you! Don't you live in Ibuki anymore? What happened to your mother?" His questions were like barbs, the worst being the mention of Okō, which led naturally to his old friend. "Are you still living with Matahachi? He was supposed to come here this morning. You haven't by any chance seen him, have you?"

Every word added to Akemi's misery. Nestled in his arms, she could do no more than shake her weeping head.

"Isn't Matahachi coming?" he persisted. "What happened to him? How will I ever know if you just stand here and cry?"

"He . . . he . . . he's not coming. He never . . . he never got your message." Akemi pressed her face against Musashi's chest and went into a new spasm of tears.

She thought of saying this, of saying that, but each idea died in her feverish brain. How could she tell him of the horrid fate she had suffered because of her mother? How could she put into words what had happened in Sumiyoshi or in the days since then?

The bridge was bathed in the New Year's sun, and more and more people were passing by—girls in bright new kimono going to make their New Year's obeisance at Kiyomizudera, men in formal robes starting their rounds of New Year's calls. Almost hidden among them was Jōtarō, his gnomish thatch of hair in the same disheveled state as on any other day. He was nearly in the middle of the bridge when he caught sight of Musashi and Akemi.

"What's all this?" he asked himself. "I thought he'd be with Otsū. That's not Otsū!" He stopped and made a peculiar face.

He was shocked to the core. It might have been all right if no one were watching, but there they were chest to chest, embracing each other on a busy thoroughfare. A man and a woman hugging each other in public? It was shameless. He couldn't believe any grownup could act so disgracefully, much less his own, revered *sensei*. Jōtarō's heart throbbed violently, he was both sad and a little jealous. And angry, so angry that he wanted to pick up a rock and throw it at them.

"I've seen that woman somewhere," he thought. "Ah! She's the one who took Musashi's message for Matahachi. Well, she's a teahouse girl, so what could you expect? But how on earth did they get to know one another? I think I should tell Otsū about this!"

He looked up and down the street and peered over the railing, but there was no sign of her.

The previous night, confident that she would be meeting Musashi the next day, Otsū had washed her hair and stayed up till the early hours doing it up in proper fashion. Then she had put on a kimono given her by the Karasumaru family and, before dawn, set out to pay her respects at Gion Shrine and Kiyomizudera before proceeding to Gojō Avenue. Jōtarō had wanted to accompany her, but she had refused.

Normally it would be all right, she had explained, but today Jōtarō would be in the way. "You stay here," she said. "First I want to talk to Musashi alone. You can come along to the bridge after it gets light, but take your time. And don't worry; I promise I'll be waiting there with Musashi when you come."

Jōtarō had been more than a little peeved. Not only was he old enough to understand Otsū's feelings; he also had a certain appreciation of the attraction men and women felt for each other. The experience of rolling about in the straw with Kocha in Koyagyū had not faded from his mind. Even so, it remained a mystery to him why a grown woman like Otsū went around moping and weeping all the time over a man.

Search as he might, he could not find Otsū. While he fretted, Musashi and Akemi moved to the end of the bridge, presumably to avoid being so conspicuous. Musashi folded his arms and leaned on the railing. Akemi, at his

363

side, looked down at the river. They did not notice Jōtarō when he slipped by on the opposite side of the bridge.

"Why is she taking so much time? How long can you pray to Kannon?" Grumbling to himself, Jōtarō stood on tiptoe and strained his eyes toward the hill at the end of Gojō Avenue.

About ten paces from where he was standing, there were four or five leafless willow trees. Often a flock of white herons gathered here along the river to catch fish, but today none were to be seen. A young man with a long forelock leaned against a willow branch, which stretched out toward the ground like a sleeping dragon.

On the bridge, Musashi nodded as Akemi whispered fervently to him. She had thrown pride to the winds and was telling him everything in the hope that she could persuade him to be hers alone. It was difficult to discern whether her words penetrated beyond his ears. Nod though he might, his look was not that of a lover saying sweet nothings to his beloved. On the contrary, his pupils shone with a colorless, heatless radiance and focused steadily on some particular object.

Akemi did not notice this. Completely absorbed, she seemed to choke slightly as she tried to analyze her feelings.

"Oh," she sighed, "I've told you everything there is to tell. I haven't hidden anything." Edging closer to him, she said wistfully, "It's been more than four years since Sekigahara. I've changed both in body and in spirit." Then, with a burst of tears: "No! I haven't really changed. My feeling toward you hasn't changed a bit. I'm absolutely sure of that! Do you understand, Musashi? Do you understand how I feel?"

"Mm."

"Please try to understand! I've told you everything. I'm not the innocent wild flower I was when we met at the foot of Mount Ibuki. I'm just an ordinary woman who's been violated. . . . But is chastity a thing of the body, or of the mind? Is a virgin who has lewd thoughts really chaste? . . . I lost my virginity to—I can't say his name, but to a certain man—and yet my heart is pure."

"Mm. Mm."

"Don't you feel anything for me at all? I can't keep secrets from the person I love. I wondered what to say when I saw you: should I say anything or not? But then it became clear. I couldn't deceive you even if I wanted to. Please understand! Say something! Say you forgive me. Or do you consider me despicable?"

"Mm. Ah . . ."

"When I think of it again, it makes me so furious!" She put her face down on the railing. "You see, I'm ashamed to ask you to love me. I haven't the right to do that. But . . . but . . . I'm still a virgin at heart. I still treasure my first love like a pearl. I haven't lost that treasure, and I won't, no matter what kind of life I lead, or what men I'm thrown together with!"

Each hair of her head trembled with her sobbing. Under the bridge where her tears fell, the river, glistening in the New Year's sun, flowed on like Akemi's dreams toward an eternity of hope.

364

"Mm." While the poignance of her story elicited frequent nods and grunts, Musashi's eyes remained fixed on that point in the distance. His father had once remarked, "You're not like me. My eyes are black, but yours are dark brown. They say your granduncle, Hirata Shōgen, had terrifying brown eyes, so maybe you take after him." At this moment, in the slanting rays of the sun, Musashi's eyes were a pure and flawless coral.

"That has to be him," thought Sasaki Kojirō, the man leaning against the willow. He had heard of Musashi many times, but this was the first time he had set eyes on him.

Musashi was wondering: "Who could he be?"

From the instant their eyes met, they had silently been searching, each sounding the depths of the other's spirit. In practicing the Art of War, it is said that one must discern from the point of the enemy's sword the extent of his ability. This is exactly what the two men were doing. They were like wrestlers, sizing each other up before coming to grips. And each had reasons to regard the other with suspicion.

"I don't like it," thought Kojirō, seething with displeasure. He had taken care of Akemi since rescuing her from the deserted Amida Hall, and this patently intimate conversation between her and Musashi upset him. "Maybe he's the kind who preys on innocent women. And her! She didn't say where she was going, and now she's up there weeping on a man's shoulder!" He himself was here because he'd followed her.

The enmity in Kojirō's eyes was not lost on Musashi, and he was also conscious of that peculiar instant conflict of wills that arises when one *shugyōsha* encounters another. Nor was there any doubt that Kojirō felt the spirit of defiance conveyed in Musashi's expression.

"Who could he be?" thought Musashi again. "He looks like quite a fighter. But why the malicious look in his eye? Better watch him closely."

The intensity of the two men came not from their eyes but from deep inside. Fireworks seemed about to shoot from their pupils. From appearances, Musashi might be a year or two younger than Kojirō, but then again it might be the other way around. In either case, they shared one similarity: both were at that age of maximum impudence when they were certain they knew everything there was to know about politics, society, the Art of War and all other subjects. As a vicious dog snarls when it sees another vicious dog, so both Musashi and Kojirō knew instinctively that the other was a dangerous fighter.

Kojirō was the first to disengage his eyes, which he did with a slight grunt. Musashi, despite the touch of contempt he could see in Kojirō's profile, was convinced deep down that he'd won. The opponent had given in to his eyes, to his willpower, and this made Musashi happy.

"Akemi," he said, putting his hand on her shoulder.

Still sobbing with her face to the railing, she did not reply.

"Who's that man over there? He's somebody who knows you, isn't he? I mean the young man who looks like a student warrior. Just who is he?"

Akemi was silent. She had not seen Kojirō until now, and the sight threw her tear-swollen face into confusion. "Uh . . . you mean that tall man over there?"

"Yes. Who is he?"

"Oh, he's . . . well . . . he's . . . I don't know him very well."

"But you do know him, don't you?"

"Uh, yes."

"Carrying that great long sword and dressed to attract attention—he must think he's quite a swordsman! How do you happen to know him?"

"A few days ago," Akemi said quickly, "I was bitten by a dog, and the bleeding wouldn't stop, so I went to a doctor in the place where he happened to be staying. He's been looking after me the past few days."

"In other words, you're living in the same house with him?"

"Yes, well, I'm living there, but it doesn't mean anything. There's nothing between us." She spoke with more force now.

"In that case, I suppose you don't know much about him. Do you know his name?"

"His name is Sasaki Kojirō. He's also called Ganryū."

"Ganryū?" He had heard that name before. Though not exceptionally famous, it was known among the warriors in a number of provinces. He was younger than Musashi had imagined him to be; he took another look at him.

An odd thing happened then. A pair of dimples appeared in Kojirō's cheeks.

Musashi smiled back. Yet this silent communication was not full of peaceful light and friendship, like the smile exchanged between the Buddha and his disciple Ananda as they rubbed flowers between their fingers. In Kojirō's smile were both a challenging jeer and an element of irony.

Musashi's smile not only accepted Kojirō's challenge but conveyed a fierce will to fight.

Caught between these two strong-willed men, Akemi was about to start pouring out her feelings again, but before it came to that, Musashi said, "Now, Akemi, I think it'd be best for you to go back with that man to your lodgings. I'll come to see you soon. Don't worry."

"You'll really come?"

"Why, yes, of course."

"The name of the inn, it's the Zuzuya, in front of the Rokujō Avenue monastery."

"I see."

The casual manner of his reply was not enough for Akemi. She grabbed his hand from the railing and squeezed it passionately in the shadow of her sleeve. "You'll really come, won't you? Promise?"

Musashi's reply was drowned by a burst of belly-splitting laughter.

"Ha, ha, ha, ha, ha! Oh! Ha, ha, ha, ha! Oh . . ." Kojirō turned his back and walked away as best he could in view of his uncontrollable mirth.

Looking on acidly from one end of the bridge, Jōtarō thought: "Nothing could possibly be that funny!" He himself was disgusted with the world, and particularly with his wayward teacher and with Otsū.

"Where could she have got to?" he asked again as he started tramping angrily toward town. He had taken only a few steps when he spied Otsū's white face between the wheels of an oxcart standing at the next corner over. "There she is!" he shouted, then bumped into the ox's nose in his hurry to reach her.

Today, for a change, Otsū had applied a little rouge to her lips. Her makeup was somewhat amateurish, but there was a pleasant scent about her, and her kimono was a lovely spring outfit with a white and green pattern embroidered on a deep pink background. Jōtarō hugged her from behind, not caring whether he mussed her hair or smeared the white powder on her neck.

"Why are you hiding here? I've been waiting for hours. Come with me, quick!"

She made no reply.

"Come on, right now!" he pleaded, shaking her by the shoulders. "Musashi's here too. Look, you can see him from here. I'm mad at him myself, but let's go anyway. If we don't hurry, he'll be gone!" When he took her wrist and tried to pull her to her feet, he noticed her arm was damp. "Otsū! Are you crying?"

"Jō, hide behind the wagon like me. Please!"

"Why?"

"Never mind why!"

"Well, of all—" Jōtarō made no attempt to conceal his wrath. "That's what I hate about women. They do crazy things! You keep saying you want to see Musashi and go weeping all over the place looking for him. Now that he's right in front of you, you decide to hide. You even want me to hide with you! Isn't that funny? Ha— Oh, I can't even laugh."

The words stung like a whip. Lifting her swollen red eyes, she said, "Please don't talk that way. I beg you. Don't you be mean to me too!"

"Why accuse me of being mean? What have I done?"

"Just be quiet, please. And stoop down here with me."

"I can't. There's ox manure on the ground. You know, they say if you cry on New Year's Day, even the crows will laugh at you."

"Oh, I don't care. I'm just—"

"Well, then, I'll laugh at you! Laugh like that samurai a few minutes ago. My first laugh of the New Year. Would that suit you?"

"Yes. Laugh! Laugh hard!"

"I can't," he said, wiping his nose. "I'll bet I know what's wrong. You're jealous because Musashi was talking to that woman."

"It's . . . it's not that! It's not that at all!"

"Yes it is! I know it is. It made me mad too. But isn't that all the more reason for you to go and talk to him? You don't understand anything, do you?"

Otsū showed no signs of rising, but he tugged so hard at her wrist that she was forced to. "Stop!" she cried. "That hurts! Don't be so spiteful. You say I don't understand anything, but you don't have the slightest idea how I feel."

"I know exactly how you feel. You're jealous!"

"That's not the only thing."

"Quiet. Let's go!"

She emerged from behind the wagon, but not voluntarily. The boy pulled; her feet scraped the ground. Still tugging, Jōtarō craned his neck and looked toward the bridge.

"Look!" he said. "Akemi's not there anymore."

"Akemi? Who's Akemi?"

"The girl Musashi was talking to. . . . Oh, oh! Musashi's walking away. If you don't come right now, he'll be gone." Jōtarō let go of Otsū and started toward the bridge.

"Wait!" cried Otsū, sweeping the bridge with her eyes to make sure Akemi wasn't lurking about somewhere. Assured that her rival was really gone, she appeared immensely relieved and her eyebrows unfurrowed. But back she went, behind the oxcart, to dry her puffy eyes with her sleeve, smooth her hair and straighten her kimono.

"Hurry, Otsū!" Jōtarō called impatiently. "Musashi seems to have gone down to the riverbank. This is no time to primp!"

"Where?"

"Down to the riverbank. I don't know why, but that's where he went."

The two of them ran together to the end of the bridge, and Jōtarō, with perfunctory apologies, made a way for them through the crowd to the railing.

Musashi was standing by the boat where Osugi was still squirming around, trying to free her bonds.

"I'm sorry, Granny," he said, "but it seems Matahachi's not coming after all. I hope to see him in the near future and try to drum some courage into him. In the meantime, you yourself should try to find him and take him home to live with you, like a good son. That'd be a far better way to express your gratitude to your ancestors than by trying to cut off my head."

He put his hand under the rush mats and with a small knife cut the rope.

"You talk too much, Musashi! I don't need any advice from you. Just make up your stupid mind what you're going to do. Are you going to kill me or be killed?"

Bright blue veins stood out all over her face as she struggled out from under the mats, but by the time she stood up, Musashi was crossing the river, jumping like a wagtail across the rocks and shoals. In no time he reached the opposite side and climbed to the top of the dike.

Jōtarō caught sight of him and cried, "See, Otsū! There he is!" The boy went straight down the dike, and she did the same.

To Jōtarō's nimble legs, rivers and mountains meant nothing, but Otsū, because of her fine kimono, came to a dead halt at the river's edge. Musashi was now out of sight, but there she stood, screaming his name at the top of her lungs.

"Otsū!" came a reply from an unexpected quarter. Osugi was not a hundred feet away.

When Otsū saw who it was, she uttered a cry, covered her face with her hands for a moment and ran.

The old woman lost no time in giving chase, white hair flying in the wind. "Otsū!" she screamed, in a voice that might have parted the waters of the Kamo. "Wait! I want to talk to you."

An explanation for Otsū's presence was already taking shape in the old woman's suspicious mind. She felt sure Musashi had tied her up because he had a rendezvous with the girl today and had not wanted her to see this. Then, she reasoned, something Otsū said had annoyed him, and he had abandoned her. That, no doubt, was why she was wailing for him to come back.

"That girl is incorrigible!" she said, hating Otsū even more than she hated Musashi. In her mind, Otsū was rightfully her daughter-in-law, never mind whether the nuptials had actually taken place or not. The promise had been made, and if his fiancée had come to hate her son, she must also hate Osugi herself.

"Wait!" she shrieked again, opening her mouth almost from ear to ear.

The force of the scream startled Jōtarō, who was right beside her. He grabbed hold of her and shouted, "What are you trying to do, you old witch?"

"Get out of my way!" cried Osugi, shoving him aside.

Jōtarō did not know who she was, or why Otsū had fled at the sight of her, but he sensed that she meant danger. As the son of Aoki Tanzaemon and the sole student of Miyamoto Musashi, he refused to be pushed aside by an old hag's scrawny elbow.

"You can't do that to me!" He caught up with her and leapt squarely on her back.

She quickly shook him off, and taking his neck in the crook of her left arm, dealt him several sharp slaps. "You little devil! This'll teach you to butt in!"

While Jōtarō struggled to free himself, Otsū ran on, her mind in turmoil. She was young, and like most young people, full of hope, not in the habit of bemoaning her unhappy lot. She savored the delights of each new day as though they were flowers in a sunny garden. Sorrows and disappointments were facts of life, but they did not get her down for long. Likewise, she could not conceive of pleasure as completely divorced from pain.

But today she had been jolted out of her optimism, not once but twice. Why, she wondered, had she ever come here this morning?

Neither tears nor anger could nullify the shock. After thinking fleetingly of suicide, she had condemned all men as wicked liars. She had been by turns furious and miserable, hating the world, hating herself, too overcome to find release in tears or to think clearly about anything. Her blood boiled with jealousy, and the insecurity it caused made her scold herself for her many shortcomings, including her lack of poise at the moment. She told herself repeatedly to keep cool and gradually repressed her impulses beneath the veneer of dignity that women were supposed to maintain.

The entire time that strange girl was at Musashi's side, Otsū had not been able to move. When Akemi left, however, forbearance was no longer possible and Otsū felt irresistibly compelled to face Musashi and pour out how she felt. Although she had no idea where to begin, she resolved to open her heart and tell him everything.

But life is full of tiny accidents. One small misstep—a minute miscalculation made in the heat of the moment—can, in many instances, alter the shape of things to come for months or years. It was by letting Musashi out of her sight for a second that Otsū exposed herself to Osugi. On this glorious New Year's morning, Otsū's garden of delights was overrun by snakes.

369

It was a nightmare come true. In many a frenzied dream, she had encountered Osugi's leering face, and here was the stark reality bearing down on her.

Completely winded after running several hundred yards, she halted and looked back. For a moment, her breath stopped altogether. Osugi, about a hundred yards away, was hitting Jōtarō and swinging him around, this way and that.

He fought back, kicking the ground, kicking the air, landing an occasional blow on his captor.

Otsū saw that it would be only a matter of moments before he succeeded in drawing his wooden sword. And when he did, it was a dead certainty the old woman would not only unsheath her short sword but show no compunction about using it. At a time like this, Osugi was not one to show mercy. Jōtarō might well be killed.

Otsū was in a terrible predicament: Jōtarō had to be rescued, but she dared not approach Osugi.

Jōtarō did succeed in getting his wooden sword free of his obi but not in extracting his head from Osugi's viselike grip. All his kicking and flailing were working against him, because they increased the old woman's self-confidence.

"Brat!" she cried snidely. "What're you trying to do, imitate a frog?" The way her front teeth jutted out made her look harelipped, but her expression was one of hideous triumph. Step by scraping step, she pressed on toward Otsū.

As she glared at the terrified girl, her natural cunning asserted itself. In a flash it came to her that she was going about this the wrong way. If the opponent had been Musashi, trickery would not work, but the enemy before her was Otsū—tender, innocent Otsū—who could probably be made to believe anything, provided it was put to her gently and with an air of sincerity. First tie her up with words, thought Osugi, then roast her for dinner.

"Otsū!" she called in an earnestly poignant tone. "Why are you running away? What makes you flee the minute you lay eyes on me? You did the same thing at the Mikazuki Teahouse. I can't understand it. You must be imagining things. I haven't the slightest intention of doing you any harm."

An expression of doubt crept over Otsū's face, but Jōtarō, still captive, asked, "Is that true, Granny? Do you mean it?"

"Why, of course. Otsū doesn't understand how I really feel. She seems to be afraid of me."

"If you mean that, let go of me, and I'll go get her."

"Not so fast. If I let you go, how do I know you won't hit me with that sword of yours and run away?"

"Do you think I'm a coward? I'd never do anything like that. It looks to me as though we're fighting over nothing. There's been a mistake somewhere."

"All right. You go to Otsū and tell her I'm not angry at her anymore. There was a time when I was, but that's all over. Since Uncle Gon died, I've been wandering around all by myself, carrying his ashes at my side—a lonely old

370

lady with no place to go. Explain to her that whatever my feelings about Musashi, I still look upon her as a daughter. I'm not asking her to come back and be Matahachi's bride. I only hope she'll take pity on me and listen to what I have to say."

"That's enough. Any more and I won't be able to remember it all."

"All right, just tell her what I've said so far."

While the boy ran to Otsū and repeated Osugi's message, the old woman, pretending not to watch, sat down on a rock and gazed toward a shoal where a school of minnows were making patterns in the water. Would Otsū come, or would she not? Osugi stole a glance, faster than the lightning movements of the tiny fish.

Otsū's doubts were not easily dispelled, but eventually Jōtarō convinced her there was no danger. Timidly she began walking toward Osugi, who, reveling in her victory, smiled broadly.

"Otsū, my dear girl," she said in a motherly tone.

"Granny," replied Otsū, bowing to the ground at the old woman's feet. "Forgive me. Please, forgive me. I don't know what to say."

"There's no need for you to say anything. It's all Matahachi's fault. Apparently he still resents your change of heart, and at one time I'm afraid I thought ill of you too. But that's all water under the bridge."

"Then you'll pardon me for the way I acted?"

"Well, now," said Osugi, introducing a note of uncertainty, but at the same time squatting down beside Otsū.

Otsū picked at the sand with her fingers, scratching a small hole in the cold surface. Tepid water bubbled to the surface.

"As Matahachi's mother, I suppose I can say that you've been forgiven, but then there's Matahachi to consider. Won't you see him and talk to him again? Since he ran off with another woman of his own free will, I don't think he'd ask you to come back to him. In fact, I wouldn't permit him to do anything so selfish, but . . . "

"Yes?"

"Well, won't you at least agree to seeing him? Then, with the two of you there side by side, I'll tell him exactly what's what. That way, I'll be able to fulfill my duty as a mother. I'll feel I've done everything I could."

"I see," replied Otsū. From the sand beside her, a baby crab crawled out and scurried behind a rock. Jōtarō latched on to it, went behind Osugi and dropped it on the top of her head.

Otsū said, "But I can't help feeling that after all this time it would be better for me not to see Matahachi."

"I'll be right there with you. Wouldn't you feel better if you saw him and made a clean break of it?"

"Yes, but—"

"Then do it. I say this for the sake of your own future."

"If I agree . . . how are we to find Matahachi? Do you know where he is?"

"I can, uh, I can find him very quickly. Very quickly. You see, I saw him quite recently in Osaka. He got into one of his willful moods and went off and left me in Sumiyoshi, but when he does things like that, he always regrets them later. It won't be long before he shows up in Kyoto looking for me."

Despite Otsū's uncomfortable feeling that Osugi wasn't telling the truth, she was swayed by the old woman's faith in her worthless son. What led to her final surrender, however, was the conviction that the course proposed by Osugi was right and proper. "How would it be," she asked, "if I went and helped you look for Matahachi?"

"Oh, would you?" cried Osugi, taking the girl's hand in her own.

"Yes. Yes, I think I should."

"All right, come with me now to my inn. Ouch! What's this?" Standing up, she put her hand to the back of her collar and caught the crab. With a shiver, she exclaimed, "Now, how did that get there?" She held out her hand and shook it loose from her fingers.

Jōtarō, who was behind her, suppressed a snicker, but Osugi was not fooled. With flashing eyes, she turned and glared at him. "Some of your mischief, I suppose!"

"Not me. I didn't do it." He ran up the dike for safety and called, "Otsū, are you going with her to her inn?"

Before Otsū could answer for herself, Osugi said, "Yes, she's coming with me. I'm staying at an inn near the foot of Sannen Hill. I always stay there when I come to Kyoto. We won't be needing you. You go back to wherever you came from."

"All right, I'll be at the Karasumaru house. You come too, Otsū, when you've finished your business."

Otsū felt a twinge of anxiety. "Jō, wait!" She ran quickly up the dike, reluctant to let him go. Osugi, fearing the girl might change her mind and flee, was quick to follow, but for a few seconds Otsū and Jōtarō were alone.

"I think I ought to go with her," said Otsū. "But I'll come to Lord Karasumaru's whenever I have a chance. Explain everything to them, and get them to let you stay until I've finished what I have to do."

"Don't worry. I'll wait as long as necessary."

"Look for Musashi while you're waiting, won't you?"

"There you go again! When you finally find him, you hide. And now you're sorry. Don't say I didn't warn you."

"It was very foolish of me."

Osugi arrived and inserted herself between the two. The trio started walking back to the bridge, Osugi's needlelike glance darting frequently toward Otsū, whom she dared not trust. Although Otsū had not the slightest inkling of the perilous fate that lay before her, she nevertheless had the feeling of being trapped.

When they arrived back at the bridge, the sun was high above the willows and the pines and the streets well filled with the New Year's throng. A sizable group had congregated before the sign posted on the bridge.

"Musashi? Who's that?"

"Do you know any great swordsman by that name?"

"Never heard of him."

"Must be quite a fighter if he's taking on the Yoshiokas. That should be something to see."

Otsū came to a halt and stared. Osugi and Jōtarō, too, stopped and looked, listening to the softly reverberating whisper. Like the ripples caused by minnows in the shoal, the name *Musashi* spread through the crowd.

Book IV   WIND

The Withered Field

The swordsmen from the Yoshioka School assembled in a barren field overlooking the Nagasaka entrance to the Tamba highroad. Beyond the trees edging the field, the glistening of the snow in the mountains northwest of Kyoto struck the eye like lightning.

One of the men suggested making a fire, pointing out that their sheathed swords seemed to act like conduits, transmitting the cold directly to their bodies. It was the very beginning of spring, the ninth day of the new year. A frigid wind blew down from Mount Kinugasa and even the birds sounded forlorn.

"Burns nice, doesn't it?"

"Um. Better be careful. Don't want to start a brush fire."

The crackling fire warmed their hands and faces, but before long, Ueda Ryōhei, waving smoke from his eyes, grumbled, "It's too hot!" Glaring at a man who was about to throw more leaves on the fire, he said, "That's enough! Stop!"

An hour passed uneventfully.

"It must be past six o'clock already."

To a man, without giving it a thought, they lifted their eyes toward the sun.

"Closer to seven."

"The Young Master should be here by now."

"Oh, he'll show up any minute."

Faces tense, they anxiously watched the road from town; not a few were swallowing nervously.

"What could have happened to him?"

A cow lowed, breaking the silence. The field had once been used as pasture for the Emperor's cows, and there were still untended cows in the vicinity. The sun rose higher, bringing with it warmth and the odor of manure and dried grass.

"Don't you suppose Musashi's already at the field by the Rendaiji?"

"He may be."

"Somebody go and take a look. It's only about six hundred yards."

No one was eager to do this; they lapsed into silence again, their faces smoldering in the shadows cast by the smoke.

"There's no misunderstanding about the arrangements, is there?"

"No. Ueda got it directly from the Young Master last night. There couldn't be any mistake."

Ryōhei confirmed this. "That's right. I wouldn't be surprised if Musashi's there already, but maybe the Young Master's deliberately coming late to make Musashi nervous. Let's wait. If we make a false move and give people the impression we're going to the aid of the Young Master, it'll disgrace the school. We can't do anything until he arrives. What's Musashi anyway? Just a rōnin. He can't be that good."

The students who had seen Musashi in action at the Yoshioka dōjō the previous year knew otherwise, but even to them it was unthinkable that Seijūrō would lose. The consensus was that though their master was bound to win, accidents do happen. Moreover, since the fight had been publicly announced, there would be a lot of spectators, whose presence, they felt, would not only add to the prestige of the school but enhance the personal reputation of their teacher.

Despite Seijūrō's specific instructions that they were under no circumstances to assist him, forty of them had gathered here to await his arrival, give him a rousing send-off, and be on hand—just in case. Besides Ueda, five of the other Ten Swordsmen of the House of Yoshioka were present.

It was now past seven, and as the spirit of calm enjoined upon them by Ryōhei gave way to boredom, they mumbled discontentedly.

Spectators on their way to the bout were asking if there had been some mistake.

"Where's Musashi?"

"Where's the other one—Seijūrō?"

"Who are all those samurai?"

"Probably here to second one side or the other."

"Strange way to have a duel! The seconds are here, the principals aren't."

Though the crowd grew bigger and the buzz of voices louder, the onlookers were too prudent to approach the Yoshioka students, who, for their part, took no notice of the heads peering through the withered miscanthus or looking down from tree branches.

Jōtarō padded around in the midst of the mob, leaving a trail of little puffs of dust. Carrying his larger-than-life wooden sword and wearing sandals too big for him, he was going from woman to woman, checking one face after another. "Not here, not here," he murmured. "What could have happened to Otsū? She knows about the fight today." She had to be here, he thought. Musashi might be in danger. What could possibly keep her away?

But his search was fruitless, though he trudged about until he was dead tired. "It's so strange," he thought. "I haven't seen her since New Year's Day. I wonder if she's sick. . . . That old hag she went away with talked nice, but maybe it was a trick. Maybe she's done something awful to Otsū."

This worried him terribly, far more than the outcome of today's bout. He had no misgivings about that. Of the hundreds of people in the crowd, there was hardly one who did not expect Seijūrō to win. Only Jōtarō was sustained by unshakable faith in Musashi. Before his eyes was a vision of his teacher facing the lances of the Hōzōin priests at Hannya Plain.

Finally, he stopped in the middle of the field. "There's something else strange," he mused. "Why are all these people here? According to the sign, the fight is to take place in the field by the Rendaiji." He seemed to be the only person puzzled by this.

Out of the milling crowd came a surly voice. "You there, boy! Look here!"

Jōtarō recognized the man; he was the one who had been watching Musashi and Akemi whispering on the bridge on New Year's morning.

"What do you want, mister?" asked Jōtarō.

Sasaki Kojirō came up to him, but before speaking, slowly eyed him from head to toe. "Didn't I see you on Gojō Avenue recently?"

"Oh, so you remember."

"You were with a young woman."

"Yes. That was Otsū."

"Is that her name? Tell me, does she have some connection with Musashi?"

"I should say so."

"Is she his cousin?"

"Unh-unh."

"Sister?"

"Unh-unh."

"Well?"

"She likes him."

"Are they lovers?"

"I don't know. I'm only his pupil." Jōtarō nodded his head proudly.

"So that's why you're here. Look, the crowd's getting restless. You must know where Musashi is. Has he left his inn?"

"Why ask me? I haven't seen him for a long time."

Several men pushed their way through the crowd and approached Kojirō.

He turned a hawklike eye on them.

"Ah, so there you are, Sasaki!"

"Why, it's Ryōhei."

"Where've you been all this time?" Ryōhei demanded, grabbing Kojirō's hand as though taking him prisoner. "You haven't been to the dōjō for more than ten days. The Young Master wanted to get in some practice with you."

"So what if I stayed away? I'm here today."

Placing themselves discreetly around Kojirō, Ryōhei and his comrades led him off to their fire.

The whisper went around among those who had seen Kojirō's long sword and his flashy outfit. "That's Musashi, for sure!"

"Is that him?"

"It must be."

"Pretty loud clothing he's got on. He doesn't look weak, though."

"That's not Musashi!" Jōtarō cried disdainfully. "Musashi's not like that at all! You'd never catch him dressed up like a Kabuki actor!"

Presently even those who could not hear the boy's protest realized their mistake and went back to wondering what was going on.

Kojirō was standing with the Yoshioka students, regarding them with obvious contempt. They listened to him in silence, but their faces were sullen.

"It was a blessing in disguise for the House of Yoshioka that neither Seijūrō nor Musashi arrived on time," said Kojirō. "What you'd better do is split up into groups, head Seijūrō off and take him home quickly before he gets hurt."

This cowardly proposal enraged them, but he went further. "What I'm advising would do Seijūrō more good than any assistance he could possibly get from you." Then, rather grandly: "Heaven sent me here as a messenger for the sake of the House of Yoshioka. I shall give you my prediction: if they fight, Seijūrō will lose. I'm sorry to have to say this, but Musashi will certainly defeat him, maybe kill him."

Miike Jūrōzaemon thrust his chest against the younger man's and shouted, "That's an insult." His right elbow between his own face and Kojirō's, he was prepared to draw and strike.

Kojirō looked down and grinned, "I take it you don't like what I said."

"Ugh!"

"In that case, I'm sorry," said Kojirō blithely. "I won't attempt to be of further assistance."

"Nobody asked for your help in the first place."

"That's not quite right. If you had no need of my support, why did you insist that I come from Kema to your house? Why were you trying so hard to keep me happy? You, Seijūrō, all of you!"

"We were simply being polite to a guest. You think a lot of yourself, don't you?"

"Ha, ha, ha, ha! Let's stop all this, before it ends up with my having to fight all of you. But I warn you, if you don't heed my prophecy, you'll regret it! I've compared the two men with my own eyes, and I say the chances Seijūrō will lose are overwhelming. Musashi was at the Gojō Avenue bridge on New Year's morning. As soon as I laid eyes on him, I knew there was danger. To me, that sign you put up looks more like an announcement of mourning for the House of Yoshioka. It's very sad, but it seems to be the way of the world that people never realize when they're finished."

"That's enough! Why come here if your only purpose is to talk like that?"

Kojirō's tone became snide. "It also seems to be typical of people on the way down that they won't accept an act of kindness in the spirit in which it's offered. Go on! Think what you like! You won't even have to wait the day out. You'll know in an hour or less how wrong you are."

"Yech!" Jūrōzaemon spat at Kojirō. Forty men moved a step forward, their anger radiating darkly over the field.

Kojirō reacted with self-assurance. Jumping quickly to one side, he demonstrated by his stance that if they were looking for a fight, he was ready. The goodwill he had professed earlier now seemed a sham. An observer might well have asked if he wasn't using mob psychology to create an opportunity for himself to steal the show from Musashi and Seijūrō.

A stir of excitement spread through those close enough to see. This was not the fight they had come to watch, but it promised to be a good one.

Into the midst of this murder-charged atmosphere ran a young girl. Speeding along behind her like a rolling ball was a small monkey. She rushed in between Kojirō and the Yoshioka swordsmen and screamed, "Kojirō! Where's Musashi! Isn't he here?"

Kojirō turned on her angrily. "What is this?" he demanded.

"Akemi!" said one of the samurai. "What's she doing here?"

"Why did you come?" Kojirō snapped. "Didn't I tell you not to?"

"I'm not your private property! Why can't I be here?"

"Shut up! And get out of here! Go on back to the Zuzuya," shouted Kojirō, pushing her away gently.

Akemi, panting heavily, shook her head adamantly. "Don't order me around! I stayed with you, but I don't belong to you. I—" She choked and began to sob noisily. "How can you tell me what to do after what you did to me? After tying me up and leaving me on the second floor of the inn? After bullying and torturing me when I said I was worried about Musashi?"

Kojirō opened his mouth, ready to speak, but Akemi didn't give him the chance. "One of the neighbors heard me scream and came and untied me. I'm here to see Musashi!"

"Are you out of your mind? Can't you see the people around you? Shut up!"

"I won't! I don't care who hears. You said Musashi would be killed today— if Seijūrō couldn't handle him, you'd act as his second and kill Musashi yourself. Maybe I'm crazy, but Musashi's the only man in my heart! I must see him. Where is he?"

Kojirō clicked his tongue but was speechless before her vitriolic attack.

To the Yoshioka men, Akemi seemed too distraught to be believed. But maybe there was some truth in what she said. And if there was, Kojirō had used kindness as a lure, then tortured her for his own pleasure.

Embarrassed, Kojirō glared at her with unconcealed hate.

Suddenly their attention was diverted by one of Seijūrō's attendants, a youth by the name of Tamihachi. He was running like a wild man, waving his arms and shouting. "Help! It's the Young Master! He's met Musashi. He's injured! Oh, it's awful! A-w-w-ful!"

"What're you babbling about?"

"The Young Master? Musashi?"

"Where? When?"

"Tamihachi, are you telling the truth?"

Shrill questions poured from faces suddenly drained of blood.

Tamihachi went on screaming inarticulately. Neither answering their questions nor pausing to catch his breath, he ran stumbling back to the Tamba highroad. Half believing, half doubting, not really knowing what to think, Ueda, Jūrōzaemon and the others chased after him like wild beasts charging across a burning plain.

Running north about five hundred yards, they came to a barren field *381* stretching out beyond the trees to the right, quietly basking in the spring sunlight, on the surface serene and undisturbed. Thrushes and shrikes, chirping as though nothing had happened, hastily took to the air as Tamihachi scrambled wildly through the grass. He climbed up a knoll that looked like an ancient burial mound and fell to his knees. Clutching at the earth, he moaned and screamed, "Young Master!"

The others caught up with him, then stood nailed to the ground, gaping at the sight before their eyes. Seijūrō, clad in a kimono with a blue flowered design, a leather strap holding back his sleeves and a white cloth tied around his head, lay with his face buried in the grass.

"Young Master!"

"We're here! What happened?"

There was not a drop of blood on the white headband, nor on his sleeve or the grass around him, but his eyes and forehead were frozen in an expression of excruciating pain. His lips were the color of wild grapes.

"Is . . . is he breathing?"

"Barely."

"Quick, pick him up!"

One man knelt and took hold of Seijūrō's right arm, ready to lift him. Seijūrō screamed in agony.

"Find something to carry him on! Anything!"

Three or four men, shouting confusedly, ran down the road to a farmhouse and came back with a rain shutter. They gently rolled Seijūrō onto it, but though he seemed to revive a little, he was still writhing in pain. To keep him quiet, several men removed their obis and tied him to the shutter.

With one man at each corner, they lifted him up and began walking in funereal silence.

Seijūrō kicked violently, almost breaking the shutter. "Musashi . . . is he gone? . . . Oh, it hurts! . . . Right arm—shoulder. The bone . . . O-w-w-w! . . . Can't stand it. Cut it off! . . . Can't you hear? Cut the arm off!"

The horror of his pain caused the men carrying the improvised stretcher to avert their eyes. This was the man they respected as their teacher; it seemed indecent to look at him in this condition.

Pausing, they called back to Ueda and Jūrōzaemon. "He's in terrible pain, asking us to cut off his arm. Wouldn't it be easier on him if we did?"

"Don't talk like fools," roared Ryōhei. "Of course it's painful, but he won't die from that. If we cut his arm off and can't stop the bleeding, it'll be the end of him. What we've got to do is get him home and see how badly he's injured. If the arm has to come off, we can do it after proper steps have been taken to keep him from bleeding to death. A couple of you go on ahead and bring the doctor to the school."

There were still a lot of people about, standing silently behind the pine trees along the road. Annoyed, Ryōhei scowled blackly and turned to the men behind him. "Chase those people away," he ordered. "The Young Master's not a spectacle to be stared at."

Most of the samurai, grateful for a chance to work off their pent-up anger, took off on the run, making vicious gestures at the onlookers. The latter scattered like locusts.

"Tamihachi, come here!" called Ryōhei angrily, as if blaming the young attendant for what had happened.

The youth, who had been walking tearfully beside the stretcher, shrank in terror. "Wh-what is it?" he stammered.

"Were you with the Young Master when he left the house?"

"Y-y-yes."

"Where did he make his preparations?"

"Here, after we reached the field."

"He must have known where we were waiting. Why didn't he go there first?"

"I don't know."

"Was Musashi already there?"

"He was standing on the knoll where ... where ... "

"Was he alone?"

"Yes."

"How did it go? Did you just stand there and watch?"

"The Young Master looked straight at me and said ... he said if by any chance he should lose, I was to pick up his body and take it to the other field. He said you and the others had been there since dawn, but I wasn't under any circumstances to let anyone know anything until the bout was over. He said there were times when a student of the Art of War had no choice but to risk defeat, and he didn't want to win by dishonorable, cowardly means. After that, he went forward to meet Musashi." Tamihachi spoke rapidly, relieved to get the story told.

"Then what?"

"I could see Musashi's face. He seemed to be smiling slightly. The two of them exchanged some sort of greeting. Then ... then there was a scream. It carried from one end of the field to the other. I saw the Young Master's wooden sword fly into the air, and then ... only Musashi was standing. He had on an orange headband, but his hair was on end."

The road had been cleared of the curious. The men carrying the shutter were dejected and subdued but kept scrupulously in step so as to avoid causing further pain to the injured man.

"What's that?"

They halted, and one of the men in front raised his free hand to his neck. Another looked up at the sky. Dead pine needles were fluttering down on Seijūrō. Perched on a limb above them was Kojirō's monkey, staring vacantly and making obscene gestures.

"Ouch!" cried one of the men as a pine cone struck his upturned face. Cursing, he whipped his stiletto from his scabbard and sent it flying with a flash of light at the monkey, but missed his target.

At the sound of his master's whistle, the monkey somersaulted and bounced lightly onto his shoulder. Kojirō was standing in the shadows, Akemi at his side. While the Yoshioka men directed resentful eyes at him, Kojirō stared fixedly at the body on the rain shutter. His supercilious smile had deserted his face, which now bore a look of reverence. He grimaced at Seijūrō's agonized moans. With his recent lecture still fresh in mind, the samurai could only assume that he had come to have the last laugh.

Ryōhei urged the stretcher bearers on, saying, "It's only a monkey, not even a human being. Forget it, get moving."

"Wait," Kojirō said, then went to Seijūrō's side and spoke directly to him. "What happened?" he asked, but did not wait for an answer. "Musashi got the better of you, didn't he? Where did he hit you? Right shoulder? . . . Oh, this is bad. The bone's shattered. Your arm's like a sack of gravel. You shouldn't be lying on your back, being bounced along on the shutter. The blood might go to your brain."

Turning to the others, he commanded arrogantly, "Put him down! Go ahead, put him down! . . . What are you waiting for? Do as I say!"

Seijūrō seemed on the verge of death, but Kojirō ordered him to stand up. "You can if you try. The wound isn't all that serious. It's only your right arm. If you try walking, you can do it. You've still got the use of your left arm. Forget about yourself! Think of your dead father. You owe him more respect than you're showing now, a lot more. Being carried through the streets of Kyoto—what a sight that would be. Think what it would do to your father's good name!"

Seijūrō stared at him, his eyes white and bloodless. Then with one quick motion, he lifted himself to his feet. His useless right arm looked a foot longer than his left.

"Miike!" cried Seijūrō.

"Yes, sir."

"Cut it off!"

"Huh-h-h!"

"Don't just stand there! Cut off my arm!"

"But . . ."

"You gutless idiot! Here, Ueda, cut it off! Right now!"

"Y-y-yes, sir."

But before Ueda moved, Kojirō said, "I'll do it if you want."

"Please!" said Seijūrō.

Kojirō went to his side. Grasping Seijūrō's hand firmly, he lifted the arm high, at the same time unsheathing his small sword. With a quick, startling sound, the arm fell to the ground, and blood spurted from the stump.

When Seijūrō staggered, his students rushed to his support and covered the wound with cloth to stop the blood.

"From now on I'll walk," said Seijūrō. "I'll walk home on my own two feet." His face waxen, he took ten steps. Behind him, the blood dripping from the wound oozed blackly into the ground.

"Young Master, be careful!"

His disciples clung to him like hoops to a barrel, their voices filled with solicitude, which turned rapidly to anger.

One of them cursed Kojirō, saying, "Why did that conceited ass have to butt in? You'd have been better off the way you were."

But Seijūrō, shamed by Kojirō's words, said, "I said I'll walk, and walk I will!" After a short pause, he proceeded another twenty paces, carried more by his willpower than by his legs. But he could not hold on for long; after fifty or sixty yards, he collapsed.

"Quick! We've got to get him to the doctor."

They picked him up and made quickly for Shijō Avenue. Seijūrō no longer had the strength to object.

Kojirō stood for a time under a tree, watching grimly. Then, turning to Akemi, he said with a smirk, "Did you see that? I imagine it made you feel good, didn't it?" Her face deadly white, Akemi regarded his sneer with loathing, but he went on. "You've done nothing but talk about how you'd like to get back at him. Are you satisfied now? Is this enough revenge for your lost virginity?"

Akemi was too confused to speak. Kojirō seemed at this moment more frightening, more hateful, more evil than Seijūrō. Though Seijūrō was the cause of her troubles, he was not a wicked man. He was not blackhearted, not a real villain. Kojirō, on the other hand, was genuinely evil—not the type of sinner most people envisioned but a twisted, perverse fiend, who, far from rejoicing in the happiness of others, delighted in standing by and watching them suffer. He would never steal or cheat, yet he was more dangerous by far than the ordinary crook.

"Let's go home," he said, putting the monkey back on his shoulder. Akemi longed to flee but could not muster the courage. "It won't do you any good to go on looking for Musashi," mumbled Kojirō, talking to himself as much as to her. "There's no reason for him to linger around here."

Akemi asked herself why she did not take this opportunity to make a dash for freedom, why she seemed unable to leave this brute. But even as she cursed her own stupidity, she could not prevent herself from going with him.

The monkey turned its head and looked at her. Chattering derisively, it bared its white teeth in a broad grin.

Akemi wanted to scold it, but couldn't. She felt she and the monkey were bound together by the same fate. She recalled how pitiful Seijūrō had looked, and despite herself, her heart went out to him. She despised men like Seijūrō and Kojirō, and yet she was drawn to them like a moth to a red-hot flame.

A Man of Parts

Musashi left the field thinking, "I won." He told himself: "I defeated Yoshioka Seijūrō, brought down the citadel of the Kyoto Style!"

But he knew his heart was not in it. His eyes were downcast, and his feet seemed to sink into the dead leaves. A small bird on the wing, rising, exposing its underside, reminded him of a fish.

Looking back, he could see the slender pines on the mound where he had fought Seijūrō. "I only struck once," he thought. "Maybe it didn't kill him." He examined his wooden sword to assure himself there was no blood on it.

This morning, on his way to the appointed place, he had been expecting to find Seijūrō accompanied by a host of students, who might very well resort to some underhanded maneuver. He had squarely faced the possibility that he himself might be killed, and to avoid looking unkempt at the end had carefully brushed his teeth with salt and washed his hair.

Seijūrō fell far short of Musashi's preconception. He had asked himself if this could really be the son of Yoshioka Kempō. He could not perceive in the urbane and obviously well-bred Seijūrō the leading master of the Kyoto Style. He was too slender, too subdued, too gentlemanly, to be a great swordsman.

When the greetings were exchanged, Musashi thought uncomfortably: "I should never have gotten into this fight."

His regrets were sincere, because his aim was always to take on opponents who were better than he. One good look was sufficient; there had been no need to train for a year just to have this bout. Seijūrō's eyes betrayed a lack of self-confidence. The necessary fire was absent, not only from his face but from his whole body.

"Why did he come here this morning," wondered Musashi, "if he has no more faith in himself than this?" But Musashi was aware of his opponent's predicament and sympathized. Seijūrō was in no position to call the fight off, even if he wanted to. The disciples he'd inherited from his father looked up to him as their mentor and guide; he had no choice but to go through the motions. As the two men stood poised for battle, Musashi cast about for an excuse to call the whole thing off, but the opportunity did not present itself.

Now that it was all over, Musashi thought: "It's too bad! I wish I hadn't had to do it." And in his heart he prayed, for Seijūrō's sake, that the wound would heal quickly.

But the day's work was done, and it was not the mark of a mature warrior to stand around moping over the past.

As he quickened his pace, the startled face of an elderly woman appeared above a patch of grass. She'd been scratching about on the ground, apparently looking for something, and the sound of his footsteps brought a gasp to her lips. Dressed in a light, plain kimono, she would have been almost indistinguishable from the grass, except for the purple cord holding her cloak in place. Though her clothing was that of a layman, the kerchief hiding her round head was that of a nun. She was small of build and genteel in appearance.

Musashi was as astonished as the woman. Another three or four steps and he might have trampled on her.

"What are you looking for?" he asked genially. He glimpsed a string of coral prayer beads on her arm, just inside her sleeve, and a basket of tender wild plants in one hand. Her fingers and the beads trembled slightly.

To put her at her ease, Musashi said easily, "I'm surprised to see the greens up so early. I guess it's really getting to be spring. Hmm, I see you have some nice parsley there, and some rape and cottonweed. Did you pick them all yourself?"

The old nun dropped the basket and ran, shouting, "Kōetsu! Kōetsu!"

Musashi watched bemused as the little form retreated toward a slight rise in the otherwise flat field. From behind it rose a wisp of smoke.

Thinking it would be a shame for her to lose her vegetables after going to all the trouble of finding them, he picked them up and, basket in hand, started off after her. After a minute or so, two men came into view.

They had spread a rug on the sunny southern side of a gentle slope. There were also various implements used by devotees of the tea cult, including an iron kettle hanging over a fire and a pitcher of water to one side. Taking the natural surroundings for their garden, they had made themselves an open-air tea room. It all looked rather stylish and elegant.

One of the men seemed to be a servant, while the other's white skin, smooth complexion and well-composed features brought to mind a large china doll representing a Kyoto aristocrat. He had a contented paunch; self-assurance was reflected in his cheeks and in his posture.

"Kōetsu." The name rang a bell, for there was at this time a very famous Hon'ami Kōetsu living in Kyoto. It was rumored, with considerable envy, that he had been granted an annual stipend of one thousand bushels by the very wealthy Lord Maeda Toshiie of Kaga. As an ordinary townsman, he could have lived magnificently on this alone, but in addition he enjoyed the special favor of Tokugawa Ieyasu and was frequently received in the homes of high noblemen. The greatest warriors of the land, it was said, felt constrained to dismount and walk by his shop on foot, so as not to give the impression that they were looking down on him.

The family name came from their having taken up residence on Hon'ami Lane, and Kōetsu's business was the cleaning, polishing and appraising of swords. His family had gained a reputation as early as the fourteenth century and had flourished during the Ashikaga period. They had later been patronized by such leading daimyō as Imagawa Yoshimoto, Oda Nobunaga and Toyotomi Hideyoshi.

Kōetsu was known as a man of many talents. He painted, excelled as a ceramist and lacquer-maker and was regarded as a connoisseur of art. He himself considered calligraphy to be his forte; in this field he was generally ranked with acknowledged experts like Shōkadō Shōjō, Karasumaru Mitsuhiro and Konoe Nobutada, the creator of the famous Sammyakuin Style, which was so popular these days.

Despite his fame, Kōetsu felt that he was not fully appreciated, or so it would seem from a story that was going around. According to this tale, he often visited the mansion of his friend Konoe Nobutada, who was not only a nobleman but currently Minister of the Left in the Emperor's government. During one of these visits, the story went, the talk turned naturally to calligraphy and Nobutada asked, "Kōetsu, who would you select as the three greatest calligraphers in the country?"

Without the slightest hesitation, Kōetsu answered, "The second is yourself, and then I suppose Shōkadō Shōjō."

A little puzzled, Nobutada asked, "You start with the second best, but who is the best?"

Kōetsu, without so much as a smile, looked directly into his eyes and replied, "I am, of course."

Lost in thought, Musashi stopped a short distance from the group.

Kōetsu was holding a brush in his hand, and on his knees were several sheets of paper. He was studiously sketching the flow of water in a stream close by. This drawing, as well as earlier efforts lying scattered about on the ground, consisted solely of watery lines of a sort that, to Musashi's eye, any novice might be able to draw.

Looking up, Kōetsu said quietly, "Is something wrong?" Then, with steady eyes, he took in the scene: Musashi on one side and on the other his mother trembling behind the servant.

Musashi felt calmer in the presence of this man. He was clearly not the sort of person he came into contact with every day, but somehow he found him appealing. His eyes held a profound light. After a moment they began to smile at Musashi, as if he were an old acquaintance.

"Welcome, young man. Has my mother done something wrong? I'm forty-eight myself, so you can imagine how old she is. She's very healthy, but there are times when she complains about her eyesight. If she's done anything she shouldn't, I hope you'll accept my apologies." Placing his brush and pad on the small rug he was sitting on, he started to put his hands on the ground and make a deep bow.

Hurriedly dropping to his knees, Musashi stopped Kōetsu from bowing. "Then you're her son?" he asked in confusion.

"Yes."

"It is I who must apologize. I don't really know what made your mother afraid, but as soon as she saw me, she dropped her basket and ran off. Seeing she'd spilled her greens made me feel guilty. I've brought the things she dropped. That's all. There's no need for you to bow."

Laughing pleasantly, Kōetsu turned to the nun and said, "Did you hear that, Mother? You had the wrong impression entirely."

Immensely relieved, she ventured out from her place of refuge behind the servant. "Do you mean the rōnin didn't intend to harm me?"

"Harm? No, not at all. See, he's even brought back your basket. Wasn't that considerate of him?"

"Oh, I'm sorry," said the nun, bowing deeply, her forehead touching the prayer beads on her wrist. Quite cheerful now, she laughed as she turned to her son. "I'm ashamed to admit it," she said, "but when I first saw the young man, I thought I detected the smell of blood. Oh, it was frightening! I broke out in goose pimples. Now I see how foolish I was."

The old woman's insight amazed Musashi. She had seen right through him and without really knowing, had put it very candidly. To this woman's delicate senses, he must indeed have seemed a terrifying, gory apparition.

Kōetsu, too, must have taken in his intense, penetrating look, his menacing mane of hair, that prickly, dangerous element that said he was ready to strike at the slightest provocation. Still, Kōetsu seemed inclined to search out the good in him.

"If you're in no hurry," he said, "stay and rest awhile. It's so quiet and peaceful here. Just sitting silently in these surroundings, I feel clean and fresh."

"If I pick a few more greens, I can make some nice gruel for you," said the nun. "And some tea. Or don't you like tea?"

In the company of mother and son, Musashi felt at peace with the world. He sheathed his bellicose spirit, like a cat retracting its claws. In this pleasant atmosphere, it was hard to believe he was among perfect strangers. Before he realized it, he had removed his straw sandals and taken a seat on the rug.

Taking the liberty of asking some questions, he learned that the mother, whose religious name was Myōshū, had been a good and faithful wife before becoming a nun, and that her son was indeed the celebrated aesthete and craftsman. Among swordsmen, there was not one worth his salt who did not know the name Hon'ami—such was the family's reputation for sound judgment with regard to swords.

Musashi found it difficult to associate Kōetsu and his mother with the picture he had of how such famous people should look. To him they were simply ordinary people he had met by accident in a deserted field. This was the way he wanted it to be, for otherwise he himself might grow tense and spoil their picnic.

Bringing the kettle for the tea, Myōshū asked her son, "How old do you suppose this lad is?"

With a glance at Musashi, he replied, "Twenty-five or -six, I imagine."

Musashi shook his head. "No, I'm only twenty-three."

"Only twenty-three," exclaimed Myōshū. She then proceeded to ask the usual questions: where his home was, whether his parents were still alive, who had taught him swordsmanship, and so on.

She addressed him gently, as though he were her grandson, and this brought out the boy in Musashi. His manner of speech slipped into the youthful and informal. Accustomed as he was to discipline and rigorous training, to spending all his time forging himself into a fine steel blade, he knew nothing of the more civilized side of life. As the old nun talked, warmth spread through his weather-beaten body.

Myōshū, Kōetsu, the things on the rug, even the tea bowl, subtly fused into the atmosphere and became part of nature. But Musashi was impatient, his body too restless, to sit still for long. It was pleasant enough while they were chatting, but when Myōshū began staring silently at the teakettle and Kōetsu turned his back to continue his sketching, Musashi became bored. "What," he asked himself, "do they find so entertaining about coming out here like this? Spring's only barely begun. It's still cold."

If they wanted to pick wild greens, why not wait until it was warmer and more people were around? There would be lots of flowers and fresh green plants then. And if they wanted to enjoy a tea ceremony, why go to the trouble of lugging the kettle and tea bowls all the way out here? A well-known, prosperous family like theirs would surely have an elegant tea room in their house.

Was it to sketch?

Staring at Kōetsu's back, he found that by twisting a little to the side he could see the moving brush. Drawing nothing but the lines of flowing water, the artist kept his eyes on the narrow brook wending its way through the dry grass. He concentrated solely on the movement of the water, again and again trying to capture the flowing motion, but the exact feel seemed to elude him. Undeterred, he went on drawing the lines over and over.

"Um," thought Musashi, "drawing's not as easy as it looks, I guess." His ennui receding for the moment, he watched Kōetsu's brush strokes with fascination. Kōetsu, he thought, must feel very much as he himself did when he faced an enemy swordpoint to swordpoint. At some stage he would rise above himself and sense that he had become one with nature—no, not "sense," because all sensation would be obliterated at that moment when his sword cut through his opponent. That magic instant of transcendence was all.

"Kōetsu's still looking at the water as an enemy," he mused. "That's why he can't draw it. He has to become one with it before he'll succeed."

With nothing to do, he was sliding from boredom into lethargy and this worried him. He must not let himself go slack, even for a moment. He had to get away from here.

"I'm sorry I disturbed you," he said brusquely, and started retying his sandals.

"Oh, are you leaving so soon?" asked Myōshū.

Kōetsu turned around quietly and said, "Can't you stay a little longer? Mother is going to make the tea now. I gather you're the one who had a bout with the master of the House of Yoshioka this morning. A little tea after a fight does you good, or at least that's what Lord Maeda says. Ieyasu, too. Tea is good for the spirit. I doubt whether there's anything better. In my opinion, action is born of quiet. Stay and talk. I'll join you."

So Kōetsu knew about the fight! But maybe that was not so strange; the Rendaiji wasn't far away, only the next field over. A more interesting question was why he had said nothing about it so far. Was it simply that he regarded such matters as belonging to a world different from his own? Musashi took a second look at mother and son, then sat down again.

"If you insist," he said.

"We haven't much to offer, but we enjoy having you with us," said Kōetsu. He put the cover on his ink box and placed it on his sketches to keep them from blowing away. In his hands, the lid glittered like fireflies. It seemed to be sheathed in thick gold, with silver and mother-of-pearl inlay.

Musashi leaned forward to inspect it. Now that it was resting on the carpet, it no longer gleamed so brightly. He could see that there was nothing at all gaudy about it; its beauty was that of the gold-leaf and color paintings in Momoyama castles, reduced many times in size. There was also a hint of something very ancient about it, a dull patina suggestive of faded glories. Musashi stared intently. There was something comforting about the box.

"I made that myself," said Kōetsu modestly. "Do you like it?"

"Oh, can you make lacquerware too?"

Kōetsu merely smiled. As he looked at this youth, who seemed to admire the artifice of man more than the beauty of nature, he was thinking with amusement: "After all, he is from the country."

Musashi, unaware of Kōetsu's lofty attitude, said with great sincerity, "It's really beautiful." He couldn't take his eyes off the ink box.

"I said I made it myself, but actually the poem on it is the work of Konoe Nobutada, so I should say we made it together."

"Is that the Konoe family the imperial regents come from?"

"Yes. Nobutada's the son of the former regent."

"My aunt's husband has served the Konoe family for many years."

"What's his name?"

"Matsuo Kaname."

"Oh, I know Kaname well. I see him whenever I go to the Konoe house, and he sometimes comes to visit us."

"Is that so?"

"Mother, it's a small world, isn't it? His aunt is the wife of Matsuo Kaname."

"You don't say!" exclaimed Myōshū.

She moved away from the fire and placed the vessels for tea before them. There could be no doubt that she was perfectly at home with the tea ceremony. Her movements were elegant yet natural, her delicate hands graceful. Even at seventy, she seemed to be the epitome of feminine grace and beauty.

Musashi, uncomfortably out of his depth, sat politely on his haunches, in what he hoped was the same fashion as Kōetsu. The tea cake was a plain bun known as Yodo *manjū*, but it rested prettily on a green leaf of a variety not found in the surrounding field. Musashi knew there were set rules of etiquette for serving the tea, just as there were for using the sword, and as he watched Myōshū, he admired her mastery of them. Judging her in terms of swordsmanship, he thought to himself, "She's perfect! She doesn't leave herself open anywhere." As she whisked the tea, he sensed in her the same unearthly proficiency that one might observe in a master swordsman poised to strike. "It's the Way," he thought, "the essence of art. One has to have it to be perfect at anything."

He turned his attention to the tea bowl in front of him. This was the first time he had been served in this fashion, and he had not the slightest notion of what to do next. The tea bowl surprised him, for it resembled something that might have been made by a child playing in the mud. Yet seen against the color of this bowl, the deep green of the foam on the tea was more serene and ethereal than the sky.

He looked helplessly at Kōetsu, who had already eaten his tea cake and was holding his tea bowl lovingly in both hands, as one might fondle a warm object on a cold night. He drank down the tea in two or three sips.

"Sir," began Musashi hesitantly, "I'm just an ignorant country boy, and I don't know the first thing about the tea ceremony. I'm not even certain how to drink the tea."

Myōshū chided him gently. "Hush, my dear, it doesn't make any difference. There shouldn't be anything sophisticated or esoteric about drinking tea. If you're a country boy, then drink it the way you would in the country."

"It is really all right?"

"Of course. Manners are not a matter of rules. They come from the heart. It's the same with swordsmanship, isn't it?"

"When you put it that way, yes."

"If you become self-conscious about the proper way to drink, you won't enjoy the tea. When you use a sword, you can't let your body become too tense. That would break the harmony between the sword and your spirit. Isn't that right?"

"Yes, ma'am." Musashi unconsciously bowed his head and waited for the old nun to continue the lesson.

She laughed, a little tinkling laugh. "Listen to me! Talking about swordsmanship, when I know nothing at all about it."

"I'll drink my tea now," said Musashi with renewed confidence. His legs were tired from sitting in formal style, so he crossed them in front of him in a more comfortable position. Swiftly, he emptied the tea bowl and set it down again. The tea was very bitter. Not even for the sake of politeness could he force himself to say it was good.

"Will you have another cup?"

"No, thank you, that's quite enough."

What did these people find good about this bitter liquid? Why did they talk on so seriously about the "simply purity" of its flavor and all that sort of thing? Though understanding eluded him, he found it impossible to regard his host with anything but admiration. After all, he reflected, there must be more to tea than he himself had detected; otherwise it could not have become the focal point for a whole philosophy of aesthetics and life. Nor would great men like Hideyoshi and Ieyasu have displayed such interest in it.

Yagyū Sekishūsai, he recalled, was devoting his old age to the Way of Tea, and Takuan also had spoken of its virtues. Looking down at the tea bowl and the cloth beneath it, he suddenly envisioned the white peony from Sekishū-sai's garden and felt again the thrill it had given him. Now, inexplicably, the tea bowl struck him in the same forceful way. He wondered for a moment if he had gasped out loud.

He reached out, picked up the bowl lovingly and placed it on his knee. His eyes shone as he examined it; he felt an excitement he had never experienced before. As he studied the bottom of the vessel and the traces of the potter's spatula, he realized that the lines had the same keenness as Sekishūsai's slicing of the peony stem. This unpretentious bowl, too, had been made by a genius. It revealed the touch of the spirit, the mysterious insight.

He could hardly breathe. Why, he knew not, but he sensed the strength of the master craftsman. It came to him silently but unmistakably, for he was far more sensitive to the latent force that resided here than most people would have been. He rubbed the bowl, unwilling to lose physical contact with it.

"Kōetsu," he said, "I don't know any more about the utensils than I know about tea, but I would guess that this vessel was made by a very skillful potter."

"Why do you say that?" The artist's words were as gentle as his face, with its sympathetic eyes and well-formed mouth. The corners of his eyes turned down a bit, giving him an air of gravity, but there were teasing wrinkles around the edges.

"I don't know how to explain it, but I feel it."

"Exactly what do you feel? Tell me."

Musashi thought for a moment and said, "Well, I can't express it very clearly, but there's something superhuman about this sharp cut in the clay. . . ."

"Hmm." Kōetsu had the attitude of the true artist. He did not suppose for a moment that other people knew much about his own art, and was reasonably certain Musashi was no exception. His lips tightened. "What about the cut, Musashi?"

"It's extremely clean."

"Is that all?"

"No, no . . . it's more complicated than that. There's something big and daring about the man who made this."

"Anything else?"

"The potter himself was as sharp as a sword from Sagami. Yet he enveloped the whole thing in beauty. This tea bowl looks very simple, but there's a certain haughtiness about it, something regal and arrogant, as though he didn't regard other people as being quite human."

"Mm."

"As a person, the man who made this would be difficult to fathom, I think.

But whoever he is, I'd bet he's famous. Won't you tell me who it was?"

Kōetsu's heavy lips broke into a laugh. "His name is Kōetsu. But this is just something I made for fun."

Musashi, not knowing he had been undergoing a test, was genuinely surprised and impressed to hear that Kōetsu was able to make his own ceramics. What affected him more than the man's artistic versatility, however, was the human profundity concealed within this ostensibly plain tea bowl. It disturbed him a little to recognize the depth of Kōetsu's spiritual resources. Accustomed to measuring men in terms of their swordsmanship, he suddenly decided that his yardstick was too short. The thought humbled him; here was yet another man before whom he must admit defeat. For all his splendid victory of the morning, he was now no more than a bashful youth.

"You like ceramics too, don't you?" Kōetsu said. "You seem to have a good eye for pottery."

"I doubt whether that's true," Musashi replied modestly. "I was only saying what came into my head. Please forgive me if I said something foolish."

"Well, of course, you couldn't be expected to know a great deal about the subject, because to make a single good tea bowl involves a lifetime of experience. But you do have a feeling for aesthetics, a rather firm instinctive grasp. I suppose studying swordsmanship has developed your eye to a slight extent." There seemed to be something close to admiration in Kōetsu's remark, but as an older man, he could not bring himself to praise the boy. Not only would it not be dignified, it might also go to his head.

Presently, the servant returned with more wild greens, and Myōshū prepared the gruel. As she took it up on small plates, which also appeared to have been made by Kōetsu, a jar of fragrant sake was heated, and the picnic feast began.

The tea ceremony food was too light and delicate for Musashi's taste. His constitution craved more body and stronger flavor. Yet he made a dutiful attempt to savor the thin aroma of the leafy mixture, for he acknowledged that there was much he could learn from Kōetsu and his charming mother.

As the time passed, he began to look nervously about the field. Eventually, he turned to his host and said, "It's been very pleasant, but I should go now. I'd like to stay, but I'm afraid my opponent's men might come and cause trouble. I don't want to involve you in anything like that. I hope I'll have the opportunity to see you again."

Myōshū, rising to see him off, said, "If you're ever in the vicinity of Hon'ami Lane, don't fail to stop in to see us."

"Yes, please come and visit us. We can have a nice long talk," Kōetsu added.

Despite Musashi's fears, there was no sign of the Yoshioka students. Having taken his leave, he paused to look back at his two new friends on their rug. Yes, theirs was a world apart from his. His own long, narrow road would never lead him to Kōetsu's sphere of peaceful pleasures. He walked silently toward the edge of the field, his head bowed in thought.

Too Many Kojirōs

In the little drinking shop on the city's outskirts, the smell of burning wood and boiling food filled the air. It was only a shack—floorless, with a plank for a table and a few stools scattered about. Outside, the last glow of sunset made it seem that some distant building was on fire, and crows circling the Tōji pagoda looked like black ashes rising from the flames.

Three or four shopkeepers and an itinerant monk sat at the makeshift table, while in a corner several workmen gambled for drinks. The top they spun was a copper coin with a stick stuck through the hole in the middle.

"Yoshioka Seijūrō's really got himself in a mess this time!" said one of the shopkeepers. "And I, for one, couldn't be happier! A toast!"

"I'll drink to that," said another man.

"More sake!" another called to the proprietor.

The shopkeepers drank at a steady, fast pace. Gradually, only a faint light outlined the shop's curtain, and one of them bellowed, "I can't see whether I'm raising my cup to my nose or my mouth, it's so dark in here. How about some light!"

"Hold on a minute. I'm taking care of it," the proprietor said wearily.

Flames were soon shooting from the open earthenware oven. The darker it grew outside, the redder were the rays from the fire.

"I get mad every time I think of it," said the first man. "The money those people owed me for fish and charcoal! It came to quite a bit, I can tell you. Just look at the size of the school! I swore I'd get it at year end, so what happened when I got down there? Those Yoshioka bullies were blocking the entrance, blustering and threatening everybody. The nerve, throwing every bill collector out, honest shopkeepers who'd been giving them credit for years!"

"No use crying about it now. What's done is done. Besides, after that fight at the Rendaiji, they're the ones with reason to cry, not us."

"Oh, I'm not mad anymore. They got what was coming to them."

"Imagine, Seijūrō going down with hardly a fight!"

"Did you see it?"

"No, but I heard about it from someone who did. Musashi knocked him down with a single blow. And with a wooden sword, too. Crippled for life, he is."

"What'll become of the school?"

"It doesn't look good. The students are out for Musashi's blood. If they don't 395 kill him, they'll lose face completely. The Yoshioka name will have to come down. And Musashi's so strong, everyone figures the only person who might be able to beat him is Denshichirō, the younger brother. They're looking all over for him."

"I didn't know there was a younger brother."

"Hardly anyone did, but he's the better swordsman, according to what I heard. He's the black sheep of the family. Never shows his face at the school unless he needs money. Spends all his time eating and drinking on his name. Sponges off people who respected his father."

"They make quite a pair. How did an outstanding man like Yoshioka Kempō wind up with two sons like that?"

"It just goes to show that blood isn't everything!"

A rōnin was slumped in a stupor next to the oven. He'd been there for quite a while and the proprietor had left him alone, but now he roused him. "Sir, please move back a little," he said as he put more kindling on the fire. "The fire might burn your kimono."

Matahachi's sake-reddened eyes opened slowly. "Mm, mm. I know, I know. Just leave me alone."

This sake shop wasn't the only place where Matahachi had heard about the bout at the Rendaiji. It was on everyone's tongue, and the more famous Musashi became, the more wretched his wayward friend felt.

"Hey, bring me another," he called. "You don't have to heat it; just pour it in my cup."

"Are you all right, sir? Your face is awful pale."

"What's that to you! It's my face, isn't it?"

He leaned against the wall again and folded his arms.

"I'll show them one of these days." he thought. "Swordsmanship's not the only road to success. Whether you get there by being rich, or having a title, or becoming a gangster, so long as you get to the top you're all right. Musashi and I are both twenty-three. Not many of these fellows who make names for themselves at that age end up amounting to much. By the time they're thirty, they're old and tottering—'aging child prodigies.'"

Word of the duel at the Rendaiji had spread to Osaka, bringing Matahachi immediately to Kyoto. Though he had no clear purpose in mind, Musashi's triumph weighed so heavily on his spirit that he had to see for himself what the situation was. "He's riding high now," thought Matahachi antagonistically, "but he's due for a fall. There are plenty of good men at the Yoshioka School—the Ten Swordsmen, Denshichirō, lots of others. . . ." He could hardly wait for the day Musashi would receive his comeuppance. In the meantime, his own luck was bound to change.

"Oh, I'm thirsty!" he said aloud. By sliding his back up the wall, he managed to stand. All eyes watched as he bent over a water barrel in the corner, almost dunking his head, and drank several giant gulps from a dipper. Flinging the dipper aside, he pushed back the shop curtain and staggered out.

The proprietor soon recovered from his gaping surprise and ran after the wobbly figure. "Sir, you haven't paid yet!" he called.

"What's that?" Matahachi was barely articulate.

"I think you've forgotten something, sir."

"I didn't forget anything."

"I mean the money for your sake. Ha, ha!"

"Is that so?"

"Sorry to bother you."

"I don't have any money."

"No money?"

"Yeah, I don't have any at all. I did until a few days ago, but—"

"You mean you were sitting there drinking— Why, you . . . you . . ."

"Shut up!" After fishing around in his kimono, Matahachi came up with the dead samurai's pillbox, which he flung at the man. "Stop kicking up such a fuss! I'm a samurai with two swords. You see that, don't you? I haven't sunk low enough to sneak away without paying. That thing's worth more than the sake I had. You can keep the change!"

The pillbox struck the man squarely in the face. He squealed with pain and covered his eyes with his hands. The other customers, who had stuck their heads through slits in the shop curtain, shouted in indignation. Like many a drunk, they were indignant at seeing another of their kind welsh on his bill.

"The bastard!"

"Rotten cheat!"

"Let's teach him a lesson!"

They ran out and surrounded Matahachi.

"Bastard! Pay up! You're not going to get away with this."

"Crook! You probably pull the same stunt all the time. If you can't pay, we'll hang you by the neck!"

Matahachi put his hand to his sword to scare them off.

"You think you can?" he snarled. "That should be fun. Just try it! Do you know who I am?"

"We know *what* you are—a filthy rōnin from the garbage heap, with less pride than a beggar and more gall than a thief!"

"You're asking for it!" cried Matahachi, glaring and knitting his brow fiercely. "You'd sing a different tune if you knew my name."

"Your name? What's so special about it?"

"I am Sasaki Kojirō, fellow student of Itō Ittōsai, swordsman of the Chūjō Style. You must have heard of me!"

"Don't make me laugh! Never mind the fancy names; just pay up."

One man stretched out his hand to grab at Matahachi, who cried, "If the pillbox isn't enough, I'll give you a bit of my sword too!" Quickly drawing the weapon, he struck at the man's hand, cutting it clean off.

The others, seeing that they had underestimated their adversary, reacted as if it were their blood that had been spilled. They sprinted off into the darkness.

A look of triumph on his face, Matahachi challenged them anyway. "Come back, you vermin! I'll show you how Kojirō uses his sword when he's serious. Come on, I'll take your heads off for you."

He looked up at the heavens and giggled, his white teeth gleaming in the darkness as he exulted over his success. Then abruptly his mood changed. His face wrapped in sadness, he seemed on the verge of tears. Ramming his sword clumsily back into its scabbard, he started walking unsteadily away.

The pillbox on the ground sparkled under the stars. Made of black sandalwood, with a shell inlay, it didn't look very valuable, but a glint of the blue nacre gave it the subtle beauty of a tiny cluster of fireflies.

Coming out of the shack, the itinerant monk saw the pillbox and picked it up. He started to walk on but then went back and stood under the shop's eaves. In the dim light from a crack in the wall, he examined the design and the cord carefully. "Hmm," he thought. "This is definitely the master's. He must have had it with him when he was killed at Fushimi Castle. Yes, here's his name, Tenki, written on the bottom."

The monk hurried off after Matahachi. "Sasaki!" he called. "Sasaki Kojirō!"

Matahachi heard the name, but in his befuddled condition, failed this time to connect it with himself. He stumbled on from Kujō Avenue up Horikawa Street.

The monk caught up with him and took hold of the end of his scabbard. "Wait, Kojirō," he said. "Wait just a moment."

"Eh?" Matahachi hiccuped. "Do you mean me?"

"You're Sasaki Kojirō, aren't you?" A severe light shone in the monk's eyes.

Matahachi became slightly more sober. "Yes, I'm Kojirō. What's that got to do with you?"

"I want to ask you a question."

"Well, what is it?"

"Just where did you get this pillbox?"

"Pillbox?" he asked vacantly.

"Yes. Where did you get it? That's all I want to know. How did it come into your possession?" The monk spoke rather formally. He was still young, perhaps twenty-six or so, and did not appear to be one of the spiritless beggar monks who wandered from temple to temple living on charity. In one hand he had a round oak staff, more than six feet long.

"Who are you anyway?" demanded Matahachi, concern beginning to show on his face.

"That doesn't matter. Why don't you just tell me where this came from?"

"It didn't come from anywhere. It's mine, always has been."

"You're lying! Tell me the truth."

"I've told you the truth already."

"You refuse to confess?"

"Confess to what?" asked Matahachi innocently.

"You're not Kojirō!" Immediately the staff in the monk's hand split the air.

Matahachi's instincts pulled him backward, but he was still too groggy to react quickly. The staff connected, and with a shriek of pain, he staggered back fifteen or twenty feet before landing on his backside. On his feet again, he took off.

The monk gave chase and after a few paces hurled the oak staff. Matahachi heard it coming and lowered his head. The flying missile sailed past his ear. Terrified, he doubled his speed.

When the monk reached the fallen weapon, he seized it, and taking careful aim, threw it again, but again Matahachi ducked.

Running at full speed for more than a mile, Matahachi passed Rokujō Avenue and approached Gojō, finally decided he'd lost his pursuer and stopped. Rapping his chest, he panted, "That staff—terrible weapon! A man has to be careful these days."

Cold sober and burning with thirst, he began searching for a well. He found one at the far end of a narrow alley. He pulled up the bucket and guzzled his fill, then put the bucket on the ground and splashed water on his sweaty face.

"Who can that have been?" he wondered. "And what did he want?" But as soon as he began to feel normal again, dejection set in. Before his eyes he saw the agonized chinless face of the corpse at Fushimi.

That he had used up the dead man's money hurt his conscience, and not for the first time he thought about atoning for his misdeeds. "When I have money," he vowed, "the first thing I'm going to do is pay back what I borrowed. Maybe after I'm successful, I'll put up a memorial stone to him.

"The certificate is all that's left. Maybe I should get rid of it. If the wrong person found out I have it, it might lead to complications." He reached inside his kimono and touched the scroll, which he always kept tucked in the stomach wrapper under his obi, though this was rather uncomfortable.

Even if he couldn't convert it into a vast amount of money, it might lead to some opening, to that magic first rung on the ladder of success. The unfortunate experience with Akakabe Yasoma hadn't cured him of dreaming.

The certificate had already come in handy, for he had found that by showing it at small, nameless dōjōs or to innocent townspeople with an urge to learn swordsmanship, he could not only command their respect but receive a free meal and a place to sleep, without so much as asking. This was the way he had survived during the past six months.

"No reason to throw it away. What's wrong with me? I seem to be getting more and more timid. Maybe that's what keeps me from getting ahead in the world. From now on, I'm not going to be like that! I'll be big and bold, like Musashi. I'll show them!"

He looked around at the shanties surrounding the well. The people living here struck him as enviable. Their houses sagged under the weight of the mud and weeds on their roofs, but at least they had shelter. Somewhat abjectly, he peeped in on some of the families. In one dwelling, he saw a husband and wife facing each other over the single pot that held their meager dinner. Near them were a son and daughter, together with their grandmother, doing some piecework.

Despite the paucity of worldly goods, there existed a spirit of family unity, a treasure that even great men like Hideyoshi and Ieyasu lacked. Matahachi reflected that the more poverty-stricken people were, the stronger their mutual affection grew. Even the poor could know the joy of being human.

With a tinge of shame, he recalled the clash of wills that had led him to 399 stalk angrily away from his own mother at Sumiyoshi. "I shouldn't have done that to her," he thought. "Whatever her faults, there'll never be anyone else who loves me the way she does."

During the week they had been together, going, to his great annoyance, from shrine to temple and temple to shrine, Osugi had told him time and time again about the miraculous powers of the Kannon at Kiyomizudera. "No boddhisattva in the world works greater wonders," she had assured him. "Less than three weeks after I went there to pray, Kannon led Takezō to me—brought him right to the temple. I know you don't care much for religion, but you'd better have faith in that Kannon."

Now that he thought of it, she had mentioned that after the beginning of the new year, she planned to go to Kiyomizu and ask Kannon's protection for the Hon'iden family. There's where he should go! He had no place to sleep tonight; he could spend the night on the porch, and there was a chance he'd see his mother again.

As he headed down dark streets toward Gojō Avenue, he was joined by a pack of barking stray mongrels, not, unfortunately, of the sort that could be silenced by throwing a rock or two at them. But he was used to being barked at, and it didn't bother him when the dogs came up snarling and baring their teeth.

At Matsubara, a pine woods near Gojō Avenue, he saw another pack of curs gathered around a tree. The ones escorting him loped off to join them. There were more than he could count, all raising a great racket, some jumping five and six feet up the tree trunk.

Straining his eyes, he could barely make out a girl crouched trembling on a branch. Or at least he was fairly sure it was a girl.

He shook his fist and shouted to drive the dogs away. When this had no effect, he threw rocks, also to no avail. Then he remembered having heard that the way to scare dogs away was to get down on all fours and roar loudly, so he tried that. But this did not work either, possibly because there were so many of them, jumping about like fish in a net, wagging their tails, scratching the bark of the tree and howling viciously.

It suddenly occurred to him that a woman might consider it ludicrous for a young man with two swords to be down on all fours acting like an animal. With a curse, he jumped to his feet. The next instant, one dog gave a final howl and died. When the others saw Matahachi's bloody sword hanging above the body, they drew together, their bony backs heaving up and down like ocean waves.

"You want more, uh?"

Sensing the threat of the sword, the dogs scattered in all directions.

"You up there!" he called. "You can come down now."

He heard a pretty little metallic tinkle among the pine needles. "It's Akemi!" he gasped. "Akemi, is that you?"

And it was Akemi's voice that called down, "Who are you?"

"Matahachi. Can't you tell from my voice?"

"It couldn't be! Did you say Matahachi?"

"What are you doing up there? You're not the type to be frightened by dogs."

"I'm not up here because of the dogs."

"Well, whatever you're hiding from, come down."

From her perch on the limb, Akemi peered around into the silent darkness. "Matahachi!" she said urgently. "Get away from here. I think he's come looking for me."

"He? Who's he?"

"There's no time to talk about it. A man. He offered to help me at the end of last year, but he's a beast. At first I thought he was kind, then he did all sorts of cruel things to me. Tonight I saw a chance to get away."

"It's not Okō who's after you?"

"No, not Mother; it's a man!"

"Gion Tōji, maybe?"

"Don't be ridiculous. I'm not afraid of *him.* . . . Oh, oh—he's right over there. If you stay here, he'll find me. He'll do something awful to you too! Hide quick!"

"Do you expect me to run just because some man has turned up?" He stood where he was, fidgeting with indecision. He had half a mind to perform a valiant deed. He was a man. He had a woman in distress on his hands. And he would have liked to make up for the mortification of having been on his hands and knees trying to scare the dogs away. The more Akemi urged him to hide, the more he longed to demonstrate his virility, both to her and to himself.

"Who's there?"

The words were spoken simultaneously by Matahachi and Kojirō. Kojirō glared at Matahachi's sword and the blood dripping from it. "Who are you?" he demanded belligerently.

Matahachi remained silent. Having heard the fear in Akemi's voice, he grew tense. But after a second look, he relaxed. The stranger was tall and well built, but no older than Matahachi himself. From his boyish hairdo and outfit, Matahachi took him to be a rank novice, and contempt came into his eyes. The monk had given him a real scare, but he was sure he could not lose to this young fop.

"Could this be the brute who was tormenting Akemi?" he wondered. "He looks green as a gourd to me. I haven't heard what it's all about yet, but if he's causing her a lot of trouble, I guess I'll just have to give him a lesson or two."

"Who are you?" Kojirō asked again. The force of the utterance was such as to roll away the darkness around them.

"Me?" Matahachi answered teasingly. "I am merely a human being." He grinned deliberately.

The blood rushed to Kojirō's face. "So you have no name," he said. "Or could it be that you're ashamed of your name?"

Provoked but unafraid, Matahachi retorted, "I see no need to give my name to a stranger, who probably wouldn't recognize it anyway."

"Watch how you talk!" snapped Kojirō. "But let's leave the fight between you and me until later. I'm going to get that girl down from the tree and take her back where she belongs. You wait here."

"Don't talk like a fool! What makes you think I'll let you have her?"

"What's it got to do with you?"

"That girl's mother used to be my wife, and I'm not going to let her be harmed. If you lay one finger on her, I'll slice you to bits."

"Now, this is interesting. You seem to fancy yourself to be a samurai, though I must say I haven't seen such a bony one for many a day. But there's something you should know. This Drying Pole on my back has been weeping in its sleep, because not once since it was passed on as a family heirloom has it gotten its fill of blood. It's getting a little rusty too, so now I think I'll polish it a bit on that scrawny carcass of yours. And don't try to run away!"

Matahachi, lacking the sense to see that this was no bluff, said scornfully, "Stop talking so big! If you want to reconsider, now's the time. Just leave, while you can still see where you're going. I'll spare your life."

"The same to you. But listen, my fine human being. You boasted that your name was too good to mention to the likes of me. Pray, just what is that illustrious name? It's part of the etiquette of fighting to declare yourself. Or don't you know that?"

"I don't mind telling it, but don't be startled when you hear it."

"I shall steel myself against surprise. But first, what is your style of swordsmanship?"

Matahachi figured that no one who prattled on in this fashion could be much of a swordsman; his estimation of his opponent dropped even lower.

"I," he informed Kojirō, "hold a certificate in the Chūjō Style, which branched off from the style of Toda Seigen."

Kojirō, astonished, tried to hide a gasp.

Matahachi, believing that he had the advantage, decided it would be foolish not to press it. Mimicking his questioner, he said, "Now would you tell me your style? It's part of the etiquette of fighting, you know."

"Later. Just who did you learn the Chūjō Style from?"

"From Kanemaki Jisai, of course," Matahachi answered glibly. "Who else?"

"Oh?" exclaimed Kojirō, now really puzzled. "And do you know Itō Ittōsai?"

"Naturally." Interpreting Kojirō's questions as proof his story was taking effect, Matahachi felt sure the young man would soon propose a compromise. Laying it on a bit thicker, he said, "I supposed there's no reason to hide my connection with Itō Ittōsai. He was a predecessor of mine. By that, I mean that we both studied under Kanemaki Jisai. Why do you ask?"

Kojirō ignored the question. "Then may I ask again, just who are you?"

"I am Sasaki Kojirō."

"Say that again!"

"I am Sasaki Kojirō," Matahachi repeated very politely.

After a moment of dumbfounded silence, Kojirō uttered a low hum and showed his dimples.

402

Matahachi glared at him. "Why do you look at me that way? Does my name take you by surprise?"

"I should say it does."

"All right then—go away!" Matahachi commanded menacingly, raising his chin.

"Ha, ha, ha, ha, ha! Oh! Ha, ha, ha!" Kojirō held his stomach to keep from collapsing with laughter. When he finally brought himself under control, he said, "I've met many people in the course of my travels, but never have I heard anything to compare with this. Now, Sasaki Kojirō, would you kindly tell me who *I* am?"

"How should I know?"

"But you must know! I hope I don't seem to be rude, but just to be sure I heard you right, would you repeat your name one more time?"

"Haven't you got ears? I'm Sasaki Kojirō."

"And I am . . . ?"

"Another human being, I suppose."

"No question about that, but what's my name?"

"Look, you bastard, are you making fun of me?"

"No, of course not. I'm quite serious. I've never been more serious in my life. Tell me, Kojirō, what's my name?"

"Why make a nuisance of yourself? You answer the question."

"All right. I shall ask myself my name, and then, at the risk of seeming presumptuous, I shall tell it to you."

"Good, let's have it."

"Don't be startled!"

"Idiot!"

"I am Sasaki Kojirō, also known as Ganryū."

"Wh-what?"

"Since the days of my ancestors, my family has lived in Iwakuni. The name Kojirō I received from my parents. I am also the person known among swordsmen as Ganryū. Now, when and how do you suppose it came about that there are two Sasaki Kojirōs in this world?"

"Then you . . . you're . . ."

"Yes, and even though a great number of men are traveling about the countryside, you're the first I've ever encountered with my name. The very first. Isn't it a strange coincidence that has brought us together?"

Matahachi was thinking rapidly.

"What's the matter? You seem to be trembling."

Matahachi cringed.

Kojirō came closer, slapped him on the shoulder, and said, "Let's be friends."

Matahachi, face dead white, jerked away and yelped.

"If you run, I'll kill you." Kojirō's voice thrust like a lance straight into Matahachi's face.

The Drying Pole screaming over Kojirō's shoulder was a silver snake. Only one strike, no more. In one bound Matahachi covered nearly ten feet. Like an insect blown from a leaf, he turned three somersaults and stretched out on the ground unconscious.

Kojirō did not even look his way. The three-foot sword, still bloodless, slid back into its scabbard.

"Akemi!" called Kojirō. "Come down! I won't do that sort of thing anymore, so come back to the inn with me. Oh, I knocked your friend down, but I didn't really hurt him. Get down here and take care of him."

No answer. Seeing nothing among the dark branches, Kojirō climbed up the tree and found himself alone. Akemi had run away from him again.

The breeze blew softly through the pine needles. He sat quietly on the limb, asking himself where his little sparrow could have flown. He simply could not fathom why she was so afraid of him. Had he not given her his love in the best way he knew how? He might have been willing to agree that his way of showing affection was a little rough, but he did not appreciate how different it was from the way other people made love.

A clue might be found in his attitude toward swordsmanship. When he had entered Kanamaki Jisai's school as a child, he had displayed great ability and was treated as a prodigy. His use of the sword was quite extraordinary. Even more extraordinary was his tenacity. He absolutely refused to give up. If he faced a stronger opponent, he clung on all the tighter.

In this day and age, the manner in which a fighter won was far less significant than the fact of winning. No one questioned methods very closely, and Kojirō's proclivity to hang on by hook or crook until he finally conquered was not considered dirty fighting. Opponents complained of his harassing them when others would have admitted defeat, but no one considered this unmanly.

Once when he was still a boy, a group of older students, whom he openly despised, pummeled him senseless with wooden swords. Taking pity on him, one of his attackers gave him some water and stayed with him until he revived, whereupon Kojirō seized his benefactor's wooden sword and beat him to death with it.

If he did lose a bout, he never forgot it. He would lie in wait until his enemy was off guard—in a dark place, asleep in bed, even in the toilet—and then attack with full force. To defeat Kojirō was to make an implacable enemy.

As he grew older, he took to speaking of himself as a genius. There was more than braggadocio in this, both Jisai and Ittōsai having acknowledged the truth of it. Nor was he making anything up when he claimed to have learned how to cut down flying sparrows and to have created his own style. This led the people in the neighborhood to regard him as a "wizard," an appraisal with which he heartily concurred.

Exactly what form his tenacious will to dominate took when Kojirō was in love with a woman, no one knew. But there could be no doubt that he would have his way. He himself, however, saw no connection whatever between his swordsmanship and his love-making. He couldn't begin to understand why Akemi disliked him, when he loved her so much.

As he pondered his love problems, he noticed a figure moving about under the tree, oblivious of his presence.

"Why, there's a man lying there," said the stranger. He stooped over for a closer look and exclaimed, "It's that rascal from the sake shop!"

It was the itinerant monk. Taking the pack off his back, he remarked, "He doesn't seem to be wounded. And his body's warm." He felt around and found the cord underneath Matahachi's obi, undid it, and tied Matahachi's hands behind his back. He then put his knees in the small of Matahachi's back and jerked his shoulders backward, putting considerable pressure on the solar plexus. Matahachi came to with a muffled groan. The monk carried him like a sack of potatoes to a tree and propped him up against the trunk.

"Stand up!" he said sharply, underscoring the point with a kick. "On your feet!"

Matahachi, who had been halfway to hell, began to regain his senses, but could not quite take in what was going on. Still in a stupor, he dragged himself into a standing position.

"That's fine," said the monk. "Just stay that way." He then tied Matahachi's legs and chest to the tree.

Matahachi opened his eyes slightly and uttered a cry of astonishment.

"Now, you phony," said his captor, "you led me quite a chase, but that's all over." Slowly he began working Matahachi over, slapping his forehead several times, sending his head thudding against the tree. "Where did you get the pillbox?" he demanded. "Tell me the truth. Now!"

Matahachi did not answer.

"So you think you can brazen it out, uh?" Infuriated, the monk clamped his thumb and forefinger on Matahachi's nose and shook his head back and forth.

Matahachi gasped, and since he seemed to be trying to speak, the monk let go of his nose.

"I'll talk," said Matahachi desperately. "I'll tell you everything." Tears streamed from his eyes. "What happened was, last summer . . ." he began, and then he told the whole story, ending with a plea for mercy. "I can't pay the money back right now, but I promise, if you don't kill me, I'll work hard and return it someday. I'll give you a written promise, signed and sealed."

Confessing was like letting the pus out of a festering wound. Now there was nothing more to hide, nothing more to fear. Or so he thought.

"Is that the absolute truth?" asked the monk.

"Yes." Matahachi bowed his head contritely.

After a few minutes of silent reflection, the monk drew his short sword and pointed it at Matahachi's face.

Quickly turning his head aside, Matahachi cried, "Are you going to kill me?"

"Yes, I think you'll have to die."

"I've told you everything in perfect honesty. I've returned the pillbox. I'll give you the certificate. One of these days I'll pay back the money. I swear I will! Why do you have to kill me?"

"I believe you, but my position is difficult. I live in Shimonida in Kōzuke, 405 and I was a retainer of Kusanagi Tenki. He was the samurai who died at Fushimi Castle. Though I'm dressed as a monk, I'm actually a samurai. My name is Ichinomiya Gempachi."

Matahachi, trying to wriggle free and escape, did not really hear any of this. "I apologize," he said abjectly. "I know I did the wrong thing, but I didn't mean to steal anything. I was going to deliver everything to his family. Then, well, I ran short of money and, well, I knew I shouldn't, but I used his. I'll apologize all you want, but please don't kill me."

"I'd rather you didn't apologize," said Gempachi, who seemed to be going through an emotional struggle of his own. Shaking his head sadly, he continued, "I've been to Fushimi to investigate. Everything fits in with what you said. Still, I must take something in the way of consolation back to Tenki's family. I don't mean money. I need something to show that vengeance has been done. But there's no villain—no single person killed Tenki. So how can I take them the head of his murderer?"

"I . . . I . . . I didn't kill him. Don't make any mistake about that."

"I know you didn't. But his family and friends don't know he was mobbed and murdered by common laborers. That's not the sort of story that would do him honor, either. I'd hate to have to tell them the truth. So though I feel sorry for you, I think you'll have to be the culprit. It'd help if you'd consent to my killing you."

Straining at his ropes, Matahachi cried, "Let me loose! I don't want to die."

"That's quite natural, but look at it another way. You couldn't pay for the sake you drank. That means you don't have the ability to take care of yourself. Rather than starve or lead a shameful existence in this cruel world, wouldn't it be better to rest in peace in another? If it's money you're worried about, I have a little. I'd be glad to send it to your parents as a funeral gift. If you prefer, I could send it to your ancestral temple as a memorial donation. I assure you it would be delivered in good order."

"That's insane. I don't want money; I want to live! . . . Help!"

"I've explained everything carefully. Whether you agree or not, I'm afraid you'll have to stand in as my master's slayer. Give up, my friend. Consider it an appointment with destiny." He gripped his sword and stepped back to give himself room to strike.

"Gempachi, wait!" called Kojirō.

Gempachi looked up and shouted, "Who's there?"

"Sasaki Kojirō."

Gempachi repeated the name slowly, suspiciously. Was another fake Kojirō about to descend on him from the sky? Still, the voice was too human to belong to a ghost. He jumped well away from the tree and raised his sword straight up in the air.

"This is absurd," he said, laughing. "It looks like everybody's calling himself Sasaki Kojirō these days. There's another one down here, looking very sad. Ah! I'm beginning to understand. You're one of this man's friends, aren't you?"

"No, I'm Kojirō. Look, Gempachi, you're ready to cut me in two the minute I
come down from here, aren't you?"

"Yes. Bring on all the phony Kojirōs you like. I'll take care of every one of them."

"That's fair enough. If you cut me down, you'll know I was a fake, but if you wake up dead, you can be sure I was the real Kojirō. I'm coming down now, and I warn you, if you don't slice me in midair, the Drying Pole will split you like a piece of bamboo."

"Wait. I seem to remember your voice, and if your sword is the famous Drying Pole, you must be Kojirō."

"You believe me now?"

"Yes, but what are you doing up there?"

"We'll talk about that later."

Kojirō passed over Gempachi's upturned face and landed behind him in a flurry of pine needles. The transformation amazed Gempachi. The Kojirō he remembered seeing at Jisai's school had been a dark-skinned, gawky boy; his only job had been drawing water, and in accordance with Jisai's love of simplicity, he had never worn any but the plainest of clothing.

Kojirō seated himself at the foot of the tree and motioned to Gempachi to do likewise. Gempachi then related how Tenki had been mistaken for an Osaka spy and stoned to death and how the certificate had come into Matahachi's hands. Though Kojirō was vastly amused to learn how he had acquired a namesake, he said that there was nothing to be gained by killing a man so lacking in strength as to impersonate him. There were other ways of punishing Matahachi. If Gempachi was worried about Tenki's family or reputation, Kojirō himself would go to Kōzuke and see to it that Gempachi's master was recognized as a brave and honorable warrior. There was no need to make Matahachi the scapegoat.

"Don't you agree, Gempachi?" concluded Kojirō.

"If you put it that way, I guess so."

"All right, that's that. I have to leave now, but I think you should go back to Kōzuke."

"I will. I'll go directly."

"To tell the truth, I'm rather in a hurry. I'm trying to find a girl who left me rather suddenly."

"Aren't you forgetting something?"

"Not that I know of."

"What about the certificate?"

"Oh, that."

Gempachi reached under Matahachi's kimono and took out the scroll. Matahachi felt light and unencumbered. Now that it seemed that his life would be spared, he was glad to be rid of the document.

"Hmm," said Gempachi. "Come to think of it, maybe this incident tonight was arranged by the spirits of Jisai and Tenki so that I could recover the certificate and give it to you."

"I don't want it," said Kojirō.

"Why?" asked Gempachi incredulously.

"I don't need it."

"I don't understand."

"I don't have any use for a piece of paper like that."

"What a thing to say! Don't you feel any gratitude toward your teacher? It took Jisai years to decide whether to give you the certificate. He didn't make up his mind until he was on his deathbed. He charged Tenki with delivering it to you, and look what happened to Tenki. You should be ashamed."

"What Jisai did was his business. I have ambitions of my own."

"That's no way to talk."

"Don't misunderstand me."

"You'd insult the man who taught you?"

"Of course not, but not only was I born with greater talents than Jisai; I intend to go farther than he did. Being an unknown swordsman somewhere off in the sticks is no aim of mine."

"Do you really mean that?"

"Every word of it." Kojirō had no compunction about revealing his ambitions, outrageous though they were by ordinary standards. "I'm grateful to Jisai, but being saddled with a certificate from a little-known country school would do me more harm than good. Itō Ittōsai accepted his, but he didn't carry on the Chūjō Style. He created a new style. I intend to do the same. My interest is the Ganryū Style, not the Chūjō Style. One of these days, the name Ganryū will be very famous. So you see, the document means nothing to me. Take it back to Kōzuke and ask the temple there to preserve it along with its records of births and deaths." There was not a trace of modesty or humility in Kojirō's speech.

Gempachi stared at him resentfully.

"Please give my regards to the Kusanagi family," Kojirō said politely. "One of these days I'll go east and visit them, of that you can be sure." He ended these words of dismissal with a broad smile.

To Gempachi, this final display of courtesy smacked of patronization. He thought seriously of taking Kojirō to task for his ungrateful and disrespectful attitude toward Jisai, but a moment's consideration told him it would be a waste of time. Walking over to his pack, he put the certificate in it, said a curt good-bye and took his leave.

After he was gone, Kojirō had a good laugh. "My, he was angry, wasn't he? Ha, ha, ha, ha!" Then he turned to Matahachi. "Now, what have you got to say for yourself, you worthless fake?"

Matahachi, of course, had nothing to say.

"Answer me! You admit that you tried to impersonate me, don't you?"

"Yes."

"I know you're called Matahachi, but what's your full name?"

"Hon'iden Matahachi."

"Are you a rōnin?"

"Yes."

"Take a lesson from me, you spineless ass. You saw me return that certificate, didn't you? If a man doesn't have enough pride to do a thing like that, he'll never be able to do anything on his own. But look at you! You use another man's name, steal his certificate, go about living on his reputation.

Could anything be more despicable? Maybe your experience tonight will teach you a lesson: a house cat may put on a tiger's skin, but it's still a house cat."

"I'll be very careful in the future."

"I'm going to refrain from killing you, but I think I'll leave you here to get free by yourself, if you can manage." On a sudden impulse, Kojirō slipped the dagger from his scabbard and began scraping off the bark above Matahachi's head. The chips tumbled down onto Matahachi's neck. "I need something to write with," grumbled Kojirō.

"There's a kit with a brush and ink stone in my obi," said Matahachi obligingly.

"Good! I'll just borrow them for a moment."

Kojirō inked the brush and wrote on the patch of tree trunk from which he had shaved the bark. Then he backed off and admired his handiwork. "This man," it said, "is an impostor who, using my name, has gone about the countryside committing dishonorable deeds. I have caught him, and I leave him here to be ridiculed by one and all. My name and my sword name, which belong to me and to no other man, are Sasaki Kojirō, Ganryū."

"That should do it," said Kojirō contentedly.

In the black forest, the wind was moaning like the tide. Kojirō left off thinking about his ambition for the future and returned to his immediate course of action. His eyes lit up as he bounded off through the trees like a leopard.

The Younger Brother

Since ancient times, people of the highest classes had been able to ride in palanquins, but it was only recently that a simplified type had become available to the common people. It was little more than a large, low-sided basket suspended from a horizontal carrying pole, and to avoid falling out, the passenger had to hold on tightly to straps in front and back. The bearers, chanting rhythmically to keep in step, had a tendency to treat their customers like so much cargo. Those who chose this form of conveyance were advised to adjust their breathing to the rhythm of the bearers, especially when they were running.

The palanquin moving rapidly toward the pine woods on Gojō Avenue was accompanied by seven or eight men. Both the bearers and the other men were panting as though they were about to spit up their hearts.

"We're on Gojō Avenue."

"Isn't this Matsubara?"

"Not much farther."

Though the lanterns they carried bore a crest used by courtesans in the licensed quarter in Osaka, the passenger was no lady of the night.

"Denshichirō!" called one of the attendants in front. "We're almost at Shijō Avenue."

Denshichirō did not hear; he was asleep, his head bobbing up and down like a paper tiger's. Then the basket lurched, and a bearer put his hand out to keep his passenger from being spilled onto the ground.

Opening his large eyes, Denshichirō said, "I'm thirsty. Give me some sake!"

Thankful for a chance to rest, the bearers lowered the palanquin to the ground and began wiping the clammy sweat off their faces and hairy chests with hand towels.

"There's not much sake left," said an attendant, handing the bamboo tube to Denshichirō.

He emptied it in one draft, then complained, "It's cold—sets my teeth on edge." But it woke him up enough to observe, "It's still dark. We must have made very good time."

"As far as your brother is concerned, it must seem a long time. He's so eager to see you that each minute is like a year."

"I hope he's still alive."

"The doctor said he would be. He's restless, though, and his wound hemorrhages. That could be dangerous."

Denshichirō lifted the empty tube to his lips and turned it upside down. "Musashi!" he said disgustedly, throwing the tube away. "Let's go!" he bellowed. "Hurry up!"

Denshichirō, a strong drinker, an even stronger fighter and a quick-tempered man, was almost the perfect antithesis of his brother. There were some who, even when Kempō was still alive, had had the audacity to assert that he was more capable than his father. The young man himself shared this view of his talents. During their father's lifetime, the two brothers worked out together in the dōjō and somehow managed to get along, but as soon as Kempō died, Denshichirō stopped participating in the activities of the school and had gone so far as to tell Seijūrō to his face that he should retire and leave matters concerning swordsmanship to him.

Since his departure for Ise the previous year, it had been rumored that he was whiling away his time in Yamato Province. It was only after the disaster at the Rendaiji that men were sent in search of him. Denshichirō, despite his distaste for Seijūrō, readily consented to return.

In the impatient rush back to Kyoto, he had driven the bearers so hard that they had had to be changed three or four times. But he had found time to stop at each station on the highway to buy sake. Perhaps the alcohol was needed to quiet his nerves, for he was definitely in a state of extreme agitation.

As they were about to get under way again, barking dogs in the dark woods attracted their attention.

410   "What do you suppose is going on?"

"Nothing but a pack of dogs."

The city was full of stray dogs, great numbers of them coming in from the outlying districts, now that there were no longer any battles to furnish them with a supply of human meat.

Denshichirō shouted angrily to stop dawdling, but one of the students said, "Wait; there's something funny about what's going on over there."

"Go see what it is," said Denshichirō, who then proceeded to take the lead himself.

After Kojirō left, the dogs had come back. The three or four circles of canines around Matahachi and his tree were raising a tremendous racket. If dogs were capable of the higher sentiments, it might be imagined that they were taking revenge for the death of one of their flock. It is far more likely, however, that they were merely tormenting a victim they sensed to be in an impossible position, all of them being as hungry as wolves—their bellies concave, backbones sharp as knives, and teeth so keen they might have been filed.

Matahachi was far more afraid of them than he had been of Kojirō and Gempachi. Unable to use his arms and legs, he had for weapons only his face and his voice.

After first having naively tried to reason with the animals, he switched tactics. He howled like a wild beast. The dogs grew timid and backed off a little. But then his nose started running, and the effect was immediately spoiled.

Next he had opened his mouth and eyes as wide as he could and glared—somehow managing not to blink. He'd wrinkled his face and stuck his tongue out far enough to touch the tip of his nose, only to become quickly exhausted. Ransacking his brain, he had resorted again to pretending that he himself was just one of their number but had nothing against the rest of them. He barked, even imagined that he had a tail to wag.

The howling grew louder, the dogs closest to him baring their teeth in his face and licking his feet.

Hoping to soothe them with music, he began singing a famous passage from *Tales of the Heike*, imitating the bards who went about reciting this story to the accompaniment of the lute.

> Then the cloistered Emperor decided
> In the spring of the second year
> To see the country villa of Kenreimon'in,
> In the mountains near Ōhara.
> But throughout the second and third months
> The wind was violent, the cold lingered on,
> Nor did the white snows on the mountain peaks melt.

Eyes closed, face strained in a painful grimace, Matahachi sang almost loudly enough to deafen himself.

He was still singing when the arrival of Denshichirō and his companions sent the dogs scurrying.

Matahachi, beyond any pretense of dignity, cried, "Help! Save me!"

411

"I've seen that guy at the Yomogi," said one of the samurai.

"Yeah, that's Okō's husband."

"Husband? She's not supposed to have a husband."

"That's the story she told Tōji."

Denshichirō, taking pity on Matahachi, ordered them to stop gossiping and set him free.

In response to their questions, Matahachi made up a story in which his sterling qualities figured prominently and his weaknesses not at all. Taking advantage of the fact that he was talking to Yoshioka partisans, he brought up Musashi's name. They had been childhood friends, he revealed, until Musashi had abducted his fiancée and covered his family with unspeakable shame. His valiant mother had vowed not to return home; both his mother and himself were bent on finding Musashi and destroying him. As for being Okō's husband, this was far from the truth. His long stay at the Yomogi Teahouse was not because of any personal connection with the proprietress, and the proof of this was in her having fallen in love with Gion Tōji.

Then he explained why he was tied to a tree. He had been set upon by a band of robbers, who had stolen his money. He had put up no resistance, of course; he had to be careful not to be injured because of his obligation to his mother.

Hoping they were taking it all in, Matahachi said, "Thank you. I feel that perhaps there is some fate that links us together. We regard one man as our common enemy, an enemy we cannot live under the same sky with. Tonight you came along at just the right moment. I am eternally grateful.

"I would judge, sir, from your appearance that you are Denshichirō. I feel certain you plan to meet Musashi. Which one of us will kill him first I cannot say, but I hope I shall have the opportunity of seeing you again."

He did not want to give them a chance to ask questions, so he hurried on. "Osugi, my mother, is on a pilgrimage to Kiyomizudera to pray for success in our battle against Musashi. I'm on my way to meet her now. I shall certainly call soon at the house on Shijō Avenue to pay my respects. In the meantime, let me apologize for holding you up when you are in such a hurry."

And off he went, leaving his listeners to wonder how much truth there was in what he had said.

"Who on earth is that buffoon anyway?" snorted Denshichirō, clicking his tongue over the time they had wasted.

As the doctor had said, the first few days would be the worst. This was the fourth day, and since the night before, Seijūrō felt a little better.

Slowly he opened his eyes, wondering whether it was day or night. The paper-covered lamp by his pillow was nearly out. From the next room came the sound of snoring; the men watching over him had dropped off to sleep.

"I must still be alive," he thought. "Alive and in complete disgrace!" He pulled the quilt over his face with quivering fingers. "How can I face anyone after this?" He swallowed hard to stifle his tears. "It's all over," he moaned. "The end of me and the end of the House of Yoshioka."

A cock crowed and the lamp went out with a sputter. As the pale light of dawn crept into the room, he was taken back to that morning at the Rendaiji. The look in Musashi's eyes! The memory made him shiver. He had to admit he'd been no match for that man. Why hadn't he thrown down his wooden sword, accepted defeat and made an attempt to save the family's reputation?

"I had too high an opinion of myself," he moaned. "Besides being the son of Yoshioka Kempō, what have I ever done to distinguish myself?"

Even he had come to realize that sooner or later, time would have caught up with the House of Yoshioka if he had stayed in charge. With everything else changing, it could not continue to prosper.

"My bout with Musashi only hastened the collapse. Why couldn't I have died there? Why do I have to live?"

He knitted his brows. His armless shoulder throbbed with pain.

Only seconds after the banging on the front gate, a man came to wake up the samurai in the room next to Seijūrō's.

"Denshichirō?" exclaimed a startled voice.

"Yes; he just arrived."

Two men rushed out to meet him, another ran to Seijūrō's side.

"Young Master! Good news! Denshichirō's back."

The rain shutters were opened, charcoal put in the brazier, and a cushion spread on the floor. After a moment, Denshichirō's voice came from beyond the shoji. "Is my brother in here?"

Seijūrō thought nostalgically: "It's been a long time." Though he had asked to see Denshichirō, he dreaded being seen in his present state even by his brother—no, especially by his brother. As Denshichirō entered, Seijūrō looked up wanly and tried, unsuccessfully, to smile.

Denshichirō spoke with gusto. "See?" He laughed. "When you're in trouble, your good-for-nothing brother comes back to help you. I dropped everything and came as fast as I could. We stopped in Osaka for provisions, then traveled all night. I'm here now, so you can stop worrying. Whatever happens, I won't let a soul lay a finger on the school. . . .

"What's this?" he said gruffly, turning to a servant who had brought tea. "I don't need any tea! Go and get some sake ready." Then he shouted for someone to close the outside doors. "Are you all crazy? Can't you see my brother's cold?"

Sitting down, he leaned over the brazier and stared silently at the sick man's face. "Just what kind of stance did you take in the fight?" he asked. "Why did you lose? Maybe this Miyamoto Musashi's making name for himself, but he's no more than a rank beginner, is he? How could you let yourself be taken off guard by a nobody like him?"

From the doorway, one of the students called Denshichirō's name.

"Well, what is it?"

"The sake is ready."

"Bring it in!"

"I've set a place in the other room. You'll be wanting a bath first, won't you?"

"I don't want a bath! Bring the sake in here."

"Right by the Young Master's bedside?"

"Why not? I haven't seen him for a few months, and I want to talk to him. We haven't always been on the best of terms, but there's nothing like a brother when you need one. I'll drink it here with him."

He poured himself a cupful, then another and another. "Ah, this is good. If you were well, I'd pour some for you too."

Seijūrō put up with this for a few minutes, then raised his eyes and said, "Would you mind not drinking here?"

"Uh?"

"It brings back a lot of unpleasant memories."

"Oh?"

"I'm thinking of our father. He wouldn't be pleased at the way you and I have always indulged ourselves. And what good has it ever done either one of us?"

"What's the matter with you?"

"Maybe you don't see it yet, but lying here, I've had time to regret my wasted life."

Denshichirō laughed. "Speak for yourself! You've always been a nervous, sensitive type. That's why you've never become a real swordsman. If you want the truth, I think it was a mistake for you to take Musashi on. But then it doesn't make much difference whether it's Musashi or somebody else. Fighting's just not in your blood. You should let this defeat be a lesson to you and forget about swordsmanship. As I told you a long time ago, you should retire. You could still preside over the House of Yoshioka, and if there's anyone so intent on challenging you that you can't get out of it, I'll fight in your stead.

"Leave the dōjō to me from now on. I'll prove I can make it several times as successful as it was in our father's time. If you'll just put aside your suspicions that I'm trying to take your school away from you, I'll show you what I can do." He poured the last of the sake into his cup.

"Denshichirō!" cried Seijūrō. He tried to rise from his pallet, but couldn't even push aside the covers. Falling back, he reached out and grasped his brother's wrist.

"Watch out!" sputtered Denshichirō. "You'll make me spill this." He shifted his cup to his other hand.

"Denshichirō, I'll gladly let you have the school, but you'll have to take over my position as head of the house too."

"All right, if that's the way you want it."

"You shouldn't undertake the burden so lightly. You'd better give it some thought. I'd rather . . . close the place down than have you make the same mistakes I did and bring greater disgrace on our father's name."

"Don't be ridiculous. I'm not like you."

"Do you promise to mend your ways?"

"Hold on! I'll drink if I want—if that's what you mean."

"I don't care about your drinking, if you don't carry it to excess. After all, the mistakes I made didn't really come from sake."

"Ah, I'll bet your trouble was women. You always did like them too much. What you should do when you get well is marry and settle down."

"No. I'm giving up the sword, but it's no time to think about taking a wife. Yet there is one person I must do something for. If I can be sure she's happy, I'll ask for nothing more. I'll be content to live by myself in a thatched hut in the woods."

"Who is she?"

"Never mind; it doesn't concern you. As a samurai, I feel I should hang on and try to redeem myself. But I can swallow my pride. You take charge of the school."

"I'll do that. You have my promise. I also swear that before long I'll clear your name too. Just where is Musashi now?"

"Musashi?" Seijūrō choked. "You're not thinking of fighting Musashi! I've just warned you not to make the same mistakes I did."

"What else could I be thinking of? Isn't that why you sent for me? We have to find Musashi before he escapes. If it weren't for that, what point was there in my coming home so fast?"

"You don't know what you're talking about." Seijūrō shook his head. "I forbid you to fight Musashi!"

Denshichirō's tone became resentful. Taking orders from his elder brother had always annoyed him.

"And why not?"

A tinge of pink appeared on Seijūrō's pale cheeks. "You can't win!" he said curtly.

"Who can't?" Denshichirō's face was livid.

"*You* can't. Not against Musashi."

"Why can't I?"

"You're not good enough!"

"Nonsense!" Denshichirō deliberately broke into a laugh that shook his shoulders. Pulling his hand loose from Seijūrō's, he upended the sake jar. "Somebody bring sake," he bellowed. "There's none left."

By the time a student came with the sake, Denshichirō was no longer in the room, and Seijūrō was lying face down under the covers. When the student straightened him around and put his head on the pillow, he said softly, "Call him back. I've something more to say to him."

Relieved that the Young Master was speaking clearly, the man ran out to look for Denshichirō. He found him seated on the floor of the dōjō, with Ueda Ryōhei and Miike Jūrōzaemon, Nampo Yoichibei, Ōtaguro Hyōsuke and a few more of the senior disciples.

One was asking, "Have you seen the Young Master?"

"Mm. I just came from his room."

"He must have been happy to see you."

"He didn't seem too pleased. Until I went to his room, I'd been eager to see him. But he was dejected and cross, so I said what I had to say. We got into a quarrel, as usual."

"You argued with him? You shouldn't have done that. He's only just beginning to recover."

"Wait till you hear the whole story."

Denshichirō and the senior disciples were like old chums. He grabbed the reproachful Ryōhei by the shoulder and shook him in a friendly way.

"Listen to what my brother said," he began. "He said I shouldn't try to clear his name by fighting Musashi, because I couldn't win! And if I was defeated, the House of Yoshioka would be ruined. He told me he'd retire and accept sole responsibility for the disgrace. He doesn't expect me to do any more than carry on in his place and work hard to put the school back on its feet."

"I see."

"What do you mean by that?"

Ryōhei didn't answer.

As they sat there in silence, the student came in and said to Denshichirō, "The Young Master wants you to come back to his room."

Denshichirō scowled. "What happened to the sake?" he snapped.

"I left it in Seijūrō's room."

"Well, bring it here!"

"What about your brother?"

"He seems to be suffering from a case of the jitters. Do as I say."

The protestations of the others that they did not want any, that this was no time to be drinking, annoyed Denshichirō and he lashed out at them. "What's the matter with all of you? Are you afraid of Musashi too?"

Shock, pain and bitterness were evident in their faces. To their dying day, they would remember how with a single blow of a wooden sword their master had been crippled and the school disgraced. Still, they had been unable to agree on a plan of action. Every discussion over the past three days had split them into two factions, some favoring a second challenge, others arguing for leaving bad enough alone. Now a few of the older men looked approvingly at Denshichirō, but the rest, Ryōhei included, were inclined to agree with their defeated master. Unfortunately, it was one thing for Seijūrō to urge forbearance and quite another for the students to agree, particularly in the presence of this hotheaded younger brother.

Denshichirō, observing their hesitancy, declared, "Even if my brother is injured, he has no business behaving like a coward. Just like a woman! How could I be expected to listen, let alone agree?"

The sake had been brought, and he proceeded to pour each man a cup. Now that he was going to be running things, he intended to set the tone he himself liked: this would be a real man's outfit.

"This is what I'm going to do," he announced. "I'll fight Musashi and defeat him! It doesn't matter what my brother says. If he thinks we should let this man get away with what he did, it's no wonder he got beaten. Don't any of you make the mistake of thinking I'm yellow like him."

Nampo Yoichibei spoke up. "There's no question about your ability. We all have confidence in that, but still . . ."

416

"But still what? What's on your mind?"

"Well, your brother seems to be of the opinion that Musashi isn't important. He's right, isn't he? Think of the risk—"

"Risk?" howled Denshichirō.

"I didn't mean it that way! I take it back," stammered Yoichibei.

But the damage was done. Denshichirō, jumping up and seizing him by the scruff of the neck, threw him violently against the wall.

"Get out of here! Coward!"

"It was a slip of the tongue. I didn't mean to—"

"Shut up! Out! Weaklings aren't fit to drink with me."

Yoichibei turned pale, then quietly sank to his knees, facing the others. "I thank you all for letting me stay among you so long," he said simply. He went to the small Shinto shrine in the back of the room, bowed and left.

Without so much as a glance in his direction, Denshichirō said, "Now let's all drink together. After that, I want you to find Musashi. I doubt that he's left Kyoto yet. He's probably swaggering around town boasting of his victory.

"And another thing. We're going to put some life back into this dōjō. I want each of you to practice hard and see that your fellow students do too. As soon as I've had a rest, I'll start practicing myself. And remember one thing. I'm not soft like my brother. I want even the youngest to go at it for all they're worth."

Exactly a week later, one of the younger students came running into the dōjō with the news: "I've found him!"

Denshichirō, true to his word, had been training relentlessly day after day. His seemingly inexhaustible energy came as a surprise to the disciples, a group of whom were now watching him take care of Ōtaguro, one of the most experienced among them, as though he were a child.

"We'll stop now," said Denshichirō, withdrawing his sword and sitting down at the edge of the practice area. "You say you've found him?"

"Yes." The student came and knelt before Denshichirō.

"Where?"

"East of Jissōin, in Hon'ami Lane. Musashi's staying at the house of Hon'ami Kōetsu. I'm sure of it."

"Strange. How would a rustic like Musashi get to know a man like Kōetsu?"

"I don't know, but that's where he is."

"All right, let's go after him. Now!" barked Denshichirō, striding off to make his preparations. Ōtaguro and Ueda, trailing along behind, tried to dissuade him.

"Taking him by surprise would make it look like a common brawl. People would disapprove, even if we carried it off."

"Never mind. Etiquette is for the dōjō. In a real battle, he who wins, wins!"

"True, but that isn't the way that oaf defeated your brother. Don't you think it would be more befitting a swordsman to send him a letter specifying the time and place, then beat him fair and square?"

"Um, maybe you're right. All right, we'll do it that way. In the meantime I don't want any of you to let my brother talk you into opposing me. I'll fight Musashi whatever Seijūrō or anybody else says."

"We've gotten rid of all the men who disagreed with you, as well as the ingrates who wanted to leave."

"Good! We're that much stronger. We have no need of crooks like Gion Tōji or timid souls like Nampo Yoichibei."

"Should we mention it to your brother before sending the letter?"

"Not you, no! I'll do it myself."

As he went off toward Seijūrō's room, the others prayed there wouldn't be another fraternal clash; neither brother had budged an inch on the question of Musashi. When after a time no loud voices were heard, the students took up the matter of time and place for this second confrontation with their mortal foe.

Then Denshichirō's voice rang out. "Ueda! Miike! Ōtaguro . . . all of you! Come here!"

Denshichirō was standing in the middle of the room with a clouded look on his face and tears in his eyes. No one had ever seen him like this.

"Take a look at this, all of you."

He held up a long, long letter and said, with forced anger, "See what my idiot brother has done now. He had to tell me his opinions again, but he's gone for good. . . . Didn't even say where he's going."

A Mother's Love

Otsū put down her sewing and called, "Who's there?"

She slid open the shoji onto the veranda, but no one was in sight. Her spirits sank. She had hoped it was Jōtarō. She needed him now more than ever.

Another day of utter loneliness. She could not keep her mind on her needlework.

Here below Kiyomizudera, at the bottom of Sannen Hill, the streets were squalid, but behind the houses and shops were bamboo groves and small fields, camellias blooming and plum blossoms beginning to fall. Osugi was very fond of this particular inn. She stayed here whenever she was in Kyoto, and the innkeeper always let her have this small, quiet separate house. Behind it was a stand of trees, part of the garden next door; in front was a small vegetable garden, beyond which was the always bustling kitchen of the inn.

"Otsū!" called a voice from the kitchen. "It's time for lunch. May I bring it to you now?"

"Lunch?" said Otsū. "I'll eat with the old woman when she comes back."

"She said she wouldn't be back until late. We probably won't see her before evening."

"I'm not hungry."

"I don't see how you can go on, eating so little."

Pine smoke billowed into the enclosure from potters' kilns in the neighborhood. On the days when they were fired, there was always a lot of smoke. But after the air cleared, the early spring sky was bluer than ever.

From the street came the sound of horses and the footsteps and voices of pilgrims on their way to the temple. It was from the passersby that the story of Musashi's victory over Seijūrō had reached Otsū's ears. Musashi's face appeared before her eyes. "Jōtarō must have been at the Rendaiji that day," she thought. "If only he'd come and tell me about it!"

She couldn't believe the boy had looked for her and not been able to find her. Twenty days had passed, and he knew she was staying at the foot of Sannen Hill. He might be sick, but she did not really believe this either; Jōtarō was not the type to be ill. "He's probably out flying a kite somewhere, having a good time," she said to herself. The idea made her a little peevish.

Maybe he was the one who was doing the waiting. She had not been back to the Karasumaru house, though she had promised him she would return soon.

She was unable to go anywhere, for she had been forbidden to leave the inn without Osugi's permission. Osugi had obviously told the innkeeper and servants to keep an eye on her. Whenever she so much as glanced toward the street, someone would ask, "Are you going out, Otsū?" The question, the tone of voice, sounded innocent, but she comprehended the meaning. And the only way she could send a letter was by entrusting it to the people at the inn, who had been instructed to keep any message she might try to send.

Osugi was something of a celebrity in this area, and people were easily persuaded to do her bidding. Quite a few of the shopkeepers, palanquin bearers and draymen in the neighborhood had seen her in action the year before, when she challenged Musashi at Kiyomizudera, and, for all her irascibility, regarded her with a certain affectionate awe.

As Otsū made yet another attempt to finish reassembling Osugi's travel outfit, which had been taken apart at the seams to be washed, a shadow appeared outside. She heard an unfamiliar voice say, "I wonder if I'm in the wrong place."

A young woman had come through the passageway from the street and was standing under a plum tree between two patches of scallions. She seemed nervous, a little embarrassed, but reluctant to turn back.

"Isn't this the inn? There's a lantern at the entrance of the passageway saying it is," she said to Otsū.

Otsū could hardly believe her eyes, so painful was the suddenly reawakened memory.

Thinking she had made a mistake, Akemi asked diffidently, "Which building is the inn?" Then, looking around, she noticed the plum blossoms and exclaimed, "My, aren't they pretty!"

Otsū looked at the girl without answering.

A clerk, summoned by one of the kitchen girls, came hurrying around the corner of the inn. "Are you looking for the entrance?" he asked.

"Yes."

"It's on the corner just to the right of the passageway."

"The inn faces directly on the street?"

"It does, but the rooms are quiet."

"I'd like a place where I can come and go without people watching me. I thought the inn was away from the street. Isn't that little house part of the inn?"

"Yes."

"It looks like a nice quiet place."

"We also have some very nice rooms in the main building."

"There seems to be a woman staying there now, but couldn't I stay too?"

"Well, there's another lady. I'm afraid she's old and rather nervous."

"Oh, I don't mind, if it's all right with her."

"I'll have to ask her when she comes back. She's out now."

"May I have a room to rest in till then?"

"By all means."

The clerk led Akemi down the passageway, leaving Otsū to regret that she had not taken the opportunity to ask a few questions. If only she could learn to be a little more aggressive, she reflected sadly.

To assuage her jealous suspicions, Otsū had assured herself time and time again that Musashi was not the kind of man who played around with other women. But ever since that day, she had been discouraged. "She's had more opportunities to be near Musashi. . . . She's probably much cleverer than I— knows better how to win a man's heart."

Until that day, the possibility of another woman had never crossed her mind. Now she brooded over what she considered to be her own weaknesses. "I'm just not beautiful. . . . I'm not very bright either. . . . I have neither parents nor relatives to back me in marriage." Comparing herself with other women, it seemed that the great hope of her life was ridiculously beyond her reach, that it was presumptuous to dream that Musashi could be hers. She could no longer summon up the bravery that had enabled her to climb the old cryptomeria tree during a blinding storm.

"If only I had Jōtarō's help!" she lamented. She even imagined she had lost her youthfulness. "At the Shippōji, I still had some of the innocence Jōtarō has now. That was why I was able to free Musashi." She began to weep into her sewing.

"Are you here, Otsū?" Osugi asked imperiously. "What are you doing, sitting there in the dark?"

Twilight had descended without the girl's noticing it. "Oh, I'll light a lamp right away," she said apologetically, rising and going to a small room in the rear.

420

As she came in and sat down, Osugi cast a cold look at Otsū's back.

Otsū placed the lamp by Osugi's side and bowed. "You must be worn out," she said. "What did you do today?"

"You should know without asking."

"Shall I massage your legs for you?"

"My legs aren't so bad, but my shoulders have been stiff the last four or five days. Probably the weather. If you feel like it, massage them a little." To herself, she was saying that she had to put up with this dreadful girl only a little while longer, until she found Matahachi and got him to set right the evils of the past.

Otsū knelt behind her and started to work on her shoulders. "They're really stiff, aren't they? It must hurt to breathe."

"It does feel as though my chest is clogged up sometimes. But I'm old. One of these days I'll probably have some sort of seizure and die."

"Oh, that's not going to happen to you. You've got more vitality than most young people."

"Maybe, but think of Uncle Gon. He was as lively as could be, but then it was all over in an instant. People don't know what's going to happen to them. There's no mistake about one thing, though. All I have to do to be myself is think about Musashi."

"You're wrong about Musashi. He's not a wicked man."

"Yes, yes, that's right," said the old woman with a slight snort. "After all, he's the man you love so much you threw my son over for him. I shouldn't say bad things about him to you."

"Oh, it's not like that!"

"Isn't it? You do love Musashi more than Matahachi, don't you? Why not admit it?"

Otsū was silent, and the old woman went on: "When we find Matahachi, I'll have a talk with him and fix everything up the way you want it. But I suppose after that you'll run straight to Musashi, and the two of you will malign us for the rest of your lives."

"Why do you think that? I'm not that kind of person. I won't forget the many things you've done for me in the past."

"The way you young girls talk these days! I don't know how you manage to sound so sweet. I'm an honest woman myself. I can't conceal my feelings with a lot of clever words. You know, if you marry Musashi, you'll be my enemy. Ha, ha, ha! It must be annoying to massage my shoulders."

The girl did not answer.

"What are you crying about?"

"I'm not crying."

"What's that water falling on my neck?"

"I'm sorry. I couldn't help it."

"Stop it! It feels like a bug crawling around. Quit pining over Musashi and put some strength into your arms!"

A light appeared in the garden. Otsū thought it was probably the maid, who usually brought their evening meal about this time, but it turned out to be a priest.

421

"I beg your pardon," he said, stepping up onto the veranda. "Is this the room of the Hon'iden dowager? Ah, there you are." The lantern he held bore the legend "Kiyomizudera on Mount Otowa."

"Let me explain," he began. "I'm a priest from the Shiandō, up the hill." He put the lantern down and took a letter from his kimono. "I don't know who it was, but this evening just before sunset a young rōnin came to the temple and asked if an elderly lady from Mimasaka was doing her devotions there. I told him no, but a devoted worshiper answering that description did come occasionally. He asked for a brush and wrote this letter. He wanted me to give it to the lady the next time she came. I'd heard that you were staying here, and since I was on my way to Gojō Avenue, I dropped in to deliver it."

"That was very kind of you," said Osugi cordially. She offered him a cushion, but he took his leave immediately.

"Now what?" thought Osugi. She unfolded the letter; as she read, her color changed.

"Otsū," she called.

"Yes, what is it?" replied the girl from the back room.

"There's no need to prepare tea. He's already gone."

"Has he? Why don't you drink it, then?"

"How dare you think of serving me tea you made for him? I'm not a drainpipe! Forget about the tea and get dressed!"

"Are we going out?"

"Yes. Tonight we'll reach the settlement you've been hoping for."

"Oh, then the letter was from Matahachi."

"That doesn't concern you."

"Very well; I'll go and ask for our dinner to be brought now."

"Haven't you eaten yet?"

"No; I was waiting for you to come back."

"You're always doing foolish things. I ate while I was out. Well, have some rice and pickles. But be quick about it!"

As Otsū started for the kitchen, the old woman said, "It'll be cold on the mountain tonight. Have you finished sewing up my cloak?"

"I still have a little more to do on your kimono."

"I didn't say kimono, I said cloak. I put that out for you to work on too. And have you washed my socks? The cords on my sandals are loose. Have some new ones brought."

The orders came so fast Otsū didn't have time to answer, let alone comply, but she felt powerless to rebel. Her spirit seemed to crouch in fear and dismay before this gnarled old harridan.

Food was out of the question. In a matter of minutes, Osugi declared she was ready to leave.

Placing new sandals by the veranda, Otsū said, "You go ahead. I'll catch up."

"Did you bring a lantern?"

"No—"

"Nitwit! Were you expecting me to stumble around on the mountainside
without a light? Go borrow one from the inn."

422

"I'm sorry. I didn't think."

Otsū wanted to know where they were going but did not ask, knowing it would provoke Osugi's anger. She fetched the lantern and led the way silently up Sannen Hill. For all the harassment, she felt cheerful. The letter must have been from Matahachi, and this meant the problem that had vexed her for so many years would be solved tonight. "As soon as everything has been talked over," she thought, "I'll go to the Karasumaru house. I must see Jōtarō."

It was not an easy climb. They had to walk carefully to avoid fallen rocks and holes in the path. In the deep silence of night, the waterfall sounded louder than in the daytime.

After a time, Osugi said, "I'm sure this is the place sacred to the god of the mountain. Ah, here's the sign: 'Cherry Tree of the Mountain God.'

"Matahachi!" she called into the darkness. "Matahachi! I'm here." The trembling voice and face brimming with maternal affection came as a revelation to Otsū. She had never expected to see Osugi overcome by concern for her son.

"Don't let the lantern go out!" snapped Osugi.

"I'll take care," replied Otsū dutifully.

The old woman grumbled under her breath. "He's not here. He's simply not here." She had made a round of the temple grounds, but made another one. "He said in the letter I should come to the hall of the mountain god."

"Did he say tonight?"

"He didn't say tonight or tomorrow or any particular time. I wonder if he'll ever grow up. I don't see why he couldn't come to the inn, but maybe he's embarrassed about what happened in Osaka."

Otsū pulled at her sleeve and said, "Shh! That could be him. Someone's coming up the hill."

"Son, is that you?" Osugi called.

The man passed them without a glance and went straight to the back of the little temple. He returned shortly and stopped beside them, staring boldly at Otsū's face. When he had first passed, she had not recognized him, but she did now—the samurai who had been sitting beneath the bridge on New Year's Day.

"Have you two just come up the hill?" asked Kojirō.

The question came so unexpectedly that neither Otsū nor Osugi answered. Their surprise was compounded by the sight of Kojirō's gaudy clothes.

Pointing his finger at Otsū's face, he went on, "I'm looking for a girl about your age. Her name's Akemi. She's a little smaller than you, and her face is a little rounder. She was trained in a teahouse and acts a little old for her age. Have either of you seen her around here?"

They shook their heads in silence.

"Very peculiar. Somebody told me she'd been seen in the neighborhood. I felt sure she'd spend the night in one of the temple halls." For all the attention he was paying to them, he might as well have been talking to himself. He mumbled a few more words, then left.

Osugi clicked her tongue. "There's another good-for-nothing. He has two swords, so I suppose he's a samurai, but did you see that outfit? And up here 423 looking for a woman at this time of night! Well, I guess he saw it was neither of us."

Though she did not mention it to Osugi, Otsū had a strong suspicion that the girl he was searching for was the one who had wandered into the inn that afternoon. What on earth could be the tie that linked Musashi with the girl and the girl with this man?

"Let's go back," said Osugi, her voice both disappointed and resigned.

In front of the Hongandō, where Osugi's confrontation with Musashi had taken place, they ran into Kojirō again. He looked at them, and they at him, but no words were exchanged. Osugi watched as he went up to the Shiandō, then turned away and walked straight down Sannen Hill.

"That man has scary eyes," Osugi murmured, "like Musashi." Just then her own eyes caught a shadowy movement and her bent shoulders jerked up. "Oww!" She hooted like an owl. From behind a large cryptomeria, a hand beckoned. "Matahachi," murmured Osugi, thinking it was very touching that he did not want to be seen by anyone but her

She called to Otsū, now fifty or sixty feet farther down the slope. "Go on ahead, Otsū. But not too far. Wait for me at the place they call Chirimazuka. I'll be with you in a few minutes."

"All right," said Otsū.

"Now, don't go off anywhere! I've got my eye on you. You needn't try to run away."

Osugi ran swiftly to the tree. "Matahachi, it's you, isn't it?"

"Yes, Mother." His hands came out of the darkness and clasped hers as though he had been waiting for years to see her.

"What are you doing behind this tree? My, your hands are as cold as ice!" She was almost moved to tears by her own solicitude.

"I had to hide," said Matahachi, his eyes shifting nervously. "That man who passed here a minute ago. You saw him, didn't you?"

"The man with the long sword on his back?"

"Yes."

"Do you know him?"

"Sort of. That's Sasaki Kojirō."

"What! I thought you were Sasaki Kojirō."

"Huh?"

"In Osaka you showed me your certificate. That was the name written on it. You said it was the name you'd taken, didn't you?"

"Did I? Uh, that wasn't true. . . . Today, on my way up here, I caught sight of him. Kojirō gave me a bad time a couple of days ago, so I've been hiding, to keep out of his way. If he comes back this way, I might be in trouble."

Osugi was so shocked words failed her. But she noticed that Matahachi was thinner than he had been. This and his agitated state made her love him all the more—for the time being at least.

With a look that told him she did not want to hear the details, she said, "All that doesn't matter. Tell me, son, did you know that Uncle Gon died?"

424   "Uncle Gon . . . ?"

"Yes, Uncle Gon. He died right there, on the beach at Sumiyoshi, just after you left us."

"I hadn't heard."

"Well, it happened. The question is whether you understand the reason for his tragic death and for my continuing this long, sad mission, even at my age."

"Yes; it's been engraved on my mind since that night in Osaka when you . . . reminded me of my shortcomings."

"You remember that, do you? Well, I have news for you, news that'll make you happy."

"What's that?"

"It concerns Otsū."

"Oh! That was the girl with you."

Matahachi started around her, but Osugi blocked his way and asked reproachfully, "Where do you think you're going?"

"If that was Otsū, I want to see her. It's been a long time."

Osugi nodded. "I brought her here for the purpose of letting you see her. But would you mind telling your mother just what you plan to do?"

"I'll tell her I'm sorry, I treated her very badly, and I hope she'll forgive me."

"And then?"

"Then . . . well, then I'll tell her I'll never make a mistake like that again. You tell her that too, Mother, for me."

"Then what?"

"Then it'll be just like before."

"What will?"

"Me and Otsū. I want to be friends with her again. I want to marry her. Oh, Mother, do you think she still—"

"You fool!" She dealt him a resounding slap.

He staggered back and put his hand to his stinging cheek. "Wh-why, Mother, what's the matter?" he stammered.

Osugi, looking angrier than he had ever seen her since the day he was weaned, growled, "You just now assured me you'd never forget what I said in Osaka, didn't you?"

He hung his head.

"Did I ever say a word about apologizing to that worthless bitch? How could you conceivably beg forgiveness from that she-monster after she threw you over and went off with another man? You'll see her, all right, but apologize you shall not! Now, listen to me!" Osugi collared him with both hands and shook him back and forth. Matahachi, head bobbing, closed his eyes and listened meekly to a long string of angry rebukes.

"What's this?" she screamed. "You're crying? Do you still love that tramp enough to weep over her? If you do, you're no son of mine!" As she threw him to the ground, she collapsed too.

For several minutes, both of them sat there and wept.

But Osugi's bitterness could not stay submerged for long. Straightening up, she said, "You've reached a point where you must make a decision. I may not live much longer. And when I'm dead, you won't be able to talk with me like this, even if you want to.

"Think, Matahachi. Otsū's not the only girl in the world." Her voice became calmer. "You mustn't let yourself feel any attachment to someone who's acted the way she has. Find a girl you like, and I'll get her for you, even if I have to visit her parents a hundred times—even if it wears me out and I die."

He remained sullen and silent.

"Forget about Otsū, for the sake of the Hon'iden name. Whatever you think, she's unacceptable from the family's viewpoint. So if you absolutely cannot do without her, then cut off this old head of mine. After that you can do as you please. But so long as I'm alive—"

"Mother, stop!"

The virulence of his tone made her bristle. "You have your nerve, shouting at me!"

"Just tell me this: Is the woman I marry to be my wife or yours?"

"What a silly thing to say!"

"Why can't I choose by myself?"

"Now, now. You're always saying headstrong things. How old do you think you are? You're not a child anymore, or have you forgotten?"

"But . . . well, even if you are my mother, you're asking too much of me. It's not fair."

Their disagreements were often like this, beginning with a violent clash of emotions, a locking of horns in implacable antagonism. Mutual understanding was undermined before it ever had a chance to grow.

"It's not fair?" Osugi hissed. "Whose son do you think you are? Whose belly do you think you came from?"

"There's no point talking about that. I want to marry Otsū! She's the one I love!" Unable to endure his mother's ashen scowl, he directed his words to the sky.

"Son, do you mean that?" Osugi drew her short sword and pointed the blade at her throat.

"Mother, what are you doing?"

"I've had enough. Don't try to stop me! Just have the decency to give me the final blow."

"Don't do this to me! I'm your son! I can't stand here and let you do that!"

"All right. Will you give up Otsū—right now?"

"If that's what you wanted me to do, why did you bring her here? Why tantalize me by parading her in front of me? I don't understand you."

"Well, it'd be simple enough for me to kill her, but you're the one she's wronged. As your mother, I thought I should leave her punishment for you to carry out. It seems to me you should be grateful for that."

"You expect me to kill Otsū?"

"Don't you want to? If you don't, say so! But make up your mind!"

"But . . . but, Mother . . ."

426   "So you still can't get over her, eh? Well, if that's the way you feel, you're

not my son, and I'm not your mother. If you can't cut off that hussy's head, at least cut mine off! The final blow, please."

Children, Matahachi reflected, are wont to make trouble for their parents, but sometimes it is the other way around. Osugi wasn't simply browbeating him; she'd thrust him into the most difficult situation in his life. The wild look on her face shook him to the core.

"Mother, stop! Don't do it! All right, I'll do what you want. I'll forget about Otsū!"

"Is that all?"

"I'll punish her. I promise to punish her with my own hands."

"You'll kill her?"

"Uh, yes, I'll kill her."

Osugi triumphantly burst into tears of joy. Putting away her sword, she clutched her son's hand. "Good for you! Now you sound like the future head of the House of Hon'iden. Your ancestors will be proud of you."

"Do you really think so?"

"Go and do it now! Otsū's waiting down there, at Chirimazuka. Hurry!"

"Mm."

"We'll write a letter to send back to the Shippōji with her head. Then everyone in the village will know our shame has been halved. And when Musashi hears she's dead, his pride will force him to come to us. How glorious! . . . Matahachi, hurry up!"

"You'll wait here, won't you?"

"No. I'll follow you but stay out of sight. If Otsū sees me, she'll start whining that I went back on my promise. That would be awkward."

"She's only a defenseless woman," said Matahachi, getting up slowly. "It's no problem to do away with her, so why don't you wait here? I'll bring her head back. There's nothing to worry about. I won't let her get away."

"Well, you can't be too careful. She may be only a woman, but when she sees the blade of your sword, she'll put up a fight."

"Stop worrying. There's nothing to it."

Bracing himself, he started down the hill, his mother behind him, an anxious look on her face. "Remember," she said, "don't let your guard down!"

"Are you still following me? I thought you were going to stay out of sight."

"Chirimazuka is farther down the path."

"I know, Mother! If you insist on going, go by yourself. I'll wait here."

"Why are you hanging back?"

"She is a human being. It's difficult to attack her when I have the feeling it's like killing an innocent kitten."

"I can see your point. No matter how faithless she's been, she was your fiancée. All right; if you don't want me to watch, go by yourself. I'll stay here."

He went, silently.

Otsū had first thought of running away, but if she did, all the patience she had exercised in the previous twenty days would come to naught. She decided 427 to bear it a little longer. To pass the time, she thought of Musashi, then Jōtarō. Her love for Musashi set millions of bright stars shining in her heart. As if in a dream, she counted the many hopes she had for the future and recalled the vows he had made to her—at the pass at Nakayama, on Hanada Bridge. Though many years might pass, she believed with all her heart that in the end he would not forsake her.

Then the image of Akemi came to haunt her, darkening her hopes and making her uneasy. But only for a moment. Her fears about Akemi were insignificant in comparison with her unbounded confidence in Musashi. She recalled, too, Takuan's saying that she was to be pitied, but that made no sense. How could he regard her self-perpetuating joy in that light?

Even now, waiting in this dark, lonely spot for a person she did not want to see, her rapturous dream of the future made any amount of suffering bearable.

"Otsū!"

"Who . . . is it?" she called back.

"Hon'iden Matahachi."

"Matahachi?" she gasped.

"Have you forgotten my voice?"

"No, I recognize it now. Did you see your mother?"

"Yes, she's waiting for me. You haven't changed, have you? You look just the way you did back in Mimasaka."

"Where are you? It's so dark I can't see."

"May I come closer? I've been standing here. I'm so ashamed to face you. What were you thinking about?"

"Oh, nothing; nothing in particular."

"Were you thinking of me? Not a day has gone by I didn't think of you."

As he slowly approached her, Otsū felt a little apprehensive. "Matahachi, did your mother explain everything to you?"

"Uh-huh."

"Since you've heard everything," she said, immensely relieved, "you understand my sentiments, but I'd like to ask you myself to see things from my viewpoint. Let's forget the past. It was never intended to be."

"Now, Otsū, don't be like that." He shook his head. Though he had no idea what his mother had told Otsū, he was fairly certain it had been intended to deceive her. "It hurts me to have the past mentioned. It's difficult for me to hold my head up in front of you. If it were possible to forget, heaven knows I'd be glad to. But for some reason, I can't bear the thought of giving you up."

"Matahachi, be sensible. There is nothing between your heart and mine. We're separated by a great valley."

"That's true. And more than five years have flowed through that valley."

"Exactly. Those years will never come back. There's no way to recapture the feelings we once had."

"Oh, no! We can recapture them! We can!"

"No, they're gone forever."

He stared at her, stunned by the coolness in her face and the finality of her tone, asking himself if this was the girl who, when she allowed herself to reveal her passions, was like spring sunlight? He had the feeling he was rubbing a piece of snowy white alabaster. Where had this severity been hidden in the past?

He recalled the porch of the Shippōji and how she had sat there with limpid, dreamy eyes, often for half a day or more, silently looking off into space, as though she saw in the clouds mother and father, brothers and sisters.

He drew closer, and as timidly as he might have reached among thorns for a white rosebud, whispered, "Let's try again, Otsū. There's no way to bring back five years, but let's begin again, now, just the two of us."

"Matahachi," she said dispassionately, "are you imagining things? I wasn't talking about the length of time; I was talking about the abyss that separates our hearts, our lives."

"I know that. What I mean is that beginning right now I'll win your love back. Maybe I shouldn't say it, but isn't the mistake I made one almost any young man might be guilty of?"

"Talk if you like, but I'll never again be able to take your word seriously."

"Oh, but, Otsū, I know I was wrong! I'm a man, but here I am, apologizing to a woman. Don't you understand how difficult that is for me?"

"Stop it! If you're a man, you should act like one."

"But there's nothing in the world more important to me. If you want, I'll get down on my knees and beg forgiveness. I'll give you my oath. I'll swear to anything you wish."

"I don't care what you do!"

"Please don't be angry. Look, this is no place to talk. Let's go somewhere else."

"No."

"I don't want my mother to find us. Come on, let's go. I can't kill you. I couldn't possibly kill you!"

He took her hand, but she wrenched it away from him. "Don't touch me!" she cried angrily. "I'd rather be killed than spend my life with you!"

"You won't come with me?"

"No, no, no."

"Is that final?"

"Yes!"

"Does that mean you're still in love with Musashi?"

"Yes, I love him. I'll love him throughout this life and the next."

His body trembled. "That's the wrong thing to say, Otsū."

"Your mother already knows. She said she'd tell you. She promised we could talk it over together and put an end to the past."

"I see. And I suppose Musashi ordered you to find me and tell me that. Is that what happened?"

"No, it is not! Musashi doesn't have to tell me what to do."

"I've got pride too, you know. All men have pride. If that's the way you feel about me—"

"What are you doing?" she cried.

"I'm as much a man as Musashi, and if it takes my whole life, I'll keep you 429 from him. I won't permit it, do you hear? I won't permit it!"

"And just who are you to give permission?"

"I won't allow you to marry Musashi! Remember, Otsū, it wasn't Musashi you were engaged to."

"You're hardly the one to bring that up."

"But I am! You were promised to me as my bride. Unless I consent, you can't marry anyone."

"You're a coward, Matahachi! I pity you. How can you debase yourself like this? I long ago received letters from you and some woman named Okō, breaking our engagement."

"I don't know anything about that. I didn't send any letter. Okō must have done it on her own."

"That's not true. One letter was in your own hand and said I should forget about you and find somebody else to marry."

"Where's the letter? Show it to me."

"I don't have it anymore. When Takuan read it, he laughed, then blew his nose on it and threw it away."

"In other words, you have no proof, so nobody is going to believe you. Everybody in the village knows you were engaged to me. I've got all the proof and you have none. Think, Otsū: if you cut yourself off from everybody else in order to be with Musashi, you'll never be happy. The thought of Okō seems to upset you, but I swear I have absolutely nothing to do with her anymore."

"You're wasting your time."

"You won't listen, even when I apologize?"

"Matahachi, didn't you just now brag that you were a man? Why don't you act like one? No woman is going to lose her heart to a weak, shameless, lying coward. Women don't admire weaklings."

"Watch what you're saying!"

"Let me go! You'll tear my sleeve."

"You . . . you fickle whore!"

"Stop it!"

"If you won't listen to me, I don't care what happens."

"Matahachi!"

"If you care about living, swear you'll give up Musashi!"

He let go of her sleeve to draw his sword. Once drawn, the sword seemed to take control of him. He was like a man possessed, a wild light in his eyes.

Otsū screamed, not so much because of the weapon as because of the way he looked.

"You bitch!" he shouted as she turned to flee. His sword descended, grazing the knot of her obi. "I mustn't let her escape!" he thought, and started after her, calling over his shoulder to his mother.

Osugi came racing down the hill. "Has he bungled it?" she wondered, drawing her own sword.

"She's over there. Catch her, Mother!" called Matahachi. But he soon ran back and came to a halt just before colliding with the old woman. Saucer-eyed, he asked, "Where did she go?"

430

"You didn't kill her?"

"No, she got away."

"Fool!"

"Look, she's down below. That's her. There!"

Otsū, scampering down a steep bank, had had to stop to get her sleeve loose from a branch. She knew she must be near the waterfall, because the sound was very loud. As she rushed on, holding her torn sleeve, Matahachi and Osugi closed in on her, and when Osugi cried, "We've got her trapped now," the sound was right behind her.

At the bottom of a ravine, the darkness loomed like a wall around Otsū.

"Matahachi, kill her! There she is, lying on the ground."

Matahachi gave himself over to the sword completely. Jumping forward, he aimed at the dark form and brought the blade down savagely. "She-devil!" he screamed.

With the cracking of twigs and branches came a screeching death cry.

"Take this, and this!" Matahachi struck three times, four—again and again until it seemed the sword would break in two. He was drunk with blood; his eyes spat fire.

Then it was over. Silence ensued.

Holding the bloody sword listlessly, he returned slowly to his senses, and his face went blank. He looked at his hands and saw the blood on them, felt his face, and there was blood there too, and all over his clothes. He blanched and grew dizzy, sick with the thought that each drop of blood was Otsū's.

"Splendid, son! You've finally done it." Panting more from exhilaration than from exertion, Osugi stood behind him, and leaning over his shoulder, peered down at the torn and battered foliage. "How happy I am to see this," she exulted. "We did it, my son. I've been relieved of half my burden, and now I can hold up my head in the village again. What's the matter with you? Quick! Cut off her head!"

Noticing his queasiness, she laughed. "You don't have any guts. If you can't bring yourself to cut off her head, I'll do it for you. Get out of the way."

He stood stark still until the old woman started toward the bushes, then raised his sword and jabbed the hilt into her shoulder.

"Watch what you're doing!" cried Osugi as she stumbled forward. "Have you lost your mind?"

"Mother!"

"What?"

Strange sounds gurgled from Matahachi's throat. He wiped his eyes with his bloody hands. "I've . . . I've killed her. I've murdered Otsū!"

"And it was a praiseworthy deed too. Why, you're crying."

"I can't help it. Oh, you fool. You crazy, fanatic old fool!"

"Are you sorry?"

"Yes . . . yes! If it hadn't been for you—you ought to be dead by now—I'd have somehow gotten Otsū back. You and your family honor!"

"Stop your blabbering. If she meant that much to you, why didn't you kill me and protect her?"

431

"If I'd been able to do that, I— Could there be anything worse than having a pigheaded maniac for a mother?"

"Stop carrying on like that. And how dare you speak to me that way!"

"From now on I'll live my life the way I want. If I make a mess of it, that's nobody's business but mine."

"That's always been a failing of yours, Matahachi. You get excited and make scenes just to cause your mother trouble."

"I'll cause you trouble, all right, you old sow. You're a witch. I hate you!"

"My, my! Isn't he angry. . . . Get out of the way. I'll take Otsū's head, and then I'll teach you a few things."

"More talk? I'm not listening."

"I want you to take a good look at that girl's head. You'll see then just how pretty she is. I want you to see with your own eyes what a woman is like after she dies. Nothing but bones. I want you to know the folly of passion."

"Shut up!" Matahachi shook his head violently. "When I think of it, all I've ever wanted was Otsū. When I told myself I couldn't go on as I was, tried to find a way to succeed, start out again on the right path—it was all because I wanted to marry her. It wasn't family honor, and it wasn't for the sake of a horrible old woman."

"How long are you going to go on about something that's already finished? You'd do yourself more good chanting sutras. Hail to Amida Buddha!"

She fumbled among the broken branches and dry grass, which were liberally sprinkled with blood, then bent some grass over and knelt on it. "Otsū," she said, "don't hate me. Now that you're dead, I have no more grudge against you. It was all a matter of necessity. Rest in peace."

She felt around with her left hand and got hold of a mass of black hair.

Takuan's voice rang out. "Otsū!" Carried down into the hollow by the dark wind, it seemed as if its source was the trees and the stars themselves.

"Have you found her yet?" he called, his voice sounding rather strained.

"No, she's not around here." The keeper of the inn where Osugi and Otsū had been staying wiped the sweat wearily from his brow.

"Are you sure you heard right?"

"Quite sure. After the priest came from Kiyomizudera in the evening, the old lady left suddenly, saying she was going to the hall of the mountain god. The girl was with her."

Both of them folded their arms in thought.

"Maybe they went on up the mountain or some place off the main path," said Takuan.

"Why are you so worried?"

"I think Otsū's been tricked."

"Is the old woman really that wicked?"

"No," said Takuan enigmatically. "She's a very good woman."

"Not from what you told me. Oh, I just remembered something."

"What's that?"

"Today I saw the girl crying in her room."

"That may not mean much."

"The old woman told us she was her son's bride."

"She would say that."

"From what you said, it sounds like some terrible hatred made the old woman torment the girl."

"Still, that's one thing, and taking her up into the mountains on a dark night is another. I'm afraid Osugi's been planning to murder her."

"Murder! How can you say she's a good woman?"

"Because she is without a doubt what the world calls good. She often goes to Kiyomizudera to worship, doesn't she? And when she's seated before Kannon with her prayer beads in her hand, she must be very close to Kannon in spirit."

"I hear she also prays to the Buddha Amida."

"There are lots of Buddhists like that in this world. The faithful, they're called. They do something they shouldn't, go to the temple and pray to Amida. They seem to dream up diabolical deeds for Amida to forgive. They'll quite cheerfully strike a man dead, perfectly confident that if they call on Amida afterward, their sins will be absolved and they'll go to the Western Paradise when they die. These good people are something of a problem."

Matahachi looked around fearfully, wondering where the voice had come from.

"Hear that, Mother?" he asked excitedly.

"Do you recognize the voice?" Osugi raised her head, but the interruption did not disturb her greatly. Her hand still grasped the hair; her sword was poised to strike.

"Listen! There it is again."

"That's strange. If anybody came looking for Otsū, it'd be that boy named Jōtarō."

"This is a man's voice."

"Yes, I know, and I think I've heard it somewhere before."

"This looks bad. Mother, forget about the head. Bring the lantern. Somebody's coming!"

"This way?"

"Yes, two men. Come on, let's run."

Danger united mother and son in the twinkling of an eye, but Osugi couldn't tear herself away from her gory task.

"Just a minute," she said. "After coming this far, I'm not going back without the head. If I don't have it, how can I prove I took vengeance on Otsū? I'll be through in no time."

"Oh," he moaned with revulsion.

A horrified cry sprang from Osugi's lips. She dropped the head, half stood, staggered, and collapsed on the ground.

'It's not her!' she screamed. She flailed her arms and tried to stand up, but again fell down.

Matahachi jumped forward to look and stammered, "Wh-wh-what?"

433

"See, it's not Otsū! It's a man—beggar—invalid—"

"This couldn't be," exclaimed Matahachi. "I know this man."

"What? Some friend of yours?"

"Oh, no! He tricked me into giving him all my money," he blurted out. "What was a dirty swindler like Akakabe Yasoma doing here, so near a temple?"

"Who's there?" called Takuan. "Otsū, is that you?" Suddenly he was standing right behind them.

Matahachi was fleeter of foot than his mother. As he dashed out of sight, Takuan caught up with her and took a firm grip on her collar.

"Just as I thought. And I trust it was your loving son who fled. Matahachi! What do you mean by running away and leaving your mother behind? Ungrateful lout! Come back here!"

Osugi, though squirming miserably at his knees, had lost none of her spunk. "Who are you?" she demanded angrily. "What do you want?"

Takuan released her and said, "Don't you remember me, Granny? You must be getting senile after all."

"Takuan!"

"Are you surprised?"

"I don't see why I should be. A beggar like you, going wherever he pleases. Sooner or later, you were bound to float into Kyoto."

"You're right," he agreed with a grin. "It's just as you say. I was roaming about in Koyagyū Valley and Izumi Province, but I came up to the capital and last night at a friend's house heard some disturbing news. I decided it was too important not to act on."

"What does that have to do with me?"

"I thought Otsū would be with you, and I'm looking for her."

"Hmph!"

"Granny."

"What?"

"Where's Otsū?"

"I don't know."

"I don't believe you."

"Sir," said the innkeeper. "Blood has been spilled here. It's still fresh." He moved his lantern closer to the corpse.

A stony frown came to Takuan's face. Osugi, seeing him preoccupied, jumped up and started running away. Without moving, the priest shouted, "Wait! You left home to clear your name, didn't you? Are you going back now with it more sullied than ever? You said you loved your son. Do you plan to desert him now that you've made him miserable?" The force of his booming voice wrapped itself around Osugi, bringing her to an abrupt halt.

Her face distorted by defiant wrinkles, she cried, "Soiled my family's name, made my son unhappy—what do you mean?"

"Exactly what I said."

"Fool!" She gave a short, scornful laugh. "Who are you? You go around
434 eating other people's food, living in other people's temples, relieving your

bowels in the open field. What do you know about family honor? What do you know of a mother's love for her son? Have you ever once borne the hardships ordinary people bear? Before telling everybody else how to act, you should try working and feeding yourself, like everybody else."

"You strike a sore spot, and I feel it. There are priests in this world to whom I'd like to say the same thing. I've always said I was no match for you in a battle of words, and I see you still have command of a sharp tongue."

"And I still have important things to do in this world. You needn't think the only thing I can do is talk."

"Never mind that. I want to discuss other matters with you."

"And what might they be?"

"You put Matahachi up to killing Otsū tonight, didn't you? The two of you murdered her, I suspect."

Stretching her wrinkled neck, Osugi laughed contemptuously. "Takuan, you can carry a lantern through this life, but it won't do you any good unless you open your eyes. What are they anyway? Just holes in your head, funny ornaments?"

Takuan, feeling slightly uneasy, finally turned his attention to the scene of the murder.

When he looked up in relief, the old woman said, not without a touch of rancor, "I suppose you're happy it's not Otsū, but don't think I've forgotten that you were the unholy matchmaker who threw her together with Musashi and caused all this trouble in the first place."

"If that's the way you feel, fine. But I know you're a woman with religious faith, and I say you shouldn't go away and leave this body lying here."

"He was stretched out there, on the verge of death anyway. Matahachi killed him, but it wasn't Matahachi's fault."

"This rōnin," said the innkeeper, "*was* a little peculiar in the head. For the last few days, he's been staggering around town drooling at the mouth. He had a huge lump on his head."

Displaying an absolute lack of concern, Osugi turned to leave. Takuan asked the innkeeper to take care of the corpse and followed her, much to Osugi's annoyance. But as she turned to unleash her poisonous tongue again, Matahachi called softly, "Mother."

She went happily toward the voice. He was a good son after all; he had stayed to make sure his mother was safe. Whispering a few words to each other, they apparently decided they were not completely free from danger in the priest's presence and ran as fast as they could toward the foot of the hill.

"It's no use," murmured Takuan. "To judge from that performance, they wouldn't listen to anything I have to say. If only the world could be rid of silly misunderstandings, how much less people would suffer."

But right now, he had to find Otsū. She had discovered some means of escaping. His spirits rose a little, but he could not really relax until he was sure she was safe. He decided to continue his search despite the darkness.

The innkeeper had gone up the hill a while earlier. He came back down, accompanied by seven or eight men with lanterns. The night watchmen at the temple, having agreed to help with the burial, brought shovels and spades. Presently Takuan heard the unpleasant sound of gravedigging.

About the time the hole was deep enough, someone cried, "Look, over here, another body. This one's a pretty young girl." The man was about ten yards from the grave, on the edge of a marsh.

"Is she dead?"

"No, just unconscious."

The Urbane Craftsman

Until his dying day, Musashi's father had never stopped reminding him of his ancestry. "I may be only a country samurai," he'd say, "but never forget, the Akamatsu clan was once famous and powerful. It should be a source of strength and pride to you."

Since he was in Kyoto, Musashi decided to visit a temple called the Rakanji, near which the Akamatsus had once had a house. The clan had long since fallen, but it was just possible he might find at the temple some record of his ancestors. Even if he didn't, he could burn some incense in their memory.

Arriving at the Rakan Bridge over the Lower Kogawa, he thought that he must be near the temple, for it was said to be located a little east of where the Upper Kogawa became the Lower Kogawa. His inquiries in the neighborhood, however, drew a complete blank. No one had ever heard of it.

Returning to the bridge, he stood and gazed at the clear, shallow water flowing beneath it. Though it wasn't so many years since Munisai's death, it appeared that the temple had been either moved or destroyed, leaving neither trace nor memory.

He watched idly as a whitish eddy formed and disappeared, formed and disappeared again. Noticing mud dripping from a grassy spot on the left bank, he concluded that it came from a sword polisher's shop.

"Musashi!"

He looked around and saw the old nun Myōshū returning from an errand.

"How good of you to come," she exclaimed, thinking he was there to pay a call. "Kōetsu's at home today. He'll be glad to see you." She led him through the gate of a nearby house and sent a servant to fetch her son.

After warmly welcoming his guest, Kōetsu said, "At the moment, I'm busy with an important polishing job, but later we can have a nice long chat."

It pleased Musashi to see that both mother and son were as friendly and natural as they had been the first time he met them. He spent the afternoon and evening chatting with them, and when they urged him to spend the night, he accepted. The next day, while Kōetsu showed him the workshop and explained the technique of sword polishing, he begged Musashi to stay on as long as he wished.

The house, with its deceptively modest gate, stood on a corner southeast of the remains of the Jissōin. In the neighborhood were several houses belonging to Kōetsu's cousins and nephews, or to other men engaged in the same profession; all the Hon'amis lived and worked here, after the fashion of the large provincial clans of the past.

The Hon'amis were descended from a fairly distinguished military family, and had been retainers to the Ashikaga shōguns. In the present social hierarchy, the family belonged to the artisan class, but insofar as wealth and prestige were concerned, Kōetsu might have been taken for a member of the samurai class. He hobnobbed with high court nobles and had on occasion been invited by Tokugawa Ieyasu to Fushimi Castle.

The Hon'amis' position was not unique; most of the wealthy artisans and merchants of the day—Suminokura Soan, Chaya Shirōjirō and Haiya Shōyū, among others—were of samurai descent. Under the Ashikaga shōguns, their ancestors had been assigned work related to manufacture or trade. Success in these fields led to a gradual severing of connections with the military class, and as private enterprise became profitable, they were no longer dependent on their feudal emoluments. Although their social rank was technically lower than that of the warriors, they were very powerful.

When it came to business, not only was samurai status more of a hindrance than a help, there were definite advantages to being a commoner, chief of which was stability. When fighting erupted, the great merchants were patronized by both sides. True, they were sometimes forced to furnish military supplies for little or nothing, but they had come to regard this onus as no more than a fee paid in lieu of having their property destroyed during wartime.

During the Ōnin War of the 1460s and '70s, the whole district around the ruins of the Jissōin had been razed, and even now people planting trees often dug up rusted fragments of swords or helmets. The Hon'ami residence had been one of the first built in the vicinity after the war.

A branch of the Arisugawa flowed through the compound, meandering first through a quarter acre or so of vegetable garden, then disappearing into a grove, to emerge again near the well by the front entrance of the main house. There was a branch flowing off toward the kitchen, another toward the bath, and still another toward a simple, rustic teahouse, where the clear water was used for the tea ceremony. The river was the source of water for the workshop, where swords forged by master craftsmen like Masamune, Muramasa and Osafune were expertly polished. Since the workshop was sacred to the family, a rope was suspended over the entranceway in the manner of Shinto shrines.

Almost before he knew it, four days passed, and Musashi made up his mind to take his leave. But before he'd had a chance to mention this, Kōetsu said, "We're not doing much to entertain you, but if you're not bored, please stay as long as you like. There are some old books and curios in my study. If you'd like to look them over, feel free to do so. And in a day or two, I'm going to fire some tea bowls and dishes. You might enjoy watching. You'll find ceramics almost as interesting as swords. Maybe you could model a piece or two yourself."

Touched by the graciousness of the invitation and his host's assurance that no one would take offense if he decided to leave on a moment's notice, Musashi allowed himself to settle down and enjoy the relaxed atmosphere. He was far from bored. The study contained books in Chinese and Japanese, scroll paintings from the Kamakura period, rubbings of calligraphy by ancient Chinese masters and dozens of other things, any one of which Musashi could happily have pored over for a day or so. He was particularly attracted by a painting hanging in the alcove. Called *Chestnuts*, it was by the Sung master Liang-k'ai. It was small, about two feet high by two and a half wide, and so old that it was impossible to tell what sort of paper it was drawn on.

He sat and gazed at it by the hour. Finally, one day, he remarked to Kōetsu, "I'm sure no rank amateur could paint the sort of pictures you paint, but I wonder if maybe even I couldn't draw something as simple as this work."

"It's the other way around," Kōetsu informed him. "Anybody could learn to paint as well as I, but there is a degree of profundity and spiritual loftiness in Liang-k'ai's painting that cannot be acquired merely by studying art."

"Is that really true?" Musashi asked in surprise. He was assured that it was.

It showed nothing but a squirrel looking at two fallen chestnuts, one split open and the other tightly closed, as if it wanted to follow its natural impulse and eat the chestnuts but hesitated for fear of the thorns. Since the painting was executed very freely in black ink, Musashi had thought it looked naive. But the more he looked at it after talking to Kōetsu, the more clearly he saw that the artist was right.

One afternoon, Kōetsu came in and said, "Are you staring at Liang-k'ai's picture again? You seem to have taken a great liking to it. When you leave, roll it up and take it with you. I'd like you to have it."

Musashi demurred. "I couldn't possibly accept it. It's bad enough for me to stay here in your house so long. Why, that must be a family heirloom!"

"But you do like it, don't you?" The older man smiled indulgently. "You may have it if you want it. I really don't need it. Pictures should be owned by the people who really love and appreciate them. I'm sure that's what the artist would want."

"If you put it that way, I'm not the one to own a painting like this. To tell the truth, I've thought several times it'd be nice to have it, but if I did, what would I do with it? I'm only a wandering swordsman. I never stay in the same place very long."

"I suppose it would be a nuisance, carrying a painting around with you wherever you go. At your age, you probably don't even want a house of your own, but I think every man should have a place he can regard as home, even if it's nothing more than a little shack. Without a house, a person gets lonely— feels lost somehow. Why don't you find some logs and build a cabin in some quiet corner of the city?"

"I never thought about it. I'd like to travel to a lot of distant places, go to the farthest end of Kyushu and see how people live under the foreign influences in Nagasaki. And I'm eager to see the new capital the shōgun is building in Edo and the great mountains and rivers in northern Honshu. Maybe I'm just a vagabond at heart."

"You're not the only one, by any means. It's only natural, but you should avoid the temptation of thinking that your dreams can be realized only in some far-off place. If you think that way, you'll neglect the possibilities in your immediate surroundings. Most young people do, I fear, and become dissatisfied with their lives." Kōetsu laughed. "But an idle old man like myself has no business preaching to the young. Anyway, I didn't come here to talk about that. I came to invite you out this evening. Have you ever been to the licensed quarter?"

"The geisha district?"

"Yes. I've a friend named Haiya Shōyū. Despite his age, he's always up to some mischief or other. I just received a note inviting me to join him near Rokujō Avenue this evening, and I wondered if you'd like to come along."

"No, I don't think so."

"If you really don't want to, I'll not insist, but I think you'd find it interesting."

Myōshū, who had crept in silently and was listening with obvious interest, put in, "I think you should go, Musashi. It's an opportunity to see something you haven't seen. Haiya Shōyū's not the kind of man you have to be stiff and formal with, and I believe you'd enjoy the experience. By all means, go!"

The old nun went to the chest of drawers and began taking out a kimono and obi. As a rule, older people were at pains to prevent young men from frittering away their time and money at geisha houses, but Myōshū seemed as enthusiastic as if she herself were getting ready to go somewhere.

"Now let's see, which of these kimonos do you like?" she asked. "Will this obi do?" Chattering away, she busied herself getting out things for Musashi as if he were her son. She chose a lacquered pillbox, a decorative short sword and a brocade wallet, then took some gold coins from the money chest and slipped them into the wallet.

"Well," said Musashi, with only a trace of reluctance, "if you insist, I'll go, but I wouldn't look right in all that finery. I'll just wear this old kimono I have on. I sleep in it when I'm out in the open. I'm used to it."

"You'll do no such thing!" Myōshū said sternly. "You yourself may not mind, but think of the other people. In those nice pretty rooms, you'd look no better than a dirty old rag. Men go there to have a good time and forget their troubles. They want to be surrounded by beautiful things. Don't think of it as dressing up to make yourself look like something you're not. Anyway, these clothes aren't nearly as fancy as some men wear; they're just clean and neat. Now, put them on!"

Musashi complied.

When he was dressed, Myōshū remarked cheerfully, "There, you look very handsome."

As they were about to leave, Kōetsu went to the household Buddhist altar   *439* and lit a candle on it. Both he and his mother were devout members of the Nichiren sect.

At the front entrance, Myōshū had laid out two pairs of sandals with new thongs. While they were putting them on, she whispered with one of the servants, who was waiting to shut the front gate after them.

Kōetsu said good-bye to his mother, but she looked up at him quickly and said, "Wait just a minute." Her face was creased in a worried frown.

"What's the matter?" he asked.

"This man tells me three rough-looking samurai were just here and spoke very rudely. Do you suppose it's anything important?"

Kōetsu looked questioningly at Musashi.

"There's no reason to be afraid," Musashi assured him. "They're probably from the House of Yoshioka. They may attack me, but they don't have anything against you."

"One of the workmen said the same sort of thing happened a couple of days ago. Only one samurai, but he came through the gate without being asked and looked over the hedge by the teahouse path, toward the part of the house where you're staying."

"Then I'm sure it's the Yoshioka men."

"I think so too," agreed Kōetsu. He turned to the trembling gateman. "What did they say?"

"The workmen had all left, and I was about to close the gate when these three samurai suddenly surrounded me. One of them—he looked mean—took a letter out of his kimono and ordered me to hand it to the guest staying here."

"He didn't say 'Musashi'?"

"Well, later on he did say 'Miyamoto Musashi.' And he said Musashi'd been staying here for several days."

"What did you say?"

"You said not to tell anyone about Musashi, so I shook my head and said there was no one here by that name. He got angry and called me a liar, but one of the others—a somewhat older man, with a smirk on his face—calmed him down and said they'd find a way to deliver the letter directly. I'm not sure what he meant, but it sounded like a threat. They went off toward the corner down there."

"Kōetsu, you walk on a little ahead of me," said Musashi. "I don't want you to get hurt or become involved in any trouble because of me."

Kōetsu replied with a laugh, "There's no need to worry about me, particularly if you're sure they're Yoshioka men. I'm not the least bit afraid of them. Let's go."

After they were outside, Kōetsu put his head back through the small door in the gate and called, "Mother!"

"Did you forget something?" she asked.

"No, I was just thinking: if you're worried about me, I could send a messenger to Shōyū and tell him I can't come this evening."

"Oh, no. I'm more afraid something might happen to Musashi. But I don't think he'd come back if you tried to stop him. Go on, and have a good time!"

Kōetsu caught up with Musashi and as they ambled along the riverbank said, "Shōyū's house is just down the road, at Ichijō Avenue and Horikawa Street. He's probably getting ready now, so let's stop in for him. It's right on the way."

It was still light, and the walk along the river was pleasant, all the more so because they were completely at leisure at an hour when everybody else was busy.

Musashi remarked, "I've heard Haiya Shōyū's name, but I really don't know anything about him."

"I'd be surprised if you hadn't heard of him. He's a well-known expert at composing linked verse."

"Ah! So he's a poet."

"He is, but of course he doesn't make his living writing verse. He comes from an old Kyoto merchant family."

"How did he get the name Haiya?"

"It's the name of his business."

"What does he sell?"

"His name means 'ash salesman,' and that's what he sells—ashes."

"Ashes?"

"Yes, they're used in dyeing cloth. It's a big business. He sells to dyers' guilds all over the country. At the beginning of the Ashikaga period, the ash trade was controlled by an agent of the shōgun, but later it was turned over to private wholesalers. There are three big wholesale houses in Kyoto, and Shōyū's is one of them. He himself doesn't have to work, of course. He's retired and living a life of ease. Look over there; you can see his house. It's the one with the stylish gate."

Musashi nodded as he listened, but his attention was distracted by the feel of his sleeves. While the right one was waving lightly in the breeze, the left did not move at all. Slipping his hand in, he drew out an object enough to see what it was—a well-tanned purple leather thong of the type warriors used to tie up their sleeves when fighting. "Myōshū," he thought. "Only she could have put it there."

He looked backed and smiled at the men behind them, who, as he was already aware, had been trailing along at a discreet distance ever since he and Kōetsu had turned out of Hon'ami Lane.

His smile seemed to relieve the three men. They whispered a few words to each other and began taking longer strides.

Coming to the Haiya house, Kōetsu sounded the clapper on the gate, and a servant carrying a broom came to admit them. Kōetsu was through the gate and in the front garden before he noticed Musashi was not with him. Turning back toward the gate, he called, "Come in, Musashi. There's nothing to be hesitant about."

Having closed in on Musashi, the three samurai had their elbows thrust out and their hands on their swords. Kōetsu couldn't catch what they said to Musashi, nor the latter's soft reply.

441

Musashi told him not to wait, and Kōetsu answered with an air of complete calm. "All right, I'll be in the house. Join me as soon as you've finished your business."

"We're not here," one of the men said, "to argue about whether you ran away to hide or not. I'm Ōtaguro Hyōsuke. I'm one of the Ten Swordsmen of the House of Yoshioka. I've brought a letter from Seijūrō's younger brother, Denshichirō." Taking the letter out, he held it up for Musashi to see. "Read it and give us your answer immediately."

Opening the letter in an offhand manner, Musashi read it quickly and said, "I accept."

Hyōsuke looked at him suspiciously. "Are you sure?"

Musashi nodded. "Absolutely sure."

Musashi's casualness took them off guard.

"If you don't keep your word, you'll never be able to show your face in Kyoto again. We'll see to that!"

Musashi's stare was accompanied by a slight smile, but he said nothing.

"Are you satisfied with the conditions? There's not much time left to prepare yourself."

"I'm quite ready," Musashi answered calmly.

"Then we'll see you later this evening."

As Musashi started through the gate, Hyōsuke approached him again and asked, "Will you be here until the time agreed on?"

"No. My host is taking me to the licensed quarter near Rokujō Avenue."

"The licensed quarter?" Hyōsuke was surprised. "Well, I assume you'll be either here or there. If you're late, I'll send someone for you. I trust you won't try any tricks."

Musashi had already turned his back and entered the front garden, a step that took him into a different world.

The irregularly shaped, artlessly spaced stepping-stones of the garden path appeared to have been put there by nature. On either side were moist clumps of low fernlike bamboo, interspersed with taller bamboo shoots, no thicker than a writing brush. As he walked on, the roof of the main house came into view, then the front entrance, a small separate house and a garden bower, each contributing to the atmosphere of venerable age and long tradition. Around the buildings, tall pines suggested wealth and comfort.

He could hear people playing the game of kickball called *kemari*, a soft sporadic thump, often heard from behind the walls of the mansions of court nobles. Hearing it in a merchant's establishment surprised him.

Once in the house, he was shown into a room looking out onto the garden. Two servants entered with tea and cakes, one informing them that their host would be with them shortly. Musashi could tell from the servants' manner that they were impeccably trained.

Kōetsu murmured, "It's quite cold, isn't it, now that the sun's gone down?" He wanted to have the shoji closed but didn't ask because Musashi appeared to be enjoying the view of the plum blossoms. Kōetsu also turned his eyes toward the view. "I see there are clouds above Mount Hiei," he remarked. "I'd guess they're from the north. Aren't you chilly?"

442

"No, not especially," answered Musashi honestly, serenely ignorant of what his companion was hinting at.

A servant brought a candlestick, and Kōetsu took the opportunity to close the shoji. Musashi became conscious of the atmosphere within the household, which was peaceful and genial. Relaxing and listening to the laughing voices coming from the inner part of the house, he was struck by the complete absence of ostentation. It was as though the decor and surroundings had deliberately been made as simply as possible. He could imagine himself in the guest room of a large farmhouse in the country.

Haiya Shōyū entered the room and proclaimed, "I'm sorry to have kept you waiting so long." His voice, open, friendly, youthful, was just the opposite of Kōetsu's soft drawl. Thin as a crane, he was perhaps ten years older than his friend, yet far more jovial. When Kōetsu explained who Musashi was, he said, "Oh, so you're a nephew of Matsuo Kaname? I know him quite well."

Shōyū's acquaintance with his uncle must have been through the noble House of Konoe, thought Musashi, beginning to sense the close ties between the wealthy merchants and the palace courtiers.

Without further ado, the spry old merchant said, "Let's be on our way. I'd intended to go while it was still light, so that we could stroll over. But since it's already dark, I think we should call for palanquins. This young man's coming with us, I assume."

Palanquins were summoned, and the three set off, Shōyū and Kōetsu in front, Musashi behind. It was the first time he had ever ridden in one.

By the time they reached the Yanagi Riding Grounds, the bearers were already puffing white steam.

"Oh, it's cold," one complained.

"The wind cuts into you, doesn't it?"

"And it's supposed to be spring!"

Their three lanterns swung to and fro, flickering in the wind. Dark clouds above the city hinted ominously of still worse weather before the night was out. Beyond the riding field, the lights of the city shone in dazzling splendor. Musashi had the impression of a great swarm of fireflies glowing cheerfully in the cold, clear breeze.

"Musashi!" Kōetsu called from the middle palanquin. "That's where we're going, over there. It's quite an experience to come upon it suddenly, isn't it?" He explained that until three years ago the licensed district had been at Nijō Avenue, near the palace, then the magistrate, Itakura Katsushige, had had it moved, because the nightly singing and carousing was a nuisance. He said the whole area was thriving and that all new fashions originated within those rows of lights.

"You could almost say that a whole new culture has been created there." Pausing and listening carefully for a moment, he added, "You can just hear it, can't you? The sound of strings and singing?"

It was music Musashi had never heard before.

"The instruments are shamisen. They're an improved version of a three-stringed instrument brought from the Ryukyu Islands. A great many new songs have been composed for them, all right here in the quarter, then spread

443

out among the common people. So you can see how influential this district is, and why certain standards of decency have to be maintained, even though it's rather cut off from the rest of the city."

They turned into one of the streets; the light from countless bright lamps and lanterns hanging from the willow trees reflected in Musashi's eyes. The district had kept its old name when it was moved: Yanagimachi, the Town of Willows, willows having long been associated with drinking and dalliance.

Kōetsu and Shōyū were well known at the establishment they entered. The greetings were obsequious yet jocular, and it soon became apparent that here they used nicknames—"play names," as it were. Kōetsu was known as Mizuo-chi-sama—Mr. Falling Water—because of the streams traversing his estate, and Shōyū was Funabashi-sama—Mr. Boat Bridge—after a pontoon bridge in the vicinity of his house.

If Musashi was to become a habitué, he would certainly acquire a nickname soon, for in this never-never land, few used their real names. Hayashiya Yoji-bei was only the pseudonym of the proprietor of the house they were visiting, but more often than not he was called Ōgiya, the name of the establishment. Along with the Kikyōya, it was one of the two best-known houses in the district, the only two, in fact, with the reputation of being absolutely first class. The reigning beauty at the Ōgiya was Yoshino Dayū, and her counterpart at the Kikyōya, Murogimi Dayū. Both ladies enjoyed a degree of fame in the city rivaled only by that of the greatest daimyō.

Although Musashi studiously attempted not to gape, he was astonished by the elegance of his surroundings, which approached that of the most opulent palaces. The reticular ceilings, ornately carved openwork transoms, exquisite curved railings, fastidiously tended inner gardens—everything was a feast for the eye. Absorbed in a painting on a wooden door panel, he did not notice that his companions had gone on ahead until Kōetsu came back for him.

The silver-colored doors of the room they entered were transformed into a hazy liquid by the light of the lamps. One side opened onto a garden in the style of Kobori Enshū, well-raked sand and a rock arrangement suggestive of Chinese mountain scenery, such as one might see in a Sung painting.

Shōyū, complaining of the cold, sat down on a cushion and drew his shoulders together. Kōetsu also seated himself and bade Musashi to do likewise. Serving girls soon arrived with warm sake.

Seeing that the cup he had urged on Musashi had cooled off, Shōyū became insistent. "Drink up, young man," he said, "and have a hot cup."

After this refrain had been repeated two or three times, Shōyū's manner began to border on rudeness. "Kobosatsu!" he said to one of the serving girls. "Make him drink! You, Musashi! What's the matter with you? Why aren't you drinking?"

"I am," protested Musashi.

The old man was already a little tipsy. "Well, you're not doing very well. You don't have any spirit!"

"I'm not much of a drinker."

444   "What you mean is that you're not a strong swordsman, isn't it?"

"Maybe that's true," said Musashi mildly, laughing off the insult.

"If you're worried about drinking interfering with your studies, or throwing you off balance, or weakening your willpower, or preventing you from making a name for yourself, then you haven't got the pluck to be a fighter."

"Oh, it's not that. There's only one small problem."

"What might that be?"

"It makes me sleepy."

"Well, you can go to sleep here or anywhere else in the place. No one will mind." Turning to the girls, he said, "The young man's afraid he'll get drowsy if he drinks. If he gets sleepy, put him to bed!"

"Oh, we'll be glad to!" chorused the girls, smiling coyly.

"If he goes to bed, someone will have to keep him warm. Kōetsu, which one should it be?"

"Which one indeed?" said Kōetsu noncommittally.

"It can't be Sumigiku Dayū; she's my little wife. And you yourself wouldn't want it to be Kobosatsu Dayū. There's Karakoto Dayū. Um, she won't do. She's too hard to get along with."

"Isn't Yoshino Dayū going to put in an appearance?" asked Kōetsu.

"That's it! She's just the one! Even our reluctant guest should be happy with her. I wonder why she isn't here now. Someone go call her. I want to show her to the young samurai here."

Sumigiku objected. "Yoshino's not like the rest of us. She has many clients, and she won't come running at just anyone's beck and call."

"Oh, yes she will—for me! Tell her I'm here, and she'll come, no matter who she happens to be with. Go and call her!" Shōyū reared up, looked around and called to the young girls who attended the courtesans and were now playing in the next room: "Is Rin'ya there?"

Rin'ya herself answered.

"Come here a minute. You wait on Yoshino Dayū, don't you? Why isn't she here? Tell her Funabashi is here, she should come right away. If you bring her back with you, I'll give you a present."

Rin'ya looked a little puzzled. Her eyes opened wide, but after a moment she signaled her assent. She already showed signs of becoming a great beauty, and it was almost certain she would be the successor in the next generation to the famous Yoshino. But she was only eleven years old. Barely had she gone into the outside corridor and slid the door shut when she clapped her hands and called loudly, "Uneme, Tamami, Itonosuke! Look out here!"

The three girls rushed out and began clapping their hands and shrieking joyfully, delighted by the discovery of snow outside.

The men looked out to see what the commotion was about and, except for Shōyū, were amused by the sight of the young attendants chattering excitedly, trying to decide whether the snow would still be on the ground in the morning. Rin'ya, her mission forgotten, rushed out into the garden to play in the snow.

Impatient, Shōyū sent one of the courtesans in search of Yoshino Dayū.

She returned and whispered into his ear, "Yoshino said she would like more than anything to join you, but her guest won't permit it."

"Won't permit it! That's ridiculous! Other women here may be forced to do their customers' bidding, but Yoshino can do as she pleases. Or is she allowing herself to be bought for money these days?"

"Oh, no. But the guest she's with tonight is particularly stubborn. Every time she says she'd like to leave, he insists more adamantly that she stay."

"Um. I suppose none of her customers ever wants her to go. Who is she with tonight?"

"Lord Karasumaru."

"Lord Karasumaru?" repeated Shōyū with an ironic smile. "Is he alone?"

"No."

"He's with some of his usual cronies?"

"Yes."

Shōyū slapped his knee. "This might turn out to be interesting. The snow is good, the sake is good, and if we just had Yoshino, everything would be perfect. Kōetsu, let's write his lordship a letter. You, young lady, bring me an ink stone and brush."

When the girl placed the writing materials before Kōetsu, he said, "What shall I write?"

"A poem would be good. Prose might do, but verse would be better. Lord Karasumaru is one of our more celebrated poets."

"I'm not sure I know how to go about it. Let's see, we want the poem to persuade him to let us have Yoshino, isn't that right?"

"That's it."

"If it's not a good poem, it won't make him change his mind. Good poems are not easy to write on the spur of the moment. Why don't you write the first lines, and I'll write the rest?"

"Hmm. Let's see what we can do." Shōyū took the brush and wrote:

> To our humble hut
> Let there come one cherry tree,
> One tree from Yoshino.

"So far, so good," said Kōetsu, and wrote:

> The flowers shiver from cold
> In the clouds above the peaks.

Shōyū was immensely pleased. "Marvelous," he said. "That ought to take care of his lordship and his noble companions—the 'people above the clouds.'" He neatly folded the paper, then handed it to Sumigiku, saying gravely, "The other girls don't seem to have the dignity you have, so I appoint you my envoy to Lord Kangan. If I'm not mistaken, that's the name he's known by in these parts." The nickname, meaning "Frigid Mountain Crag," was a reference to Lord Karasumaru's exalted status.

Sumigiku was not long in returning. "Lord Kangan's reply, if you please," she said, reverentially placing a gorgeously wrought letter box before Shōyū and Kōetsu. They looked at the box, which implied formality, then at each other. What had started as a little joke was taking on more serious overtones.

"My word," said Shōyū. "We must be more careful next time. They must have been surprised. Surely they couldn't have known we'd be here tonight."

Still hoping to get the better of the exchange, Shōyū opened the box and unfolded the answer. To his dismay, he saw nothing but a piece of cream-colored paper, devoid of writing.

Thinking he must have dropped something, he looked around for a second sheet, then glanced again into the box.

"Sumigiku, what does this mean?"

"I have no idea. Lord Kangan handed me the box and told me to give it to you."

"Is he trying to make asses of us? Or was our poem too clever for him and he's raising the white flag of surrender?" Shōyū had a way of interpreting things to suit his own convenience, but this time he appeared uncertain. He handed the paper to Kōetsu and asked, "What do you make of it?"

"I think he intends us to read it."

"Read a blank piece of paper?"

"I should think it can be construed somehow."

"Do you? What could it possibly mean?"

Kōetsu thought for a moment. "Snow . . . snow covering everything."

"Hmm. Maybe you're right."

"In answer to our request for a cherry tree from Yoshino, it could mean:

> If you gaze at snow
> And fill your cup with sake,
> Even without flowers . . .

In other words, he's telling us that since it's snowing tonight, we should forget about love, open the doors and admire the snow as we drink. Or at least, that's my impression."

"How annoying!" exclaimed Shōyū with distaste. "I have no intention of drinking in such a heartless fashion. Not going to sit here and be silent either. One way or another, we'll transplant the Yoshino tree to our room and admire her blossoms." Excited now, he moistened his lips with his tongue.

Kōetsu humored him, hoping he would calm down, but Shōyū kept after the girls to bring Yoshino and refused to allow the subject to be changed for very long. Though his persistence did not secure his wish, it eventually became comical, and the girls rolled on the floor with laughter.

Musashi quietly left his seat. He had chosen the right time. No one noticed his departure.

Reverberations in the Snow

Musashi wandered about the many hallways, avoiding the brightly lit front parlors. He came upon one dark room where bedding was kept and another full of tools and implements. The walls seemed to exude the warmish odor of food being prepared, but still he could not find the kitchen.

An attendant came out of one room and held out her arms to block his way. "Sir, guests aren't supposed to come back here," she said firmly, with none of the childish cuteness she might have affected in the guest rooms.

"Oh! Shouldn't I be here?"

"Certainly not!" She gave him a shove toward the front and walked in the same direction herself.

"Aren't you the girl who fell in the snow a while ago? Rin'ya, isn't it?"

"Yes, I'm Rin'ya. I suppose you got lost trying to find the toilet. I'll show you where it is." She took his hand and pulled.

"That's not it. I'm not drunk. I'd like you to do me a favor. Take me to an empty room and bring me some food."

"Food? If that's what you want, I'll take it to your parlor."

"No, not there. Everybody's having a good time. They don't want to be reminded of dinner yet."

Rin'ya cocked her head. "I suppose you're right. I'll bring you something here. What would you like?"

"Nothing special; two large rice balls will do."

She returned in a few minutes with the rice balls and served them to him in an unlit room.

When he had finished, he said, "I guess I can get out of the house through the inner garden there." Without waiting for a reply, he stood up and walked to the veranda.

"Where are you going, sir?"

"Don't worry, I'll be back soon."

"Why are you leaving by the back way?"

"People would make a fuss if I went out the front way. And if my hosts saw me, it would upset them and spoil their fun."

"I'll open the gate for you, but be sure to come back right away. If you don't, they'll blame me."

"I understand. If Mr. Mizuochi should ask about me, tell him I went to the neighborhood of the Rengeōin to see a man I know. I intend to return shortly."

"You must come back soon. Your companion for the evening is to be Yoshino Dayū." She opened the snow-laden folding wooden gate and let him out.

Directly opposite the main entrance to the gay quarter was a tea shop called the Amigasa-jaya. Musashi stopped and asked for a pair of straw sandals, but they had none. As the name implied, their chief business was selling basket hats to men who wished to conceal their identity when entering the quarter.

After sending the shopgirl to buy sandals, he sat down on the edge of a stool and tightened his obi and the cord under it. Removing his loose-fitting coat and folding it neatly, he borrowed paper and brush and wrote a brief note, folded it and slipped it into the sleeve of the coat. He then called to the old man crouched beside the hearth in the room behind the shop, whom he took to be the proprietor. "Would you keep this coat for me? If I don't return by eleven o'clock, please take it to the Ōgiya and give it to a man called Kōetsu. There's a letter for him inside the sleeve."

The man said he'd be glad to help, and on being asked, informed Musashi it was only about seven o'clock, the watchman having just passed and announced the hour.

When the girl returned with the sandals, Musashi examined the thongs to make sure the plait was not too tight, then tied them on over his leather socks. Handing the shopkeeper more money than was necessary, he picked up a new basket hat and went outside. Instead of tying the hat on, he held it over his head to keep off the snow, which fell in flakes softer than cherry blossoms.

Lights were visible along the riverbank at Shijō Avenue, but to the east, in the Gion woods, it was pitch black, except for widely scattered patches of light from stone lanterns. The deathly stillness was broken only sporadically, by the noise of snow sliding off a branch.

In front of a shrine gate about twenty men knelt in prayer, facing the deserted buildings. The temple bells in the nearby hills had just pealed five times, marking the hour of eight. On this particular night the loud, clear sound of the bells seemed to penetrate to the pit of the stomach.

"That's enough praying," said Denshichirō. "Let's be on our way."

As they started off, one of the men asked Denshichirō if the thongs of his sandals were all right. "On a freezing night like this, if they're too tight, they'll break."

"They're fine. When it's this cold, the only thing to do is use cloth thongs. You'd better remember that."

At the shrine, Denshichirō had completed his battle preparations, down to the headband and the leather sleeve thong. Surrounded by his grim-faced retinue, he strode across the snow, taking long deep breaths and emitting puffs of white vapor.

The challenge delivered to Musashi had specified the area behind the Ren-

449

geōin at nine o'clock. Fearing, or professing to fear, that if they gave Musashi any extra time he might flee, never to return, the Yoshiokas had decided to act quickly. Hyōsuke had remained in the vicinity of Shōyū's house, but had sent his two comrades to report on the situation.

Approaching the Rengeōin, they saw a bonfire near the back of the temple.

"Who's that?" asked Denshichirō.

"It's probably Ryōhei and Jūrōzaemon."

"They're here too?" said Denshichirō with a trace of annoyance. "There are too many of our men present. I don't want people saying Musashi lost only because he was attacked by a large force."

"When the time comes, we'll go away."

The main temple building, the Sanjūsangendō, extended through thirty-three column spans. Behind it was a large open space ideal for practicing archery and long used for that purpose. This association with one of the martial arts was what had induced Denshichirō to choose the Rengeōin for his encounter with Musashi. Denshichirō and his men were satisfied with the choice. There were some pine trees, enough to keep the landscape from being barren, but no weeds or rushes to get in the way during the course of the fight.

Ryōhei and Jūrōzaemon rose to greet Denshichirō, Ryōhei saying, "You've had a cold walk, I imagine. There's still plenty of time. Sit down and warm yourself."

Silently, Denshichirō seated himself in the place Ryōhei had vacated. He stretched his hands out over the flames and cracked his knuckles, one finger at a time. "I guess I'm too early," he said. His face, warmed by the fire, had already taken on a bloodthirsty look. Frowning, he asked, "Didn't we pass a teahouse on the way?"

"Yes, but it was closed."

"One of you go and get some sake. If you knock long enough, they'll answer."

"Sake, now?"

"Yes, now. I'm cold." Moving closer to the fire, Denshichirō squatted, almost hugging it.

Since no one could remember a time, morning, noon or night, when he had appeared at the dōjō not smelling of alcohol, his drinking had come to be accepted as a matter of course. Though the fate of the whole Yoshioka School was at stake, one man wondered fuzzily if it wouldn't be better for him to warm his body with a little sake than to try to wield the sword with freezing arms and legs. Another quietly pointed out that it would be risky to disobey him, even for his own good, and a couple of the men ran off to the teahouse. The sake they brought was piping hot.

"Good!" said Denshichirō. "My very best friend and ally."

They watched nervously as he imbibed, praying he wouldn't consume as much as usual. Denshichirō, however, stopped well short of his normal quota. Despite his show of nonchalance, he well knew that his life was in the balance.

"Listen! Could that be Musashi?"

Ears pricked up.

As the men around the fire rapidly got to their feet, a dark figure appeared around the corner of the building. He waved his hand and shouted, "Don't worry; it's only me."

Though gallantly attired, with his *hakama* tucked up for running, he could not disguise his age. His back was bent into the shape of a bow. When the men could see him more clearly, they informed each other that it was only the "old man from Mibu," and the excitement died down. The old man was Yoshioka Genzaemon, Kempō's brother and Denshichirō's uncle.

"Why, if it isn't Uncle Gen! What brings you here?" exclaimed Denshichirō.

It had not occurred to him that his uncle might consider his assistance needed tonight.

"Ah, Denshichirō," said Genzaemon, "you're really going through with it. I'm relieved to find you here."

"I meant to go and discuss the matter with you first, but—"

"Discuss? What is there to discuss? The Yoshioka name has been dragged through the mud, your brother's been made a cripple! If you'd taken no action, you'd have had me to answer to!"

"There's nothing to worry about. I'm not weak-kneed like my brother."

"I'll take your word for that. And I know you'll win, but I thought I'd better come and give you some encouragement. I ran all the way from Mibu. Denshichirō, let me warn you, you shouldn't take this opponent too lightly, from what I hear."

"I'm aware of that."

"Don't be in too much of a hurry to win. Be calm, leave it to the gods. If by any chance you get killed, I'll take care of your body."

"Ha, ha, ha, ha! Come, Uncle Gen, warm yourself by the fire."

The old man silently drank a cup of sake, then addressed the others reproachfully. "What are you doing here? Certainly you don't intend to back him up with your swords, do you? This match is between one swordsman and another, and it looks cowardly to have a lot of supporters around. It's almost time now. Come with me, all of you. We'll go far enough away so it doesn't look as though we were planning a mass attack."

The men did as they were commanded, leaving Denshichirō alone. He sat close to the fire, thinking: "When I heard the bells, it was eight o'clock. It must be nine by now. Musashi's late."

The only trace of his disciples was their black footprints in the snow; the only sound, the crack of icicles breaking off the eaves of the temple. Once, the branch of a tree snapped under the weight of the snow. Each time the silence was disturbed, Denshichirō's eyes darted about like a falcon's.

And like a falcon, a man came kicking through the snow.

Nervous and panting, Hyōsuke said between breaths, "He's coming."

Denshichirō knew the message before he heard it and was already on his feet. "He's coming?" he asked parrotlike, but his feet were automatically stamping out the last embers of the fire.

Hyōsuke reported that Musashi had taken his time after leaving the Ōgiya, as if oblivious of the heavy snowfall. "Just a few minutes ago he climbed the stone steps of the Gion Shrine. I took a back street and came as fast as I could, but even dawdling the way he was, he couldn't be far behind me. I hope you're ready."

"Hmm, this is it. . . . Hyōsuke, get away from here."

"Where are the others?"

"I don't know, but I don't want you here. You make me nervous."

"Yes, sir." Hyōsuke's tone was obedient, but he did not want to leave and made up his mind not to. After Denshichirō had trampled the fire into the slush and turned with a tremor of excitement toward the courtyard, Hyōsuke ducked under the floor of the temple and squatted in the darkness. Though he had not particularly noticed the wind out in the open, here underneath the building it whipped frigidly. Chilled to the bone, he hugged his knees and tried to deceive himself into thinking that the chattering of his teeth and the painful shiver running up and down his spine came from the cold alone and had nothing to do with his fear.

Denshichirō walked about a hundred paces from the temple and took a solid stance, bracing one foot against the root of a tall pine tree and waiting with palpable impatience. The warmth of the sake had worn off rapidly, and Denshichirō felt the cold biting into his flesh. That his temper was growing shorter was evident even to Hyōsuke, who could see the courtyard as clearly as if it were daylight.

A pile of snow cascaded off the branch of a tree. Denshichirō started nervously.

Still Musashi did not appear.

Finally, unable to sit still any longer, Hyōsuke came out of his hiding place and shouted, "What happened to Musashi?"

"Are you still here?" Denshichirō asked angrily, but he was as irritated as Hyōsuke and did not order him away. By tacit mutual consent, the two walked toward each other. They stood there, looking around in all directions, time and again one or the other saying, "I can't see him." Each time the tone grew both angrier and more suspicious.

"That bastard—he's run away!" exclaimed Denshichirō.

"He couldn't have," insisted Hyōsuke, launching into an earnest recapitulation of all he had seen and why he was sure Musashi would eventually come.

Denshichirō interrupted him. "What's that?" he asked, looking quickly at one end of the temple.

A candle was emerging shakily from the kitchen building behind the long hall. It was in the hands of a priest, that much was clear, but they could not make out the dim figure behind him.

Two shadows and the speck of light, passing through the gate between the kitchen and the main building, ascended the long veranda of the Sanjūsangendō.

The priest was saying in a subdued voice, "Everything here is shut up at
night, so I can't say. This evening there were some samurai warming them-

selves in the courtyard. They may have been the people you're asking about, but they're gone now, as you can see."

The other man spoke quietly. "I'm sorry to have intruded while you were asleep. Ah, aren't there two men over there under that tree? They may be the ones who sent word they'd wait for me here."

"Well, it wouldn't do any harm to ask them and see."

"I'll do that. I can find my way by myself now, so please feel free to go back to your room."

"Are you joining your friends for a snow-viewing party?"

"Something like that," said the other man with a slight laugh.

Putting out the candle, the priest said, "I suppose I needn't say this, but if you build a fire near the temple, as those men did earlier, please be careful and extinguish it when you leave."

"I'll do so without fail."

"Very well, then. Please excuse me."

The priest went back through the gate and shut it. The man on the veranda stood still for a time, looking intently toward Denshichirō.

"Hyōsuke, who is it?"

"I can't tell, but he came from the kitchen."

"He doesn't seem to belong to the temple."

The two of them walked about twenty paces nearer the building. The shadowy man moved to a point near the middle of the veranda, stopped and tied up his sleeve. The men in the courtyard unconsciously approached close enough to see this, but then their feet refused to go any nearer.

After an interval of two or three breaths, Denshichirō shouted, "Musashi!" He was well aware that the man standing several feet above him was in a very advantageous position. Not only was he perfectly safe from the rear, but anyone trying to attack him from either the right or the left would first have to climb up to his level. He was thus free to devote his entire attention to the enemy before him.

Behind Denshichirō was open ground, snow and wind. He felt sure Musashi would not bring anyone with him, but he could not afford to ignore the wide space to his rear. He made a motion as though brushing something off his kimono and said urgently to Hyōsuke, "Get away from here!" Hyōsuke moved to the back edge of the courtyard.

"Are you ready?" Musashi's question was calm but trenchant, falling like so much ice water on his opponent's feverish excitement.

Denshichirō now got his first good look at Musashi. "So this is the bastard!" he thought. His hatred was total; he resented the maiming of his brother, he was vexed at being compared with Musashi by the common people, and he had an ingrained contempt for what he regarded as a country upstart posing as a samurai.

"Who are you to ask, 'Are you ready'? It's well past the hour of nine!"

"Did I say I'd be here exactly at nine?"

"Don't make excuses! I've been waiting a long time. As you can see, I'm fully prepared. Now come down from there!" He did not underestimate his opponent to the extent of daring to attack from his present position.

"In a minute," answered Musashi with a slight laugh.

There was a difference between Musashi's idea of preparation and his opponent's. Denshichirō, though physically prepared, had only begun to pull himself together spiritually, whereas Musashi had started fighting long before he presented himself to his enemy. For him, the battle was now entering its second and central phase. At the Gion Shrine, he had seen the footprints in the snow, and at that moment his fighting instinct had been aroused. Knowing that the shadow of the man following him was no longer there, he had boldly entered the front gate of the Rengeōin and made a quick approach to the kitchen. Having wakened the priest, he struck up a conversation, subtly questioning the man as to what had been going on earlier in the evening. Disregarding the fact that he was a little late, he had had some tea and warmed himself. Then when he made his appearance, it was abrupt and from the relative safety of the veranda. He had seized the initiative.

His second opportunity came in the form of Denshichirō's attempt to draw him out. One way of fighting would be to accept this; the other would be to ignore it and create an opening of his own. Caution was in order; in a case like this, victory is like the moon reflected on a lake. If one jumps for it impulsively, one can drown.

Denshichirō's exasperation knew no bounds. "Not only are you late," he shouted; "you aren't ready. And I haven't got a decent footing here."

Musashi, still perfectly calm, replied, "I'm coming. Just a minute."

Denshichirō did not have to be told that anger could result in defeat, but in the face of this deliberate effort to annoy him, he was unable to control his emotions. The lessons he had learned in strategy deserted him.

"Come down!" he screamed. "Here, into the courtyard! Let's stop the tricks and fight bravely! I am Yoshioka Denshichirō! And I have nothing but spit for makeshift tactics or cowardly attacks. If you're frightened before the match begins, you're not qualified to confront me. Get down from there!"

Musashi grinned. "Yoshioka Denshichirō, eh? What do I have to fear from you? I cut you in half in the spring of last year, so if I do it again tonight, it's only repeating what I've done before."

"What are you talking about? Where? When?"

"At Koyagyū in Yamato."

"Yamato?"

"In the bath at the Wataya Inn, to be exact."

"Were you there?"

"I was. We were both naked, of course, but with my eyes I calculated whether I could cut you down or not. And with my eyes I slew you then and there, in rather splendid fashion, if I may say so myself. You probably didn't notice, because there were no scars left on your body, but you were defeated, no question about it. Other people may be willing to listen to you brag about your ability as a swordsman, but from me you'll get nothing but a laugh."

"I was curious as to how you'd talk, and now I know—like an idiot. But your babbling intrigues me. Come down from there, and I'll open your conceited eyes for you!"

"What's your weapon? Sword? Wooden sword?"

"Why ask when you don't have a wooden sword? You came expecting to use a sword, didn't you?"

"I did, but I thought if you wanted to use a wooden sword, I'd take yours away from you and fight with that."

"I don't have one, you fool! Enough big talk. Fight!"

"Ready?"

"No!"

Denshichirō's heels made a black slanted line about nine feet long as he opened a space for Musashi to land in. Musashi quickly sidestepped twenty or thirty feet along the veranda before jumping down. Then when they had moved, swords sheathed, eyeing each other warily, about two hundred feet from the temple, Denshichirō lost his head. Abruptly he drew and swung. His sword was long, just the right size for his body. Making only a slight whistling sound, it went through the air with amazing lightness, straight to the spot where Musashi had been standing.

Musashi was faster than the sword. Even quicker was the springing of the glittering blade from his own scabbard. It looked as though they were too close together for both of them to emerge unscathed, but after a moment of dancing reflected light from the swords, they backed off.

Several tense minutes passed. The two combatants were silent and motionless, swords stationary in the air, point aimed at point but separated by a distance of about nine feet. The snow piled on Denshichirō's brow dropped to his eyelashes. To shake it off, he contorted his face until his forehead muscles looked like countless moving bumps. His bulging eyeballs glowed like the windows of a smelting furnace, and the exhalations of his deep, steady breathing were as hot and gusty as those from a bellows.

Desperation had entered his thinking, for he realized how bad his position was. "Why am I holding the sword at eye level when I always hold it above my head for the attack?" he asked himself. He was not thinking in the ordinary sense of the word. His very blood, palpitating audibly through his veins, told him that. But his whole body, down to his toenails, was concentrated in an effort to present an image of ferocity to the enemy.

The knowledge that the eye-level stance was not one in which he excelled nagged him. Any number of times he itched to raise his elbows and get the sword above his head, but it was too risky. Musashi was on the alert for just such an opening, that tiny fraction of a second when his vision would be blocked by his arms.

Musashi held his sword at eye level too, with his elbows relaxed, flexible and capable of movement in any direction. Denshichirō's arms, held in an unaccustomed stance, were tight and rigid, and his sword unsteady. Musashi's was absolutely still; snow began to pile up on its thin upper edge.

As he watched hawklike for the slightest slip on his opponent's part, Musashi counted the number of times he breathed. He not only wanted to win, he *had* to win. He was acutely conscious of once again standing on the borderline—on one side life, on the other, death. He saw Denshichirō as a gigantic boulder, an overpowering presence. The name of the god of war, Hachiman, passed through his mind.

"His technique is better than mine," Musashi thought candidly. He had had the same feeling of inferiority at Koyagyū Castle, when he had been encircled by the four leading swordsmen of the Yagyū School. It was always this way when he faced swordsmen of the orthodox schools, for his own technique was without form or reason, nothing more, really, than a do-or-die method. Staring at Denshichirō, he saw that the style Yoshioka Kempō had created and spent his life developing had both simplicity and complexity, was well ordered and systematic, and was not to be overcome by brute strength or spirit alone.

Musashi was cautious about making any unnecessary movements. His primitive tactics refused to come into play. To an extent that surprised him, his arms rebelled against being extended. The best he could do was to maintain a conservative, defensive stance and wait. His eyes grew red searching for an opening, and he prayed to Hachiman for victory.

With swelling excitement, his heart began to race. If he had been an ordinary man, he might have been sucked into a whirlpool of confusion and succumbed. Yet he remained steady, shaking off his sense of inadequacy as if it were no more than snow on his sleeve. His ability to control this new exhilaration was the result of having already survived several brushes with death. His spirit was fully awake now, as though a veil had been removed from before his eyes.

Dead silence. Snow accumulated on Musashi's hair, on Denshichirō's shoulders.

Musashi no longer saw a great boulder before him. He himself no longer existed as a separate person. The will to win had been forgotten. He saw the whiteness of the snow falling between himself and the other man, and the spirit of the snow was as light as his own. The space now seemed an extension of his own body. He had become the universe, or the universe had become him. He was there, yet not there.

Denshichirō's feet inched forward. At the tip of his sword, his willpower quivered toward the start of a movement.

Two lives expired with two strokes of a single sword. First, Musashi attacked to his rear, and Ōtaguro Hyōsuke's head, or a piece of it, sailed past Musashi like a great crimson cherry, as the body staggered lifelessly toward Denshichirō. The second horrendous scream—Denshichirō's cry of attack—was cut short midway, the broken-off sound thinning out into the space around them. Musashi leapt so high that he appeared to have sprung from the level of his opponent's chest. Denshichirō's big frame reeled backward and dropped in a spray of white snow.

Body pitifully bent, face buried in the snow, the dying man cried, "Wait! Wait!"

Musashi was no longer there.

"Hear that?"

"It's Denshichirō!"

"He's been hurt!"

The black forms of Genzaemon and the Yoshioka disciples rushed across the courtyard like a wave.

"Look! Hyōsuke's been killed!"

"Denshichirō!"

"Denshichirō!"

Yet they knew there was no use calling, no use thinking about medical treatment. Hyōsuke's head had been sliced sideways from the right ear to the middle of the mouth, Denshichirō's from the top down to the right cheekbone. All in a matter of seconds.

"That's . . . that's why I warned you," sputtered Genzaemon. "That's why I told you not to take him lightly. Oh, Denshichirō, Denshichirō!" The old man hugged his nephew's body, trying in vain to console it.

Genzaemon clung to Denshichirō's corpse, but it angered him to see the others milling about in the blood-reddened snow. "What happened to Musashi?" he thundered.

Some had already started searching; they saw no sign of Musashi.

"He's not here," came the answer, timid and obtuse.

"He's around somewhere," barked Genzaemon. "He hasn't got wings. If I don't get in a blow of revenge, I can never again hold my head up as a member of the Yoshioka family. Find him!"

One man gasped and pointed. The others fell back a pace and stared in the direction indicated.

"It's Musashi."

"Musashi?"

As the idea sank in, silence filled the air, not the tranquillity of a place of worship, but an ominous, diabolical silence as though ears, eyes and brains had ceased to function.

Whatever the man had seen, it was not Musashi, for Musashi was standing under the eaves of the nearest building. His eyes fixed on the Yoshioka men and his back pressed to the wall, he edged his way along until he reached the southwest corner of the Sanjūsangendō. He climbed onto the veranda and crept, slowly and quietly, to the center.

"Will they attack?" he asked himself. When they made no move in his direction, he continued stealthily on to the north side of the building and, with a bound, disappeared into the darkness.

The Elegant People

"No impudent nobleman's going to get the best of me! If he thinks he can put me off by sending a blank piece of paper, I'll just have to have a word with him. And I'll bring Yoshino back, if only for the sake of my pride."

It is said that one need not be young to enjoy playing games. When Haiya Shōyū was in his cups, there was no holding him back.

"Take me to their room!" he ordered Sumigiku. He put a hand on her shoulder to prop himself into a standing position.

In vain, Kōetsu admonished him to be calm.

"No! I'm going to get Yoshino.... Standard bearers, ho! Your general is moving into action! Those with heart, follow!"

A peculiar characteristic of the inebriated is that though they appear to be in constant danger of falling, or suffering some worse mishap, if left alone they usually escape harm. Still, if no one took measures to protect them, it would be a cold world indeed. With all his years of experience, Shōyū was able to draw a fine line between amusing himself and entertaining others. When they thought him tipsy enough to be easy to handle, he would contrive to be as difficult as possible, staggering and tottering until someone came to his rescue, at which point there would be a meeting of spirits on the boundary where drunkenness evokes sympathetic response.

"You'll fall," cried Sumigiku, rushing to prevent this.

"Don't be silly. My legs may wobble a bit, but my spirit's firm!" He sounded peevish.

"Try walking alone."

She let go, and he immediately slumped to the floor.

"I guess I'm a little tired. Someone'll have to carry me."

On the way to Lord Kangan's parlor, appearing to know nothing, yet perfectly conscious of everything, he staggered, swayed, turned into jelly, and otherwise kept his companions on edge from one end of the long hallway to the other.

At stake was whether or not "insolent, half-baked noblemen," as he called them, were going to monopolize Yoshino Dayū. The great merchants, who were nothing more than rich commoners, did not stand in awe of the Emperor's courtiers. True, they were appallingly rank-conscious, but this counted for little because they had no money. By spreading around enough gold to keep them happy, participating in their elegant pastimes, making a show of deference to their status and allowing them to maintain their pride, it was possible to manipulate them like puppets. No one knew this better than Shōyū.

Light danced gaily on the shoji of the anteroom to Lord Karasumaru's parlor as Shōyū fumbled to open it.

Abruptly the door was opened from inside. "Why, Shōyū, it's you!" exclaimed Takuan Sōhō.

Shōyū's eyes widened, first in astonishment, then in delight. "Good priest," he sputtered, "what a pleasant surprise! Have you been here all along?"

"And you, good sir, have you been here all along?" mimicked Takuan. He put his arm around Shōyū's neck, and the two drunkenly embraced like a pair of lovers, cheek against stubbled cheek.

"Are you well, you old scoundrel?"

"Yes, you old fraud. And you?"

"I've been hoping to see you."

"And I you."

Before the maudlin greeting had run its course, the two were patting each other on the head and licking each other on the nose.

Lord Karasumaru turned his attention from the anteroom to Lord Konoe Nobutada, who sat opposite him, and said with a sardonic grin, "Ha! Just as I expected. The noisy one has arrived."

Karasumaru Mitsuhiro was still young, perhaps thirty. Even without his impeccable dress, he would have had an aristocratic air about him, for he was handsome and light-complexioned, with thick eyebrows, crimson lips and intelligent eyes. While he gave the impressison of being a very gentle man, beneath the polished surface lurked a strong temper, fed by pent-up resentment against the military class. Often he had been heard to say, "Why, in this age when only the warriors are deemed to be full-fledged human beings, did I have to be born a nobleman?"

In his opinion, the warrior class should concern itself with military matters and nothing else, and any young courtier with intelligence who did not bridle at the current state of affairs was a fool. The warriors' assumption of absolute control reversed the ancient principle that government should be carried on by the Imperial Court with the aid of the military. The samurai no longer made any attempt to maintain harmony with the nobility; they ran everything, treating members of the court as though they were mere ornaments. Not only were the ornate headdresses the courtiers were allowed to wear meaningless, but the decisions they were allowed to make could have been made by dolls.

Lord Karasumaru considered it a grave mistake on the part of the gods to have made a man like himself a nobleman. And, though a servant of the Emperor, he saw only two paths open to him: to live in constant misery or to spend his time carousing. The sensible choice was to rest his head on the knees of a beautiful woman, admire the pale light of the moon, view the cherry blossoms in season and die with a cup of sake in his hand.

Having advanced from Imperial Minister of Finance to Assistant Vice Minister of the Right and then to Imperial Councillor, he was a high official in the

459

Emperor's impotent bureaucracy, but he spent a great deal of time in the licensed quarter, where the atmosphere was conducive to forgetting the insults he had to endure when attending to more practical affairs. Among his habitual companions were several other disgruntled young noblemen, all of them poor in comparison with the military rulers but somehow able to raise the money for their nightly excursions to the Ōgiya—the only place, they averred, where they were free to feel human.

Tonight he had as his guest a man of another sort, the taciturn, well-mannered Konoe Nobutada, who was about ten years older. Nobutada, too, had an aristocratic demeanor and a grave look in his eyes. His face was full and his eyebrows thick, and though his darkish complexion was marred by shallow pockmarks, the pleasant modesty of the man made the blemishes seem somehow appropriate. In places like the Ōgiya, an outsider would never have guessed he was one of Kyoto's highest-ranking noblemen, the head of the family from which imperial regents were chosen.

Smiling affably by Yoshino's side, he turned to her and said, "That's Mr. Funabashi's voice, isn't it?"

She bit her lips, already redder than plum blossoms, and her eyes betrayed embarrassment at the awkwardness of the situation. "What shall I do if he comes in?" she fretted.

Lord Karasumaru commanded, "Don't stand up!" and grasped the hem of her kimono.

"Takuan, what are you doing out there? It's cold with the door open. If you're going out, go, and if you're coming back, come back, but close the door."

Swallowing the bait, Takuan said to Shōyū, "Come on in," and pulled the old man into the room.

Shōyū walked over and sat down directly in front of the two noblemen.

"My, what a pleasant surprise!" exclaimed Mitsuhiro with feigned sincerity.

Shōyū, on his bony knees, edged closer. Sticking his hand out toward Nobutada, he said, "Give me some sake." Having received the cup, he bowed with exaggerated ceremony.

"Good to see you, Old Man Funabashi," said Nobutada with a grin. "You always seem to be in high spirits."

Shōyū drained the cup and returned it. "I didn't dream that Lord Kangan's companion was your excellency." Still pretending to be drunker than he actually was, he shook his thin, wrinkled neck like an ancient manservant and said in mock fear, "Forgive me, esteemed excellency!" Then, in a different tone, "Why should I be so polite? Ha, ha! Isn't that so, Takuan?" He put his arm around Takuan's neck, pulled the priest toward him and pointed a finger at the two courtiers. "Takuan," he said, "the people in this world I feel sorriest for are the noblemen. They bear resounding titles like Councillor or Regent, but there's nothing to go with the honors. Even the merchants are better off, don't you think?"

"I do indeed," replied Takuan, contriving to disengage his neck.

"Say," said Shōyū, placing a cup directly beneath the priest's nose. "I haven't received a drink from you yet."

Takuan poured him some sake. The old man drank.

"You're a wily man, Takuan. In the world we live in, priests like you are cunning, merchants smart, warriors strong and noblemen stupid. Ha, ha! Isn't that so?"

"It is, it is," agreed Takuan.

"The noblemen can't do as they please because of their rank, but they're shut out of politics and the government. So all that's left for them to do is compose poetry or become experts at calligraphy. Isn't that the truth?" He laughed again.

Though Mitsuhiro and Nobutada were as fond of fun as Shōyū, the bluntness of the ridicule was embarrassing. They responded with stony silence.

Taking advantage of their discomfort, Shōyū pressed on. "Yoshino, what do you think? Do you fancy noblemen, or do you prefer merchants?"

"Hee-hee," tittered Yoshino. "Why, Mr. Funabashi, what a strange question!"

"I'm not joking. I'm trying to peer deep into a woman's heart. Now I can see what's there. You really prefer merchants, don't you? I think I'd better take you away from here. Come with me to my parlor." He took her by the hand and stood up, a shrewd look on his face.

Mitsuhiro, startled, spilled his sake. "A joke can be carried too far," he said, yanking Yoshino's hand from Shōyū's and pulling her closer to his side.

Caught between the two, Yoshino laughed and tried to make the best of it. Taking Mitsuhiro's hand in her right hand and Shōyū's in her left, she put on a worried look and said, "What am I ever going to do with you two?"

For the two men, though they neither disliked each other nor were serious rivals in love, the rules of the game dictated that they do everything in their power to make Yoshino Dayū's position more embarrassing.

"Come now, my good lady," said Shōyū. "You must decide for yourself. You must choose the man whose room you will grace, the one to whom you will give your heart."

Takuan jumped into the fray. "A very interesting problem, isn't it? Tell us, Yoshino, which one is your choice?"

The only person not participating was Nobutada. After a time, his sense of propriety moved him to say, "Come now, you're guests; don't be rude. The way you're acting, I daresay Yoshino would be delighted to be rid of you both. Why don't we all enjoy ourselves and stop bothering her? Kōetsu must be all by himself. One of you girls go and invite him to come here."

Shōyū waved his hand. "No reason to fetch him. I'll just go back to my room with Yoshino."

"You will not," said Mitsuhiro, hugging her tighter.

"The insolence of the aristocracy!" exclaimed Shōyū. Eyes sparkling, he offered Mitsuhiro a cup, saying, "Let's decide who gets her by holding a drinking contest—right before her eyes."

"Why, of course; that sounds like good fun." Mitsuhiro took a large cup and placed it on a small table between them. "Are you sure you're young enough to stand it?" he asked playfully.

"Don't have to be young to compete with a skinny nobleman!"

"How are we going to decide whose turn it is? It's no fun just swilling. We   461 should play a game. Whoever loses has to drink a cupful. What game shall we play?"

"We could try staring each other down."

"That would involve looking at your ugly merchant's face. That's not play; it's torture."

"Don't be insulting! Um, how about the stone-scissors-paper game?"

"Fine!"

"Takuan, you be referee."

"Anything to oblige."

With earnest faces, they began. After each round, the loser complained with appropriate bitterness and everyone laughed.

Yoshino Dayū slipped quietly out of the room, gracefully trailing the bottom of her long kimono behind her, and walked at a stately pace down the hallway. Not long after she left, Konoe Nobutada said, "I must go too," and took his leave unnoticed.

Yawning shamelessly, Takuan lay down and without so much as a by-your-leave, rested his head on Sumigiku's knee. Though it felt good to doze here, he also felt a pang of guilt. "I should go home," he thought. "They're probably lonely without me." He was thinking of Jōtarō and Otsū, who were together again at Lord Karasumaru's house. Takuan had taken Otsū there after her ordeal at Kiyomizudera.

Takuan and Lord Karasumaru were old friends with many interests in common—poetry, Zen, drinking, even politics. Toward the end of the previous year, Takuan had received a letter inviting him to spend the New Year's holidays in Kyoto. "You seem to be cooped up in a little temple in the country," Mitsuhiro wrote. "Don't you long for the capital, for some good Nada sake, for the company of beautiful women, for the sight of the little plovers by the Kamo River? If you like to sleep, I suppose it's all right to practice your Zen in the country, but if you want something more lively, then come here and be among people. Should you feel any nostalgia for the capital, by all means pay us a visit."

Shortly after his arrival, early in the new year, Takuan was quite surprised to see Jōtarō playing in the courtyard. He learned in detail from Mitsuhiro what the boy was doing there and then heard from Jōtarō that there had been no news of Otsū since Osugi got her clutches into the girl on New Year's Day.

The morning after her return, Otsū had come down with a fever, and she was still in bed, with Jōtarō nursing her, sitting by her pillow all day, cooling her forehead with wet towels and measuring out her medicine at the proper times of the day.

As much as Takuan wanted to leave, he could hardly do so before his host did, and Mitsuhiro seemed to be more and more absorbed in the drinking contest.

Both combatants being veterans, the contest seemed destined to end in a draw, which it did. They went on drinking anyway, facing each other knee to knee and chatting animatedly. Takuan could not tell whether the subject was

government by the military class, the inherent worth of the nobility, or the role of merchants in the development of foreign trade, but evidently it was something very serious. He lifted his head from Sumigiku's knee and, eyes still closed, leaned against a post of the alcove, every once in a while grinning at a snatch of conversation.

Presently Mitsuhiro asked, in an injured tone, "Where's Nobutada? Did he go home?"

"Never mind him. Where's Yoshino?" Shōyū asked, suddenly looking quite sober.

Mitsuhiro told Rin'ya to go and bring Yoshino back.

As she passed the room where Shōyū and Kōetsu had started out the evening, Rin'ya looked in. Musashi was sitting there alone, his face next to the white light of the lamp.

"Why, I didn't know you were back," said Rin'ya.

"I haven't been here long."

"Did you come in by the back way?"

"Yes."

"Where did you go?"

"Umm, outside the district."

"I bet you had an engagement with a beautiful girl. Shame on you! Shame on you! I'm going to tell my mistress," she said saucily.

Musashi laughed. "No one's here," he said. "What happened to them?"

"They're in another room, playing games with Lord Kangan and a priest."

"Kōetsu too?"

"No. I don't know where he is."

"Maybe he went home. If he did, I should go too."

"You mustn't say that. When you come to this house, you can't leave without Yoshino Dayū's consent. If you just sneak away, people will laugh at you. And I'll be scolded."

Not being attuned to the humor of the courtesans, he received this news with serious countenance, thinking: "So that's the way they do things here."

"You absolutely mustn't go without taking your leave properly. Just wait here until I come back."

A few minutes later Takuan appeared. "And where did you come from?" he asked, with a tap on the rōnin's shoulder.

"What?" gasped Musashi. Slipping off his cushion, he put both hands on the floor and bowed deeply. "What a long time since I saw you last!"

Lifting Musashi's hands from the floor, Takuan said, "This place is for fun and relaxation. No need for formal greetings.... I was told Kōetsu was here too, but I don't see him."

"Where do you suppose he could have gone?"

"Let's find him. I do have a number of things to talk to you about privately, but they can wait until a more suitable occasion."

Takuan opened the door into the next room. There, with his feet in the covered *kotatsu* and a quilt over him, lay Kōetsu, sequestered from the rest of the room by a small gold screen. He was sleeping peacefully. Takuan could not bring himself to wake him.

Kōetsu opened his eyes of his own accord. He stared for a moment at the priest's face, then at Musashi's, not quite knowing what to make of it.

After they had explained the situation to him, Kōetsu said, "If it's only you and Mitsuhiro in the other room, I have no objection to going there."

They found that Mitsuhiro and Shōyū, having finally talked themselves out, had sunk into melancholy. They had reached the stage where the sake begins to taste bitter, the lips feel parched, and a sip of water evokes thoughts of home. Tonight the aftereffects were worse; Yoshino had deserted them.

"Why don't we all go home?" someone suggested.

"We might as well," agreed the others.

Though not really eager to leave, they were afraid that if they stayed longer, nothing would be left of the evening's mellowness. But as they stood up to go, Rin'ya came running into the room with two younger girls. Clasping Lord Kangan's hands, Rin'ya said, "We're sorry to have kept you waiting. Please don't leave. Yoshino Dayū is ready to receive you in her private quarters. I know it's late, but it's light outside—because of the snow—and in this cold you should at least warm yourselves properly before getting in your palanquins. Come with us."

None of them felt like playing anymore. The spirit, once gone, was difficult to summon back.

Noting their hesitation, one of the attendants said, "Yoshino said she was sure you all thought her rude for leaving, but she saw nothing else to do. If she gave in to Lord Kangan, Mr. Funabashi would be hurt, and if she went away with Mr. Funabashi, Lord Kangan would be lonesome. She doesn't want either of you to feel slighted, so she's inviting you for a nightcap. Please understand how she feels, and stay a little longer."

Sensing that a refusal would be ungallant—and more than a little curious to see the leading courtesan in her own living quarters—they allowed themselves to be persuaded. Guided by the girls, they found five pairs of rustic straw sandals at the top of the garden steps. Donning these, they made their way soundlessly across the soft snow. Musashi had no idea of what was going on, but the others assumed they were to take part in a tea ceremony, for Yoshino was known to be an ardent devotee of the tea cult. Since there was something to be said for a bowl of tea after all the drinking they had done, no one was upset until they were led on past the teahouse and into an overgrown field.

"Where are you taking us?" asked Lord Kangan in an accusing tone. "This is a mulberry patch!"

The girls giggled, and Rin'ya hastened to explain. "Oh, no! This is our peony garden. In the early summer, we put out stools, and everybody comes here to drink and admire the blossoms."

"Mulberry patch or peony garden, it's not very pleasant being out here in the snow. Is Yoshino trying to make us catch cold?"

"I'm sorry. It's only a little farther."

In the corner of the field was a little cottage with a thatched roof, which,

from the looks of it, was probably a farmhouse that had been here since before the area was built up. There was a grove of trees behind it, and the yard was cut off from the well-cared-for garden of the Ōgiya.

"This way," urged the girls, leading them into a dirt-floored room whose walls and posts were black with soot.

Rin'ya announced their arrival, and from the interior Yoshino Dayū answered, "Welcome! Please come in."

The fire in the hearth cast a soft, red glow on the shoji paper. The atmosphere seemed utterly remote from the city. As the men looked around the kitchen and noticed straw rain capes hanging on one wall, they wondered what sort of entertainment Yoshino had planned for them. The shoji slid open, and one by one they stepped up into the hearth room.

Yoshino's kimono was a pale solid yellow, her obi of black satin. She wore the minimum of makeup and had rearranged her hair into a simple housewifely style. Her guests stared at her with admiration.

"How unusual!"

"How charming!"

In her unpretentious outfit, set off by the blackened walls, Yoshino was a hundred times more beautiful than she was in the elaborately embroidered Momoyama-style costumes she wore at other times. The gaudy kimonos the men were accustomed to, the iridescent lipstick and the setting of gold screens and silver candlesticks were necessary for a woman in her business. But Yoshino had no need for props to enhance her beauty.

"Hmm," said Shōyū, "this is something quite special." Not one to offer praise lightly, the old man, with his acerbic tongue, seemed temporarily tamed.

Without spreading cushions, Yoshino invited them to sit down by the hearth.

"I live here, as you can see, and I can't offer you much, but at least there's a fire. I hope you agree, a fire is the most excellent feast one can present on a cold snowy night, whether one's guest is prince or pauper. There's a good supply of kindling, so even if we talk the night out, I won't have to use the potted plants for fuel. Please, make yourselves comfortable."

The nobleman, the merchant, the artist and the priest sat cross-legged by the hearth, with their hands over the fire. Kōetsu reflected on the cold walk from the Ōgiya and the invitation to the cheery fire. It actually was like a feast, the essence, really, of entertaining.

"You come up by the fire too," said Yoshino. She smiled invitingly at Musashi and moved slightly to make a place for him.

Musashi was struck by the exalted company he was in. Next to Toyotomi Hideyoshi and Tokugawa Ieyasu, she was probably the most famous person in Japan. Of course, there was Okuni of Kabuki fame and Hideyoshi's mistress Yodogimi, but Yoshino was regarded as having more class than the former and more wit, beauty and kindness than the latter. The men who associated with Yoshino were known as the "buyers," while she herself was called "the Tayū." Any courtesan of the first class was known as Tayū, but to say "the Tayū" meant Yoshino and no one else. Musashi had heard that she had seven attendants to bathe her and two to cut her nails.

This evening, for the first time in his life, Musashi found himself in the company of painted and polished ladies, and he reacted by becoming stiffly formal. This was partly because he could not help wondering what men found so extraordinary about Yoshino.

"Please, relax," she said. "Come sit here."

After the fourth or fifth invitation, he capitulated. Taking his place beside her, he imitated the others, extending his hands awkwardly over the fire.

Yoshino glanced at his sleeve and saw a spot of red. While the others were immersed in conversation, she quietly took a piece of paper from her sleeve and wiped it off.

"Uh, thank you," said Musashi. If he had remained silent, no one would have noticed, but the moment he spoke, every eye went to the crimson stain on the paper in Yoshino's hand.

Opening his eyes wide, Mitsuhiro said, "That's blood, isn't it?"

Yoshino smiled. "No, of course not. It's a petal from a red peony."

The Broken Lute

The four or five sticks of wood in the hearth burned softly, giving off a pleasant aroma and lighting up the small room as if it were noon. The gentle smoke did not cause the eyes to smart; it looked like white peony petals billowing in the breeze, flecked now and again with sparks of purple-gold and crimson. Whenever the fire showed signs of dying down, Yoshino added foot-long strips of kindling from the scuttle.

The men were too captivated by the beauty of the flames to ask about the firewood, but eventually Mitsuhiro said, "What sort of wood are you using? It's not pine."

"No," replied Yoshino. "It's peony wood."

They were mildly surprised, for the peony, with its thin, bushy branches, hardly seemed suitable for firewood. Yoshino took a stick that had been only slightly charred and handed it to Mitsuhiro.

She told them that the peony stumps in the garden had been planted more than a hundred years earlier. At the beginning of winter, the gardeners pruned them very closely, cutting off the worm-eaten upper parts. The trimmings were saved for firewood. Though the quantity was small, it was sufficient for Yoshino.

The peony, remarked Yoshino, was the king of flowers. Perhaps it was only

466

natural that its withered branches had a quality not to be found in ordinary wood, just as certain men had a worth not displayed by others. "How many men are there," she mused, "whose merit endures after the blossoms have faded and died?" With a melancholy smile, she answered her own question. "We human beings blossom only during our youth, then become dry, odorless skeletons even before we die."

A little later, Yoshino said, "I'm sorry I have nothing more to offer you than the sake and the fire, but at least there's wood, enough to last until sunrise."

"You shouldn't apologize. This is a feast fit for a prince." Shōyū, though accustomed to luxury, was sincere in his praise.

"There is one thing I'd like you to do for me," said Yoshino. "Will you please write a memento of this evening?"

While she was rubbing the ink stone, the girls spread a woolen rug in the next room and laid out several pieces of Chinese writing paper. Being made of bamboo and paper mulberry, it was tough and absorbent, just right for calligraphic inscriptions.

Mitsuhiro, assuming the role of host, turned to Takuan and said, "Good priest, since the lady requests it, will you write something appropriate? Or perhaps we should first ask Kōetsu?"

Kōetsu moved silently on his knees. He took up the brush, thought for a moment and drew a peony blossom.

Above this, Takuan wrote:

> Why should I cling to
> A life so far removed from
> Beauty and passion?
> Peonies though lovely
> Shed their bright petals and die.

Takuan's poem was in the Japanese style. Mitsuhiro chose to write in the Chinese manner, setting down lines from a poem by Tsai Wen:

> When I am busy, the mountain looks at me.
> When I am at leisure, I look at the mountain.
> Though it seems the same, it is not the same,
> For busy-ness is inferior to leisure.

Under Takuan's poem, Yoshino wrote:

> Even as they bloom
> A breath of sadness hangs
> Over the flowers.
> Do they think of the future,
> When their petals will be gone?

Shōyū and Musashi looked on in silence, the latter greatly relieved when no one insisted that he write something too.

They returned to the hearth and chatted for a while, until Shōyū, noticing a *biwa*, a kind of lute, next to the alcove in the inner room, asked Yoshino to play for them. The others seconded his suggestion.

Yoshino, displaying no trace of timidity, took up the instrument and sat down in the middle of the dimly lit inner room. Her manner was not that of a virtuoso proud of her skills, nor did she attempt to be unduly modest. The men cleared their minds of random thoughts, the better to give their attention to her rendition of a section from *Tales of the Heike*. Soft, gentle tones gave way to a turbulent passage, then to staccato chords. The fire dwindled and the room darkened. Entranced by the music, no one stirred until a tiny explosion of sparks brought them back to earth.

As the music ended, Yoshino said, with a slight smile, "I'm afraid I didn't play very well." She replaced the lute and returned to the fire. When the men stood up to take their leave, Musashi, happy to be saved from further boredom, was the first to reach the door. Yoshino said farewell to the others one by one but said nothing to him. As he turned to go, she quietly took hold of his sleeve.

"Musashi, spend the night here. Somehow . . . I don't want to let you go home."

The face of an importuned virgin couldn't have been redder. He tried to cover up by pretending not to hear, but it was plain to the others that he was too flustered to speak.

Turning to Shōyū, Yoshino said, "It'll be all right if I keep him here, won't it?"

Musashi removed Yoshino's hand from his sleeve. "No, I'm going with Kōetsu."

As he made hastily for the door, Kōetsu stopped him. "Don't be like that, Musashi. Why don't you stay here tonight? You can come back to my house tomorrow. After all, the lady has been kind enough to show her concern for you." He pointedly went to join the other two men.

Musashi's cautiousness warned him that they were deliberately trying to trick him into staying for what laughs they might derive from it later. Still, the seriousness he saw written on the faces of Yoshino and Kōetsu argued against its being only a joke.

Shōyū and Mitsuhiro, vastly amused by his discomfort, persisted in teasing him, one saying, "You're the most fortunate man in the country," and the other volunteering to stay in his stead.

The joking stopped with the arrival of a man Yoshino had sent out to take a look around the quarter. He was breathing heavily, and his teeth were chattering with fright.

"The other gentlemen can leave," he said, "but Musashi shouldn't think of it. Only the main gate is open now, and on either side of it, around the Amigasa teahouse and along the street, are swarms of samurai, heavily armed, roaming around in small bands. They're from the Yoshioka School. The tradesmen are afraid something awful might happen, so they all closed early. Beyond the quarter, toward the riding ground, I was told there are at least a hundred men."

The men were impressed, not only by the report but by the fact that

Yoshino had taken such a precaution. Only Kōetsu had any inkling that some incident might have occurred.

Yoshino had guessed something was afoot when she saw the spot of blood on Musashi's sleeve.

"Musashi," she said, "now that you've heard what it's like out there, you may be more determined than ever to leave, just to prove you're not afraid. But please don't do anything rash. If your enemies think you're a coward, you can always prove to them tomorrow that you aren't. Tonight, you came here to relax, and it's the mark of a real man to enjoy himself to his heart's content. The Yoshiokas want to kill you. Certainly it's no disgrace to avoid that. In fact, many people would condemn you for poor judgment if you insisted on walking into their trap.

"There's the matter of your personal honor, of course, but please stop to consider the trouble a battle would cause to the people in the quarter. Your friends' lives would be endangered too. Under the circumstances, the only wise thing for you to do is stay here."

Without waiting for his reply, she turned to the other men and said, "I think it's all right for the rest of you to go, if you're careful along the way."

A couple of hours later, the clock struck four. The distant sound of music and singing had died out. Musashi was seated on the threshold of the hearth room, a lonely prisoner waiting for the dawn. Yoshino remained by the fire.

"Aren't you cold there?" she asked. "Do come over here, where it's warm."

"Never mind me. Go to bed. When the sun comes up, I'll let myself out."

The same words had been exchanged quite a number of times already, but to no effect.

Despite Musashi's lack of polish, Yoshino was attracted to him. Though it had been said that a woman who thought of men as men, rather than as sources of income, had no business seeking employment in the gay quarters, this was merely a cliché repeated by the patrons of brothels—men who knew only common prostitutes and had no contact with the great courtesans. Women of Yoshino's breeding and training were quite capable of infatuation. She was only a year or two older than Musashi, but how different they were in their experience of love. Watching him sit so stiffly, restraining his emotions, avoiding her face as though a look at her might blind him, she felt once again like a sheltered maiden experiencing the first pangs of love.

The attendants, ignorant of the psychological tension, had spread luxurious pallets, fit for the son and daughter of a daimyō, in the adjoining room. Little golden bells gleamed softly on the corners of the satin pillows.

The sound of snow sliding off the roof was not unlike that of a man jumping down from the fence into the garden. Each time he heard it, Musashi bristled like a hedgehog. His nerves seemed to reach to the very tips of his hair.

Yoshino felt a shiver run through her. It was the coldest part of the night, the hour just before dawn, yet her discomfort was not due to the cold. It came from the sight of this fierce man and clashed in an intricate rhythm with her natural attraction to him.

The kettle over the fire began to whistle, a cheerful sound that calmed her. Quietly she poured some tea.

"It'll be daylight soon. Have a cup of tea and warm yourself by the fire."

"Thank you," said Musashi, without moving.

"It's ready now," she said again, and gave up trying. The last thing she wanted to do was make a nuisance of herself. Still, she was slightly offended at seeing the tea go to waste. After it was too cold to drink, she poured it into a small pail kept for that purpose. What is the use, she thought, of offering tea to a rustic like him, for whom the niceties of tea-drinking have no meaning?

Though his back was to her, she could see that his whole body was as taut as steel armor. Her eyes grew sympathetic.

"Musashi."

"What?"

"Who are you on guard against?"

"No one. I'm just trying to keep myself from relaxing too much."

"Because of your enemies?"

"Of course."

"In your present state, if you were suddenly attacked in force, you'd be killed immediately. I'm sure of it, and it makes me sad."

He did not answer.

"A woman like myself knows nothing of the Art of War, but from watching you tonight, I have the terrible feeling I've seen a man who was about to be cut down. Somehow there's the shadow of death about you. Is that really safe for a warrior who may at any minute have to face dozens of swords? Can such a man expect to win?"

The question sounded sympathetic, but it unsettled him. He whirled around, moved to the hearth and sat facing her.

"Are you saying I'm immature?"

"Did I make you angry?"

"Nothing a woman ever said would make me angry. But I am interested in knowing why you think I act like a man who's about to be killed."

He was painfully conscious of the web of swords and strategies and maledictions being woven around him by the Yoshioka partisans. He had anticipated an attempt at revenge, and in the courtyard of the Rengeōin, had considered going away to hide. But this would have been rude to Kōetsu and would have meant breaking his promise to Rin'ya. Far more decisive, however, was his desire not to be accused of running away because he was afraid.

After returning to the Ōgiya, he thought he had displayed an admirable degree of composure. Now Yoshino was laughing at his immaturity. This would not have upset him had she been bantering in the fashion of courtesans, but she seemed perfectly serious.

He professed not to be angry, but his eyes were as keen as sword tips. He stared straight into her white face. "Explain what you said." When she did not answer immediately, he said, "Or maybe you were just joking."

Her dimples, which had deserted her for a moment, reappeared. "How can you say that?" She laughed, shaking her head. "Do you think I'd joke about something so serious to a warrior?"

"Well, what did you mean? Tell me!"

"All right. Since you seem so eager to know, I'll try to explain. Were you listening when I played the lute?"

"What does that have to do with it?"

"Perhaps it was foolish of me to ask. Tense as you are, your ears could hardly have taken in the fine, subtle tones of the music."

"No, that's not true. I was listening."

"Did it occur to you to wonder how all those complicated combinations of soft and loud tones, weak and strong phrases, could be produced from only four strings?"

"I was listening to the story. What else was there to hear?"

"Many people do that, but I'd like to draw a comparison between the lute and a human being. Rather than go into the technique of playing, let me recite a poem by Po Chü-i in which he describes the sounds of the lute. I feel sure you know it."

She wrinkled her brow slightly as she intoned the poem in a low voice, her style somewhere between singing and speaking.

> The large strings hummed like rain,
> The small strings whispered like a secret,
> Hummed, whispered—and then were intermingled
> Like a pouring of large and small pearls into a plate of jade.
> We heard an oriole, liquid, hidden among flowers.
> We heard a brook bitterly sob along a bank of sand. . . .
> By the checking of its cold touch, the very string seemed broken
> As though it could not pass; and the notes, dying away
> Into a depth of sorrow and concealment of lament,
> Told even more in silence than they had told in sound. . . .
> A silver vase abruptly broke with a gush of water,
> And out leapt armored horses and weapons that clashed and smote—
> And before she laid her pick down, she ended with one stroke,
> And all four strings made one sound, as of rending silk.

"And so, you see, one simple lute can produce an infinite variety of tonalities. Since the days when I was an apprentice, this puzzled me. Finally, I broke a lute apart to see what was inside. Then I attempted to make one myself. After trying a number of things, I finally understood that the secret of the instrument is in its heart."

Breaking off, she went and got the lute from the next room. Once reseated, she held the instrument by the neck and stood it up in front of him.

"If you examine the heart inside, you can see why the tonal variations are possible." Taking a fine, keen knife in her lithe hand, she brought it down quickly and sharply on the pear-shaped back of the lute. Three or four deft strokes and the work was done, so quickly and decisively that Musashi half expected to see blood spurt from the instrument. He even felt a slight twinge of pain, as though the blade had nicked his own flesh. Placing the knife behind her, Yoshino held the lute up so he could see its structure.

Looking first at her face, then at the broken lute, he wondered whether she actually possessed the element of violence seemingly displayed in her handling of the weapon. The smarting pain from the screech of the cuts lingered.

"As you can see," she said, "the inside of the lute is almost completely hollow. All the variations come from this single crosspiece near the middle. This one piece of wood is the instrument's bones, its vital organs, its heart. If it were absolutely straight and rigid, the sound would be monotonous, but in fact it has been shaved into a curved shape. This alone would not create the lute's infinite variety. That comes from leaving the crosspiece a certain amount of leeway to vibrate at either end. To put it another way, the tonal richness comes from there being a certain freedom of movement a certain relaxation, at the ends of the core.

"It's the same with people. In life, we must have flexibility. Our spirits must be able to move freely. To be too stiff and rigid is to be brittle and lacking in responsiveness."

His eyes did not move from the lute, nor did his lips open.

"This much," she continued, "should be obvious to anybody, but isn't it characteristic of people to become rigid? With one stroke of the pick, I can make the four strings of the lute sound like a lance, like a sword, like the rending of a cloud, because of the fine balance between firmness and flexibility in the wooden core. Tonight, when I first saw you, I could detect no trace of flexibility—only stiff, unyielding rigidity. If the crosspiece were as taut and unbending as you are, one stroke of the pick would break a string, perhaps even the sounding board itself. It may have been presumptuous of me to say what I did, but I was worried about you. I wasn't joking or making fun of you. Do you understand that?"

A cock crowed in the distance. Sunlight, reflected by the snow, came through the slits in the rain shutters. Musashi sat and stared at the maimed body of the lute and the chips of wood on the floor. The crow of the cock escaped him. He did not notice the sunlight.

"Oh," said Yoshino, "it's daylight." She seemed sorry that the night had passed. She reached out her hand for more firewood before realizing there was none.

The sounds of morning—doors rattling open, the twitter of birds—infiltrated the room, but Yoshino made no move to open the rain shutters. Though the fire was cold, the blood coursed warmly in her veins.

The young girls who waited on her knew better than to open the door to her little house until they were summoned.

A Sickness of the Heart

Within two days, the snow had melted, and warm spring breezes were encouraging a myriad of fresh buds to swell to their fullest. The sun was strong and even cotton garments were uncomfortable.

A young Zen monk, mud spattered up the back of his kimono as high as the waist, stood before the entrance of Lord Karasumaru's residence. Getting no answer to his repeated calls for admission, he walked around to the servants' quarters and stood on tiptoe to peek through a window.

"What is it, priest?" asked Jōtarō.

The monk whirled around and his mouth fell open. He couldn't imagine what such a ragamuffin could be doing in the courtyard of Karasumaru Mitsuhiro's house. "If you're begging, you'll have to go around to the kitchen," said Jōtarō.

"I'm not here for alms," replied the monk. He took a letter box from his kimono. "I'm from the Nansōji in Izumi Province. This letter is for Takuan Sōhō, and I understand he's staying here. Are you one of the delivery boys?"

"Of course not. I'm a guest, like Takuan."

"Is that so? In that case, would you please tell Takuan I'm here?"

"Wait here. I'll call him."

As he jumped into the entrance hall, Jōtarō tripped over the foot of a standing screen and the tangerines cradled in his kimono tumbled to the floor. Retrieving them rapidly, he sped off toward the inner rooms.

He came back a few minutes later to inform the monk that Takuan was out. "They say he's over at the Daitokuji."

"Do you know when he'll be back?"

"They said 'pretty soon.'"

"Is there someplace I could wait without inconveniencing anyone?"

Jōtarō bounded into the courtyard and led the monk straight to the barn. "You can wait here," he said. "You won't be in anybody's way."

The barn was littered with straw, cart wheels, cow manure and a variety of other things, but before the priest could say anything, Jōtarō was running across the garden toward a small house at the west end of the compound.

"Otsū!" he cried. "I've brought you some tangerines."

Lord Karasumaru's doctor had told Otsū there was nothing to worry about. She believed him, though she herself could tell how thin she was just by putting her hand to her face. Her fever persisted and her appetite had not returned, but this morning she had murmured to Jōtarō that she would like a tangerine.

Leaving his post at her bedside, he went first to the kitchen, only to learn there were no tangerines in the house. Finding none at the greengrocers or other food shops, he went to the open marketplace in Kyōgoku. A wide variety of goods was available there—silk thread, cotton goods, lamp oil, furs and so on—but no tangerines. After he left the market, his hopes were raised a couple of times by the sight of orange-colored fruit beyond the walls of private gardens—bitter oranges and quinces, as it turned out.

Having covered nearly half of the city, he met with success only by turning thief. The offering in front of the Shinto shrine consisted of small piles of potatoes, carrots and tangerines. He stuffed the fruit into his kimono and glanced around to make sure no one was watching. Fearful that the outraged god would materialize at any minute, he prayed all the way back to the Karasumaru house: "Please don't punish me. I'm not going to eat them myself."

He lined the tangerines up in a row, offered Otsū one and peeled it for her. She turned away, refusing to touch it.

"What's the matter?"

When he leaned forward to look at her face, she buried her head deeper in the pillow. "Nothing's the matter," she sobbed.

"You've started crying again, haven't you?" said Jōtarō, clicking his tongue.

"I'm sorry."

"Don't apologize; just eat one of these."

"Later."

"Well, eat the one I've peeled, at least. Please."

"Jō, I appreciate your thoughtfulness, but I can't eat anything just now."

"It's because you cry so much. Why are you so sad?"

"I'm crying because I'm happy—that you're so good to me."

"I don't like to see you like this. It makes me want to cry too."

"I'll stop, I promise. Now will you forgive me?"

"Only if you eat the tangerine. If you don't eat something, you'll die."

"Later. You eat this one."

"Oh, I can't." He swallowed hard, imagining the wrathful eyes of the god. "Oh, all right, we'll each have one."

She turned over and began removing the stringy white fibers from the pulp with her delicate fingers.

"Where's Takuan?" she asked absently.

"They told me he's at the Daitokuji."

"Is it true he saw Musashi the night before last?"

"You heard about that?"

"Yes. I wonder if he told Musashi I'm here."

"I suppose so."

"Takuan said he'd invite Musashi to come here one of these days. Did he say anything to you about that?"

"No."

"I wonder if he's forgotten."

"Shall I ask him?"

"Please do," she replied, smiling for the first time. "But don't ask him in front of me."

"Why not?"

"Takuan's awful. He keeps saying I'm suffering from 'Musashi sickness.'"

"If Musashi came, you'd be up and about in no time, wouldn't you?"

"Even you have to say things like that!" But she seemed genuinely happy.

"Is Jōtarō there?" called one of Mitsuhiro's samurai.

"Here I am."

"Takuan wants to see you. Come with me."

"Go and see what he wants," urged Otsū. "And don't forget what we were talking about. Ask him, won't you?" A tinge of pink crept into her pale cheeks as she pulled the cover halfway up over her face.

Takuan was in the sitting room talking with Lord Mitsuhiro. Jōtarō flung open the sliding door and said, "Did you want me?"

"Yes. Come in here."

Mitsuhiro watched the boy with an indulgent smile, ignoring his lack of manners.

As Jōtarō sat down, he said to Takuan, "A priest just like you came here a while ago. He said he was from the Nansōji. Shall I go get him?"

"Never mind. I know about that already. He was complaining about what a wicked little boy you are."

"Me?"

"Do you think it's proper to put a guest in the barn and leave him there?"

"He said he wanted to wait someplace where he wouldn't be in anyone's way."

Mitsuhiro laughed until his knees shook. Recovering his composure almost immediately, he asked Takuan, "Are you going directly to Tajima, without returning to Izumi?"

The priest nodded. "The letter was rather disturbing, so I think I should. I don't have to make any preparations. I'll leave today."

"You're going away?" asked Jōtarō.

"Yes; I must return home as quickly as possible."

"Why?"

"I've just heard that my mother's condition is very serious."

"*You* have a mother?" The boy couldn't believe his ears.

"Of course."

"When are you coming back?"

"That depends on my mother's health."

"What . . . what am I going to do without you here?" grumbled Jōtarō. "Does that mean we won't see you anymore?"

"Of course not. We'll meet again soon. I've arranged for you two to stay on here, and I'm counting on you to look after Otsū. Try to make her stop brooding and get well. What she needs more than medicine is greater fortitude."

"I'm not strong enough to give her that. She won't get well until she sees Musashi."

475

"She's a difficult patient, I'll grant you. I don't envy you a traveling companion like her."

"Takuan, where was it you met Musashi?"

"Well . . . " Takuan looked at Lord Mitsuhiro and laughed sheepishly.

"When's he coming here? You said you'd bring him, and that's the only thing Otsū has thought about since."

"Musashi?" Mitsuhiro said casually. "Isn't he the rōnin who was with us at the Ōgiya?"

Takuan said to Jōtarō, "I haven't forgotten what I told Otsū. On my way back from the Daitokuji, I stopped in at Kōetsu's house to see if Musashi was there. Kōetsu hasn't seen him and thinks he must still be at the Ōgiya. He said his mother was so worried she wrote a letter to Yoshino Dayū asking her to send Musashi home right away."

"Oh?" exclaimed Lord Mitsuhiro, raising his eyebrows half in surprise and half in envy. "So he's still with Yoshino?"

"It would appear that Musashi's only a man, like any other. Even if they seem to be different when they're young, they always turn out to be the same."

"Yoshino's a strange woman. What does she see in that uncouth swordsman?"

"I don't pretend to understand her. Nor do I understand Otsū. What it comes down to is, I don't understand women in general. As far as I'm concerned, they all seem a little sick. As for Musashi, I suppose it's about time he reached the springtime of life. His real training starts now, and let's hope that he gets it through his head that women are more dangerous than swords. Still, other people can't solve his problems for him, and I see nothing for me to do but leave him alone."

A little uncomfortable about having said so much in front of Jōtarō, he hastened to offer his thanks and bid farewell to his host, requesting him a second time to allow Otsū and Jōtarō to stay a little longer.

The old saying that journeys should be commenced in the morning meant nothing to Takuan. He was ready to depart, and depart he did, though the sun was well into the west and twilight already descending.

Jōtarō ran along beside him, pulling at his sleeve. "Please, please, come back and say a word to Otsū. She's been crying again, and I can't do anything to cheer her up."

"Did you two talk about Musashi?"

"She told me to ask you when he's coming. If he doesn't come, I'm afraid she might die."

"You don't have to worry about her dying. Just leave her alone."

"Takuan, who's Yoshino Dayū?"

"Why do you want to know that?"

"You said Musashi was with her. Didn't you?"

"Um. I have no intention of going back and trying to heal Otsū's illness, but I want you to tell her something for me."

"What is it?"

476   "Tell her to eat properly."

"I've told her that a hundred times."

"You have? Well, that's the best thing she could possibly be told. But if she won't listen, you may as well give her the whole truth."

"What's that?"

"Musashi is infatuated with a courtesan named Yoshino, and he hasn't left the brothel for two nights and two days. She's a fool to go on loving a man like that!"

"That's not true!" protested Jōtarō. "He's my *sensei!* He's a samurai! He's not like that. If I told Otsū that, she might commit suicide. You're the one who's a fool, Takuan. A great big old fool!"

"Ha, ha, ha!"

"You have no business saying bad things about Musashi or saying Otsū is foolish."

"You're a good boy, Jōtarō," said the priest, patting him on the head.

Jōtarō ducked from under his hand. "I've had enough of you, Takuan. I'll never ask for your help again. I'll find Musashi myself. I'll bring him back to Otsū!"

"Do you know where the place is?"

"No, but I'll find it."

"Be sassy if you like, but it's not going to be easy for you to find Yoshino's place. Shall I tell you how?"

"Don't bother."

"Jōtarō, I'm no enemy of Otsū's, nor do I have anything against Musashi. Far from it! I've been praying for years that both of them would be able to make good lives for themselves."

"Then why are you always saying such mean things?"

"Does it seem that way to you? Maybe you're right. But just at the moment, both of them are sick people. If Musashi is left alone, his illness will go away, but Otsū needs help. Being a priest, I've tried to help her. We're supposed to be able to cure sicknesses of the heart, just as doctors cure illnesses of the body. Unfortunately, I haven't been able to do anything for her, so I'm giving up. If she can't realize that her love is one-sided, advising her to eat properly is the best I can do."

"Don't worry about it. Otsū is not going to ask a big phony like you for help."

"If you don't believe me, go to the Ōgiya in Yanagimachi and see for yourself what Musashi is up to. Then go back and tell Otsū what you saw. She'll be heartbroken for a while, but it just might open her eyes."

Jōtarō put his fingers in his ears. "Shut up, you acorn-headed old fraud!"

"You're the one who came chasing after me, or have you forgotten?"

As Takuan walked off and left him, Jōtarō stood in the middle of the street, repeating a very disrespectful chant with which street urchins were wont to taunt beggar priests. But the moment Takuan was out of sight, he choked up, burst into tears and wept hopelessly. When he finally pulled himself together, he wiped his eyes and, like a lost puppy suddenly remembering the way home, began his search for the Ōgiya.

The first person he saw was a woman. Head covered by a veil, she ap- 477 peared to be an ordinary housewife. Jōtarō ran up to her and asked, "How do you get to Yanagimachi?"

"That's the licensed quarter, isn't it?"

"What's a licensed quarter?"

"Goodness!"

"Well, tell me, what do they do there?"

"Why, you—!" She glared at him indignantly for a moment before hastening on.

Undaunted, Jōtarō went steadfastly on his way, asking one person after another where the Ōgiya was.

The Scent of Aloeswood

The lights in the windows of the houses of pleasure burned brightly, but it was still too early for many customers to be prowling the three main alleys of the district.

At the Ōgiya, one of the younger servants happened to glance toward the entrance. There was something strange about the eyes peeping through a slit in the curtain, below which a pair of feet in dirty straw sandals and the tip of a wooden sword were visible. The young man gave a little jump of surprise, but before he could open his mouth, Jōtarō had entered and stated his business.

"Miyamoto Musashi is in this house, isn't he? He's my teacher. Will you please tell him Jōtarō is here. You might ask him to come out."

The servant's look of surprise was replaced by a stern frown. "Who are you, you little beggar?" he growled. "There's nobody here by that name. What do you mean, sticking your dirty face in here just as business is about to begin? Out!" Clutching Jōtarō's collar, he gave him a hard shove.

Angry as a puffed-up blowfish, Jōtarō screamed, "Stop it! I came here to see my teacher."

"I don't care why you're here, you little pack rat. This Musashi's already caused a lot of trouble. He's not here."

"If he's not here, why can't you just say so? Take your hands off me!"

"You look sneaky. How do I know you're not a spy from the Yoshioka School?"

"That's got nothing to do with me. When did Musashi leave? Where did he go?"

478   "First you order me around; now you ask for information. You should learn

to keep a civil tongue in your head. How should I know where he is?"

"If you don't know, all right, but let go of my collar!"

"I'll let go, all right—like this!" He pinched Jōtarō's ear hard, swung him around and pitched him toward the gateway.

"Ouch!" screamed Jōtarō. Crouching, he drew his wooden sword and struck the servant in the mouth, breaking his front teeth.

"O-w-w!" The young man put one hand to his bloody mouth, and with the other, he knocked Jōtarō down.

"Help! Murder!" yelled Jōtarō.

He mustered his strength, as he had when he killed the dog at Koyagyū, and brought his sword down on the servant's skull. Blood spurted from the young man's nose, and with a sound no louder than an earthworm's sigh, he collapsed under a willow tree.

A prostitute on display behind a grille window on the opposite side of the street raised her head and shouted to the next window over: "Look! Can you see! That boy with the wooden sword just killed a man from the Ōgiya! He's getting away!"

In no time the street was filled with people running hither and thither, and the air echoed with bloodthirsty shouts.

"Which way did he go?"

"What did he look like?"

As suddenly as it had started, the hubbub died down, and by the time merrymakers began arriving, the incident had ceased to be a topic of conversation. Fights were common occurrences, and the denizens of the quarter settled or covered up the bloodier ones in short order, so as to avoid investigations by the police.

While the main alleys were lit up like daylight, there were byways and vacant lots where all was completely dark. Jōtarō found a hiding place, then changed it for another. Innocently enough, he thought he'd be able to get away, but in fact the whole quarter was surrounded by a ten-foot wall, made of charred logs sharpened to a point at the top. Having come up against this, he felt his way along it but could not find even a large crack, let alone a gate. As he turned back to avoid one of the alleys, he caught sight of a young girl. As their eyes met, she called softly and beckoned with a delicate white hand.

"Are you calling me?" he asked guardedly. He saw no evil intent in her thickly powdered face, so he went a little nearer. "What is it?"

"Aren't you the boy who came to the Ōgiya and asked for Miyamoto Musashi?" she asked gently.

"Yes."

"Your name's Jōtarō, isn't it?"

"Uh-huh."

"Come with me. I'll take you to Musashi."

"Where is he?" Jōtarō asked, growing suspicious again.

The girl stopped and explained that Yoshino Dayū, seriously concerned about the incident with the servant, had sent her to look for Jōtarō and take him to Musashi's place of hiding.

With a look of gratitude, he asked, "Are you Yoshino Dayū's servant?"

"Yes. And you can relax now. If she stands up for you, no one in the quarter can touch you."

"Is my teacher really there?"

"If he wasn't, why would I be showing you the way?"

"What's he doing in a place like this?"

"If you open the door of that little farmhouse right over there, you can see for yourself. Now I have to go back to my work." She disappeared quietly beyond the shrubbery in the neighboring garden.

The farmhouse seemed too modest to be the end of his search, but he could not leave without making sure. To reach a side window, he rolled a rock from the garden over to the wall, perched on it and pressed his nose against the bamboo grille.

"He is there!" he said, keeping his voice down and concealing his presence with some difficulty. He yearned to reach out and touch his master. It had been so long!

Musashi was asleep by the hearth, his head resting on his arm. His attire was like nothing Jōtarō had ever seen him in before—a silk kimono with large figured designs, of the sort favored by the stylish young men about town. Spread out on the floor was a red woolen cloth; on it lay a painter's brush, an ink box and several pieces of paper. On one sheet Musashi had practiced sketching an eggplant, on another, the head of a chicken.

Jōtarō was shaken. "How can he waste his time drawing pictures?" he thought angrily. "Doesn't he know Otsū is sick?"

A heavy embroidered cloak half covered Musashi's shoulders. It was unquestionably a woman's garment, and the gawdy kimono—disgusting. Jōtarō sensed an aura of voluptuousness, in which there lurked evil. As had happened on New Year's Day, a wave of bitter indignation at the corrupt ways of adults swept over him. "There's something wrong with him," he thought. "He's not himself."

As vexation slowly turned to mischievousness, he decided he knew what to do. "I'll give him a good scare," he thought. Very quietly, he started to lower himself from the rock.

"Jōtarō," Musashi called. "Who brought you here?"

The boy caught himself and looked through the window again. Musashi was still lying down, but his eyes were half open and he was grinning.

Jōtarō sped around to the front of the house, ran in through the front door, and threw his arms around Musashi's shoulders.

"Sensei!" he burbled happily.

"So you've come, have you?" Lying on his back, Musashi stretched out his arms and hugged the boy's dirty head to his chest. "How did you know I was here? Did Takuan tell you? It's been a long time, hasn't it?" Without loosening his embrace, Musashi sat up. Jōtarō, nestled against the warm chest he had almost forgotten, wiggled his head like a Pekingese.

Jōtarō moved his head to Musashi's knee and lay still. "Otsū's sick in bed. You can't imagine how badly she wants to see you. She keeps saying she'd be all right if only you'd come. Just once, that's all she wants."

"Poor Otsū."

"She saw you on the bridge on New Year's Day, talking with that crazy girl. Otsū got angry and shut herself up in her shell, like a snail. I tried to drag her to the bridge, but she wouldn't come."

"I don't blame her. I was upset with Akemi that day too."

"You have to go see her. She's at Lord Karasumaru's house. Just go in and say, 'Look, Otsū, I'm here.' If you do that, she'll get well right away."

Jōtarō, eager to get his point across, said much more, but this was the substance of it. Musashi grunted occasionally, once or twice saying, "Is that so?" but for reasons the boy could not fathom, he did not come out and say in so many words that he would do what he was asked, despite the boy's begging and pleading. Jōtarō, for all his devotion to his teacher, began to feel a dislike for him, an itch to have a real fight with his teacher.

His belligerence boiled higher, to the point where it was held in check only by his respect. He lapsed into silence, his disapproval written large on his face, his eyes sullen and his lips twisted as though he had just drunk a cup of vinegar.

Musashi took up his drawing manual and brush and began adding strokes to one of his sketches. Jōtarō, glaring distastefully at the eggplant drawing, thought: "What makes him think he can paint pictures? He's awful!"

Presently Musashi lost interest and began washing out his brush. Jōtarō was about to make one more appeal, when they heard wooden sandals on the stepping-stones outside.

"Your wash is dry," said a girlish voice. The attendant who had been Jōtarō's guide entered with a kimono and a cloak, both neatly folded. Placing them in front of Musashi, she invited him to inspect them.

"Thank you," he said. "They look as good as new."

"Bloodstains don't come out easily. You have to scrub and scrub."

"They seem to be gone now, thank you. . . . Where's Yoshino?"

"Oh, she's terribly busy, going from one guest to another. They don't give her a moment's rest."

"It's been very pleasant here, but if I stay longer, I'll be a burden on people. I plan to slip away as soon as the sun comes up. Would you tell Yoshino that and convey my deepest thanks to her?"

Jōtarō relaxed. Musashi must certainly be planning to see Otsū. This was the way his master should be, a good upright man. He broke into a happy smile.

As soon as the girl left, Musashi laid the clothes before Jōtarō and said, "You came at just the right time. These must be returned to the woman who lent them to me. I want you to take them to the house of Hon'ami Kōetsu—it's in the north part of the city—and bring back my own kimono. Will you be a good boy and do this for me?"

"Certainly," said Jōtarō with a look of approval. "I'll go now."

He wrapped the garments in a piece of cloth, along with a letter from Musashi to Kōetsu, and swung the parcel onto his back.

The attendant arrived just then with dinner and threw up her hands in horror.

"What are you doing?" she gasped. When Musashi explained, she cried, *481*

"Oh, you can't let him go!" and told him what Jōtarō had done. Fortunately, Jōtarō's aim had not been perfect, so the servant had survived. She assured Musashi that since this was only one fight among many, the matter had ended there, Yoshino having personally warned the owner and the younger people in the establishment to keep quiet. She also pointed out that by unwittingly proclaiming himself to be Miyamoto Musashi's student, Jōtarō had lent credence to the rumor that Musashi was still at the Ōgiya.

"I see," said Musashi simply. He looked inquisitively at Jōtarō, who scratched his head, retreated to a corner and made himself as small as possible.

The girl went on: "I don't need to tell you what would happen if he tried to leave. There are still a lot of Yoshioka men around waiting for you to show your face. It's very difficult for Yoshino and the proprietor, because Kōetsu begged us to take good care of you. The Ōgiya can't possibly let you walk straight into their clutches. Yoshino's resolved to protect you.

"Those samurai are so persistent. They've kept constant watch and sent men around several times accusing us of hiding you. We've gotten rid of them, but they're still not convinced. I don't understand it, really. They act as if they were on a major campaign. Beyond the gate to the quarter, there are three or four ranks of them, and lookouts everywhere, and they're armed to the teeth.

"Yoshino thinks you should stay here another four or five days, or at least until they tire of waiting."

Musashi thanked her for her kindness and concern, but added cryptically, "I'm not without a plan of my own."

He readily agreed to have a servant sent to Kōetsu's house in Jōtarō's stead. The servant returned in less than an hour with a note from Kōetsu: "When we have another chance, let us meet again. Life, though it may seem long, is in truth all too short. I beg you to take the best possible care of yourself. My regards from afar." Though few in number, the words seemed warm and very much in character.

"Your clothing is in this package," said the servant. "Kōetsu's mother asked me particularly to convey her best wishes." He bowed and left.

Musashi looked at the cotton kimono, old, ragged, so often exposed to dew and rain, spotted with sweat stains. It would feel better on his skin than the fine silks lent him by the Ōgiya; surely this was the outfit for a man engaged in the serious study of swordsmanship. Musashi neither needed nor wanted anything better.

He expected it to be smelly after being folded up for a few days, but as he slipped his arms into the sleeves, he found it to be quite fresh. It had been washed; the creases stood out neatly. Thinking Myōshū had washed it herself, he wished he, too, had a mother and thought of the long, solitary life ahead of him, with no relatives except his sister, living in mountains to which he himself could not return. He looked down at the fire for a time.

"Let's go," he said. He tightened his obi and slid his beloved sword between it and his ribs. As he did so, the loneliness fell away as quickly as it had come. This sword, he reflected, would have to be his mother, his father, his brothers and sisters. That was what he had vowed to himself years earlier, and that was the way it would have to be.

Jōtarō was already outside, gazing up at the stars, thinking that no matter how late they arrived at Lord Karasumaru's house, Otsū would be awake.

"My, won't she be surprised," he said to himself. "She'll be so happy she'll probably start crying again."

"Jōtarō," said Musashi, "did you come in through the wooden gate in back?"

"I don't know if it's in back. It's that one over there."

"Go there and wait for me."

"Aren't we going together?"

"Yes, but first I want to say good-bye to Yoshino. I won't be long."

"All right; I'll be by the gate." He felt a twinge of anxiety at having Musashi leave him even for a few moments, but on this particular night, he would have done anything his teacher asked him to do.

The Ōgiya had been a haven, pleasant but only temporary. Musashi reflected that being shut off from the outside world had done him good, for until now his body and mind had been like ice, a thick, frigid mass insensitive to the beauty of the moon, heedless of the flowers, unresponsive to the sun. He had no doubts about the rectitude of the ascetic life he led, but now he could see how his self-denial might make him narrow, small-minded and stubborn. Takuan had told him years ago that his strength was no different from that of a wild beast; Nikkan had warned him about being too strong. After his fight with Denshichirō, body and soul had been too tense and strained. These past two days, he had let himself go and allowed his spirit to expand. He had drunk a little, dozed when he felt like it, read, dabbled at painting, yawned and stretched at will. Taking a rest had been of immense value, and he had decided that it was important, and would continue to be important, for him occasionally to have two or three days of completely carefree leisure.

Standing in the garden watching the lights and shadows in the front parlors, he thought: "I must say just one word of thanks to Yoshino Dayū for all she's done." But he changed his mind. He could easily hear the plinking of shamisen and the raucous singing of the buyers. He saw no way to sneak in to see her. Better to thank her in his heart and hope she would understand. Having bowed toward the front of the house, he made his departure.

Outside, he beckoned to Jōtarō. As the boy ran to him, they heard Rin'ya coming with a note from Yoshino. She pressed it into Musashi's hand and left.

The notepaper was small and beautifully colored. As he unfolded it, the scent of aloeswood came to his nostrils. The message said: "More memorable than the luckless flowers that wither and disintegrate night after night is a glimpse of moonlight through the trees. Though they laugh as I weep into another's cup, I send you this one word of remembrance."

"Who's the note from?" asked Jōtarō.

"Nobody in particular."

"A woman?"

"Does it make any difference?"

"What does it say?"

"You don't need to know that." Musashi folded up the paper.

Jōtarō leaned toward it and said, "It smells good. That's aloeswood."

483

The Gate

Jōtarō thought their next move would be to get out of the quarter without being detected.

"Going this way will take us to the main gate," he said. "That would be dangerous."

"Mm."

"There must be another way out."

"Aren't all the entrances except the main one closed at night?"

"We could climb the wall."

"That would be cowardly. I do have a sense of honor, you know, as well as a reputation to maintain. I'll walk straight out the main entrance, when the time is right."

"You will?" Though uneasy, the boy didn't argue, for he was well aware that according to the rules of the military class, a man without pride was worthless.

"Of course," replied Musashi. "But not you. You're still a child. You can go out some safer way."

"How?"

"Over the wall."

"By myself?"

"By yourself."

"I can't do that."

"Why not?"

"I'd be called a coward."

"Don't be foolish. They're after me, not you."

"But where will we meet?"

"The Yanagi Riding Grounds."

"You're sure you'll come?"

"Absolutely."

"Promise you won't run off again?"

"I won't run away. One of the things I don't intend to teach you is lying. I said I'll meet you, and I will. Now, while nobody's around, let's get you over the wall."

Jōtarō looked about cautiously before making a run for the wall, where he stopped dead, looking wistfully upward. It was more than double his height. Musashi joined him, carrying a sack of charcoal. He dropped the sack and peered through a crack in the wall.

"Can you see anyone out there?" Jōtarō asked.

"No; nothing but rushes. There may be water underneath, so you'll have to be careful when you land."

"I don't care about getting wet, but how am I going to get to the top of this wall?"

Musashi ignored the question. "We have to assume guards have been stationed at strategic points besides the main gate. Take a good look around before you jump, or you may find a sword pointed at you."

"I understand."

"I'll throw this charcoal over the wall as a decoy. If nothing happens, you can go ahead."

He stooped and Jōtarō jumped onto his back. "Stand on my shoulders."

"My sandals are dirty."

"Never mind."

Jōtarō hoisted himself to a standing position.

"Can you reach the top?"

"No."

"If you jumped, could you make it?"

"I don't think so."

"All right; stand on my hands." He stretched his arms straight above his head.

"I've got it!" Jōtarō said in a loud whisper.

Musashi took the sack of charcoal in one hand and lobbed it as high as he could. It thudded into the rushes. Nothing happened.

"There's no water here," Jōtarō reported after he jumped down.

"Take care of yourself."

Musashi kept one eye to the crack until he could no longer hear Jōtarō's footsteps, then walked quickly and lightheartedly to the busiest of the main alleys. None of the many revelers milling about paid any attention to him.

When he went out the main gate, the Yoshioka men uttered a collective gasp, and all eyes focused on him. Besides the guards at the gate, there were samurai squatting around the bonfires where the palanquin bearers passed the time while they waited, and relief guards in the Amigasa teahouse and the drinking shop across the street. Their vigilance had never relaxed. Basket hats had been unceremoniously lifted and faces examined; palanquins had been stopped and their occupants examined.

Several times negotiations had been started with the Ōgiya to search the premises, but these had come to naught. As far as the management was concerned, Musashi was not there. The Yoshiokas could not act on the rumor that Yoshino Dayū was protecting Musashi. She was too highly admired, both within the district and in the city itself, to be assailed without serious repercussions.

Obliged to fight a waiting war, the Yoshiokas had encircled the quarter at a distance. They didn't rule out the possibility that Musashi might try to escape over the wall, but most expected him to leave by the gate, either in disguise or in a closed palanquin. The one contingency they were unprepared for was the one they were faced with now.

No one made a move to block Musashi's path, nor did he pause to acknowledge them. He covered a hundred paces with bold strides before a samurai shouted, "Stop him!"

"After him!"

Eight or nine shouting men filled the street behind Musashi and began stalking him.

"Musashi, wait!" called an angry voice.

"What is it?" he replied immediately, startling all with the force of his voice.

He moved to the side of the road and backed up against the wall of a shanty. The shanty was part of a sawmill, and a couple of the mill hands slept there. One of them opened the door a crack, but after a quick glance slammed the door and bolted it.

Yelping and howling like a pack of stray dogs, the Yoshioka men gradually formed a black crescent around Musashi. He stared intently at them, gauging their strength, assessing their position, anticipating where a move might come from. The thirty men were quickly losing the use of their thirty minds. It was not difficult for Musashi to read the workings of this communal brain.

As he had anticipated, not one came forward alone to challenge him. They babbled and hurled insults, most of which sounded like the barely articulate name-calling of common tramps.

"Bastard!"

"Coward!"

"Amateur!"

They themselves were far from realizing that their bravado was merely vocal and revealed their weakness. Until the horde achieved a degree of cohesion, Musashi had the upper hand. He examined their faces, singled out the ones who might be dangerous, picked out the weak spots in the formation, and prepared himself for battle.

He took his time, and after slowly scrutinizing their faces, declared, "I am Musashi. Who called to me to wait?"

"We did. All of us!"

"I take it that you're from the Yoshioka School."

"That's right."

"What business do you have with me?"

"You know! Are you prepared?"

"Prepared?" Musashi's lips twisted into a sardonic grin. The laugh that issued from his white teeth chilled their excitement. "A real warrior is prepared even in his sleep. Come forward when you wish! When you're picking a meaningless fight, what sense is there in trying to talk like a human being or in observing the etiquette of the sword? But tell me one thing. Is your objective only to see me dead? Or do you want to fight like men?"

No answer.

"Are you here to settle a grudge or challenge me to a return bout?"

Had Musashi, by the slightest false movement of eye or body, given them an opening, their swords would have rushed at him like air into a vacuum, but he maintained perfect poise. No one moved. The entire group stood as still and silent as prayer beads.

Out of the confused silence came a loud shout: "You should know the answer without asking."

Musashi, shooting a glance at the speaker, Miike Jūrōzaemon, judged from the man's appearance that he was a samurai worthy to uphold Yoshioka Kempō's reputation. He alone seemed willing to end the stalemate by striking the first blow. His feet edged forward in a sliding motion.

"You maimed our teacher Seijūrō and killed his brother Denshichirō. How can we hold up our heads if we let you live? Hundreds of us who are loyal to our master have vowed to remove the source of his humiliation and restore the name of the Yoshioka School. It's not a matter of grudges or lawless violence. But we will vindicate our master and console the spirit of his slain brother. I don't envy you your position, but we're going to take your head. On guard!"

"Your challenge is worthy of a samurai," replied Musashi. "If this is your true purpose, I may lose my life to you. But you talk of discharging your duty, you speak of revenge according to the Way of the Samurai. Why, then, do you not challenge me properly, as Seijūrō and Denshichirō did? Why do you attack en masse?"

"You're the one who's been hiding!"

"Nonsense! You're merely proving that a coward attributes cowardice to others. Am I not standing here before you?"

"Because you were afraid of being caught when you tried to escape!"

"Not so! I could have escaped any number of ways."

"And did you think the Yoshioka School would have let you?"

"I assumed that you would greet me one way or another. But wouldn't it disgrace us, not only as individuals but as members of our class, to brawl here? Should we disturb the people here, like a pack of wild beasts or worthless tramps? You speak of your obligation to your master, but wouldn't a fight here heap still greater shame on the Yoshioka name? If that's what you've decided on, then that's what you shall have! If you've resolved to destroy your teacher's work, disband your school and abandon the Way of the Samurai, I have nothing more to say—save this: Musashi will fight so long as his limbs hold together."

"Kill him!" cried the man next to Jūrōzaemon, whipping out his sword.

A distant voice cried, "Watch out! It's Itakura!"

As magistrate of Kyoto, Itakura Katsushige was a powerful man, and though he governed well, he did so with an iron fist. Even children sang songs about him. "Whose chestnut roan is that,/clopping down the street?/Itakura Katsushige's?/Run, everyone, run." Or: "Itakura, Lord of Iga, has/more hands than the Thousand-armed Kannon,/more eyes than the three-eyed Temmoku./His constables are everywhere."

Kyoto was not an easy city to rule. While Edo was well on the way to replacing it as the country's greatest city, the ancient capital was still a center for economic, political and military life. And as the place where culture and education were most highly advanced, it was also the one where criticism of the shogunate was most articulate. The townspeople had, from about the fourteenth century, given up all military ambition and taken to trades and crafts. They were now recognized as a class apart, and on the whole a conservative one.

Also among the populace were many samurai who sat on the fence, waiting to see whether the Tokugawas would be upset by the Toyotomis, as well as a number of upstart military leaders who, while lacking both background and lineage, managed to maintain personal armies of considerable size. There was also a considerable number of rōnin like those in Nara.

Libertines and hedonists were plentiful in all classes, so that the number of drinking shops and brothels was disproportionate to the city's size.

Considerations of expediency rather than political convictions tended to govern the allegiance of a substantial portion of the people. They swam with the current and grasped any opportunity seemingly favorable to themselves.

A story circulated in the city at the time of Itakura's appointment, in 1601, said that before accepting, he asked Ieyasu if he might first consult his wife. When he returned home, he said to her: "Since ancient times, there have been innumerable men in positions of honor who have performed outstanding deeds but have ended up bringing disgrace upon themselves and their families. Most often the source of their failure is to be found in their wives or family connections. Thus I consider it most important to discuss this appointment with you. If you will swear that you won't interfere with my activities as magistrate, I will accept the post."

His wife readily consented, avowing that "wives have no business interfering in matters of this sort." Then the next morning, as Itakura was about to leave for Edo Castle, she noticed that the collar of his underrobe was askew. She had barely touched it when he admonished her: "You've forgotten your oath already." She was made to swear again that she would not meddle. It was generally agreed that Itakura was an effective deputy, strict but fair, and that Ieyasu had been wise to choose him.

At the mention of his name, the samurai shifted their eyes away from Musashi. Itakura's men patrolled the quarter regularly, and everyone gave them a wide berth.

A young man pushed his way into the open space in front of Musashi. "Wait!" he cried in the booming voice that had given the alarm.

Smirking, Sasaki Kojirō said, "I was just getting out of my palanquin when I heard a fight was to break out. I've been afraid for some time this might happen. I'm appalled to see it take place here and now. I'm not a partisan of the Yoshioka School. Still less am I a supporter of Musashi. Nevertheless, as a warrior and visiting swordsman, I believe I am qualified to make an appeal in the name of the warrior's code and the warrior class as a whole." He spoke forcefully and eloquently, but in a patronizing tone and with uncompromising arrogance.

"I want to ask you what you're going to do when the police get here. Wouldn't you be ashamed to be picked up in a common street brawl? If you force the authorities to take notice, it won't be treated like an ordinary fight among townspeople. But that is another question.

"Your timing is bad. So is the place. It's a disgrace to the entire military class for samurai to disturb the public order. As one of your number, I enjoin you to cease this unseemly behavior immediately. If you must cross swords to settle your grievance, then in the name of heaven, abide by the rules of swordsmanship. Choose a time and place!"

"Fair enough!" said Jūrōzaemon. "But if we set a time and place, can you guarantee Musashi will appear?"

"I'd be willing to, but—"

"Can you guarantee it?"

"What can I say? Musashi can speak for himself!"

"Perhaps you have in mind helping him to escape!"

"Don't be an ass! If I were to show partiality to him, the rest of you would challenge me. He's no friend of mine. There's no reason for me to protect him. And if he leaves Kyoto, you only have to put up notices all over town to expose his cowardice."

"That's not enough. We aren't leaving here tonight unless you guarantee to take custody of him until the bout."

Kojirō spun around. He thrust out his chest and walked closer to Musashi, who had been staring fixedly at his back. Their eyes locked, like those of two wild beasts watching each other. There was an inevitability in the way their youthful egos were pitted one against the other, a recognition of the other man's ability and, perhaps, a mote of fear.

"Do you consent, Musashi, to meet as I have proposed?"

"I accept."

"Good."

"However, I take exception to your involvement."

"You're not willing to put yourself in my custody?"

"I resent the implication. In my bouts with Seijūrō and Denshichirō, I have done absolutely nothing cowardly. Why should their followers think I'd flee in the face of a challenge from them?"

"Well spoken, Musashi. I won't forget that. Now, my guarantee aside, would you name the time and place?

"I agree to any time and place they choose."

"That, too, is a gallant answer. Where will you be between now and the time of the fight?"

"I don't have an address."

"If your opponents don't know where you are, how can they send a written challenge?"

"Decide the time and place now. I'll be there."

Kojirō nodded. After consulting with Jūrōzaemon and a few of the others, he came back to Musashi and said, "They want the time to be five o'clock in the morning the day after tomorrow."

"I accept."

"The place is to be the spreading pine at the foot of Ichijōji Hill, on the road   *489* to Mount Hiei. The nominal representative of the House of Yoshioka will be Genjirō, the eldest son of Yoshioka Genzaemon, uncle of Seijurō and Denshichirō. Genjirō being the new head of the House of Yoshioka, the bout will be conducted in his name. But he is still a child, so it is stipulated that a number of the Yoshioka disciples will accompany him as his seconds. I tell you this to preclude any misunderstanding."

After promises had been formally exchanged, Kojirō knocked on the door of the shanty. The door was gingerly opened and the mill hands peeped out.

"There must be some wood you don't need around here," Kojirō said gruffly. "I want to put up a sign. Find me a suitable board and nail it to a post about six feet long."

While the board was being planed, Kojirō sent a man for brush and ink. Materials assembled, he wrote the time, place and other details in an expert hand. As before, the notice was being made public, for this was a better guarantee than a private exchange of oaths. To dishonor the pledge would be to bring on public ridicule.

Musashi watched the Yoshioka men erect the signboard at the most conspicuous corner in the neighborhood. He turned away nonchalantly and walked rapidly to the Yanagi Riding Grounds.

All alone in the dark, Jōtarō was fidgety. Eyes and ears were alert, but he saw only the occasional light of a palanquin and heard only fleeting echoes of men singing songs on their way home. Dreading the thought that Musashi might have been injured or even killed, he eventually lost patience and started off at a run toward Yanagimachi.

Before he had gone a hundred yards, Musashi's voice came through the darkness. "Hey! What's this?"

"Oh, there you are!" the boy exclaimed with relief. "It took you so long, I decided to go have a look."

"That wasn't very smart. We might have missed each other."

"Were there lots of Yoshioka men outside the gate?"

"Um, quite a few."

"Didn't they try to capture you?" Jōtarō looked quizzically up at Musashi's face. "Nothing at all happened?"

"That's right."

"Where are you going? Lord Karasumaru's house is this way. I bet you're eager to see Otsū, aren't you?"

"I want to see her very badly."

"At this time of night, she'll be terribly surprised."

An awkward silence ensued.

"Jōtarō, do you remember that little inn where we first met? What was the name of the village?"

"Lord Karasumaru's house is much nicer than that old inn."

"I'm sure there's no comparison."

"Everything's closed up for the night, but if we go around to the servants' gate, they'll let us in. And when they find out I've brought you, Lord Karasumaru himself may come to greet you. Oh, I meant to ask you, what's wrong with that crazy monk Takuan? He was so mean it made me sick. He told me the best thing to do with you was leave you alone. And he didn't want to tell me where you were, though he knew perfectly well all along."

Musashi made no comment. Jōtarō prattled on as they walked.

"There it is," said Jōtarō, pointing at the back gate. Musashi stopped but said nothing. "See that light above the fence? That's the north wing, where Otsū's staying. She must be waiting up for me."

As he made a quick move toward the gate, Musashi gripped his wrist tightly and said, "Not just yet. I'm not going into the house. I want you to give Otsū a message for me."

"Not going in? Isn't that why you're here?"

"No. I only wanted to see that you arrived safely."

"You must come in! You can't leave now!" He tugged frantically at Musashi's sleeve.

"Keep your voice down," said Musashi, "and listen."

"I won't listen! I won't! You promised to come with me."

"And I did come, didn't I?"

"I didn't invite you to look at the gate. I asked you to visit Otsū."

"Calm down. . . . For all I know, I may be dead in a very short time."

"That's nothing new. You're always saying a samurai must be prepared to die at any time."

"That's true, and I think it's a good lesson for me to hear you repeat my words. But this time isn't like the others. I already know I don't have one chance in ten of surviving. That's why I don't think I should see Otsū."

"That doesn't make sense."

"You wouldn't understand now if I explained. When you grow older, though, you will."

"Are you telling the truth? Do you really think you're going to die?"

"I do. But you can't tell Otsū that, not while she's sick. Tell her to be strong, to choose a path that will lead to her future happiness. That's the message I want you to give her. You mustn't mention anything about my being killed."

"I will tell her! I'll tell her everything! How can I lie to Otsū? Oh, please, please come with me."

Musashi pushed him away. "You're not listening."

Jōtarō couldn't hold back the tears. "But . . . but I feel so sorry for her. If I tell her you refused to see her, she'll get worse. I know she will."

"That's why you have to give her my message. Tell her it won't do either of us any good to see each other as long as I'm still training to be a warrior. The way I've chosen is one of discipline. It requires me to overcome my sentiments, lead a stoic life, immerse myself in hardship. If I don't, the light I seek will escape me. Think, Jōtarō. You yourself are going to have to follow the same path, or you'll never become a self-respecting warrior."

The boy was quiet, except for his weeping. Musashi put his arm around him and hugged him.

"The Way of the Samurai—one never knows when it will end. When I'm gone, you must find yourself a good teacher. I can't see Otsū now, because I know that in the long run she'll be happier if we don't meet. And when she finds happiness, she'll understand how I feel now. That light—are you sure it's coming from her room? She must be lonely. You must go and get some sleep."

Jōtarō was beginning to understand Musashi's dilemma, but there was a trace of sullenness in his attitude as he stood with his back to his teacher. He realized he could press Musashi no further.

Lifting his tearful face, he grasped at the last faint ray of hope. "When your studies are finished, will you see Otsū and make up with her? You will, won't you? When you think you've studied long enough."

"Yes, when that day comes."

"When will that be?"

"It's difficult to say."

"Two years, maybe?"

Musashi did not answer.

"Three years?"

"There's no end to the path of discipline."

"Aren't you ever going to see Otsū again, for the rest of your life?"

"If the talents I was born with are the right ones, I may someday achieve my goal. If not, I may go through life being as stupid as I am now. But now I'm faced with the possibility of dying soon. How can a man with that prospect make vows for the future to a woman as young as Otsū?"

He had said more than he'd intended to. Jōtarō looked bewildered, but then said triumphantly, "You don't have to promise Otsū anything. All I'm asking is that you see her."

"It's not as simple as that. Otsū's a young woman. I'm a young man. I dislike admitting this to you, but if I met her, I'm afraid her tears would defeat me. I wouldn't be able to stick to my decision."

Musashi was no longer the impetuous youth who had spurned Otsū at Hanada Bridge. He was less self-centered and reckless, more patient and much more gentle. Yoshino's charm might have reawakened the fires of passion, had he not rejected love in much the same way that fire repels water. Still, when the woman was Otsū, he lacked confidence in his ability to practice self-control. He knew that he must not think of her without considering the effect he might have on her life.

Jōtarō heard Musashi's voice close to his ear. "Do you understand now?"

The boy wiped the tears from his eyes, but when he took his hand away from his face and looked around, he saw nothing but thick black mist.

"Sensei!" he cried.

Even as he ran to the corner of the long earthen wall, he knew his cries would never bring Musashi back. He pressed his face to the wall; the tears came afresh. He felt utterly defeated, again by adult reasoning. He wept until his throat tightened and no sound came out, but his shoulders went on shaking with convulsive sobs.

492   Noticing a woman outside the servants' gate, he thought it must be one of

the kitchen girls returning from a late errand and wondered if she had heard him crying.

The shadowy figure raised her veil and walked slowly toward him.

"Jōtarō? Jōtarō, is that you?"

"Otsū! What are you doing out here? You're sick."

"I was worried about you. Why did you leave without saying anything to anyone? Where have you been all this time? The lamps were lit and the gate closed and still you didn't return. I can't tell you how worried I was."

"You're crazy. What if your fever goes up again? Go back to bed, right now!"

"Why were you crying?"

"I'll tell you later."

"I want to know now. There must have been something to upset you so. You went chasing after Takuan, didn't you?"

"Hmm. Yes."

"Did you find out where Musashi is?"

"Takuan's evil. I hate him!"

"He didn't tell you?"

"Uh, no."

"You're hiding something from me."

"Oh, you're both impossible!" wailed Jōtarō. "You and that stupid teacher of mine. I can't tell you anything before you lie down and I put a cold towel on your head. If you don't go back to the house now, I'm going to drag you there."

Seizing her wrist with one hand and beating on the gate with the other, he called furiously, "Open up! The sick girl's out here. If you don't hurry up, she'll freeze!"

A Toast to the Morrow

Matahachi paused on the pebbled road and wiped the sweat from his forehead. He had run all the way from Gojō Avenue to Sannen Hill. His face was quite red, but this was due more to the sake he'd drunk than to the rare physical exertion. Ducking through the dilapidated gate, he trotted round to the little house beyond the vegetable garden.

"Mother!" he called urgently. Then he glanced into the house and muttered, "Is she sleeping again?"

After stopping by the well to wash his hands and feet, he entered the house. 493

Osugi stopped snoring, opened one eye and roused herself. "Why are you making such a racket?" she asked grumpily.

"Oh, are you finally awake?"

"What do you mean by that?"

"All I have to do is sit down for a minute and you start griping about how lazy I am, nagging at me to search for Musashi."

"Well, pardon me," Osugi said indignantly, "for being old. I have to sleep for my health, but nothing's wrong with my spirit. I haven't felt well since the night Otsū got away. And my wrist, where Takuan grabbed it, is still sore."

"Why is it every time I feel good, you start complaining about something?"

Osugi glared. "You don't often hear me complain, in spite of my age. Have you found out anything about Otsū or Musashi?"

"The only people in town who haven't heard the news are old women who sleep all day."

"News! What news?" Osugi was immediately on her knees, crawling closer to her son.

"Musashi's going to have a third bout with the Yoshioka School."

"When? Where?"

"There's a sign at Yanagimachi with all the details. It's going to be in Ichijōji Village early tomorrow morning."

"Yanagimachi! That's the licensed quarter." Osugi's eyes narrowed. "What were you doing loafing in the middle of the day in a place like that?"

"I wasn't loafing," Matahachi said defensively. "You always take things the wrong way. I was there because it's a good place to pick up news."

"Never mind; I was just teasing. I'm satisfied you've settled down and won't go back to the wicked life you were leading. But did I hear you right? Did you say tomorrow morning?"

"Yes, at five o'clock."

Osugi thought. "Didn't you tell me you knew somebody at the Yoshioka School?"

"Yes, but I didn't meet them under very favorable circumstances. Why?"

"I want you to take me to the school, right now. Get yourself ready."

Matahachi was again struck by the impetuousness of the aged. Without making a move, he said coolly, "Why get excited? Anybody would think the house was on fire. What do you expect to accomplish by going to the Yoshioka School?"

"Volunteer our services, of course."

"Huh?"

"They're going out to kill Musashi tomorrow. I'll ask them to let us join them. We may not be much help, but we can probably get in at least one good blow."

"Mother, you must be joking!" Matahachi laughed.

"What do you find so funny?"

"You're so simple-minded."

"How dare you speak that way! You're the one who's simple-minded."

"Instead of arguing, go out and look around. The Yoshiokas are out for blood; this is their last chance. The rules of fighting aren't going to mean anything to them. The only way they can possibly save the House of Yoshioka is by killing Musashi—any way they can. It's no secret they're going to attack in force."

"Is that so?" Osugi purred. "Then Musashi's bound to be killed. . . . Isn't he?"

"I'm not so sure. He may bring men to help him. And if he does, it'll be quite a battle. That's what a lot of people think will happen."

"They may be right, but it's still annoying. We can't just sit on our hands and let somebody else kill him after searching for him all this time."

"I agree, and I've got a plan," Matahachi said excitedly. "If we get there before the battle, we can present ourselves to the Yoshiokas and tell them why we're after Musashi. I'm sure they'll let us strike a blow at the corpse. Then we can take some of his hair, or a sleeve, or something like that, and use it to prove to the people back home that we killed him. That would restore our standing, wouldn't it?"

"That's a good plan, my son. I doubt if there's any better way." Apparently forgetting that she had once suggested the same thing to him, she sat straight and squared her shoulders. "Not only would it clear our name, but with Musashi dead, Otsū would be like a fish out of water."

His mother's calm restored, Matahachi felt relieved—but also thirsty again. "Well, that's settled. We have a few hours to wait. Don't you think we should have some sake before dinner?"

"Hmm; all right. Have some brought out here. I'll have a little myself to celebrate our approaching victory."

As he put his hands on his knees and started to get up, he glanced to one side, blinked and stared.

"Akemi!" he cried, and ran to the small window.

She was cowering under a tree just outside, like a guilty cat that had not quite managed to flee in time. Staring with disbelieving eyes, she gasped, "Matahachi, is that you?"

"What brought you here?"

"Oh, I've been staying here for some time."

"I had no idea. Are you with Okō?"

"No."

"Don't you live with her anymore?"

"No. You know Gion Tōji, don't you?"

"I've heard of him."

"He and Mother ran away together." Her little bell tinkled as she raised her sleeve to hide her tears.

The light in the shade of the tree had a bluish tinge; the nape of her neck, her delicate hand, everything about her looked very different from the Akemi he remembered. The girlish glow that had so enchanted him at Ibuki and relieved his gloom at the Yomogi was no longer in evidence.

"Matahachi," said Osugi suspiciously, "who's that you're talking to?"

"It's the girl I told you about before. Okō's daughter."

"Her? What was she doing, eavesdropping?"

Matahachi turned, saying heatedly, "Why do you always jump to conclusions? She's staying here too. She just happened to be passing by. Right, Akemi?"

"Yes, I didn't dream you were here, though I saw that girl named Otsū here once."

"Did you talk to her?"

"Not really, but later I got to wondering. Isn't she the girl you were engaged to?"

"Yes."

"I thought so. My mother caused you a lot of trouble, didn't she?"

Matahachi ignored the question. "Are you still single? You look different somehow."

"Mother made life miserable for me after you left. I put up with it as long as I could, because she is my mother. But last year, when we were in Sumiyoshi, I ran away."

"She messed up both our lives, didn't she? But you just wait and see. In the end, she'll get what she deserves."

"I don't even care if she doesn't. I just wish I knew what I'm going to do from now on."

"Me too. The future doesn't look very bright. I'd like to get even with Okō, but I suppose all I'll ever do is think about it."

While they were complaining about their difficulties, Osugi had busied herself with her travel preparations. Now, with a click of her tongue, she said sharply, "Matahachi! Why are you standing there grumbling to somebody who has nothing to do with us? Come help me pack!"

"Yes, Mother."

"Good-bye, Matahachi. See you again." Looking dejected and ill at ease, Akemi hurried away.

Presently a lamp was lit, and the maid appeared with dinner trays and sake. Mother and son exchanged cups without looking at the bill, which lay on the tray between them. The servants, who came one by one to pay their respects, were followed by the innkeeper himself.

"So you're leaving tonight?" he said. "It's been good having you with us for so long. I'm sorry we haven't been able to give you the special treatment you deserve. We hope to see you again when you're next in Kyoto."

"Thank you," replied Osugi. "I may very well come again. Let's see, it's been three months, hasn't it—since the end of the year?"

"Yes, about that. We'll miss you."

"Won't you have a little sake with us?"

"That's very kind of you. It's quite unusual to be leaving at night. What made you decide to do that?"

"To tell the truth, some important business came up very suddenly. By the way, do you happen to have a map of Ichijōji Village?"

"Let's see, that's a little place on the other side of Shirakawa, near the top of

Mount Hiei. I don't think you'd better be going there in the middle of the night. It's quite deserted and—"

"That doesn't matter," interrupted Matahachi. "Would you please just draw us a map?"

"I'll be glad to. One of my servants comes from there. He can furnish me with the information I need. Ichijōji, you know, doesn't have many people, but it's spread out over quite a large area."

Matahachi, a little drunk, said curtly, "Don't worry about where we're going. We just want to know how to get there."

"Oh, forgive me. Take your time with your preparations." Rubbing his hands together obsequiously, he bowed his way out onto the veranda.

As he was about to step down into the garden, three or four of his employees came running up, the chief clerk saying excitedly, "Didn't she come this way?"

"Who?"

"That girl, the one who was staying in the back room."

"Well, what about her?"

"I'm sure I saw her earlier in the evening, but then I looked in her room, and—"

"Get to the point!"

"We can't find her."

"You idiot!" shouted the innkeeper, his outraged face devoid of the oily servility he had shown a few moments ago. "What's the use of running around like this after she's gone? You should have known from her looks there was something wrong. You let a week go by without making sure she had money? How can I stay in business with you doing stupid things like that?"

"I'm sorry, sir. She seemed decent."

"Well, it's too late now. You'd better see whether anything's missing from the other guest rooms. Oh, what a pack of dunces!" He stormed off toward the front of the inn.

Osugi and Matahachi drank a little more sake, then the old woman switched to tea and advised her son to do likewise.

"I'll just finish what's here," he said, pouring himself another cup. "I don't want anything to eat."

"It's not good for you not to eat. Have a little rice and some pickles at least."

Clerks and servants were running about in the garden and passageways, waving their lanterns.

"They don't seem to have caught her," said Osugi. "I don't want to get involved, so I kept quiet in front of the innkeeper, but don't you think the girl they're looking for is the one you were talking to earlier?

"I wouldn't be surprised."

"Well, you couldn't expect much from somebody with a mother like hers. Why on earth were you so friendly with her?"

"I feel kind of sorry for her. She's had a hard life."

"Well, be careful and don't let on that you know her. If the innkeeper thinks she has some connection with us, he'll demand that we pay her bill."

Matahachi had other things on his mind. Clutching the back of his head, he lay back and grumbled, "I could kill that whore! I can see her face now. Musashi's not the one who led me astray. It was Okō!"

Osugi rebuked him sharply. "Don't be stupid! Supposing you killed Okō—what good would it do our reputation? Nobody in the village knows or cares about her."

At two o'clock the innkeeper came to the veranda with a lantern and announced the time.

Matahachi stretched and asked, "Did you catch the girl?"

"No; no sign of her." He sighed. "She was pretty, so the clerks thought that even if she couldn't pay her bill, we could get back the money by having her live here for a while, if you see what I mean. Unfortunately, she was a bit too fast for us."

Sitting on the edge of the veranda, Matahachi tied his sandals. After waiting a minute or so, he called irritably, "Mother, what are you doing in there? You're always hurrying me up, but at the last minute you're never ready!"

"Just hold on. Matahachi, did I give you the money pouch I carry in my traveling bag? I paid the bill with some cash from my stomach wrapper, but our travel money was in the pouch."

"I haven't seen it."

"Come here a minute. Here's a scrap of paper with your name on it. What! ... Why, of all the nerve! It says ... it says that because of her long acquaintance with you, she hopes you'll pardon her for borrowing the money. Borrowing ... borrowing!"

"That's Akemi's writing."

Osugi turned on the innkeeper. "Look here! If a guest's property is stolen, the responsibility is yours. You'll have to do something about this."

"Is that so?" He smiled broadly. "Ordinarily, that would be the case, but since it appears you knew the girl, I'm afraid I'll have to ask you to take care of her bill first."

Osugi's eyes darted back and forth wildly, as she stammered, "Wh-what are you talking about? Why, I never saw that thieving wench before in my life. Matahachi! Stop fooling around! If we don't get started, the cock will be crowing."

The Death Trap

With the moon still high in the early morning sky, the shadows of the men climbing the white mountain path collided eerily, making the climbers feel even more uneasy.

"This isn't what I expected," said one.

"Me either. There are lots of faces missing. I thought for sure there'd be a hundred and fifty of us at least."

"Um. Doesn't look like half that many."

"I guess when Genzaemon arrives with his men, we'll total about seventy in all."

"It's too bad. The House of Yoshioka certainly isn't what it used to be."

From another group: "Who cares about the ones who aren't here? With the dōjō closed, a lot of men have to think first about making a living. The proudest and most loyal are here. That's more important than numbers!"

"Right! If there were a hundred or two hundred men here, they'd just get in each other's way."

"Ha, ha! Talking brave again. Remember the Rengeōin. Twenty men standing around, and Musashi still got away!"

Mount Hiei and the other peaks were still fast asleep in the folds of the clouds. The men were gathered at the fork of a little country road, where one path led to the top of Hiei and the other branched off toward Ichijōji. The road was steep, rocky and deeply furrowed by gullies. Around the most prominent landmark, a great pine tree spreading out like a gigantic umbrella, was a group of the senior disciples. Seated on the ground like so many night-crawling crabs, they were discussing the terrain.

"The road has three branches, so the question is which one Musashi will use. The best strategy is to divide the men into three squads and station one at each approach. Then Genjirō and his father can stay here with a corps of about ten of our strongest men—Miike, Ueda and the others."

"No, the ground's too rugged to have a large number of men in one place. We should spread them out along the approaches and have them stay hidden until Musashi is halfway up. Then they can attack from front and rear simultaneously."

There was a good deal of coming and going among the groups, moving shadows appearing to be skewered on lances or long scabbards. Despite a tendency to underestimate their enemy, there were no cowards among them.

"He's coming!" a man on the outer rim shouted.

Shadows came to a dead standstill. An icy twinge ran through the veins of every sumurai.

"Take it easy. It's only Genjirō."

"Why, he's riding in a palanquin!"

"Well, he's only a child!"

The slowly approaching lanterns, swinging to and fro in the chilly winds from Mount Hiei, seemed dull in comparison with the moonlight.

A few minutes later, Genzaemon alighted from his palanquin and declared, "I guess we're all here now."

Genjirō, a boy of thirteen, emerged from the next palanquin. Father and son both wore tightly tied white headbands and had their *hakama* hitched up high.

Genzaemon instructed his son to go and stand under the pine. The boy nodded silently as his father gave him an encouraging pat on the head, saying, "The battle is being carried out in your name, but the fighting will be done by the disciples. Since you're too young to take part, you don't have to do anything but stand there and watch."

Genjirō ran straight to the tree, where he assumed a pose as stiff and dignified as a samurai doll at the Boys' Festival.

"We're a little early," said Genzaemon. "The sun won't be up for a while." Fumbling around his waist, he pulled out a long pipe with a large bowl. "Does anyone have a light?" he asked casually, letting the others know that he was in complete command of himself.

A man stepped forward and said, "Sir, before you settle down for a smoke, don't you think we should decide how to divide up the men?"

"Yes, I guess we should. Let's station them quickly, so we'll be prepared. How are you going to do it?"

"There'll be a central force here by the tree. Other men will be hiding at intervals of about twenty paces on both sides of the three roads."

"Who'll be here by the tree?"

"You and I and about ten others. By being here, we can protect Genjirō and be ready to join in when the signal comes that Musashi has arrived."

"Wait just a minute," said Genzaemon, thinking over the strategy with judicious caution. "If the men are spread out like that, there'll be only about twenty in a position to attack him at the outset."

"True, but he'll be surrounded."

"Not necessarily. You can be sure he'll bring help. And you have to remember, he's as good at extracting himself from a tight spot as he is at fighting, if not better. Don't forget the Rengeōin. He might strike at a point where our men are thinly dispersed, wound three or four, then leave. Then he'd go around bragging he'd taken on more than seventy members of the Yoshioka School and come out the victor."

"We'll never let him get away with that."

"It'd be his word against ours. Even if he brings supporters, people are going to regard this match as being between him personally and the Yoshioka School as a whole. And their sympathies are going to be with the lone swordsman."

"I think," said Miike Jūrōzaemon, "it goes without saying that if he escapes again, we'll never live it down, no matter what we say. We're here to kill Musashi, and we can't be too fussy about how we do it. Dead men tell no tales."

Jūrōzaemon summoned four men in the nearest group to come forward. Three of them carried small bows, the fourth a musket. He had them face Genzaemon. "Perhaps you'd like to see what precautions we've taken."

"Ah! Flying weapons."

"We can station them on high ground or in trees."

"Won't people say we're using dirty tactics?"

"We care less about what people say than about making sure Musashi is dead."

"All right. If you're prepared to face the criticism, I have nothing more to add," the old man said meekly. "Even if Musashi brings along five or six men, he's not likely to escape when we have bows and arrows and a gun. Now, if we go on standing here, we may find ourselves taken by surprise. I leave the disposition of the men to you, but get them to their posts immediately."

The black shadows dispersed like wild geese in a marsh, some diving into copses of bamboo, others disappearing behind trees or flattening themselves out on the ridges between the rice paddies. The three archers ascended to a higher point overlooking the field. Below, the musketeer climbed into the upper branches of the spreading pine. As he squirmed about to conceal himself, pine needles and bark cascaded onto Genjirō.

Noticing the boy wriggling around, Genzaemon said reprovingly, "You're not nervous already, are you? Don't be such a coward!"

"It's not that. I've got pine needles down my back."

"Stand still and bear it. This will be a good experience for you. Watch closely when the actual fighting begins."

Along the easternmost approach, a great shout went up. "Stop, you crazy fool!"

The bamboo rustled loud enough to let any but the deaf know men were hiding all along the roads.

Genjirō cried, "I'm scared!" and hugged his father around the waist.

Jūrōzaemon immediately set off toward the commotion, though somehow sensing that this was a false alarm.

Sasaki Kojirō was bawling out one of the Yoshioka men. "Haven't you got eyes? The idea of mistaking me for Musashi! I've come here to act as a witness, and you come running at me with a lance. What an ass!"

The Yoshioka men, too, were angry, some of them suspecting he might be spying on them. They held themselves back but continued to block his way.

As Jūrōzaemon broke through the circle, Kojirō lit into him. "I came here to stand as witness, but your men are treating me as an enemy. If they're acting on instructions from you, I'll be more than happy, clumsy swordsman that I am, to take you on. I have no reason to help Musashi, but I do have my honor to uphold. Besides, this would be a welcome opportunity for me to dampen my Drying Pole with some fresh blood, something I've neglected to do for some time now." He was a tiger spitting fire. Those of the Yoshioka men who had been deceived by his foppish appearance were taken aback by his sheer nerve.

Jūrōzaemon, determined to show that he was not frightened by Kojirō's tongue, laughed. "Ha, ha! You're really riled, aren't you? But tell me, just who asked you to be a witness? I don't remember any such request. Did Musashi?"

"Don't talk nonsense. When we posted the sign at Yanagimachi, I told both parties I would act as witness."

"I see. *You* said that. In other words, Musashi didn't ask you, nor did we. You took it upon yourself to be an observer. Well, the world is full of people who butt into affairs that don't concern them."

"That's an insult!" snapped Kojirō.

Spit flying from his mouth, Jūrōzaemon cried, "Go away! We're not here to put on a show."

Kojirō, blue with rage, deftly detached himself from the group and ran a short distance back down the path. "Watch out, you bastards!" he shouted, preparing to attack.

Genzaemon, who had trailed after Jūrōzaemon, said, "Wait, young man!"

"*You* wait!" shouted Kojirō. "I have no business with you. But I'll show you what happens to people who insult me!"

The old man ran up to him. "Now, now, you're taking this too seriously! Our men are keyed up. I'm Seijūrō's uncle, and I heard from him that you're an outstanding swordsman. I'm sure there's been some mistake. I hope you'll forgive me personally for our men's conduct."

"I'm grateful to you for greeting me in this fashion. I've been on good terms with Seijūrō, and I wish the House of Yoshioka well, though I do not feel I can act as a second. But that is no reason for your men to insult me."

Kneeling in a formal bow, Genzaemon said, "You're quite right. I hope you'll forget what happened, for the sake of Seijūrō and Denshichirō." The old man chose his words tactfully, worried that Kojirō, if offended, might advertise the cowardly strategy they had adopted.

Kojirō's anger subsided. "Stand up, sir. I'm embarrassed to have an older man bow before me." In a swift about-face, the wielder of the Drying Pole now put his eloquent tongue to work encouraging the Yoshioka men and vilifying Musashi. "I have for some time been friendly with Seijūrō, and as I said before, I have no connection with Musashi. It is only natural that I favor the House of Yoshioka.

"I have seen many conflicts among warriors, but never have I witnessed a tragedy such as has befallen you. It is incredible that the house that served the Ashikaga shōguns as instructors in the martial arts should be brought into disrepute by a mere country bumpkin."

His words, spoken as though he were deliberately trying to make their ears burn, were received with rapt attention. On Jūrōzaemon's face was a look of regret for having spoken so rudely to a man who had nothing but goodwill for the House of Yoshioka.

The reaction was not lost on Kojirō. He picked up momentum. "In the future, I plan to establish a school of my own. It is therefore not out of curiosity that I make a practice of observing bouts and studying the tactics of other fighters. This is part of my education. I do not believe, however, that I've ever witnessed or heard of a bout that irritated me more than your two encounters with Musashi. Why, when so many of you were at the Rengeōin, and before that at the Rendaiji, did you allow Musashi to escape, so that he could swagger about the streets of Kyoto? This I cannot comprehend."

Licking his dry lips, he went on: "There's no doubt Musashi is a surprisingly tenacious fighter, as vagabond swordsmen go. I know that myself just from having seen him a couple of times. But at the risk of seeming meddlesome, I want to tell you what I've found out about Musashi." Without mentioning Akemi's name, he elaborated. "The first information came to me when I happened to meet a woman who had known him since he was seventeen. Filling out what she told me with other bits of information picked up here and there, I can give you a fairly complete outline of his life.

"He was born the son of a provincial samurai in Mimasaka Province. He ran away to the Battle of Sekigahara, and after returning home, committed so many atrocities that he was driven out of the village. Since then, he's been roaming about the countryside.

"Though he's a man of worthless character, he possesses a certain talent for the sword. And physically he's extremely strong. Moreover, he fights with no regard for his own life. Because of this, orthodox methods of swordsmanship are ineffective against him, just as reason is ineffective against insanity. You must trap him as you would a vicious animal, or you will fail. Now consider what your enemy is like and make your plans accordingly!"

Genzaemon, with great formality, thanked Kojirō and proceeded to describe the precautions that had been taken.

Kojirō nodded his approval. "If you've been that thorough, he probably hasn't a chance of getting away alive. Still, it seems to me you could devise a more effective trick."

"Trick?" repeated Genzaemon, taking a fresh and somewhat less admiring look at Kojirō's cocky face. "Thank you, but I think we've done enough already."

"No, my friend, you haven't. If Musashi comes walking up the path in an honest, straightforward manner, there's probably no way he can escape. But what if he should find out about your strategy in advance and not show up at all? Then all your planning will have been in vain, won't it?"

"If he does that, we only have to put up signs all over the city to make him the laughingstock of Kyoto."

"That would no doubt restore your face to some degree, but don't forget he'd still be free to go around saying your tactics were dirty. In that case, you wouldn't have cleared your master's name completely. Your preparations are meaningless unless you kill Musashi here today. To be sure of doing that, you must take steps to ensure that he actually comes here and falls into the death trap you have set."

"Is there any way of doing that?"

"Certainly. In fact, I can think of several ways." Kojirō's voice was full of   *503* confidence. He bent forward and, with a look of friendliness not often observed on his proud face, whispered a few words in Genzaemon's ear. "How about that?" he asked out loud.

"Hmm. I see what you mean." The old man nodded several times, then turned to Jūrōzaemon and whispered the scheme to him.

A Meeting in the Moonlight

It was already past midnight when Musashi arrived at the small inn north of Kitano where he had first met Jōtarō. The astonished innkeeper welcomed him cordially and quickly prepared a place for him to sleep.

Musashi went out early in the morning and returned late in the evening, presenting the old man with a sack of Kurama sweet potatoes. He also showed him a bolt of bleached Nara cotton, purchased at a nearby shop, and asked if he could have it made up into an undershirt, a stomach wrapper and a loincloth.

The innkeeper obligingly took the cloth to a neighborhood seamstress and on his way back bought some sake. He made a stew with the sweet potatoes and chatted with Musashi over the stew and sake until midnight, when the seamstress came with the clothes. Musashi folded the clothing neatly and placed it beside his pillow before retiring.

The old man was awakened long before dawn by the sound of splashing water. Looking out, he saw that Musashi had bathed with cold well water and was standing in the moonlight wearing his new underwear and just putting on his old kimono.

Musashi, remarking that he was a little tired of Kyoto and had decided to go to Edo, promised that when he came to Kyoto again, in three or four years, he would stay at the inn.

The innkeeper having tied his obi in the back for him, Musashi set off at a fast pace. He took the narrow path through the fields to the Kitano highroad, carefully picking his way through the piles of ox dung. The old man watched sadly as the darkness swallowed him.

Musashi's mind was as clear as the sky above him. Physically refreshed, his body seemed to grow more buoyant with each step.

"There's no reason to walk so fast," he said out loud, slackening his pace. "I suppose this will be my last night in the realm of the living." This was neither exclamation nor lament, merely a statement coming unbidden to his lips. He had no sense as yet of actually staring death in the face.

He had spent the previous day meditating under a pine tree at the inner temple at Kurama, hoping to achieve that state of bliss in which body and soul no longer matter. Unsuccessful in his effort to rid himself of the idea of death, he was now ashamed of having wasted his time.

The night air was invigorating. The sake, just the right amount, a short but sound sleep, the bracing well water, new clothing—he did not feel like a man about to die. He recalled the night in the dead of winter when he had forced himself to the top of Eagle Mountain. Then, too, the stars had been dazzling, and the trees had been festooned with icicles. The icicles would now have given way to budding flowers.

His head full of stray thoughts, he found it impossible to concentrate on the vital problem facing him. What purpose, he wondered, would be served at this stage by pondering questions that a century of thinking would not solve—the meaning of death, the agony of dying, the life that would follow afterward?

The district he was in was inhabited by noblemen and their retainers. He heard the doleful sound of a flageolet, accompanied by the slow strains of a reed mouth organ. In his mind's eye he saw mourners seated around a coffin, waiting for the dawn. Had the dirge penetrated his ears before he actually became aware of it? Perhaps it had aroused a subconscious memory of the dancing virgins of Ise and his experience on Eagle Mountain. Doubt gnawed at his mind.

As he paused to give the matter some thought, he noticed that he had passed the Shōkokuji and was now only about a hundred yards from the silvery Kamo River. In the light reflected on a dirt wall, he caught sight of a still, dark figure. The man walked toward him, followed by a smaller shadow, a dog on a leash. Satisfied by the presence of the animal that the man was not one of his enemies, he relaxed and walked on by.

The other man took a few steps, turned and said, "Can I trouble you, sir?"

"Me?"

"Yes, if it's all right." His cap and *hakama* were of the sort worn by artisans.

"What is it?" asked Musashi.

"Forgive me a peculiar question, but did you notice a house all lit up along this street?"

"I wasn't paying much attention, but no, I don't think I did."

"I guess I'm on the wrong street again."

"What are you looking for?"

"A house where there's just been a death."

"I didn't see the house, but I heard a mouth organ and a flageolet about a hundred yards back."

"That must be the place. The Shinto priest probably arrived before me and began the wake."

"Are you attending the wake?"

"Not exactly. I'm a coffin-maker from Toribe Hill. I was asked to go to the Matsuo house, so I went to Yoshida Hill. They don't live there anymore."

"The Matsuo family on Yoshida Hill?"

"Yes; I didn't know they'd moved. I went a long way for nothing. Thank you."

"Wait," said Musashi. "Would that be Matsuo Kaname, who's in the service of Lord Konoe?"

"That's right. He fell sick only about ten days before he died."

Musashi turned and walked on; the coffin-maker hurried off in the opposite direction.

"So my uncle's dead," thought Musashi matter-of-factly. He recalled how his uncle had scraped and saved to accumulate a small sum of money. He thought of the rice cakes he had received from his aunt and devoured on the bank of the freezing river on New Year's morning. He wondered vacantly how his aunt would get along now that she was all alone.

He stood on the bank of the Upper Kamo and regarded the looming dark panorama of the thirty-six hills of Higashiyama. Each peak seemed to stare back at him with enmity. Then he ran down to a pontoon bridge. From the northern part of the city, it was necessary to cross here to reach the road to Mount Hiei and the pass leading to Ōmi Province.

He was halfway across when he heard a voice, loud but indistinct. He stopped and listened. The rapidly flowing water gurgled cheerfully, while a cold wind swept through the valley. He couldn't locate the source of the cry and after a few more steps paused again at the sound of the voice. Still unable to tell where it came from, he hurried on to the other bank. As he left the bridge, he spied a man with upraised arms running toward him from the north. The figure seemed familiar.

It was—Sasaki Kojirō, the ubiquitous fixer.

As he approached, he greeted Musashi in an all too friendly way. After a glance across the bridge, he asked, "Are you alone?"

"Yes, of course."

"I hope you will pardon me for the other night," said Kojirō. "Thank you for putting up with my interference."

"I think it is I who should thank you," replied Musashi with equal politeness.

"Are you on your way to the bout?"

"Yes."

"All alone?" Kojirō asked again.

"Yes, of course."

"Hmm. I wonder, Musashi, if you've misunderstood the sign we put up at Yanagimachi."

"I don't think so."

"You're fully aware of the conditions? This isn't to be a simple man-to-man fight as it was in the case of Seijūrō and Denshichirō."

"I know that."

"Though the battle will be fought in the name of Genjirō, he'll be aided by members of the Yoshioka School. Do you understand that 'members of the Yoshioka School' could be ten men, or a hundred, even a thousand?"

"Yes; why do you ask?"

"Some of the weaker men have run away from the school, but the stronger and more courageous have all gone up to the spreading pine. Right now they're stationed all over the hillside, waiting for you."

"Have you been to take a look?"

"Um. I decided I'd better come back and warn you. Knowing you'd cross the pontoon bridge, I waited here. I consider this my duty, since I wrote the sign."

"That's very thoughtful of you."

"Well, that's the situation. Are you really intending to go alone, or do you have supporters going by another route?"

"I will have one companion."

"Is that so? Where is he now?"

"Right here!" Musashi, his laughing teeth shining in the moonlight, pointed to his shadow.

Kojirō bristled. "This is no laughing matter."

"I didn't mean it as a joke."

"Oh? It sounded as though you were making fun of my advice."

Musashi, assuming an attitude even graver than Kojirō's, countered, "Do you think the great saint Shinran was joking when he said that any believer has the strength of two, because the Buddha Amida walks with him?"

Kojirō did not answer.

"From all appearances, it seems the Yoshiokas have the upper hand. They're out in force. I'm alone. Without a doubt, you're assuming I'll be beaten. But I beg you not to worry on my behalf. Supposing I knew they had ten men and took ten men with me. What would happen? They'd throw in twenty men, rather than ten. If I took twenty, they'd increase the number to thirty or forty, and the battle would create an even greater public disturbance. Many people would be killed or injured. The result would be a serious infringement against the principles of government, with no compensating advancement for the cause of swordsmanship. In other words, there'd be much to lose and little to gain by my calling in assistance."

"True as that may be, it's not in accordance with *The Art of War* to enter into a battle you know you're going to lose."

"There are times when it's necessary."

"No! Not according to *The Art of War*. Abandoning yourself to rash action is quite a different matter."

"Whether or not my method is in accordance with *The Art of War*, I know what's necessary for me."

"You're breaking all the rules."

Musashi laughed.

"If you insist on going against the rules," argued Kojirō, "why don't you at least choose a line of action that will give you a chance to go on living?"

"The path I'm following is, for me, the way toward a fuller life."

"You'll be lucky if it doesn't lead you straight to hell!"

"This river, you know, may be the three-pronged river of hell; this road, the mile-long road to perdition; the hill I'll soon climb, the mountain of needles on which the damned are impaled. Nevertheless, this is the only path toward true life."

"The way you talk, you may already be possessed by the god of death."

"Think what you like. There are people who die by remaining alive and others who gain life by dying."

"You poor devil!" said Kojirō, half in derision.

"Tell me, Kojirō—if I follow this road, where will it take me?"

"To Hananoki Village and then to the spreading pine at Ichijōji, where you've chosen to die."

"How far is it?"

"Only about two miles. You have plenty of time."

"Thank you. I'll see you later," said Musashi breezily, as he turned and started down a side road.

"That's not the way!"

Musashi nodded.

"That's the wrong way, I tell you."

"I know."

He went on down the slope. Beyond the trees on either side of the road were tiered rice paddies, off in the distance a few thatched farmhouses. Kojirō watched Musashi stop, look up at the moon and stand still for a time.

Kojirō broke into laughter as it dawned on him that Musashi was urinating. He himself looked up at the moon, thinking that before it had set, a lot of men would be dead or dying.

Musashi didn't come back. Kojirō sat down on the root of a tree and contemplated the coming fight with a sentiment approaching glee. "To judge from Musashi's calmness, he's already resigned to dying. Still, he'll put up a tremendous struggle. The more of them he cuts down, the more fun it'll be to watch. Ah, but the Yoshiokas have flying weapons. If he's hit by one of them, the show will be over right then. That would spoil everything. I think I'd better tell him about them."

There was now a little mist and a predawn chill in the air.

Standing up, Kojirō called, "Musashi, what's taking you so long?"

A sense that something was off key sent a pang of anxiety through him. He walked rapidly down the slope and called again. The only sound was the turning of a waterwheel.

"The silly bastard!"

Racing back to the main road, he looked around in all directions, seeing only the temple roofs and forests of Shirakawa, rising on the slopes of Higashiyama, and the moon. Jumping to the conclusion that Musashi had run away, he rebuked himself for not seeing through his calmness and took off at a flying pace for Ichijōji.

Grinning, Musashi emerged from behind a tree and stood where Kojirō had been standing. He was glad to be rid of him. He had no use for a man who took pleasure in watching other people die, who watched impassively while other men staked their lives on causes that were important to them. Kojirō was no innocent spectator, motivated only by the desire to learn. He was a deceitful, scheming interloper, always out to ingratiate himself with both sides, always presenting himself as the splendid chap who wants to help everybody.

Perhaps Kojirō had thought that if he told Musashi how strong the enemy was, Musashi would get down on his hands and knees and ask him to serve as his second. And, conceivably, if Musashi's first objective had been to preserve his own life, he would have welcomed assistance. But even before meeting Kojirō, he had picked up enough information to know he might have to face a hundred men.

It wasn't that he had forgotten the lesson Takuan had taught him: the truly brave man is one who loves life, cherishing it as a treasure that once forfeited can never be recovered. He well knew that to live was more than merely to survive. The problem was how to imbue his life with meaning, how to ensure that his life would cast a bright ray of light into the future, even if it became necessary to give up that life for a cause. If he succeeded in doing this, the length of his life—twenty years or seventy—made little difference. A lifetime was only an insignificant interval in the endless flow of time.

To Musashi's way of thinking, there was one way of life for ordinary people, another for the warrior. It was vitally important for him to live like a samurai and to die like one. There was no turning back from the path he had chosen. Even if he was hacked to pieces, the enemy could not obliterate the fact of his having responded fearlesssly and honestly to the challenge.

He gave his attention to the routes available. The shortest, as well as the widest and easiest to travel, was the road Kojirō had taken. Another, not quite so direct, was a path leading along the Takano River, a tributary of the Kamo, to the Ōhara highroad and then by way of the Shugakuin imperial villa to Ichijōji. The third route went east for a short distance, then north as far as the foothills of Uryū and finally across a path into the village.

The three roads met at the spreading pine; the difference in distance was insignificant. Yet from the viewpoint of a small force attacking a much larger one, the approach was all-important. The choice itself could decide victory or defeat.

Instead of weighing the problem at some length, after only a momentary pause he started running in a direction almost opposite from that of Ichijōji. First he crossed over the foot of Kagura Hill to a point behind the tomb of the Emperor Go-Ichijō. Then, passing through a thick bamboo grove, he came to a mountain stream flowing through a village in the northwest. Looming above him was the north shoulder of Mount Daimonji. Silently he began climbing.

Through the trees on his right he could see a garden wall, apparently belonging to the Ginkakuji. Almost directly beneath him, the jujube-shaped pond in the garden shone like a mirror. As he went farther up, the pond was lost in the trees, and the rippling Kamo River came into view. He felt as though he held the whole city in the palm of his hand.

He stopped for a moment to check his position. By proceeding horizontally across the sides of four hills, he could reach a point above and behind the spreading pine, where he could command a bird's-eye view of the enemy's position. Like Oda Nobunaga at the Battle of Okehazama, he had spurned the usual routes in favor of a difficult detour.

"Who goes there?"

Musashi froze and waited. Footsteps approached cautiously. Seeing a man dressed like a samurai in the service of a court noble, Musashi decided he was not a member of the Yoshioka forces.

The man's nose was smudged from the smoke of his torch; his kimono was damp and mud-spattered. He uttered a little cry of surprise.

Musashi stared at him suspiciously.

"Aren't you Miyamoto Musashi?" the man asked with a low bow, his eyes tinged with fright.

Musashi's eyes brightened in the light of the torch.

"Are you Miyamoto Musashi?" Terrified, the samurai seemed to wobble slightly on his feet. The fierceness in Musashi's eyes was something not often encountered in human beings.

"Who are you?" Musashi asked crisply.

"Er, I . . . I . . ."

"Stop stammering. Who are you?"

"I'm . . . I'm from the house of Lord Karasumaru Mitsuhiro."

"I'm Miyamoto Musashi, but what's a retainer of Lord Karasumaru's doing up here in the middle of the night?"

"Then you are Musashi!" He sighed with relief. The next instant, he was running at breakneck speed down the mountain, his torch trailing light behind him. Musashi turned and continued on his way across the mountainside.

When the samurai reached the vicinity of the Ginkakuji, he shouted, "Kura, where are you?"

"We're here. Where are you?" It wasn't the voice of Kura, another retainer of Karasumaru, but that of Jōtarō.

"Jō-ta-rō! Is that you?"

"Y-e-e-s!"

"Come up here fast!"

"I can't. Otsū can't walk any farther."

The samurai swore under his breath, raised his voice even higher and shouted, "Come quick! I found Musashi! Mu-sa-shi! If you don't hurry, we'll lose him!"

Jōtarō and Otsū were about two hundred yards farther down the path; it took a while for their two long shadows, seemingly linked together, to hobble up to the samurai. He waved his torch to hurry them on, and in a matter of seconds could hear for himself Otsū's labored breathing. Her face looked whiter than the moon; the travel paraphernalia on her thin arms and legs seemed cruel and absurd. But when the light fell full upon her, her cheeks took on a ruddy hue.

"Is it true?" she panted.

"Yes, I just saw him." Then, in a more urgent tone: "If you hurry, you should be able to catch him. But if you waste time—"

"Which way?" asked Jōtarō, exasperated at being caught between an agitat-
510 ed man and an ailing woman.

Otsū's physical condition had by no means improved, but once Jōtarō had divulged the news of Musashi's impending battle, there was no way of keeping her in bed, even if that might prolong her life. Disregarding all entreaties, she had tied up her hair, laced on her straw sandals and all but staggered out of Lord Karasumaru's gate. Once the impossibility of stopping her had become apparent, Lord Karasumaru did all he could to help. He took charge of the operation himself, and while she was limping slowly toward the Ginkakuji, sent his men to scour the various approaches to Ichijōji Village. The men walked until their feet ached and had been on the verge of giving up when the quarry was found.

The samurai pointed, and Otsū started resolutely up the hill.

Jōtarō, fearing she might collapse, asked at every other step, "Are you all right? Can you make it?"

She did not reply. Truth to tell, she did not even hear him. Her emaciated body was responsive only to the need to reach Musashi. Though her mouth was parched, cold sweat poured from her ashen forehead.

"This must be the way," said Jōtarō, hoping to encourage her. "This road goes to Mount Hiei. It's all flat from now on. No more climbing. Do you want to rest for a moment?"

Silently she shook her head, clinging firmly to the stick they were carrying between them, struggling for breath as though all life's difficulties were compressed into this one journey.

When they'd managed to cover nearly a mile, Jōtarō shouted, "Musashi! *Sensei!*" and went on shouting.

His strong voice bolstered Otsū's courage, but before long her strength was gone. "Jō-Jōtarō," she whispered weakly. She let go of the stick and sank into the grass by the road. Face to the ground, she clasped her delicate fingers over her mouth. Her shoulders jerked convulsively.

"Otsū! It's blood! You're spitting up blood! Oh, Otsū!" On the brink of tears, he clasped his arms around her waist and held her up. She shook her head slowly from side to side. Not knowing what else to do, Jōtarō patted her gently on the back. "What do you want?" he asked.

She was beyond replying.

"I know! Water! Is that it?"

She nodded feebly.

"Wait here. I'll get some."

He stood up and looked around, listened for a moment and went to a nearby ravine, where he heard water running. With little difficulty, he found a spring bubbling forth from the rocks. As he started to scoop up some water with his hands, he hesitated, eyes fixed on the tiny crabs at the bottom of the pristine pool. The moon wasn't shining directly on the water, but the reflection of the sky was more beautiful than the silver-white clouds themselves. Deciding to take a sip himself before carrying out his task, he moved a few feet to one side and bent down on his hands and knees, craning his neck like a duck.

Then he gasped—apparition?—and his body bristled like a chestnut in its burr. Reflected in the small pool was a striped pattern, half a dozen trees on the other side. Right beside them was the image of Musashi.

Jōtarō thought his imagination was playing tricks on him, that the reflection would soon dissolve. When it failed to go away, he raised his eyes very slowly.

"You're here!" he cried. "You're really here!" The peaceful reflection of the sky turned to mud as he splashed across to the other side, wetting his kimono to the shoulders.

"You're here!" He threw his arms around Musashi's legs.

"Quiet," said Musashi softly. "It's dangerous here. Come back later."

"No! I've found you. I'm staying with you."

"Quiet. I heard your voice. I've been waiting here. Now take Otsū some water."

"It's muddy now."

"There's another brook over there. See? Here, take this with you." He held out a bamboo tube.

Jōtarō raised his face and said, "No! You take it to her."

They stood like that for a few seconds, then Musashi nodded and went to the other brook. Having filled the tube, he carried it to Otsū's side. He put his arm around her gently and held the tube to her mouth.

Jōtarō stood beside them. "Look, Otsū! It's Musashi. Don't you understand? Musashi!"

As Otsū sipped the cool water, her breath came a little more easily, though she remained limp in Musashi's arm. Her eyes seemed to be focused on something very far away.

"Don't you see, Otsū? Not me, Musashi! It's Musashi's arm around you, not mine."

Burning tears gathered in her vacant eyes until they looked like glass. Two streams sparkled down her cheeks. She nodded.

Jōtarō was beside himself with joy. "You're happy now, aren't you? This is what you wanted, isn't it?" Then, to Musashi: "She's been saying, over and over, that whatever happened, she had to see you. She wouldn't listen to anybody! Please tell her, if she keeps on acting like this, she'll die. She won't pay any attention to me. Maybe she'll do what you tell her."

"It was all my fault," said Musashi. "I'll apologize and tell her to take better care of herself. Jōtarō . . ."

"Yes?"

"Would you leave us alone, just for a little while?"

"Why? Why can't I stay here?"

"Don't be that way, Jōtarō," Otsū said pleadingly. "Just for a few minutes. Please."

"Oh, all right." He couldn't refuse Otsū, even if he didn't understand. "I'll be up the hill. Call me when you're through."

Otsū's natural shyness was magnified by her illness, and she could not decide what to say.

Musashi, embarrassed, turned his face away from her. With her back to him, she stared at the ground. He gazed up at the sky.

He feared instinctively that no words existed to tell her what was in his heart. All that had happened since the night she had freed him from the cryptomeria tree passed through his mind, and he recognized the purity of the love that had kept her searching for him these five long years.

Who was stronger, who had suffered more? Otsū, her life difficult and complex, burning with a love she could not conceal? Or he himself, hiding his feelings behind a stony face, burying the embers of his passion under a layer of cold ashes? Musashi had thought before, and thought now, that his way was the more painful. Yet there was strength and valor in Otsū's constancy. The burden she had borne was too heavy for most men to bear alone.

"Only a short time to go," thought Musashi.

The moon was low in the sky, the light whiter now. Dawn was not far away. Soon both the moon and he himself would fade behind the mountain of death. He must, in the short time remaining, tell Otsū the truth. He owed her that much, for her devotion and her faithfulness. But the words would not come. The harder he tried to speak, the more tongue-tied he became. He watched the sky helplessly, as though inspiration might descend from it.

Otsū stared at the ground and wept. Within her heart was a flaming love, a love so strong that it had driven everything else out. Principles, religion, concern for her own welfare, pride—all paled beside this one consuming passion. In some way, she believed, this love simply had to overcome Musashi's resistance. Somehow, through her tears, a way must be found for them to live together, apart from the world of ordinary people. But now that she was with him, she was helpless. She could not bring herself to describe the pain of being away from him, the misery of traveling through life alone, the agony she suffered over his lack of feeling. If only she had a mother to whom she could pour out all her sorrows . . .

The long silence was broken by the honking of a flock of geese. Attuned to the approach of dawn, they rose above the trees and flew off over the mountaintops.

"The geese are flying north," said Musashi, conscious of the irrelevance.

"Musashi . . ."

Their eyes met in a shared memory of the years in the village, when the geese had passed high above each spring and fall.

Everything had been so simple then. She had been friendly with Matahachi. Musashi she had disliked because of his roughness, but she had never been afraid to talk back to him when he said insulting things to her. Each now thought of the mountain where the Shippōji stood and the banks of the Yoshino River below. And both knew they were squandering precious moments—moments that would never return.

"Jōtarō said you were ill. Is it very bad?"

"It's nothing serious."

"Are you feeling better now?"

"Yes, but it's of no importance. Are you really expecting to be killed today?"

"I'm afraid so."

"If you die, I can't go on living. Perhaps that's why it's so easy to forget about my sickness now."

A certain light came into her eyes, and it made him feel the weakness of his 513 own determination as compared to hers. To acquire even a degree of self-control, he had had to ponder the question of life and death for many years, discipline himself at every turn of the road, force himself to undergo the rigors of a samurai's training. With no training or conscious self-discipline, this woman was able to say without the slightest hesitation that she, too, was prepared to die if he did. Her face expressed perfect serenity, her eyes telling him she was neither lying nor speaking impulsively. She seemed almost happy over the prospect of following him in death. He wondered, with a tinge of shame, how women could be so strong.

"Don't be a fool, Otsū!" he suddenly blurted. "There's no reason why you should die." The strength of his own voice and the depth of his feeling surprised even him. "It's one thing for me to die fighting against the Yoshiokas. Not only is it right for a man who lives by the sword to die by the sword; I have a duty to remind those cowards of the Way of the Samurai. Your willingness to follow me in death is deeply touching, but what good would it do? No more than the pitiful death of an insect."

Seeing her burst into tears again, he regretted the brutality of his words.

"Now I understand how over the years I've lied to you, and I've lied to myself. I didn't intend to deceive you when we ran away from the village or when I saw you at Hanada Bridge, but I did—by pretending to be cold and indifferent. That wasn't the way I really felt.

"In a little while, I'll be dead. What I'm about to say is the truth. I love you, Otsū. I'd throw everything to the four winds and live out my life with you, if only . . ."

After a moment's pause, he continued in a more forceful vein. "You must believe every word I say, because I'll never have another chance to tell you this. I speak with neither pride nor pretense. There have been days when I couldn't concentrate for thinking about you, nights I couldn't sleep for dreaming of you. Hot, passionate dreams, Otsū, dreams that nearly drove me mad. Often I've hugged my pallet, pretending it was you.

"But even when I felt like that, if I took out my sword and looked at it, the madness evaporated and my blood cooled."

Her face turned toward him, tearful but as radiant as a morning glory, she started to speak. Seeing the fervor in his eyes, her words caught in her throat and she looked at the ground again.

"The sword is my refuge. Any time my passion threatens to overcome me, I force myself back into the world of swordsmanship. This is my fate, Otsū. I'm torn between love and self-discipline. I seem to be traveling on two paths at once. Yet when the paths diverge, I invariably manage to keep myself on the right one.

"I know myself better than anyone else does. I'm neither a genius nor a great man."

He became silent again. Despite his desire to express his feelings honestly, his words seemed to him to be concealing the truth. His heart told him to be even more candid.

514 "That's the kind of man I am. What else can I say? I think of my sword, and

you disappear into some dark corner of my mind—no, disappear altogether, leaving no trace. At times like that I'm happiest and most satisfied with my life. Do you understand? All this time you've suffered, you've risked body and soul on a man who loves his sword more than he loves you. I'll die to vindicate my sword, but I wouldn't die for the love of a woman. Not even you. As much as I'd like to fall on my knees and beg your forgiveness, I can't."

He felt her sensitive fingers tighten on his wrist. She was no longer crying. "I know all that," she said emphatically. "If I didn't know it, I wouldn't love you as I do."

"But can't you see the foolishness of dying on my account? For this one moment, I'm yours, body and soul. But once I've left you . . . You mustn't die for the love of a man like me. There's a good way, a proper way, for a woman to live, Otsū. You must search for it, make a happy life for yourself. These must be my parting words. It's time for me to go."

Gently he removed her hand from his wrist and stood up. She caught his sleeve and cried, "Musashi, just one minute more!"

There were so many things she wanted to tell him: she did not care if he forgot her when he was not with her, she did not mind being called insignificant, she'd had no delusions about his character when she fell in love with him. She caught his sleeve again, her eyes searching his, trying to prolong this last moment, to keep it from ever ending.

Her silent appeal nearly undid him. There was beauty even in the weakness that prevented her from speaking. Overcome by his own weakness and fear, he felt himself to be a tree with brittle roots, menaced by a raging wind. He wondered if his chaste devotion to the Way of the Sword would crumble, like a landslide, under the weight of her tears.

To break the silence, he asked, "Do you understand?"

"Yes," she said weakly. "I understand perfectly, but if you die, I'll die too. My dying will have a meaning to me, just as yours has to you. If you can face the end calmly, so can I. I won't be trampled down like an insect, or drown in a moment of grief. I have to decide for myself. Nobody else can do it for me, not even you."

With great strength and perfect calm, she went on. "If in your heart you'll consider me to be your bride, that's enough, a joy and a blessing that only I, of all the women in the world, possess. You said you didn't want to make me unhappy. I can assure you I won't die because of unhappiness. There are people who seem to consider me unfortunate, yet I don't feel that way in the least. I look forward with pleasure to the day when I die. It will be like a glorious morning when the birds are singing. I'll go as happily as I would to my wedding."

Nearly out of breath, she folded her arms over her breast and gazed up contentedly, as though captivated by a delightful dream.

The moon seemed to be sinking rapidly. Though it was still not daybreak, mist had begun to rise through the trees.

The silence was shattered by a horrifying scream that rent the air like the screech of a mythical bird. It came from the cliff Jōtarō had climbed earlier. 515

Startled out of her dreams, Otsū directed her eyes to the top of the cliff.

Musashi chose this moment to leave. Without a word, he simply withdrew from her side and walked away, toward his appointment with death.

Otsū, with a stifled cry, ran a few steps after him.

Musashi ran farther ahead, then turned back and said, "I understand your feelings, Otsū, but please don't die a cowardly death. Don't, because of your sorrow, allow yourself to sink into the valley of death and succumb like a weakling. Get well first, then think about it. I'm not throwing my life away for a useless cause. I've chosen to do what I'm doing because by dying I can achieve eternal life. Depend on one thing: my body may turn to dust, but I'll still be alive."

Catching his breath, he added a warning. "Are you listening? By attempting to follow me in death, you may find that you're dying alone. You may look for me in the world beyond only to find I'm not there. I intend to live on for a hundred or a thousand years—in the hearts of my countrymen, in the spirit of Japanese swordsmanship."

He was out of hearing before she could speak again. She felt her very soul had left her, but she did not think of this as a parting. It was more as though the two of them were being engulfed in a great wave of life and death.

A cascade of dirt and pebbles came to rest at the foot of the cliff, followed closely by Jōtarō, wearing the grotesque mask he had received from the widow in Nara.

Throwing his hands up, he said, "I've never been so surprised in my life!"

"What happened?" whispered Otsū, not quite recovered from the shock of seeing the mask.

"Didn't you hear it? I don't know why, but all of a sudden there was this horrible scream."

"Where were you? Were you wearing that mask?"

"I was above the cliff. There's a path up there about as wide as this one. After I climbed up a little way, I found a nice big rock, so I was just sitting there looking at the moon."

"The mask—did you have it on?"

"Yes. I could hear foxes howling, and maybe badgers or something rustling around near me. I thought the mask would scare them away. Then I heard this shriek, bloodcurdling, like it was coming from a ghost in hell!"

516

Stray Geese

"Wait for me, Matahachi. Why do you have to walk so fast?" Osugi, far behind and completely winded, had forfeited both patience and pride.

Matahachi, in a voice calculated to be heard, grumbled, "She was in such a hurry when we left the inn, but listen to her now. She talks better than she walks."

As far as the foot of Mount Daimonji, they had been on the road to Ichijōji, but now, deep in the mountains, they were lost.

Osugi would not give up. "The way you keep picking on me," she rasped, "anybody would think you had a terrible grudge against your own mother." By the time she had wiped the sweat from her wrinkled face, Matahachi was off again.

"Won't you slow down?" she cried. "Let's sit here for a while."

"If you keep stopping every ten feet to rest, we won't be there before sunrise."

"The sun won't be up for a long time yet. Ordinarily I wouldn't have any trouble on a mountain road like this, but I'm coming down with a cold."

"You'll never admit you're wrong, will you? Back there, when I woke up the innkeeper so you could rest, you couldn't sit still for a minute. You didn't want anything to drink, so you started carrying on about how we'd be late. I hadn't had two sips before you dragged me out of the place. I know you're my mother, but you're a hard woman to get along with."

"Ha! Still peeved because I wouldn't let you drink yourself silly. Is that it? Why can't you exercise a little restraint? We have important things to do today."

"It's not as if we're going to whip out our swords and do the job ourselves. All we have to do is get a lock of Musashi's hair or something off the body. There's nothing so hard about that."

"Have it your way! No use fighting with each other like this. Let's go."

As they started walking again, Matahachi resumed his disgruntled soliloquy. "The whole thing's stupid. We take a lock of hair back to the village and offer it as proof that our great mission in life had been accomplished. Those bumpkins have never been out of the mountains, so they'll be impressed. Oh, how I hate that village!"

Not only had he not lost his fondness for the good sake of Nada, the pretty girls of Kyoto and a number of other things, he still believed the city was where he would get his lucky break. Who could deny that one morning he mightn't wake up with everything he'd ever wanted? "I'll never go back to that piddling village," he vowed silently.

Osugi, again lagging a good distance behind, cast dignity to the winds. "Matahachi," she wheedled, "carry me on your back, won't you? Please. Just for a short while?"

He frowned, said nothing, but stopped to let her catch up. Just as she reached him, their ears were assaulted by the shriek of terror that had jolted Otsū and Jōtarō. Faces blankly curious, they stood still, listening keenly. A moment later, Osugi uttered a cry of dismay, as Matahachi ran abruptly to the edge of the cliff.

"Wh-where are you going?"

"It must be down there!" he said, and disappeared over the edge of the cliff. "Stay there. I'll see who it is."

Osugi recovered in no time. "Fool!" she shouted. "Where are you going?"

"You deaf? Didn't you hear that scream?"

"What's that got to do with you? Come back! Come back here!"

Ignoring her, he rapidly made his way from tree root to tree root to the bottom of the little ravine.

"Fool! Numskull!" she cried. She might as well have been barking at the moon.

Matahachi again shouted to her to stay where she was, but he was so far down that Osugi barely heard him. "Now what?" he thought, beginning to regret his impulsiveness. If he was wrong about where the cry had come from, he was wasting time and energy.

Though no moonlight penetrated the foliage, his eyes gradually became accustomed to the dark. He came upon one of the many shortcuts crisscrossing the mountains east of Kyoto and leading to Sakamoto and Ōtsu. Walking alongside a brook with tiny waterfalls and rapids, he found a hut, probably a shelter for men who came to spear mountain trout. It was too small to hold more than one person, and obviously empty, but behind it he spotted a crouching figure, face and hands starkly white.

"It's a woman," he thought with satisfaction, and concealed himself behind a large rock.

After a couple of minutes, the woman crept from behind the hut, went to the edge of the stream and scooped up some water to drink. He took a step forward. As though warned by animal instinct, the girl looked around furtively and started to flee.

"Akemi!"

"Oh, you frightened me!" But there was relief in her voice. She swallowed the water that had caught in her throat and heaved a deep sigh.

After eyeing her up and down, Matahachi asked, "What happened? What are you doing here at this hour of the night dressed in traveling clothes?"

"Where's your mother?"

"She's up there." He waved his arm.

"I bet she's furious."

"About the money?"

"Yes. I'm really sorry, Matahachi. I had to leave in a hurry, and I didn't have enough to pay my bill, and nothing to travel on. I know it was wrong, but I panicked. Please forgive me! Don't make me go back! I promise I'll return the money someday." She melted into tears.

"Why all the apologies? Oh, I see. You think we came up here to catch you!"

"Oh, I don't blame you. Even if it was just a wild impulse, I did run away with the money. If I'm caught and treated like a thief, I guess I can't really complain."

"That's the way Mother would look at it, but I'm not like that. Anyway, it wasn't very much. If you really needed it, I'd have been glad to give it to you. I'm not angry. I'm much more interested in why you left so suddenly and what you're doing up here."

"I overheard you and your mother talking tonight."

"Oh? About Musashi?"

"Uh, yes."

"And you decided all of a sudden to go to Ichijōji?"

She didn't answer.

"Oh, I forgot!" he exclaimed, recalling his purpose in coming down into the ravine. "Were you the one who screamed a few minutes ago?"

She nodded, then quickly stole a frightened glance at the slope above them. Satisfied that nothing was there, she told him how she had crossed the stream and was climbing a steep crag when she looked up and saw an incredibly evil-looking ghost sitting on a high rock, staring at the moon. It had the body of a midget, but the face, that of a woman, was an eerie color, whiter than white, with a mouth that slashed up on one side to the ear. It seemed to be laughing grotesquely at her and had frightened her out of her wits. Before she came to her senses, she had already slid back down into the ravine.

Though the tale sounded absurd, she told it with deadly seriousness. Matahachi tried to listen politely, but was soon overcome with laughter.

"Ha, ha! You're making it all up! You probably frightened the ghost. Why, you used to roam the battlefields and didn't even wait for the dead spirits to leave before you started stripping the corpses."

"I was only a child then. I didn't know enough to be afraid."

"You weren't all that young. . . . I gather you're still pining over Musashi."

"No. . . . He was my first love, but—"

"Then why go to Ichijōji?"

"I don't really know myself. I just thought that if I went, I might see him."

"You're wasting your time," he said emphatically, then told her Musashi didn't have a chance in a thousand of coming out of the battle alive.

After what had happened to her at the hands of Seijūrō and Kojirō, thoughts of Musashi could no longer conjure up images of the bliss she had once imagined sharing with him. Having neither died nor found a life that appealed to her, she felt like a soul in limbo—a goose separated from the flock and lost.

As he stared at her profile, Matahachi was struck by the similarity between her situation and his. They had both been cut adrift from their moorings.   *519*

Something in her powdered face suggested that she was looking for a companion.

He put his arm around her, brushed his cheek against hers and whispered, "Akemi, let's go to Edo."

"To . . . to Edo? You must be joking," she said, but the idea shook her out of her trance.

Tightening his hold on her shoulders, he said, "It doesn't necessarily have to be Edo, but everybody says it's the city of the future. Osaka and Kyoto are old now. Maybe that's why the shōgun's building a new capital in the east. If we go there now, there should still be lots of good jobs, even for a couple of stray geese like you and me. Come on, Akemi, say you'll go." Encouraged by the growing spark of interest in her face, he went on more fervently.

"We could have fun, Akemi. We could do the things we want to do. Why live if you can't do that? We're young. We've got to learn to be bold and clever. Neither of us will get anywhere acting like weaklings. The more you try to be good and honest and conscientious, the harder fate kicks you in the teeth and laughs at you. You end up crying your heart out, and where does that get you?

"Look, that's the way it's always been for you, isn't it? You've done nothing but let yourself be devoured by that mother of yours and some brutal men. From now on, you've got to be the one who eats, rather than the one who gets gobbled up."

She was beginning to be swayed. Her mother's teahouse had been a cage from which they had both fled. Since then the world had shown her nothing but cruelty. She sensed that Matahachi was stronger and better able to cope with life than she. After all, he was a man.

"Will you go?" he asked.

Even though she knew it was as if the house had burned down and she was trying to rebuild it with the ashes, it took some effort to shake off her fantasy, the rapturous daydream in which Musashi was hers and hers alone. But finally she nodded without speaking.

"Then it's settled. Let's go, now!"

"What about your mother?"

"Oh, her?" He sniffed. He glanced up at the cliff. "If she manages to lay hands on something to prove that Musashi's dead, she'll go back to the village. No doubt she'll be mad as a hornet when she finds I'm not around. I can hear her now, telling everybody how I left her on the mountain to die, the way they used to throw away old women in some parts of the country. But if I make a success of myself, that'll make up for everything. Anyway, we've made up our minds. Let's go!"

He strode off ahead, but she hung back.

"Matahachi, not that way!"

"Why?"

"We'll have to pass that rock again."

"Ha, ha! And see the midget with a woman's face? Forget it! I'm with you now. Oh, listen—isn't that my mother calling? Hurry up, before she comes looking for me. She's a lot worse than a small ghost with a scary face."

The Spreading Pine

The wind soughed in the bamboo. Though it was still too dark to take flight, birds were awake and chirping.

"Don't attack! It's me—Kojirō!" Having run like a demon for more than a mile, he was breathing heavily when he reached the spreading pine.

The faces of the men who emerged from their hiding places to encircle him were numb from waiting.

"Didn't you find him?" Genzaemon asked impatiently.

"I found him, all right," replied Kojirō with an inflection that turned every eye upon him. Looking around coolly, he said, "I found him and we walked together up the Takano River for a way, but then he—"

"He ran away!" exclaimed Miike Jūrōzaemon.

"No!" Kojirō said emphatically. "To judge from his calmness and from what he said, I don't think he did. At first it seemed that way, but on second thought I decided he was just trying to get rid of me. He's probably devised some strategy he wanted to conceal from me. Better keep your guard up!"

"Strategy? What kind of strategy?"

They jostled closer to avoid missing a word.

"I suspect he's enlisted several seconds. He was probably on his way to meet them so they could attack all at once."

"Uh," groaned Genzaemon. "That seems likely. It also means it won't be long before they arrive."

Jūrōzaemon separated himself from the group and ordered the men back to their stations. "If Musashi attacks while we're scattered like this," he warned, "we may lose the first skirmish. We don't know how many men he'll have with him, but it can't be very many. We'll stick to our original plan."

"He's right. Mustn't be caught off guard."

"It's easy to make a mistake when you're tired of waiting. Be careful!"

"Get to your posts!"

Gradually they dispersed. The musketeer resettled himself in the upper branches of the pine tree.

Kojirō, noticing Genjirō standing stiffly with his back to the trunk, asked, "Sleepy?"

"No!" the boy replied pluckily.

Kojirō patted him on the head. "Your lips have turned blue! You must be cold. Since you're the representative of the House of Yoshioka, you have to be brave and strong. Be patient a little longer and you'll see some interesting things happen." Walking away, he added, "Now I have to find a good place for myself."

The moon had traveled with Musashi from the hollow between Shiga Hill and Uryū Hill, where he'd left Otsū. Now it sank behind the mountain, as a gradual upward movement of the clouds resting on the thirty-six peaks served notice that the world would soon be beginning its daily chores.

He quickened his pace. Directly below him, a temple roof came into view. "It's not far now," he thought. He looked up and reflected that in only a short time—a few breaths—his spirit would join the clouds in their skyward flight. To the universe, the death of one man could hardly have any more significance than that of a butterfly, but in the realm of mankind, a single death could affect everything, for better or worse. Musashi's only concern now was how to die a noble death.

The welcome sound of water struck his ears. Stopping and kneeling at the foot of a tall rock, he scooped some water from the brook and drank quickly. His tongue smarted from its freshness, an indication, he hoped, that his spirit was calm and collected and his courage had not deserted him.

Taking a moment to rest, he seemed to hear voices calling him. Otsū? Jōtarō? He knew it couldn't be Otsū; she was not the kind to lose control of herself and chase after him at a time like this. She knew him too well for that. Still, he couldn't rid himself of the notion that he was being beckoned. He looked back several times, hoping to see someone. The thought that he might be having delusions was unnerving.

But he couldn't afford to waste any more time. Being late would not only mean breaking his promise but put him at a considerable disadvantage. For a lone warrior attempting to take on an army of opponents, the ideal time, he surmised, was the brief interval after the moon had set but before the sky was completely light.

He recalled the old saying "It is easy to crush an enemy outside oneself but impossible to defeat an enemy within." He had vowed to expel Otsū from his thoughts, had even bluntly told her this as she had clung to his sleeve. Yet he seemed unable to shake her voice from his mind.

He cursed softly. "I'm acting like a woman. A man on a man's mission has no business thinking about frivolities like love!"

He spurred himself on, running as fast as he could. Then all at once he caught sight, below him, of a white ribbon rising from the foot of the mountain through the bamboo and trees and fields, one of the roads to Ichijōji. He was only about four hundred yards from the point where it met with the other two roads. Through the milky mist he could make out the branches of the great spreading pine.

He dropped to his knees, his body tense. Even the trees around him seemed transformed into potential enemies. As nimbly as a lizard, he left the path and made his way to a point directly above the pine tree. A gust of cold wind swept down from the mountaintop, pushing the mist in a great rolling wave over the pine trees and bamboo. The branches of the spreading pine quivered, as though to warn the world of impending disaster.

Straining his eyes, he could just discern the figures of ten men standing perfectly still around the pine tree, their lances poised. The presence of others elsewhere on the mountain he could feel, even though he couldn't see them. Musashi knew he had now entered the province of death. A feeling of awe brought goose pimples even to the backs of his hands, but his breathing was deep and steady. Down to the tips of his toes, he was keyed for action. As he crept slowly forward, his toes gripped the ground with the strength and sureness of fingers.

A stone embankment that might once have been part of a fortress was nearby. On an impulse, he made his way among the rocks to the eminence on which it had stood. There he found a stone *torii* looking straight down on the spreading pine. Behind it was the sacred precinct, protected by rows of tall evergreens, among which he could see a shrine building.

Though he had no idea which deity was honored here, he ran through the grove to the shrine gate and knelt before it. With death so near, he could not keep his heart from trembling at the thought of the sacred presence. The shrine was dark inside, save for a holy lamp, swaying in the wind, threatening to expire, then miraculously recapturing its full brightness. The plaque above the door read "Hachidai Shrine."

Musashi took comfort from the thought that he had a powerful ally, that if he charged down the mountain, the god of war would be behind him. The gods, he knew, always supported the side that was right. He recalled how the great Nobunaga, on his way to the Battle of Okehazama, had paused to pay his respects at the Atsuta Shrine. The discovery of this holy place seemed felicitous indeed.

Just inside the gate was a stone basin, where supplicants could cleanse themselves before praying. He rinsed out his mouth, then took a second mouthful and sprayed water on the hilt of his sword and the cords of his sandals. Thus purified, he hitched up his sleeves with a leather thong and tied on a cotton headband. Flexing his leg muscles as he walked, he went to the steps of the shrine and put his hand on the rope hanging from the gong above the entrance. In time-honored fashion, he was about to give the gong a rap and say a prayer to the deity.

Catching himself, he quickly withdrew his hand. "What am I doing?" he thought in horror. The rope, plaited with red and white cotton cord, seemed to be inviting him to take hold of it, sound the gong and make his supplication. He stared at it. "What was I going to request?" he asked himself. "What need have I of the help of the gods? Am I not already one with the universe? Haven't I always said I must be prepared to face death at any time? Haven't I trained myself to face death calmly and confidently?"

He was appalled. Without thinking, without remembering his years of training and self-discipline, he had been on the brink of begging for supernatural assistance. Something was wrong, for deep down he knew that the samurai's true ally was not the gods but death itself. Last night and earlier this morning, he had felt confident that he had come to terms with his fate. And yet, there he was within a hairbreadth of forgetting all he had ever learned, beseeching aid from the deity. Head drooped in shame, he stood there like a rock.

"What a fool I am! I thought I'd achieved purity and enlightenment, but there is still, within me, something that longs to go on living. Some delusion stirring up thoughts of Otsū or my sister. Some false hope leading me to clutch at any straw. A diabolical yearning, causing me to forget myself, tempting me to pray to the gods for help."

He was disgusted, exasperated, with his body, with his soul, with his failure to master the Way. The tears he had held back in Otsū's presence poured from his eyes.

"It was all unconscious. I had no intention of praying, hadn't even thought of what I was going to pray for. But if I'm doing things unconsciously, that makes it all the worse."

Racked by doubt, he felt foolish and inadequate. Had he ever had the ability to become a warrior in the first place? If he had achieved the state of calm he had aspired to, there should have been no need, not even a subconscious need, for prayers or supplications. In one shattering moment, only minutes before the battle, he had discovered in his heart the true seeds of defeat. It was impossible now to regard his approaching death as the culmination of a samurai's life!

In the next breath a surge of gratitude swept over him. The presence and magnanimity of the deity enveloped him. The battle had not yet begun; the real test still lay before him. He had been warned in time. By recognizing his failure, he had overcome it. Doubt vanished; the deity had guided him to this place to teach him this.

While believing sincerely in the gods, he did not consider it the Way of the Samurai to seek their aid. The Way was an ultimate truth transcending gods and Buddhas. Stepping back a pace, he folded his hands and, rather than ask for protection, thanked the gods for their timely help.

After a quick bow, he hurried out of the shrine compound and down the narrow, steep path, the sort of path which a heavy downpour would quickly convert into a rushing stream. Pebbles and brittle clumps of dirt tumbled down at his heels, breaking the silence. When the spreading pine came into view again, he leaped off the path and crouched in the bushes. Not a drop of dew had yet fallen from the leaves, and his knees and chest were soon drenched. The pine tree was no more than forty or fifty paces below him. He could see the man with the musket in its branches.

His anger flashed. "Cowards!" he said, almost out loud. "All this against one man."

In a way he felt a little sorry for an enemy who had to go to such extremes. Still, he had expected something like this and was, insofar as possible, prepared for it. Since they would naturally assume that he was not alone, prudence would dictate that they have at least one flying weapon, and probably more. If they were also using short bows, the archers were probably hidden behind rocks or on lower ground.

Musashi had one great advantage: both the man in the tree and the men underneath it had their backs to him. Stooping so low that the hilt of his sword rose above his head, he crept, almost crawled, forward. Then he covered about twenty paces at a dead run.

The musketeer twisted his head around, spotted him and shouted, "There he is!"

Musashi ran on another ten paces, knowing that the man would have to reverse his position to aim and fire.

"Where?" cried the men nearest the tree.

"Behind you!" came the throat-splitting reply.

The musketeer had his weapon trained on Musashi's head. While sparks from the fuse showered down, Musashi's right elbow described an arc in the air. The rock he hurled hit the fuse squarely with terrific force. The musketeer's scream mingled with the sound of cracking branches as he plunged to the ground.

In an instant Musashi's name was on every man's lips. Not one of them had taken the trouble to think the situation through, to imagine that he might devise a means of attacking the central corps first. Their confusion was all but total. In their rush to reorient themselves, the ten men bumped into each other, got their weapons tangled, tripped each other with their lances and otherwise displayed a perfect picture of disorder, all the while screaming at each other not to let Musashi escape.

Just as they sorted themselves out and began to form a semicircle, they were challenged: "I am Miyamoto Musashi, the son of Shimmen Munisai of Mimasaka Province. I have come in accordance with our agreement made the day before yesterday at Yanagimachi.

"Genjirō, are you there? I beg you not to be careless like Seijūrō and Denshichirō before you. I understand that, because of your youth, you have several score men to support you. I, Musashi, have come alone. Your men may attack individually or in a group, as they wish.

"Now, fight!"

Another total surprise: no one expected Musashi to deliver a formal challenge. Even those who would desperately have liked to reply in kind lacked the necessary composure.

"Musashi, you're late!" cried a hoarse voice.

Many took encouragement from Musashi's declaration that he was alone, but Genzaemon and Jūrōzaemon, believing it was a trick, started looking around for phantom seconds.

A loud twang off to one side was followed a split second later by the glint of Musashi's sword flashing through the air. The arrow aimed at his face broke, half falling behind his shoulder, the other half near the tip of his lowered sword.

Or rather where his sword had just been, for Musashi was already on the move. His hair bristling like a lion's mane, he was bounding toward the shadowy form behind the spreading pine.

Genjirō hugged the trunk, screaming, "Help! I'm scared!"

Genzaemon jumped forward, howling as though the blow had struck him, but he was too late. Musashi's sword sliced a two-foot strip of bark off the trunk. It fell to the ground by Genjirō's blood-covered head.

It was the act of a ferocious demon. Musashi, ignoring the others, had made straight for the boy. And it seemed he had had this in mind from the beginning.

The assault was of a savagery beyond conception. Genjirō's death did not reduce the Yoshiokas' fighting capacity in the slightest. What had been nervous excitement rose to the level of murderous frenzy.

"Beast!" screamed Genzaemon, face livid with grief and rage. He rushed headlong at Musashi, wielding a sword somewhat too heavy for a man of his age. Musashi shifted his right heel back a foot or so, leaned aside and struck upward, grazing Genzaemon's elbow and face with the tip of his sword. It was impossible to tell who wailed, for at that moment a man attacking Musashi from the rear with a lance stumbled forward and fell on top of the old man. The next instant, a third swordsman coming from the front was sliced from shoulder to navel. His head sagged and his arms went limp as his legs carried his lifeless body forward a few more steps.

The other men near the tree screamed their lungs out, but the calls for help were lost in the wind and trees. Their comrades were too far away to hear and couldn't have seen what happened even if they'd been looking toward the pine tree instead of watching the roads.

The spreading pine had been standing for hundreds of years. It had witnessed the retreat of the defeated Taira troops from Kyoto to Ōmi in the wars of the twelfth century. Innumerable were the times it had seen the warrior-priests of Mount Hiei descend on the capital to put pressure on the Imperial Court. Whether out of gratitude for the fresh blood seeping through to its roots or out of anguish over the carnage, its branches stirred in the misty wind and scattered drops of cold dew on the men beneath. The wind gave rise to a medley of sounds, from the branches, from the swaying bamboo, from the mist, from the tall grass.

Musashi took a stance with his back against the tree trunk, whose girth could hardly be spanned by two men with outstretched arms. The tree made an ideal shield for his rear, but he seemed to consider it hazardous to stay there long. As his eye traveled down the top edge of his sword and fastened on his opponents, his brain reviewed the terrain, searched for a better position.

"Go to the spreading pine! The pine tree! The fighting's there!" The shout came from the top of the rise from which Sasaki Kojirō had chosen to view the spectacle.

Then came a deafening report from the musket, and at last the samurai of the House of Yoshioka grasped what was going on. Swarming like bees, they left their hiding places and hurtled toward the crossroads.

Musashi slipped deftly sideways. The bullet lodged in the tree trunk, inches from his head. On guard, the seven men facing him edged around a couple of feet to compensate for his change in position.

Without warning, Musashi darted toward the man at the extreme left, his sword held at eye level. The man—Kobashi Kurando, one of the Yoshioka Ten—was taken completely by surprise. With a low cry of dismay, he whirled on one foot, but he was not quick enough to escape the blow to his side. Musashi, sword still extended, continued running straight ahead.

"Don't let him get away!"

The other six rushed after him. But the attack had again thrown them into perilous disarray, all coordination lost. In a flash, Musashi spun around, striking laterally at the nearest man, Miike Jūrōzaemon. Experienced swordsman that he was, Jūrōzaemon had anticipated this and left some play in his legs, so that he was able to quickly move backward. The tip of Musashi's sword barely grazed his chest.

Musashi's use of his weapon differed from that of the ordinary swordsman of his time. By normal techniques, if the first blow did not connect, the force of the sword was spent in the air. It was necessary to bring the blade back before striking again. This was too slow for Musashi. Whenever he struck laterally, there was a return blow. A slice to the right was followed in essentially the same motion by a return strike to the left. His blade created two streaks of light, the pattern very much like two pine needles joined at one end.

The unexpected return stroke slashed upward through Jūrōzaemon's face, turning his head into a large red tomato.

Not having studied under a teacher, Musashi found himself occasionally at a disadvantage, but there were also times when he had profited from this. One of his strengths was that he had never been pressed into the mold of any particular school. From the orthodox point of view, his style had no discernible form, no rules, no secret techniques. Created by his own imagination and his own needs, it was hard to define or categorize. To an extent, he could be challenged effectively using conventional styles, if his opponent was highly skilled. Jūrōzaemon had not anticipated Musashi's tactic. Anyone adept at the Yoshioka Style, or for that matter at any of the other Kyoto styles, would probably have been taken unawares in similar fashion.

If, following through on his fatal blow to Jūrōzaemon, Musashi had charged the motley group that remained around the tree, he would certainly have slain several more of them in short order. Instead he ran toward the crossroads. But then, just as they thought he was about to flee, he suddenly turned and attacked again. By the time they had regrouped to defend themselves, he was gone again.

"Musashi!"

"Coward!"

"Fight like a man!"

"We're not through with you yet!"

The usual imprecations filled the air, as furious eyes threatened to pop out of their sockets. The men were drunk on the sight and smell of blood, as drunk as if they had swallowed a storehouseful of sake. The sight of blood, which makes a brave man cooler, has the opposite effect on cowards. These men were like goblins surfacing from a lake of gore.

Leaving the shouts behind him, Musashi reached the crossroads and plunged immediately into the narrowest of the three paths of exit, the one leading toward the Shugakuin. Coming helter-skelter from the opposite direction were the men who had been stationed along the path. Before he had gone forty paces, Musashi saw the first man in this contingent. By the ordinary laws of physics, he would soon be trapped between these men and those pursuing him. In fact, when the two forces collided, he was no longer there.

"Musashi! Where are you?"

"He came this way. I saw him!"

"He must have!"

"He's not here!"

Musashi's voice broke through the confused babble. "Here I am!"

He jumped from the shadow of a rock to the middle of the road behind the returning samurai, so that he had them all to one side. Dumbfounded by this lightning change of position, the Yoshioka men moved on him as rapidly as they could, but in the narrow path they could not concentrate their strength. Considering the space needed to swing a sword, it would have been dangerous for even two of them to try to move forward abreast.

The man nearest Musashi stumbled backward, pushing the man behind him back into the oncoming group. For a time, they all floundered about helplessly, legs clumsily entwined. But mobs do not give up easily. Though frightened by Musashi's speed and ferocity, the men soon gained confidence in their collective strength. With a stirring roar, they moved forward, again convinced that no single swordsman was a match for all of them.

Musashi fought like a swimmer battling giant waves. Striking once, then retreating a step or two, he had to give more attention to his defense than to his attack. He even refrained from cutting down men who stumbled into range and were easy prey, both because their loss would only result in meager gains and because, if he missed, he would have been exposed to the thrusts of the enemy's lances. It was possible to judge the range of a sword accurately, but not that of a lance.

As he continued his slow retreat, his attackers pressed on relentlessly. His face was bluish-white; it seemed inconceivable that he was breathing adequately. The Yoshioka men hoped that he would eventually stumble on a tree root or trip on a rock. At the same time, none of them was eager to get too close to a man fighting desperately for his life. The nearest of the swords and lances pressing in on him were always two or three inches short of their target.

The tumult was punctuated by the whinnying of a packhorse; people were up and about in the nearby hamlet. This was the hour when early-rising priests passed by on their way to and from the top of Mount Hiei, clopping along on raised wooden sandals, their shoulders proudly squared. As the battle progressed, woodcutters and farmers joined the priests on the road to witness the spectacle, and then excited cries set up an answering response from every chicken and horse in the village. A crowd of bystanders collected around the shrine where Musashi had prepared for battle. The wind had dropped and the mist descended again like a thick white veil. Then all of a sudden it lifted, giving the spectators a clear view.

During the few minutes of fighting, Musashi's appearance had changed completely. His hair was matted and gory; blood mixed with sweat had dyed his headband pink. He looked like the devil incarnate, charging up from hell. He was breathing with his whole body, his shieldlike chest heaving like a volcano. A rip in his *hakama* exposed a wound on his left knee; the white ligaments visible at the bottom of the gash were like seeds in a split pomegranate. There was also a cut on his forearm, which, though not serious, had spattered blood from his chest to the small sword in his obi. His whole kimono appeared to have been tie-dyed with a crimson design. Onlookers who had a clear view of him covered their eyes in horror.

More ghastly still was the sight of the dead and wounded left in his wake. As he continued his tactical retreat up the path, he reached a patch of open land where his pursuers surged forward in a mass attack. In a matter of seconds, four or five men had been cut down. They lay scattered over a wide area, moribund testimony to the speed with which Musashi struck and moved on. He seemed to be everywhere at once.

But for all his agile shifts and dodges, Musashi clung to one basic strategy. He never attacked a group from the front or the side—always obliquely at an exposed corner. Whenever a battery of samurai approached him head on, he somehow contrived to shift like lightning to a corner of their formation, from which he could confront only one or two of them at a time. In this way, he managed to keep them in essentially the same position. But eventually, Musashi was bound to be worn down. Eventually, too, his opponents seemed bound to find a way to thwart his method of attack. To do this, they would need to form themselves into two large forces, before and behind him. Then he would be in even greater danger. It took all Musashi's resourcefulness to stop that from happening.

At some point, Musashi drew his smaller sword and started to fight with both hands. While the large sword in his right hand was smeared with blood, up to the hilt and the fist that held it, the small sword in his left hand was clean. And though it picked up a bit of flesh the first time it was used, it continued to sparkle, greedy for blood. Musashi himself was not yet fully aware that he had drawn it, even though he was wielding it with the same deftness as the larger sword.

When not actually striking, he held the left sword so that it was pointed directly at his opponent's eyes. The right sword extended out to the side, forming a broad horizontal arc with his elbow and shoulder, and was largely outside the enemy's line of vision. If the opponent moved to Musashi's right, he could bring the right sword into play. If the attacker moved the other way, Musashi could shift the small sword in to his left and trap him between the two swords. By thrusting forward, he could pin the man in one place with the smaller sword and, before there was time to dodge, attack with the large sword. In later years, this method came to be formally named the Two-Sword Technique Against a Large Force, but at this moment he was fighting by pure instinct.

By all accepted standards, Musashi was not a great sword technician. Schools, styles, theories, traditions—none of these meant anything to him. His mode of fighting was completely pragmatic. What he knew was only what he had learned from experience. He wasn't putting theory into practice; he fought first and theorized later.

The Yoshioka men, from the Ten Swordsmen on down, had all had the theories of the Kyōhachi Style pounded thoroughly into their skulls. Some of them had even gone on to create stylistic variations of their own. Despite being highly trained and highly disciplined fighters, they had no way of gauging a swordsman like Musashi, who had spent his time as an ascetic in the mountains, exposing himself to the dangers presented by nature as often as to those presented by man. To the Yoshioka men, it was incomprehensible that Musashi, with his breathing so erratic, face ashen, eyes bleary with sweat and body covered with gore, was still able to wield two swords and threaten to make short work of anyone who came within range. But he fought on like a god of fire and fury. They themselves were dead tired, and their attempts to pin down this bloody specter were becoming hysterical.

All at once, the tumult increased.

"Run!" cried a thousand voices.

"You, fighting by yourself, run!"

"Run while you can!"

The shouts came from the mountains, the trees, the white clouds above. Spectators on all sides saw the Yoshioka forces actually closing in on Musashi. The impending peril moved them all to try to save him, if only with their voices.

But their warnings made no impression. Musashi would not have noticed if the earth had split asunder or the heavens cast down crackling bolts of lightning. The uproar reached a crescendo, shaking the thirty-six peaks like an earthquake. It issued simultaneously from the spectators and the jostling throng of Yoshioka samurai.

Musashi had finally taken off across the mountainside with the speed of a wild boar. In no time, five or six men were on his heels, trying desperately to get in a solid blow.

Musashi, with a vicious howl, suddenly wheeled, crouched and swung his sword sideways at shin level, stopping them in their tracks. One man brought his lance down from above, only to see it knocked into the air by a powerful counterblow. They shrank back. Musashi swung fiercely with the left sword, then the right, then the left again. Moving like a combination of fire and water, he had his enemies reeling and cowering, tottering and stumbling in his wake.

Then he was gone again. He had leapt from the open land across which the battle had been raging into a green field of barley below.

530   "Stop!"

"Come back and fight!"

Two men in hot pursuit jumped blindly after Musashi. A second later, there were two death screams, two lances flying through the air and coming to rest upright in the middle of the field. Musashi was slithering like a great ball of mud through the far end of the field. Already a hundred yards away, he was rapidly widening the gap.

"He's going toward the village."

"He's heading for the main road."

But in fact he had crawled rapidly and invisibly up the far edge of the field and was now hidden in the woods above. He watched his pursuers dividing up to continue their chase in several directions.

It was daylight, a sunny morning, much like any other.

An Offering for the Dead

When Oda Nobunaga finally lost patience with the priests' political machinations, he attacked the ancient Buddhist establishment on Mount Hiei, and in one horrendous night, all but a few of its three thousand temples and shrines had gone up in flames. Though four decades had passed and the main hall and a number of secondary temples had been rebuilt, the memory of that night hung like a shroud over the mountain. The establishment was now stripped of its temporal powers, and the priests devoted their time once again to religious duties.

Situated on the southernmost peak, commanding a view of the other temples and of Kyoto itself, was a small, secluded temple known as the Mudōji. It was rare for the stillness to be broken by any sound less peaceful than the rippling of a brook or the chirping of small birds.

From the inner recesses of the temple came a masculine voice reciting the words of Kannon, the Goddess of Mercy, as revealed in the Lotus Sutra. The monotone would rise gradually for a time, then, as if the chanter had suddenly remembered himself, sink abruptly.

Along the jet black floor of the corridor walked a white-robed acolyte, carrying at eye level a tray on which had been placed the meager, meatless meal customarily served in religious establishments. Entering the room from which the voice was coming, he placed the tray in one corner, knelt politely and said, "Good day, sir."

Leaning slightly forward, absorbed in his work, the guest did not hear the boy's greeting.

531

"Sir," said the acolyte, raising his voice slightly, "I've brought your lunch. I'll leave it here in the corner, if you wish."

"Oh, thank you," replied Musashi, straightening up. "That's very kind of you." He turned and bowed.

"Would you like to eat now?"

"Yes."

"Then I'll serve you your rice."

Musashi accepted the bowl of rice and began eating. The acolyte stared first at the block of wood by Musashi's side, then at the small knife behind him. Chips and slivers of fragrant white sandalwood lay scattered about.

"What are you carving?" he asked.

"It's to be a sacred image."

"The Buddha Amida?"

"No. Kannon. Unfortunately, I don't know anything about sculpture. I seem to be cutting my hands more than the wood." He held out a couple of well-nicked fingers as evidence, but the boy seemed more interested in the white bandage around his forearm.

"How are your wounds?" he asked.

"Thanks to the good treatment I've received here, they're about healed now. Please tell the head priest I am very grateful."

"If you're carving an image of Kannon, you should visit the main hall. There's a statue of Kannon by a very famous sculptor. If you'd like, I'll take you there. It's not far—only half a mile or so."

Delighted by the offer, Musashi finished his meal, and the two of them started for the main hall. Musashi had not been outdoors in the ten days since he'd arrived, covered with blood and using his sword as a cane. He'd barely begun to walk when he discovered his wounds were not so thoroughly healed as he had thought. His left knee ached, and the breeze, though light and cool, seemed to cut into the gash on his arm. But it was pleasant outside. Blossoms falling from the gently swaying cherry trees danced in the air like snowflakes. The sky showed signs of the azure hue of early summer. Musashi's muscles swelled as if they were buds about to burst open.

"Sir, you're studying the martial arts, aren't you?"

"That's right."

"Then why are you carving an image of Kannon?"

Musashi did not answer immediately.

"Instead of carving, wouldn't it be better to spend your time practicing swordsmanship?"

The question pained Musashi more than his wounds. The acolyte was about the same age as Genjirō, and about the same size.

How many men had been killed or wounded on that fateful day? He could only guess. He had no clear memory even of how he had extricated himself from the fighting and found a place to hide. The only two things that stuck quite clearly in his mind, haunting him in his sleep, were Genjirō's terrified scream and the sight of his mutilated body.

He thought again, as he had several times in the past few days, of the resolution in his notebook: he would do nothing that he would later regret. If he took the view that what he had done was inherent in the Way of the Sword, a bramble lying on his chosen path, then he would have to assume that his future would be bleak and inhuman.

In the peaceful atmosphere of the temple, his mind had cleared. And once the memory of spilled blood and gore began to fade, he was overcome by grief for the boy he had slaughtered.

His mind coming back to the acolyte's question, he said, "Isn't it true that great priests, like Kōbō Daishi and Genshin, made lots of images of the Buddha and bodhisattvas? I understand quite a few statues here on Mount Hiei were carved by priests. What do you think of that?"

Cocking his head, the boy said uncertainly, "I'm not sure, but priests do make religious paintings and statues."

"Let me tell you why. It's because by painting a picture or carving an image of the Buddha, they draw closer to him. A swordsman can purify his spirit in the same way. We human beings all look up at the same moon, but there are many roads we may travel to reach the top of the peak nearest it. Sometimes, when we lose our way, we decide to try someone else's, but the ultimate aim is to find fulfillment in life."

Musashi paused, as though he might have more to say, but the acolyte ran ahead and pointed to a rock almost hidden in the grass. "Look," he said. "This inscription is by Jichin. He was a priest—a famous one."

Musashi read the words carved on the moss-covered stone:

> The water of the Law
> Will presently run shallow.
> At the very end
> A cold, bleak wind will blow on
> The barren peaks of Hiei.

He was impressed by the writer's powers of prophecy. The wind on Mount Hiei had indeed been cold and bleak since Nobunaga's merciless raid. There were rumors that some of the clergy longed for the old days, for a powerful army, political influence and special privileges, and it was a fact that they never selected a new abbot without a lot of intrigue and ugly internal conflict. While the holy mountain was dedicated to the salvation of the sinful, it actually depended on the alms and donations of the sinful for its survival. Altogether not a very happy state of affairs, mused Musashi.

"Let's go," said the boy impatiently.

As they started to walk on, one of the priests from the Mudōji came running after them. "Seinen!" he called to the boy. "Where are you going?"

"To the main hall. He wants to see a statue of Kannon."

"Couldn't you take him some other time?"

"Forgive me for bringing the boy with me when he probably has work to do," said Musashi. "By all means take him back with you. I can go to the main hall anytime."

"I didn't come for him. I'd like you to come back with me, if you don't mind."

"Me?"

533

"Yes, I'm sorry to bother you, but . . . "

"Has somebody come looking for me?" asked Musashi, not at all surprised.

"Well, yes. I told them you weren't in, but they said they'd just seen you with Seinen. They insisted I come and get you."

On the way back to the Mudōji, Musashi asked the priest who his visitors were and learned that they were from the Sannōin, another of the subsidiary temples.

There were about ten of them, dressed in black robes and wearing brown headbands. Their angry faces might well have belonged to the dreaded warrior-priests of old, a haughty race of bullies in clerical robes who had had their wings clipped but apparently had rebuilt their nest. Those who had failed to profit from Nobunaga's lesson swaggered about with great swords at their sides, lording it over others, calling themselves scholars of the Buddhist Law but being in fact intellectual ruffians.

"There he is," said one.

"Him?" asked another contemptuously.

They stared with undisguised hostility.

A burly priest, motioning to Musashi's guides with his lance, said, "Thanks. You're not needed. Go inside the temple!" Then, very gruffly, "Are you Miyamoto Musashi?"

There was no courtesy in the words. Musashi replied curtly, without bowing.

Another priest, appearing from behind the first, declaimed, as though reading from a text, "I shall convey to you the decision handed down by the tribunal of the Enryakuji. It is this: 'Mount Hiei is a pure and sacred precinct, which must not be used as a haven by those who harbor enmities and grudges. Nor can it be offered as a refuge to base men who have engaged in dishonorable conflicts. The Mudōji has been instructed to send you away from the mountain immediately. If you disobey, you shall be strictly punished in accordance with the laws of the monastery.'"

"I shall do as the monastery directs," Musashi replied in a mild tone. "But since it is well past midday and I've made no preparations, I should like to ask that you permit me to stay until tomorrow morning. Also, I'd like to inquire whether this decision came from the civil authorities or from the clergy itself. The Mudōji reported my arrival. I was told there was no objection to my staying. I don't understand why this has changed so suddenly."

"If you really want to know," the first priest replied, "I'll tell you. At first we were glad to extend our hospitality because you fought alone against a large number of men. Later, however, we received bad reports concerning you, which forced us to reconsider. We decided we could no longer afford to provide refuge for you."

"Bad reports?" Musashi thought resentfully. He might have expected that. It required no stretch of the imagination to guess that the Yoshioka School would be vilifying him all over Kyoto. But he saw no point in trying to defend himself. "Very well," he said coldly. "I shall leave tomorrow morning, without fail."

534

As he entered the temple gate, the priests started to malign him.

"Look at him, the evil wretch!"

"He's a monster!"

"Monster? Simple-minded is what he is!"

Turning and glaring at the men, Musashi asked sharply, "What did you say?"

"Oh, you heard, did you?" asked a priest defiantly.

"Yes. And there's one thing I would like you to know. I'll comply with the wishes of the priesthood, but I'm not going to put up with abuse from the likes of you. Are you looking for a fight?"

"As servants of the Buddha, we do not pick fights," came the sanctimonious reply. "I opened my mouth, and the words came out naturally."

"It must be the voice of heaven," said another priest.

The next instant they were all around Musashi, cursing, taunting, even spitting at him. He wasn't sure how long he'd be able to restrain himself. Despite the power the warrior-priests had lost, these latter-day embodiments had lost none of their arrogance.

"Look at him!" sneered one of the priests. "From what the villagers said, I thought he was a self-respecting samurai. Now I see he's only a brainless oaf! He doesn't get angry; he doesn't even know how to speak on his own behalf."

The longer Musashi remained silent, the more viciously the tongues wagged. Finally, his face reddening slightly, he said, "Didn't you say something about the voice of heaven speaking through a man?"

"Yes; what of it?"

"Are you suggesting heaven has spoken out against me?"

"You've heard our decision. Don't you understand yet?"

"No."

"I guess you wouldn't. Having no more sense than you do, you deserve to be pitied. But I daresay in the next life you'll come to your senses!"

When Musashi said nothing, the priest continued, "You'd better be careful after you leave the mountain. Your reputation is nothing to be proud of."

"What does it matter what people say?"

"Listen to him! He still thinks he's right."

"What I did was right! I did nothing base or cowardly in my fight with the Yoshiokas."

"You're talking nonsense!"

"Did I do anything to be ashamed of? Name one thing!"

"You have the gall to say that?"

"I'm warning you. I'll overlook other things, but I won't permit anyone to belittle my sword!"

"Very well, see if you can answer one question. We know you put up a brave fight against overwhelming odds. We admire your brute strength. We praise your courage in holding out against so many men. But why did you murder a boy only thirteen years old? How could you be so inhuman as to slaughter a mere child?"

Musashi's face turned pale; his body suddenly felt weak.

535

The priest went on. "After he lost his arm, Seijūrō became a priest. Denshi-chirō you killed outright. Genjirō was the only person left to succeed them. By murdering him, you put an end to the House of Yoshioka. Even if it was done in the name of the Way of the Samurai, it was cruel, dastardly. You're not good enough to be described as a monster or a demon. Do you consider your-self human? Do you imagine you should be ranked as a samurai? Do you even belong in this great land of the cherry blossoms?

"No! And this is why the priesthood is expelling you. Whatever the circum-stances, slaying the child is unforgivable. A real samurai would commit no crime like that. The stronger a samurai is, the gentler and more considerate he is to the weak. A samurai understands and practices compassion.

"Now go away from here, Miyamoto Musashi! As fast as you can! Mount Hiei rejects you!"

Their anger spent, the priests marched off in a body.

Though he'd borne this last torrent of abuse silently, it wasn't because he had no answer to their charges. "Whatever they say, I was right," he thought. "I did the only thing I could to protect my convictions, which are not mistaken."

He honestly believed in the validity of his principles and in the necessity of upholding them. Once the Yoshiokas had set Genjirō up as their standard-bearer, there had been no alternative to killing him. He was their general. So long as he lived, the Yoshioka School would remain undefeated. Musashi could have killed ten, twenty or thirty men, but unless Genjirō died, the survi-vors would always claim victory. Killing the boy first made Musashi the vic-tor, even if he'd later been killed in the fighting.

By the laws of swordsmanship, there was no flaw in this logic. And to Mu-sashi those laws were absolute.

Nevertheless, the memory of Genjirō disturbed him profoundly, giving rise to doubt, grief and pain. The cruelty of his act was repellent, even to himself.

"Should I throw away my sword and live like an ordinary man?" he asked himself, not for the first time. In the clear, early evening sky, the white petals of the cherry blossoms fell randomly, like flakes of snow, leaving the trees looking as vulnerable as he now felt, vulnerable to doubts about whether he should not change his way of life. "If I give up the sword, I could live with Otsū," he thought. But then he remembered the easygoing lives of the Kyoto townspeople and the world inhabited by Kōetsu and Shōyū.

"That's not for me," he said decisively.

He went through the gate and entered his room. Seated by the lamp, he took up his half-finished work and began carving rapidly. It was vitally im-portant to finish the statue. Whether the craftsmanship was expert or not, he wanted desperately to leave something here to comfort the spirit of the de-parted Genjirō.

The lamp dimmed; he trimmed the wick. In the dead stillness of evening, the sound of tiny chips falling on the tatami was audible. His concentration was total, his whole being focused with perfect intensity on the point of con-tact with the wood. Once he had set himself a task, it was his nature to lose himself in it until it was completed, unmindful of boredom or fatigue.

The tones of the sutra rose and fell.

After each trimming of the wick, he resumed his work with an air of devotion and reverence, like the ancient sculptors who were said to have bowed three times to the Buddha before picking up their chisels to carve an image. His own statue of Kannon would be like a prayer for Genjirō's happiness in the next life and, in a sense, a humble apology to his own soul.

Finally, he mumbled, "I guess this will do." As he straightened up and examined the statue, the bell in the eastern pagoda sounded the second watch of the night, which began at ten o'clock. "It's getting late," he thought, and left immediately to pay his respects to the head priest and ask him to take custody of the statue. The image was roughly carved, but he had put his soul into it, weeping tears of repentance as he prayed for the dead boy's spirit.

No sooner was he out of the room than Seinen came in to sweep the floor. When the room was again tidy, he laid out Musashi's pallet and, broom over shoulder, sauntered back to the kitchen. Unknown to Musashi, while he was still carving, a catlike figure had crept into the Mudōji, through doors that were never locked, and onto the veranda. After Seinen was out of sight, the shoji onto the veranda slid silently open and just as silently shut.

Musashi returned with his going-away presents, a basket hat and a pair of straw sandals. Placing them beside his pillow, he extinguished the lamp and crawled into bed. The outer doors were open and a breeze blew softly through the corridors. There was just enough moonlight to give the white paper of the shoji a dull gray hue. Tree shadows swayed gently, like waves on a calm, open sea.

He snored softly, breathing more slowly as he sank deeper into sleep. Silently, the edge of a small screen in the corner shifted forward, and a dark figure crawled stealthily out on hands and knees. The snoring halted, and the black form quickly spread itself flat on the floor. Then, as the breathing steadied, the intruder advanced inch by inch, patiently, cautiously, coordinating his movements with the rhythmical breathing.

All at once, the shadow rose like a cloud of black floss and descended on Musashi, crying, "Now I'll teach you!" A short sword swept toward Musashi's neck. But the weapon clattered to one side as the black form flew back through the air and landed with a crash against the shoji. The invader emitted one loud wail before tumbling, along with the shoji, into the darkness outside.

At the instant Musashi made his throw, it crossed his mind that the person in his hands was as light as a kitten. Though the face had been swathed in cloth, he thought he had caught a glimpse of white hair. Without pausing to analyze these impressions, he grabbed his sword and ran out onto the veranda.

"Stop!" he shouted. "Since you've gone to the trouble of coming here, give me a chance to greet you properly!" Leaping to the ground, he ran swiftly toward the sound of retreating footsteps. But his heart was not in it. After a few seconds, he stopped and watched laughingly as some priests disappeared into the darkness.

Osugi, after her bone-jarring landing, lay on the ground groaning with pain.

"Why, Granny, it's you!" he exclaimed, surprised that his attacker was neither a Yoshioka man nor one of the irate priests. He put his arm around her to help her up.

"Now I begin to understand," he said. "You're the one who told the priests a lot of bad things about me, aren't you? And since the story came from a courageous, upright old lady, they believed every word of it, I suppose."

"Oh, my back hurts!" Osugi neither confirmed nor denied his accusation. She squirmed a bit but lacked the strength to put up much resistance. Feebly she said, "Musashi, since it's come to this, it's no use worrying about right and wrong. The House of Hon'iden has been unlucky in war, so just cut off my head now."

It seemed unlikely to Musashi that she was merely being dramatic. Hers sounded like the honest words of a woman who had gone as far as she could and wanted to put an end to it.

"Are you in pain?" he asked, refusing to take her seriously. "Where does it hurt? You can stay here tonight, so there's nothing to worry about." He lifted her in his arms, carried her inside and laid her on his pallet. Sitting by her side, he nursed her through the night.

When the sky lightened, Seinen brought the lunch box Musashi had requested, along with a message from the head priest, who, while apologizing for being rude, urged Musashi to be on his way as quickly as possible.

Musashi sent word explaining that he now had an ailing old woman on his hands. The priest, not wanting Osugi at the temple, offered a suggestion. It seemed that a merchant from the town of Ōtsu had come to the temple with a cow and left the animal in the head priest's care while he went off on a side trip. The priest offered Musashi the use of the animal, saying that Musashi could let the woman ride it down the mountain. In Ōtsu, the cow could be left at the wharf or at one of the wholesale houses in the vicinity.

Musashi accepted the offer gratefully.

A Drink of Milk

The road descending along a ridge from Mount Hiei came out in Ōmi Province, at a point just beyond the Miidera.

Musashi was leading the cow by a rope. Looking over his shoulder, he said gently, "If you want, we can stop and rest. It's not as though either of us is in a hurry." But at least, he thought, they were on their way. Osugi, unused to cows, had at first flatly refused to get on the animal. It had taken all his ingenuity to persuade her, the argument that worked being that she could not remain indefinitely in a priestly bastion of celibacy.

Face down on the cow's neck, Osugi groaned painfully and readjusted herself. At every sign of solicitude on Musashi's part, she reminded herself of her hatred, silently conveying her contempt at being cared for by her mortal enemy.

Though he was well aware that she lived for no other reason than to take revenge on him, he found himself unable to regard her as a genuine foe. No one, not even enemies much stronger than she was, had ever caused him so much trouble or embarrassment. Her trickery had brought him to the brink of disaster in his own village; because of her he had been jeered and reviled at Kiyomizudera; time and again she had tripped him up and thwarted his plans. There had been times, such as the previous night, when he had cursed her and very nearly given in to the urge to slice her in two.

Still, he could not bring himself to lay a hand on her, especially now, when she was ailing and bereft of her customary verve. Oddly, the inactivity of her vicious tongue depressed him, and he longed to see her restored to health, even if this meant more trouble for him.

"Riding that way must be pretty uncomfortable," he said. "Try to bear up a little longer. When we get to Ōtsu, I'll think of something."

The view to the northeast was magnificent. Lake Biwa was spread out placidly below them, Mount Ibuki was just beyond, and the peaks of Echizen rose in the distance. On the near side of the lake, Musashi could make out each of the famous Eight Views of Karasaki in the village of Seta.

"Let's stop for a while," he said. "You'll feel better if you get off and lie down for a few minutes." Tying the animal to a tree, he put his arms around her and lifted her down.

Face down on the ground, Osugi pushed his hands away and let out a groan. Her face was feverishly hot and her hair was a mess.

"Don't you want some water?" Musashi asked, not for the first time, rubbing her on the back. "You should eat something too." She shook her head stubbornly. "You haven't drunk a drop of water since last night," he said pleadingly. "If you keep this up, you'll just make yourself worse. I'd like to get some medicine for you, but there aren't any houses around here. Look, why don't you eat half of my lunch?"

"How disgusting!"

"Huh?"

"I'd rather die in some field and get eaten by the birds. I'd never sink so low as to accept food from an enemy!" She shook his hand off her back and clutched at the grass.

Wondering if she would ever get over her basic misunderstanding, he treated her as tenderly as he would his own mother, patiently trying to soothe her each time she lashed out at him.

"Now, Granny, you know you don't want to die. You've got to live. Don't you want to see Matahachi make something of himself?"

She bared her teeth and snarled, "What's that got to do with you? Mataha- 539 chi'll get ahead one of these days without your help, thank you."

"I'm sure he will. But you must get well so that you yourself can encourage him."

"You hypocrite!" the old woman screamed. "You're wasting your time if you think you can flatter me into forgetting how much I hate you."

Realizing that anything he said would be taken the wrong way, Musashi stood up and walked away. He chose a spot behind a rock and began eating his lunch of rice balls stuffed with a dark, sweetish bean paste and individually wrapped in oak leaves. Half of them he left uneaten.

Hearing voices, he looked around the rock and saw a country woman talking with Osugi. She was dressed in the *hakama* worn by the women of Ōhara, and her hair hung down around her shoulders. In stentorian tones, she was saying, "I've got this sick person at my place. She's better now, but she'd recover even quicker if I could give her some milk. May I milk the cow?"

Osugi lifted her face and looked at the woman inquiringly. "We don't have many cows where I come from. Can you actually get milk from her?"

The two exchanged a few more words as the woman squatted down and began squirting milk into a sake jar. When it was full, she stood up, clutching it tightly in her arms, and said, "Thanks. I'll be going now."

"Wait!" cried Osugi in a raspy voice. She stretched out her arms and glanced around to make sure Musashi was not watching. "Give me some milk first. Just a sip or two will be enough."

The woman watched, astonished, as Osugi put the jar to her lips, closed her eyes and gulped greedily, dribbling milk down her chin.

When she was through, Osugi shuddered, then grimaced as though she might vomit. "What a nasty taste!" she whined. "But maybe it'll make me better. It's awful, though; viler than medicine."

"Is something the matter? Are you sick?"

"Nothing serious. Cold and a little fever." She stood up briskly, as though all her ailments had dropped away, and after again reassuring herself that Musashi wasn't looking, drew closer to the woman and asked in a low voice, "If I go straight down this road, where will it take me?"

"Just above the Miidera."

"That's in Ōtsu, isn't it? Is there a back way I could take?"

"Well, yes, but where do you want to go?"

"I don't care. I just want to get away from that villain!"

"About eight or nine hundred yards down this road, there's a path going off to the north. If you keep on that, you'll end up between Sakamoto and Ōtsu."

"If you meet a man looking for me," Osugi said furtively, "don't tell him you saw me." She bumbled off, like a lame praying mantis in a hurry, brushing clumsily past the woman.

Musashi chuckled and came out from behind his rock. "I suppose you live around here," he said amicably. "Your husband, he's a farmer, woodcutter, something like that?"

The woman cowered, but answered, "Oh, no. I'm from the inn at the top of
540   the pass."

"So much the better. If I gave you some money, would you run an errand for me?"

"I'd be glad to, but you see, there's this sick person at the inn."

"I could take the milk back for you and wait for you there. How would that be? If you go now, you should be back before dark."

"In that case, I guess I could go, but—"

"Nothing to worry about! I'm not the villain the old woman said I am. I was only trying to help her. If she can get about on her own, there's no reason for me to worry about her. Now I'll just write a note. I want you to take it to the house of Lord Karasumaru Mitsuhiro. That's in the north part of the city."

With the brush from his writing kit, he quickly scribbled the words he had been longing to write to Otsū during his recuperation at the Mudōji. Having entrusted his letter to the woman, he mounted the cow and lumbered off, repeating the words he had written and speculating on how Otsū would feel when she read them. "And I thought I'd never see her again," he mumbled, suddenly coming to life.

"Considering how weak she was," he mused, "she may be sick in bed again. But when she receives my letter, she'll get up and come as fast as she can. Jōtarō too."

He allowed the cow to proceed at her own pace, stopping from time to time to let her nibble grass. His letter to Otsū was simple, but he was rather pleased with it: "At Hanada Bridge, it was you who waited. This time, let it be me. I've gone on ahead. I'll wait for you in Ōtsu, at Kara Bridge in the village of Seta. When we're together again, we'll talk of many things." He had tried to give the matter-of-fact message a poetic cast. He recited it again to himself, pondering the "many things" they had to discuss.

When he reached the inn, he got off the cow and, holding the jar of milk in both hands, called, "Anybody here?"

As was usual in roadside establishments of this sort, there was an open area under the front eaves for travelers who stopped to have tea or a light meal. Inside was a tea room, a section of which formed the kitchen. Rooms for guests were in the rear. An old woman was putting wood into an earthen oven, on top of which was a wooden steamer.

As he took a seat on a bench out front, she came and poured him a cup of lukewarm tea. He then explained himself and handed her the jar.

"What's this?" she asked, eyeing him dubiously.

Thinking that perhaps she was deaf, he slowly repeated what he had said.

"Milk, you say? Milk? What for?" Still puzzled, she turned toward the interior and called, "Sir, can you come out here a minute? I don't know what this is all about."

"What?" A man ambled around the corner of the inn and asked, "What's the trouble, ma'am?"

She thrust the jar into his hands, but he neither looked at it nor heard what she was saying. His eyes were glued on Musashi, his face a study in disbelief.

Musashi, equally astounded, cried, "Matahachi!"

"Takezō!"

The two rushed at each other, stopping just before they collided. When Musashi held out his arms, Matahachi did the same thing, letting go of the jar.

"How many years?"

"Not since Sekigahara."

"That makes it . . . "

"Five years. It must be. I'm twenty-two now."

As they hugged each other, the sweet odor of the milk from the broken jar enveloped them, evoking the time when they had both been babes in arms.

"You've become very famous, Takezō. But I guess I shouldn't be calling you Takezō. I'll call you Musashi, like everyone else. I've heard many stories about your success at the spreading pine—and about some things you did before that too."

"Don't embarrass me. I'm still an amateur. But the world's full of people who don't seem to be as good as I am. Say, are you staying here?"

"Yes, I've been here about ten days. I left Kyoto with the idea of going to Edo, but something came up."

"I'm told somebody's sick. Oh, well, can't do anything about it now, but that's why I brought the milk."

"Sick? Oh, yeah . . . my traveling companion."

"That's too bad. Anyway, it's good to see you. The last I heard from you was the letter Jōtarō brought when I was on my way to Nara."

Matahachi hung his head, hoping Musashi wouldn't mention the boastful predictions he'd made at the time.

Musashi put his hand on Matahachi's shoulder, thinking how good it was to see him again and how he'd like to have a good long talk.

"Who's traveling with you?" he asked innocently.

"Oh, it's nobody, nobody you'd be interested in. It's just—"

"It doesn't matter. Let's go somewhere where we can talk."

As they walked away from the inn, Musashi asked, "What are you doing for a living?"

"Work, you mean?"

"Yes."

"I don't have any special talents or skills, so it's hard to get a position with a daimyō. I guess I can't say I do anything in particular."

"You mean you've been loafing all these years?" asked Musashi, vaguely suspecting the truth.

"Stop it. Saying things like that brings back all sorts of unpleasant memories." His mind seemed to drift back to those days in the shadow of Mount Ibuki. "Where I made my great mistake was in taking up with Okō."

"Let's sit down," said Musashi, crossing his legs and dropping to the grass. He felt a twinge of exasperation. Why did Matahachi persist in considering himself inferior? And why did he attribute his troubles to others? "You blame everything on Okō," he said firmly, "but is that any way for a full-grown man to talk? Nobody can create a worthwhile life for you but you yourself."

"I admit I was wrong, but . . . how can I put it? I just don't seem able to alter my fate."

542 "In times like these, you'll never get anywhere thinking that way. Go to Edo

if you want, but when you get there, you're going to find people from all over the country, everyone hungry for money and position. You won't make a name for yourself just doing what the next man does. You'll have to distinguish yourself in some way."

"I should have taken up swordsmanship when I was young."

"Now that you mention it, I wonder if you're cut out to be a swordsman. Anyway, you're just starting out. Maybe you should think of becoming a scholar. I suspect that'd be the best way for you to find a position with a daimyō."

"Don't worry. I'll do something." Matahachi broke off a blade of grass and put it between his teeth. His shame weighed him down. It was mortifying to realize what five years of idleness had done. He'd been able to brush off stories he'd heard about Musashi with comparative ease; confronting him in the flesh like this drove home the contrast between them. In Musashi's overpowering presence, Matahachi had trouble remembering they had once been the best of friends. Even the man's dignity was somehow oppressive. Neither envy nor his competitive urge could save him from the painful awareness of his own inadequacy.

"Cheer up!" said Musashi. But even as he slapped Matahachi on the shoulder, he sensed the man's weakness. "What's done is done. Forget about the past," he urged. "If you killed five years, so what? All it means is you're starting out five years later. Those five years may in their own way hold a valuable lesson."

"They were lousy."

"Oh, I forgot! I just left your mother a little while ago."

"You saw my mother?"

"Yes. I must say, I can't understand why you weren't born with more of her strength and tenacity." Nor, he thought to himself, could he understand why Osugi had a son like this, so shiftless and full of self-pity. He felt like shaking him and reminding him how lucky he was to have a mother at all. Staring at Matahachi, he asked himself how Osugi's wrath could be assuaged. The answer came immediately: if Matahachi would only make something of himself . . .

"Matahachi," he said solemnly. "Why, when you have a mother like yours, don't you try to do something to make her happy? Having no parents, I can't help feeling you're not as grateful as you ought to be. It's not that you don't show her enough respect. But somehow, even though you're blessed with the best thing a person can have, you seem to think no more of it than of so much dirt. If I had a mother like yours, I'd be much more eager to improve myself and do something really worthwhile simply because there'd be someone to share my happiness. Nobody rejoices over a person's accomplishments as much as his parents.

"Maybe it sounds like I'm just spouting moral platitudes. But from a vagabond like me, it's not that. I can't begin to tell you how lonely I feel when I come across a beautiful view, then suddenly realize there's no one to enjoy it with me."

Musashi paused to catch his breath and took hold of his friend's hand. "You 543 yourself know what I'm saying is true. You know I'm speaking as an old friend, a man from the same village. Let's try to recapture the spirit we had when we went off to Sekigahara. There are no more wars now, but the struggle to survive in a peaceful world is no less difficult. You have to fight; you have to have a plan. If you'd give it a try, I'd do anything I could to help."

Matahachi's tears dropped onto their clutched hands. Despite the resemblance of Musashi's words to one of his mother's tiresome sermons, he was deeply moved by his friend's concern.

"You're right," he said, wiping away his tears. "Thanks. I'll do what you say. I'll become a new man, right now. I agree, I'm not the type to succeed as a swordsman. I'll go to Edo and find a teacher. Then I'll study hard. I swear I will."

"I'll keep my eyes open for a good teacher, as well as a good master you might work for. You could even work and study at the same time."

"It'll be like starting life over again. But there's something else that bothers me."

"Well? As I said, I'll do anything I can to help. That's the least I can do to make up for making your mother so angry."

"It's sort of embarrassing. You see, my companion is a woman.... Not just any woman. It's—oh, I can't say it."

"Come on, act like a man!"

"Don't get angry. It's somebody you know."

"Who?"

"Akemi."

Startled, Musashi thought: "Could he have picked anybody worse?" but he caught himself before saying it out loud.

True, Akemi was not as sexually depraved as her mother, not yet at least, but she was well on her way—a bird on the wing with a destructive torch in its mouth. Besides the incident with Seijūrō, Musashi strongly suspected there had been something going on between her and Kojirō. He wondered what perverse fate led Matahachi to women like Okō and her daughter.

Matahachi misinterpreted Musashi's silence as a sign of jealousy. "Are you angry? I told you honestly, because I didn't think I should hide it."

"You simpleton, it's you I'm worried about. Have you been cursed since birth, or do you go out of your way to find bad luck? I thought you'd learned your lesson from Okō."

In reply to Musashi's questions, Matahachi told him how he and Akemi happened to be together. "Maybe I'm being punished for deserting Mother," he concluded. "Akemi hurt her leg when she fell into the ravine, and it began to get worse, so—"

"Oh, here you are, sir!" said the old woman from the inn in the local dialect. Vague and senile, she put her arms behind her back and looked up at the sky, as though checking on the weather. "The sick woman isn't with you," she added, her flat inflection leaving it unclear as to whether she was asking or telling.

Flushing slightly, Matahachi said, "Akemi? Has something happened to her?"

"She's not in bed."

"Are you sure?"

"She was there a while ago, but she isn't now."

Though a sixth sense told Musashi what had happened, he merely said, "We'd better go see."

Akemi's bedding was still spread out on the floor, but otherwise the room was bare.

Matahachi cursed and made a futile circuit of the room. Face burning with rage, he said, "No obi, no money! Not so much as a comb or hairpin! She's crazy! What's wrong with her—deserting me like this!"

The old woman was standing in the doorway. "Terrible thing to do," she said, as if to herself. "That girl—maybe I shouldn't say it—but she wasn't sick. Putting on, she was, so she could stay in bed. I may be old, but I can see through things like that."

Matahachi ran out and stood staring down the white road curving along the ridge. The cow, lying under a peach tree whose blossoms had already darkened and fallen, broke the silence with a long, sleepy-sounding moo.

"Matahachi," said Musashi, "why stand there moping? Let's pray she finds a place where she can settle down and lead a peaceful life, and let it go at that."

A single yellow butterfly was tossed high in the swirling breeze before plummeting over the edge of a cliff.

"Your promise made me very happy," said Musashi. "Now, isn't it time to do something about it, really try and make something of yourself?"

"Yes, I have to, don't I?" mumbled Matahachi without enthusiasm, biting his lower lip to keep it from trembling.

Musashi swung him around, diverting his eyes from the deserted road. "Look here," he said cheerfully. "Your path has opened up of its own accord. Wherever Akemi's headed, it isn't right for you. Go now, before it's too late. Take the path that comes out between Sakamoto and Ōtsu. You should catch up with your mother before the day is out. Once you've found her, don't ever lose sight of her again."

To emphasize the point, he brought Matahachi's sandals and leggings, then went into the inn and came back with his other belongings.

"Do you have any money?" he asked. "I don't have much myself, but you can have part of it. If you think Edo's the place for you, I'll go there with you. Tonight I'll be at the Kara Bridge in Seta. After you find your mother, look for me there. I'm counting on you to bring her."

After Matahachi left, Musashi settled down to wait for twilight and the reply to his letter. Stretching out on the bench in the back of the tea room, he closed his eyes and was soon dreaming. Of two butterflies, drifting in the air, frolicking among intertwining branches. One of the butterflies he recognized . . . Otsū.

When he awoke, the slanting rays of the sun had reached the back wall of the tea room. He heard a man say, "However you look at it, it was a shoddy performance."

"You mean the Yoshiokas?"

"That's right."

"People had too much regard for the school, because of Kempō's reputation. Looks like in any field only the first generation counts for much. The next generation gets lackluster, and by the third, everything falls apart. You don't often see the head of the fourth generation buried by the side of the founder."

"Well, I intend to be buried right next to my great-grandfather."

"You're nothing but a stonecutter anyway. I'm talking about famous people. If you think I'm wrong, just look what happened to Hideyoshi's heir."

The stonecutters worked in a quarry in the valley and around three o'clock every afternoon came up to the inn for a cup of tea. Earlier, one of them, who lived near Ichijōji, had claimed that he saw the battle from beginning to end. Having already told his story dozens of times, he could now deliver it with stirring eloquence, embroidering skillfully on facts and mimicking Musashi's movements.

While the stonecutters were listening raptly to this recital, four other men had arrived and taken seats out front: Sasaki Kojirō and three samurai from Mount Hiei. Their scowling faces made the workmen uneasy, so they'd picked up their teacups and retreated inside. But as the saga gathered steam, they began laughing and commenting, repeating Musashi's name frequently and with obvious admiration.

When Kojirō reached the limit of his forbearance, he called loudly, "You, there!"

"Yes, sir," they chorused, automatically bowing their heads.

"What's going on here? You!" He pointed his steel-ribbed fan at the man. "Talking as if you knew so much. Come out here! The rest of you too! I'm not going to hurt you."

As they shuffled outdoors again, he continued: "I've been listening to you sing the praises of Miyamoto Musashi, and I've had enough. You're talking nonsense!"

There were questioning looks and murmurs of puzzlement.

"Why do you consider Musashi a great swordsman? You—you say you saw the fight the other day, but let me assure you, I, Sasaki Kojirō, also saw it. As the official witness, I observed every detail. Later, I went to Mount Hiei and lectured to the student priests on what I'd seen. Moreover, at the invitation of some eminent scholars, I visited several subsidiary temples and gave more lectures.

"Now, unlike me, you men know nothing about swordsmanship." Condescension was creeping into Kojirō's voice. "You see only who won and who lost, then you join the herd and praise Miyamoto Musashi as though he were the greatest swordsman who ever lived.

"Ordinarily, I wouldn't bother to refute the prattle of ignoramuses, but I feel it's necessary now, because your erroneous opinions are harmful to society at large. Moreover, I wish to expose your fallacies for the benefit of these distinguished scholars who accompany me today. Clean out your ears and listen carefully! I'll tell you what actually happened at the spreading pine and what kind of man Musashi is."

546   Obedient noises issued from the captive audience.

"In the first place," declaimed Kojirō, "let us consider what Musashi really has in mind—his ulterior purpose. To judge from the way he provoked this last bout, I can only conclude that he was trying desperately to sell his name, to make a reputation for himself. To do this, he singled out the House of Yoshioka, the most famous school of swordsmanship in Kyoto, and cleverly picked a fight. By falling victim to this ruse, the House of Yoshioka became Musashi's stepping-stone to fame and success.

"What he did was dishonest. It was already common knowledge that the days of Yoshioka Kempō were over, that the Yoshioka School had fallen into decline. It was like a withered tree, or an invalid close to death. All Musashi had to do was give a push to an empty hulk. Anyone could have done the same, but no one did. Why? Because those of us who understand *The Art of War* already knew the school was powerless. Second, because we did not wish to sully the honored name of Kempō. Yet Musashi chose to provoke an incident, to place challenging signs on the streets of Kyoto, to spread rumors and finally to make a great spectacle of doing what any reasonably skillful swordsman could have done.

"I couldn't begin to enumerate all the cheap, cowardly tricks he resorted to. Consider, for example, that he contrived to be late both for his bout with Yoshioka Seijūrō and for his encounter with Denshichirō. Instead of meeting his enemies head on at the spreading pine, he came by a roundabout way and employed all sorts of base stratagems.

"It's been pointed out that he was only one man fighting against many. That's true, but it's only part of his devilish scheme for promoting his name. He knew full well that because he was outnumbered, the public would sympathize with him. And when it comes to the actual fighting, I can tell you—I observed it personally—it was little more than child's play. Musashi managed to survive for a time with his clever tricks, then, when the chance to flee presented itself, he ran. Oh, I have to admit that to a certain extent he displayed a kind of brute strength. But that doesn't make him an expert swordsman. No, not at all. Musashi's greatest claim to fame is his ability to run fast. At making a rapid getaway, he is without equal."

The words were now streaming from Kojirō's mouth like water over a dam.

"Ordinary people think it's difficult for a lone swordsman to fight against a great number of opponents, but ten men are not necessarily ten times stronger than one man. To the expert, numbers are not always important." Kojirō then gave a professional critique of the battle. It was easy to belittle Musashi's feat, for despite his valor, any knowledgeable observer could have picked out flaws in his performance. When he got around to mentioning Genjirō, Kojirō was scathing. He said the boy's murder was an atrocity, a violation of the ethics of swordsmanship, that could not be condoned from any point of view.

"And let me tell you about Musashi's background," he cried indignantly. He then revealed that within the past few days he'd met Osugi herself on Mount Hiei and had heard the whole, long story of Musashi's duplicity. Sparing no details, he recounted the wrongs suffered by this "sweet old woman."

He ended by saying, "I shudder to think that there are people who shout 547 the praises of this rogue. The effect on public morals is terrifying to contemplate! And this is the reason I've spoken at some length. I have no connection with the House of Yoshioka, nor do I have any personal grudge against Musashi. I've spoken to you fairly and impartially, as a man devoted to the Way of the Sword and as one determined to follow righteously in that Way! I've told you the truth. Remember it!"

Falling silent, he eased his thirst with a cup of tea, then turned to his companions and remarked very quietly, "Ah, the sun's already low in the sky. If you don't start soon, it'll be dark before you reach the Miidera."

The samurai from the temple rose to take their leave.

"Take good care of yourself," said one of them.

"We look forward to seeing you again when you return to Kyoto."

The stonecutters saw their chance and, like prisoners freed by a tribunal, hastened back to the valley, which was now cloaked in purplish shadows and echoed with the singing of nightingales.

Kojirō watched them go, then called into the inn, "I'll put the money for the tea here on the table. By the way, do you have any matchlock fuses?"

The old woman was squatting before the earthen oven, preparing the evening meal. "Fuses?" she said. "There's a bunch hanging in the corner back there. Take as many as you want."

He strode to the corner. As he was pulling two or three of them out of a sheaf, the rest fell on the bench below. Reaching to retrieve them, he couldn't help noticing the two legs stretched out on the bench. His eyes traveled slowly from legs to body to face. The shock was like a solid blow to the solar plexus.

Musashi stared straight at him.

Kojirō sprang back a step.

"Well, well," said Musashi, grinning broadly. Unhurriedly he stood up and went to Kojirō's side, where he stood silently, an amused and knowing expression on his face.

Kojirō tried to smile back, but his facial muscles refused to obey. He realized instantly that Musashi must have overheard every word he'd said, and his embarrassment was all the more unbearable because he felt Musashi was laughing at him. It took him only a moment to recover his usual aplomb, but during that brief interval his confusion was unmistakable.

"Why, Musashi, I didn't expect to find you here," he said.

"Nice to see you again."

"Yes, yes, indeed." Regretting the words even as he spoke them, yet somehow unable to help himself, he went on: "I must say, you've really distinguished yourself since I last saw you. It's hard to believe a mere human being could have fought the way you did. Let me congratulate you. You don't even seem to be any the worse for it."

The trace of a smile still on his lips, Musashi said, with exaggerated politeness, "Thank you for acting as witness that day. And thank you also for the critique you've just given of my performance. Not often are we allowed to see ourselves as others see us. I am much indebted to you for your comments. I assure you I won't forget them."

Despite the quiet tone and lack of rancor, the last statement sent a chill through Kojirō. He recognized it for what it was, a challenge that would have to be met at some future date.

These two men, both proud, both headstrong, both convinced of their own rectitude, were bound to clash head on, sooner or later. Musashi was content to wait, but when he said, "I won't forget," he was only speaking the simple truth. He already regarded his most recent victory as a milestone in his career as a swordsman, a high point in his struggle to perfect himself. Kojirō's calumnies would not go unchallenged indefinitely.

Though Kojirō had embellished his speech to sway his listeners, he actually saw the event very much as he had described it, and his honest opinion was not substantially different from what he had stated. Nor did he doubt for a moment the fundamental accuracy of his appraisal of Musashi.

"I'm glad to hear you say that," said Kojirō. "I wouldn't want you to forget. Nor will I."

Musashi was still smiling as he nodded his agreement.

Entwining Branches

"Otsū, I'm back," Jōtarō called as he swept through the rustic front gate.

Otsū sat just inside the veranda with her arms propped on a low writing table, staring at the sky as she had been since morning. Under the gable was a wooden plaque bearing an inscription in white characters: "Hermitage of the Mountain Moon." The little cottage belonging to a priestly official at the Ginkakuji had, at Lord Karasumaru's request, been lent to Otsū.

Jōtarō plopped down in a clump of blossoming violets and began splashing his feet in the brook to wash off the mud. The water, which flowed directly from the garden of the Ginkakuji, was purer than fresh snow. "Water's freezing," he observed with a frown, but the earth was warm and he was happy to be alive and in this beautiful spot. Swallows sang as if they, too, were pleased with the day.

He rose, wiped his feet on the grass and walked over to the veranda. "Don't you get bored?" he asked.

"No; I have many things to think about."

"Wouldn't you like to hear some good news?"

"What news?"

"It's about Musashi. I heard he's not so far from here."

"Where?"

"I've been wandering around for days asking if anyone knew where he was, and today I heard he's staying at the Mudōji on Mount Hiei."

"In that case, I suppose he's all right."

"Probably, but I think we should go there right away, before he goes off someplace. I'm hungry. Why don't you get ready while I have something to eat?"

"There are some rice dumplings wrapped in leaves. They're in that three-tiered box over there. Help yourself."

When Jōtarō finished the dumplings, Otsū hadn't moved from the table.

"What's the matter?" he asked, eyeing her suspiciously.

"I don't think we ought to go."

"Of all the stupid . . . One minute you're dying to see Musashi, and the next you start pretending you don't want to."

"You don't understand. He knows how I feel. That night when we met on the mountain, I told him everything, said all there was to say. We thought we'd never see each other alive again."

"But you can see him again, so what are you waiting for?"

"I don't know what he's thinking, whether he's satisfied with his victory or just staying out of danger. When he left me I resigned myself to never being with him again in this life. I don't think I should go unless he sends for me."

"What if he doesn't do that for years?"

"I'll go on doing what I'm doing right now."

"Sit there and look at the sky?"

"You don't understand. But never mind."

"What don't I understand?"

"Musashi's feelings. I really feel I can trust him now. I used to love him heart and soul, but I don't think I believed in him completely. Now I do. Everything's different.

"We're closer than the branches of the same tree. Even if we're separated, even if we die, we'll still be together. So nothing can make me lonely anymore. Now I only pray he'll find the Way he's searching for."

Jōtarō exploded. "You're lying!" he shouted. "Can't women even tell the truth? If you want to act that way, all right, but don't ever mention to me again how much you long to see Musashi. Cry your eyes out! It's all the same to me." He'd put a lot of effort into finding out where Musashi had gone from Ichijōji—and now this! He ignored Otsū and didn't say a word the rest of the day.

Just after dusk, a reddish torchlight crossed the garden, and one of Lord Karasumaru's samurai knocked on the door. He handed a letter to Jōtarō, saying, "It's from Musashi to Otsū. His lordship said Otsū should take good care of herself." He turned and left.

"It's Musashi's handwriting, all right," thought Jōtarō. "He must be alive." Then, with a trace of indignation: "It's addressed to Otsū, not to me, I see."

Emerging from the rear of the cottage, Otsū said, "That samurai brought a letter from Musashi, didn't he?"

"Yes, but I don't suppose you'd be interested," he replied with a pout, hiding the letter behind his back.

"Oh, stop it, Jōtarō. Let me see it," Otsū implored.

He resisted for a time, but at the first hint of tears thrust the envelope at her. "Ha!" he gloated. "You pretend you don't want to see him, but you can't wait to read his letter."

As she crouched by the lamp, the paper trembling in her white fingers, the flame seemed to have a special gaiety, a portent almost of happiness and good fortune.

The ink sparkled like a rainbow, the tears on her eyelashes like jewels. Otsū, suddenly transported to a world she hadn't dared hope existed, recalled the ecstatic passage in Po Chü-i's poem where the departed spirit of Yang Kuei-fei rejoiced over a message of love from her bereaved emperor.

She read the short message, then again read it. "He must be waiting this very minute. I must hurry." Though she thought she said the words aloud, she uttered not a sound.

Flying into action, she wrote thank-you notes to the owner of the cottage, to other priests at the Ginkakuji and to all those who had been kind to her during her stay. She had gathered her belongings together, tied on her sandals and was out in the garden before she noticed that Jōtarō was still sitting inside nursing his pique.

"Come on, Jō! Hurry up!"

"Going somewhere?"

"Are you still angry?"

"Who wouldn't be? You never think of anybody but yourself. Is there something so secret about Musashi's letter you can't even show it to me?"

"I'm sorry," she said apologetically. "There's no reason you shouldn't see it."

"Forget it. I'm not interested now."

"Don't be so difficult. I want you to read it. It's a wonderful letter, the first he's ever sent me. And this is the first time he's asked me to come and join him. I've never been so happy in my life. Stop pouting, and come with me to Seta. Please."

On the road through Shiga Pass, Jōtarō maintained a grumpy silence, but eventually he plucked a leaf to use as a whistle and hummed a few popular ditties to relieve the nocturnal stillness.

Eventually, too, Otsū, prompted to make a peace offering, said, "There are some sweets left from the box Lord Karasumaru sent the day before yesterday."

But dawn was breaking and clouds beyond the pass were turning pink before he became his normal self again.

"Are you all right, Otsū? Aren't you tired?"

"A little. It's been uphill all the way."

"It'll be easier from now on. Look, you can see the lake."

551

"Yes; Lake Biwa. Where's Seta?"

"Over that way. Musashi wouldn't be there this early, would he?"

"I really don't know. It'll take us half the day to get there ourselves. Shall we take a rest?"

"Okay," he replied, his good humor restored. "Let's sit down under those two big trees over there."

The smoke of early morning cooking fires rose in strands, like vapors ascending from a battlefield. Through the mist stretching from the lake to the town of Ishiyama, the streets of Ōtsu were becoming visible. As he approached, Musashi drew his hand across his brow and looked around, glad to be back among people.

Near the Miidera, as he started up the Bizōji slope, he had wondered idly which road Otsū would take. He had imagined earlier he might meet her on the way but later decided this was unlikely. The woman who had taken his letter to Kyoto had informed him that though Otsū was no longer at the Karasumaru residence, his letter would be delivered to her. Since she would have received it no sooner than late evening and would have had various things to do before leaving, it seemed probable that she would wait until morning before setting out.

Passing a temple with a fine stand of old cherry trees—no doubt famous, he thought, for their spring blossoms—he had noticed a stone monument standing on a mound. Though he had caught only a glimpse of the poem inscribed thereon, it came back to him a few hundred yards farther down the road. It was from the *Taiheiki*. Recalling that the poem was connected with a tale he had once memorized, he began reciting it slowly to himself.

" 'A venerable priest from the temple of Shiga—leaning on a six-foot staff and so old that his white eyebrows grew together in a frosty peak on his forehead—was contemplating the beauty of Kannon in the waters of the lake when he chanced to catch sight of an imperial concubine from Kyōgoku. She was on her way back from Shiga, where there was a great field of flowers, and when he saw her, he was overcome with passion. The virtue that he had so arduously accumulated over the years deserted him. He was engulfed in the burning house of desire and . . .'

"Now, how did that go? I seem to have forgotten some of it. Ah!

" ' . . . and he returned to his hut made of sticks and prayed before the image of the Buddha, but a vision of the woman persisted. Though he called on the Buddha's name, his own voice sounded like the breath of delusion. In the clouds above the mountains at twilight, he seemed to see the combs in her hair. This made him sad. When he raised his eyes to the lonely moon, her face smiled back at him. He was perplexed and ashamed.

" 'Fearing that such thoughts would prevent him from going to paradise when he died, he resolved to meet the damsel and reveal his feelings to her. In this way, he hoped to die a peaceful death.

" 'So he went to the Imperial Palace and, planting his staff firmly in the ground, stood waiting in the kickball court for an entire day and night—' "

"Pardon me, sir! You, on the cow!"

The man seemed to be a day laborer of the sort found in the wholesale district. Coming around in front of the cow, he patted her nose and looked over her head at the rider.

"You must have come from the Mudōji," he said.

"I did, as a matter of fact. How did you know?"

"I lent this cow to a merchant. I guess he must have left her there. I rent her out, so I'll have to ask you to pay me for the use of her."

"I'll be happy to pay. But tell me, how far would you let me take her?"

"So long as you pay, you can take her anywhere. All you have to do is turn her over to a wholesaler in the town nearest where you're going. Then somebody else'll rent her. Sooner or later she'll get back here."

"How much would it cost me if I took her to Edo?"

"I'll have to check that at the stable. It's right on your way anyhow. If you decide to rent her, you just have to leave your name at the office."

The wholesale district was near the ford at Uchidegahama. Since many travelers passed through there, Musashi thought it was just the place to freshen up and buy some things he needed.

After the arrangements for the cow had been made, he had a leisurely breakfast and set out for Seta, savoring the prospect of seeing Otsū again. He no longer had any misgivings about her. Until their meeting on the mountain, she had always elicited a certain fear in him, but this time it was different: her purity, intelligence and devotion on that moonlit night had made his confidence in her deeper than love.

Not only did he trust her; he knew she trusted him. He had vowed that once they were together again, he would refuse her nothing—provided, of course, it did not jeopardize his way of life as a swordsman. What had worried him before was the dread that if he allowed himself to love her, his sword would be blunted. Like the old priest in the story, he might lose the Way. That she was well disciplined was now evident; she would never become a hindrance or a fetter holding him back. His only problem now was to make sure that he himself did not drown in the deep pool of love.

"When we get to Edo," he thought, "I'll see she gets the type of training and education a woman needs. While she studies, I'll take Jōtarō with me, and together we'll find a still higher plane of discipline. Then one day, when the time comes . . ." Light reflected from the lake bathed his face in a gently flickering glow.

The two sections of Kara Bridge, one ninety-six column spans and the other twenty-three column spans, were linked by a small island. On the island was an ancient willow tree, a landmark for travelers. The bridge itself was often called Willow Bridge.

"He's coming!" cried Jōtarō, dashing out of the tea shop onto the shorter section of the bridge, where he stood beckoning to Musashi with one hand and pointing to the tea shop with the other. "There he is, Otsū! See? Riding a cow." He broke into a little dance. Soon Otsū was standing beside him, she waving her hand, he waving his basket hat. A broad grin lit Musashi's face as he drew near.

He tied the cow to a willow tree, and the three of them entered the tea   553

shop. Though Otsū had called wildly to Musashi while he was still on the far
side of the bridge, now that he was beside her, words failed her. Beaming
happily, she left the talking to Jōtarō.

"Your wound's healed," said the boy, almost rhapsodically. "When I saw
you on the cow, I thought maybe it was because you couldn't walk. But we
still managed to get here first, didn't we? As soon as Otsū got your letter, she
was ready to leave."

Musashi smiled, nodded, murmured "oh"s and "ah"s, but Jōtarō's talk about
Otsū and her love in front of strangers made him uncomfortable. At his insistence, they moved to a little porch in back, which was shaded by a wisteria
trellis. Otsū remained too diffident to speak, and Musashi grew taciturn. But
Jōtarō paid no heed; his rapid chatter mingled with the buzzing of bees and
the whir of gadflies.

He was interrupted by the proprietor's voice, saying, "You'd better come
inside. A storm's brewing. Look how dark the sky's getting above Ishiyamadera." He bustled about, putting away straw blinds and placing wooden rain
shutters around the sides of the porch. The river had turned gray; gusts of
wind set the lavender wisteria blossoms into wild motion. All at once, a flash
of light streaked through the sky, and the rain came pouring down in great
torrents.

"Lightning!" cried Jōtarō. "The first this year. Hurry up, get inside, Otsū.
You'll get soaked. Hurry, *Sensei*. Oh, the rain came at just the right time. It's
perfect."

But if the shower was "perfect" for Jōtarō, it meant embarrassment for Musashi and Otsū, for going back inside together would make them feel like
starry-eyed lovers. Musashi held back, and Otsū, blushing, stood at the edge of
the porch, no better protected from the elements than the wisteria blossoms.

The man holding a piece of straw matting over his head as he ran through
the blinding rain looked like a large self-propelled umbrella. Dashing under
the eaves of a shrine gate, he smoothed his wet, rumpled hair and looked up
questioningly at the swiftly moving clouds. "It's just like midsummer," he
grumbled. No sound was audible above the pounding of the rain, but an
abrupt flash of light sent his hands to his ears. Matahachi squatted fearfully
near a statue of the god of thunder, which stood beside the gate.

As suddenly as it had begun, the rain ceased. The black clouds parted, the
sunshine streamed through, and before long the street had returned to normal. Somewhere in the distance Matahachi could hear the plinking of shamisen. As he started to move on, a woman dressed like a geisha crossed the
street and walked directly up to him.

"Your name's Matahachi, isn't it?" she said.

"It is," he answered suspiciously. "How did you know?"

"A friend of yours is at our shop now. He saw you from the window and
told me to come get you."

Glancing around, he saw that there were several brothels in the neighborhood. Though he hesitated, the woman hurried him along toward her own.

"If you have other business," she said, "you don't have to stay long."

When they entered, the girls virtually fell all over him, wiping off his feet, removing his wet kimono and insisting that he go to the parlor upstairs. When he asked who this friend was, they laughed and told him he would find out soon enough.

"Well," said Matahachi, "I've been out in the rain, so I'll stay until my clothes dry, but don't try to keep me here any longer than that. There's a man waiting for me at the bridge in Seta."

With much tittering, the women promised him he could leave in good time, meanwhile almost pushing him up the stairs.

At the threshold of the parlor, he was greeted by a man's voice. "Well, well, if it isn't my friend Inugami *Sensei!*"

For a moment, Matahachi thought it was a case of mistaken identity, but when he looked into the room, the face seemed vaguely familiar.

"Who are you?" he asked.

"Have you forgotten Sasaki Kojirō?"

"No," Matahachi replied quickly. "But why do you call me Inugami? My name's Hon'iden, Hon'iden Matahachi."

"I know, but I always remember you as you were that night on Gojō Avenue, making funny faces at a pack of stray curs. I think Inugami—god of the dogs—is a good name for you."

"Cut it out! That's nothing to joke about. I had a terrible time that night, thanks to you."

"I don't doubt it. In fact, I sent for you today because I want to do you a good turn for a change. Come in, have a seat. Give the man some sake, girls."

"I can't stay. I have to meet someone in Seta. I can't afford to get drunk today."

"Who are you meeting?"

"A man by the name of Miyamoto. He's a childhood friend of mine, and—"

"Miyamoto Musashi? Did you make an appointment with him when you were at the inn in the pass?"

"How did you know?"

"Oh, I've heard all about you, all about Musashi too. I met your mother—Osugi, is it?—at the main hall on Mount Hiei. She told me about all the troubles she's gone through."

"You talked to my mother?"

"Yes. She's a splendid woman. I admire her, and so do all the priests on Mount Hiei. I tried to give her some encouragement." Rinsing his cup in a bowl of water, he offered it to Matahachi and continued: "Here, let's drink together and wash away our old enmity. There's no reason to worry about Musashi if you've got Sasaki Kojirō on your side."

Matahachi refused the cup.

"Why don't you drink?"

"I can't. I have to go."

As Matahachi started to get up, Kojirō grabbed him tightly by the wrist, saying, "Sit down!"

555

"But Musashi's waiting."

"Don't be an ass! If you attack Musashi by yourself, he'll kill you instantly."

"You've got it all wrong! He promised to help me. I'm going with him to Edo to make a new start in life."

"You mean you'd rely on a man like Musashi?"

"Oh, I know, a lot of people say he's no good. But that's because my mother's gone around slandering him. But she's wrong, has been all along. Now that I've talked to him, I'm more sure of that than ever. He's my friend, and I'm going to learn from him so that I can make something of myself too. Even if it is a little late in the day."

Roaring with laughter, Kojirō slapped the tatami with his hand. "How could you be so innocent? Your mother told me you were unusually naive, but to be taken in by—"

"That's not true! Musashi's—"

"Just be quiet! Listen. In the first place, how could you think of betraying your own mother by siding with her enemy? It's inhuman. Even I, a total stranger, was so moved by that valiant old lady that I swore to give her all the support I can."

"I don't care what you think. I'm going to meet Musashi, and don't try to stop me. You, girl, bring my kimono! It should be dry by now."

Raising his drunken eyes, Kojirō commanded, "Don't touch it until I tell you to. Now look, Matahachi, if you plan to go with Musashi, you should at least talk to your mother first."

"I'm going on to Edo with Musashi. If I make something of myself there, the whole problem will solve itself."

"That sounds like something Musashi would say. In fact, I'd bet he put the words in your mouth. Anyway, wait till tomorrow, and I'll go with you to look for your mother. You have to listen to her opinion before you do anything. In the meantime, let's enjoy ourselves. Like it or not, you're going to stay here and drink with me."

This being a brothel, and Kojirō the paying guest, the women all came to his support. Matahachi's kimono was not forthcoming, and after a few drinks, he stopped asking for it.

Sober, Matahachi was no match for Kojirō. Inebriated, he could be something of a menace. By the time day faded into night, he was demonstrating to one and all how much he could drink, demanding more, saying everything he should not say, airing all his resentments—in short, being a complete nuisance. It was dawn before he passed out and noon before he came to again.

The sun seemed all the brighter for the rain the previous afternoon. With Musashi's words echoing in his head, Matahachi longed to throw up every drop he had drunk. Fortunately, Kojirō was still asleep in another room. Matahachi slipped downstairs, made the women give him his kimono, and set off at a run for Seta.

The muddy red water under the bridge was liberally sprinkled with Ishiyamadera's fallen cherry blossoms. The storm had broken the wisteria vines and strewn yellow kerria flowers everywhere.

After a lengthy search, Matahachi asked at the tea shop and was told that the man with the cow had waited until the shop closed for the night, then had gone to an inn. He had returned in the morning, but not finding his friend, had left a note tied to a willow branch.

The note, which looked like a large white moth, said, "Sorry I couldn't wait longer. Catch up with me on the way. I'll be looking for you."

Matahachi made good time along the Nakasendō, the highroad leading through Kiso to Edo, but he had still not caught up with Musashi when he reached Kusatsu. After passing through Hikone and Toriimoto, he began to suspect he had missed him on the way, and when he reached Suribachi Pass, he waited half a day, keeping his eyes on the road the whole time.

It wasn't until he reached the road for Mino that Kojirō's words came back to him.

"Was I taken in after all?" he asked himself. "Did Musashi really have no intention of going with me?"

After much doubling back and investigation of side roads, he finally caught sight of Musashi just outside the town of Nakatsugawa. At first he was elated, but when he got close enough to see that the person on the cow was Otsū, jealousy took instant and complete control of him.

"What a fool I've been," he growled, "from the day that bastard talked me into going to Sekigahara until this very minute! Well, he can't walk all over me this way forever. I'll get even with him somehow—and soon!"

The Male and Female Waterfalls

"Whew, it's hot!" Jōtarō exclaimed. "I've never sweated like this on a mountain road before. Where are we?"

"Near Magome Pass," said Musashi. "They say it's the most difficult section of the highroad."

"Well, I don't know about that, but I've had enough of this. I'll be glad to get to Edo. Lots of people there—right, Otsū?"

"There are, but I'm in no hurry to get there. I'd rather pass the time traveling on a lonely road like this."

"That's because you're riding. You'd feel different if you were walking. Look! There's a waterfall over there."

"Let's take a rest," said Musashi.

The three of them made their way along a narrow path. All around, the 557 ground was covered with wild flowers, still damp with morning dew. Coming to a deserted hut on a cliff overlooking the falls, they stopped. Jōtarō helped Otsū off the cow, then tied the animal to a tree.

"Look, Musashi," said Otsū. She was pointing at a sign that read: "Meoto no Taki." The reason for the name, "Male and Female Waterfalls," was easy to understand, for rocks split the falls into two sections, the larger one looking very virile, the other one small and gentle.

The roiling basin and rapids below the falls fired Jōtarō with renewed energy. Half jumping, half dancing down the steep bank, he called up excitedly, "There're fish down here!"

A few minutes later, he cried, "I can catch them! I threw a rock and one rolled over dead."

Not long after that, his voice, barely audible above the roar of the falls, echoed back from still another direction.

In the shadow of the little hut, Musashi and Otsū sat among countless tiny rainbows made by the sun shining on the wet grass.

"Where has that boy gone, do you suppose?" she asked, adding, "He's really impossible to manage."

"Do you think so? I was worse than that at his age. Matahachi, though, was just the opposite, really very well behaved. I wonder where he is. He worries me far more than Jōtarō."

"I'm glad he's not here. I'd have to hide if he was."

"Why? I think he'd understand if we explained."

"I doubt it. He and his mother aren't like other people."

"Otsū, are you sure you won't change your mind?"

"About what?"

"I mean, mightn't you decide you really want to marry Matahachi?"

Her face twitched with shock. "Absolutely not!" she replied indignantly. Her eyelids turned orchid pink, and she covered her face with her hands, but the slight trembling of her white collar almost seemed to cry out, "I'm yours, no one else's!"

Regretting his words, Musashi turned his eyes toward her. For several days now he had watched the play of light on her body—at night, the flickering glow of a lamp; in the daytime, the warm rays of the sun. Seeing her skin glisten with perspiration, he'd thought of the lotus blossom. Separated from her pallet by only a flimsy screen, he'd inhaled the faint scent of her black tresses. Now the roar of the water became one with the throbbing of his blood, and he felt himself being swallowed up by a powerful impulse.

Abruptly he stood up and moved to a sunny spot where the winter grass was still high, then sat down heavily and heaved a sigh.

Otsū came and knelt at his side, put her arms around his knees and twisted her neck to look up into his silent, frightened face.

"What is it?" she asked. "Did something I said make you angry? Forgive me. I'm sorry."

The more tense he became—and the harsher the look in his eyes—the more closely she clung to him. Then all at once she threw her arms around him. Her fragrance, the warmth of her body, overwhelmed him.

"Otsū!" he cried impetuously as he seized her in his brawny arms and threw her backward onto the grass.

The roughness of the embrace took her breath away. She struggled free and crouched beside him.

"You mustn't! You mustn't do that!" she shrieked hoarsely. "How could you? You, of all people—" She broke off, sobbing.

His burning passion suddenly chilled by the pain and horror in her eyes, Musashi came to himself with a jolt. "Why?" he cried. "Why?" Overcome by shame and anger, he himself was on the verge of tears.

Then she was gone, leaving behind only a sachet, which had broken loose from her kimono. Staring blankly at it, Musashi groaned, then turned his face to the ground and let the tears of pain and frustration flow into the withered grass.

He felt she'd made a fool of him—deceived, defeated, tortured and shamed him. Hadn't her words—her lips, her eyes, her hair, her body—been calling out to him? Hadn't she labored to light a fire in his heart, then when the flames burst forth, fled in terror?

By some perverse logic, it seemed that all his efforts to become a superior person had been defeated, all his struggles and privations had been rendered utterly meaningless. His face buried in the grass, he told himself he'd done nothing wrong, but his conscience wasn't satisfied.

What a girl's virginity, vouchsafed to her for only a short period of her life, meant to her—how precious and sweet it was—was a question that never entered his mind.

But as he breathed in the smell of the earth, he gradually regained his self-control. When he eventually dragged himself to his feet, the raging fire was gone from his eyes and his face was devoid of passion. Trampling the sachet underfoot, he stood looking intently at the ground, listening, it seemed, to the voice of the mountains. His heavy black eyebrows were knit together just as they had been when he threw himself into battle under the spreading pine.

The sun went behind a cloud, and the sharp screech of a bird split the air. The wind changed, subtly altering the sound of the falling water.

Otsū, her heart fluttering like a frightened sparrow's, observed his agony from behind a birch tree. Realizing how deeply she had hurt him, she now longed to have him at her side again, but as much as she wanted to run to him and beg forgiveness, her body would not obey. For the first time, she realized that the lover she had given her heart to was not the vision of masculine virtues she had imagined. Discovering the naked beast, the flesh and blood and passions, clouded her eyes with sadness and fear.

She had started to run away, but after twenty paces, her love caught and held her. Now, a little calmer, she began to imagine that Musashi's lust was different from that of other men. More than anything else in the world, she wanted to apologize and assure him she harbored no resentment for what he'd done.

"He's still angry," she thought fearfully, suddenly realizing he was no longer before her eyes. "Oh, what'll I do?"

Nervously, she went back to the little hut, but there was only a cold white mist and the thundering of the water, which seemed to shake the trees and stir up vibrations all around her.

"Otsū! Something awful's happened! Musashi's thrown himself into the water!" Jōtarō's frantic cry came from a promontory overlooking the basin, just a second before he grabbed a wisteria vine and began descending, swinging from branch to branch like a monkey.

Though she hadn't caught the actual words, Otsū heard the urgency in his voice. She raised her head in alarm and began clambering down the steep path, slipping on the moss, then clinging to rocks to steady herself.

The figure just visible through the spray and mist resembled a large rock but was actually Musashi's naked body. Hands clasped in front of him, head bowed, he was dwarfed by the fifty-foot flood cascading down on him.

Halfway down, Otsū stopped and stared in horror. Across the river, Jōtarō stood similarly transfixed.

"*Sensei!*" he cried.

"Musashi!"

Their shouts never reached Musashi's ears. It was as though a thousand silver dragons were nipping at his head and shoulders, the eyes of a thousand water demons exploding around him. Treacherous eddies tugged at his legs, ready to pull him to his death. One false rhythm in breathing, one faltering heartbeat, and his heels would lose their tenuous hold on the algae-covered bottom, his body would be swept up in a violent current from which there was no return. His lungs and heart seemed to be collapsing under the incalculable weight—the total mass of the Magome mountains—falling on him.

His desire for Otsū died a slow death, for it was closely akin to the hot-blooded temperament without which he would never have gone to Sekigahara or accomplished any of his extraordinary feats. But the real danger lay in the fact that at a certain point, all his years of training became powerless against it and he sank again to the level of a wild, mindless beast. And against an enemy like this, formless and hidden, the sword was utterly useless. Bewildered, perplexed, conscious of the devastating defeat he'd suffered, he prayed that the raging waters might bring him back to his quest for discipline.

"*Sensei! Sensei!*" Jōtarō's shouts had become a tearful wailing. "You mustn't die! Please don't die!" He, too, had clasped his hands in front of his chest, and his face was contorted, as if he, too, were bearing the weight of the water, the sting, the pain, the cold.

Glancing across the river, Jōtarō suddenly felt himself go limp.

He couldn't make any sense out of what Musashi was doing; apparently he was determined to stay under the torrent until he died, but now Otsū—Where was she? He was sure she'd leaped to her death in the river below.

Then, above the sound of the water, he heard Musashi's voice. The words weren't clear. He thought it might be a sutra, but then . . . maybe they were angry oaths of self-recrimination.

The voice was full of strength and life. Musashi's broad shoulders and muscular body exuded youth and vigor, as if his soul had been cleansed and was now ready to begin life afresh.

Jōtarō began to feel that whatever had been wrong had passed. As the light of the evening sun made a rainbow above the falls, he called, "Otsū!" and dared to hope that she had left the cliffside simply because she thought Musashi was in no real danger. "If she's confident he's all right," he thought, "there's nothing for me to worry about. She knows him better than I do, right down to the bottom of his heart."

Jōtarō skipped lightly down to the river, found a narrow place, crossed it and climbed up the other side. Approaching silently, he saw that Otsū was inside the hut, huddled on the floor with Musashi's kimono and swords clutched to her bosom.

Jōtarō sensed that her tears, which she made no effort to hide, were somehow not ordinary tears. And without really understanding what had happened, he felt it was of grave concern to Otsū. After a couple of minutes, he slipped quietly back to where the cow lay in the whitish grass and sprawled out beside her.

"At this rate, we'll never get to Edo," he said.

Book V   SKY

The Abduction

Beyond the pass, the snow on Mount Koma glistened in lancelike streaks, while on Mount Ontake, visible through the faintly reddish tree buds, it lay in scattered patches. The light green heralding the growing season seemed to shimmer along the highroad and in the fields.

Otsū daydreamed. Jōtarō was like a new plant—stubborn and hardy. It would take an awful lot to trample him, to keep him down for long. He was growing fast these days; occasionally she thought she caught a glimpse of the man he would one day be.

The line between rambunctiousness and insolence was a fine one, however, and even making allowances for his unorthodox upbringing, Otsū was growing more and more dismayed with Jōtarō's behavior. His demands, particularly for food, were unending. Every time they came to a food shop, he stopped dead and wouldn't budge until she'd bought him something.

After buying rice crackers at Suhara, she vowed, "This is the very last time." But before they'd gone a mile farther, the crackers were gone, and he was claiming to be half starved. The next crisis was only just averted by stopping at a tea shop in Nezame for an early lunch; by the time they'd crossed another pass, he was famished again.

"Look, Otsū! That shop has dried persimmons. Shouldn't we get some, just to carry with us?"

Pretending not to hear, Otsū rode on.

When they arrived at Fukushima, in Shinano Province, a place famous for the variety and abundance of its food products, it was midafternoon, about the time they were in the habit of having a snack.

"Let's rest awhile," he whined. "Please."

She paid no attention.

"Come on, Otsū! Let's have some of those rice cakes coated with soybean flour. The ones they make here are famous. Don't you want any?" Since he

565

now had hold of the cow's rope, Otsū saw it was going to be difficult to get past the shop.

"Haven't you had enough?" she said with annoyance.

The cow, as if in secret alliance with Jōtarō, stopped and began munching grass by the roadside.

"All right!" snapped Otsū. "If that's the way you're going to act, I'll go on ahead and tell Musashi." When she made as if to dismount, Jōtarō burst into laughter, knowing perfectly well she wouldn't carry out her threat.

Her bluff called, Otsū resignedly got off the cow, and together they went into the open-sided lean-to in front of the shop. Jōtarō shouted an order for two servings, then went out to tether the cow.

When he returned, Otsū said, "You shouldn't have ordered any for me. I'm not hungry."

"You don't want anything to eat?"

"No. People who eat too much turn into stupid pigs."

"Ah, I guess I'll have to eat yours too."

"You are shameless!"

His mouth was too full for his ears to hear. Presently, however, he paused long enough to shift his wooden sword to his back, where it wouldn't interfere with his expanding ribs. He began eating again, but all at once stuffed the last rice cake in his mouth and bolted for the exit.

"Through already?" Otsū called after him. She laid some money on the table and started to follow him, but he returned and roughly shoved her back inside.

"Wait!" he said excitedly. "I just saw Matahachi."

"You couldn't have." She turned pale. "What would he be doing around here?"

"I have no idea. Didn't you see him? He had on a basket hat, and he was staring straight at us."

"I don't believe it."

"Want me to bring him in here and prove it?"

"You'll do no such thing!"

"Oh, don't worry. If anything happens, I'll go get Musashi."

Otsū's pulse was beating wildly, but realizing that the longer they stood there, the farther ahead Musashi would have gone, she got back on the cow.

As they started off, Jōtarō said, "I can't figure it out. Until we got to the waterfall at Magome, we were all as friendly as could be. Since then, Musashi's hardly said a word, and you haven't been talking to him either. What's the matter?"

When she said nothing, he went on: "Why is he walking on ahead of us? Why do we sleep in different rooms now? Did you have a fight or something?"

Otsū couldn't bring herself to give him an honest answer, for she hadn't been able to give herself one. Did all men treat women the way Musashi had treated her, openly trying to force his love on her? And why had she rejected him so vehemently? Her distress and confusion now were, in a way, more

566

painful than the illness from which she had but recently recovered. The fountain of love that had comforted her for years had suddenly turned into a raging waterfall.

The memory of that other waterfall resounded in her ears, along with her own cry of distress and Musashi's angry protest.

She could ask herself whether they would go on like this forever, never understanding each other, but why she was now trailing along behind him, trying not to lose sight of him, struck even her as illogical. Though, out of embarrassment, they kept apart and spoke rarely, Musashi showed no signs of breaking his promise to go with her to Edo.

At the Kōzenji they turned onto another road. There was a barrier at the top of the first hill. Otsū had heard that ever since the Battle of Sekigahara, government officials had been examining travelers, particularly women, on this road with great thoroughness. But Lord Karasumaru's letter of introduction worked like a charm, and they passed the checkpoint without difficulty.

As they reached the last of the tea shops on the far side of the barrier, Jōtarō asked, "Otsū, what does 'Fugen' mean?"

"Fugen?"

"Yeah. Back there, in front of a tea shop, a priest pointed at you and said you 'looked like Fugen on a cow.' What does that mean?"

"I suppose he was referring to the Bodhisattva Fugen."

"That's the bodhisattva that rides on an elephant, isn't it? In that case, I must be the Bodhisattva Monju. They're always together."

"A very gluttonous Monju, I should say."

"Good enough for a crybaby Fugen!"

"Oh, you would say that!"

"Why are Fugen and Monju always together? They're not a man and a woman."

Intentionally or not, he was striking close again. Having heard much about these things while she was living at the Shippōji, Otsū could have answered the question in some detail, but she replied simply, "Monju represents wisdom, Fugen, devoted conduct."

"Stop!" The voice was Matahachi's and it came from behind them.

Sick with revulsion, Otsū thought: "The coward!" She turned and stared frigidly at him.

Matahachi glared back, his feelings more muddled than ever. At Nakatsugawa, it had been pure jealousy, but he'd continued to spy on Musashi and Otsū. When he saw that they were keeping apart, he interpreted this as an attempt to deceive people and imagined all sorts of scandalous goings-on when they were alone.

"Get down!" he commanded.

Otsū stared at the cow's head, unable to speak. Her feeling toward him had settled once and for all into hatred and contempt.

"Come on, woman, get down!"

Though she burned with indignation, she spoke coldly. "Why? I have no business with you."

567

"Is that so?" he growled menacingly, taking hold of her sleeve. "You may not have any business with me, but I have business with you. Get down!"

Jōtarō let go of the rope and shouted, "Leave her alone! If she doesn't want to get off, why should she?" Holding his arms straight out, he butted Matahachi's chest.

"What do you think you're doing, you little bastard?" Thrown off balance, Matahachi readjusted his feet in his sandals and raised his shoulders threateningly. "I thought I'd seen your ugly face somewhere. You're the tramp from the sake shop in Kitano."

"Yeah, and now I know why you were drinking yourself silly. You were living with some old bitch and you didn't have the guts to stand up to her. Isn't that the truth?"

Jōtarō couldn't have touched a more tender spot.

"You snot-nosed runt!" Matahachi snatched at his collar, but Jōtarō ducked and came up on the other side of the cow.

"If I'm a snot-nosed runt, what does that make you? Snot-nosed oaf! Scared of a woman!"

Matahachi darted around the cow, but again Jōtarō slipped under the animal's belly and came up on the other side. This happened three or four times before Matahachi finally managed to latch on to the boy's collar.

"All right, just say that one more time."

"Snot-nosed oaf! Scared of a woman!"

Jōtarō's wooden sword was only half drawn when Matahachi got a good grip and sent him sailing well away from the road into a clump of bamboo. He landed on his back in a small stream, stunned and only barely conscious.

By the time he recovered enough to crawl like an eel back to the road, it was too late. The cow was loping heavily along the road, Otsū still on her back, Matahachi running ahead with the rope in his hand.

"Bastard!" moaned Jōtarō, stung by his own helplessness. Too dazed to get to his feet, he lay there fuming and cursing.

On a hill a mile or so ahead, Musashi was resting his feet and idly wondering whether the clouds were moving or, as they seemed, were permanently suspended between Mount Koma and the broad foothills below.

He started, as though at some wordless communication, shook himself and straightened up.

His thoughts were really on Otsū, and the more he thought, the angrier he became. Both his shame and his resentment had been washed away in the swirling basin under the falls, but as the days passed the doubts kept coming back. Had it been wicked of him to reveal himself to her? Why had she rebuffed him, shrunk from him as though she despised him?

"Leave her behind," he said out loud. Yet he knew he was only deceiving himself. He had told her that when they reached Edo, she could study what was best for her, while he followed his own path. Implicit in this was a promise for the more distant future. He had left Kyoto with her. He had a responsibility to stay with her.

"What will happen to me? With two of us, what will happen to my sword?" He raised his eyes to the mountain and bit his tongue, ashamed of his pettiness. To look at the great peak was humbling.

He wondered what could be keeping them and stood up. He could see the forest a mile back, but no people.

"Could they have been held up at the barrier?"

The sun would be setting soon; they should have caught up long ago.

Suddenly, he felt alarmed. Something must have happened. Before he knew it, he was tearing down the hill so fast that the animals in the fields scurried off in all directions.

The Warrior of Kiso

Musashi had not run very far when a traveler called to him, "Hey, weren't you with a young woman and a boy before?"

Musashi stopped abruptly. "Yes," he said with sinking heart. "Has something happened to them?"

Apparently he was about the only person who had not heard the story that was fast becoming common gossip along the highroad. A young man had approached the girl . . . kidnapped her. He had been seen whipping the cow . . . driving her down a side road near the barrier. The traveler had barely finished repeating the tale before Musashi was on his way.

Racing at top speed, he still took an hour to reach the barrier, which had closed at six, and with it the tea shops on either side. Looking rather frantic, Musashi approached an old man who was piling up stools in front of his shop.

"What's the matter, sir? Forget something?"

"No. I'm looking for a young woman and a boy who passed here a few hours ago."

"Would that be the girl who looked like Fugen on a cow?"

"That's the one!" Musashi answered without thinking. "I'm told a rōnin took her off somewhere. Do you know which way they went?"

"I didn't actually see the incident myself, but I heard they left the main road at the head-burying mound. That'd take them toward Nobu Pond."

For the life of him, Musashi had no idea who might have kidnapped Otsū or why. Matahachi's name never entered his mind. He imagined it might be a good-for-nothing rōnin, like the ones he had encountered in Nara. Or perhaps one of the freebooters reputed to be hanging out in the woods hereabouts. He only hoped it was a petty crook, rather than one of the hoodlums who made a business of abducting and selling women and were known to be vicious on occasion.

He ran on and on in his search for Nobu Pond. After the sun went down, he could hardly see a foot ahead, though the stars were bright above. The road began to slope upward; he assumed he was entering the foothills of Mount Koma.

Having seen nothing resembling a pond and fearing he was on the wrong road, he stopped and looked around. In the vast sea of blackness, he was able to make out a lone farmhouse, a windbreak of trees, and looming darkly above these, the mountain.

When he got closer, he saw that the house was large and sturdily built, though moss grew on the thatched roof and the thatch itself was rotting. There was a light outside—whether torch or fire, he couldn't tell—and near the kitchen, a spotted cow. He was sure it was the animal Otsū had been riding.

He approached stealthily, keeping to the shadows. When he was close enough to see into the kitchen, he heard a loud male voice coming from a shed on the other side of some piles of straw and firewood.

"Put up your work, Mother," the man was saying. "You're always complaining about your eyes being bad, but you go on working practically in the dark."

There was a fire in the hearth room next to the kitchen, and Musashi thought he heard the whir of a spinning wheel. After a moment or two, the sound stopped, and he heard someone moving about.

The man came out of the shed and closed the door behind him. "I'll be in as soon as I've washed my feet," he called. "You can go ahead and put dinner on."

He placed his sandals on a rock by a stream flowing behind the kitchen. As he sat wiggling his feet in the water, the cow put her head close to his shoulder. He rubbed her nose.

"Mother," he called, "come here a minute. I made a real find today. What do you think it is? . . . It's a cow; a really fine one too."

Musashi made his way quietly past the front door of the house. Crouching on a stone beneath a side window, he looked into what turned out to be a hearth room. The first object he saw was a lance hanging from a blackened rack near the top of the wall, a fine weapon that had been polished and lovingly cared for. Bits of gold shone dully on the leather of its scabbard. Musashi did not know what to make of it; it was not the sort of thing usually found in a farmer's house. Farmers were forbidden to have weapons, even if they could afford them.

The man appeared for a moment in the light of the outside fire. At a glance, Musashi knew he was no ordinary peasant. His eyes were too bright, too alert. He wore a knee-length work kimono and mud-spattered leggings. His face was round, and his bushy hair was tied in back with two or three lengths of straw. Though he was short—no more than five feet six—he was thick-chested and solidly built. He walked with firm, decisive steps.

570

Smoke began to escape from the window. Musashi raised his sleeve to cover his face, but too late; he inhaled a lungful of smoke and couldn't stop himself from coughing.

"Who's there?" the old woman called from the kitchen. She came into the hearth room and said, "Gonnosuke, did you shut the shed? There seems to be a millet thief around. I heard him cough."

Musashi slipped away from the window and hid himself among the trees of the windbreak.

"Where?" shouted Gonnosuke, striding rapidly from behind the house.

The old woman appeared at the little window. "He must be right around here. I heard him cough."

"Are you sure it's not just your ears?"

"My hearing's all right. And I'm sure I saw a face at the window. The smoke from the fire must have made him cough."

Slowly, suspiciously, Gonnosuke advanced fifteen or twenty paces, looking carefully to right and left, as though he were a sentinel guarding a fortress. "You may be right," he said. "I seem to smell a human being."

Taking his cue from the look in Gonnosuke's eyes, Musashi bided his time. There was something about the man's posture, something that said it was best to be cautious. He seemed to be leaning slightly forward from the waist. Musashi could not make out what sort of weapon he was carrying, but when he turned, Musashi saw he had a four-foot staff behind his back. No ordinary pole, it had the sheen of a much-used weapon and seemed to be an integral part of the man's body. There was no question in Musashi's mind but that he lived with it day in and day out and knew exactly how to use it.

Moving into view, Musashi shouted, "You—whoever you are! I've come for my companions!"

Gonnosuke glared silently at him.

"Give me back the woman and boy you kidnapped on the highroad. If they're unharmed, we'll let it go at that. But if they've been injured, you're in for it."

The snowmelt feeding the streams in this area gave the breeze a sharp edge, which somehow emphasized the silence.

"Turn them over to me. Now!" Musashi's voice bit more sharply than the wind.

Gonnosuke had what was called a reverse hold on his staff. His hair standing up like a hedgehog's, he straightened to his full height and shouted, "You horse's turd! Who are you calling a kidnapper?"

"You! You must have seen the boy and woman were unprotected, so you kidnapped them and took them here. Bring them out!"

The staff came away from Gonnosuke's side in a movement so rapid Musashi could not tell where the man's arm ended and the weapon began.

Musashi jumped aside. "Don't do anything you'll regret," he warned, then withdrew several paces.

"Who do you think you are, you crazy bastard!" As Gonnosuke spat out his reply, he moved swiftly into action again, determined not to give Musashi a moment's rest. When the latter shifted ten paces, he covered the same distance simultaneously.

Twice Musashi started to move his right hand to the hilt of his sword, but both times he stopped. During the instant when he grasped his sword, his elbow would be exposed. Musashi had seen the swiftness of Gonnosuke's staff and knew he wouldn't have time to complete the movement. He saw, too, that if he allowed himself to make light of his stocky opponent, he'd be in trouble. And if he didn't remain calm, even taking a breath could endanger him.

Musashi had yet to size up this enemy, who at the moment had his legs and torso in a splendid stance of the Indestructible-Perfect type. Musashi was already beginning to feel that this farmer had a technique superior to that of any expert swordsman he had encountered so far, and a look in his eyes suggested he had mastered that Way which Musashi was forever seeking.

But he had little time for assessment. Strike followed strike, almost by the second, as one curse after another poured from Gonnosuke's mouth. Sometimes he used both hands, sometimes only one, executing with flowing dexterity the overhead strike, the lateral strike, the thrust and the shift. A sword, being distinctly divided into blade and hilt, has only one point, but either end of a staff can be applied lethally. Gonnosuke was wielding the staff with the same agility as a candy-maker handling taffy: now it was long, now short, now invisible, now high, now low—seemingly everywhere at once.

From the window, the old woman urged her son to be careful. "Gonnosuke! He doesn't look like an ordinary samurai!" She seemed to be as involved in the fight as he was.

"Don't worry!" The knowledge that she was watching appeared to raise Gonnosuke's fighting spirit to an even higher pitch.

At this point, Musashi ducked a blow to his shoulder, and in the same movement slid in close to Gonnosuke and seized his wrist. The next instant, the farmer was flat on his back, his feet kicking at the stars.

"Wait!" shouted the mother, breaking the lattice of the window in her excitement. Her hair stood on end; she seemed thunderstruck to see her son downed.

The wild look on her face kept Musashi from taking the next logical step, which would have been to whip out his sword and finish Gonnosuke off. "All right, I'll wait," he shouted, straddling Gonnosuke's chest and pinning him to the ground.

Gonnosuke was struggling valiantly to free himself. His legs, over which Musashi had no control, flew in the air, then crashed into the earth as he arched his back. It was all Musashi could do to keep him down.

The mother came rushing out the kitchen door, screaming vituperously, "Look at you! How did you get into a mess like that?" But she added, "Don't give up. I'm here to help you."

Since she had asked Musashi to wait, he expected her to fall down on her knees and beg him not to kill her son. But a glance told him that he was sadly mistaken. She held the lance, now unsheathed, behind her, but he caught the glint of the blade. And he felt her eyes burning into his back.

"Filthy rōnin!" she cried. "Use a tricky throw, will you? You think we're nothing but dumb farmers, don't you?"

Musashi couldn't turn to ward off an attack from behind, because of the way Gonnosuke was squirming about, trying to put Musashi in a position advantageous to his mother.

"Don't worry, Mother!" he said. "I'll make it. Don't get too close."

"Keep calm," she cautioned. "You mustn't lose to the likes of him. Remember your ancestors! What's happened to the blood you inherited from the great Kakumyō, who fought side by side with the General of Kiso."

"I won't forget!" yelled Gonnosuke. No sooner were the words out of his mouth than he managed to raise his head and sink his teeth into Musashi's thigh, at the same time letting go of his staff and striking Musashi with both hands. The old woman chose this moment to level the lance at Musashi's back.

"Wait!" shouted Musashi.

They had reached a stage where settlement seemed possible only through the death of one of them. If Musashi had been absolutely sure that by winning he could free Otsū and Jōtarō, he would have pressed on. Now it seemed the better part of valor to call a halt and talk things over. He turned his shoulders toward the old woman and told her to put down the lance.

"What should I do, son?"

Gonnosuke was still pinned to the ground, but he was also having second thoughts. Perhaps this rōnin had some reason to think his companions were here. There was no sense in risking death over a misunderstanding.

Once they had disentangled themselves, it took only a few minutes to make it clear that it was all a mistake.

The three of them repaired to the house and the blazing fire. Kneeling by the hearth, the mother said, "Very dangerous! To think that there was no cause for a fight to begin with."

As Gonnosuke prepared to take his place beside her, she shook her head. "Before you sit down," she said, "take the samurai all through the house, so that he can be satisfied that his friends aren't here." Then, to Musashi: "I want you to look carefully and see for yourself."

"That's a good idea," agreed Gonnosuke. "Come with me, sir. Examine the house from top to bottom. I dislike being suspected of kidnapping."

Already seated, Musashi declined. "It's not necessary. From what you've told me, I'm sure you had nothing to do with the kidnapping. Forgive me for accusing you."

"I was partly to blame," Gonnosuke said apologetically. "I should have found out what you were talking about before I lost my temper."

Musashi then asked, somewhat hesitantly, about the cow, explaining that he was quite sure it was the one he had rented in Seta.

"I just happened to find her," replied Gonnosuke. "This evening, I was down at Nobu Pond netting loaches, and on my way home I saw the cow with one leg sunk in the mud. It's swampy down there. The more she struggled, the deeper she sank. She was raising an awful rumpus, so I pulled her free.

When I asked around the neighborhood, she didn't seem to belong to anybody, so I thought a thief must have stolen her and later abandoned her.

"A cow's worth about half a man on a farm, and this is a good one, with a young udder." Gonnosuke laughed. "I sort of decided that heaven must have sent the cow to me because I'm poor and can't do anything for my mother without a little supernatural help. I don't mind giving the animal back to her owner, but I don't know who that is."

Musashi noted that Gonnosuke told his story with the simple straightforward honesty of a person born and brought up in the country.

His mother became sympathetic. "I'm sure this rōnin's worried about his friends," she said. "Eat your dinner and take him to look for them. I only hope they're somewhere near the pond. The hills are no place for strangers. They're full of bandits who'll steal anything—horses, vegetables, anything! This whole business sounds like some of their work."

The breeze would begin as a whisper, mushroom into a violent gust, then roar through the trees and raise havoc with the smaller plants.

During a lull that left only the ominous silence of the stars above, Gonnosuke held the torch high and waited for Musashi to catch up with him.

"Sorry," he said, "but nobody seems to know anything about them. There's just one more house between here and the pond. It's behind those woods over there. The owner farms part of the time and hunts the rest. If he can't help us, there's nowhere else to look."

"Thanks for going to all this trouble. We've already been to more than ten houses, so I suppose there's not much hope of their being around here. If we don't find out anything at this next house, let's give up and go back."

It was past midnight. Musashi had expected they would at least find some trace of Jōtarō, but no one had seen him. Descriptions of Otsū had brought nothing but blank looks and long country pauses.

"If it's the walking you're thinking about, that's nothing to me. I could walk all night. Are the woman and boy servants of yours? Brother? Sister?"

"They're the people closest to me."

Each would have liked to ask the other more about himself, but Gonnosuke lapsed into silence, moved a pace or two ahead and guided Musashi along a narrow path toward Nobu Pond.

Musashi was curious about Gonnosuke's skill with the staff and how he had acquired it, but his sense of propriety kept him from asking about it. Musing that his meeting the man was due to a mishap—and his own rashness—he nevertheless felt extremely grateful. What a misfortune it would have been to miss seeing this great fighter's dazzling technique!

Gonnosuke stopped and said, "You'd better wait here. Those people are probably asleep, and we don't want to frighten them. I'll go alone and see if I can find out anything."

He pointed out the house, whose thatched roof seemed nearly buried in the trees. A rustling of bamboo accompanied his running footsteps. Presently Musashi heard him knocking loudly on the door.

He returned a few minutes later with a story that seemed to give Musashi his first real lead. It had taken him a while to make the man and his wife understand what he was asking about, but finally the wife told him of something that had happened to her that afternoon.

A little before sundown, on her way home from shopping, the woman had seen a boy running toward Yabuhara, hands and face covered with mud and a long wooden sword in his obi. When she stopped him and asked what was wrong, he responded by asking her where the office of the shōgun's deputy was. He went on to tell her that a bad man had carried off the person he was traveling with. She advised him that he was wasting his time; the shōgun's officers would never on their own organize a search for a person of no consequence. If it was somebody great or important, or if they had orders from above, they would turn every dollop of horse manure, every grain of sand, but they had no use for common folk. Anyway, for a woman to be kidnapped or a traveler to be stripped clean by highwaymen was nothing unusual. Things like that happened morning, noon and night.

She had told the boy to go past Yabuhara to a place called Narai. There, at an intersection it was easy to see, he would find a wholesale house dealing in herbs. It was owned by a man named Daizō, who would listen to his story and in all likelihood offer to help him. Unlike the officials, Daizō not only sympathized with the weak but would go to great lengths to help them if he thought their cause was worthy.

Gonnosuke ended by saying, "It sounded to me as though the boy was Jōtarō. What do you think?"

"I'm sure of it," said Musashi. "I suppose the best thing to do would be to go to Narai as quickly as possible and look up this man Daizō. Thanks to you, I at least have an idea what to do."

"Why not spend the rest of the night at my house? You can start out in the morning, after you've had some breakfast."

"May I do that?"

"Sure. If we cross Nobu Pond, we can get home in less than half the time it took us to get here. I asked the man and he said we could use his boat."

The pond, at the end of a short downhill walk, looked like a gigantic drumhead. Encircled by purple willow trees, it must have been twelve or thirteen hundred yards in diameter. The dark shadow of Mount Koma was reflected in the water, along with a skyful of stars.

With Musashi holding the torch and Gonnosuke poling, they slid silently across the middle of the pond. Far redder than the torch itself was its reflection in the smooth water.

Poisonous Fangs

From a distance, the torch and its reflection suggested a pair of firebirds swimming across the serene surface of Nobu Pond.

"Somebody coming!" whispered Matahachi. "All right, we'll go this way," he said, tugging at the rope he had tied Otsū with. "Come on!"

"I'm not going anywhere," protested Otsū, digging in her heels.

"Stand up!"

With the end of the rope, he lashed her across the back, then lashed and lashed again. But every stroke reinforced her resistance.

Matahachi lost heart. "Come on now," he implored. "Please walk."

When she still refused to stand, his anger flared again and he seized her by the collar. "You'll come whether you like it or not."

Otsū tried to turn toward the pond and scream, but he quickly gagged her with a hand towel. Eventually he managed to drag her to a tiny shrine hidden among the willows.

Otsū, yearning to have her hands free to attack her abductor, thought how wonderful it would be to be transformed into a snake, like the one she could see painted on a plaque. It was coiled around a willow, hissing at a man who was putting a curse on it.

"That was lucky." Sighing with relief, he pushed her into the shrine and leaned heavily against the outside of the grille door, intently watching the little boat coast into an inlet some four hundred yards away.

His day had been totally exhausting. When he'd tried to use brute force to take her, she'd made it clear she'd rather die than submit. She'd even threatened to bite off her tongue, and Matahachi knew her well enough to know it was no empty threat. His frustration brought him to the verge of committing murder, but the very notion sapped his strength and cooled his lust.

He couldn't fathom why she loved Musashi instead of him, when it had, for so long, been the other way around. Didn't women prefer him to his old friend? Hadn't they always? Hadn't Okō been immediately drawn to Matahachi when they'd first met her? Of course she had. Only one explanation was possible: Musashi was slandering him behind his back. Pondering his betrayal, Matahachi worked himself into a fury.

"What a stupid, gullible ass I am! How could I have let him make such a fool of me? To think I was in tears listening to him talk about undying friendship, about how he treasured it! Ha!"

He upbraided himself for ignoring Sasaki Kojirō's warning, which resounded in his ears. "Trust that scoundrel Musashi and you'll live to regret it."

Until today he'd wavered between liking and disliking his childhood friend, but now he loathed him. And although he couldn't bring himself to voice it, a solemn prayer for Musashi's eternal damnation took form in his heart.

He had become convinced that Musashi was his enemy, born to thwart him at every turn and eventually destroy him. "The lousy hypocrite," he thought. "He sees me after such a long time and starts preaching about being a real human being, tells me to buck up, that we'll go on from here hand in hand, friends for life. I remember every word—can see him saying it all so sincerely. It makes me sick just to think about it. He was probably laughing to himself the whole time.

"The so-called good people of this world are all phonies like Musashi," he reassured himself. "Well, I see through them now. They can't fool me anymore. Studying a lot of silly books and putting up with all sorts of hardship just to become another hypocrite is nonsense. From now on, they can tell me whatever they please. If I have to be a villain to do it, one way or another I'll stop that bastard from making a name for himself. For the rest of his life, I'll stand in his way!"

He turned around and kicked the grille door in. Then he untied her gag and said coldly, "Still crying, are you?"

She did not answer.

"Answer me! Answer the question I asked you before."

Enraged by her silence, he kicked her dark form on the floor. She moved out of range and said, "I have nothing to say to you. If you're going to kill me, do it like a man."

"Don't talk like a fool! I've made up my mind. You and Musashi have ruined my life, and I'm going to get even no matter how long it takes."

"That's nonsense. Nobody led you astray but you yourself. Of course, you may have had a little help from that Okō woman."

"Watch what you're saying!"

"Oh, you and your mother! What is it about your family? Why do you always have to go around hating somebody?"

"You talk too much! What I want to know is, are you going to marry me or not?"

"I can answer that question easily."

"Well, answer then."

"Throughout this lifetime and the eternal future, my heart is bound to one man, Miyamoto Musashi. How can I possibly care for anyone else, let alone a weakling like you. I hate you!"

A trembling swept over his body. With a cruel laugh, he said, "So you hate me, do you? Well, that's too bad, because whether you like me or not, from this night on, your body is mine!"

Otsū shook with anger.

"You still want to be difficult about it?"

577

"I was brought up in a temple. I never saw my father or mother. Death doesn't frighten me in the least."

"Are you joking?" he growled, as he dropped to the floor beside her and pressed his face toward hers. "Who said anything about death? Killing you wouldn't give me any satisfaction. This is what I'm going to do!" Seizing her shoulder and her left wrist, he sank his teeth right through her sleeve and into her upper arm.

Screaming and writhing about, she tried to free herself but only tightened the hold of his teeth on her arm. He did not release her even when blood dribbled down to the wrist he was holding.

Face stark white, she fainted from the pain. Feeling her body grow limp, he let go and hastily forced open her mouth to make sure she hadn't actually bitten off her tongue. Her face was bathed in sweat.

"Otsū," he wailed. "Forgive me!" He shook her until she came to.

The moment she was able to speak, she stretched out full length and groaned hysterically. "Oh, it hurts! It hurts so! Jōtarō, Jōtarō, help me!"

Matahachi, pale and gasping for breath, said, "Does it hurt? Too bad! Even after it heals, the mark of my teeth will be there for a long time. What'll people say when they see that? What'll Musashi think? I put that there as a brand, so everyone'll know that one of these days you'll belong to me. If you want to run away, run, but you'll never stop being reminded of me."

In the dark shrine, slightly hazy with dust, the silence was broken only by Otsū's sobbing.

"Stop blubbering. It gets on my nerves. I'm not going to touch you, so just be quiet. Do you want me to bring you some water?" He took an earthen bowl from the altar and started to go out.

He was surprised to see a man standing outside, looking in. When the man took to his heels, Matahachi bounded through the door and grabbed him.

The man, a farmer on his way to the wholesale market in Shiojiri with several sacks of grain packed on his horse's back, fell at Matahachi's feet, quaking with terror. "I wasn't going to do anything. I just heard a woman crying and looked in to see what happened."

"Is that so? Are you sure?" His manner was as stern as a local magistrate's.

"Yes; I swear it is."

"If that's the case, I'll let you off alive. Take those sacks off the horse's back and tie the woman on it. Then you'll stay with us until I'm through with you." His fingers played menacingly with his sword hilt.

The farmer, too frightened to disobey, did as he was told, and the three of them started off.

Matahachi picked up a bamboo stick to use as a whip. "We're going to Edo and we don't want any company, so stay away from the main road," he ordered. "Take a road where we won't run into anybody."

"That's very difficult."

"I don't care how difficult it is! Take a back road. We'll go to Ina and from there to Kōshū without using the main highway."

"But that means climbing a very bad mountain path from Ubagami to Gombei Pass."

"All right, start climbing! And don't try any tricks, or I'll split your skull open. I don't particularly need you. All I want is the horse. You should be thankful I'm taking you along."

The dark path seemed to get steeper with every step. By the time they reached Ubagami, about halfway up, both men and horse were ready to drop. Beneath their feet, clouds billowed like waves. A faint trace of light tinged the eastern sky.

Otsū had ridden all night without uttering a word, but when she saw the rays of the sun, she said quietly, "Matahachi, please let the man go. Give him back his horse. I promise not to run away."

Matahachi was reluctant, but she repeated her plea a third and fourth time, and he gave in. As the farmer went away, Matahachi said to Otsū, "Now, you just come along quietly, and don't try to escape."

She placed her hand over the injured arm, and biting her lip, said, "I won't. You don't think I want anyone to see the marks of your venomous fangs on me, do you?"

A Maternal Warning

"Mother," said Gonnosuke, "you're going too far. Can't you see I'm upset too?" He was weeping, and the words came in spurts.

"Shh! You'll wake him." His mother's voice was soft but stern. She might have been scolding a three-year-old. "If you feel so bad, the only thing to do is get a firm grip on yourself and follow the Way with all your heart. Crying won't do any good. Besides, it's unbecoming. Wipe your face."

"First promise you'll forgive me for that shameful performance yesterday."

"Well, I couldn't help scolding you, but I suppose after all it's a matter of skill. They say the longer a man goes without facing a challenge, the weaker he becomes. It's only natural you lost."

"Hearing that from you makes it all the worse. After all your encouragement, I still lost. I see now I don't have the talent or spirit to be a real warrior. I'll have to give up the martial arts and be content with being a farmer. I can do more for you with my hoe than I can with my staff."

Musashi was already awake. He sat straight up, amazed that the young man and his mother had taken the skirmish so seriously. He himself had already brushed it off as a mistake on his part as well as Gonnosuke's. "What a sense of honor," he mumbled as he crept quietly into the next room. He went to the far side and put his eye to the crack between the shoji panels.

Faintly lit by the rising sun, Gonnosuke's mother was seated with her back to the Buddhist altar. Gonnosuke was kneeling meekly before her, his eyes downcast and his face streaked with tears.

Grabbing the back of his collar, she said with vehemence, "What did you say? What's this about spending your life as a farmer?" Pulling him closer, until his head rested on her knees, she continued in an outraged tone. "Only one thing's kept me going all these years—the hope that I could make a samurai of you and restore our family's good name. So I had you read all those books and learn the martial arts. And that's why I've managed to live all these years on so little. And now . . . now you say you're going throw it all away!"

She, too, began to weep. "Since you let him get the best of you, you have to think of vindicating yourself. He's still here. When he wakes up, challenge him to another bout. That's the only way you can regain your self-confidence."

Gonnosuke, lifting his head, said sadly, "If I could do that, Mother, I wouldn't feel the way I do now."

"What's the matter with you? You're not acting like yourself. Where's your spirit?"

"Last night, when I went with him to the pond, I kept my eye open for a chance to attack him, but I couldn't bring myself to do it. I kept telling myself he was only a nameless rōnin. Still, when I took a good look at him, my arm refused to move."

"That's because you're thinking like a coward."

"What of it? Look, I know I've got the blood of a Kiso samurai in me. I haven't forgotten how I prayed before the god of Ontake for twenty-one days."

"Didn't you swear before the god of Ontake that you'd use your staff to create your own school?"

"Yes, but I guess I've been too complacent. I haven't considered that other men know how to fight too. If I'm as immature as I showed myself to be yesterday, how could I ever establish a school of my own? Rather than live in poverty and see you hungry, it'd be better to break my staff in half and forget about it."

"You've never lost before, and you've had a number of matches. Maybe the god of Ontake intended yesterday's defeat as a lesson to you. Maybe you're being punished for being overconfident. Giving up the staff to take better care of me isn't the way to make me happy. When that rōnin wakes up, challenge him. If you lose again, then's the time to break your staff and forget your ambitions."

Musashi went back to his room to give the matter some thought. If Gonnosuke challenged him, he'd have to fight. And if he fought, he knew he'd win. Gonnosuke would be crushed, his mother heartbroken.

"There's nothing to do but avoid it," he concluded.

Noiselessly sliding open the door to the veranda, he went out. The morning sun spilled a whitish light through the trees. In the corner of the yard near a storehouse stood the cow, grateful for another day and for the grass growing at her feet. Bidding the animal a silent farewell, Musashi went through the windbreak and strode off on a path winding through the fields.

Mount Koma today was visible from top to bottom. The clouds were countless, small and cottony, each of a different shape, all playing freely in the breeze.

"Jōtarō's young, Otsū frail," he told himself. "But there're people who have the goodness of heart to take care of the young and the frail. Some power in the universe will decide whether I find them or not." His spirit, in turmoil since that day at the waterfall, had seemed in danger of losing its way. Now it returned to the path it was meant to follow. On a morning like this, thinking solely of Otsū and Jōtarō seemed shortsighted, no matter how important they were to him. He must keep his mind on the Way he had sworn to follow throughout this life and into the next.

Narai, which he reached a little after noon, was a thriving community. One shop displayed a variety of pelts outside. Another specialized in Kiso combs.

With the intention of asking his way, Musashi stuck his head into a shop that sold medicine made from bear's gall. There was a sign reading "The Big Bear," and by the entrance a large bear in a cage.

The proprietor, his back turned, finished pouring himself a cup of tea and said, "Can I help you?"

"Could you tell me how to find the store belonging to a man named Daizō?"

"Daizō? He's down at the next crossroads." The man came out, holding his cup of tea, and pointed down the road. Catching sight of his apprentice returning from an errand, he called, "Here. This gentleman wants to go to Daizō's place. He might not recognize it, so you'd better take him there."

The apprentice, whose head was shaved so as to leave one shock of hair in front and another in back but none on top, marched off with Musashi in tow. The latter, grateful for the kindness, reflected that Daizō must enjoy the respect of his fellow townsmen.

"Over there," said the boy. He pointed at the establishment on the left and immediately took his leave.

Musashi, having expected a shop like the ones catering to travelers, was surprised. The grilled display window was eighteen feet long, and behind the shop there were two storehouses. The house, which was large and appeared to extend quite a way back from the high wall enclosing the rest of the compound, had an imposing entranceway, now closed.

With a certain hesitancy, Musashi opened the door and called, "Good day!" The large, dim interior reminded him of the inside of a sake brewery. Because of the dirt floor, the air was pleasantly cool.

A man stood in front of a bookkeeper's cabinet in the office, a room with a raised floor covered with tatami.

Shutting the door behind him, Musashi explained what he wanted. Before he finished, the clerk nodded and said, "Well, well, so you've come for the boy." He bowed and offered Musashi a cushion. "I'm sorry to say, you've just missed him. He showed up around midnight, while we were preparing for the master's trip. Seems the woman he was traveling with was kidnapped, and he wanted the master to help find her. The master told him he'd be glad to try, but he couldn't guarantee anything. If she'd been taken by a freebooter or bandit from around here, there'd be no problem. Apparently, though, it was another traveler, and he'd be sure to stay off the main roads.

"This morning, the master sent people out to look, but they didn't find any clues. The boy broke down when he heard that, so the master suggested he come along with him. Then they could look for her on the way, or they might even run into you. The boy seemed eager to go, and they left shortly after that. I guess it's been about four hours now. What a shame you missed them!"

Musashi was disappointed, though he wouldn't have been in time even if he had started earlier and traveled faster. He consoled himself with the thought that there was always tomorrow.

"Where's Daizō going?" he asked.

"It's hard to say. We don't run a shop in the ordinary sense. The herbs are prepared in the mountains and brought here. Twice a year, spring and fall, the salesmen stock up here and go out on the road. Since the master doesn't have much to keep him busy, he often takes trips, sometimes to temples or shrines, sometimes to hot-spring resorts, other times to places famous for their scenery. This time I suspect he'll go to the Zenkōji, travel around Echigo awhile and then go on to Edo. That's only a hunch, though. He never mentioned where he was going.... Wouldn't you like some tea?"

Musashi waited impatiently, ill at ease in such surroundings, while fresh tea was fetched from the kitchen. When the tea arrived, he asked what Daizō looked like.

"Oh, if you see him, you'll recognize him right off. He's fifty-two years old, quite robust—looks strong too—squarish, ruddy face with a few pockmarks. There's a balding spot on his right temple."

"How tall is he?"

"About average, I'd say."

"How does he dress?"

"Now that you ask, I imagine that's the easiest way to recognize him. He's wearing a striped Chinese cotton kimono he ordered from Sakai especially for this trip. It's a very unusual fabric. I doubt anybody else is wearing it yet."

Musashi formed an impression of the man's character, as well as his appearance. Out of politeness, he lingered long enough to finish the tea. He could not catch up with them before sundown, but he reckoned that if he traveled during the night, he'd be at Shiojiri Pass by dawn and could wait for them there.

By the time he came to the foot of the pass, the sun had disappeared, and an evening mist was descending softly over the highroad. It was late spring; lights in the houses along the road emphasized the loneliness of the mountains. It was still five miles to the top of the pass. Musashi climbed on, not stopping to relax until he reached Inojigahara, a high, level place hard by the pass. There he lay down among the stars and allowed his mind to wander. It was not long before he was sleeping soundly.

The diminutive Sengen Shrine marked the pinnacle of the rocky eminence that stood out like a carbuncle on the plateau. This was the highest point in the Shiojiri area.

Musashi's sleep was interrupted by the sound of voices. "Come up here," shouted one man. "You can see Mount Fuji." Musashi sat up and looked around without seeing anyone.

The morning light was dazzling. And there, floating on a sea of clouds, was the red cone of Mount Fuji, still wearing its winter mantle of snow. The sight brought a childish cry of delight to his lips. He had seen paintings of the famous mountain and had a mental image of it, but this was the first time he had actually seen it. It was nearly a hundred miles away but seemed to be on the same level as he was.

"Magnificent," he sighed, making no effort to wipe the tears from his unblinking eyes.

He felt awed by his own tininess, saddened by the thought of his insignificance in the vastness of the universe. Since his victory at the spreading pine, he had secretly dared to think there were few, if any, men as well qualified as he was to be called great swordsmen. His own life on earth was short, limited; the beauty and splendor of Mount Fuji eternal. Annoyed and a little depressed, he asked himself how he could possibly attach any importance to his accomplishments with the sword.

There was an inevitability in the way nature rose majestically and sternly above him; it was in the order of things that he was doomed to remain beneath it. He fell on his knees before the mountain, hoping his presumptuousness would be forgiven, and clasped his hands in prayer—for his mother's eternal rest and for the safety of Otsū and Jōtarō. He expressed his thanks to his country and begged to be allowed to become great, even if he could not share nature's greatness.

But even as he knelt, different thoughts came rushing into his mind. What had made him think man was small? Wasn't nature itself big only when it was reflected in human eyes? Didn't the gods themselves come into existence only when they communicated with the hearts of mortals? Men—living spirits, not dead rock—performed the greatest actions of all.

"As a man," he told himself, "I am not so distant from the gods and the universe. I can touch them with the three-foot sword I carry. But not so long as I feel there is a distinction between nature and humankind. Not so long as I remain distant from the realm of the true expert, the fully developed man."

His contemplation was interrupted by the chattering of some merchants who had climbed up near where he was and were gazing at the peak.

"They were right. You can see it."

"But it's not often you can bow before the sacred mountain from here."

Travelers moved in antlike streams in both directions, laden with a kaleidoscopic array of luggage. Sooner or later Daizō and Jōtarō would come up the 583 hill. If by chance he failed to pick them out from among the other travelers, surely they would see the sign he had left at the foot of the cliff: "To Daizō of Narai. I wish to see you when you pass through. I shall wait at the shrine up above. Musashi, Jōtarō's teacher."

The sun was well above the horizon now. Musashi had been watching the road like a hawk, but there was no sign of Daizō. On the other side of the pass, the road divided into three. One went through Kōshū straight to Edo. Another, the main route, crossed Usui Pass and entered Edo from the north. The third veered off to the northern provinces. Whether Daizō was going north to the Zenkōji or east to Edo, he would have to use this pass. Still, as Musashi realized, people did not always move as one might expect. The wholesaler could have gone somewhere well off the beaten path, or he could be spending an extra night at the foot of the mountain. Musashi decided it might not be a bad idea to go back there and ask about Daizō.

As he started down the path cut into the cliffside, he heard a familiar raucous voice say, "There he is, up there!" It brought to mind instantly the staff that had grazed his body two nights before.

"Come down from there!" Gonnosuke shouted. Staff in hand, he glared at Musashi. "You ran away! You figured I'd challenge you and ducked out. Come down, fight me one more time!"

Musashi stopped between two rocks, leaned against one of them and stared silently at Gonnosuke.

Taking this to mean that he was not coming, Gonnosuke said to his mother, "Wait here. I'll go up there and throw him down. Just watch."

"Stop!" scolded his mother, who was astride the cow. "That's what's wrong with you. You're impatient. You have to learn to read your enemy's thoughts before you go flying into battle. Supposing he were to throw a big rock down on you, then what?"

Musashi could hear their voices, but the words were not clear. As far as he was concerned, he'd already won; he already understood how Gonnosuke used his staff. What he found upsetting was their bitterness and their desire for revenge. If Gonnosuke lost again, they would be that much more resentful. From his experience with the House of Yoshioka, he knew the folly of fighting bouts that led to even greater hostility. And then there was the man's mother, in whom Musashi saw a second Osugi, a woman who loved her son blindly and would bear an eternal grudge against anyone who harmed him.

He turned around and began climbing.

"Wait!"

Held back by the strength of the old woman's voice, Musashi stopped and turned around.

She dismounted and walked to the foot of the cliff. When she was sure she had his attention, she knelt, put both hands on the ground and bowed deeply.

Musashi had done nothing to cause her to humble herself before him, but he bowed back as best he could from the rocky path. His hand went out as though to help her up.

584   "Good samurai!" she cried. "I am ashamed to appear before you like this.

I'm sure you have nothing but scorn for my stubbornness. But I'm not acting out of hate or spite or ill will. I ask you to take pity on my son. For ten years he's practiced all by himself—no teachers, no friends, no truly worthy opponents. I beg you to give him another lesson in the art of fighting."

Musashi listened silently.

"I would hate to see you part from us like this," she continued emotionally. "My son's performance two days ago was shoddy. If he doesn't do something to prove his ability, neither he nor I will be able to face our ancestors. Right now he's nothing more than a farmer who lost a fight. Since he's had the good fortune to meet a warrior of your stature, it would be a shame for him not to profit from the experience. That's why I've brought him here. I implore you to heed my pleas and accept his challenge."

Her speech ended, she bowed again, almost as though she were worshiping at Musashi's feet.

Coming down the hill, he took her hand and helped her back up onto the cow. "Gonnosuke," he said, "take the rope. Let's talk this over while we walk. I'll consider whether I want to fight you or not."

Musashi walked slightly ahead of them, and though he had suggested discussing the question, said not a word. Gonnosuke kept his eyes suspiciously on Musashi's back, now and again absently flicking a switch at the cow's legs. His mother looked anxious and worried.

When they had gone perhaps a mile, Musashi grunted and turned on his heel. "I'll fight you," he said.

Dropping the rope, Gonnosuke said, "Are you ready now?" He looked around to check his position, as if ready to have it out right then and there.

Ignoring him, Musashi addressed his mother. "Are you prepared for the worst? There's not a whit's difference between a bout like this and a fight to the death, even if the weapons are not the same."

For the first time, the old woman laughed. "No need to tell me that. If he loses to a younger man like you, then he may as well give up the martial arts, and if he does that, there'd be no further point in living. If it turns out that way, I'll bear you no grudge."

"If that's the way you feel, all right." He picked up the rope Gonnosuke had thrown down. "If we stay on the road, there'll be people in the way. Let's tie the cow up, then I'll fight as long as you wish."

There was a huge larch tree in the very middle of the flat area on which they stood. Pointing at it, Musashi led them there.

"Make your preparations, Gonnosuke," he said calmly.

Gonnosuke needed no urging. In a moment he was standing before Musashi with his staff pointed toward the ground.

Musashi stood empty-handed, arms and shoulders relaxed.

"Aren't you going to make any preparations?" asked Gonnosuke.

"What for?"

Gonnosuke's anger flared. "Get something to fight with. Anything you want."

"I'm ready."

585

"No weapon?"

"I have my weapon here," Musashi replied, bringing his left hand up to his sword hilt.

"You're fighting with a sword?"

Musashi's only reply was a crooked little smile at the corner of his mouth. They were already at the stage where he couldn't afford to waste breath talking.

Underneath the larch tree sat Gonnosuke's mother, looking like a stone Buddha. "Don't fight yet. Wait!" she said.

Staring at each other, not making the slightest move, neither man seemed to hear. Gonnosuke's staff was waiting under his arm for the opportunity to strike, as if it had breathed in all the air on the plateau and was about to exhale it in one great screeching blow. His hand glued to the underside of his sword hilt, Musashi's eyes seemed to pierce Gonnosuke's body. Inwardly, the battle had already begun, for the eye can damage a man more seriously than sword or staff. After the opening slice is made with the eye, the sword or staff slips in effortlessly.

"Wait!" called the mother again.

"What is it?" asked Musashi, jumping back four or five feet to a safe position.

"You're fighting with a real sword?"

"The way I fight, it doesn't make any difference whether I use a wooden sword or a real one."

"I'm not trying to stop you."

"I want to be sure you understand. The sword, wood or steel, is absolute. In a real bout, there are no halfway measures. The only way to avoid risk is to run away."

"You're perfectly right, but it occurred to me that in a match this important, you should announce yourself formally. Each of you is meeting an opponent the likes of whom he will encounter only rarely. After the fight's over, it'll be too late."

"True."

"Gonnosuke, give your name first."

Gonnosuke bowed formally to Musashi. "Our distant ancestor is said to have been Kakumyō, who fought under the banner of the great warrior of Kiso, Minamoto no Yoshinaka. After Yoshinaka's death, Kakumyō became a follower of the saint Hōnen, and it is possible that we are from the same family as he. Over the centuries, our ancestors have lived in this area, but in my father's generation we suffered dishonor, which I shall not name. In my distress, I went with my mother to Ontake Shrine and vowed in writing that I would restore our good name by following the Way of the Samurai. Before the god of Ontake Shrine, I acquired my technique for using the staff. I call it the Musō Style, that is, the Style of the Vision, for I received it in a revelation at the shrine. People call me Musō Gonnosuke."

Musashi returned his bow. "My family is descended from Hirata Shōgen, whose house was a branch of the Akamatsus of Harima. I am the only son of

Shimmen Munisai, who lived in the village of Miyamoto in Mimasaka. I have been given the name Miyamoto Musashi. I have no close relatives, and I have dedicated my life to the Way of the Sword. If I should fall before your staff, there is no need to trouble yourself about my remains."

Retaking his stance, he cried, "On guard!"

"On guard!"

The old woman seemed scarcely to breathe. Far from having danger thrust on herself and her son, she had gone out of her way to seek it out, deliberately placing her son in front of Musashi's gleaming sword. Such a course would have been unthinkable for an ordinary mother, but she was fully confident she had done the right thing. She sat now in formal style, her shoulders leaning slightly forward and her hands placed primly, one on top of the other, on her knees. Her body gave the impression of being small and shrunken; it would have been hard to believe that she had borne several children, buried all but one of them, and persevered through innumerable hardships to make a warrior out of the lone survivor.

Her eyes emitted a flash of light, as though all the gods and bodhisattvas of the cosmos had gathered in her person to witness the battle.

In the instant when Musashi unsheathed, Gonnosuke felt a chill go through his body. He sensed instinctively that his fate, exposed to Musashi's sword, had already been decided, for at this moment he saw before him a man he had not seen before. Two days earlier, he had observed Musashi in a fluid, flexible mood, one that might be likened to smooth, flowing lines of calligraphy in the cursive style.

He was unprepared for the man who faced him now, a study in austerity, like a square, immaculately written character with every line and dot in place.

Realizing that he had misjudged his adversary, he found himself unable to swing into a violent attack, as he had done before. His staff remained poised but powerless above his head.

While the two men confronted each other silently, the last of the morning mist cleared away. A bird flew indolently between them and the hazy mountains in the distance. Then all at once a shriek split the air, as though the bird had plummeted to earth. It was impossible to tell whether the sound came from the sword or the staff. It was unreal—the clapping of one hand that followers of Zen talk about.

Simultaneously, the two fighters' bodies, moving in perfect coordination with their weapons, shifted positions. The change took less time than it takes for an image to be transmitted from the eye to the brain. Gonnosuke's strike had missed. Musashi had defensively reversed his forearm and swept upward, from near Gonnosuke's side to a point above his head, narrowly missing his right shoulder and temple. Musashi then employed his masterful return strike, the one that had previously brought all opponents to grief, but Gonnosuke, seizing his staff near the ends with both hands, blocked the sword above his own head.

Had the sword not met the wood obliquely, Gonnosuke's weapon would doubtless have been split in two. In shifting, he had thrust his left elbow

587

forward and lifted his right elbow, with the intent of striking Musashi in the solar plexus, but at what should have been the moment of impact, the end of the staff was still a fraction of an inch from Musashi's body.

With sword and staff crossed above Gonnosuke's head, neither could advance or retreat. Both knew that a false move meant sudden death. Though the position was analogous to a sword-guard-to-sword-guard impasse, Musashi was aware of the important differences between sword and staff. A staff ostensibly had no guard, no blade, no hilt, no point. But in the hands of an expert like Gonnosuke, any part of the four-foot weapon could be blade, point or hilt. Thus the staff was far more versatile than the sword and could even be used as a short lance.

Unable to predict Gonnosuke's reaction, Musashi could not withdraw his weapon. Gonnosuke, on the other hand, was in an even more perilous position: his weapon was playing the passive role of blocking Musashi's blade. If he allowed his spirit to waver for so much as an instant, the sword would split open his head.

Gonnosuke's face paled, he bit his lower lip, and oily sweat glistened around the upturned corners of his eyes. As the crossed weapons began to waver, his breathing became heavier.

"Gonnosuke!" cried his mother, her face more pallid than her son's. She raised her torso and slapped her hip. "Your hip's too high!" she shouted, then fell forward. Her senses seemed to have left her; her voice had sounded as though she were spitting blood.

It had appeared that sword and staff would remain locked until the fighters turned to stone. At the sound of the old woman's cry, they came apart with a force more frightening than that of their coming together.

Musashi, slamming his heels into the ground, leaped backward a full seven feet. The interval was spanned in a flash by Gonnosuke and the length of his staff. Musashi barely managed to jump aside.

Thwarted in this do-or-die attack, Gonnosuke stumbled forward off balance, exposing his back. Musashi moved with the speed of a peregrine falcon, and a thin flash of light connected with the dorsal muscles of his adversary, who, with the bleat of a terrified calf, stumbled, and fell face down on the ground. Musashi sat down with a thud on the grass, holding his hand to his stomach.

"I give up!" he shouted.

No sound came from Gonnosuke. His mother, too stunned to speak, stared blankly at his prostrate form.

"I used the ridge of the sword," said Musashi, turning to her. Since she did not seem to comprehend, he said, "Get him some water. He's not badly hurt."

"What?" she cried in disbelief. Seeing there was no blood on her son's body, she staggered to his side and threw her arms around him. She called his name, brought him water, then shook him until he came to his senses.

Gonnosuke gazed vacantly at Musashi for a few minutes, then walked over to him and bowed his forehead to the ground. "I'm sorry," he said simply. "You're too good for me."

588   Musashi, seemingly awakening from a trance, grasped his hand and said,

"Why do you say that? You didn't lose; I did." He opened the front of his kimono. "Look at this." He pointed to a red spot where the staff had struck him. "Only a little more and I'd have been killed." There was a tremor of shock in his voice, for the truth was he had not yet figured out when or how he had suffered the wound.

Gonnosuke and his mother stared at the red mark but said nothing.

Pulling his kimono together, Musashi asked the old woman why she had cautioned her son about his hips. Had she observed something faulty or dangerous in his stance?

"Well, I'm no expert in these matters, but as I watched him using all his strength to hold your sword off, it seemed to me he was missing an opportunity. He couldn't advance, couldn't retreat, and he was too excited. But I saw that if he simply dropped his hips, holding his hands the way they were, the end of the staff would naturally strike your chest. It all happened in an instant. At the time, I wasn't really conscious of what I said."

Musashi nodded, regarding himself fortunate to have received a useful lesson without having had to pay with his life. Gonnosuke, too, listened reverently; no doubt he had also gained a new insight. What he had just experienced was no ephemeral revelation but a journey to the boundary between life and death. His mother, perceiving him to be on the brink of disaster, had taught him a lesson in survival.

Years later, after Gonnosuke had established his own style and become known far and wide, he recorded the technique his mother had discovered on this occasion. Though he wrote at some length of his mother's devotion and of his match with Musashi, he refrained from saying that he had won. On the contrary, for the rest of his life he told people that he had lost, and that the defeat had been an invaluable lesson to him.

Musashi, having wished mother and son well, proceeded on from Inojigahara to Kamisuwa, unaware that he was being followed by a samurai who inquired of all the grooms at the horse stations, as well as of other travelers, whether they had seen Musashi on the road.

A One-Night Love Affair

Musashi's injury was painful, so instead of spending time in Kamisuwa to make inquiries about Otsū and Jōtarō, he went on to the hot springs at Shimosuwa. This town, on the banks of Lake Suwa, was quite a large one, with the houses of ordinary townsmen alone numbering over a thousand.

At the inn designated for use by daimyō, the bath was covered by a roof, but otherwise the pools situated along the roadside were open to the sky and available to anyone who wanted to use them.

Musashi hung his clothes and swords on a tree and eased himself into the steaming water. As he massaged the swelling on the right side of his abdomen, he rested his head against a rock on the edge of the pool, closed his eyes and savored a groggy, pleasurable sense of well-being. The sun was beginning to set, and a reddish mist rose from the surface of the lake, which he could see between the fishermen's houses along the shore.

A couple of small vegetable plots lay between the pool and the road, where people and horses were coming and going with the usual noise and bustle. At a shop selling lamp oil and sundries, a samurai was purchasing straw sandals. Having selected a suitable pair, he sat down on a stool, took off his old ones and tied the new ones on.

"You must have heard about it," he said to the shopkeeper. "It happened under the great spreading pine at Ichijōji near Kyoto. This rōnin took on the entire House of Yoshioka all by himself and fought with a spirit you rarely hear about anymore. I'm sure he passed this way. Are you certain you didn't see him?"

For all his eagerness, the samurai seemed to know little about the man he was looking for, neither his age nor how he might be dressed. Disappointed when he received a negative reply, he repeated, "I must find him somehow," two or three times while he finished tying his sandals.

The samurai, a man of about forty, was well dressed and sunburned from traveling. The hair at his temples stood out around the cords of his basket hat, and the toughness in his facial expression matched his manly build. Musashi suspected his body bore the marks and calluses that come from wearing armor. "I don't remember ever seeing him before," he thought. "But if he's going around talking about the Yoshioka School, maybe he's one of their students. The school's had so many students; a few must have some backbone. They may be hatching another plot for revenge."

When the man had completed his business and left, Musashi dried himself and put on his clothes, thinking the coast was clear. But when he walked out onto the highroad, he almost bumped into him.

The samurai bowed and, looking intently into his face, said, "Aren't you Miyamoto Musashi?"

Musashi nodded, and the samurai, ignoring the suspicion written on his face, said, "I knew it." After a short paean to his own perspicacity, he continued familiarly, "You can't know how happy I am to meet you at last. I've had the feeling I'd run into you somewhere along the way." Without pausing to give Musashi a chance to speak, he urged him to spend the night at the same inn with him. "Let me assure you," he added, "you don't have to worry about me. My status, if you'll forgive me for saying so, is such that I usually travel with a dozen attendants and a change of horses. I'm a retainer of Date Masamune, the lord of Aoba Castle in Mutsu. My name is Ishimoda Geki."

When Musashi passively accepted the invitation, Geki decided they would stay at the inn for daimyō and led him into the place.

"How about a bath?" he asked. "But of course, you've just had one. Well, make yourself comfortable while I take one. I'll be back shortly." He took off his traveling clothes, picked up a towel and left the room.

Though the man had a winning way about him, Musashi's head was full of questions. Why would this well-placed warrior be looking for him? Why was he being so friendly?

"Wouldn't you like to change into something more comfortable?" asked the maid, proffering one of the cotton-stuffed kimonos furnished to guests.

"No, thank you. I'm not sure I'll be staying."

Musashi stepped out onto the veranda. Behind him he heard the maid quietly setting the dinner trays. As he watched the ripples on the lake change from deep indigo to black, the image of Otsū's sad eyes formed in his mind. "I suppose I'm not looking in the right place," he thought. "Anyone evil enough to kidnap a woman certainly has the instinct to avoid towns." He seemed to hear Otsū calling for help. Was it really all right to take the philosophic view that all things happen as a result of heaven's will? Standing there doing nothing, he felt guilty.

Coming back from his bath, Ishimoda Geki apologized for having left him alone and sat down before his dinner tray. Noticing that Musashi still wore his own kimono, he asked, "Why don't you change?"

"I'm comfortable in what I have on. I wear this all the time—on the road, inside the house, when I sleep on the ground under the trees."

Geki was favorably impressed. "I might have known," he said. "You want to be ready for action at any time, no matter where you are. Lord Date would admire that." He stared with unconcealed fascination at Musashi's face, which was lit from the side by the lamp. Remembering himself after a moment, he said, "Come. Sit down and have some sake." He rinsed off a cup in a bowl of water and offered it to Musashi.

Musashi seated himself and bowed. Resting his hands on his knees, he asked, "Could you tell me, sir, why you're treating me in such a friendly manner? And if you don't mind, why you were inquiring about me out on the highroad."

"I suppose it's only natural for you to wonder, but there's really very little to explain. Perhaps the simplest way to put it is that I have a sort of crush on you." He paused for a moment, laughed and went on: "Yes, it's a matter of infatuation, a case of one man being attracted to another."

Geki seemed to feel this was sufficient explanation, but Musashi was more mystified than ever. While it did not seem impossible for one man to be enamored of another, he himself had never experienced such an attachment. Takuan was too severe to inspire strong affection. Kōetsu lived in an entirely different world. Sekishūsai occupied a plane so far above Musashi's that either liking or disliking was inconceivable. Though it could be Geki's way of flattering him, a man who made such statements opened himself to the charge of insincerity. Still, Musashi doubted that this samurai was a sycophant; he was too solid, too manly in appearance, for that.

"Precisely what do you mean," Musashi asked with a sober air, "when you say you are attracted to me?"

"Perhaps I'm being presumptuous, but ever since I heard of your feat at Ichijōji, I've been convinced that you're a man I would like, and like very much."

"Were you in Kyoto then?"

"Yes, I arrived during the first month of the year and was staying at Lord Date's residence on Sanjō Avenue. When I happened to drop in on Lord Karasumaru Mitsuhiro the day after the fight, I heard quite a bit about you. He said he'd met you and remarked on your youth and what you'd been doing in the past. Feeling this strong attraction, I resolved that I must make an effort to meet you. On my way from Kyoto, I saw the sign you put up at Shiojiri Pass."

"Oh, you saw that?" Ironic, thought Musashi, that instead of bringing him Jōtarō, the sign had brought him someone of whose existence he had never dreamed.

But the more he considered the matter, the less he felt he deserved the esteem in which Geki seemed to hold him. Painfully conscious of his own mistakes and failures, he found Geki's adulation embarrassing.

With perfect honesty, he said, "I think you're rating me too highly."

"There are a number of outstanding samurai serving under Lord Date—his fief has an income of five million bushels, you know—and in time I've met many a skilled swordsman. But from what I've heard, it would seem that few can be compared with you. What's more, you're still very young. You have your whole future before you. And that, I suppose, is why you appeal to me. Anyway, now that I've found you, let's be friends. Have a drink, and talk about anything that interests you."

Musashi accepted the sake cup in good humor and began matching his host drink for drink. Before long, his face was bright red.

Geki, still going strong, said, "We samurai from the north can drink a lot. We do it to stay warm. Lord Date can outdrink any of us. With a strong general in the lead, it wouldn't do for the troops to fall behind."

The maid kept bringing more sake. Even after she'd trimmed the lamp wick several times, Geki showed no inclination to stop. "Let's drink all night," he suggested. "That way, we can talk all night."

"Fine," agreed Musashi. Then, with a smile: "You said you'd talked to Lord Karasumaru. Do you know him well?"

"You couldn't say we're close friends, but over the years I've been to his house any number of times on errands. He's very friendly, you know."

"Yes, I met him on the introduction of Hon'ami Kōetsu. For a nobleman, he seemed remarkably full of life."

Looking somewhat dissatisfied, Geki asked, "Is that your only impression? If you'd talked with him at any length, I'd think you'd have been struck by his intelligence and sincerity."

"Well, we were in the licensed quarter at the time."

"In that case, I suppose he refrained from revealing his true self."

"What's he really like?"

Geki settled himself in more formal fashion and in a rather grave tone said, "He's a troubled man. A man of sorrows, if you will. The shogunate's dictatorial ways disturb him greatly."

For a moment, Musashi was conscious of a lilting sound coming from the lake and the shadows cast by the white light of the lamp.

Abruptly Geki asked, "Musashi, my friend, for whose sake are you trying to perfect your swordsmanship?"

Never having considered the question, Musashi replied with guileless candor, "For my own."

"That's all right as far as it goes, but for whose sake are you trying to improve yourself? Surely your aim is not merely personal honor and glory. That's hardly sufficient for a man of your stature." By accident or design, Geki had come around to the subject he really wanted to talk about. "Now that the whole country's under Ieyasu's control," he declared, "we have a semblance of peace and prosperity. But is it real? Can the people actually live happily under the present system?

"Over the centuries, we've had the Hōjōs, the Ashikagas, Oda Nobunaga, Hideyoshi—a long string of military rulers consistently oppressing not only the people but the Emperor and the court as well. The imperial government has been taken advantage of, and the people mercilessly exploited. All the benefits have gone to the military class. This has been going on since Minamoto no Yoritomo, hasn't it? And the situation today is unchanged.

"Nobunaga seems to have had some idea of the injustice involved; at least he built a new palace for the Emperor. Hideyoshi not only honored the Emperor Go-Yōzei by requiring all the daimyō to pay obeisance to him, but even tried to provide a measure of welfare and happiness for the common people. But what of Ieyasu? To all intents and purposes, he has no interest beyond the fortunes of his own clan. So again, the happiness of the people and the well-being of the imperial family are being sacrificed to create wealth and power for a military dictatorship. We seem to be at the threshold of another age of tyranny. No one worries about this state of affairs more than Lord Date Masamune or, among the nobility, Lord Karasumaru."

Geki paused, waiting for a response, but none was forthcoming except for a barely articulate, "I see."

Like anyone else, Musashi was aware of the drastic political changes that had occurred since the Battle of Sekigahara. Yet he had never paid any attention to activities of the daimyō in the Osaka faction, or the ulterior motives of the Tokugawas, or the stands taken by powerful outside lords like Date and Shimazu. All he knew about Date was that his fief officially had an income of three million bushels per year but in fact probably yielded five million, as Geki had mentioned.

"Twice every year," Geki went on, "Lord Date sends produce from our fief to Lord Konoe in Kyoto for presentation to the Emperor. He's never failed to do this, even in times of war. That's why I was in Kyoto.

"Aoba Castle is the only one in the country to have a special room reserved for the Emperor. It's unlikely, of course, that it'll ever be used, but Lord Date set it aside for him anyway, built it out of wood taken from the old Imperial Palace when that was rebuilt. He had the wood brought from Kyoto to Sendai by boat.

"And let me tell you about the war in Korea. During the campaigns there, Katō, Konishi and other generals were competing for personal fame and triumph. Not Lord Date. Instead of his own family crest, he wore the crest of the rising sun and told everyone he'd never have led his men to Korea for the glory of his own clan or for that of Hideyoshi. He went out of love for Japan itself."

While Musashi listened attentively, Geki became absorbed in his monologue, describing his master in glowing terms and assuring Musashi that he was unexcelled in his single-minded devotion to the nation and the Emperor.

For a time he forgot about drinking but then suddenly looked down and said, "The sake's cold." Clapping his hands for the maid, he was about to order more.

Musashi hurriedly interrupted. "I've had more than enough. If you don't mind, I'd rather have some rice and tea now."

"Already?" mumbled Geki. He was obviously disappointed but, out of deference to his guest, told the girl to bring the rice.

Geki continued to talk as they ate. The impression Musashi formed of the spirit that seemed to prevail among the samurai of Lord Date's fief was that, as individuals and as a group, they were vitally concerned with the Way of the Samurai and with the problem of disciplining themselves in accordance with the Way.

This Way had existed since ancient times, when the warrior class had come into being, but its moral values and obligations were now little more than a vague memory. During the chaotic domestic strife of the fifteenth and sixteenth centuries, the ethics of the military man had been distorted, if not totally ignored, and now almost anyone who could wield a sword or shoot an arrow from a bow was regarded as a samurai, regardless of the attention—or lack of it—given to the deeper meaning of the Way.

The self-styled samurai of the day were often men of lower character and baser instincts than common peasants or townsmen. Having nothing but brawn and technique to command the respect of those beneath them, they were in the long run doomed to destruction. There were few daimyō capable of seeing this, and only a handful of the higher vassals of the Tokugawas and the Toyotomis gave any thought to establishing a new Way of the Samurai, which could become the foundation of the nation's strength and prosperity.

Musashi's thoughts returned to the years when he had been confined in Himeji Castle. Takuan, remembering that Lord Ikeda had in his library a handwritten copy of *Nichiyō Shūshin-kan* by Fushikian, had taken it out for Musashi to study. Fushikian was the literary name of the celebrated general Uesugi Kenshin; in his book, he recorded points of daily ethical training for the guidance of his chief vassals. From this, Musashi had not only learned about Kenshin's personal activities but also gained an understanding of why Kenshin's fief in Echigo had come to be known throughout the country for its wealth and military prowess.

Swayed by Geki's enthusiastic descriptions, he began to feel that Lord Date, besides equaling Kenshin in integrity, had created in his domain an atmosphere in which samurai were encouraged to develop a new Way, one that would enable them to resist even the shogunate, should that become necessary.

"You must forgive me for going on and on about matters of personal interest," said Geki. "What do you think, Musashi? Wouldn't you like to come to Sendai, see for yourself? His lordship is honest and straightforward. If you're striving to find the Way, your present status doesn't matter to him. You can talk with him as you would with any other man.

"There's a great need for samurai who will devote their lives to their country. I'll be more than happy to recommend you. If it's all right with you, we can go to Sendai together."

By this time the dinner trays had been removed, but Geki's ardor was in no way diminished. Impressed, but still cautious, Musashi replied, "I'll have to give it some thought before I can reply."

After they had said good night, Musashi went to his room, where he lay awake in the dark, his eyes glistening.

The Way of the Samurai. He concentrated on this concept as it applied to himself and to his sword.

Suddenly he saw the truth: the techniques of a swordsman were not his goal; he sought an all-embracing Way of the Sword. The sword was to be far more than a simple weapon; it had to be an answer to life's questions. The Way of Uesugi Kenshin and Date Masamune was too narrowly military, too hidebound. It would be up to him to add to its human aspect, to give it greater profundity, greater loftiness.

For the first time, he asked whether it was possible for an insignificant human being to become one with the universe.

A Gift of Money

Musashi's first waking thought was of Otsū and Jōtarō, and though he and Geki carried on a convivial conversation over breakfast, the problem of how to find them was very much on his mind. After emerging from the inn, he unconsciously scrutinized every face he encountered on the highroad. Once or twice he thought he saw Otsū ahead, only to find he was mistaken.

"You seem to be looking for someone," said Geki.

"I am. My companions and I got separated along the way, and I'm worried about them. I think I'd better give up the idea of going to Edo with you and search some of the other roads."

Disappointed, Geki said, "That's too bad. I was looking forward to traveling with you. I hope the fact that I talked too much last night won't change your mind about visiting Sendai."

Geki's manner, straightforward and masculine, appealed to Musashi. "That's very kind of you," he said. "I hope I have the chance someday."

"I want you to see for yourself how our samurai conduct themselves. And if you're not interested in that, then just regard it as a sightseeing trip. You can listen to the local songs and visit Matsushima. It's famous for its scenery, you know." Geki took his leave and headed briskly for Wada Pass.

Musashi turned around and went back to where the Kōshū highroad branched off from the Nakasendō. As he stood there mapping out his strategy, a group of day laborers from Suwa came up to him. Their dress suggested they were porters or grooms or bearers of the primitive palanquins used in these parts. They approached slowly, arms folded, looking like an army of crabs.

As their eyes rudely sized him up, one of them said, "Sir, you seem to be looking for someone. A beautiful lady, is it, or only a servant?"

Musashi shook his head, waved them off with a slightly disdainful gesture and turned away. He did not know whether to go east or west, but finally made up his mind to spend the day seeing what he could find out in the neighborhood. If his inquiries led nowhere, he could then proceed to the shōgun's capital with a clear conscience.

One of the laborers broke in upon his thoughts. "If you're looking for somebody, we could help you," he said. "It's better than standing around under the hot sun. What does your friend look like?"

Another added, "We won't even set a rate for our services. We'll leave it up to you."

Musashi relented to the extent of describing Otsū and Jōtarō in detail.

After consulting with his fellows, the first man said, "We haven't seen them, but if we split up we're sure to find them. The kidnappers must've taken one of the three roads between Suwa and Shiojiri. You don't know this area, but we do."

None too optimistic about his chances of success in such difficult terrain, Musashi said, "All right, go look for them."

"Done," shouted the men.

Again they huddled, ostensibly deciding who was to go where. Then the ringleader came forward, rubbing his hands together deferentially. "There's just one little thing, sir. You see . . . I don't like to mention it, but we're just penniless laborers. Why, not one of us has had anything to eat yet today. Wonder if you couldn't advance us half a day's pay and, say, a little something extra. I guarantee we'll find your companions before sundown."

"Of course. I was planning to give you something."

The man named a figure, which Musashi found, after counting his money, was more than he had. He was not unmindful of the value of money, but being alone, with no one to support, his attitude was on the whole indifferent. Friends and admirers sometimes donated travel funds, and there were temples where he could often obtain free lodging. At other times, he slept in the open or went without ordinary food. One way or another, he had always managed to get by.

On this trip, he had left the finances to Otsū, who had received a sizable gift of travel money from Lord Karasumaru. She had been paying the bills and giving him a certain amount of spending money each morning, as any ordinary housewife might do.

Keeping only a little for himself, he distributed the rest of his money among the men, and though they'd expected more, they agreed to undertake the search as a "special favor."

"Wait for us by the two-story gate of the Suwa Myōjin Shrine," the spokesman advised. "By evening we'll be back with some news." They made off in several directions.

Rather than waste the day doing nothing, Musashi went to see Takashima Castle and the town of Shimosuwa, stopping here and there to note features of the local topography, which might come in handy at some future date, and to observe the methods of irrigation. He asked several times whether there were any outstanding military experts in the area, but heard nothing of interest.

As sundown drew near, he went to the shrine and sat down, tired and dispirited, on the stone stairway leading up to the two-story gate. No one showed up, so he took a turn around the spacious shrine grounds. But when he returned to the gate, there was still no one there.

Though not loud, the sound of horses stamping the ground began to get on his nerves. Descending the steps, he came upon a shed, obscured by the trees, where an ancient horsekeeper was feeding the shrine's sacred white horse.

He glanced at Musashi accusingly. "Can I help you?" he asked brusquely. "Do you have some business with the shrine?"

Upon hearing why Musashi was there, he broke out in uncontrollable laughter. Musashi, seeing nothing at all funny about his predicament, made no attempt to conceal a scowl. Before he spoke, however, the old man said, "You've no business being on the road by yourself. You're too innocent. Did you really believe roadside vermin would spend the whole day looking for your friends? If you paid them in advance, you'll never see them again."

"You mean you think they were just putting on an act when they divided up and left?"

The horsekeeper's expression changed to one of sympathy. "You've been robbed!" he said. "I heard there were about ten vagrants drinking and gambling in the grove on the other side of the mountain all day today. They're most likely the ones. These things happen all the time." He went on to tell some stories of travelers being cheated out of their money by unscrupulous laborers, but concluded mildly, "That's the way the world is. You'd better be more careful from now on."

With this sage advice, he picked up his empty pail and departed, leaving Musashi feeling foolish. "It's too late to do anything now," he sighed. "I pride myself on my ability not to give my opponent any opening, and then get taken in by a gang of illiterate workmen!" This evidence of his gullibility came like a slap in the face. Such lapses could easily muddy his practice of the Art of War. How could a man so easily deceived by his inferiors effectively command an army? As he climbed slowly toward the gate, he resolved to henceforth pay more attention to the ways of the world about him.

One of the laborers was peering around in the dark, and as soon as he caught sight of Musashi, he called to him and ran partway down the steps.

"Glad I found you, sir," he said. "I've got news about one of the people you're looking for."

"Oh?" Musashi, having just reprimanded himself for his naiveté, was astonished but gratified to know that not everyone in the world was a swindler. "By one of them, do you mean the boy or the woman?"

"The boy. He's with Daizō of Narai, and I've found out where Daizō is, or at least where he's headed."

"Where might that be?"

"I didn't think that bunch I was with this morning would do what they promised. They took the day off to gamble, but I felt sorry for you. I went from Shiojiri to Seba, asking everybody I ran into. Nobody knew anything about the girl, but I heard from the maid at the inn where I ate that Daizō passed through Suwa about noon today on his way to Wada Pass. She said he had a young boy with him."

Embarrassed, Musashi said rather formally, "It was good of you to let me know." He took out his money pouch, knowing it contained only enough for his own meal. He hesitated a moment, but reflecting that honesty should not go unrewarded, gave the laborer his last bit of cash.

Pleased with the tip, the man raised the money to his forehead in a gesture of thanks and went happily on his way.

Watching his money go down the road, Musashi felt he had used it for a purpose worthier than that of filling his stomach. Perhaps the laborer, having learned that right conduct can be profitable, would go out on the road the next day and help another traveler.

It was already dark, but he decided that instead of sleeping under the eaves of some peasant's house, he would cross Wada Pass. By traveling all night, he should be able to catch up with Daizō. He started off, savoring once again the satisfaction of being on a deserted road at night. Something about it appealed to his nature. Counting his footsteps, listening to the silent voice of the heavens above, he could forget everything and rejoice in his own being. When he was surrounded by crowds of busy people, his spirit often seemed sad and isolated, but now he felt alive and buoyant. He could think about life coolly and objectively, even appraise himself as he might appraise a total stranger.

A little after midnight, his musings were distracted by a light in the distance. He had been climbing steadily since crossing the bridge over the Ochiai River. One pass was behind him; the next one, at Wada, loomed up in the starry sky ahead, and beyond that the even higher crossing at Daimon. The light was in a hollow that ran parallel to the two ridges.

"It looks like a bonfire," he thought, feeling pangs of hunger for the first time in hours. "Maybe they'll let me dry off my sleeves, give me a bit of gruel or something."

As he drew near, he saw that it wasn't an outdoor fire but the light from a small roadside teahouse. There were four or five stakes for tying horses, but no horses. It seemed incredible that there would be anyone in such a place at this hour, yet he could hear the sound of raucous voices mingling with the crackling of the fire. He stood hesitantly under the eaves for a few minutes. If it had been a farmer's or a woodcutter's hut, he would have had no qualms about asking for shelter and some leftovers, but this was a place of business.

The smell of food made him hungrier than ever. The warm smoke enveloped him; he could not tear himself away. "Well, if I explain my situation to them, maybe they'll accept the statue as payment." The "statue" was the small image of Kannon he had carved from the wood of an ancient plum tree.

When he barged into the shop, the startled customers stopped talking. The interior was simple, a dirt floor with a hearth and fire hood in the middle, around which huddled three men on stools. Stewing in a pot was a mixture of boar's meat and giant radish. A jar of sake was warming in the ashes. Standing with his back to them, slicing pickles and chatting good-naturedly, was the proprietor.

"What do you want?" asked one of the customers, a keen-eyed man with long sideburns.

Too hungry to hear, Musashi passed by the men and, seating himself on the edge of a stool, said to the proprietor, "Give me something to eat, quick. Rice and pickles'll do. Anything."

The man poured some of the stew over a bowl of cold rice and set it before him. "Are you planning to cross the pass tonight?" he asked.

"Um," mumbled Musashi, who had already seized some chopsticks and was attacking the food with gusto. After his second mouthful, he asked, "Do you know if a man named Daizō—he comes from Narai—passed here this afternoon, going toward the pass? He has a young boy with him."

"I'm afraid I can't help you." Then, to the other men, "Tōji, did you or your friends see an older man traveling with a boy?"

After a bit of whispering, the three replied in the negative, shaking their heads in unison.

Musashi, filled and warmed by the hot food, began to worry about the bill. He'd hesitated discussing it with the proprietor first, due to the presence of the other men, but he didn't for a moment feel he was begging. It had simply seemed more important to tend to his stomach's needs first. He made up his mind that if the shopkeeper would not accept the statue, he'd offer him his dagger.

"I'm sorry to have to tell you this," he began, "but I don't have any cash at all. I'm not asking for a free meal, mind you. I have something here to offer in payment, if you'll take it."

With unexpected amiability, the proprietor replied, "I'm sure that'll be all right. What is it?"

"A statue of Kannon."

"A real statue?"

"Oh, it's not the work of a famous sculptor—just something I carved myself. It may not be worth even the price of a bowl of rice, but take a look at it anyway."

As he began untying the cords of his bag, the one he had carried for years, the three men left off drinking and focused their attention on his hands. Besides the statue, the bag contained a single change of underwear and a writing set. When he emptied out the contents, something fell with a clunk to the ground. The others gasped, for the object that lay at Musashi's feet was a money pouch, from which several gold and silver coins had spilled out. Musashi himself stared in speechless amazement.

"Where did that come from?" he wondered.

The other men craned their necks to gape at the treasure.

Feeling something else in the bag, Musashi pulled out a letter. It consisted of a single line, saying, "This should take care of your travel expenses for the time being," and was signed "Geki."

Musashi had a pretty clear idea of what it meant: it was Geki's way of trying to buy his services for Lord Date Masamune of Sendai and Aoba Castle. The increasing probability of a final clash between the Tokugawas and the Toyotomis made it imperative for the great daimyō to maintain sizable numbers of able fighters. A favorite method used in the cutthroat competition for the few really outstanding samurai was to attempt to get such men in debt, even for a small sum, and then forge a tacit agreement for future cooperation.

It was common knowledge that Toyotomi Hideyori was providing large sums of money to Gotō Matabei and Sanada Yukimura. Though Yukimura was ostensibly in retirement on Mount Kudo, so much gold and silver was being sent to him from Osaka Castle that Ieyasu had undertaken a full-scale investigation. Since the personal requirements of a retired general living in a hermitage were fairly modest, it was all but certain that the money was being passed on to several thousand indigent rōnin, who were idling away their time in nearby towns and cities waiting for the outbreak of hostilities.

Finding an able warrior, as Geki believed he had, and somehow enticing him into his lord's service was one of the most valuable services a retainer could perform. And it was for just this reason that Musashi had no interest in Geki's money: using it would incur an unwanted obligation. In a matter of seconds, he decided to ignore the gift, to pretend it did not exist.

Without a word he reached down, picked up the pouch and restored it to his bag. Addressing the proprietor as though nothing had happened, he said, "All right then, I'll leave the statue here in payment."

But the man balked. "I can't accept that now, sir!"

"Is there something wrong with it? I don't claim to be a sculptor, but—"

"Oh, it's not bad, and I would have taken it if you didn't have any money, like you said, but you've got plenty. Why do you throw your cash around for people to see if you want them to think you're broke?"

The other customers, sobered and thrilled by the sight of the gold, vigorously nodded their agreement. Musashi, recognizing the futility of arguing that the money was not his, took out a piece of silver and handed it to the man.

"This is far too much, sir," complained the proprietor. "Don't you have anything smaller?"

A cursory examination revealed some variation in the worth of the pieces, but nothing less valuable. "Don't worry about the change," Musashi said. "You can keep it."

No longer able to maintain the fiction that the money didn't exist, Musashi tucked the pouch into his stomach wrapper for safekeeping.

Then, despite urgings to linger awhile, he shouldered his pack and went out into the night. Having eaten and restored his strength, he calculated that he could make it to Daimon Pass by sunrise. By day, he would have seen around him an abundance of highland flowers—rhododendrons, gentians, wild chrysanthemums—but at night there in the immense sea of darkness he could see only a cottonlike mist clinging to the earth.

He was about two miles from the teahouse when one of the men he'd seen there hailed him, saying, "Wait! You forgot something." Catching up with Musashi, the man puffed, "My, you walk fast! After you left, I found this money, so I brought it to you. It must be yours."

He held out a piece of silver, which Musashi refused, saying it certainly wasn't his. The man insisted that it was. "It must have rolled into the corner when you dropped your money pouch."

Not having counted the money, Musashi was in no position to prove the man wrong. With a word of thanks, he took the silver and put it in his kimono sleeve. Yet for some reason he found himself unmoved by this display of honesty.

Though the man's errand had been completed, he fell in alongside Musashi and began making small talk.

"Perhaps I shouldn't ask, but are you studying swordsmanship under a well-known teacher?"

601

"No. I use my own style."

The perfunctory answer failed to discourage the man, who declared that he had been a samurai himself, adding, "But for the time being I'm reduced to living here in the mountains."

"Is that so?"

"Um. Those two back there too. We were all samurai. Now we make our living cutting trees and gathering herbs. We're like the proverbial dragon biding its time in a pond. I can't pretend to be Sano Genzaemon, but when the time comes, I'll grab my old sword and put on my threadbare armor and go fight for some famous daimyō. I'm just waiting for that day to come!"

"Are you for Osaka or Edo?"

"Doesn't matter. The main thing is to be on somebody's side, or else I'll waste my life hanging around here."

Musashi laughed politely. "Thanks for bringing the money."

Then, in an effort to lose the man, he started taking long, rapid strides. The man stayed right beside him, step for step. He also kept pressing in on Musashi's left side, an encroachment that any experienced swordsman would regard as suspicious. Rather than reveal his wariness, however, Musashi did nothing to protect his left side, leaving it wide open.

The man became increasingly friendly. "May I make a suggestion? If you'd like, why don't you come spend the night at our place? After Wada Pass, you've still got Daimon ahead of you. You might make it by morning, but it's very steep—a difficult road for a man not familiar with these parts."

"Thanks. I think I'll take you up on that."

"You should, you should. Only thing is, we don't have anything to offer in the way of food or entertainment."

"I'd be happy to have a place to lie down. Where is your house?"

"About a half mile off to the left and a little higher up."

"You really are deep in the mountains, aren't you?"

"As I said, until the proper time comes, we're lying low, gathering herbs, hunting, doing things like that. I share a house with the other two men."

"Now that you mention it, what became of them?"

"They're probably still drinking. Every time we go there, they get drunk, and I wind up lugging them home. Tonight I decided to just leave them. . . . Watch out! There's a sharp drop there—stream down below. It's dangerous."

"Do we cross the stream?"

"Yes. It's narrow here, and there's a log across it just below us. After we cross, we turn right and climb up along the riverbank."

Musashi sensed that the man had stopped walking, but he did not look back. He found the log and started across. A moment later, the man leaped forward and lifted the end of the log in an attempt to throw Musashi into the stream.

"What are you up to?"

The shout came from below, but the man jerked his head upward in astonishment. Musashi, having anticipated his treacherous move, had already jumped from the log and lit as lightly as a wagtail on a large rock. His startled attacker dropped the log into the stream. Before the curtain of flying water had fallen back to earth, Musashi had jumped back onto the bank, sword unsheathed, and cut his assailant down. It all happened so quickly that the man did not even see Musashi draw.

The corpse wriggled for a moment or two before subsiding into stillness. Musashi did not deign to give it a glance. He had already taken a new stance in preparation for the next attack, for he was sure there would be one. As he steeled himself for it, his hair stood up like an eagle's crown feathers.

A short silence ensued, followed by a boom loud enough to split the gorge asunder. The gunshot seemed to have come from somewhere on the other side. Musashi dodged, and the well-aimed slug hissed through the space he had been occupying, burying itself in the embankment behind him. Falling as though wounded, Musashi looked across to the opposite side, where he saw red sparks flying through the air like so many fireflies. He could just make out two figures creeping cautiously forward.

A Cleansing Fire

Clenching his teeth tightly on the sputtering fuse, the man made ready to fire his musket again. His confederate crouched down, and squinting into the distance, whispered, "Do you think it's safe?"

"I'm sure I got him with the first shot," came the confident reply.

The two crept cautiously forward, but no sooner had they reached the edge of the bank than Musashi jumped up. The musketeer gasped and fired but lost his balance, sending the bullet uselessly skyward. As the echo reverberated through the ravine, both men, the other two from the teahouse, fled up the path.

Suddenly one of them stopped in his tracks and roared, "Wait! What are we running for? There's two of us and only one of him. I'll take him on and you can back me up."

"I'm with you!" shouted the musketeer, letting go of the fuse and aiming the butt of his weapon at Musashi.

They were definitely a cut above ordinary hoodlums. The man Musashi took to be the leader wielded his sword with genuine finesse; nonetheless, he was a poor match for Musashi, who sent them both flying through the air with a single sword stroke. The musketeer, sliced from shoulder to waist, fell dead to the ground, his upper torso hanging over the bank as if by a thread. The other man sped up the slope, clutching a wounded forearm, with Musashi in hot 603 pursuit. Showers of dirt and gravel rose and fell in his wake.

The ravine, Buna Valley, lay midway between Wada and Daimon passes and took its name from the beech trees that seemed to fill it. On its highest point stood an exceptionally large mountaineer's cabin surrounded by trees and itself crudely fashioned of beech logs.

Scrambling rapidly toward the tiny flame of a torch, the bandit shouted, "Douse the lights!"

Protecting the flame with an outstretched sleeve, a woman exclaimed, "Why, you— Oh! You're covered with blood!"

"Sh-shut up, you fool! Put out the lights—the ones inside too." He could hardly get the words out from panting, and with a last look behind him, he hurtled past her. The woman blew out the torch and rushed after him.

By the time Musashi arrived at the cabin, not a trace of light was visible anywhere.

"Open up!" he bellowed. He was indignant, not for being taken to be a fool, nor because of the cowardly attack, but because men like these daily inflicted great harm on innocent travelers.

He might have broken open the wooden rain shutters, but rather than make a frontal attack, which would have left his back dangerously exposed, he cautiously kept at a distance of four or five feet.

"Open up!"

Getting no answer, he picked up the largest rock he could handle and hurled it at the shutters. It struck the crack between the two panels, sending both the man and the woman reeling into the house. A sword flew out from beneath them and was followed by the man crawling on his knees. He quickly regained his feet and retreated into the house. Musashi bounded forward and seized him by the back of his kimono.

"Don't kill me! I'm sorry!" pleaded Gion Tōji, his whining tone exactly that of a petty crook.

He was soon back on his feet again, trying to find Musashi's weak point. Musashi parried each of his moves, but when he pressed forward to hem in his opponent, Tōji, mustering all his strength, pulled his short sword and made a powerful thrust. Dodging adroitly, Musashi swept him up in his arms and with a cry of contempt sent him crashing into the next room. Either an arm or a leg struck the pot hanger, for the bamboo pole from which it hung broke with a loud crack. White ashes billowed up from the hearth like a volcanic cloud.

A barrage of missiles coming through the smoke and ashes kept Musashi at bay. As the ashes settled, he saw that his adversary was no longer the bandits' chief, who was flat on his back near the wall. The woman, between curses, was throwing everything she could lay her hands on—pot lids, kindling, metal chopsticks, tea bowls.

Musashi leapt forward and quickly pinned her to the floor, but she managed to pull a bodkin from her hair and take a stab at him. When he brought his foot down on her wrist, she gnashed her teeth, then cried out in anger and disgust at the unconscious Tōji, "Haven't you any pride? How can you lose to a nobody like this?"

Hearing the voice, Musashi abruptly drew in his breath and let her go. She jumped to her feet, grabbed up the short sword and lunged at him.

"Stop it, ma'am," said Musashi.

Startled by the oddly courteous tone, she paused and gaped at him. "Why, it's . . . it's Takezō!"

His hunch was right. Apart from Osugi, the only woman who would still call him by his childhood name was Okō.

"It *is* Takezō," she exclaimed, her voice growing syrupy. "Your name's Musashi now, isn't it? You've become quite a swordsman, haven't you?"

"What are you doing in a place like this?"

"I'm ashamed to say."

"Is that man lying over there your husband?"

"You must know him. He's what's left of Gion Tōji."

"That's Tōji?" murmured Musashi. He had heard in Kyoto what a reprobate Tōji was, and how he had pocketed the money collected to enlarge the school and absconded with Okō. Still, as he looked at the human wreck by the wall, he couldn't help feeling sorry for him. "You'd better tend to him," he said. "If I'd known he was your husband, I wouldn't have been so rough with him."

"Oh, I want to crawl in a hole and hide," simpered Okō.

She went to Tōji's side, gave him some water, bound his wounds, and when he had begun to come around, told him who Musashi was.

"What?" he croaked. "Miyamoto Musashi? The one who . . . Oh, this is awful!" Placing his hands over his face, he doubled up abjectly.

Forgetting his anger, Musashi allowed himself to be treated as an honored guest. Okō swept the floor, tidied up the hearth, put on new kindling and heated some sake.

Handing him a cup, she said, in accordance with the accepted rules of etiquette, "We haven't a thing to offer, but . . ."

"I had quite enough at the teahouse," Musashi replied politely. "Please don't go to any trouble."

"Oh, I hope you can eat the food I've prepared. It's been such a long time." Having hung a pot of stew on the pot hanger, she sat down beside him and poured his sake.

"It reminds me of old times at Mount Ibuki," said Musashi amiably.

A strong wind had come up, and though the shutters were again securely in place, it came in through various cracks and teased the smoke from the hearth as it rose to the ceiling.

"Please don't remind me of that," said Okō. "But tell me, have you heard anything of Akemi? Do you have any idea where she is?"

"I heard she spent several days at the inn on Mount Hiei. She and Matahachi were planning to go to Edo. Seems she ran away with all his money."

"Oh?" said Okō disappointedly. "Her too." She gazed at the floor, sadly comparing her daughter's life with her own.

When Tōji had recovered sufficiently, he joined them and begged Musashi's forgiveness. He had, he avowed, acted on a sudden impulse, which he now deplored. There would come a day, he assured his guest, when he would reenter society as the Gion Tōji the world had known before.

Musashi kept quiet, but he would have liked to say that there didn't seem to be much to choose from between Tōji the samurai and Tōji the bandit, but if he did return to the life of a warrior, the roads would be that much safer for travelers.

Somewhat mellowed by the sake, he said to Okō, "I think you'd be wise to give up this dangerous way of life."

"You're quite right, but of course, it's not as though I'm living this way out of choice. When we left Kyoto, we were going to try our luck in Edo. But in Suwa, Tōji got to gambling and lost everything we had—travel money, everything. I thought of the moxa business, so we started gathering herbs and selling them in the town. Oh, I've had enough of his get-rich-quick schemes to last a lifetime. After tonight, I'm through." As always, a few drinks had introduced a coquettish note into her speech. She was beginning to turn on the charm.

Okō was one of those women of indeterminate age, and she was still dangerous. A house cat will romp coyly on its master's knees so long as it is well fed and cared for, but turn it loose in the mountains, and in no time it will be prowling the night with flaming eyes, ready to feast off a corpse or tear the living flesh off travelers who have fallen sick by the wayside. Okō was very much like that.

"Tōji," she said lovingly, "according to Takezō, Akemi was headed for Edo. Couldn't we go there too and live more like human beings again? If we found Akemi, I'm sure we'd think of some profitable business to go into."

"Well, maybe," was the unenthusiastic reply. His arms were wrapped pensively around his knees; perhaps the implied idea—peddling Akemi's body—was a little raw even for him. Tōji, after living with this predatory woman, was beginning to have the same regrets as Matahachi.

To Musashi, the expression on Tōji's face seemed pathetic. It reminded him of Matahachi. With a shudder, he recalled how he himself had once been enticed by her charms.

"Okō," said Tōji, lifting his head. "It won't be long till daylight. Musashi's probably tired. Why don't you fix a place for him in the back room, so he can get some rest?"

"Yes, of course." With a tipsy sidelong glance at Musashi, she said, "You'll have to be careful, Takezō. It's dark back there."

"Thanks. I could use some sleep."

He followed her down a dark corridor to the back of the house. The room seemed to be an addition to the cabin. It was supported by logs and projected out over the valley, with a drop of about seventy feet from the outer wall to the river. The air was damp from the mist and the spray blowing in from a waterfall. Each time the groaning of the wind rose a trifle, the little room rocked like a boat.

Okō's white feet retreated across the slatted floor of the outdoor hallway to the hearth room.

"Has he gone to sleep?" asked Tōji.

"I think so," she replied, kneeling by his side. She whispered in his ear, "What are you going to do?"

"Go call the others."

"You're going through with it?"

"Absolutely! It's not just a matter of money. If I kill the bastard, I'll have taken revenge for the House of Yoshioka."

Tucking up the skirt of her kimono, she went outside, Under the starless sky, deep in the mountains, she sped through the black wind like a feline demon, her long hair streaming out behind.

The nooks and crevices on the mountainside were not inhabited solely by birds and beasts. As Okō raced along, she made contact with more than twenty men, all members of Tōji's band. Trained for night forays, they moved more quietly than floating leaves to a spot just in front of the cabin.

"Only one man?"

"A samurai?"

"Does he have money?"

The whispered exchanges were accompanied by explanatory gestures and eye movements. Carrying muskets and daggers and the type of lances used by boar hunters, a few of them surrounded the back room. About half went down into the valley, while a couple stopped halfway down, directly below the room.

The floor of the room was covered with reed mats. Along one wall were neat little piles of dried herbs and a collection of mortars and other tools used to make medicine. Musashi found the pleasant aroma of the herbs soothing; it seemed to beckon him to close his eyes and sleep. His body felt dull and swollen to the tips of his extremities. But he knew better than to give in to the sweet temptation.

He was aware there was something afoot. The herb gatherers of Mimasaka never had storage sheds like this; theirs were never located where dampness accumulated and were always at some distance from dense foliage. By the dim light of a small lamp resting on a mortar stand beside his pillow, he could see something else that disturbed him. The metal brackets holding the room together at the corners were surrounded by numerous nail holes. He could also discern fresh wooden surfaces that must previously have been covered by joinery. The implication was unmistakable: the room had been rebuilt, probably a number of times.

A tiny smile came to his lips, but he did not stir.

"Takezō," Okō called softly. "Are you asleep?" Gently sliding the shoji aside, she tiptoed to his pallet and placed a tray near his head. "I'll put some water here for you," she said. He gave no sign of being awake.

When she was back in the cabin itself, Tōji whispered, "Is everything all right?"

Closing her eyes for emphasis, she replied, "He's sound asleep."

With a satisfied look, Tōji hurried outside, went to the back of the cabin and waved a lighted musket fuse, whereupon the men below pulled the supports out from under the room, sending it crashing down into the valley—walls, frame, ridgepole and all.

With a triumphant roar, the others sprang from their hiding places, like hunters from behind portable blinds, and rushed down to the riverbank. The 607 next step was to extricate the corpse and the victim's belongings from the debris. After that, it would be a simple matter to gather up the pieces and rebuild the room.

The bandits jumped into the pile of planks and posts like dogs falling on bones.

Arriving from above, others asked, "Have you found the body?"

"No, not yet."

"It's got to be here somewhere."

Tōji shouted raucously, "Maybe he struck a rock or something on the way down and bounced off to the side. Look all around."

Rocks, water, the trees and plants of the valley, were taking on a bright reddish cast. With startled exclamations, Tōji and his henchmen looked toward the sky. Seventy feet above, bright flames spouted from the doors, windows, walls and roof of the cabin. It had turned into a huge ball of fire.

"Quick! Hur-r-ry! Get back up here!" The piercing summons came from Okō, and sounded like the howl of a woman gone mad.

By the time the men had made their way up the cliff, the flames were dancing wildly in the wind. Unprotected from the shower of sparks and embers, Okō stood tied securely to a tree trunk.

To a man, they were dumbfounded. Musashi gone? How? How could he conceivably have outwitted them all?

Tōji lost heart; he did not even send his men in pursuit. He had heard enough about Musashi to know they'd never catch him. On their own, however, the bandits quickly organized search parties and flew off in all directions.

They found no trace of Musashi.

Playing with Fire

Unlike the other principal routes, there were no trees lining the Kōshū highroad, which joined Shiojiri and Edo by way of Kai Province. Used for military transport during the sixteenth century, it lacked the Nakasendō's network of back roads and had only recently been upgraded to the status of a main artery.

For travelers coming from Kyoto or Osaka, its least agreeable feature was a dearth of good inns and eating places. A request for a box lunch was likely to bring forth nothing more appetizing than flat rice cakes wrapped in bamboo leaves or, even less appealing, balls of plain rice done up in dried oak leaves. Despite the primitive fare—probably not much different from that of the

Fujiwara period, hundreds of years earlier—the rustic hostelries swarmed with guests, most of them bound for Edo.

A group of travelers was taking a rest above Kobotoke Pass. One of them exclaimed, "Look, there's another batch," referring to a sight he and his companions had been enjoying almost daily—a group of prostitutes on their way from Kyoto to Edo.

The girls numbered about thirty, some old, some in their twenties or early thirties, at least five in their middle teens. Together with about ten men who managed or served them, they resembled a large patriarchal family. There were in addition several packhorses loaded down with everything from small wicker baskets to man-sized wooden chests.

The head of the "family," a man of about forty, was addressing his girls. "If your straw sandals are giving you blisters, change into zōri, but tie them tight so they don't slip around. And stop complaining that you can't walk any farther. Just look at the children on the road, the children!" It was clear from his acid tone that he was having a hard time forcing his usually sedentary charges to keep moving.

The man, whose name was Shōji Jinnai, was a native of Fushimi, a samurai by birth, who had for reasons of his own abandoned the military life to become a brothel keeper. Being both quick-witted and resourceful, he had succeeded in gaining the support of Tokugawa Ieyasu, who often took up residence at Fushimi Castle, and had not only obtained permission to move his own business to Edo but had also persuaded many of his colleagues in the trade to do likewise.

Near the crest of Kobotoke, Jinnai brought his procession to a halt, saying, "It's still a little early, but we can have our lunch now." Turning to Onao, an old woman who functioned as a sort of mother hen, he ordered her to pass out the food.

The basket containing the box lunches was duly unloaded from one of the horses and a leaf-wrapped ball of rice dealt out to each of the women, who scattered themselves about and relaxed. The dust that had yellowed their skin had also turned their black hair nearly white, though they wore broad-brimmed traveling hats or had tied hand towels around their heads. There being no tea, eating entailed a good deal of lip smacking and tooth sucking. There was no suggestion of sexual wiles or amorous thrills. "Whose arms will embrace this red, red blossom tonight?" seemed utterly beside the point.

"Oh, this is delicious!" cried one of Jinnai's younger charges ecstatically. Her tone of voice would have brought tears to her mother's eyes.

The attention of two or three others wandered from their lunch to focus on a young samurai passing by.

"Isn't he handsome?" whispered one.

"Umm, not bad," replied another, of more worldly outlook.

A third volunteered, "Oh, I know him. He used to come to our place with men from the Yoshioka School."

"Which one are you talking about?" asked one lustful-eyed creature.

"The young one, strutting along there with the long sword on his back."

Unaware of the admiration, Sasaki Kojirō was pushing his way through a throng of porters and packhorses.

A high, flirtatious voice called, "Mr. Sasaki! Over here, Mr. Sasaki!"

Since there were lots of people named Sasaki, he didn't even turn.

"You with the forelock!"

Kojirō's eyebrows shot up, and he spun around.

"Watch your tongues!" Jinnai shouted angrily. "You're being rude." Then, glancing up from his lunch, he recognized Kojirō.

"Well, well," he said, rising quickly. "If it isn't our friend Sasaki! Where are you headed, if I may ask?"

"Why, hello. You're the master of the Sumiya, aren't you? I'm going to Edo. And what about you? You seem to be engaged in a full-scale move."

"That we are. We're moving to the new capital."

"Really? Do you think you can make a go of it there?"

"Nothing grows in stagnant waters."

"The way Edo's growing, I imagine there's plenty of work for construction workers and gunsmiths. But elegant entertainment? It seems doubtful there's much demand for it yet."

"You're wrong, though. Women made a city out of Osaka before Hideyoshi got around to taking any notice of it."

"Maybe, but in a place as new as Edo, you probably won't even be able to find a suitable house."

"Wrong again. The government's set aside some marshland in a place called Yoshiwara for people in my business. My associates have already started filling it in, putting in streets and building houses. From all reports, I should be able to find a good street-front location fairly easily."

"You mean the Tokugawas are giving the land away? For free?"

"Of course. Who'd pay for marshland? The government's even providing some of the construction materials."

"I see. No wonder you're all abandoning the Kyoto area."

"And what about you? Or do you have some prospect of a position with a daimyō?"

"Oh, no; nothing like that. I wouldn't take one if it was offered. I just thought I'd see what's going on up there, since it's the shōgun's residence and the place where orders are going to come from in the future. Of course, if I were asked to be one of the shōgun's instructors, I might accept."

Though no judge of swordsmanship, Jinnai had a good eye for people. Thinking it just as well not to comment on Kojirō's unbridled egotism, he averted his eyes and began prodding his troop into movement. "Everybody up now! It's time we were going."

Onao, who had been counting heads, said, "We seem to be missing one girl. Which one is it, now? Kichō? Or maybe Sumizome? No; they're both over there. This is strange. Who could it be?"

Kojirō, disinclined to have a party of prostitutes for traveling companions, went on his way.

A couple of the girls who had gone back down the road to search returned to where Onao was.

Jinnai joined them. "Here, here, Onao, which one is it?"

"Ah, I know now. It was that girl named Akemi," she replied contritely, as if the fault were hers. "The one you picked up on the road in Kiso."

"She must be around here somewhere."

"We've looked everywhere. I think she must have run away."

"Well, I didn't have a written commitment from her, and I didn't lend her any 'body money.' She said she was willing, and since she was good-looking enough to be marketable, I took her on. I suppose she's cost me a bit in traveling expenses, but not enough to worry about. Never mind her. Let's get moving."

He began hustling his group along. Even if it meant traveling after sundown, he wanted to reach Hachiōji within the day. If they could get that far before stopping, they could be in Edo the next day.

A short way down the road, Akemi reappeared and fell in with them.

"Where have you been?" Onao demanded angrily. "You can't just wander off without telling anyone where you're going. Unless, of course, you're planning to leave us." The old woman went on to explain self-righteously how they had all been so worried about her.

"You don't understand," said Akemi, from whom the scolding brought nothing but giggles. "There was a man I know on the road, and I didn't want him to see me. I ran into a clump of bamboo, not knowing there was a sudden drop-off there. I slid all the way down to the bottom." She corroborated this by holding up her torn kimono and a skinned elbow. But all the time she was begging forgiveness, her face showed not the slightest sign of contrition.

From his position near the front, Jinnai caught wind of what had happened and summoned her. Sternly he said, "Your name's Akemi, isn't it? Akemi— that's hard to remember. If you're really going to succeed in this business, you'll have to find a better name. Tell me, have you really resolved to go through with this?"

"Does it require resolution to become a whore?"

"It's not something you can take up for a month or so and then quit. And if you become one of my girls, you'll have to give the customers what they ask for, like it or not. Don't make any mistake about that."

"What difference does it make now? Men have already made a mess of my life."

"That's not the right attitude at all. Now, you give this some careful thought. If you change your mind before we reach Edo, that's all right. I won't ask you to pay me back for your food and lodging."

That same day, at the Yakuōin in Takao, an older man, apparently free of the pressures of business, was about to resume his leisurely journey. He, his servant and a boy of about fifteen had arrived the previous evening and requested overnight accommodations. He and the boy had been touring the temple grounds since early morning. It was now about noon.

"Use this for roof repairs, or whatever is necessary," he said, offering one of the priests three large gold coins.

The head priest, immediately apprised of the gift, was so overwhelmed by 611 the donor's generosity that he personally hastened out to exchange greetings. "Perhaps you would like to leave your name," he said.

Another priest, saying this had already been done, showed him the entry in the temple registry, which read: "Daizō of Narai, dealer in herbs, resident at the foot of Mount Ontake in Kiso."

The head priest apologized profusely for the poor quality of the fare served by the temple, for Daizō of Narai was known throughout the country as a lavish contributor to shrines and temples. His gifts always took the form of gold coins—in some cases, it was said, as many as several dozen. Only he himself knew whether he did this for amusement, to acquire a reputation, or out of piety.

The priest, eager to have him stay longer, begged him to inspect the temple's treasures, a privilege accorded to few.

"I'll be in Edo awhile," said Daizō. "I'll come see them another time."

"By all means, but at least let me accompany you to the outer gate," insisted the priest. "Are you planning to stop in Fuchū tonight?"

"No; Hachiōji."

"In that case, it'll be an easy trip."

"Tell me, who's the lord of Hachiōji now?"

"It's recently been put under the administration of Ōkubo Nagayasu."

"He was magistrate of Nara, wasn't he?"

"Yes, that's the man. The gold mines on Sado Island are also under his control. He's very rich."

"A very able man, it would appear."

It was still daylight when they came to the foot of the mountains and stood on the busy main street of Hachiōji, where reportedly there were no fewer than twenty-five inns.

"Well, Jōtarō, where shall we stay?"

Jōtarō, who had stuck to Daizō's side like a shadow, let it be known in no uncertain terms that he preferred "anywhere—as long as it's not a temple."

Choosing the largest and most imposing inn, Daizō entered and requested a room. His distinguished appearance, together with the elegant lacquered traveling case his servant carried on his back, made a dazzling impression on the head clerk, who said fawningly, "You're stopping quite early, aren't you?" Inns along the highroads were accustomed to having hordes of travelers tumble in at dinnertime or even later.

Daizō was shown to a large room on the first floor, but shortly after sundown, both the innkeeper and the head clerk came to Daizō's room.

"I'm sure it's a great inconvenience," the innkeeper began abjectly, "but a large party of guests has come in very suddenly. I'm afraid it'll be terribly noisy here. If you wouldn't mind moving to a room on the second floor . . ."

"Oh, that's perfectly all right," replied Daizō good-naturedly. "Glad to see your business is thriving."

Signaling Sukeichi, his servant, to take care of the luggage, Daizō proceeded upstairs. He had no sooner left the room than it was overrun by women from the Sumiya.

The inn wasn't just busy; it was frenetic. What with the hubbub downstairs, the servants did not come when called. Dinner was late, and when they had eaten, no one came to clear away the dishes. On top of that, there was the constant tramping of feet on both floors. Only Daizō's sympathy for the hired help kept him from losing his temper. Ignoring the litter in the room, he stretched out to take a nap, using his arm for a pillow. After only a few minutes, a sudden thought came to him, and he called Sukeichi.

When Sukeichi failed to materialize, Daizō opened his eyes, sat up and shouted, "Jōtarō, come here!"

But he, too, had disappeared.

Daizō got up and went to the veranda, which he saw was lined with guests, excitedly gaping with delight at the prostitutes on the first floor.

Spying Jōtarō among the spectators, Daizō swiftly yanked him back into the room. With a forbidding eye, he demanded, "What were you staring at?"

The boy's long wooden sword, which he did not take off even indoors, scraped the tatami as he sat down. "Well," he said, "everyone else is looking."

"And just what are they looking at?"

"Oh, there're a lot of women in the back room downstairs."

"Is that all?"

"Yes."

"What's so entertaining about that?" The presence of the whores didn't bother Daizō, but for some reason he found the intense interest of the men gawking at them annoying.

"I don't know," replied Jōtarō honestly.

"I'm going for a walk around town," Daizō said. "You stay here while I'm gone."

"Can't I go with you?"

"Not at night."

"Why not?"

"As I told you before, when I go for a walk, it's not simply to amuse myself."

"Well, what's the idea, then?"

"It has to do with my religion."

"Don't you get enough of shrines and temples during the daytime? Even priests have to sleep at night."

"Religion has to do with more than shrines and temples, young man. Now go find Sukeichi for me. He has the key to my traveling case."

"He went downstairs a few minutes ago. I saw him peeking into the room where the women are."

"Him too?" exclaimed Daizō with a click of his tongue. "Go get him, and be quick about it." After Jōtarō had left, Daizō began retying his obi.

Having heard the women were Kyoto prostitutes, famous for their beauty and savoir faire, the male guests were unable to leave off feasting their eyes. Sukeichi was so absorbed with the sight that his mouth was still hanging open when Jōtarō located him.

"Come on, you've seen enough," snapped the boy, giving the servant's ear a tug.

"Ouch!" squealed Sukeichi.

"Your master's calling you."

"That's not true."

"It is too. He said he was going for a walk. He's always taking walks, isn't he?"

"Eh? Oh, all right," said Sukeichi, tearing his eyes away reluctantly.

The boy had turned to follow him when a voice called, "Jōtarō? You're Jō-tarō, aren't you?"

The voice was that of a young woman. He looked around searchingly. The hope that he would find his lost teacher and Otsū never left him. Could it be? He peered tensely through the branches of a large evergreen shrub.

"Who is it?"

"Me."

The face that emerged from the foliage was familiar.

"Oh, it's only you."

Akemi slapped him roughly on the back. "You little monster! And it's been such a long time since I saw you. What are you doing here?"

"I could ask you the same question."

"Well, I . . . Oh, it wouldn't mean anything to you anyway."

"Are you traveling with those women?"

"I am, but I haven't made up my mind yet."

"Made up your mind about what?"

"Whether to become one of them or not," she replied with a sigh. After a long pause, she asked, "What's Musashi doing these days?"

This, Jōtarō perceived, was what she really wanted to know. He only wished he could answer the question.

"Otsū and Musashi and I . . . we got separated on the highroad."

"Otsū? Who's she?" She had hardly spoken before she remembered. "Oh, never mind; I know. Is she *still* chasing after Musashi?" Akemi was in the habit of thinking of Musashi as a dashing *shugyōsha*, wandering about as the mood suited him, living in the forest, sleeping on bare rocks. Even if she succeeded in catching him, he'd see right away how dissolute her life had become and shun her. She had long since resigned herself to the idea that her love would go unrequited.

But the mention of another woman awoke feelings of jealousy and rekindled the dying embers of her amorous instinct.

"Jōtarō," she said, "there're too many curious eyes around here. Let's go out somewhere."

They left via the garden gate. Out in the street, their eyes were regaled by the lights of Hachiōji and its twenty-five hostelries. It was the liveliest town either had seen since leaving Kyoto. To the northwest rose the dark, silent forms of the Chichibu Range and the mountains marking the boundary of Kai Province, but here the atmosphere was replete with the aroma of sake, noisy with the clicking of weavers' reeds, the shouts of market officials, the excited voices of gamblers and the dispirited whining songs of local street singers.

"I often heard Matahachi mention Otsū," Akemi lied. "What kind of person is she?"

"She's a very good person," Jōtarō said soberly. "Sweet and gentle and considerate and pretty. I really like her."

The threat Akemi felt hanging over her grew heavier, but she cloaked her feelings with a benign smile. "Is she really so wonderful?"

"Oh, yes. And she can do anything. She sings; she writes well. And she's good at playing the flute."

Now visibly ruffled, Akemi said, "I don't see what good it does a woman to be able to play the flute."

"If you don't, you don't, but everybody, even Lord Yagyū Sekishūsai, speaks highly of Otsū. There's only one little thing I don't like about her."

"All women have their faults. It's just a question of whether they honestly admit to them, the way I do, or try to hide them behind a ladylike pose."

"Otsū's not like that. It's just this one weakness of hers."

"What's that?"

"She's always breaking into tears. She's a regular crybaby."

"Oh? Why is that?"

"She cries whenever she thinks of Musashi. That makes being around her pretty gloomy, and I don't like it." Jōtarō expressed himself with youthful abandon, heedless of the effect this might have.

Akemi's heart, her whole body, was afire with raging jealousy. It showed in the depths of her eyes, even in the color of her skin. But she continued her interrogation. "Tell me, how old is she?"

"About the same."

"You mean the same age as me?"

"Um. But she looks younger and prettier."

Akemi plunged on, hoping to turn Jōtarō against Otsū. "Musashi's more masculine than most men. He must hate having to watch a woman carry on all the time. Otsū probably thinks tears will win a man's sympathy. She's like the girls working for the Sumiya."

Jōtarō, very much irked, retorted, "That's not true at all. In the first place, Musashi likes Otsū. He never shows his feelings, but he's in love with her."

Akemi's flushed face grew bright crimson. She longed to throw herself into a river to quench the flames that were consuming her.

"Jōtarō, let's go this way." She pulled him toward a red light in a side street.

"That's a drinking place."

"Well, what of it?"

"Women have no business in a place like that. You can't go in there."

"All of a sudden I have the urge to drink, and I can't go in alone. I'd be embarrassed."

"*You'd* be embarrassed. What about me?"

"They'll have things to eat. You can have anything you want."

At first glance, the shop seemed empty. Akemi walked right in, then, facing the wall rather than the counter, said, "Bring me some sake!"

One cup after another went down as fast as was humanly possible. Jōtarō, frightened by the quantity, tried to slow her down, but she elbowed him out of the way.

"Quiet!" she yelped. "What a nuisance you are! Bring some more sake! Sake!"

Jōtarō, insinuating himself between her and the sake jar, pleaded, "You've got to stop. You can't go on drinking here like this."

"Don't worry about me," she slurred. "You're a friend of Otsū's, aren't you? I can't stand women who try to win a man with tears!"

"Well, I dislike women who get drunk."

"I'm so sorry, but how could a runt like you understand why I drink?"

"Come on, just pay the bill."

"You think I've got money?"

"Don't you?"

"No. Maybe he can collect from the Sumiya. I've already sold myself to the master anyway." Tears flooded her eyes. "I'm sorry . . . I'm really sorry."

"Weren't you the one who was making fun of Otsū for crying? Look at yourself."

"My tears aren't the same as hers. Oh, life's too much trouble. I might as well be dead."

With that, she stood up and lurched out into the street. The shopkeeper, having had other female customers like this in his time, merely laughed it off, but a rōnin who had until then been sleeping quietly in a corner opened his bleary eyes and stared at her retreating back.

Jōtarō darted after her and grabbed her around the waist, but he lost his hold. She started running down the darkened street, Jōtarō close behind.

"Stop!" he cried with alarm. "You mustn't even think of it. Come back!"

Though she seemed not to care whether she ran into something in the dark or fell into a swamp, she was fully conscious of Jōtarō's pleading. When she had plunged into the sea at Sumiyoshi, she had wanted to kill herself, but she was no longer so lacking in guile. She got a certain thrill from having Jōtarō so worried about her.

"Watch out!" he screamed, seeing that she was headed straight toward the murky water of a moat. "Stop it! Why do you want to die? It's crazy."

As he caught her around the waist again, she wailed, "Why shouldn't I die? You think I'm wicked. So does Musashi. Everybody does. There's nothing I can do but die, embracing Musashi in my heart. Never will I let him be taken from me by a woman like that!"

"You're pretty mixed up. How did you get this way?"

"It doesn't matter. All you have to do is push me into the moat. Go ahead, Jōtarō, push." Covering her face with her hands, she burst into frenzied tears. This awakened a strange fear in Jōtarō. He, too, felt the urge to cry.

"Come on, Akemi. Let's go back."

"Oh, I yearn so to see him. Find him for me, Jōtarō. Please find Musashi for me."

"Stand still! Don't move; it's dangerous."

"Oh, Musashi!"

"Watch out!"

616 At that moment the rōnin from the sake shop stepped out of the darkness.

"Go away, boy," he commanded. "I'll take her back to the inn." He put his hands under Jōtarō's arms and roughly lifted him aside.

He was a tall man, thirty-four or -five years old, with deep-set eyes and a heavy beard. A crooked scar, no doubt left by a sword, ran from below his right ear to his chin. It looked like the jagged tear that appears when a peach is broken open.

Swallowing hard to overcome his fear, Jōtarō tried coaxing. "Akemi, please come with me. Everything'll be all right."

Akemi's head was now resting on the samurai's chest.

"Look," the man said, "she's gone to sleep. Off with you! I'll take her home later."

"No! Let go of her!"

When the boy refused to budge, the rōnin slowly reached out with one hand and grabbed his collar.

"Hands off!" screamed Jōtarō, resisting with all his strength.

"You little bastard! How'd you like to get thrown into the moat?"

"Who's going to do it?" He wriggled loose, and as soon as he was free, his hand found the end of his wooden sword. He swung it at the man's side, but his own body did a somersault and landed on a rock by the roadside. He moaned once, then remained still.

Jōtarō had been out for some time before he began hearing voices around him.

"Wake up, there."

"What happened?"

Opening his eyes, he vaguely took in a small crowd of people.

"Are you awake?"

"Are you all right?"

Embarrassed by the attention he was attracting, he picked up his wooden sword and was trying to get away when a clerk from the inn grabbed his arm. "Wait a minute," he barked. "What happened to the woman you were with?"

Looking around, Jōtarō got the impression that the others were also from the inn, guests as well as employees. Some of the men were carrying sticks; others were holding round paper lanterns.

"A man came and said you'd been attacked and a rōnin had carried the woman off. Do you know which way they went?"

Jōtarō, still dazed, shook his head.

"That's impossible. You must have some idea."

Jōtarō pointed in the first direction that came to hand. "Now I remember. It was that way." He was reluctant to say what really happened, fearing a scolding from Daizō for getting involved, but also dreading to admit in front of these people that the rōnin had thrown him.

Despite the vagueness of his reply, the crowd rushed off, and presently a cry went up: "Here she is. Over here."

The lanterns gathered in a circle around Akemi, whose disheveled form lay where she had been abandoned, on a stack of hay in a farmer's shed. Prodded back to reality by the clatter of running feet, she dragged herself to her feet.

The front of her kimono was open; her obi lay on the ground. Hay clung to her hair and clothing.

"What happened?"

While the word "rape" was on the tip of everyone's tongue, no one said it. Nor did it even cross their minds to chase the villain. Whatever had happened to Akemi, they felt, she had brought on herself.

"Come on, let's go back," said one of the men, taking her hand.

Akemi pulled away quickly. Resting her face forlornly against the wall, she broke down in bitter tears.

"Seems to be drunk."

"How'd she get that way?"

Jōtarō had been watching the scene from a distance. What had befallen Akemi was not clear to him in detail, but somehow he was reminded of an experience that had nothing to do with her. The titillation of lying in the fodder shed in Koyagyū with Kocha came back to him, along with the strangely exciting fear of approaching footsteps. But his pleasure quickly evaporated. "I better get back," he said decisively.

As his pace quickened, his spirit, back from its trip to the unknown, moved him to break into song.

> Old metal Buddha, standing in the field,
> Have you seen a girl of sixteen?
> Don't you know a girl who's strayed?
> When asked, you say "Clang."
> When struck, you say "Bong."

A Cricket in the Grass

Jōtarō jogged along at a good pace, paying little attention to the road. Suddenly he halted and looked around, wondering if he'd lost his way. "I don't remember passing here before," he thought nervously.

Samurai houses fringed the remains of an old fortress. One section of the compound had been rebuilt to serve as the official residence of the recently appointed Ōkubo Nagayasu, but the rest of the area, rising like a natural mound, was covered with weeds and trees. The stone ramparts were crumbling, having been ravaged many years earlier by an invading army. The fortification looked primitive compared to the castle complexes of the last forty to fifty years. There was no moat, no bridge, nothing that could properly be described as a castle wall. It had probably belonged to one of the local gentry in the days before the great civil war daimyō incorporated their rural domains into larger feudal principalities.

On one side of the road were paddies and marshland; on the other, walls; and beyond, a cliff, atop which the fortress must once have stood.

As he tried to get his bearings, Jōtarō's eyes traveled along the cliff. Then he saw something move, stop, and move again. At first it looked like an animal, but soon the stealthily moving silhouette became the outline of a man. Jōtarō shivered but stood riveted to the spot.

The man lowered a rope with a hook attached to the top. After he had slid down the full length of the rope and found a foothold, he shook the hook loose and repeated the process. When he reached the bottom, he disappeared into a copse.

Jōtarō's curiosity was thoroughly aroused.

A few minutes later, he saw the man walking along the low rises separating the paddies and apparently heading straight for him. He nearly panicked, but relaxed when he could make out the bundle on the man's back. "What a waste of time! Nothing but a farmer stealing kindling." He thought the man must have been crazy to risk scaling the cliff for nothing more than some firewood. He was disappointed too; his mystery had become unbearably humdrum. But then came his second shock. As the man strolled up the road past the tree Jōtarō was hiding behind, the boy had to stifle a gasp. He was sure the dark figure was Daizō.

"It couldn't be," he told himself.

The man had a black cloth around his face and wore peasant's knickers, leggings and light straw sandals.

The mysterious figure turned off onto a path skirting a hill. No one with such sturdy shoulders and buoyant stride could be in his fifties, as Daizō was. Having convinced himself that he was mistaken, Jōtarō followed. He had to get back to the inn, and the man just might, unwittingly, help him find his way.

When the man came to a road marker, he set down his bundle, which appeared to be very heavy. As he leaned over to read the writing on the stone, something about him again struck Jōtarō as familiar.

While the man climbed the path up the hill, Jōtarō examined the marker, on which were carved the words "Pine Tree on Head-burying Mound—Above." This was where the local inhabitants buried the severed skulls of criminals and defeated warriors.

The branches of an immense pine were clearly visible against the night sky. By the time Jōtarō reached the top of the rise, the man had seated himself by the roots of the tree and was smoking a pipe.

Daizō! No question about it now. A peasant would never carry tobacco with him. Some had been successfully grown domestically, but on such a limited scale that it was still very expensive. Even in the relatively well-off Kansai district, it was considered a luxury. And up in Sendai, when Lord Date smoked, his scribe felt constrained to make an entry in his daily journal: "Morning, three smokes; afternoon, four smokes; bedtime, one smoke."

Financial considerations aside, most people who had a chance to try tobacco found it made them dizzy or even nauseated. Though appreciated for its flavor, it was generally regarded as a narcotic.

Jōtarō knew that smokers were few; he also knew that Daizō was one of them, for he had frequently seen him drawing on a handsomely made ceramic pipe. Not that this had ever before struck him as strange. Daizō was wealthy and a man of expensive tastes.

"What's he up to?" he thought impatiently. Accustomed now to the danger of the situation, he gradually crept closer.

Having finished his pipe, the merchant got to his feet, removed his black kerchief and tucked it into his waist. Then slowly he walked around the pine. The next thing Jōtarō knew, he was holding a shovel in his hands. Where had that come from? Leaning on the shovel, Daizō looked around at the night scenery for a moment, apparently fixing the location in his mind.

Seemingly satisfied, Daizō rolled aside a large rock on the north side of the tree and began digging energetically, looking neither right nor left. Jōtarō watched the hole grow nearly deep enough for a man to stand in. Finally, Daizō stopped and wiped the sweat from his face with his kerchief. Jōtarō remained as still as a rock and totally baffled.

"This'll do," the merchant murmured softly, as he finished trampling down the soft dirt at the bottom of the hole. For an instant, Jōtarō had a peculiar impulse to call out and warn him not to bury himself, but he held back.

Jumping up to the surface, Daizō proceeded to drag the heavy bundle from the tree to the edge of the hole and undo the hempen cord around the top. At first Jōtarō thought the sack was made of cloth, but now he could see that it was a heavy leather cloak, of the sort generals wore over their armor. Inside was another sack, made of tenting or some similar fabric. When this was opened, the top of an incredible stack of gold came into view—semi-cylindrical ingots made by pouring the molten metal into half sections of bamboo, split lengthwise.

There was more to come. Loosening his obi, Daizō unburdened himself of several dozen large, newly minted gold pieces, which had been stuffed into his stomach wrapper, the back of his kimono and other parts of his clothing. Having placed these neatly on top of the ingots, he tied both containers securely and dropped the bundle into the pit, as he might have dumped the carcass of a dog. He then shoveled the dirt back in, stamped on it with his feet, and replaced the rock. He finished off by scattering dry grass and twigs around the rock.

Then he set about transforming himself back into the well-known Daizō of Narai, affluent dealer in herbs. The peasant's garb, wrapped around the shovel, went into a thicket not likely to be explored by passersby. He donned his traveling cloak and hung his money pouch around his neck in the manner of itinerant priests. As he slipped his feet into his zōri, he mumbled with satisfaction, "Quite a night's work."

When Daizō was out of hearing range, Jōtarō emerged from his hiding place and went to the rock. Though he scrutinized the spot carefully, he could discern no trace of what he had just witnessed. He stared at the ground as if at a magician's empty palm.

"I'd better get moving," he thought suddenly. "If I'm not there when he gets back to the inn, he'll be suspicious." Since the lights of the town were now visible beneath him, he had no trouble setting his course. Running like the wind, he somehow contrived to stay on back roads and keep well out of Daizō's path.

It was with an expression of perfect innocence that he climbed the stairs at the inn and entered their room. He was in luck; Sukeichi was slumped against the lacquered traveling case, alone and sound asleep. A thin trickle of saliva ran down his chin.

"Hey, Sukeichi, you'll catch cold there." Purposely Jōtarō shook him to wake him up.

"Oh, it's you, is it?" drawled Sukeichi, rubbing his eyes. "What were you doing out this late without telling the master?"

"Are you crazy? I've been back for hours. If you'd been awake, you'd have known that."

"Don't try to fool me. I know you went out with that woman from the Sumiya. If you're running around after a whore now, I hate to think what you'll be acting like when you grow up."

Just then, Daizō open the shoji. "I'm back," was all he said.

An early morning start was necessary in order to make Edo before nightfall. Jinnai had his troupe, Akemi restored to it, on the road well before sunrise. Daizō, Sukeichi and Jōtarō, however, took their time over breakfast and were not ready to leave until the sun was fairly high in the sky.

Daizō led the way, as usual, but Jōtarō trailed behind with Sukeichi, which was unusual.

Finally Daizō stopped, asking, "What's the matter with you this morning?"

"Pardon?" Jōtarō did his best to appear nonchalant.

"Is something wrong?"

"No, nothing at all. Why do you ask?"

"You look glum. Not like you."

"It's nothing, sir. I was just thinking. If I stay with you, I don't know whether I'll ever find my teacher or not. I'd like to go and look for him on my own, if it's all right with you."

Without a moment's hesitation, Daizō replied, "It isn't!"

Jōtarō had sidled up and started to take hold of the man's arm, but now he withdrew his hand and asked nervously, "Why not?"

"Let's rest here awhile," said Daizō, lowering himself onto the grassy plain for which the province of Musashi was famous. Once seated, he gestured to Sukeichi to go on ahead.

"But I have to find my teacher—as soon as possible," pleaded Jōtarō.

"I told you, you're not going off by yourself." Looking very stern, Daizō put his ceramic pipe to his lips and took a puff. "As of today, you're my son."

He sounded serious. Jōtarō swallowed hard, but then Daizō laughed, and the boy, assuming it was all a joke, said, "I couldn't do that. I don't want to be your son."

"What?"

621

"You're a merchant. I want to be a samurai."

"I'm sure you'll find that Daizō of Narai is no ordinary townsman, without honor or background. Become my adopted son, and I'll make a real samurai out of you."

Jōtarō realized with dismay that he meant what he was saying. "May I ask why you decided this so suddenly?" the boy asked.

In a trice, Daizō seized him and pinioned him to his side. Putting his mouth to the boy's ear, he whispered, "You saw me, didn't you, you little bastard?"

"Saw you?"

"Yes; you were watching, weren't you?"

"I don't know what you're talking about. Watching what?"

"What I did last night."

Jōtarō tried his best to stay calm.

"Why did you do that?"

The boy's defenses were close to collapse.

"Why were you prying into my private affairs?"

"I'm sorry!" blurted Jōtarō. "I'm really sorry. I won't tell a soul."

"Keep your voice down! I'm not going to punish you, but in return, you're going to become my adopted son. If you refuse, you give me no choice but to kill you. Now, don't force me to do that. I think you're a fine boy, very likable."

For the first time in his life, Jōtarō began to feel real fear. "I'm sorry," he repeated fervently. "Don't kill me. I don't want to die!" Like a captured sky-lark, he wriggled timidly in Daizō's arms, afraid that if he really struggled, the hand of death would descend on him forthwith.

Although the boy felt his grip to be viselike, Daizō was not holding him tightly at all. In fact, when he pulled the boy onto his lap, his touch was almost tender. "Then you'll be my son, won't you?" His stubbly chin scratched Jōtarō's cheek.

Though he couldn't have identified it, what fettered Jōtarō was an adult, masculine scent. He was like an infant on Daizō's knee, unable to resist, unable even to speak.

"It's for you to decide. Will you let me adopt you, or will you die? Answer me, now!"

With a wail, the boy burst into tears. He rubbed his face with dirty fingers until muddy little puddles formed on both sides of his nose.

"Why cry? You're lucky to have such an opportunity. I guarantee you'll be a great samurai when I finish with you."

"But . . ."

"What is it?"

"You're . . . you're . . ."

"Yes?"

"I can't say it."

"Out with it. Speak. A man should state his thoughts simply and clearly."

"You're . . . well, your business is stealing." Had it not been for the hands resting lightly on him, Jōtarō would have been off like a gazelle. But Daizō's

622

lap was a deep pit, the walls of which prevented him from moving.

"Ha, ha," chortled Daizō, giving him a playful slap on the back. "Is that all that's bothering you?"

"Y-y-yes."

The big man's shoulders shook with laughter. "I might be the sort of person who'd steal the whole country, but a common burglar or highwayman I am not. Look at Ieyasu or Hideyoshi or Nobunaga—they're all warriors who stole or tried to steal the whole nation, aren't they? Just stick with me, and one of these days you'll understand."

"Then you're not a thief?"

"I wouldn't bother with a business that's so unprofitable." Lifting the boy off his knee, he said, "Now stop blubbering, and let's be on our way. From this moment on, you're my son. I'll be a good father to you. Your end of the bargain is that you never breathe a word to anyone about what you think you saw last night. If you do, I'll wring your neck."

Jōtarō believed him.

The Pioneers

On the day near the end of the fifth month when Osugi arrived in Edo, the air was steamingly sultry, the way it was only when the rainy season failed to bring rain. In the nearly two months since she had left Kyoto, she had traveled at a leisurely pace, taking time to pamper her aches and pains or to visit shrines and temples.

Her first impression of the shōgun's capital was distasteful. "Why build houses in a swamp like this?" she remarked disdainfully. "The weeds and rushes haven't even been cleared away yet."

Because of the unseasonable drought, a pall of dust hung over the Takanawa highroad, with its newly planted trees and recently erected milestones. The stretch from Shioiri' to Nihombashi was crowded with oxcarts loaded with rocks or lumber. All along the way, new houses were going up at a furious clip.

"Of all the—!" gasped Osugi, looking up angrily at a half-finished house. A gob of wet clay from a plasterer's trowel had accidentally landed on her kimono.

The workmen exploded with laughter.

"How dare you throw mud on people and then stand there laughing? You should be on your knees, apologizing!"

623

Back in Miyamoto, a few sharp words from her would have had her tenants or any of the other villagers cowering. These laborers, among the thousands of newcomers from all over the country, barely looked up from their work.

"What's the old hag babbling about?" a worker asked.

Osugi, incensed, shouted, "Who said that? Why, you . . ."

The more she sputtered, the harder they laughed. Spectators began to gather, asking each other why the old woman wasn't acting her age and taking the matter in stride.

Storming into the house, Osugi seized the end of the plank the plasterers were standing on and yanked it off its supports. Men and buckets full of wet clay clattered to the floor.

"You old bitch!"

Jumping to their feet, they surrounded her threateningly.

Osugi did not flinch. "Come outside!" she commanded grimly as she placed her hand on her short sword.

The workmen had second thoughts. The way she looked and carried on, she had to be from a samurai family; they might get into trouble if they weren't careful. Their manner softened noticeably.

Observing the change, Osugi declared grandly, "Henceforward, I'll not countenance rudeness from the likes of you." With a look of satisfaction on her face, she went out and started up the road again, leaving the spectators to gape at her stubborn, straight back.

She was hardly on her way again before an apprentice, his muddy feet grotesquely covered with shavings and sawdust, ran up behind her, carrying a bucket of mucky clay.

Shouting, "How do you like this, you old witch?" he slung the contents of his pail at her back.

"O-w-w-w!" The howl did credit to Osugi's lungs, but before she could turn around, the apprentice had vanished. When she realized the extent of the damage, she scowled bitterly and tears of sheer vexation filled her eyes.

The merriment was general.

"What're you nincompoops laughing at?" raged Osugi, baring her teeth. "What's so funny about an old woman being splattered with grime? Is this the way you welcome elderly people to Edo? You're not even human! Just remember, you'll all be old one day."

This outburst attracted even more onlookers.

"Edo, indeed!" she snorted. "To hear people talk, you'd think it was the greatest city in the whole country. And what is it? A place full of dirt and filth, where everybody's pulling down hills and filling in swamps and digging ditches and piling up sand from the seaside. Not only that, it's full of riffraff, like you'd never find in Kyoto or anywhere in the west." Having got that off her chest, she turned her back on the sniggering crowd and went rapidly on her way.

To be sure, the city's newness was its most remarkable feature. The wood and plaster of the houses was all bright and fresh, many building sites were only partially filled in, and ox and horse dung assailed the eyes and nostrils.

Not so long ago, this road had been a mere footpath through the rice paddies between the villages of Hibiya and Chiyoda. Had Osugi gone a little to the west, nearer Edo Castle, she would have found an older and more sedate district, where daimyō and vassals of the shōgun had begun building residences soon after Tokugawa Ieyasu occupied Edo in 1590.

As it was, absolutely nothing appealed to her. She felt ancient. Everyone she saw—shopkeepers, officials on horseback, samurai striding by in basket hats—all were young, as were laborers, craftsmen, vendors, soldiers, even generals.

The front of one house, where plasterers were still at work, bore a shop sign, behind which sat a heavily powdered woman, brushing her eyebrows as she awaited customers. In other half-finished buildings, people were selling sake, setting up displays of dry goods, laying in supplies of dried fish. One man was hanging out a sign advertising medicine.

"If I weren't looking for someone," Osugi mumbled sourly, "I wouldn't stay in this garbage dump a single night."

Coming to a hill of excavated dirt blocking the road, she halted. At the foot of a bridge crossing the as yet waterless moat stood a shanty. Its walls consisted of reed matting held in place by strips of bamboo, but a banner proclaimed that this was a public bath. Osugi handed over a copper coin and went in to wash her kimono. After cleaning it as well as she could, she borrowed a drying pole and hung the garment up by the side of the shanty. Clothed in her underwear, with a light bathrobe draped over her back, she squatted in the shadow of the bathhouse and gazed absently at the road.

Across the street, half a dozen men stood in a circle, haggling in voices loud enough for Osugi to hear what they were saying.

"How many square feet is it? I wouldn't mind considering it if the price is right."

"There's two thirds of an acre. The price is what I mentioned before. I can't come down from that."

"It's too much. You must know that yourself."

"Not at all. It costs a lot of money to fill in land. And don't forget, there's no more available around here."

"Oh, there must be. They're filling in everywhere."

"Already sold. People are snatching it up as it is, swamp and all. You won't find three hundred square feet for sale. Of course, if you're willing to go way over toward the Sumida River, you might be able to get something cheaper."

"Do you guarantee there's two thirds of an acre?"

"You don't have to take my word for it. Get a rope and measure it off yourself."

Osugi was astounded; the figure quoted for a hundred square feet would have been sufficient for tens of acres of good rice land. But essentially the same conversation was taking place all over the city, for many a merchant speculated in land. Osugi was also mystified. "Why would anybody want land here? It's no good for rice, and you can't call this place a city."

By and by the deal across the street was sealed with a ritual hand clapping intended to bring good luck to all concerned.

As she idly watched the departing shadows, Osugi became conscious of a hand on the back of her obi. "Thief!" she shrieked as she made a grab for the pickpocket's wrist. But her coin purse had already been removed, and the thief was already in the street.

"Thief!" Osugi screamed again. Flying after the man, she managed to throw her arms around his waist. "Help! Thief!"

The pickpocket struggled, striking her several times in the face without being able to break her grip. "Let go of me, you cow!" he shouted, kicking her in the ribs. With a loud grunt, Osugi fell down, but she had her short sword out and slashed at the man's ankle.

"Ow!" Blood pouring from the wound, he limped a few steps, then flopped down on the ground.

Startled by the commotion, the land dealers turned around, and one of them exclaimed, "Hey, isn't that that good-for-nothing from Kōshū?" The speaker was Hangawara Yajibei, master of a large gang of construction workers.

"Looks like him," agreed one of his henchmen. "What's that in his hand? Looks like a purse."

"It does, doesn't it? And somebody just yelled thief. Look! There's an old woman sprawled out on the ground. Go see what's the matter with her. I'll take care of him."

The pickpocket was on his feet and running again, but Yajibei caught up with him and slapped him to the ground as he might have swatted a grasshopper.

Returning to his boss, the henchman reported, "Just as we thought. He stole the old lady's purse."

"I have it here. How is she?"

"Not hurt bad. She fainted, but came to screaming bloody murder."

"She's still sitting there. Can't she stand up?"

"I guess not. He kicked her in the ribs."

"You son of a bitch!" Still glaring at the pickpocket, Yajibei issued a command to his underling. "Ushi, put up a stake."

The words set the thief to trembling as though the point of a knife were being pressed against his throat. "Not that," he pleaded, groveling in the dirt at Yajibei's feet. "Let me off just this once. I promise I won't do it again."

Yajibei shook his head. "No. You'll get what you deserve."

Ushi, who had been named after the zodiac sign under which he was born, a not uncommon practice among farmers, returned with two workmen from the nearby bridge site.

"Over there," he said, pointing toward the middle of a vacant lot.

After the workmen had driven a heavy post into the ground, one of them asked, "This good enough?"

"That's fine," said Yajibei. "Now tie him to it, and nail a board above his head."

When this had been done, Yajibei borrowed a carpenter's ink pot and brush and wrote on the board: "This man is a thief. Until recently, he worked for me, but he has committed a crime for which he must be punished. He is to be tied here, exposed to rain and sun, for seven days and seven nights. By order of Yajibei of Bakurōchō."

"Thanks," he said, returning the ink pot. "Now, if it's not too much trouble, give him a bite to eat every once in a while. Just enough to keep him from starving. Anything left over from your lunch will do."

The two workmen, along with others who had congregated in the meantime, signified their assent. Some of the laborers promised that they would see to it that the thief got his share of ridicule. It wasn't just samurai who feared public exposure of their misdeeds or weaknesses. Even for ordinary townspeople in these times, to be laughed at was the worst of all punishments.

Punishing criminals without reference to law was a firmly established practice. In the days when the warriors were too busy with warfare to maintain order, townsmen had, for the sake of their own safety, taken it upon themselves to deal with miscreants. Though Edo now had an official magistrate and a system was developing whereby leading citizens in each district functioned as government representatives, the summary administration of justice still occurred. With conditions still being a bit chaotic, the authorities saw little reason to interfere.

"Ushi," said Yajibei, "take the old lady her purse. Too bad this had to happen to somebody her age. She seems to be all alone. What happened to her kimono?"

"She says she washed it and hung it up to dry."

"Go get it for her, then bring her along. We might as well take her home with us. There's little point in punishing the thief if we're going to leave her here for some other ruffian to prey on."

Moments later, Yajibei strode away. Ushi was close behind, the kimono over his arm and Osugi on his back.

They soon reached Nihombashi, the "Bridge of Japan" from which all distances along the roads leading out of Edo were now measured. Stone parapets supported the wooden arch, and since the bridge had been constructed only about a year before, the railings still preserved a feeling of newness. Boats from Kamakura and Odawara were moored along one riverbank. On the other was the city's fish market.

"Oh, my side hurts," Osugi said with a loud groan.

The fishmongers looked up to see what was going on.

Being gaped at was not to Yajibei's liking. Glancing back at Osugi, he said, "We'll be there soon. Try to hold on. Your life's not in danger."

Osugi laid her head on Ushi's back and became as quiet as a baby.

In the downtown area, tradesmen and artisans had formed their own neighborhoods. There was a blacksmiths' district, one for lance-makers, others for dyers, tatami weavers, and so on. Yajibei's house stood out prominently from those of the other carpenters because the front half of the roof was covered with tiles; all the other houses had board roofs. Until a fire a couple of years before, nearly all the roofs had been made of thatch. As it happened, Yajibei had acquired what passed for his surname from his roof, Hangawara meaning "half tiled."

He had come to Edo as a rōnin, but being both clever and warmhearted, he had proved to be a skillful manager of men. Before long he set himself up as a contractor employing a sizable crew of carpenters, roofers and unskilled workers. From building projects carried out for various daimyō, he acquired enough capital to branch out into the real estate business as well. Too affluent now to have to work with his own hands, he played the role of local boss. Among Edo's numerous self-appointed bosses, Yajibei was one of the best known and most highly respected.

The townspeople looked up to the bosses as well as to the warriors, but of the two, the bosses were the more highly admired, because they usually stood up for the common people. Although those of Edo had a style and spirit of their own, the bosses were not unique to the new capital. Their history went back to the troubled latter days of the Ashikaga shogunate, when gangs of thugs roamed the countryside like prides of lions, pillaging at will and submitting to no restraints.

According to a writer of that era, they wore little more than vermilion loincloths and wide stomach wrappers. Their long swords were very long—nearly four feet—and even their short swords were more than two feet in length. Many used other weapons, of a cruder type, such as battle-axes and "iron rakes." They let their hair grow wild, using thick strips of rope for headbands, and leather leggings often covered their calves.

Having no fixed loyalties, they operated as mercenaries, and after peace was restored, were ostracized by both farmers and samurai alike. By the Edo era, those not content with being bandits or highwaymen often sought their fortunes in the new capital. More than a few succeeded, and this breed of leaders was once described as having "righteousness for bones, love of the people for flesh and gallantry for skin." In short, they were popular heroes par excellence.

Slaughter by the Riverside

Life under Yajibei's half-tiled roof agreed so much with Osugi that a year and a half later she was still there. After the first few weeks, during which she rested and recovered her health, hardly a day passed without her telling herself she should be on her way.

Whenever she broached the subject to Yajibei, whom she didn't see often, he urged her to stay on. "What's the hurry?" he would ask. "There's no reason for you to go anywhere. Bide your time until we find Musashi. Then we can serve as your seconds." Yajibei knew nothing of Osugi's enemy except what she herself had told him—that he was, in so many words, the blackest of blackguards—but since the day of her arrival, all of his men had been under instructions to report immediately anything they heard or saw of Musashi.

After initially detesting Edo, Osugi had mellowed in attitude to the point where she was willing to admit that the people were "friendly, carefree and really very kind at heart."

The Hangawara household was a particularly easygoing place and something of a haven for social misfits; country boys too lazy to farm, displaced rōnin, profligates who had run through their parents' money and tattooed ex-convicts made up a coarse and motley crew, whose unifying esprit de corps curiously resembled that of a well-run school for warriors. The ideal here, however, was blustering masculinity rather than spiritual manliness; it was really a "dōjō" for thugs.

As in the martial arts dōjō, there was a rigid class structure. Under the boss, who was the ultimate temporal and spiritual authority, came a group of seniors, usually referred to as the "elder brothers." Below them were the ordinary henchmen—the *kobun*—whose ranking was determined largely by length of service. There was also a special class of "guests"; their status depended on such factors as their ability with weapons. Bolstering the hierarchical organization was a code of etiquette, of uncertain origin but strictly adhered to.

At one point, Yajibei, thinking Osugi might be bored, suggested that she take care of the younger men. Since then, her days had been fully occupied with sewing, mending, washing and straightening up after the *kobun*, whose slovenliness gave her plenty of work.

For all their lack of breeding, the *kobun* recognized quality when they saw it. They admired both Osugi's spartan habits and the efficiency with which she went about her chores. "She's a real samurai lady," they were wont to say. "The House of Hon'iden must have very good blood in it."

Osugi's unlikely host treated her with consideration and had even built her separate living quarters on the vacant lot behind his house. And whenever he was at home, he went to pay his respects each morning and evening. When asked by one of his underlings why he displayed such deference toward a stranger, Yajibei confessed that he had acted very badly toward his own father and mother while they were still alive. "At my age," he said, "I feel I have a filial duty to all older people."

Spring came, and the wild plum blossoms fell, but the city itself had as yet almost no cherry blossoms. Apart from a few trees in the sparsely settled hills to the west, there were only the saplings that Buddhists had planted along the road leading to the Sensōji, in Asakusa. Rumor had it that this year they were sprouting buds and would blossom for the first time.

One day Yajibei came to Osugi's room and said, "I'm going to the Sensōji. Do you feel like coming along?"

"I'd love to. That temple's dedicated to Kanzeon, and I'm a great believer in her powers. She's the same bodhisattva as the Kannon I prayed to at Kiyomizudera in Kyoto."

With Yajibei and Osugi went two of the *kobun*, Jūrō and Koroku. Jūrō bore the nickname "Reed Mat," for reasons no one knew, but it was obvious why Koroku was called the "Acolyte." He was a small, compact man with a distinctly benign face, if one overlooked the three ugly scars on his forehead, evidence of a proclivity for street brawls.

They first made their way to the moat at Kyōbashi, where boats were available for hire. After Koroku had skillfully sculled them out of the moat and into the Sumida River, Yajibei ordered the box lunches opened.

"I'm going to the temple today," he explained, "because it's the anniversary of my mother's death. I really should go back home and visit her grave, but it's too far, so I compromise by going to the Sensōji and making a donation. But that's neither here nor there; just think of it as a picnic." He reached over the side of the boat, rinsed off a sake cup and offered it to Osugi.

"It's very fine of you to remember your mother," she said as she accepted the cup, all the while wondering fretfully if Matahachi would do the same when she was gone. "I wonder, though, is drinking sake on the anniversary of your poor mother's passing the thing to do?"

"Well, I'd rather do that than hold some pompous ceremony. Anyway, I believe in the Buddha; that's all that counts for ignorant louts like me. You know the saying, don't you? 'He who has faith need have no knowledge.'"

Osugi, letting it go at that, proceeded to have several refills. After a time she remarked, "I haven't drunk like this for ages. I feel like I'm floating on air."

"Drink up," urged Yajibei. "It's good sake, isn't it? Don't worry about being out on the water. We're here to take care of you."

The river, flowing south from the town of Sumida, was broad and placid. On the Shimōsa side, the east bank opposite Edo, stood a luxuriant forest. Tree roots jutting into the water formed nests holding limpid pools, which shone like sapphires in the sunlight.

"Oh," said Osugi. "Listen to the nightingales!"

"When the rainy season comes, you can hear cuckoos all day long."

"Let me pour for you. I hope you don't mind my joining in your celebration."

"I like to see you having a good time."

From the stern, Koroku called out lustily, "Say, boss, how about passing the sake around?"

"Just pay attention to your work. If you start now, we'll all drown. On the way back you can have all you want."

"If you say so. But I just want you to know the whole river's beginning to look like sake."

"Stop thinking about it. Here, pull over to that boat next to the bank so we can buy some fresh fish."

Koroku did as he was told. After a bit of haggling, the fisherman, flashing a happy smile, lifted the cover off a tank built into the deck and told them to take anything they wanted. Osugi had never seen anything like it. The tank was full to the brim with wriggling, flapping fish, some from the sea, some from the river. Carp, prawns, catfish, black porgies, gobies. Even trout and sea bass.

Yajibei sprinkled soy sauce on some whitebait and began eating it raw. He offered some to Osugi, but she declined, with a look of dread on her face.

When they drew up on the west side of the river and disembarked, Osugi seemed a little wobbly on her feet.

"Be careful," warned Yajibei. "Here, take my hand."

"No, thank you. I don't need any help." She waved her own hand before her face indignantly.

After Jūrō and Koroku had moored the boat, the four of them crossed a broad expanse of stones and puddles to get to the riverbank proper.

A group of small children were busily turning over stones, but seeing the unusual foursome, they stopped and flocked around, chattering excitedly.

"Buy some, sir. Please."

"Won't you buy some, Granny?"

Yajibei seemed to like children; at least, he showed no signs of annoyance. "What have you got there—crabs?"

"Not crabs; arrowheads," they cried, producing handfuls of them from their kimonos.

"Arrowheads?"

"That's right. A lot of men and horses are buried in a mound by the temple. People coming here buy arrowheads to offer to the dead. You should too."

"I don't think I want any arrowheads, but I'll give you some money. How'll that do?"

That, it appeared, would do admirably, and as soon as Yajibei had passed out a few coins, the children ran off to resume their digging. But even as he watched, a man emerged from a thatched-roof house nearby, took the coins away from them and went back inside. Yajibei clicked his tongue and turned away in disgust.

Osugi was gazing out over the river, fascination in her eyes. "If there are a lot of arrowheads lying around," she observed, "there must have been a big battle."

"I don't really know, but it seems there were quite a few battles here in the days when Edo was only a provincial estate. That was four or five hundred years ago. I've heard that Minamoto no Yoritomo came up here from Izu to organize troops in the twelfth century. When the Imperial Court was divided—when was that, fourteenth century?—Lord Nitta of Musashi was defeated by the Ashikagas somewhere in the neighborhood. Just in the last couple of centuries, Ōta Dōkan and other local generals are said to have fought many battles not far up the river."

While they were talking, Jūrō and Koroku went on ahead to make a place for them to sit on the veranda of the temple.

The Sensōji turned out to be a terrible disappointment to Osugi. In her eyes it was nothing more than a large, run-down house, the priest's residence a mere shack. "Is this it?" she wanted to know, with more than a hint of deprecation. "After all I've heard about the Sensōji . . ."

The setting was a splendidly primeval forest of large, ancient trees, but not only did the Kanzeon hall look shabby; when the river flooded, the water came through the woods right up to the veranda. Even at other times, small tributaries washed over the grounds.

"Welcome. Good to see you again."

Glancing up in surprise, Osugi saw a priest kneeling on the roof.

"Working on the roof?" asked Yajibei amiably.

"Have to, because of the birds. The oftener I mend it, the oftener they steal the thatch to make nests with. There's always a leak somewhere. Make yourselves comfortable. I'll be down shortly."

Yajibei and Osugi picked up votive candles and went into the dim interior. "No wonder it leaks," she thought, looking at the starlike holes above her.

Kneeling beside Yajibei, she took out her prayer beads and with a dreamy look in her eye chanted the Vow of Kanzeon from the Lotus Sutra.

> You will reside in the air like the sun.
> And if you are pursued by evil men
> And pushed off the Diamond Mountain,
> Reflect on the power of Kanzeon
> And you will not lose a hair from your head.
> And if bandits surround you
> And threaten you with swords,
> If you reflect on the power of Kanzeon,
> The bandits will take pity on you.
> And if the king sentences you to death
> And the sword is about to behead you,
> Reflect on the power of Kanzeon.
> The sword will break into pieces.

She recited softly at first, but as she became oblivious to the presence of Yajibei, Jūrō and Koroku, her voice rose and grew resonant; a rapt expression came to her face.

> The eighty-four thousand sentient beings
> Began to aspire in their hearts
> For *anuttara-samyak-sambodhi*,
> The unsurpassed Wisdom of the Buddhas.

Prayer beads trembling in her fingers, Osugi went without a break from the recitation into a personal supplication of her own.

> Hail to Kanzeon, World-Honored One!
> Hail to the Bodhisattva of Infinite Mercy and Infinite Compassion!
> Look favorably on this old woman's one wish.
> Let me strike Musashi down, and very soon!
> Let me strike him down!
> Let me strike him down!

Abruptly lowering her voice, she bowed to the floor. "And make Matahachi a good boy! Cause the House of Hon'iden to prosper!"

632

After the long prayer ended, there was a moment's silence before the priest invited them outside to have some tea. Yajibei and the two younger men, who had knelt in proper fashion throughout the invocation, got up rubbing their tingly legs and went out on the veranda.

"I can have some sake now, can't I?" Jūrō asked eagerly. Permission having been granted, he hastened to the priest's house and arranged their lunch on the porch. By the time the others joined him, he was sipping sake with one hand and broiling the fish they had bought with the other. "Who cares if there aren't any cherry blossoms?" he remarked. "Feels just like a flower-viewing picnic anyway."

Yajibei handed the priest an offering, delicately wrapped in paper, and told him to use it for the roof repairs. As he did so, he happened to notice a row of wooden plaques on which were written donors' names, together with the amounts they had contributed. Nearly all were about the same as Yajibei's, some less, but one stood out conspicuously. "Ten gold coins, Daizō of Narai, Province of Shinano."

Turning to the priest, Yajibei remarked, somewhat diffidently, "Perhaps it's crass of me to say so, but ten gold coins is a considerable sum. Is this Daizō of Narai as rich as all that?"

"I really couldn't say. He appeared out of the blue one day toward the end of last year and said it was a disgrace that the most famous temple in the Kanto district was in such bad shape. He told me the money should be added to our fund for buying lumber."

"Sounds like an admirable sort of man."

"He also donated three gold coins to Yushima Shrine and no fewer than twenty to Kanda Myōjin Shrine. He wanted the latter to be kept in good condition because it enshrines the spirit of Taira no Masakado. Daizō insists that Masakado was not a rebel. He thinks he should be revered as the pioneer who opened up the eastern part of the country. You'll find there are some very unusual donors in this world."

Hardly had he finished speaking when a crowd of children came running helter-skelter toward them.

"What're you doing here?" shouted the priest sternly. "If you want to play, go down by the river. You mustn't run wild in the temple grounds."

But the children swept on like a school of minnows until they reached the veranda.

"Come quick," cried one. "It's awful!"

"There's a samurai down there. He's fighting."

"One man against four."

"Real swords!"

"Praise to Buddha, not again!" lamented the priest as he hurriedly slipped on his sandals. Before running off, he took a moment to explain. "Forgive me. I'll have to leave you for a while. The riverbank is a favorite place for fights. Every time I turn around, somebody's down there cutting people to pieces or beating them to a pulp. Then men from the magistrate's office come to me for a written report. I'll have to go see what it is this time."

"A fight?" chorused Yajibei and his men, and off they raced. Osugi followed 633 but was so much slower on her feet that by the time she got there the fight was over. The children and some onlookers from a nearby fishing village all stood around in silence, swallowing hard and looking pale.

At first Osugi thought the silence strange, but then she, too, caught her breath, and her eyes opened wide. Across the ground flitted the shadow of a swallow. Walking toward them was a young, smug-faced samurai clad in a purplish-red warrior's cloak. Whether or not he noticed the spectators, he paid them no heed.

Osugi's gaze shifted to four bodies lying in a tangle some twenty paces behind the samurai.

The victor paused. As he did so, a low gasp went up from several lips, for one of the vanquished had moved. Struggling to his feet, he cried, "Wait! You can't run away."

The samurai assumed a waiting stance while the wounded man ran forward, gasping, "This . . . fight's . . . not over yet."

When he leapt weakly to the attack, the samurai retreated a step, allowing the man to stumble forward. Then he struck. The man's head split in two.

"Now is it over?" he shouted viciously.

No one had even seen the Drying Pole drawn.

Having wiped off his blade, he stooped to wash his hands in the river. Though the villagers were accustomed to fights, they were astonished at the samurai's sangfroid. The last man's death had been not only instantaneous but inhumanly cruel. Not a word was uttered.

The samurai stood up and stretched. "It's just like the Iwakuni River," he said. "Reminds me of home." For a few moments he gazed idly at the wide stream and a flock of white-bellied swallows swooping and skimming the water. Then he turned and walked rapidly downstream.

He made straight for Yajibei's boat, but as he began untying it, Jūrō and Koroku came running out of the forest.

"Wait! What do you think you're doing?" shouted Jūrō, who was now close enough to see the blood on the samurai's *hakama* and sandal thongs but took no notice of it.

Dropping the rope, the samurai grinned and asked, "Can't I use the boat?"

"Of course not," snapped Jūrō.

"Suppose I paid to use it?"

"Don't talk nonsense." The voice brusquely refusing the samurai's request was Jūrō's, but in a sense, it was the whole brash new city of Edo speaking fearlessly through his mouth.

The samurai did not apologize, but neither did he resort to force. He turned and walked off without another word.

"Kojirō! Kojirō! Wait!" Osugi called at the top of her lungs.

When Kojirō saw who it was, the grimness vanished from his face and he broke into a friendly smile. "Why, what are you doing here? I've been wondering what happened to you."

"I'm here to pay my respects to Kanzeon. I came with Hangawara Yajibei and these two young men. Yajibei's letting me stay at his house in Bakurōchō."

"When was it I saw you last? Let's see—Mount Hiei. You said then you were going to Edo, so I thought I might run into you. I hardly expected it to be here." He glanced at Jūrō and Koroku, who were in a state of shock. "You mean those two there?"

"Oh, they're just a couple of ruffians, but their boss is a very fine man."

Yajibei was just as thunderstruck as everybody else to see his guest chatting amiably with the awesome samurai. He was on the spot in no time, bowing to Kojirō and saying, "I'm afraid my boys spoke very rudely to you, sir. I hope you'll forgive them. We're just ready to leave. Perhaps you'd like to ride downstream with us."

Shavings

Like most people thrown together by circumstance, who ordinarily have little or nothing in common, the samurai and his host soon found mutual ground. The supply of sake was plentiful, the fish fresh, and Osugi and Kojirō had an odd spiritual kinship that kept the atmosphere from getting stickily formal. It was with genuine concern that she inquired about his career as a *shugyōsha* and he about her progress in achieving her "great ambition."

When she told him she'd had no word of Musashi's whereabouts for a long time, Kojirō offered a ray of hope. "I heard a rumor that he visited two or three prominent warriors last fall and winter. I have a hunch he's still in Edo."

Yajibei wasn't so sure, of course, and told Kojirō that his men had learned absolutely nothing. After they had discussed Osugi's predicament from every angle, Yajibei said, "I hope we can count on your continued friendship."

Kojirō responded in the same vein and made rather a display of rinsing out his cup and offering it not only to Yajibei but to his two minions, for each of whom he poured a drink.

Osugi was positively exhilarated. "They say," she observed gravely, "that good is to be found wherever one looks. Even so, I'm exceptionally lucky! To think that I have two strong men like you on my side! I'm sure the great Kanzeon is looking after me." She made no attempt to conceal her sniffling or the tears that came to her eyes.

Not wanting the conversation to get maudlin, Yajibei said, "Tell me, Kojirō, who were the four men you cut down back there?"

This seemed to be the opportunity Kojirō had been waiting for, for his agile tongue set to work without delay. "Oh, them!" he began with a nonchalant laugh. "Just some rōnin from Obata's school. I went there five or six times to discuss military matters with Obata, and those fellows kept butting in with impertinent remarks. They even had the nerve to spout off on the subject of swordsmanship, so I told them that if they'd come to the banks of the Sumida, I'd give them a lesson in the secrets of the Ganryū Style, along with a demonstration of the Drying Pole's cutting edge. I let them know I didn't care how many of them came.

"When I got there, there were five of them, but the minute I took a stance, one turned tail and ran. I must say, Edo has no shortage of men who talk better than they fight." He laughed again, this time boisterously.

"Obata?"

"You don't know him? Obata Kagenori. He comes from the lineage of Obata Nichijō, who served the Takeda family of Kai. Ieyasu took him on, and now he's a lecturer in military science to the shōgun, Hidetada. He also has his own school."

"Oh, yes, I remember now." Yajibei was surprised and impressed by Kojirō's apparent familiarity with such a celebrated person. "The young man still has his forelock," he marveled to himself, "but he must be somebody if he associates with samurai of that rank." The carpenter boss was, after all, a simple soul, and the quality he most admired in his fellow man was clearly brute strength. His admiration for Kojirō intensified.

Leaning toward the samurai, he said, "Let me make you a proposition. I've always got forty or fifty young louts lying around my house. How would it be if I built a dōjō for you and asked you to train them?"

"Well, I wouldn't mind giving them lessons, but you must understand that so many daimyō are tugging at my sleeve with offers—two, three thousand bushels—that I don't know what to do. Frankly, I wouldn't seriously consider going into anyone's service for less than five thousand. Also, I'm rather obligated, just for the sake of courtesy, to stay where I'm living now. Still, I've no objection to coming to your place."

With a low bow, Yajibei said, "I'd greatly appreciate that."

Osugi chimed in, "We'll be expecting you."

Jūrō and Koroku, far too naive to recognize the condescension and self-serving propaganda lacing Kojirō's speech, were bowled over by the great man's largesse.

When the boat rounded the turn into the Kyōbashi moat, Kojirō said, "I'll be getting off here." He then leapt onto the bank and in a matter of seconds was lost in the dust hovering over the street.

"Very impressive young man," said Yajibei, still under the spell.

"Yes," Osugi agreed with conviction. "He's a real warrior. I'm sure plenty of daimyō would pay him a handsome stipend." After a moment's pause, she added wistfully, "If only Matahachi were like that."

About five days later, Kojirō breezed into Yajibei's establishment and was ushered into the guest room. There, the forty or fifty henchmen on hand paid their respects, one by one. Kojirō, delighted, remarked to Yajibei that he seemed to lead a very interesting life.

Pursuing his earlier idea, Yajibei said, "As I told you, I'd like to build a dōjō. Would you care to take a look at the property?"

The field in back of the house measured nearly two acres. Freshly dyed cloth hung in one corner, but Yajibei assured Kojirō the dyer he had rented the plot to could easily be evicted.

"You don't really need a dōjō," observed Kojirō. "The area's not open to the street; no one's likely to intrude."

"Whatever you say, but what about rainy days?"

"I won't come if the weather's bad. I should warn you, though: the practice sessions will be rougher than the ones held by the Yagyū or other schools around town. If your men aren't careful, they might wind up crippled, or worse. You'd better make that clear to them."

"There'll be no misunderstanding about that. Feel free to conduct classes as you see fit."

They agreed on having lessons three times a month, on the third, the thirteenth and the twenty-third, weather permitting.

Kojirō's appearances in Bakurōchō were a source of endless gossip. One neighbor was heard to say, "Now they've got a show-off over there worse than all the others put together." His boyish forelock also came in for considerable comment, the general opinion being that since he must be in his early twenties, it was high time he conformed to the samurai practice of shaving his pate. But only those inside the Hangawara household were treated to the sight of Kojirō's brightly embroidered underrobe, which they got to see every time he bared his shoulder to give his arm free play.

Kojirō's demeanor was quite what might be expected. Though this was practice and many of his students were inexperienced, he gave no quarter. By the third session, the casualties already included one man permanently deformed, plus four or five suffering from lesser injuries. The wounded were not far off; their moans could be heard coming from the back of the house.

"Next!" shouted Kojirō, brandishing a long sword made of loquat wood. At the beginning he had told them that a blow struck with a loquat sword "will rot your flesh to the bone."

"Ready to quit? If you're not, come forward. If you are, I'm going home," he taunted contemptuously.

Out of pure chagrin, one man said, "All right, I'll give it a try." He disengaged himself from the group, walked toward Kojirō, then leaned over to pick up a wooden sword. With a sharp crack, Kojirō flattened him.

"That," he declared, "is a lesson in why not to leave yourself open. It's the worst thing you can do." With obvious self-satisfaction, he looked around at the faces of the others, thirty to forty in number, most of them all but visibly trembling.

The latest victim was carried to the well, where water was poured over him. He did not come to.

"Poor guy's done for."

"You mean . . . he's dead?"

"He's not breathing."

Others ran up to stare at their slain comrade. Some were angry, some resigned, but Kojirō didn't give the corpse a second glance.

"If something like this frightens you," he said menacingly, "you'd better forget about the sword. When I think that any one of you would be itching to fight if somebody on the street called you a thug or a braggart . . ." He didn't finish the sentence, but as he walked across the field in his leather socks, he continued his lecture. "Give the matter some thought, my fine hoodlums. You're ready to draw the minute a stranger steps on your toes or brushes against your scabbard, but you're tied up in knots when the time comes for a real bout. You'll throw your lives away cheerfully over a woman or your own petty pride, but you haven't the guts to sacrifice yourself in a worthy cause. You're emotional, you're moved only by vanity. That's not enough, nowhere near enough."

Throwing his chest out, he concluded, "The truth is simple. The only real bravery, the only genuine self-confidence, comes from training and self-discipline. I dare any one of you: stand up and fight me like a man."

One student, hoping to make him eat his words, attacked from behind. Kojirō bent double, almost touching the ground, and the assailant flew over his head and landed in front of him. The next instant, there was the loud crack of Kojirō's loquat sword against the man's hipbone.

"That'll be all for today," he said, tossing the sword aside and going to the well to wash his hands. The corpse was lying in a flaccid heap beside the sink. Kojirō dipped his hands in the water and splashed some on his face without a word of sympathy.

Slipping his arm back into his sleeve, he said, "I hear a lot of people go to this place called Yoshiwara. You men must know the district pretty well. Wouldn't you like to show me around?" Bluntly announcing that he wanted to have a good time or go drinking was a habit of Kojirō's, but it was a matter of conjecture whether he was being deliberately impudent or disarmingly candid.

Yajibei chose the more charitable interpretation. "Haven't you been to Yoshiwara yet?" he asked with surprise. "We'll have to do something about that. I'd go with you myself, but, well, I have to be here this evening for the wake and so on."

He singled out Jūrō and Koroku and gave them some money. Also a warning. "Remember, you two—I'm not sending you out to play around. You're only going along to take care of your teacher and see that he has a good time."

Kojirō, a few steps in front of the other two, soon found he had trouble staying on the road, for at night most of Edo was pitch black, to an extent unimaginable in cities like Kyoto, Nara and Osaka.

"This road's terrible," he said. "We should have brought a lantern."

"People'd laugh if you went around the licensed quarter carrying a lantern," said Jūrō. "Watch out, sir. That pile of dirt you're on came out of the new moat. You'd better come down before you fall in."

Presently the water in the moat took on a reddish cast, as did the sky beyond the Sumida River. A late spring moon hung like a flat white cake above the roofs of Yoshiwara.

"That's it over there, across the bridge," said Jūrō. "Shall I lend you a hand towel?"

"What for?"

"To hide your face a little—like this." Jūrō and Koroku both drew red cloths from their obi and tied them kerchief-fashion over their heads. Kojirō followed suit, using a piece of russet silk crepe.

"That's the way," said Jūrō. "Stylish like."

"Looks very good on you."

Kojirō and his guides fell in with the bandannaed throng sauntering from house to house. Like Yanagimachi in Kyoto, Yoshiwara was brightly lit. The entrances to the houses were gaily decorated with curtains of red or pale yellow; some had bells at the bottom to let the girls know when customers entered.

After they had been in and out of two or three houses, Jūrō said leeringly to Kojirō, "There's no use trying to hide it, sir."

"Hide what?"

"You said you'd never been here before, but a girl in the last house recognized you. The minute we went in, she gave a little cry and hid behind a screen. Your secret's out, sir."

"I've never been here before. Who're you talking about?"

"Don't play innocent, sir. Let's go back. I'll show you."

They reentered the house, whose curtain bore a crest shaped like a bitter buckbean leaf, split in three. "Sumiya" was written in rather small characters to the left.

The house's heavy beams and stately corridors were reminiscent of Kyoto temple architecture, but the garish newness nullified the attempt to create an aura of tradition and dignity. Kojirō strongly suspected that swamp plants still thrived beneath the floor.

The large parlor they were shown to upstairs had not been straightened up after the last customers. Both table and floor were strewn with bits of food, tissue paper, toothpicks and whatnot. The maid who came to clean up performed her chore with all the finesse of a day laborer.

When Onao arrived to take their orders, she made a point of letting them know how busy she was. She claimed that she hardly had time to sleep and another three years of this hectic pace would put her in her grave. The better houses of Kyoto contrived to maintain the fiction that their raison d'être was to entertain and please their customers. Here the aim was obviously to relieve men of their money as quickly as possible.

"So this is Edo's pleasure quarter," sniffed Kojirō, with a critical glance at the knotholes in the ceiling. "Pretty shoddy, I'd say."

"Oh, this is only temporary," Onao protested. "The building we're putting up now will be finer than anything you'd see in Kyoto or Fushimi." She stared at Kojirō a moment. "You know, sir, I've seen you somewhere before. Ah, yes! It was last year on the Kōshū highroad."

639

Kojirō had forgotten the chance meeting, but reminded of it, he said with a spark of interest, "Why, yes; I guess our fates must be entwined."

"I should say they are," Jūrō said, laughing, "if there's a girl here who remembers you." While teasing Kojirō about his past, he described the girl's face and clothing and asked Onao to go find her.

"I know the one you mean," said Onao, and went to fetch her.

When some time had passed and she still hadn't come back, Jūrō and Koroku went out in the hall and clapped their hands to summon her. They had to clap several more times before she finally reappeared.

"She's not here, the one you asked for," said Onao.

"She was here only a few minutes ago."

"It's strange, just as I was saying to the master. We were at Kobotoke Pass and that samurai you're with came walking along the road, and she went off by herself that time too."

Behind the Sumiya stood the frame of the new building, roof partly finished, no walls.

"Hanagiri! Hanagiri!"

This was the name they had given Akemi, who was hiding between a stack of lumber and a small mountain of shavings. Several times the searchers had passed so close she had had to hold her breath.

"How disgusting!" she thought. For the first few minutes her wrath had been directed at Kojirō alone. By now it had expanded to embrace every member of the masculine sex—Kojirō, Seijūrō, the samurai at Hachiōji, the customers who manhandled her nightly at the Sumiya. All men were her enemies, all abominable.

Except one. The right one. The one who would be like Musashi. The one she had sought incessantly. Having given up on the real Musashi, she had now persuaded herself that it would be comforting to pretend to be in love with someone similar to him. Much to her chagrin, she found no one remotely like him.

"Ha-na-gi-ri!" It was Shōji Jinnai himself, first shouting from the back of the house, now drawing closer to her hiding place.

He was accompanied by Kojirō and the other two men. They had complained at tiresome length, making Jinnai repeat his apologies over and over, but finally they went off toward the street.

Akemi, seeing them go, breathed a sigh of relief and waited until Jinnai went back inside, then ran straight to the kitchen door.

"Why, Hanagiri, were you out there all the time?" the kitchen maid asked hysterically.

"Shh! Be quiet, and give me some sake."

"Sake? Now?"

"Yes, sake!" Since coming to Edo, the times when Akemi had sought solace in sake had become more and more frequent.

The frightened maid poured her a large cupful. Shutting her eyes, Akemi drained the vessel dry, her powdered face tilted back until it was almost parallel with the white bottom of the cup.

As she turned away from the door, the maid cried in alarm, "Where're you off to now?"

"Shut up. I'll just wash my feet, then go back inside."

Taking her at her word, the maid shut the door and returned to her work.

Akemi slipped her feet into the first pair of zōri she saw and walked somewhat unsteadily to the street. "How good to be out in the open!" was her first reaction, but this was followed very closely by revulsion. She spat in the general direction of the pleasure-seekers strolling along the brightly lit road and took to her heels.

Coming to a place where stars were reflected in a moat, she stopped to look. She heard running feet behind her. "Oh, oh! Lanterns this time. And they're from the Sumiya. Animals! Can't they even let a girl have a few minutes' peace? No. Find her! Put her back to making money! Turning flesh and blood into a little lumber for their new house—that's the only thing that'll satisfy them. Well, they won't get me back!"

The curled wood shavings hanging loosely in her hair bobbed up and down as she ran as fast as her legs would carry her into the darkness. She had no idea where she was going, and couldn't have cared less, so long as it was away, far away.

The Owl

When they finally forsook the teahouse, Kojirō was barely able to stand.

"Shoulder . . . shoulder," he gurgled, grabbing onto both Jūrō and Koroku for support.

The three lumbered uncertainly down the dark, deserted street.

Jūrō said, "Sir, I told you we should spend the night."

"In that dive? Not on your life! I'd rather go back to the Sumiya."

"I wouldn't, sir."

"Why not?"

"That girl, she ran away from you. If they find her, she could be forced to go to bed with you, but for what? You wouldn't enjoy it then."

"Umm. Maybe you're right."

"Do you want her?"

"Nah."

"But you can't quite get her out of your mind, can you?"

"I've never fallen in love in my life. I'm not the type. I've got more important things to do."

"What, sir?"

"Obvious, my boy. I'm going to be the best, most famous swordsman ever, and the quickest way to do that is to be the shōgun's teacher."

"But he already has the House of Yagyū to teach him. And I hear he recently hired Ono Jirōemon."

"Ono Jirōemon! Who gives a fart about him? The Yagyūs don't impress me much either. You watch me. One of these days . . ."

They had reached the stretch of road along which the new moat was being dug, and soft dirt was piled halfway up the willow trees.

"Watch out, sir; it's very slippery," said Jūrō as he and Koroku tried to help their teacher down from the pile of dirt.

"Hold it!" Kojirō shouted, abruptly shoving the two men away. He slid rapidly down the dirt pile. "Who's there?"

The man who had just lunged at Kojirō's back lost his balance and tumbled headfirst into the moat.

"Have you forgotten, Sasaki?"

"You killed four of our comrades!"

Kojirō jumped to the top of the dirt pile, from where he could see that there were at least ten men among the trees, partly hidden by rushes. Swords pointed at him, they slowly began closing in.

"So you're from the Obata School, are you?" he said in a contemptuous tone. The sudden action had sobered him completely. "Last time, you lost four men out of five. How many of you came tonight? How many want to die? Just give me the number, and I'll oblige. Cowards! Attack if you dare!" His hand went deftly over his shoulder to the hilt of the Drying Pole.

Obata Nichijō, before taking the tonsure, had been one of the most celebrated warriors in Kai, a province famous for its heroic samurai. After the defeat of the House of Takeda by Tokugawa Ieyasu, the Obata family had lived in obscurity until Kagenori distinguished himself at the Battle of Sekigahara. He had subsequently been summoned into service by Ieyasu himself and had gained fame as a teacher of military science. He had, however, refused the shogunate's offer of a choice plot of land in central Edo with the plea that a country warrior like himself would feel out of place there. He preferred a wooded lot adjoining Hirakawa Tenjin Shrine, where he had established his school in an ancient thatched farmhouse to which had been added a new lecture hall and a rather imposing entrance.

Now advanced in years and suffering from a neural disorder, Kagenori had been confined to his sickroom in recent months, appearing only rarely in the lecture hall. The woods were full of owls, and he had taken to signing his name as "Old Man Owl." Sometimes he'd smile weakly and say, "I'm an owl, like the others."

Not infrequently, the pain from the waist up was agonizing. Tonight had been one of those times.

"Feel a little better? Would you like some water?" The speaker was Hōjō Shinzō, son of Hōjō Ujikatsu, the celebrated military strategist.

"I'm much more comfortable now," said Kagenori. "Why don't you go to bed? It'll soon be light." The invalid's hair was white, his frame as skinny and angular as an aged plum tree.

"Don't worry about me. I get plenty of sleep during the day."

"You can't have much time left for sleeping when you spend your days taking over my lectures. You're the only one who can do that."

"Sleeping too much isn't good discipline."

Noticing that the lamp was about to go out, Shinzō stopped rubbing the old man's back and went to fetch some oil. When he returned, Kagenori, still lying on his stomach, had raised his bony face from the pillow. The light was reflected eerily in his eyes.

"What is it, sir?"

"Don't you hear it? It sounds like splashing water."

"It seems to be coming from the well."

"Who would it be at this hour? Do you suppose some of the men have been out drinking again?"

"That's probably it, but I'll take a look anyhow."

"Give them a good scolding while you're at it."

"Yes, sir. You'd better go to sleep. You must be tired."

When Kagenori's pain had subsided and he had dropped off to sleep, Shinzō carefully tucked the covers up around his shoulders and went to the back door. Two students were leaning over the well bucket, washing blood off their faces and hands.

He ran toward them with a scowl on his face. "You went, didn't you?" he said curtly. "After I pleaded with you not to!" The exasperation in his voice faded when he saw a third man lying in the shadow of the well. From the way he was groaning, it sounded as if he might die from his wounds at any moment.

Like little boys begging for help from an older brother, both men, their faces oddly twisted, sobbed uncontrollably.

"Fools!" Shinzō had to restrain himself from giving them a thrashing. "How many times did I warn you you were no match for him? Why didn't you listen?"

"After he dragged our master's name through the mud? After he killed four of our men? You keep saying we're not being reasonable. Aren't you the one who's lost his reason? Controlling your temper, holding yourself back, bearing insults in silence! Is that what you call reasonable? That's not the Way of the Samurai."

"Isn't it? If confronting Sasaki Kojirō was the thing to do, I'd have challenged him myself. He went out of his way to insult our teacher and commit other outrages against us, but that's no excuse for losing our sense of proportion. I'm not afraid to die, but Kojirō is not worth risking my life or anybody else's over."

"That's not the way most people see it. They think we're afraid of him. Afraid to stand up for our honor. Kojirō's been maligning Kagenori all over Edo."

643

"If he wants to run off at the mouth, let him. Do you think anybody who knows Kagenori is going to believe he lost an argument to that conceited novice?"

"Do as you please, Shinzō. The rest of us are not going to sit by and do nothing."

"Just exactly what do you have in mind?"

"Only one thing. Kill him!"

"You think you can? I told you not to go to the Sensōji. You wouldn't listen. Four men died. You've just returned after being defeated by him again. Isn't that piling shame on dishonor? It's not Kojirō who's destroying Kagenori's reputation, it's you. I have one question. Did you kill him?"

There was no answer.

"Of course not. I'll bet anything he doesn't have a scratch on him. The trouble with you is you don't have enough sense to avoid meeting him on his own terms. You don't understand his strength. True, he's young, he's of low character, he's coarse, he's arrogant. But he's an outstanding swordsman. How he learned his skill, I don't know, but there's no denying he has it. You underestimate him. That's your first mistake."

One man pressed in on Shinzō as though ready to attack him physically. "You're saying that whatever the bastard does, there's nothing we can do about it."

Shinzō nodded defiantly. "Exactly. There's nothing we can do. We're not swordsmen; we're students of military science. If you think my attitude is cowardly, then I'll just have to put up with being called a coward."

The wounded man at their feet moaned. "Water . . . water . . . please."

His two comrades knelt and propped him into a sitting position.

Seeing they were about to give him some water, Shinzō cried in alarm, "Stop! If he drinks water, it'll kill him!"

As they hesitated, the man put his mouth to the bucket. One swallow and his head collapsed into it, bringing the night's death toll to five.

While the owls hooted at the morning moon, Shinzō silently returned to the sickroom. Kagenori was still asleep, breathing deeply. Reassured, Shinzō went to his own cubicle.

Works on military science lay open on his desk, books he had begun reading but had had no time to finish. Though well born, as a child he had done his share of splitting firewood, carrying water and studying long hours by candlelight. His father, a great samurai, did not believe that young men of his class should be pampered. Shinzō had entered the Obata School with the ultimate aim of strengthening military skills in his family's fief, and though one of the younger students, he ranked highest in his teacher's estimation.

These days, caring for his ailing master kept him awake most of the night. He sat now with his arms folded and heaved a deep sigh. Who would look after Kagenori if he were not there? All the other students living at the school were of an uncouth type typically attracted to military matters. The men who came to the school only for classes were even worse. They blustered about, voicing opinions on the masculine subjects that samurai habitually discussed;

none of them really understood the spirit of the lonely man of reason who was their teacher. The finer points of military science went over their heads. Far more comprehensible was any kind of slur, either real or fancied, against their pride or their ability as samurai. Insulted, they became mindless instruments of vengeance.

Shinzō had been away on a trip when Kojirō arrived at the school. Since Kojirō had claimed that he wanted to ask some questions about military textbooks, his interest seemed genuine and he had been introduced to the master. But then, without asking a single question, he began arguing with Kagenori presumptuously and arrogantly, which suggested that his real purpose was to humiliate the old man. When some students finally got him into another room and demanded an explanation, he reacted with a flood of invective and an offer to fight any of them at any time.

Kojirō had then spread allegations that Obata's military studies were superficial, that they were no more than a rehash of the Kusunoki Style or the ancient Chinese military text known as the *Six Secrets*, and that they were spurious and unreliable. When his malicious pronouncements got back to the ears of the students, they vowed to make him pay with his life.

Shinzō's opposition—the problem was trivial, their master ought not to be disturbed by matters of this sort, Kojirō was not a serious student of military science—had proved futile, though he had also pointed out that before any decisive step was taken, Kagenori's son Yogorō, who was away on a long journey, should be consulted.

"Can't they see how much useless trouble they're causing?" lamented Shinzō. The fading light of the lamp dimly illuminated his troubled face. Still racking his brain for a solution, he laid his arms across the open books and dozed off.

He awoke to the murmur of indistinct voices.

Going first to the lecture hall and finding it empty, he slipped on a pair of zōri and went outside. In a bamboo grove that was part of the sacred compound of the Hirakawa Tenjin Shrine, he saw what he had expected: a large group of students holding an emotion-charged council of war. The two wounded men, their faces ashen, their arms suspended in white slings, stood side by side, describing the night's disaster.

One man asked indignantly, "Are you saying ten of you went and half were killed by this one man?"

"I'm afraid so. We couldn't even get close to him."

"Murata and Ayabe were supposed to be our best swordsmen."

"They were the first to go. Yosobei managed by sheer guts to get back here, but he made the mistake of drinking some water before we could stop him."

A grim silence descended over the group. As students of military science, they were concerned with problems of logistics, strategy, communications, intelligence and so on, not with the techniques of hand-to-hand combat. Most of them believed, as they had been taught, that swordsmanship was a matter for ordinary soldiers, not generals. Yet their samurai pride stood in the way of their accepting the logical corollary, which was that they were helpless against an expert swordsman like Sasaki Kojirō.

"What can we do?" asked a mournful voice. For a time the only answer was the hooting of the owls.

Then one student said brightly, "I have a cousin in the House of Yagyū. Maybe through him we could get them to help us."

"Don't be stupid!" shouted several others.

"We can't ask for outside help. It'd only bring more shame on our teacher. It'd be an admission of weakness."

"Well, what can we do?"

"The only way is to confront Kojirō again. But if we do it on a dark road again, it'll only do more damage to the school's reputation. If we die in open battle, we die. At least we won't be thought of as cowards."

"Should we send him a formal challenge?"

"Yes, and we have to keep at it, no matter how many times we lose."

"I think you're right, but Shinzō isn't going to like this."

"He doesn't have to know about it, nor does our master. Remember that, all of you. We can borrow brush and ink from the priest."

They started quietly for the priest's house. Before they had gone ten paces, the man in the lead gasped and stepped back. The others instantly came to a dead halt, their eyes riveted on the back veranda of the timeworn shrine building. There, against a backdrop formed by the shadow of a plum tree laden with green fruit, stood Kojirō, one foot propped on the railing and a malevolent grin on his face. To a man, the students turned pale; some had trouble breathing.

Kojirō's voice was venomous. "I gather from your discussion that you still haven't learned, that you've decided to write a letter of challenge and have it delivered to me. Well, I've saved you the trouble. I'm here, ready to fight.

"Last night, before I'd even washed the blood off my hands, I came to the conclusion there'd be a sequel, so I followed you sniveling cowards home."

He paused to let this sink in, then continued in an ironic tone. "I was wondering how you decide on the time and place to challenge an enemy. Do you consult a horoscope to pick the most propitious day? Or do you consider it wiser not to draw your swords until there comes a dark night when your opponent is drunk and on his way home from the licensed quarter?"

He paused again, as though waiting for an answer.

"Have you nothing to say? Isn't there a single red-blooded man among you? If you're so eager to fight me, come on. One at a time, or all at once—it's all the same to me! I wouldn't run from the likes of you if you were in full armor and marching to the beat of drums!"

No sound came from the cowed men.

"What's the matter with you?" The pauses grew longer. "Have you decided not to challenge me? . . . Isn't there even one among you with some backbone?"

"All right, it's time now to open your stupid ears and listen.

"I am Sasaki Kojirō. I learned the art of the sword indirectly from the great Toda Seigen after his death. I know the secrets of unsheathing invented by Katayama Hisayasu, and I have myself created the Ganryū Style. I'm not like those who deal in theory, who read books and listen to lectures on Sun-tzu or the *Six Secrets.* In spirit, in will, you and I have nothing in common.

"I don't know the details of your daily study, but I'm showing you now what the science of fighting is all about in real life. I'm not bragging. Think! When a man is set upon in the dark as I was last night, if he has the good fortune to win, what does he do? If he's an ordinary man, he goes as quickly as he can to a safe place. Once there, he thinks back over the incident and congratulates himself on having survived. Isn't that right? Isn't that what you would do?

"But did I do that? No! Not only did I cut down half of your men, I followed the stragglers home and waited here, right under your noses. I listened while you tried to make up your weak minds, and I took you completely by surprise. If I wanted to, I could attack now and smash you to bits. That's what it means to be a military man! That's the secret of military science!

"Some of you have said Sasaki Kojirō is just a swordsman, that he had no business coming to a military school and shooting off his mouth. How far do I have to go to convince you how wrong you are? Perhaps today I'll also prove to you that I'm not only the greatest swordsman in the country but also a master of tactics!

"Ha, ha! This is turning into quite a little lecture, isn't it? I'm afraid if I continue to pour out my fund of knowledge, poor Obata Kagenori may find himself out of a stipend. That wouldn't do, would it?

"Oh, I'm thirsty, Koroku! Jūrō! Get me some water!"

"Right away, sir!" they replied in unison from beside the shrine, where they had been watching in rapt admiration.

Having brought him a large earthen cup of water, Jūrō asked eagerly, "What are you going to do, sir?"

"Ask them!" Kojirō sneered. "Your answer's in those weasely, empty faces."

"Did you ever see men look so stupid?" Koroku laughed.

"What a gutless bunch," said Jūrō. "Come on, sir, let's go. They're not going to stand up to you."

While the three of them swaggered through the shrine gate, Shinzō, concealed among the trees, muttered through clenched teeth, "I'll get you for this."

The students were despondent. Kojirō had outwitted and defeated them; then he'd gloated, leaving them frightened and humiliated.

The silence was broken by a student running up and asking in a bewildered tone, "Did we order coffins?" When no one replied, he said, "The coffin-maker's just arrived with five coffins. He's waiting."

Finally, one of the group answered dispiritedly, "The bodies have been sent for. They haven't arrived yet. I'm not sure, but I think we'll need one more coffin. Ask him to make it, and put the ones he brought in the storehouse."

That night a wake was held in the lecture hall. Though everything was done quietly, in the hope that Kagenori would not hear, he was able to guess more or less what had occurred. He refrained from asking questions, nor did Shinzō make any comment.

From that day, the stigma of defeat hung over the school. Only Shinzō, who had urged restraint and been accused of cowardice, kept alive the desire for revenge. His eyes harbored a glint that none of the others could fathom.

In early fall, Kagenori's illness worsened. Visible from his bedside was an owl perched on a limb of a large zelkova tree, staring, never moving, hooting at the moon in the daytime. Shinzō now heard in the owl's hoot the message that his master's end was near.

Then a letter arrived from Yogorō, saying he had heard about Kojirō and was on his way home. For the next few days, Shinzō wondered which would come first, the arrival of the son or the death of the father. In either case, the day for which he was waiting, the day of his release from his obligations, was at hand.

On the evening before Yogorō was expected, Shinzō left a farewell letter on his desk and took his leave of the Obata School. From the woods near the shrine, he faced Kagenori's sickroom and said softly, "Forgive me for leaving without your permission. Rest at ease, good master. Yogorō will be home tomorrow. I don't know if I can present Kojirō's head to you before you die, but I must try. If I should die trying, I shall await you in the land of the dead."

A Plate of Loaches

Musashi had been roaming the countryside, devoting himself to ascetic practices, punishing his body to perfect his soul. He was more resolved than ever to go it alone: if that meant being hungry, sleeping out in the open in cold and rain and walking about in filthy rags, then so be it. In his heart was a dream that would never be satisfied by taking a position in Lord Date's employ, even if his lordship were to offer him his entire three-million-bushel fief.

After the long trip up the Nakasendō, he had spent only a few nights in Edo before taking to the road again, this time north to Sendai. The money given him by Ishimoda Geki had been a burden on his conscience; from the moment he'd discovered it, he'd known he'd find no peace until it was returned.

Now, a year and a half later, he found himself on Hōtengahara, a plain in Shimōsa Province, east of Edo, little changed since the rebellious Taira no Masakado and his troops had rampaged through the area in the tenth century. The plain was a dismal place still, sparsely settled and growing nothing of value, only weeds, a few trees and some scrubby bamboo and rushes. The sun, low on the horizon, reddened the pools of stagnant water but left the grass and brush colorless and indistinct.

648   "What now?" Musashi mumbled, resting his weary legs at a crossroads. His

body felt listless and still waterlogged from the cloudburst he'd been caught in a few days earlier at Tochigi Pass. The raw evening damp made him eager to find human habitation. For the past two nights he'd slept under the stars, but now he longed for the warmth of a hearth and some real food, even simple peasant fare such as millet boiled with rice.

A touch of saltiness in the breeze suggested that the sea was near. If he headed toward it, he reasoned, he just might find a house, perhaps even a fishing village or small port. If not, then he'd have to resign himself to yet another night in the autumn grasses, under the great autumn moon.

He realized with no small hint of irony that were he a more poetic type, he might savor these moments in a poignantly lonely landscape. As it was, he wanted only to escape it, to be with people, to have some decent food and get some rest. Yet the incessant buzzing of the insects seemed to be reciting a litany to his solitary wandering.

Musashi stopped on a dirt-covered bridge. A definite splashing noise seemed to rise above the peaceful rippling of the narrow river. An otter? In the fading daylight, he strained his eyes until he could just make out a figure kneeling in the hollow by the water's edge. He chuckled to note that the face of the young boy peering up at him was distinctly otter-like.

"What are you up to down there?" Musashi called in a friendly voice.

"Loaches," was the laconic reply. The boy was shaking a wicker basket in the water to clean the mud and sand off his wriggling catch.

"Catch many?" Musashi inquired, loath to sever this newly found bond with another human.

"Aren't many around. It's already fall."

"How about letting me have some?"

"My loaches?"

"Yes, just a handful. I'll pay you for them."

"Sorry. These are for my father." Hugging the basket, he leapt nimbly up the bank and was off like a shot into the darkness.

"Speedy little devil, I must say." Musashi, alone once again, laughed. He was reminded of his own childhood and of Jōtarō. "I wonder what's become of him," he mused. Jōtarō had been fourteen when Musashi had last seen him. Soon he would be sixteen. "Poor boy. He accepted me as his teacher, loved me as his teacher, served me as his teacher, and what did I do for him? Nothing."

Absorbed in his memories, he forgot his fatigue. He stopped and stood still. The moon had risen, bright and full. It was on nights like this that Otsū liked to play the flute. In the insects' voices he heard the sound of laughter, Otsū's and Jōtarō's together.

Turning his head to one side, he spotted a light. He turned the rest of his body in the same direction and made straight for it.

Lespedeza grew all around the isolated shack, almost as high as the lopsided roof. The walls were covered with calabash vines, the blossoms looking from a distance like enormous dewdrops. As he drew nearer, he was startled by the great angry snort of an unsaddled horse tied up beside the hovel.

"Who's there?"

Musashi recognized the voice coming from the shack as that of the boy with *649* the loaches. Smiling, he called, "How about putting me up for the night? I'll leave first thing in the morning."

The boy came to the door and looked Musashi over carefully. After a moment, he said, "All right. Come in."

The house was as rickety as any Musashi had ever seen. Moonlight poured through cracks in the walls and roof. After removing his cloak, he couldn't find even a peg to hang it on. Wind from below made the floor drafty, despite the reed mat covering it.

The boy knelt before his guest in formal fashion and said, "Back there at the river you said you wanted some loaches, didn't you? Do you like loaches?"

In these surroundings, the boy's formality so surprised Musashi that he merely stared.

"What are you looking at?"

"How old are you?"

"Twelve."

Musashi was impressed by his face. It was as dirty as a lotus root just pulled out of the ground, and his hair looked and smelled like a bird's nest. Yet there was character in his expression. His cheeks were chubby, and his eyes, shining like beads through the encircling grime, were magnificent.

"I have a little millet and rice," said the boy hospitably. "And now that I've given some to my father, you can have the rest of the loaches, if you want them."

"Thanks."

"I suppose you'd like some tea too."

"Yes, if it's not too much trouble."

"Wait here." He pushed open a screechy door and went into the next room.

Musashi heard him breaking firewood, then fanning the flame in an earthen hibachi. Before long, the smoke filling the shack drove a host of insects outdoors.

The boy came back with a tray, which he placed on the floor in front of Musashi. Falling to immediately, Musashi devoured the salty broiled loaches, the millet and rice and the sweetish black bean paste in record time.

"That was good," he said gratefully.

"Was it really?" The boy seemed to take pleasure in another person's happiness.

A well-behaved lad, thought Musashi. "I'd like to express my thanks to the head of the house. Has he gone to bed?"

"No; he's right in front of you." The boy pointed at his own nose.

"Are you here all alone?"

"Yes."

"Oh, I see." There was an awkward pause. "And what do you do for a living?" Musashi asked.

"I rent out the horse and go along as a groom. We used to farm a little too. . . . Oh, we've run out of lamp oil. You must be ready for bed anyway, aren't you?"

Musashi agreed that he was and lay down on a worn straw pallet spread next to the wall. The hum of the insects was soothing. He fell asleep, but perhaps because of his physical exhaustion, he broke into a sweat. Then he dreamed he heard rain falling.

The sound in his dream made him sit up with a start. No mistake about it. What he heard now was a knife or sword being honed. As he reached reflexively for his sword, the boy called in to him, "Can't you sleep?"

How had he known that? Amazed, Musashi said, "What are you doing sharpening a blade at this hour?" The question was uttered so tensely that it sounded more like the counterblow of a sword than an inquiry.

The boy broke into laughter. "Did I scare you? You look too strong and brave to be frightened so easily."

Musashi was silent. He wondered if he had come upon an all-seeing demon in the guise of a peasant boy.

When the scraping of the blade on the whetstone began again, Musashi went to the door. Through a crack, he could see that the other room was a kitchen with a small sleeping space at one end. The boy was kneeling in the moonlight next to the window with a large jug of water at his side. The sword he was sharpening was of a type farmers used.

"What do you intend to do with that?" asked Musashi.

The boy glanced toward the door but continued with his work. After a few more minutes, he wiped the blade, which was about a foot and a half long, and held it up to inspect it. It glistened brightly in the moonlight.

"Look," he said, "do you think I can cut a man in half with this?"

"Depends on whether you know how."

"Oh, I'm sure I do."

"Do you have someone particular in mind?"

"My father."

"Your *father*?" Musashi pushed open the door. "I hope that's not your idea of a joke."

"I'm not joking."

"You can't mean you intend to kill your father. Even the rats and wasps in this forsaken wilderness have better sense than to kill their parents."

"But if I don't cut him in two, I can't carry him."

"Carry him where?"

"I have to take him to the burial ground."

"You mean he's dead?"

"Yes."

Musashi looked again at the far wall. It had not occurred to him that the bulky shape he had seen there might be a body. Now he saw that it was indeed the corpse of an old man, laid out straight, with a pillow under its head and a kimono draped over it. By its side was a bowl of rice, a cup of water and a helping of broiled loaches on a wooden plate.

Recalling how he had unwittingly asked the boy to share the loaches intended as an offering to the dead man's spirit, Musashi felt a twinge of embarrassment. At the same time, he admired the boy for having the coolness to conceive of cutting the body into pieces so as to be able to carry it. His eyes riveted on the boy's face, for a few moments he said nothing.

"When did he die?"

651

"This morning."

"How far away is the graveyard?"

"It's up in the hills."

"Couldn't you have got somebody to take him there for you?"

"I don't have any money."

"Let me give you some."

The boy shook his head. "No. My father didn't like to accept gifts. He didn't like to go to the temple either. I can manage, thank you."

From the boy's spirit and courage, his stoic yet practical manner, Musashi suspected that his father had not been born an ordinary peasant. There had to be something to explain the son's remarkable self-sufficiency.

In deference to the dead man's wishes, Musashi kept his money and instead offered to contribute the strength needed to transport the body in one piece. The boy agreed, and together they loaded the corpse on the horse. When the road got steep, they took it off the horse, and Musashi carried it on his back. The graveyard turned out to be a small clearing under a chestnut tree, where a solitary round stone served as a marker.

After the burial, the boy placed some flowers on the grave and said, "My grandfather, grandmother and mother are buried here too." He folded his hands in prayer. Musashi joined him in silent supplication for the family's repose.

"The gravestone doesn't seem to be very old," he remarked. "When did your family settle here?"

"During my grandfather's time."

"Where were they before that?"

"My grandfather was a samurai in the Mogami clan, but after his lord's defeat, he burned our genealogy and everything else. There was nothing left."

"I don't see his name carved on the stone. There's not even a family crest or a date."

"When he died, he ordered that nothing appear on the stone. He was very strict. One time some men came from the Gamō fief, another time from the Date fief, and offered him a position, but he refused. He said a samurai shouldn't serve more than one master. That was the way he was about the stone too. Since he'd become a farmer, he said putting his name on it would reflect shame on his dead lord."

"Do you know your grandfather's name?"

"Yes. It was Misawa Iori. My father, since he was only a farmer, dropped the surname and just called himself San'emon."

"And your name?"

"Sannosuke."

"Do you have any relatives?"

"An older sister, but she went away a long time ago. I don't know where she is."

"No one else?"

"No."

"How do you plan to make your living now?"

652   "Same as before, I guess." But then he added hurriedly, "Look, you're a

shugyōsha, aren't you? You must travel around just about everywhere. Take me with you. You can ride my horse and I'll be your groom."

As Musashi turned the boy's request over in his mind, he gazed out upon the land below them. Since it was fertile enough to support a plethora of weeds, he could not understand why it was not cultivated. It was certainly not because the people hereabouts were well off; he had seen evidence of poverty everywhere.

Civilization, Musashi was thinking, does not flourish until men have learned to exercise control over the forces of nature. He wondered why the people here in the center of the Kanto Plain were so powerless, why they allowed themselves to be oppressed by nature. As the sun rose, Musashi caught glimpses of small animals and birds reveling in the riches that man had not yet learned to harvest. Or so it seemed.

He was soon reminded that Sannosuke, despite his courage and independence, was still a child. By the time the sunlight made the dewy foliage glisten and they were ready to start back, the boy was no longer sad, seemed in fact to have put all thoughts of his father completely out of mind.

Halfway down the hill, he began badgering Musashi for an answer to his proposal. "I'm ready to start today," he declared. "Just think, anywhere you go, you'll be able to ride the horse, and I'll be there to wait on you."

This elicited a noncommittal grunt. While Sannosuke had much to recommend him, Musashi questioned whether he should again put himself in the position of being responsible for a boy's future. Jōtarō—he had natural ability, but how had he benefited by attaching himself to Musashi? And now that he had disappeared to heaven knew where, Musashi felt his responsibility even more keenly. Still, Musashi thought, if a man dwells only on the dangers ahead, he cannot advance a single step, let alone make his way through life successfully. Furthermore, in the case of a child, no one, not even his parents, can actually guarantee his future. "Is it really possible to decide objectively what's good for a child and what's not?" he asked himself. "If it's a matter of developing Sannosuke's talents and guiding him in the right direction, I can do that. I guess that's about as much as anyone can do."

"Promise, won't you? Please," the boy insisted.

"Sannosuke, do you want to be a groom all your life?"

"Of course not. I want to be a samurai."

"That's what I thought. But if you come with me and become my pupil, you'll be in for a lot of rough times, you know."

The boy threw down the rope and, before Musashi knew what he was up to, knelt on the ground below the horse's head. Bowing deeply, he said, "I beg you, sir, make a samurai of me. That's what my father wanted, but there was no one we could ask for help."

Musashi dismounted, looked around for a moment, then picked up a stick and handed it to Sannosuke. He found another one for himself and said, "I want you to strike me with that stick. After I've seen how you handle it, I can decide whether you have the talent to be a samurai."

"If I hit you, will you say yes?"

"Try it and see." Musashi laughed.

653

Sannosuke took a firm grip on his weapon and rushed forward as if possessed. Musashi showed no mercy. Time and again the boy was struck—on the shoulders, in the face, on the arms. After each setback, he staggered away but always came back to the attack.

"Pretty soon he'll be in tears," thought Musashi.

But Sannosuke would not give up. When his stick broke in two, he charged empty-handed.

"What do you think you're doing, you runt?" Musashi snapped with deliberate meanness. He seized the boy by his obi and threw him flat on the ground.

"You big bastard!" shouted Sannosuke, already on his feet and attacking again.

Musashi caught him by the waist and held him up in the air. "Had enough?"

"No!" he shouted defiantly, though the sun was in his eyes and he was reduced to uselessly waving his arms and legs.

"I'm going to throw you against that rock over there. It'll kill you. Ready to give up?"

"No!"

"Stubborn, aren't you? Can't you see you're beaten?"

"Not as long as I'm alive I'm not! You'll see. I'll win in the end."

"How do you expect to do that?"

"I'll practice, I'll discipline myself."

"But while you're practicing for ten years, I'll be doing the same thing."

"Yes, but you're a lot older than I am. You'll die first."

"Hmm."

"And when they put you in a coffin, I'll strike the final blow and win!"

"Fool!" shouted Musashi, tossing the boy to the ground.

When Sannosuke stood up, Musashi looked at his face for a moment, laughed and clapped his hands together once. "Good. You can be my pupil."

Like Teacher, Like Pupil

On the short journey back to the shack, Sannosuke rattled on and on about his dreams for the future.

But that night, when Musashi told him he should be ready to bid farewell to the only home he had ever known, he became wistful. They sat up late, and Sannosuke, misty-eyed and speaking in a soft voice, shared his memories of parents and grandparents.

In the morning, while they were preparing to move out, Musashi announced that henceforth he would call Sannosuke Iori. "If you're going to become a samurai," he explained, "it's only proper that you take your grandfather's name." The boy was not yet old enough for his coming-of-age ceremony, when he would normally have been given his adult name; Musashi thought taking his grandfather's name would give him something to live up to.

Later, when the boy seemed to be lingering inside the house, Musashi said quietly but firmly, "Iori, hurry up. There's nothing in there you need. You don't want reminders of the past."

Iori came flying out in a kimono barely covering his thighs, a groom's straw sandals on his feet and a cloth wrapper containing a box lunch of millet and rice in his hand. He looked like a little frog, but he was ready and eager for a new life.

"Pick a tree away from the house and tie the horse up," Musashi commanded.

"You may as well mount it now."

"Do as I say."

"Yes, sir."

Musashi noted the politeness; it was a small but encouraging sign of the boy's readiness to adopt the ways of the samurai in place of the slovenly speech of peasants.

Iori tied up the horse and came back to where Musashi was standing under the eaves of the old shack, gazing at the surrounding plain. "What's he waiting for?" wondered the boy.

Putting his hand on Iori's head, Musashi said, "This is where you were born and where you acquired your determination to win."

Iori nodded.

"Rather than serve a second lord, your grandfather withdrew from the warrior class. Your father, true to your grandfather's dying wish, contented himself with being a mere farmer. His death left you alone in the world, so the time has come for you to stand on your own feet."

"Yes, sir."

"You must become a great man!"

"I'll try." Tears sprang to his eyes.

"For three generations this house sheltered your family from wind and rain. Say your thanks to it, then say good-bye, once and for all, and have no regrets."

Musashi went inside and set fire to the hovel.

When he came out, Iori was blinking back his tears.

"If we left the house standing," said Musashi, "it'd only become a hideout for highwaymen or common thieves. I'm burning it to keep men like that from desecrating the memory of your father and grandfather."

"I'm grateful."

The shack turned into a small mountain of fire, then collapsed.

"Let's go," said Iori, no longer concerned with relics of the past.

"Not yet."

"There's nothing else to do here, is there?"

Musashi laughed. "We're going to build a new house on that knoll over there."

"New house? What for? You just burned the old one down."

"That belonged to your father and grandfather. The one we build will be for us."

"You mean we're going to stay here?"

"That's right."

"We're not going away somewhere and train and discipline ourselves?"

"We'll do that here."

"What can we train ourselves for here?"

"To be swordsmen, to be samurai. We'll discipline our spirits and work hard to make ourselves into real human beings. Come with me, and bring that ax with you." He pointed to a clump of grass where he had put the farm tools.

Shouldering the ax, Iori followed Musashi to the knoll, where there were a few chestnut trees, pines and cryptomerias.

Musashi, stripping to the waist, took the ax and went to work. Soon he was sending up a veritable shower of white chips of raw wood.

Iori watched, thinking: "Maybe he's going to build a dōjō. Or are we going to practice out in the open?"

One tree fell, then another and another. Sweat poured down Musashi's ruddy cheeks, washing away the lethargy and loneliness of the past few days.

He had conceived of his present plan while standing by the farmer's fresh grave in the tiny burial ground. "I'll lay down my sword for a time," he had decided, "and work with a hoe instead." Zen, calligraphy, the art of tea, painting pictures and carving statues were all useful in perfecting one's swordsmanship. Couldn't tilling a field also contribute to his training? Wasn't this broad tract of earth, waiting for someone to bring it under cultivation, a perfect training hall? By changing inhospitable flatlands into ·farmlands, he would also be promoting the welfare of future generations.

He'd lived his whole life like a mendicant Zen priest—on the receiving end, so to speak, depending on other people for food, shelter and donations. He wanted to make a change, a radical one, since he'd long suspected that only those who had actually grown their own grain and vegetables really understood how sacred and valuable they were. Those who hadn't were like priests who did not practice what they preached or swordsmen who learned combat techniques but knew nothing of the Way.

As a boy, he had been taken by his mother into the fields and had worked alongside the tenants and villagers. His purpose now, however, was more than just to produce food for his daily meals; he sought nourishment for his soul. He wanted to learn what it meant to work for a living, rather than beg for one. He also wanted to implant his own way of thinking among the people of the district. As he saw it, by surrendering the land to weeds and thistles and giving in to storms and floods, they were passing on their hand-to-mouth existence from generation to generation without ever opening their eyes to their own potentialities and those of the land around them.

656

"Iori," he called, "get some rope and tie up this timber. Then drag it down to the riverbank."

When that was done, Musashi propped his ax against a tree and wiped the sweat off his forehead with his elbow. He then went down and stripped the bark off the trees with a hatchet. When darkness fell, they built a bonfire with the scraps and found blocks of wood to use as pillows.

"Interesting work, isn't it?" said Musashi.

With perfect honesty, Iori answered, "I don't think it's interesting at all. I didn't have to become your pupil to learn how to do this."

"You'll like it better as time goes on."

As autumn waned, the insect voices faded into silence. Leaves withered and fell. Musashi and Iori finished their cabin and addressed themselves to the task of making the land ready for planting.

One day while he was surveying the land, Musashi suddenly found himself thinking it was like a diagram of the social unrest that lasted for a century after the Ōnin War. Such thoughts aside, it was not an encouraging picture.

Unknown to Musashi, Hōtengahara had over the centuries been buried many times by volcanic ash from Mount Fuji, and the Tone River had repeatedly flooded the flatlands. When the weather was fair, the land became bone dry, but whenever there were heavy rains, the water carved out new channels, carrying great quantities of dirt and rock along with it. There was no principal stream into which the smaller ones flowed naturally, the nearest thing to this being a wide basin that lacked sufficient capacity to either water or drain the area as a whole. The most urgent need was obvious: to bring the water under control.

Still, the more he had looked, the more he had questioned why the area was undeveloped. "It won't be easy," he thought, excited by the challenge it posed. Joining water and earth to create productive fields was not much different from leading men and women in such a way that civilization might bloom. To Musashi it seemed that his goal was in complete agreement with his ideals of swordsmanship.

He had come to see the Way of the Sword in a new light. A year or two earlier, he had wanted only to conquer all rivals, but now the idea that the sword existed for the purpose of giving him power over other people was unsatisfying. To cut people down, to triumph over them, to display the limits of one's strength, seemed increasingly vain. He wanted to conquer himself, to make life itself submit to him, to cause people to live rather than die. The Way of the Sword should not be used merely for his own perfection. It should be a source of strength for governing people and leading them to peace and happiness.

He realized his grand ideals were no more than dreams, and would remain so as long as he lacked the political authority to implement them. But here in this wasteland, he needed neither rank nor power. He plunged into the struggle with joy and enthusiasm.

Day in and day out, stumps were uprooted, gravel sifted, land leveled, soil   *657* and rocks made into dikes. Musashi and Iori worked from before dawn until after the stars were shining bright in the sky.

Their relentless toil attracted attention. Villagers passing by often stopped, stared, and commented.

"What do they think they're doing?"

"How can they live in a place like that?"

"Isn't the boy old San'emon's son?"

Everyone laughed, but not all let it go at that. One man came out of genuine kindness and said, "I hate to tell you this, but you're wasting your time. You can break your backs making a field here, but one storm and it'll be gone overnight."

When he saw they were still at it several days later, he seemed a bit offended. "All you're doing here, I tell you, is making a lot of water holes where they won't do any good."

A few days later he concluded that the strange samurai was short on brains. "Fools!" he shouted in disgust.

The next day brought a whole group to heckle.

"If anything could grow here, we wouldn't sweat under the blazing sun working our own fields, poor as they are. We'd sit home and play the flute."

"And there wouldn't be any famines."

"You're digging up the place for nothing."

"Got the sense of a pile of manure."

Still hoeing, Musashi kept his eyes on the ground and grinned.

Iori was less complacent, though Musashi had earlier scolded him for taking the peasants seriously. "Sir"—he pouted—"they all say the same thing."

"Pay no attention."

"I can't help it," he cried, seizing a rock to throw at their tormentors.

An angry glare from Musashi stopped him. "Now, what good do you think that would do? If you don't behave yourself, I'm not going to have you as my pupil."

Iori's ears burned at the rebuke, but instead of dropping the rock, he cursed and hurled it at a boulder. The rock gave off sparks as it cracked in two. Iori tossed his hoe aside and began to weep.

Musashi ignored him, though he wasn't unmoved. "He's all alone, just as I am," he thought.

As though in sympathy with the boy's grief, a twilight breeze swept over the plain, setting everything astir. The sky darkened and raindrops fell.

"Come on, Iori, let's go in," called Musashi. "Looks like we're in for a squall." Hurriedly collecting his tools, he ran for the house. By the time he was inside, the rain was coming down in gray sheets.

"Iori," he shouted, surprised that the boy had not come with him. He went to the window and strained his eyes toward the field. Rain spattered from the sill into his face. A streak of lightning split the air and struck the earth. As he shut his eyes and put his hands over his ears, he felt the force of the thunder.

In the wind and rain, Musashi saw the cryptomeria tree at the Shippōji and heard the stern voice of Takuan. He felt that whatever he had gained since then he owed to them. He wanted to possess the tree's immense strength as well as Takuan's icy, unwavering compassion. If he could be to Iori what the old cryptomeria had been to him, he would feel he'd succeeded in repaying a part of his debt to the monk.

"Iori! . . . Iori!"

There was no answer, only thunder and the rain pounding on the roof.

"Where could he have gone?" he wondered, still unwilling to venture outside.

When the rain slackened to a drizzle, he did go out. Iori had not moved an inch. With his clothing clinging to his body and his face still screwed up in an angry frown, he looked rather like a scarecrow. How could a child be so stubborn?

"Idiot!" Musashi chided. "Get back into the house. Being drenched like that's not exactly good for you. Hurry up, before rivers start forming. Then you won't be able to get back."

Iori turned, as though trying to locate Musashi's voice, then started laughing. "Something bothering you? This kind of rain doesn't last. See, the clouds are breaking up already."

Musashi, not expecting to receive a lesson from his pupil, was more than a little put out, but Iori didn't give the matter a second thought. "Come on," the boy said, picking up his hoe. "We can still get quite a bit done before the sun's gone."

For the next five days, bulbuls and shrikes conversed hoarsely under a cloudless blue sky, and great cracks grew in the earth as it caked around the roots of the rushes. On the sixth day, a cluster of small black clouds appeared on the horizon and rapidly spread across the heavens until the whole plain seemed to be under an eclipse.

Iori studied the sky briefly and said in a worried tone, "This time it's the real thing." Even as he spoke, an inky wind swirled around them. Leaves shook and little birds dropped to the earth as if felled by a silent and invisible horde of hunters.

"Another shower?" Musashi asked.

"Not with the sky like that. I'd better go to the village. And you'd better gather up the tools and get inside as fast as you can." Before Musashi could ask why, Iori took off across the flatlands and was quickly lost in a sea of high grass.

Again, Iori's weather sense was accurate. The sudden downpour, driven by a raging, gusty wind, that sent Musashi scurrying for shelter developed its own distinctive rhythms. The rain fell in unbelievable quantity for a time, stopped suddenly, then recommenced with even greater fury. Night came, but the storm continued unabated. It began to seem as though the heavens were set on making the entire earth into an ocean. Several times Musashi feared that the wind would rip off the roof; the floor was already littered with shingles torn off its underside.

Morning came, gray and formless and with no sign of Iori. Musashi stood by the window, and his heart sank: he could do nothing. Here and there a tree or a clump of grass was visible; all else was a vast muddy swamp. Luckily, the cabin was still above water level, but in what had been a dry riverbed immediately below it, there was now a rushing torrent, carrying along everything in its path.

Not knowing for sure that Iori hadn't fallen into the water and drowned, Musashi felt time drag on, until finally he thought he heard Iori's voice calling, "*Sensei!* Here!" He was some distance beyond the river, riding a bullock, with a great bundle tied behind him.

Musashi watched in consternation as Iori rode straight into the muddy flow, which seemed about to suck him under at every step.

When he gained the other bank, he was quaking from the cold and wet, but he calmly guided the bullock to the side of the cabin.

"Where have you been?" demanded Musashi, his voice both angry and relieved.

"To the village, of course. I brought back lots of food. It'll rain half a year's worth before this storm's over, and when it is, we'll be trapped by the floodwaters."

After they had taken the straw bundle inside, Iori untied it and removed the items one by one from the inner wrapping of oiled paper. "Here are some chestnuts . . . lentil beans . . . salted fish. . . . We shouldn't run out of food even if it takes a month or two for the water to go down."

Musashi's eyes misted over with gratitude, but he said nothing. He was too abashed at his own lack of common sense. How could he guide humanity if he was careless about his own survival? Were it not for Iori, he would now be facing starvation. And the boy, having been raised in a remote rural area, must have known about laying in supplies since he was two years old.

It struck Musashi as odd that the villagers had agreed to furnish all this food. They couldn't have had very much for themselves. When he recovered his voice and raised the question, Iori replied, "I left my money pouch in hock and borrowed from the Tokuganji."

"And what's the Tokuganji?"

"It's the temple about two miles from here. My father told me there was some powdered gold in the pouch. He said if I got into difficulty, I should use it a little at a time. Yesterday, when the weather turned bad, I remembered what he said." Iori wore a smile of triumph.

"Isn't the pouch a keepsake from your father?"

"Yes. Now that we've burned the old house down, that and the sword are the only things left." He rubbed the hilt of the short weapon in his obi. Though the tang bore no craftsman's signature, Musashi had noted when he'd examined the blade earlier that it was of excellent quality. He also had the feeling that the inherited pouch had some significance beyond that of the powdered gold it contained.

"You shouldn't hand keepsakes over to other people. One of these days, I'll get it back for you, but after that you must promise not to let go of it."

660   "Yes, sir."

"Where did you spend the night?"

"The priest told me I'd better wait there till morning."

"Have you eaten?"

"No. You haven't either, have you?"

"No, but there's no firewood, is there?"

"Oh, there's plenty." He pointed downward, indicating the space under the cabin, where he'd stored a good supply of sticks and roots and bamboo picked up while he worked in the fields.

Holding a piece of straw matting over his head, Musashi crawled under the cabin and again marveled at the boy's good sense. In an environment like this, survival depended on foresight and a small mistake could spell the difference between life and death.

When they had finished eating, Iori brought out a book. Then, kneeling formally before his teacher, he said, "While we're waiting for the water to go down so we can work, would you teach me some reading and writing?"

Musashi agreed. On such a dismal stormy day, it was a good way to pass the time. The book was a volume of the *Analects of Confucius*. Iori said it had been given to him at the temple.

"Do you really want to study?"

"Yes."

"Have you done much reading?"

"No; only a little."

"Who taught you?"

"My father."

"What have you read?"

"*The Lesser Learning*."

"Did you enjoy it?"

"Yes, very much," he said eagerly, his eyes brightening.

"All right then. I'll teach you all I know. Later on, you can find somebody better educated to teach you what I don't know."

They devoted the rest of the day to a study session, the boy reading aloud, Musashi stopping him to correct him or explain words he did not understand. They sat in utter concentration, oblivious of the storm.

The deluge lasted two more days, by which time there was no land visible anywhere.

On the following day, it was still raining. Iori, delighted, took out the book again and said, "Shall we begin?"

"Not today. You've had enough of reading for a while."

"Why?"

"If you do nothing but read, you'll lose sight of the reality around you. Why don't you take the day off and play? I'm going to relax too."

"But I can't go outside."

"Then just do like me," said Musashi, sprawling on his back and crossing his arms under his head.

"Do I have to lie down?"

"Do what you want. Lie down, stand up, sit—whatever's comfortable."

661

"Then what?"

"I'll tell you a story."

"I'd like that," said Iori, flopping down on his stomach and wiggling his legs in the air. "What kind of story?"

"Let me see," said Musashi, going over the tales he had liked to hear as a child. He chose the one about the battles between the Genji and the Heike. All boys loved that.

Iori proved to be no exception. When Musashi came to the part about the Genji being defeated and the Heike taking over the country, the boy's face became gloomy. He had to blink to keep from crying over Lady Tokiwa's sad fate. But his spirits rose as he heard about Minamoto no Yoshitsune learning swordsmanship from the "long-nosed goblins" on Mount Kurama and later making his escape from Kyoto.

"I like Yoshitsune," he said, sitting up. "Are there really goblins on Mount Kurama?"

"Maybe. Anyway, there're people in this world who might as well be goblins. But the ones who taught Yoshitsune weren't real goblins."

"What were they?"

"Loyal vassals of the defeated Genji. They couldn't come out in the open while the Heike were in power, so they stayed hidden in the mountains until their chance came."

"Like my grandfather?"

"Yes, except he waited all his life, and his chance never came. After Yoshitsune grew up, the faithful Genji followers who had looked after him during his childhood got the opportunity they had prayed for."

"I'll have a chance to make up for my grandfather, won't I?"

"Hmm. I think it's possible. Yes, I really think so."

He pulled Iori to him, lifted him up and balanced him on his hands and feet like a ball. "Now try being a great man!" He laughed.

Iori giggled, and stammered, "You . . . you're a gob-goblin too! Stop . . . it. I'll fa-fall." He reached down and pinched Musashi's nose.

On the eleventh day, it finally stopped raining. Musashi chafed to be out in the open, but it was another week before they were able to return to work under a bright sun. The field they had so arduously carved out of the wilderness had disappeared without a trace; in its place were rocks, and a river where none had been before. The water seemed to mock them just as the villagers had.

Iori, seeing no way to reclaim their loss, looked up and said, "This place is beyond hope. Let's look for better land somewhere else."

"No," Musashi said firmly. "With the water drained off, this would make excellent farmland. I examined the location from every angle before I chose it."

"What if we have another heavy rain?"

"We'll fix it so the water doesn't come this way. We'll lay a dam from here all the way to that hill over there."

662

"That's an awful lot of work."

"You seem to forget that this is our dōjō. I'm not giving up a foot of this land until I see barley growing on it."

Musashi carried on his stubborn struggle throughout the winter, into the second month of the new year. It took several weeks of strenuous labor to dig ditches, drain the water off, pile dirt for a dike and then cover it with heavy rocks.

Three weeks later everything was again washed away.

"Look," Iori said, "we're wasting our energy on something impossible. Is that the Way of the Sword?" The question struck close to the bone, but Musashi would not give in.

Only a month passed before the next disaster, a heavy snowfall followed by a quick thaw. Iori, on his return from trips to the temple for food, inevitably wore a long face, for the people there rode him mercilessly about Musashi's failure. And finally Musashi himself began to lose heart.

For two full days and on into a third, he sat silently brooding and staring at his field.

Then it dawned on him suddenly. Unconsciously, he had been trying to create a neat, square field like those common in other parts of the Kanto Plain, but this was not what the terrain called for. Here, despite the general flatness, there were slight variations in the lay of the land and the quality of the soil that argued for an irregular shape.

"What a fool I've been," he exclaimed aloud. "I tried to make the water flow where I thought it should and force the dirt to stay where I thought it ought to be. But it didn't work. How could it? Water's water, dirt's dirt. I can't change their nature. What I've got to do is learn to be a servant to the water and a protector of the land."

In his own way, he had submitted to the attitude of the peasants. On that day he became nature's manservant. He ceased trying to impose his will on nature and let nature lead the way, while at the same time seeking out possibilities beyond the grasp of other inhabitants of the plain.

The snow came again, and another thaw; the muddy water oozed slowly over the plain. But Musashi had had time to work out his new approach, and his field remained intact.

"The same rules must apply to governing people," he said to himself. In his notebook, he wrote: "Do not attempt to oppose the way of the universe. But first make sure you know the way of the universe."

Mountain Devils

"Let me make myself clear. I don't want you to go to any trouble on my account. Your hospitality, which I appreciate greatly, is quite sufficient."

"Yes, sir. That's very considerate of you, sir," replied the priest.

"I'd just like to relax. That's all."

"By all means."

"Now I hope you'll forgive my rudeness," said the samurai, stretching out casually on his side and propping his graying head on his forearm.

The guest who'd just arrived at the Tokuganji was Nagaoka Sado, a high-ranking vassal of Lord Hosokawa Tadaoki of Buzen. He had little time for personal matters, but he invariably came on such occasions as the anniversary of his father's death, usually staying overnight, since the temple was some twenty miles from Edo. For a man of his rank, he traveled unostentatiously, accompanied this time by only two samurai and one young personal attendant.

To get away from the Hosokawa establishment even for a short time, he had had to trump up an excuse. He rarely had the chance to do as he pleased, and now that he did, he was fully enjoying the local sake while listening to the croaking of frogs. Briefly he could forget about everything—the problems of administration and the constant need to be attuned to the nuances of daily affairs.

After dinner, the priest quickly cleared the dishes and left. Sado was chatting idly with his attendants, who were seated next to the wall, only their faces showing in the light of the lamp.

"I could just lie here forever and enter Nirvana, like the Buddha," Sado said lazily.

"Careful you don't catch cold. The night air is damp."

"Oh, leave me alone. This body's survived a few battles. It can hold its own against a sneeze or two. But just smell those ripe blossoms! Nice fragrance, isn't it?"

"I don't smell anything."

"Don't you? If your sense of smell is that poor . . . you sure you don't have a cold yourself?"

They were engrossed in this kind of seemingly light banter when suddenly the frogs fell silent, and a loud voice shouted, "You devil! What're you doing here, staring into the guest room?"

Sado's bodyguards were on their feet instantly.

"What is it?"

"Who's out there?"

As their cautious eyes scanned the garden, the clatter of small feet receded in the direction of the kitchen.

A priest looked in from the veranda, bowed and said, "Sorry for the disturbance. It's only one of the local children. There's nothing to worry about."

"Are you sure?"

"Yes, of course. He lives a couple of miles from here. His father worked as a groom, until he died recently, but his grandfather is said to have been a samurai, and every time he sees one, he stops and stares—with his finger in his mouth."

Sado sat up. "You mustn't be too hard on him. If he wants to be a samurai, bring him in. We'll have some sweets and talk it over."

By now Iori had reached the kitchen. "Hey, Granny," he shouted. "I've run out of millet. Fill this up for me, will you?" The sack he thrust out to the wrinkled old woman who worked in the kitchen would have held half a bushel.

She shouted right back. "Watch your tongue, you beggar! You talk as if we owe you something."

"You've got a lot of nerve to begin with!" said a priest who was washing dishes. "The head priest took pity on you, so we're giving you food, but don't be insolent. When you're asking a favor, do it politely."

"I'm not begging. I gave the priest the pouch my father left me. There's money in it, plenty of money."

"And how much could a groom living out in the sticks leave his son?"

"Are you going to give me the millet? Yes or no?"

"There you go again. Just look at yourself. You're crazy, taking orders from that fool rōnin. Where did he come from anyway? Who is he? Why should he be eating your food?"

"None of your business."

"Hmph. Digging around in that barren plain where there's never going to be a field or a garden or anything else! The whole village is laughing at you."

"Who asked for your advice?"

"Whatever's wrong with that rōnin's head must be catching. What do you expect to find up there—a pot of gold, like in a fairy tale? You're not even dry behind the ears, and you're already digging your own grave."

"Shut up and give me the millet. The millet! Now."

The priest was still teasing Iori a couple of minutes later when something cold and slimy hit his face. His eyes popped, then he saw what it was—a warty toad. He screamed and lunged for Iori, but just as he collared him, another priest arrived to announce that the boy was wanted in the samurai's room.

The head priest had also heard the commotion and rushed to the kitchen. "Did he do something to upset our guest?" he asked worriedly.

"No. Sado just said he'd like to talk to him. He'd like to give him some sweets too."

The head priest hurriedly took Iori by the hand and delivered him personally to Sado's room.

As Iori timidly sat down beside the priest, Sado asked, "How old are you?"

"Thirteen."

"And you want to become a samurai?"

"That's right," replied Iori, nodding vigorously.

"Well, well. Why don't you come and live with me, then? You'd have to help with the housework at the beginning, but later I'd make you one of the apprentice samurai."

Iori shook his head silently. Sado, taking this for bashfulness, assured him that the offer was serious.

Iori, flashing an angry look, said, "I heard you wanted to give me some sweets. Where are they?"

Paling, the head priest slapped him on the wrist.

"Don't scold him," Sado said reprovingly. He liked children and tended to indulge them. "He's right. A man should keep his word. Have the sweets brought in."

When they arrived, Iori began stuffing them into his kimono.

Sado, a little taken aback, asked, "Aren't you going to eat them here?"

"No. My teacher's waiting for me at home."

"Oh? You have a teacher?"

Without bothering to explain himself, Iori bolted from the room and disappeared through the garden.

Sado thought his behavior highly amusing. Not so the head priest, who bowed to the floor two or three times before going to the kitchen in pursuit of Iori.

"Where is that insolent brat?"

"He picked up his sack of millet and left."

They listened for a moment but heard only a discordant screeching. Iori had plucked a leaf from a tree and was trying to improvise a tune. None of the few songs he knew seemed to work. The grooms' chantey was too slow, the *Bon* festival songs too complicated. Finally, he settled on a melody resembling the sacred dance music at the local shrine. This suited him well enough, for he liked the dances, which his father had sometimes taken him to see.

About halfway to Hōtengahara, at a point where two streams joined to make a river, he gave a sudden start. The leaf flew from his mouth, along with a spray of saliva, and he leapt into the bamboo beside the road.

Standing on a crude bridge were three or four men, engaged in a furtive conversation. "It's them," Iori exclaimed softly.

A remembered threat rang in his frightened ears. When mothers in this region scolded their children, they were apt to say, "If you're not good, the mountain devils will come down and get you." The last time they had actually come had been in the fall of the year before last.

Twenty miles or so from here, in the mountains of Hitachi, there was a shrine dedicated to a mountain deity. Centuries earlier, the people had so feared this god that the villages had taken turns making annual offerings of grain and women to him. When a community's turn came, the inhabitants had assembled their tribute and gone in a torchlight procession to the shrine. As time went on and it became evident that the god was really only a man, they became lax in making their offerings.

During the period of the civil wars, the so-called mountain god had taken to having his tribute collected by force. Every two or three years, a pack of brigands, armed with halberds, hunting spears, axes—anything to strike terror into the hearts of peaceful citizens—would descend on first one community, then the next, carrying away everything that caught their fancy, including wives and daughters. If their victims put up any resistance, the plundering was accompanied by slaughter.

Their last raid still vivid in his memory, Iori cringed in the underbrush. A group of five shadows came running across the field to the bridge. Then, through the night mist, another small band, and still another, until the bandits numbered between forty and fifty.

Iori held his breath and stared while they debated a course of action. They soon reached a decision. Their leader issued a command and pointed toward the village. The men rushed off like a swarm of locusts.

Before long, the mist was rent by a great cacophony—birds, cattle, horses, the wailing of people young and old.

Iori quickly made up his mind to get help from the samurai at the Tokuganji, but the minute he left the shelter of the bamboo, a shout came from the bridge: "Who's there?" He had not seen the two men left behind to stand guard. Swallowing hard, he ran for all he was worth, but his short legs were no match for those of grown men.

"Where do you think you're going?" shouted the man who got hold of him first.

"Who are you?"

Instead of crying like a baby, which might have thrown the men off guard, Iori scratched and fought against the brawny arms imprisoning him.

"He saw all of us together. He was going to tell somebody."

"Let's beat him up and dump him in a rice field."

"I've got a better idea."

They carried Iori to the river, threw him down the bank and jumping down after him, tied him to one of the bridge posts.

"There, that takes care of him." The two ruffians climbed back up to their station on the bridge.

The temple bell tolled in the distance. Iori watched horrified as the flames rising from the village dyed the river a bloody red. The sound of babies crying and women wailing came closer and closer. Then wheels rumbled onto the bridge. Half a dozen of the bandits were leading oxcarts and horses loaded with loot.

"Filthy scum!" screamed a masculine voice.

"Give me back my wife!"

667

The scuffle on the bridge was brief but fierce. Men shouted, metal clanged, a shriek went up, and a bloody corpse landed at Iori's feet. A second body splashed into the river, spraying his face with blood and water. One by one farmers fell from the bridge, six of them in all. The bodies rose to the surface and floated slowly downstream, but one man, not quite dead, grasped at the reeds and clawed the earth until he had pulled himself halfway out of the water.

"You!" cried Iori. "Untie this rope. I'll go for help. I'll see that you get your revenge." Then his voice rose to a bellow. "Come on. Untie me. I've got to save the village."

The man lay motionless.

Straining at his bonds with all his might, Iori finally loosened them enough to squirm down and kick the man in the shoulder.

The face that turned toward his was blotched with mud and gore, the eyes dull and uncomprehending.

The man crawled painfully closer; with his last ounce of strength, he undid the knots. As the rope fell loose, he collapsed and died.

Iori looked cautiously up at the bridge and bit his lip. There were more bodies up there. But luck was with him. A cartwheel had broken through a rotten plank. The thieves, hurrying to pull it out, didn't notice his escape.

Realizing he couldn't make it to the temple, Iori tiptoed along in the shadows until he reached a place shallow enough to cross. When he gained the other bank, he was on the edge of Hōtengahara. He covered the remaining mile to the cabin as though lightning was nipping at his heels.

As he neared the knoll where the cabin stood, he saw that Musashi was standing outside, looking at the sky. "Come quick!" he shouted.

"What happened?"

"We have to go to the village."

"Is that where the fire is?"

"Yes. The mountain devils have come again."

"Devils? . . . Bandits?"

"Yes, at least forty of them. Please hurry. We have to rescue the villagers."

Musashi ducked into the cabin and emerged with his swords. While he was tying his sandals, Iori said, "Follow me. I'll show you the way."

"No. You stay here."

Iori couldn't believe his ears.

"It's too dangerous."

"I'm not scared."

"You'd be in the way."

"You don't even know the shortest way there!"

"The fire's all the guide I need. Now just be a good boy and stay right here."

"Yes, sir." Iori nodded obediently, but with deep misgivings. He turned his head toward the village and watched somberly as Musashi streaked off in the direction of the red glow.

668   The bandits had tied their female captives, moaning and screaming, in a

row and were pulling them mercilessly toward the bridge.

"Stop your squawking!" shouted one bandit.

"You act like you don't know how to walk. Move!"

When the women held back, the ruffians lashed them with whips. One woman fell, dragging down others. Seizing the rope and forcing them back on their feet, one man snarled, "Stubborn bitches! What have you got to groan about? Stay here and you work like slaves the rest of your lives, all for a bit of millet. Look at you, nothing but skin and bones! You'll be a lot better off having fun with us."

Picking one of the healthier-looking animals, which were all heavily loaded with booty, they tied the rope to it and gave it a sharp slap on the rump. The slack in the rope was snapped up suddenly and fresh shrieks rent the air as the women were yanked forward again. Those who fell were dragged along, with their faces scraping the ground.

"Stop!" screamed one. "My arms're coming off!"

A wave of raucous laughter swept through the brigands.

At that moment, horse and women came to a dead halt.

"What's going on? . . . Somebody's up ahead!"

All eyes strained to see.

"Who's there?" roared one bandit.

The silent shadow walking toward them carried a white blade. The bandits, trained to be sensitive to odors, instantly recognized the one they smelled now—blood, dripping from the sword.

As the men in front fell back clumsily, Musashi sized up the enemy force. He counted twelve men, all hard-muscled and brutish-looking. Recovering from the initial shock, they readied their weapons and took defensive stances. One ran forward with an ax. Another, carrying a hunter's spear, approached diagonally, keeping his body low and aiming at Musashi's ribs. The man with the ax was the first to go.

"A-w-w-k!" Sounding as though he'd bitten his own tongue off, he weaved crazily and collapsed in a heap.

"Don't you know me?" Musashi's voice rang out sharply. "I am the protector of the people, a messenger from the god who watches over this village." In the same breath, he seized the spear pointed at him, wrested it from its owner's hands and threw it violently to the ground.

Moving swiftly into the band of ruffians, he was kept busy countering thrusts from all sides. But after the first surge, made while they still fought with confidence, he had a good idea of what lay ahead. It was a matter not of numbers but of the opposition's cohesiveness and self-control.

Seeing one man after another turned into a blood-spurting missile, the bandits were soon falling back to ever greater distances, until finally they panicked and lost all semblance of organization.

Musashi was learning even as he fought, acquiring experience that would lead him to specific methods to be used by a smaller force against a larger one. This was a valuable lesson and couldn't be learned in a fight with a single enemy.

669

His two swords were in their scabbards. For years, he'd practiced to master the art of seizing his opponent's weapon and turning it against him. Now he'd put study into practice, taking the sword away from the first man he'd encountered. His reason wasn't that his own sword, which he thought of as his soul, was too pure to be sullied by the blood of common brigands. He was being practical; against such a motley array of weapons, a blade might get chipped, or even broken.

When the five or six survivors fled toward the village, Musashi took a minute or two to relax and catch his breath, fully expecting them to return with reinforcements. Then he freed the women and ordered those who could stand to take care of the others.

After some words of comfort and encouragement, he told them it was up to them to save their parents and children and husbands.

"You'd be miserable if you survived and they perished, wouldn't you?" he asked.

There was a murmur of agreement.

"You yourselves have the strength to protect yourselves and save the others. But you don't know how to use that strength. That's why you're at the mercy of outlaws. We're going to change that. I'm going to help you by showing you how to use the power you have. The first thing to do is arm yourselves."

He had them collect the weapons lying about and distributed one to each of the women.

"Now follow me and do just as I say. You mustn't be afraid. Try to believe that the god of this district is on your side."

As he led the women toward the burning village, other victims emerged from the shadows and joined them. Soon the group had grown into a small army of nearly a hundred people. Women tearfully hugged loved ones: daughters were reunited with parents, wives with husbands, mothers with children.

At first, as the women described how Musashi had dealt with the bandits, the men listened with shocked expressions on their faces, not believing that this could be the idiot rōnin of Hōtengahara. When they did accept it, their gratitude was obvious, despite the barrier imposed by their dialect.

Turning to the men, Musashi told them to find weapons. "Anything'll do, even a good, heavy stick or a length of fresh bamboo."

No one disobeyed, or even questioned his orders.

Musashi asked, "How many bandits are there in all?"

"About fifty."

"How many houses in the village?"

"Seventy."

Musashi calculated that there was probably a total of seven or eight hundred people. Even allowing for old people and children, the brigands would still be outnumbered by as much as ten to one.

He smiled grimly at the thought that these peaceful villagers had believed they had no recourse but to throw up their hands in despair. He knew that if something was not done, the atrocity would be repeated. Tonight he wanted to accomplish two things: show the villagers how to protect themselves and see that the brigands were banished forever.

"Sir," cried a man who had just come from the village. "They're on their way here."

Though the villagers were armed now, the news made them uneasy. They showed signs of breaking and running.

To restore confidence, Musashi said loudly, "There's nothing to be alarmed about. I was expecting this. I want you to hide on both sides of the road, but first listen to my instructions." He talked rapidly but calmly, briefly repeating points for emphasis. "When they get here, I'll let them attack me. Then I'll pretend to run away. They'll follow me. You—all of you— stay where you are. I won't need any help.

"After a time, they'll come back. When they do, attack. Make lots of noise; take them by surprise. Strike at their sides, legs, chests—any area that's unguarded. When you've taken care of the first bunch, hide again and wait for the next one. Keep doing this until they're all dead."

He barely had time to finish and the peasants to disperse before the marauders appeared. From their dress and lack of coordination, Musashi guessed that theirs was a primitive fighting force, of a sort that might have been common long ago, when men hunted and fished for sustenance. The name Tokugawa meant nothing to them, no more than did Toyotomi. The mountains were their tribal home; the villagers existed to provide them with food and supplies.

"Stop!" ordered the man at the head of the pack. There were about twenty of them, some with crude swords, some with lances, one with a battle-ax, another with a rusty spear. Silhouetted against the glow of the fire, their bodies looked like demonic, jet-black shadows.

"Is he the one?"

"Yeah, that's him, all right."

Some sixty feet ahead of them, Musashi stood his ground, blocking the road. Disconcerted, they began to doubt their own strength, and for a short time none of them moved.

But only for a moment. Then Musashi's blazing eyes started to pull them inexorably toward him.

"You the son of a bitch trying to get in our way?"

"Right!" roared Musashi, raising his sword and tearing into them. There was a loud reverberation, followed by a whirlwind fray in which it was impossible to make out individual movements. It was like a spinning swarm of winged ants.

The rice fields on one side of the road and the embankment lined with trees and bushes on the other were ideal for Musashi, since they provided a measure of cover, but after the first skirmish, he executed a strategic withdrawal.

"See that?"

"The bastard's running away!"

"After him!"

They pursued him to a far corner of the nearest field, where he turned and faced them. With nothing behind him, his position seemed worse, but he kept his opponents at bay by moving swiftly to right and left. Then the moment one of them made a false move, Musashi struck.

His dark form seemed to flit from place to place, a geyser of blood rising before him each time he paused. The bandits who were not killed were soon too dazed to fight, while Musashi grew sharper with every strike. It was a different sort of battle from the one at Ichijōji. He did not have the feeling of standing on the border between life and death, but he had reached a plane of selflessness, body and sword performing without the need of conscious thought. His attackers fled in complete disarray.

A whisper went along the line of villagers. "They're coming." Then a group of them jumped out of hiding and fell upon the first two or three bandits, killing them almost effortlessly. The farmers melted into the darkness again, and the process was repeated until all the bandits had been ambushed and slain.

Counting the corpses bolstered the villagers' confidence.

"They're not so strong after all," gloated one man.

"Wait! Here comes another one."

"Get him!"

"No, don't attack. It's the rōnin."

With a minimum of confusion, they lined up along the road like soldiers being reviewed by their general. All eyes were fixed on Musashi's bloody clothing and dripping sword, whose blade was chipped in a dozen places. He threw it away and picked up a lance.

"Our work's not done," he said. "Get yourselves some weapons and follow me. By combining your strength, you can drive the marauders out of the village and rescue your families."

Not one man hesitated. The women and children also found weapons and followed along.

The damage to the village was not as extensive as they had feared, because the dwellings were set well apart. But the terrified farm animals were raising a great ruckus, and somewhere a baby was crying its lungs out. Loud popping noises came from the roadside, where the fire had spread to a grove of green bamboo.

The bandits were nowhere in sight.

"Where are they?" asked Musashi. "I seem to smell sake. Where would there be a lot of sake in one place?"

The villagers were so absorbed in gaping at the fires that nobody had noticed the smell, but one of them said, "Must be the village headman's house. He's got barrels of sake."

"Then that's where we'll find them," said Musashi.

As they advanced, more men came out of hiding and joined their ranks. Musashi was gratified by the growing spirit of unity.

"That's it, there," said one man, pointing out a large house surrounded by an earthen wall.

While the peasants were getting themselves organized, Musashi scaled the wall and invaded the bandits' stronghold. The leader and his chief lieutenants were ensconced in a large dirt-floored room, swilling sake and forcing their attentions on young girls they were holding captive.

"Don't get excited!" the leader shouted angrily in a rough, mountain dialect. "He's only one man. I shouldn't have to do anything myself. The rest of you take care of him." He was upbraiding an underling who had rushed in with the news of the defeat outside the village.

As their chief fell silent, the others became aware of the hum of angry voices beyond the wall and stirred uneasily. Dropping half-eaten chickens and sake cups, they jumped to their feet and instinctively reached for their weapons. Then they stood there, staring at the entrance to the room.

Musashi, using his lance as a pole, vaulted through a high side window, landing directly behind the chief. The man whirled around, only to be impaled on the lance. Letting out a fearsome "A-w-r-g," he grabbed with both hands the lance lodged in his chest. Musashi calmly let go of the lance, and the man toppled face down on the ground, the blade and most of the shaft projecting from his back.

The second man to attack Musashi was relieved of his sword. Musashi sliced him through, brought the blade down on the head of a third man, and thrust it into the chest of a fourth. The others made helter-skelter for the door. Musashi hurled the sword at them and in a continuation of the same motion extricated the lance from the chief's body.

"Don't move!" he bellowed. He charged with the lance held horizontally, parting the bandits like water struck with a pole. This gave him enough room to make effective use of the long weapon, which he now swung with a deftness that tested the very resiliency of its black oak shaft, striking sideways, slicing downward, thrusting viciously forward.

The bandits attempting to get out the gate found their way blocked by the armed villagers. Some climbed the wall. When they hit the ground, most were slaughtered on the spot. Of the few who succeeded in escaping, nearly all received crippling wounds.

For a time the air was filled with shouts of triumph from young and old, male and female, and as the first flush of victory subsided, man and wife, parents and children, hugged each other and shed tears of joy.

In the midst of this ecstatic scene, someone asked, "What if they come back?"

There was a moment of sudden, anxious stillness.

"They won't be back," Musashi said firmly. "Not to this village. But don't be overconfident. Your business is using plows, not swords. If you grow too proud of your fighting ability, the punishment heaven will mete out to you will be worse than any raid by mountain devils."

"Did you find out what happened?" Nagaoka Sado asked his two samurai when they got back to the Tokuganji. In the distance, across field and swamp, he could see that the light of the fires in the village was fading.

"Everything's quieted down now."

673

"Did you chase the bandits away? How much damage was done in the village?"

"The villagers killed all but a few of them before we got there. The others got away."

"Well, that's odd." He looked surprised, for if this was true, he had some thinking to do about the way of governing in his own lord's district.

On leaving the temple the following day, he directed his horse toward the village, saying, "It's out of the way, but let's have a look."

A priest came along to show them the way, and while they rode, Sado observed, "Those bodies along the roadside don't look to me as though they were cut down by farmers," and asked his samurai for more details.

The villagers, forgoing sleep, were hard at work, burying corpses and cleaning up debris from the conflagration. But when they saw Sado and the samurai, they ran inside their houses and hid.

"Get one of the villagers to come here, and let's find out exactly what happened," he said to the priest.

The man who came back with the priest gave them a fairly detailed account of the night's events.

"Now it begins to make sense," Sado said, nodding. "What's this rōnin's name?"

The peasant, never having heard Musashi's name, cocked his head to one side. When Sado insisted on knowing it, the priest asked about for a time and came up with the required information.

"Miyamoto Musashi?" Sado said thoughtfully. "Is he the man the boy spoke of as his teacher?"

"That's right. From the way he's been trying to develop a piece of waste land on Hōtengahara, the villagers thought he was a little soft in the head."

"I'd like to meet him," said Sado, but then he remembered the work waiting for him in Edo. "Never mind; I'll talk to him the next time I come out here." He turned his horse around and left the peasant standing by the road.

A few minutes later, he reined up in front of the village headman's gate. There, written in shiny ink on a fresh board, hung a sign: "Reminder for the People of the Village: Your plow is your sword. Your sword is your plow. Working in the fields, don't forget the invasion. Thinking of the invasion, don't forget your fields. All things must be balanced and integrated. Most important, do not oppose the Way of successive generations."

"Hmm. Who wrote this?"

The headman had finally come out and was now bowing on the ground before Sado. "Musashi," he answered.

Turning to the priest, Sado said, "Thank you for bringing us here. It's too bad I couldn't meet this Musashi, but just now I don't have the time. I'll be back this way before long."

First Planting

The management of the palatial Hosokawa residence in Edo, as well as the performance of the fief's duties to the shōgun, was entrusted to a man still in his early twenties, Tadatoshi, the eldest son of the daimyō, Hosokawa Tadaoki. The father, a celebrated general who also enjoyed a reputation as a poet and master of the tea ceremony, preferred to live at the large Kokura fief in Buzen Province on the island of Kyushu.

Though Nagaoka Sado and a number of other trusted retainers were assigned to assist the young man, this was not because he was in any way incompetent. He was not only accepted as a peer by the powerful vassals closest to the shōgun but had distinguished himself as an energetic and farsighted administrator. In fact, he seemed more in tune with the peace and prosperity of the times than the older lords, who had been nurtured on constant warfare.

At the moment, Sado was walking in the general direction of the riding ground. "Have you seen the Young Lord?" he asked of an apprentice samurai coming toward him.

"I believe he's at the archery range."

As Sado threaded his way down a narrow path, he heard a voice asking, "May I have a word with you?"

Sado stopped, and Iwama Kakubei, a vassal respected for his shrewdness and practicality, came up to him. "You're going to talk with his lordship?" he asked.

"Yes."

"If you're not in a hurry, there's a little matter I'd like to consult with you about. Why don't we sit down over there?" As they walked the few steps to a rustic arbor, Kakubei said, "I have a favor to ask. If you have a chance during your talk, there's a man I'd like to recommend to the Young Lord."

"Someone wanting to serve the House of Hosokawa?"

"Yes. I know all sorts of people come to you with the same request, but this man's very unusual."

"Is he one of those men interested only in security and a stipend?"

"Definitely not. He's related to my wife. He's been living with us since he came up from Iwakuni a couple of years ago, so I know him quite well."

"Iwakuni? The House of Kikkawa held Suō Province before the Battle of Sekigahara. Is he one of their rōnin?"

"No. He's the son of a rural samurai. His name's Sasaki Kojirō. He's still   675 young, but he was trained in the Tomita Style of Kanemaki Jisai, and he learned the techniques of drawing a sword with lightning swiftness from Lord Katayama Hisayasu of Hōki. He's even created a style of his own, which he calls Ganryū." Kakubei went on, listing in detail Kojirō's various exploits and accomplishments.

Sado was not really listening. His mind had gone back to his last visit to the Tokuganji. Though he was sure, even from the little he'd seen and heard, that Musashi was the right sort of man for the House of Hosokawa, he had intended to meet him personally before recommending him to his master. In the meantime, a year and a half had slipped by without his finding an opportunity to visit Hōtengahara.

When Kakubei finished, Sado said, "I'll do what I can for you," and continued on to the archery range.

Tadatoshi was engaged in a contest with some vassals of his own age, none of whom was remotely a match for him. His shots, unerringly on target, were executed with flawless style. A number of retainers had chided him for taking archery so seriously, arguing that in an age of gun and lance, neither sword nor bow was any longer of much use in actual combat. To this he had replied cryptically, "My arrows are aimed at the spirit."

The Hosokawa retainers had the highest respect for Tadatoshi, and would have served under him with enthusiasm even if his father, to whom they were also devoted, had not been a man of substantial accomplishments. At the moment, Sado regretted the promise he'd just made to Kakubei. Tadatoshi was not a man to whom one lightly recommended prospective retainers.

Wiping the sweat off his face, Tadatoshi walked past several young samurai with whom he'd been talking and laughing. Catching sight of Sado, he called, "How about it, Ancient One? Have a shot?"

"I make it a rule to compete only against adults," Sado replied.

"So you still think of us as little boys with our hair tied up on our heads?"

"Have you forgotten the Battle of Yamazaki? Nirayama Castle? I have been commended for my performance on the battlefield, you know. Besides, I go in for real archery, not—"

"Ha, ha. Sorry I mentioned it. I didn't mean to get you started again." The others joined in the laughter. Slipping his arm out of his sleeve, Tadatoshi became serious and asked, "Did you come to discuss something?"

After going over a number of routine matters, Sado said, "Kakubei says he has a samurai to recommend to you."

For a moment there was a faraway look in Tadatoshi's eyes. "I suppose he's talking about Sasaki Kojirō. He's been mentioned several times."

"Why don't you call him in and have a look at him?"

"Is he really good?"

"Shouldn't you see for yourself?"

Tadatoshi put on his glove and accepted an arrow from an attendant. "I'll take a look at Kakubei's man," he said. "I'd also like to see that rōnin you mentioned. Miyamoto Musashi, was it?"

"Oh, you remember?"

676   "I do. You're the one who seems to have forgotten."

"Not at all. But being so busy, I haven't had a chance to go out to Shimōsa."

"If you think you've found someone, you should take the time. I'm surprised at you, Sado, letting something so important wait until you've got other business to take you out there. It's not like you."

"I'm sorry. There're always too many men looking for positions. I thought you'd forgotten about it. I suppose I should have brought it up again."

"Indeed you should have. I don't necessarily accept other people's recommendations, but I'm eager to see anyone old Sado considers suitable. Understand?"

Sado apologized again before taking his leave. He went directly to his own house and without further ado had a fresh horse saddled and set out for Hōtengahara.

"Isn't this Hōtengahara?"

Satō Genzō, Sado's attendant, said, "That's what I thought, but this is no wilderness. There're rice fields all over. The place they were trying to develop must be nearer the mountains."

They had already gone a good distance beyond the Tokuganji and would soon be on the highroad to Hitachi. It was late afternoon, and the white herons splashing about in the paddies made the water seem like powder. Along the riverbank and in the shadows of hillocks grew patches of hemp and waving stalks of barley.

"Look over there, sir," said Genzō.

"What is it?"

"There's a group of farmers."

"So there is. They seem to be bowing to the ground, one by one, don't they?"

"It looks like some sort of religious ceremony."

With a snap of the reins, Genzō forded the river first, making sure it was safe for Sado to follow.

"You, there!" called Genzō.

The farmers, looking surprised, spread out from their circle to face the visitors. They were standing in front of a small cabin, and Sado could see that the object they'd been bowing before was a tiny wooden shrine, no larger than a birdcage. There were about fifty of them, on their way home from work, it appeared, for their tools had all been washed.

A priest came forward, saying, "Why, it's Nagaoka Sado, isn't it? What a pleasant surprise!"

"And you're from the Tokuganji, aren't you? I believe you're the one who guided me to the village after the bandit raid."

"That's right. Have you come to pay a call at the temple?"

"No, not this time. I'll be going back right away. Could you tell me where I might find that rōnin named Miyamoto Musashi?"

"He's not here anymore. He left very suddenly."

"Left suddenly? Why should he do that?"

"One day last month, the villagers decided to take a day off and celebrate the progress that's been made here. You can see for yourself how green it is 677 now. Well, the morning after that, Musashi and the boy, Iori, were gone." The priest looked around, as though half expecting Musashi to materialize out of the air.

In response to Sado's prompting, the priest filled in the details of his story. After the village had strengthened its defenses under Musashi's leadership, the farmers were so thankful for the prospect of living in peace that they practically deified him. Even the ones who had ridiculed him most cruelly had come forward to help with the development project.

Musashi treated them all fairly and equally, first convincing them that it was pointless to live like animals. He then tried to impress upon them the importance of exerting a little extra effort so as to give their children a chance for a better life. To be real human beings, he told them, they must work for the sake of posterity.

With forty or fifty villagers pitching in to help each day, by fall they were able to keep the floodwaters under control. When winter came, they plowed. And in the spring, they drew water from the new irrigation ditches and transplanted the rice seedlings. By early summer the rice was thriving, while in the dry fields, hemp and barley were already a foot high. In another year, the crop would double; the year after that, triple.

Villagers began to drop in at the cabin to pay their respects, thanking Musashi from the bottom of their hearts, the women bearing gifts of vegetables. On the day of the celebration, the men arrived with great jars of sake, and all took part in performing a sacred dance, accompanied by drums and flutes.

With the villagers gathered around him, Musashi had assured them that it was not his strength, but theirs. "All I did was show you how to use the energy you possess."

Then he had taken the priest aside to tell him that he was concerned about their relying on a vagabond like him. "Even without me," he said, "they should have confidence in themselves and maintain solidarity." He had then taken out a statue of Kannon he'd carved and given it to the priest.

The morning after the celebration, the village was in an uproar.

"He's gone!"

"He can't be."

"Yes, he's disappeared. The cabin's empty."

Grief-stricken, none of the farmers went near the fields that day.

When he heard about it, the priest reproached them sharply for their ingratitude, urging them to remember what they'd been taught and subtly coaxing them to carry on the work that had been started.

Later, the villagers had built the tiny shrine and placed the treasured image of Kannon in it. They paid their respects to Musashi morning and evening, on their way to and from the fields.

Sado thanked the priest for the information, concealing the fact that he was disconsolate as only a man of his position could do.

As his horse made its way back through the evening mist of late spring, he thought uneasily: "I shouldn't have put off coming. I was derelict in my duty, and now I've failed my lord."

The Flies

On the east bank of the Sumida River where the road from Shimōsa converged with a branch of the Ōshū highroad rose a great barrier with an imposing gate, ample evidence of the firm rule of Aoyama Tadanari, the new magistrate of Edo.

Musashi stood in line, idly waiting his turn, Iori at his side. When he had passed through Edo three years earlier, entering and leaving the city had been a simple matter. Even at this distance, he could see that there were far more houses than before, fewer open spaces.

"You there, rōnin. You're next."

Two officials in leather *hakama* began frisking Musashi with great thoroughness, while a third glared at him and asked questions.

"What business do you have in the capital?"

"Nothing specific."

"No special business, eh?"

"Well, I'm a *shugyōsha*. I suppose it could be said that studying to be a samurai is my business."

The man was silent. Musashi grinned.

"Where were you born?"

"In the village of Miyamoto, district of Yoshino, Mimasaka Province."

"Your master?"

"I have none."

"Who furnishes your travel money?"

"No one. I carve statues and draw pictures. Sometimes I can exchange them for food and lodging. Often I stay at temples. Occasionally I give lessons in the sword. One way or another, I manage."

"Where are you coming from?"

"For the past two years, I've been farming in Hōtengahara in Shimōsa. I decided I didn't want to do that for the rest of my life, so I've come here."

"Do you have a place to stay in Edo? No one can enter the city unless he has relatives or a place to live."

"Yes," replied Musashi on the spur of the moment. He saw that if he tried to stick to the truth, there was going to be no end to it.

"Well?"

"Yagyū Munenori, Lord of Tajima."

The official's mouth dropped open.

Musashi, amused at the man's reaction, congratulated himself. The risk of being caught in a lie did not trouble him greatly. He felt that the Yagyūs must have heard about him from Takuan. It seemed unlikely they would deny all acquaintance with him if questioned. It might even be that Takuan was in Edo now. If so, Musashi had his means of introduction. It was too late to have a bout with Sekishūsai, but he longed to have one with Munenori, his father's successor in the Yagyū Style and a personal tutor of the shōgun.

The name acted like magic. "Well, well," said the official amiably. "If you're connected with the House of Yagyū, I'm sorry to have troubled you. As you must realize, there are all sorts of samurai on the road. We have to be particularly careful about anyone who appears to be a rōnin. Orders, you know." After a few more questions for the sake of form or face, he said, "You can go now," and personally escorted Musashi to the gate.

"Sir," Iori asked when they were on the other side, "why are they so careful about rōnin and nobody else?"

"They're on the lookout for enemy spies."

"What spy would be stupid enough to come here looking like a rōnin? The officials are pretty dumb—them and their stupid questions! They made us miss the ferry!"

"Shh. They'll hear you. Don't worry about the ferry. You can look at Mount Fuji while we're waiting for the next one. Did you know you could see it from here?"

"So what? We could see it from Hōtengahara too."

"Yes, but it's different here."

"How?"

"Fuji's never the same. It varies from day to day, hour to hour."

"Looks the same to me."

"It's not, though. It changes—time, weather, season, the place you're looking at it from. It differs, too, according to the person who's looking at it, according to his heart."

Unimpressed, Iori picked up a flat stone and sent it skimming across the water. After amusing himself in this fashion for a few minutes, he came back to Musashi and asked, "Are we really going to Lord Yagyū's house?"

"I'll have to think about that."

"Isn't that what you told the guard?"

"Yes. I intend to go, but it's not all that simple. He's a daimyō, you know."

"He must be awfully important. That's what I want to be when I grow up."

"Important?"

"Umm."

"You shouldn't aim so low."

"What do you mean?"

"Look at Mount Fuji."

"I'll never be like Mount Fuji."

"Instead of wanting to be like this or that, make yourself into a silent, immovable giant. That's what the mountain is. Don't waste your time trying to impress people. If you become the sort of man people can respect, they'll respect you, without your doing anything."

Musashi's words didn't have time to sink in, for just then Iori shouted, "Look, here comes the ferry," and ran ahead to be the first one on board.

The Sumida River was a study in contrasts, wide in places, narrow in others, shallow here and deep there. At high tide, the waves washing the banks took on a muddy hue. Sometimes the estuary swelled to twice its normal width. At the point where the ferry crossed, it was virtually an inlet of the bay.

The sky was clear, the water transparent. Looking over the side, Iori could see schools of countless tiny fish racing about. Among the rocks he also spotted the rusty remains of an old helmet. He had no ears for the conversation going on around him.

"What do you think? Is it going to stay peaceful, the way it is now?"

"I doubt it."

"You're probably right. Sooner or later, there'll be fighting. I hope not, but what else can you expect?"

Other passengers kept their thoughts to themselves and stared dourly at the water, afraid an official, possibly in disguise, might overhear and connect them with the speakers. Those who did take the risk seemed to enjoy flirting with the ubiquitous eyes and ears of the law.

"You can tell from the way they're checking everybody that we're heading for war. It's only very recently they've been clamping down like that. And there're a lot of rumors about spies from Osaka."

"You also hear about burglars breaking into daimyō's houses, though they try to hush it up. It must be embarrassing being robbed when you're supposed to be the enforcers of law and order."

"You'd have to be after more than money to take that kind of risk. It's got to be spies. No ordinary crook would have the nerve."

As he looked around, it occurred to Musashi that the ferry was transporting a fair cross section of Edo society. A lumberman with sawdust clinging to his work clothes, a couple of cheap geisha who might have come from Kyoto, a broad-shouldered roughneck or two, a group of well-diggers, two openly coquettish whores, a priest, a beggar monk, another rōnin like himself.

When the boat reached the Edo side and they all piled out, a short, heavy-set man called to Musashi, "Hey, you. The rōnin. You forgot something." He held out a reddish brocade pouch, so old that the dirt seemed to shine more brightly than the few gold threads left in it.

Musashi, shaking his head, said, "It's not mine. It must belong to one of the other passengers."

Iori piped up, "It's mine," snatched the pouch from the man's hand and stuffed it into his kimono.

The man was indignant. "What're you doing, grabbing like that! Give it here! Then you're going to bow three times before you get it back. If you don't, you're going to get thrown in the river!"

Musashi intervened, asking the man to excuse Iori's rudeness because of his age.

"What are you?" the man asked roughly. "Brother? Master? What's your name!"

"Miyamoto Musashi."

"What!" exclaimed the ruffian, staring hard at Musashi's face. After a moment he said to Iori, "You'd better be more careful from now on." Then, as though eager to escape, he turned away.

"Just a moment," said Musashi. The gentleness of his tone took the man completely by surprise.

He whirled around, his hand going to his sword. "What do you want?"

"What's your name?"

"What's it to you?"

"You asked mine. As a matter of courtesy, you should tell me yours."

"I'm one of Hangawara's men. My name's Jūrō."

"All right. You can go," said Musashi, pushing him away.

"I won't forget that!" Jūrō stumbled a few steps before he found his feet and fled.

"Serves him right, the coward," said Iori. Satisfied that he'd been vindicated, he looked up worshipfully at Musashi's face and moved closer to him.

As they walked into the city, Musashi said, "Iori, you have to realize that living here is not like being out in the country. There, we had only foxes and squirrels for neighbors. Here, there're lots of people. You'll have to be more careful about your manners."

"Yes, sir."

"When people live together in harmony, the earth is a paradise," Musashi went on gravely. "But every man has a bad side as well as a good side. There are times when only the bad comes out. Then the world's not paradise, but hell. Do you understand what I'm saying?"

"Yes, I think so," said Iori, more subdued now.

"There's a reason we have manners and etiquette. They keep us from letting the bad side take over. This promotes social order, which is the objective of the government's laws." Musashi paused. "The way you acted ... It was a trivial matter, but your attitude couldn't help but make the man angry. I'm not at all happy about it."

"Yes, sir."

"I don't know where we'll be going from here. But wherever we are, you'd better follow the rules and act courteously."

The boy bobbed his head a couple of times and made a small, stiff bow. They walked on in silence for a short while.

"Sir, would you carry my pouch for me? I don't want to lose it again."

Accepting the small brocade bag, Musashi inspected it closely before tucking it into his kimono. "Is this the one your father left you?"

"Yes, sir. I got it back from the Tokuganji at the beginning of the year. The priest didn't take any of the money. You can use some of it if you need to."

"Thanks," Musashi said lightly. "I'll take good care of it."

"He has a talent I don't have," mused Musashi, thinking ruefully of his own indifference to personal finances. The boy's innate prudence had taught Musashi the meaning of economics. He appreciated the boy's trust and was growing fonder of him by the day. He looked forward with enthusiasm to the task of helping him develop his native intelligence.

"Where would you like to stay tonight?" he asked.

Iori, who had been looking at his new surroundings with great curiosity, remarked, "I see lots of horses over there. It looks like a marketplace, right here in town." He spoke as though he had run across a long-lost friend in a strange country.

They had reached Bakurōchō, where there was a large and diverse selection of tea shops and hostelries catering to the equine professions—sellers, buyers, draymen, grooms, a variety of lesser factotums. Men in small groups haggled and babbled in a welter of dialects, the most prominent being the tangy, irate-sounding speech of Edo.

Among the rabble was a well-groomed samurai, searching for good horses. With a disgruntled look, he said, "Let's go home. There's nothing here but nags, nothing worth recommending to his lordship."

Striding briskly between the animals, he came face to face with Musashi, blinked, and stepped back in surprise. "You're Miyamoto Musashi, aren't you?"

Musashi looked at the man for an instant, then broke into a grin. It was Kimura Sukekurō. Although the two men had come within inches of locking swords at Koyagyū Castle, Sukekurō's manner was cordial. He seemed to bear no lingering rancor from that encounter.

"I certainly didn't expect to see you here," he said. "Have you been in Edo long?"

"I've just come from Shimōsa," replied Musashi. "How's your master? Is he still in good health?"

"Yes, thank you, but of course at Sekishūsai's age . . . I'm staying with Lord Munenori. You must come to visit; I'd be glad to introduce you. Oh, there's something else, too." He flashed a meaningful look and smiled. "We have a beautiful treasure that belongs to you. You must come as soon as you can."

Before Musashi could inquire what the "beautiful treasure" might be, Sukekurō made a slight bow and walked rapidly away, his attendant trailing along behind.

The guests staying at the inexpensive inns of Bakurōchō were mostly horse traders in from the provinces. Musashi decided to take a room there rather than in another part of town, where the rates would most likely be higher. Like the other inns, the one he chose had a large stable, so large in fact that the rooms themselves seemed rather like an annex. But after the rigors of Hōtengahara, even this third-rate hostelry seemed luxurious.

Despite his feeling of well-being, Musashi found the horseflies annoying and began grumbling.

The proprietress heard him. "I'll change your room," she offered solicitously. "The flies aren't so bad on the second floor."

Once resettled, Musashi found himself exposed to the full strength of the western sun and felt like grumbling again. Only a few days ago, the afternoon sun would have been a source of cheer, a bright ray of hope shedding nourishing warmth on the rice plants and portending good weather for the morrow. As for the flies, when his sweat had attracted them while he worked in the fields, he had taken the view that they were only going about their chores, just as he was going about his. He had even regarded them as fellow creatures. Now, having crossed one wide river and entered the maze of the city, he found the heat of the sun anything but comforting, the flies only an irritation.

His appetite took his mind off the inconveniences. He glanced at Iori and saw symptoms of lassitude and gluttony in his face too. Small wonder, for a party in the next room had ordered a great pot of steaming food and was now attacking it ravenously, amid much talk, laughter and drinking.

Buckwheat noodles—*soba*—that's what he wanted! In the country, if a man wanted *soba*, he planted buckwheat in the early spring, watched it flower in the summer, dried the grain in the fall, ground the flour in the winter. Then he could make *soba*. Here it required no more effort than clapping one's hands for service.

"Iori, shall we order some *soba*?"

"Yes," came the eager reply.

The proprietress came and took their order. While they waited, Musashi propped his elbows on the windowsill and shaded his eyes. Diagonally across the way was a signboard reading: "Souls polished here. Zushino Kōsuke, Master in the Hon'ami Style."

Iori had noticed it too. After staring for a moment in bewilderment, he said, "That sign says 'Souls polished.' What sort of business is that?"

"Well, it also says the man works in the Hon'ami Style, so I suppose he's a sword polisher. Come to think of it, I ought to have my sword worked on."

The *soba* was slow to arrive, so Musashi stretched out on the tatami for a nap. But the voices in the next room had risen several decibels and become quarrelsome. "Iori," he said, opening one eye, "will you ask the people next door to be a little quieter?"

Only shoji separated the two rooms, but instead of opening them, Iori went out into the hall. The door to the other room was open. "Don't make so much noise," he shouted. "My teacher's trying to sleep."

"Hunh!" The squabble came to an abrupt halt. The men turned and stared angrily at him.

"You say something, shrimp?"

Pouting at the epithet, Iori said, "We came upstairs because of the flies. Now you're yelling so much he can't rest."

"Is this your idea, or did your master send you?"

"He sent me."

"Did he? Well, I'm not wasting my time talking to a little turd like you. Go tell your master Kumagorō of Chichibu will give him his answer later. Now beat it!"

Kumagorō was a great brute of a man, and the two or three others in the room were not much smaller. Cowed by the menace in their eyes, Iori quickly retreated. Musashi had dropped off to sleep; not wanting to disturb him, Iori sat down by the window.

684 Presently, one of the horse traders opened the shoji a crack and peeked in at

Musashi. There followed much laughter, accompanied by loud and insulting remarks.

"Who does he think he is, butting into our party? Dumb rōnin! No telling where he comes from. Just barges in and starts acting like he owns the place."

"We'll have to show him what's what."

"Yeah, we'll make sure he knows what the horse traders of Edo are made of."

"Talking's not going to show him. Let's haul him out back and throw a bucket of horse piss in his face."

Kumagorō spoke up. "Hold on, now. Let me handle this. Either I'll get an apology in writing or we'll wash his face with horse piss. Enjoy your sake. Leave everything to me."

"This should be good," said one man, as Kumagorō, with a confident smirk, tightened his obi.

"I beg your pardon," said Kumagorō, sliding the shoji open. Without standing up, he shuffled into Musashi's room on his knees.

The *soba*, six helpings in a lacquered box, had finally arrived. Musashi was sitting up now, addressing his chopsticks to his first helping.

"Look, they're coming in," said Iori under his breath, moving slightly to get out of the way.

Kumagorō seated himself behind and to Iori's left, legs crossed, elbows resting on his knees. With a fierce scowl, he said, "You can eat later. Don't try to hide the fact that you're scared by sitting there playing with your food."

Though he was grinning, Musashi gave no indication that he was listening. He stirred the *soba* with his chopsticks to separate the strands, lifted a mouthful and swallowed with a joyous slurp.

The veins in Kumagorō's forehead nearly popped. "Put that bowl down," he said angrily.

"And who are you?" Musashi asked mildly, making no move to comply.

"You don't know who I am? The only people in Bakurōchō who haven't heard my name are good-for-nothings and deaf-mutes."

"I'm a little hard of hearing myself. Speak up, tell me who you are and where you come from."

"I'm Kumagorō from Chichibu, the best horse trader in Edo. When children see me coming, they get so scared they can't even cry."

"I see. Then you're in the horse business?"

"You bet I am. I sell to the samurai. You'd better remember that when you're dealing with me."

"In what way am I dealing with you?"

"You sent that runt there to complain about the noise. Where do you think you are? This is no fancy inn for daimyō, nice and quiet and all. We horse traders like noise."

"I gathered that."

"Then why were you trying to bust up our party? I demand an apology."

"Apology?"

"Yes, in writing. You can address it to Kumagorō and his friends. If we   *685* don't get one we'll take you outside and teach you a thing or two."

"What you say is interesting."

"Hunh!"

"I mean your way of speaking is interesting."

"Cut out the nonsense! Do we get the apology or don't we? Well?" Kumagorō's voice had gone from a growl to a roar, and the sweat on his crimson forehead glistened in the evening sun. Looking ready to explode, he bared his hairy chest and took a dagger from his stomach wrapper.

"Make up your mind! If I don't hear your answer soon, you're in big trouble." He uncrossed his legs and held the dagger vertically beside the lacquered box, its point touching the floor.

Musashi, restraining his mirth, said, "Well, now how should I respond to that?"

Lowering his bowl, he reached out with his chopsticks, removed a dark speck from the soba in the box and threw it out the window. Still silent, he reached out again and picked off another dark speck, then another.

Kumagorō's eyes bugged; his breath halted.

"There's no end to them, is there?" remarked Musashi casually. "Here, Iori, go give these chopsticks a good washing."

As Iori went out, Kumagorō faded silently back into his own room and in a hushed voice told his companions of the incredible sight he had just witnessed. After first mistaking the black spots on the soba for dirt, he had realized they were live flies, plucked so deftly they had had no time to escape. Within minutes, he and his fellows transferred their little party to a more remote quarter, and silence reigned.

"That's better, isn't it?" said Musashi to Iori. The two of them grinned at one another.

By the time they'd finished their meal, the sun was down, and the moon was shining wanly above the roof of the "soul polisher's" shop.

Musashi stood up and straightened his kimono. "I think I'll see about having my sword taken care of," he said.

He picked up the weapon and was about to leave when the proprietress came halfway up the blackened staircase and called, "A letter's come for you."

Puzzled that anyone should know his whereabouts so soon, Musashi went down, accepted the missive and asked, "Is the messenger still here?"

"No; he left immediately."

The outside of the letter bore only the word "Suke," which Musashi took to stand for Kimura Sukekurō. Unfolding it, he read: "I informed Lord Munenori that I saw you this morning. He seemed happy to receive word of you after all this time. He instructed me to write and ask when you will be able to visit us."

Musashi descended the remaining steps and went to the office, where he borrowed ink and brush. Seating himself in a corner, he wrote on the back of Sukekurō's letter: "I shall be happy to visit Lord Munenori whenever he wishes to have a bout with me. As a warrior, I have no other purpose in calling on him." He signed the note "Masana," a formal name he seldom used.

"Iori," he called from the bottom of the stairs. "I want you to run an errand for me."

"Yes, sir."

"I want you to deliver a letter to Lord Yagyū Munenori."

"Yes, sir."

According to the proprietress, everybody knew where Lord Munenori lived, but she offered directions anyway. "Go down the main street until you come to the highroad. Go straight along that as far as Nihombashi. Then bear to the left and go along the river until you get to Kobikichō. That's where it is; you can't miss it."

"Thanks," said Iori, who already had his sandals on. "I'm sure I can find it." He was delighted at the opportunity to go out, particularly since his destination was the home of an important daimyō. Giving no thought to the hour, he walked away quickly, swinging his arms and holding his head up proudly.

As Musashi watched him turn the corner, he thought: "He's a little too self-confident for his own good."

The Soul Polisher

"Good evening," called Musashi.

Nothing about Zushino Kōsuke's house suggested it was a place of business. It lacked the grilled front of most shops, and there was no merchandise on display. Musashi stood in the dirt-floored passageway running down the left side of the house. To his right was a raised section, floored with tatami and screened off from the room beyond it.

The man sleeping on the tatami with his arms resting on a strongbox resembled a Taoist sage Musashi had once seen in a painting. The long, thin face was the grayish color of clay. Musashi could detect in it none of the keenness he associated with sword craftsmen.

"Good evening," Musashi repeated, a little louder.

When his voice penetrated Kōsuke's torpor, the craftsman raised his head very slowly; he might have been awakening from centuries of slumber.

Wiping the saliva from his chin and sitting up straight, he asked lackadaisically, "Can I help you?" Musashi's impression was that a man like this might make swords, as well as souls, duller, but he nevertheless held out his own weapon and explained why he was there.

"Let me take a look at it." Kōsuke's shoulders perked up smartly. Placing his left hand on his knee, he reached out with his right to take the sword, simultaneously bowing his head toward it.

"Strange creature," thought Musashi. "He barely acknowledges the presence of a human being but bows politely to a sword."

687

Holding a piece of paper in his mouth, Kōsuke quietly slid the blade out of the scabbard. He stood it vertically in front of him and examined it from hilt to tip. His eyes took on a bright glitter, reminding Musashi of glass eyes in a wooden Buddhist statue.

Snapping the weapon back into its scabbard, Kōsuke looked up inquiringly at Musashi. "Come, have a seat," he said, moving back to make room and offering Musashi a cushion.

Musashi removed his sandals and stepped up into the room.

"Has the sword been in your family for some generations?"

"Oh, no," said Musashi. "It's not the work of a famous swordsmith, nothing like that."

"Have you used it in battle, or do you carry it for the usual purposes?"

"I haven't used it on the battlefield. There's nothing special about it. The best you could say is that it's better than nothing."

"Mm." Looking directly into Musashi's eyes, Kōsuke then asked, "How do you want it polished?"

"How do I want it polished? What do you mean?"

"Do you want it sharpened so it'll cut well?"

"Well, it is a sword. The cleaner it cuts, the better."

"I suppose so," agreed Kōsuke with a defeated sigh.

"What's wrong with that? Isn't it the business of a craftsman to sharpen swords so they'll cut properly?" As Musashi spoke, he squinted curiously into Kōsuke's face.

The self-proclaimed polisher of souls shoved the weapon toward Musashi and said, "I can't do anything for you. Take it to somebody else."

Strange, indeed, thought Musashi. He could not disguise a certain vexation, but he said nothing. Kōsuke, his lips tightly set, made no attempt to explain.

While they sat silently staring at each other, a man from the neighborhood stuck his head in the door. "Kōsuke, have you got a fishing pole? It's high tide, and the fish are jumping. If you'll lend me a pole, I'll divide my catch with you."

Kōsuke plainly regarded the man as one more burden he ought not to have to bear. "Borrow one somewhere else," he rasped. "I don't believe in killing, and I don't keep instruments for murder in my house."

The man went quickly away, leaving Kōsuke looking grumpier than ever.

Another man might have become discouraged and left, but Musashi's curiosity held him there. There was something appealing about this man—not wit nor intelligence, but a rough natural goodness like that of a Karatsu sake jar or a tea bowl by Nonkō. Just as pottery often has a blemish evocative of its closeness to the earth, Kōsuke had, in a semi-bald spot on his temple, a lesion of some sort, which he'd covered with salve.

While attempting to conceal his growing fascination, Musashi said, "What is there to keep you from polishing my sword? Is it of such poor quality you can't put a good edge on it?"

"Of course not. You're the owner. You know as well as I do it's a perfectly good Bizen sword. I also know you want it sharpened for the purpose of cutting people."

"Is there anything wrong with that?"

"That's what they all say—what's wrong with wanting me to fix a sword so it'll cut better? If the sword cuts, they're happy."

"But a man bringing in a sword to be polished naturally wants—"

"Just a minute." Kōsuke raised his hand. "It'll take some time to explain. First, I'd like you to take another look at the sign on the front of my shop."

"It says 'Souls polished,' or at least I think so. Is there any other way of reading the characters?"

"No. You'll notice it doesn't say a word about polishing swords. My business is polishing the souls of the samurai who come in, not their weapons. People don't understand, but that's what I was taught when I studied sword polishing."

"I see," said Musashi, although he didn't really.

"Since I try to abide by my master's teachings, I refuse to polish the swords of samurai who take pleasure in killing people."

"Well, you have a point there. But tell me, who was this master of yours?"

"That's written on the sign too. I studied in the House of Hon'ami, under Hon'ami Kōetsu himself." Kōsuke squared his shoulders proudly as he uttered his master's name.

"That's interesting. I happen to have made the acquaintance of your master and his excellent mother, Myōshū." Musashi went on to tell how he had met them in the field near the Rendaiji and later spent a few days at their house.

Kōsuke, astonished, scrutinized him closely for a moment. "Are you by any chance the man who caused a great stir in Kyoto some years ago by defeating the Yoshioka School at Ichijōji? Miyamoto Musashi was the name, I believe."

"That is my name." Musashi's face reddened slightly.

Kōsuke moved back a bit and bowed deferentially, saying, "Forgive me. I shouldn't have been lecturing you. I had no idea I was talking to the famous Miyamoto Musashi."

"Don't give it a second thought. Your words were very instructive. Kōetsu's character comes through in the lessons he teaches his disciples."

"As I'm sure you know, the Hon'ami family served the Ashikaga shōguns. From time to time they've also been called upon to polish the Emperor's swords. Kōetsu was always saying that Japanese swords were created not to kill or injure people but to maintain the imperial rule and protect the nation, to subdue devils and drive out evil. The sword *is* the samurai's soul; he carries it for no other purpose than to maintain his own integrity. It is an ever-present admonition to the man who rules over other men and seeks in doing so to follow the Way of Life. It's only natural that the craftsman who polishes the sword must also polish the swordsman's spirit."

"How true," agreed Musashi.

"Kōetsu said that to see a good sword is to see the sacred light, the spirit of the nation's peace and tranquillity. He hated touching a bad sword. Even being near one used to nauseate him."

"I see. Are you saying you sensed something evil in my sword?"

"No, not in the least. I just felt a little depressed. Since coming to Edo, I've worked on any number of weapons, but none of their owners seem to have an

689

inkling of the sword's true meaning. I sometimes doubt they have souls to polish. All they care about is quartering a man or splitting his head open—helmet and all. It got so tiresome. That's why I put up a new sign a few days ago. It doesn't seem to have had much effect, though."

"And I came in asking for the same thing, didn't I? I understand how you feel."

"Well, that's a beginning. Things may turn out a little differently with you. But frankly, when I saw that blade of yours, I was shocked. All those nicks and stains, stains made by human flesh. I thought you were just one more senseless rōnin, proud of himself for committing a number of meaningless murders."

Musashi bowed his head. It was the voice of Kōetsu, coming from Kōsuke's mouth. "I'm grateful for this lesson," he said. "I've carried a sword since I was a boy, but I've never really given sufficient thought to the spirit that resides in it. In the future, I'll pay heed to what you've said."

Kōsuke appeared vastly relieved. "In that case, I'll polish the sword for you. Or perhaps I should say I consider it a privilege for one in my profession to be able to polish the soul of a samurai like yourself."

Twilight had faded, and the lights had been lit. Musashi decided it was time to go.

"Wait," said Kōsuke. "Do you have another sword to carry while I'm working on this one?"

"No; I have only the one long sword."

"In that case, why don't you pick out a replacement? None of the swords I have here now are very good, I'm afraid, but come and take a look."

He guided Musashi into the back room, where he took several swords out of a cabinet and lined them up on the tatami. "You can take any one of these," he offered.

Despite the craftsman's modest disavowal, they were all weapons of excellent quality. Musashi had difficulty choosing from the dazzling display, but finally he selected one and immediately fell in love with it. Just holding it in his hands, he sensed its maker's dedication. Drawing the blade from the scabbard confirmed his impression; it was indeed a beautiful piece of workmanship, probably dating from the Yoshino period in the fourteenth century. Nagged by the doubt that it was too elegant for him, once he had brought it close to the light and examined it, he found his hands reluctant to let it go.

"May I take this one?" he asked. He could not bring himself to use the word "borrow."

"You have the eye of an expert," observed Kōsuke, as he put away the other swords.

For once in his life, Musashi was swamped by covetousness. He knew it was futile to mention buying the sword outright; the price would be far beyond his means. But he couldn't help himself.

"I don't suppose you'd consider selling me this sword, would you?" he asked.

"Why not?"

"How much are you asking for it?"

"I'll let you have it for what I paid for it."

"How much was that?"

"Twenty pieces of gold."

An almost inconceivable sum to Musashi. "I'd better give it back," he said hesitantly.

"Why?" asked Kōsuke with a puzzled look. "I'll lend it to you for as long as you wish. Go on, take it."

"No; that'd make me feel even worse. Wanting it the way I do is bad enough. If I wore it for a while, it would be torture to part with it."

"Are you really so attached to it?" Kōsuke looked at the sword, then at Musashi. "All right then, I'll give it to you—in wedlock, as it were. But I expect an appropriate gift in exchange."

Musashi was baffled; he had absolutely nothing to offer.

"I heard from Kōetsu that you carve statues. I'd be honored if you'd make me an image of Kannon. That would be sufficient payment."

The last Kannon Musashi had carved was the one he'd left in Hōtengahara. "I have nothing on hand," he said. "But in the next few days, I can carve something for you. May I have the sword then?"

"Certainly. I didn't mean to imply I expected it this minute. By the way, instead of putting up at that inn, why don't you come and stay with us? We have a room we're not using."

"That would be perfect," said Musashi. "If I moved in tomorrow, I could start on the statue right away."

"Come and take a look at it," urged Kōsuke, who was also happy and excited.

Musashi followed him down the outside passageway, at the end of which was a flight of half a dozen steps. Tucked in between the first and second floors, not quite belonging to either, was an eight-mat room. Through the window Musashi could see the dew-laden leaves of an apricot tree.

Pointing at a roof covered with oyster shells, Kōsuke said, "That's my workshop there."

The craftsman's wife, as if summoned by a secret signal, arrived with sake and some tidbits. When the two men sat down, the distinction between host and guest seemed to evaporate. They relaxed, legs stretched out, and opened their hearts to each other, oblivious of the restraints normally imposed by etiquette. The talk, of course, turned to their favorite subject.

"Everybody pays lip service to the importance of the sword," said Kōsuke. "Anybody'll tell you the sword's the 'soul of the samurai' and that a sword is one of the country's three sacred treasures. But the way people actually treat swords is scandalous. And I include samurai and priests, as well as townsmen. I took it upon myself at one time to go around to shrines and old houses where there were once whole collections of beautiful swords, and I can tell you the situation is shocking."

Kōsuke's pale cheeks were ruddy now. His eyes burned with enthusiasm, and the saliva that gathered at the corners of his mouth occasionally flew in a spray right into his companion's face.

"Almost none of the famous swords from the past are being properly taken care of. At Suwa Shrine in Shinano Province there are more than three hundred swords. They could be classed as heirlooms, but I found only five that weren't rusted. Ōmishima Shrine in Iyo is famous for its collection—three thousand swords dating back many centuries. But after spending a whole month there, I found only ten that were in good condition. It's disgusting!" Kōsuke caught his breath and continued. "The problem seems to be that the older and more famous the sword is, the more the owner is inclined to make sure it's stored in a safe place. But then nobody can get at it to take care of it, and the blade gets rustier and rustier.

"The owners are like parents who protect their children so jealously that the children grow up to be fools. In the case of children, more are being born all the time—doesn't make any difference if a few are stupid. But swords . . ."

Pausing to suck in the spit, he raised his thin shoulders even higher and with a gleam in his eyes declared, "We already have all the good swords there'll ever be. During the civil wars, the swordsmiths got careless—no, downright sloppy! They forgot their techniques, and swords have been deteriorating ever since.

"The only thing to do is to take better care of the swords from the earlier periods. The craftsmen today may try to imitate the older swords, but they'll never turn out anything as good. Doesn't it make you angry to think about it?"

Abruptly he stood up and said, "Just look at this." Bringing out a sword of awesome length, he laid it down for his guest to inspect. "It's a splendid weapon, but it's covered with the worst kind of rust."

Musashi's heart skipped a beat. The sword was without doubt Sasaki Kojirō's Drying Pole. A flood of memories came rushing back.

Controlling his emotions, he said calmly, "That's really a long one, isn't it? Must take quite a samurai to handle it."

"I imagine so," agreed Kōsuke. "There aren't many like it." Taking the blade out, he turned the back toward Musashi and handed it to him by the hilt. "See," he said. "It's rusted badly—here and here and here. But he's used it anyway."

"I see."

"This is a rare piece of workmanship, probably forged in the Kamakura period. It'll take a lot of work, but I can probably fix it up. On these ancient swords, the rust is only a relatively thin film. If this were a new blade, I'd never be able to get the stains off. On new swords, rust spots are like malignant sores; they eat right into the heart of the metal."

Reversing the sword's position so that the back of the blade was toward Kōsuke, Musashi said, "Tell me, did the owner of this sword bring it in himself?"

"No. I was at Lord Hosokawa's on business, and one of the older retainers, Iwama Kakubei, asked me to drop in at his house on the way back. I did, and he gave it to me to work on. Said it belonged to a guest of his."

"The fittings are good too," remarked Musashi, his eyes still focused on the weapon.

"It's a battle sword. The man's been carrying it on his back up till now, but he wants to carry it at his side, so I've been asked to refit the scabbard. He must be a very large man. Either that or he has a very practiced arm."

Kōsuke had begun to feel his sake. His tongue was becoming a little thick. Musashi concluded it was time to take his leave, which he did with a minimum of ceremony.

It was much later than he thought. There were no lights in the neighborhood.

Once inside the inn, he groped through the darkness to the stairway and up to the second floor. Two pallets had been spread, but both were empty. Iori's absence made him uncomfortable, for he suspected the boy was wandering about lost on the streets of this great unfamiliar city.

Going back downstairs, he shook the night watchman awake. "Isn't he back yet?" asked the man, who seemed more surprised than Musashi. "I thought he was with you."

Knowing he would only stare at the ceiling until Iori came back, Musashi went out into the black-lacquer night again and stood with arms crossed under the eaves.

The Fox

"Is this Kobikichō?"

In spite of repeated assurances that it was, Iori still had his doubts. The only lights visible on the broad expanse of land belonged to the makeshift huts of woodworkers and stonemasons, and these were few and far between. Beyond them, in the distance, he could just make out the foaming white waves of the bay.

Near the river were piles of rocks and stacks of lumber, and although Iori knew that buildings were going up at a furious pace all over Edo, it struck him as unlikely that Lord Yagyū would build his residence in an area like this.

"Where to next?" he thought dejectedly as he sat down on some lumber. His feet were tired and burning. To cool them he wiggled his toes in the dewy grass. Soon his tension ebbed away and the sweat dried, but his spirits remained decidedly damp.

"It's all the fault of that old woman at the inn," he muttered to himself. "She didn't know what she was talking about." The time he himself had spent gawking at the sights in the theater district at Sakaichō conveniently slipped his mind.

The hour was late, and there was no one around from whom he could ask directions. Yet the idea of spending the night in these unfamiliar surroundings made him uneasy. He had to complete his errand and return to the inn before daybreak, even if it meant waking up one of the workers.

As he approached the nearest shack where a light showed, he saw a woman with a strip of matting tied over her head like a shawl.

"Good evening, auntie," he said innocently.

Mistaking him for the helper at a nearby sake shop, the woman glared and sniffed, "You, is it? You threw a rock at me and ran away, didn't you, you little brat?"

"Not me," protested Iori. "I've never seen you before!"

The woman came hesitantly toward him, then burst out laughing. "No," she said, "you're not the one. What's a cute little boy like you doing wandering around here at this time of night?"

"I was sent on an errand, but I can't find the house I'm looking for."

"Whose house is it?"

"Lord Yagyū of Tajima's."

"Are you joking?" She laughed. "Lord Yagyū is a daimyō, and a teacher to the shōgun. Do you think he'd open his gate to *you*?" She laughed again. "You know somebody in the servants' quarters perhaps?"

"I've brought a letter."

"Who to?"

"A samurai named Kimura Sukekurō."

"Must be one of his retainers. But you, you're so funny—throwing Lord Yagyū's name around like you knew him."

"I just want to deliver this letter. If you know where the house is, tell me."

"It's on the other side of the moat. If you cross that bridge over there, you'll be in front of Lord Kii's house. The next one is Lord Kyōgoku, then Lord Katō, then Lord Matsudaira of Suō." Holding up her fingers, she counted off the sturdy storehouses on the opposite bank. "I'm sure the one after that is the one you want."

"If I cross the moat, will I still be in Kobikichō?"

"Of course."

"Of all the stupid—"

"Here now, that's no way to talk. Hmm, you seem such a nice boy, I'll come along and show you Lord Yagyū's place."

Walking in front of him with the matting on her head, she looked to Iori rather like a ghost.

They were in the middle of the bridge when a man coming toward them brushed against her sleeve and whistled. He reeked of sake. Before Iori knew what was going on, the woman turned and made for the drunk. "I know you," she warbled. "Don't just pass me by like that. It isn't nice." She grabbed his sleeve and started toward a place from which they could go below the bridge.

"Let go," he said.

"Wouldn't you like to go with me?"

"No money."

"Oh, I don't care." Latching on to him like a leech, she looked back at Iori's startled face and said, "Run along now. I've got business with this gentleman."

Iori watched in bewilderment as the two of them tugged back and forth. After a few moments, the woman appeared to get the upper hand, and they disappeared below the bridge. Still puzzled, Iori went to the railing and looked over at the grassy riverbank.

Glancing up, the woman shouted, "Nitwit!" and picked up a rock.

Swallowing hard, Iori dodged the missile and made for the far end of the bridge. In all his years on the barren plain of Hōtengahara, he had never seen anything so frightening as the woman's angry white face in the dark.

On the other side of the river, he found himself before a storehouse. Next to that was a fence, then another storehouse, then another fence, and so on down the street. "This must be it," he said when he came to the fifth building. On the gleaming white plaster wall was a crest in the form of a two-tiered woman's hat. This, Iori knew from the words of a popular song, was the Yagyū family crest.

"Who's there?" demanded a voice from inside the gate.

Speaking as loudly as he dared, Iori announced, "I'm the pupil of Miyamoto Musashi. I've brought a letter."

The sentry said a few words Iori could not catch. In the gate was a small door, through which people could be let in and out without opening the great gate itself. After a few seconds, the door slowly opened, and the man asked suspiciously, "What are you doing here at this hour?"

Iori thrust the letter at the guard's face. "Please deliver this for me. If there's an answer, I'll take it back."

"Hmm," mused the man, taking the letter. "This is for Kimura Sukekurō, is it?"

"Yes, sir."

"He's not here."

"Where is he?"

"He's at the house in Higakubo."

"Huh? Everybody told me Lord Yagyū's house was in Kobikichō."

"People say that, but there're only storehouses here—rice, lumber and a few other things."

"Lord Yagyū doesn't live here?"

"That's right."

"How far is it to the other place—Higakubo?"

"Pretty far."

"Just where is it?"

"In the hills outside the city, in Azabu Village."

"Never heard of it." Iori sighed disappointedly, but his sense of responsibility prevented him from giving up. "Sir, would you draw me a map?"

"Don't be silly. Even if you knew the way, it'd take you all night to get there."

"I don't mind."

"Lot of foxes in Azabu. You don't want to be bewitched by a fox, do you?"

"No."

"Do you know Sukekurō well?"

"My teacher does."

"I'll tell you what. Since it's so late, why don't you catch some sleep over there in the granary, and go in the morning?"

"Where am I?" exclaimed Iori, rubbing his eyes. He jumped up and ran outside. The afternoon sun made him dizzy. Squinting his eyes against the glare, he went to the gatehouse, where the guard was eating his lunch.

"So you're finally up."

"Yes, sir. Could you draw me that map now?"

"You in a hurry, Sleepyhead? Here, you'd better have something to eat first. There's enough for both of us."

While the boy chewed and gulped, the guard sketched a rough map and explained how to get to Higakubo. They finished simultaneously, and Iori, fired up with the importance of his mission, set off at a run, never thinking that Musashi might be worried about his failure to return to the inn.

He made good time through the busy thoroughfares until he reached the vicinity of Edo Castle, where the imposing houses of the leading daimyō stood on the land built up between the crisscross system of moats. As he looked around, his pace slowed. The waterways were jammed with cargo boats. The stone ramparts of the castle itself were half covered with log scaffolding, which from a distance resembled the bamboo trellises used for growing morning glories.

He dawdled again in a broad, flat area called Hibiya, where the scraping of chisels and the thud of axes raised a dissonant hymn to the power of the new shogunate.

Iori stopped. He was mesmerized by the spectacle of the construction work: the laborers hauling huge rocks, the carpenters with their planes and saws and the samurai, the dashing samurai, who stood proudly supervising it all. How he wanted to grow up and be like them!

A lusty song rose from the throats of the men hauling rocks:

> We'll pluck the flowers
> In the fields of Musashi—
> The gentians, the bellflowers,
> Wild blossoms splashed
> In confusing disarray.
> And that lovely girl,
> The flower unpluckable,
> Moistened by the dew—
> 'Twill only dampen your sleeve, like falling tears.

He stood enchanted. Before he realized it, the water in the moats was taking on a reddish cast and the evening voices of crows reached his ears.

"Oh, no, it's nearly sundown," he chastised himself. He sped away and for a time moved along at full speed, paying attention to nothing save the map the guard had drawn for him. Before he knew it, he was climbing the path up Azabu Hill, which was so thickly overhung with trees it might as well have been midnight. Once he reached the top, however, he could see the sun was still in the sky, though low on the horizon.

There were almost no houses on the hill itself, Azabu Village being a mere scattering of fields and farm dwellings in the valley below. Standing in a sea of grass and ancient trees, listening to the brooks gurgling down the hillside, Iori felt his fatigue give way to a strange refreshment. He was vaguely aware that the spot where he was standing was historic, although he didn't know why. In fact it was the very place that had given birth to the great warrior clans of the past, both the Taira and the Minamoto.

He heard the loud booming of a drum being beaten, the kind often used at Shinto festivals. Down the hill, visible in the forest, were the sturdy cross-logs atop the ridgepole of a religious sanctuary. Had Iori but known, it was the Great Shrine of Iigura he'd studied about, the famous edifice sacred to the sun goddess of Ise.

The shrine was a far cry from the enormous castle he had just seen, even from the stately gates of the daimyō. In its simplicity it was almost indistinguishable from the farmhouses around it, and Iori thought it puzzling that people talked more reverently about the Tokugawa family than they did about the most sacred of deities. Did that mean the Tokugawas were greater than the sun goddess? he wondered. "I'll have to ask Musashi about that when I get back."

Taking out his map, he pored over it, looked about him and stared at it again. Still there was no sign of the Yagyū mansion.

The evening mist spreading over the ground gave him an eerie feeling. He'd felt something similar before, when in a room with the shoji shut the setting sun's light played on the rice paper so that the interior seemed to grow lighter as the outside darkened. Of course, such a twilight illusion is just that, but he felt it so strongly, in several flashes, that he rubbed his eyes as if to erase his light-headedness. He knew he wasn't dreaming and looked around suspiciously.

"Why, you sneaky bastard," he cried, jumping forward and whipping out his sword. In the same motion he cut through a clump of tall grass in front of him.

With a yelp of pain, a fox leapt from its hiding place and streaked off, its tail glistening with blood from a cut on its hindquarters.

"Devilish beast!" Iori set off in hot pursuit, and though the fox was fast, Iori was too. When the limping creature stumbled, Iori lunged, confident of victory. The fox, however, slipped nimbly away, to surge ahead several yards, and no matter how fast Iori attacked, the animal managed to get away each time.

On his mother's knee, Iori had heard countless tales proving beyond a shadow of a doubt that foxes had the power to bewitch and possess human beings. He was fond of most other animals, even wild boar and noisome possums, but foxes he hated. He was also afraid of them. To his way of thinking, coming across this wily creature lurking in the grass could mean only one thing—it   *697* was to blame for his not finding his way. He was convinced it was a treacherous and evil being that had been following him since the night before and had, just moments before, cast its malevolent spell over him. If he didn't slay it now, it was sure to hex him again. Iori was prepared to pursue his quarry to the end of the earth, but the fox, bounding over the edge of a drop, was lost to sight in a thicket.

Dew glistened on the flowers of the dog nettle and spiderwort. Exhausted and parched, Iori sank down and licked the moisture from a mint leaf. Shoulders heaving, he finally caught his breath, whereupon sweat poured copiously from his forehead. His heart thumped violently. "Where did it go?" he asked, his voice halfway between a scream and a choke.

If the fox had really gone, so much the better, but Iori didn't know what to believe. Since he had injured the animal, he felt it was certain to take revenge, one way or another. Resigning himself, he sat still and waited.

Just as he was beginning to feel calmer, an eerie sound floated to his ears. Wide-eyed, he looked around. "It's the fox, for sure," he said, steeling himself against being bewitched. Rising quickly, he moistened his eyebrows with saliva—a trick thought to ward off the influence of foxes.

A short distance away, a woman came floating through the evening mist, her face half hidden by a veil of silk gauze. She was riding a horse sidesaddle, the reins lying loosely across the low pommel. The saddle was made of lacquered wood with mother-of-pearl inlay.

"It's changed into a woman," thought Iori. This vision in a veil, playing a flute and silhouetted against the thin rays of the evening sun, could by no stretch of the imagination be a creature of this world.

As he squatted in the grass like a frog, Iori heard an otherworldly voice call, "Otsū!" and was sure it had come from one of the fox's companions.

The rider had nearly reached a turnoff, where a road diverged to the south, and the upper part of her body glowed reddish. The sun, sinking behind the hills of Shibuya, was fringed by clouds.

If he killed her, he could expose her true fox form. Iori tightened his grip on the sword and braced himself, thinking: "Lucky it doesn't know I'm hiding here." Like all those acquainted with the truth about foxes, he knew the animal's spirit would be situated a few feet behind its human form. He swallowed hard in anticipation, while waiting for the vision to proceed and make the turn to the south.

But when the horse reached the turnoff, the woman stopped playing, put her flute in a cloth wrapper and tucked it into her obi. Lifting her veil, she peered about with searching eyes.

"Otsū!" the voice called again.

A pleasant smile came to her face as she called back, "Here I am, Hyōgo. Here."

Iori watched as a samurai came up the road from the valley. "Oh, oh!" he gasped when he noticed that the man walked with a slight limp. *This* was the fox he had wounded; no doubt about it! Disguised not as a beautiful temptress but as a handsome samurai. The apparition terrified Iori. He shivered violently and wet himself.

After the woman and the samurai had exchanged a few words, the samurai took hold of the horse's bit and led it right past the place where Iori was hiding.

"Now's the time," he decided, but his body would not respond.

The samurai noticed a slight motion and looked around, his gaze falling squarely on Iori's petrified face. The light from the samurai's eyes seemed more brilliant than the edge of the setting sun. Iori prostrated himself and buried his face in the grass. Never in his entire fourteen years had he experienced such terror.

Hyōgo, seeing nothing alarming about the boy, walked on. The slope was steep, and he had to lean back to keep the horse in check. Looking over his shoulder at Otsū, he asked gently, "Why are you so late? You've been gone a long time just to have ridden to the shrine and back. My uncle got worried and sent me to look for you."

Without answering, Otsū jumped down from the horse.

Hyōgo stopped. "Why are you getting off? Something wrong?"

"No, but it's not fitting for a woman to ride when a man's walking. Let's walk together. We can both hold the bit." She took her place on the other side of the horse.

They descended into the darkening valley and passed a sign reading: "Sendan'en Academy for Priests of the Sōdō Zen Sect." The sky was filling with stars, and the Shibuya River could be heard in the distance. The river divided the valley into North Higakubo and South Higakubo. Since the school, established by the monk Rintatsu, lay on the north slope, the priests were casually referred to as the "fellows of the north." The "fellows of the south" were the men studying swordsmanship under Yagyū Munenori, whose establishment was directly across the valley.

As Yagyū Sekishūsai's favorite among his sons and grandsons, Yagyū Hyōgo enjoyed a special status among the "fellows of the south." He had also distinguished himself in his own right. At the age of twenty, he had been summoned by the famous general Katō Kiyomasa and given a position at Kumamoto Castle in Higo Province at a stipend of fifteen thousand bushels. This was unheard of for a man so young, but after the Battle of Sekigahara, Hyōgo began to have second thoughts about his status, because of the danger inherent in having to side with either the Tokugawas or the Osaka faction. Three years earlier, using his grandfather's illness as a pretext, he had taken a leave of absence from Kumamoto and returned to Yamato. After that, saying he needed more training, he had traveled about the countryside for a time.

He and Otsū had been thrown together by chance the previous year, when he had come to stay with his uncle. For more than three years prior to that, Otsū had led a precarious existence, never quite able to escape from Matahachi, who had dragged her along everywhere, glibly telling prospective employers that she was his wife. Had he been willing to work as an apprentice to a carpenter or a plasterer or a stonemason, he could have found employment on the day they arrived in Edo, but he preferred to imagine they could work together at softer jobs, she as a domestic servant perhaps, he as a clerk or accountant.

Finding no takers for his services, they had managed to survive by doing odd jobs. And as the months passed, Otsū, hoping to lull her tormentor into complacency, had given in to him in every way short of surrendering her body.

Then one day they had been walking along the street when they encountered a daimyō's procession. Along with everyone else, they moved to the side of the road and assumed a properly respectful attitude.

The palanquins and lacquered strongboxes bore the Yagyū crest. Otsū had raised her eyes enough to see this, and memories of Sekishūsai and the happy days at Koyagyū Castle flooded her heart. If only she were back in that peaceful land of Yamato now! With Matahachi at her side, she could only stare blankly after the passing retinue.

"Otsū, isn't that you?" The conical sedge hat came low over the samurai's face, but as he drew closer, Otsū had seen that it was Kimura Sukekurō, a man she remembered with affection and respect. She couldn't have been more amazed or thankful if he had been the Buddha himself, surrounded by the wondrous light of infinite compassion. Slipping away from Matahachi's side, she had hurried to Sukekurō, who promptly offered to take her home with him.

When Matahachi had opened his mouth to protest, Sukekurō said peremptorily, "If you have anything to say, come to Higakubo and say it there."

Powerless before the prestigious House of Yagyū, Matahachi held his tongue, biting his lower lip in angry frustration as he sullenly watched his precious treasure escape from him.

An Urgent Letter

At thirty-eight, Yagyū Munenori was regarded as the best swordsman of them all. This hadn't kept his father from constantly worrying about his fifth son. "If only he can control that little quirk of his," he often said to himself. Or: "Can anybody that self-willed manage to keep a high position?"

It was now fourteen years since Tokugawa Ieyasu had commanded Sekishūsai to provide a tutor for Hidetada. Sekishūsai had passed over his other sons, grandsons and nephews. Munenori was neither particularly brilliant nor heroically masculine, but he was a man of good, solid judgment, a practical man not likely to get lost in the clouds. He possessed neither his father's towering stature nor Hyōgo's genius, but he was reliable, and most important, he understood the cardinal principle of the Yagyū Style, namely that the true value of the Art of War lay in its application to government.

Sekishūsai had not misinterpreted Ieyasu's wishes; the conquering general had no use for a swordsman to teach his heir only technical skills. Some years before Sekigahara, Ieyasu himself had studied under a master swordsman named Okuyama, his objective being, as he himself frequently expressed it, "to acquire the eye needed to oversee the country."

Still, Hidetada was now shōgun, and it would not do for the shōgun's instructor to be a man who lost in actual combat. A samurai in Munenori's position was expected to excel over all challengers and to demonstrate that Yagyū swordsmanship was second to none. Munenori felt he was constantly being scrutinized and tested, and while others might regard him as lucky to have been singled out for this distinguished appointment, he himself often envied Hyōgo and wished he could live the way his nephew did.

Hyōgo, as it happened, was now walking down the outside passageway leading to his uncle's room. The house, though large and sprawling, was neither stately in appearance nor lavish in its appointments. Instead of employing carpenters from Kyoto to create an elegant, graceful dwelling, Munenori had deliberately entrusted the work to local builders, men accustomed to the sturdy, spartan warrior style of Kamakura. Though the trees were relatively sparse, and the hills of no great height, Munenori had chosen the solid rustic style of architecture exemplified by the old Main House at Koyagyū.

"Uncle," called Hyōgo softly and politely, as he knelt on the veranda outside Munenori's room.

"Is that you, Hyōgo?" asked Munenori without removing his eyes from the garden.

"May I come in?"

Having received permission to enter, Hyōgo made his way into the room on his knees. He had taken quite a few liberties with his grandfather, who was inclined to spoil him, but he knew better than to do that with his uncle. Munenori, though no martinet, was a stickler for etiquette. Now, as always, he was seated in strict formal fashion. At times Hyōgo felt sorry for him.

"Otsū?" asked Munenori, as though reminded of her by Hyōgo's arrival.

"She's back. She'd only gone to Hikawa Shrine, the way she often does. On the way back, she let her horse wander around for a while."

"You went looking for her?"

"Yes, sir."

Munenori remained silent for a few moments. The lamplight accented his tight-lipped profile. "It worries me to have a young woman living here indefinitely. You never know what might happen. I've told Sukekurō to look for an opportunity to suggest she go elsewhere."

His tone slightly plaintive, Hyōgo said, "I'm told she has no place to go." His uncle's change of attitude surprised him, for when Sukekurō had brought

Otsū home and introduced her as a woman who had served Sekishūsai well, Munenori had welcomed her cordially and said she was free to stay as long as she wished. "Don't you feel sorry for her?" he asked.

"Yes, but there's a limit to what you can do for people."

"I thought you yourself thought well of her."

"It has nothing to do with that. When a young woman comes to live in a house full of young men, tongues are apt to wag. And it's difficult for the men. One of them might do something rash."

This time Hyōgo was silent, but not because he took his uncle's remarks personally. He was thirty and, like the other young samurai, single, but he firmly believed his own feelings toward Otsū were too pure to raise doubts about his intentions. He had been careful to allay his uncle's misgivings by making no secret of his fondness for her, while at the same time not once letting on that his feeling went beyond friendship.

Hyōgo felt that the problem might lie with his uncle. Munenori's wife came from a highly respected and well-placed family, of the sort whose daughters were delivered to their husbands on their wedding day in curtained palanquins lest they be seen by outsiders. Her chambers, together with those of the other women, were well removed from the more public parts of the house, so virtually no one knew whether relations between the master and his wife were harmonious. It was not difficult to imagine that the lady of the house might take a dim view of beautiful and eligible young women in such proximity to her husband.

Hyōgo broke the silence, saying, "Leave the matter to Sukekurō and me. We'll work out some solution that won't be too hard on Otsū."

Munenori nodded, saying, "The sooner the better."

Sukekurō entered the anteroom just then, and placing a letter box on the tatami, knelt and bowed. "Your lordship," he said respectfully.

Turning his eyes toward the anteroom, Munenori asked, "What is it?"

Sukekurō moved forward on his knees.

"A courier from Koyagyū has just arrived by fast horse."

"Fast horse?" said Munenori quickly, but without surprise.

Hyōgo accepted the box from Sukekurō and handed it to his uncle. Munenori opened the letter, which was from Shōda Kizaemon. Written in haste, it said: "The Old Lord has had another spell, worse than any previous. We fear he may not last long. He stoutly insists his illness is not sufficient reason for you to leave your duties. However, after discussing the matter among ourselves, we retainers decided to write and inform you of the situation."

"His condition is critical," said Munenori.

Hyōgo admired his uncle's ability to remain calm. He surmised that Munenori knew exactly what was to be done and had already made the necessary decisions.

After some minutes of silence, Munenori said, "Hyōgo, will you go to Koyagyū in my stead?"

"Of course, sir."

"I want you to assure my father there's nothing to worry about in Edo. And I want you to look after him personally."

"Yes, sir."

"I suppose it's all in the hands of the gods and the Buddha now. All you can do is hurry and try to get there before it's too late."

"I'll leave tonight."

From Lord Munenori's room, Hyōgo went immediately to his own. During the short time it took him to lay out the few things he would need, the bad news spread to every corner of the house.

Otsū quietly went to Hyōgo's room, dressed, to his surprise, for traveling. Her eyes were moist. "Please take me with you," she pleaded. "I can never hope to repay Lord Sekishūsai for taking me into his home, but I'd like to be with him and see if I can be of some assistance. I hope you won't refuse."

Hyōgo considered it possible that his uncle might have refused her, but he himself did not have the heart to. Perhaps it was a blessing that this opportunity to take her away from the house in Edo had presented itself.

"All right," he agreed, "but it'll have to be a fast journey."

"I promise I won't slow you down." Drying her tears, she helped him finish packing and then went to pay her respects to Lord Munenori.

"Oh, are you going to accompany Hyōgo?" he said, mildly surprised. "That's very kind of you. I'm sure my father will be pleased to see you." He made a point of giving her ample travel money and a new kimono as a going-away present. Despite his conviction that it was for the best, her departure saddened him.

She bowed herself out of his presence. "Take good care of yourself," he said with feeling, as she reached the anteroom.

The vassals and servants lined up along the path to the gate to see them off, and with a simple "Farewell" from Hyōgo, they were on their way.

Otsū had folded her kimono up under her obi, so the hem reached only five or six inches below her knees. On her head was a broad-brimmed lacquered traveling hat and in her right hand she carried a stick. Had her shoulders been draped with blossoms, she would have been the image of the Wisteria Girl so often seen in woodblock prints.

Since Hyōgo had decided to hire conveyances at the stations along the highroad, their goal tonight was the inn town of Sangen'ya, south of Shibuya. From there, his plan was to proceed along the Ōyama highroad to the Tama River, take the ferry across, and follow the Tōkaidō to Kyoto.

In the night mist, it was not long before Otsū's lacquered hat glistened with moisture. After walking through a grassy river valley, they came to a rather wide road, which since the Kamakura period had been one of the most important in the Kantō district. At night it was lonely and deserted, with trees growing thickly on both sides.

"Gloomy, isn't it?" said Hyōgo with a smile, again slowing down his naturally long strides to let Otsū catch up with him. "This is Dōgen Slope. There used to be bandits around here," he added.

"Bandits?" There was just enough alarm in her voice to make him laugh.

"That was a long time ago, though. A man by the name of Dōgen Tarō, who was related to the rebel Wada Yoshimori, is supposed to have been the head of a band of thieves who lived in the caves around here."

"Let's not talk about things like that."

Hyōgo's laughter echoed through the dark, and hearing it made him feel guilty for acting frivolous. He couldn't help himself, however. Though sad, he looked forward with pleasure to being with Otsū these next few days.

"Oh!" cried Otsū, taking a couple of steps backward.

"What's the matter?" Instinctively, Hyōgo's arm went around her shoulders.

"There's somebody over there."

"Where?"

"It's a child, sitting there by the side of the road, talking to himself and crying. The poor thing!"

When Hyōgo got close enough, he recognized the boy he had seen earlier that evening, hiding in the grass in Azabu.

Iori leaped to his feet with a gasp. An instant later, he uttered an oath and pointed his sword at Hyōgo. "Fox!" he cried. "That's what you are, a fox!"

Otsū caught her breath and stifled a scream. The look on Iori's face was wild, almost demonic, as if he were possessed by an evil spirit. Even Hyōgo drew back cautiously.

"Foxes!" Iori shouted again. "I'll take care of you!" His voice cracked hoarsely, like an old woman's. Hyōgo stared at him in puzzlement but was careful to steer clear of his blade.

"How's this?" shouted Iori, whacking off the top of a tall shrub not far from Hyōgo's side. Then he sank to the ground, exhausted by his effort. Breathing hard, he asked, "What did you think of that, fox?"

Turning to Otsū, Hyōgo said with a grin, "Poor little fellow. He seems to be possessed by a fox."

"Maybe you're right. His eyes are ferocious."

"Just like a fox's."

"Isn't there something we can do to help him?"

"Well, they say there's no cure for either madness or stupidity, but I suspect there's a remedy for his ailment." He walked up to Iori and glared sternly at him.

Glancing up, the boy hastily gripped his sword again. "Still here, are you?" he cried. But before he could get to his feet, his ears were assailed by a fierce roar coming from the pit of Hyōgo's stomach.

"Y-a-a-w-r!"

Iori was scared witless. Hyōgo picked him up by the waist, and holding him horizontally, strode back down the hill to the bridge. He turned the boy upside down, grasped him by the ankles and held him out over the railing.

"Help! Mother! Help, help! Sensei! Save me!" The screams gradually changed to a wail.

Otsū hastened to the rescue. "Stop that, Hyōgo. Let him go. You shouldn't be so cruel."

"I guess that's enough," said Hyōgo, setting the boy down gently on the bridge.

Iori was in a terrible state, bawling and choking, convinced there was not a soul on earth who could help him. Otsū went to his side and put her arm affectionately around his drooping shoulders. "Where do you live, child?" she asked softly.

Between sobs, Iori stammered, "O-over th-th-that way," and pointed.

"What do you mean, 'that way'?"

"Ba-ba-bakurōchō."

"Why, that's miles away. How did you get all the way out here?"

"I came on an errand. I got lost."

"When was that?"

"I left Bakurōchō yesterday."

"And you've been wandering around all night and all day?" Iori half shook his head, but didn't say anything. "Why, that's terrible. Tell me, where were you supposed to go?"

A little calmer now, he replied promptly, as though he'd been waiting for the question. "To the residence of Lord Yagyū Munenori of Tajima." After feeling around under his obi, he clutched the crumpled letter and waved it proudly in front of his face. Bringing it close to his eyes, he said, "It's for Kimura Sukekurō. I'm to deliver it and wait for an answer."

Otsū saw that Iori took his mission very seriously and was ready to guard the missive with his life. Iori, for his part, was determined to show the letter to no one before he reached his destination. Neither had any inkling of the irony of the situation—a missed chance, a happening rarer than the coming together across the River of Heaven of the Herdboy and the Spinning Maiden.

Turning to Hyōgo, Otsū said, "He seems to have a letter for Sukekurō."

"He's wandered off in the wrong direction, hasn't he? Fortunately, it's not very far." Calling Iori to him, he gave him directions. "Go along this river to the first crossroads, then go left and up the hill. When you get to a place where three roads come together, you'll see a pair of large pine trees off to your right. The house is to the left, across the road."

"And watch out you don't get possessed by a fox again," added Otsū.

Iori had regained his confidence. "Thanks," he called back, already running along the river. When he reached the crossroads, he half turned and shouted, "To the left here?"

"That's it," answered Hyōgo. "The road's dark, so be careful." He and Otsū stood watching from the bridge for a minute or two. "What a strange child," he said.

"Yes, but he seems rather bright." In her mind she was comparing him with Jōtarō, who had been only a little bigger than Iori when she had last seen him. Jōtarō, she reflected, must be seventeen now. She wondered what he was like and felt an inevitable pang of yearning for Musashi. So many years since she'd had any word of him! Though now accustomed to living with the suffering that love entails, she dared hope that leaving Edo might bring her closer to him, that she might even meet him somewhere along the road.

"Let's get on," Hyōgo said brusquely, to himself as much as to Otsū. "There's nothing to be done about tonight, but we'll have to be careful not to waste any more time."

Filial Piety

"What're you doing, Granny, practicing your handwriting?" Jūrō the Reed Mat's expression was ambiguous; it might have been admiration, or simply shock.

"Oh, it's you," said Osugi with a trace of annoyance.

Sitting down beside her, Jūrō mumbled, "Copying a Buddhist sutra, are you?" This elicited no reply. "Aren't you old enough so you don't have to practice your writing anymore? Or are you thinking of becoming a calligraphy teacher in the next world?"

"Be quiet. To copy the holy scriptures, one has to achieve a state of selflessness. Solitude is best for that. Why don't you go away?"

"After I hurried home just to tell you what happened to me today?"

"It can wait."

"When will you be finished?"

"I have to put the spirit of the Buddha's enlightenment into each character I write. It takes me three days to make one copy."

"You've got a lot of patience."

"Three days is nothing. This summer I'm going to make dozens of copies. I've made a vow to make a thousand before I die. I'll leave them to people who don't have proper love for their parents."

"A thousand copies? That's a lot."

"It's my sacred vow."

"Well, I'm not very proud of it, but I guess I've been disrespectful to my parents, like the rest of these louts around here. They forgot about them a long time ago. The only one who cares for his mother and father is the boss."

"It's a sad world we live in."

"Ha, ha. If it upsets you that much, you must have a good-for-nothing son too."

"I'm sorry to say, mine has caused me a lot of grief. That's why I took the vow. This is the *Sutra on the Great Love of Parents.* Everyone who doesn't treat his mother or father right should be forced to read it."

"You're really giving a copy of whatever-you-call-it to a thousand people?"

"They say that by planting one seed of enlightenment you can convert a hundred people, and if one sprout of enlightenment grows in a hundred hearts, ten million souls can be saved." Laying down her brush, she took a finished copy and handed it to Jūrō. "Here, you can have this. See that you read it when you have time."

She looked so pious Jūrō nearly burst out laughing, but he managed to contain himself. Overcoming his urge to stuff it into his kimono like so much tissue paper, he lifted it respectfully to his forehead and placed it on his lap.

"Say, Granny, you sure you wouldn't like to know what happened today? Maybe your faith in the Buddha gets results. I ran into somebody pretty special."

"Who might that be?"

"Miyamoto Musashi. I saw him down at the Sumida River, getting off the ferry."

"You saw Musashi? Why didn't you say so!" She pushed the writing table away with a grunt. "Are you sure? Where is he now?"

"There, now, take it easy. Your old Jūrō doesn't do things halfway. After I found out who he was, I followed him without him knowing it. He went to an inn in Bakurōchō."

"He's staying near here?"

"Well, it's not all that close."

"It may not seem that way to you, but it does to me. I've been all over the country looking for him." Springing to her feet, she went to her clothes cabinet and took out the short sword that had been in her family for generations.

"Take me there," she ordered.

"Now?"

"Of course now."

"I thought you had a lot of patience, but . . . Why do you have to go now?"

"I'm always ready to meet Musashi, even on a moment's notice. If I get killed, you can send my body back to my family in Mimasaka."

"Couldn't you wait until the boss comes home? If we go off like this, all I'll get for finding Musashi is a bawling out."

"But there's no telling when Musashi might go somewhere else."

"Don't worry about that. I sent a man to keep an eye on the place."

"Can you guarantee Musashi won't get away?"

"What? I do you a favor, and you want to tie me up with obligations! Oh, all right. I guarantee it. Absolutely. Look, Granny, now's the time when you should be taking it easy, sitting down copying sutras or something like that."

"Where is Yajibei?"

"He's on a trip to Chichibu with his religious group. I don't know exactly when he'll be back."

"I can't afford to wait."

"If that's the way it is, why don't we get Sasaki Kojirō to come over? You can talk to him about it."

The next morning, after contacting his spy, Jūrō informed Osugi that Musashi had moved from the inn to the house of a sword polisher.

"See? I told you," declared Osugi. "You can't expect him to sit still in one place forever. The next thing you know, he'll be gone again." She was seated at her writing table but hadn't written a word all morning.

"Musashi hasn't got wings," Jūrō assured her. "Just be calm. Koroku's going to see Kojirō today."

707

"Today? Didn't you send somebody last night? Tell me where he lives. I'll go myself."

She started getting ready to go out, but Jūrō suddenly disappeared and she had to ask a couple of the other henchmen for directions. Having seldom left the house during her more than two years in Edo, she was quite unfamiliar with the city.

"Kojirō's living with Iwama Kakubei," she was told.

"Kakubei's a vassal of the Hosokawas, but his own house is on the Takanawa highroad."

"It's about halfway up Isarago Hill. Anybody can tell you where that is."

"If you have any difficulty, ask for Tsukinomisaki. That's another name for Isarago Hill."

"The house is easy to recognize, because the gate is painted bright red. It's the only place around there with a red gate."

"All right, I understand," said Osugi impatiently, resenting the implication that she was senile, or stupid. "It doesn't sound difficult, so I'll just be on my way. Take care of things while I'm out. Be careful about fire. We don't want the place to burn down while Yajibei's away." Having put on her zōri, she checked to make sure her short sword was at her side, took a firm grip on her staff and marched off.

A few minutes later, Jūrō reappeared and asked where she was.

"She asked us how to get to Kakubei's house and went out by herself."

"Oh, well, what can you do with a pigheaded old woman?" Then he shouted in the direction of the men's quarters, "Koroku!"

The Acolyte abandoned his gambling and answered the summons posthaste.

"You were going to see Kojirō last night, then you put it off. Now look what's happened. The old woman's gone by herself."

"So?"

"When the boss gets back, she'll blab to him."

"You're right. And with that tongue of hers, she'll make us look real bad."

"Yeah. If she could only walk as well as she talks, but she's thin as a grasshopper. If she gets run into by a horse, that'll be the end of her. I hate to ask you, but you better go after her and see she gets there in one piece."

Koroku ran off, and Jūrō, ruminating on the absurdity of it all, appropriated a corner of the young men's room. It was a big room, perhaps thirty by forty feet. The floor was covered with thin, finely woven matting, and a wide variety of swords and other weapons were lying about. Hanging from nails were hand towels, kimono, underwear, fire hats and other items of the sort a band of ne'er-do-wells might require. There were two incongruous articles. One was a woman's kimono, in bright colors with a red silk lining; the other was the gold-lacquered mirror stand over which it was suspended. They had been placed there on the instructions of Kojirō, who explained to Yajibei, somewhat mysteriously, that if a group of men lived together in one room with no feminine touch, they were apt to get out of hand and fight each other, rather than save their energies for meaningful battles.

708   "You're cheating, you son of a bitch!"

"Who's cheating? You're nuts."

Jūrō cast a disdainful look at the gamblers and lay down with his legs crossed comfortably. With all the rumpus going on, sleep was out of the question, but he wasn't going to demean himself by joining one of the card or dice games. No competition, as he saw it.

As he closed his eyes, he heard a dejected voice say, "It's no good today—no luck at all." The loser, with the sad eyes of the utterly defeated, dropped a pillow on the floor and stretched out beside Jūrō. They were joined by another, then another and another.

"What's this?" asked one of them, reaching out for the sheet of paper that had fallen from Jūrō's kimono. "Well, I'll be—it's a sutra. Now, what would a mean cuss like you be carrying a sutra for? "

Jūrō opened one sleepy eye and said lazily, "Oh, that? It's something the old woman copied. She said she'd sworn to make a thousand of them."

"Let me see it," said another man, making a grab for it. "What do you know? It's written out nice and clear. Why, anybody could read it."

"Does that mean you think *you* can read it?"

"Of course. It's child's play."

"All right then, let's hear some of it. Put a nice tune to it. Chant it like a priest."

"Are you joking? It's not a popular song."

"What difference does that make? A long time ago they used to sing sutras. That's how Buddhist hymns got started. You know a hymn when you hear one, don't you?"

"You can't chant these words to the tune of a hymn."

"Well, use any tune you like."

"You sing, Jūrō."

Encouraged by the enthusiasm of the others, Jūrō, still lying on his back, opened the sutra above his face and began:

"The Sutra on the Great Love of Parents.

Thus have I heard.
Once when the Buddha was on the Sacred Vulture Peak
In the City of Royal Palaces,
Preaching to bodhisattvas and disciples,
There gathered a multitude of monks and nuns and lay believers, both male and
    female,
All the people of all the heavens, dragon gods and demons,
To hear the Sacred Law.
Around the jeweled throne they gathered
And gazed, with unwavering eyes,
At the holy face—"

"What's all that mean?"

"When it says 'nuns,' does it mean the girls we call nuns? You know, I heard some of the nuns from Yoshiwara have started powdering their faces gray and will give it to you for less than in the whorehouses—"

"Quiet!"

> "At this time the Buddha
> Preached the Law as follows:
> 'All ye good men and good women,
> Acknowledge your debt for your father's compassion,
> Acknowledge your debt for your mother's mercy.
> For the life of a human being in this world
> Has karma as its basic cause,
> But parents as its immediate means of origin.'"

"It's just talking about being good to your mama and daddy. You've already heard it a million times."

"Shh!"

"Sing some more. We'll be quiet."

> "'Without a father, the child is not born.
> Without a mother, the child is not nourished.
> The spirit comes from the father's seed;
> The body grows within the mother's womb.'"

Jūrō paused to rearrange himself and pick his nose, then resumed.

> "'Because of these relationships,
> The concern of a mother for her child
> Is without comparison in this world. . . .'"

Noticing how silent the others were, Jūrō asked, "Are you listening?"

"Yes. Go on."

> "'From the time when she receives the child in her womb,
> During the passage of nine months,
> Going, coming, sitting, sleeping,
> She is visited by suffering.
> She ceases to have her customary love for food or drink or clothing
> And worries solely about a safe delivery.'"

"I'm tired," complained Jūrō. "That's enough, isn't it?"

"No. Keep singing. We're listening."

> "'The months are full, and the days sufficient.
> At the time of birth, the winds of karma hasten it on,
> Her bones are racked with pain.
> The father, too, trembles and is afraid.
> Relatives and servants worry and are distressed.
> When the child is born and dropped upon the grass,
> The boundless joy of the father and mother
> Match that of a penurious woman
> Who has found the omnipotent magic jewel.
> When the child utters its first sounds,
> The mother feels that she herself is born anew.
> Her chest becomes the child's place of rest;
> Her knees, its playground,

710

Her breasts, its source of food.
Her love, its very life.
Without its mother, the child cannot dress or undress.
Though the mother hungers,
She takes the food from her own mouth and gives it to her child.
Without the mother, the child cannot be nourished. . . .'"

"What's the matter? Why'd you stop?"
"Wait a minute, will you?"
"Will you look at that? He's crying like a baby."
"Aw, shut up!"

It had all begun as an idle way to pass the time, almost a joke, but the meaning of the words of the sutra was sinking in. Three or four others besides the reader had unsmiling faces, their eyes a faraway look.

"'The mother goes to the neighboring village to work.
She draws water, builds the fire,
Pounds the grain, makes the flour.
At night when she returns,
Before she reaches the house,
She hears the baby's crying
And is filled with love.
Her chest heaves, her heart cries out,
The milk flows forth, she cannot bear it.
She runs to the house.
The baby, seeing its mother approach from afar,
Works its brain, shakes its head,
And wails for her.
She bends her body,
Takes the child's two hands,
Places her lips upon its lips.
There is no greater love than this.
When the child is two,
He leaves the mother's breast.
But without his father, he would not know that fire can burn.
Without his mother, he would not know that a knife can cut off fingers.
When he is three, he is weaned and learns to eat.
Without his father, he would not know that poison can kill.
Without his mother, he would not know that medicine cures.
When the parents go to other houses
And are presented with marvelous delicacies,
They do not eat but put the food in their pockets
And take it home for the child, to make him rejoice. . . .'"

"You blubbering again?"
"I can't help it. I just remembered something."
"Cut it out. You'll have me doing it too."

Sentimentality with regard to parents was strictly taboo among these denizens of society's outer edge, for to express filial affection was to invite charges of weakness, effeminacy or worse. But it would have done Osugi's aging heart   *711* good to see them now. The sutra reading, possibly because of the simplicity of the language, had reached the core of their being.

"Is that all? Isn't there any more?"

"There's lots more."

"Well?"

"Wait a minute, will you?" Jūrō stood up, blew his nose loudly and sat down to intone the rest.

> "'The child grows.
> The father brings cloth to clothe him.
> The mother combs his locks.
> The parents give every beautiful thing they possess to him,
> Keeping for themselves only that which is old and worn.
> The child takes a bride
> And brings this stranger into the house.
> The parents become more distant.
> The new husband and wife are intimate with each other.
> They stay in their own room, talking happily with each other.'"

"That's the way it works, all right," broke in a voice.

> "'The parents grow old.
> Their spirits weaken, their strength diminishes.
> They have only the child to depend on,
> Only his wife to do things for them.
> But the child no longer comes to them,
> Neither at night nor in the daytime.
> Their room is cold.
> There is no more pleasant talk.
> They are like lonely guests at an inn.
> A crisis arises, and they call their child.
> Nine times in ten, he comes not,
> Nor does he serve them.
> He grows angry and reviles them,
> Saying it would be better to die
> Than to linger on unwanted in this world.
> The parents listen, and their hearts are filled with rage.
> Weaping, they say, "When you were young,
> Without us, you would not have been born,
> Without us, you could not have grown.
> Ah! How we—"'"

Jūrō broke off abruptly and threw the text aside. "I . . . I can't. Somebody else read it."

But there was no one to take his place. Lying on their backs, sprawled out on their bellies, sitting with their legs crossed and their heads drooping between their knees, they were as tearful as lost children.

Into the middle of this unlikely scene walked Sasaki Kojirō.

712

Spring Shower in Red

"Isn't Yajibei here?" Kojirō asked loudly.

The gamblers were so absorbed in their play, and the weepers in their memories of childhood, that no one replied.

Going over to Jūrō, who was lying on his back with his arms over his eyes, Kojirō said, "May I ask what's going on?"

"Oh, I didn't know it was you, sir." There was a hasty wiping of eyes and blowing of noses as Jūrō and the others pulled themselves to their feet and bowed sheepishly to their sword instructor.

"Are you crying?" he asked.

"Unh, yes. I mean, no."

"You're an odd one."

While the others drifted off, Jūrō began telling about his chance encounter with Musashi, happy to have a subject that might distract Kojirō's attention from the state of the young men's room. "Since the boss is away," he said, "we didn't know what to do, so Osugi decided to go and talk to you."

Kojirō's eyes flared brightly. "Musashi's putting up at an inn in Bakurōchō?"

"He was, but now he's staying at Zushino Kōsuke's house."

"That's an interesting coincidence."

"Is it?"

"It just happens I sent my Drying Pole to Zushino to work on. As a matter of fact, it should be ready now. I came this way today to pick it up."

"You've been there already?"

"Not yet. I thought I'd drop in here for a few minutes first."

"That's lucky. If you'd showed up suddenly, Musashi might have attacked you."

"I'm not afraid of him. But how can I confer with the old lady when she's not here?"

"I don't imagine she's reached Isarago yet. I'll send a good runner to bring her back."

At the council of war held that evening, Kojirō expressed the opinion that there was no reason to wait for Yajibei's return. He himself would serve as Osugi's second, so that she might, at long last, take her proper revenge. Jūrō and Koroku asked to go along too, more for the honor than to help. Though

713

aware of Musashi's reputation as a fighter, they never imagined he might be a match for their brilliant instructor.

Nothing could be done tonight, however. For all her enthusiasm, Osugi was dead tired and complained of a backache. They decided they would carry out their plan the following night.

The next afternoon, Osugi bathed under cold water, blackened her teeth and dyed her hair. At twilight, she made her preparations for battle, first donning a white underrobe she had bought to be buried in and had carried around with her for years. She had had it stamped for good luck at every shrine and temple she visited—Sumiyoshi Shrine in Osaka, Oyama Hachiman Shrine and Kiyomizudera in Kyoto, the Kannon Temple in Asakusa, and dozens of less prominent religious establishments in various parts of the country. The sacred imprints made the robe resemble a tie-dyed kimono; Osugi felt safer than she would have in a suit of mail.

She carefully tucked a letter to Matahachi into the sash under her obi, together with a copy of the *Sutra on the Great Love of Parents*. There was also a second letter, which she always carried in a small money pouch; this said: "Though I am old, it has become my lot to wander about the country in an effort to realize one great hope. There is no way of knowing but that I may be slain by my sworn enemy or die of illness by the wayside. Should this be my fate, I ask the officials and people of goodwill to use the money in this purse to send my body home. Sugi, widow of Hon'iden, Yoshino Village, Mimasaka Province."

With her sword in place, her shins wrapped in white leggings, fingerless gloves on her hands and a blind-stitched obi snugly holding her sleeveless kimono in place, her preparations were nearly complete. Placing a bowl of water on her writing table, she knelt before it and said, "I'm going now." She then closed her eyes and sat motionless, addressing her thoughts to Uncle Gon.

Jūrō opened the shoji a crack and peeked in. "Are you ready?" he asked. "It's about time we were leaving. Kojirō's waiting."

"I'm ready."

Joining the others, she went to the place of honor they had left open for her before the alcove. The Acolyte took a cup from the table, put it in Osugi's hand and carefully poured her a cupful of sake. Then he did the same for Kojirō and Jūrō. When each of the four had drunk, they extinguished the lamp and set forth.

Quite a few of the Hangawara men clamored to be taken along, but Kojirō refused, since a large group would not only attract attention but encumber them in a fight.

As they were going out the gate, one young man called to them to wait. He then struck sparks from a flint to wish them luck. Outside, under a sky murky with rain clouds, nightingales were singing.

As they made their way through the dark, silent streets, dogs started barking, set off, perhaps, by some instinctive sense that these four human beings were on a sinister mission.

"What's that?" Koroku asked, staring back along a narrow lane.

"Did you see something?"

"Somebody's following us."

"Probably one of the fellows from the house," said Kojirō. "They were all so eager to come with us."

"They'd rather brawl than eat."

They turned a corner, and Kojirō stopped under the eaves of a house, saying, "Kōsuke's shop's around here, isn't it?" Their voices dropped to whispers.

"Down the street, there, on the other side."

"What do we do now?" asked Koroku.

"Proceed according to plan. The three of you hide in the shadows. I'll go to the shop."

"What if Musashi tries to sneak out the back door?"

"Don't worry. He's no more likely to run away from me than I am from him. If he ran away, he'd be finished as a swordsman."

"Maybe we should position ourselves on opposite sides of the house anyway—just in case."

"All right. Now, as we agreed, I'll bring Musashi outside and walk along with him. When we get near Osugi, I'll draw my sword and take him by surprise. That's the time for her to come out and strike."

Osugi was beside herself with gratitude. "Thank you, Kojirō. You're so good to me. You must be an incarnation of the great Hachiman." She clasped her hands and bowed, as if before the god of war himself.

In his heart, Kojirō was thoroughly convinced that he was doing the right thing. Indeed, it is doubtful that ordinary mortals could imagine the vastness of his self-righteousness at the moment he stepped up to Kōsuke's door.

At the beginning, when Musashi and Kojirō had been very young, full of spirit and eager to demonstrate their superiority, there had existed no deep-seated cause for enmity between them. There had been rivalry, to be sure, but only the friction that normally arose between two strong and almost equally matched fighters. What had subsequently rankled with Kojirō was seeing Musashi gradually gaining fame as a swordsman. Musashi, for his part, respected Kojirō's extraordinary skill, if not his character, and always treated him with a certain amount of caution. As the years passed, however, they found themselves at odds over various matters—the House of Yoshioka, the fate of Akemi, the affair of the Hon'iden dowager. Conciliation was by now out of the question.

And now that Kojirō had taken it upon himself to become Osugi's protector, the trend of events bore the unmistakable seal of fate.

"Kōsuke!" Kojirō rapped lightly on the door. "Are you awake?" Light seeped through a crack, but there was no other sign of life inside.

After a few moments, a voice asked, "Who's there?"

"Iwama Kakubei gave you my sword to work on. I've come for it."

"The great long one—is that the one?"

"Open up and let me in."

"Just a moment."

The door slid open, and the two men eyed each other. Blocking the way, Kōsuke said curtly, "The sword's not ready yet."

"I see." Kojirō brushed past Kōsuke and seated himself on the step leading up to the shop. "When will it be ready?"

"Well, let's see. . . ." Kōsuke rubbed his chin, pulling the corners of his eyes down and making his long face seem even longer.

Kojirō had the feeling he was being made fun of. "Don't you think it's taking an awful long time?"

"I told Kakubei very clearly I couldn't promise when I'd finish."

"I can't do without it much longer."

"In that case, take it back."

"What's this?" Kojirō was taken aback. Artisans didn't talk that way to samurai. But instead of trying to ascertain what might be behind the man's attitude, he jumped to the conclusion that his visit had been anticipated. Thinking it best to act quickly, he said, "By the way, I heard Miyamoto Musashi, from Mimasaka, is staying here with you."

"Where did you hear that?" Kōsuke said, looking anxious. "As it happens, he is staying with us."

"Would you mind calling him? I haven't seen him for a long time, since we were both in Kyoto."

"What's your name?"

"Sasaki Kojirō. He'll know who I am."

"I'll tell him you're here, but I don't know whether he can see you or not."

"Just a moment."

"Yes?"

"Perhaps I'd better explain. I happened to hear at Lord Hosokawa's house that a man of Musashi's description was living here. I came with the idea of inviting Musashi out to drink a little and talk a little."

"I see." Kōsuke turned and went toward the back of the house.

Kojirō mulled over what to do if Musashi smelled a rat and refused to see him. Two or three stratagems came to mind, but before he had come to a decision, he was startled by a horrendous howling scream.

He jumped like a man who had been savagely kicked. He had miscalculated. His strategy had been seen through—not only seen through but turned against him. Musashi must have sneaked out the back door, gone around to the front and attacked. But who had screamed? Osugi? Jūrō? Koroku?

"If that's the way it is . . ." thought Kojirō grimly, as he ran out into the street. Muscles taut, blood racing, in an instant he was ready for anything. "I have to fight him sooner or later anyway," he thought. He had known this since that day at the pass on Mount Hiei. The time had come! If Osugi had already been struck down, Kojirō swore that Musashi's blood would become an offering for the eternal peace of her soul.

He had covered about ten paces when he heard his name called from the side of the road. The painfully forced voice seemed to clutch at his running footsteps.

716   "Koroku, is that you?"

"I-I-I've b-been h-h-hit."

"Jūrō! Where's Jūrō?"

"H-him too."

"Where is he?" Before the answer came, Kojirō spotted Jūrō's blood-soaked form about thirty feet away. His entire body bristling with vigilance for his own safety, he thundered, "Koroku! Which way did Musashi go?"

"No . . . not . . . Musashi." Koroku, unable to lift his head, rolled it from side to side.

"What are you saying? Are you telling me it wasn't Musashi who attacked you?"

"Not . . . not . . . Musa—"

"Who was it?"

It was a question Koroku would never answer.

His thoughts in a turmoil, Kojirō ran to Jūrō and pulled him up by the red, sticky collar of his kimono. "Jūrō, tell me. Who did it? Which way did he go?"

But Jūrō, instead of answering, used his last tearful breath to say, "Mother . . . sorry . . . shouldn't have . . ."

"What are you talking about?" snorted Kojirō, letting go of the bloody garment.

"Kojirō! Kojirō, is that you?"

Running in the direction of Osugi's voice, he saw the old woman lying helpless in a ditch, straw and vegetable peelings clinging to her face and hair. "Get me out of here," she pleaded.

"What are you doing in that filthy water?"

Kojirō, sounding more angry than sympathetic, yanked her unceremoniously out onto the road, where she collapsed like a rag.

"Where did the man go?" she asked, taking the words out of his mouth.

"What man? Who attacked you?"

"I don't know exactly what happened, but I'm sure it was the man who was following us."

"Did he attack suddenly?"

"Yes! Out of nowhere, like a gust of wind. There was no time to speak. He jumped out of the shadows and got Jūrō first. By the time Koroku drew his sword, he was wounded too."

"Which way did he go?"

"He shoved me aside, so I didn't even see him, but the footsteps went that way." She pointed toward the river.

Running across a vacant lot where the horse market was held, Kojirō came to the dike at Yanagihara and stopped to look around. Some distance away, he could see piles of lumber, lights and people.

When he got closer, he saw they were palanquin bearers. "My two companions have been struck down in a side street near here," he said. "I want you to pick them up and take them to the house of Hangawara Yajibei in the carpenters' district. You'll find an old woman with them. Take her too."

"Were they attacked by robbers?"

"Are there robbers around here?"

"Packs of them. Even we have to be careful."

"Whoever it was must have come running out from that corner over there. Didn't you see anyone?"

"Just now, you mean?"

"Yes."

"I'm leaving," said the bearer. He and the others picked up three palanquins and prepared to depart.

"What about the fare?" asked one.

"Collect it when you get there."

Kojirō made a quick search of the riverbank and around the stacks of lumber, deciding as he did so that he'd do just as well to go back to Yajibei's house. There was little point in meeting Musashi without Osugi; it also seemed unwise to face the man in his present state of mind.

Starting back, he came to a firebreak, along one side of which grew a row of paulownia trees. He looked at it for a minute, then as he turned away, he saw the glint of a blade among the trees. Before he knew it, half a dozen leaves fell. The sword had been aimed at his head.

"Yellow-livered coward!" he shouted.

"Not me!" came the reply as the sword struck out a second time from the darkness.

Kojirō whirled and jumped back a full seven feet. "If you're Musashi, why don't you use the proper—" Before he could finish, the sword was at him again. "Who are you?" he shouted. "Aren't you making a mistake?"

He dodged a third stroke successfully, and the attacker, badly winded, realized before attempting a fourth that he was wasting his effort. Changing tactics, he began inching forward with his blade extended before him. His eyes were shooting fire. "Silence," he growled. "There's no mistake at all. Perhaps it'll refresh your memory if you know my name. I'm Hōjō Shinzō."

"You're one of Obata's students, aren't you?"

"You insulted my master and killed several of my comrades."

"By the warrior's code, you're free to challenge me openly at any time. Sasaki Kojirō doesn't play hide-and-seek."

"I'll kill you."

"Go ahead and try."

As Kojirō watched him close the distance—twelve feet, eleven, ten—he quietly loosened the upper part of his kimono and placed his right hand on his sword. "Come on!" he cried.

The challenge caused an involuntary hesitation on Shinzō's part, a momentary wavering. Kojirō's body bent forward, his arm snapped like a bow, and there was a metallic ring. The next instant, his sword clicked sharply back into its scabbard. There had been only a thin flashing thread of light.

Shinzō was still standing, his legs spread apart. There was no sign of blood yet, but it was plain that he'd been wounded. Though his sword was still stretched out at eye level, his left hand had gone reflexively to his neck.

"Oh!" Gasps went up on both sides of Shinzō at the same time—from Kojirō and from a man running up behind Shinzō. The sound of footsteps, together with the voice, sent Kojirō off into the darkness.

"What happened?" cried Kōsuke. He reached out to support Shinzō, only to have the full weight of the other man's body fall into his arms. "Oh, this looks bad!" cried Kōsuke. "Help! Help, somebody!"

A piece of flesh no larger than a clamshell fell from Shinzō's neck. The blood gushing out soaked first Shinzō's arm, then the skirts of his kimono all the way to his feet.

A Block of Wood

Plunk. Another green plum fell from the tree in the dark garden outside. Musashi ignored it, if he heard it at all. In the bright but unsteady lamplight, his disheveled hair appeared heavy and bristly, lacking in natural oil and reddish in color.

"What a difficult child!" his mother had often complained. The stubborn disposition that had so often reduced her to tears was still with him, as enduring as the scar on his head left by a large carbuncle during childhood.

Memories of his mother now floated through his mind; at times the face he was carving closely resembled hers.

A few minutes earlier Kōsuke had come to the door, hesitated and called in: "Are you still working? A man named Sasaki Kojirō says he'd like to see you. He's waiting downstairs. Do you want to speak to him, or shall I tell him you've already gone to bed?"

Musashi had the vague impression Kōsuke had repeated his message but wasn't sure whether he himself had answered.

The small table, Musashi's knees and the floor immediately around him were littered with wood chips. He was trying to finish the image of Kannon he had promised Kōsuke in exchange for the sword. His task had been made even more challenging because of a special request by Kōsuke, a man of pronounced likes and dislikes.

When Kōsuke had first taken the ten-inch block out of a cupboard and very gently handed it to him, Musashi saw that it must have been six or seven hundred years old. Kōsuke treated it like an heirloom, for it had come from an eighth-century temple at the tomb of Prince Shōtoku in Shinaga. "I was on a trip there," he explained, "and they were repairing the old buildings. Some stupid priests and carpenters were axing up the old beams for firewood. I couldn't stand seeing the wood wasted that way, so I got them to cut off this block for me."

The grain was good, as was the feel of the wood to the knife, but thinking of how highly Kōsuke valued his treasure made Musashi nervous. If he made a slip, he would ruin an irreplaceable piece of material.

He heard a bang, which sounded like the wind blowing open the gate in the garden hedge. Looking up from his work, for almost the first time since he had begun carving, he thought: "Could that be Iori?" and cocked his head, waiting for confirmation.

"What're you standing there gaping for?" Kōsuke shouted at his wife. "Can't you see the man's badly wounded? It doesn't make any difference which room!"

Behind Kōsuke, the men carrying Shinzō excitedly offered to help.

"Any spirits to wash the wound with? If there aren't, I'll go home for some."

"I'll fetch the doctor."

After the commotion died down a bit, Kōsuke said, "I want to thank all of you. I think we saved his life; no more need to worry." He bowed deeply to each man as he left the house.

Finally it penetrated Musashi's consciousness that something had happened and Kōsuke was involved. Brushing the chips from his knees, he descended the staircase formed by the tops of tiered storage chests and went to the room where Kōsuke and his wife stood staring down at the wounded man.

"Oh, are you still awake?" asked the sword polisher, moving over to make a place for Musashi.

Sitting down near the man's pillow, Musashi looked closely at his face and inquired, "Who is he?"

"I couldn't have been more surprised. I didn't recognize him until we got him back here, but it's Hōjō Shinzō, the son of Lord Hōjō of Awa. He's a very dedicated young man who's been studying under Obata Kagenori for several years."

Musashi carefully lifted the edge of the white bandage around Shinzō's neck and examined the wound, which had been cauterized, then washed with alcohol. The clam-sized piece of flesh had been sliced out cleanly, exposing the pulsating carotid artery. Death had come that close. "Who?" Musashi wondered. From the shape of the wound, it seemed probable the sword had been on the upswing of a swallow-flight stroke.

Swallow-flight stroke? Kojirō's specialty.

"Do you know what happened?" Musashi asked.

"Not yet."

"Neither do I, of course, but I can tell you this much." He nodded his head confidently. "It's the work of Sasaki Kojirō."

Back in his own room, Musashi lay down on the tatami with his hands under his head, ignoring the mess around him. His pallet had been spread, but he ignored that too, despite his fatigue.

720   He had been working on the statue for nearly forty-eight hours straight.

Not being a sculptor, he lacked the technical skills necessary to solve difficult problems, nor could he execute the deft strokes that would cover up a mistake. He had nothing to go on but the image of Kannon he carried in his heart, and his sole technique was to clear his mind of extraneous thoughts and do his best to faithfully transfer this image to the wood.

He would think for a time that the sculpture was taking form, but then somehow it would go wrong, some slip would occur between the image in his mind and the hand working with the dagger. Just as he felt he was making progress again, the carving would get out of hand again. After many false starts, the ancient piece of wood had shrunk to a length of no more than four inches.

He heard a nightingale call twice, then dropped off to sleep for perhaps an hour. When he awoke, his strong body was surging with energy, his mind perfectly clear. As he arose, he thought: "I'll make it this time." Going to the well behind the house, he washed his face and swilled water through his teeth. Refreshed, he sat down by the lamp again and took up his work with renewed vigor.

The knife had a different feel to it now. In the grain of the wood he sensed the centuries of history contained within the block. He knew that if he did not carve skillfully this time, there would be nothing left but a pile of useless chips. For the next few hours, he concentrated with feverish intensity. Not once did his back unbend, nor did he stop for a drink of water. The sky grew light, the birds began to sing, all the doors in the house save his were thrown open for the morning's cleaning. Still, his attention remained focused on the tip of his knife.

"Musashi, are you all right?" asked his host in a worried tone, as he slid open the shoji and entered the room.

"It's no good," Musashi sighed. He straightened up and tossed his dagger aside. The block of wood was no larger than a man's thumb. The wood around his legs lay like fallen snow.

"No good?"

"No good."

"How about the wood?"

"Gone. . . . I couldn't get the bodhisattva's form to emerge." Placing his hands behind his head, he felt himself returning to earth after having been suspended for an indeterminate length of time between delusion and enlightenment. "No good at all. It's time to forget and to meditate."

He lay on his back. When he closed his eyes, distractions seemed to fade away, to be replaced by a blinding mist. Gradually, his mind filled with the single idea of the infinite void.

Most of the guests leaving the inn that morning were horse traders, going home after the four-day market that had ended the day before. For the next few weeks, the inn would see few customers.

Catching sight of Iori going up the stairs, the proprietress called out to him from the office.

"What do you want?" asked Iori. From his vantage point, he could see the woman's artfully disguised bald spot.

"Where do you think you're going?"

"Upstairs, where my teacher is. Something wrong?"

"More than you know," replied the woman with an exasperated glance. "Just when did you leave here?"

Counting on his fingers, Iori answered, "The day before the day before yesterday, I think."

"Three days ago, wasn't it?"

"That's right."

"You certainly took your time, didn't you? What happened? Did a fox bewitch you or something?"

"How'd you know? You must be a fox yourself." Giggling at his own riposte, he started for the top of the stairs again.

"Your teacher's not here anymore."

"I don't believe you." He ran up the stairs, but soon came back with a dismayed look on his face. "Has he changed rooms?"

"What's the matter with you? I told you he left."

"Really gone?" There was alarm in the boy's voice.

"If you don't believe me, look at the account book. See?"

"But why? Why would he leave before I got back?"

"Because you were gone too long."

"But . . . but . . ." Iori burst into tears. "Where did he go? Please tell me."

"He didn't tell me where he was going. I imagine he left you behind because you're so useless."

His color changing, Iori charged out into the street. He looked east, west, then he gazed up at the sky. Tears poured down his cheeks.

Scratching the bald spot with a comb, the woman broke into raucous laughter. "Stop your bawling," she called. "I was only fooling. Your teacher's staying at the sword polisher's, over there." She had barely finished speaking when a straw horseshoe came sailing into the office.

Meekly, Iori sat down in formal fashion at Musashi's feet and in a subdued voice announced, "I'm back."

He'd already noticed the atmosphere of gloom hanging over the house. The wood chips had not been cleaned up, and the burned-out lamp was still sitting where it had been the night before.

"I'm back," Iori repeated, no more loudly than before.

"Who is it?" mumbled Musashi, slowly opening his eyes.

"Iori."

Musashi sat up quickly. Although relieved to see the boy back safe, his only greeting was: "Oh, it's you."

"I'm sorry I took so long." This met with silence. "Forgive me." Neither his apology nor a polite bow elicited a response.

Musashi tightened his obi and said, "Open the windows and tidy up the room."

He was out the door before Iori had time to say, "Yes, sir."

Musashi went to the room downstairs at the back and asked Kōsuke how the invalid was this morning.

"He seems to be resting better."

"You must be tired. Shall I come back after breakfast so you can have a rest?"

Kōsuke answered that there was no need. "There is one thing I would like to see done," he added. "I think we should let the Obata School know about this, but I don't have anybody to send."

Having offered to either go himself or send Iori, Musashi went back to his own room, which was now in good order. As he sat down, he said, "Iori, was there an answer to my letter?"

Relieved at not being scolded, the boy broke into a smile. "Yes, I brought a reply. It's right here." With a look of triumph, he fished the letter from his kimono.

"Let me have it."

Iori advanced on his knees and placed the folded paper in Musashi's outstretched hand. "I am sorry to say," Sukekurō had written, "that Lord Munenori, as tutor to the shōgun, cannot engage in a bout with you, as you requested. If, however, you should visit us for some other purpose, there is a possibility that his lordship may greet you in the dōjō. If you still feel strongly about trying your hand against the Yagyū Style, the best plan, I think, would be for you to confront Yagyū Hyōgo. I regret to say, however, that he left yesterday for Yamato to be at the bedside of Lord Sekishūsai, who is gravely ill. Such being the case, I must ask you to postpone your visit until a later day. I shall be happy to make arrangements at that time."

As he slowly refolded the lengthy scroll, Musashi smiled. Iori, feeling more secure, extended his legs comfortably and said, "The house is not in Kobiki-chō; it's at a place called Higakubo. It's very large, very splendid, and Kimura Sukekurō gave me lots of good things to eat—"

His eyebrows arching in disapproval at this display of familiarity, Musashi said gravely, "Iori."

The boy's legs quickly shot back to their proper place under him. "Yes, sir."

"Even if you did get lost, don't you think three days is a rather long time? What happened?"

"I was bewitched by a fox."

"A fox?"

"Yes, sir, a fox."

"How could a boy like you, born and raised in the country, be bewitched by a fox?"

"I don't know, but afterward I couldn't remember where I'd been for half a day and half a night."

"Hmm. Very strange."

"Yes, sir. I thought so myself. Maybe foxes in Edo have it in for people more than the ones in the country do."

"I suspect that's true." Taking into account the boy's seriousness, Musashi   723 did not have the heart to scold him, but he did feel it necessary to pursue his point. "I also suspect," he continued, "you were up to something you shouldn't have been up to."

"Well, the fox was following me, and to keep it from bewitching me, I cut it with my sword. Then the fox punished me for that."

"No, it didn't."

"Didn't it?"

"No. It wasn't the fox punishing you; it was your own conscience, which is invisible. Now, you sit there and think about that for a while. When I come back, you can tell me what you think it means."

"Yes, sir. Are you going somewhere?"

"Yes; to a place near the Hirakawa Shrine in Kōjimachi."

"You'll be back by evening, won't you?"

"Ha, ha. I should be, unless a fox gets me."

Musashi departed, leaving Iori to ponder his conscience. Outside, the sky was obscured by the dull, sullen clouds of the summer rainy season.

The Deserted Prophet

The forest around the Hirakawa Tenjin Shrine was alive with the hum of cicadas. An owl hooted as Musashi walked from the gate to the entrance hall of the Obata house.

"Good day!" he called, but his greeting echoed back as though from an empty cavern.

After a time, he heard footsteps. The young samurai who emerged wearing his two swords was clearly no mere underling assigned to answer the door.

Without bothering to kneel, he said, "May I ask your name?" Though no more than twenty-four or -five, he gave the impression of being someone to be reckoned with.

"My name is Miyamoto Musashi. Am I correct in thinking this is Obata Kagenori's academy of military science?"

"That's right," came the reply, in clipped tones. From the samurai's manner, it was evident he expected Musashi to explain how he was traveling around to perfect his knowledge of the martial arts, and so on.

"One of the students from your school has been wounded in a fight," said Musashi. "He's now being cared for by the sword polisher Zushino Kōsuke, whom I believe you know. I came at Kōsuke's request."

"It must be Shinzō!" There were fleeting signs of severe shock, but the youth recovered immediately. "Forgive me. I'm Kagenori's only son, Yogorō. Thank you for taking the trouble to come and tell us. Is Shinzō's life in danger?"

"He seemed better this morning, but it's still too early for him to be moved. I think it'd be wise to let him stay at Kōsuke's house for the time being."

"I hope you'll convey our thanks to Kōsuke."

"I'd be happy to."

"To tell the truth, since my father is bedridden, Shinzō was lecturing in his stead, until last fall when he suddenly left. As you can see, there's almost nobody here now. I regret we're not able to receive you properly."

"Of course; but tell me, is there a feud going on between your school and Sasaki Kojirō?"

"Yes. I was away when it started, so I don't know all the details, but apparently Kojirō insulted my father, which of course incited the students. They took it upon themselves to punish Kojirō, but he killed several of them. As I understand it, Shinzō left because he finally came to the conclusion that he himself should take revenge."

"I see. It's beginning to make sense. I'd like to give you a bit of advice. Don't fight Kojirō. He can't be beaten by ordinary sword techniques, and he's even less vulnerable to clever strategy. As a fighter, as a speaker, as a strategist, he's without rival, even among the greatest masters alive today."

This assessment brought a burst of angry fire to Yogorō's eyes. Observing this, Musashi felt it prudent to repeat his warning. "Let the proud have their day," he added. "It's senseless to risk disaster over a trivial grievance. Don't entertain the idea that Shinzō's defeat makes it necessary for you to settle the score. If you do, you'll simply follow in his footsteps. That would be foolish, very foolish."

After Musashi was out of sight, Yogorō leaned against the wall with his arms folded. Softly, in a faintly tremulous voice, he muttered, "To think it's come to this. Even Shinzō has failed!" Gazing vacantly at the ceiling, he thought of the letter Shinzō had left for him, in which he'd said that his purpose in leaving was to kill Kojirō and that if he did not succeed, Yogorō would probably never see him alive again.

That Shinzō was not dead did not make his defeat any less humiliating. With the school forced to suspend operations, the public in general had concluded that Kojirō was right: the Obata Academy was a school for cowards, or at best for theoreticians devoid of practical ability. This had led to the desertion of some of the students. Others, apprehensive over Kagenori's illness or the apparent decline of the Kōshū Style, had switched to the rival Naganuma Style. Only two or three were still in residence.

Yogorō decided not to tell his father about Shinzō. It seemed that the only course open to him was to nurse the old man as best he could, although the doctor's opinion was that recovery was out of the question.

"Yogorō, where are you?"

It was a source of constant amazement to Yogorō that although Kagenori was at death's door, when an impulse moved him to summon his son, his voice became that of a perfectly healthy man.

"Coming." He ran to the sickroom, fell to his knees and said, "You called?"

As he often did when he was tired of lying flat on his back, Kagenori had propped himself up by the window, using his pillow as an armrest. "Who was the samurai who just went out the gate?" he asked.

"Huh," said Yogorō, somewhat flustered. "Oh, him. Nobody in particular. He was just a messenger."

"Messenger from where?"

"Well, it seems Shinzō has had an accident. The samurai came to tell us. He gave his name as Miyamoto Musashi."

"Mm. He wasn't born in Edo, was he?"

"No. I've heard he's from Mimasaka. He's a rōnin. Did you think you recognized him?"

"No," Kagenori replied with a vigorous shake of his thin gray beard. "I don't recall ever having seen or heard of him. But there's something about him. . . . I've met a lot of people during my lifetime, you know, on the battlefield as well as in ordinary life. Some were very good people, people I valued greatly. But the ones I could consider to be genuine samurai, in every sense of the term, were very few. This man—Musashi, did you say?—appealed to me. I'd like to meet him, talk to him a little. Go bring him back."

"Yes, sir," Yogorō answered obediently, but before getting to his feet, he continued in a slightly puzzled tone: "What was it you noticed about him? You only saw him from a distance."

"You wouldn't understand. When you do, you'll be old and withered like me."

"But there must have been something."

"I admired his alertness. He wasn't taking any chances, even on a sick old man like me. When he came through the gate, he paused and looked around—at the layout of the house, at the windows, whether they were open or closed, at the path to the garden—everything. He took it all in at a single glance. There was nothing unnatural about it. Anyone would have assumed he was simply halting for a moment as a sign of deference. I was amazed."

"Then you believe he's a samurai of real merit?"

"Perhaps. I'm sure he'd be a fascinating man to talk to. Call him back."

"Aren't you afraid it'll be bad for you?" Kagenori had become quite excited, and Yogorō was reminded of the doctor's warning that his father shouldn't talk for any length of time.

"Don't worry your head about my health. I've been waiting for years to meet a man like that. I didn't study military science all this time to teach it to children. I grant that my theories of military science are called the Kōshū Style, but they're not simply an extension of the formulas used by the famous Kōshū warriors. My ideas differ from those of Takeda Shingen, or Uesugi Kenshin, or Oda Nobunaga, or the other generals who were fighting for control of the country. The purpose of military science has changed since then.

My theory is directed toward the achievement of peace and stability. You know some of these things, but the question is, whom can I entrust my ideas to?"

Yogorō was silent.

"My son, while there are many things I want to pass on to you, you're still immature, too immature to recognize the remarkable qualities of the man you just met."

Yogorō dropped his eyes but endured the criticism in silence.

"If even I, inclined as I am to look favorably on everything you do, see you as immature, then there's no doubt in my mind. You're not yet the person who can carry on my work, so I must find the right man and entrust your future to him. I've been waiting for the right person to come along. Remember, when the cherry blossom falls, it must rely on the wind to spread its pollen."

"You mustn't fall, Father. You must try to live."

The old man glared and raised his head. "Talk like that proves you're still a child! Now go quickly and find the samurai!"

"Yes, sir!"

"Don't push him. Just tell him roughly what I've told you, and bring him back with you."

"Right away, Father."

Yogorō departed on the run. Once outside, he first tried the direction he'd seen Musashi take. Then he looked all over the shrine grounds, even went out to the main street running through Kōjimachi, but to no avail.

He was not unduly disturbed, for he was not as thoroughly convinced as his father of Musashi's superiority, nor was he grateful for Musashi's warning. The talk about Kojirō's unusual ability, about the folly of "risking disaster over a trivial grievance" had stuck in his craw. It was as though Musashi's visit had been for the express purpose of singing Kojirō's praises.

Even while listening submissively to his father, he had been thinking to himself: "I'm not as young and immature as you say." And the truth was that just then, he really couldn't have cared less what Musashi thought.

They were about the same age. Even if Musashi's talent was exceptional, there were limits to what he could know and what he could do. In the past, Yogorō had gone away for a year, two years, even three, to lead the life of the ascetic *shugyōsha*. He had lived and studied for a while at the school of another military expert, and he had studied Zen under a strict master. Yet his father, after merely catching a glimpse of the man, had not only formed what Yogorō suspected was an exaggerated opinion of the unknown rōnin's worth but had gone so far as to suggest that Yogorō take Musashi as a model.

"May as well go back," he thought sadly. "I suppose there's no way to convince a parent that his son is no longer a child." He longed desperately for the day when Kagenori would look at him and suddenly see that he was both a grown man and a brave samurai. It pained him to think that his father might die before that day arrived.

"Hey, Yogorō! It is Yogorō, isn't it?"

Yogorō turned on his heel and saw that the voice belonged to Nakatogawa Handayū, a samurai from the House of Hosokawa. They had not seen each other recently, but there had been a time when Handayū had attended Kagenori's lectures regularly.

"How's our revered teacher's health? Official duties keep me so busy I haven't had time to call."

"He's about the same, thanks."

"Say, I hear Hōjō Shinzō attacked Sasaki Kojirō and was beaten."

"You've heard that already?"

"Yes; they were talking about it at Lord Hosokawa's this morning."

"It only happened last night."

"Kojirō's a guest of Iwama Kakubei. Kakubei must have passed the word around. Even Lord Tadatoshi knew about it."

Yogorō was too young to listen with detachment, yet he was loath to reveal his anger by some involuntary twitch. Taking leave of Handayū as quickly as possible, he hurried home.

His mind was made up.

The Talk of the Town

Kōsuke's wife was in the kitchen making gruel for Shinzō when Iori came in.

"The plums are turning yellow," he said.

"If they're almost ripe, that means the cicadas will be singing soon," she answered absently.

"Don't you pickle the plums?"

"No. There aren't many of us here, and pickling all those plums would take several pounds of salt."

"The salt wouldn't go to waste, but the plums will if you don't pickle them. And if there was a war or a flood, they'd come in handy, wouldn't they? Since you're busy taking care of the wounded man, I'll be happy to pickle them for you."

"My, what a funny child you are, worrying about floods and such. You think like an old man."

Iori was already getting an empty wooden bucket out of the closet. With this in hand, he sauntered out into the garden and looked up at the plum tree. Alas, though sufficiently grown up to worry about the future, he was still young enough to be easily distracted by the sight of a buzzing cicada. Sneaking closer, he captured it and held it in his cupped hands, making it screech like a terrified hag.

Peeking between his thumbs, Iori experienced a strange sensation. Insects were supposed to be bloodless, he thought, but the cicada felt warm. Perhaps even cicadas when faced with the peril of death gave off body heat. Suddenly he was seized by a mixture of fear and pity. Spreading his palms, he tossed the cicada into the air and watched it fly off toward the street.

The plum tree, which was quite large, was the home of a sizable community—fat caterpillars with surprisingly beautiful fur, ladybirds, tiny blue frogs clinging to the undersides of leaves, small sleeping butterflies, dancing gadflies. Gazing in fascination at this little corner of the animal kingdom, he thought it would be inhuman to throw these ladies and gentlemen into consternation by shaking a branch. Carefully, he reached out, picked a plum and bit into it. Then he shook the nearest branch gently and was surprised when the fruit did not fall off. Reaching out, he picked a few plums and dropped them into the bucket below.

"Son of a bitch!" shouted Iori, abruptly firing three or four plums into the narrow lane next to the house. The clothes-drying pole between the house and the fence fell to the ground with a clatter, and footsteps hastily retreated from the lane into the street.

Kōsuke's face appeared at the bamboo grille of his workroom window. "What was that noise?" he asked, his eyes wide with astonishment.

Jumping down from the tree, Iori cried, "Another strange man was hiding in the shadows, squatting right there in the lane. I threw some plums at him, and he ran away."

The sword polisher came outside, wiping his hands on a towel. "What sort of man?"

"A thug."

"One of Hangawara's men?"

"I don't know. Why do those men come snooping around here?"

"They're looking for a chance to get back at Shinzō."

Iori looked toward the back room, where the injured man was just finishing his gruel. His wound had healed to the extent that the bandage was no longer necessary.

"Kōsuke," called Shinzō.

The craftsman walked to the edge of the veranda and asked, "How are you feeling?"

Pushing his tray aside, Shinzō reseated himself more formally. "I want to apologize for causing you so much trouble."

"Don't mention it. I'm sorry I've been too busy to do more for you."

"I notice that besides worrying about me, you're being annoyed by those Hangawara hoodlums. The longer I stay, the more danger there is that they'll come to regard you as an enemy too. I think I should be leaving."

"Don't give it a thought."

"I'm much better now, as you can see. I'm ready to go home."

"Today?"

"Yes."

"Don't be in such a hurry. At least wait until Musashi comes back."

"I'd rather not, but please thank him for me. He's been very kind to me too. I can walk all right now."

"You don't seem to understand. Hangawara's men are watching this house day and night. They'll pounce on you the minute you step outside. I can't possibly let you leave alone."

"I had a good reason for killing Jūrō and Koroku. Kojirō started all this, not me. But if they want to attack me, let them attack."

Shinzō was on his feet and ready to go. Sensing there was no way of holding him back, Kōsuke and his wife went to the front of the shop to see him off.

Musashi appeared at the door just then, his sunburned forehead moist with sweat. "Going out?" he asked. "Going home? . . . Well, I'm glad to see you feel well enough, but it'd be dangerous to go alone. I'll go with you."

Shinzō tried to refuse, but Musashi insisted. Minutes later, they set off together.

"It must be difficult to walk after being in bed so long."

"Somehow the ground seems higher than it really is."

"It's a long way to Hirakawa Tenjin. Why don't we hire a palanquin for you?"

"I suppose I ought to have mentioned it before. I'm not going back to the school."

"Oh? Where then?"

Casting his eyes downward, Shinzō answered, "It's rather humiliating, but I think I'll go to my father's house for a while. It's in Ushigome."

Musashi stopped a palanquin and virtually forced Shinzō into it. Despite the insistence of the bearers, Musashi refused one for himself—to the disappointment of the Hangawara men watching from around the next corner.

"Look, he put Shinzō into a palanquin."

"I saw him glance this way."

"It's too early to do anything yet."

After the palanquin turned right by the outer moat, they hitched up their skirts, pulled back their sleeves, and followed along behind, their glittering eyes seemingly ready to pop out and shoot toward Musashi's back.

Musashi and Shinzō had reached the neighborhood of Ushigafuchi when a small rock glanced off the palanquin pole. At the same time, the gang started shouting and moved in to surround its prey.

"Wait!" called one of them.

"Just stay where you are, you bastard!"

The bearers, terrified, dropped the palanquin and fled. Shinzō crawled out of the palanquin, hand on sword. Pulling himself to his feet, he assumed a stance and cried, "Is it me you're telling to wait?"

Musashi jumped in front of him and shouted, "State your business!"

The hoodlums inched closer, cautiously, as though feeling their way through shallow water.

"You know what we want!" spat one of them. "Turn over that yellowbelly you're protecting. And don't try anything funny, or you'll be dead too."

Encouraged by this bravado, they seethed with bloodthirsty fury, but none advanced to strike with his sword. The fire in Musashi's eyes was sufficient to hold them at bay. They howled and cursed, from a safe distance.

Musashi and Shinzō glared at them in silence. Moments passed before Musashi took them unawares by shouting, "If Hangawara Yajibei is among you, let him come forward."

"The boss isn't here. But if you have anything to say, speak to me, Nembutsu Tazaemon, and I'll do you the favor of listening." The elderly man who stepped forward wore a white hemp kimono and had Buddhist prayer beads hung around his neck.

"What do you have against Hōjō Shinzō?"

Squaring his shoulders, Tazaemon replied, "He slaughtered two of our men."

"According to Shinzō, your two louts helped Kojirō kill a number of Obata's students."

"That was one thing. This is another. If we don't settle our score with Shinzō, we'll be laughed off the streets."

"That may be the way things are done in the world you live in," Musashi said in a conciliatory tone. "But it's different in the world of the samurai. Among warriors, you can't fault a man for seeking and taking his proper revenge. A samurai may take revenge for the sake of justice or to defend his honor, but not to satisfy a personal grudge. It's not manly. And what you're trying to do right now isn't manly."

"Not manly? You're accusing us of being unmanly?"

"If Kojirō came forward and challenged us in his own name, that'd be all right. But we can't get involved in a squabble raised by Kojirō's minions."

"There you go, preaching self-righteously, just like any other samurai. Say what you please. We still have to protect our name."

"If samurai and outlaws fight over whose rules are to prevail, the streets will be filled with blood. The only place to settle this is at the magistrate's office. How about it, Nembutsu?"

"Horse manure. If it was something the magistrate could settle, we wouldn't be here to begin with."

"Listen, how old are you?"

"What business is it of yours?"

"I'd say you look old enough to know you shouldn't be leading a group of young men to a meaningless death."

"Ah, keep your smart talk to yourself. I'm not too old for a fight!" Tazaemon drew his sword, and the hoodlums moved forward, jostling and shouting.

Musashi dodged Tazaemon's thrust and grabbed him by the back of his gray head. Covering the ten paces or so to the moat in great strides, he summarily

731

dumped him over the edge. Then, as the mob closed in, he dashed back, picked Shinzō up by the waist and made off with him.

He ran across a field, toward the middle reaches of a hill. Below them a stream flowed into the moat and a bluish marsh was visible at the bottom of the slope. Halfway up, Musashi stopped and stood Shinzō on his feet. "Now," he said, "let's run." Shinzō hesitated, but Musashi prodded him into motion.

The hoodlums, having recovered from their shock, were giving chase.

"Catch him!"

"No pride!"

"*That's* a samurai?"

"He can't throw Tazaemon in the moat and get away with it!"

Ignoring the taunts and slurs, Musashi said to Shinzō, "Don't even consider getting involved with them. Run! It's the only thing to do in a case like this." With a grin, he added, "It's not so easy to make good time on this terrain, is it?" They were passing through what would someday be known as Ushigafuchi and Kudan Hill, but now the area was heavily wooded.

By the time they lost their pursuers, Shinzō's face was deathly pale.

"Worn out?" Musashi asked solicitously.

"It's . . . it's not so bad."

"I suppose you don't like the idea of letting them insult us like that without fighting back."

"Well . . ."

"Ha, ha! Think about it quietly and calmly, and you'll see why. There're times when it makes you feel better to run away. There's a stream over there. Rinse your mouth out, and then I'll take you to your father's house."

In a few minutes, the forest around the Akagi Myōjin Shrine came into view. Lord Hōjō's house was just below.

"I hope you'll come in and meet my father," Shinzō said when they came to the earthen wall surrounding the house.

"Some other time. Get plenty of rest and take care of yourself." With that, he was off.

After this incident, Musashi's name was heard quite frequently in the streets of Edo, far more frequently than he would have wished. People were calling him "a fake," "the coward to end all cowards," and saying, "shameless . . . a disgrace to the samurai class. If a fraud like that defeated the Yoshiokas in Kyoto, they must have been hopelessly weak. He must have challenged them knowing they couldn't protect themselves. And then he probably ran away before he was in any real danger. All that phony wants to do is sell his name to people who don't know swordsmanship." Before long, it was impossible to find anyone who would put in a good word for him.

The crowning insult was signs posted all over Edo: "Here's a word to Miyamoto Musashi, who turned tail and ran. The Hon'iden dowager is eager for revenge. We, too, would like to see your face instead of your back for a change. If you are a samurai, come out and fight. The Hangawara Association."

Book VI   SUN AND MOON

A Chat with the Men

Before having breakfast, Lord Hosokawa Tadatoshi began his day with the study of the Confucian classics. Official duties, which often required his attendance at Edo Castle, consumed most of his time, but when he could fit it into his schedule, he practiced the martial arts. Evenings, whenever possible, he liked to spend in the company of the young samurai in his service.

The atmosphere was rather like that of a harmonious family seated around its patriarch, not completely informal, to be sure, for the idea that his lordship was just one of the boys was not encouraged, but the usually rigorous etiquette was relaxed a bit. Tadatoshi, lounging in a lightweight hemp kimono, encouraged an exchange of views, which often included the latest gossip.

"Okatani," said his lordship, singling out one of the more robust men.

"Yes, sir."

"I hear you're pretty good with the lance now."

"That's right. Very good, in fact."

"Ha, ha. You certainly don't suffer from false modesty."

"Well, sir, with everybody else saying so, why should I deny it?"

"One of these days I'll find out for myself how advanced your technique really is."

"I've been looking forward to that day, but it never seems to come."

"You're lucky it doesn't."

"Tell me, sir, have you heard the song everybody's singing?"

"What's that?"

"It goes like this:

> There're lancers and lancers,
> All sorts of lancers,
> But the greatest one of all is
> Okatani Gorōji—"

Tadatoshi laughed. "You can't take me in that easily. That song's about Nagoya Sanzō."

735

The others joined in the laughter.

"Oh, you knew?"

"You'd be surprised at what I know." He was on the verge of giving further evidence of this but thought better of it. He enjoyed hearing what his men were thinking and talking about and considered it his duty to keep himself well informed, but it would hardly do to reveal just how much he actually knew. Instead he asked, "How many of you are specializing in the lance, how many in the sword?"

Out of seven, five were studying the lance, only two the sword.

"Why do so many of you prefer the lance?" asked Tadatoshi.

The consensus among the lancers was that it was more effective in battle.

"And what do the swordsmen think about that?"

One of the two replied, "The sword is better. Swordsmanship prepares you for peace as well as for war."

This was a perennial subject for discussion and the debate was usually lively.

One of the lancers asserted, "The longer the lance is, the better, provided it's not too long to handle efficiently. The lance can be used for striking, thrusting or slicing, and if you fail with it, you can always fall back on your sword. If you have only a sword and it gets broken, that's it."

"That may be true," rejoined an exponent of sword fighting, "but a samurai's work isn't limited to the battlefield. The sword is his soul. To practice its art is to refine and discipline your spirit. In the broadest sense, the sword is the basis for all military training, whatever drawbacks it may have in battle. If you master the inner meaning of the Way of the Samurai, the discipline can be applied to the use of the lance, or even guns. If you know the sword, you don't make silly mistakes or get taken unawares. Swordsmanship is an art with universal applications."

The argument might have gone on indefinitely, had not Tadatoshi, who had been listening without taking sides, said, "Mainosuke, what you just said sounds to me like something you heard somebody else say."

Matsushita Mainosuke grew defensive. "No, sir. That's my own opinion."

"Come now, be honest."

"Well, to tell the truth, I heard something similar when I was visiting Kakubei recently. Sasaki Kojirō said about the same thing. But it fitted in so well with my own idea . . . I wasn't trying to deceive anyone. Sasaki just put it into words better than I could."

"I thought as much," said Tadatoshi with a knowing smile. The mention of Kojirō's name reminded him that he had not yet made a decision as to whether to accept Kakubei's recommendation.

Kakubei had suggested that since Kojirō was not very old, he might be offered a thousand bushels or so. But much more than the matter of the stipend was involved. Tadatoshi had been told by his father many times that it was of prime importance to first exercise good judgment in hiring samurai and then to treat them well. Before accepting a candidate, it was imperative to assess not only his skills but also his character. No matter how desirable a man might seem to be, if he could not work together with the retainers who had made the House of Hosokawa what it was today, he would be virtually useless.

A fief, the elder Hosokawa had advised, was like a castle wall built of many rocks. A rock that could not be cut to fit in comfortably with the others would weaken the whole structure, even though the rock itself might be of admirable size and quality. The daimyō of the new age left the unsuitable rocks in the mountains and fields, for there was an abundance of them. The great challenge was to find one great rock that would make an outstanding contribution to one's own wall. Thought of in this way, Tadatoshi felt, Kojirō's youth was in his favor. He was still in his formative years and consequently susceptible to a certain amount of molding.

Tadatoshi was also reminded of the other rōnin. Nagaoka Sado had first mentioned Musashi at one of these evening get-togethers. Though Sado had allowed Musashi to slip through his fingers, Tadatoshi had not forgotten him. If Sado's information was accurate, Musashi was both a better fighter than Kojirō and a man of sufficient breadth to be valuable in government.

As he compared the two, he had to admit that most daimyō would prefer Kojirō. He came from a good family and had studied the Art of War thoroughly. Despite his youth, he had developed a formidable style of his own, and he had gained considerable fame as a fighter. The story of his "brilliant" defeat of men from the Obata Academy on the banks of the Sumida River and again at the dike on the Kanda River was already well known.

Nothing had been heard of Musashi for some time. His victory at Ichijōji had made his reputation. But that had been years ago, and soon afterward word had spread that the story was exaggerated, that Musashi was a seeker after fame who had trumped up the fight, made a flashy attack and then fled to Mount Hiei. Every time Musashi did something praiseworthy, a spate of rumors followed, denigrating his character and ability. It had reached the point where even the mention of his name usually met with critical remarks. Or else people ignored him entirely. As the son of a nameless warrior in the mountains of Mimasaka, his lineage was insignificant. Though other men of humble origin—most notably Toyotomi Hideyoshi, who came from Nakamura in Owari Province—had risen to glory in recent memory, people were on the whole class-conscious and not given to paying much heed to a man of Musashi's background.

As Tadatoshi mulled over the question, he looked around and asked, "Do any of you know of a samurai named Miyamoto Musashi?"

"Musashi?" replied a surprised voice "It'd be impossible not to hear of him. His name's all over town." It was evident that they were all familiar with the name.

"Why is that?" A look of anticipation came over Tadatoshi's face.

"There are signs up about him," offered one young man, with a slight air of reticence.

Another man, whose name was Mori, chimed in, "People were copying the signs, so I did too. I've got it with me now. Shall I read it?"

"Please do."

737

"Ah, here it is," said Mori, unfolding a crumpled scrap of paper. " 'Here's a word to Miyamoto Musashi, who turned tail and ran—' "

Eyebrows were raised and smiles began to appear, but Tadatoshi's face was grave. "Is that all?"

"No." He read the rest of it and said, "The signs were put up by a gang from the carpenters' district. People find it amusing because it's a case of street ruffians tweaking the nose of a samurai."

Tadatoshi frowned slightly, feeling that the words maligning Musashi called his own judgment into question. This was a far cry from the image he had formed of Musashi. Still, he was not ready to accept what he had heard at face value. "Hmm," he murmured. "I wonder if Musashi is really that sort of man."

"I gather he's a worthless lout," volunteered Mori, whose opinion was shared by the others. "Or at least a coward. If he wasn't, why would he allow his name to be dragged through the mud?"

The clock struck, and the men departed, but Tadatoshi sat on, thinking: "There's something interesting about this man." Not one to be swayed by the prevailing opinion, he was curious to know Musashi's side of the story.

The next morning, after listening to a lecture on the Chinese classics, he emerged from his study onto the veranda and caught sight of Sado in the garden. "Good morning, my elderly friend," he called.

Sado turned and politely bowed his morning greeting.

"Are you still on the lookout?" asked Tadatoshi.

Puzzled by the question, Sado merely stared back.

"I mean, are you still keeping an eye out for Miyamoto Musashi?"

"Yes, my lord." Sado lowered his eyes.

"If you do find him, bring him here. I want to see what he's like."

Shortly after noon on the same day, Kakubei approached Tadatoshi at the archery range and pressed his recommendation of Kojirō.

As he picked up his bow, the Young Lord said quietly, "Sorry, I'd forgotten. Bring him any time you wish. I'd like to have a look at him. Whether he becomes a retainer or not is another matter, as you well know."

738

Buzzing Insects

Seated in a back room of the small house Kakubei had lent him, Kojirō was examining the Drying Pole. After the incident with Hōjō Shinzō, he had requested Kakubei to press the craftsman for the return of the weapon. It had come back this morning.

"It won't be polished, of course," Kojirō had predicted, but in fact the sword had been worked on with an attention and care that were beyond his wildest hopes. From the blue-black metal, rippling like the current of a deep-running stream, there now sprang a brilliant white glow, the light of centuries past. The rust spots, which had seemed like leprous blemishes, were gone; the wavy tempering pattern between the blade's edge and the ridge line, hitherto smudged with bloodstains, was now as serenely beautiful as a misty moon floating in the sky.

"It's like seeing it for the first time," marveled Kojirō. Unable to take his eyes from the sword, he didn't hear the visitor calling from the front of the house: "Are you here? . . . Kojirō?"

This part of the hill had been given the name Tsukinomisaki because of the magnificent view it afforded of the rising moon. From his sitting room, Kojirō could see the stretch of bay from Shiba to Shinagawa. Across the bay, frothy clouds appeared to be on a level with his eyes. At this moment, the white of the distant hills and the greenish blue of the water seemed fused with the blade.

"Kojirō! Isn't anybody here?" This time the voice came from the grass-woven side gate.

Coming out of his reverie, he shouted, "Who is it?" and returned the sword to its scabbard. "I'm in the back. If you want to see me, come around to the veranda."

"Oh, here you are," said Osugi, walking around to where she could see into the house.

"Well, this is a surprise," said Kojirō cordially. "What brings you out on a hot day like this?"

"Just a minute. Let me wash my feet. Then we can talk."

"The well's over there. Be careful. It's quite deep. You, boy—go with her and see she doesn't fall in." The man addressed as "boy" was a low-ranking member of Hangawara's gang who had been sent along to guide Osugi.

After washing her sweaty face and rinsing her feet, Osugi entered the house and exchanged a few words of greeting. Noticing the pleasant breeze coming off the bay, she squinted and said, "The house is nice and cool. Aren't you afraid you'll get lazy, staying in a comfortable place like this?"

Kojirō laughed. "I'm not like Matahachi."

The old woman blinked her eyes sadly but ignored the barb. "Sorry I didn't bring you a real gift," she said. "In place of one I'll give you a sutra I copied." As she handed him the *Sutra on the Great Love of Parents*, she added, "Please read it when you have time."

After a perfunctory glance at her handiwork, Kojirō turned to her guide and said, "That reminds me. Did you put up the signs I wrote for you?"

"The ones telling Musashi to come out of hiding?"

"Yes, those."

"It took us two whole days, but we put one up at almost every important intersection."

Osugi said, "We passed some on the way here. Everywhere they're posted, people are standing around gossiping. It made me feel good to hear the things they're saying about Musashi."

"If he doesn't answer the challenge, he's finished as a samurai. The whole country'll be laughing at him. That should be ample revenge for you, Granny."

"Not on your life. Being laughed at isn't going to get through to him. He's shameless. And it won't satisfy me either. I want to see him punished once and for all."

"Ha, ha," laughed Kojirō, amused by her tenacity. "You get older, but you never give up, do you? By the way, did you come about anything in particular?"

The old lady rearranged herself and explained that after more than two years with Hangawara she felt she should be moving on. It was not right for her to live on Yajibei's hospitality indefinitely; besides, she was tired of mothering a houseful of roughnecks. She had seen a nice litle place for rent in the vicinity of Yoroi Ferry.

"What do you think?" Her face was serious, questioning. "It doesn't look like I'll find Musashi soon. And I have a feeling Matahachi's somewhere in Edo. I think I should have some money sent from home and stay on for a while. But by myself, as I said."

There being no reason for Kojirō to object, he quickly agreed with her. His own connection with the Hangawara ménage, entertaining and useful at the beginning, was now a little embarrassing. It was certainly no asset to a rōnin looking for a master. He had already decided to discontinue the practice sessions.

Kojirō summoned one of Kakubei's subordinates and had him bring a watermelon from the patch behind the house. They chatted while it was being cut and served, but before long he showed his guest out, his manner rather suggesting he preferred to have her out of the way before sundown.

When they had left, he himself swept his rooms and sprinkled the garden with well water. The morning glory and yam vines growing on the fence had reached the top and returned to the ground again, threatening to ensnare the foot of the stone water basin. Their white flowers waved in the evening breeze.

In his room again, he lay down and wondered idly if his host would be on duty that night at the Hosokawa house. The lamp, which would probably have been blown out by the wind anyway, was unlit. The light of the moon, rising beyond the bay, was already on his face.

At the bottom of the hill, a young samurai was breaking through the cemetery fence.

Kakubei stabled the horse he rode to and from the Hosokawa mansion at a florist's shop at the foot of Isarago Hill.

This evening, curiously enough, there was no sign of the florist, who always came out promptly to take charge of the animal. Not seeing him inside the shop, Kakubei went around to the back and started to tether his horse to a tree. As he did so, the florist came running out from behind the temple.

Taking the reins from Kakubei's hands, he panted, "Sorry, sir. There was a strange man in the cemetery, on his way up the hill. I shouted, told him there was no pathway there. He turned and stared at me—angry he was—then disappeared." He paused for a moment, peered up into the dark trees and added worriedly, "Do you think he could be a burglar? They say a lot of daimyō houses have been broken into recently."

Kakubei had heard the rumors, but he replied with a short laugh, "That's all talk, nothing more. If the man you saw was a burglar, I daresay he was a petty thief or one of the rōnin who waylay people on the streets."

"Well, we're right here at the entrance to the Tōkaidō, and lots of travelers have been attacked by men fleeing to other provinces. It makes me nervous when I see suspicious-looking men around at night."

"If anything happens, run up the hill and knock at my gate. The man staying with me is chafing at the bit, always complaining there's never any action around here."

"You mean Sasaki Kojirō? He's got quite a reputation as a swordsman here in the neighborhood."

Hearing this did Kakubei's self-esteem no harm. Apart from liking young people, he knew quite well that it was regarded as both admirable and wise for established samurai like himself to take on promising younger men as protégés. Should an emergency arise, there could be no more persuasive proof of his loyalty than to be able to furnish his lord with good fighters. And if one of them turned out to be outstanding, due credit would be given to the retainer who had recommended him. One of Kakubei's beliefs was that self-interest was an undesirable trait in a vassal; nevertheless, he was realistic. In a large fief, there were few retainers willing to disregard their own interests entirely.

Despite the fact that he held his position through heredity, Kakubei was as loyal to Lord Tadatoshi as the other retainers, without being the sort who would strive to outdo others in demonstrating his fealty. For purposes of routine administration, men of his type were on the whole much more satisfac-

741

tory than the firebrands who sought to perform spectacular feats.

"I'm back," he called on entering the gate to his house. The hill was quite steep, and he was always a little winded when he reached this point. Since he had left his wife in the country and the house was populated mostly by men, with only a few woman servants, feminine touches tended to be lacking. Yet on evenings when he had no night duty, he invariably found the stone path from the red gate to the entrance inviting, for it had been freshly watered down in anticipation of his return. And no matter how late the hour, someone always came to the front door to greet him.

"Is Kojirō here?" he asked.

"He's been in all day," replied the servant. "He's lying down in his room, enjoying the breeze."

"Good. Get some sake ready and ask him to come in to see me."

While preparations were being made, Kakubei took off his sweaty clothes and relaxed in the bath. Then, donning a light kimono, he entered his sitting room, where Kojirō sat waving a fan.

The sake was brought in. Kakubei poured, saying, "I called you because something encouraging happened today that I wanted to tell you about."

"Good news?"

"Since I mentioned your name to Lord Tadatoshi, he seems to have heard of you from other sources as well. Today he told me to bring you to see him sometime soon. As you know, it's not easy to arrange these matters. There are dozens of retainers with someone they want to suggest." His expectation that Kojirō would be immensely pleased showed clearly in his tone and manner.

Kojirō put his cup to his lips and drank. When he did speak, his expression was unchanged and he said only, "Let me pour you one now."

Kakubei, far from being put out, admired the young man for being able to conceal his emotions. "This means I've been successful in carrying out what you requested of me. I think that calls for a celebration. Have another."

Kojirō bowed his head slightly and mumbled, "I'm grateful for your kindness."

"I was only doing my duty, of course," Kakubei replied modestly. "When a man is as capable and talented as you, I owe it to my lord to see that you're given consideration."

"Please don't overestimate me. And let me reemphasize one point. It's not the stipend I'm interested in. I simply think the House of Hosokawa is a very good one for a samurai to serve. It's had three outstanding men in a row." The three men were Tadatoshi and his father and grandfather, Sansai and Yūsai.

"You needn't think I've talked you up to the high heavens. I didn't have to. The name Sasaki Kojirō is known throughout the capital."

"How could I be famous when all I do is loaf around here all day long? I don't see that I'm outstanding in any way. It's just that there are so many fakes around."

"I was told that I could bring you anytime. When would you like to go?"

"Any time suits me too."

"How about tomorrow?"

"That's all right with me." His face revealed no eagerness, no anxiety, only calm self-confidence.

Kakubei, even more impressed at his sangfroid, chose this time to say matter-of-factly, "You understand, of course, his lordship won't be able to make a final decision until he's seen you. You needn't let that worry you. It's only a matter of form. I have no doubt but what the position will be offered."

Kojirō set his cup down on the table and stared straight into Kakubei's face. Then, very coldly and defiantly, he said, "I've changed my mind. Sorry to have put you to so much trouble." Blood seemed about to burst from his earlobes, already bright red from the drink.

"Wh-what?" stammered Kakubei. "You mean you're giving up the chance for a position with the House of Hosokawa?"

"I don't like the idea," answered his guest curtly, offering no further explanation. His pride told him there was no reason for him to submit to an inspection; dozens of other daimyō would snap him up sight unseen for fifteen hundred, even twenty-five hundred, bushels.

Kakubei's puzzled disappointment seemed to make no impression on him whatsoever, nor did it matter that he would be regarded as a willful ingrate. Without the least suggestion of doubt or repentance, he finished off his food in silence and returned to his own quarters.

The moonlight fell softly on the tatami. Stretching out drunkenly on the floor, arms under his head, he began to laugh quietly to himself. "Honest man, that Kakubei. Good, old, honest Kakubei." He knew his host would be at a loss to explain this sudden shift to Tadatoshi, but he knew also that Kakubei would not be angry at him for very long, no matter how outrageously he behaved.

While he had piously denied interest in the stipend, he was in fact consumed with ambition. He wanted a stipend and much more—every ounce of fame and success he could possibly achieve. Otherwise, what would be the purpose of persevering through years of arduous training?

Kojirō's ambition was different from that of other men only by dint of its magnitude. He wanted to be known throughout the country as a great and successful man, to bring glory to his home in Iwakuni, to enjoy every one of the benefits that can possibly derive from being born human. The quickest road to fame and riches was to excel in the martial arts. He was fortunate in having a natural talent for the sword; he knew this and derived no small measure of self-satisfaction from it. He had planned his course intelligently and with remarkable foresight. Every action of his was calculated to put him closer to his goal. To his way of thinking, Kakubei, though his senior, was naive and a little sentimental.

He fell asleep dreaming of his brilliant future.

Later, when the moonlight had edged a foot across the tatami, a voice no louder than the breeze whispering through the bamboo said, "Now." A shadowy form, crouching among the mosquitoes, crept forward like a frog to the eaves of the unlighted house.

743

The mysterious man seen earlier at the foot of the hill advanced slowly, silently, until he reached the veranda, where he stopped and peered into the room. Stooping in the shadows, out of the moonlight, he might have remained undiscovered indefinitely had he himself made no sound.

Kojirō snored on. The soft hum of insects, briefly interrupted as the man moved into position, came again across the dew-covered grass.

Minutes passed. Then the silence was broken by the clatter the man made as he whipped out his sword and jumped up onto the veranda.

He leapt toward Kojirō and cried, "Arrgh!" an instant before he clenched his teeth and struck.

There was a sharp hissing as a long black object descended heavily on his wrist, but the original force of his strike had been powerful. Instead of falling from his hand, his sword sank into the tatami, where Kojirō's body had been.

Like a fish darting away from a pole striking water, the intended victim had streaked to the wall. He now stood facing the intruder, the Drying Pole in one hand, its scabbard in the other.

"Who are you?" Kojirō's breathing was calm. Alert as always to the sounds of nature's creatures, to the falling of a dewdrop, he was unperturbed.

"I-it-it's me!"

"'Me' doesn't tell me anything. I know you're a coward, attacking a man in his sleep. What's your name?"

"I am Yogorō, the only son of Obata Kagenori. You took advantage of my father when he was sick. And you spread gossip about him all over the city."

"I wasn't the one who spread the gossip. It was the gossipers—the people of Edo."

"Who was it who lured his students into a fight and killed them?"

"I did that, no doubt about it. I, Sasaki Kojirō. How can I help it if I'm better than they? Stronger. Braver. More knowledgeable in the Art of War."

"How can you have the gall to say that when you called on Hangawara's vermin to help you?"

With a snarl of disgust, Kojirō took a step forward. "If you want to hate me, go ahead! But any man who carries a personal grudge into a test of strength in the Art of War isn't even a coward. He's worse than that, more pitiable, more laughable. So once again I have to take the life of an Obata man. Are you resigned to that?"

No answer.

"I said, are you resigned to your fate?" He moved another step forward. As he did so, the light of the moon reflecting off the newly polished blade of his sword blinded Yogorō.

Kojirō stared at his prey as a starving man stares at a feast.

The Eagle

Kakubei regretted having allowed himself to be used shabbily and vowed to have nothing more to do with Kojirō. Yet deep down, he liked the man. What he didn't like was being caught between his master and his protégé. Then he began to rethink the matter.

"Maybe Kojirō's reaction proves how exceptional he is. The ordinary samurai would have jumped at the chance to be interviewed." The more he reflected on Kojirō's fit of pique, the more the rōnin's independent spirit appealed to him.

For the next three days Kakubei was on night duty. He did not see Kojirō until the morning of the fourth day, when he walked casually over to the young man's quarters.

After a short but awkward silence, he said, "I want to talk to you for a minute, Kojirō. Yesterday, when I was leaving, Lord Tadatoshi asked me about you. He said he'd see you. Why don't you drop in at the archery range and have a look at the Hosokawa technique?"

When Kojirō grinned without replying, Kakubei added, "I don't know why you insist on thinking it's demeaning. It's usual to interview a man before offering him an official position."

"I know, but supposing he rejects me, then what? I'd be a castoff, wouldn't I? I'm not so hard up that I have to go around peddling myself to the highest bidder."

"Then the fault is mine. I put it the wrong way. His lordship never meant to imply any such thing."

"Well, what answer did you give him?"

"None yet. But he seems a little impatient."

"Ha, ha. You've been very thoughtful, very helpful. I suppose I shouldn't put you in such a difficult position."

"Wouldn't you reconsider—go and call on him, just once?"

"All right, if it means so much to you," Kojirō said patronizingly, but Kakubei was nonetheless pleased.

"How about today?"

"So soon?"

"Yes."

"What time?"

"How about a little after noon? That's when he practices archery."

"All right, I'll be there."

745

Kojirō set about making elaborate preparations for the meeting. The kimono he chose was of excellent quality, and the *hakama* was made of imported fabric. Over the kimono he wore a formal vestlike garment of sheer silk, sleeveless but with stiff flaring shoulders. To complement his finery, he had the servants provide him with new zōri and a new basket hat.

"Is there a horse I can use?" he inquired.

"Yes. The master's spare horse, the white one, is at the shop at the bottom of the hill."

Failing to find the florist, Kojirō glanced toward the temple compound across the way, where a group of people was gathering around a corpse covered with reed matting. He went over to have a look.

They were discussing plans for burial with the local priest. The victim had no identifying possessions on him; no one knew who he was, only that he was young and of the samurai class. The blood around the deep gash extending from the tip of one shoulder to his waist was dried and black.

"I've seen him before. About four days ago, in the evening," said the florist, who went on talking excitedly until he felt a hand on his shoulder.

When he looked to see who it was, Kojirō said, "I'm told Kakubei's horse is kept at your place. Get him ready for me, please."

Bowing hastily, the florist asked perfunctorily, "Are you going out?" and hurried off.

He patted the dappled-gray steed on the neck as he led it out of his stable.

"Quite a good horse," Kojirō remarked.

"Yes, indeed. A fine animal."

Once Kojirō was in the saddle, the florist beamed and said, "It's a good match."

Taking some money from his purse, Kojirō threw it to the man. "Use this for flowers and incense."

"Huh? Who for?"

"The dead man over there."

Beyond the temple gate, Kojirō cleared his throat and spat, as if to eject the bitter taste left by the sight of the corpse. But he was pursued by the feeling that the youth he had cut down with the Drying Pole had thrown aside the reed matting and was following him. "I did nothing he could hate me for," he told himself, and felt better for the thought.

As horse and rider moved along the Takanawa highroad under the boiling sun, townsmen and samurai alike stood aside to make way. Heads turned in admiration. Even on the streets of Edo, Kojirō cut an impressive figure, causing people to wonder who he was and where he came from.

At the Hosokawa residence, he turned the horse over to a servant and entered the house. Kakubei rushed to meet him. "My thanks for coming. It's just the right time too," he said, as though Kojirō were doing him a great personal favor. "Rest awhile. I'll tell his lordship you're here." Before doing so, he made sure the guest was provided with cool water, barley tea and a tobacco tray.

When a retainer came to show him to the archery range, Kojirō handed over his beloved Drying Pole and followed along wearing only his short sword.

Lord Tadatoshi had resolved to shoot a hundred arrows a day during the summer months. A number of close retainers were always there, watching each shot with bated breath and making themselves useful retrieving arrows.

"Give me a towel," his lordship commanded, standing his bow beside him.

Kneeling, Kakubei asked, "May I trouble you, sir?"

"What is it?"

"Sasaki Kojirō is here. I would appreciate your seeing him."

"Sasaki? Oh, yes."

He fitted an arrow to the bowstring, took an open stance, and raised his shooting arm above his eyebrows. Neither he nor any of the others so much as glanced in Kojirō's direction until the hundred shots were finished.

With a sigh Tadatoshi said, "Water. Bring me some water."

An attendant brought some from the well and poured it into a large wooden tub at Tadatoshi's feet. Letting the upper part of his kimono hang loose, he wiped off his chest and washed his feet. His men assisted by holding his sleeves, running to fetch more water and wiping off his back. There was nothing formal in their manner, nothing to suggest to an observer that this was a daimyō and his retinue.

Kojirō had supposed that Tadatoshi, a poet and an aesthete, the son of Lord Sansai and the grandson of Lord Yūsai, would be a man of aristocratic bearing, as refined in his conduct as the elegant courtiers of Kyoto. But his surprise did not show in his eyes as he watched.

Slipping his still damp feet into his zōri, Tadatoshi looked at Kakubei, who was waiting off to one side. With the air of one who has suddenly recalled a promise, he said, "Now, Kakubei, I'll see your man." He had a stool brought and placed in the shade of a tent, where he sat down in front of a banner bearing his crest, a circle surrounded by eight smaller circles, representing the sun, moon and seven planets.

Beckoned by Kakubei, Kojirō came forward and knelt before Lord Tadatoshi. As soon as the formal greeting was completed, Tadatoshi invited Kojirō to sit on a stool, thus signifying that he was an honored guest.

"By your leave," said Kojirō, as he rose and took a seat facing Tadatoshi.

"I've heard about you from Kakubei. I believe you were born in Iwakuni, weren't you?"

"That is correct, sir."

"Lord Kikkawa Hiroie of Iwakuni was well known as a wise and noble ruler. Were your ancestors retainers of his?"

"No, we never served the House of Kikkawa. I've been told we're descended from the Sasakis of Ōmi Province. After the fall of the last Ashikaga shōgun, my father seems to have retired to my mother's village."

After a few more questions concerning family and lineage, Lord Tadatoshi asked, "Will you be going into service for the first time?"

"I do not yet know whether I am going into service."

"I gathered from Kakubei you wish to serve the House of Hosokawa. What are your reasons?"

"I believe it is a house I would be willing to live and die for."

Tadatoshi seemed pleased with this answer. "And your style of fighting?"

"I call it the Ganryū Style."

" 'Ganryū'?"

"It's a style I invented myself."

"Presumably it has antecedents."

"I studied the Tomita Style, and I had the benefit of lessons from Lord Katayama Hisayasu of Hōki, who in his old age retired to Iwakuni. I've also mastered many techniques on my own. I used to practice cutting down swallows on the wing."

"I see. I suppose the name Ganryū comes from the name of that river near where you were born?"

"Yes, sir."

"I'd like to see a demonstration." Tadatoshi looked around at the faces of his samurai. "Which one of you would like to take this man on?"

They had been watching the interview in silence, thinking that Kojirō was remarkably young to have acquired the reputation he had. Now all looked first at each other, then at Kojirō, whose flushed cheeks proclaimed his willingness to face any challenger.

"How about you, Okatani?"

"Yes, sir."

"You're always claiming the lance is superior to the sword. Now's your chance to prove it."

"I shall be glad to, if Sasaki is willing."

"By all means," Kojirō answered with alacrity. In his tone, which was polite but extremely cool, there was a hint of cruelty.

The samurai who had been sweeping the sand on the archery range and putting away the equipment assembled behind their master. Although weapons were as familiar to them as chopsticks, their experience had been primarily in the dōjō. The chance to witness, much less have, a real bout would occur only a few times throughout their lives. They would readily agree that a man-to-man fight was a greater challenge than going out on the battlefield, where it was sometimes possible for a man to pause and get his wind while his comrades fought on. In hand-to-hand combat, he had only himself to rely on, only his own alertness and strength from beginning to end. Either he won, or he was killed or maimed.

They watched Okatani Gorōji solemnly. Even among the lowest-ranking foot soldiers there were quite a few who were adept with the lance; Gorōji was generally conceded to be the best. He had not only been in battle but had practiced diligently and devised techniques of his own.

"Give me a few minutes," said Gorōji, bowing toward Tadatoshi and Kojirō before withdrawing to make his preparations. It pleased him that today, as on other days, he had on spotless underwear, in the tradition of the good samurai, who started each day with a smile and an uncertainty: by evening he might be a corpse.

After borrowing a three-foot wooden sword, Kojirō selected the ground for the match. His body seemed relaxed and open, the more so since he didn't hitch up his pleated *hakama*. His appearance was formidable; even his enemies would have had to admit that. There was an eaglelike air of valor about him, and his handsome profile was serenely confident.

Worried eyes began to turn toward the canopy behind which Gorōji was adjusting his clothing and equipment.

"What's taking him so long?" someone asked.

Gorōji was calmly wrapping a piece of damp cloth around the point of his lance, a weapon he had used to excellent effect on the battlefield. The shaft was nine feet long, and the tapering blade alone, at eight or nine inches, was the equivalent of a short sword.

"What are you doing?" called Kojirō. "If you're worried about hurting me, save yourself the trouble." Again, though the words were courteous, the implication was arrogant. "I don't mind if you leave it unwrapped."

Looking sharply at him, Gorōji said, "Are you sure?"

"Perfectly."

Though neither Lord Tadatoshi nor his men spoke, their piercing eyes told Gorōji to go ahead. If the stranger had the gall to ask for it, why not run him through?

"In that case . . ." Gorōji tore off the wrapping and advanced holding the lance midway along the shaft. "I'm happy to comply, but if I use a naked blade, I want you to use a real sword."

"This wooden one's fine."

"No; I can't agree to that."

"Certainly you wouldn't expect me, an outsider, to have the audacity to employ a real sword in the presence of his lordship."

"But—"

With a touch of impatience, Lord Tadatoshi said, "Go ahead, Okatani. Nobody will consider you cowardly for complying with the man's request." It was obvious Kojirō's attitude had affected him.

The two men, faces flushed with determination, exchanged greetings with their eyes. Gorōji made the first move, leaping to the side, but Kojirō, like a bird stuck to a limed fowling pole, slipped under the lance and struck directly at his chest. Lacking time to thrust, the lancer whirled sideways and tried to jab the nape of Kojirō's neck with the butt of his weapon. With a resounding crack, the lance flew back up into the air, as Kojirō's sword bit into Gorōji's ribs, which had been exposed by the momentum of the rising lance. Gorōji slid to one side, then leapt away, but the attack continued without letup. With no time to catch his breath, he jumped aside again, then again and again. The first few dodges were successful, but he was like a peregrine falcon trying to fend off an eagle. Hounded by the raging sword, the lance shaft snapped in two. At the same instant, Gorōji emitted a cry; it sounded as though his soul was being torn from his body.

The brief battle was ended. Kojirō had hoped to take on four or five men, but Tadatoshi said that he had seen enough.

When Kakubei came home that evening, Kojirō asked him, "Did I go a little too far? In front of his lordship, I mean."

"No, it was a magnificent performance." Kakubei felt rather ill at ease. Now that he could assess the full extent of Kojirō's ability, he felt like a man who had hugged a tiny bird to his chest, only to see it grow up to be an eagle.

"Did Lord Tadatoshi say anything?"

"Nothing in particular."

"Come now, he must have said something."

"No; he left the archery range without a word."

"Hmm." Kojirō looked disappointed but said, "Oh, it doesn't matter. He impressed me as a greater man than he's usually made out to be. I was thinking if I had to serve anyone, it might as well be him. But of course I have no control over how things turn out." He didn't reveal how carefully he had thought about the situation. After the Date, Kuroda, Shimazu and Mōri clans, the Hosokawa was the most prestigious and secure. He felt sure this would continue to be true so long as Lord Sansai held the Buzen fief. And sooner or later, Edo and Osaka would clash once and for all. There was no way of predicting the outcome; a samurai who had chosen the wrong master might easily find himself a rōnin again, his whole life sacrificed for a few months' stipend.

The day after the bout, word came that Gorōji had survived, though his pelvis or left thighbone had been smashed. Kojirō accepted the news calmly, telling himself that even if he did not receive a position, he had given a good enough account of himself.

A few days later he abruptly announced he was going to pay a call on Gorōji. Offering no explanation for this sudden display of kindness, he set out alone and on foot for Gorōji's house near Tokiwa Bridge.

The unexpected visitor was received cordially by the injured man.

"A match is a match," said Gorōji, a smile on his lips and moistness in his eyes. "I may deplore my own lack of skill, but I certainly hold nothing against you. It was good of you to come to see me. Thank you."

After Kojirō left, Gorōji remarked to a friend, "Now, there's a samurai I can admire. I thought he was an arrogant son of a bitch, but he turns out to be both friendly and polite."

This was precisely the reaction Kojirō had hoped for. It was part of his plan; other visitors would hear him praised by the defeated man himself. Calling once every two or three days, he made three more visits to Gorōji's house. On one occasion he had a live fish delivered from the fish market as a get-well present.

Green Persimmons

In the dog days after the summer rainy season, the land crabs crawled slug-
gishly in the parched street, and the signs taunting Musashi to "come out and
fight" were no longer visible. The few that hadn't fallen in the rain-softened
earth or been stolen for firewood were obscured by weeds and tall grass.

"There must be something somewhere," thought Kojirō, looking around for
a place to eat. But this was Edo, not Kyoto, and the cheap rice-and-tea shops so
common in the older city had not yet made their appearance here. The only
likely place stood in a vacant lot, screened off with reed blinds. Smoke rose
lazily from behind the blinds, and on a vertical banner was the word "Donjiki." The word immediately reminded him of *tonjiki*, which in the distant past
had meant the rice balls used as military rations.

As he approached, he heard a masculine voice ask for a cup of tea. Inside,
two samurai were energetically gobbling rice, one from an ordinary rice bowl,
the other from a sake bowl.

Kojirō seated himself on the edge of a bench across from them and asked the
proprietor, "What do you have?"

"Rice dishes. I also have sake."

"On the banner it says 'Donjiki.' What does that mean?"

"As a matter of fact, I don't know."

"Didn't you write it?"

"No. It was written by a retired merchant who stopped in to rest."

"I see. Good calligraphy, I must say."

"He said he was on a religious pilgrimage, said he'd visited Hirakawa Tenjin Shrine, Hikawa Shrine, Kanda Myōjin, all sorts of places, making big contributions to each of them. Very pious and generous, he seemed."

"Do you know his name?"

"He told me it was Daizō of Narai."

"I've heard the name."

"Donjiki—well, I don't understand it. But I figured if a fine man like him
wrote it, it might help keep the god of poverty away." He laughed.

After a look into several large china bowls, Kojirō took some rice and fish,
poured tea over the rice, brushed a fly away with his chopsticks and began
eating.

One of the other customers stood up and peered through a broken slat in the blind. "Take a look out there, Hamada," he said to his companion. "Isn't that the watermelon vendor?"

The other man went quickly to the blind and looked out. "Yeah, that's him all right."

The vendor, shouldering a pole with baskets at either end, was walking languidly past the Donjiki. The two samurai ran out of the shop and caught up with him. Drawing their swords, they cut the ropes supporting the baskets. The vendor stumbled forward, along with the melons.

Hamada yanked him up by the scruff of his neck. "Where did you take her?" he demanded angrily. "Don't lie. You must be hiding her somewhere."

The other samurai thrust the tip of his sword under the captive's nose.

"Out with it! Where is she?"

The sword blade tapped menacingly against the man's cheek. "How could anybody with a face like yours think of going off with somebody else's woman?"

The vendor, cheeks flushed with anger and fear, shook his head, but then, seeing an opening, shoved one of his captors out of the way, picked up his pole and took a swing at the other one.

"So you want to fight, do you? Careful, Hamada, this guy's not just an ordinary melon vendor."

"What can this ass do?" sneered Hamada, snatching the pole and knocking the vendor to the ground. Straddling him, he used the ropes to tie him to the pole.

A cry like that of a stuck pig went up behind him. Hamada turned his face around, right into a spray of fine red mist. Looking totally dumbfounded, he jumped up, screaming, "Who are you? What—"

The adderlike blade moved directly toward him. Kojirō laughed, and as Hamada shrank back, followed him relentlessly. The two moved in a circle through the grass. When Hamada moved back a foot, Kojirō moved forward the same distance. When Hamada leapt to one side, the Drying Pole followed, pointing unwaveringly at its prospective victim.

The melon vendor cried out in astonishment, "Kojirō! It's me. Save me!"

Hamada blanched with terror and gasped, "Ko-ji-rō!" Then he wheeled around and tried to flee.

"Where do you think you're going?" barked Kojirō. The Drying Pole flashed through the sultry stillness, lopping off Hamada's ear and lodging deep in the flesh under the shoulders. He died on the spot.

Kojirō promptly cut the melon vendor's bonds. Rearranging himself into a proper sitting posture, the man bowed, and stayed bowed, too embarrassed to show his face.

Kojirō wiped and resheathed his sword. Amusement playing faintly around his lips, he said, "What's the matter with you, Matahachi? Don't look so miserable. You're still alive."

"Yes, sir."

"None of this 'yes, sir' business. Look at me. It's been a long time, hasn't it?"

"I'm glad you're well."

"Why wouldn't I be? But I must say you've taken to an unusual trade."

"Let's not talk about it."

"All right. Pick up your melons. Then—I know, why don't you leave them at the Donjiki?" With a loud shout, he summoned the proprietor, who helped them stack the melons behind the blinds.

Kojirō took out his brush and ink and wrote on one of the shoji: "To whom it may concern: I certify that the person who killed the two men lying on this vacant lot was myself, Sasaki Kojirō, a rōnin residing at Tsukinomisaki."

To the proprietor, he said, "This should fix it so no one'll bother you about the killings."

"Thank you, sir."

"Think nothing of it. If friends or relatives of the dead men should come around, please deliver this message for me. Tell them I won't run away. If they want to see me, I'm ready to greet them anytime."

Outside again, he said to Matahachi, "Let's go."

Matahachi walked beside him but would not take his eyes off the ground. Not once since coming to Edo had he held a steady job. Whatever his intention—to become a *shugyōsha* or to go into business—when he found the going rough, he changed jobs. And after Otsū slipped away from him, he felt less and less like working. He'd slept in first one place, then another, sometimes at flophouses populated by hoodlums. The past few weeks, he had been making his living as a common peddler, trudging from one part of the castle wall to another, hawking watermelons.

Kojirō wasn't particularly interested in what Matahachi had been doing, but he had written the sign at the Donjiki and he might later be questioned about the incident. "Why did those samurai have it in for you?" he asked.

"To tell the truth, it had to do with a woman. . . ."

Kojirō smiled, thinking wherever Matahachi went, there soon arose some difficulty connected with women. Perhaps this was his karma. "Mm," he mumbled. "The great lover in action again, eh?" Then, more loudly, "Who is the woman, and what exactly happened?"

It took some prodding, but eventually Matahachi gave in and told his tale, or part of it. Near the moat, there were dozens of tiny tea shops catering to construction workers and passersby. In one of these there had been a waitress who caught everybody's eyes, enticing men who did not want tea to step in for a cup and men who were not hungry to order bowls of sweet jelly. One regular customer had been Hamada; Matahachi, too, dropped in occasionally.

One day this waitress whispered to him that she needed his help. "That rōnin," she had said. "I don't like him, but every night after the shop closes, the master orders me to go home with him. Won't you let me come and hide in your house? I won't be a burden. I'll cook for you, and mend your clothes."

Since her plea seemed reasonable, Matahachi had agreed. That was all there was to it, he insisted.

Kojirō was unconvinced. "It sounds fishy to me."

"Why?" Matahachi asked.

Kojirō could not decide whether Matahachi was trying to make himself appear innocent or whether he was bragging about an amorous conquest. Without even smiling, he said, "Never mind. It's hot out here under the sun. Let's go to your house, and you can tell me about it in more detail."

Matahachi stopped in his tracks.

"Is there anything wrong with that?" asked Kojirō.

"Well, my place is—it's not the sort of place I'd want to take you to."

Seeing the distressed look in Matahachi's eyes, Kojirō said lightly, "Never mind. But one of these days soon you must come to see me. I'm staying with Iwama Kakubei, about halfway up Isarago Hill."

"I'd like that."

"By the way, did you see the signs posted around the city recently, the ones addressed to Musashi?"

"Yes."

"They said your mother was looking for him too. Why don't you go to see her?"

"Not the way I am now!"

"Idiot. You don't have to put on a great show for your own mother. There's no way of knowing just when she might find Musashi, and if you're not there at the time, you'll lose the chance of a lifetime. You'd regret that, wouldn't you?"

"Yes, I'll have to do something about that soon," Matahachi said noncommittally, thinking resentfully that other people, including the man who had just saved his life, did not understand the feelings between mothers and their offspring.

They parted, Matahachi ambling down a grassy lane, Kojirō ostensibly setting out in the opposite direction. Kojirō soon doubled back and followed Matahachi, taking care to stay out of sight.

Matahachi arrived presently at a motley collection of "long houses," one-story tenements, each containing three or four small apartments under a single roof. Since Edo had grown rapidly and not everybody could be choosy about where he lived, people cleared land as the necessity arose. Streets came into existence afterward, developing naturally from pathways. Drainage, too, came about by accident, as waste water cut its own path to the nearest stream. Had it not been for these jerry-built slums, the influx of newcomers could not have been absorbed. The majority of the inhabitants of such places were, of course, workmen.

Near his home, Matahachi was greeted by a neighbor named Umpei, the boss of a crew of well diggers. Umpei was seated cross-legged in a large wooden tub, only his face showing above the rain shutter placed sideways in front of the tub for privacy.

"Good evening," said Matahachi. "I see you're having your bath."

"I'm about to get out," replied the boss genially. "Would you like to use it next?"

"Thanks, but I think Akemi's probably heated water for me."

"You two are very fond of each other, aren't you? Nobody around here seems to know whether you're brother and sister or husband and wife. Which is it?"

Matahachi giggled sheepishly. The appearance of Akemi saved him from having to answer.

She placed a tub under a persimmon tree and brought pailfuls of hot water from the house to fill it. When she was done, she said, "Feel it, Matahachi. See if it's hot enough."

"It's a little too hot."

There was the squeaking of the well pulley, and Matahachi, stripped to his loincloth, brought up a bucket of cold water and poured it into the bath before climbing in himself. "Ah-h-h," he sighed contentedly. "This feels good."

Umpei, wearing a cotton summer kimono, placed a bamboo stool under a gourd trellis and sat down. "Did you sell lots of melons?" he inquired.

"Not many. I never sell very many." Noticing dried blood between his fingers, he hastily wiped it off.

"I don't imagine you would. I still think your life would be easier if you went to work on a well-digging gang."

"You're always saying that. Don't think I'm ungrateful, but if I did that, they wouldn't let me off the castle grounds, would they? That's why Akemi doesn't want me to take the job. She says she'd be lonesome without me."

"Happily married couple, eh? Well, well."

"Ouch!"

"What's the matter?"

"Something fell on my head."

A green persimmon landed on the ground just behind Matahachi.

"Ha, ha! Punishment for bragging about your wife's devotion, that's what it is." Still laughing, Umpei rapped his tannin-coated fan on his knee.

Over sixty years old, with a shaggy, hemplike mane of white hair, Umpei was a man who enjoyed the respect of his neighbors and the admiration of the young people, whom he bigheartedly treated as his own children. Each morning he could be heard chanting *Namu Myōhō Rengekyō*, the sacred invocation of the Nichiren sect.

A native of Itō in Izu Province, he had a sign in front of his house saying: "Idohori no Umpei, Well Digger for the Shōgun's Castle." To build the many wells necessary for the castle involved technical skills beyond those of ordinary laborers. Umpei had been hired as a consultant and recruiter of workers because of his long experience in the gold mines of Izu Peninsula. He enjoyed nothing more than sitting under his beloved gourd trellis, spinning yarns and drinking his nightly cup of cheap but potent *shōchū*, the poor man's sake.

After Matahachi emerged from the bath, Akemi surrounded the washtub with rain shutters and had hers. Later, the matter of Umpei's proposal came up once again. Besides having to stay on the castle grounds, the workers were watched very closely, and their families were virtually hostages of the bosses of the areas where they lived. On the other hand, the work was easier than on the outside and paid at least twice as much.

Leaning over a tray on which there was a dish of cold bean curd, garnished with fresh, fragrant basil leaf, Matahachi said, "I don't want to become a prisoner just to earn a little money. I'm not going to sell melons all my life, but bear with me a little longer, Akemi."

755

"Umm," she replied between mouthfuls of tea-and-rice gruel. "I'd rather you tried just once to do something really worthwhile, something that would make people take notice."

Though nothing was ever said or done to discourage the idea that she was Matahachi's legal wife, she wasn't about to marry anyone who shilly-shallied the way he did. Fleeing the world of play at Sakaimachi with Matahachi had been only an expedient; he was the perch from which she intended, at the first opportunity, to fly once more into the open sky. But it did not suit her purposes for Matahachi to go off to the castle to work. She felt being left alone would be dangerous; specifically, she was afraid Hamada might find her and force her to live with him.

"Oh, I forgot," said Matahachi, as they finished their frugal meal. He then told her about his experiences that day, adjusting the details in a fashion calculated to please her. By the time he had finished, her face was ashen.

Taking a deep breath, she said, "You saw Kojirō? Did you tell him I was here? You didn't, did you?"

Matahachi took her hand and placed it on his knee. "Of course not. Do you think I'd let that bastard know where you are? He's the kind that never gives up. He'd be after you—"

He broke off with an inarticulate shout and pressed his hand to the side of his face. The green persimmon that smashed against his cheek broke and spattered its whitish meat in Akemi's face.

Outside, in the shadows of a moonlit bamboo grove, a form not unlike that of Kojirō could be seen walking nonchalantly away in the direction of town.

Eyes

"*Sensei!*" called Iori, who was not yet tall enough to see over the tall grass. They were on Musashino Plain, which was said to cover ten counties.

"I'm right here," replied Musashi. "What's taking you so long?"

"I guess there's a path, but I keep losing it. How much farther do we have to go?"

"Till we find a good place to live."

"Live? We're going to stay around here?"

"Why shouldn't we?"

Iori gazed up at the sky, thought of its vastness and the emptiness of the land around him and said, "I wonder."

"Think what it'll be like in the fall. Clear, beautiful skies, fresh dew on the grass. Doesn't it make you feel cleaner just thinking about it?"

"Well, maybe, but I'm not against living in the city, like you."

"I'm not, really. In a way, it's nice to be among people, but even with my thick skin I couldn't stand being there when those signs were put up. You saw what they said."

Iori grimaced. "I get mad just thinking about it."

"Why let yourself get angry over that?"

"I couldn't help it. No matter where I went, there wasn't anybody who'd say anything good about you."

"Nothing I could do about that."

"You could have cut down the men spreading the rumors. You could have put up your own signs challenging them."

"There's no point in starting fights you can't win."

"You wouldn't have lost to that scum. You couldn't have."

"No, you're wrong. I would have."

"How?"

"Sheer numbers. If I beat ten, there'd be a hundred more. If I defeated a hundred, there'd be a thousand. There's no possibility of winning in that kind of situation."

"But does that mean you're going to be laughed at for the rest of your life?"

"Of course not. I'm as determined as the next person to have a good name. I owe it to my ancestors. And I intend to become a man who's never laughed at. That's what I came out here to learn."

"We can walk all we want, but I don't think we're going to find any houses. Shouldn't we try to find a temple to stay in again?"

"That's not a bad idea, but what I really want is to find someplace with a lot of trees and build a house of our own."

"It'll be like Hōtengahara again, won't it?"

"No. This time we're not going to farm. I think maybe I'll practice Zen meditation every day. You can read books, and I'll give you some lessons in the sword."

Entering the plain at the village of Kashiwagi, the Kōshū entrance to Edo, they had come down the long slope from Jūnisho Gongen and followed a narrow path that repeatedly threatened to disappear among the waving summer grasses. When they finally reached a pine-covered knoll, Musashi made a quick survey of the terrain and said, "This'll do fine." To him, any place could serve as home—more than that: wherever he happened to be was the universe.

They borrowed tools and hired a laborer at the nearest farmhouse. Musashi's approach to building a house was not at all sophisticated; in fact, he could have learned quite a bit from watching birds build a nest. The result, finished a few days later, was an oddity, less substantial than a hermit's mountain retreat but not so crude as to be described as a shed. The posts were logs with the bark left on, the remainder a rough alliance of boards, bark, bamboo and miscanthus.

Standing back to take a good look, Musashi remarked thoughtfully, "This must be like the houses people lived in back in the age of the gods." The only relief from the primitiveness were scraps of paper lovingly fashioned to make small shoji.

In the days following, the sound of Iori's voice, floating from behind a reed blind as he recited his lessons, rose above the buzz of the cicadas. His training had become very strict in every respect.

With Jōtarō, Musashi had not insisted on discipline, thinking at the time that it was best to let growing boys grow naturally. But with the passage of time, he had observed that, if anything, bad traits tended to develop and good ones to be repressed. Similarly, he had noticed that trees and plants he wanted to grow would not grow, while weeds and brush flourished no matter how often he cut them down.

During the hundred years after the Ōnin War, the nation had been like a tangled mass of overgrown hemp plants. Then Nobunaga had cut the plants down, Hideyoshi had bundled them up, and Ieyasu had broken and smoothed the ground to build a new world. As Musashi saw it, warriors who placed a high value only on martial practices and whose most noticeable characteristic was unbounded ambition were no longer the dominant element in society. Sekigahara had put an end to that.

He had come to believe that whether the nation remained in the hands of the Tokugawas or reverted to the Toyotomis, people in general already knew the direction they wanted to move in: from chaos toward order, from destruction toward construction.

At times, he'd had the feeling he had been born too late. No sooner had Hideyoshi's glory penetrated into remote rural areas and fired the hearts of boys like Musashi than the possibility of following in Hideyoshi's footsteps evaporated.

So it was his own experience that led to his decision to emphasize discipline in Iori's upbringing. If he was going to create a samurai, he should create one for the coming era, not for the past.

"Iori."

"Yes, sir." The boy was kneeling before Musashi almost before the words were out.

"It's almost sunset. Time for our practice. Bring the swords."

"Yes, sir." When he placed them in front of Musashi, he knelt and formally requested a lesson.

Musashi's sword was long, Iori's short, both wooden practice weapons. Teacher and pupil faced each other in tense silence, swords held at eye level. A rim of sunlight hovered on the horizon. The cryptomeria grove behind the cabin was already sunk in gloom, but if one looked toward the voices of the cicadas, a sliver of moon was visible through the branches.

"Eyes," said Musashi.

Iori opened his eyes wide.

"*My* eyes. Look at them."

Iori did his best, but his eyes seemed to literally bounce away from Musashi's. Instead of glaring, he was being defeated by his opponent's eyes. When he tried again, he was seized by giddiness. His head began to feel as if it were no longer his own. His hands, his feet, his whole body felt wobbly.

"Look at my eyes!" Musashi commanded with great sternness. Iori's look had strayed again. Then, concentrating on his master's eyes, he forgot the sword in his hand. The short length of curved wood seemed to become as heavy as a bar of steel.

"Eyes, eyes!" said Musashi, advancing slightly.

Iori checked the urge to fall back, for which he had been scolded dozens of times. But when he attemped to follow his opponent's lead and move forward, his feet were nailed to the ground. Unable either to advance or to retreat, he could feel his body temperature rise. "What's the matter with me?" The thought exploded like fireworks inside him.

Sensing this burst of mental energy, Musashi yelled, "Charge!" At the same time he lowered his shoulders, dropped back and dodged with the agility of a fish.

With a gasp, Iori sprang forward, spun around—and saw Musashi standing where he himself had been.

Then the confrontation began again, just as before, both teacher and pupil maintaining strict silence.

Before long the grass was soaked with dew, and the eyebrow of a moon hung above the cryptomerias. Each time the wind gusted, the insects stopped singing momentarily. Autumn had come, and the wild flowers, though not spectacular in the daytime, now quivered gracefully, like the feathered robe of a dancing deity.

"Enough," said Musashi, lowering his sword.

As he handed it to Iori, they became conscious of a voice coming from the direction of the grove.

"I wonder who that is," said Musashi.

"Probably a lost traveler wanting to put up for the night."

"Run and see."

As Iori sped around to the other side of the building, Musashi seated himself on the bamboo veranda and gazed out over the plain. The eulalias were tall, their tops fluffy; the light bathing the grass had a peculiar autumn sheen.

When Iori returned, Musashi asked, "A traveler?"

"No, a guest."

"Guest? Here?"

"It's Hōjō Shinzō. He tied his horse up and he's waiting for you in back."

"This house doesn't really have any back or front, but I think it'd be better to receive him here."

Iori ran round the side of the cabin, shouting, "Please come this way."

"This is a pleasure," said Musashi, his eyes expressing his delight at seeing Shinzō completely recovered.

"Sorry to have been out of touch so long. I suppose you live out here to get away from people. I hope you'll forgive me for dropping in unexpectedly like this."

Greetings having been exchanged, Musashi invited Shinzō to join him on 759 the veranda. "How did you find me? I haven't told anyone where I am."

"Zushino Kōsuke. He said you'd finished the Kannon you promised him and sent Iori to deliver it."

"Ha, ha. I suppose Iori let the secret out. It doesn't matter. I'm not old enough to abandon the world and retire. I did think, though, that if I left the scene for a couple of months, the malicious gossip would quiet down. Then there'd be less danger of reprisals against Kōsuke and my other friends."

Shinzō lowered his head. "I owe you an apology—all this trouble because of me."

"Not really. That was a minor thing. The real root of the matter has to do with the relationship between Kojirō and me."

"Did you know he killed Obata Yogorō?"

"No."

"Yogorō, when he heard about me, decided to take revenge himself. He was no match for Kojirō."

"I warned him. . . ." The image of the youthful Yogorō standing in the entrance of his father's house was still vivid in Musashi's mind. "What a pity," he thought to himself.

"I can understand how he felt," continued Shinzō. "The students had all left, and his father had died. He must have thought he was the only one who could do it. In any case, he appears to have gone to Kojirō's house. Still, no one saw them together; there's no real proof."

"Mm. Maybe my warning had the opposite effect from what I intended—stirred up his pride so he felt he had to fight. It's a shame."

"It is. Yogorō was *Sensei's* only blood relation. With his death the House of Obata ceased to exist. However, my father discussed the matter with Lord Munenori, who somehow managed to institute adoption proceedings. I'm to become Kagenori's heir and successor and carry on the Obata name. . . . I'm not sure I'm mature enough yet. I'm afraid I may end up bringing further disgrace to the man. After all, he was the greatest proponent of the Kōshū military tradition."

"Your father's the Lord of Awa. Isn't the Hōjō military tradition considered to be on a par with the Kōshū School? And your father as great a master as Kagenori?"

"That's what they say. Our ancestors came from Tōtōmi Province. My grandfather served Hōjō Ujitsuna and Hōjō Ujiyasu of Odawara, and my father was selected by Ieyasu himself to succeed them as head of the family."

"Coming from a famous military family, isn't it unusual for you to have become a disciple of Kagenori's?"

"My father has his disciples, and he's given lectures before the shōgun on military science. But instead of teaching me anything, he told me to go out and learn from somebody else. Find out the hard way! That's the kind of man he is."

Musashi sensed an element of intrinsic decency, even nobility, in Shinzō's demeanor. And it was probably natural, he thought, for his father, Ujikatsu, was an outstanding general, and his mother was the daughter of Hōjō Ujiyasu.

"I'm afraid I've been talking too much," said Shinzō. "Actually, my father sent me out here. Of course, it would have been only proper for him to come and express his gratitude to you in person, but just now he has a guest, who's quite eager to see you. My father told me to bring you back with me. Will you come?" He peered inquiringly into Musashi's face.

"A guest of your father's wants to see me?"

"That's right."

"Who could it be? I know almost no one in Edo."

"A person you've known since you were a boy."

Musashi couldn't imagine who it might be. Matahachi, perhaps? A samurai from Takeyama Castle? A friend of his father's?

Maybe even Otsū . . . But Shinzō refused to divulge his secret. "I was instructed not to tell you who it is. The guest said it would be better to surprise you. Will you come?"

Musashi's curiosity was piqued. He told himself it couldn't be Otsū, but in his heart hoped it was.

"Let's go," he said, rising to his feet. "Iori, don't wait up for me."

Shinzō, pleased that his mission was successful, went behind the house and brought his horse. Saddle and stirrups were dripping with dew. Holding the bit, he offered the horse to Musashi, who proceeded without further ado to mount it.

As they left, Musashi said to Iori, "Take care of yourself. I may not be back until tomorrow." It was not long before he was swallowed up by the evening mist.

Iori sat quietly on the veranda, lost in thought.

"Eyes," he thought. "Eyes." Innumerable times he had been ordered to keep his eyes on his opponent's, but as yet he could neither understand the import of the instruction nor get the idea out of his mind. He gazed vacantly up at the River of Heaven.

What was wrong with him? Why was it that when Musashi stared at him, he couldn't stare straight back? More vexed by his failure than an adult would have been, he was trying very hard to find the explanation when he became conscious of a pair of eyes. They were aimed at him from the branches of a wild grapevine, which twined around a tree in front of the cabin.

"What's that?" he thought.

The brightly shining eyes reminded him strongly of Musashi's eyes during practice sessions.

"Must be a possum." He had seen one several times, eating the wild grapes. The eyes were like agate, the eyes of a fierce hobgoblin.

"Beast!" cried Iori. "You think I don't have any courage, think even you can outstare me. Well, I'll show you! I'm not about to lose to you."

With grim determination, he tensed his elbows and glared back. The possum, whether out of stubbornness or curiosity, made no move to flee. Its eyes took on an even more lustrous brilliance.

The effort so absorbed Iori that he forgot to breathe. He swore again not to lose, not to this lowly beast. After what seemed like hours, he realized with a 761 flash that he had triumphed. The leaves of the grapevine shook and the possum vanished.

"That'll show you!" exulted Iori. He was drenched with sweat, but he felt relieved and refreshed. He only hoped he would be able to repeat the performance the next time he confronted Musashi.

Having lowered a reed blind on the window and snuffed out the lamp, he went to bed. A bluish-white light reflected from the grass outside. He dozed off, but inside his head he seemed to see a tiny spot, shining like a jewel. In time, the spot grew into the vague outline of the possum's face.

Tossing and moaning, he was suddenly overwhelmed by the conviction that there were eyes at the foot of his pallet. He roused himself with difficulty. "Bastard," he cried, reaching for his sword. He took a murderous swing but ended up doing a somersault. The shadow of the possum was a moving spot on the blind. He slashed at it wildly, then ran outside and hacked fiercely at the grapevine. His eyes rose skyward in search of the eyes.

There came into focus, slowly, two large, bluish stars.

Four Sages with a Single Light

"Here we are," Shinzō said as they reached the foot of Akagi Hill.

From the flute music, which sounded like the accompaniment to a sacred shrine dance, and the bonfire visible through the woods, Musashi thought a night festival must be in progress. The trip to Ushigome had taken two hours.

On one side was the spacious compound of Akagi Shrine; across the sloping street stood the earthen wall of a large private residence and a gate of magnificent proportions. When they reached the gate, Musashi dismounted and handed the reins to Shinzō, thanking him as he did so.

Shinzō led the horse inside and handed the reins to one of a group of samurai waiting near the entrance with paper lanterns in their hands. They all came forward, welcomed him back and led the way through the trees to a clearing in front of the imposing entrance hall. Inside, servants holding lanterns were lined up on both sides of the hallway.

The chief steward greeted them, saying, "Come in. His lordship is expecting you. I'll show you the way."

"Thank you," replied Musashi. He followed the steward up a stairway and into a waiting room.

The design of the house was unusual; one stairway after another led to a series of apartments, which gave the impression of being stacked one above another all the way up Akagi Hill. As he seated himself, Musashi noted that the room was well up the slope. Beyond a drop at the edge of the garden, he could just make out the northern part of the castle moat and the woods framing the escarpment. He found himself thinking that the view from the room in the daytime must be breathtaking.

Noiselessly, the door in an arched doorway slid open. A beautiful serving girl came gracefully in and placed a tray bearing cakes, tea and tobacco in front of him. Then she slipped out as quietly as she had entered. It seemed as if her colorful kimono and obi had emerged from and melted into the wall itself. A faint fragrance lingered after her, and suddenly Musashi was reminded of the existence of women.

The master of the house appeared shortly after that, attended by a young samurai. Dispensing with formalities, he said, "Good of you to come." In good soldierly fashion, he seated himself cross-legged on a cushion spread by the attendant and said, "From what I hear, my son is much indebted to you. I hope you'll pardon my asking you to come here rather than visiting your house to express my thanks." With his hands resting lightly on the fan in his lap, he inclined his prominent forehead ever so slightly.

"I'm honored to be invited to meet you," said Musashi.

It was not easy to estimate Hōjō Ujikatsu's age. Three front teeth were missing, but his smooth, shiny skin testified to a determination never to grow old. The heavy black mustache, streaked with only a few white hairs, had been allowed to grow out on both sides to conceal any wrinkles resulting from the lack of teeth. Musashi's first impression was of a man who had many children and got along well with young people.

Sensing that his host wouldn't object, Musashi went straight to the point. "Your son tells me that you have a guest who knows me. Who might that be?"

"Not one but two. You'll see them by and by."

"Two people?"

"Yes. They know each other very well, and both are good friends of mine. I happened to meet them at the castle today. They came back with me, and when Shinzō came in to greet them, we started chatting about you. One of them said he hadn't seen you for a long time and would like to. The other, who knows you only by reputation, expressed the desire to be introduced."

Smiling broadly, Musashi said, "I think I know. One is Takuan Sōhō, isn't it?"

"That's right," exclaimed Lord Ujikatsu, slapping his knee in surprise.

"I haven't seen him since I came east several years ago."

Before Musashi had time to make a guess at who the other man was, his lordship said, "Come with me," and went out into the corridor.

They climbed a short stairway and walked down a long, dark corridor. Rain shutters were in place on one side. Suddenly Musashi lost sight of Lord Ujikatsu. He stopped and listened.

After a few moments, Ujikatsu called, "I'm down here." His voice seemed to come from a well-lit room that was situated across an open space from the corridor.

"I understand," Musashi called back. Instead of heading directly for the light, he stood where he was. The space outside the corridor was openly inviting, but something told him danger lurked in that stretch of darkness.

"What are you waiting for, Musashi? We're over here."

"Coming," answered Musashi. He was in no position to reply otherwise, but his sixth sense had warned him to be on the alert. Stealthily, he turned and walked back about ten paces to a small door, which let out onto the garden. Slipping on a pair of sandals, he made his way around the garden to the veranda of Lord Ujikatsu's parlor.

"Oh, you came that way, did you?" said his lordship, looking around from the other end of the room. He sounded disappointed.

"Takuan!" called Musashi as he entered the room, a radiant smile on his face. The priest, seated in front of the alcove, stood up to greet him. To meet again—and under the roof of Lord Hōjō Ujikatsu—seemed almost too fortuitous. Musashi had trouble convincing himself that it was really happening.

"We'll have to bring each other up to date," said Takuan. "Shall I begin?" He was clad in the plain robes he always wore. No finery, not so much as prayer beads. Yet he seemed mellower than before, more soft-spoken. Just as Musashi's rural upbringing had been leached out of him by strenuous attempts at self-discipline, Takuan, too, seemed to have had the sharper corners rounded off and to have become more deeply endowed with the wisdom of Zen. To be sure, he was no longer a youth. Eleven years older than Musashi, he was now approaching forty.

"Let's see. Kyoto, wasn't it? Ah, I remember. It was shortly before I went back to Tajima. After my mother died, I spent a year in mourning. Then I traveled for a while, spent some time at the Nansōji in Izumi, then at the Daitokuji. Later, I saw a good deal of Lord Karasumaru—composed poetry with him, had tea ceremonies, fended off the cares of this world. Before I knew it, I'd spent three years in Kyoto. Recently I became friendly with Lord Koide of Kishiwada Castle and came with him to have a look at Edo."

"Then you've been here only a short time?"

"Yes. Although I've met Hidetada twice at the Daitokuji and been summoned into Ieyasu's presence a number of times, this is my first trip to Edo. And what about you?"

"I've been here only since the beginning of this summer."

"It seems you've made quite a name for yourself in this part of the country."

Musashi didn't try to justify himself. He hung his head and said, "I suppose you've heard about that."

Takuan stared at him for a few moments, seemingly comparing him with the Takezō of old. "Why worry about that? It'd be strange if a man your age had too good a reputation. So long as you haven't done anything disloyal or ignoble or rebellious, what does it matter? I'm more interested in hearing about your training."

Musashi gave a brief account of his recent experiences and ended by saying, "I'm afraid I'm still immature, imprudent—far from being truly enlightened. The more I travel, the longer the road becomes. I have the feeling I'm climbing an endless mountain path."

"That's the way it has to be," said Takuan, clearly pleased with the youth's integrity and humility. "If a man not yet thirty claims to know the least bit about the Way, it's an unmistakable sign his growth has stopped. Even I still shudder with embarrassment when anyone suggests that an uncouth priest like me could know the ultimate meaning of Zen. It's disconcerting, the way people are always asking me to tell them about the Buddhist Law or explain the true teachings. People try to look up to a priest as a living Buddha. Be thankful that others don't overestimate you, that you don't have to pay attention to appearances."

While the two men happily renewed their friendship, servants arrived with food and drink. Presently Takuan said, "Forgive me, your lordship. I'm afraid we're forgetting something. Why don't you call your other guest in?"

Musashi was certain now that he knew who the fourth person was, but elected to remain silent.

Hesitating slightly, Ujikatsu said, "Shall I call him?" Then, to Musashi, "I'll have to admit you saw through our little trick. As the one who planned it, I feel rather ashamed."

Takuan laughed. "Good for you! I'm glad to see you're up to admitting defeat. But why not? It was only a game to amuse everybody anyway, wasn't it? Certainly nothing for the master of the Hōjō Style to lose face over."

"Well, no doubt I was defeated," murmured Ujikatsu, reluctance still in his voice. "The truth is that although I've heard what sort of man you are, I had no way of knowing just how well trained and disciplined you are. I thought I'd see for myself, and my other guest agreed to cooperate. When you stopped in the passageway, he was waiting in ambush, ready to draw his sword." His lordship seemed to regret having had to put Musashi to the test. "But you perceived you were being lured into a trap and came across the garden." Looking directly at Musashi, he asked, "May I ask why you did that?"

Musashi merely grinned.

Takuan spoke up. "It's the difference, your lordship, between the military strategist and the swordsman."

"Is it, now?"

"It's a matter of instinctive responses—that of a military scholar, based on intellectual principles, versus that of a man who follows the Way of the Sword, based on the heart. You reasoned that if you led Musashi on, he'd follow. Yet without being able to actually see, or to put his finger on anything definite, Musashi sensed danger and moved to protect himself. His reaction was spontaneous, instinctive."

"Instinctive?"

"Like a Zen revelation."

"Do you have premonitions like that?"

"I can't really say."

"In any case, I've learned a lesson. The average samurai, sensing danger, might have lost his head, or perhaps seized upon the trap as an excuse to display his prowess with the sword. When I saw Musashi go back, put on the sandals and cross the garden, I was deeply impressed."

Musashi kept his silence, his face revealing no special pleasure at Lord Ujikatsu's words of praise. His thoughts turned to the man still standing outside in the dark, stranded by the victim's failure to fall into the trap.

Addressing his host, he said, "May I request that the Lord of Tajima take his place among us now?"

"What's that?" Ujikatsu was astonished, as was Takuan. "How did you know?"

Moving back to give Yagyū Munenori the place of honor, Musashi said, "Despite the darkness, I felt the presence of peerless swordsmanship. Taking into consideration the other faces present, I don't see how it could be anyone else."

"You've done it again!" Ujikatsu was amazed.

At a nod from him, Takuan said, "The Lord of Tajima. Quite right." Turning to the door, he called, "Your secret is out, Lord Munenori. Won't you join us?"

There was a loud laugh, and Munenori appeared in the doorway. Instead of arranging himself comfortably in front of the alcove, he knelt in front of Musashi and greeted him as an equal, saying, "My name is Mataemon Munenori. I hope you will remember me."

"It is an honor to meet you. I am a rōnin from Mimasaka, Miyamoto Musashi by name. I pray for your guidance in the future."

"Kimura Sukekurō mentioned you to me some months ago, but at the time I was busy because of my father's illness."

"How is Lord Sekishūsai?"

"Well, he's very old. There's no way of knowing . . ." After a brief pause, he continued with warm cordiality: "My father told me about you in a letter, and I've heard Takuan speak of you several times. I must say your reaction a few minutes ago was admirable. If you don't mind, I think we should regard the bout you requested as having taken place. I hope you're not offended by my unorthodox way of carrying it out."

Musashi's impression was of intelligence and maturity quite in accordance with the daimyō's reputation.

"I'm embarrassed by your thoughtfulness," he replied, bowing very low. His show of deference was natural, for Lord Munenori's status was so far above Musashi's as to put him virtually in another world. Though his fief amounted to only fifty thousand bushels, his family had been famous as provincial magistrates since the tenth century. To most people, it would have seemed odd to find one of the shōgun's tutors in the same room with Musashi, let alone talking to him in a friendly, informal fashion. It was a relief to Musashi to note that neither Ujikatsu, a scholar and member of the shōgun's banner guard, nor Takuan, a country priest by origin, felt any constraint because of Munenori's rank.

Warm sake was brought, cups were exchanged, talk and laughter ensued. Differences in age and class were forgotten. Musashi knew he was being accepted in this select circle not because of who he was. He was seeking the Way, just as they were. It was the Way that permitted such free camaraderie.

At one point, Takuan set down his cup and asked Musashi, "What's become of Otsū."

766

Reddening slightly, Musashi said he hadn't seen or heard anything of her for some time.

"Nothing at all?"

"Nothing."

"That's unfortunate. You can't leave her in the lurch forever, you know. It's not good for you, either."

"By Otsū," asked Munenori, "do you mean the girl who once stayed with my father in Koyagyū?"

"Yes," replied Takuan on Musashi's behalf.

"I know where she is. She went to Koyagyū with my nephew Hyōgo to help nurse my father."

With a noted military scientist and Takuan present, thought Musashi, they could be talking about strategy or discussing Zen. With both Munenori and Musashi present, the subject could have been swords.

With a nod of apology to Musashi, Takuan told the others about Otsū and her relationship with Musashi. "Sooner or later," he concluded, "someone will have to bring the two of you together again, but I fear it's no task for a priest. I ask the assistance of you two gentlemen." What he was actually suggesting was that Ujikatsu and Munenori act as Musashi's guardians.

They seemed willing to accept this role, Munenori observing that Musashi was old enough to have a family and Ujikatsu saying that he had reached a satisfactorily high level of training.

Munenori suggested that one of these days Otsū should be summoned back from Koyagyū and given in marriage to Musashi. Then Musashi could set himself up in Edo, where his house, along with those of Ono Tadaaki and Yagyū Munenori, would form a triumvirate of the sword and usher in a golden age of swordsmanship in the new capital. Both Takuan and Ujikatsu concurred.

Specifically, Lord Ujikatsu, eager to reward Musashi for his kindness to Shinzō, wanted to recommend him as a tutor to the shōgun, an idea the three of them had explored before sending Shinzō for Musashi. And having seen how Musashi reacted to their test, Munenori himself was now ready to give his approval to the plan.

There were difficulties to be overcome, one being that a teacher in the shōgun's household also had to be a member of the honor guard. Since many of its members were faithful vassals of the Tokugawas from the days when Ieyasu had held the Mikawa fief, there was a reluctance to appoint new people, and all candidates were investigated with great thoroughness. However, it was felt that with recommendations from Ujikatsu and Munenori, together with a letter of guarantee from Takuan, Musashi would get by.

The sticky point was his ancestry. There was no written record tracing his ancestry back to Hirata Shōgen of the Akamatsu clan, nor even a genealogical chart to prove he was of good samurai stock. He assuredly had no family connections with the Tokugawas. On the contrary, it was an undeniable fact that as a callow youth of seventeen he had fought against the Tokugawa forces at Sekigahara. Still, there was a chance; other rōnin from former enemy clans had joined the House of Tokugawa after Sekigahara. Even Ono Tadaaki, a rōnin from the Kitabatake clan, which was at present in hiding in Ise Matsuzaka, held an appointment as tutor to the shōgun despite his undesirable connections.

After the three men had again gone over the pros and cons, Takuan said, "All right then, let's recommend him. But perhaps we should find out what he himself thinks about it."

The question was put to Musashi, who replied mildly, "It's kind and generous of you to suggest this, but I'm nothing but an immature young man."

"Don't think of it in that way," said Takuan with an air of candor. "What we're advising you to do is become mature. Will you establish a house of your own, or do you plan to make Otsū go on indefinitely living as she is now?"

Musashi felt hemmed in. Otsū had said she was willing to bear any hardship, but this would in no way lessen Musashi's responsibility for any grief that might befall her. While it was acceptable for a woman to act in accordance with her own feelings, if the outcome was not a happy one, the man would be blamed.

Not that Musashi was unwilling to accept the responsibility. On the whole, he yearned to accept. Otsū had been guided by love, and the onus of that love belonged to him as much as to her. Nevertheless, he felt it was still too early to marry and have a family. The long, hard Way of the Sword stretched before him yet; his desire to follow it was undiminished.

It did not simplify matters that his attitude toward the sword had changed. Since Hōtengahara, the sword of the conqueror and the sword of the killer were things of the past, no longer of any use or meaning.

Nor did being a technician, even one who gave instruction to men of the shōgun's retinue, excite his interest. The Way of the Sword, as he had come to see it, must have specific objectives: to establish order, to protect and refine the spirit. The Way had to be one men could cherish as they did their lives, until their dying day. If such a Way existed, could it not be employed to bring peace to the world and happiness to all?

When he had answered Sukekurō's letter with a challenge to Lord Munenori, his motive had not been the shallow urge to score a victory that had led him to challenge Sekishūsai. Now his wish was to be engaged in the business of governing. Not on any grand scale, of course; a small, insignificant fief would suffice for the activities he imagined would promote the cause of good government.

But he lacked the confidence to express these ideas, feeling that other swordsmen would dismiss his youthful ambitions as being absurd. Or, if they took him seriously, they would feel compelled to warn him: politics leads to destruction; by going into government he would sully his beloved sword. They would do this out of genuine concern for his soul.

He even believed that if he spoke his mind truthfully, the two warriors and the priest would react either with laughter or with alarm.

When he did get around to speaking, it was to protest—he was too young, too immature, his training was inadequate. . . .

At length, Takuan cut him off, saying, "Leave it to us."

Lord Ujikatsu added, "We'll see that it turns out all right for you."

The matter was decided.

Coming in periodically to trim the lamp, Shinzō had caught the gist of the conversation. He quietly let his father and the guests know that what he had heard pleased him immensely.

The Locust Tree

Matahachi opened his eyes and looked around, got up and poked his head out the back door.

"Akemi!" he called.

There was no answer.

Something prompted him to open the closet. She had recently finished making a new kimono. It was gone.

Going next door first, to Umpei's, he then walked through the alley toward the street, anxiously asking everyone he met if they'd seen her.

"I saw her this morning," said the charcoal vendor's wife.

"You did? Where?"

"She was all dressed up. I asked her where she was off to, and she said to see relatives in Shinagawa."

"Shinagawa?"

"Doesn't she have relatives there?" she asked skeptically.

He started to say no, but caught himself. "Uh, yes, of course. That's where she's gone."

Run after her? In truth, his attachment to her was not particularly strong, and he was more annoyed than anything else. Her disappearance left a bittersweet taste.

He spat and gave vent to an oath or two, then strolled down to the beach, just on the other side of the Shibaura highroad. A little back from the water stood a scattering of fishermen's houses. It was his habit to come here every morning while Akemi was cooking rice and look for fish. Usually at least five or six had fallen from the nets, and he would return just in time to have them cooked for breakfast. Today he ignored the fish.

"What's the matter, Matahachi?" The pawnbroker from the main street tapped him on the shoulder.

"Good morning," said Matahachi.

"It's nice to be out early, isn't it? I'm glad to see you come out for a walk every morning. Great for your health!"

"You're joking, I suppose. Maybe if I was rich like you, I'd be walking for my health. For me, walking's work."

"You don't look too well. Something happen?"

Matahachi picked up a handful of sand and cast it bit by bit into the wind. Both he and Akemi were well acquainted with the pawnbroker, who had tided them over several emergencies.

Undaunted, the man continued: "You know, there's something I've been meaning to talk to you about, but I never seem to have the chance. Are you going out to work today?"

"Why bother? It's not much of a living, selling watermelons."

"Come fishing with me."

Matahachi scratched his head and looked apologetic. "Thanks, but I really don't like to fish."

"Well, you don't have to fish if you don't want to. But come along anyway. It'll make you feel better. That's my boat over there. You can scull a boat, can't you?"

"I guess so."

"Come along. I'm going to tell you how to make a lot of money—maybe a thousand pieces of gold. How would you like that?"

Suddenly Matahachi had a great interest in going fishing.

About a thousand yards offshore, the water was still shallow enough to touch bottom with the scull. Letting the boat drift, Matahachi asked, "Just how do I go about making this money?"

"I'll tell you soon enough." The pawnbroker readjusted his bulky frame on the seat at the waist of the boat. "I'd appreciate it if you'd hold a fishing pole out over the water."

"Why?"

"It's better if people think we're fishing. Two people rowing out this far just to talk would look suspicious."

"How's this?"

"Fine." He took out a pipe with a ceramic bowl, packed it with expensive tobacco and lit it. "Before I tell you what I have in mind, let me ask you a question. What do your neighbors say about me?"

"About you?"

"Yes, about Daizō of Narai."

"Well, pawnbrokers are supposed to be skinflints, but everybody says you're very good about lending money. They say you're a man who understands life."

"I don't mean my business practices. I want to know their opinion of me personally."

"They think you're a good man, a man with a heart. I'm not just flattering you. That's really what they say."

"Don't they ever comment on what a religious man I am?"

"Oh, yes, of course. Everybody's amazed at how charitable you are."

"Have men from the magistrate's office ever come around inquiring about me?"

770

"No. Why should they?"

Daizō gave a little laugh. "I suppose you think my questions are foolish, but the truth of the matter is that I'm not really a pawnbroker."

"What?"

"Matahachi, you may never have another chance to make so much money all at once."

"You're probably right."

"Do you want to catch hold?"

"Of what?"

"The money vine."

"Wh-what do I have to do?"

"Make a promise to me and carry it out."

"That's all?"

"That's all, but if you change your mind later, you're as good as dead. I know the money interests you, but think hard before you give your final answer."

"Just what do I have to do?" Matahachi asked suspiciously.

"You have to become a well digger. There's nothing to it."

"At Edo Castle?"

Daizō gazed out over the bay. Cargo boats loaded with building materials and bearing the flags of several great clans—Tōdō, Arima, Katō, Date, Hosokawa—were lined up almost prow to stern.

"You catch on quick, Matahachi." The pawnbroker refilled his pipe. "Edo Castle is precisely what I have in mind. If I'm not mistaken, Umpei's been trying to persuade you to dig wells for him. It'd be perfectly natural for you to decide to take him up on the offer."

"That's all I have to do? . . . How is becoming a well digger going to bring me that much money?"

"Be patient. I'll tell you all about it."

When they returned to shore, Matahachi was euphoric. They parted with a promise. That evening he was to slip away unobserved and go to Daizō's house to receive an advance payment of thirty pieces of gold.

He went home, took a nap and awoke a few hours later with the image of the vast sum that would soon be his dancing before his eyes.

Money, a fantastic amount, enough to compensate for all the bad luck he had had up till then. Enough to last him for the rest of his life. Even more exciting was the prospect of being able to show people that they were wrong, that he had what it took after all.

With the money fever upon him, he could not calm down. His mouth still felt dry, even a little numb. Going outside, he stood in the deserted alleyway facing the bamboo grove behind the house and thought: "Who is he, anyway? Just what is he up to?" Then he began to go over the conversation with Daizō.

The well diggers were presently working at the Goshinjō, the new castle in the western encirclement. Daizō had told him, "You're to bide your time until the chance presents itself, and then you're to shoot the new shōgun with a 771 musket." The gun and ammunition would be on the castle grounds, under a huge, centuries-old locust tree near the back gate at the bottom of Momiji Hill.

Needless to say, the laborers were under close surveillance, but Hidetada liked going around with his attendants to inspect the work. It would be simple enough to accomplish the objective. In the ensuing uproar, Matahachi could escape by jumping into the outer moat, from which Daizō's accomplices would rescue him—"without fail," he had said.

Back in his room, Matahachi stared at the ceiling. He seemed to hear Daizō's voice whispering certain words over and over and recalled how his own lips had trembled when he'd said, "Yes, I'll do it." His skin covered with goose pimples, he jumped to his feet. "This is awful! I'm going over there right now and tell him I don't want any part of it."

Then he remembered something else Daizō had said: "Now that I've told you all this, you're committed. I'd hate to see anything happen to you, but if you try to back out, my friends will have your head within—oh, three days at the outside." Daizō's piercing stare as he had said this flashed before Matahachi's eyes.

Matahachi walked the short distance down Nishikubo Lane to the corner of the Takanawa highroad, where the pawnshop stood. The bay, cloaked in darkness, was at the end of a side street. He entered the alley alongside the familiar storehouse, went to the inconspicuous back door of the shop and knocked softly.

"It's not locked," came the immediate response.

"Daizō?"

"Yes. Glad you came. Let's go into the storehouse."

A rain shutter had been left open. Matahachi went into the outer corridor and followed the pawnbroker.

"Sit down," said Daizō, placing a candle on a long wooden clothes chest. Sitting down himself and crossing his arms, he asked, "Did you see Umpei?"

"Yes."

"When will he take you to the castle?"

"The day after tomorrow, when he has to bring ten new laborers. He said he'd include me."

"Then everything's set?"

"Well, we still have to get the district headman and the five-man neighborhood association to put their seals on the documents."

"No problem. It so happens I'm a member of the association."

"Really? You?"

"What's so surprising about that? I'm one of the more influential businessmen in the neighborhood. Last spring, the headman insisted I join."

"Oh, I wasn't surprised. I . . . I just didn't know, that's all."

"Ha, ha. I know exactly what you thought. You thought it was scandalous for a man like me to be on the committee that looks after neighborhood affairs. Well, let me tell you, if you have money, everybody'll say you're a fine man. You can't avoid becoming a local leader even if you try. Think, Matahachi. Before long you're going to have lots of money too."

"Y-y-yes," stammered Matahachi, unable to suppress a shiver. "W-w-will you give me the advance now?"

"Wait a minute."

Picking up the candle, he went to the rear of the storehouse. From a casket on the shelf, he counted out thirty pieces of gold. He came back and said, "Do you have anything to wrap them in?"

"No."

"Use this." He snatched a cotton rag from the floor and threw it to Matahachi. "You'd better put it in your stomach wrapper and make sure it's done up tight."

"Should I give you a receipt?"

"Receipt?" echoed Daizō with an involuntary laugh. "My, aren't you the honest one! But no, I don't need one. If you make a mistake, I'll confiscate your head."

Matahachi blinked and said, "I suppose I'd better be going now."

"Not so fast. Some obligations go with that money. Do you remember everything I told you this morning?"

"Yes. Well, there is one thing. You said the musket would be under the locust tree. Who's going to put it there?" Considering how difficult it was for ordinary workers to enter the castle grounds, he wondered how anyone could possibly manage to sneak in a musket and ammunition. And how could anyone without supernatural powers bury them so they'd be ready and waiting half a month from now?

"That doesn't concern you. You just do what you've agreed to do. You're nervous now because you're not used to the idea. After you've been there a couple of weeks, you'll be all right."

"I hope so."

"First you have to make up your mind you're going through with it. Then you have to be on the lookout for the right moment."

"I understand."

"Now, I don't want any slipups. Hide that money where no one can find it. And leave it there until after you've carried out your mission. When projects like this fall through, it's always because of money."

"Don't worry. I've thought about that already. But let me ask you this: How can I be sure that after I've done my job you won't refuse to pay me the rest?"

"Hmph! It may seem like bragging, but money's the least of my worries. Feast your eyes on those boxes." He held the candle up so Matahachi could see better. All over the room were boxes—for lacquered trays, for armor, for many other purposes. "Every one of them contains a thousand pieces of gold."

Without looking very closely, Matahachi said apologetically, "I don't doubt your word, of course."

The secret conversation went on for another hour or so. Matahachi, feeling somewhat more confident, left by the back way.

Daizō went to a nearby room and looked in. "Akemi, are you there?" he called. "I think he'll go straight from here to hide the money. You'd better follow him."

773

After a few visits to the pawnshop, Akemi, enthralled with Daizō's personality, had unburdened herself, complaining about her present circumstances and expressing her desire to move on to something better. A couple of days earlier, Daizō had remarked that he was in need of a woman to run his house. Akemi had shown up at his door very early this morning. When he'd let her in, he'd told her not to worry, he'd "take care of" Matahachi.

The prospective assassin, serenely unaware he was being followed, returned home. Hoe in hand, he then climbed through the dark grove behind the house to the top of Nishikubo Hill and buried his treasure.

Having observed all this, Akemi reported to Daizō, who immediately set out for Nishikubo Hill. It was almost dawn when he returned to the storehouse and counted the gold pieces he had dug up. He counted them a second time, and a third, but there was no mistake. Only twenty-eight.

Daizō cocked his head and frowned. He profoundly disliked people who stole his money.

Tadaaki's Madness

Osugi was not one to be driven to despair by the sorrows and bitter disappointments of unrequited maternal devotion, but here, with the insects singing amid the lespedeza and eulalia plants, with the great river flowing slowly by, she was not unmoved by feelings of nostalgia and the impermanence of life.

"Are you home?" The rough voice sounded harsh in the still evening air.

"Who is it?" she called.

"I'm from Hangawara's. A lot of fresh vegetables came in from Katsushika. The boss told me to bring you some."

"Yajibei's always so thoughtful."

She was seated at a low table, candle beside her and writing brush in hand, copying the *Sutra on the Great Love of Parents*. She had moved into a small rented house in the sparsely populated district of Hamachō and was making a reasonably comfortable living treating other people's aches and pains with moxa. She had no physical complaints to speak of. Since the beginning of autumn, she had felt quite young again.

"Say, Granny, did a young man come to see you earlier this evening?"

"For a moxa treatment, you mean?"

"Unh-unh. He came to Yajibei's, seemed to have something important on his mind. He asked where you were living now, and we told him."

"How old was he?"

"Twenty-seven or -eight, I guess."

"What did he look like?"

"Sort of round-faced. Not very tall."

"Mm, I wonder. . . ."

"He had an accent like yours. I thought maybe he came from the same place. Well, I'll be going. Good night."

As the footsteps faded, the voices of the insects rose again like the sound of drizzling rain. Putting down her brush, Osugi gazed at the candle, thinking of the days when she was young and people had read portents in the halo of the candlelight. Those left behind had no way of knowing how husbands, sons and brothers who'd gone off to war were faring, or what fate might lie in their own uncertain futures. A bright halo was taken as a sign of good fortune, purplish shadows as an indication that someone had died. When the flame crackled like pine needles, a person they were expecting was sure to come.

Osugi had forgotten how to interpret the omens, but tonight the cheerful halo, as colorfully beautiful as a rainbow, suggested something splendid in the offing.

Could it have been Matahachi? Her hand reached toward the brush once but drew back. As though entranced, she forgot herself and her surroundings and for the next hour or two thought only of her son's face, which seemed to float about in the darkness of the room.

A rustling noise at the back entrance brought her out of her reverie. Wondering if a weasel was playing havoc with her kitchen, she took the candle and went to investigate.

The sack of vegetables was by the sink; on top of the sack was a white object. Picking it up, she found it was heavy—as heavy as two pieces of gold. On the white paper in which they were wrapped, Matahachi had written: "I still don't have the heart to face you. Please forgive me if I neglect you for another six months. I'll just leave this note, without coming in."

A samurai with murder in his eyes was crashing through the tall grass to reach two men standing on the riverbank. Gasping for breath, he called, "Hamada, was it him?"

"No," groaned Hamada. "Wrong man." But his eyes sparkled as he continued to survey the surroundings.

"I'm sure it was."

"It wasn't. It was a boatman."

"Are you sure?"

"When I ran after him, he climbed into that boat over there."

"That doesn't make him a boatman."

"I checked."

"I must say, he's fast on his feet."

Turning away from the river, they started back through the fields of Hamachō.

"Matahachi . . . Matahachi!"

At first, the sound barely rose above the murmuring of the river, but as it was repeated and became unmistakable, they stopped and looked at one another in astonishment.

"Somebody's calling him! How could that be?"

"Sounds like an old woman."

With Hamada in the lead, they quickly traced the sound to its source, and when Osugi heard their footsteps, she ran toward them.

"Matahachi? Is one of you—"

They surrounded her and pinioned her arms behind her.

"What are you doing to me?" Puffing up like an enraged blowfish, she shouted, "Who are you anyway?"

"We're students of the Ono School."

"I don't know anybody named Ono."

"You never heard of Ono Tadaaki, tutor to the shōgun?"

"Never."

"Why, you old—"

"Wait. Let's see what she knows about Matahachi."

"I'm his mother."

"You're the mother of Matahachi, the melon vendor?"

"What do you mean, you pig! Melon vendor! Matahachi is a descendant of the House of Hon'iden, and that's an important family in the province of Mimasaka. I'll have you know the Hon'idens are high-ranking retainers of Shimmen Munetsura, lord of Takeyama Castle in Yoshino."

"Enough of this," said one man.

"What should we do?"

"Pick her up and carry her."

"Hostage? Do you think it'll work?"

"If she's his mother, he'll have to come for her."

Osugi pulled her scrawny body together and fought like a cornered tigress, but to no avail.

Bored and dissatisfied these past several weeks, Kojirō had fallen into the habit of sleeping a lot, in the daytime as well as at night. At the moment, he was lying on his back, grumbling to himself, hugging his sword to his chest.

"It's enough to make my Drying Pole weep. A sword like this, a swordsman like myself—rotting away in another man's house!"

There was a loud click and a metallic flash.

"Stupid fool!"

Striking in a great arc above him, the weapon slithered back into its scabbard like a living creature.

"Splendid!" cried a servant from the edge of the veranda. "Are you practicing a technique for striking from a supine position?"

"Don't be silly," sniffed Kojirō. He turned over onto his stomach, picked up two specks and flicked them toward the veranda. "It was making a nuisance of itself."

The servant's eyes widened. The insect, resembling a moth, had had both its soft wings and tiny body sliced neatly in two.

"Are you here to lay out my bedding?" asked Kojirō.

"Oh, no! Sorry! There's a letter for you."

Kojirō unhurriedly unfolded the letter and began to read. As he read, a touch of excitement came to his face. According to Yajibei, Osugi had been missing since the night before. Kojirō was requested to come at once and confer on a course of action.

The letter explained in some detail how they had learned where she was. Yajibei had had all his men out searching for her all day long, but the crux of the matter was the message Kojirō had left at the Donjiki. It had been crossed out and beside it was written: "To Sasaki Kojirō: The person holding Matahachi's mother in custody is Hamada Toranosuke of the House of Ono."

"Finally," said Kojirō, the words coming from deep in his throat. At the time he'd rescued Matahachi, he'd suspected that the two samurai he cut down had some connection with the Ono School.

He chuckled and said, "Just what I was waiting for." Standing on the veranda, he glanced up at the night sky. There were clouds, but it didn't look like rain.

Very shortly afterward, he was seen riding up the Takanawa highroad on a rented packhorse. It was late when he reached the Hangawara house. After questioning Yajibei in detail, he made up his mind to spend the night there and move into action the next morning.

Ono Tadaaki had received his new name not long after the Battle of Sekigahara. It was as Mikogami Tenzen that he'd been summoned to Hidetada's encampment to lecture on swordsmanship, which he did with distinction. Along with bestowal of the name came his appointment as a direct vassal of the Tokugawas and the granting of a new residence on Kanda Hill in Edo.

Since the hill afforded an excellent view of Mount Fuji, the shogunate designated it as a residential district for retainers from Suruga, the province in which Fuji was situated.

"I was told the house is on Saikachi Slope," said Kojirō.

He and one of Hangawara's men were at the top of the hill. In the deep valley below them, they could see Ochanomizu, a section of river from which water for the shōgun's tea was said to be drawn.

"Wait here," said Kojirō's guide. "I'll see where it is." He returned shortly with the information that they had already passed it.

"I don't remember any place that looked as though it might belong to the shōgun's tutor."

"Neither did I. I thought he'd have a big mansion, like Yagyū Munenori. But his house is that old one we saw on the right. I've heard it used to belong to the shōgun's stable keeper."

"I suppose it's nothing to be surprised about. Ono's only worth fifteen hundred bushels. Most of Munenori's income was earned by his ancestors."

"This is it," said the guide, pointing.

Kojirō stopped to inspect the general layout of the buildings. The old earthen wall extended back from the middle section of the slope to a thicket on a hill beyond. The compound appeared to be quite large. From the doorless gate he could see, beyond the main house, a building he took to be the dōjō and an annex, apparently of more recent construction.

"You can go back now," said Kojirō. "And tell Yajibei if I don't return with the old lady by evening, he can assume I've been killed."

"Yes, sir." The man ran swiftly down Saikachi Slope, stopping several times to look back.

Kojirō hadn't wasted any time trying to get near Yagyū Munenori. There was no way to defeat him and thereby take for himself the other man's glory, for the Yagyū Style was the one actually employed by the Tokugawas. That in itself was sufficient excuse for Munenori to refuse to take on ambitious rōnin. Tadaaki was inclined to take on all comers.

Compared with the Yagyū Style, Ono's was more practical, the aim being not to make a great display of skill but to actually kill. Kojirō had heard of no one who had succeeded in attacking the House of Ono and putting it to shame. While Munenori was in general the more highly respected, Tadaaki was considered the stronger.

Ever since coming to Edo and learning of this situation, Kojirō had told himself that one of these days he would be knocking on the Ono gate.

Numata Kajūrō glanced out the window of the dōjō's dressing room. He did a double take and his eyes swept the room, looking for Toranosuke. Spotting him in the middle of the room, giving a lesson to a younger student, he ran to his side and, in a low voice, sputtered, "He's here! Out there, in the front yard!"

Toranosuke, his wooden sword poised in front of him, shouted to the student, "On guard." Then he pressed forward, his footsteps resounding sharply on the floor. Just as the two reached the north corner, the student did a somersault and his wooden sword went sailing through the air.

Toranosuke turned and said, "Who are you talking about? Kojirō?"

"Yes, he's just inside the gate. He'll be here any minute."

"Much sooner than I expected. Taking the old lady hostage was a good idea."

"What do you plan to do now? Who's going to greet him? It should be someone who's prepared for anything. If he has the nerve to come here alone, he may try a surprise move."

"Have him brought to the dōjō. I'll greet him myself. The rest of you stay in the background and keep quiet."

"At least there're plenty of us here," said Kajūrō. Looking around, he was encouraged to see the faces of stalwarts like Kamei Hyōsuke, Negoro Hachikurō and Itō Magobei. There were also about twenty others; they had no idea of Kojirō's way of thinking, but they all knew why Toranosuke wanted him here.

One of the two men Kojirō had killed near the Donjiki was Toranosuke's elder brother. Though he was a good-for-nothing, not well thought of at school, his death nevertheless had to be avenged because of the blood relationship.

Despite his youth and his modest income, Toranosuke was a samurai to be reckoned with in Edo. Like the Tokugawas, he came originally from Mikawa Province, and his family was numbered among the oldest of the shōgun's hereditary vassals. He was also one of the "four generals of Saikachi Slope," the others being Kamei, Negoro and Itō.

When Toranosuke had come home the night before with Osugi, the consensus was that he had scored a noteworthy coup. Now it would be difficult for Kojirō not to show his face. The men vowed that if he did appear, they would beat him within an inch of his life, cut off his nose and hang him on a tree by the Kanda River for all to see. But they were by no means certain he'd show up; in fact, they had placed wagers on it, the majority betting that he wouldn't.

Assembling in the main room of the dōjō, they left the floor space open in the middle and waited anxiously.

After a time, one man asked Kajūrō, "Are you sure it was Kojirō you saw?"

"Absolutely sure."

They sat in formidable array. Their faces, woodenly stiff at first, were now showing signs of strain. Some feared that if this kept up much longer, they would fall victim to their own tenseness. Just as the breaking point seemed near, the rapid patter of sandals came to a halt outside the dressing room, and the face of another student, standing on tiptoe, appeared in the window.

"Listen! There's no sense in waiting here. Kojirō's not coming."

"What do you mean? Kajūrō just saw him."

"Yes, but he went straight to the house. How he got admitted, I don't know, but he's in the guest room talking with the master."

"The master?" echoed the group with a collective gasp.

"Are you telling the truth?" demanded Toranosuke, the look on his face close to consternation. He strongly suspected that if the circumstances of his brother's death were investigated, it would turn out that he'd been up to no good, but he'd glossed over this in relating the incident to Tadaaki. And if his master knew he'd abducted Osugi, it wasn't because he himself had told him.

"If you don't believe me, go look."

"What a mess!" groaned Toranosuke.

Far from sympathizing with him, his fellow students were annoyed by his lack of decisiveness.

Advising the others to keep cool while they went to see what the situation was, Kamei and Negoro were just stepping into their zōri when an attractive, light-complexioned girl came running out of the house. Recognizing Omitsu, they stopped where they were and the others rushed to the doorway.

"All of you," she cried in an excited, shrill voice. "Come right away! Uncle and the guest have drawn swords. In the garden. They're fighting!"

Though Omitsu was officially regarded as Tadaaki's niece, it had been whispered about that she was really the daughter of Itō Ittōsai by a mistress. Rumor had it that since Ittōsai was Tadaaki's teacher, Tadaaki must have agreed to rear the girl.

The look of fear in her eyes was most unusual. "I heard Uncle and the guest talking—their voices got louder and louder—and the next thing I knew . . . I don't suppose Uncle's in danger, but—"

The four generals emitted a collective yelp and lit out for the garden, which was set off from the outer compound by a shrub fence. The others caught up with them at the woven-bamboo gate.

"The gate's locked."

"Can't you force it?"

This proved unnecessary. The gate gave way under the weight of the samurai pressing against it. As it fell, a spacious area backed by a hill came into view. Tadaaki, his faithful Yukihira sword held at eye level, stood in the middle. Beyond him, at a fair distance, was Kojirō, the great Drying Pole rising above his head, fire shooting from his eyes.

The charged atmosphere seemed to create an invisible barrier. For men raised in the strict tradition of the samurai class, the awe-inspiring solemnity surrounding the combatants, the dignity of the deadly unsheathed swords, was inviolable. Despite their agitation, the spectacle momentarily deprived the students both of their mobility and of their emotions.

But then two or three of them started toward Kojirō's rear.

"Stay back!" cried Tadaaki angrily. His voice, harsh and chilling, not at all the fatherly voice they were accustomed to, arrested all movement on the part of his students.

People were apt to guess Tadaaki's age to be as much as ten years less than his fifty-four or -five years and take his height for average, whereas actually it was somewhat less than that. His hair was still black, his body small but solidly built. There was nothing stiff or awkward in the movements of his long limbs.

Kojirō had not yet made one strike—had not, in fact, been able to.

Yet Tadaaki had had to face one fact instantly: he was up against a terrific swordsman. "He's another Zenki!" he thought with an imperceptible shudder.

Zenki was the last fighter he had encountered to have such scope and driving ambition. And that had been long ago, in his youth, when he traveled with Ittōsai, living the life of a *shugyōsha*. Zenki, the son of a boatman in Kuwana Province, had been Ittōsai's senior disciple. As Ittōsai aged, Zenki began to look down on him, even proclaiming that the Ittō Style was his own invention.

Zenki had caused Ittōsai much grief, for the more adept he became with the sword, the more harm he caused other people. "Zenki," Ittōsai had lamented, "is the greatest mistake in my life. When I look at him, I see a monster embodying all the bad qualities I ever had. It makes me hate myself to watch him."

Ironically, Zenki served the youthful Tadaaki well—as a bad example—spurring him to higher achievements than might otherwise have been possible. Eventually, Tadaaki clashed with the evil prodigy at Koganegahara in Shimōsa and killed him, whereupon Ittōsai awarded him his certificate in the Ittō Style and gave him the book of secret instructions.

Zenki's one flaw had been that his technical capability was marred by a lack of breeding. Not so Kojirō. His intelligence and education were evident in his swordsmanship.

"I can't win this fight," thought Tadaaki, who felt himself in no way inferior to Munenori. In fact, his assessment of Munenori's skill was not very high.

While he stared at his awesome opponent, another truth came home to rest. "Time appears to have passed me by," he thought ruefully.

They stood motionless; not the slightest change was evident. But both Tadaaki and Kojirō were expending vital energy at a fearful rate. The physiological toll took the form of sweat pouring copiously from their foreheads, air rushing through flaring nostrils, skin turning white, then bluish. Though a move seemed imminent, the swords remained poised and unwavering.

"I give up," said Tadaaki, abruptly dropping back several paces. They had agreed it was not to be a fight to the finish. Either man could withdraw by acknowledging defeat.

Springing like a beast of prey, Kojirō brought the Drying Pole into action with a downward stroke of whirlwind force and speed. Though Tadaaki ducked just in time, his topknot flew up and was lopped off. Tadaaki himself, while dodging, executed a brilliant reprisal, slicing off some six inches of Kojirō's sleeve.

"Coward!" rose the cry from the students, whose faces burned with rage. By seizing on his opponent's capitulation as the opening for an attack, Kojirō had violated the samurai's code of ethics.

Every one of the students started for Kojirō.

He responded by flying with the speed of a cormorant to a large jujube tree at one end of the garden and half hiding himself behind the trunk. His eyes shifted with intimidating rapidity.

"Did you see it?" he shouted. "Did you see who won?"

"They saw it," said Tadaaki. "Hold off!" he told his men, sheathing his sword and returning to the veranda of his study.

Summoning Omitsu, he told her to tie up his hair. While she was doing this, he caught his breath. His chest glistened with rivulets of sweat.

An old saying came back to his mind: it is easy to surpass a predecessor, but difficult to avoid being surpassed by a successor. He'd been enjoying the fruits of hard training in his youth, complacent in the knowledge that his Ittō Style was no less flourishing than the Yagyū Style. Meanwhile society was giving birth to new geniuses like Kojirō. The realization came as a bitter shock, but he was not the sort of man to ignore it.

When Omitsu was finished, he said, "Give our young guest some water to rinse his mouth out with and show him back to the guest room."

The faces of the students around him were white with shock. Some were forcing back tears; others stared resentfully at their master.

"We'll assemble in the dōjō," he said. "Now." He himself led the way.

Tadaaki took his place on the raised seat in front and silently contemplated the three rows of his followers sitting facing him.

At length he lowered his eyes and said quietly, "I fear that I, too, have become old. As I look back, it seems to me my best days as a swordsman were when I defeated that devil Zenki. By the time this school was opened and people began talking about the Ono group on Saikachi Slope, calling the Ittō Style unbeatable, I'd already passed my peak as a swordsman."

The meaning of the words was so alien to their customary way of thinking that the students could not believe their ears.

His voice became firmer, and he looked directly at their doubting, discontented faces. "In my opinion, this is something that happens to all men. Age creeps up on us while we're not looking. Times change. The followers surpass their leaders. A younger generation opens up a new way. . . . This is the way it ought to be, for the world advances only through change. Yet this is inadmissible in the field of swordsmanship. The Way of the Sword must be a way that does not permit a man to age.

"Ittōsai . . . I don't know if he's still alive. I've had no word from my master for years. After Koganegahara, he took the tonsure and retreated to the mountains. His aim, he said, was to study the sword, to practice Zen, to search for the Way of Life and Death, to climb the great peak of perfect enlightenment.

"Now it's my turn. After today, I could no longer hold my head up before my master. . . . I regret I haven't lived a better life."

"M-m-master!" broke in Negoro Hachikurō. "You say you lost, but we don't believe you'd lose to a man like Kojirō under normal circumstances, even if he is young. There must have been something wrong today."

"Something wrong?" Tadaaki shook his head and chuckled. "Nothing wrong. Kojirō's young. But that's not why I lost. I lost because the times have changed."

"What does that mean?"

"Listen and see." He looked from Hachikurō to the other silent faces. "I'll try to make it brief, because Kojirō is waiting for me. I want you to listen carefully to my thoughts and my hopes for the future."

He then informed them that as of this day, he was retiring from the dōjō. His intention was not to retire in the ordinary sense but to follow in the footsteps of Ittōsai and go out in search of great enlightenment.

"That is my first great hope," he told them.

Next, he requested Itō Magobei, his nephew, to take charge of his only son, Tadanari. Magobei was also enjoined to report the day's happenings to the shogunate and explain that Tadaaki had decided to become a Buddhist priest.

Then he said, "I have no deep regrets over my defeat by a younger man. What does trouble and shame me is this: new fighters like Sasaki are appearing in other quarters, but not a single swordsman of his caliber has come out of the Ono School. I think I know why. A lot of you are hereditary vassals of the shōgun. You've let your status go to your heads. After a bit of training, you begin congratulating yourselves on being masters of the 'invincible Ittō Style.' You're too self-satisfied."

"Wait, sir," Hyōsuke protested in a trembling voice. "That's not fair. Not all of us are lazy and arrogant. We don't all neglect our studies."

"Shut up!" Tadaaki glared at him fiercely. "Laxness on the part of students is a reflection of laxness on the part of the teacher. I'm confessing my own shame now, passing judgment on myself.

782

"The task ahead of you is to eliminate laxness, to make the Ono School a center where youthful talent can develop correctly. It must become a training ground for the future. Unless it does, my leaving and making way for a reform will accomplish nothing."

At last, the sincerity of his statement began to take effect. His students hung their heads, pondering his words, each reflecting on his own shortcomings.

"Hamada," said Tadaaki.

Toranosuke replied, "Yes, sir," but he was obviously taken by surprise. Under Tadaaki's cold stare, his own eyes dropped to the floor.

"Stand up."

"Yes, sir," he said, without rising.

"Stand up! This instant."

Toranosuke rose to his feet. The others looked on mutely.

"I'm expelling you from the school." He paused to let this sink in. "But in doing so, I hope there will come a day when you'll have mended your ways, learned discipline and grasped the meaning of the Art of War. Perhaps at that time we can be together again as teacher and student. Now get out!"

"M-master, why? I don't remember doing anything to deserve this."

"You don't remember because you don't understand the Art of War. If you think about it long and carefully, you'll see."

"Tell me, please. I can't leave until you do." The veins stood out on his forehead.

"All right. Cowardice is the most shameful weakness a samurai can be accused of. The Art of War admonishes strictly against it. It is an ironclad rule at this school that any man guilty of a cowardly act must be expelled.

"Nevertheless, you, Hamada Toranosuke, let several weeks pass after your brother's death before challenging Sasaki Kojirō. In the meantime, you ran around trying to take revenge on some insignificant melon vendor. And yesterday you took this man's aged mother captive and brought her here. Do you call that conduct becoming a samurai?"

"But, sir, you don't understand. I did it to draw Kojirō out." He was about to launch into a spirited defense, but Tadaaki cut him short.

"That's precisely what I mean by cowardice. If you wanted to fight Kojirō, why didn't you go directly to his house? Why didn't you send him a message challenging him? Why didn't you declare your name and your purpose?"

"W-w-well, I did consider those things, but—"

"Consider? There was nothing to stop you from doing that. But you adopted the cowardly ruse of getting others to help you lure Kojirō here so you could attack him en masse. By comparison, Kojirō's attitude was admirable." Tadaaki paused. "He came alone, to see me personally. Refusing to have anything to do with a coward, he challenged me, on the grounds that a student's misconduct is his teacher's misconduct.

"The result of the confrontation between his sword and mine revealed a shameful crime. I now humbly confess that crime."

The room was deathly quiet.

"Now, Toranosuke, upon reflection, do you still believe yourself to be a samurai without shame?"

783

"Forgive me."

"Get out."

Eyes downcast, Toranosuke walked backward ten paces and knelt on the floor with his arms before him, preparatory to bowing.

"I wish you the best of health, sir. . . . And the same to the rest of you." His voice was dark.

He rose and walked sadly from the dōjō.

Tadaaki stood up. "I, too, must take my leave of the world." Suppressed sobs were audible. His final words were stern, yet full of affection. "Why mourn? Your day has come. It's up to you to see that this school advances into a new age with honor. Beginning now, be humble, work hard and try with all your might to cultivate your spirit."

Returning to the guest room, Tadaaki appeared quite unperturbed as he quietly took a seat and addressed Kojirō.

After apologizing for keeping him waiting, he said, "I've just expelled Hamada. I advised him to change his ways, to try to understand the real meaning of the samurai's discipline. I intend, of course, to release the old woman. Would you like to take her back with you, or should I arrange for her to go later?"

"I'm satisfied with what you've done. She can go with me." Kojirō moved as though to rise. The bout had completely drained him, and the subsequent wait had seemed very, very long.

"Don't go yet," said Tadaaki. "Now that it's all over, let's have a cup together and let bygones be bygones." Clapping his hands, he called, "Omitsu! Bring some sake."

"Thank you," said Kojirō. "It's kind of you to ask me." He smiled and said hypocritically, "I know now why Ono Tadaaki and the Ittō Style are so famous." He had no respect whatsoever for Tadaaki.

"If his natural talents are developed in the right way," thought Tadaaki, "the world will bow at his feet. But if he takes the wrong turn, there's another Zenki in the making."

"If you were my student—" The words were on the tip of Tadaaki's tongue. Instead of saying them, he laughed and replied modestly to Kojirō's flattery.

In the course of their conversation, Musashi's name came up and Kojirō learned he was under consideration to become one of the select group of men who gave lessons to the shōgun.

Kojirō merely said, "Oh?" But his expression betrayed his displeasure. Turning his eyes quickly toward the setting sun, he insisted it was time for him to go.

Not many days after that, Tadaaki vanished from Edo. He had the reputation of being a simple, straightforward warrior, the embodiment of honesty and selflessness, but a man who lacked Munenori's knack for politics. Not understanding why a man who could apparently accomplish anything he set his mind to would flee the world, people were consumed with curiosity and read all sorts of meanings into his disappearance.

As a result of his failure, Tadaaki, it was said, had lost his mind.

The Poignancy of Things

Musashi said it was the worst storm he'd ever seen.

Iori gazed wistfully at the sodden, tattered book pages scattered hither and yon, and thought sadly: "No more studying."

Two days of autumn—the two hundred tenth and two hundred twentieth days of the year—were especially dreaded by farmers. It was on these two days that typhoons were most likely to destroy the rice crop. Iori, more attuned to the dangers than his master, had taken the precaution of tying down the roof and weighting it with rocks. Nevertheless, during the night, the wind had ripped the roof off, and when it was light enough to inspect the damage, it was evident that the cabin was beyond any hope of repair.

With his experience at Hōtengahara in mind, Musashi set off shortly after dawn. Watching him go, Iori thought: "What good will it do him to look at the neighbors' paddies? Of course they're flooded. Doesn't his own house mean anything to him?"

He built a fire, using bits and pieces of the walls and floor, and roasted some chestnuts and dead birds for breakfast. The smoke stung his eyes.

Musashi came back a little after noon. About an hour later, a group of farmers wearing thick straw rain capes arrived to offer their thanks—for assistance to a sick person, for help in draining off the flood water, for a number of other services. As one old man admitted, "We always get into quarrels at times like these, what with everybody in a hurry to take care of his own problems first. But today we followed your advice and worked together."

They also brought gifts of food—sweets, pickles and, to Iori's delight, rice cakes. As he thought about it, Iori decided that that day he'd learned a lesson: if one forgot about oneself and worked for the group, food would naturally be forthcoming.

"We'll build you a new house," one farmer promised. "One that won't be blown down." For the present, he invited them to stay at his house, the oldest in the village. When they got there, the man's wife hung their clothes out to dry, and when they were ready to go to bed, they were shown to separate rooms.

Before he fell asleep, Iori became aware of a sound that stirred his interest. Turning over to face Musashi's room, he whispered through the shoji, "Do you hear that, sir?"

"Umm?"

"Listen. You can just hear them—drums from the shrine dances. Strange, isn't it, having religious dances the night after a typhoon?"

The only reply was the sound of deep breathing.

The next morning, Iori got up early and asked the farmer about the drums. Coming back to Musashi's room, he said brightly, "Mitsumine Shrine in Chichibu isn't so far from here, is it?"

"I shouldn't think so."

"I wish you'd take me there. To pay my respects."

Puzzled, Musashi asked why the sudden interest and was told that the drummers had been musicians in a neighboring village, practicing for the Asagaya Sacred Dance, which their household had specialized in since the distant past. They went every month to perform at the Mitsumine Shrine Festival.

The beauty of music and the dance was known to Iori only through these Shinto dances. He was inordinately fond of them, and having heard that the Mitsumine dances were one of the three great types in this tradition, he had his heart set on seeing them.

"Won't you take me?" he pleaded. "It'll be five or six days, at least, before our house is ready."

Iori's fervency reminded Musashi of Jōtarō, who had often made a nuisance of himself—whining, pouting, purring—to get what he wanted. Iori, so grown up and self-sufficient for his age, rarely resorted to such tactics. Musashi wasn't thinking about it particularly, but an observer might have noticed the effects of his influence. One thing he had deliberately taught Iori was to make a strict distinction between himself and his teacher.

At first he replied noncommittally, but after a little thought, he said, "All right, I'll take you."

Iori jumped in the air, exclaiming, "The weather's good too." Within five minutes, he'd reported his good fortune to their host, requested box lunches and procured new straw sandals. Then he was in front of his teacher again, asking, "Shouldn't we get started?"

The farmer saw them off with the promise that their house would be finished by the time they returned.

They passed places where the typhoon had left ponds, small lakes almost, in its wake, but otherwise it was difficult to believe the heavens had unleashed their fury only two days earlier. Shrikes flew low in the clear blue sky.

The first night, they chose a cheap inn in the village of Tanashi and went to bed early. The next day, their road led them farther into the great Musashino Plain.

Their journey was interrupted for several hours at the Iruma River, which was swollen to three times its normal size. Only a short section of the dirt bridge stood, uselessly, in the middle of the stream.

While Musashi watched a group of farmers carrying new piling out from both sides to make a temporary crossing, Iori noticed some old arrowheads and remarked on them, adding, "There's tops of helmets too. There must have been a battle here." He amused himself along the riverbank, digging up arrowheads, rusted fragments of broken swords and miscellaneous pieces of old, unidentifiable metal.

Suddenly he snatched his hand away from a white object he'd been about to pick up.

"It's a human bone," he cried.

"Bring it over here," said Musashi.

Iori had no stomach for touching it again. "What are you going to do with it?"

"'Bury it where it won't be walked on."

"It's not just a couple of bones. There're lots of them."

"Good. It'll give us something to do. Bring all you can find." Turning his back to the river, he said, "You can bury them over there, where those gentians are blooming."

"I don't have a spade."

"You can use a broken sword."

When the hole was deep enough, Iori put the bones in it, then gathered up his collection of arrowheads and bits of metal and buried them with the bones. "Is that all right?" he asked.

"Put some rocks over it. Make it into a proper memorial."

"When was there a battle here?"

"Have you forgotten? You must have read about it. The *Taiheiki* tells about two fierce battles, in 1333 and 1352, in a place called Kotesashigahara. That's about where we are now. On one side was the Nitta family, supporting the Southern Court, and on the other a huge army led by Ashikaga Takauji."

"Oh, the battles of Kotesashigahara. I remember now."

At Musashi's urging, Iori continued. "The book tells us Prince Munenaga lived in the eastern region for a long time and studied the Way of the Samurai, but was astonished when the Emperor appointed him shōgun."

"What was the poem he composed on that occasion?" Musashi asked.

Iori glanced up at a bird soaring through the azure sky and recited:

> "How could I have known
> I'd ever be master of
> The catalpa bow?
> Had I not passed through
> life
> Without touching it?"

"And the poem in the chapter telling how he crossed into Musashi Province and fought at Kotesashigahara?"

The boy hesitated, biting his lip, then began, in phrasing largely of his own making:

> "Why, then, should I cling
> To a life that is fulfilled
> When nobly given
> For the sake of our great
> lord,
> For the sake of the people?"

"And the meaning?"

"I understand that."

"Are you sure?"

"Anyone who can't understand without having it explained to him isn't really Japanese, even if he is a samurai. Isn't that true?"

"Yes. But tell me, Iori, if that's the case, why are you behaving as though handling those bones made your hands dirty?"

"Would it make you feel good to handle the bones of dead people?"

"The men who died here were soldiers. They'd fought and perished for the sentiments expressed in Prince Munenaga's poem. The number of samurai like that is uncountable; their bones, buried in the earth, are the foundation on which this country is built. Were it not for them, we'd still have neither peace nor the prospect of prosperity.

"Wars, like the typhoon we had, pass. The land as a whole is unchanged, but we must never forget the debt we owe to the white bones under the ground."

Iori nodded at almost every word. "I understand now. Shall I make an offering of flowers and bow before the bones I buried?"

Musashi laughed. "Bowing's not really necessary, if you keep the memory alive in your heart."

"But . . ." Not quite satisfied, the boy picked some flowers and placed them before the pile of stones. He was about to clasp his hands together in obeisance when another troubling thought came to him. "Sir, it's all well and good if these bones really belonged to samurai who were loyal to the Emperor. But what if they're the remains of Ashikaga Takauji's men? I wouldn't want to pay respect to them."

Iori stared at him, waiting for his answer. Musashi fixed his eyes on the thin sliver of daylight moon. But no satisfactory reply came to mind.

At length, he said, "In Buddhism there is salvation even for those guilty of the ten evils and the five deadly sins. The heart itself is enlightenment. The Buddha forgives the wicked if only they'll open their eyes to his wisdom."

"Does that mean loyal warriors and evil rebels are the same after they die?"

"No!" Musashi said emphatically. "A samurai holds his name to be sacred. If he sullies it, there's no redress throughout all generations."

"Then why does the Buddha treat bad people and loyal servants alike?"

"Because people are all fundamentally the same. There are those who are so blinded by self-interest and desire that they become rebels or brigands. The Buddha is willing to overlook this. He urges all to accept enlightenment, to open their eyes to true wisdom. This is the message of a thousand scriptures. Of course, when one dies, all becomes void."

"I see," said Iori, without really seeing. He pondered the matter for a few minutes and then asked, "But that's not true of samurai, is it? Not *everything* becomes void when a samurai dies."

"Why do you say that?"

"His name lives on, doesn't it?"

"That's true."

"If it's a bad name, it stays bad. If it's a good name, it stays good, even when the samurai is reduced to bones. Isn't that the way it is?"

"Yes, but it isn't really quite so simple," said Musashi, wondering if he could successfully guide his pupil's curiosity. "In the case of a samurai, there is such a thing as an appreciation of the poignancy of things. A warrior lacking this sensitivity is like a shrub in a desert. To be a strong fighter and nothing more is to be like a typhoon. It's the same with swordsmen who think of nothing but swords, swords, swords. A real samurai, a genuine swordsman, has a compassionate heart. He understands the poignancy of life."

Silently, Iori rearranged the flowers and clasped his hands.

Two Drumsticks

Halfway up the mountain, antlike human figures, climbing in continual procession, were swallowed up by a thick ring of clouds. Emerging near the summit, where Mitsumine Shrine was situated, they were greeted by a cloudless sky.

The mountain's three peaks, Kumotori, Shiraiwa and Myōhōgatake, straddled four eastern provinces. Within the Shinto complex there were Buddhist temples, pagodas, various other buildings and gates. Outside was a flourishing little town, with teahouses and souvenir shops, the offices of the high priests and the houses of some seventy farmers whose produce was reserved for the shrine's use.

"Listen! They've started playing the big drums," Iori said excitedly, gobbling down his rice and red beans. Musashi sat opposite, enjoying his repast at a leisurely pace.

Iori threw down his chopsticks. "The music's started," he said. "Let's go and watch."

"I had enough last night. You go alone."

"But they only did two dances last night. Don't you want to see the others?"

"Not if it means hurrying."

Seeing his master's wooden bowl was still half full, Iori said in a calmer tone, "Thousands of people have arrived since yesterday. It'd be a shame if it rained."

"Oh?"

When Musashi finally said, "Shall we go now?" Iori bounded for the front door like a dog unleashed, borrowed some straw sandals, and set them in place on the doorstep for his master.

In front of the Kannon'in, the subtemple where they were staying, and on both sides of the shrine's main gate, great bonfires blazed. Every house had a lighted torch in front of it, and the whole area, several thousand feet above sea level, was as bright as day. Overhead, in a sky the color of a deep lake, the River of Heaven glittered like magic smoke, while in the street swarms of men and women, oblivious of the chill in the mountain air, surged toward the stage where the sacred dances were performed. Flutes and great drums echoed on the mountain breeze. The stage itself was empty, except for the gently fluttering banners that would soon serve as a backdrop.

Jostled by the mob, Iori got separated from Musashi but quickly pushed his way through the crowd until he spied him standing near a building, staring up at a list of donors. Iori called his name, ran up to him, tugged at his sleeve, but Musashi's attention was riveted on one plaque, larger than the others. It stood out from all the rest because of the size of the contribution made by "Daizō of Narai, Shibaura Village, Province of Musashi."

The booming of the drums built to a crescendo.

"They've started the dance," squealed Iori, his heart flying to the sacred dance pavilion. "*Sensei*, what are you looking at?"

Musashi, stirred from his reverie, said, "Oh, nothing special. . . . I just remembered something I have to do. You go watch the dances. I'll be along later."

Musashi sought out the office of the Shinto priests, where he was greeted by an old man.

"I'd like to inquire about a donor," said Musashi.

"Sorry, we don't have anything to do with that here. You'll have to go to the residence of the chief Buddhist priest. I'll show you where it is."

Though Mitsumine Shrine was Shinto, general supervision of the whole establishment was in the hands of a Buddhist prelate. The plaque over the gate read: "Office of the High Priest in Charge," in suitably large characters.

At the entrance hall, the old man talked at some length with the priest on duty. When they were finished, the priest invited Musashi inside and very politely led him to an inner room. Tea was served, along with a tray of splendid cakes. Next came a second tray, followed shortly by a handsome young acolyte bearing sake. Presently no less a personage than a provisional bishop appeared.

"Welcome to our mountain," he said. "I fear we have only simple country fare to offer you. I trust you'll forgive us. Please make yourself comfortable."

Musashi was at a loss to understand the solicitous treatment. Without touching the sake, he said, "I came to make an inquiry about one of your donors."

"What?" The benign countenance of the priest, a rotund man of about fifty, underwent a subtle alteration. "An inquiry?" he asked suspiciously.

In rapid succession, Musashi asked when Daizō had come to the temple, whether he came there often, whether he ever brought anyone with him, and if so, what sort of person.

With every question the priest's displeasure grew, until finally he said,

"Then you're not here to make a contribution but merely to ask questions about someone who did?" His face was a study in exasperation.

"The old man must have misunderstood me. I never intended to make a donation. I only wanted to ask about Daizō."

"You could have made that perfectly clear at the entrance," the priest said haughtily. "From all I can see, you're a rōnin. I don't know who you are or where you come from. You must understand that I can't give out information about our donors to just anyone."

"I assure you nothing will happen."

"Well, you'll have to see the priest in charge of such matters." Looking as though he felt he'd been robbed, he dismissed Musashi.

The register of contributors turned out to be no more helpful, for it recorded only that Daizō had been there several times. Musashi thanked the priest and left.

Near the dance pavilion, he looked around for Iori without seeing him. If he'd looked up, he would have. The boy was almost directly over his head, having climbed a tree to get a better view.

Watching the scene unfolding on the stage, Musashi was transported back to his childhood, to the night festivals at the Sanumo Shrine in Miyamoto. He saw phantom images of the crowds, of Otsū's white face in their midst. Of Matahachi, always chewing food, of Uncle Gon, walking about importantly. Vaguely he sensed the face of his mother, worried about his being out so late, coming to look for him.

The musicians, clad in unusual costumes intended to simulate the elegance of the imperial guards of old, took their places on the stage. In the light of the fire, their tawdry finery, glittering with patches of gold brocade, was suggestive of the mythical robes of the age of the gods. The beating of the slightly slack drumheads reverberated through the forest of cryptomeria, then the flutes and well-seasoned boards, clapped rhythmically with small blocks, sounded the prelude. The master of the dance came forward, wearing the mask of an ancient man. This unearthly face, from whose cheeks and chin much of the lacquer had peeled, moved slowly as he sang the words of *Kamiasobi*, the dance of the gods.

> On sacred Mount Mimuro
> With its godly fence,
> Before the great deity,
> The leaves of the sakaki tree
> Grow in profuse abundance,
> Grow in profuse abundance.

The tempo of the drums picked up and other instruments joined in. Soon song and dance melded in a lively, syncopated rhythm.

> Whence came this spear?
> It is the spear of the sacred dwelling
> Of the Princess Toyooka who is in Heaven—
> The spear of the sacred dwelling.

Musashi knew some of the songs. As a child, he had sung them and donned a mask and taken part in the dancing at Sanumo Shrine.

> The sword that protects the people,
> The people of all lands.
> Let's hang it festively before the deity,
> Hang it festively before the deity.

The revelation struck like lightning. Musashi had been watching the hands of one of the drummers, wielding two short, club-shaped drumsticks. He sucked in his breath and fairly shouted, "That's it! Two swords!"

Startled by the voice, Iori took his eyes away from the stage just long enough to look down and say, "Oh, there you are."

Musashi didn't even glance up. He stared straight ahead, not in dreamy rapture like the others but with a look of almost frightening penetration.

"Two swords," he repeated. "It's the same principle. Two drumsticks, but only one sound." He folded his arms more tightly and scrutinized the drummer's every movement.

From one point of view, it was simplicity itself. People were born with two hands; why not use both of them? As it was, swordsmen fought with only one sword, and often one hand. This made sense, so long as everybody followed the same practice. But if one combatant were to employ two swords at once, what chance would an opponent using only one have of winning?

Against the Yoshioka School at Ichijōji, Musashi had discovered his long sword in his right hand, his short sword in his left. He had grasped both weapons instinctively, unconsciously, each arm involved to the utmost in protecting him. In a life-and-death struggle, he had reacted in an unorthodox fashion. Now, all of a sudden, the rationale seemed natural, if not inevitable.

If two armies were facing each other in battle, it would be unthinkable under the rules of the Art of War for either to make use of one flank while allowing the other to stand idle. Was there not a principle here that the lone swordsman could not afford to ignore? Ever since Ichijōji, it had seemed to Musashi that to use both hands and both swords was the normal, human way. Only custom, followed unquestioningly over the centuries, had made it seem abnormal. He felt he had arrived at an undeniable truth: custom had made the unnatural appear natural, and vice versa.

While custom was bred by daily experience, being on the boundary between life and death was something that occurred only a few times during a lifetime. Yet the ultimate aim of the Way of the Sword was to be able to stand on the brink of death at any time: facing death squarely, unflinchingly, should be as familiar as all other daily experiences. And the process had to be a conscious one, though movement should be as free as if it were purely reflexive.

The two-sword style had to be of this nature—conscious but at the same time as automatic as a reflex, completely free of the restrictions inherent in conscious action. Musashi had been trying for some time to unite in a valid principle what he knew instinctively with what he had learned by intellectual means. Now he was close to formulating it in words, and it would make him famous throughout the country for generations to come.

Two drumsticks, one sound. The drummer was conscious of left and right, right and left, but at the same time unconscious of them. Here, before his eyes, was the Buddhist sphere of free interpenetration. Musashi felt enlightened, fulfilled.

The five sacred dances, having begun with the song of the master of the dance, continued with performances by the dancers. There was the broad, sweeping Dance of Iwato, then the Dance of Ara Mikoto no Hoko. The melodies of the flutes quickened; bells rang in lively rhythm.

Musashi looked up at Iori and said, "Aren't you ready to leave?"

"Not yet," came the absentminded reply. Iori's spirit had become part of the dance; he felt himself to be one of the performers.

"Come back before it gets too late. Tomorrow we're going to climb the peak to the inner shrine."

The Demon's Attendant

The dogs of Mitsumine were a feral breed, said to result from the crossing of dogs brought by immigrants from Korea more than a thousand years earlier with the wild dogs of the Chichibu Mountains. Only a step removed from the wild stage, they roamed the mountainside and fed like wolves on the other wildlife in the region. But since they were regarded as messengers of the deity and were spoken of as his "attendants," worshipers often took home printed or sculptured images of them as good-luck charms.

The black dog with the man following Musashi was the size of a calf.

As Musashi entered the Kannon'in, the man turned, said, "This way," and beckoned with his free hand.

The dog growled, tugged at his leash—a piece of thick rope—and began sniffing.

Flicking the leash across the dog's back, the man said, "Shh, Kuro, be quiet."

The man was about fifty, solidly but supplely built, and like his dog, he seemed not quite tame. But he was well dressed. With his kimono, which looked like a priest's robe or a samurai's formal wear, he wore a narrow, flat obi and a hemp *hakama*. His straw sandals, of the sort men wore at festivals, were fitted with new thongs.

"Baiken?" The woman held back, to keep away from the dog.

"Down," commanded Baiken, rapping the animal sharply on the head. "I'm glad you spotted him, Okō."

"Then it was him?"

"No doubt about it."

For a moment, they stood silently looking through a break in the clouds at the stars, hearing but not really listening to the sacred dance music.

"What'll we do?" she asked.

"I'll think of something."

"We can't let this chance go to waste."

Okō stared expectantly at Baiken.

"Is Tōji at home?" he asked.

"Yes; he got drunk on the festival sake and fell asleep."

"Get him up."

"What about you?"

"I've got work to do. After I make my rounds, I'll come to your place."

Outside the main shrine gate, Okō broke into a trot. Most of the twenty or thirty houses were souvenir shops or teahouses. There were also a few small eating establishments, from which emanated the cheerful voices of revelers. From the eaves of the shack Okō entered hung a sign saying "Rest House." On one of the stools in the dirt-floored front room sat a young servant enjoying a catnap.

"Still sleeping?" asked Okō.

The girl, expecting a scolding, shook her head vigorously.

"I don't mean you—my husband."

"Oh, yes, he's still asleep."

With a disapproving click of her tongue, Okō grumbled, "A festival's going on, and he's sleeping. This is the only shop that isn't full of customers."

Near the door, a man and an old woman were steaming rice and beans in an earthen oven. The flames struck the only cheerful note in the otherwise gloomy interior.

Okō walked over to where a man was sleeping on a bench by the wall, tapped him on the shoulder and said, "Get up, you! Open your eyes for a change."

"Huh?" he mumbled, raising himself slightly.

"Oh, my," she exclaimed, as she backed away. Then she laughed and said, "I'm sorry. I thought you were my husband."

A piece of matting had slipped to the ground. The man, a round-faced youth with large, questioning eyes, picked it up, pulled it over his face and stretched out again. His head rested on a wooden pillow and his sandals were spattered with mud. On the table next to him were a tray and an empty rice bowl; by the wall, a travel pack, a basket hat and a staff.

Turning back to the girl, Okō said, "I suppose he's a customer?"

"Yes. He said he's planning to go up to the inner shrine early in the morning and asked if it was all right to take a nap here."

"Where's Tōji?"

"I'm over here, stupid." His voice came from behind a torn shoji. Reclining in the next room, with one foot hanging out into the shop, he said sullenly, "And why carry on about me taking a little snooze? Where've you been all this time, when you should have been tending to business?"

In many ways, the years had been even less kind to Okō than they had to Tōji. Not only was the charm of her earlier years no longer evident, but running the Oinu Teahouse required her to do a man's work to make up for her shiftless spouse, since Tōji made a pittance hunting in the winter but did little else. After Musashi burned down their hideout with its trick room at Wada Pass, their henchmen had all deserted them.

Tōji's bleary red eyes gradually focused on a barrel of water. Pulling himself to his feet, he went over to it and gulped down a dipperful.

Okō leaned on a bench and looked over her shoulder at him. "I don't care if there is a festival going on. It's about time you learned when to stop. You're lucky you didn't get run through by a sword while you were out."

"Huh?"

"I'm telling you you'd better be more careful."

"I don't know what you're talking about."

"Did you know Musashi's here at the festival?"

"Musashi? Miyamoto . . . Musashi?" Jolted into wakefulness, he said, "Are you serious? Look, you'd better go hide in the back."

"Is that all you can think of—hiding?"

"I don't want what happened at Wada Pass to happen again."

"Coward. Aren't you eager to get even with him, not only for that but for what he did to the Yoshioka School? I am, and I'm only a woman."

"Yeah, but don't forget, we had lots of men to help us then. Now there's just the two of us." Tōji hadn't been at Ichijōji, but he had heard how Musashi had fought and had no illusions about who would end up dead if the two of them ran into each other again.

Sidling up to her husband, Okō said, "That's where you're wrong. There's another man here, isn't there? A man who hates Musashi as much as you do."

Tōji knew she was referring to Baiken, whom they had become acquainted with when their wanderings brought them to Mitsumine.

Since there were no more battles, being a freebooter was no longer profitable, so Baiken had opened a smithy in Iga, only to be driven out when Lord Tōdō tightened his rule over the province. Intending to seek his fortune in Edo, he had disbanded his gang, but then, through the introduction of a friend, had become the watchman at the temple's treasure house.

Even now, the mountains between the provinces of Musashi and Kai were infested with bandits. In hiring Baiken to guard the treasure house, with its religious treasures and donated cash, the temple elders were fighting fire with fire. He had the advantage of being intimately familiar with the ways of bandits, and he was also an acknowledged expert with the chain-ball-sickle. As the originator of the Yaegaki Style, he might possibly have attracted the attention of a daimyō, had it not been for the fact that his brother was Tsujikaze Temma. In years long past, the two of them had terrorized the region between Mount Ibuki and the Yasugawa district. Changing times meant nothing to Baiken. To his way of thinking, Temma's death at the hands of Takezō had been the ultimate cause of all his subsequent difficulties.

Okō had long since told Baiken about their grievance against Musashi, exaggerating her rancor in order to cement her friendship with him. He had responded by scowling and saying, "One of these days . . ."

Okō had just finished telling Tōji how she had caught sight of Musashi from the teahouse, then lost him in the crowd. Later, on a hunch, she had gone to the Kannon'in, arriving just as Musashi and Iori were leaving for the outer shrine. This information she had promptly imparted to Baiken.

"So that's the way it is," said Tōji, taking courage from the knowledge that a dependable ally had already been lined up. He knew Baiken, using his favorite weapon, had beaten every swordsman at the recent shrine tournament. If he attacked Musashi, there was a good chance of winning. "What did he say when you told him?"

"He'll come as soon as he finishes his rounds."

"Musashi's no fool. If we're not careful—" Tōji shuddered and uttered a gruff, unintelligible sound. Okō followed his eyes to the man sleeping on the bench.

"Who's that?" asked Tōji.

"Just a customer," answered Okō.

"Wake him up and get him out of here."

Okō delegated this task to the girl servant, who went to the far corner and shook the man until he sat up.

"Get out," she said bluntly. "We're closing up now."

He stood up, stretched and said, "That was a nice nap." Smiling to himself and blinking his large eyes, he moved quickly but smoothly, wrapping the matting around his shoulders, donning his basket hat and adjusting his pack. He placed his staff under his arm, said, "Thanks a lot," with a bow and walked quickly out the door.

Okō judged from his clothing and accent that he was not one of the local farmers, but he seemed harmless enough. "Funny-looking man," she said. "I wonder if he paid his bill."

Okō and Tōji were still rolling up blinds and straightening up the shop when Baiken came in with Kuro.

"Good to see you," said Tōji. "Let's go to the back room."

Baiken silently removed his sandals and followed them, while the dog nosed around for scraps of food. The back room was only a broken-down lean-to with a first coat of rough plaster on the walls. It was out of earshot of anyone in the shop.

When a lamp had been lit, Baiken said, "This evening in front of the dance stage, I overheard Musashi tell the boy they'd go up to the inner shrine tomorrow morning. Later I went to the Kannon'in and checked it out."

Both Okō and Tōji swallowed and looked out the window; the peak on which the inner shrine stood was dimly outlined against the starry sky.

Knowing whom he was up against, Baiken had made a plan of attack and mobilized reinforcements. Two priests, guards at the treasure house, had already agreed to help and had gone on ahead with their lances. There was also a man from the Yoshioka School, who ran a small dōjō at the shrine. Baiken calculated he could mobilize perhaps ten freebooters, men he'd known in Iga who were now working in the vicinity. Tōji would carry a musket, while Baiken would have his chain-ball-sickle.

"You've done all this already?" asked Tōji in disbelief.

Baiken grinned but said nothing more.

A diminutive sliver of moon hung high above the valley, hidden from view by a thick fog. The great peak was still sleeping, with only the gurgling and roaring of the river to accentuate the silence. A group of dark figures huddled on the bridge at Kosaruzawa.

"Tōji?" Baiken whispered hoarsely.

"Here."

"Be sure to keep your fuse dry."

Conspicuous among the motley crew were the two lancer priests, who had the skirts of their robes tucked up ready for action. The others were dressed in a variety of outfits, but all were shod so as to be able to move nimbly.

"Is this everybody?"

"Yes."

"How many altogether?"

They counted heads: thirteen.

"Good," said Baiken. He went over their instructions again. They listened in silence, nodding occasionally. Then, at a signal, they scurried into the fog to take up positions along the road. At the end of the bridge, they passed a milestone saying: "Six Thousand Yards to the Inner Shrine."

When the bridge was empty again, a great company of monkeys emerged from hiding, jumping from limbs, climbing vines, converging on the road. They ran out onto the bridge, crawled under it, threw stones into the ravine. The fog toyed with them, as if encouraging their frolic. Had a Taoist Immortal appeared and beckoned, perhaps they would have been transformed into clouds and flown off with him to heaven.

The barking of a dog echoed through the mountains. The monkeys vanished, like sumac leaves before an autumn wind.

Kuro came up the road, dragging Okō along with him. He'd somehow broken loose, and though Okō had eventually got hold of the leash, she hadn't been able to make him go back. She knew Tōji didn't want the dog around to make noise, so she thought maybe she could get him out of the way by letting him go up to the inner shrine.

As the restlessly shifting fog began to settle in the valleys like snow, the three peaks of Mitsumine and the lesser mountains between Musashino and Kai rose against the sky in all their grandeur. The winding road stood out white, and birds began to ruffle their feathers and chirp a greeting to the dawn.

Iori said, half to himself, "Why is that, I wonder?"

"Why is what?" asked Musashi.

"It's getting light, but I can't see the sun."

"For one thing, you're looking toward the west."

"Oh." Iori gave the moon, sinking behind the distant peaks, a cursory glance.

"Iori, a lot of your friends seem to live here in the mountains."

"Where?"

"Over there." Musashi laughed and pointed to some monkeys clustered around their mother.

"I wish I was one of them."

"Why?"

"At least they have a mother."

They climbed a steep part of the road in silence and came to a relatively flat stretch. Musashi noticed the grass had been trampled by a large number of feet.

After winding around the mountain for a while more, they reached a level area where they were facing east.

"Look," cried Iori, looking over his shoulder at Musashi. "The sun's coming up."

"So it is."

From the sea of clouds beneath them, the mountains of Kai and Kōzuke jutted up like islands. Iori stopped and stood stock still, feet together, arms at his sides, lips tightly set. He stared in rapt fascination at the great golden sphere, imagining himself to be a child of the sun. All at once he exclaimed in a very loud voice, "It's Amaterasu Ōmikami! Isn't it?" He looked to Musashi for confirmation.

"That's right."

Raising his arms high above his head, the boy filtered the brilliant light through his fingers. "My blood!" he cried. "It's the same color as the sun's blood." Clapping his hands, as he would at a shrine to summon the deity, he bowed his head in silent obeisance, thinking: "The monkeys have a mother. I have none. But I have this goddess. They have none."

The revelation filled him with joy, and as he burst into tears, he seemed to hear from beyond the clouds the music of the shrine dances. The drums boomed in his ears, while the counterpoint of the flutes hovered around the melody of the Dance of Iwato. His feet caught the rhythm; his arms swayed gracefully. From his lips came the words he had memorized only the night before:

> "The catalpa bow—
> With each coming of spring,
> I hope to see the dancing
> Of the myriad of gods,
> Oh, how I hope to see their dancing—"

Suddenly realizing Musashi had gone on ahead, he abandoned his dance and ran to catch up.

The morning light barely penetrated the forest they now entered. Here, in the approach to the inner shrine, the cryptomerias were of enormous circumference and all about the same height. Tiny white flowers grew in the thick patches of moss clinging to the trees. Suspecting the trees were ancient—five hundred years old, perhaps even a thousand—Iori had an urge to bow to them. Here and there, bright red vine maple caught his eye. Low striped bamboo encroaching on the road narrowed it to a path.

Without warning, the earth seemed to tremble under their feet. Close upon the thunderous report came an unnerving scream and a cascade of sharp echoes. Iori covered his ears with his hands and dived into the bamboo.

"Iori! Stay down!" Musashi commanded from the shadow of a large tree. "Don't move even if they trample on you!"

The gloomy half light seemed infested with lances and swords. Because of the scream, the attackers thought at first the bullet had found its mark, but there was no body in sight. Uncertain as to what had happened, they froze.

Iori was at the center of a circle of eyes and unsheathed blades. In the deathly silence that followed, curiosity got the better of him. He slowly raised his head above the bamboo. Only a few feet away, a sword blade, extending from behind a tree, caught a flash of sunlight.

Losing all control, Iori screamed at the top of his lungs, "*Sensei!* Somebody's hiding there!" As he shouted, he jumped to his feet and made a dash for safety.

The sword leapt from the shadows and hung like a demon above his head. But only for an instant. Musashi's dagger flew straight to the swordsman's head and lodged in the temple.

"Ya-a-h!"

One of the priests charged at Musashi with his lance. Musashi caught the lance and held it tightly with one hand.

Another death cry sounded, as if the man's mouth were full of rocks. Wondering if his attackers could be fighting among themselves, Musashi strained his eyes to see. The other priest took careful aim with his lance and hurtled toward him. Musashi caught this lance too and held it securely under his right arm.

"Jump him now!" screamed one of the priests, realizing that Musashi had his hands full.

His voice stentorian, Musashi shouted, "Who are you? Identify yourselves, or I'll assume you're all enemies. It's a shame to spill blood on this holy ground, but I may have no choice."

Whirling the lances around and sending the two priests off on different tangents, Musashi whipped out his sword and finished off one of them before he had stopped tumbling. Spinning around, he found himself confronting three more blades, lined up across the narrow path. Without pausing, he moved toward them threateningly, one step at a time. Two more men came out and took their places shoulder to shoulder beside the first three.

As Musashi advanced and his opponents retreated, he caught a glimpse of the other lancer priest, who had recovered his weapon and was chasing Iori. "Stop, you cutthroat!" But the moment Musashi turned to go to Iori's rescue, the five men let out a howl and charged. Musashi rushed head on to meet them. It was like the collision of two raging waves, but the spray was blood, not brine. Musashi kept whirling from opponent to opponent with the speed of a typhoon. Two bloodcurdling cries, then a third. They fell like dead trees, each sliced through the middle of the torso. In Musashi's right hand was his long sword, in his left the short one.

With cries of terror, the last two turned and ran, Musashi close behind them.

"Where do you think you're going?" he shouted, splitting one man's head open with the short sword. The black spurt of blood caught Musashi in the eye. Reflexively, he raised his left hand to his face and, in that instant, heard a strange metallic sound behind him.

He swung his long sword to deflect the object, but the effect of the action was very different from the intention. Seeing the ball and chain wrapped around the blade near the sword guard, he was seized with alarm. Musashi had been taken off guard.

"Musashi!" shouted Baiken. He pulled the chain taut. "Have you forgotten me?"

Musashi stared for a moment before exclaiming, "Shishido Baiken, from Mount Suzuka!"

"That's right. My brother Temma's calling you from the valley of hell. I'll see that you get there quick!"

Musashi could not free his sword. By slow degrees, Baiken was taking in the chain and moving closer, to make use of the razor-sharp sickle. As Musashi looked for an opening for his short sword, he realized with a start that if he had been fighting with only his long sword, he would be utterly defenseless now.

Baiken's neck was so swollen it was nearly as thick as his head. With a strained cry, he jerked powerfully on the chain.

Musashi had blundered; he knew that. The ball-chain-sickle was an unusual weapon, but not unfamiliar to him. Years earlier, he had been struck by admiration when he had first seen the hellish device in the hands of Baiken's wife. But it was one thing to have seen it, something else to know how to counter it.

Baiken gloated, a broad, evil grin spreading over his face. Musashi knew there was only one course open to him: he had to let go of his long sword. He looked for the right moment.

With a ferocious howl, Baiken leapt and swept the sickle toward Musashi's head, missing by only a hair's breadth. Musashi released the sword with a loud grunt. No sooner had the sickle been withdrawn than the ball came whirring through the air. Then the sickle, the ball, the sickle . . .

Dodging the sickle put Musashi right in the path of the ball. Unable to get close enough to strike, he wondered frantically how long he could keep it up. "Is this it?" he asked. The question was conscious, but as the tension increased, his body became difficult to control and his responses purely physiological. Not only his muscles but his very skin was struggling instinctively; concentration became so intense the flow of oily sweat stopped. Every hair on his body stood on end.

It was too late to get behind a tree. If he made a dash for it now, he'd probably run into another foe.

He heard a clear, plaintive cry, and thought: "Uh-oh. Iori?" He wanted to look but in his heart gave the boy up for lost.

"Die! You son of a bitch!" The cry came from behind Musashi, then: "Musashi, why're you taking so much time? I'm taking care of the vermin behind you."

Musashi didn't recognize the voice but decided he could focus his attention on Baiken alone.

To Baiken, the most important factor was his distance from his opponent; his effectiveness depended on manipulating the length of the chain. If Musashi could move a foot beyond the reach of the chain or approach a foot nearer, Baiken would be in trouble. He had to make sure that Musashi did neither.

Musashi marveled at the man's secret technique, and as he marveled, it suddenly struck him that here was the principle of the two swords. The chain was a single length, the ball functioned as the right sword, the sickle as the left.

"Of course!" he cried triumphantly. "That's it—that's the Yaegaki Style." Now confident of victory, he leapt back, putting five feet between the two of them. He transferred his sword to his right hand and hurled it straight as an arrow.

Baiken twisted his body, and the sword glanced off, burying itself in the root of a nearby tree. But as he twisted, the chain wrapped itself around his torso. Before he could even cry out, Musashi slammed his full weight into him. Baiken got his hand as far as the hilt of his sword, but Musashi broke his hold with a sharp chop to the wrist. In a continuation of the same motion, he drew the weapon and split Baiken open, like lightning splitting a tree. As he pulled the blade down, he twisted ever so slightly.

"What a pity," thought Musashi. As the story was later told, he even uttered a sigh of compassion as the originator of the Yaegaki Style breathed his last.

"The *karatake* slice," exclaimed an admiring voice. "Straight down the trunk. No different from splitting bamboo. It's the first time I've ever seen it."

Musashi turned and said, "Why, if it isn't ... Gonnosuke from Kiso. What are you doing here?"

"It's been a long time, hasn't it? The god of Mitsumine must have arranged it, perhaps with the aid of my mother, who taught me so much before she died."

They fell to chatting, but Musashi suddenly stopped and cried, "Iori!"

"He's all right. I rescued him from that pig of a priest and had him climb a tree."

Iori, watching them from a high branch, started to speak but instead shaded his eyes and looked toward a small flat area beyond the edge of the forest. Kuro, tied to a tree, had caught Okō's kimono sleeve with his teeth. She yanked desperately at the sleeve. In a trice, it tore off, and she ran away.

The lone survivor, the other priest, was hobbling along, leaning heavily on his lance, blood flowing from a head wound. The dog, perhaps crazed by the smell of blood, started making a terrible racket. The noise echoed and re-echoed for a time, but then the rope gave way, and the dog went after Okō. When he reached him, the priest lifted his lance and aimed for the dog's head. Wounded in the neck, the beast ran into the woods.

"That woman's getting away," cried Iori.

"Never mind. You can come down now."

"There's an injured priest over there. Shouldn't you catch him?"

"Forget it. He doesn't matter anymore."

"The woman's probably the one from the Oinu Teahouse," said Gonnosuke. He explained his presence, the heaven-sent coincidence that had enabled him to come to Musashi's assistance.

Deeply grateful, Musashi said, "You killed the man who fired the gun?"

"No." Gonnosuke smiled. "Not me; my staff. I knew ordinarily you could take care of men like that, but if they were going to use a gun, I decided I'd better do something. So I came here ahead of them and slipped up behind the man while it was still dark."

They checked the corpses. Seven had been killed with the staff, only five with the sword.

Musashi said, "I haven't done anything except defend myself, but this area belongs to the shrine. I feel I should explain things to the government official in charge. Then he can ask his questions and get the incident cleared up."

On their way down the mountain, they ran into a contingent of armed officials at the bridge at Kosaruzawa. Musashi told his story. The captain in charge listened, seemingly puzzled, but nevertheless ordered Musashi tied up.

Shocked, Musashi wanted to know why, since he was on his way to report to them in the first place.

"Get moving," ordered the captain.

Angry as Musashi was about being treated as an ordinary criminal, there was still another surprise coming. There were more officials farther down the mountain. By the time they arrived in the town, his guard numbered no fewer than a hundred.

Brother Disciples

"Come now, no more tears." Gonnosuke hugged Iori to his chest. "You're a man, aren't you?"

"It's because I'm a man . . . that I'm crying." He lifted his head, opened his mouth wide and bawled at the sky.

"They didn't arrest Musashi. He gave himself up." Gonnosuke's mild words masked his own deep concern. "Come on, let's go now."

"No! Not until they bring him back."

"They'll let him go soon. They'll have to. Do you want me to leave you here by yourself?" Gonnosuke walked a few paces away.

Iori didn't move. Just then, Baiken's dog came charging out of the woods, his muzzle a dull, bloody red.

"Help!" screamed Iori, running to Gonnosuke's side.

"You're worn out, aren't you? Look, would you like me to carry you piggyback?"

Iori, pleased, mumbled his thanks, climbed on the proffered back and wrapped his arms around the broad shoulders.

With the festival over the night before, the visitors had departed. A gentle breeze wafted bits of bamboo wrapping and scraps of paper along the deserted streets.

Passing the Oinu Teahouse, Gonnosuke glanced inside, intending to go by unnoticed.

But Iori piped out, "There's the woman who ran away!"

"I imagine that's where she'd be." He stopped and wondered aloud, "If the officials dragged in Musashi, why didn't they arrest her too?"

When Okō saw Gonnosuke, her eyes blazed with anger.

Seeing she seemed to be hurriedly gathering her belongings together, Gonnosuke laughed. "Going on a trip?" he asked.

"None of your business. Don't think I don't know you, you meddling scoundrel. You killed my husband!"

"You brought it on yourselves."

"I'll get even one of these days."

"She-demon!" Iori shouted over Gonnosuke's head.

Retreating into the back room, Okō laughed scornfully. "You're fine ones to be saying bad things about me when you're the thieves who broke into the treasure house."

"What's this?" Gonnosuke let Iori slide to the ground and went into the teahouse. "Who are you calling thieves?"

"You can't fool me."

"Say that again, and—"

"*Thieves!*"

As Gonnosuke grabbed her arm, she turned and stabbed at him with a dagger. Not bothering with his staff, he wrested the dagger from her hand and sent her sprawling through the front door.

Okō jumped up and screamed, "Help! Thieves! I'm being attacked."

Gonnosuke took aim and hurled the dagger. It entered her back and the point came out in front. Okō pitched forward onto her face.

From nowhere, Kuro bounded forth and was at the body, first slurping blood hungrily, then lifting his head to howl at the sky.

"Look at those eyes!" exclaimed Iori in horror.

Okō's cry of "Thieves!" had caught the ears of the excited villagers. Sometime before dawn, someone had broken into the temple treasure house. It was clearly the work of outsiders, for the religious treasures—old swords, mirrors and the like—had been left untouched, but a fortune in gold dust, bullion and cash, accumulated over a period of many years, was missing. The news had leaked out slowly and was still unconfirmed. The effect of Okō's scream, the most tangible proof so far, was electric.

"There they are!"

"Inside the Oinu!"

The cries attracted a still larger mob, armed with bamboo spears, boar guns, sticks and rocks. In no time it seemed that the whole village was surrounding the teahouse, thirsty for blood.

Gonnosuke and Iori ducked out the back and for the next several hours were driven from hiding place to hiding place. But now they had an explanation: Musashi had been arrested not for the "crime" he was about to confess but as a thief. It was not until they reached Shōmaru Pass that they shook off the last of the search parties.

"You can see Musashino Plain from here," said Iori. "I wonder if my teacher's all right."

"Hmm. I imagine he's in prison by now and being questioned."

"Isn't there any way to save him?"

"There must be."

"Please do something. Please."

"You don't have to beg. He's like a teacher to me too. But, Iori, there's not much you can do here. Can you make it back home by yourself?"

"I suppose so, if I have to."

"Good."

"What about you?"

"I'm going back to Chichibu. If they refuse to release Musashi, I'll get him out some way. Even if I have to tear the prison down." For emphasis, he thumped the ground once with his staff. Iori, who had seen the power of this weapon, quickly nodded his agreement. "That's a boy. You go back and watch over things until I bring Musashi home safe and sound." Placing his staff under his arm, he turned back toward Chichibu.

Iori didn't feel lonely or afraid, nor did he worry about getting lost. But he was dreadfully sleepy, and as he walked along under the warm sun, he could hardly keep his eyes open. At Sakamoto, he saw a stone Buddha by the wayside and lay down in its shadow.

The evening light was fading when he awoke and heard soft voices on the other side of the statue. Feeling rather guilty about eavesdropping, he pretended he was still asleep.

There were two of them, one sitting on a tree stump, the other on a rock. Tied to a tree a little distance away were two horses with lacquered boxes suspended from both sides of their saddles. A wooden tag attached to one of the boxes said: "From Shimotsuke Province. For use in the construction of the west encirclement. Lacquerware Supplier to the Shōgun."

To Iori, who now peeked around the statue, they did not look like the normal run of well-fed castle officials. Their eyes were too sharp, their bodies too muscular. The older one was a vigorous-looking man of more than fifty. The last rays of the sun reflected strongly from his bonnetlike hat, which came down over both ears and projected out in front, concealing his features.

His companion was a slender, wiry youth wearing a forelock that suited his boyish face. His head was covered with a Suō-dyed hand towel, tied beneath his chin.

"How about the lacquerware boxes?" the younger one asked. "That was pretty good, wasn't it?"

"Yes, that was clever, making people think we're connected with the work going on at the castle. I wouldn't have thought of that myself."

"I'll have to teach you these things little by little."

"Careful now. Don't start making fun of your elders. But who knows? Maybe in four or five years, old Daizō will be taking orders from you."

"Well, young people do grow up. Old people just get older, no matter how hard they work at staying young."

"Do you think that's what I'm doing?"

"It's obvious, isn't it? You're always thinking of your age, and that's what makes you so devoted to seeing your mission accomplished."

"You know me pretty well, I guess."

"Shouldn't we be going?"

"Yes; night's catching up with us."

"I don't like the idea of being caught up with."

"Ha, ha. If you scare easily, you can't have much confidence in what you're doing."

"I haven't been at this business very long. Even the sound of the wind makes me nervous sometimes."

"That's because you still think of yourself as an ordinary thief. If you keep in mind that you're doing it for the good of the country, you'll be all right."

"You always say that. I believe you, but something keeps telling me I'm not doing the right thing."

"You have to have the courage of your convictions." But the admonition sounded slightly unconvincing, as though Daizō was reassuring himself.

The youth jumped lightly into the saddle and rode on ahead. "Keep your eye on me," he called back over his shoulder. "If I see anything, I'll signal."

The road made a long descent to the south. Iori watched from behind the stone Buddha for a minute, then decided to follow them. Somehow the idea had formed in his mind that these were the treasure house thieves.

Once or twice they looked back cautiously. Apparently finding nothing to warrant alarm, they seemed to forget about him after a time. Before long, the evening glow was gone, and it was too dark to see more than a few yards ahead.

The two riders were almost at the edge of Musashino Plain when the youth pointed and said, "There, Chief, you can see the lights of Ōgimachiya." The road was flattening out. A short distance ahead, the Iruma River, twisting like a discarded obi, shone silvery in the moonlight.

Iori was now being careful to remain inconspicuous. His idea that these men were the thieves had become a conviction, and he knew all about bandits from his days in Hōtengahara. Bandits were vicious men who would commit mayhem over a single egg or a handful of red beans. Unprovoked murder was nothing to them.

By and by, they entered the town of Ōgimachiya. Daizō lifted his arm and said, "Jōta, we'll stop here and have a bite to eat. The horses have to be fed, and I'd like a smoke."

805

They tied the horses in front of a dimly lit shop and went inside. Jōta stationed himself by the door, keeping his eyes on the boxes the whole time he was eating. When he was finished, he went out and fed the horses.

Iori went into a food shop across the street, and when the two men rode off, he grabbed the last handful of his rice and ate it as he walked.

They rode side by side now; the road was dark but level.

"Jōta, did you send a courier to Kiso?"

"Yes, I took care of that."

"What time did you tell them?"

"Midnight. We should be there on schedule."

In the still night, Iori caught enough of their conversation to know that Daizō called his companion by a boy's name, while Jōta addressed the older man as "Chief." This might mean nothing more than that he was the head of a gang, but somehow Iori got the impression they were father and son. This made them not mere bandits but hereditary bandits, very dangerous men he would never be able to capture by himself. But if he could stick with them long enough, he could report their whereabouts to the officials.

The town of Kawagoe was fast asleep, as soundless as a swamp in the dead of night. Having passed rows of darkened houses, the two riders turned off the highway and began climbing a hill. A stone marker at the bottom said: "Forest of the Head-burying Mound—Above."

Climbing up through the bushes alongside the path, Iori reached the top first. There was a lone pine tree of great size, to which a horse was tied. Squatting at the base were three men dressed like rōnin, arms folded on their knees, looking expectantly toward the path.

Iori had hardly ensconced himself in a hiding place before one of the men stood up and said, "It's Daizō, all right." All three ran forward and exchanged jovial salutations. Daizō and his confederates had not met for nearly four years.

Before long, they got down to work. Under Daizō's direction, they rolled a huge stone aside and began digging. Dirt was piled to one side, a great store of gold and silver to the other. Jōta unloaded the boxes from the horses and dumped out their contents, which, as Iori had suspected, consisted of the missing treasure from Mitsumine Shrine. Added to the previous cache, the total booty must have had a value of many tens of thousands of *ryō*.

The precious metals were poured into plain straw sacks and loaded on three horses. The empty lacquered boxes, along with other objects that had served their purpose, were dumped into the hole. After the ground had been smoothed over, the stone was restored to its original position.

"That should do it," said Daizō. "Time for a smoke." He sat down by the pine tree and took out his pipe. The others brushed off their clothes and joined him.

During the four years of his so-called pilgrimage, Daizō had covered the Kantō Plain very thoroughly. There were few temples or shrines without a plaque attesting to his generosity, the extent of which was no secret. Strangely, though, no one had thought to ask how he had come by all this money.

Daizō, Jōtarō and the three men from Kiso sat in a circle for about an hour, discussing future plans. That it was now risky for Daizō to return to Edo was not in doubt, but one of them had to go. There was gold in the storehouse at Shibaura to be recovered and documents to be burned. And something had to be done about Akemi.

Just before sunup, Daizō and the three men began the journey down the Kōshū highroad to Kiso. Jōtarō, on foot, set off in the opposite direction.

The stars Iori was gazing at offered no answer to his question: "Who to follow?"

Under the transparently blue autumn sky, the strong rays of the afternoon sun seemed to sink right into Jōtarō's skin. His head filled with thoughts of his role in the coming age, he was strolling across the Musashino Plain as though he owned it.

Casting a somewhat apprehensive glance behind him, he thought: "He's still there." Thinking the boy might want to talk to him, he'd already stopped a couple of times, but the boy had made no attempt to catch up with him.

Deciding to find out what was going on, Jōtarō chose a clump of eulalia and hid in it.

When Iori reached the stretch of road where he'd last seen Jōtarō, he began looking around worriedly.

Abruptly Jōtarō stood up and called out, "You there, runt!"

Iori gasped but recovered quickly. Knowing he couldn't get away, he walked on past and asked nonchalantly, "What do you want?"

"You've been following me, haven't you?"

"Unh-unh." Iori shook his head innocently. "I'm on my way to Jūnisō Nakano."

"You're lying! You were following me."

"I don't know what you're talking about." Iori started to break and run, but Jōtarō caught him by the back of his kimono.

"Out with it!"

"But . . . I . . . I don't know anything."

"Liar!" said Jōtarō, tightening his grip. "Somebody sent you after me. You're a spy!"

"And you—you're a lousy thief!"

"What?" Jōtarō shouted, his face almost touching Iori's.

Iori bent nearly to the ground, broke loose and took off.

Jōtarō hesitated a minute, then set off after him.

Off to one side, Iori could see thatched roofs scattered about like wasp nests. He ran through a field of reddish autumn grass, kicking apart several dusty molehills.

"Help! Help! Thief!" cried Iori.

The small village he was entering was inhabited by families charged with fighting fires on the plain. Iori could hear a blacksmith's hammer and anvil. People came running out of dark stables and houses where persimmons had been hung to dry. Waving his arms, Iori panted, "The man with the bandanna

. . . chasing me . . . is a thief. Capture him. Please! . . . Oh, oh! Here he comes."

The villagers stared in bewilderment, some looking fearfully at the two youths, but to Iori's dismay they made no move to capture Jōtarō.

"He's a thief! He stole from the temple!"

He stopped halfway through the village, conscious that the only thing disturbing the peaceful atmosphere was his own shouting. Then he took to his heels again and found a place to hide and catch his breath.

Jōtarō cautiously slowed down to a dignified walk. The villagers watched in silence. He certainly didn't look like either a robber or a rōnin up to no good; in fact, he seemed like a clean-cut youth incapable of committing any kind of crime.

Disgusted that the villagers—grownups!—wouldn't stand up to a thief, Iori made up his mind to hurry back to Nakano, where he could at least present his case to people he knew.

He left the road and struck out across the plain. When he could see the cryptomeria grove behind the house, there was only a mile to go. Filled with relief, he changed his pace, from a trot to a full run.

Suddenly he saw that his way was blocked by a man with both arms outstretched.

He didn't have time to figure out how Jōtarō had got ahead of him, but he was on home ground now. He jumped back and drew his sword.

"You bastard," he screamed.

Jōtarō rushed forward empty-handed and caught Iori's collar, but the boy pulled free and jumped ten feet to the side.

"Son of a bitch," muttered Jōtarō, feeling warm blood running down his right arm from a two-inch cut.

Iori took a stance and fixed his mind on the lesson Musashi had drummed into him. Eyes . . . Eyes . . . Eyes . . . His strength concentrated in his bright pupils, his whole being seemed to be channeled into a pair of fiery eyes.

Outstared, Jōtarō whipped out his own sword. "I'll have to kill you," he snarled.

Iori, taking fresh courage from the strike he had scored, charged, his attack the one he always employed against Musashi.

Jōtarō was having second thoughts. He hadn't believed Iori could use a sword; now he put his full strength into the fight. For the sake of his comrades, he had to get this meddling child out of the way. Seemingly ignoring Iori's attack, he pressed forward and swung viciously, but unsuccessfully.

After two or three parries, Iori turned around, ran, stopped, and charged again. When Jōtarō countered, he retreated again, encouraged to see that his strategy was working. He was drawing the opponent into his own territory.

Pausing to catch his breath, Jōtarō looked around the dark grove and shouted, "Where are you, you stupid little bastard?" The answer was a shower of bark and leaves. Jōtarō raised his head and shouted, "I see you," though all he could actually see through the foliage was a couple of stars.

Jōtarō started climbing toward the rustling sound Iori made as he moved out on a limb. From there, unfortunately, there was nowhere to go.

"I've got you now. Unless you can grow wings, you'd better give up. Otherwise you're dead."

Iori moved silently back to the fork of two limbs. Jōtarō climbed slowly and carefully. When Jōtarō reached out to grab him, Iori again moved out on one of the limbs. With a grunt, Jōtarō caught hold of a branch with both hands and started to pull himself up, giving Iori the chance he'd been waiting for. With a resounding whack, his sword connected with the branch Jōtarō was on. It broke, and Jōtarō plummeted to the ground.

"How do you like that, thief!" gloated Iori.

His fall broken by lower branches, Jōtarō wasn't seriously injured, except for his pride. He cursed and started back up the tree, this time with the speed of a leopard. When he was under Iori's feet again, Iori slashed back and forth with his sword to keep him from getting any nearer.

While they were locked in stalemate, the plaintive tones of a *shakuhachi* came to their ears. For a moment, they both stopped and listened.

Then Jōtarō decided to try reasoning with his adversary. "All right," he said, "you put up a better fight than I expected. I admire you for that. If you'll tell me who asked you to follow me, I'll let you go."

"Admit you're licked!"

"Are you crazy?"

"I may not be very big, but I'm Misawa Iori, the only disciple of Miyamoto Musashi. Begging mercy would be an insult to my master's reputation. Give up!"

"Wh-what?" said Jōtarō incredulously. "S-say that once more." His voice was shrill and unsteady.

"Listen carefully," Iori said proudly. "I am Misawa Iori, the only pupil of Miyamoto Musashi. Does that surprise you?"

Jōtarō was ready to admit defeat. With a mixture of doubt and curiosity, he asked, "How is my teacher? Is he well? Where is he?"

Astonished, but keeping a safe distance from Jōtarō, who was moving closer, Iori said, "Ha! *Sensei* would never have a thief for a disciple."

"Don't call me that. Didn't Musashi ever mention Jōtarō?"

"Jōtarō?"

"If you're really Musashi's pupil, you must've heard him mention my name sometime or other. I was about your age then."

"That's a lie."

"No it isn't. It's the truth."

Overcome with nostalgia, Jōtarō reached out to Iori and tried to explain that they should be friends because they were disciples of the same teacher. Still wary, Iori took a swipe at his ribs.

Squeezed precariously between two limbs, Jōtarō barely succeeded in clasping his hand around Iori's wrist. For some reason, Iori let go of the branch he was holding on to. When they fell, they fell together, one landing on top of the other, both knocked senseless.

The light in Musashi's new house was visible from all directions, since,   *809* though the roof was in place, the walls hadn't been built yet.

Takuan, arriving the day before for an after-the-storm call, had decided to wait for Musashi's return. Today, just after nightfall, his enjoyment of his solitary surroundings had been interrupted by a mendicant priest asking for hot water to go with his supper.

After his meager meal of rice balls, the aged priest had taken it upon himself to play his *shakuhachi* for Takuan, fingering his instrument in a halting, amateurish fashion. Yet as Takuan listened, the music struck him as having genuine feeling, albeit of the artless sort often expressed in poems by nonpoets. He thought, too, that he could recognize the emotion the player was attempting to wring from his instrument. It was remorse, from the first off-key note to the last—a wailing cry of repentance.

It seemed to be the story of the man's life, but then, Takuan reflected, that couldn't have been too different from his own. Whether people were great or not, there was not much variety in their inner life experience. Any difference lay merely in how they dealt with common human weaknesses. To Takuan, both he and the other man were basically a bundle of illusions wrapped in human skin.

"I do believe I've seen you before somewhere," Takuan murmured thoughtfully.

The priest blinked his almost sightless eyes and said, "Now that you mention it, I thought I recognized your voice. Aren't you Takuan Sōhō from Tajima?"

Takuan's memory cleared. Moving the lamp closer to the man's face, he said, "You're Aoki Tanzaemon, aren't you?"

"Then you *are* Takuan. Oh, I wish I could crawl into a hole and hide this miserable flesh of mine!"

"How strange we should meet in a place like this. It's been nearly ten years since that time at the Shippōji, hasn't it?"

"Thinking of those days gives me a chill." Then he said stiffly, "Now that I'm reduced to wandering about in darkness, this wretched sack of bones is sustained only by thoughts of my son."

"Do you have a son?"

"I've been told he's with that man who was tied up in the old cryptomeria tree. Takezō, was it? I hear he's called Miyamoto Musashi now. The two of them are said to have come east."

"You mean your son is Musashi's disciple?"

"That's what they say. I was so ashamed. I couldn't face Musashi, so I resolved to put the boy out of my mind. But now . . . he's seventeen this year. If only I could have one look at him and see what kind of a man he's growing up to be, I'd be ready and willing to die."

"So Jōtarō's your son. I didn't know that," said Takuan.

Tanzaemon nodded. There was no hint in his shriveled form of the proud captain filled with lust for Otsū. Takuan gazed at him with pity, pained to see Tanzaemon so tormented by guilt.

Seeing that despite his priestly garb he lacked even the comfort of religious faith, Takuan decided the first thing he should do was bring him face to face with the Buddha Amida, whose infinite mercy saves even those guilty of the ten evils and the five deadly sins. There would be time enough after he'd recovered from his despair to look for Jōtarō.

Takuan gave him the name of a Zen temple in Edo. "If you tell them I sent you, they'll let you stay as long as you wish. As soon as I have time, I'll come and we'll have a long talk. I have an idea where your son might be. I'll do everything I can to make sure you see him in the not too distant future. In the meantime, give up brooding. Even after a man's fifty or sixty, he can still know happiness, even do useful work. You may live for many more years. Talk it over with the priests when you get to the temple."

Takuan shooed Tanzaemon out the door, unceremoniously and without showing any sympathy, but Tanzaemon seemed to appreciate the unsentimental attitude. After numerous bows of gratitude, he picked up his reed hat and *shakuhachi* and left.

For fear of slipping, Tanzaemon chose to go through the woods, where the path sloped more gently. Presently his cane struck an obstacle. Feeling around with his hands, he was surprised to find two bodies lying motionless on the damp ground.

He hurried back to the cabin. "Takuan! Can you help me? I came across two unconscious boys in the woods." Takuan roused himself and came outside. Tanzaemon continued: "I don't have any medicine with me, and I can't see well enough to get water for them."

Takuan slipped on his sandals and shouted toward the bottom of the hill. His voice carried easily. A farmer answered, asking him what he wanted. Takuan told him to bring a torch, some men and some water. While he waited, he suggested to Tanzaemon that the road was the better way to go, described it in detail and sent him on his way. Halfway down the hill, Tanzaemon passed the men coming up.

When Takuan arrived with the farmers, Jōtarō had come to and was sitting underneath the tree, looking dazed. One hand resting on Iori's arm, he was debating whether to revive him and find out what he wanted to know or to get away from there. He reacted to the torch like a nocturnal animal, tensing his muscles, ready to run.

"What's going on here?" asked Takuan. As he looked more closely, inquisitive interest turned to surprise, a surprise matched by Jōtarō's. The young man was much taller than the boy Takuan had known, and his face had changed quite a bit.

"You're Jōtarō, aren't you?"

The youth placed both hands on the ground and bowed. "Yes, I am," he replied haltingly, almost fearfully. He'd recognized Takuan instantly.

"Well, I must say, you've grown up to be a fine young man." Turning his attention to Iori, he put his arm around him and ascertained that he was still alive.

Iori revived, and after looking around curiously for a few seconds, burst into tears.

"What's the matter?" Takuan asked soothingly. "Are you hurt?"

Iori shook his head and blubbered, "I'm not hurt. But they took my teacher away. He's in the prison in Chichibu." With Iori bawling the way he was, Takuan had trouble understanding him, but soon the basic facts of the story became clear. Takuan, realizing the seriousness of the situation, was nearly as grieved as Iori.

Jōtarō, too, was deeply agitated. In a shaky voice, he said abruptly, "Takuan, I have something to tell you. Could we go somewhere where we can talk?"

"He's one of the thieves," said Iori. "You can't trust him. Anything he says will be a lie." He pointed accusingly at Jōtarō, and they glared at each other.

"Shut up, both of you. Let me decide who's right and who's wrong." Takuan led them back to the house and ordered them to build a fire outside.

Seating himself by the fire, Takuan commanded them to do likewise. Iori hesitated, his expression saying very plainly he had no intention of being friendly with a thief. But seeing Takuan and Jōtarō talking amiably over old times, he felt a pang of jealousy and grudgingly took a seat near them.

Jōtarō lowered his voice, and like a woman confessing her sins before the Buddha, became very earnest.

"For four years now, I've been receiving training from a man named Daizō. He comes from Narai in Kiso. I've learned about his aspirations and what he wants to do for the world. I'd be willing to die for him, if necessary. And that's why I've tried to help him with his work. . . . Well, it does hurt to be called a thief. But I'm still Musashi's disciple. Even though I'm separated from him, I've never been apart from him in spirit, not even for a day."

He hurried on, not waiting to be asked questions. "Daizō and I have sworn by the gods of heaven and earth not to tell anyone what our aim in life is. I can't even tell you. Still, I can't stand by when Musashi's been thrown in prison. I'll go to Chichibu tomorrow and confess."

Takuan said, "Then it was you and Daizō who robbed the treasure house."

"Yes," Jōtarō replied without the slightest sign of contrition.

"So you *are* a thief," said Takuan.

Jōtarō lowered his head to avoid Takuan's eyes. "No . . . no," he murmured lamely. "We're not just common burglars."

"I was not aware that thieves came in different varieties."

"Well, what I'm trying to say is we don't do these things for our own gain. We do them for the people. It's a matter of moving public property for the good of the public."

"I don't understand reasoning like that. Are you telling me your robberies are righteous crimes? Are you saying you're like the bandit heroes in Chinese novels? If so, it's a poor imitation."

"I can't answer that without revealing my secret agreement with Daizō."

"Ha, ha. You aren't going to let yourself be taken in, are you?"

"I don't care what you say. I'll confess only to save Musashi. I hope you'll put in a good word for me with him later."

"I wouldn't be able to think of a good word to put in. Musashi's innocent.

812

Whether you confess or not, he'll be freed eventually. It seems to me it's far more important for you to take yourself to the Buddha. Use me as an intermediary and confess everything to him."

"Buddha?"

"That's what I said. To hear you tell it, you're doing something grand for the sake of other people. In fact, you're putting yourself before others. Has it not occurred to you that you leave quite a number of people unhappy?"

"One can't consider himself when one is working on behalf of society."

"Stupid fool!" He struck Jōtarō soundly on the cheek with his fist. "One's self is the basis of everything. Every action is a manifestation of the self. A person who doesn't know himself can do nothing for others."

"What I meant—I wasn't acting to satisfy my own desires."

"Shut up! Don't you see you're barely grown? There's nothing more frightening than a half-baked do-gooder who knows nothing of the world but takes it upon himself to tell the world what's good for it. You needn't say any more about what you and Daizō are doing; I have a very good idea already. . . . What are you crying about? Blow your nose."

Ordered to bed, Jōtarō lay down obediently but couldn't get to sleep for thinking of Musashi. He clasped his hands together over his chest and silently begged forgiveness. Tears dribbled into his ears. He turned on his side and began thinking about Otsū. His cheek hurt; Otsū's tears would hurt worse. Still, revealing his secret promise to Daizō was inconceivable, even if Takuan tried to get it out of him in the morning, as he was sure to do.

He got up without making a sound, went outside and looked up at the stars. He would have to hurry; the night was nearly gone.

"Stop!" The voice froze Jōtarō where he was. Behind him, Takuan was a huge shadow.

The priest came to his side and put his arm around him. "Are you determined to go and confess?"

Jōtarō nodded.

"That's not very intelligent," said Takuan sympathetically. "You'll die a dog's death. You seem to think that if you give yourself up, Musashi will be set free, but it isn't that simple. The officials will keep Musashi in prison until you tell them everything you've been refusing to tell me. And you—you'll be tortured until you talk, whether it takes a year, two years or more."

Jōtarō hung his head.

"Is that what you want, to die a dog's death? But you have no choice now: either you confess everything under torture or you tell me everything. As a disciple of the Buddha, I'll not sit in judgment. I'll relay it to Amida."

Jōtarō said nothing.

"There is one other way. By the sheerest chance, I happened to meet your father last night. He now wears the robes of a mendicant priest. Of course, I never dreamed you were here too. I sent him to a temple in Edo. If you've made up your mind to die, it'd be good for you to see him first. And when you see him, you can ask him if I'm not right.

"Jōtarō, there're three paths open to you. You must decide for yourself which one to follow." He turned away and started back into the house.

Jōtarō realized that the *shakuhachi* he had heard the night before must have belonged to his father. Without being told, he could imagine how his father must look and feel as he wandered around from place to place.

"Takuan, wait! I'll talk. I'll tell everything to the Buddha, including my promise to Daizō." He caught hold of the priest's sleeve, and the two went into the grove.

Jōtarō confessed in a long monologue, omitting nothing. Takuan neither moved a muscle nor spoke.

"That's all," said Jōtarō.

"Everything?"

"Every single thing."

"Good."

Takuan remained silent for fully an hour. Dawn came. Crows began cawing; dew glistened everywhere. Takuan sat on the root of a cryptomeria. Jōtarō leaned against another tree, head bowed, waiting for the tongue-lashing he knew was coming.

When Takuan finally spoke, he appeared to have no more doubts. "I must say, you got mixed up with quite a crowd. Heaven help them. They don't understand which way the world is turning. It's a good thing you told me before matters got worse." Reaching into his kimono, he produced, surprisingly enough, two gold coins and handed them to Jōtarō. "You'd better get away as fast as you can. The slightest delay may bring disaster not only to you but to your father and your teacher. Get as far away as possible but don't go near the Kōshū highroad or the Nakasendō. By noon today, they'll be carrying out a rigid check on all travelers."

"What'll happen to *Sensei?* I can't go away and leave him where he is."

"Leave that to me. After a year or two, when things have quieted down, you can go to see him and make your apologies. *Then* I'll put in a good word for you."

"Good-bye."

"Just a minute."

"Yes?"

"Go to Edo first. In Azabu there's a Zen temple called Shōjuan. Your father should be there by now. Take this seal I received from the Daitokuji. They'll know it's mine. Get them to give you and your father priests' hats and robes, as well as the necessary credentials. Then you can travel in disguise."

"Why do I have to pretend to be a priest?"

"Is there no end to your naiveté? You, my silly young friend, are an agent of a group planning to kill the shōgun, set fire to Ieyasu's castle in Suruga, throw the whole Kantō district into confusion and take over the government. In short, you're a traitor. If you're caught, the mandatory punishment is death by hanging."

Jōtarō's mouth fell open.

814   "Now go."

"May I ask one question? Why should men who want to overthrow the Tokugawas be considered traitors? Why aren't the ones who overthrew the Toyotomis and seized control of the country traitors?"

"Don't ask me," Takuan answered with a cold stare.

The Pomegranate

Takuan and Iori arrived at Lord Hōjō Ujikatsu's mansion in Ushigome later the same day. A young retainer stationed at the gate went to announce Takuan, and a few minutes later Shinzō came out.

"My father is at Edo Castle," said Shinzō. "Won't you come in and wait?"

"At the castle?" said Takuan. "I'll go on then, since that's where I was headed anyway. Would you mind if I left Iori here with you?"

"Not at all," replied Shinzō with a smile and a quick glance at Iori. "May I order a palanquin for you?"

"If you would."

The lacquered palanquin was barely out of sight before Iori was at the stables, inspecting Lord Ujikatsu's well-fed chestnut browns and dappled grays one by one. He particularly admired their faces, which he thought much more aristocratic than those of workhorses of his acquaintance. There was a mystery here, though: how could the warrior class afford to keep large numbers of horses standing idle, instead of having them out working the fields?

He was just beginning to imagine cavalrymen riding into battle when Shinzō's loud voice distracted him. He looked toward the house, expecting a scolding, but saw that the object of Shinzō's wrath was a thin old woman with a staff and a stubbornly set face.

"Pretending to be out!" shouted Shinzō. "Why would my father have to pretend to an old hag he doesn't even know?"

"My, aren't you angry?" Osugi said sarcastically. "I gather you're his lordship's son. Do you know how many times I've come here trying to see your father? Not a few, I'll tell you, and every time I've been told he's out."

A little rattled, Shinzō said, "It doesn't have anything to do with how many times you come. My father doesn't like to receive people. If he doesn't want to see you, why do you keep coming back?"

Undaunted, Osugi cackled, "Doesn't like to see people! Why does he live among them, then?" She bared her teeth.

The idea of calling her a dirty name and letting her hear the click of his sword being released crossed Shinzō's mind, but he didn't want to make an unseemly show of temper, nor was he sure it would work.

"My father is not here," he said in an ordinary tone of voice. "Why don't you sit down and tell me what this is all about?"

"Well, I think I'll accept your kind offer. It's been a long walk and my legs are tired." She sat down on the edge of the step and began rubbing her knees. "When you speak softly to me, young man, I feel ashamed for raising my voice. Now, I want you to convey what I say to your father when he comes home."

"I'll be glad to do that."

"I came to tell him about Miyamoto Musashi."

Puzzled, Shinzō asked, "Has something happened to Musashi?"

"No, I want your father to know what kind of man he is. When Musashi was seventeen, he went to Sekigahara and fought against the Tokugawas. *Against* the Tokugawas, do you hear? What's more, he's done so many evil deeds in Mimasaka that no one there has anything good to say about him. He killed any number of people, and he's been running away from me for years because I've been trying to take my rightful revenge on him. Musashi's a useless vagabond, and he's dangerous!"

"Now, wait—"

"No, just listen! Musashi started playing around with the woman my son was engaged to. He actually stole her and made off with her."

"Hold on now," said Shinzō, raising his hand in protest. "Why tell such stories about Musashi?"

"I'm doing it for the sake of the country," Osugi said smugly.

"What good will it do the country to slander Musashi?"

Osugi rearranged herself and said, "I hear that slick-tongued rogue is soon to be appointed an instructor in the shōgun's house."

"Where did you hear that?"

"A man who was at the Ono dōjō. I heard it with my own ears."

"Did you, now?"

"A swine like Musashi shouldn't even be allowed in the shōgun's presence, let alone be appointed tutor. A teacher to the House of Tokugawa is a teacher to the nation. It makes me sick just to think of it. I'm here to warn Lord Hōjō, because I hear he recommended Musashi. Do you understand now?" She sucked in the saliva at the corners of her mouth and went on: "I'm sure it's to the country's benefit to warn your father. And let me warn you too. Be careful you don't get taken in by Musashi's smooth talk."

Fearing she might go on in this vein for hours, Shinzō summoned his last ounce of patience, swallowed hard and said, "Thank you. I understand what you've said. I'll pass it on to my father."

"Please do!"

With the air of someone who has finally achieved a cherished goal, Osugi got up and walked toward the gate, her sandals flopping noisily on the path.

"Filthy old hag!" cried a boyish voice.

Startled, Osugi barked, "What? . . . What?" and looked around until she
spotted Iori among the trees, showing his teeth like a horse.

"Eat that!" he shouted, and flung a pomegranate at her. It struck so hard it broke.

"Ow-w-w!" screamed Osugi, clutching at her chest.

She bent to pick up something to throw at him, but he ran out of sight. She ran to the stable and was looking inside when a large, soft lump of horse manure struck her squarely in the face.

Sputtering and spitting, Osugi wiped the mess from her face with her fingers, and the tears began to flow. To think that traveling about the country on her son's behalf had led to this sort of thing!

Iori watched at a safe distance from behind a tree. Seeing her weeping like an infant, he was suddenly very ashamed of himself. He half wanted to go and apologize to her before she got out the gate, but his fury at hearing her malign Musashi had not subsided. Caught between pity and hatred, he stood there for a time biting his fingernails.

"Come up here, Iori. You can see the red Fuji." Shinzō's voice came from a room high up on the hill.

With a great sense of relief, Iori ran off. "Mount Fuji?" The vision of the peak dyed crimson in the evening light emptied his mind of all other thoughts.

Shinzō, too, seemed to have forgotten his conversation with Osugi.

Land of Dreams

Ieyasu turned the office of shōgun over to Hidetada in 1605 but continued to govern from his castle in Suruga. Now that the work of laying the foundations for the new regime was largely completed, he was beginning to let Hidetada take over his rightful duties.

When he yielded his authority, Ieyasu had asked his son what he intended to do.

Hidetada's reply, "I'm going to build," was said to please the old shōgun immensely.

In contrast to Edo, Osaka was still preoccupied with preparations for the final battle. Illustrious generals laid secret plots, couriers carried messages to certain fiefs, displaced military leaders and rōnin were provided with solace and compensation. Ammunition was stockpiled, lances polished, moats deepened.

And more and more townsmen deserted the western cities for the booming city in the east, frequently changing loyalties, for the fear lingered that a

Toyotomi victory might mean a reversion to chronic strife.

To the daimyō and higher-ranking vassals who had yet to decide whether to entrust the fate of their children and grandchildren to Edo or Osaka, the impressive construction program in Edo was an argument in favor of the Tokugawas.

Today, as on many other days, Hidetada was engaged in one of his favorite pastimes. Dressed as though for a country outing, he left the main encirclement and went to the hill at Fukiage to inspect the construction work.

At about the time the shōgun and his retinue of ministers, personal attendants and Buddhist priests stopped for a rest, a commotion broke out at the bottom of Momiji Hill.

"Stop the son of a bitch!"

"Catch him!"

A well digger was running around in circles, trying to shake off the carpenters who were chasing him. He darted like a hare between stacks of lumber and hid briefly behind a plasterers' hut. Then he made a dash for the scaffolding on the outer wall and began climbing.

Cursing loudly, a couple of the carpenters climbed after him and caught hold of his feet. The well digger, arms waving frantically, fell back into a pile of shavings.

The carpenters fell on him, kicking and beating him from all sides. For some strange reason, he neither cried out nor attempted to resist, but clung as tightly as he could to the ground, as if that was his only hope.

The samurai in charge of the carpenters and the inspector of workmen came running up.

"What's going on here?" asked the samurai.

"He stepped on my square, the filthy pig!" one carpenter whined. "A square is a carpenter's soul!"

"Get hold of yourself."

"What would you do if he walked on your sword?" demanded the carpenter.

"All right, that's enough. The shōgun is resting up there on the hill."

Hearing the shōgun mentioned, the first carpenter quieted down, but another man said, "He's got to go wash. Then he's got to bow to the square and apologize!"

"We'll take care of the punishment," said the inspector. "You men go back to work."

He seized the prostrate man by the collar and said, "Lift your face."

"Yes, sir."

"You're one of the well diggers, aren't you?"

"Yes, sir."

"What are you doing down here? This isn't where you work."

"He was around here yesterday too," said the carpenter.

"Was he?" said the inspector, staring at Matahachi's pale face and noticing that for a well digger he was a little too delicate, a little too refined.

He conferred with the samurai for a minute, then led Matahachi away.

Matahachi was locked in a woodshed behind the Office of the Inspector of

Workmen and for the next several days had nothing to look at but some firewood, a sack or two of charcoal and barrels for making pickles. Fearing the plot would be discovered, he was soon in a state of terror.

Once inside the castle, he'd reconsidered and decided that if it meant being a well digger the rest of his life, he wasn't going to become an assassin. He'd seen the shōgun and his entourage several times and done nothing.

What took him to the foot of Momiji Hill whenever he could manage it during his rest periods was an unforeseen complication. A library was to be built, and when it was, the locust tree would be moved. Matahachi guiltily supposed the musket would be uncovered and this would link him directly to the plot. But he hadn't been able to find a time when no one was around to dig up the musket and throw it away.

Even when sleeping, he'd break out in a sweat. Once he dreamed he was in the land of the dead, and wherever he looked there were locust trees. A few nights after his confinement in the woodshed, in a vision as clear as day, he dreamed of his mother. Instead of taking pity on him, Osugi shouted angrily and threw a basketful of cocoons at him. When the cocoons rained down on his head, he tried to run away. She pursued him, her hair mysteriously transformed into white cocoons. He ran and ran, but she was always behind him. Bathed in sweat, he jumped off a cliff and began falling through the darkness of hell, falling endlessly through blackness.

"Mother! Forgive me," he cried out like a hurt child, and the sound of his own voice awakened him. The reality he woke to—the prospect of death—was more terrifying than the dream.

He tried the door, which was locked, as he already knew. In desperation he climbed up a pickle barrel, broke a small window near the roof and squeezed through. Using piles of lumber and rock and small hills of excavated dirt for cover, he made his way stealthily to the vicinity of the western rear gate. The locust tree was still there. He sighed with relief.

He found a hoe and started digging as if he expected to discover his own life. Unnerved by the noise he was making, he stopped and looked all around him. Seeing no one, he began again.

The fear that someone had already found the musket made him swing the hoe frantically. His breathing became rapid and uneven. Sweat and grime mixed, making him look as if he'd just come from a mud bath. He was beginning to get dizzy, but he could not stop.

The blade struck something long. Casting the hoe aside, he reached down to pull it out, thinking: "I've got it."

His relief was short-lived. The object wasn't wrapped in oil paper, there was no box, and it wasn't cool like metal. He took hold, held it up and dropped it. It was a slender white wristbone or shinbone.

Matahachi did not have the heart to pick up the hoe again. It seemed like another nightmare. But he knew he was awake; he could count every leaf of the locust tree.

"What would Daizō have to gain by lying?" he wondered, as he walked around the tree, kicking at the dirt.

He was still circling the tree when a figure walked quietly up behind him *819* and slapped him lightly on the back. With a loud laugh, right beside Matahachi's ear, he said, "You won't find it."

Matahachi's whole body went limp. He almost fell into the hole. Turning his head toward the voice, he stared blankly for several minutes before uttering a little croak of astonishment.

"Come with me," said Takuan, taking him by the hand.

Matahachi could not move. His fingers went numb, and he clawed at the priest's hand. A chill of abject horror spread from his heels upward.

"Didn't you hear? Come with me," said Takuan, scolding with his eyes.

Matahachi's tongue was almost as useless as a mute's. "Th-this . . . fix . . . dirt . . . I—"

In a pitiless tone, Takuan said, "Leave it. It's a waste of time. The things people do on this earth, good or bad, are like ink on porous paper. They cannot be erased, not in a thousand years. You imagine that kicking a little dirt around will undo what you've done. It's because you think like that that your life is so untidy. Now come with me. You're a criminal, your crime heinous. I'm going to cut off your head with a bamboo saw and cast you into the Pool of Blood in hell." He seized Matahachi's earlobe and pulled him along.

Takuan rapped on the door of the shed where the kitchen helpers slept.

"One of you boys come out here," he said.

A boy came out, rubbing the sleep from his eyes. When he recognized the priest he'd seen talking with the shōgun, he came awake and said, "Yes, sir. Can I do something for you?"

"I want you to open that woodshed."

"There's a well digger locked up in there."

"He isn't in there. He's right here. There's no point in putting him back in through the window, so open the door."

The boy hastened to fetch the inspector, who rushed out, apologizing and begging Takuan not to report the matter.

Takuan shoved Matahachi into the shed, went inside and closed the door. A few minutes later, he poked his head out and said, "You must have a razor somewhere. Sharpen it and bring it here."

The inspector and the kitchen helper looked at each other, neither daring to ask the priest why he wanted the razor. Then they honed the razor and handed it over to him.

"Thanks," said Takuan. "Now you can go back to bed."

The inside of the shed was pitch black, only a glimpse of starlight being visible through the broken window. Takuan seated himself on a pile of kindling. Matahachi slumped down on a reed mat, hanging his head in shame. For a long time there was silence. Unable to see the razor, Matahachi wondered nervously whether Takuan was holding it in his hand.

At last Takuan spoke. "Matahachi, what did you dig up under the locust tree?"

Silence.

"I could show you how to dig up something. It would mean extracting something from nothingness, recovering the real world from a land of dreams."

"Yes, sir."

"You haven't the least idea what the reality I'm talking about is. No doubt you are still in your world of fantasy. Well, since you're as naive as an infant, I suppose I'll have to chew your intellectual food for you. . . . How old are you?"

"Twenty-eight."

"The same age as Musashi."

Matahachi put his hands to his face and wept.

Takuan did not speak until he had cried himself out. Then he said, "Isn't it frightening to think that the locust tree nearly became the grave marker of a fool? You were digging your own grave, actually on the verge of putting yourself into it."

Matahachi flung his arms around Takuan's legs and pleaded, "Save me. Please save me. My eyes . . . my eyes are open now. I was taken in by Daizō of Narai."

"No, your eyes are not open. Nor did Daizō deceive you. He simply tried to make use of the biggest fool on earth—a greedy, unsophisticated, petty-minded dolt who nevertheless had the temerity to take on a task any sensible man would shrink from."

"Yes . . . yes . . . I was a fool."

"Just who did you think this Daizō was?"

"I don't know."

"His real name is Mizoguchi Shinano. He was a retainer of Ōtani Yoshitsugu, who's a close friend of Ishida Mitsunari. Mitsunari, you will remember, was one of the losers at Sekigahara."

"N-no," gasped Matahachi. "He's one of the warriors the shogunate is trying to track down?"

"What else would a man out to assassinate the shōgun be? Your stupidity is appalling."

"He didn't tell me that. He just said he hated the Tokugawas. He thought it'd be better for the country if the Toyotomis were in power. He was talking about working for the sake of everybody."

"You didn't bother to ask yourself who he really was, did you? Without once using your head, you went boldly about the business of digging your own grave. Your kind of courage is frightening, Matahachi."

"What am I to do?"

"Do?"

"Please, Takuan, please, help me!"

"Let go of me."

"But . . . but I didn't actually use the gun. I didn't even find it!"

"Of course you didn't. It didn't arrive on time. If Jōtarō, whom Daizō duped into becoming a part of this dreadful plot, had reached Edo as planned, the musket might very well have been buried under the tree."

"Jōtarō? You mean the boy—"

"Never mind. That doesn't concern you. What does concern you is the crime of treason, which you have committed and which cannot be pardoned. Nor can it be condoned by the gods and the Buddha. You may as well stop thinking about being saved."

"Isn't there any way . . . ?"

"Certainly not!"

"Have mercy," sobbed Matahachi, clinging to Takuan's knees.

Takuan stood up and kicked him away. "Idiot!" he shouted in a voice that threatened to lift the roof off the shed. The ferocity of his glare was beyond description—a Buddha refusing to be clung to, a terrifying Buddha unwilling to save even the penitent.

For a second or two, Matahachi met the look resentfully. Then his head dropped in resignation, and his body was racked with sobs.

Takuan took the razor from the top of the woodpile and touched Matahachi's head with it lightly.

"As long as you're going to die, you may as well die looking like a disciple of the Buddha. Out of friendship, I'll help you do that. Close your eyes and sit quietly with your legs crossed. The line between life and death is not thicker than an eyelid. There is nothing frightening about death, nothing to cry over. Don't weep, child, don't weep. Takuan will prepare you for the end."

The room where the shōgun's Council of Elders met to discuss matters of state was isolated from other parts of Edo Castle. This secret chamber was completely enclosed by other rooms and hallways. Whenever it was necessary to receive a decision from the shōgun, the ministers would either go to his audience chamber or send a petition in a lacquered box. Notes and replies had been going back and forth with unusual frequency, and Takuan and Lord Hōjō had been admitted to the room several times, often remaining there for day-long deliberations.

On this particular day, in another room, less isolated but no less well guarded, the ministers had heard the report of the envoy sent to Kiso.

He said that though there had been no delay in acting on the order for Daizō's arrest, Daizō had escaped after closing up his establishment in Narai, taking his entire household with him. A search had brought to light a substantial supply of arms and ammunition, together with a few documents that had escaped destruction. The papers included letters to and from Toyotomi supporters in Osaka. The envoy had arranged for shipment of the evidence to the shōgun's capital and then rushed back to Edo by fast horse.

The ministers felt like fishermen who had cast a big net and not caught so much as a single minnow.

The very next day, a retainer of Lord Sakai, who was a member of the Council of Elders, made a report of a different sort: "In accordance with your lordship's instructions, Miyamoto Musashi has been released from prison. He was handed over to a man named Musō Gonnosuke, to whom we explained in detail how the misunderstanding came about."

Lord Sakai promptly informed Takuan, who said lightly, "Very good of you."

"Please ask your friend Musashi not to think too badly of us," said Lord Sakai apologetically, uncomfortably aware of the error made in the territory under his jurisdiction.

One of the problems solved most quickly was that of Daizō's base of operations in Edo. Officials under the Commissioner of Edo descended on the pawnshop in Shibaura and in one swift move confiscated everything, both property and secret documents. In the process, the unlucky Akemi was taken into custody, though she was completely in the dark regarding her patron's treacherous plans.

Received in audience by the shōgun one evening, Takuan related events as he knew them and told him how everything had turned out. He ended by saying, "Please do not forget for a moment that there are many more Daizōs of Narai in this world."

Hidetada accepted the warning with a vigorous nod.

"If you attempt to search out all such men and bring them to justice," Takuan continued, "all your time and effort will be consumed in coping with insurgents. You won't be able to carry out the great work expected of you as your father's successor."

The shōgun perceived the truth of Takuan's words and took them to heart. "Let the punishments be light," he directed. "Since you reported the conspiracy, I leave it to you to decide the penalties."

After expressing his heartfelt thanks, Takuan said, "Quite without intending to, I see I've been here at the castle for more than a month. It's time to leave now. I'll go to Koyagyū in Yamato to visit Lord Sekishūsai. Then I'll return to the Daitokuji, traveling by way of the Senshū district."

Mention of Sekishūsai seemed to evoke a pleasant memory for Hidetada. "How is old Yagyū's health?" he asked.

"Unfortunately, I'm told that Lord Munenori thinks the end is near."

Hidetada recalled a time when he had been at the Shōkokuji encampment and Sekishūsai had been received by Ieyasu. Hidetada had been a child at the time, and Sekishūsai's manly bearing had made a deep impression on him.

Takuan broke the silence. "There is one other matter," he said. "In consultation with the Council of Elders and with their permission, Lord Hōjō of Awa and I have recommended a samurai by the name of Miyamoto Musashi to be a tutor in your excellency's household. I hope that you will look favorably upon this recommendation."

"I've been informed of that. It's said that the House of Hosokawa is interested in him, which is very much to his favor. I have decided it would be all right to appoint one more tutor."

It was a day or two before Takuan left the castle, and in the time he acquired a new disciple. Going to the woodshed behind the inspector's office, he had one of the kitchen helpers open the door for him, letting the light fall on a freshly shaven head.

Temporarily blinded, the novice, who thought himself a condemned man, slowly lifted his downcast eyes and said, "Ah!"

"Come," said Takuan.

823

Wearing the priest's robe Takuan had sent him, Matahachi stood up unsteadily on legs that felt as if they had begun to decay. Takuan gently put his arm around him and helped him out of the shed.

The day of retribution had arrived. Behind his eyelids, closed in resignation, Matahachi could see the reed mat on which he would be forced to kneel before the executioner raised his sword. Apparently he had forgotten that traitors faced an ignominious death by hanging. Tears trickled down his clean-shaven cheeks.

"Can you walk?" asked Takuan.

Matahachi thought he was replying; in fact, no sound came out. He was barely conscious of going through the castle gates and crossing the bridges spanning the inner and outer moats. Trudging along dolefully beside Takuan, he was the perfect image of the proverbial sheep being led to slaughter. "Hail to the Buddha Amida, hail to the Buddha Amida. . . ." Silently he repeated the invocation to the Buddha of Eternal Light.

Matahachi squinted and looked beyond the outer moat at stately daimyō mansions. Farther to the east lay Hibiya Village; beyond, the streets of the downtown district were visible.

The floating world called out to him anew, and along with his yearning for it, fresh tears came to his eyes. He closed them and rapidly repeated, "Hail to the Buddha Amida, hail to the Buddha Amida. . . ." The supplication became first audible, then louder and louder, faster and faster.

"Hurry up," Takuan said sternly.

From the moat, they turned toward Ōtemachi and cut diagonally across a large vacant lot. Matahachi felt he had walked a thousand miles already. Would the road simply go on like this all the way to hell, daylight gradually giving way to utter darkness?

"Wait here," commanded Takuan. They were in the middle of a flat open area; to the left, muddy water came down the moat from Tokiwa Bridge.

Directly across the street was an earthen wall, only recently covered with white plaster. Beyond this was the stockade of the new prison and a group of black buildings, which looked like ordinary town houses but was actually the official residence of the Commissioner of Edo.

His legs quaking, Matahachi could no longer support himself. He plopped down on the ground. Somewhere in the grass, the cry of a quail suggested the pathway to the land of the dead.

Run for it? His feet were not bound, nor were his hands. But no, he thought, he couldn't get away with it. If the shōgun decided he was worth finding, there would not be a leaf, a blade of grass, to hide behind.

In his heart, he cried out to his mother, who at this moment seemed very dear to him. If only he had never left her side, he wouldn't be here now. He recalled other women too: Okō, Akemi, Otsū, others he had been fond of or dallied with. But his mother was the only woman he genuinely longed to see. If only he were given the opportunity to go on living, he was certain he would never again go against her will, never again be an unfilial son.

He felt a damp chill on the back of his neck. He looked up at three wild geese winging their way toward the bay and envied them.

The urge to take flight was like an itch. And why not? He had nothing to lose. If he were caught, he would be no worse off than he was now. With a desperate look in his eyes, he glanced toward the gate across the street. No sign of Takuan.

He jumped up and started to run.

"Stop!"

The loud voice alone was enough to break his spirit. He looked around and saw one of the commissioner's executioners. The man stepped forward and brought his long staff down on Matahachi's shoulder, felling him with one blow, then pinned him down with the staff, as a child might pin down a frog with a stick.

When Takuan came out of the commissioner's residence, he was accompanied by several guards, including a captain. They led out another prisoner, who was tied up with a rope.

The captain selected the place where the punishment would be carried out, and two freshly woven reed mats were spread on the ground.

"Shall we get on with it?" he asked Takuan, who nodded his assent.

As captain and priest sat down on stools to watch, the executioner shouted, "Stand up!" and lifted his staff. Matahachi dragged himself to his feet but was too weak to walk. The executioner seized him angrily by the back of his robe and half dragged him to one of the mats.

He sat. His head dropped. He could no longer hear the quail. Though he was conscious of voices, they sounded indistinct, as though separated from him by a wall.

Hearing his name whispered, he looked up in surprise.

"Akemi!" he gasped. "What are you doing here?"

She was kneeling on the other mat.

"No talking!" Two of the guards made use of their staffs to separate them.

The captain stood up and began reading the official judgments and sentences in stern, dignified tones. Akemi held back her tears, but Matahachi wept shamelessly. The captain finished, sat down and shouted, "Strike."

Two low-ranking guards carrying long switches of split bamboo pranced into position and began systematically lashing the prisoners across the back.

"One. Two. Three," they counted.

Matahachi moaned. Akemi, head bowed and face ashen, clamped her teeth together with all her might in an effort to bear the pain.

"Seven. Eight. Nine." The switches frayed; smoke seemed to rise from their tips.

A few passersby stopped at the edge of the lot to watch.

"What's going on?"

"Two prisoners being punished, it looks like."

"A hundred lashes, probably."

"They're not even to fifty yet."

"Must hurt."

A guard approached and startled them by thumping the ground sharply   *825* with his staff. "Off with you. You're not allowed to stand here."

The gawkers moved to a safer distance and, looking back, saw that the punishment was over. The guards discarded their switches, which were now only bundles of flabby strands, and wiped the sweat off their faces.

Takuan stood up. The captain was already on his feet. They exchanged amenities, and the captain led his men back toward the commissioner's compound. Takuan stood still for several minutes, looking at the bowed figures on the mats. He said nothing before walking away.

The shōgun had bestowed a number of gifts on him; these he had donated to various Zen temples in the city. Yet the gossips of Edo were soon at it again. According to which rumor one heard, he was an ambitious priest who meddled in politics. Or one the Tokugawas had persuaded to spy on the Osaka faction. Or a "black-robed" conspirator.

The rumors meant nothing to Takuan. Though he cared very much about the welfare of the nation, it made little difference to him whether the gaudy flowers of the time—the castles at Edo and Osaka—blossomed or fell.

A few thin rays of sunlight filtered through the clouds; the voice of the quail was audible again. Neither of the forms moved for quite some time, though neither had completely lost consciousness.

Finally Akemi mumbled, "Matahachi, look—water." Before them were two wooden pails of water, each with a dipper, placed there as evidence that the Office of the Commissioner was not entirely heartless.

After gulping down several mouthfuls, Akemi offered the dipper to Matahachi. When he failed to respond, she asked, "What's the matter? Don't you want any?"

Slowly he reached out and took the dipper. Once it touched his lips, he drank ravenously.

"Matahachi, have you become a priest?"

"Huh? . . . Is that all?"

"Is what all?"

"Is the punishment over? They haven't cut off our heads yet."

"They weren't supposed to. Didn't you hear the man read the sentences?"

"What did he say?"

"He said we were to be banished from Edo."

"I'm alive!" he shrieked. Almost insane with joy, he jumped up and walked away without so much as a backward glance at Akemi.

She put her hands to her head and began to fuss with her hair. Then she adjusted her kimono and tightened her obi. "Shameless," she muttered through crooked lips. Matahachi was only a speck on the horizon.

The Challenge

Iori was bored after only a few days at the Hōjō residence. There was nothing to do but play.

"When's Takuan coming back?" he asked Shinzō one morning, really wanting to know what had happened to Musashi.

"My father is still at the castle, so I suppose Takuan is too," said Shinzō. "They'll be back sooner or later. Why don't you amuse yourself with the horses?"

Iori raced to the stable and threw a lacquer and mother-of-pearl saddle on his favorite steed. He had ridden the horse both the day before and the day before that without telling Shinzō. Receiving permission made him feel proud. He mounted and tore out the back gate at full gallop.

The houses of daimyō, the paths through the fields, the rice paddies, the forests—the sights came at him in rapid succession and were left behind just as rapidly. Bright red snake gourds and russet grass proclaimed that autumn was at its height. The Chichibu Range rose beyond Musashino Plain. "He's in those mountains somewhere," thought Iori. He envisioned his beloved master in jail, and the tears on his cheeks made the wind feel soothingly cool.

Why not go see Musashi? Without giving the matter further thought, he whipped the horse, and horse and rider surged through the silvery sea of fluffy eulalia.

After covering a mile at breakneck speed, he reined in the horse, thinking: "Maybe he's gone back to the house."

He found the new house finished but unlived in. At the nearest paddy, he called out to the farmers harvesting their rice, "Has anyone seen my teacher?" They shook their heads sadly in reply.

Then it had to be Chichibu. On horseback, he could make the journey in a day.

After a time he came to the village of Nobidome. The entrance to the village was virtually blocked by samurai's mounts, packhorses, traveling chests, palanquins and between forty and fifty samurai having their lunch. He turned around to look for a way around the village.

Three or four samurai's attendants came running after him.

"Hey, you rascal, wait!"

"What're you calling me?" Iori asked angrily.

"Off the horse!" They were on either side of him now.

"Why? I don't even know you."

"Just keep your mouth shut and get off."

"No! You can't make me!"

Before he knew what was happening, one of the men lifted Iori's right leg high in the air, tumbling him off the other side of the horse.

"Someone wants to see you. Come along with me." He took hold of Iori's collar and pulled him toward a roadside teahouse.

Osugi stood outside, a cane in one hand. With a wave of her other hand, she dismissed the attendants. She was dressed for traveling and in the company of all those samurai. Iori didn't know what to make of it, nor did he have time to give it much thought.

"Brat!" said Osugi, then she whacked him across the shoulder with her cane. He went through the motions of taking a stance, though he knew he was hopelessly outnumbered. "Musashi has only the best of disciples. Ha! I hear you're one of them."

"I . . . I wouldn't say things like that if I were you."

"Oh, wouldn't you now?"

"I . . . I don't have any business with you."

"Oh, yes you do. You're going to tell us a few things. Who sent you to follow us?"

"Follow you?" Iori asked with a snort of disdain.

"How dare you talk that way!" the old woman screeched. "Hasn't Musashi taught you any manners?"

"I don't need any lessons from you. I'm leaving."

"No you aren't!" cried Osugi as she caught him on the shin with her cane.

"O-w-w!" Iori collapsed to the ground.

Attendants grabbed the boy and marched him over to the miller's shop by the village gate, where sat a samurai of obviously high rank. He had finished eating and was sipping hot water. Seeing Iori's predicament, he broke into a grin.

"Dangerous," thought the boy, as his eyes met Kojirō's.

With a look of triumph, Osugi thrust out her chin and said, "See! Just as I thought—it was Iori. What's Musashi got up his sleeve now? Who else could have sent him to follow us?"

"Umm," mumbled Kojirō, nodding and dismissing his attendants, one of whom asked if he wanted the boy tied up.

Kojirō smiled and shook his head. Held by Kojirō's eyes, Iori was unable to stand straight, let alone run away.

Kojirō said, "You heard what she said. Is it true?"

"No; I just came out for a ride. I wasn't following you or anybody else."

"Hmm, could be. If Musashi's any kind of a samurai, he wouldn't resort to cheap tricks." Then he began thinking out loud. "On the other hand, if he heard we'd suddenly left on a trip with a contingent of Hosokawa samurai, he might get suspicious and send someone to check on our movements. It would only be natural."

828 The change in Kojirō's circumstances was striking. Instead of the forelock,

his head was shaved in proper samurai fashion. And in place of the loud clothing he used to wear, he had on a solid black kimono, which together with his rustic *hakama* made a most conservative impression. The Drying Pole he now carried at his side. His hope of becoming a vassal in the House of Hosokawa had been realized—not for the five thousand bushels he had wanted but for a stipend about half that large.

The present entourage, under the command of Kakubei, was an advance party on the way to Buzen to make things ready for Hosokawa Tadatoshi's return. With his father's age foremost in his mind, he had submitted his request to the shogunate quite some time earlier. Permission had finally been granted, an indication that the shogunate had no qualms about the Hosokawas' loyalty.

Osugi had asked to come along because she felt it imperative to return home. She had not relinquished her position as head of the family, yet she had been absent for nearly ten years. Uncle Gon might have looked after things for her if he were still alive. As it was, she suspected there were a number of family matters awaiting her attention.

They would be going through Osaka, where she had left Uncle Gon's ashes. She would be able to carry them to Mimasaka and hold a memorial service. It had been a long time, too, since she'd held a service for her neglected ancestors. She could return to her quest after she had straightened out affairs at home.

Recently she'd felt pleased with herself, believing she had struck a strong blow against Musashi. On first hearing of his recommendation from Kojirō, she had fallen into a state of extreme depression. If Musashi were to receive the appointment, he would be that much farther from her reach.

She'd taken it upon herself to prevent this disaster to the shogunate and the nation from happening. She hadn't seen Takuan, but she visited the House of Yagyū as well as the House of Hōjō, denouncing Musashi, claiming that it would be a dangerous folly to raise him to a high station. Not content with that, she reiterated her calumnies at the house of every government minister whose servants allowed her through the gate.

Kojirō, of course, made no effort to stop her, but he offered no special encouragement either, knowing that she wouldn't rest until she had done a thorough job. And thorough it was: she even wrote malicious letters about Musashi's past and threw them into the compounds of the Commissioner of Edo and the members of the Council of Elders. Before she was done, even Kojirō wondered if she hadn't gone too far.

Kojirō encouraged Osugi to make the journey, believing it would be better for him if she was back in the country where she could do a minimum of harm. If Osugi had any regret, it was only that Matahachi was not going with her, for she was still convinced that someday he would see the light and return to her.

Iori had no way of knowing the circumstances. Unable to flee, loath to cry for fear it would discredit Musashi, he felt trapped among enemies.

Deliberately, Kojirō stared directly into the boy's eyes and to his surprise *829* found his stare returned. Not once did Iori's eyes waver.

"Do you have brush and ink?" Kojirō asked Osugi.

"Yes, but the ink's all dried up. Why?"

"I want to write a letter. The signs Yajibei's men put up didn't draw Musashi out, and I don't know where he is. Iori is the best messenger one could ask for. I think I should send Musashi a note on the occasion of my departure from Edo."

"What are you going to write?"

"Nothing elaborate. I'll tell him to practice his swordsmanship and visit me in Buzen one of these days. I'll let him know I'm willing to wait the rest of my life. He can come whenever he has the necessary confidence."

Osugi threw up her hands in horror. "How can you talk like that? The rest of your life, indeed! I haven't got that much time to wait. I must see Musashi dead within the next two or three years at most."

"Leave it to me. I'll take care of your problem at the same time I take care of mine."

"Can't you see I'm getting old? It has to be done while I'm still alive."

"If you look after yourself, you'll be around when my invincible sword does its work."

Kojirō took the writing kit and walked to a nearby stream, where he wet his finger to moisten the ink stick. Still standing, he took some paper from his kimono. He wrote quickly, but both his calligraphy and his composition were those of an expert.

"You can use this for paste," said Osugi, taking a few grains of cooked rice and placing them on a leaf. Kojirō mashed them between his fingers, spread the stuff along the edge of the letter and sealed it. On the back, he wrote: "From Sasaki Ganryū, Retainer to the House of Hosokawa."

"Come here, you. I'm not going to hurt you. I want you to take this letter to Musashi. Make sure he gets it, because it's important."

Iori hung back a minute but then grunted his assent and snatched the letter from Kojirō's hand. "What's written in it?"

"Just what I told the old lady."

"May I look at it?"

"You aren't to break the seal."

"If you wrote something insulting, I won't take it."

"There's nothing rude in it. I asked him to remember our promise for the future and told him I look forward to seeing him again, perhaps in Buzen, if he should happen to come there."

"What do you mean by 'seeing him again'?"

"I mean meeting him on the boundary between life and death." Kojirō's cheeks reddened slightly.

Stuffing the letter into his kimono, Iori said, "All right, I'll deliver it," and ran off. About thirty yards away, he stopped, turned and stuck out his tongue at Osugi. "Crazy old witch!" he shouted.

"Wh-what?" She was ready to go after him, but Kojirō took her arm and held her back.

"Let it pass," he said with a rueful smile. "He's only a child." Then to Iori he shouted, "Don't you have anything better to say?"

"No . . ." Tears of anger rose from his chest. "You'll be sorry, though. There isn't any way Musashi could lose to the likes of you."

"Just like him, aren't you? Never say die. But I like the way you stick up for him. If he ever dies, come to me. I'll put you to work sweeping the garden or something."

Not knowing Kojirō was only teasing, Iori was insulted to the marrow. He picked up a rock. When he raised his arm to throw it, Kojirō fixed his eyes on him.

"Don't do that," he said in a calm but forceful voice.

Iori, feeling the eyes had hit him like two bullets, dropped the stone and ran. He ran on and on until, completely exhausted, he collapsed in the middle of Musashino Plain.

He sat there for two hours thinking about the man he looked up to as his teacher. Though he knew Musashi had many enemies, he thought of him as a great man and wanted to become a great man himself. Believing he had to do something to fulfill his obligations to his master and ensure his safety, he resolved to develop his own strength as quickly as possible.

Then the memory of the terrifying light in Kojirō's eyes came back to haunt him. Wondering whether Musashi could defeat a man that strong, he pessimistically decided even his master would have to study and practice harder. He got to his feet.

The white mist rolling down from the mountains spread over the plain. Deciding he should go on to Chichibu and deliver Kojirō's letter, he suddenly remembered the horse. Fearing bandits might have got hold of it, he searched frantically, calling and whistling at every other step.

He seemed to hear the sound of hooves coming from the direction of what he took to be a pond. He ran toward it. But there was no horse, no pond. The shimmering mist receded into the distance.

Seeing a moving black object, he approached it. A wild boar stopped rooting for food and charged dangerously close to him. The boar was swallowed up in the reeds and in its wake the mist formed a white line, looking as if it had been spread by a magician's wand. As he gazed at it, he became conscious of gurgling water. Going closer, he saw the reflection of the moon in a rocky brook.

He had always been sensitive to the mysteries of the open plain. He firmly believed that the tiniest ladybird possessed the spiritual power of the gods. In his eyes, nothing was without a soul, neither fluttering leaves nor beckoning water nor driving wind. Surrounded now by nature, he experienced the tremulous loneliness of autumn nearly gone, the sad wistfulness that must be felt by grasses and insects and water.

He sobbed so hard his shoulders shook—sweet tears, not bitter ones. If some being other than a human—a star perhaps, or the spirit of the plain—had asked him why he was weeping, he wouldn't have been able to say. If the

831

inquiring spirit had persisted, soothing and coaxing him, he might finally have said, "I often cry when I'm out in the open. I always have the feeling the house in Hōtengahara is somewhere near."

Crying was refreshment for his soul. After he had cried to his heart's content, heaven and earth would comfort him. When the tears were dry, his spirit would come forth from the clouds clean and fresh.

"That's Iori, isn't it?"

"I believe it is."

Iori turned toward the voices and the two human figures standing out blackly against the evening sky.

"*Sensei!*" cried Iori, stumbling as he ran toward the man on horseback. "It's you!" Beside himself with joy, he clung to the stirrup and looked up to make sure he wasn't dreaming.

"What happened?" asked Musashi. "What are you doing out here alone?" Musashi's face seemed to be very thin—was it the moonlight?—but the warmth of the voice was what Iori had hungered for weeks to hear.

"I thought I'd go to Chichibu—" The saddle caught Iori's eye. "Why, this is the horse I was riding!"

Gonnosuke, laughing, said, "Is it yours?"

"Yes."

"We didn't know who it belonged to. It was wandering around near the Iruma River, so I regarded it as a gift from heaven to Musashi."

"The god of the plain must have sent the horse to meet you," said Iori with perfect sincerity.

"Your horse, you say? That saddle couldn't belong to a samurai getting less than five thousand bushels."

"Well, it's really Shinzō's."

Dismounting, Musashi asked, "You've been staying at his house, then?"

"Yes. Takuan took me there."

"What about our new house?"

"It's finished."

"Good. We can go back there."

"*Sensei...*"

"Yes."

"You're so thin. Why's that?"

"I've spent quite a bit of time meditating."

"How did you get out of prison?"

"You can hear about it from Gonnosuke later. For now, let's say the gods were on my side."

"You don't have to worry anymore, Iori," said Gonnosuke. "No one has any doubts about his innocence."

Relieved, Iori became quite talkative, telling them about his meeting with Jōtarō and Jōtarō's going to Edo. When he came to the "repulsive old woman" who had showed up at the Hōjō mansion, he remembered Kojirō's letter.

"Oh, I forgot something important," he exclaimed, and handed the letter to Musashi.

"A letter from Kojirō?" Surprised, he held it in his hand for a moment as though it were a missive from a long-lost friend. "Where did you see him?" he asked.

"At the village of Nobidome. That mean old woman was with him. He said he was going to Buzen."

"Oh?"

"He was with a lot of Hosokawa samurai. . . . *Sensei*, you better be on your toes and not take any chances."

Musashi stuffed the unopened letter into his kimono and nodded.

Not certain his meaning had got through, Iori said, "That Kojirō's very strong, isn't he? Has he got something against you?" He related to Musashi every detail of his encounter with the enemy.

When they reached the cabin, Iori went down to the bottom of the hill to get food, and Gonnosuke gathered wood and fetched water.

They sat down around the fire burning brightly in the hearth, and savored the pleasure of seeing each other safe and sound again. It was then that Iori noticed the fresh scars and bruises on Musashi's arms and neck.

"How did you get all those marks?" he asked. "You're covered with them."

"It's nothing important. Did you feed the horse?"

"Yes, sir."

"Tomorrow you must return it."

Early the next morning, Iori mounted the horse and galloped off for a short ride before breakfast. When the sun was above the horizon, he brought the horse to a halt and gaped in awe.

Racing back to the cabin, he yelled, *"Sensei*, get up. Quick! It's like when we saw it from the mountain in Chichibu. The sun—it's huge, and it looks like it's going to roll over the plain. Get up, Gonnosuke."

"Good morning," said Musashi from the grove, where he was taking a stroll.

Too excited to think about breakfast, Iori said, "I'm going now," and rode off.

Musashi watched as boy and horse took on the semblance of a crow at the very center of the sun. The black spot grew smaller and smaller, until at last it was absorbed by the great flaming orb.

The Gateway to Glory

Before sitting down to breakfast, the gateman raked the garden, set fire to the leaves and opened the gate. Shinzō had been up for some time too. He started his day as he always did, by reading a selection from the Chinese classics. This was followed by sword practice.

From the well, where he'd gone to wash, he walked to the stable to have a look at the horses.

"Groom," he called.

"Yes, sir."

"Isn't the chestnut roan back yet?"

"No, but it isn't the horse I'm worried about so much as the boy."

"Don't worry about Iori. He grew up in the country. He can take care of himself."

The elderly gateman came up to Shinzō and informed him that some men had come to see him and were waiting in the garden.

Walking toward the house, Shinzō waved, and as he came up to them, one man said, "It's been a long time."

"It's good to see you all together again," said Shinzō.

"How's your health?"

"Splendid, as you can see."

"We heard you'd been wounded."

"It didn't amount to much. What brings you here at this early hour?"

"There's a little matter we'd like to talk over with you."

The five former students of Obata Kagenori, all handsome sons of banner guards or Confucian scholars, exchanged significant glances.

"Let's go over there," said Shinzō, indicating a maple-covered hillock in one corner of the garden.

Coming to the gateman's fire, they stopped and stood around it.

Shinzō put his hand to his neck, then noticing the others were looking at him, said, "When it's cold, it does ache a little." They took turns examining the scar.

"I heard that was the work of Sasaki Kojirō."

There was a short, tense silence.

"As it happens, our purpose in coming today was to talk about Kojirō. Yesterday we learned he was the man who killed Yogorō."

"I suspected that. Do you have any proof?"

"Circumstantial, but convincing. Yogorō's body was found at the bottom of Isarago Hill, behind the temple. Kakubei's house is halfway up the hill. Kojirō was living there."

"Hmm. I wouldn't be surprised if Yogorō went alone to see Kojirō."

"We're pretty sure that's what happened. Three or four nights before the body was found, a florist saw a man answering to Yogorō's description climbing the hill. Kojirō must've killed him and carried the body down the hill."

The six men stared solemnly at each other, their eyes reflecting their silent anger.

Shinzō, his face reddened by the fire, asked, "Is that all?"

"No. We wanted to talk about the future of the House of Obata and how we're going to take care of Kojirō."

Shinzō stood lost in thought. The man who had spoken first said, "You may have heard this already. Kojirō's become a vassal of Lord Hosokawa Tadatoshi. He's on his way to Buzen now, and he hasn't paid for what he did—ruin our master's reputation, kill his only son and heir and slaughter our comrades."

"Shinzō," urged a third man, "as disciples of Obata Kagenori, we have to do something."

Bits of white ash drifted up from the fire. One man caught a whiff of smoke and coughed.

After listening to them for a few minutes, as they expressed their bitter indignation, Shinzō said, "I'm one of the victims, of course, and I have a plan of my own. But tell me just what you have in mind."

"We're thinking of lodging a protest with Lord Hosokawa. We'll tell him the whole story and ask that Kojirō be turned over to us."

"Then what?"

"We'll see his head up on a pike in front of the graves of our teacher and his son."

"You might be able to do that if he were turned over to you tied up. But the Hosokawas aren't likely to do that. Even though he's only recently been engaged, he is their vassal, and it's his skill they're interested in. Your complaint would only be taken as further proof of his ability. What daimyō is going to turn over one of his vassals to anyone without compelling reasons?"

"Then we'll have to take extreme measures."

"Such as?"

"The group he's traveling with is fairly large. We could easily catch up with them. With you as our leader, the six of us and other loyal disciples—"

"Are you suggesting attacking him?"

"Yes. Go with us, Shinzō."

"I don't like it."

"Aren't you the one who's been chosen to carry on the Obata name?"

"Admitting an enemy is better than we are is difficult," Shinzō said thoughtfully. "Still, objectively, Kojirō's the better swordsman. Even with dozens of men, I'm afraid we'd only end up adding to our shame."

"You're going to stand by and do nothing?" asked one man indignantly.

"No, I resent Kojirō's getting away with what he's done as much as any of you. But I'm willing to wait until the time is right."

"You're awfully patient," one man said sarcastically.

"Aren't you evading your responsibility?" asked another.

When Shinzō made no reply, the five men decided further talk was useless and departed in haste.

On the way they passed Iori, who had dismounted at the gate and was leading the horse to the stable. After tying the animal up, he saw Shinzō by the fire and went to join him.

"Oh, so you're back," said Shinzō.

"Yes," said Iori. "Say, did you have a quarrel?"

"Why do you ask?"

"When I came in just now, I passed some samurai. They seemed angry. They were saying strange things, like 'I overestimated him,' and 'He's a weakling.'"

"That doesn't mean anything," said Shinzō with a little laugh. "Come closer and warm yourself."

"Who needs a fire? I rode all the way from Musashino without stopping."

"You seem in good spirits. Where did you stay last night?"

"At the house. *Sensei*'s back!"

"I heard he was or soon would be."

"You already knew?"

"Takuan told me. Iori, have you heard the news?"

"What news?"

"Your teacher's going to be a great man. It's a wonderful stroke of luck for him. He's going to be one of the shōgun's teachers. He'll be the founder of his own school of swordsmanship."

"Do you mean that?"

"Does it make you happy?"

"Of course—happier than anything. Can I borrow the horse?"

"Now? You just came back."

"I'll go and tell him."

"You don't have to do that. Before the day's out, the Council of Elders will issue a formal summons. As soon as we receive word, I'll go myself and tell Musashi."

"Will he come here?"

"Yes," Shinzō assured him. With a last look at the dying fire, he started toward the house, cheered a bit by Iori but worried about the fate of his angry friends.

The summons was not long in coming. A messenger arrived about two hours later with a letter for Takuan and an order for Musashi to appear the following day at the Reception Pavilion just outside Wadakura Gate. After his appointment was confirmed, he would be received in audience by the shōgun.

When Shinzō, with an attendant, reached the house on Musashino Plain, he found Musashi sitting in the sun with a kitten on his lap, talking with Gonnosuke.

836

Words were few. Shinzo said only, "I've come for you."

"Thanks," said Musashi. "I was about to call you to thank you for looking after Iori."

Without further ado, he mounted the horse Shinzō had brought along for him and they returned to Ushigome.

That evening, as he sat with Takuan and Lord Ujikatsu, he felt immensely fortunate to be able to regard these men, as well as Shinzō, as true friends.

In the morning, Musashi awoke to find clothes suitable to the occasion already laid out for him, together with such things as a fan and tissue paper. And at breakfast, Lord Ujikatsu said to him, "It's a great day. You should rejoice." The meal included rice with red beans, a whole sea bream for each person and other dishes served only on festive occasions. The menu was very much as it would have been for a coming-of-age ceremony in the Hōjō family.

Musashi wanted to refuse the appointment. In Chichibu, he had reconsidered his two years in Hōtengahara and his ambition to put his swordsmanship to work in the interest of good government. Now the belief that Edo, not to speak of the rest of the country, was ready for the type of ideal government he envisioned seemed less tenable. The sanctity of the Way and the application of the principles of swordsmanship for the sake of peace seemed no more than lofty ideals, at least until either Edo or Osaka succeeded in consolidating its rule over the whole country. And he hadn't made up his mind on another point: if the final battle were to come tomorrow, should he support the Eastern Army or the Western Army? Or should he leave the world behind and survive on mountain grasses until peace was restored?

Even on this morning, he could not escape the feeling that if he contented himself with a high position, his pursuit of the Way would be aborted.

But he couldn't refuse. What finally swayed him was the trust in him shown by his supporters. There was no way to say no; he could not break faith with Takuan, his old friend and stern mentor, and Lord Ujikatsu, now a valued acquaintance.

Dressed in formal attire and riding a splendid horse with a beautiful saddle, he set forth on a brilliantly sunlit road for the castle, each step supposedly carrying him closer to the gateway to glory.

In front of the Reception Pavilion was a graveled courtyard and, on a high post, a sign saying: "Dismount." As Musashi got off the horse, an official and one of the stablemen came forward.

"My name is Miyamoto Musashi," he announced in a formal tone of voice. "I have come in response to a summons issued yesterday by the Council of Elders. May I request that you show me to the official in charge of the waiting room?" He had come alone, as was expected of him. Another official came and escorted him to the waiting room, where he was advised to stay "until there is word from within."

It was a large room, more than twenty mats in size, known as the "Orchid Room," after the paintings of birds and spring orchids on the walls and door panels. Before long, a servant came with tea and cakes, but that was Musashi's only contact with human beings for nearly half a day. The little birds in the pictures did not sing, the orchids gave off no fragrance. Musashi began to yawn.

He assumed that the ruddy-faced, white-haired man who eventually appeared was one of the ministers. Perhaps in his prime he had been a distinguished warrior.

"You're Musashi, are you?" Lord Sakai Tadakatsu said lightly as he sat down. "Forgive us for making you wait so long." Though Lord of Kawagoe and a well-known daimyō, in the shōgun's castle he was merely another official, attended by only one samurai. His manner suggested he cared little about pomp or protocol.

Musashi bowed to the floor and remained in this position as he announced in stiffly formal language: "My name is Miyamoto Musashi. I am a rōnin from Mimasaka, the son of Munisai, who was descended from the Shimmen family. I have come to the castle gate in compliance with the shōgun's will, as stated in the summons sent to me."

Tadakatsu nodded several times, causing his double chin to shake. "Many thanks for your trouble," he said, but then went on in an apologetic vein: "With regard to your appointment to official position, for which you were recommended by the priest Takuan and Lord Hōjō of Awa, there was, last evening, a sudden change in the shōgun's plans. As a result, you will not be engaged. Since several of us were not satisfied with this decision, the Council of Elders reviewed this matter today. In fact, we have been discussing it until just now. We took the question to the shōgun again. I am sorry to say that we were unable to alter this latest decision."

There was sympathy in his eyes, and he seemed for a moment to be searching for words of consolation. "In our fleeting world," he went on, "this sort of thing happens all the time. You mustn't let yourself be annoyed by what people say about you. In matters having to do with official appointments, it is often difficult to tell whether one has been fortunate or unfortunate."

Musashi, still bowing, said, "Yes, sir."

Tadakatsu's words were music to his ears. Gratitude swelled from the bottom of his heart, filling his whole body.

"I understand the decision, sir. I am grateful to you." The words came out naturally. Musashi was not concerned with face, nor was he being ironic. He felt that a being greater than the shōgun had just bestowed on him an appointment much higher than that of official tutor. The word of the gods had been vouchsafed to him.

"He took it well," thought Tadakatsu, gazing rather pointedly at Musashi. Aloud he said, "Perhaps it is presumptuous of me, but I've been told you have artistic interests unusual in a samurai. I would like to show an example of your work to the shōgun. Replying to the malicious gossip of ordinary people is unimportant. I think it would be more befitting a noble samurai to rise above the babble of the crowd and leave behind a wordless testimony to the purity of his heart. A work of art would be appropriate, don't you think?"

While Musashi was still pondering the meaning of this, Tadakatsu said, "I hope I will see you again," and left the room.

Musashi raised his head and sat up straight. It was a couple of minutes before he grasped the meaning of Tadakatsu's words—that is, there was no need to answer malicious gossip, but he had to give evidence of his character. If he could do this, his honor would be unsullied, and the men who had recommended him would suffer no loss of face.

Musashi's eye fell on a six-panel screen in one corner of the room. It was invitingly blank. Summoning a young samurai from the guard room, he explained that Lord Sakai had asked him to draw a picture and requested materials with which to comply—brushes, ink of good quality, some aged cinnabar and a bit of blue pigment.

It occurred to Musashi what an odd fact it was that most children could draw—and sing, for that matter—but that they forgot how to as they grew older. Perhaps the little bit of wisdom they acquired inhibited them. He himself was no exception. As a child he had often drawn pictures, this having been one of his favorite ways of overcoming loneliness. But from the age of thirteen or fourteen until he was past twenty, he gave up drawing almost entirely.

In the course of his travels he had often stopped over at temples or the houses of the wealthy, where he had the opportunity to see good paintings—murals, or scrolls hanging in alcoves—and this had given him a lively interest in art.

The aristocratic simplicity and subtle profundity of Liang-k'ai's painting of chestnuts had made an especially deep impression. After seeing that work at Kōetsu's house, he had availed himself of every opportunity to view rare Chinese paintings of the Sung dynasty, the works of the fifteenth-century Japanese Zen masters and the paintings of contemporary masters of the Kanō School, particularly Kanō Sanraku and Kaihō Yūshō. Naturally, he had his likes and dislikes. Liang-k'ai's bold, virile brushwork, as seen by a swordsman's eye, struck him as revealing the prodigious strength of a giant. Kaihō Yūshō, possibly because he was of samurai origin, had in his old age achieved such a high degree of purity that Musashi considered him a worthy man to take as a model. He was also attracted by the light impromptu effects in the works of the hermit priest and aesthete Shōkadō Shōjō, whom he liked all the more because he was reputed to be a close friend of Takuan.

Painting, which seemed far removed from the path he had chosen, was hardly an art for a person who rarely spent a full month in any one place. Yet he did paint from time to time.

As in the case of other adults who have forgotten how to draw, his mind would work, but not his spirit. Intent upon drawing skillfully, he was unable to express himself naturally. Many had been the times he'd become discouraged and quit. Then, sooner or later, some impulse invariably moved him to pick up the brush again—in secret. Being ashamed of his paintings, he never showed them to others, though he allowed people to inspect his sculpture.

Until now, that is. To commemorate this fateful day, he resolved to paint a picture fit for the shōgun, or anyone else, to see.

He worked rapidly and without interruption until it was finished. Then he quietly put the brush in a jar of water and left, without a single backward glance at his work.

In the courtyard, he did turn around for one last look at the imposing gate, one question filling his mind: Did glory lie inside or outside the gate?

Sakai Tadakatsu returned to the waiting room and sat for some time gazing at the still damp painting. The picture was of Musashino Plain. In the middle, appearing very large, was the rising sun. This, symbolizing Musashi's confidence in his own integrity, was vermilion. The rest of the work was executed in ink to capture the feeling of autumn on the plain.

Tadakatsu said to himself, "We've lost a tiger to the wilds."

The Sound of Heaven

"Back already?" asked Gonnosuke, blinking his eyes at the sight of Musashi in stiffly starched formal dress.

Musashi went inside the house and sat down. Gonnosuke knelt at the edge of the reed matting and bowed. "Congratulations," he said warmly. "Will you have to go to work right away?"

"The appointment was canceled," Musashi said with a laugh.

"Canceled? Are you joking?"

"No. And I consider it a good thing, too."

"I don't understand. Do you know what went wrong?"

"I saw no reason to ask. I'm grateful to heaven for the way it turned out."

"But it seems a pity."

"Are even you of the opinion I can find glory only within the walls of Edo Castle?"

Gonnosuke did not answer.

"For a time, I had such an ambition. I dreamed of applying my understanding of the sword to the problem of providing peace and happiness for the people, making the Way of the Sword the Way of Government. I thought being an official would give me a chance to test my idea."

"Somebody slandered you. Is that it?"

"Perhaps, but don't give it another thought. And don't misunderstand me. My ideas, I've learned, particularly today, are little more than dreams."

"That's not true. I've had the same idea; the Way of the Sword and the spirit of good government ought to be one and the same."

"I'm glad we agree. But in fact, the truth of the scholar, alone in his study, does not always accord with what the world at large considers to be true."

"Then you think the truth you and I are searching for is of no use in the real world."

"No, it's not that," said Musashi impatiently. "As long as this country exists, no matter how things change, the brave man's Way of the Spirit will never cease to be useful. . . . If you give the matter some thought, you'll see that the Way of Government is not concerned with the Art of War alone. A flawless political system must be based on a perfect blending of military and literary arts. To cause the world to live in peace is the ultimate Way of the Sword. That's why I've come to the conclusion that my thoughts are only dreams, childish dreams at that. I must learn to be a humble servant of two gods, one of the sword, one of the pen. Before I attempt to govern the nation, I must learn what the nation has to teach." He concluded with a laugh but abruptly stopped and asked Gonnosuke if he had an ink box or a writing kit.

When he finished writing, he folded up his letter and said to Gonnosuke, "I'm sorry to trouble you, but I'd like to ask you to deliver this for me."

"To the Hōjō residence?"

"Yes. I've written fully about my feelings. Give Takuan and Lord Ujikatsu my warmest greetings. . . . Oh, there's one more thing. I've been keeping something of Iori's. Please give it to him." He pulled out the pouch Iori's father had left him and placed it beside the letter.

With an anxious look on his face, Gonnosuke moved forward on his knees and said, "Why are you returning this to Iori now?"

"I'm going to the mountains."

"Mountains or city, wherever you go, Iori and I want to be with you as your disciples."

"I won't be away forever. While I am, I'd like you to take care of Iori, say for the next two or three years."

"What? Are you going into retirement?"

Musashi laughed, uncrossed his legs and leaned back on his arms. "I'm much too young for that. I'm not giving up my great hope. Everything's still ahead of me: desire, illusion, everything. . . . There's a song. I don't know who wrote it, but it goes like this:

> While yearning to gain
> The depths of the mountains,
> I'm drawn against my will
> To the places
> Where people reside."

Gonnosuke lowered his head as he listened. Then he stood up and put the letter and pouch in his kimono. "I'd better go now," he said quietly. "It's getting dark."

"All right. Please return the horse, and tell Lord Ujikatsu that since the clothes are soiled from travel, I'll keep them."

"Yes, of course."

"I don't think it would be discreet for me to go back to Lord Ujikatsu's house. The cancellation of the appointment must mean that the shogunate regards me as unreliable or suspicious. It might cause Lord Ujikatsu trouble to be associated any more closely with me. I didn't write that in the letter, so I want you to explain it to him. Tell him I hope he's not offended."

"I understand. I'll be back before morning."

The sun was rapidly setting. Gonnosuke took the horse's bit and led the animal down the path. Since it had been lent to Musashi, the idea of riding it never crossed his mind.

It was about two hours later when he reached Ushigome. The men were sitting around, wondering what had become of Musashi. Gonnosuke joined them and gave the letter to Takuan.

An official had already been there to inform them of unfavorable reports on Musashi's character and past activities. Of all the points against him, the most damaging was that he had an enemy who had sworn vengeance. According to the rumors, Musashi was in the wrong.

After the official left, Shinzō had told his father and Takuan about Osugi's visit. "She even tried to sell her wares here," was the way he put it.

What was left unexplained was why people accepted so unquestioningly what they were told. Not just ordinary people—women gossiping around the well or laborers drinking in cheap sake shops—but men who had the intelligence to sift fact from fabrication. The shōgun's ministers had discussed the matter for many long hours, but even they had ended up giving credence to Osugi's calumnies.

Takuan and the others half expected Musashi's letter to express his discontent, but in fact it said little beyond giving his reason for going away. He began by saying that he had asked Gonnosuke to tell them how he felt. Then came the song he had sung for Gonnosuke. The short letter ended: "Indulging my chronic wanderlust, I am setting out on another aimless journey. On this occasion, I offer the following poem, which may amuse you:

> If the universe
> Is indeed my garden,
> When I look at it,
> I stand at the exit of
> The house called the Floating World."

Though Ujikatsu and Shinzō were deeply touched by Musashi's consideration, Ujikatsu said, "He's too self-effacing. I'd like to see him once more before he goes away. Takuan, I doubt that he'd come if we sent for him, so let's go to him." He got to his feet, ready to leave immediately.

"Could you wait a moment, sir?" asked Gonnosuke. "I'd like to go with you, but Musashi asked me to give something to Iori. Could you have him brought here?"

When Iori came in, he asked, "Did you want me?" His eyes went immediately to the pouch in Gonnosuke's hand.

"Musashi said you were to take good care of this," said Gonnosuke, "since it's the only keepsake you have from your father." He then explained that the two of them would be together until Musashi's return.

Iori couldn't hide his disappointment, but not wanting to appear weak, he nodded halfheartedly.

In answer to Takuan's inquiries, Iori told all he knew about his parents. When there were no more questions, he said, "One thing I've never known is what became of my sister. My father didn't say much about her, and my mother died without telling me anything I can remember. I don't know where she lives, or whether she's alive or dead."

Takuan placed the pouch on his knee and took out a crumpled piece of paper. As he read the cryptic message Iori's father had written, his eyebrows shot up in surprise. Staring hard at Iori, he said, "This tells us something about your sister."

"I thought maybe it did, but I didn't understand it and neither did the priest at the Tokuganji."

Skipping over the first part, Takuan read aloud: "'Since I had resolved to die of starvation before serving a second lord, my wife and I wandered around for many years, living in the humblest circumstances. One year we had to abandon our daughter at a temple in the central provinces. We put 'one sound of heaven' in her baby clothes and entrusted her future to the threshold of compassion. Then we went on to another province.

"'Later, I acquired my thatched house in the fields of Shimōsa. I thought back to that earlier time, but the place was far away and we had had no word, so I feared it might not be in the girl's interest to try to find her. I consequently left matters as they were.

"'How cruel parents can be! I am reproved by the words of Minamoto no Sanetomo:

> Even the animals,
> Which cannot speak their feelings,
> Are not bereft of
> The tender generous love
> Of parents for their offspring.

"'May my ancestors take pity on me for refusing to sully my honor as a samurai by taking a second lord. You are my son. No matter how much you crave success, do not eat dishonorable millet!'"

As he placed the paper back in the pouch, Takuan said, "You'll be able to see your sister. I've known her since I was a young man. Musashi knows her too. Come with us, Iori." He gave no hint as to why he said this, nor did he mention Otsū or the "sound of heaven," which he recognized to be her flute.

They all left together and hurried to the cabin, arriving shortly after the first rays of the rising sun touched it. It stood empty. On the edge of the plain was one white cloud.

Book VII   THE PERFECT LIGHT

The Runaway Ox

The shadow of the plum branch cast on the white plaster wall by the pallid sun was beautiful in a restrained way evocative of monochrome ink painting. It was early spring in Koyagyū, and quiet, the branches of the plum trees seemingly beckoning southward to the nightingales that would soon flock to the valley.

Unlike the birds, the *shugyōsha* who presented themselves at the castle gate knew no season. They came in a constant stream, seeking either to receive instruction from Sekishūsai or to try their hand against him. The litany varied little: "Please, just one bout"; "I beg you, let me see him"; "I'm the only true disciple of so-and-so, who teaches at such-and-such a place." For the past ten years, the guards had been giving the same reply: because of their master's advanced age, he was unable to receive anyone. Few swordsmen, or would-be swordsmen, would let it go at that. Some launched diatribes on the meaning of the true Way and how there should be no discrimination between young and old, rich and poor, beginner and expert. Others simply pleaded, while still others rashly tried to offer bribes. Many went away muttering angry imprecations.

Had the truth been generally known, namely that Sekishūsai had passed away late the previous year, matters might have been greatly simplified. But it had been decided that since Munenori couldn't get away from Edo until the fourth month, the death should be kept secret until the funeral service had been held. One of the handful of people outside the castle who knew the circumstances now sat in a guest room asking rather insistently to see Hyōgo.

It was Inshun, the elderly abbot of the Hōzōin, who throughout In'ei's dotage and after his death had upheld the temple's reputation as a martial arts center. Many even believed he had improved it. He had done everything possible to maintain the close ties between the temple and Koyagyū that had existed since the days of In'ei and Sekishūsai. He wanted to see Hyōgo, he said, because he wanted to have a talk about the martial arts. Sukekurō knew what he really wanted—to have a bout with the man whom his grandfather had privately regarded as a better swordsman than either himself or Munenori. Hyōgo, of course, would have no part in such a match, since he thought it would benefit neither side and was therefore senseless.

Sukekurō assured Inshun that word had been sent. "I'm sure Hyōgo would come to greet you if he were feeling better."

"So you mean to say he still has a cold?"

"Yes; he can't seem to get rid of it."

"I didn't know his health was so frail."

"Oh, it isn't really, but he's been in Edo for some time, you know, and he can't quite get used to these cold mountain winters."

While the two men chatted, a servant boy was calling Otsū's name in the garden of the innermost encirclement. A shoji opened, and she emerged from one of the houses, trailing a wisp of incense smoke. She was still in mourning more than a hundred days since Sekishūsai's passing, and her face looked as white as a pear blossom.

"Where've you been? I've been looking everywhere," asked the boy.

"I've been in the Buddhist chapel."

"Hyōgo's asking for you."

When she entered Hyōgo's room, he said, "Ah, Otsū, thank you for coming. I'd like you to greet a visitor for me."

"Yes, of course."

"He's been here quite a while. Sukekurō went to keep him company, but listening to him go on and on about the Art of War must have Sukekurō pretty exhausted by now."

"The abbot of the Hōzōin?"

"Um."

Otsū smiled faintly, bowed and left the room.

Meanwhile, Inshun was not too subtly feeling Sukekurō out regarding Hyōgo's past and character.

"I'm told that when Katō Kiyomasa offered him a position, Sekishūsai refused to consent unless Kiyomasa agreed to an unusual condition."

"Really? I don't recall ever hearing of any such thing."

"According to In'ei, Sekishūsai told Kiyomasa that since Hyōgo was extremely quick-tempered, his lordship would have to promise in advance that if Hyōgo committed any capital offenses, he would pardon the first three. Sekishūsai was never known to condone impetuosity. He must have had rather a special feeling about Hyōgo."

This came as such a surprise that Sukekurō was still at a loss for words when Otsū entered. She smiled at the abbot and said, "How good to see you again. Unfortunately, Hyōgo is tied up preparing a report which must be sent to Edo immediately, but he asked me to convey his apologies at not being able to see you this time." She busied herself serving tea and cakes to Inshun and the two young priests attending him.

The abbot looked disappointed, though he politely ignored the discrepancy between Sukekurō's excuse and Otsū's. "I'm sorry to hear that. I had some important information for him."

"I'll be happy to pass it on," said Sukekurō, "and you can rest assured Hyōgo's ears alone will hear it."

"Oh, I'm sure of that," said the old priest. "I just wanted to warn Hyōgo in person."

Inshun then repeated a rumor he'd heard about some samurai from Ueno Castle in Iga Province. The dividing line between Koyagyū and the castle lay in a sparsely inhabited area about two miles to the east, and ever since Ieyasu had confiscated it from the Christian daimyō Tsutsui Sadatsugu and reassigned it to Tōdō Takatora, many changes had been taking place. Takatora had, since taking up residence the previous year, repaired the castle, revised the tax system, improved the irrigation facilities and carried out other measures to consolidate his holdings. All this was common knowledge. What Inshun had got wind of was that Takatora was in the process of trying to expand his lands by pushing back the boundary line.

According to the reports, Takatora had dispatched a number of samurai to Tsukigase, where they were building houses, cutting down plum trees, waylaying travelers and openly trespassing on Lord Yagyū's property.

"It could be," observed Inshun, "Lord Takatora is taking advantage of your being in mourning. You may think I'm an alarmist, but it looks as though he's planning to push the boundary back in this direction and put up a new fence. If he is, it'd be a lot easier to attend to things now than after he's finished. If you sit back and do nothing, you'll regret it later, I'm afraid."

Speaking as one of the senior retainers, Sukekurō thanked Inshun for the information. "I'll have the situation investigated, and lodge a complaint if one is warranted." Expressing thanks on behalf of Hyōgo, Sukekurō bowed as the abbot took his leave.

When Sukekurō went to inform Hyōgo of the rumors, Hyōgo just laughed. "Let it be," he said. "When my uncle gets back, he can look into it."

Sukekurō, who knew the importance of guarding every foot of land, wasn't quite satisfied with Hyōgo's attitude. He conferred with the other ranking samurai and together they agreed that, though discretion was called for, something should be done. Tōdō Takatora was one of the most powerful daimyō in the country.

The following morning, as Sukekurō was leaving the dōjō above the Shinkagedō after sword practice, he ran into a boy of thirteen or fourteen.

The lad bowed to Sukekurō, who said jovially, "Hello there, Ushinosuke. Peeking into the dōjō again? Did you bring me a present? Let's see . . . wild potatoes?" He was only half teasing, since Ushinosuke's potatoes were always better than anyone else's. The boy lived with his mother in the isolated mountain village of Araki and often came to the castle to sell charcoal, boar meat and other things.

"No potatoes today, but I brought this for Otsū." He held up a package wrapped in straw.

"What's that, now—rhubarb?"

"No, it's alive! In Tsukigase, I sometimes hear nightingales singing. I caught one!"

"Hmm, you always come by way of Tsukigase, don't you?"

"That's right. That's the only road."

"Let me ask you a question. Have you seen a lot of samurai in that area lately?"

"Some."

"What are they doing there?"

"Building cabins . . ."

"Have you seen them putting up fences, anything like that?"

"No."

"Have they been cutting down plum trees?"

"Well, besides the cabins, they've been fixing bridges, so they've been cutting down all kinds of trees. For firewood too."

"Are they stopping people on the road?"

"I don't think so. I haven't seen them do that."

Sukekurō cocked his head. "I've heard those samurai are from Lord Tōdō's fief, but I don't know what they're doing in Tsukigase. What do people in your village say?"

"They say they're rōnin chased out of Nara and Uji. They didn't have anyplace to live, so they came to the mountains."

Despite what Inshun had said, Sukekurō thought this a not unreasonable explanation. Ōkubo Nagayasu, the magistrate of Nara, had not relaxed his efforts to keep his jurisdiction free of indigent rōnin.

"Where's Otsū?" asked Ushinosuke. "I want to give her her present." He always looked forward to seeing her, but not just because she gave him sweets and said nice things to him. There was something about her beauty that was mysterious, otherworldly. At times, he couldn't decide whether she was human or a goddess.

"She's in the castle, I imagine," said Sukekurō. Then, looking toward the garden, he said, "Oh, you seem to be in luck. Isn't that her over there?"

"Otsū!" Ushinosuke called loudly.

She turned and smiled. Running breathlessly to her side, he held up his package.

"Look! I caught a nightingale. It's for you."

"A nightingale?" Frowning, she kept her hands close to her sides.

Ushinosuke looked disappointed. "It has a beautiful voice," he said. "Wouldn't you like to hear it?"

"I would, but only if it's free to fly wherever it wants to. Then it'll sing pretty songs for us."

"I guess you're right," he said with a little pout. "Do you want me to turn it loose?"

"I appreciate your wanting to give me a present, but yes, that'd make me happier than keeping it."

Silently, Ushinosuke split open the straw package, and like an arrow the bird flew away over the castle wall.

"There, you see how glad it is to be free?" said Otsū.

"They call nightingales harbingers of spring, don't they? Maybe some-body'll bring you good news."

"A messenger bringing news as welcome as the coming of spring? It's true there's something I'm longing to hear."

As Otsū started walking toward the woods and bamboo grove in back of the castle, Ushinosuke fell in at her side.

"Where are you going?" he asked.

"I've been inside a lot lately. I thought I'd go up the hill and look at the plum blossoms for a change."

"Plum blossoms? Those up there aren't much to look at. You should go to Tsukigase."

"That might be nice. Is it far?"

"A couple of miles or so. Why don't you go? I brought firewood today, so I have the ox with me."

Having scarcely been outside the castle all winter, Otsū made up her mind quickly. Without telling anyone where she was going, the two of them strolled down to the back gate, which was used by tradesmen and others hav-ing business at the castle. It was guarded by a samurai armed with a lance. He nodded and smiled at Otsū. Ushinosuke, too, was a familiar figure, and he let them out the gate without checking the boy's written permission to be in the castle grounds.

People in the fields and on the road spoke a friendly greeting to Otsū, whether they knew her or not. When the dwellings became sparser, she looked back at the white castle nestled on the skirt of the mountain and said, "Can I get back home while it's still light?"

"Sure, but I'll come back with you anyway."

"Araki Village is beyond Tsukigase, isn't it?"

"It doesn't matter."

Chatting about various things, they passed a salt shop, where a man was bartering some boar meat for a sack of salt. He finished his transaction, came out and walked along the road behind them. With the snow melting, the road grew worse and worse. There were few travelers.

"Ushinosuke," said Otsū, "you always come to Koyagyū, don't you?"

"Yes."

"Isn't Ueno Castle closer to Araki Village?"

"It is, but there's no great swordsman like Lord Yagyū at Ueno Castle."

"Do you like swords?"

"Uh-huh."

He stopped the ox, let go of the rope and ran down to the edge of the stream. There was a bridge from which a log had fallen. He put it back in place and waited for the man behind them to cross first.

The man looked like a rōnin. As he walked by Otsū, he eyed her brazenly, then glanced back several times from the bridge and from the other side, be-fore disappearing into a fold of the mountain.

"Who do you suppose that is?" asked Otsū nervously.

"Did he frighten you?"

"No, but . . ."

"There're lots of rōnin in the mountains around here."

"Are there?" she said uneasily.

Over his shoulder, Ushinosuke said, "Otsū, I wonder if you'd help me. Do you think you could ask Master Kimura to hire me? I mean, you know, I could sweep the garden, draw water—do things like that."

It was only recently that the boy had received special permission from Sukekurō to enter the dōjō and watch the men at practice, but already he had only one ambition. His ancestors bore the surname Kikumura; the head of the family for several generations had used the given name Mataemon. Ushinosuke had decided that when he became a samurai he would take the name Mataemon, but none of the Kikumuras had done anything of particular note. He'd change his surname to that of his village, and if his dream came true, become famous far and wide as Araki Mataemon.

As Otsū listened, she thought of Jōtarō and was seized by a sense of loneliness. She was twenty-five now; he must be nineteen or twenty. Looking around at the plum blossoms—not yet in full bloom—she couldn't help but feel that spring had already passed for her.

"Let's go back, Ushinosuke," she said suddenly.

He gave her a questioning look but obediently turned the ox around.

"Stop!" shouted a loud male voice.

Two other rōnin had joined the one from the salt shop. All three came and stood around the ox with their arms folded.

"What do you want?" asked Ushinosuke.

The men kept their eyes fixed on Otsū.

"I see what you mean," said one.

"She's a beauty, isn't she?"

"I've seen her somewhere before," said the third man. "In Kyoto, I think."

"She must be from Kyoto, certainly not from any of the villages around here."

"I don't remember whether it was at the Yoshioka School or somewhere else, but I know I've seen her."

"Were you at the Yoshioka School?"

"For three years, after Sekigahara."

"If you've got any business with us, say what it is!" Ushinosuke said angrily. "We want to get back before dark."

One of the rōnin glared at him, as if noticing him for the first time. "You're from Araki, aren't you? One of the charcoal-makers?"

"Yes. So what?"

"We don't need you. Run along home."

"That's just what I'm going to do."

He pulled the rope taut, and one man gave him a look that would have had most boys trembling with fright.

"Get out of the way," said Ushinosuke.

"This lady's going with us."

"Going where?"

852   "What difference does it make to you? Give me that rope."

"No!"

"Say, he doesn't think I mean it."

The other two men, squaring their shoulders and glowering, moved in on Ushinosuke. One presented a fist as hard as a pine knot in front of his chin.

Otsū clutched the ox's back. The tilt of Ushinosuke's eyebrows said very clearly something was going to happen.

"Oh, no, stop!" she cried, hoping to keep the boy from doing anything rash. But the plaintive note in her voice just spurred him to action. He lashed out swiftly with one leg, caught the man in front of him, sending him staggering backward. No sooner was Ushinosuke's foot in contact with the ground again than he rammed his head into the gut of the man on his left. Simultaneously he got a grip on the man's sword and pulled it from its scabbard. Then he began swinging.

He moved with lightning quickness. He whirled and seemed to be attacking in every direction at the same time, all three opponents at once, with equal force. Whether he was acting brilliantly out of instinct or out of childish recklessness, his unorthodox tactics took the rōnin by surprise.

The reverse swing of the sword drove forcefully into the chest of one man. Otsū cried out, but her voice was drowned by the scream of the wounded man. He fell toward the ox, a geyser of blood spurting into the animal's face. Terrified, the ox let out an indescribable shriek. Just then, Ushinosuke's sword cut deeply into its rump. With another shriek, the ox set off at a near gallop.

The other two rōnin rushed at Ushinosuke, who was leaping nimbly from rock to rock in the stream bed. "I didn't do anything wrong! It was you!" he shouted.

Realizing he was out of their reach, the two rōnin started after the ox.

Ushinosuke jumped back onto the road and took after them, shouting, "Running away? You running away?"

One man stopped and half turned.

"You little bastard!"

"Leave him till later!" shouted the other man.

The ox, blind with fear, left the valley road and ran up a low hill, traveled a short distance along the crest and plunged down the other side. In a very short time, it covered a considerable distance, reaching a point not far from the Yagyū fief.

Otsū, her eyes shut in resignation, managed to keep from being thrown by clinging to the packsaddle. She could hear the voices of the people they were passing but was too stunned to utter a cry for help. Not that it would have done any good. None of the people commenting on the spectacle had the courage to stop the demented beast.

When they were almost to Hannya Plain, a man came from a side road into the middle of the main road, which, though very narrow, was the Kasagi highroad. He had a letter case slung from his shoulder and appeared to be a servant of some sort.

People were shouting, "Watch out! Get out of the way!" but he walked on, right in the path of the ox.

Then there was a terrible cracking sound.

"He's been gored!"

"The idiot!"

But it wasn't as the bystanders first thought. The sound they'd heard was not that of the ox striking the man but of the man landing a stunning blow on the side of the animal's head. The ox lifted its heavy neck sideways, turned halfway around and started back the other way. It hadn't gone ten feet before it came to a dead halt, saliva streaming from its mouth, its whole body shaking.

"Get down quick," the man said to Otsū.

Onlookers crowded around excitedly, staring at the man's foot, which was firmly planted on the rope.

Once she was safely on the ground, Otsū bowed to her rescuer, though she was still too dazed to know where she was or what she was doing.

"Why should a gentle animal like this go mad?" asked the man, as he led the ox to the side of the road and tied it to a tree. Catching sight of the blood on the animal's legs, he said, "What's this, now. Why, it's been cut—with a sword!"

While he was examining the wound and muttering to himself, Kimura Sukekurō pushed through the ring of people and sent them on their way.

"Aren't you Abbot Inshun's attendant?" he asked, even before he'd had a chance to catch his breath.

"How fortunate to meet you here, sir. I have a letter for you from the abbot. If you don't mind, I'd like to ask you to read it immediately." He took the letter from the case and handed it to Sukekurō.

"For me?" Sukekurō asked with surprise. Having ascertained there was no mistake, he opened it and read: "Regarding the samurai at Tsukigase, I have, since our conversation yesterday, verified that they are not Lord Tōdō's men. They are riffraff, rōnin expelled from the cities, who have holed up there for the winter. I hasten to inform you of this unfortunate error on my part."

"Thank you," said Sukekurō. "This agrees with what I've learned from another source. Tell the abbot I am much relieved and trust that he is too."

"Forgive me for delivering the letter in the middle of the road. I'll convey your message to the abbot. Good-bye."

"Wait a minute. How long have you been at the Hōzōin?"

"Not long."

"What's your name?"

"I'm called Torazō."

"I wonder," mumbled Sukekurō, scrutinizing the man's face. "Are you by any chance Hamada Toranosuke?"

"No."

"I've never met Hamada, but there's a man at the castle who insists Hamada's now serving as Inshun's attendant."

"Yes, sir."

"Is it a case of mistaken identity?"

Torazō, red in the face, lowered his voice. "Actually, I am Hamada. I've come to the Hōzōin for reasons of my own. To avoid further disgrace to my teacher and greater shame to myself, I'd like to keep my identity secret. If you don't mind . . ."

"Don't worry. I had no intention of prying into your affairs."

"I'm sure you've heard about Tadaaki. His abandoning his school and retiring to the mountains was due to a mistake of mine. I've given up my status. Doing menial tasks at the temple will be good discipline. I didn't give the priests my real name. It's all very embarrassing."

"The outcome of Tadaaki's fight with Kojirō is no secret. Kojirō told everyone he met between Edo and Buzen. I take it you've resolved to clear your teacher's name."

"One of these days . . . I'll see you again, sir." Torazō took his leave swiftly, as though unable to endure another moment.

Hemp Seed

Hyōgo was growing concerned. After going to Otsū's room with a letter from Takuan in his hand, he'd searched for her all over the castle grounds, more and more urgently as the hours passed.

The letter, dated the tenth month of the previous year but inexplicably delayed, told of Musashi's pending appointment as an instructor to the shōgun. Takuan had asked that Otsū come to the capital as soon as possible, since Musashi would soon need a house as well as "someone to look after it." Hyōgo couldn't wait to see her face light up.

Not finding her, he finally went to question the guard at the gate and was told men were out looking for her. Hyōgo took a deep breath, thinking how unlike Otsū it was to cause people to worry, how unlike her not to leave word. She rarely acted impulsively, even in the smallest matters.

Before he began to imagine the worst, however, news came that they were back, Otsū with Sukekurō, and Ushinosuke with the men sent to Tsukigase. The boy, apologizing to everyone for no one knew what, was obviously in a hurry to be on his way.

"Where do you think you're going?" asked one of the attendants.

"I've got to get back to Araki. My mother will worry if I don't."

"If you try to go back now," said Sukekurō, "those rōnin will get you, and it's not likely they'd let you go alive. You can stay here tonight and go home in the morning."

Ushinosuke mumbled something vaguely acquiescent and was told to go to a wood storehouse in the outer encirclement, where the apprentice samurai slept. *855*

Beckoning to Otsū, Hyōgo took her aside and told her what Takuan had written. He wasn't surprised when she said, "I'll leave in the morning," a deep blush revealing her feelings.

Hyōgo then reminded her of Munenori's coming visit and suggested she return to Edo with him, though he knew quite well what her answer would be. She was in no mood to wait two more days, much less two more months. He made another attempt, saying that if she waited until after the funeral service, she could travel with him as far as Nagoya, since he'd been invited to become a vassal of Lord Tokugawa of Owari. When she again demurred, he told her how much the idea of her making the long journey alone displeased him. In every town and inn along the way she would encounter inconveniences, if not actual danger.

She smiled. "You seem to forget. I'm used to traveling. There's nothing for you to worry about."

That evening, at a modest farewell party, everyone expressed his affection for Otsū, and the next morning, which was bright and clear, family and servants gathered at the front gate to see her off.

Sukekurō sent a man to fetch Ushinosuke, thinking that Otsū could ride his ox as far as Uji. When the man returned and reported the boy had gone home the night before after all, Sukekurō ordered a horse to be brought.

Otsū, feeling she was of too low a status to be so favored, refused the offer, but Hyōgo insisted. The horse, a dapple gray, was led by an apprentice samurai down the gentle slope to the outer gate.

Hyōgo went partway, then stopped. He couldn't deny it. At times he envied Musashi, as he would have envied any man whom Otsū loved. That her heart belonged to another did not diminish his affection for her. She'd been a delightful companion on the trip down from Edo, and in the subsequent weeks and months he had marveled at the devotion with which she had cared for his grandfather. Though deeper than ever, his love for her was selfless. Sekishūsai had instructed him to deliver her to Musashi safely; Hyōgo intended to do just that. It wasn't his nature to covet another man's good fortune nor to think of depriving him of it. He could not think of any act as being apart from the Way of the Samurai; carrying out his grandfather's wish would in itself have been an expression of his love.

He was lost in reverie when Otsū turned and bowed her thanks to her well-wishers. As she set off, she brushed against some plum blossoms. Unconsciously watching the petals fall, Hyōgo could almost smell the fragrance. He felt he was seeing her for the last time and took comfort in a silent prayer for her future life. He stood and stared as she disappeared from sight.

"Sir."

Hyōgo turned around and a smile came slowly to his face. "Ushinosuke. Well, well. I hear you went home last night after I told you not to."

"Yes, sir; my mother . . ." He was still at an age when mention of separation from his mother brought him to the verge of tears.

"That's all right. It's good for a boy to take care of his mother. But how did you get by those rōnin at Tsukigase?"

"Oh, that was easy."

"Was it, now?"

The boy smiled. "They weren't there. They heard Otsū was from the castle, so they were afraid of being attacked. I guess they must've gone to the other side of the mountain."

"Ha, ha. We don't have to worry about them anymore, do we? Have you had breakfast?"

"No," said Ushinosuke, slightly embarrassed. "I got up early to dig some wild potatoes for Master Kimura. If you like them, I'll bring you some too."

"Thank you."

"Do you know where Otsū is?"

"She just left for Edo."

"Edo? . . ." Hesitantly he said, "I wonder if she asked you or Master Kimura what I wanted her to."

"And what was that?"

"I've been hoping you'd let me become a samurai's attendant."

"You're still a little too young for that. Maybe when you're older."

"But I want to learn swordsmanship. Won't you teach me, please. I have to learn while my mother's still alive."

"Have you been studying under someone?"

"No, but I've practiced using my wooden sword on trees and animals."

"That's a good way to start. When you get a little older, you can come and join me in Nagoya. I'm going there to live soon."

"That's way off in Owari, isn't it? I can't go so far away, not while my mother's still alive."

Hyōgo, not unmoved, said, "Come with me." Ushinosuke followed along silently. "We'll go to the dōjō. I'll see if you have the natural ability to become a swordsman."

"The dōjō?" Ushinosuke wondered if he was dreaming. Since early childhood, he'd regarded the ancient Yagyū dōjō as symbolizing everything he aspired to in the world. Though Sukekurō had said he could enter, he had not done so yet. But now, to be invited inside by a member of the family!

"Rinse your feet."

"Yes, sir." Ushinosuke went to a small pond near the entrance and very carefully washed his feet, taking care to remove the dirt from under his toenails.

Once inside, he felt small and insignificant. The beams and rafters were old and massive, the floor polished to a sheen he could see his reflection in. Even Hyōgo's voice when he said, "Get a sword," sounded different.

Ushinosuke selected a black-oak sword from among the weapons hanging on one wall. Hyōgo took one too, and with the point directed toward the floor, walked to the middle of the room.

"Are you ready?" he asked coldly.

"Yes," said Ushinosuke, raising his weapon to chest level.

Hyōgo opened his stance slightly on the diagonal. Ushinosuke was puffed up like a hedgehog. His eyebrows were raised, his face was set in a fierce frown, and his blood raced. When Hyōgo signaled with his eyes that he was about to attack, Ushinosuke grunted loudly. Feet pounding the floor, Hyōgo advanced rapidly and struck laterally at Ushinosuke's waist.

"Not yet!" shouted the boy. As though kicking the floor away from him, he leaped high in the air, clearing Hyōgo's shoulder. Hyōgo reached out with his left hand and lightly pushed the boy's feet upward. Ushinosuke did a somersault and landed behind Hyōgo. He was up in a split second, running to retrieve his sword.

"That's enough," said Hyōgo.

"No; once more!"

Grabbing his sword, Ushinosuke held it high over his head with both hands and flew like an eagle toward Hyōgo. Hyōgo's weapon, aimed straight at him, stopped him dead in his tracks. He saw the look in Hyōgo's eyes and his own filled with tears.

"This boy has spirit," thought Hyōgo, but he pretended to be angry. "You're fighting dirty," he shouted. "You jumped over my shoulder."

Ushinosuke did not know what to say to that.

"You don't understand your status—taking liberties with your betters! Sit down, right there." The boy knelt and put his hands out in front of him to bow in apology. As he came toward him, Hyōgo dropped the wooden sword and drew his own weapon. "I'll kill you now. Don't bother to scream."

"K-k-kill me?"

"Stick out your neck. For a samurai, *nothing* is more important than abiding by the rules of proper conduct. Even if you are only a farm boy, what you did is unforgivable."

"You're going to kill me just for doing something rude?"

"That's right."

After looking up at the samurai for a moment, Ushinosuke, resignation in his eyes, lifted his hands in the direction of his village and said, "Mother, I'm going to become part of the soil here at the castle. I know how sad you'll feel. Forgive me for not being a good son." Then he obediently extended his neck.

Hyōgo laughed and put his sword back in its scabbard. Patting Ushinosuke on the back, he said, "You don't think I'd really kill a boy like you, do you?"

"You weren't serious?"

"No."

"You said proper conduct is important. Is it all right for a samurai to play jokes like that?"

"It wasn't a joke. If you're going to train to become a samurai, I have to know what you're made of."

"I thought you meant it," said Ushinosuke, his breathing returning to normal.

"You told me you hadn't had lessons," said Hyōgo. "But when I forced you to the edge of the room, you jumped over my shoulder. Not many students, even with three or four years of training, could execute that ploy."

"I never studied with anyone, though."

"It's nothing to hide. You must have had a teacher, and a good one. Who was he?"

The boy thought for a moment, then said, "Oh, I remember how I learned that."

"Who taught you?"

"It wasn't a human being."

"A goblin maybe?"

"No, a hemp seed."

"What?"

"A hemp seed."

"How could you learn from a hemp seed?"

"Well, way up in the mountains there are some of those fighters—you know, the ones who seem to disappear right in front of your eyes. I watched them train a couple of times."

"You mean the *ninja*, don't you? It must have been the Iga group you saw. But what does that have to do with a hemp seed?"

"Well, after hemp's planted in the spring, it doesn't take long before a little sprout comes up."

"Yes?"

"You jump over it. Every day you practice jumping back and forth. When it gets warmer, the sprout grows fast—nothing else grows as fast—so you have to jump higher every day. If you don't practice every day, it's not long before the hemp is so high you can't jump over it."

"I see."

"I did it last year, and the year before that. From spring till fall."

Sukekurō came into the dōjō just then and said, "Hyōgo, here's another letter from Edo."

After Hyōgo read it, he said, "Otsū couldn't have gone very far, could she?"

"Not more than five miles, probably. Has something come up?"

"Yes. Takuan says Musashi's appointment has been canceled. They seem to have doubts about his character. I don't think we should let Otsū go on to Edo without telling her."

"I'll go."

"No. I'll go myself."

With a nod to Ushinosuke, Hyōgo left the dōjō and went directly to the stable.

He was halfway to Uji when he began to have second thoughts. Musashi's not receiving the appointment would make no difference to Otsū; she was thinking of the man himself, not his status. Even if Hyōgo managed to persuade her to stay a while longer in Koyagyū, she would no doubt want to go on to Edo. Why spoil her journey by telling her the bad news?

He turned back toward Koyagyū and slowed down to a trot. Though he appeared to be at peace with the world, a fierce battle raged in his heart. If only he could see Otsū once more! While he had to admit to himself this was the real reason for going after her, he would not have admitted it to anyone else.

Hyōgo tried to rein in his emotions. Warriors had weak moments, foolish moments, like everybody else. Still, his duty, that of every samurai, was clear: to persevere until he reached a state of stoic balance. Once he had crossed the   *859* barrier of illusion, his soul would be light and free, his eyes open to the green willows around him, to every blade of grass. Love was not the only emotion capable of firing a samurai's heart. His was another world. In an age hungry for young men of talent, this was no time to be distracted by a flower along the wayside. What was important, as Hyōgo saw it, was to be in the right place to ride the wave of the times.

"Quite a crowd, isn't it?" Hyōgo remarked lightheartedly.
"Yes; Nara doesn't have many days as fine as this," replied Sukekurō.
"It's like an outing."
Following a few steps behind them was Ushinosuke, for whom Hyōgo was developing quite a fondness. The boy came to the castle more frequently now and was on his way to becoming a regular attendant. He carried their lunches on his back and had an extra pair of sandals for Hyōgo tied to his obi.
They were in an open field in the middle of town. On one side, the five-story pagoda of the Kōfukuji rose above the surrounding woods; visible across the field were the houses of the Buddhist and Shinto priests. Though the day was bright and the air springlike, a thin mist hung over the lower areas, where townsmen lived. The crowd, numbering between four and five hundred people, did not seem that large because of the vastness of the field. Some of the deer, for which Nara was famous, were nosing their way among the spectators, sniffing out tasty morsels of food here and there.
"They haven't finished already, have they?" asked Hyōgo.
"No," said Sukekurō. "They seem to be taking time off for lunch."
"So even priests have to eat!"
Sukekurō laughed.
The occasion was a show of sorts. The larger cities had theaters, but in Nara and the smaller towns, shows were held in the open air. Magicians, dancers, puppeteers, as well as archers and swordsmen, all performed outdoors. Today's attraction was more than mere entertainment, though. Each year the lancer-priests of the Hōzōin held a tournament, at which they decided the order of seating at the temple. Since they were performing in public, the competitors fought hard, and the bouts were often violent and spectacular. There was a sign in front of the Kōfukuji, clearly stating that the tournament was open to all who were devoted to the martial arts, but the outsiders who dared face the lancer-priests were very, very few.
"Why don't we sit down somewhere and have our lunch?" said Hyōgo. "We seem to have plenty of time."
"Where would be a good spot?" said Sukekurō, looking around.
"Over here," called Ushinosuke. "You can sit on this." He indicated a piece of reed matting he had picked up somewhere and spread on a pleasant knoll. Hyōgo admired the boy's resourcefulness and, in general, was pleased by the way his needs were looked after, although he did not regard solicitousness as an ideal quality for a future samurai.
After they had arranged themselves, Ushinosuke passed out their simple fare: balls of unpolished rice, sour plum pickles and sweetish bean paste, all

860

wrapped in dried bamboo to make them easier to carry.

"Ushinosuke," said Sukekurō, "run over to those priests there and get some tea. But don't tell them who it's for."

"It'd be a nuisance if they came over to pay their respects," added Hyōgo, who had a basket hat pulled down over his face. Sukekurō's features were more than half hidden by a bandanna of the type worn by priests.

As Ushinosuke got to his feet, another boy, about fifty feet away, was saying, "I can't understand it. The matting was right here."

"Forget it, Iori," said Gonnosuke. "It's no great loss."

"Somebody must have swiped it. Who do you suppose would do a thing like that?"

"Don't worry about it." Gonnosuke sat down on the grass, took out his brush and ink and began listing his expenses in a small notebook, a habit he had recently acquired from Iori.

In some ways, Iori was too serious for his years. He paid close attention to his personal finances, never wasted a thing, was meticulously neat, and felt grateful for every bowl of rice, every fair day. He was, in short, fastidious, and he looked down on people who were not.

For anyone who'd walk off with another person's property, even if it was only a cheap piece of matting, he had only contempt.

"Oh, there it is," he cried. "Those men over there took it. Hey, you!"

He ran toward them, but stopped about ten paces short to consider what he was going to say and found himself face to face with Ushinosuke.

"What do you want?" growled Ushinosuke.

"What do you mean, what do I want?" snapped Iori.

Regarding him with the coldness country folk reserve for outsiders, Ushinosuke said, "You're the one who called to us!"

"Anybody who goes off with somebody else's things is a thief!"

"Thief? Why, you son of a bitch!"

"That matting belongs to us."

"Matting? I found it lying on the ground. Is that all you're upset about?"

"A mat's important to a traveler," said Iori rather pompously. "It protects him from the rain, provides him with something to sleep on. Lots of things. Give it back!"

"You can have it, but first take back what you said about me being a thief!"

"I don't have to apologize to get back what belongs to us. If you don't give it back, I'll take it back!"

"Just try it. I'm Ushinosuke of Araki. I have no intention of losing to a runt like you. I'm the disciple of a samurai."

"I bet you are," said Iori, standing a little straighter. "You talk big with all these people around, but you wouldn't dare fight if we were by ourselves."

"I won't forget that!"

"Come over there later."

"Where?"

"By the pagoda. Come alone."

They parted, Ushinosuke went for the tea, and by the time he came back with an earthenware teapot, the matches were under way again. Standing in a large circle with the other spectators, Ushinosuke looked pointedly at Iori, challenging him with his eyes. Iori's eyes answered. Both believed that winning was all that counted.

The noisy crowd pushed this way and that, raising yellow clouds of dust. In the center of the circle stood a priest with a lance as long as a fowling pole. One after another, rivals stepped forward and challenged him. One after another, they were struck to the ground or sent flying through the air.

"Come forward," he cried, but eventually no more came. "If there's no one else, I'm going to leave. Is there any objection to declaring me, Nankōbō, the winner?" After studying under In'ei, he had created a style of his own and was now the chief rival of Inshun, who was absent today on the pretext of illness. No one knew whether he was afraid of Nankōbō or preferred to avoid conflict.

When no one came forward, the burly priest lowered his lance, holding it horizontally, and announced, "There's no challenger."

"Wait," called a priest, running out in front of Nankōbō. "I'm Daun, a disciple of Inshun. I challenge you."

"Get ready."

After bowing to each other, the two men jumped apart. Their two lances stared at each other like living beings for such a long time that the crowd, bored, began shouting for action. Then all at once the shouting ceased. Nankōbō's lance thudded into Daun's head, and, like a scarecrow toppled by the wind, his body leaned slowly to the side, then fell suddenly to the ground. Three or four lancers ran forward, not to take revenge but merely to drag the body away.

Nankōbō arrogantly threw back his shoulders and surveyed the crowd. "There seem to be a few brave men left. If indeed there are, come ahead."

A mountain priest stepped out from behind a tent, took his traveling chest off his back and asked, "Is the tournament open only to lancers of the Hōzōin?"

"No," chorused the Hōzōin priests.

The priest bowed. "In that case, I'd like to try my hand. Can anyone lend me a wooden sword?"

Hyōgo glanced at Sukekurō and said, "This is getting interesting."

"It is, isn't it?"

"No question about the outcome."

"I don't suppose there's any chance of Nankōbō's losing."

"That's not what I meant. I don't think Nankōbō will agree to fight. If he does, he'll lose."

Sukekurō looked puzzled but didn't ask for an explanation.

Someone handed the vagabond priest a wooden sword. He walked up to Nankōbō, bowed and issued his challenge. He was a man of about forty, but his body, like spring steel, strongly suggested training not in the ascetic fashion of mountain priests but on the battlefield, a man who must have faced death many times and would be prepared to accept it philosophically. His manner of speaking was soft, his eyes placid.

Despite his arrogance, Nankōbō was no fool. "Are you an outsider?" he asked pointlessly.

"Yes," replied the challenger with another bow.

"Wait just a minute." Nankōbō saw two things clearly: His technique might be better than the priest's. He couldn't win in the long run. Quite a few celebrated warriors, defeated at Sekigahara, were still masquerading as wandering priests. There was no telling who this man was.

"I can't take on an outsider," he said, shaking his head.

"I just asked the rules and was told it was all right."

"It may be all right with others, but I prefer not to fight outsiders. When I fight, it's not for the purpose of defeating my opponent. It's a religious activity, in which I discipline my soul by means of the lance."

"I see," said the priest with a little laugh. He seemed to have something more to say, but hesitated. After mulling it over for a moment, he retired from the ring, returned the wooden sword and disappeared.

Nankōbō chose this time to make his exit, ignoring the whispered comments that it was cowardly of him to back out. Trailed by two or three disciples, he strode away grandly, like a conquering general.

"What did I tell you?" said Hyōgo.

"You were absolutely right."

"That man is without a doubt one of those hiding out on Mount Kudo. Change his white robe and bandanna for a helmet and armor, and you'll find you're looking at one of the great swordsmen of a few years ago."

When the crowd thinned out, Sukekurō began looking around for Ushinosuke. He didn't find him. At a signal from Iori, he had gone over to the pagoda, where now they stood glaring fiercely at each other.

"Don't blame me if you get killed," said Iori.

"You talk big," said Ushinosuke, picking up a stick to use as a weapon.

Iori, sword held high, rushed to the attack. Ushinosuke jumped back. Thinking he was afraid, Iori ran straight at him. Ushinosuke leaped over him, kicking him in the side of the head. Iori's hand went to his head, and he crashed to the ground. Recovering quickly, he was on his feet again in no time. The two boys faced each other with their weapons raised.

Forgetting what Musashi and Gonnosuke had taught him, Iori charged with his eyes shut. Ushinosuke moved slightly to one side and knocked him down with his stick.

Iori lay on his stomach, moaning, sword still in hand.

"Ha! I won," shouted Ushinosuke. Then, noticing that Iori was not moving at all, he grew frightened and ran.

"No you don't!" roared Gonnosuke, his four-foot staff catching the boy on the hip.

Ushinosuke fell with a shriek of pain, but after one look at Gonnosuke, he got to his feet and bounded off like a rabbit, only to collide head on with Sukekurō.

"Ushinosuke! What's going on here?"

Ushinosuke quickly hid behind Sukekurō, leaving the samurai face to face with Gonnosuke. For a moment, it appeared that a clash was inevitable. Sukekurō's hand went to his sword; Gonnosuke tightened his grip on the staff.

"Would you mind telling me," asked Sukekurō, "why you're chasing a mere child as though you wanted to kill him?"

"Before I answer, let me ask a question. Did you see him knock that boy down?"

"Is he with you?"

"Yes. Is this one of your attendants?"

"Not officially." Looking sternly at Ushinosuke, he asked, "Why did you hit the boy and run away? Tell the truth, now."

Before Ushinosuke could open his mouth, Iori raised his head and shouted, "It was a bout." Rising painfully to a sitting position, he said, "We had a bout and I lost."

"Did you two challenge each other in the proper way and agree to fight it out?" asked Gonnosuke. There was a trace of amusement in his eyes as he looked from one to the other.

Ushinosuke, deeply embarrassed, said, "I didn't know it was his mat when I picked it up."

The two men grinned at each other, both aware that if they had not acted with restraint themselves, a trivial, childish affair could have ended in bloodshed.

"I'm very sorry about this," said Sukekurō.

"So am I. I hope you'll forgive me."

"Don't mention it. My master's waiting for us, so I think we'd better go."

They went out the gate laughing, Gonnosuke and Iori going to the left, Sukekurō and Ushinosuke to the right.

Then Gonnosuke turned and said, "Could I ask you something? If we go straight down this road, will it take us to Koyagyū Castle?"

Sukekurō walked over to Gonnosuke and some minutes later, when Hyōgo joined them, told him who the travelers were and why they were here.

Hyōgo sighed sympathetically. "That's too bad. If only you'd come three weeks ago, before Otsū left to join Musashi in Edo."

"He's not in Edo," said Gonnosuke. "No one knows where he is, not even his friends."

"What'll she do now?" said Hyōgo, regretting he hadn't brought Otsū back to Koyagyū.

Though he held back his tears, Iori really wanted to go somewhere all alone and cry his heart out. On the way down, he'd talked incessantly of meeting Otsū, or so it had seemed to Gonnosuke. As the men's conversation shifted to events in Edo, he slowly drifted away. Hyōgo asked Gonnosuke for more information about Musashi, for news about his uncle, for details about the disappearance of Ono Tadaaki. There seemed to be no end either to his questions or to Gonnosuke's supply of information.

"Where're you going?" Ushinosuke asked Iori, coming up behind him and laying a sympathetic hand on his shoulder. "Are you crying?"

"Of course not." But as he shook his head, the tears flew.

"Hmm. . . . Do you know how to dig wild potatoes?"

"Sure."

"There are some potatoes over there. You want to see who can dig the fastest?"

Iori accepted the challenge, and they began digging.

It was getting late in the day, and since there was still much to talk about, Hyōgo urged Gonnosuke to spend a few days at the castle. Gonnosuke, however, said he preferred to continue his journey.

While they were saying their farewells, they noticed the boys were missing again. After a moment, Sukekurō pointed and said, "There they are, over there. They seem to be digging."

Iori and Ushinosuke were absorbed in their work, which because of the brittleness of the roots, involved digging carefully to a great depth. The men, amused at their concentration, walked quietly up behind them and watched for several minutes before Ushinosuke looked up and saw them. He gasped slightly, and Iori turned around and grinned. Then they redoubled their efforts.

"I've got it," cried Ushinosuke, pulling up a long potato and laying it on the ground.

Seeing Iori's arm sunk in the hole up to his shoulder, Gonnosuke said impatiently, "If you don't finish soon, I'm going on by myself."

Placing his hand on his hip like an aged farmer, Iori forced himself to a standing position and said, "I can't do it. It'd take me the rest of the day." With a look of resignation, he brushed the dirt off his kimono.

"You can't get the potato out after you've dug that far?" asked Ushinosuke. "Here, I'll pull it out for you."

"No," said Iori, pulling back Ushinosuke's hand. "It'll break." He gently pushed the dirt back in the hole and packed it down.

"Bye," called Ushinosuke, proudly shouldering his potato and accidentally revealing that the tip was broken off.

Seeing that, Hyōgo said, "You lost. You may have won the fight, but you're disqualified from the potato-digging contest."

Sweepers and Salesmen

The cherry blossoms were pale, past their prime, and the thistle blossoms were wilting, hinting nostalgically of the time centuries ago when Nara had been the capital. It was a little warm for walking, but neither Gonnosuke nor Iori tired of the road.

Iori tugged at Gonnosuke's sleeve and said worriedly, "That man's still following us."

Keeping his eyes straight ahead, Gonnosuke said, "Pretend you don't see him."

"He's been behind us ever since we left the Kōfukuji."

"Umm."

"And he was at the inn where we stayed, wasn't he?"

"Don't let it worry you. We don't have anything worth stealing."

"We have our lives! They're not nothing."

"Ha, ha. I keep my life locked up. Don't you?"

"I can take care of myself." Iori tightened the grip of his left hand on his scabbard.

Gonnosuke knew the man was the mountain priest who had challenged Nankōbō the previous day, but couldn't imagine why he'd be tailing them.

Iori looked around again and said, "He's not there anymore."

Gonnosuke looked back too. "He probably got tired." He took a deep breath and added, "But it does make me feel better."

They put up at a farmer's house that night and early the next morning reached Amano in Kawachi. This was a small village of low-eaved houses, behind which ran a stream of pristine mountain water. Gonnosuke had come to have the memorial tablet to his mother placed in the Kongōji, the so-called Women's Mount Kōya. But first he wanted to look up a woman named Oan, whom he had known since childhood, so there would be someone to burn incense before the tablet from time to time. If she could not be found, he intended to go on to Mount Kōya, the burial place of the rich and the mighty. He hoped he wouldn't have to; going there would make him feel like a beggar.

Asking directions from a shopkeeper's wife, he was told that Oan was the wife of a brewer named Tōroku and their house was the fourth one on the right inside the temple gate.

As he went through the gate, Gonnosuke wondered if the woman knew

866

what she was talking about, for there was a sign saying that bringing sake and leeks into the sacred compound was prohibited. How could there be a brewery there?

This little mystery was cleared up that evening by Tōroku, who had made them feel welcome and readily agreed to talk to the abbot about the memorial tablet. Tōroku said that Toyotomi Hideyoshi had once tasted and expressed admiration for the sake made for use by the temple. The priests had then established the brewery to make sake for Hideyoshi and the other daimyō who contributed to the temple's support. Production had fallen off somewhat after Hideyoshi's death, but the temple still supplied a number of special patrons.

When Gonnosuke and Iori awoke the next morning, Tōroku was already gone. He returned a little past noon and said that arrangements had been made.

The Kongōji was situated in the Amano River valley, amid peaks the color of jade. Gonnosuke, Iori and Tōroku stopped for a minute on the bridge leading to the main gate. Cherry blossoms floated in the water beneath the bridge. Gonnosuke straightened his shoulders and an air of reverence seemed to settle over him. Iori rearranged his collar.

Approaching the main hall, they were greeted by the abbot, a tall, rather stout man wearing an ordinary priest's robe. A torn basket hat and a long staff would not have seemed unnatural.

"Is this the man who wants to have a service said for his mother?" he asked in a friendly voice.

"Yes, sir," replied Tōroku, prostrating himself on the ground.

Having expected a stern-visaged cleric in gold brocade, Gonnosuke was somewhat confused in his greeting. He bowed and watched as the abbot came down from the porch, slipped his big feet into dirty straw sandals and came to a halt in front of him. Prayer beads in hand, the abbot directed them to follow him and a young priest fell in behind them.

They passed the Hall of Yakushi, the refectory, the one-story treasure pagoda and the priests' living quarters. When they reached the Hall of Dainichi, the young priest came forward and spoke to the abbot. The latter nodded and the priest opened the door with an enormous key.

Entering the large hall together, Gonnosuke and Iori knelt before the priests' dais. Fully ten feet above this was a huge golden statue of Dainichi, the universal Buddha of the esoteric sects. After a few moments, the abbot appeared from behind the altar, attired in his cassock, and arranged himself on the dais. The chanting of the sutra began, and he seemed to be subtly transformed into a dignified high priest, his authority evident in the set of his shoulders.

Gonnosuke clasped his hands in front of him. A small cloud seemed to pass before his eyes and from it emerged an image of Shiojiri Pass, where he and Musashi had tested each other. His mother was sitting to one side, straight as a board, looking worried, just as she had been when she called out the word that saved him in that fight.

867

"Mother," he thought, "you don't have to worry about my future. Musashi has consented to be my teacher. The day is not far off when I'll be able to establish my own school. The world may be in turmoil, but I won't stray from the Way. Nor will I neglect my duties as a son. . . ."

By the time Gonnosuke came out of his reverie, the chanting had stopped and the abbot was gone. Beside him, Iori sat transfixed, his eyes glued to the face of Dainichi, a miracle of sculptural sensitivity carved by the great Unkei in the thirteenth century.

"Why are you staring so, Iori?"

Without moving his eyes, the boy said, "It's my sister. That Buddha looks like my sister."

Gonnosuke burst out laughing. "What are you talking about? You've never even seen her. Anyway, no human could ever have the compassion and serenity of Dainichi."

Iori shook his head vigorously. "I have seen her. Near Lord Yagyū's residence in Edo. And talked to her. I didn't know she was my sister then, but just now, while the abbot was chanting, the Buddha's face turned into hers. She seemed to be saying something to me."

They went out and sat down on the porch, reluctant to break the spell of the visions they had experienced.

"The memorial service was for my mother," said Gonnosuke pensively. "But it's been a good day for the living too. Sitting here like this, it's hard to believe fighting and bloodshed exist."

The metal spire of the treasure pagoda glistened like a jeweled sword in the rays of the setting sun; all the other buildings stood in deep shadow. Stone lanterns lined the darkened path leading up the steep hill to a Muromachi-style teahouse and a small mausoleum.

Near the teahouse, an old nun, her head covered with a white silk bandanna, and a plump man of about fifty were sweeping leaves with straw brooms.

The nun sighed and said, "I guess it's better than it was." Few people came to this part of the temple, even to clear away the winter's accumulation of leaves and bird skeletons.

"You must be tired, Mother," said the man. "Why don't you sit down and rest? I'll finish up." He was dressed in a simple cotton kimono, sleeveless cloak, straw sandals, and leather socks with a cherry blossom design, and carried a short sword with an unadorned hilt made of sharkskin.

"I'm not tired," she replied with a little laugh. "But what about you? You're not used to this. Aren't your hands chapped?"

"No, not chapped, but they're covered with blisters."

The woman laughed again, saying, "Now, isn't that a nice reminder to take home with you?"

"I don't mind. I feel my heart's been purified. I hope that means our little offering of labor has pleased the gods."

"Oh, it's getting so dark. Let's leave the rest for tomorrow morning."

Gonnosuke and Iori were standing by the porch now. Kōetsu and Myōshū came down the path slowly, hand in hand. When they got near the Dainichi Hall, both started and cried, "Who's there?"

Then Myōshū said, "It's been a lovely day, hasn't it? Have you come for sightseeing?"

Gonnosuke bowed and said, "No, I've had a sutra read for my mother."

"It's nice to meet young people who are grateful to their parents." She gave Iori a maternal pat on the head. "Kōetsu, do you have any of those wheat cakes left?"

Taking a small package from his sleeve, Kōetsu offered it to Iori, saying, "Forgive me for offering you leftovers."

"Gonnosuke, may I accept it?" asked Iori.

"Yes," said Gonnosuke, thanking Kōetsu on Iori's behalf.

"From the way you talk, you seem to be from the east," said Myōshū. "May I ask where you're going?"

"It seems to be on an endless journey on a never-ending road. This boy and I are fellow disciples in the Way of the Sword."

"It's an arduous path you've chosen. Who is your teacher?"

"His name is Miyamoto Musashi."

"Musashi? You don't say!" Myōshū gazed into space, as though conjuring up a pleasant memory.

"Where is Musashi now?" asked Kōetsu. "It's been a long time since last we saw him."

Gonnosuke told them of Musashi's fortunes during the past couple of years. As he listened, Kōetsu nodded and smiled, as if to say: "That's what I'd expect of him."

When he finished, Gonnosuke asked, "May I inquire who you are?"

"Oh, forgive me for not telling you before." Kōetsu introduced himself and his mother. "Musashi stayed with us for a while, several years ago. We're very fond of him and often talk about him even now." He then told Gonnosuke about two or three incidents that had occurred when Musashi was in Kyoto.

Gonnosuke had long known of Kōetsu's reputation as a sword polisher, and more recently he had heard of Musashi's relationship with the man. But he'd never expected to run into this wealthy townsman tidying up neglected temple grounds.

"Is there a grave of someone close to you here?" he asked. "Or perhaps you've come for an outing?"

"No, nothing so frivolous as an outing," exclaimed Kōetsu. "Not in a holy place like this. . . . Have you heard from the priests something of the history of the Kongōji?"

"No."

"In that case allow me, in the priests' stead, to tell you a little about it. Please understand, however, that I'm merely repeating what I've heard." Kōetsu paused and looked around slowly, then said, "We have just the right moon tonight," and pointed out the landmarks: above them the mausoleum, Mieidō and Kangetsutei; below, the Taishidō, Shinto shrine, treasure pagoda, refectory and two-story gate.

"Look carefully," he said, seemingly under the spell of the lonely setting. "That pine tree, those rocks, every tree, every blade of grass here, partake of the invisible constancy, the elegant tradition of our country."

He went on in this vein, solemnly telling how in the fourteenth century, during a conflict between southern and northern courts, the mountain had been a stronghold of the southern court. How Prince Morinaga, known also as Daitō no Miya, had held secret conferences to plan the overthrow of the Hōjō regents. How Kusunoki Masashige and other loyalists had fought the armies of the northern court. Later the Ashikagas had come to power, and Emperor Go-Murakami, driven from Mount Otoko, had been forced to flee from place to place. Finally he took refuge at the temple and for many years lived the same sort of life as the mountain priests, suffering the same deprivations. Using the refectory as his seat of government, he had worked tirelessly to recover the imperial prerogatives seized by the military.

At an earlier time, when samurai and courtiers had gathered around the ex-emperors Kōgon, Kōmyō and Sukō, the monk Zen'e had written poignantly: "The priests' quarters and mountain temples were all swept away. The loss is indescribable."

Gonnosuke listened humbly, respectfully. Iori, awed by the gravity of Kōetsu's voice, could not take his eyes from the man's face.

Kōetsu took a deep breath and went on: "Everything here is a relic of that age. The mausoleum is the last resting place of the Emperor Kōgon. Since the decline of the Ashikagas, nothing's been properly taken care of. That's why my mother and I decided to do a little cleaning up, as a gesture of reverence."

Pleased by the attentiveness of his audience, Kōetsu searched diligently for words to express his heartfelt emotions.

"While we were sweeping, we found a stone with a poem carved on it, perhaps by a soldier-priest of that age. It said:

> Though the war goes on,
> Even for a hundred years,
> Spring will return.
> Live with a song in your hearts,
> You, the Emperor's people.

"Think of the bravery, the largeness of spirit it took for a simple soldier, after fighting for years, perhaps decades, to protect the emperor, to be able to rejoice and sing. I'm sure it's because the spirit of Masashige communicated itself to him. Though a hundred years of fighting have passed, this place remains a monument to the imperial dignity. Isn't this something for which we should be very grateful?"

"I didn't know this was the site of a sacred battle," said Gonnosuke. "I hope you'll forgive my ignorance."

"I'm glad I had a chance to share with you some of my thoughts on the history of our country."

The four of them strolled down the hill together. In the moonlight, their shadows seemed thin and unsubstantial.

As they passed the refectory, Kōetsu said, "We've been here seven days. We'll be leaving tomorrow. If you see Musashi, please tell him to come see us again."

Gonnosuke assured him that he would.

The shallow, swift-flowing stream along the outer temple wall was like a natural moat and was crossed by a dirt-floored bridge.

Gonnosuke and Iori had hardly set foot on the bridge when a large white figure armed with a staff emerged from the shadows and flew at Gonnosuke's back. Gonnosuke evaded the attack by sliding to one side, but Iori was knocked off the bridge.

The man plunged on past Gonnosuke to the road on the other side of the bridge. Turning around, he took a solid stance, his legs resembling small tree trunks. Gonnosuke saw it was the priest who had been following him the previous day.

"Who are you?" shouted Gonnosuke.

The priest said nothing.

Gonnosuke moved his staff into striking position and shouted, "Who are you? What reason do you have for attacking Musō Gonnosuke?"

The priest acted as if he hadn't heard. His eyes spat fire as his toes, protruding from heavy straw sandals, inched forward like a centipede in motion.

Gonnosuke growled and cursed under his breath. His short, heavy limbs bursting with the will to fight, he too inched forward.

The priest's staff broke in two with a resounding crack. One part flew through the air; the other the priest hurled with all his might at Gonnosuke's face. It missed, but while Gonnosuke was recovering his balance, his opponent drew his sword and stomped out onto the bridge.

"You bastard!" shouted Iori.

The priest gasped and put his hand to his face. The small stones Iori had thrown had found their mark, one hitting him squarely in the eye. He spun around and ran down the road.

"Stop!" shouted Iori, scrambling up the bank with a handful of stones.

"Never mind," said Gonnosuke, putting his hand on Iori's arm.

"I guess that'll show him," gloated Iori, casting the stones toward the moon.

Soon after they returned to Tōroku's house and went to bed, a squall came up. The wind roared through the trees, threatening to tear the roof off the house, but this was not the only thing that kept them from falling asleep right away.

Gonnosuke lay awake thinking about past and present, wondering if the world was really better off now than it had been in bygone ages. Nobunaga, Hideyoshi and Ieyasu had won the hearts of the people, as well as the authority to govern, but, he wondered, hadn't the true sovereign been virtually forgotten, the people led to worship false gods? The age of the Hōjōs and Ashikagas had been a hateful one, blatantly contradicting the very principle on which the country was founded. Still, even then, great warriors, like Masashige and his son, and loyalists from many provinces had followed the true warrior's code. What had become of the Way of the Samurai? Gonnosuke asked himself. Like the Way of the Townsman and the Way of the Farmer, it seemed to exist now only for the sake of the military ruler.

Gonnosuke's thoughts made his body feel warm all over. The peaks of Kawachi, the woods around the Kongōji, the howling storm, seemed to become living beings, calling to him in a dream.

Iori could not get the unknown priest out of his mind. He was still thinking of the ghostly white figure much later when the storm intensified. He pulled the covers over his eyes and fell into a deep, dreamless sleep.

When they set out the next day, the clouds above the mountains were rainbow-colored. Just outside the village, a traveling merchant materialized from the morning mist and wished them a jovial good morning.

Gonnosuke replied perfunctorily. Iori, absorbed in the thoughts that had kept him awake the night before, was no more talkative.

The man tried to strike up a conversation. "You stayed at Tōroku's house last night, didn't you? I've known him for years. Fine people, him and his wife."

This elicited only a mild grunt from Gonnosuke.

"I also call at Koyagyū Castle from time to time," said the merchant. "Kimura Sukekurō had done me a lot of favors."

This met with another grunt.

"I see you've been to the 'Women's Mount Kōya.' I suppose now you'll be going to Mount Kōya itself. It's just the right time of the year. The snow's gone, and all the roads have been repaired. You can take your time crossing Amami and Kiimi passes, spend the night at Hashimoto or Kamuro—"

The man's probing about their itinerary made Gonnosuke suspicious. "What business are you in?" he asked.

"I sell braided cord," said the man, pointing to the small bundle on his back. "The cord's made of flat-braided cotton. It was only invented recently, but it's getting popular fast."

"I see," said Gonnosuke.

"Tōroku's helped me a lot, telling worshipers at the Kongōji about my cord. As a matter of fact, I was planning to stay at his house last night, but he said he already had two guests. That was sort of a disappointment. When I stay with him, he always fills me up with good sake." He laughed.

Relaxing a bit, Gonnosuke began asking questions about places along the way, for the merchant was quite familiar with the local countryside. By the time they reached Amami plateau, the conversation had grown fairly friendly.

"Hey, Sugizō!"

A man came trotting along the road to catch up with them.

"Why did you go off and leave me? I was waiting at Amano Village. You said you'd stop by for me."

"Sorry, Gensuke," said Sugizō. "I fell in with these two and we got to talking. I forgot all about you." He laughed and scratched his head.

Gensuke, who was dressed like Sugizō, turned out to be a cord salesman too. As they walked, the two merchants fell to discussing business.

Coming to a gully about twenty feet deep, Sugizō suddenly stopped talking and pointed.

"Oh, that's dangerous," he said.

Gonnosuke stopped and looked at the gully, which might have been a gap left by an earthquake, perhaps one that happened a very long time ago.

"What seems to be the trouble?" he asked.

"Those logs, they're not safe to cross. See, there—some of the rocks supporting them have been washed away. We'll fix it so the logs are steady." Then he added, "We should do that for the sake of other travelers."

Gonnosuke watched as they squatted at the edge of the cliff and began packing rocks and dirt under the logs. While thinking that these two merchants traveled a great deal, and thus knew the difficulties of travel as well as anybody, he was a little surprised. It was unusual for men like them to care enough about others to go to the trouble of repairing a bridge.

Iori didn't give the matter any thought. Impressed by their show of concern, he contributed by gathering rocks for them.

"That should do it," said Gensuke. He took a step on the bridge, decided it was safe and said to Gonnosuke, "I'll go first." Holding his arms out for balance, he crossed quickly to the other side, then beckoned for the others to follow.

At Sugizō's urging, Gonnosuke went next, Iori just behind him. They were not quite to the middle when they let out a shout of surprise. Ahead of them, Gensuke had a lance pointed at them. Gonnosuke looked back and saw Sugizō had also acquired a lance.

"Where did the lances come from?" thought Gonnosuke. He swore, bit his lip angrily and considered the awkwardness of his position.

"Gonnosuke, Gonnosuke . . ." Taken off guard, Iori clung to Gonnosuke's waist, while Gonnosuke, holding his arm around the boy, shut his eyes for an instant, entrusting his life to the will of heaven.

"You bastards!"

"Shut up!" shouted the priest, who stood higher up on the road, behind Gensuke, his left eye swollen and black.

"Keep calm," Gonnosuke told Iori in a soothing voice. Then he shouted. "So you're behind this! Well, watch out, you thieving bastards! You've tangled with the wrong man this time!"

The priest stared coldly at Gonnosuke. "You're not worth robbing. We know that. If you're no smarter than that, what are you doing trying to be a spy?"

"You calling me a spy?"

"Tokugawa dog! Throw that staff away. Put your hands behind your back. And don't try anything funny."

"Ah!" sighed Gonnosuke, as though the will to fight was deserting him. "Look, you're making a mistake. I did come from Edo, but I'm not a spy. My name is Musō Gonnosuke. I'm a *shūgyosha*."

"Never mind the lies."

"What makes you think I'm a spy?"

"Our friends in the east told us some time ago to be on the lookout for a man traveling with a young boy. You were sent down here by Lord Hōjō of Awa, weren't you?"

"No."

"Drop the staff and come along peacefully."

"I'm not going anywhere with you."

"Then you'll die right here."

Gensuke and Sugizō began to close in from front and back, lances ready for action.

To keep Iori out of harm's way, Gonnosuke slapped him on the back. With a loud shriek, Iori dived into the bushes covering the bottom of the gully.

Thundering "Y-a-a-h!" Gonnosuke rushed Sugizō.

The lance requires some space and good timing to be effective. Sugizō extended his arm to thrust his weapon forward but missed the exact moment. A loud croak came from his throat as the blade cut through thin air. Gonnosuke slammed into him, and he fell backward, with Gonnosuke on top of him. When Sugizō attempted to rise, Gonnosuke rammed his right fist into his face. Sugizō bared his teeth but the effect was ludicrous, for his face was already a bloody mess. Gonnosuke stood up, used Sugizō's head for a springboard and cleared the distance to the end of the bridge.

Staff poised, he shouted, "I'm here waiting, you cowards!"

Even as he shouted, three ropes came slithering across the top of the grass, one weighted with a sword guard, another with a short sword in its scabbard. One rope looped around Gonnosuke's arm, another around his legs and the third around his neck. In a moment, still another rope wound around his staff.

Gonnosuke wriggled like an insect caught in a spiderweb, but not for long. Half a dozen men ran out of the woods behind him. By the time they were finished, he lay helpless on the ground, trussed up tighter than a bundle of straw. With the exception of the surly priest, all his captors were dressed as cord salesmen.

"No horses?" asked the priest. "I don't want to walk him all the way to Mount Kudo."

"We can probably hire a horse in Amami Village."

A Pear Blossom

In the dark, solemn forest of cryptomerias, the voices of the lowly shrike, mingling with those of the celestial bulbul, sounded like the jeweled tones of the mythical Kalavinka bird.

Two men, coming down from the top of Mount Kōya, where they had visited the halls and pagodas of the Kongōbuji and paid their respects at the inner shrine, stopped on a small arched bridge between the inner and outer temple precincts.

"Nuinosuke," said the older man pensively, "the world is indeed fragile and impermanent, isn't it?" From his heavy homespun cloak and utilitarian *hakama*, he might have been taken for a country samurai, were it not for his swords, which were of outstanding quality, and the fact that his companion was far too suave and well-groomed for a provincial samurai's attendant.

"You saw them, didn't you?" he continued. "The graves of Oda Nobunaga, Akechi Mitsuhide, Ishida Mitsunari, Kobayakawa Kingo—all brilliant, famous generals only a few years ago. And over there, those moss-covered stones mark the burial places of great members of the Minamoto and Taira clans."

"Friend and foe . . . all together here, aren't they?"

"All of them nothing more than lonely stones. Were names like Uesugi and Takeda really great, or were we only dreaming?"

"It gives me an odd feeling. Somehow it seems the world we live in is unreal."

"Is it that? Or is it this place that's unreal?"

"Umm. Who knows?"

"Who do you suppose thought of calling this the Bridge of Illusions?"

"It's a well-chosen name, isn't it?"

"I think illusion is truth, just as enlightenment is reality. If illusion were unreal, the world couldn't exist. A samurai who devotes his life to his master cannot—not for an instant—allow himself to be nihilistic. That's why the Zen I practice is living Zen. It's the Zen of the tainted world, the Zen of hell. A samurai who trembles at the thought of impermanence or despises the world cannot perform his duties. . . . Enough of this place. Let's go back to the other world."

He walked quickly, with a remarkably firm step for a man of his age.

Catching sight of priests from the Seiganji, he frowned and grumbled, "Why did they have to do that?" He'd stayed at the temple the night before; now about twenty young priests were lined up along the pathway, waiting to see him off, though he had said his farewells that morning with the intention of avoiding a display of this sort.

He ran the gauntlet, saying polite good-byes, and hurried on down the road overlooking the patchwork of valleys known as Kujūkutani. Only when he regained the ordinary world did he relax. Conscious as he was of his own fallible human heart, the odor of this world came as relief.

"Hello, who are you?" The question came at him like a shot as they rounded a bend in the road.

"Who are you?" asked Nuinosuke.

The well-built, light-complexioned samurai standing in the middle of the road said politely, "Forgive me if I'm mistaken, but aren't you Lord Hosokawa Tadatoshi's senior retainer, Nagaoka Sado?"

"I'm Nagaoka, to be sure. Who are you, and how did you know I was in the vicinity?"

"My name is Daisuke. I'm the only son of Gessō, who lives in retirement on Mount Kudo."

Seeing the name did not ring a bell, Daisuke said, "My father has long since discarded his former name, but until the Battle of Sekigahara he was known as Sanada Saemonnosuke."

"Do you mean Sanada Yukimura?"

"Yes, sir." With a bashfulness seemingly at odds with his appearance, Daisuke said, "A priest from the Seiganji dropped in at my father's house this morning. He said you'd come to Mount Kōya for a short visit. Though we heard you were traveling incognito, my father thought it'd be a pity not to invite you to have a cup of tea with him."

"That's very kind of him," replied Sado. He squinted for a minute, then said to Nuinosuke, "I think we ought to accept, don't you?"

"Yes, sir," replied Nuinosuke without enthusiasm.

Daisuke said, "It's still fairly early in the day, but my father would be honored if you'd spend the night with us."

Sado hesitated a moment, wondering if it was wise to accept the hospitality of a man regarded as an enemy of the Tokugawas, then nodded and said, "We can decide about that later, but I'll be delighted to join your father for a cup of tea. Don't you agree, Nuinosuke?"

"Yes, sir."

Nuinosuke seemed a bit on edge, but as they started down the road behind Daisuke, master and attendant exchanged knowing glances.

From the village of Mount Kudo, they climbed a little farther up the mountain to a residence set apart from the other houses. The enclosure, surrounded by a low stone wall topped by a fence of woven grass, resembled the semifortified house of a lesser provincial warlord, but all in all one got the impression of refinement rather than military preparedness.

"My father's over there, by that thatched building," said Daisuke as they went through the gate.

There was a small vegetable garden, sufficient to provide onions and greens for the morning and evening soup. The main house stood in front of a cliff; near the side veranda was a bamboo grove, beyond which two more houses were just visible.

Nuinosuke knelt on the veranda outside the room Sado was shown to.

Sado sat down and remarked, "It's very quiet here."

A few minutes later, a young woman who appeared to be Daisuke's wife quietly served tea and left.

While Sado waited for his host, he took in the view—the garden and the valley. Below was the village, and in the distance the inn town of Kamuro. Tiny flowers bloomed on the moss clinging to the overhanging thatched roof, and there was the pleasant fragrance of a rare incense. Though he could not see it, he could hear the stream running through the bamboo grove.

The room itself evoked a feeling of quiet elegance, a gentle reminder that the owner of this unpretentious dwelling was the second son of Sanada Masayuki, lord of Ueda Castle and recipient of an income of 190,000 bushels.

The posts and beams were thin, the ceiling low. The wall behind the small, rustic alcove was of roughly finished red clay. The flower arrangement in the alcove consisted of a single sprig of pear blossoms in a slender yellow and light green ceramic vase. Sado thought of Po Chü-i's "solitary pear blossom bathed by the spring rain" and of the love that united the Chinese emperor and Yang Kuei-fei, as described in the *Chang He Ke*. He seemed to hear a voiceless sob.

His eye moved to the hanging scroll above the flower arrangement. The characters, large and naive, spelled out "Hōkoku Daimyōjin," the name Hideyoshi was given when he was elevated to the rank of a god after his death. To one side, a notation in much smaller characters said that this was the work of Hideyoshi's son Hideyori at the age of eight. Feeling it discourteous to Hideyoshi's memory to have his back turned to the scroll, Sado shifted a little to the side. As he did so, he realized suddenly that the pleasant smell came not from incense burning right then but from the walls and shoji, which must have absorbed the fragrance when incense was placed there morning and evening to purify the room in Hideyoshi's honor. Presumably an offering of sake was also made daily, as to established Shinto deities.

"Ah," he thought, "Yukimura's as devoted to Hideyoshi as they say." What he could not fathom was why Yukimura did not hide the scroll. He had the reputation of being an unpredictable man, a man of the shadows, lurking and waiting for a propitious moment to return to the center of the country's affairs. It took no stretch of the imagination to conceive of guests later reporting his sentiments to the Tokugawa government.

Footsteps approached along the outside corridor. The small, thin man who entered the room wore a sleeveless cloak, with only a short sword in the front of his obi. There was an air of modesty about him.

Dropping to his knees and bowing to the floor, Yukimura said, "Forgive me for sending my son to bring you and for interrupting your journey."

This show of humility made Sado uncomfortable. From the legal viewpoint, Yukimura had given up his status. He was now only a rōnin who had taken the Buddhist name Denshin Gessō. Nevertheless, he was the son of Sanada Masayuki, and his older brother, Nobuyuki, was a daimyō and had close connections with the Tokugawas. Being only a retainer, Sado was of much lower rank.

"You shouldn't bow to me that way," he said, returning the greeting. "It's an unexpected honor and pleasure to meet you again. I'm glad to see you're in good health."

"You seem to be too," replied Yukimura, relaxing while Sado was still bowing. "I'm pleased to hear Lord Tadatoshi has returned to Buzen safely."

"Thank you. This is the third year since Lord Yūsai passed away, so he thought it was time."

"Has it been that long?"

"Yes. I've been in Buzen myself, though I have no idea what use Lord Tadatoshi might have for a relic like myself. I served his father and grandfather too, as you know."

When the formalities were over and they began talking of this and that, Yukimura asked, "Have you seen our Zen master recently?"

"No, I've seen or heard nothing of Gudō for some time. That reminds me, it was in his meditation room that I first saw you. You were only a boy then, and you were with your father." Sado smiled happily as he reminisced about the time he had been put in charge of constructing the Shumpoin, a building the Hosokawas had donated to the Myōshinji.

"A lot of hellions came to Gudō to get the rough edges smoothed off," said Yukimura. "He accepted them all, not caring whether they were old or young, daimyō or rōnin."

"Actually, I think he particularly liked young rōnin," mused Sado. "He used to say that a true rōnin did not seek fame or profit, did not curry favor with the powerful, did not attempt to use political power for his own ends, did not exempt himself from moral judgments. Rather he was as broad-minded as floating clouds, as quick to act as the rain and quite content in the midst of poverty. He never set himself any targets and never harbored any grudges."

"You remember that after all these years?" asked Yukimura.

Sado nodded ever so slightly. "He also maintained that a true samurai was as hard to find as a pearl in the vast blue sea. The buried bones of the innumerable rōnin who sacrificed their lives for the good of the country he likened to pillars supporting the nation." Sado looked straight into Yukimura's eyes as he said this, but the latter did not seem to notice the allusion to men of his own adopted status.

"That reminds me," he said. "One of the rōnin who sat at Gudō's feet in those days was a young man from Mimasaka named Miyamoto . . ."

"Miyamoto Musashi?"

"That's it, Musashi. He impressed me as being a man of great depth, even though he was only about twenty at the time, and his kimono was always filthy."

"It must be the same man."

"Then you do remember him?"

"No; I didn't hear of him until recently, when I was in Edo."

"He's a man to watch. Gudō said that his approach to Zen was promising, so I kept an eye on him. Then he suddenly disappeared. A year or two later, I heard he'd won a brilliant victory against the House of Yoshioka. I remember thinking at the time that Gudō must have a very good eye for people."

"I came across him quite by accident. He was in Shimōsa and gave some villagers a lesson in how to protect themselves from bandits. Later he helped them turn a tract of wasteland into paddy."

"I think he may be the true rōnin Gudō had in mind—the pearl in the vast blue sea."

"Do you really think so? I recommended him to Lord Tadatoshi, but I'm afraid finding him is as hard as discovering a pearl. One thing you can be sure of. If a samurai like that took an official position, it wouldn't be for the sake of the income. He'd be concerned with how his work measured up to his ideals. It may be that Musashi would prefer Mount Kudo to the House of Hosokawa."

"What?"

Sado brushed off his remark with a short laugh, as if it were a slip of the tongue.

"You're joking, of course," said Yukimura. "In my present circumstances, I can hardly afford to hire a servant, let alone a well-known rōnin. I doubt whether Musashi would come even if I did invite him."

"There's no need to deny it," said Sado. "It's no secret the Hosokawas are on the side of the Tokugawas. And everybody knows you are the support on which Hideyori leans most heavily. Looking at the scroll in the alcove, I was impressed by your loyalty."

Seemingly offended, Yukimura said, "The scroll was given to me by a certain person at Osaka Castle in lieu of a memorial portrait of Hideyoshi. I try to take good care of it. But Hideyoshi is dead." He swallowed and went on. "Times change, of course. It doesn't take an expert to see that Osaka has fallen on bad days, while the power of the Tokugawas continues to grow. But I'm not able by nature to change my loyalty and serve a second lord."

"I wonder if people will believe it's that simple. If I may speak candidly, everybody says Hideyori and his mother furnish you great sums every year and at a wave of the hand you could muster five or six thousand rōnin."

Yukimura laughed deprecatingly. "Not a word of truth in it. I tell you, Sado, there's nothing worse than having people make you out to be more than you are."

"You can't blame them. You went to Hideyoshi when you were young, and he liked you better than anyone else. I understand your father's been heard to say you're the Kusunoki Masashige or the K'ung-ming of our times."

"You embarrass me."

"Isn't it true?"

"I want to spend the rest of my days here, quietly, in the shadow of the mountain where the Buddha's Law is preserved. That's all. I'm not a man of refinement. It's enough for me if I can expand my fields a little, live to see my son's child born, have freshly made buckwheat noodles in the fall, eat fresh greens in the spring. Beyond that, I'd like to live a long life, far removed from wars or rumors of war."

"Is that really all there is to it?" Sado asked mildly.

"Laugh if you will, but I've been spending my free time reading Lao-tsu and Chuang-tsu. The conclusion I've come to is that life is enjoyment. Without enjoyment, what use is there in living?"

"Well, well," exclaimed Sado, feigning surprise.

They talked for another hour or so, over cups of fresh tea served by Daisuke's wife.

Eventually Sado said, "I fear I've stayed too long, wasting your time with my chatter. Nuinosuke, shall we be going?"

"Don't hurry off," said Yukimura. "My son and his wife have made some noodles. Poor country food, but I wish you'd have some with us. If you're planning to stop over at Kamuro, you have plenty of time."

Daisuke appeared just then to ask his father if he was ready to have the meal served. Yukimura stood up and led the way down a corridor to the back part of the house.

When they were seated, Daisuke offered Sado a pair of chopsticks, saying, "I'm afraid the food isn't too good, but try some anyway."

His wife, not accustomed to having strangers around, diffidently held out a sake cup, which Sado politely refused. Daisuke and his wife lingered a moment longer before excusing themselves.

"What's that noise I can hear?" asked Sado. It sounded rather like a loom, though louder and with a slightly different quality.

"Oh, that? It's a wooden wheel for making cord. I'm sorry to say, I've had to put the family and servants to work braiding cord, which we sell to help with the finances." Then he added, "We're all used to it, but I suppose it might be annoying to anyone who's not. I'll send word to have it stopped."

"No, that's all right. It doesn't bother me. I'd hate to think I was holding up your work."

As he started to eat, Sado thought about the food, which sometimes provides insight into a man's condition. But he found nothing revealing there. Yukimura was not at all like the young samurai he had known years before, but he seemed to have shrouded his present circumstances in ambiguity.

Sado then thought about the sounds he heard—kitchen noises, people coming and going, and a couple of times the clink of money being counted. The dispossessed daimyō were not accustomed to physical labor, and sooner or later they would run out of treasures to sell. It was conceivable that Osaka Castle had ceased to be a source of funds. Still, the idea of Yukimura in tight straits was oddly disturbing.

He had been aware that his host might be trying to piece together bits of conversation to form a picture of how things were going with the House of Hosokawa, but there was no indication of this. What stood out about his recollections of their meeting was that Yukimura had not asked about his visit to Mount Kōya. Sado would have answered readily, for there was nothing mysterious about it. Many years ago, Hosokawa Yūsai had been sent by Hideyoshi to the Seiganji and had stayed for quite some time. He had left behind books, some writings and some personal effects, which had become important keepsakes. Sado had gone through them, sorted them out and arranged for the temple to turn them over to Tadatoshi.

Nuinosuke, who hadn't moved from the veranda, cast an anxious look toward the back of the house. Relations between Edo and Osaka were strained, to say the least. Why was Sado taking a risk like this? He didn't imagine Sado to be in any immediate danger, but he'd heard that the lord of Kii Province, Asano Nagaakira, had instructions to keep a strict watch on Mount Kudo. If one of Asano's men reported that Sado had paid a secret visit to Yukimura, the shogunate would become suspicious of the House of Hosokawa.

"Now's my chance," he thought, as the wind suddenly swept through the forsythia and kerria blossoms in the garden. Black clouds were forming rapidly, and it began to sprinkle.

He hurried down the corridor and announced, "It's starting to rain, sir. If we're going to leave, I think now is the time."

Grateful for the opportunity to break away, Sado stood up immediately. "Thank you, Nuinosuke," he said. "By all means, let's be on our way."

Yukimura refrained from urging Sado to stay overnight. He called Daisuke and his wife and said, "Give our guests some straw rain capes. And you, Daisuke, go with them to Kamuro."

At the gate, after expressing thanks for Yukimura's hospitality, Sado said, "I'm sure we'll meet again one of these days. Maybe it'll be another day of rain, or maybe there'll be a strong wind blowing. Until then, I wish you the best of health."

Yukimura grinned and nodded. Yes, one of these days . . . For an instant each man saw the other in his mind's eye, mounted on horseback and carrying a lance. But for the present there was only the host bowing amidst falling apricot petals and the departing guest in a straw cape streaked with rain.

As they walked slowly down the road, Daisuke said, "It won't rain much. At this time of year, we have a little shower like this every day."

Still, the clouds above Senjō Valley and the peaks of Kōya looked threatening, and they unconsciously quickened their pace.

Entering Kamuro, they were greeted by the sight of a man sharing the back of a horse with bundles of firewood and tied so tightly he couldn't move. Leading the horse was a white-robed priest, who called Daisuke's name and ran toward him. Daisuke pretended not to notice.

"Someone's calling you," said Sado, exchanging glances with Nuinosuke.

Forced to take notice of the priest, Daisuke said, "Oh, Rinshōbō. Sorry, I didn't see you."

"I've come straight from Kiimi Pass," said the priest in a loud, excited voice. "The man from Edo—the one we were told to watch for—I spotted him in Nara. He put up quite a fight, but we took him alive. Now, if we take him to Gessō and force him to talk, we'll find out—"

"'What are you talking about?" broke in Daisuke.

"The man on the horse. He's a spy from Edo."

"Can't you shut up, you fool!" hissed Daisuke. "Do you know who the man with me is? Nagaoka Sado of the House of Hosokawa. We rarely have the privilege of seeing him, and I'll not have you disturbing us with your silly joke."

Rinshōbō's eyes, turning to the two travelers, betrayed his shock, and he barely caught himself before blurting out, "House of Hosokawa?"

Sado and Nuinosuke were trying to look poised and indifferent, but the wind whipped at their rain capes, making them flap out like the wings of a crane and rather spoiling their efforts.

"Why?" asked Rinshōbō in a low voice.

Daisuke drew him a little to one side and spoke in a whisper. When he returned to his guests, Sado said, "Why don't you go back now? I'd hate to put you to any more trouble."

After watching them until they were out of sight, Daisuke said to the priest, "How could you be so stupid? Don't you know enough to open your eyes before you open your mouth? My father wouldn't be pleased to hear about this."

"Yes, sir. I'm sorry. I didn't know."

Despite his robes, the man was no priest. He was Toriumi Benzō, one of Yukimura's leading retainers.

The Port

"Gonnosuke! . . . Gonnosuke! . . . Gonnosuke!"

Iori couldn't seem to stop himself. He called the name over and over and over. Having found some of Gonnosuke's belongings lying on the ground, he was convinced the man was dead.

A day and a night had passed. He'd been in a walking daze, oblivious of his weariness. His legs, hands and head were spattered with blood, his kimono badly torn.

Seized by a spasm, he would look up at the sky and cry, "I'm ready." Or stare at the ground and curse.

"Have I gone crazy?" he thought, suddenly feeling cold. Looking into a puddle of water, he recognized his own face and felt relieved. But he was alone, with no one to turn to, only half believing he was still alive. When he'd awoken at the bottom of the ravine, he couldn't remember where he'd been the past several days. It didn't occur to him to try to go back to the Kongōji or Koyagyū.

An object glinting with the colors of the rainbow caught his eye—a pheasant. He became aware of the fragrance of wild wisteria in the air and sat down. As he tried to make sense of his situation, thoughts of the sun captured his mind. He imagined it as being everywhere—beyond the clouds, among the peaks, in the valleys. He shifted to a kneeling position, clasped his hands, shut his eyes and began praying. When he opened his eyes a few minutes later, the first thing he saw was a glimpse of ocean, blue and misty, between two mountains.

"Little boy," said a motherly voice. "Are you all right?"

"Hunh?" With a start, Iori turned his hollow eyes toward the two women who were staring at him curiously.

"What do you suppose is wrong with him, Mother?" asked the younger woman, regarding Iori with distaste.

Looking puzzled, the older woman walked over to Iori, and seeing the blood on his clothes, she frowned. "Don't those cuts hurt?" she asked. Iori shook his head. She turned to her daughter and said, "He seems to understand what I say."

They asked his name, where he had come from, where he had been born, what he was doing here, and whom he had been praying to. Little by little, as he searched around for the answers, his memory came back.

More sympathetic now, the daughter, whose name was Otsuru, said, "Let's take him back to Sakai with us. Maybe he'd be useful in the shop. He's just the right age."

"That might be a good idea," said her mother, Osei. "Will he come?"

"He'll come.... Won't you?"

Iori nodded and said, "Uh-huh."

"Come along then, but you'll have to carry our luggage."

"Uh."

Iori acknowledged their remarks with a grunt but otherwise said nothing on the journey down the mountain, along a country road and into Kishiwada. But among people again, he became talkative.

"Where do you live?" he asked.

"In Sakai."

"Is that near here?"

"No, it's near Osaka."

"Where's Osaka?"

"We'll take a ship from here and go to Sakai. Then you'll know."

"Really! A ship?" Excited by the prospect, he rattled on for several minutes, telling them how he'd ridden any number of ferryboats on the way from Edo to Yamato, but though the ocean wasn't far from his birthplace in Shimōsa, he'd never been out to sea in a ship.

"That'll make you happy, then, won't it?" said Otsuru. "But you mustn't call my mother 'Auntie.' Say 'Madam' when you speak to her."

"Uh."

"And you mustn't answer 'Uh.' Say 'Yes, ma'am.'"

"Yes, ma'am."

"That's better. Now, if you stay with us and work hard, I'll see you're made a shop assistant."

"What does your family do?"

"My father's a shipping broker."

"What's that?"

"He's a merchant. He owns a lot of ships, and they sail all over western Japan."

"Oh, just a merchant?" sniffed Iori.

"'Just a merchant'! Why—!" exclaimed the girl. The mother was inclined to overlook Iori's bluntness, but the daughter was indignant. Then she hesitated, saying, "I suppose he's never seen merchants other than candy sellers or clothing salesmen." The fierce pride of the Kansai merchants took over, and she informed him that her father had three warehouses, large ones, in Sakai

883

and several tens of vessels. She gave him to understand that there were branch offices in Shimonoseki, Marukame and Shikama, and that the services performed for the House of Hosokawa in Kokura were of such great importance that her father's ships had the status of official vessels.

"And," she went on, "he's allowed to have a surname and carry two swords, like a samurai. Everyone in western Honshu and Kyushu knows the name of Kobayashi Tarōzaemon of Shimonoseki. In time of war, daimyō like Shimazu and Hosokawa never have enough ships, so my father is just as important as a general."

"I didn't mean to make you angry," said Iori.

The two women laughed.

"We're not angry," said Otsuru. "But a boy like you, what do you know of the world?"

"I'm sorry."

Turning a corner, they were greeted by the tang of salt air. Otsuru pointed to a ship tied up at Kishiwada Pier. It had a capacity of five hundred bushels and was loaded with local produce.

"That's the ship we'll go home in," she said proudly.

The ship captain and a couple of Kobayashi agents came out of a dockside teahouse to meet them.

"Did you have a nice walk?" asked the captain. "I'm sorry to say we're very heavily loaded, so I couldn't keep much space open for you. Shall we go on board?"

He led the way to the stern of the ship, where a space had been partitioned off with curtains. A red rug had been spread, and elegant Momoyama-style lacquered utensils contained an abundance of food and sake. Iori had the feeling he was entering a small, well-appointed room in a daimyō's mansion.

The ship reached Sakai in the evening, after an uneventful voyage up Osaka Bay. The travelers went directly to the Kobayashi establishment, facing the wharf, where they were welcomed by the manager, a man named Sahei, and a large group of assistants who had gathered at the spacious entrance.

As Osei was going into the house, she turned and said, "Sahei, will you look after the child, please?"

"You mean the dirty little urchin who came off the ship?"

"Yes. He seems quick-witted, so you should be able to put him to work. . . . And do something about his clothes. He may have lice. See that he washes well and give him a new kimono. Then he can go to bed."

Iori didn't see the mistress of the house or her daughter for the next few days. There was a half-length curtain separating the office from the living quarters in the back. It was like a wall. Without special permission, not even Sahei dared go beyond it.

Iori was given a corner of the "shop," as the office was called, in which to sleep, and though he was grateful for being rescued, he soon became dissatisfied with his new way of life.

The cosmopolitan atmosphere into which he'd been dropped had a certain fascination. He gaped at the foreign innovations he saw on the streets, at the ships in the harbor and the signs of prosperity evident in the way people lived. But it was always, "Hey, boy! Do this!... Do that!" From the lowest assistant to the manager, they made him chase around like a dog, not at all like their attitude when speaking to a member of the household or a customer. Then they turned into fawning sycophants. And from morning to night, they talked of money, money. If it was not that, it was work, work.

"And they call themselves human beings!" thought Iori. He longed for the blue sky and the smell of warm grass under the sun and decided any number of times to run away. The yearning was strongest when he remembered Musashi talking about ways of nourishing the spirit. He visualized how Musashi had looked, and the face of the departed Gonnosuke. And Otsū.

Matters came to a head one day when Sahei called, "Io! Io, where are you?" Getting no answer, he stood up and walked to the black-lacquered *keyaki* beam forming the threshold of the office. "You there, the new boy," he shouted. "Why don't you come when you're called?"

Iori was sweeping the walk between the office and the storehouse. He looked up and asked, "Were you calling me?"

"Were you calling me, *sir!*"

"I see."

"I see, *sir!*"

"Yes, sir."

"Don't you have ears? Why didn't you answer me?"

"I heard you say 'Io.' That couldn't be me. My name's Iori . . . sir."

"Io's enough. And another thing. I told you the other day to stop wearing that sword."

"Yes, sir."

"Give it to me."

Iori hesitated a moment, then said, "It's a keepsake from my father. I couldn't let go of it."

"Impudent brat! Give it to me."

"I don't want to be a merchant anyway."

"If it weren't for merchants, people couldn't live," Sahei said forcefully. "Who'd bring in goods from foreign countries? Nobunaga and Hideyoshi are great men, but they couldn't have built all those castles—Azuchi, Jurakudai, Fushimi—without the help of merchants. Just look at the men here in Sakai—Namban, Ruzon, Fukien, Amoi. They're all carrying on trade on a large scale."

"I know that."

"How would you know?"

"Anybody can see the big weaving houses at Ayamachi, Kinumachi and Nishikimachi, and up on the hill Ruzon'ya's establishment looks like a castle. There are rows and rows of warehouses and mansions belonging to rich merchants. This place—well, I know madam and Otsuru are proud of it, but it doesn't amount to anything by comparison."

"Why, you little son of a bitch!"

Sahei was barely out the door before Iori had dropped his broom and fled. Sahei summoned some dock workers and ordered them to catch him.

When Iori was dragged back, Sahei was fuming. "What can you do with a boy like that? He talks back and makes fun of all of us. Punish him good today." Going back into the office, he added, "Take that sword away from him."

They removed the offending weapon and tied Iori's hands behind him. When they fastened the rope to a large crate of cargo, Iori looked like a monkey on a leash.

"Stay there awhile," said one of the men, smirking. "Let people make fun of you." The others guffawed and went back to their work.

There was nothing Iori hated more than this. How often Musashi and Gonnosuke had admonished him not to do things he might be ashamed of.

First he tried pleading, then promised to mend his ways. When this proved ineffective, he switched to invective.

"The manager's a fool—crazy old fart! Let me loose and give me back my sword! I won't stay in a house like this."

Sahei came out and shouted, "Quiet!" He then tried to gag Iori, but the boy bit his finger, so he gave up and had the dock workers do it.

Iori tugged at his bonds, pulling this way and that. Already under a terrible strain from being exposed to public view, he burst into tears when a horse urinated and the foamy liquid trickled toward his feet.

As he was quieting down, he saw something that almost made him faint. On the other side of a horse was a young woman, her head protected from the sweltering sun by a broad-brimmed lacquered hat. Her hemp kimono was tied up for traveling, and she carried a thin bamboo pole.

In vain, he tried to cry out her name. Stretching his neck out, he almost choked with the effort. His eyes were dry, but his shoulders shook with his sobbing. It was maddening, Otsū was so near. Where was she going? Why had she left Edo?

Later in the day, when a ship tied up at the pier, the neighborhood became even busier.

"Sahei, what's this boy doing out here, looking like a trained bear on exhibit? It's cruel to leave him like that. It's also bad for business." The man calling into the office was a cousin of Tarōzaemon. He was usually called Namban'ya, the name of the shop where he worked. Black pockmarks added a certain sinisterness to the anger in his face. Despite his appearance, he was a friendly man and often gave sweets to Iori. "I don't care if you are punishing him," he continued. "It's not right to do it out on the street. It's bad for the Kobayashi name. Untie him."

"Yes, sir." Sahei complied immediately, all the while regaling Namban'ya with a detailed account of how useless Iori was.

"If you don't know what to do with him," said Namban'ya, "I'll take him home with me. I'll speak to Osei about it today."

The manager, fearing the consequences when the mistress of the house heard what had happened, suddenly had an urge to soothe Iori's feelings. Iori, for his part, wouldn't have anything to do with the man for the rest of the day.

On his way out that evening, Namban'ya stopped in Iori's corner of the shop. A little drunk but in high spirits, he said, "Well, you won't be going with me after all. The women wouldn't hear of it. Ha!"

His conversation with Osei and Otsuru did have one salutary effect, however. The very next day Iori entered a temple school in the neighborhood. He was allowed to wear his sword to school, and neither Sahei nor the others gave him further trouble.

But still he was unable to settle down. When he was inside, his eyes often strayed to the street. Every time a young woman even remotely like Otsū passed, his color changed. Sometimes he ran out for a closer look.

One morning toward the beginning of the ninth month, a prodigious quantity of luggage began arriving by riverboat from Kyoto. By midday, chests and baskets were piled high in front of the office. Tags identified the property as that of samurai in the House of Hosokawa. They had been in Kyoto on business similar to that which had brought Sado to Mount Kōya, looking after the posthumous affairs of Hosokawa Yūsai. Now they sat drinking barley tea and fanning themselves, some in the office, some under the eaves outside.

Coming back from school, Iori got as far as the street. He stopped and turned pale.

Kojirō, seated atop a large basket, was saying to Sahei, "It's too hot out here. Hasn't our ship docked yet?"

Sahei looked up from the manifest in his hands and pointed toward the pier. "Your ship is the *Tatsumimaru*. It's right over there. As you can see, they haven't finished loading, so your places on board aren't ready yet. I'm sorry."

"I'd much prefer to wait on board. It should be a little cooler there."

"Yes, sir. I'll go and see how things are coming along." Too rushed to wipe the sweat from his forehead, he scurried out to the street, where he caught sight of Iori.

"What're you doing there, looking as though you'd swallowed a ramrod? Go and wait on the passengers. Barley tea, cold water, hot water—give them whatever they want."

Iori went to a shed at the entrance of the alley by the storehouse, where a kettle of water was kept boiling. But instead of going about his business, he stood glaring at Kojirō.

He was usually called Ganryū now, the rather scholarly-sounding name seeming more appropriate to his present age and status. He was heavier and more solid. His face had filled out; his once piercing eyes were serene and untroubled. He no longer made frequent use of his rapier tongue, which in the past had caused so much injury. Somehow the dignity of his sword had become a part of his personality.

One result was that he had gradually been accepted by his fellow samurai. They not only spoke highly of him but actually respected him.

Pouring sweat, Sahei returned from the ship, apologized again for the long wait and announced, "The seats amidship are still not ready, but those in the prow are." This meant the foot soldiers and younger samurai could go on board. They proceeded to gather up their belongings and left in a group. *887*

There remained only Kojirō and six or seven older men, all officials of some importance in the fief.

"Sado hasn't come yet, has he?" said Kojirō.

"No, but he should be here before long."

"We'll be getting the sun from the west soon," Sahei said to Kojirō. "It'll be cooler if you move inside."

"The flies are terrible," complained Kojirō. "And I'm thirsty. Could I have another cup of tea?"

"Right away, sir." Without getting up, Sahei shouted toward the hot-water shed. "Io, what are you doing? Bring some tea for our guests." He busily addressed himself to his manifest again, but realizing Iori had not answered, he started to repeat his order. Then he saw the boy approaching slowly with several cups of tea on a tray.

Iori offered tea to each of the samurai, bowing politely each time. Standing before Kojirō with the last two cups, he said, "Please have some tea."

Kojirō absentmindedly extended his hand but abruptly withdrew it as his eyes met Iori's. Startled, he exclaimed, "Why, it's—"

Breaking into a grin, Iori said, "The last time I had the bad luck to run into you was in Musashino."

"What's that?" rasped Kojirō, in a tone hardly appropriate to his present status.

He was about to say something else when Iori shouted, "Oh, you remember me?" and slung the tray at his face.

"Oh!" cried Kojirō, grabbing Iori by the wrist. Though the tray missed him, a bit of hot tea caught him in the left eye. The rest of the tea spilled onto his chest and lap. The tray crashed into a corner post.

"You little bastard!" shouted Kojirō. He threw Iori onto the dirt floor and planted one foot on top of him. "Manager," he called angrily. "This brat is one of your boys, isn't he? Come here and hold him down. Even if he is only a child, I won't stand for this."

Frightened out of his wits, Sahei rushed to do as he was told. But somehow Iori managed to draw his sword and take a swing at Kojirō's arm. Kojirō kicked him to the middle of the room and jumped back a pace.

Sahei turned and rushed back, screaming his lungs out. He reached Iori just as the boy jumped to his feet.

"You keep out of this!" Iori cried, then, looking Kojirō straight in the face, he spat out, "Serves you right!" and ran outside.

Kojirō picked up a carrying pole that happened to be handy and threw it at the boy, scoring a perfect hit behind his knee. Iori landed flat on his face.

At Sahei's command, several men fell on Iori and hauled him back to the hot-water shed, where a servant was wiping off Kojirō's kimono and *hakama*.

"Please forgive this outrage," pleaded Sahei.

"We don't know how to apologize," said one of the assistants.

Without looking at them, Kojirō took a damp towel from the servant and wiped off his face.

Iori had been forced to the ground, his arms bent tightly behind him. "Let me go," he begged, his body writhing in pain. "I won't run away. I'm a samurai's son. I did it on purpose and I'll take my punishment like a man."

Kojirō finished straightening his clothing and smoothed his hair. "Let him go," he said quietly.

Not knowing what to make of the placid expression on the samurai's face, Sahei stammered, "Are . . . are you sure it's all right?"

"Yes. But"—the word sounded like a nail being driven into a board—"although I have no intention of becoming involved with a mere child, if you feel he should be punished, I can suggest a method. Pour a dipperful of boiling water over his head. It won't kill him."

"Boiling water!" Sahei recoiled at the suggestion.

"Yes. If you want to let him go, that's all right too."

Sahei and his men looked at each other uncertainly.

"We can't let something like that go unpunished."

"He's always up to no good."

"He's lucky he didn't get killed."

"Bring a rope."

When they started to tie him, Iori fought off their hands. "What are you doing?" he screamed. Sitting on the ground, he said, "I told you I wouldn't run away, didn't I? I'll take my punishment. I had a reason for doing what I did. A merchant might apologize. Not me. The son of a samurai is not going to cry over a little hot water."

"All right," said Sahei. "You asked for it." He rolled up his sleeve, filled a dipper with boiling water and walked slowly toward Iori.

"Shut your eyes, Iori. If you don't, you'll go blind." The voice came from across the street.

Not daring to look to see whose voice it was, Iori shut his eyes. He recalled a story Musashi had told him once in Musashino. It was about Kaisen, a Zen priest highly revered by the warriors of Kai Province. When Nobunaga and Ieyasu attacked Kaisen's temple and put it to the torch, the priest seated himself calmly in the upper floor of the gate and, while burning to death, uttered the words: "If your heart is obliterated through enlightenment, the fire is cool."

"It's only a little dipper of hot water," Iori told himself. "I mustn't think that way." He tried desperately to become a selfless void, free of delusion, without sorrows. Perhaps, if he had been younger, or much older . . . but at his age, he was too much a part of the world he lived in.

When was it coming? For a giddy moment, he thought the sweat dripping from his forehead was boiling water. A minute seemed like a hundred years.

"Why, it's Sado," said Kojirō.

Sahei and all the others turned and stared at the old samurai.

"What's going on here?" Sado asked, coming across the street with Nuinosuke at his side.

Kojirō laughed and said lightly, "You caught us at an odd moment. They're punishing the boy."

Sado looked intently at Iori. "Punishing him? Well, if he's done something

889

bad, he should be punished. Go right ahead. I'll watch."

Sahei glanced out of the corner of his eye at Kojirō, who sized the situation up immediately and knew he was the one who would be held responsible for the severity of the punishment. "That's enough," he said.

Iori opened his eyes. He had a little trouble focusing them, but when he recognized Sado, he said happily, "I know you. You're the samurai who came to the Tokuganji in Hōtengahara."

"You remember me?"

"Yes, sir."

"What's happened to your teacher, Musashi?"

Iori sniffled and put his hands to his eyes.

Sado's knowing the boy came as a shock to Kojirō. Thinking about it for a moment, he decided it must have something to do with Sado's search for Musashi. But he certainly didn't want Musashi's name to come up in a conversation between himself and the senior retainer. He knew that one of these days he would have to fight Musashi, but it was no longer a strictly private matter.

In fact, a split had developed in both the main line and the branches of the House of Hosokawa, one faction thinking highly of Musashi, the other partial to the former rōnin who was now the clan's chief sword instructor. Some said the real reason the fight was inevitable was behind-the-scenes rivalry between Sado and Kakubei.

To Kojirō's relief, the boatswain of the *Tatsumimaru* arrived just then with word that the ship was ready.

Sado, remaining behind, said, "The ship doesn't leave till sundown, does it?"

"That's right," replied Sahei, who was pacing about the office worrying about the consequences of today's affair.

"I have time for a little rest, then?"

"Plenty of time. Please, have some tea."

Otsuru appeared at the inner door and beckoned to the manager. After listening to her for a couple of minutes, Sahei came back to Sado and said, "The office is not really the place to receive you. It's only a step through the garden to the house. Would you mind going there?"

"That's very kind," replied Sado. "To whom am I indebted? The lady of the house?"

"Yes. She said she'd like to thank you."

"What for?"

Sahei scratched his head. "I, eh, I imagine for seeing that Iori came to no harm. Since the master isn't here . . ."

"Speaking of Iori, I'd like to talk to him. Would you call him?"

The garden was what Sado would have expected in the house of a rich Sakai merchant. Though bounded on one side by a storehouse, it was a world apart from the hot, noisy office. Rocks and plants were all freshly watered and there was a running brook.

Osei and Otsuru were kneeling in a small, elegant room facing the garden.

There was a wool rug on top of the tatami and trays of cakes and tobacco. Sado noticed the spicy fragrance of mixed incense.

Sitting down at the edge of the room, he said, "I won't come in. My feet are dirty."

While serving him tea, Osei apologized for her employees and thanked him for saving Iori.

Sado said, "I had occasion some time ago to meet that boy. I'm happy to have found him again. How does it happen he's staying in your house?"

After hearing her explanation, Sado told her about his long search for Musashi. They chatted amiably for a while, then Sado said, "I was watching Iori from across the street for several minutes. I admired his ability to remain calm. He conducted himself very well. As a matter of fact, I think it's a mistake to raise a boy with that much spirit in a merchant's establishment. I wonder if you wouldn't consent to turning him over to me. In Kokura, he could be brought up as a samurai."

Osei agreed readily, saying, "It would be the best thing that could possibly happen to him."

Otsuru got up to go look for Iori, but just then he emerged from behind a tree, where he had overheard the whole conversation.

"Do you object to going with me?" asked Sado.

Bursting with happiness, Iori begged to be taken to Kokura.

While Sado drank his tea, Otsuru got Iori ready for the trip: kimono, *hakama*, leggings, basket hat—all new. It was the first time he had ever worn a *hakama*.

That evening, as the *Tatsumimaru* spread its black wings and sailed forth under clouds turned golden by the setting sun, Iori looked back at a sea of faces—Otsuru's, her mother's, Sahei's, those of a large group of well-wishers, the face of the city of Sakai.

With a broad smile on his face, he took off his basket hat and waved at them.

The Writing Teacher

The sign at the entrance to a narrow alley in the fishmongers' district of Okazaki read: "Enlightenment for the Young. Lessons in Reading and Writing," and bore the name Muka, who was from all appearances one of the many impoverished but honest rōnin making a living by sharing his warrior-class education with the children of commoners.

The curiously amateurish calligraphy brought a smile to the lips of passersby, but Muka said he wasn't ashamed of it. Whenever it was mentioned, he always replied in the same way: "I'm still a child at heart. I'm practicing along with the children."

The alley ended in a bamboo grove, beyond which was the riding ground of the House of Honda. In fair weather it was always covered by a cloud of dust, since the cavalrymen often practiced from dawn to dusk. The military lineage they were so proud of was that of the famous Mikawa warriors, the tradition that had produced the Tokugawas.

Muka stirred from his midday nap, went to the well and drew water. His solid-gray unlined kimono and gray hood might well have been the dress of a man of forty, but he was in fact not yet thirty. After washing his face, he walked into the grove, where he cut down a thick bamboo with a single sword stroke.

After washing the bamboo at the well, he went back inside. Blinds hanging on one side kept out the dust from the riding ground, but since this was the direction from which light came, the one room seemed smaller and darker than it actually was. A board lay flat in one corner; above it hung an anonymous portrait of a Zen priest. Muka set the piece of bamboo on the board and tossed a bindweed flower into the hollow center.

"Not bad," he thought, as he backed away to examine his work.

Sitting down in front of his table, he took his brush and began practicing, using as models a manual on squarish, formal characters by Ch'u Sui-liang and a rubbing of the priest Kōbō Daishi's calligraphy. He had evidently been progressing steadily during the year he had lived there, for the characters he wrote now were far superior to the ones on the sign.

"May I trouble you?" asked the woman from next door, the wife of a man who sold writing brushes.

"Come in, please," said Muka.

"I only have a minute. I was just wondering. . . . A few minutes ago I heard a loud noise. It sounded like something breaking. Did you hear it?"

Muka laughed. "That was only me, cutting down a piece of bamboo."

"Oh. I was worried. I thought something might have happened to you. My husband says the samurai prowling around here are out to kill you."

"It wouldn't matter if they did. I'm not worth three coppers anyway."

"You shouldn't be so easygoing. Lots of people get killed for things they don't even remember doing. Think how sad all the girls would be if some harm came to you."

She went on her way, not asking, as she often did, "Why don't you take a wife? It isn't that you don't like women, is it?" Muka never gave a clear answer, though he'd brought it on himself by carelessly revealing enough to suggest that he would make a fine catch. His neighbors knew he was a rōnin from Mimasaka, who liked to study and had lived for a time in Kyoto and in and around Edo. He professed to want to settle down in Okazaki and run a good school. Since his youth, diligence and honesty were apparent, it wasn't surprising that a number of girls had shown an interest in marriage, as well as several parents with eligible daughters.

This small corner of society had a certain fascination for Muka. The brush seller and his wife treated him kindly, the wife teaching him how to cook and sometimes doing his washing and sewing. All in all, he enjoyed living in the neighborhood. Everybody knew everybody else, and all sought out new ways to make their lives interesting. There was always something going on, if not a festival or street dances or a religious celebration, then a funeral or a sick person to be cared for.

That evening he passed the brush seller's house as he and his wife were having dinner. With a click of her tongue, the wife said, "Where does he go? He teaches the children in the morning, takes a nap or studies in the afternoon, then in the evening he's gone. He's just like a bat."

Her husband chuckled. "What's wrong with that? He's single. You ought not to begrudge him his nightly excursions."

In the streets of Okazaki, the sounds of a bamboo flute mingled with the buzzing of captive insects in wooden cages, the rhythmical wail of blind street singers, the cries of vendors of melons and sushi. There was nothing here of the frantic bustle that characterized Edo. Lanterns flickered; people strolled about in summer kimono. In the lingering heat of a summer day, everything seemed relaxed and in its place.

As Muka passed, the girls whispered.

"There he goes again."

"Hmph—paying no attention to anybody, as usual."

Some of the young women bowed to him, then turned to their friends and speculated on his destination.

Muka walked straight on, past the side streets where he might have purchased the favors of the Okazaki harlots, regarded by many to be one of the chief local attractions along the Tōkaidō highroad. At the western edge of town he stopped and stretched, letting the heat out of his sleeves. Ahead of him were the rushing waters of the Yahagi River and the 208-span Yahagi Bridge, the longest on the Tōkaidō. He walked toward the thin figure waiting for him at the first post.

"Musashi?"

Musashi smiled at Matahachi, who was wearing his priest's robe. "Has the master returned?" he asked.

"No."

They walked across the bridge shoulder to shoulder. On a pine-covered hill on the opposite bank stood an old Zen temple. Since the hill was known as Hachijō, the temple had come to be called Hachijōji. They climbed up the dark slope in front of the gate.

"How are things?" asked Musashi. "Practicing Zen must be difficult."

"It is," replied Matahachi, bowing his bluish shaved head dejectedly. "I've often thought of running away. If I have to go through mental torture to become a decent human being, I might as well put my head in a noose and forget about it."

"Don't let it discourage you. You're still only at the beginning. Your real

893

training won't come until after you've appealed to the master and persuaded him to take you as a disciple."

"It's not always impossible. I've learned to discipline myself a little. And whenever I feel low, I think of you. If you can overcome your difficulties, I should be able to overcome mine."

"That's the way it should be. There's nothing I can do that you can't do too."

"Remembering Takuan helps. If it hadn't been for him, I'd have been executed."

"If you can bear up under hardship, you can experience a pleasure greater than the pain," Musashi said solemnly. "Day and night, hour by hour, people are buffeted by waves of pain and pleasure, one after the other. If they try to experience only pleasure, they cease to be truly alive. Then the pleasure evaporates."

"I'm beginning to understand."

"Think of a simple yawn. The yawn of a person who's been working hard is different from the yawn of a lazy man. Lots of people die without knowing the pleasure yawning can bring."

"Umm. I hear talk like that at the temple."

"I hope the day soon comes when I turn you over to the master. I want to ask him for guidance too. I need to know more about the Way."

"When do you suppose he'll come back?"

"It's hard to say. Zen masters sometimes float around the country like a cloud for two or three years at a time. Now that you're here, you should resolve to wait four or five years for him, if it comes to that."

"You, too?"

"Yes. Living in that back alley, among poor and honest people, is good training—part of my education. It's not time wasted."

After leaving Edo, Musashi had passed through Atsugi. Then, driven by doubts about his future, he had disappeared into the Tanzawa Mountains, to emerge two months later more worried and haggard than ever. Solving one problem only led him to another. At times he was so tortured his sword seemed like a weapon turned against him.

Among the possibilities he had considered was choosing the easy way. If he could bring himself to live in a comfortable, ordinary way with Otsū, life would be simple. Almost any fief would be willing to pay him enough to live on, perhaps five hundred to a thousand bushels. But when he put it to himself in the form of a question, the answer was always no. An easy existence imposed restrictions; he could not submit to them.

At other times he felt as lost in base, craven illusions as the hungry demons in hell; then, for a time, his mind would clear, and he would bask in the pleasure of his proud isolation. In his heart there was a continual struggle between light and dark. Night and day, he wavered between exuberance and melancholy. He'd think of his swordsmanship and be dissatisfied. Thinking of how long the Way was, how far he was from maturity, a sickness came over his heart. Other days, the mountain life cheered him and his thoughts strayed to Otsū.

Coming down from the mountains, he'd gone to the Yugyōji in Fujisawa for a few days, then on to Kamakura. It was here that he'd met Matahachi. Determined not to return to a life of indolence, Matahachi was in Kamakura because of the many Zen temples there, but he was suffering from an even deeper sense of malaise than Musashi.

Musashi reassured him, "It's not too late. If you learn self-discipline, you can make a fresh start. It's fatal to tell yourself that it's all over, that you're no good."

He felt constrained to add, "To tell the truth, I myself have run up against a wall. There are times when I wonder if I have any future. I feel completely empty. It's like being confined in a shell. I hate myself. I tell myself I'm no good. But by chastising myself and forcing myself to go on, I manage to kick through the shell. Then a new path opens up before me.

"Believe me, it's a real struggle this time. I'm floundering around inside the shell, unable to do a thing. I came down from the mountains because I remembered a person who I think can help me."

The person was the priest Gudō.

Matahachi said, "He's the one who helped you when you were first seeking the Way, isn't he? Couldn't you introduce me and ask him to accept me as his disciple?"

At first, Musashi was skeptical about Matahachi's sincerity, but after hearing of the trouble he'd been in in Edo, he decided that he really meant it. The two of them made inquiries about Gudō at a number of Zen temples, but learned little. Musashi knew the priest was no longer at the Myōshinji in Kyoto. He had left several years earlier and traveled for some time in the east and northeast. He also knew he was a most erratic man, who might be in Kyoto giving lectures on Zen to the Emperor one day and out wandering the countryside the next. Gudō had been known to stop several times at the Hachijōji in Okazaki, and one priest suggested that might be the best place to wait for him.

Musashi and Matahachi sat in the little shed where Matahachi slept. Musashi often visited him here and they talked late into the night. Matahachi wasn't allowed to sleep in the dormitory, which, like the other buildings of the Hachijōji, was a rustic, thatched-roof affair, since he had not yet been officially accepted as a priest.

"Oh, these mosquitoes!" said Matahachi, waving away smoke from the insect repellent, then rubbing his irritated eyes. "Let's go outside."

They walked to the main hall and sat down on the porch. The grounds were deserted and there was a cool breeze.

"Reminds me of the Shippōji," said Matahachi, his voice barely audible.

"It does, doesn't it," said Musashi.

They fell silent. They always did at times like this, thoughts of home invariably bringing back memories of Otsū or Osugi or events neither of them wanted to talk about for fear of upsetting their present relationship.

But after a few moments, Matahachi said, "The hill the Shippōji was on was higher, wasn't it? There isn't any ancient cryptomeria here, though." He paused, stared for a time at Musashi's profile, then said diffidently, "There's a request I've been wanting to make, but . . ."

"What is it?"

"Otsū—" Matahachi began, but immediately choked up. When he thought he could manage it, he went on: "I wonder what Otsū's doing right now, and what will happen to her. I think of her often these days, apologizing in my heart for what I did. I'm ashamed to admit it, but in Edo I made her live with me. Nothing happened, though. She refused to let me touch her. I guess after I went to Sekigahara, Otsū must have been like a fallen blossom. Now she's a flower blooming on a different tree, in different soil." His face showed his earnestness and his voice was grave.

"Takezō—no . . . Musashi: I beg you, marry Otsū. You're the only person who can save her. I've never been able to bring myself to say that, but now that I've decided to become a disciple of Gudō, I'm resigned to the fact that Otsū is not mine. Even so I worry about her. Won't you look for her and give her the happiness she longs for?"

It was about three o'clock in the morning when Musashi started down the dark mountain path. His arms were folded, his head was bowed; Matahachi's words rang in his ears. Anguish seemed to tug at his legs. He wondered how many nights of torment Matahachi must have spent mustering up the courage to speak. Yet it seemed to Musashi that his own dilemma was uglier and more painful.

Matahachi, he thought, was hoping to flee from the flames of the past to the cool salvation of enlightenment—trying, like a baby being born, to find in the twofold mysterious pain of sadness and ecstasy a life worth living.

Musashi had not been able to say, "I can't do that," much less, "I don't want to marry Otsū. She's your fiancée. Repent, purify your heart and win her back." In the end, he had said nothing, for anything he might have said would have been a lie.

Matahachi had pleaded fervently, "Unless I'm sure Otsū will be cared for, it'll do me no good to become a disciple. You're the one who urged me to train and discipline myself. If you're my friend, save Otsū. That's the only way to save me."

Musashi had been surprised when Matahachi had broken down and wept. He hadn't suspected he was capable of such depth of feeling. And when he'd stood up to leave, Matahachi clutched his sleeve and begged for an answer. "Let me think about it," was all Musashi could say. Now he cursed himself for being a coward and lamented his inability to overcome his inertia.

Musashi thought sadly that those who have not suffered from this malady cannot know its agony. It was not a matter merely of being idle, which is often a pleasant state, but of wanting desperately to do something and not being able to. Musashi's mind and eyes seemed dull and empty. Having gone as far as he could in one direction, he found himself powerless either to retreat or to embark on a new path. It was like being imprisoned in a place with no exit. His frustration bred self-doubt, recrimination, tears.

Getting angry with himself, recalling all the things he had done wrong, did not help. It was because he was experiencing early symptoms of his ailment that he had parted with Iori and Gonnosuke and severed ties with his friends in Edo. But his intention to kick through the shell before it was well formed had failed. The shell was still there, enclosing his empty self like the abandoned skin of a cicada.

He walked on irresolutely. The wide expanse of the Yahagi River came into view, and the wind coming off the river felt cool on his face.

Suddenly, warned by a piercing whistle, he leapt to one side. The shot passed within five feet of him, and the report of a musket reverberated across the river. Counting two breaths between the bullet and the sound, Musashi concluded the gun had been fired from quite a distance. He jumped under the bridge and clung batlike to a post.

Several minutes passed before three men came running down Hachijō Hill like pine cones driven by the wind. Near the end of the bridge, they stopped and began searching for the body. Convinced he'd scored a hit, the musketeer threw away the fuse. He was dressed in darker clothes than the other two and masked, only his eyes visible.

The sky had lightened a little and brass ornaments on the gun butt gave off a soft glow.

Musashi couldn't imagine who in Okazaki wanted him dead. Not that there was any shortage of candidates. In the course of his battles, he had defeated many men who might still burn with the desire for revenge. He had killed many others whose families or friends might wish to pursue a vendetta.

Any person who followed the Way of the Sword was constantly in danger of being killed. If he survived one close call, chances were that by that very act he made new enemies or created a new peril. Danger was the grindstone on which the swordsman whetted his spirit. Enemies were teachers in disguise.

To be taught by danger to be alert even when asleep, to learn from enemies at all times, to use the sword as a means of letting people live; governing the realm, achieving enlightenment, sharing one's joys in life with others—they were all inherent in the Way of the Sword.

As Musashi crouched under the bridge, the cold reality of the situation stimulated him and his lassitude evaporated. Breathing very shallowly, noiselessly, he let his attackers approach. Failing to find the corpse, they searched the deserted road and the space under the end of the bridge.

Musashi's eyes widened. Though dressed in black, like bandits, the men carried samurai swords and were well shod. The only samurai in the district were those serving the House of Honda in Okazaki and the Owari House of Tokugawa in Nagoya. He was not aware of having enemies in either fief.

One man dived into the shadows and recovered the fuse, then lit it and waved it, leading Musashi to think there were more men across the bridge. He couldn't move, not now anyway. If he showed himself, he would invite more musket fire. Even if he gained the opposite bank, danger, perhaps greater danger, lay waiting. But he couldn't stay where he was much longer, either. Knowing he had not crossed the bridge, they would move in on him and possibly discover his hiding place.

His plan came to him like a flash of light. It was not reasoned out by the theories of the Art of War, which constituted the fiber of the trained warrior's intuition. To reason out a mode of attack was a dilatory process, often resulting in defeat in situations where speed was of the essence. The warrior's instinct was not to be confused with animal instinct. Like a visceral reaction, it came from a combination of wisdom and discipline. It was an ultimate reasoning that went beyond reason, the ability to make the right move in a split second without going through the actual process of thinking.

"There's no point in your trying to hide," he shouted. "If you're looking for me, I'm right here." The wind was fairly strong now; he wasn't sure whether his voice carried or not.

The question was answered by another shot. Musashi, of course, was no longer there. While the bullet was still in the air, he jumped nine feet nearer the end of the bridge.

He rushed into their midst. They separated slightly, facing him from three directions but totally lacking in coordination. He struck downward at the man in the middle with his long sword, simultaneously slicing laterally with his short sword at the man on his left. The third man fled across the bridge, running, stumbling and bouncing off the railing.

Musashi followed at a walk, keeping to one side and stopping from time to time to listen. When nothing more happened, he went home and to bed.

The next morning two samurai appeared at his house. Finding the entranceway full of children's sandals, they went around to the side.

"Are you Muka *Sensei?*" asked one. "We're from the House of Honda."

Musashi looked up from his writing and said, "Yes, I'm Muka."

"Is your real name Miyamota Musashi? If it is, don't try to conceal it."

"I'm Musashi."

"I believe you're acquainted with Watari Shima."

"I don't think I know him."

"He says he's been at two or three haiku parties when you were present."

"Now that you mention it, I do remember him. We met at the house of a mutual friend."

"He was wondering if you wouldn't come and spend an evening with him."

"If he's looking for someone to compose haiku with, he has the wrong man. Though it's true I've been invited to a few such parties, I'm a simple man with little experience in such matters."

"I think what he has in mind is discussing the martial arts with you."

Musashi's pupils were staring worriedly at the two samurai. For a few moments, Musashi gazed at them too, then said, "In that case, I shall be delighted to call on him. When?"

"Could you come this evening?"

"Fine."

"He'll send a palanquin for you."

"That's very kind of him. I'll be waiting."

After they'd gone, he turned back to his pupils. "Come, now," he said. "You mustn't let yourselves be distracted. Get back to work. Look at me. I'm practicing too. You have to learn to concentrate so completely that you don't even hear people talking or cicadas singing. If you're lazy when you're young, you'll turn out like me and have to practice after you're grown." He laughed and looked around at the ink-smeared faces and hands.

By twilight, he had donned a *hakama* and was ready to go. Just as he was reassuring the brush seller's wife, who looked ready to cry, that he would be safe, the palanquin arrived—not the simple basket type seen around town but a lacquered sedan chair, which was accompanied by two samurai and three attendants.

Neighbors, dazzled by the sight, crowded around and whispered. Children called their friends and chattered excitedly.

"Only great people ride in palanquins like that."

"Our teacher must be somebody."

"Where's he going?"

"Will he ever come back?"

The samurai closed the door of the palanquin, cleared the people out of the way, and they set off.

While not knowing what to expect, Musashi suspected there was a connection between the invitation and the incident at Yahagi Bridge. Perhaps Shima was going to take him to task for killing two Honda samurai. Then again, maybe Shima was the person behind the spying and the surprise attack and was now ready to confront Musashi openly. Not believing any good could come from tonight's meeting, Musashi resigned himself to facing a difficult situation. Speculation wouldn't get him very far. The Art of War demanded that he find out where he stood and act accordingly.

The palanquin rocked gently, like a boat at sea. Hearing the wind soughing through the pines, he thought they must be in the forest near the north castle wall. He did not look like a man bracing himself for an unpredictable onslaught. Eyes half shut, he appeared to be dozing.

After the castle gate grated open, the pace of the bearers was slower, the samurai's tones more subdued. They passed flickering lanterns and came to the castle buildings. When Musashi alighted, servants ushered him silently but politely to an open pavilion. Since the blinds were rolled up on all four sides, the breeze wafted through in pleasant waves. The lamps dimmed and flared riotously. It did not seem like the sweltering summer night it was.

"I am Watari Shima," said his host. He was a typical Mikawa samurai—sturdy, virile, alert but not ostensibly so, betraying no signs of weakness.

"I am Miyamoto Musashi." The equally simple reply was accompanied by a bow.

Shima returned the bow, said, "Make yourself comfortable," and proceeded to the point without further formalities. "I'm told you killed two of our samurai last night. Is that true?"

"Yes, it is." Musashi stared at Shima's eyes.

"I owe you an apology," said Shima gravely. "I heard about the incident today when the deaths were reported. There was an investigation, of course. Though I've known your name for a long time, I did not know until now that you were living in Okazaki.

"As for the attack, I was told you were fired on by a group of our men, one of whom is a disciple of Miyake Gumbei, a martial expert of the Tōgun Style."

Musashi, sensing no subterfuge, accepted Shima's words at face value, and the story unfolded gradually. Gumbei's disciple was one of several Honda samurai who had studied at the Yoshioka School. The firebrands among them got together and decided to kill the man who had put an end to the glory of the Yoshioka School.

Musashi knew Yoshioka Kempō's name was still revered throughout the country. In western Japan, particularly, it would have been difficult to find a fief in which there were no samurai who had not studied under him. Musashi told Shima he understood their hatred of him but regarded it as a personal grudge rather than a legitimate reason for revenge in accordance with the Art of War.

Shima apparently agreed. "I called the survivors in and reprimanded them. I hope you'll forgive us and forget the matter. Gumbei, too, was very displeased. If you don't mind, I'd like to introduce him to you. He would like to offer his apologies."

"That's not necessary. What happened was a common occurrence for any man committed to the martial arts."

"Even so—"

"Well, let's dispense with the apologies. But if he'd like to talk about the Way, I'd be delighted to meet him. The name is familiar."

A man was sent for Gumbei, and when the introductions were over, the talk turned to swords and swordsmanship.

Musashi said, "I'd like to hear about the Tōgun Style. Did you create it?"

"No," replied Gumbei. "I learned it from my teacher, Kawasaki Kaginosuke, from Echizen Province. According to the manual he gave me, he developed it while living as a hermit on Mount Hakuun in Kōzuke. He seems to have learned many of his techniques from a Tendai monk named Tōgumbo.... But tell me about yourself. I've heard your name mentioned a number of times. I had the impression you were older. And since you're here, I wonder if you'd favor me with a lesson." The tone was friendly. Nevertheless, this was an invitation to battle.

"Some other time," Musashi replied lightly. "I should be going now. I don't really know the way home."

"When you go," said Shima, "I'll send someone with you."

"When I heard two men had been cut down," Gumbei went on, "I went over to take a look. I found I couldn't reconcile the positions of the bodies with the wounds, so I questioned the man who escaped. His impression was that you were using two swords at once. Could that be true?"

With a smile, Musashi said he had never done so consciously. He regarded what he was doing as fighting with one body and one sword.

"You shouldn't be so modest," said Gumbei. "Tell us about it. How do you practice? What do the weights have to be for you to use two swords freely?"

Seeing he wasn't going to be able to leave before he gave some sort of explanation, he directed his eyes around the room. They came to rest on two muskets in the alcove and he asked to borrow them. Shima consented, and Musashi went to the middle of the room holding the two weapons by the barrels, one in each hand.

Musashi raised one knee and said, "Two swords are as one sword. One sword is as two swords. One's arms are separate; they both belong to the same body. In all things, the ultimate reasoning is not dual but single. All styles and all factions are alike in this respect. I will show you."

The words came out spontaneously and when they stopped, he raised his arm and said, "By your leave." Then he began twirling the muskets. They spun around like reels, creating a small whirlwind. The other men blanched.

Musashi stopped and drew his elbows to his sides. He walked over to the alcove and put the muskets back. With a slight laugh, he said, "Perhaps that will help you to understand." Offering no further explanation, he bowed to his host and took his leave. Astounded, Shima forgot all about sending someone with him.

Outside the gate, Musashi turned for a final look, relieved to be out of Watari Shima's grasp. He still did not know the man's real intentions, but one thing was clear. Not only was his identity known; he had become involved in an incident. The wisest thing would be to leave Okazaki this very night.

He was thinking about his promise to Matahachi to wait for Gudō's return when the lights of Okazaki came into view and a voice called to him from a small roadside shrine.

"Musashi, it's me, Matahachi. We were worried about you, so we came out here to wait."

"Worried?" said Musashi.

"We went to your house. The woman next door said people had been spying on you recently."

"We?"

"The master came back today."

Gudō was seated on the veranda of the shrine. He was a man of unusual mien, his skin as black as a giant cicada's, his deep-set eyes shining brilliantly under high eyebrows. He looked to be somewhere between forty and fifty, but it was impossible to tell with a man like this. Thin and wiry, he had a booming voice.

Musashi went over, knelt and lowered his forehead to the ground. Gudō regarded him silently for a minute or two. "It's been a long time," he said.

Lifting his head, Musashi said quietly, "A very long time." Gudō or Takuan—Musashi had long been convinced that only one or the other of these two men could deliver him from his present impasse. Here, at last, after a wait of a whole year, was Gudō. He gazed at the priest's face as he might at the moon on a dark night.

Suddenly and forcefully, he cried out, "*Sensei!*"

"What is it?" Gudō had no need to ask; he knew what Musashi wanted, anticipated it as a mother divines a child's needs.

Musashi, head to the ground again, said, "It's been nearly ten years since I studied under you."

"Is it that long?"

"Yes. But even after all those years, I doubt my progress along the Way is measurable."

"You still talk like a child, don't you? You couldn't have come very far."

"I'm full of regrets."

"Are you?"

"My training and self-discipline have accomplished so little."

"You're always talking about such things. So long as you do that, it's futile."

"What would happen if I gave up?"

"You'd be tied up in knots again. You'd be human rubbish, worse off than before, when you were merely an ignorant fool."

"If I desert the Way, I fall into the depths. Yet when I try to pursue it to the peak, I find I'm not up to the task. I'm twisting in the wind halfway up, neither the swordsman nor the human being I want to be."

"That seems to sum it up."

"You can't know how desperate I've been. What should I do? Tell me! How can I free myself from inaction and confusion?"

"Why ask me? You can only rely on yourself."

"Let me sit at your feet again and receive your chastisement. Me and Matahachi. Or give me a blow with your staff to awaken me from this dark emptiness. I beg you, *Sensei*, help me." Musashi had not lifted his head. He shed no tears, but his voice choked up.

Completely unmoved, Gudō said, "Come, Matahachi," and together they walked away from the shrine.

Musashi ran after the priest, grabbed his sleeve, pleaded and begged.

The priest shook his head silently. When Musashi persisted, he said, "Not one thing!" Then, angrily: "What have I to tell you? What more have I to give you? There is only a blow on the head." He waved his fist in the air but did not strike.

Musashi, letting go of his sleeve, was about to say something else. The priest walked rapidly away, not pausing to look back.

At Musashi's side, Matahachi said, "When I saw him at the temple and explained our feelings and why we wanted to become his disciples, he barely listened. When I finished, he said, 'Oh?' and told me I could follow along and wait on him. Maybe if you just follow us, whenever he seems to be in a good mood you can ask him what you want to ask."

Gudō turned and called Matahachi.

"Coming," said Matahachi. "Do what I told you," he advised Musashi as he rushed off to catch up with the priest.

Thinking that letting Gudō out of his sight again would be fatal, Musashi decided to follow Matahachi's advice. In the flow of universal time, a man's life of sixty or seventy years was only a lightning flash. If in that brief span he was privileged to meet a man like Gudō, it would be foolish to let the chance slip by.

"It's a sacred opportunity," he thought. Warm tears gathered at the corners of his eyes. He had to follow Gudō, to the end of the earth if need be, pursue him until he heard the word he longed for.

Gudō walked away from Hachijō Hill, apparently no longer interested in the temple there. His heart had already begun to flow with the water and the clouds. When he reached the Tōkaidō, he turned west, toward Kyoto.

The Circle

The Zen master's approach to travel was whimsically eccentric. One day when it rained he stayed inside the inn all day and had Matahachi give him a moxa treatment. In Mino Province, he stopped over at the Daisenji for seven days and then spent a few days at a Zen temple in Hikone, so it was only gradually that they approached Kyoto.

Musashi slept wherever he could find a place. When Gudō stayed at an inn he spent the night either outdoors or at another inn. If the priest and Matahachi were stopping at a temple, Musashi took shelter under the gate. Privations were as nothing compared to his need for a word from Gudō.

One night outside a temple by Lake Biwa, suddenly aware of the coming of autumn, he took a look at himself and saw that he resembled nothing so much as a beggar. His hair, of course, was a rat's nest, since he'd resolved not to comb it until the priest relented. It was weeks since he'd had a bath and a shave. His clothes were quickly being reduced to tatters; they felt like pine bark rubbing against his skin.

The stars seemed ready to fall from the sky. He looked at his reed mat and thought: "What a fool I am!" All at once, his attitude appeared insane. He laughed bitterly. He'd stuck to his goal doggedly, silently, but what was it he was seeking from the Zen master? Was it impossible to go through life without torturing himself so? He even began to feel sorry for the lice inhabiting his body.

Gudō had stated unequivocally that he had "not one thing" to offer. It was unreasonable to press him for something he did not possess, wrong to resent him, even though he showed less consideration than he might have for a stray dog along the wayside.

Musashi gazed upward through the hair hanging over his eyes. No doubt about it—it was an autumn moon. But the mosquitoes. His skin, already peppered with red welts, was no longer sensitive to their bites.

He was quite prepared to admit to himself that there was something he did not understand, but he thought of it as being one thing. If only he could figure out what it was, his sword would be released from its bonds. Everything else would be solved in an instant. Then just as he felt on the verge of grasping it, it always eluded him.

If his pursuit of the Way was to end here, he would prefer to die, for he saw nothing else to live for. He stretched out under the roof of the gate. When sleep would not come, he asked what it could be. A sword technique? No; not only that. A secret for getting on in the world? No; more than that. A solution to the problem of Otsū? No; no man could be this miserable over the love of a woman. It had to be one all-encompassing answer, yet for all its magnitude, it could, at the same time, be no larger than a poppy seed.

Wrapped in his matting, he looked like a caterpillar. He wondered if Matahachi was sleeping well. Comparing himself with his friend, he felt envious. Matahachi's problems did not seem to disable him. Musashi always seemed to be searching out new problems with which to torture himself.

His eyes fell on a plaque hanging on a gatepost. He got up and went up to it for a closer look. By the light of the moon, he read:

> I beg you, try to find the fundamental source.
> Pai-yün was moved by the merits of Pai-ch'ang;
> Hu-ch'iu sighed over the teachings left by Pai-yün.
> Like our great predecessors,
> Do not merely pinch off the leaves
> Or concern yourselves only with the branches.

It appeared to be a quotation from the *Testament* of Daitō Kokushi, the founder of the Daitokuji.

Musashi reread the last two lines. Leaves and branches . . . How many people were thrown off course by irrelevant matters? Was he himself not an example? While the thought seemed to lighten his burden, his doubts would not go away. Why would his sword not obey him? Why did his eyes wander from his goal? What prevented him from achieving serenity?

Somehow it all seemed so unnecessary. He knew that it was when one had pursued the Way as far as possible that vacillation set in and one was attacked by fretfulness—leaves and branches. How did one break through the cycle? How did one get at the core and destroy it?

> I laugh at my ten-year pilgrimage—
> Wilted robe, tattered hat, knocking at Zen gates.
> In reality, the Buddha's Law is simple:
> Eat your rice, drink your tea, wear your clothes.

Musashi recalled this verse written by Gudō in self-mockery. Gudō had been about the same age Musashi was now when he composed it.

On Musashi's first visit to the Myōshinji, the priest had all but kicked him away from the door. "What strange line of thinking leads you to my house?" he had shouted. But Musashi persisted, and later, after he'd gained admittance, Gudō regaled him with this ironic verse. And he laughed at him, saying the same thing he had said a few weeks ago: "You're always talking. . . . It's futile."

Thoroughly disheartened, Musashi gave up the idea of sleep and walked around the gate, just in time to see two men emerge from the temple.

Gudō and Matahachi were walking at an unusually rapid pace. Perhaps an urgent summons had come from the Myōshinji, the head temple of Gudō's sect. In any event, he brushed past the monks gathered to see him off and headed straight for the Kara Bridge in Seta.

Musashi followed, through the town of Sakamoto, which was asleep, the woodblock print shops, the greengrocer's, even the bustling inns, all tightly shuttered. The only presence was the ghostly moon.

Leaving the town, they climbed Mount Hiei, past the Miidera and the Sekiji in their veils of mist. They met almost no one. When they reached the pass, Gudō stopped and said something to Matahachi. Below them lay Kyoto, in the other direction the tranquil expanse of Lake Biwa. Aside from the moon itself, everything was like mica, a sea of soft silvery mist.

Reaching the pass a few moments later, Musashi was startled to find himself only a few feet from the master. Their eyes met for the first time in weeks.

Gudō said nothing.

Musashi said nothing.

"Now . . . it has to be now," thought Musashi. If the priest got as far as the Myōshinji, it might be necessary to wait many weeks for the opportunity to see him again.

"Please, sir," he said. His chest swelled and his neck twisted. His voice sounded like that of a frightened child, attempting to tell his mother something he really did not want to say. He edged forward timidly.

The priest did not condescend to ask what he wanted. His face might have belonged to a dry-lacquer statue. The eyes alone stood out whitely, glaring angrily at Musashi.

"Please, sir." Musashi, oblivious of everything save the flaming impulse propelling him forward, fell to his knees and bowed his head. "One word of wisdom. Just one word . . ."

He waited for what seemed like hours. When he was unable to restrain himself any longer, he started to renew his plea.

"I've heard all that," Gudō interrupted. "Matahachi talks about you every night. I know all there is to know, even about the woman."

The words were like slivers of ice. Musashi could not have lifted his head if he had wanted to.

"Matahachi, a stick!"

Musashi shut his eyes, steeling himself for the blow, but instead of striking, Gudō drew a circle around him. Without another word, he threw the stick away and said, "Let's go, Matahachi." They walked away quickly.

Musashi was incensed. After the weeks of cruel mortification he'd undergone in a sincere effort to receive a teaching, Gudō's refusal was far more than a lack of compassion. It was heartless, brutal. He was toying with a man's life.

"Swine of a priest!"

Musashi glared viciously at the departing pair, his lips set tightly in an angry scowl.

"Not one thing." Reflecting on Gudō's words, he decided they were deceitful, suggesting the man had something to offer when in fact there was "not one thing" in his foolish head.

"Wait and see," thought Musashi. "I don't need you!" He would rely on no one. In the final analysis, there *was* no one to rely on but himself. He was a man, just as Gudō was a man and all the earlier masters had been men.

He stood up, half lifted by his own rage. For several minutes, he stared at the moon, but as his anger cooled, his eyes fell to the circle. Still inside it, he turned all the way around. As he did so, he remembered the stick that had not struck him.

"A circle? What could it mean?" He let his thoughts flow.

A perfectly round line, no beginning, no end, no deviation. If expanded infinitely, it would become the universe. If contracted, it would become co-equal with the infinitesimal dot in which his soul resided. His soul was round. The universe was round. Not two. One. One entity—himself and the universe.

With a click, he drew his sword and held it out diagonally. His shadow resembled the symbol for "o" [オ]. The universal circle remained the same. By the same token, he himself was unchanged. Only the shadow had changed.

"Only a shadow," he thought. "The shadow is not my real self." The wall against which he had been beating his head was a mere shadow, the shadow of his confused mind.

He raised his head and a fierce shout broke from his lips.

With his left hand, he held out his short sword. The shadow changed again, but the image of the universe—not by one whit. The two swords were but one. And they were part of the circle.

He sighed deeply; his eyes had been opened. Looking up at the moon again, he saw that its great circle could be regarded as identical with the sword or with the soul of one who treads the earth.

"*Sensei!*" he cried, bounding off after Gudō. He sought nothing more from the priest, but he owed him an apology for having hated him with such vehemence.

After a dozen steps, he halted. "It's only leaves and branches," he thought.

Shikama Blue

"Is Otsū here?"

"Yes, here I am."

A face appeared above the top of the hedge.

"You're the hemp dealer Mambei, aren't you?" said Otsū.

"That's right. Sorry to bother you when you're busy, but I heard some news that might interest you."

"Come in." She gestured toward the wooden door in the fence.

As was evident from the cloth hanging from branches and poles, the house belonged to one of the dyers who made the sturdy fabric known throughout the country as "Shikama Blue." This involved immersing the cloth in indigo dye several times and pounding it in a large mortar after each immersion. The thread became so saturated with dye that it wore out long before it faded.

Otsū was not yet used to handling the mallet, but she worked hard and her fingers were stained blue. In Edo, after learning Musashi was gone, she had called at the Hōjō and Yagyū residences, then immediately set out on her search again. In Sakai the previous summer, she boarded one of Kobayashi Tarōzaemon's ships and came to Shikama, a fishing village situated on the triangular estuary where the Shikama River flows into the Inland Sea.

Remembering that her wet nurse was married to a dyer from Shikama, Otsū had looked her up and was living with her. Since the family was poor, Otsū felt obliged to help with the dyeing, which was the work of the young unmarried women. They often sang as they worked, and villagers said they could tell from the sound of a girl's voice whether she was in love with one of the young fishermen.

Having washed her hands and wiped the sweat from her forehead, Otsū invited Mambei to sit down and rest on the veranda.

He declined with a wave of his hand and said, "You came from the village of Miyamoto, didn't you?"

"Yes."

"I go up that way on business, to buy hemp, and the other day I heard a rumor. . . ."

"Yes?"

"About you."

"Me?"

"I also heard something about a man named Musashi."

907

"Musashi?" Otsū's heart was in her throat and her cheeks flushed.

Mambei gave a little laugh. Though it was autumn, the sun was still fairly strong. He folded a hand towel, put it on his head and squatted on his heels. "Do you know a woman named Ogin?" he asked.

"You mean Musashi's sister?"

Mambei nodded vigorously. "I ran into her at Mikazuki Village in Sayo. I happened to mention your name. She looked very surprised."

"Did you tell her where I was?"

"Yes. I didn't see any harm in that."

"Where's she living now?"

"She's staying with a samurai named Hirata—a relative of hers, I think. She said she'd like very much to see you. She said several times how much she missed you, how much she had to tell you. Some of it was secret, she said. I thought she was going to start crying."

Otsū's eyes reddened.

"There in the middle of the road was no place to write a letter, of course, so she asked me to tell you to come to Mikazuki. She said she'd like to come here, but couldn't just now." Mambei paused. "She didn't go into details, but she said she'd had word from Musashi." He added that he was going to Mikazuki the next day and suggested she go with him.

Though Otsū's mind was made up right then, she felt she should talk it over with the dyer's wife. "I'll let you know this evening," she said.

"Fine. If you decide to go, we should get an early start." With the sea murmuring in the background, his voice sounded particularly loud, and even Otsū's soft reply seemed rather shrill.

As Mambei went out the gate, a young samurai who had been sitting on the beach rubbing a handful of sand stood up and watched him with piercing eyes, as if to verify his thoughts about the man. Handsomely attired and wearing a straw basket hat shaped like a ginkgo leaf, he appeared to be eighteen or nineteen years old. When the hemp dealer was out of sight, he turned and stared at the dyer's house.

Despite the excitement caused by Mambei's news, Otsū picked up her mallet and resumed her work. The sounds of other mallets, accompanied by singing, floated through the air. No sound came from Otsū's lips when she worked, but in her heart was a song of her love for Musashi. Now she silently whispered a poem from an ancient collection:

> Since our first meeting,
> My love has been more profound
> Than that of others,
> Though it matches not the hues
> Of the cloth from Shikama.

She felt sure that if she visited Ogin, she would learn where Musashi was. And Ogin was a woman too. It would be easy to tell her her feelings.

The beats of her mallet slowed to an almost languid pace. Otsū was happier than she had been for a long time. She understood the feelings of the poet.

Often the sea seemed melancholy and alien; today it was dazzling, and the waves, though gentle, appeared to be bursting with hope.

She hung the cloth on a high drying pole and, heart still singing, wandered out through the open gate. Out of the corner of her eyes, she caught sight of the young samurai strolling unhurriedly along the water's edge. She had no idea who he was, but somehow he held her attention, and she noticed nothing else, not so much as a bird riding the salty breeze.

Their destination was not very far; even a woman could walk the distance with little difficulty, stopping over once on the way. It was nearly noon now.

"I'm sorry to put you to all this trouble," said Otsū.

"No trouble. You seem to have good walking legs," said Mambei.

"I'm used to traveling."

"I heard you've been to Edo. That's quite a journey for a woman traveling alone."

"Did the dyer's wife tell you that?"

"Yes. I've heard everything. The people in Miyamoto talk about it too."

"Oh, they would," said Otsū with a little frown. "It's so embarrassing."

"You shouldn't feel embarrassed. If you love a person that much, who's to say whether you're to be pitied or congratulated. But it seems to me this Musashi is a little coldhearted."

"Oh, he's not—not at all."

"You don't resent the way he's acted?"

"I'm the one to blame. His training and discipline are his only interest in life, and I can't resign myself to that."

"I don't see anything wrong with the way you feel."

"But it seems to me I've caused him a lot of trouble."

"Hmph. My wife should hear that. That's the way women ought to be."

"Is Ogin married?" asked Otsū.

"Ogin? Oh, I'm not quite sure," said Mambei, and changed the subject. "There's a teahouse. Let's rest awhile."

They went inside and ordered tea to go with their box lunches. As they were finishing, some passing grooms and porters called out in familiar tones to Mambei.

"Hey, you, why don't you drop in on the game in Handa today? Everybody's complaining—you left with all our money the other day."

In some confusion, he shouted back, as though he hadn't understood them, "I don't have any use for your horses today." Then quickly, to Otsū, "Shall we be going?"

As they hurried out of the shop, one of the grooms said, "No wonder he's giving us the brush-off. Take a look at the girl!"

"I'm going to tell your old woman on you, Mambei."

They heard more comments of this sort as they walked quickly on ahead. Asaya Mambei's shop in Shikama was certainly not among the more prominent business establishments there. He bought hemp in the nearby villages and parceled it out to the fishermen's wives and daughters to make into sails, *909* nets and other things. But he was the proprietor of his own enterprise, and his being on such friendly terms with common porters struck Otsū as strange.

As if to dispel her unspoken doubts, Mambei said, "What can you do with riffraff like that? Just because I do them the favor of asking them to carry stuff from the mountains, that's no reason for them to get familiar!"

They spent the night in Tatsuno, and when they left the next morning, Mambei was as kind and solicitous as ever. By the time they reached Mikazuki, it was getting dark in the foothills.

"Mambei," asked Otsū anxiously, "isn't this Mikazuki? If we cross the mountain we'll be in Miyamoto." She had heard that Osugi was in Miyamoto again.

Mambei halted. "Why, yes, it's just on the other side. Does it make you homesick?"

Otsū lifted her eyes to the black, wavy crest of the mountains and the evening sky. The area seemed very desolate, as if somehow the people who should be there were missing.

"It's only a little farther," said Mambei, walking on ahead. "Are you tired?"

"Oh, no. Are you?"

"No. I'm used to this road. I come this way all the time."

"Just where is Ogin's house?"

"Over that way," he replied, pointing. "She's sure to be waiting for us."

They walked a little faster. When they reached the place where the slope became steeper, there was a scattering of houses. This was a stopover on the Tatsuno highroad. It was hardly large enough to be described as a town, but it boasted a cheap "one-tray" eating place, where grooms hung out, and a few low-priced inns strung out on both sides of the road.

Once they were past the village, Mambei declared, "We have to climb a little now." Turning off the road, he started up a steep flight of stone stairs leading to the local shrine.

Like a small bird chirping because of a sudden drop in the temperature, Otsū sensed something out of the ordinary. "Are you sure we haven't come the wrong way? There're no houses around here," she said.

"Don't worry. It's a lonely place, but you just sit down and rest on the shrine porch. I'll go and fetch Ogin."

"Why should you do that?"

"Have you forgotten? I'm sure I mentioned it. Ogin said there might be guests it would be inconvenient for you to run into. Her house is on the other side of this grove. I'll be back very soon." He hurried off along a narrow path through the dark cryptomerias.

As the evening sky grew darker, Otsū began to feel distinctly ill at ease. Dead leaves stirred by the wind came to rest in her lap. Idly she picked one up and turned it around in her fingers. Foolishness or purity—something made her the perfect picture of virginity.

A loud cackling came suddenly from behind the shrine. Otsū jumped to the ground.

"Don't move, Otsū!" commanded a hoarse, scary voice.

Otsū gasped and put her hands over her ears.

Several shadowy shapes came from behind the shrine and surrounded her quaking form. Though her eyes were shut, she could clearly see one of them, more frightening and seemingly larger than the others, the white-haired hag she had so often seen in nightmares.

"Thank you, Mambei," said Osugi. "Now gag her before she starts screaming and take her to Shimonoshō. Be quick about it!" She spoke with the fearsome authority of the King of Hell condemning a sinner to the inferno.

The four or five men were apparently village toughs having some connection with Osugi's clan. Shouting their assent, they went at Otsū like wolves fighting over prey and tied her up so that only her legs were free.

"Take the shortcut."

"Move!"

Osugi remained behind to settle with Mambei. As she fished the money from her obi, she said, "Good of you to bring her. I was afraid you might not be able to manage it." Then she added, "Don't say a word to anybody."

With a satisfied look, Mambei tucked the money into his sleeve. "Oh, it wasn't so hard," he said. "Your plan worked just fine."

"Ah, that was something to see. Frightened, wasn't she?"

"She couldn't even run. Just stood there. Ha, ha. But maybe . . . it was rather wicked of us."

"What's wicked about it? If you only knew what I've been through."

"Yes, yes; you told me all about it."

"Well, I can't be wasting time here. I'll see you again one of these days. Come visit us in Shimonoshō."

"Be careful. That path's not easy walking," he called over his shoulder as he started back down the long, dark steps.

Hearing a gasp, Osugi whirled and shouted, "Mambei! Was that you? What's wrong?"

There was no answer.

Osugi ran to the top of the steps. She let out a little cry, then swallowed her breath as she squinted at the shadow standing beside the fallen body and the sword, dripping blood, slanting downward from the shadow's hand.

"Wh-who's there?"

There was no reply.

"Who are you?" Her voice was dry and strained, but the years had not diminished her blustering bravado.

The man's shoulders shook slightly with laughter. "It's me, you old hag."

"Who are you?"

"Don't you recognize me?"

"I never heard your voice before. A robber, I suppose."

"No robber'd bother with an old woman as poor as you."

"But you've been keeping an eye on me, haven't you?"

"I have."

"On me?"

"Why ask twice? I wouldn't come all the way to Mikazuki to kill Mambei. I come to teach you a lesson."

"Ech?" It sounded as though Osugi's windpipe had burst. "You've got the wrong person. Who are you anyway? My name is Osugi. I'm the dowager of the Hon'iden family."

"Oh, how good to hear you say that! It brings back all my hatred. Witch! Have you forgotten Jōtarō?"

"Jō-jō-tarō?"

"In three years, a newborn babe ceases to be a baby and becomes a three-year-old. You're an old tree; I'm a sapling. Sorry to say, you can't treat me like a sniveling brat anymore."

"Surely it can't be true. Are you really Jōtarō?"

"You ought to have to pay for all the grief you've caused my teacher over the years. He avoided you only because you're old and he didn't want to harm you. You took advantage of that, traveling around everywhere, even to Edo, spreading malicious rumors about him and acting as though you had a legitimate reason to take revenge on him. You even went so far as to prevent his appointment to a good post."

Osugi was silent.

"Your spite didn't end there, either. You bedeviled Otsū and tried to injure her. I thought at last you'd given up and retired to Miyamoto. But you're still at it, using that Mambei to carry out some scheme against Otsū."

Still Osugi did not speak.

"Don't you ever tire of hating? It'd be easy to slice you in two, but fortunately for you, I'm no longer the son of a wayward samurai. My father, Aoki Tanzaemon, has returned to Himeji and, since last spring, is serving the House of Ikeda. To avoid bringing dishonor on him, I shall refrain from killing you."

Jōtarō took a couple of steps toward her. Not knowing whether to believe him or not, Osugi moved back and cast about for a way to escape. Thinking she saw one, she bolted toward the path the men had taken. Jōtarō caught up with her in one leap and grabbed her by the neck.

She opened her mouth wide and cried, "What do you think you're doing?" She turned around and drew her sword in the same motion, struck at him and missed.

While dodging, Jōtarō pushed her violently forward. Her head struck hard against the ground.

"So you've learned a thing or two, have you?" she moaned, her face half buried in the grass. She seemed unable to dislodge from her mind the idea that Jōtarō was still a child.

With a growl, he placed his foot on her spine, which seemed very fragile, and pitilessly wrenched her arm around her back.

Dragging her in front of the shrine, he pinned her down with his foot, but couldn't decide what to do with her.

There was Otsū to think about. Where was she? He had come to know of her presence in Shikama largely by accident, though it may have been because their karmas were intertwined. Along with his father's reinstatement, Jōtarō had been given an appointment. It was while he was on one of his errands that he had caught a glimpse through a gap in the fence of a woman who looked like Otsū. Returning to the beach two days ago, he had verified his impression.

While he was grateful to the gods for leading him to Otsū, his long-dormant hatred of Osugi for the way she had persecuted Otsū had been rekindled. If the old woman was not disposed of, it would be impossible for Otsū to live in peace. The temptation was there. But killing her would embroil his father in a dispute with a family of country samurai. They were troublesome people at the best of times; if offended by a daimyō's direct vassal, they were certain to cause trouble.

Finally, he decided the best way was to punish Osugi quickly and then turn his attention to rescuing Otsū.

"I know the place for you," he said. "Come along."

Osugi clung fiercely to the ground, despite his attempts to yank her along. Seizing her by the waist, he carried her under his arm around to the back of the shrine. The hillside had been shaved off when the shrine was built, and there was a small cave there, the entrance to which was just big enough for a person to crawl through.

Otsū could see a single light in the distance. Otherwise, everything was pitch black—mountains, fields, streams, Mikazuki Pass, which they had just crossed by a rocky path. The two men in front were leading her by a rope, as they would a criminal.

When they neared the Sayo River, the man behind her said, "Stop a minute. What do you suppose happened to the old woman? She said she'd be right along."

"Yeah; she should have caught up by now."

"We could stop here a few minutes. Or go on to Sayo and wait at the teahouse. They're probably all in bed, but we could wake them up."

"Let's go there and wait. We can have a cup or two of sake."

They searched along the river for a shallow place and had started to cross when they heard a voice hailing them from a distance. It came again a minute or two later, from much nearer.

"The old woman?"

"No; it sounds like a man's voice."

"It can't have anything to do with us."

The water was as chillingly cold as a sword blade, especially for Otsū. By the time they heard the sound of running feet, their pursuer was almost upon them. With great splashes, he beat them to the other bank and confronted them.

"Otsū?" called Jōtarō.

Shivering from the spray of water that had fallen on them, the three men closed in around Otsū and stood where they were.

"Don't move," shouted Jōtarō, arms outstretched.

"Who are you?"

"Never mind. Release Otsū!"

"You crazy? Don't you know you can get killed meddling in other people's business?"

"Osugi said you're to hand Otsū over to me."

"You're lying through your teeth." All three men laughed.

"I'm not. Look at this." He held out a piece of tissue paper with Osugi's handwriting on it. The message was short: "Things went wrong. There's nothing you can do. Give Otsū to Jōtarō, then come back for me."

The men, brows wrinkled, looked up at Jōtarō and moved onto the bank.

"Can't you read?" taunted Jōtarō.

"Shut up. I suppose you're Jōtarō."

"That's right. My name is Aoki Jōtarō."

Otsū had been staring fixedly at him, trembling slightly from fear and doubt. Now, scarcely knowing what she was doing, she screamed, gasped and stumbled forward.

The man closest to Jōtarō shouted, "Her gag's come loose. Tighten it!" Then menacingly to Jōtarō: "This is the old woman's handwriting, no doubt about it. But what happened to her? What does she mean, 'come back for me'?"

"She's my hostage," Jōtarō said loftily. "You give me Otsū, I tell you where she is."

The three men looked at each other. "Are you trying to be funny?" asked one man. "Do you know who we are? Any samurai in Himeji, if that's where you're from, should be familiar with the House of Hon'iden in Shimonoshō."

"Yes or no—answer! If you don't surrender Otsū, I'll leave the old woman where she is until she starves to death."

"You little bastard!"

One man grabbed Jōtarō and another unsheathed his sword and took a stance. The first growled, "You keep talking nonsense like that and I'll break your neck. Where's Osugi?"

"Will you give me Otsū?"

"No!"

"Then you won't find out. Hand over Otsū, and we can put an end to this without anybody getting hurt."

The man who had grabbed Jōtarō's arm pulled him forward and tried to trip him.

Using his adversary's strength, Jōtarō threw him over his own shoulder. But the next second, he was sitting on his behind, clutching at his right thigh. The man had whipped out his sword and struck in a mowing motion. Fortunately, the wound was not deep. Jōtarō jumped to his feet at the same time as his attacker. The other two men moved in on him.

"Don't kill him. We have to take him alive if we're to get Osugi back."

Jōtarō quickly lost his reluctance to become involved in bloodshed. In the ensuing melee, the three men managed at one point to throw him to the ground. He uttered a roar and used the same tactic that moments before had been used against him. Ripping out his short sword, he jabbed straight through the belly of the man about to fall on him. Jōtarō's hand and arm, halfway up to the shoulder, came away as red as if he'd stuck them into a barrel of plum vinegar, but his head was cleared of everything save the instinct for self-preservation.

On his feet again, he shouted and struck downward at the man in front of him. The blade hit a shoulder bone, and glancing sideways, tore off a slice of meat the size of a fish fillet. Screaming, the man grabbed for his sword, but it was too late.

"Sons of bitches! Sons of bitches!" Shouting with each stroke of his sword, Jōtarō held off the other two, then managed to seriously wound one of them.

They had taken their superiority for granted, but now they lost self-control and started swinging their arms with utter abandon.

Beside herself, Otsū ran around in circles, wriggling her bound hands frantically. "Somebody come! Save him!" But her words were soon lost, drowned by the sound of the river and the voice of the wind.

Suddenly she realized that instead of calling for help, she should be relying on her own strength. With a little cry of desperation, she sank to the ground and began rubbing the rope against the sharp edge of a rock. It was only loosely woven straw rope picked up by the wayside and she was soon able to free herself.

She picked up some rocks and ran straight toward the action. "Jōtarō," she called, as she threw a rock at the face of one man. "I'm here too. It's going to be all right!" Another rock. "Keep it up!" Still another rock, but like the first two, it missed its target. She rushed back to get more.

"That bitch!" In two leaps, one man disengaged himself from Jōtarō and took after Otsū. He was about to bring the blunt edge of his sword down on her back when Jōtarō reached him. Jōtarō drove his sword so deep into the small of the man's back that the blade pointed straight out from the man's navel.

The other man, wounded and dazed, started to slink away, then broke into an unsteady run.

Jōtarō planted his feet firmly on either side of the corpse, withdrew the sword and screamed, "Stop!"

As he started to give chase, Otsū pounced forcefully on him and screamed, "Don't do it! You mustn't attack a badly wounded man when he's fleeing." The fervency of her plea astonished him. He could not imagine what psychological quirk would move her to sympathize with a man who had so recently been tormenting her.

Otsū said, "I want to hear what you've been doing all these years. I have things to tell you too. And we should get out of here as fast as we can."

Jōtarō agreed quickly, knowing that if word of the incident reached Shimonoshō, the Hon'idens would round up the whole village to come after them.

"Can you run, Otsū?"

"Yes. Don't worry about me."

And run they did, on and on through the darkness until their breath gave out. To both, it seemed like the old days when they had been a young girl and a mere boy, making their way together.

At Mikazuki, the only lights visible were at the inn. One shone in the main building, where only a little earlier a group of travelers—a metal merchant whose business took him to the local mines, a thread salesman from Tajima, an itinerant priest—had been sitting around, talking and laughing. They had all drifted off to bed.

Jōtarō and Otsū sat talking by the other light, in a small detached room where the innkeeper's mother lived with her spinning wheel and the pots in which she boiled silkworms. The innkeeper suspected the couple he was taking in were eloping, but he had the room straightened up for them anyway.

Otsū was saying, "So you didn't see Musashi in Edo either." She gave him an account of the last few years.

Saddened to hear that she had not seen Musashi since that day on the Kiso highroad, Jōtarō found it difficult to speak. Yet he thought he was able to offer a ray of hope.

"It's not much to go on," he said, "but I heard a rumor in Himeji that Musashi would be coming there soon."

"To Himeji? Could it be true?" she asked, eager to latch on to even the flimsiest straw.

"It's only what people say, but the men in our fief are talking as though it's already decided. They say he'll pass through on his way to Kokura, where he's promised to meet a challenge from Sasaki Kojirō. That's one of Lord Hosokawa's retainers."

"I heard something like that too, but I couldn't find anybody who had heard from Musashi or even knew where he was."

"Well, the word going around Himeji Castle is probably reliable. It seems the Hanazono Myōshinji in Kyoto, which has close connections with the House of Hosokawa, informed Lord Hosokawa of Musashi's whereabouts, and Nagaoka Sado—he's a senior retainer—delivered the letter of challenge to Musashi."

"Is it supposed to happen soon?"

"I don't know. Nobody seems to know exactly. But if it's to be in Kokura, and if Musashi's in Kyoto, he'll pass through Himeji on the way."

"He might go by boat "

Jōtarō shook his head. "I don't think so. The daimyō at Himeji and Okayama and other fiefs along the Inland Sea will ask him to stop over for a night or so. They want to see what kind of man he really is and sound him out about whether he's interested in a position. Lord Ikeda wrote to Takuan. Then he made inquiries at the Myōshinji and instructed the wholesalers in his area to report if they see anyone answering Musashi's description."

"That's all the more reason to suppose he won't go by land. There's nothing he hates worse than a lot of fuss. If he knows about it, he'll do his best to avoid it." Otsū seemed depressed, as if she'd suddenly lost all hope. "What do you think, Jōtarō?" she asked pleadingly. "If I went to the Myōshinji, do you think I'd be able to find out anything?"

"Well, maybe, but you have to remember it's only gossip."

"But there must be something to it, don't you think?"

"Do you feel like going to Kyoto?"

"Oh, yes. I'd like to leave right away. . . . Well, tomorrow."

"Don't be in such a hurry. That's why you're always missing Musashi. The minute you hear a rumor, you accept it as fact and go flying off. If you want to spot a nightingale, you have to look at a point in front of where its voice comes from. It seems to me you're always trailing along behind Musashi, rather than anticipating where he might be next."

"Well, maybe, but love's not logical." Not having stopped to think of what she was saying, she was surprised to see his face go crimson at the mention of the word "love." Recovering quickly, she said, "Thank you for the advice. I'll think it over."

"Do that, but in the meantime, come back to Himeji with me."

"All right."

"I want you to come to our house."

Otsū was silent.

"From the way my father talks, I guess he knew you fairly well until you left the Shippōji. . . . I don't know what he has in mind, but he said he'd like to see you once more and talk with you."

The candle was threatening to go out. Otsū turned and looked out under the tattered eaves at the sky. "Rain," she said.

"Rain? And we have to walk to Himeji tomorrow."

"What's an autumn shower? We'll wear rain hats."

"I'd like it better if it was fair."

They closed the wooden rain shutters, and the room soon became very warm and humid. Jōtarō was acutely conscious of Otsū's feminine fragrance.

"Go to bed," he said. "I'll sleep over here." Placing a wooden pillow under the window, he lay down on his side, facing the wall.

"Aren't you asleep yet?" grumbled Jōtarō. "You should go to bed." He pulled the thin covers over his head, but tossed and turned awhile longer before falling into a deep slumber.

The Mercy of Kannon

Otsū sat listening to the water dripping from a leak in the roof. Driven by the wind, the rain whipped in under the eaves and splashed against the shutters. But it was autumn, and there was no way of telling: morning might dawn bright and clear.

Then Osugi came into her thoughts. "I wonder if she's out in this storm, all wet and cold. She's old. She might not last till morning. Even if she does, it could be days before she's found. She could die of starvation."

"Jōtarō," she called softly. "Wake up." She was afraid he'd done something cruel, since she'd heard him tell the old woman's henchmen he was punishing her and had casually made a similar remark on the way to the inn.

"She's not really bad at heart." she thought. "If I'm honest with her, one of these days she'll understand me. . . . I must go to her."

Thinking: "If Jōtarō gets angry, it can't be helped," she opened a shutter. Against the blackness of the sky, the rain showed whitely. After tucking up her skirts, she took from the wall a basket hat made out of bamboo bark and tied it on her head. Then she threw a bulky straw rain cape around her shoulders, put on a pair of straw sandals and dashed through the sheet of rain pouring off the roof.

On approaching the shrine where Mambei had taken her, she saw that the stone steps leading up to it had become a many-tiered waterfall. At the top, the wind was much stronger, howling through the cryptomerias like a pack of angry dogs.

"Where can she be?" she thought, as she peered into the shrine. She called into the dark space underneath it, but no answer came.

She went around to the back of the building and stood there for a few minutes. The wailing wind swept over her like breakers on a raging sea. Gradually she became aware of another sound, almost indistinguishable from the storm. It stopped and started again.

"Oh-h-h. Hear me, somebody. . . . Isn't somebody out there? . . . Oh-h-h."

"Granny!" shouted Otsū. "Granny, where are you?" Since she was literally crying into the wind, the sound did not carry far.

But somehow the feeling communicated itself. "Oh! There's someone there. I know it. . . . Save me. Here! Save me!"

In the snatches of sound that reached her ears, Otsū heard the cry of desperation.

918

"Where are you?" she screamed hoarsely. "Granny, where are you?" She ran all the way around the shrine, stopped a moment, then ran around it again. Almost by accident, she noticed what looked like a bear's cave, about twenty paces away, near the bottom of the steep path leading up to the inner shrine.

As she drew closer, she knew for certain the old woman's voice was coming from within. Arriving at the entrance, she stopped and stared at the large rocks blocking it.

"Who is it? Who's there? Are you a manifestation of Kannon? I worship her every day. Have pity on me. Save a poor old woman who's been trapped by a fiend." Osugi's pleas took on a hysterical tone. Half crying, half begging, in the dark interval between life and death, she formed a vision of the compassionate Kannon and hurled toward it her fervent prayer for continued life.

"How happy I am!" she cried deliriously. "Kannon the all-merciful has seen the goodness of my heart and taken pity on me. She's come to rescue me! Great compassion! Great mercy! Hail to the Bodhisattva Kannon, hail to the Bodhisattva Kannon, hail to—"

Her voice broke off abruptly. Perhaps she was thinking that was sufficient, for it was only natural that in her extremity Kannon would come in some form or other to her aid. She was the head of a fine family, a good mother, and believed herself to be an upright and flawless human being. And whatever she did was, of course, morally just.

But then, sensing that whoever was outside the cave was not an apparition but a real, living person, she relaxed, and when she relaxed, she passed out.

Not knowing what the sudden cessation of Osugi's cries meant, Otsū was beside herself. Somehow, the opening to the cave had to be cleared. As she doubled her efforts, the band holding her basket hat came loose, and the hat and her black tresses tossed wildly in the wind.

Wondering how Jōtarō had been able to put the rocks in place by himself, she pushed and pulled with the strength of her whole body, but nothing budged. Exhausted by the effort, she felt a pang of hatred for Jōtarō, and the initial relief she had felt on locating Osugi turned to gnawing anxiety.

"Hold on, Granny. Just a little longer. I'll get you out," she shouted. Though she pressed her lips to a crack in the rocks, she failed to elicit a response.

By and by, she made out a low, feeble chant:

> "Or if, meeting man-eating devils,
> Venomous dragons, and demons,
> He thinks of Kannon's power,
> At once none will dare harm him.
> If, surrounded by vicious beasts,
> With sharp tusks and frightening claws,
> He thinks of Kannon's power . . ."

Osugi was intoning the *Sutra on Kannon*. Only the voice of the bodhisattva was perceptible to her. With her hands clasped together, she was at ease now, tears flowing down her cheeks, lips quivering as the sacred words poured from them.

Struck by an odd feeling, Osugi left off her chanting and put her eye to a crack between the rocks. "Who's there?" she shouted. "I ask you who's there?"

The wind had ripped off Otsū's rain cape. Bewildered, exhausted, covered with mud, she bent down and cried, "Are you all right, Granny? It's Otsū."

"Who did you say?" came the suspicious question.

"I said it's Otsū."

"I see." There was a long, dead pause before the next incredulous question. "What do you mean, you're Otsū?"

It was at this point that the first shock wave hit Osugi, rudely scattering her religious thoughts. "Wh-why have you come here? Oh, I know. You're looking for that devil Jōtarō!"

"No. I've come to rescue you, Granny. Please, forget the past. I remember how good you were to me when I was a little girl. Then you turned against me and tried to hurt me. I don't hold it against you. I admit I was very willful."

"Oh, so your eyes are open now and you can see the evil of your ways. Is that it? Are you saying you'd like to come back to the Hon'iden family as Matahachi's wife?"

"Oh, no, not that," Otsū said quickly.

"Well, why are you here?"

"I felt so sorry for you I couldn't stand it."

"And now you want to put me under obligation to you. That's what you're trying to do, isn't it?"

Otsū was too shocked to say a word.

"Who asked you to come to my rescue? Not me! And I don't need your help now. If you think by doing me a favor you can stop me from hating you, you're mistaken. I don't care how badly off I am; I'd rather die than lose my pride."

"But, Granny, how can you expect me to leave a person your age in a terrible place like this?"

"There you go, talking nice and sweet. Do you think I don't know what you and Jōtarō are up to? You two plotted to put me in this cave to make fun of me, and when I get out, I'm going to get even. You can be sure of that."

"I'm sure the day will come very soon when you'll understand how I really feel. Anyway, you can't stay in there. You'll get sick."

"Hmph. I'm tired of this nonsense."

Otsū stood up, and the obstacle that she had been unable to budge by force was dislodged as if by her tears. After the topmost rock rolled to the ground, she had surprisingly little difficulty rolling the one below it aside.

But it hadn't been Otsū's tears alone that had opened the cave. Osugi had been pushing from inside. She burst forth, her face a fiery red.

Still staggering from the exertion, Otsū uttered a cry of joy, but no sooner was Osugi in the open than she seized Otsū by the collar. From the fierceness of the attack, it looked as though her sole purpose in wanting to stay alive was to attack her benefactor.

"Oh! What are you doing? Ow!"

"Shut up!"

"Wh-wh-why—"

"What did you expect?" cried Osugi, forcing Otsū to the ground with the fury of a wild woman. Otsū was horrified beyond belief.

"Now let's go," snorted Osugi, as she started to drag the girl across the sodden ground.

Clasping her hands together, Otsū said, "Please, please. Punish me if you want, but you mustn't stay out in this rain."

"What idiocy! Have you no shame? Do you think you can make me feel sorry for you?"

"I won't run away. I won't— Oh! That hurts!"

"Of course it hurts."

"Let me—" In a sudden burst of strength, Otsū wrenched herself free and sprang to her feet.

"Oh, no you don't!" Instantly renewing the attack, Osugi clutched a fistful of Otsū's hair. Otsū's white face turned skyward; rain poured down it. She closed her eyes.

"You tramp! How I've suffered all these years because of you!"

Each time Otsū opened her mouth to speak or made an effort to wriggle free, the old woman gave a vicious tug at her hair. Without letting go of it, she threw Otsū to the ground, trampled on her and kicked her.

Then a startled look flashed across Osugi's face and she let go of the hair.

"Oh, what have I done?" she gasped in consternation. "Otsū?" she called anxiously as she looked at the limp form lying at her feet.

"Otsū!" Bending down, she stared intently at the rain-soaked face, as cold to the touch as a dead fish. As far as she could tell, the girl wasn't breathing.

"She's . . . she's dead."

Osugi was aghast. Though unwilling to forgive Otsū, she had not intended to kill her. She straightened up, moaning and backing away.

Gradually she quieted down, and it was not long before she was saying, "Well, I suppose there's nothing to be done but go for help." She started to walk away, hesitated, turned and came back. Taking Otsū's cold body in her arms, she carried it into the cave.

Though the entrance was small, the inside was roomy. Near one wall was a place where, in the distant past, religious pilgrims seeking the Way had sat for long hours in meditation.

When the rain let up, she went to the entrance and was about to crawl out, when the clouds opened again. From the stream sluicing over the mouth, water splashed nearly to the innermost part of the cave.

"It won't be long until morning," she thought. Nonchalantly she squatted and waited for the storm to die down again.

Being in total darkness with Otsū's body slowly began to work on her mind. She had the feeling that the chilly ashen face was staring accusingly at her. At first she reassured herself by saying, "Everything that happens is destined to happen. Take your place in paradise as a newborn Buddha. Don't hold a grudge against me." But before long fear and the sense of her awful responsibility prompted her to seek refuge in piety. Closing her eyes, she began to chant a sutra. Several hours passed.

When at last her lips were silent and she opened her eyes, she could hear birds chirping. The air was still; the rain had stopped. Through the mouth of the cave, a golden sun glared at her, shedding fresh white rays on the rough ground inside.

"What's that, I wonder?" she said aloud as she got to her feet and her eyes fell on an inscription carved by some unknown hand on the wall of the cave.

She stood before it and read: "In the year 1544, I sent my sixteen-year-old son, whose name was Mori Kinsaku, to fight at the battle of Tenjinzan Castle on the side of Lord Uragami. I have never seen him since. Because of my grief, I wander to various places sacred to the Buddha. Now I am placing in this cave an image of the Bodhisattva Kannon. I pray that this, and a mother's tears, will protect Kinsaku in his future life. If in later times anyone should pass here, I beg that he invoke the name of the Buddha. This is the twenty-first year since Kinsaku's death. Donor: The Mother of Kinsaku, Aita Village."

The eroded characters were difficult to read in places. It had been nearly seventy years since the villages nearby—Sanumo, Aita, Katsuta—had been attacked by the Amako family and Lord Uragami had been driven from his castle. One childhood memory that would never be erased from Osugi's memory was the burning of this fortress. She could still see the black smoke billowing up in the sky, the corpses of men and horses littering the fields and byways for days afterward. The fighting had reached almost to the houses of the farmers.

Thinking of the boy's mother, of her sorrow, her wanderings, her prayers and offerings, Osugi felt a stab of pain. "It must have been terrible for her," she said. She knelt and joined her hands together.

"Hail to the Buddha Amida. Hail to the Buddha Amida . . ."

She was sobbing, and tears fell on her hands, but not until she had cried herself out did her mind again become conscious of Otsū's face, cold and insensitive to the morning light, by the side of her knee.

"Forgive me, Otsū. It was wicked of me, terrible! Please forgive me, please." Her face twisted with remorse, she lifted Otsū's body in a gentle embrace. "Frightening . . . frightening. Blinded by motherly love. Out of devotion to my own child, I became a devil to another woman's. You had a mother too. If she had known me, she would have seen me as . . . as a vile demon. . . . I was sure I was right, but to others I'm a vicious monster."

The words seemed to fill the cave and bound back to her own ears. There was no one there, no eyes to watch, no ears to hear. The darkness of night had become the light of the Buddha's wisdom.

"How good you were, Otsū. To be tormented so many long years by this horrible old fool, yet never returning my hatred. To come in spite of everything to try to save me. . . . I see it all now. I misunderstood. All the goodness in your heart I saw as evil. Your kindness I rewarded with hatred. My mind was warped, distorted. Oh, forgive me, Otsū."

922

She pressed her damp face against Otsū's. "If only my son were as sweet and good as you. . . . Open your eyes again, see me begging for forgiveness. Open your mouth, revile me. I deserve it. Otsū . . . forgive me."

While she stared at the face and shed bitter tears, there passed before her eyes a vision of herself as she must have appeared in all those ugly past encounters with Otsū. The realization of how thoroughly wicked she had been gripped at her heart. Over and over she murmured, "Forgive me . . . forgive me." She even wondered if it wouldn't be right to sit there until she joined the girl in death.

"No!" she exclaimed decisively. "No more weeping and moaning. Maybe . . . maybe she's not dead. If I try, maybe I can nurse her back to life. She's still young. Her life is still ahead of her."

Gently she laid Otsū back on the ground and crawled out of the cave into the blinding sunlight. She shut her eyes and cupped her hands to her mouth. "Where is everybody? You people from the village, come here! Help!" Opening her eyes, she ran forward a few steps, still shouting.

There was some movement in the cryptomeria grove, then a shout: "She's here. She's all right after all!"

About ten members of the Hon'iden clan came out of the grove. After hearing the story told by the blood-smeared survivor of the fight with Jōtarō the night before, they had organized a search party and set out immediately, despite the blinding rain. Still wearing their rain capes, they had a bedraggled look about them.

"Ah, you're safe," exulted the first man to reach Osugi. They gathered around her, their faces reflecting their immense relief.

"Don't worry about me," Osugi commanded. "Quick, go and see if you can do something for that girl in the cave. She's been unconscious for hours. If we don't give her some medicine right away . . ." Her voice was thick. Almost in a trance, she pointed toward the cave. Perhaps not since Uncle Gon's death had the tears she'd shed been those of grief.

The Tides of Life

Autumn passed. And winter.

On a day early in the fourth month of 1612, passengers were arranging themselves on the deck of the regular ship from Sakai in Izumi Province to Shimonoseki in Nagato.

Informed the ship was ready to leave, Musashi got up from a bench in Kobayashi Tarōzaemon's shop and bowed to the people who had come to see him off.

"Keep your spirits up," they urged as they joined him for the short walk to the pier.

Hon'ami Kōetsu's face was among those present. His good friend Haiya Shōyū had been unable to come because of illness, but he was represented by his son Shōeki. With Shōeki was his wife, a woman whose dazzling beauty turned heads wherever she went.

"That's Yoshino, isn't it?" a man whispered, tugging at his companion's sleeve.

"From Yanagimachi?"

"Umm. Yoshino Dayū of the Ōgiya."

Shōeki had introduced her to Musashi without mentioning her former name. Her face was unfamiliar to Musashi, of course, for this was the second Yoshino Dayū. Nobody knew what had happened to the first one, where she was now, whether she was married or single. People had long since stopped talking about her great beauty. Flowers bloomed and flowers fell. In the floating world of the licensed quarter, time passed rapidly.

Yoshino Dayū. The name would have evoked memories of snowy nights, of a fire made of peony wood, of a broken lute.

"It's been eight years now since we first met," remarked Kōetsu.

"Yes, eight years," echoed Musashi, wondering where the years could have gone. He had the feeling his boarding the ship today marked the close of one phase of his life.

Matahachi was among the well-wishers, as were several samurai from the Hosokawa residence in Kyoto. Other samurai conveyed best wishes from Lord Karasumaru Mitsuhiro, and there was a group of between twenty and thirty swordsmen who, despite Musashi's protest, had been led by their acquaintance with him in Kyoto to regard themselves as his followers.

He was going to Kokura in the province of Buzen, where he would face Sasaki Kojirō in a test of skill and maturity. Due to the efforts of Nagaoka Sado, the fateful confrontation, so long in the making, was finally to take place. Negotiations had been long and difficult, necessitating the dispatch of many couriers and letters. Even after Sado had ascertained the previous autumn that Musashi was at Hon'ami Kōetsu's house, completion of the arrangements had required another half year.

Though he knew it was coming, Musashi had not in his wildest dreams been able to imagine what it would be like to set forth as the champion of a huge number of followers and admirers. The size of the crowd was an embarrassment. It also made it impossible for him to talk as he would have liked to with certain people.

What struck him most forcefully about this great send-off was its absurdity. He had no desire to be anybody's idol. Still, they were here to express their goodwill. There was no way to stop them.

Some, he felt, understood him. For their good wishes he was grateful; their admiration infused him with a sense of reverence. At the same time, he was being swept up on a wave of that frivolous sentiment called popularity. His reaction was almost one of fear, that the adulation might go to his head. He was, after all, only an ordinary man.

Another thing that upset him was the long prelude. If it could be said that both he and Kojirō saw where their relationship was leading them, it could also be said that the world had pitted them one against the other and decreed that they must decide once and for all who was the better man.

It had started with people saying, "I hear they're going to have it out."

Later, it was: "Yes, they're definitely going to face each other."

Still later: "When is the bout?"

Finally, the very day and hour were being bruited about before the principals themselves had formally decided them.

Musashi resented being a public hero. In view of his exploits, it was inevitable that he would be made one, but he did not seek this. What he really wanted was more time to himself for meditation. He needed to develop harmony, to make sure his ideas did not outpace his ability to act. Through his most recent experience with Gudō, he had advanced a step on the path toward enlightenment. And he had come to sense more keenly the difficulty of following the Way—the long Way through life.

"And yet . . ." he thought. Where would he be if it were not for the goodness of the people who supported him? Would he be alive? Would he have the clothes on his back? He was dressed in a black short-sleeved kimono sewn for him by Kōetsu's mother. His new sandals, the new basket hat in his hand, all the belongings he carried now, had been given to him by someone who valued him. The rice he ate—grown by other people. He lived on the bounties of labor not his own. How could he repay people for all they had done for him?

When his thoughts turned in this direction, his resentment at the demands made on him by his legion of supporters lessened. Nevertheless, the fear of letting them down lingered.

It was time to set sail. There were prayers for a safe voyage, final words of farewell, invisible time already flowing between the men and women on the pier and their departing hero.

The moorings were cast off, the ship drifted toward the open sea, and the great sail spread like wings against the azure sky.

A man ran out to the end of the pier, stopped and stamped his foot in disgust. "Too late!" he growled. "I shouldn't have taken a nap."

Kōetsu approached him and asked, "Aren't you Musō Gonnosuke?"

"Yes," he replied, tucking his staff under his arm.

"I met you once at the Kongōji in Kawachi."

"Yes, of course. You're Hon'ami Kōetsu."

"I'm glad to see you're well. From what I heard, I wasn't sure you were still alive."

"Heard from who?"

"Musashi."

"Musashi?"

"Yes; he was staying with me until yesterday. He had several letters from   925

Kokura. In one, Nagaoka Sado said you'd been taken prisoner on Mount Kudo. He thought you might have been injured or killed."

"It was all a mistake."

"We learned, too, that Iori is living at Sado's house."

"Then he's safe!" he exclaimed, relief flooding his face.

"Yes. Let's sit down somewhere and talk."

He steered the burly staff expert to a nearby shop. Over tea, Gonnosuke told his story. Luckily for him, after one look Sanada Yukimura had come to the conclusion he was not a spy. Gonnosuke was released, and the two men became friendly. Yukimura not only apologized for his subordinates' error, but sent a group of men to search for Iori.

When they failed to find the boy's body, Gonnosuke assumed he was still alive. He had spent his time since then searching the neighboring provinces. When he heard that Musashi was in Kyoto and a bout between him and Kojirō was imminent, he had intensified his efforts. Then, returning to Mount Kudo yesterday, he had learned from Yukimura that Musashi was to sail for Kokura today. He had dreaded facing Musashi without Iori at his side, or any news of him. But not knowing whether he would ever again see his teacher alive, he came anyway. He apologized to Kōetsu as though the latter were a victim of his negligence.

"Don't let it worry you," said Kōetsu. "There'll be another ship in a few days."

"I really wanted to travel with Musashi." He paused, then went on earnestly. "I think this trip may be the decisive point in Musashi's life. He disciplines himself constantly. He isn't likely to lose to Kojirō. Still, in a fight like that, you never know. There's a superhuman element involved. All warriors have to face it; winning or losing is partly a matter of luck."

"I don't think you need to worry. Musashi's composure was perfect. He seemed completely confident."

"I'm sure he did, but Kojirō has a high reputation too. And they say since he went into Lord Tadatoshi's service, he's been practicing and keeping himself fit."

"It'll be a test of strength between a man who's a genius, but really somewhat conceited, and an ordinary man who's polished his talents to the utmost, won't it?"

"I wouldn't call Musashi ordinary."

"But he is. That's what's extraordinary about him. He's not content with relying on whatever natural gifts he may have. Knowing he's ordinary, he's always trying to improve himself. No one appreciates the agonizing effort he's had to make. Now that his years of training have yielded such spectacular results, everybody's talking about his 'god-given talent.' That's how men who don't try very hard comfort themselves."

"Thank you for saying that," said Gonnosuke. He felt Kōetsu might have been referring to him, as well as to Musashi. Looking at the older man's broad, placid profile, he thought: "It's the same with him too."

Kōetsu looked like what he was, a man of leisure who had deliberately set himself apart from the rest of the world. At the moment, his eyes lacked that gleam that emanated from them when he concentrated on artistic creation. Now they were like a smooth sea, calm and unruffled, under a clear, bright sky.

A young man stuck his head in the door and said to Kōetsu, "Shall we go back now?"

"Ah, Matahachi," Kōetsu replied amiably. Turning to Gonnosuke, he said, "I suppose I'll have to leave you. My companions seem to be waiting."

"Are you going back by way of Osaka?"

"Yes. If we get there in time, I'd like to take the evening boat to Kyoto."

"Well, then, I'll walk that far with you." Rather than wait here for the next boat, Gonnosuke had decided to travel overland.

The three of them walked side by side, their talk rarely straying from Musashi, his present status and past exploits. At one point, Matahachi expressed concern, saying, "I hope Musashi wins, but Kojirō's sharp. His technique is terrific, you know." But his voice lacked enthusiasm; the memory of his own encounter with Kojirō was too vivid.

By twilight, they were on the crowded streets of Osaka. Simultaneously Kōetsu and Gonnosuke noticed Matahachi was no longer with them.

"Where could he have gone?" asked Kōetsu.

Retracing their steps, they found him standing by the end of the bridge. He was looking spellbound out over the riverbank, where wives from nearby dwellings, a row of broken-down shacks covered by a single roof, were washing cooking utensils, unhulled rice and vegetables.

"That's an odd expression on his face," said Gonnosuke. He and Kōetsu stood a little apart and watched.

"It is her," cried Matahachi. "Akemi!"

In the first flash of recognition, he was struck by the capriciousness of fate. But immediately it began to seem otherwise. Destiny was not playing tricks— merely confronting him with his past. She had been his common-law wife. Their karmas, too, were entwined. So long as they inhabited the same earth, they were fated to come together again, sooner or later.

He'd had trouble recognizing her. The charm and coquettishness of even two years ago had vanished. Her face was incredibly thin; her hair was unwashed and tied in a bun. She wore a tubular-sleeved cotton kimono reaching slightly below her knees, the utilitarian garment of all lower-class urban housewives. It was a far cry from the colorful silks she had donned as a prostitute.

She was crouching down in the position expected of peddlers and had in her arms a heavy-looking basket, from which she was selling clams, abalone and kelp. The things still left unsold suggested business was not very good.

Tied to her back with a soiled strip of cloth was a baby about a year old.

More than anything else, it was the child that made Matahachi's heart beat faster. Pressing his palms against his cheeks, he counted up the months. If the baby was in its second year, it had been conceived while they were in Edo ... and Akemi had been pregnant when they were publicly whipped.

The light of the evening sun, reflected from the river, danced on Mataha-chi's face, making it seem bathed in tears. He was deaf to the bustle of traffic moving along the street. Akemi was walking slowly down by the river. He started after her, waving his arms and shouting. Kōetsu and Gonnosuke followed.

"Matahachi, where are you going?"

He had forgotten all about the two men. He stopped and waited for them to catch up. "I'm sorry," he mumbled. "To tell the truth . . ." Truth? How could he explain to them what he was going to do when he couldn't explain it to himself? Sorting out his emotions was beyond him at the moment, but finally he blurted out, "I've decided not to be a priest—to return to ordinary life. I haven't been ordained yet."

"Returning to ordinary life?" exclaimed Kōetsu. "So suddenly? Hmm. You look strange."

"I can't explain it now. Even if I did, it'd probably sound crazy. I just saw the woman I used to live with. And she's carrying a baby on her back. I think it must be mine."

"Are you sure?"

"Yes, well . . ."

"Now calm down and think. Is it really your child?"

"Yes! I'm a father! . . . I'm sorry. I didn't know . . . I'm ashamed. I can't let her go through life like that—selling things out of a basket like a common tramp. I've got to go to work and help my child."

Kōetsu and Gonnosuke looked at each other in dismay. Though not quite sure whether Matahachi was still in his right mind, Kōetsu said, "I suppose you know what you're doing."

Matahachi took off the priest's robe covering his ordinary kimono and handed it to Kōetsu, together with his prayer beads. "I'm sorry to trouble you, but will you give these to Gudō at the Myōshinji? I'd appreciate it if you'd tell him I'm going to stay here in Osaka, get a job and be a good father."

"Are you sure you want to do this? Give up the priesthood, just like that?"

"Yes. Anyway, the master told me I could go back to ordinary life anytime I wanted to."

"Hmm."

"He said you don't have to be in a temple to practice religious discipline. It's more difficult, but he said it's more praiseworthy to be able to control yourself and keep your faith in the midst of lies and filth and conflict—all the ugly things in the outside world—than in the clean, pure surroundings of a temple."

"I'm sure he's right."

"I've been with him more than a year now, but he hasn't given me a priestly name. Always just calls me Matahachi. Maybe something'll come up in the future I don't understand. Then I'll go to him immediately. Tell him that for me, won't you?"

And with that, Matahachi was gone.

The Evening Boat

A single red cloud, looking like a great streamer, hung low over the horizon. Near the bottom of the glassy waveless sea was an octopus.

Around noon a small boat had tied up in the estuary of the Shikama River, discreetly out of sight. Now, as twilight deepened, a thin column of smoke rose from a clay brazier on the deck. An old woman was breaking sticks and feeding the fire.

"Are you cold?" she asked.

"No," answered the girl lying in the bottom of the boat behind some red matting. She shook her head weakly, then lifted it and looked at the old woman. "Don't worry about me, Granny. You should be careful yourself. Your voice sounds a bit husky."

Osugi put a pot of rice on the brazier to make gruel. "It's nothing," she said. "But you're sick. You have to eat properly, so you'll feel strong when the boat comes in."

Otsū held back a tear and looked out to sea. There were some boats fishing for octopus and a couple of cargo vessels. The ship from Sakai was nowhere to be seen.

"It's getting late," said Osugi. "They said the ship would be here before evening." There was a hint of complaint in her voice.

News of the departure of Musashi's ship had spread rapidly. When it reached Jōtarō in Himeji, he sent a messenger to tell Osugi. She, in turn, had hurried straight to the Shippōji, where Otsū lay ill, suffering from the effects of the beating the old woman had given her.

Since that night, Osugi had begged forgiveness so often and tearfully that listening to her had come to be rather a burden for Otsū. Otsū did not hold her responsible for her sickness; she thought it was a recurrence of the malady that had kept her confined for several months at Lord Karasumaru's house in Kyoto. In the mornings and evenings, she coughed a lot and had a slight fever. And she lost weight, which made her face more beautiful than ever, but it was an excessively delicate beauty and saddened those who met and talked with her.

Still, her eyes shone. For one thing, she was happy about the change that had come over Osugi. Having finally understood that she had been mistaken about Otsū and Musashi, the Hon'iden dowager was like a woman reborn.

And Otsū had hope, springing from the certainty that the day was near when she would see Musashi again.

Osugi had said, "To atone for all the unhappiness I've caused you, I'm going to get down on my hands and knees and beg Musashi to set things right. I'll bow. I'll apologize. I'll persuade him." After announcing to her own family and the whole village that Matahachi's betrothal to Otsū was nullified, she destroyed the document recording the promise to marry. From then on, she made it her business to tell one and all that the only person who would be a proper and fitting husband for Otsū was Musashi.

Since the village had changed, the person Otsū knew best in Miyamoto was Osugi, who took it upon herself to nurse the girl back to health, calling each morning and evening at the Shippōji with the same solicitous questions: "Have you eaten? Did you take your medicine? How do you feel?"

One day, she said with tears in her eyes, "If you hadn't come back to life that night in the cave, I would have wanted to die there too."

The old woman had never before hesitated to bend the truth or tell outright lies, one of the last of which turned out to be about Ogin's being in Sayo. In fact no one had seen or heard from Ogin for years. All that was known was that she had married and gone to another province.

So at first Otsū found Osugi's protestations unbelievable. Even if she was sincere, it seemed likely her remorse would wear off after a time. But as days turned into weeks, she grew more devoted and more attentive to Otsū.

"I never dreamed she was such a good person at heart," was how Otsū came to think of her. And since Osugi's newfound warmth and kindness extended to everyone around her, this sentiment was widely shared by both the family and the villagers, though many expressed their astonishment less delicately, saying things like, "What do you suppose got into the old hag?"

Even Osugi marveled at how kind everyone was to her now. It used to be that even those people closest to her were inclined to cringe at the very sight of her; now they all smiled and spoke cordially. At last, at an age when simply being alive was something to be thankful for, she was learning for the first time what it was like to be loved and respected by others.

One acquaintance asked frankly, "What happened to you? Your face looks more attractive every time I see you."

"Maybe so," thought Osugi later that same day, looking at herself in her mirror. The past had left its mark. When she went away from the village, there had still been black hair mixed with gray. Now it was all white. She didn't mind, for she believed that her heart, at least, was free of blackness now.

The ship Musashi was on made a regular overnight stop at Shikama to discharge and take on cargo.

Yesterday, after telling Otsū this, Osugi had asked, "What are you going to do?"

"I'm going to be there, of course."

"In that case, I'll go too."

Otsū got up from her sickbed, and they were on their way within the hour. It took them until late afternoon to walk to Himeji; all the while, Osugi hovered over Otsū as though she were a child.

At Aoki Tanzaemon's house that night, plans were laid to hold a congratulatory dinner at Himeji Castle for Musashi. It was assumed that because of his previous experience at the castle, he would now deem it an honor to be feted in this fashion. Even Jōtarō thought so.

It was also decided, in consultation with Tanzaemon's fellow samurai, that it wouldn't do for Otsū to be seen openly with Musashi. People might get the idea she was his secret lover. Tanzaemon told Otsū and Osugi the gist of this and suggested the boat as a way for Otsū to be present but at the same time not be a source of embarrassing gossip.

The sea darkened, and the color faded from the sky. Stars began to twinkle. Near the dyer's house where Otsū lived, a contingent of some twenty samurai from Himeji had been waiting since midafternoon to welcome Musashi.

"Maybe this is the wrong day," remarked one of them.

"No, don't worry," said another. "I sent a man to Kobayashi's local agent to make sure."

"Hey, isn't that it?"

"It looks like the right kind of sail."

Noisily they moved closer to the water's edge.

Jōtarō left them and ran off to the small boat in the estuary.

"Otsū! Granny! The ship's in sight—Musashi's ship!" he shouted to the excited women.

"Did you really see it? Where?" asked Otsū. She nearly fell overboard as she got to her feet.

"Be careful," warned Osugi, grabbing her from behind. They stood side by side, eyes searching the darkness. Gradually a tiny distant spot grew into a large sail, black in the starlight and seemingly gliding right into their eyes.

"That's it," cried Jōtarō.

"Hurry, grab the scull," said Otsū. "Take us out to the ship."

"There's no need to rush. One of the samurai on the beach will row out and get Musashi."

"Then we have to go now! Once he's with that bunch, there won't be a chance for Otsū to talk to him."

"We can't do that. They'll all see her."

"You spend too much time worrying about what other samurai will think. And that's the reason we're stuck away in this little boat. If you ask me, we should have waited at the dyer's house."

"No, you're wrong. You don't realize how people talk. Relax. My father and I'll find a way to bring him here." He stopped to think for a fraction of a minute. "When he gets to shore, he'll go to the dyer's house for a short rest. I'll get to him then and see to it that he comes here to you. Just wait here. I'll be back soon." He rushed off toward the beach.

"Try to get a little rest," said Osugi.

Though Otsū lay down obediently, she seemed to have trouble catching her breath.

"Cough bothering you again?" asked Osugi gently. She knelt and rubbed the girl's back. "Don't worry. Musashi'll be here before long."

"Thank you. I'm all right now." Once her coughing had subsided, she patted and smoothed her hair, trying to make herself a little more presentable.

As time passed and Musashi failed to appear, Osugi grew fidgety. Leaving Otsū in the boat, she went up on the bank.

When she was out of sight, Otsū pushed her pallet and pillow behind some matting, retied her obi and straightened her kimono. The palpitations of her heart seemed in no way different from what she had experienced as a girl of seventeen or eighteen. The red light of the small beacon fire, suspended near the prow, pierced her heart with warmth. Stretching her delicate white arm over the gunwale, she moistened her comb and ran it through her hair again. Then she applied some powder to her cheeks, but so lightly that it was nearly undetectable. After all, she thought, even samurai, when suddenly summoned from a deep sleep into their lordship's presence, would sometimes sneak into a dressing room and cover up their pallor with a little rouge.

What really troubled her was the question of what she would say to him. Fearfully she thought of becoming tongue-tied, as she had when she had seen him at other times. She didn't want to say anything that would upset him, so she had to be particularly careful about that. He was on his way to a bout. The whole country was talking about it.

At this important moment in her life, Otsū did not believe he would lose to Kojirō, yet it was not absolutely certain he would win. Accidents could happen. If she did something wrong today, and if Musashi was killed later, she would regret it for the rest of her life. Nothing would be left for her but to cry herself to death, hoping, like the ancient Chinese emperor, to be joined with her loved one in the next life.

She must say what she had to say, no matter what he himself might say or do. She had mustered the strength to come this far. Now the meeting was near at hand and her pulse raced wildly. With so many things on her mind, the words she wanted to say would not take form.

Osugi had no such problem. She was choosing the words she would use to apologize for misunderstanding and hatred, to unburden her heart and beg forgiveness. As proof of her sincerity, she would see that Otsū's life was entrusted to Musashi.

The darkness was broken only by an occasional reflection from the water. And it was quiet until Jōtarō's running footsteps became audible.

"You've finally come, have you?" said Osugi, who was still standing on the bank. "Where's Musashi?"

"Granny, I'm sorry."

"You're *sorry*? What does that mean?"

"Just listen. I'll explain everything."

"I don't want explanations. Is Musashi coming, or isn't he?"

"He's not coming."

"Not coming?" Her voice was empty and full of disappointment.

Jōtarō, looking very awkward, related what had happened, namely that when a samurai had rowed out to the ship, he was told that it wasn't stopping there. There were no passengers wanting to get off at Shikama; the cargo had been taken off by lighter. The samurai had asked to see Musashi, who came to the side of the ship and talked with the man but said disembarking was out of the question. Both he and the captain wanted to reach Kokura as quickly as possible.

By the time the samurai returned to the beach with this message, the ship was already heading out to the open sea again.

"You can't even see it anymore," said Jōtarō dejectedly. "It's already rounded the pine woods at the other end of the beach. I'm sorry. Nobody's to blame."

"Why didn't you go out in the boat with the samurai?"

"I didn't think. . . . Anyway, there's nothing we can do, no use talking about it now."

"I suppose you're right, but what a shame! What are we going to tell Otsū? You'll have to do it, Jōtarō; I haven't the heart. You can tell her exactly what happened . . . but try to calm her first, or her sickness might get worse."

But there was no need for Jōtarō to explain. Otsū, seated behind a piece of matting, had heard everything. The lapping of the water against the side of the boat seemed to resign her heart to suffering.

"If I missed him tonight," she thought, "I'll see him another day, on another beach."

She thought she understood why Musashi was set against leaving the ship. Throughout western Honshu and Kyushu, Sasaki Kojirō was acknowledged to be the greatest of all swordsmen. In challenging his primacy, Musashi would be burning with determination to win. His mind would be on that—only that.

"To think that he was so near," she sighed. Tears streaming down her cheeks, she gazed after the invisible sail, making its way slowly westward. She leaned disconsolately against the boat rail.

Then, for the first time, she became conscious of an enormous force, swelling up with her tears. Despite her frailness, somewhere deep in her being was a font of superhuman strength. Though she had not realized it, her willpower was indomitable and had enabled her to persevere through the long years of illness and anguish. Fresh blood infused her cheeks, giving them new life.

"Granny! Jōtarō!"

They came down the bank slowly, Jōtarō asking, "What is it, Otsū?"

"I heard you talking."

"Oh?"

"Yes. But I'm not going to cry about it anymore. I'll go to Kokura. I'll see the bout for myself. . . . We can't take it for granted Musashi will win. If he doesn't, I intend to receive his ashes and bring them back with me."

"But you're sick."

"Sick?" She'd pushed the very idea from her mind; she seemed filled with a   933 vitality transcending the weakness of her body. "Don't think about it. I'm perfectly all right. Well, maybe I'm still a little sick, but until I see how the bout turns out—"

"I'm determined not to die" were the words that nearly escaped her lips. She stifled them and busied herself making preparations for her journey. When she was ready, she got out of the boat all by herself, though she had to cling tightly to the rail in order to do so.

A Falcon and a Woman

At the time of the Battle of Sekigahara, Kokura had been the site of a fortress commanded by Lord Mōri Katsunobu of Iki. Since then the castle had been rebuilt and enlarged and acquired a new lord. Its towers and glistening white walls bespoke the great power and dignity of the House of Hosokawa, headed now by Tadatoshi, who had succeeded his father, Tadaoki.

In the short time since Kojirō's arrival, the Ganryū Style, developed on the foundation he had learned from Toda Seigen and Kanemaki Jisai, had swept over all Kyushu. Men even came from Shikoku to study under him, hoping that after a year or two of training they would be awarded a certificate and receive sanction to return home as teachers of this new style.

Kojirō enjoyed the esteem of those around him, including Tadatoshi, who had been heard to remark with satisfaction, "I found myself a very good swordsman." In every quarter of the extensive Hosokawa household, it was agreed that Kojirō was a person of "outstanding character." And when he traveled between his home and the castle, he did so in style, attended by seven lancers. People went out of their way to approach him and pay their respects.

Until his coming, Ujiie Magoshirō, a practitioner of the Shinkage Style, had been the clan's chief sword instructor, but his star dimmed rapidly as Kojirō's grew more brilliant. Kojirō treated him magniloquently. To Lord Tadatoshi, he had said, "You mustn't let Ujiie go. While his style is not flashy, it does have a certain maturity we younger men lack." He suggested that he and Magoshirō give lessons in the castle's dōjō on alternate days, and this was put into practice.

At one point, Tadatoshi said, "Kojirō says Magoshirō's method is not flashy, but mature. Magoshirō says Kojirō is a genius with whom he cannot match swords. Who is right? I'd like to see a demonstration."

The two men agreed to subsequently face each other with wooden swords 934 in his lordship's presence. At the first opportunity, Kojirō discarded his weapon, and seating himself at his opponent's feet, announced, "I'm no match for you. Forgive my presumption."

"Don't be modest," replied Magoshirō. "I'm the one who's not a worthy opponent."

Witnesses were divided as to whether Kojirō acted out of compassion or self-interest. In any case, his reputation rose still higher.

Kojirō's attitude toward Magoshirō remained charitable, but whenever someone made favorable mention of Musashi's growing fame in Edo and Kyoto, he was quick to set him straight.

"Musashi?" he would say with disdain. "Oh, he's been crafty enough to make something of a name for himself. He talks about his Two-Sword Style, I'm told. He's always had a certain natural ability. I doubt whether there's anybody in Kyoto or Osaka who could defeat him." He always made it appear that he was restraining himself from saying more.

An experienced warrior visiting Kojirō's house one day said, "I've never met the man, but people say this Miyamoto Musashi is the greatest swordsman since Kōizumi and Tsukahara, with the exception of Yagyū Sekishūsai, of course. Everybody seems to think that if he's not the greatest swordsman, he's at least reached the level of a master."

Kojirō laughed and the color rose in his face. "Well, people are blind,". he said bitingly. "So I suppose some consider him a great man or an expert swordsman. That just goes to show you how far the Art of War has declined, with regard to both style and personal conduct. We live in an age when a clever publicity seeker can rule the roost, at least as far as ordinary people are concerned.

"Needless to say, I look at it differently. I saw Musashi trying to sell himself in Kyoto some years ago. He gave an exhibition of his brutality and cravenness in his bout with the Yoshioka School at Ichijōji. Cravenness is not a low enough word for the likes of him. All right, so he was outnumbered, but what did he do? He showed his back at the earliest possible moment. Considering his past and his overweening ambition, I see him as a man not worth spitting on. . . . Ha, ha—if a man who spends his life trying to learn the Art of War is an expert, then I suppose Musashi's an expert. But a master of the sword—no, not that."

He obviously took praise of Musashi as a personal affront, but his insistence on winning anyone and everyone over to his point of view was so vehement that even his staunchest admirers began to wonder. Eventually the word got around that there was a long-standing enmity between Musashi and Kojirō. Before long, rumors of a match were flying.

It was at Lord Tadatoshi's order that Kojirō had finally issued a challenge. In the several months since then, the entire Hosokawa fief had buzzed with speculation as to when the fight would be held and how it would turn out.

Iwama Kakubei, now well along in years, called on Kojirō morning and evening, whenever he could find the slightest excuse. On an evening early in the fourth month, when even the pink double-petal cherry blossoms had fallen, Kakubei walked through Kojirō's front garden, past bright red azaleas blooming in the shadows of ornamental rocks. He was shown to an inner room lit only by the failing light of the evening sun.

"Ah, Master Iwama, good to see you," said Kojirō, who was standing just outside, feeding the falcon on his fist.

"I have news for you," said Kakubei, still standing. "The clan council discussed the place for the bout today in his lordship's presence and reached a decision."

"Have a seat," said an attendant from the adjacent room.

With no more than a grunt of thanks, Kakubei sat down and continued: "A number of sites were suggested, among them Kikunonagahama and the bank of the Murasaki River, but they were all rejected because they were too small or too accessible to the public. We could put up bamboo fencing, of course, but even that wouldn't prevent the riverbank from being overrun by swarms of people looking for thrills."

"I see," replied Kojirō, still intently watching the falcon's eyes and beak.

Kakubei, expecting his report to be received more or less with bated breath, was crestfallen. A guest would not normally do such a thing, but Kakubei said, "Come inside. This is nothing to be talking about while you're standing out there."

"In a minute," Kojirō said casually. "I want to finish feeding the bird."

"Is that the falcon Lord Tadatoshi gave you after you went hunting together last fall?"

"Yes. Its name is Amayumi. The more I get used to it, the better I like it." He threw away the rest of the food and, winding up the red-tasseled cord attached to the bird's neck, said to the young attendant behind him, "Here, Tatsunosuke—put it back in its cage."

The bird was passed from fist to fist, and Tatsunosuke started across the spacious garden. Beyond the customary man-made hillock was a grove of pines, bordered on the other side by a fence. The compound lay along the Itatsu River; many other Hosokawa vassals lived in the vicinity.

"Forgive me for making you wait," said Kojirō.

"Think nothing of it. I'm not exactly an outsider. When I come here, it's almost like being at my son's house."

A maid of twenty or so came in and gracefully poured tea. With a glance at the guest, she invited him to have a cup.

Kakubei shook his head admiringly. "It's good to see you, Omitsu. You're always so pretty."

She blushed down to the collar of her kimono. "And you're always making fun of me," she replied before quickly slipping out of the room.

Kakubei said, "You say the more you get used to your falcon, the better you like it. What about Omitsu? Wouldn't it be better to have her at your side, rather than a bird of prey? I've been meaning to ask you about your intentions regarding her."

"Has she by any chance secretly visited your house at one time or another?"

"I'll admit she did come to talk to me."

"Stupid woman! She hasn't said a word about it to me." He shot an angry glance at the white shoji.

"Don't let it upset you. There's no reason why she shouldn't come." He waited until he thought Kojirō's eyes had softened a little, then went on: "It's only natural for a woman to worry. I don't think she doubts your affection for her, but anybody in her position would worry about the future. I mean, what's to become of her?"

"I suppose she told you everything?"

"Why shouldn't she? It's the most ordinary thing in the world to happen between a man and a woman. One of these days you'll want to get married. You have this big house and lots of servants. Why not?"

"Can't you imagine what people would say if I married a girl I'd previously had in my house as a maid?"

"Does it really make any difference? You certainly can't throw her aside now. If she weren't a suitable bride for you, it might be awkward, but she's of good blood, isn't she? I'm told she's the niece of Ono Tadaaki."

"That's correct."

"And you met her when you went to Tadaaki's dōjō and opened his eyes to the sad state his school of swordsmanship was in."

"Yes. I'm not proud of it, but I can't keep it from someone as close to me as you are. I'd planned to tell you the whole story sooner or later. . . . As you say, it happened after my bout with Tadaaki. It was already dark when I started for home, and Omitsu—she was living with her uncle at the time—brought a small lantern and walked down Saikachi Slope with me. Without giving it a thought, I flirted with her a bit along the way, but she took me seriously. After Tadaaki disappeared, she came to see me and—"

Now it was Kakubei's turn to be embarrassed. He waved his hand to let his protégé know he had heard enough. Actually, he had not known until very recently that Kojirō had taken the girl in before leaving Edo for Kokura. He was surprised not only at his own naiveté but also at Kojirō's ability to attract a woman, have an affair with her and keep the whole thing secret.

"Leave everything to me," he said. "At the moment, it would be rather inappropriate for you to announce your marriage. First things first. It can be done after your bout." Like so many others, he was confident that final justification for Kojirō's fame and position would be forthcoming within a few days.

Remembering why he'd come, he went on: "As I said, the council has decided the location for the bout. Since one requirement was that it be within Lord Tadatoshi's domain, but somewhere that crowds can't get to easily, it was agreed that an island would be ideal. The island chosen is a small one called Funashima, between Shimonoseki and Moji."

He looked thoughtful for a minute, then said, "I wonder if it wouldn't be wise to look the terrain over before Musashi arrives. It might give you a certain advantage." His reasoning was that from a knowledge of the lay of the land, a swordsman would have an idea of how the fighting would proceed, how tightly to tie his sandals, how to make use of the terrain and the position of the sun. At the very least, Kojirō would have a sense of security, which would be impossible if he were entering the place for the first time.

He suggested they hire a fishing boat and go out to look at Funashima the next day.

937

Kojirō disagreed. "The whole point of the Art of War is to be quick to seize an opening. Even when a man takes precautions, it often happens that his opponent will have anticipated them and devised means of offsetting them. It's much better to approach the situation with an open mind and move with perfect freedom."

Seeing the logic of this argument, Kakubei made no more mention of going to Funashima.

Summoned by Kojirō, Omitsu served them sake, and the two men drank and chatted until late in the evening. From the relaxed way in which Kakubei sipped his sake, it was evident that he was pleased with life and felt that his efforts to assist Kojirō had been rewarded.

Rather like a proud father, he said, "I think it's all right to tell Omitsu. When this is over, we can invite her relatives and friends here for the marriage ceremony. It's a fine thing for you to be devoted to your sword, but you must also have a family if your name is to be carried on. When you're married, I'll feel I've done my duty by you."

Unlike the happy old retainer with many years of service, Kojirō showed no signs of drunkenness. But then he was prone to silence these days anyway. Once the bout had been decided on, Kakubei had suggested and Tadatoshi had agreed to release Kojirō from his duties. He had enjoyed the unaccustomed leisure at first, but as the day approached and more and more people came to call, he found himself forced to entertain them. Recently, times when he could rest had become few. Still, he was reluctant to shut himself away and have people turned back at the gate. If he did that, people would think he'd lost his composure.

The idea that came to him was to go out into the country every day, his falcon on his fist. In nice weather, hiking over field and mountain with only the bird for a companion did his spirit good.

When the falcon's alert azure eyes spotted a victim in the sky, Kojirō would release it. Then his own eyes, equally alert, would follow it as it rose and swooped down on its quarry. Until the feathers began to drift to earth, he remained breathless, transfixed, as though he himself were the falcon.

"Good! That's the way!" he exclaimed when the falcon made the kill. He had learned much from this bird of prey, and as a result of these hunting excursions, his face showed more confidence with the passage of each day.

Returning home in the evening, he was met by Omitsu's eyes, swollen from crying. It hurt him to observe her efforts to disguise this. To him, losing to Musashi was inconceivable. Nevertheless, the question of what would happen to her if he was killed crept into his mind.

So did the image of his dead mother, to whom he had given scarcely a thought for years. And each night as he was falling asleep, a vision of the falcon's azure eyes and the swollen eyes of Omitsu came to visit him, jumbled in an odd way with a fleeting memory of his mother's face.

Before the Thirteenth Day

Shimonoseki, Moji, the castle town of Kokura—during the past several days many travelers had come but few had left. The inns were all full, and horses were lined up side by side at the hitching posts outside.

The command issued by the castle said:

> On the thirteenth day of this month, at eight o'clock in the morning, on Funashima in the Nagato Straits of Buzen, Sasaki Kojirō Ganryū, a samurai of this fief, will at his lordship's bidding fight a bout with Miyamoto Musashi Masana, a rōnin from the province of Mimasaka.
>
> It is strictly forbidden for supporters of either swordsman to go to his aid or set forth on the water between the mainland and Funashima. Until ten o'clock on the morning of the thirteenth, no sightseeing vessels, passenger ships and fishing boats will be permitted to enter the straits. Fourth month [1612].

The announcement was posted conspicuously on bulletin boards at all major intersections, piers and gathering places.

"The thirteenth? That's the day after tomorrow, isn't it?"

"People from all over will want to see the bout, so they can go home and talk about it."

"Of course they will, but how's anybody going to see a fight taking place on an island two miles from shore?"

"Well, if you go to the top of Mount Kazashi, you can see the pine trees on Funashima. People'll come anyway, just to gawk at the boats and crowds in Buzen and Nagato."

"I hope the weather stays good."

Because of the restriction of shipping activities, boatmen who might otherwise have been turning a tidy profit were doing poorly. Travelers and townsmen, however, took it in their stride, busily searching out vantage points from which they might catch a glimpse of the excitement on Funashima.

About noon on the eleventh, a woman giving breast to her baby was pacing back and forth in front of a "one-tray" eatery where the road from Moji entered Kokura.

The baby, tired from traveling, would not stop crying. "Sleepy? Take a little nap now. There, there. Sleep, sleep." Akemi patted her foot rhythmically on the ground. She wore no makeup. With a baby to nurse, her life had changed considerably, but there was nothing in her present circumstances that she regretted.

939

Matahachi came out of the shop, wearing a sleeveless kimono of subdued color. The only hint of the days when he had aspired to becoming a priest was the bandanna on his head, hiding the once shaven head.

"Oh, my, what's this?" he said. "Still crying? You should be sleeping. Go on, Akemi. I'll take him while you eat. Eat a lot, so you'll have plenty of milk." Taking the child in his arms, he began crooning a soft lullaby.

"Well, this is a surprise!" came a voice from behind him.

"Huh?" Matahachi stared at the man, unable to place him.

"I'm Ichinomiya Gempachi. We met several years ago at the pine forest near Gojō Avenue in Kyoto. I guess you don't remember me." When Matahachi continued to stare blankly at him, Gempachi said, "You were going around calling yourself Sasaki Kojirō."

"Oh!" Matahachi gasped loudly. "The monk with the staff . . ."

"That's right. Good to see you again."

Matahachi hastened to bow, which awakened the baby. "Now, let's not start crying again," he pleaded.

"I wonder," said Gempachi, "if you could tell me where Kojirō's house is. I understand he lives here in Kokura."

"Sorry, I have no idea. I just got here myself."

Two samurais' attendants emerged from the shop, and one said to Gempachi, "If you're looking for Kojirō's house, it's right by the Itatsu River. We'll show you the way, if you like."

"Very kind of you. Good-bye, Matahachi. See you again." The samurai walked off, and Gempachi fell in step with them.

Matahachi, noticing the dirt and grime clinging to the man's clothes, thought: "I wonder if he's come all the way from Kōzuke." He was deeply impressed that news of the bout had spread to such faraway places. Then the memory of the encounter with Gempachi flowed through his mind, and he shuddered. How worthless, how shallow, how shameless he'd been in those days! To think he had actually been brazen enough to try to pass off the certificate from the Chūjō School as his own, to impersonate . . . Still, that he could see how churlish he had been was a hopeful sign. At least he'd changed since then. "I suppose," he thought, "even a stupid fool like me can improve if he stays awake and tries."

Hearing the baby crying again, Akemi bolted her meal and rushed outdoors. "Sorry," she said. "I'll take him now."

Having placed the baby on Akemi's back, Matahachi hung a candy peddler's box from his shoulder and prepared to forge on. A number of passersby looked enviously at this poor, but apparently happy, couple.

An elderly, genteel-looking woman approached and said, "What a lovely baby! How old is he? Oh, look, he's laughing." As if on command, the man-servant accompanying her stooped and peered at the baby's face.

They all walked together for a way. Then, as Matahachi and Akemi started to turn into a side street to look for an inn, the woman said, "Oh, are you going that way?" She bade them good-bye, and almost as an afterthought, asked, "You seem to be travelers, too, but would you happen to know where Sasaki Kojirō's house is?"

Matahachi imparted the information he had just heard from the two atten-dants. As he watched her go off, he mumbled gloomily, "I wonder what my mother's doing these days." Now that he had a child of his own, he had begun to appreciate her feelings.

"Come on, let's go," said Akemi.

Matahachi stood and stared vacantly at the old woman. She was about the same age as Osugi.

Kojirō's house was full of guests.

"It's a great opportunity for him."

"Yes, this'll make his reputation, once and for all."

"He'll be known everywhere."

"True enough, but we mustn't forget who his opponent is. Ganryū will have to be very careful."

Many had arrived the previous night, and callers spilled out into the great entrance hall, the side entrances, the outside corridors. Some hailed from Kyoto or Osaka, others from western Honshu, one from the village of Jōkyōji in distant Echizen. Since there weren't enough servants in the household, Ka-kubei had sent some of his to help out. Samurai who were studying under Kojirō came and went, their faces eager with anticipation.

All these friends, all these disciples, had one thing in common: whether they knew Musashi or not, he was the enemy. Particularly virulent in their hatred were the provincial samurai who had at one time or another studied the methods of the Yoshioka School. The humiliation of the defeat at Ichijōji gnawed at their minds and hearts. Moreover, the single-minded determina-tion with which Musashi had pursued his career was such that he had made himself many enemies. Kojirō's students despised him as a matter of course.

A young samurai led a recent arrival from the entrance hall into the crowd-ed parlor and announced, "This man has made the trip from Kōzuke."

The man said, "My name is Ichinomiya Gempachi," and modestly took his place among them.

A murmur of admiration and respect went around the room, for Kōzuke lay a thousand miles to the northeast. Gempachi asked that a talisman he had brought from Mount Hakuun be placed on the household altar, and there were more murmurs of approval.

"The weather will be good on the thirteenth," remarked one man, glancing out under the eaves at the flaming evening sun. "Today's the eleventh, tomor-row the twelfth, the next day . . ."

Addressing Gempachi, one guest said, "I think your coming so far to say a prayer for Kojirō's success is quite remarkable. Do you have some connection with him?"

"I'm a retainer of the House of Kusanagi in Shimonida. My late master, Kusanagi Tenki, was the nephew of Kanemaki Jisai. Tenki knew Kojirō when Kojirō was still a young boy."

"I'd heard Kojirō studied under Jisai."

"That's true. Kojirō came from the same school as Itō Ittōsai. I've heard Ittō-sai say many times that Kojirō was a brilliant fighter." He went on to recount how Kojirō had chosen to reject Jisai's certificate and create a style of his own. He told, too, of how tenacious Kojirō had been, even as a child. Meeting eager questions with detailed answers, Gempachi talked on and on.

"Isn't Ganryū *Sensei* here?" asked a young attendant, picking his way through the crowd. Not seeing him, he went from room to room. He was grumbling to himself by the time he came upon Omitsu, who was cleaning Kojirō's room. "If you're looking for the master," she said, "you'll find him at the falcon cage."

Kojirō was inside the cage, looking intently into Amayumi's eyes. He had fed the bird, brushed off loose feathers, held it for a time on his fist and was now patting it affectionately.

"*Sensei.*"

"Yes?"

"There's a woman who says she's come from Iwakuni to visit you. She said you'd know her when you see her."

"Hmm. It may be my mother's younger sister."

"Which room should I show her to?"

"I don't want to see her. I don't want to see anybody. . . . Oh, I suppose I have to. She is my aunt. Take her to my room."

The man left and Kojirō called out the door, "Tatsunosuke."

"Yes, sir." Tatsunosuke came inside the cage and knelt on one knee behind Kojirō. A student who lived at his house, he was seldom far from his master's side.

"Not long to wait now, is there?" said Kojirō.

"No, sir."

"Tomorrow I'll go to the castle and pay my respects to Lord Tadatoshi. I haven't seen him recently. After that, I want to spend a quiet night."

"There are all those guests. Why don't you refuse to see them, so you can have a good rest?"

"That's what I intend to do."

"There are so many people around here, you could be defeated by your own supporters."

"Don't talk like that. They've come from near and far. . . . Whether I win or not depends on what happens at the appointed time. It's not entirely a matter of fate, but then again . . . That's the way with warriors—sometimes win, sometimes lose. If Ganryū dies, you'll find two last testaments in my writing cabinet. Give one of them to Kakubei and the other to Omitsu."

"You've written a will?"

"Yes. It's only proper for a samurai to take that precaution. One other thing. On the day of the fight, I'm allowed one attendant. I want you to go with me. Will you come?"

"It's an honor I don't deserve."

"Amayumi too." He looked at the falcon. "It'll be a comfort to me on the boat trip."

"I understand perfectly."

"Good. I'll see my aunt now."

He found her sitting in his room. Outside, the evening clouds had blackened, like newly forged steel that has just cooled off. The white light of a candle brightened the room.

"Thank you for coming," he said as he seated himself with a great show of reverence. After his mother's death, his aunt had reared him. Unlike his mother, she had not spoiled him in the least. Conscious of her duty to her elder sister, she had striven single-mindedly to make him a worthy successor to the Sasaki name and an outstanding man in his own right. Of all his kinsmen, she was the one who had paid closest attention to his career and his future.

"Kojirō," she began solemnly, "I understand you're about to face one of the decisive moments of your life. Everybody back home is talking about it, and I felt I had to see you, one more time at least. I'm happy to see you've come as far as you have." She was silently comparing the dignified, well-to-do samurai in front of her with the youth who had left home with nothing but a sword.

Head still lowered, Kojirō replied, "It's been ten years. I hope you'll forgive me for not keeping in touch with you. I don't know whether people consider me a success or not, but I have by no means achieved all I am determined to achieve. That's why I haven't written."

"It doesn't matter. I hear news of you all the time."

"Even in Iwakuni?"

"Oh, indeed. Everyone there is for you. If you were to lose to Musashi, the whole Sasaki family—the whole province—would be disgraced. Lord Katayama Hisayasu of Hōki, who's staying as a guest in the Kikkawa fief, is planning to bring a large group of Iwakuni samurai to see the bout."

"Is he?"

"Yes. They'll be terribly disappointed, I suppose, since no boats will be allowed out. . . . Oh, I'm forgetting. Here, I brought this for you." She opened a small bundle and took out a folded underrobe. It was made of white cotton; on it were written the names of the god of war and a protective goddess worshiped by warriors. A Sanskrit good-luck charm had been embroidered on both sleeves by a hundred of Kojirō's female supporters.

He thanked her and reverently held the garment up before his forehead. Then he said, "You must be tired from your trip. You can stay here in this room and go to bed whenever you wish. Now, if you'll excuse me."

He left her and went to sit in another room, to which guests soon came offering him a variety of gifts—a sacred charm from the Hachiman Shrine on Mount Otoko, a coat of mail, an enormous sea bream, a barrel of sake. Before long, there was hardly a place to sit down.

While these well-wishers were sincere in their prayers for his victory, it was also true that eight out of ten of them, not doubting that he would win, were currying favor in the hope of advancing their own ambitions later on.

"What if I were a rōnin?" thought Kojirō. Though the sycophancy depressed him, he took satisfaction from the fact that it was he and no one else who had caused his supporters to trust him and believe in him.

"I must win. I must, I must."

Thinking of winning placed a psychological burden on him. He realized 943 this but could not help himself. "Win, win, win." Like a wind-driven wave, the word kept on repeating itself somewhere in his mind. Not even Kojirō was able to grasp why the primitive urge to conquer buffeted his brain with such persistence.

The night wore on, but quite a number of guests stayed up, drinking and talking. It was quite late when the word came.

"Musashi arrived today. He was seen getting off a boat in Moji and later walking down a street in Kokura."

The response was electric, though uttered furtively, in excited whispers.

"It stands to reason."

"Shouldn't some of us go over there and take a look around?"

At Daybreak

Musashi arrived in Shimonoseki several days early. Since he knew no one there, and no one knew him, he passed his time quietly, unbothered by sycophants and busybodies.

On the morning of the eleventh, he crossed the Kammon Strait to Moji to call on Nagaoka Sado and confirm his acceptance of the time and place of the bout.

A samurai received him at the entrance hall, staring unabashedly, one thought going through his mind: "So this is the famous Miyamoto Musashi!" All the young man said aloud, however, was: "My master is still at the castle but should be back shortly. Please come in and wait."

"No, thank you; I have no other business with him. If you'd just be so kind as to give him my message . . ."

"But you've come so far. He'll be very disappointed to have missed you. If you really have to go, please let me at least tell the others that you're here."

He'd hardly disappeared into the house when Iori came rushing out and into Musashi's arms.

"Sensei!"

Musashi patted him on the head. "Have you been studying, like a good boy?"

"Yes, sir."

"You've grown so tall!"

"Did you know I was here?"

"Yes; Sado told me in a letter. I also heard about you at Kobayashi Tarōzaemon's in Sakai. I'm glad you're here. Living in a house like this will be good for you."

Looking disappointed, Iori said nothing.

"What's the matter?" asked Musashi. "You mustn't forget that Sado's been very good to you."

"Yes, sir."

"You have to do more than just practice martial arts, you know. You have to learn from books. And although you should be the first to help when help is needed, you should try to be more modest than the other boys."

"Yes, sir."

"And don't fall into the trap of feeling sorry for yourself. Many boys like you, who've lost a father or mother, do that. You can't repay the warmheartedness of others unless you're warm and kind in return."

"Yes, sir."

"You're bright, Iori, but be careful. Don't let your rough upbringing get the best of you. Keep yourself under tight rein. You're still a child; you have a long life ahead of you. Guard it carefully. Save it until you can give it for a really good cause—for your country, your honor, the Way of the Samurai. Hold on to your life and make it honest and brave."

Iori had the sinking feeling that this was a parting, a final farewell. His intuition probably would have told him this even if Musashi hadn't spoken of such serious matters, but the mention of the word "life" left little doubt. No sooner had Musashi said it than Iori's head was buried in his chest. The child sobbed uncontrollably.

Musashi, noting that Iori was very well groomed—his hair nicely combed and tied and his white socks immaculate—now regretted his sermon. "Don't cry," he said.

"But what if you . . . "

"Stop your bawling. People will see you."

"You . . . you're going to Funashima the day after tomorrow?"

"Yes, I have to."

"Win, please win. I can't bear to think of not seeing you again."

"Ha, ha. You're crying about that?"

"Some people say you can't beat Kojirō—you shouldn't have agreed to fight him in the first place."

"I'm not surprised. People always talk like that."

"You can win, though, can't you, *Sensei?*"

"I wouldn't even waste my time thinking about it."

"You mean you're sure you won't lose?"

"Even if I do lose, I promise to do it bravely."

"But if you think you might, couldn't you just go away somewhere for a while?"

"There's always a germ of truth in the worst of gossip, Iori. I may have made a mistake, but now that it's gone this far, to run away would be to forsake the Way of the Samurai. That would bring dishonor not only on me but on many others as well."

"But didn't you say I should hang on to my life and guard it carefully?"

"Yes, I did, and if they bury me on Funashima, let that be a lesson to you and avoid getting into fights that may end in your throwing your life away." 945

Sensing that he was overdoing it, he changed the subject. "I've already asked that my respects be conveyed to Nagaoka Sado. I want you to convey them too, and tell him that I'll see him on Funashima."

Musashi gently shook himself free of the boy. As he walked toward the gate, Iori clung to the basket hat in his hand. "Don't . . . Wait . . . " was all he could say. He put his other hand to his face. His shoulders were shaking.

Nuinosuke came through a door beside the gate and introduced himself to Musashi. "Iori seems reluctant to let you go, and I'm inclined to sympathize with him. I'm sure you have other things to do, but couldn't you just stay over here one night?"

Musashi, returning his bow, said, "It's good of you to ask, but I don't think I should. In a couple of days I may be asleep for good. I don't think it'd be right for me to burden others now. It might prove to be an embarrassment later on."

"That's very considerate of you, but I'm afraid the master will be furious with us for letting you go."

"I'll send him a note explaining everything. I only came today to pay my respects. I think I should be leaving now."

Outside the gate, he turned toward the beach, but before he'd got halfway there, he heard voices calling from behind. Looking back, he saw a handful of elderly-looking samurai from the House of Hosokawa, two of whom had gray hair. Not recognizing any of them, he assumed they were shouting to someone else and walked on.

Upon reaching the shore, he stood and gazed out over the water. A number of fishing boats rested at anchor in the offing, their furled sails ashen in the misty light of early evening. Beyond the larger mass of Hikojima, the outline of Funashima was barely visible.

"Musashi!"

"You are Miyamoto Musashi, aren't you?"

Musashi turned to face them, wondering what business these aged warriors could have with him.

"You don't remember us, do you? Didn't think you would. It's been too long. My name's Utsumi Magobeinojō. All six of us are from Mimasaka. We used to be in the service of the House of Shimmen at Takeyama Castle."

"And I'm Koyama Handayū. Magobeinojō and I were close friends of your father's."

Musashi smiled broadly. "Well, this is a surprise!" Their drawl, unmistakably that of his native village, stirred up many childhood memories. After bowing to each of them, he said, "It's good to see you. But tell me, how does it happen you're all here together, so far from home?"

"Well, as you know, the House of Shimmen was disbanded after the Battle of Sekigahara. We became rōnin and fled to Kyushu, came here to Buzen Province. For a while, to keep body and soul together, we wove straw horseshoes. Later, we had a stroke of good luck."

"Is that so? Well, I must say, I never expected to meet friends of my father's in Kokura."

"It's an unexpected pleasure for us too. You're a fine-looking samurai, Musashi. Too bad your father isn't here to see you now."

For a few minutes they commented to one another on Musashi's fine appearance. Then Magobeinojō said, "Stupid of me; I'm forgetting what we came after you for. We just missed you at Sado's house. Our plan was to spend an evening with you. It's all been arranged with Sado."

Handayū chimed in, "That's right. It was very rude of you to come as far as the front door and leave without seeing Sado; you're the son of Shimmen Munisai. You should know better. Now come back with us." Apparently he felt that having been a friend of Musashi's father authorized him to issue orders to the son. Without waiting for an answer, he started walking away, expecting Musashi to follow.

Musashi, on the point of accompanying them, stopped himself.

"I'm sorry," he said. "I don't think I should go. I apologize for being so rude, but I think it'd be wrong for me to join you."

Everyone came to a halt, and Magobeinojō said, "Wrong? What's wrong about it? We want to give you a proper welcome—same village and all that, you know."

"Sado's looking forward to it too. You don't want to offend him, do you?"

Magobeinojō, sounding resentful, added, "What's the matter? Angry about something?"

"I'd like to go," Musashi said politely, "but there are other things to consider. Though it's probably just a rumor, I've heard that my bout with Kojirō is a source of friction between the two oldest retainers in the House of Hosokawa, Nagaoka Sado and Iwama Kakubei. They say Iwama's side has the approval of Lord Tadatoshi, and Nagaoka is trying to strengthen his own faction by opposing Kojirō."

This was met with murmurs of surprise.

"I feel sure," Musashi continued, "that it's no more than idle speculation, but still, public talk is a dangerous thing. What happens to a rōnin like myself doesn't matter much, but I wouldn't want to do anything to fan the rumors and raise suspicions about either Sado or Kakubei. They're both valuable men in the fief."

"I see," said Magobeinojō.

Musashi smiled. "Well, at least that's my excuse. To tell the truth, being a country boy, it's difficult for me to have to sit around and be polite all evening. I'd just like to relax."

Impressed with Musashi's consideration for others but still reluctant to part with him, they put their heads together and discussed the situation.

"This is the eleventh day of the fourth month," said Handayū. "For the past ten years, the six of us have been getting together on this date. We have an ironclad rule against inviting outsiders, but you're from the same village, you're Munisai's son, so we'd like to ask you to join us. It may not be the sort of entertainment we should provide, but you won't have to worry about having to be polite, or being seen or talked about."

"If you put it that way," said Musashi, "I don't see how I can refuse."

947

The answer pleased the old samurai immensely. After another short huddle, it was arranged that Musashi would meet one of them, a man named Kinami Kagashirō, a couple of hours later in front of a tea shop, and they went their separate ways.

Musashi met Kagashirō at the appointed hour, and they walked about a mile and a half from the center of town to a place near Itatsu Bridge. Musashi saw no samurai houses or restaurants, nothing but the lights of a solitary drinking shop and a cheap inn, both some distance away. Ever on the alert, he began turning possibilities over in his mind. There was nothing suspicious about their story; they looked the right age and their dialect fit in with their story. But why an out-of-the-way place like this?

Kagashirō left him and went toward the riverbank. Then he called Musashi, saying, "They're all here. Come on down," and led the way along the narrow path on the dike.

"Maybe the party's on a boat," thought Musashi, smiling at his own excessive cautiousness. But there was no boat. He found them sitting on reed mats in formal style.

"Forgive us for bringing you to a place like this," said Magobeinojō. "This is where we hold our meeting. We feel some special good fortune has brought you to be with us. Sit down and rest awhile." His manner grave enough to be welcoming an honored guest into a fine parlor with silver-covered shoji, he pushed a strip of matting forward for Musashi.

Musashi wondered if this was their idea of elegant restraint or if there was some particular reason for not meeting in a more public place. But as a guest, he felt constrained to act as one. Bowing, he seated himself formally on the mat.

"Make yourself comfortable," urged Magobeinojō. "We'll have a little party later, but first we have to perform our ceremony. It won't take long."

The six men rearranged themselves more informally, each man taking a sheaf of the straw they'd brought with them, and they proceeded to weave straw horseshoes. Mouths tightly closed, eyes never leaving their work, they appeared solemn, even pious. Musashi watched respectfully, sensing strength and fervor in their movements as they spat on their hands, ran the straw through their fingers and plaited it between their palms.

"I guess this'll do," said Handayū, laying down a finished pair of horseshoes and looking around at the others.

"I'm finished too."

They placed their horseshoes in front of Handayū, brushed themselves off and straightened their clothes. Handayū piled the horseshoes on a small table in the middle of the circle of samurai, and Magobeinojō, the oldest, stood up.

"It's now the twelfth year since the Battle of Sekigahara, since that day of defeat that will never be erased from our memories," he began. "We've all lived longer than we had any right to expect. This we owe to the protection and bounty of Lord Hosokawa. We must see that our sons and grandsons remember his lordship's goodness to us."

Murmurs of assent went around the group. They sat in a reverent attitude, their eyes lowered.

"We must also remember forever the largesse of successive heads of the House of Shimmen, even though that great house no longer exists. Nor should we ever forget the misery and hopelessness that were ours when we came here. It is to remind us of these three things that we hold this meeting each year. Now let us pray as one man for one another's health and welfare."

In chorus, the men replied, "The goodness of Lord Hosokawa, the largesse of the House of Shimmen, the bounty of heaven that has delivered us from distress—we will not forget for a day."

"Now make the obeisance," said Magobeinojō.

They turned toward the white walls of Kokura Castle, seen dimly against the dark sky, and bowed to the ground. Then they turned in the direction of Mimasaka Province and bowed again. Finally, they faced the horseshoes and bowed a third time. Each movement was carried out with the utmost gravity and sincerity.

To Musashi, Magobeinojō said, "Now we're going to the shrine above here and make an offering of the horseshoes. After that we can get on with the party. If you'll just wait here."

The man who led the way carried the table with the horseshoes at forehead level, the others following single file. They tied their handiwork to the branches of a tree beside the shrine entrance. Then, after clapping their hands once before the deity, they rejoined Musashi.

The fare was simple—a stew with taros, bamboo shoots with bean paste, and dried fish—the sort of meal served in local farmhouses. But there was much sake, and much laughter and talk.

When the mood became convivial, Musashi said, "It's a great honor to be asked to join you, but I've been wondering about your little ceremony. It must have some very special meaning for you."

"It does," said Magobeinojō. "When we came here as defeated warriors, we had no one to turn to. We would rather have died than steal, but we had to eat. Finally, we hit on the idea of setting up shop over there by the bridge and making horseshoes. Our hands were calloused from training with lances, so it took some effort to teach them to weave straw. We did that for three years, selling our work to passing grooms and somehow making enough to stay alive.

"The grooms came to suspect that weaving straw wasn't our usual occupation, and eventually someone told Lord Hosokawa Sansai about us. Learning we were former vassals of Lord Shimmen, he sent a man to offer us positions."

He told how Lord Sansai had offered a collective stipend of five thousand bushels, which they refused. They were willing to serve him in good faith, but they felt the lord-to-vassal relationship should be on a man-to-man basis. Sansai understood their feelings and came back with an offer of individual stipends. He had also been understanding when his retainers expressed fears that the six rōnin would not be able to attire themselves in a suitable manner to be presented to his lordship. But when a special allowance for clothes was suggested, Sansai said no, it would only cause embarrassment. Actually the fears were unwarranted, for as low as they had sunk, they were still able to dress in starched clothes and wear their two swords when they went to receive their appointments.

"It wouldn't have been difficult to forget how hard our lives were doing menial work. If we hadn't stuck together, we wouldn't have been alive for Lord Sansai to engage us. We mustn't let ourselves forget that providence took care of us during those difficult years."

Ending his recital, he held up a cup, saying, "Forgive me for talking so long about us. I just wanted you to know we're men of goodwill, even if our sake's not first class and the food not very plentiful. We want you to put up a brave fight the day after tomorrow. If you lose, we'll bury your bones for you, don't worry."

Accepting the cup, Musashi replied, "I'm honored to be here among you. It's better than drinking the very best sake in the finest mansion. I only hope I'll be as lucky as you've been."

"Don't hope that! You'll have to learn to weave horseshoes."

The sound of sliding dirt cut short their laughter. Their eyes went to the dike, where they saw the crouching batlike figure of a man.

"Who's there?" cried Kagashirō, on his feet at once. Another man rose, drawing his sword, and the two climbed the dike and peered through the mist.

Laughing, Kagashirō called down, "It seems to have been one of Kojirō's followers. He probably thinks we're Musashi's seconds and we're having a secret strategy session. He got away before we got a good look at him."

"I can see Kojirō's supporters doing that," remarked one man.

The atmosphere remained lighthearted, but Musashi decided not to linger any longer. The last thing he wanted was to do anything that might bring harm to these men later. He thanked them profusely for their kindness and left them to their party, walking casually into the darkness.

At least, he seemed casual.

Nagaoka's cold wrath for letting Musashi leave his house fell on several people, but he waited until the morning of the twelfth to dispatch men to look for him.

When the men reported they couldn't find Musashi—had no idea where he was—Sado's white eyebrows shot up anxiously. "What could have happened to him? Is it possible—" He did not want to finish the thought.

Also on the twelfth, Kojirō called at the castle and was warmly received by Lord Tadatoshi. They had some sake together, and Kojirō left in high spirits, riding his favorite pony.

By evening, the town was humming with rumors.

"Musashi probably got scared and ran away."

"No doubt about it. He's gone."

That night was a sleepless one for Sado. He tried to convince himself that it simply wasn't possible—Musashi wasn't the type to run away. . . . Still, it was not unknown for a seemingly reliable person to break down under stress. Fearing the worst, Sado foresaw having to commit seppuku, the only honorable solution if Musashi, whom he had recommended, failed to show up.

The bright, clear dawn of the thirteenth found him walking in the garden with Iori, asking himself over and over: "Was I mistaken? Did I misjudge the man?"

"Good morning, sir." Nuinosuke's tired face appeared at the side gate.

"Did you find him?"

"No, sir. None of the innkeepers have seen anyone even resembling him."

"Did you ask at the temples?"

"The temples, the dōjō, all the other places students of the martial arts go to. Magobeinojō and his group have been out all night and—"

"They haven't come back yet." Sado's brow furrowed. Through the fresh leaves of the plum trees, he could see the blue sea; the waves seemed to be beating against his very chest. "I don't understand it."

"He's nowhere to be found, sir."

One by one the searchers returned, tired and disappointed. Assembling near the veranda, they talked the situation over in a mood of anger and desperation.

According to Kinami Kagashirō, who had passed by Sasaki Kojirō's house, several hundred supporters had gathered outside the gate. The entrance was bedecked with bunting bearing a festive gentian crest, and a gold screen had been placed directly before the door from which Kojirō was to emerge. At dawn, contingents of his followers had gone to the three main shrines to pray for his victory.

Unrelieved gloom prevailed at Sado's house, the burden being especially heavy for the men who had known Musashi's father. They felt betrayed. If Musashi reneged, it would be impossible for them to face their fellow samurai or the world at large.

When Sado dismissed them, Kagashirō vowed, "We'll find the bastard. If not today, some other day. And when we do, we'll kill him."

Returning to his own room, Sado lit the incense in the incense burner, as he did every day, but Nuinosuke detected a special gravity in the deliberateness of his movements. "He's preparing himself," he thought, grieved to think that it had come to this.

Just then Iori, standing at the edge of the garden gazing at the sea, turned and asked, "Did you try the house of Kobayashi Tarōzaemon?"

Nuinosuke realized instinctively that Iori had hit on something. No one had gone to the shipping broker's establishment, but it was exactly the sort of place Musashi would choose so as to keep out of sight.

"The boy's right," exclaimed Sado, his face brightening. "How stupid of us! Get over there right away!"

"I'm going too," said Iori.

"Is it all right for him to go along?"

"Yes, he can go too. Now hurry. . . . No, wait a minute."

He dashed off a note and informed Nuinosuke of its contents: "Sasaki Kojirō will cross to Funashima in a boat provided by Lord Tadatoshi. He will arrive by eight o'clock. You can still make it by then. I suggest you come here and make your preparations. I'll provide a boat to take you to your glorious victory."

951

In Sado's name, Nuinosuke and Iori procured a fast craft from the fief's boatmaster. They made it to Shimonoseki in record time, then proceeded directly to Tarōzaemon's shop.

In response to their inquiry, a clerk said, "I don't know any details, but it appears there's a young samurai staying at the master's house."

"That's it! We've found him." Nuinosuke and Iori grinned at each other and rapidly covered the short distance between shop and house.

Confronting Tarōzaemon directly, Nuinosuke said, "This is fief business, and it's urgent. Is Miyamoto Musashi staying here?"

"Yes."

"Thank heaven. My master's been worried sick. Quick now, tell Musashi I'm here."

Tarōzaemon went into the house and reappeared a minute later, saying, "He's still in his room. He's sleeping."

"Sleeping?" Nuinosuke was appalled.

"He was up late last night, talking with me over some sake."

"This is no time to be sleeping. Wake him up. Right now!"

The merchant, refusing to be pressured, showed Nuinosuke and Iori into a guest room before going to awaken Musashi.

When Musashi joined them, he appeared well rested, eyes as clear as a baby's.

"Good morning," he said cheerfully as he seated himself. "Is there something I can do for you?"

Nuinosuke, deflated by the nonchalant greeting, silently handed him Sado's letter.

"How good of him to write," said Musashi, raising the letter to his forehead before breaking the seal and opening it. Iori was staring a hole through Musashi, who acted as if he wasn't even there. After reading the letter, he rolled it up and said, "I'm grateful for Sado's thoughtfulness." Only then did he glance at Iori, causing the boy to lower his head to hide his tears.

Musashi wrote a reply and handed it to Nuinosuke. "I've explained everything in the letter," he said, "but be sure to convey my thanks and my best wishes." He added that they were not to worry. He would go to Funashima in his own good time.

There was nothing they could do, so they left. Iori hadn't said a word to Musashi, nor Musashi to him. Yet the two had communicated to each other the mutual devotion of teacher and pupil.

As Sado read Musashi's reply, a look of relief spread across his face. The letter said:

> My deepest thanks for your offer of a boat to take me to Funashima. I do not deem myself worthy of such an honor. Moreover, I do not feel that I should accept. Please take into consideration that Kojirō and I are facing each other as opponents, and that he is using a boat provided by Lord Tadatoshi. If I were to go in your boat, it would appear that you were opposing his lordship. I do not think you should do anything on my behalf.

952

Although I should have told you this earlier, I refrained because I knew you would insist upon helping me. Rather than involve you, I came and stayed at Tarōzaemon's house. I shall also have the use of one of his boats to go to Funashima, at the hour I think appropriate. Of that you may rest assured.

Deeply impressed, Sado stared silently at the writing for a time. It was a good letter, modest, thoughtful, considerate, and he was now ashamed of his agitation of the day before.

"Nuinosuke."

"Yes, sir."

"Take this letter and show it to Magobeinojō and his comrades, as well as the others concerned."

Nuinosuke had just left, when a servant came in and said, "If your business is finished, sir, you should get ready to leave now."

"Yes, of course, but there's still plenty of time," Sado replied quietly.

"It's not early. Kakubei's already left."

"That's his business. Iori, come here a minute."

"Sir?"

"Are you a man, Iori?"

"I think so."

"Do you think you can keep from crying, whatever happens?"

"Yes, sir."

"All right then, you can go to Funashima with me as my attendant. But remember one thing: we may have to pick up Musashi's corpse and bring it back with us. Could you still keep from crying?"

"Yes, sir. I will, I swear I will."

Nuinosuke had no sooner hurried through the gate than a shabbily dressed woman called to him. "Pardon me, sir, but are you a retainer in this house?"

Nuinosuke stopped and looked at her suspiciously. "What do you want?"

"Forgive me. Looking the way I do, I shouldn't be standing in front of your gate."

"Well, why are you doing it, then?"

"I wanted to ask . . . it's about the fight today. People are saying Musashi's run away. Is that true?"

"You stupid wench! How dare you! You're talking about Miyamoto Musashi. Do you think he'd do a thing like that? Just wait until eight o'clock and you'll see. I've just been to see Musashi."

"You saw him?"

"Who are you?"

She dropped her eyes. "I'm an acquaintance of Musashi."

"Hmph. But still you worry about groundless rumors? All right—I'm in a hurry, but I'll show you a letter from Musashi." He read it aloud for her, not noticing the man with tearful eyes looking over his shoulder. When he did notice, he jerked his shoulder back and said, "Who are you? What do you think you're doing?"

Wiping the tears from his eyes, the man bowed sheepishly. "Sorry. I'm with this woman."

"Her husband?"

"Yes, sir. Thank you for showing us the letter. I feel like I've actually seen Musashi. Don't you, Akemi?"

"Yes; I feel so much better. Let's go find a place to watch."

Nuinosuke's anger evaporated. "If you go to the top of that hill over there by the shore, you should be able to see Funashima. As clear as it is today, you might even be able to make out the sandbar."

"We're sorry to have made a nuisance of ourselves when you're in a hurry. Please forgive us."

As they started to walk away, Nuinosuke said, "Just a minute—what are your names? If you don't mind, I'd like to know."

They turned and bowed. "My name's Matahachi. I was born in the same village as Musashi."

"My name's Akemi."

Nuinosuke nodded and ran off.

They watched him for a few moments, exchanged glances and hurried on to the hill. From there, they could see Funashima jutting up among a number of other islands, the mountains of Nagato in the distance beyond. They spread some reed matting on the ground and sat down. The waves rumbled below them, and a pine needle or two floated down. Akemi took the baby from her back and began nursing it. Matahachi, his hands on his knees, stared fixedly out over the water.

The Marriage

Nuinosuke went first to Magobeinojō's house, showed him the letter and explained the circumstances. He left immediately, not even taking time for a cup of tea, and made quick stops at the other five houses.

Up the beach from the shore commissioner's office, he positioned himself behind a tree and watched the bustle that had been going on since early morning. Several teams of samurai had already left for Funashima—the ground cleaners, the witnesses, the guards—each group in a separate boat. On the beach another small boat stood ready for Kojirō. Tadatoshi had had it built especially for this occasion, of new timber, with new water brooms and new hemp-palm ropes.

The people seeing Kojirō off numbered about a hundred. Nuinosuke recognized some as friends of the swordsman; many others he did not know.

Kojirō finished his tea and came out of the commissioner's office, accompanied by the officials. Having entrusted his favorite pony to friends, he walked across the sand toward the boat. Tatsunosuke followed close behind. The crowd silently arranged itself into two rows and made way for their champion. Seeing the way Kojirō was dressed made many imagine that they themselves were about to go into battle.

He had on a narrow-sleeved silk kimono, solid white with a raised figured pattern; over this, a sleeveless cloak of brilliant red. His purple leather *hakama* was of the type that is gathered just below the knees and is tight, like leggings, on the calf. His straw sandals appeared to have been dampened slightly to keep them from slipping. Besides the short sword he always carried, he had the Drying Pole, which he had not used since becoming an official in the House of Hosokawa. His white, full-cheeked face was a study in calm above the flaming red of his cloak. There was something grand, something almost beautiful, about Kojirō today.

Nuinosuke could see that Kojirō's smile was quiet and confident. Flashing his grin in all directions, he looked happy and perfectly at ease.

Kojirō stepped into the boat. Tatsunosuke got in after him. There were two crewmen, one in the prow and the other manning the scull. Amayumi perched on Tatsunosuke's fist.

Once clear of the shore, the sculler moved his arms with great languid strokes, and the little vessel glided gently forward.

Startled by the cries of the well-wishers, the falcon flapped its wings.

The crowd broke up into small groups and slowly dispersed, marveling over Kojirō's calm demeanor and praying that he would win this fight of all fights.

"I must get back," thought Nuinosuke, remembering his responsibility to see that Sado departed on time. As he turned away, he caught sight of a girl. Omitsu's body was pressed tightly against the trunk of a tree, and she was crying.

Feeling it indecent to stare, Nuinosuke averted his eyes and slipped away noiselessly. Out in the street again, he took a parting look at Kojirō's boat, then at Omitsu. "Everyone has a public and private life," he thought. "Behind all that fanfare, a woman stands weeping her heart out."

On the boat, Kojirō asked Tatsunosuke for the falcon and held out his left arm. Tatsunosuke transferred Amayumi to his fist and respectfully moved away.

The tide was flowing swiftly. The day was perfect—clear sky, crystal water—but the waves were rather high. Each time water splashed over the gunwale, the falcon, in a fighting mood, ruffled its feathers.

When they were about halfway to the island, Kojirō removed the band from its leg and threw the bird into the air, saying, "Go back to the castle."

As though hunting as usual, Amayumi attacked a fleeing seabird, sending down a flurry of white feathers. But when its master did not call it back, it swooped down low over the islands, then soared into the sky and disappeared.

After releasing the falcon, Kojirō began stripping himself of the Buddhist and Shinto good-luck charms and writings showered on him by his supporters, casting them overboard, one by one—even the cotton underrobe with the embroidered Sanskrit charm given him by his aunt.

"Now," he said softly, "I can relax." Faced with a life-or-death situation, he did not want to be bothered with memories or personalities. Being reminded of all those people who were praying for his victory was a burden. Their good wishes, no matter how sincere, were now more of a hindrance than a help. What mattered now was himself, his naked self.

The salty breeze caressed his silent face. His eyes were fixed on the green pines of Funashima.

In Shimonoseki, Tarōzaemon walked past a row of beach sheds and entered his shop. "Sasuke," he called. "Hasn't anybody seen Sasuke?" Sasuke was among the youngest of his many employees, but also one of the brightest. Treasured as a household servant, he also helped out in the shop from time to time.

"Good morning," said Tarōzaemon's manager, emerging from his station in the accounting office. "Sasuke was here just a few minutes ago." Turning to a young assistant, he said, "Go find Sasuke. Hurry."

The manager started to bring Tarōzaemon up to date on business matters, but the merchant cut him off, shaking his head as though a mosquito were after him. "What I want to know is whether anybody's been here looking for Musashi."

"As a matter of fact, there was someone here already this morning."

"The messenger from Nagaoka Sado? I know about him. Anybody else?"

The manager rubbed his chin. "Well, I didn't see him myself, but I'm told that a dirty-looking man with sharp eyes came last night. He was carrying a long oak staff and asked to see 'Musashi *Sensei*.' They had a hard time getting rid of him."

"Somebody blabbed. And after I told them how important it was to keep quiet about Musashi's being here."

"I know. I told them too, in no uncertain terms. But you can't do anything with the young ones. Having Musashi here makes them feel important."

"How did you get rid of the man?"

"Sōbei told him he was mistaken, Musashi's never been here. He finally left, whether he believed it or not. Sōbei noticed there were two or three people waiting outside for him, one a woman."

Sasuke came running up from the pier. "Do you want me, sir?"

"Yes. I wanted to make sure you're ready. It's very important, you know."

"I realize that, sir. I've been up since before sunrise. I washed in cold water and put on a new white cotton loincloth."

"Good. The boat's all ready, the way I told you last night?"

"Well, there wasn't much to do. I picked out the fastest and cleanest of the boats, sprinkled salt around to purify it and swabbed it down inside and out. I'm ready to leave whenever Musashi is."

"Where's the boat?"

"On the shore with the other boats."

After thinking a moment, Tarōzaemon said, "We'd better move it. Too many people will notice when Musashi leaves. He doesn't want that. Take it up by the big pine, the one called the Heike Pine. Hardly anyone goes by there."

"Yes, sir."

The shop, usually quite busy, was nearly deserted. Nervously upset, Tarōzaemon went out into the street. Here and in Moji, on the opposite shore, people were taking the day off—men who appeared to be samurai from neighboring fiefs, rōnin, Confucian scholars, blacksmiths, armorers, lacquer-makers, priests, townsmen of all descriptions, some farmers from the surrounding countryside. Scented women in veils and broad traveling hats. Fishermen's wives with children on their backs or clinging to their hands. They were all moving in the same general direction, trying vainly to get closer to the island, through there was no vantage point from which anything smaller than a tree could be seen.

"I see what Musashi means," thought Tarōzaemon. To be set upon by this mob of sightseers, to whom the fight was merely a spectacle, would be unendurable.

Returning to his house, he found the whole place fastidiously clean. In the room open to the beach, wave patterns flickered on the ceiling.

"Where have you been, Father? I've been looking for you." Otsuru came in with tea.

"Nowhere in particular." He lifted his teacup and gazed pensively into it.

Otsuru had come to spend some time with her beloved father. By chance, traveling from Sakai on the same vessel with Musashi, she had discovered they both had ties with Iori. When Musashi came to pay his respects to Tarōzaemon and thank him for taking care of the boy, the merchant had insisted Musashi stay at his house and had instructed Otsuru to look after him.

The night before, while Musashi talked to his host, Otsuru sat in the next room sewing the new loincloth and stomach wrapper he'd said he wanted on the day of the bout. She had already prepared a new black kimono, from which at a moment's notice she could remove the basting used to keep the sleeves and skirt properly folded until time for use.

It crossed Tarōzaemon's mind that Otsuru just might be falling in love with Musashi. There was a worried look on her face; something serious was on her mind.

"Otsuru, where Musashi? Have you given him his breakfast?"

"Oh, yes. Long ago. After that, he shut the door to his room."

"Getting ready, I suppose."

"No, not yet."

"What's he doing?"

"He seems to be painting a picture."

"Now?"

"Yes."

"Hmm. We were talking about painting, and I asked him if he'd paint a picture for me. I guess I shouldn't have done that."

"He said he'd finish it before he left. He's painting one for Sasuke too." 957

"Sasuke?" Tarōzaemon echoed incredulously. He was growing more and more nervous. "Doesn't he know it's getting late? You should see all the people milling about the streets."

"From the look on Musashi's face, you'd think he'd forgotten the bout."

"Well, it's no time to be painting. Go tell him that. Be polite, but let him know that can wait till later."

"Why me? I couldn't ... "

"And why not?" His suspicion that she was in love was confirmed. Father and daughter communicated silently but perfectly. Grumbling good-naturedly, "Silly child. Why are you crying?" he got up and went toward Musashi's room.

Musashi was kneeling silently, as though in meditation, his brush, ink box and brush pot beside him. He had already finished one painting—a heron beneath a willow tree. The paper before him now was still blank. He was considering what to draw. Or more exactly, quietly trying to put himself into the right frame of mind, for that was necessary before he could visualize the picture or know the technique he would employ.

He saw the white paper as the great universe of nonexistence. A single stroke would give rise to existence within it. He could evoke rain or wind at will, but whatever he drew, his heart would remain in the painting forever. If his heart was tainted, the picture would be tainted; if his heart was listless, so would the picture be. If he attempted to make a show of his craftsmanship, it could not be concealed. Men's bodies fade away, but ink lives on. The image of his heart would continue to breathe after he himself was gone.

He realized that his thoughts were holding him back. He was on the brink of entering the world of nonexistence, of letting his heart speak for itself, independent of his ego, free from the personal touch of his hand. He tried to be empty, waiting for that sublime state in which his heart could speak in unison with the universe, selfless and unhampered.

The sounds from the street did not reach his room. Today's bout seemed completely apart from himself. He was conscious merely of the tremulous movements of the bamboo in the inner garden.

"May I intrude?" The shoji behind him opened noiselessly, and Tarōzaemon peered in. It seemed wrong, almost evil, to barge in, but he braced himself and said, "I'm sorry to distract you when you seem to be enjoying your work so."

"Ah, please come in."

"It's nearly time to leave."

"I know."

"Everything's ready. All the things you'll need are in the next room."

"That's very kind of you."

"Please don't worry about the paintings. You can finish them when you come back from Funashima."

"Oh, it's nothing. I feel very fresh this morning. It's a good time to paint."

"But you have to think of the time."

"Yes, I know."

"Whenever you want to make your preparations, just call. We're waiting to help you."

"Thank you very much." Tarōzaemon started to leave, but Musashi said, "What time is high tide?"

"At this season, the tide's lowest between six and eight in the morning. It should be on the rise again about now."

"Thank you," Musashi said absently, again addressing his attention to the white paper.

Tarōzaemon quietly closed the shoji and went back to the parlor. He intended to sit down and wait quietly, but before long his nerves got the better of him. He rose and strode out to the veranda, from where he could see the current running through the strait. The water was already advancing on the beach.

"Father."

"What is it?"

"It's time for him to leave. I put his sandals out at the garden entrance."

"He's not ready yet."

"Still painting?"

"Yes."

"I thought you were going to make him stop and get ready."

"He knows what time it is."

A small boat pulled up on the beach nearby, and Tarōzaemon heard his name called. It was Nuinosuke, asking, "Has Musashi left yet?" When Tarōzaemon said no, Nuinosuke said rapidly, "Please tell him to get ready and start as quickly as possible. Kojirō's already left, and so has Lord Hosokawa. My master's leaving from Kokura right now."

"I'll do my best."

"Please! Maybe I sound like an old woman, but we want to be sure he's not late. It'd be a shame to bring dishonor on himself at this point." He rowed away hurriedly, leaving the shipping broker and his daughter to fret by themselves on the veranda. They counted the seconds, glancing from time to time toward the little room in the back, from which came not the slightest sound.

Soon a second boat arrived with a messenger from Funashima, sent to hurry Musashi along.

Musashi opened his eyes at the sound of shoji opening. There was no need for Otsuru to announce her presence. When she told him about the boat from Funashima, he nodded and smiled affably. "I see," he said, and left the room.

Otsuru glanced at the floor where he had been sitting. The piece of paper was now heavily blotched with ink. At first the picture looked like an indistinct cloud, but she soon saw that it was a landscape of the "broken ink" variety. It was still wet.

"Please give that picture to your father," Musashi called above the sound of splashing water. "And the other one to Sasuke."

"Thank you. You really shouldn't have done it."

"I'm sorry I don't have anything better to offer, after all the trouble you've gone to, but I hope your father will accept it as a keepsake."

Otsuru replied thoughtfully, "Tonight, by all means, come back and sit by the fire with my father, as you did last night."

Hearing the rustling of clothes in the next room, Otsuru felt pleased. At last he was getting dressed. Then there was silence again, and the next thing she knew, he was talking to her father. The conversation was very brief, only a few succinct words. As she passed through the next room, she noticed he had neatly folded his old clothes and placed them in a box in the corner. An indescribable loneliness seized her. She bent over and nestled her face against the still warm kimono.

"Otsuru!" called her father. "What are you doing? He's leaving!"

"Yes, Father." She brushed her fingers over her cheeks and eyelids and ran to join him.

Musashi was already at the garden gate, which he had chosen to avoid being seen. Father, daughter and four or five others from the house and shop came as far as the gate. Otsuru was too overwrought to utter a word. When Musashi's eyes turned toward her, she bowed like the others.

"Farewell," said Musashi. He went through the low gate of woven grass, closed it behind him and said, "Take good care of yourselves." By the time they raised their heads, he was walking rapidly away.

They stared after him, but Musashi's head did not turn.

"I guess that's the way it's supposed to be with samurai," someone mumbled. "He leaves—just like that: no speech, no elaborate good-byes, nothing."

Otsuru disappeared immediately. A few seconds later, her father retreated into the house.

The Heike Pine stood in solitude about two hundred yards up the beach. Musashi walked toward it, his mind completely at rest. He had put all his thoughts into the black ink of the landscape painting. It had felt good to be painting, and he considered his effort a success.

Now for Funashima. He was setting forth calmly, as though this were any other journey. He had no way of knowing whether he would ever return, but he had stopped thinking about it. Years ago, when at the age of twenty-two he had approached the spreading pine at Ichijōji, he had been very keyed up, shadowed by a sense of impending tragedy. He had gripped his lonely sword with intense determination. Now he felt nothing.

It was not that the enemy today was less to be feared than the hundred men he had confronted then. Far from it. Kojirō, fighting alone, was a more formidable opponent than any army the Yoshioka School could have mounted against him. There was not the least doubt in Musashi's mind but that he was going into the fight of his life.

"*Sensei!*"

"Musashi!"

Musashi's mind did a turn at the sound of the voices and the sight of two people running toward him. For an instant he was dazed.

"Gonnosuke!" he exclaimed. "And Granny! How did you two get here?"

Both, grimy from travel, knelt in the sand in front of him.

"We had to come," said Gonnosuke.

"We came to see you off," said Osugi. "And I came to apologize to you."

"Apologize? To me?"

"Yes. For everything. I must ask you to forgive me."

He looked inquiringly at her face. The words sounded unreal. "Why do you say that, Granny? Has something happened?"

She stood with her hands clasped pleadingly. "What can I say? I've done so many evil things, I can't hope to apologize for all of them. It was all . . . all a horrible mistake. I was blinded by my love for my son, but now I know the truth. Please forgive me."

He stared at her for a moment, then knelt and took her hand. He dared not raise his eyes, for fear there might be tears in them. Seeing the old woman so contrite made him feel guilty. But he felt gratitude too. Her hand trembled; even his was quivering slightly.

It took him a moment to pull himself together. "I believe you, Granny. I'm grateful to you for coming. Now I can face death without regrets, go into the bout with my spirit free and my heart untroubled."

"Then you'll forgive me?"

"Of course I will, if you'll forgive me for all the trouble I've caused you since I was a boy."

"Of course; but enough of me. There's another person who needs your help. Someone who's very, very sad." She turned, inviting him to look.

Under the Heike Pine, looking shyly at them, her face pale and dewy with anticipation, stood Otsū.

"Otsū!" he shouted. In a second, he was before her, not knowing himself how his feet had transported him there. Gonnosuke and Osugi stood where they were, wishing they could disappear into thin air and leave the shore to the couple alone.

"Otsū, you've come."

Words did not exist to bridge the chasm of years, to convey the world of feeling brimming inside him.

"You don't look well. Are you ill?" He mumbled the words, like an isolated line from a long poem.

"A little." Eyes lowered, she struggled to remain cool, to keep her wits about her. This moment—perhaps the last—must not be spoiled, nor wasted.

"Is it just a cold?" he asked. "Or something serious? What's wrong? Where have you been these past few months?"

"I went back to the Shippōji last fall."

"Back home?"

"Yes." She looked straight at him, her eyes becoming as limpid as the ocean depths, struggling to hold back the tears. "But there's no real home for an orphan like me. Only the home inside me."

"Don't talk like that. Why, even Osugi seems to have opened her heart to you. That makes me very happy. You must recover your health and learn to be happy. For me."

"I'm happy now."

"Are you? If that's true, I'm happy too. . . . Otsū . . ." He bent toward her. She stood stiffly, conscious of Osugi and Gonnosuke. Musashi, who had forgotten them, put his arm around her and brushed his cheek against hers.

"You're so thin . . . so thin." He was acutely conscious of her fevered breathing. "Otsū, please forgive me. I may seem heartless, but I'm not, not where you're concerned."

"I . . . I know that."

"Do you? Truly?"

"Yes, but I beg you, say one word for me. Just one word. Tell me that I'm your wife."

"It would spoil it if I told you what you know already."

"But . . . but . . ." She was sobbing with her whole body, but with a burst of strength, she seized his hand and cried, "Say it. Say I'm your wife throughout this life."

He nodded, slowly, silently. Then one by one he pulled her delicate fingers from his arm and stood erect. "A samurai's wife must not weep and go to pieces when he goes off to war. Laugh for me, Otsū. Send me away with a smile. This may be your husband's last departure."

Both knew the time had come. For a brief moment, he looked at her and smiled. Then he said, "Until then."

"Yes. Until then." She wanted to return his smile but only managed to hold back the tears.

"Farewell." He turned and walked with firm strides toward the water's edge. A parting word rose to her throat but refused to be uttered. The tears welled up irrepressibly. She could no longer see him.

The strong, salty wind ruffled Musashi's sideburns. His kimono flapped briskly.

"Sasuke! Bring the boat a little closer."

Though he had been waiting for over two hours and knew Musashi was on the beach, Sasuke had carefully kept his eyes averted. Now he looked at Musashi and said, "Right away, sir."

With a few strong, rapid movements, he poled the boat in. When it touched shore, Musashi jumped lightly into the prow, and they moved out to sea.

"Otsū! Stop!" The shout was Jōtarō's.

Otsū was running straight toward the water. He raced after her. Startled, Gonnosuke and Osugi joined in the chase.

"Otsū, stop! What are you doing?"

"Don't be foolish!"

Reaching her simultaneously, they threw their arms around her and held her back.

"No, no," she protested, shaking her head slowly. "You don't understand."

"Wh-what are you trying to do?"

"Let me sit down, by myself." Her voice was calm.

They released her, and she walked with dignity to a spot a few yards away, where she knelt on the sand, seemingly exhausted. But she had found her strength. She straightened her collar, smoothed her hair, and bowed toward Musashi's little craft.

"Go without regrets," she said.

Osugi knelt and bowed. Then Gonnosuke. And Jōtarō. After coming all the way from Himeji, Jōtarō had missed his chance to speak to Musashi, despite his intense yearning to say a parting word. His disappointment was softened by the knowledge that he had given his share of Musashi's time to Otsū.

The Soul of the Deep

With the tide at its peak, the water coursed through the strait like a swollen torrent in a narrow ravine. The wind was to their rear, and the boat moved swiftly across the waves. Sasuke looked proud; he intended to be praised for his work with the scull today.

Musashi was seated in the middle of the boat, his knees spread wide. "Does it take long to get there?" he asked.

"Not very long with this tide, but we're late."

"Mm."

"It's well after eight o'clock."

"Yes, it is, isn't it? What time do you think we'll get there?"

"It'll probably be ten or a little after."

"That's just right."

The sky Musashi looked at that day—the sky Ganryū looked at—was a deep azure. Snow covering the ridge of the Nagato Mountains looked like a white streamer fluttering across a cloudless sky. The houses of the city of Mojigasaki and the wrinkles and crevices of Mount Kazashi were clearly discernible. On the mountainsides, droves of people were straining their eyes toward the islands.

"Sasuke, may I have this?"

"What is it?"

"This broken oar in the bottom of the boat."

"I don't need it. Why do you want it?"

"It's about the right size," Musashi said cryptically. He held the slightly waterlogged oar out with one hand and squinted down it to see if it was straight. One edge of the blade was split off.

He placed the oar on his knee and, totally absorbed, began carving with his short sword. Sasuke cast backward glances toward Shimonoseki several times, but Musashi seemed oblivious of the people he had left behind. Was this the way a samurai approached a life-and-death battle? To a townsman like Sasuke, it seemed cold and heartless.

Musashi finished his carving and brushed the chips from his *hakama*. "Do you have something I could put around me?" he asked.

"Are you cold?"

"No, but the water's splashing in."

"There should be a quilted coat under the seat."

Musashi picked up the garment and threw it over his shoulders. Then he took some paper from his kimono and began rolling and twisting each sheet into a string. When he had accumulated more than twenty of these, he twisted them together end to end to make two cords, which he then braided to make a *tasuki*, the band used to tie sleeves back when fighting. Sasuke had heard that making *tasuki* from paper was a secret art, passed down from generation to generation, but Musashi made the process look easy. Sasuke watched with admiration the deftness of his fingers and the grace with which he slipped the *tasuki* over his arms.

"Is that Funashima?" asked Musashi, pointing.

"No. That's Hikojima, part of the Hahajima group. Funashima's a thousand yards or so to the northeast. It's easy to recognize because it's flat and looks like a long sandbar. There between Hikojima and Izaki is the Strait of Ondo. You've probably heard of it."

"To the west, then, that must be Dairinoura in Buzen Province."

"That's right."

"I remember now. The inlets and islands around here were where Yoshitsune won the last battle against the Heike."

Sasuke was growing more nervous with each stroke of the scull. He had broken out in a cold sweat; his heart was palpitating. It seemed eerie to be talking about inconsequential matters. How could a man going into battle be so calm?

It would be a fight to the death; no question about that. Would he be taking a passenger back to the mainland later? Or a cruelly maimed corpse? There was no way of knowing. Musashi, thought Sasuke, was like a white cloud floating across the sky.

This was not a pose on Musashi's part, for in fact he was thinking of nothing at all. He was, if anything, a little bored.

He looked over the side of the boat at the swirling blue water. It was deep here, infinitely deep, and alive with what seemed to be eternal life. But water had no fixed, determined form. Was it not because man had a fixed, determined form that he cannot possess eternal life? Does not true life begin only when tangible form has been lost?

To Musashi's eyes, life and death seemed like so much froth. He felt goose pimples on his skin, not from the cold water but because his body felt a premonition. Though his mind had risen above life and death, body and mind were not in accord. When every pore of his body, as well as his mind, forgot, there would remain nothing inside his being but the water and the clouds.

They were passing Teshimachi Inlet on Hikojima. Unseen by them were some forty samurai standing watch on the shore. All were supporters of Ganryū, and most were in the service of the House of Hosokawa. In violation of Tadatoshi's orders, they had crossed over to Funashima two days earlier. In the event that Ganryū was beaten, they were ready to take revenge.

This morning, when Nagaoka Sado, Iwama Kakubei and the men assigned to stand guard arrived on Funashima, they discovered this band of samurai, upbraided them severely and ordered them to go to Hikojima. But since most of the officials were in sympathy with them, they went unpunished. Once they were off Funashima, it was not the officials' responsibility what they did.

"Are you sure it's Musashi?" one of them was saying.

"It has to be."

"Is he alone?"

"He seems to be. He's got a cloak or something around his shoulders."

"He probably has on light armor and wants to hide it."

"Let's go."

Tensely eager for battle, they piled into their boats and lay in readiness. All were armed with swords, but in the bottom of each boat lay a long lance.

"Musashi's coming!"

The cry was heard around Funashima only moments later.

The sound of the waves, the voices of the pines and the rustling of the bamboo grass blended softly. Since early morning the little island had had a desolate air, despite the presence of the officials. A white cloud rising from the direction of Nagato grazed past the sun, darkening the tree and bamboo leaves. The cloud passed, and brightness returned.

It was a very small island. At the north end was a low hill, covered with pine trees. To the south the ground was level at a height about half that of the hill until the island dropped off into the shoals.

A canopy had been hung between some trees at a considerable distance from the shore. The officials and their attendants waited quietly and inconspicuously, not wishing to give Musashi the impression that they were trying to add to the dignity of the local champion.

Now, two hours past the appointed time, they were beginning to show their anxiety and resentment. Twice they had sent fast boats out to hurry Musashi on.

The lookout from the reef ran up to the officials and said, "It's him! No doubt about it."

"Has he really come?" asked Kakubei, rising involuntarily, and by doing so committing a serious breach of etiquette. As an official witness, he was expected to remain coolly reserved. His excitement was only natural, however, and was shared by others in his party, who also stood up.

Realizing his gaffe, Kakubei brought himself under control and motioned to the others to sit down again. It was essential that they not allow their personal preference for Ganryū to color their actions or their decision. Kakubei glanced toward Ganryū's waiting area. Tatsunosuke had hung a curtain with a gentian crest from several wild peach trees. Next to the curtain was a new wooden bucket with a bamboo-handled ladle. Ganryū, impatient after his long wait, had asked for a drink of water and was now resting in the shade of the curtain.

Nagaoka Sado's position was beyond Ganryū's and slightly higher. He was surrounded by guards and attendants, Iori at his side. When the lookout arrived with his news, the boy's face—even his lips—turned pale. Sado was seated in formal fashion, straight and motionless. His helmet shifted slightly to his right, as though he were looking at the sleeve of his kimono. In a low voice, he called Iori's name.

"Yes, sir." Iori bowed to the ground before looking up under Sado's helmet. Unable to control his excitement, he was trembling from head to feet.

"Iori," said Sado, looking straight into the boy's eyes. "Watch everything that happens. Don't miss a single thing. Keep in mind that Musashi has laid his life on the line to teach you what you are about to see."

Iori nodded. His eyes sparkled like flames as he fixed his gaze on the reef. The white spray of the waves breaking against it dazzled his eyes. It was about two hundred yards away, so it would be impossible for him to see the small movements and the breathing of the fighters. But it was not the technical aspects Sado wanted him to watch. It was the dramatic moment when a samurai enters a life-and-death struggle. This was what would live on in his mind and influence him throughout his life.

The waves of grass rose and fell. Greenish insects darted hither and thither. A small, delicate butterfly moved from one blade of grass to another, then was seen no more.

"He's nearly here," gasped Iori.

Musashi's boat approached the reef slowly. It was almost exactly ten o'clock.

Ganryū stood up and walked unhurriedly down the hillock behind the waiting stations. He bowed to the officials on his right and left and walked quietly through the grass to the shore.

The approach to the island was an inlet of sorts, where waves became wavelets, then mere ripples. Musashi could see the bottom through the clear blue water.

"Where should I land?" asked Sasuke, who had tempered his stroke and was scanning the shore with his eyes.

"Go straight in." Musashi threw off the quilted coat.

The bow advanced at a very restrained pace. Sasuke could not bring himself to stroke with vigor; his arms moved only slightly, exerting little force. The sound of bulbuls was in the air.

"Sasuke."

"Yes, sir."

"It's shallow enough here. There's no need to get too close. You don't want to damage your boat. Besides, it's about time for the tide to turn."

Silently, Sasuke fixed his eyes on a tall, thin pine tree, standing alone. Underneath it, the wind was playing with a brilliant red cloak.

Sasuke started to point but realized that Musashi had already seen his opponent. Keeping his eyes on Ganryū, Musashi took a russet hand towel from his

966

obi, folded it in four lengthwise, and tied it around his windblown hair. Then he shifted his short sword to the front of his obi. Taking off his long sword, he laid it in the bottom of the boat and covered it with a reed mat. In his right hand, he held the wooden sword he had made from the broken oar.

"This is far enough," he said to Sasuke.

Ahead of them was nearly two hundred feet of water. Sasuke took a couple of long strokes with the scull. The boat lurched forward and grounded on a shoal, the keel shuddering as it rose.

At that moment, Musashi, his *hakama* hitched high on both sides, jumped lightly into the sea, landing so lightly he made barely a splash. He strode rapidly toward the waterline, his wooden sword cutting through the spray.

Five steps. Ten steps. Sasuke, abandoning his scull, watched in wonderment, unconscious of where he was, what he was doing.

As Ganryū streaked away from the pine like a red streamer, his polished scabbard caught the glint of the sun.

Sasuke was reminded of a silver fox tail. "Hurry!" The word flashed through his mind, but Ganryū was already at the water's edge. Sasuke, sure that Musashi was done for, couldn't bear to watch. He fell face down in the boat, chilled and trembling, hiding his face as if he were the one who might at any moment be split in two.

"Musashi!"

Ganryū planted his feet resolutely in the sand, unwilling to give up an inch.

Musashi stopped and stood still, exposed to the water and the wind. A hint of a grin appeared on his face.

"Kojirō," he said quietly. There was an unearthly fierceness in his eyes, a force pulling so irresistibly it threatened to draw Kojirō inexorably into peril and destruction. The waves washed his wooden sword.

Ganryū's were the eyes that shot fire. A bloodthirsty flame burned in his pupils, like rainbows of fierce intensity, seeking to terrify and debilitate.

"Musashi!"

No answer.

"Musashi!"

The sea rumbled ominously in the distance; the tide lapped and murmured at the two men's feet.

"You're late again, aren't you? Is that your strategy? As far as I'm concerned, it's a cowardly ploy. It's two hours past the appointed time. I was here at eight, just as I promised. I've been waiting."

Musashi did not reply.

"You did this at Ichijōji, and before that at the Rengeōin. Your method seems to be to throw your opponent off by deliberately making him wait. That trick will get you nowhere with Ganryū. Now prepare your spirit and come forward bravely, so future generations won't laugh at you. Come ahead and fight, Musashi!" The end of his scabbard rose high behind him as he drew the great Drying Pole. With his left hand, he slid the scabbard off and threw it into the water.

Waiting just long enough for a wave to strike the reef and retreat, Musashi   *967* suddenly said in a quiet voice, "You've lost, Kojirō."

"What?" Ganryū was shaken to the core.

"The fight's been fought. I say you've been defeated."

"What are you talking about?"

"If you were going to win, you wouldn't throw your scabbard away. You've cast away your future, your life."

"Words! Nonsense!"

"Too bad, Kojirō. Ready to fall? Do you want to get it over with fast?"

"Come . . . come forward, you bastard!"

"H-o-o-o!" Musashi's cry and the sound of the water rose to a crescendo together.

Stepping into the water, the Drying Pole positioned high above his head, Ganryū faced Musashi squarely. A line of white foam streaked across the surface as Musashi ran up on shore to Ganryū's left. Ganryū pursued.

Musashi's feet left the water and touched the sand at almost the same instant that Ganryū's sword—his whole body—hurtled at him like a flying fish. When Musashi sensed that the Drying Pole was coming toward him, his body was still at the end of the motion that had taken him out of the water, leaning slightly forward.

He held the wooden sword with both hands, extended out to the right behind him and partially hidden. Satisfied with his position, he half grunted, an almost noiseless sound that wafted before Ganryū's face. The Drying Pole had appeared to be on the verge of a downward slice, but it wavered slightly, then stopped. Nine feet away from Musashi, Ganryū changed direction by leaping nimbly to the right.

The two men stared at each other. Musashi, two or three paces from the water, had the sea to his back. Ganryū was facing him, his sword held high with both hands.

Their lives were totally absorbed in deadly combat, and both were free from conscious thought.

The scene of the battle was a perfect vacuum. But in the waiting stations and beyond the sound of the waves, countless people held their breath.

Above Ganryū hovered the prayers and the hopes of those who believed in him and wanted him to live, above Musashi the prayers and hopes of others.

Of Sado and Iori, on the island.

Of Otsū and Osugi and Gonnosuke, on the beach at Shimonoseki.

Of Akemi and Matahachi, on their hill in Kokura.

All their prayers were directed to heaven.

Here, hopes, prayers and the gods were of no assistance, nor was chance. There was only a vacuum, impersonal and perfectly impartial.

Is this vacuum, so difficult of achievement by one who has life, the perfect expression of the mind that has risen above thought and transcended ideas?

The two men spoke without speaking. Then to each came the unconscious realization of the other. The pores of their bodies stood out like needles directed at the adversary.

968   Muscles, flesh, nails, hair, even eyebrows—all bodily elements that partake

of life—were united into a single force against the enemy, defending the living organism of which they were a part. The mind alone was one with the universe, clear and untroubled, like the reflection of the moon in a pond amidst the ragings of a typhoon. To reach this sublime immobility is the supreme achievement.

It seemed like eons, but the interval was in fact short—the time required for the waves to come in and recede half a dozen times.

Then a great shout—more than vocal, coming from the depths of being—shattered the instant. It came from Ganryū, and was followed immediately by Musashi's shout.

The two cries, like angry waves lashing a rocky shore, sent their spirits skyward. The challenger's sword, raised so high that it seemed to threaten the sun, streaked through the air like a rainbow.

Musashi threw his left shoulder forward, drew his right foot back and shifted his upper body into a position half-facing his opponent. His wooden sword, held in both hands, swept through the air at the same moment that the tip of the Drying Pole came down directly before his nose.

The breathing of the two combatants grew louder than the sound of the waves. Now the wooden sword was extended at eye level, the Drying Pole high above its bearer's head. Ganryū had bounded about ten paces away, where he had the sea to one side. Though he had not succeeded in injuring Musashi in his first attack, he had put himself in a much better position. Had he remained where he was, with the sun reflecting from the water into his eyes, his vision would soon have faltered, then his spirit, and he would have been at Musashi's mercy.

With renewed confidence, Ganryū began inching forward, keeping a sharp eye out for a chink in Musashi's defense and steeling his own spirit for a decisive move.

Musashi did the unexpected. Instead of proceeding slowly and cautiously, he strode boldly toward Ganryū, his sword projecting before him, ready to thrust into Ganryū's eyes. The artlessness of this approach brought Ganryū to a halt. He almost lost sight of Musashi.

The wooden sword rose straight in the air. With one great kick, Musashi leapt high, and folding his legs, reduced his six-foot frame to four feet or less.

"Y-a-a-ah!" Ganryū's sword screamed through the space above him. The stroke missed, but the tip of the Drying Pole cut through Musashi's headband, which went flying through the air.

Ganryū mistook it for his opponent's head, and a smile flitted briefly across his face. The next instant his skull broke like gravel under the blow of Musashi's sword.

As Ganryū lay where the sand met the grass, his face betrayed no consciousness of defeat. Blood streamed from his mouth, but his lips formed a smile of triumph.

"Oh, no!"

"Ganryū!"

Forgetting himself, Iwama Kakubei jumped up, and with him all his retinue, their faces distorted with shock. Then they saw Nagaoka Sado and Iori, sitting calmly and sedately on their benches. Shamed, they somehow managed to keep from running forward. They tried to regain a degree of composure, but there was no concealing their grief and disillusion. Some swallowed hard, refusing to believe what they had seen, and their minds went blank.

In an instant, the island was as quiet and still as it had ever been. Only the rustle of the pines and the swaying grasses mocked the frailty and impermanence of mankind.

Musashi was watching a small cloud in the sky. As he did, his soul returned to his body, and it became possible for him to distinguish between the cloud and himself, between his body and the universe.

Sasaki Kojirō Ganryū did not return to the world of the living. Lying face down, he still had a grip on his sword. His tenacity was still visible. There was no sign of anguish on his face. Nothing but satisfaction at having fought a good fight, not the faintest shadow of regret.

The sight of his own headband lying on the ground sent shivers up and down Musashi's spine. Never in this life, he thought, would he meet another opponent like this. A wave of admiration and respect flowed over him. He was grateful to Kojirō for what the man had given him. In strength, in the will to fight, he ranked higher than Musashi, and it was because of this that Musashi had been able to excel himself.

What was it that had enabled Musashi to defeat Kojirō? Skill? The help of the gods? While knowing it was neither of these, Musashi was never able to express a reason in words. Certainly it was something more important than either strength or godly providence.

Kojirō had put his confidence in the sword of strength and skill. Musashi trusted in the sword of the spirit. That was the only difference between them.

Silently, Musashi walked the ten paces to Kojirō and knelt beside him. He put his left hand near Kojirō's nostrils and found there was still a trace of breath. "With the right treatment, he may recover," Musashi told himself. And he wanted to believe this, wanted to believe that this most valiant of all adversaries would be spared.

But the battle was over. It was time to go.

"Farewell," he said—to Kojirō, then to the officials on their benches.

Having bowed once to the ground, he ran to the reef and jumped into the boat. There was not a drop of blood on his wooden sword.

The tiny craft moved out to sea. Who is to say where? There is no record as to whether Ganryū's supporters on Hikojima attempted to take revenge.

People do not give up their loves and hates as long as life lasts. Waves of feeling come and go with the passage of time. Throughout Musashi's lifetime, there were those who resented his victory and criticized his conduct on that day. He rushed away, it was said, because he feared reprisal. He was confused. He even neglected to administer the coup de grace.

The world is always full of the sound of waves.

The little fishes, abandoning themselves to the waves, dance and sing and play, but who knows the heart of the sea, a hundred feet down? Who knows its depth?

みやもとむさし
宮本武蔵
MUSASHI
_____

1993 年10月 1 日　第 1 刷発行
2001 年 3 月 1 日　第 8 刷発行

著　者　　　よしかわ えい じ
　　　　　吉川　英治
訳　者　　　チャールズ・S・テリー
発行者　　　野間佐和子
発行所　　　講談社インターナショナル株式会社
　　　　　〒112-8652 東京都文京区音羽 1-17-14
　　　　　電話：03-3944-6493
印刷所　　　株式会社 平河工業社
製本所　　　株式会社 堅省堂

落丁本・乱丁本は、小社業務部宛にお送りください。送料小社負担にてお取替えしま
す。なお、この本についてのお問い合わせは、編集部宛にお願いいたします。本書の
無断複写（コピー）、転載は著作権法の例外を除き、禁じられています。

定価はカバーに表示してあります。

Copyright © 1981 by Kodansha International Ltd.

Printed in Japan
ISBN 4-7700-1813-4